THE
BOOK OF THE LER

By
M. A. FOSTER

The Book of the Ler
Omnibus:
THE GAMEPLAYERS OF ZAN
THE WARRIORS OF DAWN
THE DAY OF THE KLESH

The Transformer Trilogy
Omnibus:
THE MORPHODITE
TRANSFORMER
PRESERVER

THE BOOK OF THE LER

THE GAMEPLAYERS OF ZAN
THE WARRIORS OF DAWN
THE DAY OF THE KLESH

M. A. FOSTER

DAW BOOKS, INC.

DONALD A. WOLLHEIM, FOUNDER
375 Hudson Street, New York, NY 10014
ELIZABETH R. WOLLHEIM
SHEILA E. GILBERT
PUBLISHERS
http://www.dawbooks.com

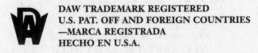

The Gameplayers of Zan

"God hath given you the stars to be your guides in the dark both by land and by sea."
—Mohammed, the *Koran*, Sura 6.

"He whose roof is heaven and over whom the stars continually rise and set in one and the same course makes the beginnings of his affairs and his knowledge of time depend on them."
—Al-Biruni

BOOK ONE

Instar Cellae Sylvestris

ONE

Processes have uses; it is also important to realize that fascination with a process can grow, there being no automatic check against this, until the bemusement obscures the intended results of the original procedure. This is the easiest trait of all to observe in others and the hardest to see and act upon in ourselves. We shall speak of obsessions with results upon another day.
—The Game Texts

ONE ALWAYS MAKES an identification of self in terms of a matrix of otherness, never saying simply "there am I," but always with the implicit definition "there am I in relation to all others I can know." And so now alone as she could not imagine anyone ever being, there was only herself. She could no longer measure who she was; only refer to a what-she-had-been, which she suspected either was no longer valid, or else was now based on distorted memories. There was herself, the memory, the whole of her life and all the things she had seen and done. There was also imagination, projections of fantasies of hopes and fears, the projections of her mind into all the places and circumstances she could never be in actuality. She balanced delicately between that which was and that which might have been. The impossible now. There was nothing else.

The present is never still, but a moving line between two points; in moving there is direction, source, destination. But with all references removed, by which one can measure motion, there was no longer any sense at all of the bridge of motion in time connecting the past with the future. They existed, of course: her memory and imagination reassured her of that; it was that she could no longer imagine quite how she related to those quantities. She was adrift in her own mind.

She could review the circumstances easily enough; in fact, she had already done so a number of times, perhaps several hundred times, seeking an alternative, a flaw, a slip, some error she could at least feel guilty about, or blame on someone else. But it was all as impervious as armor plate, there was no chink anywhere in the fearsome blankness of existentials. She imagined she felt like someone who had stepped into an elevator at exactly the moment when all of its safety devices failed: accidents happen which are in fact not the fault of their victim. She had been caught near the scene of the mission for which she had been sent. For which she had volunteered. It now seemed in hindsight that her life had always been a series of closing doors, not opening ones, of narrowing passages and shrinking rooms. And this was the last door and the last room. There was no passage. It ended here, wherever *here* was.

Near the Museum of Ancient Technologies, yes. There was nothing that could link her to the apparent vandalism that had destroyed beyond repair two obscure instruments left behind from the age of petroleum exploitation. Left behind, like astrolabes left behind from a rude era of ships powered by the wind they caught in their sails; left behind as the waves left shells, relics of life, on the beach. Artifacts of a vanished art, for there was no oil worth exploring for anymore. Yet of all those who might have been there, nearby, only she had been *ler*, deep into human lands beyond the reservation, and she had not had, even for herself, a convincing explanation for what she had been doing there. It was natural that they connect her with the damaged instruments. Her only remaining defense had been to remain quiet and somewhat passive, giving them nothing, not a name, not a reason.

They had conveyed her to their headquarters; others, in their turn, had taken her farther, to a large urban area, to a building, to a room within the building. Everything seemed unmemorable, bland; there had been no way to memorize directions or landmarks. Everything was featureless, or nearly so, as much so as could be managed. Then came the interrogators. They had been insistent, but considerate and subtle, masters of their arts. They had been firm, not especially unpleasant, and above all persuasive. She had said nothing. Only repeated in her soft voice that they should notify the Shuren Braid—hostel-keepers by the main entry into the reservation, close under the Institute—that they had picked up a lost girl. They had agreed to do so immediately, and were very polite. She knew they hadn't. No one came for her.

There had been a lack of overt threats, and there had never been any mention of anything like torture. She had not been fooled. She was too wise in her own ways not to know that people who hold all the cards have all the strengths and none of the weaknesses, and that they do not need to rant, rave, shout, pace up and down making histrionic gestures, parading about to turn suddenly, shouting bombast and threats. Or interrupting the silences with harangues and hectoring. No. They had no need to intimidate: these are acts that characterize an interrogator who is more interested in fondling the power he holds than in digging out the information he is paid to get.

Her story had been transparently flimsy, but she had repeated it anyway. She had been lost, she said, after a little exploration, and had been trying to get back by dead reckoning. She had never been in the Museum. She was sure they saw through that, but she stayed with it, however skillfully they tried to steer her into other areas. She thought that it had been easy to resist the gentle but constant, tidelike pressure, compared with other experiences in which she could draw analogs. But under her own sense of self-confidence, she could see that her visitors were in fact extraordinarily skillful among their own kind, others of the humans, the forerunners. One untrained would have broken in hours under them, and all without a single raised angry voice, a single twinge of pain. She couldn't really determine exactly how long it had gone on. There had been frosted windows, but the light shining through them was gray and never changed; she never knew if she was seeing filtered light, or some artificial light. It grew dark through those windows regularly, and there had been conspicuous clocks in the room with her, but she suspected that in a subtle world the obvious was mutable. She knew the rates of things; that had been part of her skill, her training, and she could sense subtle fluctuations of rate. But they had allowed her to sleep when she had been tired, eat when she had been hungry, wash when she had felt dirty. She learned nothing from those experiences—the noise levels were precisely uniform whatever her position.

She maintained her silence and her evasion as long as she could. After all, there had been some other close calls, and always before she had been able to bluff her way out. But perhaps those had not been so skillful as these, who seemed to sense the presence of deeper secrets in her silences, a presence that teased them, kept them at it. So despite the easy manners, the almost-pleasant sessions, the easy, relaxed interrogations, they smelled a secret. They didn't know if it had anything to do with the original issue or not—they were not, she could see, not that perceptive. That had ceased to matter. . . . The girl has secrets and will not talk: dig them out and we'll see.

Their closeness to the truth terrified her, their knowledge of the basic relational needs of people, ler and human alike (after all, they were not all that different), shook her to her foundations, and their physical presence overpowered her. To her eyes, no matter how often she had seen them before, humans were harsh, angular, hairy creatures whose tempers were at best uncertain. She herself was almost to her full bodily growth, but they were all larger than she, taller, heavier. She imagined that the larger ones must weigh almost twostone. They were wild, primitive beings who, in her view, were not yet tamed, although the logical, factual part of her mind knew well enough that most of them thought of themselves as rather effete and overcivilized. And now she was in the very midst of them, completely in their power, separated from her own intricate and carefully structured environment. One step closer to the ancient and unforgiving wild, to the primal chaos, to the world, left long ago, of tooth and claw, sinew and strength.

Here, in the city, the tooth was covered and the claw was sheathed, but neither had been removed, nor had been the will that had animated them. So, in the end, they had finally tired of her and their little game, and politely, always politely, suggested that she take a little rest, that she refresh herself, in the box. The box! Everything they did in their world revolved around a box, as it was called in the slang of the day. The box was a simulator. A training device with a controlled environment. Some were crude and simple. Others were so fearfully complex they were fully capable of denying the evidence of one's senses. So did one have a job to learn? In the box! Bad habits and antisocial traits? In the box. Criminals? Eliminate them or put them in the box. And likewise with odd suspects who are obviously covering up something, who refuse for days to answer the most simple questions. In the box. Behavior changed by the classical methodology of the cult of behaviorism, orthodox as the dawn. They never questioned ends, and why should they when they had a means that worked so well and so consistently? In the box. They could transform by their simulator alchemy a misanthrope into a philanthropist, an artist into a salesman who won prizes, a satyr or nymphomaniac into a celibate philosopher, and an autistic child into a faith healer. Those who had never been able to cope were transformed into veritable paragons of efficiency. And for those who held to their silences, there was the remedy of total isolation.

They shot her from behind with a dart; that alone, in itself, filled her with a sense of evil: they used a weapon that left the hand! The dart contained a drug that paralyzed her but left her conscious. She felt a bee sting at the back of her neck. Then, nothing. She could neither move nor feel. This part of her memory was clear and bright. Then they had gently placed her onto a little wheeled cart and rolled her down a hall into some other room, a larger one, although she could see little of its details. Her eyes could see only in the direction they were pointed. She had trained peripheral vision, as did the others of her craft, but against the bland background even that could pick up little. She sensed, rather than saw, meters, dials, instruments, switchboards. The room possessed a different odor, one that suggested machinery, electricity, not people. Then they had undressed her and looked over her body, which, judging from their expressions, seemed to them to be underdeveloped sexually; smooth and subtle of contour, hairless save some almost-invisible fine down which was all over her, undeniably female. In the eyes of one she saw the distorted longings of the child molester, but the implied assault within their imaginations did not disturb her. She did not object to nudity per se, and as for their longings, she had given a bravado mental shrug: she had given away more than all of them could take.

And after that, after they had looked enough, they had carefully and tenderly placed her within some enclosure: from its smell she thought it was a machine, but with a human fear-scent veneered over it as well, a dark place that disturbed her. She heard them refer to it as a sensory deprivation unit. She heard some more talk as they set the machine up, and fitted her into its bowels, so that she could deduce what the machine was. The unit was a life-support system that maintained a constant temperature and controlled all the inputs and outputs of the body. And some extra things: it caused total anesthesia of the sensory and motor systems, and what functions it didn't control, it monitored. It could speed or slow her heartbeat. It created and maintained a sensory environment of exactly and precisely zero.

Her universe now. Dark, odorless, weightless, sensationless. She felt nothing, was a disembodied mind. If the absence of discomfort could be said to be comfortable, then it was comfortable. There was no sensation whatsoever. She could remember being placed in it, but afterward had come the darkness and the silence. An unknowable span of time had passed since then. Sometimes she thought that it had been only minutes or at best perhaps an hour or so. Other times, she felt weary and thought of years, of growing old, of reaching elderhood in the box, or else being prolonged as an adolescent-phase infertile ler forever, as the monitoring sensors either disregarded or suppressed the hormone chemistry of her reproductive system, which she knew to be different from the human. She suspected the machine thought she had some disorder and was trying to cure her! But the time. Minutes or years. She didn't know the difference anymore. The reality of the now expanded to enormous distances, gulfs she could not imagine.

So now she could not avoid the realization that in the end it had not mattered how effective or ineffective her passive defiance had been. She had been confident at first, although she admitted to some fright and self-concern; yet she must face the fact that, to this point, she was losing this one, and that she was facing a path with only one way to go, no exit, and no place in which to turn around.

At first, the box had been easy, almost pleasant. She couldn't believe this was a threat: after all, all it did was allow one to be lazy and to daydream, which people wanted to do anyway, but somehow never found the time. She had a number of open-ended practices which were primarily cerebral in nature, and which served admirably here, in the box. So at first she renewed her sense of defiance; it had served her well before she had been caught, and so it would serve her now. After her initial adjustments to the new environment had been made, she started out by spending her waking times playing the *Zan*, a game of large scope and interesting subtleties. At first she left all the virtuoso play to herself, her side, but later this seemed too easy, no matter how complex she made the play, so she began to elaborate and embroider the antagonist side as well, carrying both sides simultaneously. This had been some challenge, for she had played before primarily in the protagonist team role; in any event, it kept her occupied.

She also tried her hand at dramatization, making up or recalling tales she had heard before. This was more challenging, as the ler did not produce plays on the stage, but either read them or listened to a storyteller, the practice of which was considered one of the ler social graces. She admitted to a deficiency at the telling end, but she had always listened well, and now the habit initially served her well. They favored tragedy, borrowing freely from human sources and presenting them as they were, or else changing the names of all the characters to ler names and proceeding from there; they also made up dramas of their own according to a complicated set of storytelling rules, and these could occur in various cultural matrices. So it was that she made up and remembered, perfecting her powers of visualization. She recalled great dramas whose roots were openly acknowledged to be from the forerunners: *Trephetas and Casilda*, essentially a tale of lust thwarted by rigid social conventions. She liked that one, for it reminded her, at a certain remove, of a situation which applied somewhat to herself. She also recalled *Thurso*, with its violet-eyed female antagonist, which always made an audience of ler listeners gasp with horror; ler eyes were invariably lightly and subtly colored, definitive colors almost never being seen, such traits indicating a force of will which could not be borne without tragic consequence to all around the possessor. *Tamar Cauldwell* and *The Women of Point Sur* pleased her with their studied intricacies and soaring flights of emotion. There was a famous ler version of *Tamar*, changed somewhat in details, called *Tamvardir the Insibling*, which in some ways was an improvement over the original.

She moved from realistic, if highly emotional tragedies, to more fantastic dramas, *Ericord the Tyrant*, the scary *Siege of Kark*, and the weirdly beautiful *The King of Shent*. And then the pure ler dramas, some of which had been adapted from human legends and tales: *The Revenge of the Hifzer Vlandimlar*, *Hunsimber the Beast*, *Schaf Meth Vor*, better known perhaps as *Science and Revolution*, and *Damvidhlan, Baethshevban, and Hurthayyan*, the last of which she found herself recoiling from somewhat, as she tended now to identify herself with the victim Hurthayyan.

Being ler, she possessed almost total recall; therefore she could also replay at her leisure pleasurable experiences, moments of beauty or sweetness in her past life. She could also project daydreams, imagined and desired scenes about herself, in the future or the past. With the memory, she could remember far back, virtually to infancy, but back of that was a feared region in which the smoothly cycling lines of memory became tangled and confused, and further back knotted, and further, blurred. The infant did not remember the womb because it had not been awake. Now, here, in this dark place—this box, this sensory deprivation unit—the lines of time had once more become confused and blurred, and she sensed that another womb had been imposed upon her. The lines were uncertain. She slept. She dreamed.

Like the rest of the lermen, her memory had always been a resource to her, a close friend, a reference. She knew that the farther up the evolutionary ladder a creature had climbed, the more it projected itself into the awareness of time. People, the natural humans and the forced ler alike, had been a giant step forward in this dimension. Yet now and here in the unmeasurable and unknowable time of the box, her memory, from overuse, had come to resemble some ancient recording—full of the noises of boredom and weariness. Scratchy and worn. The fidelity of reproduction was slipping and random noise was gradually swamping coherences. Information theory and the brain. Memory in living creatures was not a static thing, fixed in specific sites, like some mechanical computer, but a dynamic, living, moving quantity, a flying body of abstraction moving through the billions of cells and synapses exactly as a bird in the medium of air, dependent on the motion to define it in its function. Holistic.

But it was also like a recording in this way as well: in replaying the good parts so often, she had allowed herself the habit of skipping to the best scenes. This was fine, but after so much use, the scenes, extracted more or less from the matrix of reference which had made them meaningful, had become progressively more shallow and, in the end, less good. Some of them had become almost tiresome. She would find herself saying as she reviewed them, "Yes, and so what?"

As for the daydreams, the imaginings, the fantasies, she had found that it had become steadily more dangerous to allow herself to do this. *Berlethon*, she called them in her own language, paradreams. Her dreams and paradreams were becoming stronger and steadily more clear, all the while her realities were growing weaker. As her memories of the real which had been were slowly sinking into a morass, a quagmire of noise, the projections were becoming more clear and even reasonable.

At first the projected paradreams had been like dreams; the individual scenes had been highly detailed, but the scenes had permutated one into another with disregard for the laws of causality and consequence. That, after all, was what distinguished them from realities. Now, however, in the box, it was the memories of the real which had become the anticausal phantoms with the illogical shifts, while the projections had become the logical ones, vibrant and electric. Reality had become faded and meaningless. In the normal environment dreams were the mind's algorithm for sorting and placing experiences in an orderly and accessible manner in the flying holistic patterns of memory. All well and good; but there was no provision made in the program of a living brain for a zero environment. So the process of filing and sorting went on unimpeded, using that which had already been placed as an arbitrary input, feeding on images which had already been sorted and placed, resorting and refiling. At each transfer the images lost both fidelity and coherence. At every transfer noise gained on coherent content.

From the first she had encouraged visions which had been erotic in content; in her own cultural reference as it applied to her own phase, adolescence, such activities, their recollections, and their projections, were neither considered reprehensible nor undesirable, but rather encouraged by all, part of growing up. Affairs, trysts, meetings, rendezvous of variable duration, and the gatherings, where participation was not limited to a single pair, were all part of an elaborate process that instructed one in care for one's fellow creatures, intimacy, consideration. Knowledge came later; it was important to learn to relate with others and to learn to tolerate others, in view of the conditions which would come with parent phase.

So she had naturally thought of these adventures; they were pleasurable in a direct bodily manner and helped greatly to pass the time. But now, of course, they had become the worst offenders against the rule of reality. They ran away with her. In these, so great had become the confusion that she had been forced to invent an elaborate mental procedure to segregate the real and the unreal, a complication that added further waves of its own, further elaborations. Just as there was no ultimate end to the definition of meaning, and no final fraction of a transcendental number, so there was no real limit to the process of elaboration. None whatsoever. And so now she was in very deep water, being carried away from the shore by the undertow at an alarming and increasing rate. Had there ever been a shore? Had there ever been such a thing as a shore? The very projections that in the beginning of her dark journey had helped save her mind, where a lesser one would have broken, were now the very elements contaminating it.

The forerunners who had remanded her to this place and into the box knew little or nothing. They certainly did not know who she was, or else she suspected they would not have been so polite. They would not then have waited for the box to work its terrible magic on her. No, more direct methods would have been used. But their questions had reassured her of that; that they knew nothing. They did not know the right questions to ask. But they were suspicious, and of more than just the incident of the Museum. Somewhere there were other things that bothered them; there had been noises in the night, and they knew not the source, nor why. Or had it been just the settling of the house, the wind in the trees, a natural event? Obviously she had some connection with the vandalism in the Museum; at the least, she appeared to be the only suspect they had. And why those particular devices? But those questions did not bother her; she expected them. At another point, however, they had pursued other topics. For example, they had asked, quite casually, who were the ler players of the game *Zan*? What was the significance of the Game? Were the players free of other obligations, save self-support? Apparently they had several lines of inquiry going, and since she had been close to hand, they had tried a few at her. She had felt chill dread at these questions, and hoped that her projected ignorance had convinced them. Ah, indeed there was a rich area in herself for them to mine. They were closer to it than they realized; and not to solving little vandalisms, either. It was partially fortune that they did not press her there. But it disturbed her, even now. The other players needed to know this line of inquiry, the Shadow needed to know . . . and there was no way for her to tell anyone. For once set in motion, the forerunners would not ever come to a complete problem halt until they had followed every line out. Yes, they were great completers, but after all that was the true meaning of intelligence: following through. She was ler, but she had no contempt for humans. To the contrary.

Her mind wandered. After a fashion, they had been kind enough with her. They did not believe they were causing her particular harm by placing her in this sensory deprivation unit. Almost casually, yet they had no idea of the effects of it on her. Perhaps among their own kind they were pleasant enough persons. At home, or in some warm tavern, with friends, or lovers. She had heard that they did not have lovers, at least openly. And did they have taverns? She now realized that for all her previous trips outside she knew in actuality very little about how they lived, what their dreams were.

So as the interrogation had continued, she had begun to see into the basic surface smoothness of her interrogators, just as a glassy surface of water meant deeper channels; there were things they wanted to know, they had her, and she knew. Indeed did she know. And that, no matter what the cost, not a word of it could be told. The worth of it was simply too high: it was easily worth *perzhan**, one hundred and ninety-six, of her lives. It really was not even worth arguing about, even with herself, even in the box. However it went. She thought, with a certain irony, that the people who talked the most about sacrifice were always the ones who knew they would never have to make that decision. She did not particularly worry about pain, for she knew from the box that they had more sophisticated methodology at their disposal, once they had an idea who she was. That was more important than the business at the Museum. And once put into use, she was sure that these methods would leave more permanent scars on her, figuratively, than flesh would hold: they would be inside. So she kept the silence.

---

* One times fourteen to the second power. Ler use a fourteen-base number system.

At times like this, when she had to reaffirm basic quantities to herself, she allowed herself the luxury of recalling the secret, as she had come to call it. It was her only remaining source of comfort, but she only allowed herself to recall it in full when her mind felt clear, for she had no way of knowing if she was talking or not. She took great comfort in seeing how successful it would be, now that it was almost complete, how much it meant for all the people. Just a few more years. She saw the part she had played in it, more minor than it should have been, but who after all could have foreseen the exact circumstances, ridiculous as they were, and who could argue intelligently against the Great Rule, even though somewhat disadvantaged by it? But what of that? She had used the traditions herself back against the problem, and aided by a rare stroke of good fortune, had come close to regaining her place, which should have been hers by right, unquestioned. She had almost made it back . . . and now, in the box in an alien city, it pained her to know, as she had known all along, that she was not to make the contribution she knew she was capable of. They had planned things to a nicety, the elders who had guided it from the Beginning, but reality had slipped them a cruel twist. They could not have foreseen this situation, with its ironies of the best and the worst misplaced. She thought bravely, *But I have kept the faith where no one else was ever tried.* Of course, it wasn't consolation. She recalled the drama *Damvidhlan, Baethshevban, and Hurthayyan** again. Yes, she was sure of it; the plight and fate of Hurthayyan had indeed analogously applied to her, to include a match for the identity of *Hofklandor* Damvidhlan. But who or what did Baethshevban equate with? She could not be entirely certain, for it did not match a person, but rather a diffuse something, an emotion from many directed to one. And coveted, now seized. *Zakhvath-elosi.*

She could easily recall the image in her memory of the human interrogator, and his superior. The interrogator had been as bland and featureless as his surroundings, distinctly unremarkable, but the superior had been another matter; he had been tall and rather bony, and his face was angular enough to deserve the term "hatchet-faced" without further

---

* The drama referred to was a ler adaptation of the tale of *David and Bathsheba*, with the names changed to ler names. Hurthayyan was Uriah the Hittite. She could from this identification find the equal of David/Damvidhlan, but in her case, Bathsheba was not a person but rather a sense of regard or admiration.

explanation. His ears protruded after the fashion of jug handles and his jaw was long and equine. His hair was sandy-colored with reddish over-tones, cut brushy short and springing out in odd little tufts at unex-pected places. In her eyes, more accustomed to the smoother and softer lines of the ler face (which correspondingly appeared childish in the human frame of reference), he had been primitive, raw, rough-cut, homely, in fact, as an oak post. But she remembered him with dread and fear, homely as he had been, for she knew that when they came back for her, after they judged she had had enough time in the box, he'd come with them and she'd talk to him in the mode of intimacy, just to have contact with someone, some stimulus. Citizen Eykor, they had called him. She would start talking and would not be able to stop. Something would slip in her relief and the tale would start, and it would never end. She suspected she could not survive the box; she *knew* she couldn't keep the silence if they took her out and started questioning her again. A spasm of fear passed through her, gripping her momentarily; perhaps she would love him, just for talking to her after the box. Yes, that was possible. He would reassure her, probably reaching to touch her shoul-der, not realizing the overtly sexual connotations of the gesture in her reference . . . and this could not be, must not be; it must not even be al-lowed to approach the potential to be. There was nothing she could share with Citizen Eykor, and less she could allow herself to say to him.

They must not know, not one word of it, she thought. The wave had felt the first intimations of the bottom underfoot and was beginning to steepen, after a fetch of miles and years. Centuries, really, so long had it been in motion. Yes. Let it happen in its time. Then it won't matter what they know; in fact, we could even drop them off a copy of the Histo-ries; let them try to duplicate it and follow them into the night. Then it won't matter. But now? It would neither be fitting nor sufficient for her to return, broken, to the Mountain of Madness, the Holy Place, and say, to the Shadow, "I held out as long as I could, but I broke in the end. Yes, I spoke of it, and they know. They will be coming tomorrow or the next day, they will take it for themselves, and for us it will be gone forever." *And with our low birth rate and unstable genes we will be the wards of the forerunners forever, tied to old Earth with them. Intolerable.*

She stopped that line of thought, for it led to hard choices. Choices whose solutions were all too obvious. She returned once more to the present. The zero noplace nowhen, a universe in which she was the sole inhabitant. She and her memory. She was quite nude, but she could no longer perceive any sensation whatsoever; what little the box had left

her had quickly disappeared, dropped as recurring items of no consequence by her own mind, just as one ceased to hear a familiar clock, and
began to wonder if it still ran. Hard to catch even in normal circumstances, in the box these reports from oneself simply vanished, leaving
no ripples to mark the spot where they had gone under. She returned
to her nudity, tried to sense it. In some way. She couldn't. There was no
body there! She thought in anger, *I may not be able to feel it now, but I
can remember it. You can't take that away from me. It's my body and it's
my mind, you* hifzer dranloons*! She returned. Nude, yes, it was pleasant to be clothes-less, with someone exciting . . . something more than
just pleasant, a thrill. With a body-friend, a lover. Much better a
deeplover. As an adolescent ler, she did not perceive a rigid line of distinction between friends and lovers. Sex with friends of the opposite sex
was just part of the relationship. However, she did differentiate between
sex and affection. They might complement one another, or reinforce
one another, in a relationship, but in the matter of degrees of each they
operated independent of one another. Why not? One expressed one
quantity, and the other something entirely different. Where a specific
person was involved, one perceived degrees of intimacy, of both personal functions, elaborated by certain cultural reinforcements—for example, as the use of parts of one's name with persons with whom one
had such a relationship. The definitions were both complex and dynamic, possessing many variables simultaneously, and so one spent
much of one's adolescence learning the definitions. Many grew restive
and questioned the elaborate distinctions, the subtlety, the hedging. But
she knew very well what the use of it portended. Relationships among
elders were highly structured, and so after the Braid years one remembered the definitions of one's youth, and used an analog of them to
enter the elder custom.

It was as a spectrum of many colors, each shading into the next, and
no line anywhere which could be said to cause a definite distinction. It
was, in fact, a smooth continuum which went from childish games in
the woods to couples who lived together in emotional entanglements so
interpenetrating that they lay somewhere along the very borders of sanity. *I have been there. Having been to the place, with him, where the real
and the unreal are segregated. I have no respect for those who imagine that
the distinction is a casual one.* Him. Was all; she had long since ceased to
think of him-her-last as a name. One simply disregarded it. There had

* Literally, "illegitimate trash"; *loonh* is an intensifier.

been two presences in the world. Herself and him. She felt a sudden constriction somewhere indefinable in her chest, gone before she could be sure if she had felt it at all. Whisked away by the box. She thought she could detect a trace of moisture in her eyes, open in the darkness. But the sensations were gone. Had they ever been?

Nude. Yes, that. She returned to the memory, a composite of many experiences, from which she could select the specific image she wanted. The sharp thrill of slipping out of her light summer *pleth**, pulling it over her head, when their relationship had been new, turning to him smiling. Or awaking softly in the night, knowing warm breath along her neck, feeling warmth along her flank, weight . . . a wisp of memory drifted by; they had gone together down to a place they had made deep in the forests of the northeast reservation, a place where he had . . . what? It had slipped away, not forgotten, but mislaid, tangled in a thousand phantom alternatives, real and unreal, thrown up by her mind, running free. She made an effort of will: yes, down in the woods, far to the northeast, in a part of the reservation where hardly anyone made their home. This memory was a recent one, the summer just past, early in the season; the sensations came back, now vividly, now vague and evanescent, threatening to vanish in the next instant. She held on to them by a great effort of will. The rich odors of the damp forest earth, vines, and green leaves, the warm air heavy with the scent of flowers; the sunlight played in the shadows of the new foliage, the wind was in the crowns of the trees, and, listening carefully, one could hear the sound of running water. Together they had slipped their light summer pleths off over their heads, feeling the sudden rush of body feeling at the touch of cooler air, and the quick flash of goose-pimples which had disappeared as fast as it had come. He had looked deeply at her body, and she at his; he was thin, pale, and smooth, worked all over with a delicate tracery of muscle and sinew. They had laughed, and she had made him chase her running through the trees and vines and tangles, the flower scent strong in the air. The memory steadied, held firm, ran true.

There was a small treehouse, with a sun-warmed platform all around it, and when they had both climbed the rope ladder leading up to the platform, she had let him catch her and wrestle her to the warm wood:

* An "overshirt." This was an ankle-length garment superficially resembling a long shirt, but whose neck opening never extended down past the navel. A garment of general use.

touching and kissing each other lightly, childishly, like making leafprints in the fall. And then a sudden, hard embrace, and she had relaxed back on the rough wood, melting, heart pounding . . . was it pounding now?

She couldn't be sure, feeling the memory slip a little. Had the body-now responded to the memory? Had replaying it caused even a small sympathetic echo? Had indeed her heartbeat just now sped up, before the box could respond and damp it down again? She lost the image momentarily. Had it ever really happened? She went back, straining, and grasped the thread at the point she had left off, and remembered; just like it was happening now, she felt the wild surge of runaway loosed emotions, the whispers of skin on skin, the wet shoulder-kisses, the sudden warmths and hot flashes, little peaks of anticipation and the first touch *there;* then an awkward moment, followed by oneness. In the now she felt herself moving with the memory, flowing, an energy building within her greater than the box, and then she lost it, the sequence slipped away from her and swirled away quickly in the currents of her mind, fading into other erotic images, of lovers she had had, and paradreams of lovers she would like to have had. She did not know if these latter were real of imaginary. Now they were rock-hard and clear, now insubstantial and changeable as smoke, fading into other lineaments. Other images intruded as well; him again, afterward. She had let her mind go blank and had been idly following the motion of a leaf above, seen over his shoulder, and marveling at how the eye could follow and track such random motion, a leaf high in the sunlight, the strong light making it translucent and showing the pattern of veins inside.

It whipped away, pushed and pulled by the press of other images, real and unreal. Yes, that one: once in an orchard, a walled garden, the Krudhen's. There had been a rough wall, stone, unmortared, higher than their heads, and they had, after the invitations of each other's eyes, casually stepped around into the garden, not even bothering to remove their overshirts, but pulling them up about their waists and joining their bodies while leaning against the rough, bumpy surface of the wall. Some people had passed meanwhile along the path outside the wall, but they knew that the passersby did not care, even if they had noticed anything. It was doubtful they did, for they had been subtle and quiet, making a game of it. That had not been him, but another, earlier, when she had been younger, and more reckless. . . . That one vanished, replaced by another: this boy dark-haired and dark-skinned as herself. They had been swimming in the river, the muddy Hvarrif, the rich summer water leaving a sweet summer scent on their skins as they sat on the banks in the sun and air-dried. He had been so shy and tentative, younger than herself, touching her thigh accidentally, brushing against her. Sudden cool touch of skin, warmth beneath; the moment became expectant, tense, the exterior details of the instant overwhelming in their clarity. Everything registered, the sun, the still air, the heat, the clangor of the July-flies in the trees, and she had reached for the younger boy, smiling. . . .

And it vanished, leaving behind the bitter little backlash that revealed its true nature, that particular image; it had been a paradream, a projection, a hope, a fantasy, not real. She didn't know if she had imagined it earlier, or had made it up in the box. It didn't matter. It wasn't real. She savored the memory of an unreal memory and smiled mentally to herself; knowing herself as well as she did, she knew why the last one had not been real, although the one by the wall in the orchard had been. She had never been so aloof and teasing, nor had her body-friends and lovers been so innocent or shy. That was a refinement she had added herself, internally, to satisfy some deeper fantasy. Unreal, unreal. She experienced a weird emotion composed of angry chagrin and wistful sadness. There would be no more embraces by the orchard wall, no more treehouses, even no more dreams of quiet seductions along the Hvarrif banks.

That last incident broke the chain of emotional and erotic memories. She felt as if she had been on tiptoe, straining. She tried to flex her leg. No good. She couldn't feel it. With no distraction, she began to drift back from the sense of sexual anticipation she had been on, aimless, frustrated. Regretfully. She had greatly enjoyed the few moments she had had in her life, particularly the last ten years, of the adolescent phase. *And there would have been ten more of them, but for this,* she caught herself thinking. There had been fewer such events for her than for most ler girls, for during all the time, she had been busy at many other things, too serious, too bound up in the Great Work. *Now,* she thought. *Now it is time to make that decision. Time to commit oneself, time to end hesitating, time to cease waiting for a rescue that will never come because they will never know where I am. I'm getting lost in my own memory; it is a home no longer, but a labyrinth with neither way out nor way in.*

She approached the point she had been dreading; and now she was at it. Earlier, she had imagined what it would be like when she faced it: a mental image of a major forking in the path, a most remarkable intersection, a singular location at which choice, with all its terrors, was exercised. Perhaps symbolically, within this image, there would also be emblems of arresting significance: flashing lights, great illuminated signboards. Something resembling the forerunner motorways. But now that she was actually at the place, she saw with her imagination that the reality was nothing like that at all; her mind provided a symbolic image which fit better: not an intersection at all. The image was of a broad smooth road on level ground in undifferentiated country. There was not a landmark, not a reference, not even a post along the side of the road to mark the point. She was, she realized with a wistful sense of resignation, already past it and the choice had been made long ago. *The solution was obvious.* And in the middle distances, the road and the surrounding country alike ended, not with a change of conditions, but in an undefined yet total foggy nothingness. She had been on this path a long time; her life led here.

I will not speak of it, I will not talk with them, I will not even wait for them to come for me again. I am . . . She groped frantically, trying to find the name she had mislaid, burying it under tons of hopelessly tangled data, real and unreal. There were hundreds of names, and she couldn't decide which was hers; an impossible situation. Yes, apples. Something about apples. And this almost-recognition set off another train of memories and associations: apples. She could feel vividly the hard firm flesh of an apple, crisp, cool; biting the fruit, the juice had been sweet and acid on her lips. An autumn sunset, smoky orange somewhere, somewhen . . . she had been the chief player, the Center, and her team had won. And her opponent. The opponent had no identity, it was blanked into a dark shadow, a fog, a presence whose outlines gave no clue to its identity, but at the same time, she knew she could rip the curtain aside and see her antagonist in full open brightness; she could, but she recoiled from it, for she knew her opponent, in truth, better than she knew any other person, ler or forerunner, on Earth. Here an odd chuckling thought intruded, flashing by almost before she could catch it: *On Earth or off it. Why was that significant?* But before she could pursue it further, her wildly processing mind threw out another image: *And there was metal, wood, artifice, there was a sense of a construct all around her, a sense of being-inside, a great, powerful machine, a device, a Daimon, perhaps. Yet neither machine nor Daimon, but something greater and different than either, something whose operation closely paralleled life rather than mechanics or electronics.* Vanished, replaced: and once she had made bread at home with her insibling, and the warm air had been filled with the scent of dough and yeast. Another: Her first sexual experience, the first clumsy, awkward embraces (her partner had been as ignorant as she); they had felt like younger children trying to assemble some intricate toy, neither knowing where to begin nor imagining the results, but faithfully believing that if they could somehow accomplish it, they were sure to be astounded and amazed. Strange, vivid, sharply etched in her mind. And indeed they had been. *We had breathed so hard, so hotly upon each other's shoulders.* A sensation like climbing a steepening hill, ever harder, then over the top by surprise and a swift ballistic ride down, spinning, slowing. The odd, salty taste of another's mouth, the oily-sharp scent of sun-warmed skin.

Stop! She shouted into nothing, the furry all-embracing darkness that surrounded her. She could almost fleetingly feel her lips trying to verbalize the word in her own speech: *muduraile!* But the half-sensation was gone instantly, as in a nightmare when one tries to call for help, or to cry out to break the slow-motion spell, and nothing came out but incoherent, clotted throaty sounds. Croaks and gurgles. She returned to the dark. *Very well, then.* She formed letters of fire in the dark, sending them forth, changing their colors as they flew away into the night. The letters faded, leaving green afterimages which pervolved into an iridescent violet. She made the triple negative: *Dheni, dheno, dhena.* No, more no, most no. Her mind slowly responded to her Herculean efforts to bring it under control, giving in, tossing out one last image weakly: Metal, a machine, immense shifting fields of power. Metal, plastic, cloth, leather, wood. She almost had it, she could operate it and feel the control and the mastery, it had almost been hers, so close . . . and the Game. And the image was gone.

She thought clearly. She had always had, all along, one escape. But it was a drastic, irrevocable one. With total recall, the ler mind had by compensation also gained the ability to trueforget, erase data, remove it. The one balanced the other. It was something rather more than forgetting in the old sense, as the forerunners referred to it. That, in truth, was merely mislaying data. But autoforgetting was erasure. It was easy and simple to start the process—one knew instinctively how to do that, like knowing how to imagine: it was so easy and natural that one had to teach the growing child to attend to reality. But that referred only to starting the process of auto-forgetting. Stopping it was only for the experienced and the learned, enormously difficult. One could master that only after one had reached deep into elder phase, the end of one's third span*. Elders, she had heard, could do partials, forget certain sections of their memories, condense and resymbolize, making room for more raw experience . . . but she was not an elder; she was *didhosi*, adolescent, she had just celebrated her twentieth birthday this past summer. And so for her it could be only everything or nothing. She had heard that it was easy, fearless, painless. Like going to sleep. That one simply picked some point in any valid memory and undid the image, like picking a thread out of a weave: it then unraveled.

And then the ego, the persona, would be gone, vanished, as if it had never been, save for the existential traces left behind on the lives of others, on the enduring physical pieces of the world. Yes, the ego would be gone, but the body would live on, protected by its autonomic responses. The protection of secrets had not been the intent of autoforgetting, but it was of a fact one of its by-products. An ultimate protection. And afterward, her human interrogators would return and discover that all they had was an infant in a twenty-year-old's body. Hopefully, not knowing what to do with such a one, they would then return her to the people, where she would be cared for properly, washed, fed, and carefully raised to a functional persona again in the ten years remaining before she would become fertile, adult. So by then she would be conscious again, functional, a person able to breed, to be woven, to carry on the next generation as was the obligation of everyone. She felt a small pleasure in the midst of fear. And in the clear knowledge of what she had to do, there was also a confusion. She thought hard, bearing down on it. *And I will come again in this body, this sweet flesh which has given me and others so much pleasure. . . . I? No, not I, I know that. It will not be me that inhabits this skin. No, another, one who does not exist now and who will not be borne of Tlanh and Srith. She will have another name. Not mine. I take my name with me into whatever place forgetties go. Yes, another. She will be childish and absentminded, but she will function; knowing what she is, the others will love her and help her. By the time the children weave, she will be virtually complete.*

She laughed to herself in her mind, wryly, suddenly seeing it clearly, without apprehension. *Me, a forgetty. One who has autoforgotten:* Lel Ankrenamosi. She had thought in the past of autoforgetting with dread

---

* Span is a period of twenty-four years. Spans (age, pure time) and phases (body development) were not synchronized, but their interplay determined key events in one's life. Adolescents twenty-four to thirty were considered "provisional adults," even though yet adolescent in body, infertile.

and fear, feeling something unclean and wretched about being a for-getty. But there was something worse, a whole universe of somethings-worse. She balanced her distaste of the condition against what in her weakness she could reveal and therefore cause. Hobson's choice it might have been, but it was still clear: *I will be true to my oaths. Now!*

Without hesitation, she reached deep in her mind, to the very key-stone of her being, her *Klanh* role, the pivot point of all that she knew, had lived. She strained, reaching, seeking the unraveling-place deep within the complex of mnemonic tangles, found it, a knot, a nexus, pulled, felt it loosen, and unhooked it. There was a sharp, piercing pain, an acute spike of intense energy, unbearable, over before it had really began. She instantly forgot that it had hurt. Stunned and now not know-ing why, she reached again for the particular memory, which had been the time of her initiation. Initiation into what? She couldn't remember. It was gone. There were only odd little pieces left, and they were fad-ing. At the center of her mind there was an expanding blank void of un-knowledge; almost like what they called an image-reversed Game, in which one played absences, not presences. A void, expanding. Already she had to ask, most curiously, *What Game? What had been the Game?* It had been important to her, once. A puzzle, and something crucial was missing, the piece which could explain this odd lapse of memory. What was it? She stopped trying to remember and began to work on logic, working from the outside, filling in the center, and thus to recapture what it should have been. She could do it, but she found that as she did, the eradication process seemed to work faster than she could fill it back in; it was eroding her memory faster than she could fill it in at maxi-mum effort. *Useless to fight it; hopeless.* Her awareness had been like a sphere, filled from the center, always expanding outward into the empti-ness of ignorance and not-knowing, ordering. But she sensed now that she was different from everyone else in the world: she had an emptiness inside the sphere as well. And the void inside was growing, forcing her awareness first into a hollow ball, then a toroidal shape. *There's no stop-ping it now,* she thought; *I know what is doing this, but I no longer know how to start it.* After a moment, she added, wryly, *And I damn sure can't stop it.*

She had no knowledge concerning how long the process would re-quire to erase her mind. Nobody knew. Or if they did, they did not speak. Forgetties did not remember that they had forgotten. She felt tense, internally, and did not know why. Now she relaxed, letting the process play over awareness, like summer sunlight over one's bare body, something from long ago. *Now I will remember everything I can; all the sweet moments of my life.* She scanned quickly through what remained of her memories, noting what was there, the good and the bad, the pleasant and the unpleasant. There was much of both; she had had her moments, but she had also known bitter disappointments, cruel reverses which had not been her fault, but existential, circumstantial. But not accident. She settled for a sample: Name fourteen* of the most wonderful things that had happened to you. That was easy. Then, one at a time, she began to relive each of them through the magic of total recall, reseeing, reknowing, rediscovering. Under them, though, she sensed the presence of something which had not been there before: a growing void of darkness, part of her, yet not part of her either. She could not remember now why this curious condition existed. She would have to speak to someone about it.

Mornings were nicer. She had always loved the morning-time, of them all, she would always be the first of the children to wake up, seeing the firstlight turning the translucent panes of the windows of the *yos* deep violet. She would untangle herself from the others, for in cooler weather they all slept in a pile for warmth, and would then climb down out of the children's compartment, into the hearthroom. There had been four of them. Two boys, two girls. An ideal ler Braidschildren. But somehow something was wrong, there; she could no longer recall why. Now the hearthroom would be dim and dark, the hearthfire ashes dead or almost so. In her nightshift she would tiptoe barefooted through the *yos*, their home, and pass through the double entryway, pushing the doorflaps aside as she went. She would step gingerly out on the landing. The air would be cool, even in summer, and would bite at her skin through the thin nightshift, the skin beneath still sleep-warm and child-fragrant. This memory: it was winter and there was frost on the ground. Crystals of frost-heave at the bare patch by the creek. The creek by the house muttered quietly to itself, its sounds clean, precise, and clipped. The speech-of-winter. It always sounded like that in winter. In summertime its voice was rounder, looser, more flowing. She imagined that it spoke a language. No, someone had told her that. Recently. Who had it been? But the creek spoke: a running commentary on the nature of things, ground-water state, humus, moles, earthworms, new-fallen leaves of the season releasing their nutrient material to add to the rich forest soil. A sense of almost-freezing. The things water knew. She looked up.

---

* This would have the same significance as ten to a decimal user.

Farther down the creek she could make out the dim shape of the neighboring *yos* through the winter-bare brush, briars, and vine-tangles. In summer, it would have been completely hidden. And farther on, visible through a gap in the trees, was the lake, still and cold and deep blue in this early light.

She scanned again, sensing that she was losing ground more quickly than she had imagined she would. *No time for fourteen. Have time for one more replay. So let it be with him. That one will I hold, even to the end. Let it be last, and then nothingness. Even if now it is just a figment of my memory, never to be again.* Suddenly, the phantoms were gone.

The process continued inexorably, returning her mind to its entropic ground state, but as it moved, it caused ripples of pseudoknowledge to form in the central void, a logiclike action that seemed to her to be sudden flashes of insight. These momentary new forms were diverse as their origins: some were obviously invalid, others incomprehensible and alien. And some had the ring of truth. She did not know how she knew this. These last she tried to hold on to. One in particular, a towering edifice, permutating wildly. For an instant, she saw: and relief flooded through her, for she had seen the future. No fantasy, no paradream, no pseudoknowledge. Real. And that future was both true and good: There would be sorrows, caused by the very thing she had just done, but not her fault, her blame, but another's. And they would succeed in the Great Work. It would be. She saw and was happy, but she did not understand, nor did she know why the thought had pleased her. Then it was gone. And also gone was the memory that something had pleased her.

She fixed on his image. Him. Her deepest. Cool and distant at first, there had been something about him which she had not liked . . . or disapproved of. She couldn't remember. It had soon ceased to matter. And then she had discovered that he could do something she did, something . . . that was gone too. No matter. The memory of him as he had been was clear and uncluttered. If anything, the clarity of the image had been increased by the removal of the background in which they had met, and the growth of the emotional tangle which had sprung up between them, and soon tied them together. She could see him clearly: slender, wiry, almost delicate; but strong and quick. Precise movements, no wasted motions or mannerisms. A little younger than herself, but by less than a year. His hair, cut in the relaxed bowl cut common to all adolescents, was much lighter in color than hers. In a distant way, he reminded her of . . . whom? A younger child, related to her, but she couldn't remember whom. Thin, precise facial lines; tense, but not overbearing. No, not that. He had been the most tender of creatures. She knew.

She sank deeper into the memory, feeling in it a wholesome refuge from a growing dark emptiness outside it. Everything beyond this memory seemed dim, obscure, fading. That was her spatial orientation. In time, it was no better: it began with a blank and ended with one. Now she could not remember anything except the last time they had been together.

They had gone down eastward into the deep woods, in the autumn, recently. To their own secret place they had built, a treehouse. It had grown too intense between them, and they did not want others (or were afraid of them?) It had been their last time, just before she had somehow arrived in this nonplace. They had been lovers, more than that, they had touched and kissed each other's bodies, clasped one another closely with their limbs. She thought she felt a pain in her heart, wetness in her eyes. Were they real? Something oppressive was preventing her from feeling what she knew she must feel. *All gone soon. Was real? Will hold this until it is all gone. So good then. Did it in a beam of sunlight, we did. Thought my heart would burst.* She fell utterly into the memory, letting it take her, merging with the recent past, dimly sensing that somewhere she possessed a now-body which was at last beginning to respond to the then-body, as the difference between the two evaporated to her consciousness, the strength of the impulse now so strong that it was beginning to override whatever it was that had prevented her before. *It had not been designed for this.* Felt the yearning take her; she let it flow, unresisting, the undertow of the intense single-mindedness of desire, and the memory took over; in the now, in the box, she responded as one with it, synchronized with the memory, reaching, reaching, one last fractional effort and *now* the focus passed through her and for one single burning instant everything was crystal clear, gestalten, the sum of the universe and all its parts, playing over her, fire and light. She flew. Body centered, her hands wielded power. Then there was no desire, no need. She had one last thought in coherent forms, in wordlike concepts, then the words fell away. She had lost that. There were only pictorial images: She had a vision. *As from outside herself, she saw herself floating in space, looking back at her. The figure met her gaze, looking down on her from slightly above; it was wearing her own special pleth, the one to be used only for high ceremonies, with an abstract design embroidered down the front panel, odd little dots arranged in a mysterious but sensible pattern. The figure was barefoot. The sleeves dropped loosely halfway between elbow and wrist. All around outside the figure a bluish space seemed to enclose her, a cruciform shape but with an additional arm to the front and the back, precisely delineated, and everywhere with ninety-degree angles. Made up of eight cubes. The figure had extended its arms into the cubical spaces by the shoulders. And behind it, dimly in the background, there was something else, a curved screen, a large panel, immense, its true size distorted by perspective. She could not tell how far away it was. Patterns similar to the design on the pleth, but infinitely more involuted and complex, filed the screen, living, moving, changing in a way that wrenched at her mind. The girl was herself, that she knew. And now, the self she watched, who had been gazing sorrowfully back at her, turned her head slowly to the right, as if to look back just once at the design in the background. The face turned away. The pattern stopped moving, and a deadly stillness filled her mind. The vision was now lifeless, fixed forever. It lost contrast, then color, then winked out. There was only darkness absolute.*

She let it go, knowing almost nothing now. She had seen, but she had not understood. She felt fatigue, exhaustion, but completed, satisfied. She was sleepy. She had no more desires, no needs. The darkness was close, but she did not fear it; it was a friend, something she had called for. She had now forgotten a lot, and there were no more confusing images. Only some random percolating fragments. She ignored them. She had no interest in those fragments at all. She was sleepier than she had ever known, heavy, sinking. It was like swimming in a shallow summer pond at night, under an overcast sky. The warmth waited. All she had to do was kick off and flow. It was so easy. There was no longer any time, no more duration. Now that was gone, too. She was free. The universe collapsed to a point, one point, undimensional. She no longer knew who she had been. There was no past, there was nothing, and what fragments remained seemed to make little difference either way.

Either way.

Either.

Clane Oeschone, medical technician of the fourth grade, abbreviated MT4, had been working his first midnight shift of the new cycle in the Nondestructive Evaluation Facility appended to Building 8905; this was a new assignment for him, one which could be regarded as a tentative promotion. But so far his assigned duties had been absurdly simple: he was merely to attend to certain laboratory equipment, which appeared to be various Instructional Environment Enclosures. His responsibilities were limited and clearly specified, befitting to a technician of the fourth grade, although rather more than what might have been expected of the ordinary fourth. Indeed, as Oeschone thought. There was, after all, something to the acceptance of a programmed name. He had casually forgotten his old name. That person no longer existed. So one accepted, and became a cut above the average earner. It opened the doors to special assignments, and in his own case, out of the Sectional Palliatory.

However it had come to pass, his present task was simplicity itself: all he had to do was monitor the manual override panel, be alert for alarms, and tend the recording instruments, changing the paper as required, adjusting the current flow to the electrostatic needles as indicated by technical orders, and other related functions. Oeschone had received a thorough briefing on his duties here in 8905 from the evening-shift technician, including a description of patterns to watch for on the multi-encephalograph, normal patterns as well as some abnormal ones. He also had, close to hand for reference, an operating manual with hundreds of conditions and responses listed, which he was also at liberty to use. He had glanced through it; it was a heavy tome of several hundred pages. To be absolutely candid, he had not memorized all that he had seen therein; but he had noted the section dealing with emergency procedures, particularly those pages dealing with specific patterns on the graph paper: these conditions called for the standby medtech. Those called for the duty medic.

Oeschone glanced idly at the machine. It was the only one in the room he had been assigned to. Before him, needles scratched with a faint but annoyingly repetitious sound, regular as clockwork. The paper was fixed on a huge drum easy of access. It passed under the needles, and thence to an equally bulky collection reel. Oeschone made a gesture of attentiveness to the markings being made on the graph paper, although he was quick to admit privately to himself that of the data they were recording, he could interpret only the most simple and primitive portion. However his limitations, the knowledge of them did not disturb him, for Oeschone was a modest man, sure now of his career progress to come. He had no burning ambitions which could be vitalized in his day-to-day routines. He also knew that it never counted what one actually did, but rather how it was perceived. And here, a programmed name was a coin that spent well.

He bent and looked more closely, trying to see if he could read this one. He looked again; the patterns on the paper moving beneath the needles were by no means standard curves. He estimated that he could at least determine that the subject was conscious, but it appeared to be an extremely relaxed state of consciousness, almost an Alpha wave pattern. But not quite. He looked again. Yes, it was clear; he understood. He could read it: it was conscious, but there was a strong phi factor. That was one he had learned. It indicated hallucinations. Momentary, not yet of the obsessive variety. Oeschone felt uneasy, and consulted his operating instructions just to be certain. After a time, after reading the text and consulting the graph again, he relaxed. No action was called for. Abnormal, but not out of tolerances. He returned to his chair and settled himself comfortably.

So it was hallucinating, was it? Well, that was nothing to him. He did catch himself wondering briefly, without particular concern, why this one, whoever it was, had been put in the box, obviously on isolation. But after all, there was simply no telling, no telling at all. Isolation . . . Oeschone looked away from the box. This was an easy shift; nothing to it.

Even hallucinating as it obviously was, that one in the box could last for days more, weeks, before the symptoms became serious, or one of the alarms went off, and the medtech came to break open the box, carefully, of course, taking all the notes, warnings, cautions, and expansions of the operating manual in mind. But it was always the same whenever they opened up an isolation box: they invariably found an emotional beggar who would say anything, reveal any secret, no matter how trivial, just for an instant of personal contact. It was the ultimate fear, the fear of having to face the inescapable evidence of one's unique loneliness, and they had exploited it further than any previous ruling order had exploited any fear. It was physically painless and left no marks. Outside. And one who had been in the box was completely trustworthy, perhaps more so than the higher grades, if rather meek. Oeschone had heard tales . . . that after isolation, many would beg for a little light torture, just for the stimulus. For reality, however degrading.

Pitiful, such persons. Why did they allow themselves to came to such a sorry pass? Oeschone was certain that he did not know. Or if he did, he did not want to. It all worked the same in the end. But they knew the rules, they did, the order and the consequences. And after they had done whatever it was such people did, it all ended up the same way: in the box. Oeschone looked at the box. A dark gray structure somewhat higher than his height, occupying the end of the room, large enough to be a small jitney bus, almost. Silent, motionless, clean, powerful. Oeschone turned and went to his chair, sat. He pulled the narrative scanner on its telescoping mountings toward him, turned it on. He did not look back to the isolator again for a long time. . . .

Some hours later, when he had become bored with the repetitious events being depicted on the scanner programs, Oeschone looked up, rather sheepishly, wondering what the time was and thinking about a cup of coffee. He stood up, stretched, looked about the room, more to rest his eyes than anything else. The room was silent, save for the whispering of air in the circulation vents, and the faint scratching of the needles on the graph paper. That reminded him of something, after a time. He thought guiltily that he should have been checking the readout every fifteen minutes. But he wasn't particularly disturbed; it was simply a matter of adjusting his duty logs. He was sure nothing had happened worthy of note; nothing ever did. Oeschone walked over to the recording device, looked cursorily at the graph, straightened, nodding to himself. Nothing had changed.

He looked again, some subliminal cue tugging at his dimmed consciousness. He could not, however well he rationalized it, avoid the suspicion that something subtle, but not the less drastic for all that, had occurred while he had been looking at the entertainment-scanner. Oeschone looked closely, now, at the pattern still unrolling before him. There was something there, he was certain. Now he had to find it.

Each of the needles was tracing a unique pattern, and it seemed to be just as before. Just as before he had gone to his chair. Oeschone looked again, feeling that sinking feeling. No, it was not just like before. Now all of the wave-forms were perfectly regular, with no variation whatsoever being overlaid on whatever pure frequency they tapped. All of them. Regular wave-forms, as if they were being generated by a computer. He bent over the collection reel and began to unroll it frantically, looking desperately for the section in which the regular wave-forms had started. His heart leaped; then sagged again, in disappointment; he couldn't find it. Oeschone reached for the alarm button, the one which would summon the duty medic. He would know what to do.

The unexplained, unmodulated wave-forms continued without any change or deviation until the duty medic arrived, some forty minutes later. A sizable group accompanied the medic, apparently standby personnel he had called out. Oeschone tried to make himself as inconspicuous as possible.

Once he had taken stock of the general situation, the medic took charge of things in a stern manner at variance with his youthful appearance. That, at the least, did not surprise Oeschone; duty medics were a surly lot at best, and he had not yet heard of one who enjoyed being called out during his shift. It was widely believed that they napped on their shifts, and of course if they were awakened too quickly, they growled like bears. But, growling or not, Oeschone was secretly glad to have the medic here; the matter and the responsibility was now out of his hands. Perhaps there would be other circumstances as well to muddy the water and divert attention from himself.

The medic appeared to ignore Oeschone; an assistant dug into a voluminous carpetbag and extracted a weighty blue text, from which he read cryptic instructions and rejoinders, to which the medic either nodded assent or performed some action, such as turning a potentiometer, reading a meter, or flipping a toggle. They performed with an efficiency that bespoke both knowledge of the subject matter and considerable training. At several points in the sequence of actions, the medic would consult the multiencephalograph. At these occasions, he would also review Oeschone's duty log, here turning to leer knowingly at Oeschone. But he said nothing. After considerable time had been spent on the preliminaries, they began to disassemble the box, proceeding carefully in accordance with instructions so as not to disturb out of sequence the delicate life-support mechanisms. Having completed most of his preparatory actions, the duty medic then climbed up onto the box, using cleverly concealed hand- and footholds. At the top, he opened a small inspection plate, and shining a small pocket flashlamp into the opening, looked inside intently.

Oeschone knew the routine, although he had never personally observed an emergence; the medic would now climb down from the box, take a few more actions, and then stand back, grumbling, while his crew completed disassembly. But Oeschone began to feel uneasy, for it did not proceed after that fashion. The medic, instead, remained atop the box, staring intently into the opening for what seemed to be an overly long time. Then he shifted his position, and looked into the opening from several differing angles. At last, shaking his head, he climbed down from the box, very deliberately and calmly, and walked slowly over to Oeschone's console. His face looked congested, angry, although controlled.

"You have an outside line?" Indeed there was something more than irritated inconvenience in the tone of the medic's voice.

"Of course, Medic Venle," Oeschone replied, remembering to read the man's nametag so he could use the name. This always helped to allay hostility; even more so in this circumstance, since the medic was also the holder of a programmed name. Oeschone hoped that the medic would appreciate the gesture and recall that, after all, he and Oeschone alike were fellow-members of a privileged group. Oeschone also added, "Is there some problem?"

"Just get the line," answered the medic impatiently.

Oeschone complied with his request. Shortly afterward, Venle was seated at the console, looking belligerently into the viewer. The other members of the recovery team looked expectantly at Venle, as if they expected further instructions, but he waved them off, signifying they were to wait for further instructions. At the console, the Operate light flashed on.

A voice spoke from a speaker. "Operator PZ. Go ahead."

"I am Journeyman Medic Domar Venle, ranking four step C. I desire a priority conference be set up, connecting this terminal with those of, respectively, Acumen-Medic Slegele and Overgrade Eykor, the Chief of Regional Security. Precedence is flash, Authority Section B."

"Medic Venle, I understand and will comply, but the time is oh-five-three-oh local. The officials you have enumerated are, in all probability, yet sleeping. They are, of course, both dayshifters."

Venle said, calmly and deliberately, "Asleep, are they? Well, then, arouse them." Then he added, maliciously, "Wake the bastards up." While the operator hesitated, he added further, "I accept responsibility. Indeed, I demand it."

There was a pause while the operator complied with Venle's instructions and rang both mentioned parties. There was some further delay while the called parties awoke and tried to assemble some official dignity before coming on the conference call. But finally the screen before Venle divided and two faces appeared side by side. Venle spoke first. "Operator, record this."

"Recording."

"Noted. First, Acumen-Medic Slegele: Are you aware of the nature of the subject remanded to the sensory deprivation unit located in room seven-thirty-five, Building eight-nine-oh-five?"

Venle knew very well the acumen-medic did not. It was merely an opening question to put the senior man off balance. And it did. Slegele answered, "Of course I don't know at five in the morning. I don't keep rosters in my quarters. Is this why you get me out of bed at this hour?"

Venle said, "Well, let me be the first to tell you. You have a quote live unquote ler in your magic box, that's what."

The puffy face in the viewer moved, registering several emotions at once. Slegele said, "But, Venle, that's impossible. I recall the circumstance, and remember seeing the forms on info when they went through; you must be making some mistake. That particular unit holds an unknown female subject, I believe a suspect of vandalism or something similar."

"Somebody lied," Venle said sternly, not bothering to conceal his elation at confirming something he had long suspected: that Acumen-Medic Slegele was a mere paper-stamper who knew nothing about what was going on in his departments. "Yes, indeed. The forms were in error. It's a female, true enough; I looked. But not human. With them, I'd have to guess the age . . . she appears to be about middle-adolescence, over fifteen, under twenty-five. Small breasts, well-formed, no pubic hair. Second thumb on the outside of both hands. That sounds like a ler to me. And you know the terms of the Compact as well as I: No imprisonment or experimentation. All suspects are to be conveyed immediately to the Institute. You and I, we'll fry for this. How long has she been on isolation?"

Eykor broke in, his composure recovering. He was a horse-faced man with a shock of unkempt reddish hair. But despite his rude appearance, he was both suave and controlled. "There is no problem, Venle. We listed that one in that manner on the invoices. All of the extant records were paperwhipped by my people. What's the problem? More specifically, how did you come to be over there?"

"I believe I can state the reason briefly: I was called on a blankout alarm which your cretin watchman sent out six hours late. The subject, as you refer to her, has somehow managed to dismind herself. Zero. You've got a live warm body, Interrogator, but that is all you have. Apply your methodology on that. She has virtually no responses whatsoever. I should estimate early newborn, if anything."

Slegele began stammering, "But, but . . ."

Eykor interrupted Slegele. "This conference will be classified secret under the provisions of Code four-oh-one-five, section B amended, and is hereby confiscated, all recording thereof to be forwarded to this office, Organization S. Operator?"

"Noted, sir."

"Venle, complete your procedures and await me. I'll be over there immediately."

"Very well."

"And, operator, arrange an appointment for me with Chairman Parleau. Naturally, the discreet person would specify that such a meeting be at his convenience, but as early as possible."

"That is noted. It will be as you say. Shall I inform your office facilities? The Regional Chairman's unit will not be open for an hour or so yet."

"Notify me in person at room seven-thirty-five, Building eight-nine-oh-five. Venle?"

"Present."

"You verge upon insubordination."

"Others have noted that tendency, sir. But I must add that where I err in one regulation, it might be said that your office has erred in another, perhaps one with more serious consequences. I must stand upon my right to advise of error, freely and without reprisal, however subtle." Venle was quoting.

"Oh, your rights have been noted in full. Proceed with your function. Break." Eykor's half of the viewer winked out. Slegele's puffy face filled the screen. Venle was indeed sorry he had dragged the acumen-medic into this. The man simply wasn't prepared. . . .

To Slegele he said, "We'll recover her, well enough. It was fortuitous I thought to bring my own crew over here. But I will still require some assistance; can you send over the Central Palliatory and have them send me some, ah . . . pediatrics assistants?"

Slegele stammered, "Of course, if you need them. But why pediatrics? I don't understand . . ."

Venle said, patiently, "Apparently the girl, whoever she is, now has nothing but the infant responses she was born with. She breathes, she has a strong heartbeat, all the vital signs. As far as I can determine now, her blood chemistry is good, although I'll have to refer to some other manuals. But infant responses! She'll have to be cared for: she's an infant with a full set of teeth. She'll bite her tongue off before she discovers what those little pearlies are used for. And what do we tell her people when they come for her, as they surely must? That we're bloody sorry? She's obviously an adolescent. Not bred yet. They'll ransack the place when they find out." Venle mused for a moment, then added, "A shame about all this, too; she's quite attractive, if a bit childish for my tastes. . . ."

Slegele, waking up, interrupted Venle's train of thought. "How could they know she was missing? And knowing, how would they know to come here looking for her?"

"I should imagine someone will find her absence curious. They are close people, you know. And it won't take a genius to discover Building eight-nine-oh-five. Of course, we can always deny the whole thing, but that means we have to dispose of the body, also. That means that many more who know something about it. You see what I'm trying to hint at?"

"Yes . . . I think so. We could always say she did it to herself, couldn't we? We can't be held responsible for that."

"I suppose it's worth trying. But I'll say this: you and I have more to fear from our own people than from them. Get it?"

"You're cynical."

"Realistic is the terminology I prefer . . . I know that people who set events like this one in motion never pay for it. They arrange that someone else foots the bill. I'm not in danger, but you could be. Cover yourself. I'll do what I can for you."

"Let us both hope it doesn't come to that. But at any rate I appreciate the gesture."

Venle signed off disgustedly and went back to work on the occupant of the box, ignoring Oeschone entirely, save in his private thoughts, which were malevolent ones; Venle took his work more seriously than he did his status, and one of his private hates included those who applied for programmed names and then expected to ride free for the rest of their days. Careerists, he grumbled under his breath, inaudibly. There were entirely too many of them these days, and no real way to get at them, either.

Not so very long afterward, the girl was carefully lifted out of the box and almost tenderly laid on the waiting stretcher. She was, as Venle had observed earlier, lovely. Out of the box, in the open light, she was something more than that. Her hair was a lustrous dense deep brown, almost black, worn in the fashion affected by ler adolescents, a simple short style resembling a tapered bowl cut, in human eyes boyish. The face was delicate and soft at the same time, oval-triangular, rising from a small but not weak chin to large, deeply set eyes, which were an odd light brown color. She had a small nose, very straight, and her lips were pursed rather than full. There were no lines on the face whatsoever, but it was a strong face filled with myriad adult determinations, and something else as well: a sadness, something wistful, otherworldly, deeply emotional. From the head, a slender, fine neck led to a taut, athletic body, smoothly curved and completely feminine, whose skin tone was a ripe faded honey-olive. Venle looked at her long, sighing. There was only one thing out of place; she could have been human, save for the hands. The hands were narrow, three-fingered, with an opposable thumb on each side, both thumbs being narrower than the human thumb. In addition, her hands were powerful and angular, a bit at variance from the rest of her.

Venle looked back at the face, now relaxed. There was a faint shadow of a smile set along the lines and softened planes of the girl's face, something ineffably subtle, something about the set of the eyes and mouth; save for that, the face was empty of expression in the present. No one present with Venle could quite place where they had seen a smile like that before, if indeed they ever had before.

TWO

The appearance of the quality of randomness is often the most reliable indication of high and subtle systems of order.

We learn from simple analysis of the Zan (Life Game) that time is asymmetrical, one-way. To try to work time in reverse brings one immediately into the principle of uncertainty. Things may be mysterious, incomprehensible, or ineluctable, but nothing in the universe is uncertain. This is basic to understanding higher-order phenomena.

—The Game Texts

FELLIRIAN* WAS EXPLAINING, "The Four Determinants of a person are these: Aspect, Phase, Class, Position." She added fastidiously, "Gender is not a determinant. So, then; if one of us knows all four determinants of another person, we are thereby able to predict, with reasonable accuracy, what that person will do in various circumstances."

Fellirian was an adult female ler of many roles and relationships. In the present case, she was serving as resident sociologist, Visitors Bureau, at the Institute for Applied Interrelationships, a problem-solving organization which was the primary organ of human and ler interaction. Once a week, Fellirian traveled down to the Institute from her home deep inside the ler reservation, and explained an alien culture to visitors, both humble and distinguished. This particular audience appeared to be of the more humble variety, and it was close to the end of the day, and Fellirian was bored.

"Aspect," she continued, "is distantly related to your own concept of astrological sign, save that it is much simplified. We use only four: Fire, Air, Earth, Water. These correspond to the four seasons."

* Ler names in this story will be given untranslated, except for special cases.

It was autumn, on Earth, the year 2550. Fellirian lived partially in two worlds, and in the human world she visited, even the little taste she got of it at the Institute, her presence generated paperwork echoes of herself. On various rosters, lists, collations, and assorted personnel summaries, she was listed as "one each Fellirian Deren, female, ler, reservation resident, age 45, married (local custom), three offspring, two male, one female. Position: Instructor of Customs. Branch: Visitors Bureau. Supervisor: W. Vance, Director. Fertility Board Index: (not applicable).

She could, had she pondered overly long on the matter, have produced a much longer "full-name" in her own field of reference, with an even longer list of titles and identities. Her full-name, in her own environment, was Kanh Srith Fel Liryan Klan'Deren Klandormadh; which translated, more or less, to the following: Earth-Aspect's the Lady Starry Sedge-Field of the Counters Clan, Head-of-Family Foremother. But she never translated the name, as was the case with all of them. Names were names, meant to suggest in their meanings, not to describe. To friends, adult relations occasionally in the formal mode, and humans, she was simply Fellirian. That sufficed. There wasn't another; ler names never repeated that of a living person, and inasmuch as was possible, one who had ever been, although they admitted that this last would become unfeasible with time.

To her fellow Braid-members at home, in the mode of intimacy, she was Eliya, and to the Braidschildren Madheliya. Foremother Eliya. She was never called Fellir anymore, for that was an adolescent love-name. Morlenden, her insibling and co-spouse, sometimes called her Fel, the child-name, but more often he called her by an embarrassing pet name, Benon, which meant "freckles." The matter was embarrassing because the freckles were on her shoulders, which led to connotations she did not care to recall now at her age and phase.

Fellirian's phase was Kanh, the mode of the power of Earth. Her season was spring. She was saying to her audience, "Now, Phase: this is approximately how old you are. *Hazh* is a child, up to about ten years. *Didh* is adolescent: ten to twenty-nine. *Rodh* is parent, and *Starh* is elder. We are *rodhosi* until age sixty, and then we are *starosi*, although this last is somewhat arbitrary. Technically, we are only actually *rodhosi* until the end of the fertile period."

Fellirian had children, and yet lived at home, her children not yet being of weavable age; therefore she was Parent Phase. In gender, female, but sexually neuter. So it went with all after last-fertility, the so-called *hanh-dhain**.

Fellirian, being of the Earth mode, was a child born in the spring. Without being overtly obvious about it, she did in part live up to the theoretical attributes of a person of that mode, although none could consider her the prey of erratic aspectual compulsions. Spring was her preferred season as well; like her own manner, it was a direct season, things proceeding toward their due ripening, earthy, direct, practical. She did not care so much for the present season of autumn, with its *tanh* air-aspect moodiness, its constantly shifting weather, off and on again, now looking back into summer, now anticipating winter.

"There are, in theory, four social classes: Servant, Worker, Journeyman, and Grower, from the lowest to the highest; but in practice now we only use the top three, and this is of less weight than the other determinants."

One of the visitors inquired, "And what class do you belong to?"

"Worker. My Braid is part of the ler government. My family and I are, in the eyes of our peers, rather low-class, although I feel no sense of either pride or envy therefrom. Class, odd as this may sound, is only applicable to persons who are within a Braid, or family. Once you are elder and leave home, you are classless. Elders have no class. Utterly none."

She saw some expressions in the audience she did not care for. She said, "Lest you mistake me, I must define things here, although it is somewhat off the path we go upon. I am not in the government because my family and I are worker-class. It is the other way around. I derive class and status from my occupation, so to speak." She waited for a rejoinder, but there was none. Good.

She continued, "Last, and perhaps most important, is the determinant of position. What we refer to here is what place you occupied within the Braid when you were a child." Here she gestured to a chart beside her that diagrammed the intricate family relationships of the ler cultural surround. They had used it earlier. "We can be one of five different positions, with some subcategorization, of course. This measure, like class, also runs from low to high, thus: *Hifzer, Zerh, Thes, Nerh, Toorh*. You would say, Bastard, Extra, Younger Outsibling, Elder Outsibling, and

---

* Difficult to translate. *Hanh* means last, and *dhain* (pronounced "thine") is a word describing the sex act, but utterly without the connotations of vulgarity or hostility common to such terminology in English. It is purely descriptive. "Fun" might be closer to its real meaning than any other word we might use here.

highest, Insibling. These stay with you forever. They are basic identities. I was *Toorh*, and I shall always be perceived as one, no matter my age. Also this is not a smooth scale. A *Nerh* is almost equal to a *Toorh*, and a *Thes* is closer to a *Zerh*. Families do not, by definition, have *Hifzers*."

At this last, the group immediately began an argument among themselves, one faction in particular taking some exception to the concept of position being more weighty a determinant than social class. Fellirian did not know why they were arguing over this, for it did not affect them one way or another; but she did not enter the argument on either side. She felt as if she had somehow espoused a doctrine held or shared by one faction and above all she did not wish to be identified with one human faction or another. As the sides became more defined and the visitors began to polarize among themselves, she withdrew and walked slowly to the side, to the window ledge, where she settled and looked outside, leaning on one hand and half sitting on the broad metal sill.

She looked out the window, through the rain-streaked polarized glass, through the damp and rainy November airs to the wet land beyond, now taking on a bluish tint with the approach of evening. From her viewpoint, looking somewhat northeast, she could see in the land itself the clear delineation of the two cultures, human and ler. On the left, the reservation, a 4,200-square-mile forest preserve in which the ler were now allowed to pursue their own ends, whatever those ends were; and on the right, the end product of several thousand years of human culture. Both were on the same planet, Earth, the same year—2550.

To the left, the land appeared unkempt, empty, overgrown with trees and brush. To the right, as far as she could see through the light rain and foggy haze, everything was neat, orderly, trimmed, laid out, controlled. Far to the right at the edge of visibility, a manufacturing operation dominated the landscape: it appeared to be a low, rather featureless building of square ground-plan, betraying its inner activity only by the action of small vents along the roof, some of which emitted pastel clouds of vapor, while others trailed away into the rainy darkening air wisps of smoke which soon vanished. It looked dormant, inactive; but she knew this to be an illusion. Inside, unseen, it was as busy as an anthill, madly producing still more of the perishable artifacts on which their society seemed to exist. There was little traffic in or out of it; transit-ways underground handled the material flows, and the employees lived in air-conditioned cubicles in the basement. Bosses and bossed alike; it cost less to totalize their entire environment than it did to provide transportation and housing for them elsewhere.

Farther to the right, the remainder of the view through the Institute window took in agricultural fields, some smaller buildings and miscellaneous sheds, a light grid of access roads and hoverways. There was nothing but a sense of neatness and order in all that she saw, a tincture of everything calculated to a nicety; she could not help but admire it to a point. Still, a part of her insisted on another, more chaotic view: that the fine sense of order and regulation concealed something perilous. The higher the degree of apparent order, the finer the line that divided the arbitrary order from the merciless down-drag of entropy. *Nature only appears random to the unobservant*, she thought. It was one of the basic ler maxims. In reality, there was a deep and subtle order in the changes of nature, its wavelike progressions, its cycles of time.

Even so, she thought further, *eruptions are few and far between. Give them that credit*. The forerunners accepted the regimented, managed life forced upon them by overpopulation and had even managed to reduce their increase-rate to a niggling, infinitesimal amount. But they were all conscious descendants of an age, not so very far away in the historic sense of time, which was still vividly recalled by Earth's billions as The Black Hand of Malthus. The Days of the Hand. They had reduced its visibility, but never its presence: the Black Hand still awaited the unwary, offstage in the wings.

Facing to the right as she sat in the window, she had to look back over her left shoulder to see what little was visible of her own country, the sole home on Earth, or in the whole universe, for that matter, of the New Humans, *Metahomo Novalis*. There was a fence around the reservation, an ordinary chain-link barrier about eight feet high. It served no purpose save to mark a boundary, for few there were on either side of it who wished to cross to the other side. Near the fence, the land inside seemed to be empty, abandoned, allowed to be feral, half-wild, scrubby; but farther back, the forest started, here tall dark pines that concealed the inner lands. It looked ancient, a remnant of the great forests which had once covered most of the continent; but in reality most of the forest growth in the reservation was recent in terms of nature. Second-growth. The eastern sections of the reservation, in particular, where newer growth gradually extended out of the older sections farther west. It had been a forest preserve that few knew about until they had asked for it. Fellirian sighed deeply. She felt a sudden longing to be back inside, back within her own identity, in her natural surround. This room in this overbuilt Institute building was too hot, too dry, and it smelled of plastic, an odor she never found especially unpleasant, but nonetheless one she had never got used to. . . .

Chronologically, Fellirian was forty-five. Parent phase. In appearance, however, she struck most of the human visitors who met with her to be somewhere in a vague adulthood, late twenties, perhaps early thirties. A smallish, but not petite, slightly built woman with the traditional subtle figure of the ler. Somewhere along the way, she had collected an almost invisible network of fine lines along the planes of her face, lines that helped and accented the subtle beauty of the plain, almost elfin face. Fellirian was not a beauty, neither by her standards nor those of the humans, but her appearance reassured. Being relaxed and at peace with herself, she projected a reassurance that included others as well.

In her own view, her appearance fit her age, more or less; she did not ponder on the matter overly. She was not vain. She knew how others reacted to her, always had. She was satisfied; she had lived a reasonably full life, in many ways better and more fortunate than some.

Forty-five. *Almost through the second span.* Then another of the many transitions they used to mark the stages of their lives in time. Sexually, she was now, and had been for some five years, effectively neuter, although she retained her personal sense of gender unchanged. No, not unchanged. If anything, it had increased. She had been one of the minority of ler females to have a third fertile period after the second. She had been pleased with their *Zerh*, the boy Stheflannai. Third fertilities and fraternal twins were the only way the ler ever got ahead of the merciless algorithms of population increase. *And before that,* she mused, *it had been Kevlendos, one of our insiblings, who will weave in his season with the child of our others who is called Pentandrun-Toorh. And of course our firstborn Pethmirvin, a slender, fragile girl who resembles none of us.* Ages five, ten, fifteen. Twenty years hence, Kevlendos and Pentandrun would weave to become the then-Derens. And for her, Fellirian? They would then be the Derenklan; the name, the work, the family holdings—all would be theirs. She would be just herself, free. Fellirian Srith. Lady Fellirian. A new life. She could live by herself, solitary, a lonely *mnathman**, or remain with her former Braidmates, although they would have to find another place to live. They could not stay in the old Braid holding—that went to the children. Or perhaps she could join one of the lodges, communes into which most elders eventually moved. The ler analog of

* Literally, "wise person," but in actuality a hermit.

marriage was like the human model in that it had a beginning; it was utterly unlike it in that it had a predetermined end as well. It was also unlike the human model in that it was neither desirable nor optional, but mandatory. . . .

Fellirian rarely delivered her lectures, or occasional harangues, alone. Much of the time the Director of the Institute was in and out, visiting with the strangers, hobnobbing with the tourists who had come to be amazed and astounded, and have their suspicions allayed. But for all that he did with the visitors, Walter Vance admitted candidly that his primary purpose in attending the meetings was to spend a rare moment with Fellirian, who had been his friend, associate, and confidante for the more than twenty years he had been associated with the Institute. Their relationship had, like all close relationships, probably raised more questions than it answered, but at the least it satisfied a basic orientation shared by both of them in equal measure: they preferred to deal with real, though flawed in various degrees, creatures of flesh and blood and the moment, rather than a set of lifeless abstractions borrowed from a carelessly written programmed text.

With trust and a genuine fondness for each other, they could explore aspects of otherness with little fear of giving or taking offense; this was not a little thing, for the cultural gap between ler and human was an order of magnitude greater than the genetic differences, and it was growing yearly. When Vance had persuaded Fellirian to spend a little time with the Institute they had not one single ler assigned to expound on their values; all was done by humans, mostly well-intentioned but who had little direct knowledge of their subject material. They spoke skillfully, they adhered to rigorous scholarship, but they missed the feel of their subjects. Conversely, ler labored under much the same system in their view of humans. Painfully aware of their vulnerability of slow population growth, they withdrew into their reservation and further into their own identities. Vance and Fellirian could not arrest or greatly change the course of the drift of several centuries, but what little they had done they regarded as being of a value considerably above zero.

Vance now sat in a chair to one side, bored with the endless tailspin semantic arguments of the visitors among themselves, a process of which he had to endure entirely too much within his own organization. Above and below. While he waited for them to return to reality and finish the day, he watched Fellirian as she sat on the windowsill and looked into the depths of November, overcast and rain-spattered.

His perception of her was subjective, colored by memory, subtly distorted by many emotions, some of which had sources that remained concealed from him, no matter how hard he tried to dig at them. Paradoxically, he had found Fellirian to have more objective perceptions than he had, even where accustomed and familiar matters were considered. He had imagined that having total recall would muddy the image of the present even more, but, to the contrary, he had found that for them it made the present clearer. The images were distinct.

In the light of the room, and the soft overcast daylight coming in through the windows, he saw a graceful ler woman of indeterminate age sitting in the windowsill, wearing the typical general-purpose garment of males and females alike, in its winter variation, the zimpleth. This was, in essence, something resembling a loose, informally cut shirt with a very long tail that reached to the ankles. It flowed loosely around the contours of her body, terminating along her arms in wide sleeves which did not quite reach to her wrists. There was nothing under the zimpleth save Fellirian, but somehow it managed completely to conceal the shape within its lines. She was barefoot, but for the moment little showed, as she had folded her legs beneath her. He saw in her profile that she yet had the visage he knew of old, a tomboy, impudent, mischievous face, with a strong nose just slightly too large for the face, and a wide, generous soft mouth inclined to secret laughters. Her skin was light in color, even so slightly shadowed by a darker tone. Her hair was a neutral dark brown, very fine and straight, tied at her neck into a single braid which fell to the middle of her back.

Vance had met Fellirian when he had come to the Institute; they were approximately the same age in years. During the time he had known her, he had seen many aspects of her; as an adolescent, in his eyes then promiscuous and oversexed. But also as a *rodhosi*, one of parent phase, serious and practical, and as head-of-clan completely absorbed in the management and continuity of its affairs. Now, on the edge of true elderness. Ler lifespans reached to one hundred and twenty and beyond; half their lives spent in the first three phases, and the rest in the last phase. They held that one did not become oneself until elderhood, when, as they put it, the distractions fell away, and essences were revealed. In Fellirian, some creature within herself, more individual and unique than he cared to imagine, was beginning to emerge.

Twenty years. They had worked well together, learned from each other. They had become close friends and grown to enjoy one another's company as few such pairs had in the history of the Institute. Nothing had passed between them deeper than friendship, nor more intimate than a handshake, which always felt odd and unreal to Vance. One could convince oneself that ler were just other humans of small stature and almost childish appearance until one saw and felt the hand. The inner thumb was smaller and more delicate than the human thumb, and the outer opposable thumb, derived from the little finger, was stronger than its original. This change made the ler hand seem too long and narrow, and it felt *wrong*. Moreover, they seemed to lack the concept of "handedness" entirely. Ler wrote with either hand equally well, holding the writing instrument with either thumb. Still, after twenty years, it disturbed Vance's perceptions to watch Fellirian writing some office memorandum, holding the pen with an outer thumb and pulling it along the direction of writing.

If the hand had become a symbol for the alien quality, the one thing which stood out above the many ambiguities, then the reality had been more directly evoked when he had met her insibling and (then) co-parent to be. This bothered Vance, too, in some unconscious manner he could not quite fathom; the insiblings did not have common biological parents, yet they were raised together. They were always close in age, separations of more than a year being so rare as to be not worth mentioning. In some ways, closer than brother and sister in the human analog. Indeed closer, since the ler had no incest-taboo. This circumstance took the ancient argument of nature versus nurture, genetics against culture, and brought it head-on into direct opposition. The insiblings were alike, and different, all at the same time.

So Morlenden: rather alike, and totally dissimilar. In some subtle way beyond Vance's perceptions, he was most like Fellirian, in expressions, turns of speech, gestures. But he did not look like her at all. Against Fellirian's soft features, Morlenden had crisp, almost chiseled features. There was the tiniest possible suggestion of an epicanthic fold in the corners of his eyes, and his glance was direct and disturbingly contemplative. But he was neither dour of disposition nor abrupt of manner, but rather easy and sometimes inclined to elaborate pranks. His skin was darker than Fellirian's, of a tone that suggested American Indian rather than Asian. Seeing them apart was to see reflections of the other in the one at hand. Vance had come to understand that it was similar with all insiblings. Vance could not conceive of sleeping with the same person for forty-five years, growing up together, occasionally taking one another after the casual manner of ler adolescents, and then making the transition into dual heads-of-family. Humans for the most part lived in dormitories and kept the sexes separate. Nothing else had worked.

Like all poignant experiences, meeting Morlenden had caused Vance to reassess his perceptions, both of Fellirian and of the female; in both secondary sex characteristics and culture, there was almost no sex differentiation among them. Dressed, the differences almost vanished to the human eye. He thought this quality was what disturbed humans most; an internal drive. *We do not lust for the opposite sex, but for youth and innocence.* The thought formed before he had time to cut it off at the source. He refused to follow it, even to prove it false; it led into a whole world, a universe, of heresies and forbidden speculations . . . forbidden, at any rate, to a member of a culture which had been forced to become puritan, not out of religious mania but of necessity. Of all methods of contraception, only abstinence had the combination of one-hundred-percent effectiveness and zero-rate side effects. Zero? Not quite zero. There were obvious consequences, even if they were in the mind and not especially located in the body. Vance shut that one down, too. His mind was wandering in disturbing tangents today; perhaps the moody autumnal *tanh* weather. . . .

The omnipresent low buzz of conversation among the visitors had become faded and quiet in the last few moments. Vance now noticed it; Fellirian, for all her apparent inattention, had also noted it and climbed down off the windowsill, using a flowing, graceful motion Vance had always noticed in her. She went over to the chair she sometimes used, but now she did not sit in it, but stood, quietly, and nodded to the group to indicate that she was again ready to proceed.

A member of the visitors' group, a nervously aggressive woman of indeterminate middle age, wearing the heavy pleated and folded clothing of the day with indifference, and still retaining rubber covers over her heavy shoes, stood up, clearing her throat.

The woman began, "I am somewhat awkward here. I do not know how I should address you, directly." She had seen the same data as the others during her tour, and she could visualize the ler family structure as well as any of them present; yet she felt ill at ease in the presence of an active member of such a family organization. The family was now a rarity in human society. The voice which had made the tentative overture was heavy with the linguistic woodsmoke of the Balkans.

Fellirian smiled and chuckled, trying to set the woman at some ease. "Well, not Mrs. Deren, whatever you do. I suppose the nearest I could come to that would be to call myself the female half of an entity that corresponds to a Mr. Deren. I am an insibling. I retain the Braid surname. But here and for now, 'Fellirian' will be fine. It is the way we would address one another." Her voice was pleasant and clear, alto in intonation, projecting the Modanglic of the day without recognizable regional accent or mannerism. Still, there was some fleeting suggestion in the way she chose her words and enunciated them that Modanglic was a foreign language to her, however well she spoke it. It was.

The woman sighed and said, after an appreciable pause, "Very well then. So. That sounds easy enough, although I have never accustomed myself to addressing people by their first names. But I understand. The way you would use it in your own environment, I imagine it would be formal enough."

Fellirian agreed, pleasantly. "Indeed. We have a great deal of formality among ourselves, little distinctions that sometimes reflect kinship groups, or relative social status. Never fear! We make mistakes, too."

"These matters are the cause of much misunderstanding, I agree. So, then, to matters at hand. Fellirian, here you represent your people for us as people, so perhaps this is inappropriate to ask. But in my own Region* we have little contact with your people. Virtually none, as a matter of fact. And of course one hears tales. Our office has to deal with recurring questions relating to this."

Fellirian felt uncomfortable. It was a long preamble. She nodded, saying, "Please continue."

"I am very confused by what I have seen here. Out in the world, it is common belief that you are somehow superior to us, that you have an . . . ah . . . evolutionary edge on us. In short, you are greatly feared. Yet here I see a tribal, agricultural society, apparently disliking both aggressiveness and technology. Not to mention surrounded and outnumbered. In short, you do not appear to be competing with us. No competition, no threat. Can you shed any light on this . . . contradiction?"

Fellirian saw something that made her wary. At the start of her question, the woman had been tentative and embarrassed, projecting the image of a bureaucrat of some rural Region about the tatters of Europe. Yet as she had come to phrase her question, her confidence had risen noticeably, and in fact she had almost answered it herself. Somewhere in the back of Fellirian's mind, a relay clicked. She felt a sudden oppression. There was subtlety here: the woman was bait. Someone was waiting for her reaction. Her answer. She was not certain, of course. Intuition, only.

* Current political subdivision, equivalent to a large province. Regions might be geographic or ethnic in organizational basis.

She began, tentatively, "If you wish me to take the Aristotelian path and say yes or no, I must, on the balance, say no."

"No? Not superior?"

"I know from my history that such was the aim of those who manipulated human genetic material to bring us into being. True. They were after the Superman, sure enough. It is an old dream. We have not been immune to it. But they did not then have fine control. Not then and not now. They could not, for example, read the message of the genetic code and then change exact parts of it to order. They could shock or juggle or graft larger segments and then screen for viables. As you may know, mutation means only change. I cannot stress that too much. It is not a matter of one set being inferior or superior. Just different. In nature, a highly structured feedback system with the environment and with others, and in higher forms, with culture, tends to stabilize organic forms and fine-tune them. Out of their program of artifice, several forms actually appeared, all of which were equally viable, more or less. They took us because we looked the least alien. It's that simple. I am afraid that when our firstborn grew into adults, they were more than a little disappointed in us. When they discovered that no offspring results from a human-ler mating, they were doubly disappointed."

"None whatsoever? I had not known that."

"We are different, that's a fact. Conception occurs, but the female aborts within forty-eight hours. Either way you try it. We are, in a sense, a door into another possibility; but it is a door that is not open to you. Or to us. But in many ways we complement one another, so we endure. We are strong in the intuitive patterns of thought, but you outclass us in deduction. I might point out that you are physically stronger and able to endure a wider range of climatic conditions. Whereas we seem to take crowding a little better. Did you know that? Much of human aggression arises not from any genetic predisposition, but from simple overcrowding. Not recently, I mean to say. You reached that point early in your prehistory. Ten thousand years ago."

"You appear to be very knowledgeable about our history."

Fellirian answered, diplomatically, "We hoped to learn from your experiences. You are the forerunners. We have no other example to hand."

Without evoking confrontation, Fellirian had boxed the woman in, if indeed she were a provocateur for someone else. She could not rebuff her answer without making the background obvious.

"There are other differences?"

"People make much of our memory. It is a total-recall system. It sounds like an advance, I agree, but it has drawbacks. For example, we do not have a structure like your subconscious. In you, that serves as a buffer for contradictory experiences. We have to deal with the same events directly. There is a high degree of skill required, since we are now discussing basic sanity. All do not, of course, attain the preferred skill level. People envy us now for our low rate of reproduction, but it cannot be other than a serious disadvantage. And not only short, but an estrous periodic cycle as well. Twice, rarely three times, and it's over*. That basically gives us a one-to-one ratio, which is zero population growth from the beginning."

"May I ask your rate now?"

"One-to-one-point-oh-five or one-to-one-point-oh-six. Doubling every six hundred years. It was held artificially higher at first, but in the last two centuries it has been stable near that figure. Our marriage custom tends to diffuse exceptionally fertile types, so the increase is well-spread."

Fellirian paused. There was no comment. She continued: "This now means, on the average, that one Braid in six has an extra child. We cut the rate down to that. Our society is complex and delicate, and at a rate of one-to-one-point-two-five every Braid has one extra. You cannot imagine the dislocations such breeding causes. I admit that much of the problem comes from our own ordering of things. For if you have four children of the right ages, pairs five years apart, then they must go into a Braid to mate. If one does not exist, then one must be made for them. Braids have traditional basic occupations, and once set, cannot be changed, within the life of the Braid. It imposes a rate of social change upon us greater than our society has mechanism to adjust to it. We could stand an even lower rate, in my opinion."

"You said earlier that you were parent phase. You have procreated?"

Fellirian winced, internally, she hoped, at the phrasing of the question. Still, she understood it. Not many humans these days "procreated," as the woman had put it. And the strictures of the Fertility Board were by far the most exasperating regulations of all. She replied, "Yes. My Braid is one of the one-in-six five-child Braids. I had a third fertility. I have had three children, all normal and live. Their ages are fifteen, ten, and five. A girl and two boys in that order. Their names are Pethmirvin,

---

* Ler Braids ideally produced four children. Fifth children occurred in one Braid in five or six, from third-fertilities (80%) or fraternal-twinning (20%). Identical twins (clones) do not occur.

Kevlendos, and Stheflannai, in the same order. But rest assured. My days in brood are over."

She now paused to allow the idea to sink in. It was one thing to discuss such concepts in the abstract, quite another to accept such a thing personally, or in the sense of a personal interaction taking place now in the time of the real. She waited. Fellirian was patient. She knew humans well from her long association with them, and looked at none with contempt. They were always full of surprises, the inner person not always matching the outer. *Still*, she mused, *we are not so different in that*, either. . . . She also knew very well that the words of a single-channel language were also great illusions; not matching the realities they symbolized, and varying considerably in degree of variance, words tended to persuade the slow that they were one with the swift, and equally, the swift slowed to a crawl.

The woman pondered, drifted, hesitated, took another tack. "You told us about the ler family earlier, but not so much why such a structure. Is there some genetic reason for it?"

"Antigenetic, if anything. We have a small population and a high mutation rate; therefore we want a homogeneous population. We also noted that across time the family tends to become longer, more structured, more important. What we have now mixes us reasonably well, provides social stability and makes change controllable, and is the best compromise so far with our peculiar assets and liabilities. I might add here that an unforeseen consequence of the timing criteria of Braids also tends to bring, over the years, one Braid into resonance with another, and after that such groups form what we call 'partial superfamilies,' until terminated by the ending of one of the Braids involved, or the insertion of a vendetta into affairs. My own Braid is so resonant with Klanh Moren: The *Thes* of one becomes the afterparent of the other."

"You do not use human terminology to describe your relationships in a family?"

"No. Nor the concepts."

"Then the effect of resonance must be to reduce variability. It increases order, rather than continuing the randomizing you seem to value."

"This is true. We are aware of the problem. In fact, there has been consideration of declaring such a pattern to be not desirable, and prohibiting it. It is not at this time. One of the reasons why the practice continues is that with such a small population as we have we are all rather close relations anyway. In your terms, we are all not less than sixth-cousins or something very close to that. Right now, superfamily resonance with a Braid-pair has no appreciable effect. A triplet, of course, maintained over several generations, would, and is not permitted. Now, later, when our numbers are much greater, hundreds of thousands, I think resonance of any sort will be prohibited. It is, as you say, a producer of more order. But you have to realize that our oldest Braids are just now only at generation fourteen in the adults-to-be, who are now yet adolescent."

The woman seemed to be at a loss. She hesitated, as if waiting for something, moving her weight from one foot to another, a motion which produced transient heavy wrinkles to appear and fade in her garments, which were made of some heavy, stiff dark material, somewhat shiny or lustrous, which seemed more intended for use in furniture or draperies than in clothing. Additionally, the style was full of pleats, folds, tucks, darts, and gave the impression of adding bulk. The women wore skirts that fell gracelessly below the knees, while the men wore in their place heavy oversized pantaloons. The upper garments, composed of several layers of undershirts, shirts, vests, jackets, and various accessories, were similar to one another and continued the style. Fellirian watched the woman closely, sensing the others out of the corners of her eyes. The woman seemed to be waiting for some cue, to go on.

A man not far from the woman cleared his throat and asked, politely, "Fourteen? Is that all?"

The woman resumed her seat, seemingly in great relief. Fellirian answered, "Just so, fourteen. My own generation of the Derens is only generation eleven. Of the old families, we are relative newcomers."

"Let me think," the man mused, half to himself. "That would, at thirty-five years per generation, put the firstborn of the oldest generation back to, say, about 2050 or 2060. But didn't Braid family structure date from a later date, in the twenty-second century?"

Fellirian's sense of oppression increased. "True. But the two items are not contradictory. Braids were tried first on a limited scale by those who believed in them. They were adopted somewhat later by the whole of the people."

"Are those Braids still in existence now?"

"Yes. The two Player Braids, the Perklarens and the Terklarens. They were not, at the time, Players, you understand, but in fact members of a peculiar religious order, if I have my history straight. Now, I believe, the Perklarens are at *Ghen Disosi*, generation fourteen. The Terklarens are at thirteen, although due to disresonance between them individual members of equivalent ages are about ten years older."

"And fourteen has much of the same nonnumerical symbolic significance to you that ten would have, say, to us."

"Yes . . . there is a similarity, an equivalence."

"Odd, that. I have heard of a book, called *The Wisdom of the Prophets*, in which mention is made to 'marvels and wonders in the house of the last single generation.' "

Fellirian let herself drift from affirmation into ambiguity. "I have heard also of the work you mention. However, you must bear in mind that its origin has been questioned. It has not ever been accepted as cult dogma by any theosophical society of our people in my knowledge. And, of course, prophecy is always somewhat equivocal."

"You do not agree with the content of *Wisdom?*"

"I read a copy here at the Institute when I was adolescent. I found the concepts therein rather repugnant. It heavily stresses the concept of serial evolution, which is erroneous, and it injects a competitive aspect into affairs between the inhabitants of Earth which does not ring true." Fellirian felt threatened by the circumstances of the questions. Never had she faced such a situation. All her intuitions warned her; she could not resist however, letting go one last sally, just to make matters clear. "You are, sir, doubtless familiar with a similar work, I believe called *Protocols of the Elders of Zion?* I personally place *Wisdom* in the same category. Indeed, in *Wisdom* I felt an alien mind at work, one not compatible with myself."

"You don't think *Wisdom* is of ler origin?"

"I know not the number of thumbs on the hand of he who wrote. I speak of the ideals of the author, which is of the domain of the mind. And, at any rate, I know of no marvels. The Player Braids are both rather withdrawn and uncommunicative. They keep to their own affairs, which I imagine is Gameplaying. And also I am not a follower of the Game, so they could very well perform a marvel and I would be unaware of it." *Now let this one make something out of that*, she thought.

He said, "Excellent, excellent. You have clarified the matter beyond any possible doubt for me. I am doubly reassured. I do have some more questions, but they are inconsequential."

"Not at all. I am here to answer them."

"In many ways, to us, you maintain a primitive style of living. I mean no judgment of relativity here, but merely describe. You have no method of temperature control in your houses save the family hearth, and that is useful only in the winter, for example. You virtually ignore vehicular transport, when a number of sophisticated mechanisms are located only no more than fifty miles from the heart of the reservation. To the observer, if I may put it politely, you assume primitive modes by choice. May I ask why? It is a curious matter."

Fellirian paused, then began: "The first lived among you and shared your manners and styles. But they soon came to believe two things: that your culture reflects your needs, not the needs of all creatures, hence us also. And that in many instances, you had inserted the widespread use of artifacts without considering the consequences of such introductions. The classic study in this area, concerning the automobile, concentrates not on what it did to your previous value system, but in the measurable increase it caused in the size of your cities, an increase and a lowering of density which had profound, unseen effects on your society for years. These things, by the way, most conclusively did not result from increases in population. Indeed, we still feel echoes of the period in this century. It was apparent, then, that artifacts had enormous influence on culture, having the power to change many parts of it. The prediction of such effects is an arcane discipline, and in some cases not greatly more reliable than the reading of tea leaves. Therefore we had seen and were wary. We are accused of conservatism. Not so. We are merely cautious. We desire change and improvement, but we also desire that we, the objects of such change, have some willed control over the rate of change. Is this not reasonable? Therefore we moved into the woods and eschewed central heating. And vehicles. They expand the requirement for space greatly. Now we have the space to live and breathe. Why trade it for momentary and selfish conveniences?"

"You sound critical."

"Not so. You were not aware of the principle of consequence. We would not have been either, had we not seen your example and been warned. But there is more, of course. We wish to see things develop to reflect us, not a copy of you. We had to go far back, into primitiveness, if you will, to find it."

"Have you found it?'

"It is not expected for many spans."

"How long?"

"Not in my lifetime, nor that of my children's children."

The man nodded, as if he understood, and sat back in his seat. Another took his place. The latest one was rather younger than the first two, and more polished, almost offhand. Fellirian felt as if the focus of a terrible, concentrated attention suddenly had been removed from her. Not withdrawn, but no longer weighing and measuring her. Yes, that was the word. Weighing. What was the source? She glanced about the room covertly. There was no indication of anything amiss.

Vance breathed deeply, relieved also. Although the two visitors had not exceeded the lines of general propriety, they had overplayed it, he thought. Now this next fellow: probably was a regular fellow. He certainly appeared to be, although it was not out of the realm of possibility that he too was part of the act of the previous two. Two to provoke, and one to lend controlled and measured relaxation phase. It was, after all, one of the techniques of the men of history. This one seemed to be some very minor careerist out on a boondoggle, traveling around. Vance privately knew such trips to be a waste; he had seen so much even in his limited travels. Earth, at least about ninety-five percent of it, was as homogeneous as variations in climate allowed. What had been Bulgaria did not now differ appreciably from what had once been New Jersey; Vance caught himself wondering if it ever had. Surely places differed? The light must be different, the odors, the constituents of the soil? Vance thought further: few now ever saw the open sky, and when they did they disregarded it to the extent possible. The rest of objective experience was similarly shifted from the natural. Vance thought of Fellirian and what he knew of her; her perceptions were honed so fine that she could claim her nearest neighbors, the resonant-in-time Morens, actually lived in another country, one whose strangeness always amazed her. The Morens lived slightly more than a mile away. Such microprovincialization was common among them; in fact, it was a minor art form and diligently pursued, although with recognition that one of its limitations was that the "provinces" tended to grow rapidly the farther they were away from the viewer. The object of the art form was ultimately to bring everybody's perceptions into agreement and divide their whole world up into micro-provinces, purely as an exercise in perception.

Vance glanced at the roster of the visitors, to see if he could catch a hint of where the questioners had originated. He looked in vain; the whole list was comprised of programmed names, which of course gave no hint whatsoever of national or ethnic origin. Vance also felt some irritation. He was the only human in the room not having a programmed name. The visitors probably secretly regarded him as one of the obstructionists.

The most recent questioner seemed friendly, even apologetic for taking their time. He asked, "You must excuse my curiosity, but I have found today's tour fascinating. There is only one question I cannot lay to rest: what do you do for entertainment? I can imagine sleeping out of doors now and again, but after a time I should imagine becoming stifled by nothing to see but woods and nothing to do but survive."

It was tactlessly put and poorly phrased, but Fellirian thought she understood what the young man was getting at. She looked away for a moment, through the window into the deepening evening. She felt a wave of fatigue pass over her and wished to be on her way home. She turned back, her voice on the edge of a companionable chuckle: "You would be astounded to learn how much time is spent in the process of being primitive." She laughed her laugh again. "The children have to be instructed, there is the *Klanh* profession, the work of supporting the household, cleaning, washing, tending the garden and the stock. Our individual competences. Hauling water. This last is the reason for the tradition of building each *yos* close to running water. Entertainment? By the time I reach home tonight I won't need any." She became more serious. "Please don't take us for an assemblage of dour work-lovers, drudges of yard and kitchen. We have our own humors and games and pastimes, some of them subtle and intricate. And there are many other things; we tell tales to one another, sing, dance. Cultivate friendships, and enemyhoods, too. There is a whole cycle in itself on that last alone. I come here often, so I feel more at home in your house, but even so, I find myself bewildered by the entertainments you have. I would fall asleep trying to sample even a few of them."

"You don't sound bored."

"No. We have tried to order things so that ennui is at least one enemy we do not have to face. Boredom leads to revolutionary desires, not oppression, there. And change-of-boredom never improves. It gets worse. No, speaking for myself and those I know, I want no change. Only my own life."

Fellirian intended to say more, but something checked her, and she stopped. As it was, she felt naggingly that perhaps she had said more than she had intended to. *Well, too late. The words were now birds in flight.* But she thought she knew the source of the oppressive feelings during the meeting: yes, she was certain, although she could not prove it. She had been monitored. The questioners had been bait for someone else, offstage, listening, recording. She nodded to the last questioner, the young man, as if to indicate she was finished. Expressing his gratitude, he resumed his seat. Fellirian looked over the rest. They had lost interest in today's matters, and in the ler and the Institute. Now they were anxious to depart. It was an emotion she could appreciate, even share. She was anxious to leave as well. So now they had seen the famous New Humans. Well, they weren't so special after all, were they? The only thing they had really been interested in, although they went to some pains to conceal it, had been in adolescent sexual behavior and mores, which, to their minds, seemed indistinguishable from simple promiscuity. And of course that which they wanted most to see, Fellirian was unable to deliver for them.

Vance, watching the clock, was noticing that it had arrived at the proper time for the visitors to leave; in fact, several of them had also been watching the clock, as Vance had observed. They noticed him in turn, and began to busy themselves with preparations for departure, scraping chairs, arranging their coats and overcoats, retrieving rubber overshoes to put on. After a few perfunctory good-byes and appreciatory remarks, some awkward, the members of the visitors' party one by one put themselves together and filed out of the room. The last one out made some polite comment to Director Vance, and closed the door behind him as he left. The meeting room returned to silence.

Fellirian stood by her chair, Vance by the door, doing nothing, Vance remembered, turned, and turned down and then out the overhead lights. This was in deference to Fellirian who always felt uncomfortable in varying degree in any illumination other than natural light or the yellow glow of oil lamps and candles. Now she appreciated this little gallantry. The soft blue light of late November replaced the hard-emission spectrum of the overheads, flowed into the meeting room, softening it with its bluish rainy light. Outside, distant lamps began to come on, getting a headstart on piercing the darkness. Fellirian moved her chair over closer to the windows, sat.

By the door, Vance hesitated for a moment, uncertain. Then, abruptly, he called down to the canteen through the intercom for two mugs of hot tea. That done, he turned back to Fellirian, who was now rummaging through her belt pouch, retrieved from where she had laid her other things. From it, she removed a small, shallow smoking pipe, which she packed with a light brown tobacco. Vance approached, produced a lighter, held it for her, stood back to watch her get the fire up in the bowl. Started to her satisfaction, she sat back, rested an arm along the windowsill, and blew a large, roiling cloud of blue smoke at the ceiling.

"I know, I know," she said. "It will dirty up your ventilator system."

"No, no, go ahead. I don't care. Let them get dirty. Most of the visitors were dying to smoke as well but they were too shy to ask."

"Not too shy to press me closely." She paused. "But never mind." She turned to the window for a moment, looking at nothing in particular out there in the deepening blue of evening, now approaching a violet in tone. After a time, she turned back. Vance had pulled a chair over to her place, and was waiting.

Fellirian sighed deeply, as if still phrasing the words she wished to say. She began, "Walter, you have contacts there, in the real world. I mean, at Region Central. What are the changes? There is something odd in our visitors, something orchestrated that has not been there before; the last few parties of visitors and trainees have been a spooky lot, more nervous than the usual lot of sightseers we get. They seem full of odd sets of contradictions, repressed things, all under the surface, nothing out in the open. As if they suspect something, but are afraid to even inquire into it. I could feel the hostility of this last group, the looks, the attention they gave my remarks, the questions they asked. There was purpose there; someone was feeling me out. But for what? They know, those repulsive Security people, that they could ask directly and I would speak freely. I am no plotter, no member of secret covens."

Vance noted her indignation, but did not comment on it. Instead, he said, "There have been some changes recently, at Region, but I have not been able to gauge the full impact or direction of them all yet." He paused. "And of course you already know the feelings of the mass of the people. Those feelings range from outright paranoia through envy to exasperation. They say most often that you are 'a gang of oversexed mutants who refuse to save the world. . . .' "

Fellirian interrupted. "Oh, oversexed! Would that it were so, now! But it's gone . . . we were fortunate with the third child, but . . . Well, it's just gone, the way it is for all of us. Surely they know that side of us as well."

"It is your infertile adolescence that nags at them. At us," he added. "We don't have anything like it. And in this century, bastardy is a capital crime, you know. More than that, it's two for one. . . ."

"Both parents depersonified. I know. But we are no less severe with those who would outbraid mate and conceive, in our terms. But the rest is just as much nonsense. They should see me chopping wood, or Morlenden walking through the woods to the remotest districts to keep up with things. Or Kaldherman and Cannialin and Pethmirvin up to all hours out in the shed, bringing in another batch of paper for our written records; or writing entries, cross-referencing. I don't feel like *Uber-*

mensch; I feel like an overworked bureaucrat in one of your own vast civil service hierarchies."

The tea arrived, carried upward to the conference room by an automatic dumbwaiter set in an alcove in the wall. Vance went over, collected the cups. They were still steaming. Returning, he said, "Yes, I sense some of the change that you have. I know of others . . . but so far I have not been able to tie any of it to anything concrete, like a change of policy. I write it off as just a periodic mood-shift. Thrills and adventure, something to get excited about. It's the pressure, you know. We need relief. We grind away, knowing that all our best efforts are just something temporary to keep us afloat until next month, or next year. One crisis succeeds another, one shortage another. You can keep it going, but it wears hard. Even here, secluded as we are, I feel that every day."

Fellirian looked toward the window, as if looking for some hint in the darkened sky, the rain, the night-fading vistas of lights and shiny streets. She turned back, asking, "And you have heard nothing?"

"Absolutely nothing. As you know, I used to have good contacts at Region Central. Old Vaymonde, they say, wasn't much of a chairman; no charisma. But he kept the infrastructure up, he did. Always talked with the Division heads. He was liked, not tolerated."

"I remember him well. One of the few to die in office."

"Right. At his post to the end. You know, there is a vulgar story to the effect that . . . Never mind. But when Denver installed this new chairman, this Parleau, my sources dried up, one by one. Retired, replaced, shifted, reassigned. All gone. Nothing sinister; he just wants his own people. But I keep a close eye on him, this Parleau. They say that he's one of their favorites, from somewhere out west, Mojave Region, or Sonora, or even Baja. One of those desert places—solar power and mining. He's a no-nonsense type: action, long hours, clean desk, business before pleasure, the needs of society, all that. And they say at Central these days that a new broom . . ."

". . . Sweeps clean. Ugh. Tell me no more tales of brooms. That one is worn to death." She sipped her tea, nodded. "Yes. I can see that. And I also know that it has been getting harder to get off the reservation, too. More papers, forms, registrations, passports. All amply justified, of course: that's the very soul of a bureaucracy—everything has its reasons. Of course, I could say that the real reasons are never stated, and sometimes even unknown to the official; many would be offended to know them. But even so, enough. I am overly sensitive to these things because of my own role—the permitting of weavings, the allowance of names, the registration of children. Nearness breeds suspicions."

She stopped for a moment, sipped at her tea, turned and gazed once more into the distance through the windows. She turned back, saying, "Besides, it's hardly worth the trouble. We have little enough outside the reservation. And I've heard tales I'd not care to test firsthand. We've had some disappearances. . . ."

Vance looked sharply at the head of Braid Deren. "You hadn't mentioned that before. . . ."

"No."

"Who were they?"

"Not so many. No one I know personally. Elders, by the talk of it. And all very vague, you know. It's all fourth-hand stuff. So far it has apparently been only elders, who could disappear for any number of reasons. The Final Cure Cult believes in natural death, alone in the woods. No one sees *them* again. Now, if something like this were to involve someone of brood phase, or adolescent, people would be more interested."

"How interested?"

"I couldn't say, right now. If it were deliberate, and some human agency were involved, I'm sure there would be some reaction. *What*, is the question. I cannot imagine how we could threaten you; we have neither the power nor the weapons, and if we had them, I don't know the way of their use. You know the Command of Demirel—not to use that as weapon which leaves the hand. No guns, no numbers."

"But you have butter, which could be withdrawn."

"The input, through the Institute? Oh, it would have to be very serious, then. I do not wish such a confrontation."

"Nor I, Fellirian. We have learned much from you."

"Not enough, if you don't put it into practice."

"Give us time. Institutions die hard."

"You've had time: four hundred years with your backs to the wall. Twenty billion humans! I don't know what I'd do with so many bodies. The very idea gives me nightmares; we'd run out of allowable names!"

"That's your worry?"

"That's the Deren part of me speaking. The county clerk, the registrar. Just think of the awful names people would have to use: we'd use up the good ones right away. Then there would be a girl named Gallflanger and a boy named H'wilvsordwekh."

"Only one Fellirian at a time."

"Only one. As long as I live no one may have that name, no matter what aspect. But one Braid couldn't cope with that level of work, nor would the people; instead, there would be First-derens, Second-derens, Third-derens . . . not for me, such multiples. I like being unique, even if what we do is not the most desirable role in the community."

Vance returned to an older topic: "So then, you sense some hostility?"

"We always sense some. It's not a matter of none and some; it's some, and then some more. Always greater than zero."

"Do you know anything on your side that might be fueling the present feedback you are getting?"

"No. That is what makes this time so troublesome. Mind, I do not say that nothing is going on; just that I know of nothing. But I know a lot. And we can look again. Morlenden is due back late tonight or tomorrow. I'll ask him. He moves about and hears more than the rest of us. He has the bad job, you know. And you. You must have a snoop planted around Center as well. Why don't we compare notes next time I see you?"

"Probably nothing going on that some sunshine wouldn't cure."

"Indeed, it could be the season. I am moody in the rainy autumn as well. It is not my season." Fellirian finished, and sipped once more at her tea. It was gone. She returned to her pipe. It had gone out. She looked up. It was time to leave.

Vance saw the cue, and said, "Well, let it be. Don't worry about it. I know of no reason either, right now. Will you be coming next week?"

"I would like to miss next week if I can. If it's just the same with you. Why don't you see if you can get someone else to fill in for me here with the visitors. For instance, that Maellenkleth Srith Perklaren. Or the Shuren girl, Linbelleth. . . . They're both young, but they have done this before. I am far behind in Braid work, and I wish to get caught up a bit. That is also why Morlenden has been out so much lately in the field; we all have been catching up with everything that happened this summer. There is more to the role than you realize. And we were irresponsible this summer, we lazed around and played with the children, worked the garden. We got behind. So Morlenden has been out weeks at a time. I have actually begun to miss him."

"Didn't you before? I thought you were always close. . . ."

"So we have been. But you also know"—and here she slipped into her own speech, Singlespeech—"*Toli lon Tooron Mamnatheno Kurgandrozhas:* Only the insiblings know the way of incest. We are too close. We take each other for granted. It's the way. We always fought a lot when we were little; we competed. But under that, we always knew what was coming for us, so after the fights we always buried the hatchet. We never had the luxury of being able to say, 'Well, fly off, Turkey-wattle, that's the last I'll see of you.' No. We always knew that whatever happened, what had been with friends and lovers, in the end the fertility would be ours, the *Klanh*-holding ours . . . and so it's been forty-five years for us, sleeping in a pile together most of the time. A little while out for the inweaving of the afterparents. So we always took the future for granted, too; when the time came, we'd go along our own paths, as we'd waited for so long. But after Kaldherman and Cannialin, and my own third fertility . . . it changed. We found that we actually felt more right together, somehow. So now we have been talking of remaining together when the Braid unravels. This causes another problem: where do we go?"

"Of all the things you can't make up your mind about . . ."

"Morlenden wants to join an elder lodge that, as he says, has some 'rigor' to it. One which does what you would call speculating into the nature of things. Or even Beechwood Lodge, the geneticists. For myself, I'd be pleased to go off somewhere, tend a garden, eat and drink, and tell made-up adventure stories by the fire in the communal hearthroom. But he's Fire, and I'm Earth. Aspect conflict. But also I think perhaps Olede-Kadh is just kidding. When all's said and done, he's no where as rigorous as he'd like people to think."

"I'm sure you'll make up your minds by the time—after all, you've got twenty years. It isn't like it was tomorrow. At any rate, your future is either decided or decidable. As for my own . . ."

"The Fertility Board has not answered your request yet?"

"Not yet."

"What can I offer but my regrets. I should like to see you with a family as you have seen me these years."

"So should I. But time is passing."

"That it is. I have heard they only approve the best. . . ."

"Were it so there I choose to believe I should have children older than your Pethmirvin, but they choose the visible. It works out to the worst sort, by and large, of toadies and arse-kissers. My records and achievements are second to none. But this job at the Institute never has had much favor . . . and there's the matter of my turning down a programmed name back when I was a trainee. It's been no secret, but I knew then I was taking my chances. . . ."

"You know, Walter, if you had taken one of those awful random-generated tags, no better than a number, you'd not have stayed here, and that's been worth something to many of us. Many of us now work willingly here, where before we did it only out of a sense of obligation, a debt. There is a difference in the input and a measurable one in the output. They should mark that one for you."

"You'd be surprised what they dig up to hold against you, when the time comes. You know what they say over in Inspection Directorate, and in Standardization? That no matter who it is, no matter how good they look, they can always find a way to Unsat* them. It's just how far they want to go."

Fellirian looked away from Vance for a moment, something flickering across her plain, open face, too quick to be seen, something, an emotion, close to annoyance. Vance's remarks were in themselves not wrong, so much as was the emphasis he put upon them, here, now. A wave of uneasiness moved in the back of her mind, then subsided. They all knew about bureaucratic systems, and they both knew that any system applied to classifying people which advertised objectivity drifted toward the worst and most crass forms of subjectivity. They? It was common knowledge along both sides of the fence.

She commented, as neutrally as she could, "I still hope for the best for you, nevertheless." After she spoke, she turned again to the window, now rising from her chair. She looked pensively outside for a long time, and then turned and went to a recessed alcove by the door, retrieving her outer clothing. Drawing the winter overcloak about her shoulders, she stepped into her winter boots, soft, supple leather, lined with a fiber material.

"It's time to go. The mono is in and waiting for latecomers such as I."

"Of course, Fellirian. I understand about the other two, the ones you mentioned. No problem. I'll see you in a few weeks, then. Come again, and we'll visit some more over some tea."

"Oh, I'll be back. I like to study the visitors as much as they like to study me." Here she paused, as if phrasing some difficult thought into bearable language. "But you know I need to refresh myself in my own surround. You and I, we are old friends. But because of that we overlook the fact that we are really very alien to one another, that we have different perceptions. Even so, I . . . but never mind. Next time, then?"

"Next time. I shall wait."

Fellirian turned and passed through the sliding doorway, which closed behind her, leaving Director Walter Vance alone in the meeting

---

* Unsat: To give someone an unsatisfactory rating.

room. For considerable time, he sat quietly alone in the dimming evening light, now close to darkness, thinking of nothing in particular, forcing no specific pattern of coherent thoughts. He walked over to the window and looked out into the same evening landscape Fellirian had been watching not long before. The light was now a deep sourceless violet-blue, the end of another rainy November day, deep in what as a child he had thought of as the bottom of the year. Bare, dripping branches. Shiny pavements, reflecting a silvery light. Shallow puddles ruffled by a light, variable wind, their reflections broken into shards by fitful gusts of raindrops. The monorail which ran into the far reaches of the reservation was yet standing in the station, waiting. Vance watched as a hooded and cloaked figure, rather more slight in stature than a human would appear at this distance, walked over to the mono along the platform, unhurriedly. The figure slid a door back, entered a coach, and vanished from his line of sight. The pale, pastel coaches sat immobile, breathing tremulous, tentative wisps of steam from the heaters into the damp and chilly air.

Then he noticed that the mono was moving, had been moving, and it had started so subtly he had missed it. Its speed increased, and it glided effortlessly along its single, flattened concrete track, silently. It curved away to the northwest, passing through a grove of pine trees. For a time he could follow its motion behind the trees, watching the lights, but at last it vanished from view entirely, fading behind the shoulder of a low rise. Vance looked away from the window, walked back to the dumbwaiter panel, and ordered more tea. Then he returned to his seat and waited. He knew what would come.

The room was almost dark. It grew fractionally more dim, almost night-dark, and the night advanced still another increment. Vance waited. He did not wait because he was a patient man, or because he had learned the fine art of time-watching from Fellirian. Or because he was placid of disposition; rather he waited because he expected a certain specific event to occur. For a time there was no indication of any event to come. But at last a tiny sound broke the after-hours stillness of the building. It was a small noise from the ceiling, an indeterminate click whose precise location could not be pinpointed. Vance heard it. He did not look up.

He said, seemingly into empty air, in a tired voice, "To whom do I speak today?"

The voice replied with perfect fidelity, just as if it were issuing from the mouth and throat of a person physically present in the room here with him, the mechanisms transmitting even the most subtle inflections of personal mannerism which reproducers usually missed. The voice was a breathy one, a little scratchy, a voice with a bubble of confidence in it. A smug voice. A voice belonging to someone having all the high cards.

It said, "Very sly, there. As if you had known before, and so I should follow the habit. Smooth, Director. But you know that the identity is never given; against the rules, so it is. And after all, what does it matter? We all say the same things."

Vance replied, "As usual you are right. I just wondered if I would draw an inexperienced one of you, just once."

The voice chuckled, genuine humor which it deigned to share. "Hardly that, sir. We don't work that way. You wouldn't believe the training we get, the evaluations we must pass. Rigorous is simply not the proper word! We even have a simulator to reproduce this kind of environment, to prepare us for fielding these little questions, these sly feints. But, Director, I assure you, we deal with some real masters; sly indeed they are, sneakier than an agency head in budget-cutting time. But enough of the poor Controller's job, yes? We want to get to business. So I must congratulate you on an exceptionally fine performance tonight and this evening, yes, all of it. The remarks about the new staff at Region Central, the new chairman. He'll be pleased, he will, and if I may reveal a confidence, he's pleased as a rule with little enough. No nonsense, him. Why, with a bit of training I believe you could make an agent provocateur. A provoc. Or were you sincere? Impossible. But yes, indeed, they'll like all this. The chairman likes a little hostility, controlled, of course. He says that it gives his directors that cutting edge."

"I'm sure."

"So I must regretfully inform you that we shall probably stop this circuit now."

"And so you have agreed with what I first told you."

"Yes, yes, of course. This was not doubt of your word, Director Vance, just routine verification. What we derived today has already gone upchannel to Timely Analysis Branch. Real-time forwarding, or almost so, at any rate. They concur, but their concurrence returns when they send it; they have to mull things over up there, not like us front-liners down here on the killing floor, so to speak. So they agree, as did we, you and I, if I may use the pronoun loosely. There's no ore in this Fellirian for processing, neither a dram nor a scruple. Her stress index appears rather high today, but it was steady; no jumps when special tagged subject matter is introduced. We quite agree with her that she knows of no conspiracy."

"So much for what she and I know. Is there one?"

"Aha! Questions from the answerer! You'll be a Controller yet. But conspiracies? I couldn't say at this point in time. There are anomalies, peculiarities. You have no need to know them now."

"Oh."

"So this circuit will be terminated. Deactivated. If you care to forward an evaluation of the proceedings as they have occurred, please utilize form eight-four-four-A, address attention F-six-three-two. I can use index points as well as you, as everyone in this competitive world."

"Speaking of points, when do mine get registered?"

"They have already been credited with the Bonus Section. You'll get a come-back copy soon. Congratulations on your sixer."

"Six? I was told it would be twenty!"

"Who was it told you that? I . . . well, you almost never see much over a deuce for this kind of work. After all, one can demonstrate negatives all day, can't one?"

Vance had no answer. The voice paused, then added, "Do you have any final comments before I break the circuit? It's my break time now."

Vance felt, almost like a pain, a sudden surge of pure rage, of frustration, of anger, growing rapidly, a spike of clean emotion, now; but it passed, and his system of internal modulations took over without too conscious a thought, leaving behind only a bitter aftertaste. Vance, like everyone else of the day, was expert at controlling his own emotions. He had done so for years, with the system, and with individuals, such as Fellirian. He said to the bodiless voice, "Perhaps this might be considered overly bold, but I must say that spying upon one's oldest friends is a degrading act requiring great compensation. I hope you have no more of these cooperations."

"Freely said, freely taken." There was a pause. Then the voice began again, "Analysis says you get one bonus point for honesty, minus two for too great an attachment to an imaginary peer-group value." The voice hardened. "And you're too soft in that area, you know. We do. Still, you end up with a fiver for today's work. Over average. Keep working at it."

"Thank you, I will."

"I have a last word of advice. Guidelines, if you will. The first is this: if one will sell, his price can be driven down to its true value. We could have run this operation without your cooperation, entirely. But then you would have got nothing. Perhaps a minus, who knows. Consider yourself lucky that we asked first. You know the rules; we don't have to. The second thing is this: you believed the ler lady's innocence of conspiracy. So it has turned out to be no little thing to assist Control in a little surveillance when one's friends are indeed innocent. What harm does it do? We work by eliminations, by isolation of most-improbables. So now, by a little work, your friend has been eliminated as an active suspect. So states the report. That should relieve you. And then this third thing: you are director of Interface Institute, and the New People, the ler as they call themselves, are most interesting. But to us who must manage the dangerous world, they represent a greater danger than the Cro-Magnon men did to the poor Neanderthals. We never found the aliens in deep space, Director; we made them here at home—and those people are stranger than anything we could expect to find out in the stars. Fins, fur, hands, paws, flippers; air-breathers, water-filterers, ammonia processors. Those kinds of aliens we could handle. These we can't. And these we take no chances with."

"They are much like us. Almost the same, really. Could it be that we don't really understand ourselves?"

"One problem area at a time. Control doesn't work Research."

"Certainly, but . . ."

"Good evening, Director."

"Good evening." Vance never heard any audible indication that the circuit had indeed been broken. After the last parting remarks by the unnamed Controller, there passed only silence. Vance could not be sure at what moment they turned it off. If they turned it off. He got up from his chair and walked tiredly to the dumbwaiter. The tea was cold.

They were disembodied voices in the night; where they were didn't matter, couldn't matter. They could be anywhere; they were everywhere, seemingly. In the place where they were, it was always night, the lighting artificial. There were no windows. Shift relieved shift. Incoming members reviewed instructions, read notices, signed forms. Outgoing members also signed forms. Shift relieved shift. And the voices had passed and echoed through the circuits so many times that when repairmen went into the cable tunnels, they sometimes found unexplained traffic still going on what were supposed to be deactivated lines. They called these fading voices "copper ghosts," the imprints of gone and forgotten Controllers still wandering through the circuits. Voices in an eternal night.

"Sector Ten. Go ahead, there."

"Two-Alpha Control. A hard copy record format follows my voice report. Going now, there, depress your acknowledge."

"Got it there, Two-Alpha."

There was a pause, but the line remained open and live.

"And Ten here."

"Two-Alpha. Go ahead."

"Re your hard copy, noted and concur. Eval says Vance to be reassigned to a more innocuous position at the first discreet opportunity. Negative haste. Promotion category Delta. He's getting unreliable. Too specialized. Needs more generalist work. We also recommend that there be no more passives like this, permissive, you know, for not less than thirty days, as per Schedule twenty-nine, column twenty, line fifteen."

"Charlie your instructions. Have it right here. We'll set up the involuntaries, and forward tell the take to your house."

"Right that. According to schedule, there. Ten out, break."

And for a time, along a certain channel of communications, along wires, over laser beams in evacuated pipes, along wave-guides in which nothing passed save microwaves, there was silence. The line was dead. But there was not, at the ends of such channels, inaction.

THREE

The teacher instructs the student; just so the master with the novice. It is the final measure of both instructorship and masterhood how much the instructor learns from the student. We can further state that the greater the distance-of-relationship between the two, the more apparent this becomes, so that with a very young child, the best teacher actually learns more than the child in the process of instruction.

—The Game Texts

THE RESERVATION MONORAIL was their sole concession to modernity; for the rest of the space enclosed by the boundary fence, the only modes of travel available were walking, riding a pony, or driving a cart pulled either by oxen or the heavy, solid horses the ler preferred. Its track plan covered most of the reservation in a skewed figure eight, the north loop leaned sharply over into the northwest corner, and the south loop broadened and spread out to the southeast. There were two trains, which ran in the same direction twelve hours apart, each drifting around the whole of the route more or less in the course of a day.

On the days when Fellirian worked at the Institute, she had to spend almost all of the previous day traveling, spending the night at the Institute hostel (operated by Braid Shuren). Then, the next day, she would board the mono for the ride back. But where before the way of motion had been against her, so that she had to ride all the way around to get to the southeast where the Institute was located, the way back, to the contrary, was short and almost direct, straight into the center of the reservation, where lay her Braid holding.

It would be late when she arrived at last, after a lone ride, a long day, and a lone walk as well; and in the cold and damp season of the year. Still, for her, it was better than spending another night out. It would be near midnight when she finally got home, but that was fine enough—

they would save some supper for her, and some would stay up late to share some talk. She did not care so much for travel, as did her insibling and co-spouse Morlenden, who did most of the Braid's field work. That was the drudgery, the visits, the ceremonies. But Morlenden never complained, aside from some grousing which they all knew was not serious. Her work down at the Institute was tiresome; but it was a window on the outside, one of the few maintained of which she was aware. Her evaluations of that narrow view were all part of a grist constantly being fed to the lineal ruling Braid, the Revens, Pellandrey Reven, Insibling and *Klandorh* . . . the feelings and the thoughts which went with them trailed off.

Boarding the mono, which was operated by the Gruzen Braid, she could see yet, even in the deep evening light, the modest monument the people had erected for the enlightenment of the visitors; it reassured her. An inlaid woodcarving with an overlay of subtle color wash, it was supposed to be a visual image of the central doctrine of ler self-image.

Circular in outline, the bas-relief of the Emblem was divided internally into four quarters, as aligned with the four points of the compass; within each was depicted a person, highly suggestive in symbolism. The upper quarter showed a ler elder, with the long double braids characteristic of the class, wreathed in clouds bordered with lightning in the sky and flame along the base. The heraldic figure was reaching out of the clouds with its right hand toward the center of the Emblem, while its left hand, upraised, held some of the lightnings. The expression along the planes of the face appeared stern, judicial, abstract, emotionless. It was, so far as the human visitors could determine, utterly undifferentiated by sexual characteristics.

The figure depicted in the right-hand panel seemed to be a military figure, drawn with great subtlety and respect. This figure seemed mature, rather than elder; the single braid of hair falling to the middle of the back reinforced this impression. And where the elder in the upper panel had been clothed in a simple pleth, a utility garment, this one was depicted wearing a kiltlike garment about the hips and thighs, while the upper torso was covered by a light sleeveless vest or jacket. The kilt or skirt seemed to suggest leather, the vest a coarse weave, or perhaps chain mail. On the head was a light leather helmet with a stiffened ridge along the top. The Warrior, as it was known, held a short, leaf-bladed sword in its left hand, the one nearest the viewer. The point was held down, deliberately, not simply drooping. And with its right hand, it reached also for the center of the Emblem.

On the opposing left side, the figure depicted appeared to be similar in age and class to the military figure on the right, but it was dressed in a long, flowing gown, with a hood attached to the garment, but folded back. This one was shown in the act of emerging from a garden through a simple arched masonry gate, carrying a basket filled with various fruits and vegetables, some recognizable, others enigmatic. It carried the basket in the right hand, toward the viewer, and reached into the center with its left. This figure suggested a feminine nature, to the same degree that the figure to the right suggested masculinity. Subtly. One imagined, but was not quite sure.

The figure in the bottom quarter panel seemed the most striking of all: unlike the others, which were colored in a direct and naturalistic manner, she was almost completely painted in tones of blue, as were her surroundings in the panel. She: the image was of a young girl dressed in a filmy homespun shift that suggested almost every detail of the supple body beneath; and she was shown reaching upward, yearning, with both arms and hands upraised, her young and innocently lovely face also turned upward, filled with an expression of rapture. She was shown emerging from a pool of water around which water plants grew profusely. . . .

Riding along the track of the mono, Fellirian now saw full night through the windows of the coach she was riding; and little else. The mono made its deliberate and unhurried way through the nighted country of the reservation. She looked through the windows more closely; while she could not make out much of the passing unlit details, she could make out the forest silhouette of the treetops, outlined against the weak sky-glow which was always present, no matter what part of the reservation one happened to be in. There were no lights within the reservation to cause this; rather, they were all outside its borders, the signs of the industrial civilization which surrounded it on all sides. It was stronger in the west and north, but the glow was never invisible, not even in the center.

There was hardly a place on the entire planet, on the waters as well as along the lands, where it was not possible to read a newsgram from the public information agency by available light in the hours of darkness. Human society worked around the clock, in total disregard of local time. On their calendar, they still showed the ancient days of the week, but the number of people who actually used them for their schedules was very small, almost nonexistent. For the rest, the vast mass of twenty billion, they oriented themselves to their particular shift cycle. There were four of these shifts, interlaced so that each person within a shift worked, in succession, five evenings, one off, five midnights, one off, five days, followed by five days off. Four shifts, each with an identity of its own.

Fellirian continued to meditate, relaxing, letting the thoughts lead where they would. Shifter Society, they called it; its emblem was a cube with a staring brown eye upon each of its visible faces. Fellirian thought it peculiar, unnecessary. They didn't need to put the whole planet on shifts for a war footing against some invader, not for production reasons, for it took as much to sustain a twenty-four-hour-a-day operation as they gained from it. But she thought she knew. There seemed to be two main reasons; one was that by having shifts one could use space more efficiently, and hedge against the panic brought by overcrowding. It also gave the millions idled by arbitrary changes something to do while they were being reoriented.

As each man's work had become steadily more piecemeal and meaningless, so had establishments interlocked into one another and pressed into private lives. One by one, the nations had grown into one another; governments did not protect their people, but protected themselves. Some radicals hoped and strove for the day when people would wake up. But if they ever had, there had been no sign of it; the conscious decisions were no improvement over the half-asleep ones. Of course, at the very end of the old period, pre-shift, there had been some frictions, bickerings, adjustments. That had been the days of the Attitude Patrols, volunteers who did not monitor performance, but intangibles such as feelings and motivations. The end of the first population crisis had seen Shift Society emerge triumphant. And so afterward public buildings were multipurpose, used full-time, all year, every day. There was no wasted space. Every square foot which did not contain working space, contained the minuscule living quarters allotted to all. Everything left over was either power production or agriculture.

But they forgot, by will, design, or accident, that once buildings had been made to serve men, whatever perverse uses they had put them to, however seldom. The more logical and reasonable life came to be ordered, the more illogical and confusing it became; now people existed to fill buildings to maximum efficiency, just as customers in a queue existed to give the bored clerk something to do. Once buildings had been inspirational; now they were four sides and a top, functional, and reusable. Each one lasted, on the average, less than a person's lifetime. As with the buildings, so it was with everything else. If one quarter of

Earth's population was at work at a given minute, so it was also true that almost another quarter were deep in their cups, drunk as lords. And if there were no more armies, there were vast numbers of police in their place so that the actual number of armed men was greater by percentage than in the worst of previous periods of world war.

Over the shifts were the members of the hierarchy, most of whose numbers were stabilized on permanent day-shifts, although certain of their order worked other fixed shifts: midnights, eves. Recruited from the upward-striving shifters who had already demonstrated their allegiance, few had other than programmed names, and fewer still had any recognizable family ties. The organization was all.

They called this system civilization, and considered it the best of all possible circumstances; considering the chaos which it obviously held at bay, perhaps it was an excellent compromise. But to Fellirian, it suggested nature at its rawest. And the ancient dynamics of nature, the uncontrolled fears out of the past, had not been eliminated at all, but painted over with a set of new colors. There were strains and tensions everywhere, growing slowly and insidiously daily, monthly, yearly. Man's runaway population growth had been slowly braked to an agonized halt, but the price had been the complete loss of everything else. And the sad thing to her was that the people of today knew no better life, remembered no wildlife, no freedom, no open-ended self-checked ecology; they thought the ler quaint and eccentric, impractical and superstitious. . . .

The darkened coach moved on through the night. She felt at last the letdown after a full day of work, on her feet, tense with fielding question after question. The motion lulled her, and she became first relaxed, then drowsy. She began to drift in and out of a light half-sleep; there were others in the coach with her, seated away from her, in the far end, and they seemed to be absorbed in their own affairs, or perhaps also just drowsing . . . she thought she saw one of the seated figures rising, surrealistically slow, as if under water, or it might have been a dream, a daydream. She felt her head nod, and her eyelids felt heavy. Was someone now taking the seat beside her?

"Fellirian?"

She came awake instantly and the fog cleared out of her mind. She turned to her left and looked at the person who had joined her. The voice had been male, but the person was hooded. She thought that odd, for the coach was not cold. In fact, the coach was almost too warm. "Yes," she said. "I am Fellirian Deren. And who is it who speaks from within a hooded pleth in the overheated mono coach?"

The low voice from within the hood said, almost inaudibly, "One whom you once knew well."

She leaned forward to peer into the hood, caught a quick glimpse of a face, one she indeed knew well. Had known well. It had been some time since they had spoken. Her mouth started to form syllables of a name, but a finger was placed across her mouth. Within the hood was motion, a negation.

He leaned closer, saying, "And so it was, just as now. By the love I have had for you and your house, have I come this way to bring a warning to you."

She shook her head, as if unbelieving. He noted it, and continued, "One will come to your *yos*, asking a service which only your house can provide. You must neither delay, nor refuse it. Negotiate as you will, but let it not be in doubt between us now."

She answered, without hesitation, "It will be according to that you have spoken. But . . ."

"Ask no questions. They will all be answered in time. And not all the answers will be satisfying to you. Indeed, they will trouble you in your heart. I would not have had it so, but events press us, and they belong to one among the Powers. The Air element lies heavy upon us, and only Will counters it. But with this I also warn you to take care in all things relating to yourself from henceforth, and most especially to what you will do for this task, for there will be danger. It is for these reasons that I wear a hood, and ask that you not speak my name aloud. The mono is no place for such dialogue; I have risked much to come as far as I have."

"You could have met me elsewhere."

"Not so much as you imagine. I am watched. So are you, although not so much now. But do you not feel a change in the Institute, a shifting of balances?"

"Yes. Yes, I have, this last time. I was disturbed, but there was nothing I could see. What is it?"

"Times change always. There is nothing fixed; only varying degrees of the skill by which the riders ride the wave of the present. We enter different waters now, and the waves change. An accident, perhaps more malice than we anticipated, and perhaps something more—these things have made turbulence at a critical time when we do not need it. And now questions are being asked, sensors are being activated, old thoughts being rethought." He gestured at the outside, at the sky-glow visible beyond the treetops. "There, they are stirring again. Something bad has happened. We cannot make it as it was, but we can find out of it what we must, so that we may know how much has befallen us."

"What has happened?"

"I will not speak of it; to tell what I know, and to add what I suspect, is to describe something which may not be spoken of openly here, even between such as you and me. Not even hints will I give; you do not know it now: you will have to unravel it as you go along. I want no preconceptions. But you must do it, when you are asked, and you must be careful." The last word was emphasized so strongly it came out almost a hiss. Fellirian drew back.

She paused, and said, "You speak in riddles."

"I speak as only I may, now. I fear in the end of it you will know what I do. I would have spared you the weight of it." Now the hooded shape moved, as if looking away from her, to the front of the coach. "Your stop will be soon; how say you of this?"

"It will be as you have said. We shall, we Derens. I only ask why there was haste."

"Because the one who will ask of you is either approaching your *yos* now as we speak, or is already there." He added in a suppressed half-chuckle which spoke much of some private joke, "I came to use my influence and ensure your response."

Fellirian looked to the front, and glimpsed familiar landmarks passing by. She felt the mono slowing for the halt. She stood, and the hooded figure moved to allow her to pass into the aisle. She turned to him and said, "So it will be as you have asked. I wish only that we might have met more openly. We parted so."

"We will meet again, I think. And after that, who may know the future? But however the past was, we know that it is only shadows in our minds now. Pleasurable they were, but not to be repeated. We have lived other lives. And hard decisions lie ahead for me. For you. I will not trouble your heart with them now; when the time comes you will face them better with an innocent heart."

The mono stopped, fairly smoothly, but fast enough to cause Fellirian to sway slightly. He said, "And now, your stop."

"You will come with me along the long path?"

"I cannot. There are others yet to see this night, along this way, and in the north where lies my *yos*."

The coach doors opened. Outside it was so quiet the dripping of rainwater could be heard. Fellirian said quietly, "I have kept the tradition of the *vayyon*."

"As have I. But in time all secrets may have to go overboard. But think not of the past, and prepare to wrestle the future."

She nodded. "Just so . . . it was good to see you again."

"And you. I do not forget. And may it be with your *Toorh* as with you."

"And so with yours as well." She turned to depart the coach.

The doors opened, and Fellirian focused on the immediate now, where she was. Her memory had distracted her, disoriented her, reinforced by the voice of the man who had spoken. She stepped down out of the coach into the cold dampness. There was fog now; the rain had stopped, yet only recently, for all things dripped. It was almost noisy after the muffled quiet of the coach, her attention single-mindedly riveted. It was an elevated platform made of wood, shingled, charmingly rustic. To her left was the waiting-shed, open on the side facing the track; a sign, weather-beaten and stained, displayed the name of the stop: Wolgurdur, it said in the plain shapes of the Singlespeech alphabet. Flint Mountain Halt. The cold air touched her, and she shivered, adjusting from the warmth of the coach. Then she took a deep breath, clearing her head, and started slowly for the stairway which wound down to the forest floor.

At the head of the stairs she turned back to see if she could still see inside the coach. The doorway was open, and within it was the same figure, his face obscured in the shadows of his hood. She raised her voice and called to him, in a clear but still quiet voice, "Never fear! I will do it for you."

The figure answered, "Not for me, but for us all. You will see." Then he looked to his left, into the shed, back to her. "Is someone waiting there, in the shed?"

Fellirian turned back. She could not see around the corner, so she walked over to the edge of the shed, looked within. Sure enough, there was a person there, wrapped against the night damp, huddled over, apparently asleep. Fellirian shook her head, chuckling to herself. Here was some night-wanderer who had come the long walk down to Flint Mountain to await the mono, and, tired from the exertion, had taken a catnap in the corner; now not even awakened by the arrival of the train, nor their talking across the platform. The mono was waiting. Fellirian approached, and gently shook the traveler's shoulder, an adolescent by the feel of it. The person awoke, and looked up with the blankness of one awakened suddenly, undoing the hood of her overcloak.

Fellirian smiled, then laughed aloud. She said, half to herself, "Well,

well, well! Whoever should I happen upon in the mono halt waiting-shed, but my own *Nerh*, Peth-child." She turned and waved to the train, that they should depart, and turned back again to Pethmirvin. "Whatever are you doing down here in the very bowels of the night?"

While Pethmirvin collected her wits, the mono began to move. The coach in which Fellirian had been riding moved past, slowly accelerating. In a moment, it was gone. Pethmirvin, the elder outsibling of the Derens, Fellirian's firstborn and her secret favorite, looked up at her foremother blankly for a long moment, and then away, averting her eyes, deeply embarrassed to have been caught thus dozing in the shelter. Fellirian's child and favorite she might have been, but the girl resembled neither her mother nor her forefather, Morlenden. Peth was another quality. She was slender, thin as a reed, awkward, self-conscious. Her hair was a pale, washed-out light brown. She was tall already for a ler, and very pale in color. But in the summer, her hair bloomed into a warm, rich golden color, and her skin turned the color of lightly browned toast. In her face, there were faint reminders of Fellirian, in the large, expressive eyes and the broad, generous mouth; yet there was a crispness there, too, something which subtly echoed Morlenden: the long face, with its suggestions of boniness, the hard chin. Pethmirvin was variable as quicksilver: lovely one moment, homely the next.

The girl tried to speak, but since she was not yet completely awake, the words came all tumbling out, like a badly wrapped parcel suddenly coming undone, then falling completely apart. But one way or another, it somehow all got out. "Madheliya, here. I was supposed to meet you here. Am supposed. Here I am. When did you come?"

"Just now, sleepyhead."

"Oh, I'm sorry, really I am."

Fellirian reached into the hood, ruffling the girl's hair gently. "No sorries, Peth. Although you would have felt funny had you missed me, and waited all night down here." Fellirian laughed warmly. "But why have you come all the way down here, and in the cold, too? Was it to fetch me home? It's not as if I didn't know the way. Nor am I afraid of the dark. And, inasmuch as time has treated me somewhat cruelly, no lovers to make rendezvous with along the way."

Pethmirvin stood up, a little stiffly, and stretched, shivering in the damp night air, even though she was dressed quite warmly, as if she had been out for some time, and knew she was going to be. When she stretched, she was taller than Fellirian.

Fellirian watched her, thinking to herself. *Fifteen and already she's taller than me. Prettier, too, in her own way. And cast into the outsibling's lot. I worry about her, poor thing; she hasn't the temper for it.*

Pethmirvin continued, "Kadh'olede* is supposed to be at the *yos* by now; he had not yet come when I left, but he was expected at any moment. One of the Morens had seen him in a tavern by the old ferry crossing on the Hvar. They sent me down to tell you to hurry along, and not to stop along the way for tea at the Morens, nor visit with Berlargir and Darbendratht, because we have guests, important guests, and they won't talk until all the parent phase Derens are present."

Fellirian had been half listening. Morlenden seen in a tavern! Of course they saw him in a tavern! She had been hearing that kind of tale for many years now. But the words about important guests brought her to full attention, remembering what he in the mono had said. She interrupted Pethmirvin. "*Kel'ka Arnef?* Who was it?"

Pethmirvin replied, "An elder, the Perwathwiy Srith, accompanied by a didh-Srith, a bit older than me. Sanjirmil Srith Terklaren."

Fellirian leaned back. "The Perwathwiy, indeed! At our *yos*. I wonder what would bring her there."

"Madheliya, neither she nor Sanjirmil would speak of it. And you know elders; wouldn't set a foot in the *yos*. But that Sanjirmil thing did, though. Came right in and helped herself to my supper she did."

"Peth, you know the way of the hospitable. We must share with the stranger. Sanjirmil would expect supper. And as for the Perwathwiy, I'd expect the full rigor of discipline from her."

"Do you know her?"

"Only by repute. Not personally. She was a Terklaren herself, first born insibling and Klandormadh in her day . . . many years ago, of course; she is the foremother of Sanjirmil's fore-mother. If she's a day, she's *perh meth sen-dist years*."

"Yes, that's her. She's all gray. She stood outside in the rain until Kaldherman went out and unlocked the shed." Pethmirvin giggled. "He said, so Sanjirmil wouldn't hear, that if she wouldn't come in, the old bat could stand all night in rain for all he cared."

---

* Short form—"Forefather Morlenden."
† Insiblings of the previous generation of Derens. Specifically, Forefather and Foremother of both Morlenden and Fellirian.
‡ Literally, one and seven fourteens of years, in the fourteen-base number system. In decimals, ninety-nine.

"Pethmirvin Srith Deren!"

"That's what he said, Madheliya, not me! But Cannialin told him that the old woman would put a curse on him if he didn't give her some shelter. And that if she did, that she, Cannialin, would probably help her."

"Peth, you know an elder's not supposed to enter a *yos*; that's one of the Basic Arbitrations. When one's insibling children complete the weaving ceremony and the initiation, then one leaves the *yos* forever. Not just your own, anyone's!"

"I know. But a lot of them do it anyway, on the sly. And besides, it was cold and rainy."

"Doesn't matter. She would stand there anyway. But good for Ayali. So now, my sleepy girl-child; come along then. We won't get home standing here in the mono shelter and talking the night away." Fellirian put her arm around the younger girl's slender shoulders, giving her a quick hug; and so together they descended the worn, unpainted staircase to the ground, wet and quaking from the rain which had ended. They said no more, but set out directly under the bare dripping trees, northward, into the central provinces. Fellirian reflected as they began the walk homeward that in most circumstances she would have been irritated to find Peth out so late at night; yet this night she felt comforted by the girl's presence. Perhaps it was just the cold and dampness. Or more likely disturbing impressions, augmented by the cryptic rejoinder she had received riding the mono. No doubt about it: the future had become a troubled and uncertain one, and it was measurably easier to face such an uncertain future when your future could walk along for a time with you.

And her thoughts insisted, *The Perwathwiy Srith is then she of whom he spoke; she would ask something of us. Perwathwiy and her own Toorh's Toorh, Sanjirmil*. Her mind raced, seeking data: Perwathwiy was hetman of Dragonfly Lodge, the elder commune reserved for the Gameplayer Braids. And Sanjirmil? Fellirian had no knowledge of the girl directly. She recalled images of Braid Linebooks, reference logs, registered births, deaths, weaving ceremonies. There: she had it. Sanjirmil Srith Terklaren. Eldest *Toorh* and *Klandorh*-to-be of the Secondplayer Braid. Age, one and two fourteens, almost mature. Was there a connection? And was there a connection with the events in the Institute? She could see none. But that failed to comfort her, for she could see no reason why the Perwathwiy should come to her *yos*, and that what she would ask be agreed to beforehand. Fellirian shivered, and not entirely from the cold.

The path soon narrowed as they walked upward out of the valley in which the mono ran; had it been dry, it would have been wide enough for the two of them to walk abreast, but with the rain, the worn path was too slippery along the edges, so they walked single file, silently, Pethmirvin leading with her long-legged stride. Apparently the girl was taking her instructions seriously, for she wasted no time and set a steady pace. Fellirian, used to walking many miles, found that she needed her breath for the walk.

The path wound gently upward, meandering here and there, following lines of passage through the old forest that had been made long before Fellirian and Pethmirvin; indeed, before the ler had assembled and moved to this place. Game trails, the trails of humans who had lived here long ago, remnants of old logging roads. It crossed others, some broader, some equally broad, others hardly visible, mere pressed-down places that trailed off to either side. The path they followed led northward from the mono line into the heart of the reservation, the Wolguron, the Flint Mountains. The name was somewhat of a misnomer, for the range consisted of low hills of no great elevation, and no particular distinction, save that they were higher and steeper than the rolling country which surrounded them. But it was an old range, and it once had been high and proud, although no person had seen it so; now it was the gnawed and eroded wrinkle-remnants of the creases and folds made aeons ago in the collision of two great continents, North America and Africa. It had been eroded many times. Some argued that the range had never been high and great; but to the ler who now lived under its shadow this was no great matter. The Flint Mountains endured. They survived.

The rain had stopped, but under the many bare branches of November the icy water still dripped, and the creeks and streams were busy with the newly fallen water. The night was filled with water-sounds, drips, gurgles, rushing blurred sounds deeper in the woods. It was pleasant to hear, and it drowned out the distant sounds one heard when the woods were silent: the muted rumble of the civilization behind the lights. They found as they walked that they could see the path well enough, even with the overcast darkness and the weakness of the ler eye at night*, because of this very sky-glow. But they also had something more, for the night is never dark to those who allow their eyes time to adjust to it.

From time to time, they could sense they were passing either near some solitary *yos*, far off deep in the trees, or by some small elder lodge.

---

* The ler retina was more sensitive to color than the human, but it was deficient in rod cells. Their night-vision was poor.

Both of them knew the way well enough, so much of their knowledge was what they called unbidden memory. But there were other hints: woodsmoke, odors of cut wood; barnyard odors, stables, compost piles. Someone lived nearby. In this area there were few elder lodges, and all of the ones that were hereabouts were small, hardly larger than family Braid groups. Members of such lodges felt more like a contained Braid than a commune, where the Braid identities were quickly submerged. Indeed, Fellirian's own forefather and foremother lived in such a lodge; she saw them seldom now, but tried to drop in and visit from time to time on her way back from the Institute. From these visits, extended by Fellirian's talkative forefather Berlargir until nearly dawn, had come the phrase, "visiting at Berlargir's," which meant being away for an indefinite period of time.

The path passed close by one of the elder lodges, not the lodge of the former Derens, close enough that they would have been able to see it had it been daylight. Tonight they could not make out the buildings deeper down in a hollow, but before the entryway they could see flickering the ghostly blue of a spirit-lamp, a small paper lamp illuminated from within by a single tiny candle. It was a sign of mourning for the dead.

They passed by no other dwellings. Ler did not build their homes, whatever phase they were, close to path or roadway, but always at the end of dead-end paths which terminated at running water. Custom and ritual, just as there was only one doorway into a *yos*. They saw no other lights. The hour was late, now near midnight, and all the folk who lived along this creek, Thendirmon's Rivulet, had long since tumbled into sleep. Ler retired early.

"A rainy night," they would say, "and good for sleeping and dreaming under the rounded roofs while the raindrops fall from the branches overhead." And acorns would also drop in the autumn, shaken loose by a sudden gust of wind, resounding hollowly as they struck. Fellirian found herself thinking just these thoughts as she and her *nerhsrith* walked silently as ghosts through the dark, damp woods. And after they arrived? To come into the hearthroom, eat and talk a while, and then climb into the broodroom, removing clothing and wriggling a cold, tired body into a warm down-filled comforter, close to someone and the kind of warmth only a well-known, long-time close body can provide. Yes. She remembered: back when they all had been in their fertile period, the second for herself and Morlenden, first for Cannialin and Kaldherman, as they had paired off with their two new co-spouses; at night they

had hung a light print curtain across their common sleeping compartment, dividing it. Not for prudery, nor for jealousy, but for politeness
and privacy. A rare privacy. They had all as a matter of course lived ado-
lescences of active sexuality, with little hidden. But that was what one
wanted to do. Fertility was different; compulsive, driven, almost a kind
of desperate madness. The intensity of desire was of a different order entirely. Then they wanted seclusion, aloneness. It was as if children who
had played games of war had suddenly found themselves in the manic
violence, confusion, and panic of real war in all its horror. The playing
and the fun were over: the real thing had begun. Thus, the curtain. Now
it was down, packed away for the next generation. Fertility and desire
had come and gone. Not their regard for one another. "Only a Braid after
fertility," went the proverb, and indeed it was true.

She let her memory dig deeper into itself as they walked. Far back in
their past, Morlenden—Olede whom Fellirian-Eliya could not remember not-knowing—had himself suspected that after the birth of Pethmirvin, Fellirian would bring to him for second-weaving the girl
Cannialin, the *Thes*, younger outsibling of the Morens, the next Braid
down the rivulet. Their ages were right, five years apart, and the Morens
and the Derens always, rules permitting, exchanged younger outsiblings.
Their own Kaentarier Srith had already so gone to the Morens. No surprise there, and indeed they had dallied off and on for years. But Fellirian had no idea who Morlenden would bring to her second-weaving.
She had expected to be surprised, but not as astounded as she had been;
she had never let the image of that day slip from the forefront of her
memory.

. . . She had been feeling the first twinges of returning fertility, and
this aspect of herself had begun to elicit subtle responses from Morlenden and Cannialin, although at this particular time the Moren girl
had not yet moved in with them. But it had been a day late in the
spring, with heavy, wet, sagging dark clouds presaging a storm, and she
had been hoeing in the garden, all the while playing with Peth. And
Morlenden had come strolling up the path from the *yos*, with a stranger
in tow, and Fellirian, deeply embarrassed by the dust and sweat that
streaked her, caught first sight of her co-spouse-to-be. Her immediate
impression had been one of a truculent roughneck with a hard, severe
face, rusty hair with more than a hint of curl in it, and almost a swagger
to his walk. No doubt a bargeman from the River Yadh terraces.

Now at this time Fellirian had just started going down to the Institute regularly, although she had been making sporadic visits since she

had been about twenty. And as a result of her travels, she had gained a spattering of romantic ideals somewhat at variance with traditional ler visions of practicality. So in her imaginings she had wished Morlenden to bring her a poet, a dreamer, a gentle charmer. She had received, to Morlenden's apparent vast mirth, what appeared to be a hewer of timbers and a piler of stones, showing along his limbs the visible corded muscles of a wrestler. She learned later that indeed he did hold a local championship for just that. But his home was far to the northwest, and she did not know him. More, as she found out later, he was *Nerh* in his own Braid, and much accustomed to having his own way among his contemporaries. And to add insult to injury, he was already full fertile. As they were introduced, and Fellirian made the ritual responses, she could already feel her own body responding to the exaggerated maleness of him. Deep in his time, as they would say.

Later, she had abused Morlenden as she never had before, and then run away into the forest, in tears and complete exasperation. But Olede had followed, patient as he always was, and after a time explained that his choice—undeniable for her as hers had been for him, except for narrowly specified reasons which almost no one used—had been intended as a rare and subtle gift, a most high token of the regard in which he held his insibling, as she would find out, if she just would. As she did. Alone in the woods, she had stopped by a quiet pool of water, and had looked long at herself, seeing more therein than the outline and shaping of a face; and she had begun to see. And as usual, Morlenden-Olede had been right. The hints were there; for Kaldherman, Adhema she now called him, was a rare gift, indeed; for he had been as tender and giving in the reality as his apparent roughness had repulsed her at the first. Fellirian also knew herself to be no notable beauty, like, for example, the heartless flirt Cannialin; she was instead simple, direct, plain, and straightforward. But to Kaldherman, she had cast a dazzling light, Fellirian-the-wise, who walked among humans without fear, in their vast cities, levels of organization to which the ler possessed no parallel. He seemed to consider himself among the most fortunate of all outsibling *Tlanhmanon;* he had woven into a Braid containing Fellirian, a prize beyond words, and in addition the urbane Morlenden and the exotic Cannialin. And already with Pethmirvin, then a child of five, it also seemed that he would be the best of all four of them with the children.

And so it had been all these years, she thought, returning to the present. Fellirian realized with a start that she had been daydreaming, and that they had come far while her mind had been elsewhere; they had been trudging steadily through the nighted, rain-wet forest. For an instant she felt disoriented, vertiginous, lost. She looked about for a landmark, some subtle reminder; she sensed they were near home. Yes. They were already past the forking in the path which led to the *yos* of the Morens, almost at the one that led to their own, far down the steep, root-strewn path. They rounded a curve in the maul path, and Pethmirvin lengthened her stride, anticipating.

They came to the place where the path divided along a slight rise; from here, in daylight, one could catch a quick glimpse of the entire holding, the *yos* by the rivulet under a feathery canopy of ironwood, the sheds and outbuildings, the garden, the animal pens and yards, stone walls carefully laid. Now it was night and ahead of them were only suggestions of shapes, some dim lights showing in the translucent windows of the *yos*. The memory filled in what the eye did not actually see, and they felt a release, a happiness; they had arrived.

Fellirian paused for a moment at the foot of the stairs to the entryway—the hearthroom section of the *yos* looming above them like the high stern of some strange ship, its elliptical shape distorted by perspective—not climbing the narrow wooden stairs, but instead turning, reluctantly, to the wash-trough to her right, closer to the rivulet. She looked long into the dark water gurgling into the trough from a large clay pipe communicating with the rivulet, in her mind already feeling the bite of the water on her skin.

Pethmirvin did not enter either, but remained, waiting just by the foot of the stairs. Fellirian turned, not looking at the girl, and said, "Peth, dear, you don't have to wait for me; go on in and tell the rest that we've come at last."

The girl hesitated, cleared her throat. "Can't right now, Madheliya. I must take the ritual washing, too, much as I would wish not to." Already Pethmirvin's voice seemed to have the chatter of her teeth in it.

For a long-moment, they stood silently in the dark and looked at one another. They both knew the rituals and traditions and obeyed them with little hesitation. Indeed, Fellirian sometimes stressed orthodoxy, as she felt she had an example to set. Morlenden avoided the trough as much as possible, although he was fastidious and would soak for hours in a huge washtub out back while Pentandrun and Kevlendos ran relays of hot water from the hearth. But there was the wash-custom, even in winter when it was a feat of daring to address oneself to the water. Fellirian knew that she would need to wet herself with the cold creekwater before she could properly enter her own house; she had been outside. Here the purpose was not cleanliness, for any excuse would do for a bath; rather, here was ritual, magic. Fellirian had been exposed to strangeness, alien values, and the wash invoked the cleansing power of the Water elemental to remove the dross of the outside. The pollen of the strange.

Now as for Pethmirvin, she could have incurred the water obligation for any number of reasons; but Fellirian also remembered her own adolescence, and the occasions when she herself had stood before this very trough, trembling with fear of the cold water. She thought she knew the reason, although she was mildly surprised by the season and time of occurrence. Night and winter?

Fellirian addressed Peth with mock severity, "Nerh'Emivi, by some accident did you meet a *dhainman** along the way to the mono?"

The girl answered shyly, looking at the ground as she did. "In the shed by the mono line, Madheliya. Farlendur Tlanh Dalen. He walked with me when I came down to fetch you." For a moment Pethmirvin looked up and held Fellirian's eyes in her own gaze, unflinching. Then she looked down at the ground, shy again.

Fellirian threw back the hood of her overcloak, and opening the upper part of her outer garment, retrieved the long single braid of her hair from behind her and began studiously to unfasten it. She smiled at Peth.

"Well enough, for the *didhosi*. Nevertheless, I see you at least know your custom: a wash before the *yos* for each flower-fight outside it. Careful, Peth-Emivi†, that you don't grow gills from all your dunkings!"

Pethmirvin giggled, hiding her face, which was now blushing furiously. "Well enough, indeed. But now you must go first. You are *Klandorh* and Madh. You have the right of age, and besides, you've been outside."

"And warm the water for you? Certainly not! I waive my precedences and rights: into the trough with you! And by the way, was your tussling fun? This was never my season, although I never stinted in the warmer days. . . ."

Peth shifted her stance from one foot to another, saying breathlessly, "Oh, yes, except that it was too cold and we had to . . ."

Fellirian broke into the beginnings of what promised to be a long story whose purpose was to delay entry into the trough. "Never mind

---

* In this context, a casual lover, emotional relationship not specified.
† Child-name plus body-name is an address of endearment.

the details, please. If you must relate the entire circumstances, tell them to your *toorhsrith* Pentandrun. She has seemed a bit slow catching on. And for now, into the trough!"

"Oh, Madh."

"Oh, Madh, nothing. You can go to bed and sleep. I will have to stay up, probably all night, and talk nonsense with the Perwathwiy. Go on, hurry up! Waiting won't make the water any warmer."

Pethmirvin removed her outer overcloak reluctantly, stepping out of her boots and wincing at the cold touch of the wet wooden platform against her bare feet. She took a deep breath and quickly flipped off her overshift, undershift, and all with it, over her head, ruffling up the short, adolescent-cut hair, and stepped resolutely up to the trough, getting her courage up. The water in the wash-trough was nothing less than icy. Fellirian looked at the bare pale body before her. Pethmirvin was slender, graceful as a young sapling, sleek as a young squirrel. She had been well-named: Willowwand Windswaying was the sense of it, in the aspect of the Water elemental. Fellirian appreciated the young girl's grace, her small breasts, hardly more than buds, her delicate pale ribs, flat belly, lean, strong thighs. Her skin was goose-pimpled with the cold.

With no warning, Pethmirvin suddenly leaped into the wash-trough and began splashing madly, scattering water everywhere. Underneath the noise she made, Fellirian could hear the quick hissing of the girl's breath. While Peth splashed about, spilling much of the water, Fellirian began removing her own clothing; outercloak, overshirt, winter undershift. And then she stood nude, feeling the bite of the cold now in earnest, looking down at her own bare body, almost as pale and spare as Peth's, but more compact, shorter in stature, and accented with the riper curvings and lines of a longer life, of bearing children. Three, no less. Pethmirvin, Kevlendos, Stheflannai. *Not bad*, she mused. *And so I still have most of the shape of my body left to me. Not that it does me any good, as it once did, except to know that there's a lot of endurance remaining in it, a long life. But once I met lovers in the night, just as she does now, and Pentandrun will soon. Once, in the spring of my life, twenty years gone and more, boys chased me through the woods and called "Fellir" after me, as they now call "Pethmir" after her.*

Peth finished her splashing and thrashing and ran gasping from the trough, gathering her clothes hurriedly as she ran.

Fellirian, startled from her recollection, said, "Tell them I'll be along. . . ." She stopped. Pethmirvin had already run up the stairs and disappeared into the *yos*.

Fellirian shook her head, resigned. *Peth could do this in haste, for what she rinses away is nothing more than a little sly fun. The water reminds her that fun is fun, a little thrill, but that tonight, she must leave this one, this Farlendur, at the door. The mystery of the stranger. Our ties in Braid are closer than blood and genetics. But what I wash away is something more subtle, a corrosive worry about which I have seen, after all, only the tiniest part. That Vance, as long as we have known each other and been associated, could allow himself and me with him to be recorded, investigated, observed, and, well, spied upon, without a protest, a word of warning! Yes, I know. He imagined to conceal it, when his body-language shouted truth. But an obscenity. To invade the awareness is no different than to invade the home, the body.* Fellirian took a deep breath, releasing it in a long, controlled sigh, listening to the gurgling of the water in the wash-trough, allowing the random noise, the pleasant sound, to blank her mind of everything except the now, the razor-thin present, the edge between eternities. A last turbulent wave roiled the calming surface of her thought. *We live in many ways an idyllic, slow-paced life, insulated from pressure. I who see the outside know these things that I cannot tell to the others. We have pursued the silence too long, set ourselves against one temptation, one pressure, for too many summers. I sense a shift of balances, different forces. We are not now an agile people to move with them; indeed, having sought the primitive, we have attained it in all its fragility; and the world always changes. I know fear.*

When at last she felt the stillness inside, when she could hear the silences within herself, she repeated subvocally the invocation to Water, her lips moving silently, almost invisibly. Then it was time. She stepped calmly into the water, feeling the bite of its cold on her legs and feet, then her thighs as she kneeled, and then the full shock of it as she slowly, deliberately immersed herself into the water, coming to rest facedown, completely covered. *A deep fear, a corrosive worry, a mindless anger; take it all, trough-water, take it to the sea.* From the first it was painful, an assault upon the entire body, all at once, a sensory explosion blanking her mind. There was an urge to panic. She resisted, and lay still, gently thinking nonthoughts, letting the cold grip her in its teeth of iron, clamping her firmly in its clammy jaws. When she could stand it no longer, she got to her feet slowly, carefully, standing, releasing the pent breath she had been holding. Then she swiftly rubbed herself down with her hands, using the backscrubber hanging on a peg nearby to reach her back. The air now felt warm.

She was finished with the rite of Water. Still, despite the numbing cold, Fellirian forced herself to be slow, measured, deliberate. *Nothing is any good in a hurry, and rituals least of all. I must wait for the water to become still before I leave it. That is respect for what it is.* She waited, wrung out her hair, and stepped out of the trough. Then she gathered up her clothes, picked up her boots, and Pethmirvin's as well, for in her haste to get into the *yos* and warmth, Peth had left hers behind. *That scatterbrain,* Fellirian thought warmly. Only when she was completely finished did she look back to the water. It was still again, rippling only from the fresh water falling into it from the pipe. Fellirian turned away, her skin goose-pimpling violently, climbing with measured steps up the stairs to the entryway.

She brushed aside the heavy outer winter-curtain and stepped inside over the sill. As she put her old clothes down, she saw in the half-light spilling through the inner curtain that someone had left out her favorite autumn kif, a loose wraparound with wide, deep sleeves. By the light she could make out its pattern, a plain brownish hue with a pattern of cherry leaves ticked subtly throughout it. Wrapping her hair in a soft cloth, she took the kif up, putting her arms into the sleeves, wrapping it around her body, luxuriating in the feel along her skin of the smooth inner lining, already feeling it warm her. Then the wide sash belt to fasten it together, and she brushed the inner curtain aside, entering.

Inside the hearth, the others awaited her, Morlenden, Cannialin, Kaldherman. Not the children; they had all gone to bed, even Sanjirmil. Fellirian suddenly felt as if she had been gone for years, instead of the two days it had been in reality, and she looked long at them, and around the hearth, as if she wanted to reassure herself with its familiar contours. She saw its spacious roundness, the dome of the ceiling, its outlet vent blackened around the lip by the hearth-smoke of generations of Derens. To her left was the hearth proper and table, and to the other hand a cushioned shelf for sitting, all the way around the compartment. In the back, three curtained crawlways led off to other compartments, left for adults, center to the workrooms and recordium, right to the children's sleeper. Tapestries arranged behind the sitting-shelf illustrated the Salt-pilgrimage and stages along the Way. Every *yos* except the very poorest thus displayed some symbolic reminder of something great the Braid had done. Theirs was old and somewhat faded. Still, it was theirs, and this was home. It smelled of woodsmoke, clean, familiar bodies, onions.

They had kept a fire on the raised hearth, and there was a pot of stew still on it, steaming away. Nearby was the ever-present teapot. Fellirian went to her place* and sat. Morlenden ladled out a bowl of the stew, Kaldherman cut some bread from a loaf, and Cannialin stood behind her and began to braid her hair.

Fellirian, realizing how hungry she was, began to eat immediately, blowing on the spoonfuls of hot stew to cool it down. Kaldherman replaced the loaf on its shelf, sat back in his place, and leaned back expansively.

"No need to hurry, Eliya. We've bedded them all down for the night: the *starsrith* in the shed, and the little fox with the rest of the children."

"Did the Perwathwiy not wish to talk, then? Peth said she had come to talk this very night." Fellirian spoke between mouthfuls.

Cannialin answered from behind her, a soft, pleasantly hoarse throaty voice in her ear. "Oh, no. She wanted to talk, sure enough, but we convinced her it would be better to wait for daylight. One could not know when our *Klandorh* was coming home, and she did insist that you be there. I do admit we used the argument of her convenience, although it mostly is ours. But since she had to wait for morning light, she could wait to drop her secret then."

"Did she drop any hint of what it was that she wanted?" Fellirian paused, almost saying something else, then changing it. "I cannot imagine what would bring her all the way down here at night."

"And in the rain, no less," Kaldherman said. "But she never said. Although she's in a hurry, whatever, it is, and an elder in a hurry is a remarkable thing—especially out of Dragonfly *Zlos*."

"Indeed, so it is." Fellirian turned to Morlenden. "When did you arrive, Olede?"

"Not so very long before you."

"Are you tired?"

"Tired isn't the word for it. Mind, I don't mind walking in the rain all day; I'm used to that. What inconveniences one is that last evening I had to attend a weaving-party, and woke up this morn not in the best of humors."

Fellirian chuckled. "Serves you right. You're supposed to officiate at those parties, not join in them."

"Ah, who can say no to a host in his cups?" Morlenden smiled back at her. Morlenden was somewhat heavier in build than Fellirian, indeed, than any of them, and his hair was fractionally darker, now beginning to show some hints of gray. His face was more sharply drawn, full of

---

* Adults always sat around the hearth in a specific order.

planes, defined lines, demarcations. It was a harsh face in certain lights, but for the most part it was also a face animated beneath by poise, confidence, general good humor. He continued, "Well, I suppose it would have been nice enough, except for the fact, denied with vehemence and zeal by all parties concerned, that the *Toorh* were already full-fertile and obviously had no use for anybody besides themselves. Had them dressed up all in white, they did, when I, a stranger, could tell they'd been doing it a month at least. I think the girl was pregnant already, carrying the *Nerh*. And of course the potables were the vilest sort of stuff you can imagine. Homebrew! Peach brandy, they had the nerve to call it. May as well call a squeal the whole hog to be consistent. It was, so I discovered, raw corn whiskey, not even cooled decently, with some peach-pits in the bottom of the crock, or I'm a human."

Here Kaldherman interjected, "Nothing wrong with that. Just good, honest folk. Why put on airs?"

Morlenden leered askance at Kaldherman. "Even up your way they don't go so far. But this was really remote. And you know how it goes in the most distant districts; too much ag-ri-cul-ture." He drawled the last word out bawdily, making a lewd face to go with it, suggesting some yokel gaping in astonishment after the barnyard antics of bull and cow.

Fellirian laughed, waving her empty bowl. "Where was this?"

"Beshmazen's."

"You walked all the way from there?"

"Oh, indeed, all the way from the far side of the Hvar. Cleared my head, it did."

"And then you waited up for me, well knowing that the Perwathwiy would wait for the morrow?"

All of them nodded agreement.

Fellirian said, "Well, then, I am grateful to you all." She turned the teacup up, draining it. "Now you can all come to the sleeper with me and warm my body to sleep. I'm freezing!"

Fellirian arose from the hearth, placing her bowl with the others in the soak-tub by the fire, and went directly to the sleeper, pushing aside the curtain and climbing in. Morlenden and Cannialin followed her, while Kaldherman remained behind momentarily, banking the hearth-fire and blowing out lamps. One by one, they all climbed into the adult sleeper compartment, at a higher level than the rest of the *yos*, reached by a short ladder. Inside, they carefully removed their kifs and over-shirts, folded them up, and placed them on shelves that ran all around the circular wall of the compartment. Here, they did not make lights; it was a smaller compartment than the main hearth, and they all knew every inch of it, especially Morlenden and Fellirian. She reached upward to a shelf for something she knew would be there: a large double comforter, which she retrieved and with Morlenden's help spread out and buttoned the edges together. Finished, they spread it out, just so, and slid into it, moving close together for warmth, feeling the familiar bumps, angles, and contours of each other as they moved, making tiny adjustments in position until the fit was exactly right, just as they had been doing on winter nights for the greatest part of their lives. Across the compartment they could hear Cannialin and Kaldherman doing exactly likewise, rustling the comforter, arranging themselves, seeking out the most comfortable and warm position; for while the material of which the *yos* was traditionally built was a good insulator, it was also unheated inside except for what warmth from the hearth took the edge off the chill.

Fellirian moved closer to Morlenden; she was still chilled thoroughly, more than she had thought, from the long walk up from the mono line and the Water Rite as well. She felt the body next to her own; the skin was cool, but underneath he was warm. She stretched, tensing and releasing every muscle, feeling Morlenden curl around her. Across the sleeper, Cannialin whispered good night in her quiet shy voice into the darkness and the quiet, broken only by an occasional drip on the roof, and then by deep, even breathing. Kaldherman, like an animal, fell asleep instantly.

When she was sure that the others were asleep, she nudged her insibling. Morlenden nudged back. She whispered, under the covers, barely audibly, "Do you have any idea what is going on? Why the Perwathwiy, and Sanjirmil?"

"I know no more than you, Eliya. They told me naught save that it was a Braidish thing—that all of us would have to hear and judge, and agree. Sanjirmil said nothing. At any rate, when I came home she was too busy eating Peth's supper to say anything."

"Did she really?"

"Thus she did. But Peth did all well enough, I think. She wanted to go out anyway—I suspect a young buck hidden away in the brush outside."

"She had one, so it was."

"Might have known; comes from her foremother. You used to do that."

"Never mind the things I used to do. You used to bring them home, you rooster. Where you ever found such bedraggled things I'll never know. Did you scour the whole reservation looking for the poorest girls?"

"Well, as I have often averred, the wealthy give luxury, but from the destitute comes speed."

"Speed, was it? It was never speed that kept the rest of us awake half the night with your whispers and giggles under the window. And after I had spent most of the evening record-keeping so at least one of us would do it right after weaving."

"Ah, Fel, you always were too serious for your own good."

"Serious or not, what do you think of the Perwathwiy walking down here from Garkaeszlos in the rain?"

"I like it not. Nor the fact she wouldn't talk, either. It can't be a good thing, can it?"

"I see no way it could go thus."

"And you are tense, too. Something else? You spent too long in the water for things to be normal, even for a zealot like you. Have a bad time of it down there among the *Hauthpir**?"

"No, not that way. No different from other times. The same, more or less, and the same tired old provocs in the crowd. But I realized something I'd been stupid enough to overlook for some time. I really can't be sure how long it's been going on, but Vance has been having me monitored during the meetings, and after the visitors leave, when we sit and chat a bit. He hasn't been pushy, just a little more leading and curious than normal. At first I thought it was just him—he is a little erratic in behavior. But when I saw it, it was clear. I tell you, something's afoot, something's going to happen, something bad. Maybe already. But I don't know to whom, or why."

"Maybe it's already happened."

"No. If it has, that's not what we're looking for."

"That's not like Vance. He's an old friend."

"So he has been. He's been a good channel for us—working both ways. Keeps the worst of them away from us, and lets us have a freer hand than we might have had. And I know him well enough, or so I thought . . . He wouldn't without good reason."

"Perhaps. But we don't know those reasons, even assuming what you say is true."

---

* "Ancestral Primates." A derogatory epithet. Morlenden had little contact with the human world, and distrusted it greatly.

"Mor, I think there's some connection between this visit and the change at the Institute."

"Nothing we can do tonight. Unless you wish to walk out to the shed and wake the Perwathwiy."

"No. I want to sleep. By the way, did Sanjirmil say anything at all?"

Morlenden was silent for a time. Fellirian could hear only his regular breathing. She prodded him. "Morlenden?"

"Hm? Sanjirmil? No, she said nothing. Nothing at all. She was here when I arrived, but she kept her own counsel. A few pleasantries, politeness . . . no, nothing."

"Were you not as much past the Change as I, I'd suspect you of distraction."

"Distraction? Hmph. Hardly. Although you have to admit that Sanjirmil certainly possesses more erotic quality than the average girl."

"Bah. A primitive, that's all."

"Just so, just so. . . ." He mused. "And a waste too, for one hears along the road that she's a bit of a zealot, a *Zan* fanatic."

"All those players are odd, you know? Well, so be it. I leave them to their *Zan* Game, however they will. Good night."

"And you, Eliya. On the morrow."

FOUR

The more dimensions in a Game, the more complex become the factors in the surround that influence the state of a given cell. This becomes significant when we recall that only two things determine what a cell's state will be: what it was in the last temporal frame, and what the surround is. Now if we imagine that our familiar universe of three dimensions is instead a three-dimensional projection of an n-dimensional Game, then the task before us of first importance is to determine the dimensional matrix. Is this not obvious?

—*The Game Texts*

FELLIRIAN SEEMED TO drop into sleep instantly, as soon as she had moved a little, finding just the right position she wanted. Her breathing became deep, slow, and regular. Morlenden did not fall asleep. No less tired than Fellirian, something deep in his mind itched, something basically wrong. Wrong? That was not quite the proper word. Un-right might have been better. He could not place the source of these feelings. For a time, he probed at it, but he could not find the unraveling-place, so gradually he left it. He reflected on his past, keyed by the events of this night, and the visitors who had come to their holding. Perwathwiy. Sanjirmil. Yes, Sanjirmil. Morlenden reflected on his past. His, and Sanjirmil's.

It had been long ago. Two and a fourteen years ago. In 2534, in the human calendar. In the early autumn. He had been one and two fourteens, twenty-nine, and she thirteen. At this time had occurred the interplay of two separate customs, or traditions, in a most curious way he had never put away in his mind.

The first had been the Canon of Permissibility: the rules governing sexual activity among ler adolescents were few, and of those that existed fewer still were the ones restricting it. Thus, it was said that among persons of adolescent phase age of itself would be no bar, provided that all acted according to their own desires and wills. In practice, one most usually paired off with partners near one's own age, but exceptions did occur, and one was neither praised nor defamed, either way.

The other tradition was more restrictive, for it pertained only to insiblings. Normally avoiding one another somewhat as they grew up through adolescence, as fertility drew near, insiblings gradually spent more time with each other. But at the same time, the rivalries and tensions accumulated during their long childhood and adolescence began to simmer and come to the surface. Knowing how tense this period could be, and was, and knowing how important it was that the insiblings remain together, the ler had inserted a period of relief into the very last part of adolescence, so that a hostile relationship would not unravel Braid lines carefully nurtured over hundreds of years. It was custom, then, that sometime in the last year of adolescence, the insibling was allowed a *vayyon*, a walkabout, an idle wandering-off, a last adventure, a great affair. It went without saying that these walkabouts were undertaken more or less specifically for the purpose of having one last fling, something to remember and cherish for the rest of one's life.

Autumn, 2534. Fellirian had already had her adventure, her *vayyon;* in the spring of that year, in accordance with the custom, she had simply wandered off one rainy day. Three months later, in summer, she had returned, saying nothing to anyone, dropping no hints, revealing no confidences. She had been tense before, uncharacteristically sharp-tongued and acrid of remark. Now she seemed settled, placid, relaxed, at home again within herself, most of the earlier late-adolescent fidgets gone, her perplexities resolved. Or were they? Morlenden did not know. He had never known. She had never spoken of it, what she had done or with whom, if indeed anyone. That, too, was the custom: what one did on the *vayyon* was forever a secret. And so Fellirian had returned, calm as still water, silent, enigmatic.

All this time Morlenden had felt the urge to the unknown building in him, and had found the environs of the Deren Braid holding increasingly bland, unsatisfying. Fellirian had been not only *Klandorh*-to-be, but she was also eldest insibling, so it was her right to go first. But within a few days of her return, Morlenden gathered a few things and also left, as silently as had his insibling. On the way out to Main Path, they had passed, wordless. There was nothing she could say to him. One found one's own truth, and no other's words could tell it.

At first, in the first days, it had been tremendously exciting; he had never known such a sense of freedom, such a feeling of total irresponsibility. Morlenden wandered first northward, then northwestward, sleeping in the open, feeling the chill of night which was now in the air, doing an occasional odd job in exchange for a meal and a bath, or perhaps some small change, at someone's *yos*, or again, sometimes an elder lodge, where the silent inhabitants gave him knowing leers, but said nothing, made no disparagements. Those who had been insiblings in a former life had known the *vayyon*. They knew.

The great affair had not materialized. Morlenden could not put into words exactly what it was he was looking for, but whatever it had been, there seemed to be an ever-receding chance of finding it. It was not that there were no girls; there were girls in plenty, and his days and nights were not, by and large, totally devoid of dalliance, teasings, flower-fights. But somehow the connection he wanted seemed to be absent. This one was busy, house-bound, and would not wander off, though she had possibilities. One who would readily go off with him was less than hopeless; Fellirian at her worst appeared preferable, even as a companion. Others he only caught glimpses of. In earlier days, Morlenden had delighted in the busy interplay of eye and gesture, of suggestive word. Now that he was free, really free, that whole universe seemed to have dropped away and vanished; what irony—now that he was available, no one was interested. Prospects were few, and he always seemed to be arriving at the wrong place at the wrong time, too early, too late. He began drifting from place to place, becoming bored and dissatisfied, frustrated and full of an ambience he could not put a name to. More than once he had caught himself doubting that this was really the great adventure. Was it all to be summed up in the end as nothing more than the value of a long walk? An unfulfilled expectation? Was it the surrounding matrices of routine life which made momentary exceptions to it exciting? Indeed, was it rarity that gave value? And was the lesson of the *vayyon* that the adventure wasn't there, had never been, never could be, but was entangled in the slower growths and procedures of the ordinary life of managing one's holding, raising the children? To be sure, he sensed that these were basic testings of reality which all have had to learn, individually, over and over again, human and ler alike, but like everyone else he was surprised at the pain of losing many of his favorite illusions.

For a time, Morlenden grew uncaring, diffident, even a little hostile; his sight seemed to grow crystal-clear, piercing, powerful, solvent. He saw things from a distance, but in his mind the distance grew greater; he saw those ler of parent phase, *rodhosi*, at their works, in field and shop; younger adolescents, *didhosi*, learning, pursuing their affairs. And after all that, the elders, retired to their secretive lodges, deep in their own matters. He had waited all his life to be free of that endless cycle, but now free, he found little enough to stay for. The real life was there, not here.

These were bitter thoughts; Morlenden spent more time along the empty paths of the forest, lost interest in eating, let his weight drop. He became, over the weeks, rather gaunt and hungry-looking; his sharp and somewhat chiseled features became honed and sharper. At one time he tried fasting for a vision, a practice he had heard of. But there was no result there either; he grew tired of it. Either he lacked some innate sense of awe requisite to the religious experience, or perhaps he lacked some basic competence of discipline necessary to make the vision work. At any rate, one never came. He simply grew fractionally thinner, and a lot hungrier.

He returned to his old ways and returned, tentatively, to the routines of working and eating. His weight began to return. And he thought ruefully to himself that he had indeed learned the last lesson. And it was then that he turned back to the south and began his journey homeward. He tried to imagine how it would be, when he did return: Fellirian would wonder what he had done, and he would smile knowingly at her and let her draw her own conclusions, make up her own imaginings. Perhaps he could drop a cryptic remark from time to time, faintly suggesting, never saying directly, never declaiming forthrightly. It would serve her right. She had probably seen herself the same emptiness he had discovered, whose core was within himself, the basic loneliness that lies at the heart of all sapient creatures in the universe. He knew now that all of them who had been privileged to the *vayyon* were sharers of this secret.

He returned slowly. There was no hurry now. He had covered much of the distance, leaving only a few more days of leisurely travel and work, when he happened to pass close by a place called Lamkleth, meaning "resin-scented," which was a combination of many things: faded resort, hostel, elder lodge for a lodge organization which seemed to have been forgotten by most elders. It carried the name of a settled place, or town, but it seemed to be no more than a random collection of cabins, rambling wooden apartments built to a high-gabled, eccentric style, rambling worksheds, and seedy pavilions along the lake, all half hidden and subtly blended into and among the conifers of the forest. The site was a gloomy defile, a rocky, narrow valley which opened up suddenly into a wide lowland. At the mouth of the valley was a still, enigmatic lake, bordered by a mixed sand and rock beach on the east, the valley side, and on the west by a watery, tree-choked swamp. The area all around the defile and the lake was dense with pine and cedar, swamp fir and arborvitae, deodar and chamaephyte, ground yew and retinispora. A pungent, resinous odor hung in the air, and the smoke of the fires was rich, and fragrant. A moody place, which was doubtless much of the reason why it had never been popular.

Nevertheless, Lamkleth was known for one thing; adolescents gathered there, with the force of tradition behind them, to meet likeminded others, to seduce and be seduced, to dance in the night under the colored party lanterns, to sing and listen to the last heart-songs of yearning before the halter was finally put on them. Personally, Morlenden had never cared very much for the place, and as a fact, although he had passed it often, had never stopped or visited before. But this time—passing Lamkleth on the ridgeline above the valley and the lake, the dark water, the deep shadows, and the bright lanterns—he thought once again of last flings, of last opportunities. . . . He wandered slowly down into the settlement. He caught in himself the last shreds of anticipation, that here at last he would find the one, her, an insibling like himself, also in the last of the *vayyon* and likewise illuminated. He imagined. He projected images.

With the money he had accumulated, Morlenden secured for himself a small but comfortable little cabin with an attached bath and woodstove. A pile of faggots had been conveniently deposited outside by the door. The cabin was not close to the lakefront but was situated farther away, far up the valley, under the ridge, half invisible under the trees, buried in a grove of ancient arborvitae, their feathery fronds hanging over the mossy roof. The odor of resin was in everything. The elder who accompanied him to the cabin said little, noting only that the season was apparently over, and that most had already left. Remaining were only a scattered few latecomers and hangers-on. The nights were quite cool now, and this had apparently dissuaded most of the late summer visitors. Morlenden, thinking how gay and festive the lanterns and their reflections along the water had been, listened to this news with sinking heart.

Nonetheless, he was tired of walking, and a good rest here in a comfortable little cabin was an improvement over sleeping in the forest under a tree. So he bathed and dressed in the last dress-overshirt remaining to him, carefully removing it from his rucksack and pressing it out with his hands. It was his favorite, tastefully patterned with the heraldic emblem of his aspectual sign—Fire, the Salamander. It had been dusk when he had wandered down from the heights; it was fully dark when Morlenden left the cabin and wandered down the hill to the lakeshore. The path was smooth and well-tended, swept free of twig and pebble, groomed of roots and knots.

From a distance, it seemed as if the summer season were still in full swing: the lanterns still swung above the pavilions, sending brightly colored reflections dancing along the water. There was music in the air as well, floating from an unseen source, lending a further anticipation. But all these things were faded reflections and shadows; most of the painted tables were empty, the pergolas and gazebos abandoned, and the music, upon closer listening, seemed to be slow and reflective of mood rather than exciting and gay. Emerging from the pines and entering the pavilion along the shore, Morlenden was able to confirm his worst suspicions: the place was almost empty. Within sight, in an area which could easily hold a crowd of *terzhan** young adventurous bodies, there seemed to be only a handful, most of whom had already paired off for the night, or who sat quietly and rather disinterestedly looking out over the water into the darkness.

He also noted as he looked out over the whole of the pavilion that the ages of the remaining celebrants appeared to be wildly varied, as if the low density had made it more noticeable. Some were late-adolescents like himself, of comparable age. Others were obviously younger, still deep in their first span, country bumpkins down from the farm in the period between the end of the growing season and the beginning of the harvests. A scattered few were much younger, veritable urchins, playing rowdy chase-and-tumble games among the old whitewashed stands and under the trees; some of these were barely adolescent, while a few were yet little children. These he ignored.

For a time, Morlenden wandered up and down along the pavilion, looking over the prospects, as it were, hoping that certain among those he was looking at were harboring similar thoughts. If they were, none of it showed. Everyone he saw seemed to be immersed deeply in his own thoughts, his own projections of the subtle manifestations of reality, emerging from the end of summer about the precincts of a faded resort. Failure and the ambience of second thoughts lay in the lamplight like a tincture.

* Two times fourteen to the second power—196.

Morlenden, while savoring this air, was not daunted and attempted to
make the acquaintance of a pair of girls who were diffidently lounging
at one of the pavilion tables over glasses of mulled wine. The first was
convincingly uninterested, and the second hardly less so, although she
did give her name, Meydhellin. She also mentioned a certain young man
with whom she would conduct a rendezvous presently. Morlenden excused himself, after a tactful and strategic pause, and wandered some
distance away to a table of his own, where he seated himself and
brooded, watching the scanty crowd evaporate into even lower densities
as individual members of the vacationers and pleasure-seekers drifted
away one by one. The noise of the urchins behind him faded. After a
time, he observed that at the least the girl Meydhellin had been truthful; a boy appeared and joined her at the table. The other girl uttered
something rendered enigmatic by the distance, and departed. Meydhellin and her friend greeted one another with a reluctant formality.
Morlenden grew disinterested.

From the cookhouse nearby and behind him, an elder approached
Morlenden, informing him discreetly that the cookhouse was on the
verge of closing for the night, and that perhaps the discerning young
gentleman would like to order some of the remainders, at reduced
stipend. Morlenden nodded enthusiastically, for he was suddenly aware
that he hadn't eaten all day and was ravenously hungry. He inquired
into the bill of fare; unfortunately, nothing remained but some dner, a
preparation made by arranging paper-thin slices of various meats along
a vertical skewer, roasting it along the outside by rotating it past the
grates of a vertical charcoal burner, and then slicing off slivers of it. It
was a heavy, over-rich dinner, and Morlenden ordered it without great
enthusiasm, selecting to wash it down a small jug of the local wine,
Shrav Bel-lamosi, tart and resinous. Presently, with no great ceremony,
the meal arrived, along with a tray of local wild greens. Morlenden ate,
because he was still hungry, but it was with no great sense of culinary
relish. He thought, *Indeed, this is the very end of it. Tomorrow I'll go home.*

Gradually, the wine and his somber musings led him to disregard his
immediate surroundings and he ignored the comings and goings of the
few patrons and proprietors remaining. They all receded into a common
background. He no longer heard the noises of the urchins.

As Morlenden ate, thinking random and somewhat moody thoughts,
he slowly came to suspect that he was being observed closely by someone, someone nearby; in fact, someone who was standing by his own
table, cautiously positioned to his right and just out of his field of vision

to the rear. Morlenden stopped, fork halfway between plate and mouth, and looked.

It appeared to be one of the children he had noted earlier, one of the nondescript gaggle of noisy urchins playing tag and grab-'ems along the shadow line under the trees beyond. This one, he thought, seemed to be female*, and perhaps even adolescent, dressed in little more than a ragged pleth which had seen better and cleaner days. He looked at the girl again; there was immediately apparent a certain dashing quality about her, a piquancy of expression, an adventurous quality, a recklessness. Morlenden thought that she would have made a very good approximation of a bandit, but a bandit constantly poor from careless expenses. Indeed, almost a desperate look about her. A brat for sure. An urchin of dark skin, large eyes, sharp, predatory features.

Her eyes caught his glance immediately: they did not move about, looking at this or that, but seemed to stare glassily, unfocused yet intent at the same time. The set of her face showed that she missed nothing. Morlenden looked more closely at the startling expression in her eyes. He saw movement in the spaces framed by the angular face. She seemed not to regard directly, but to scan in a regular pattern, using her peripheral vision. This lent her expression a dualistic quality, glassy yet deeply animated as well.

Morlenden had quite forgotten his fork. The girl observed Morlenden's notice. She said, in a flat tone with a hint of nasality, "Enjoying yourself?"

Morlenden thought the question boorish. He recalled the fork, thoughtfully took a mouthful of dner, and answered, equally boorishly, "As a fact, no."

"How does one call you?"

"I have responded in my time to endearments and curses, anonymous hoots and hoarse whispers. I have been known to reply to 'you, there,' although I deplore the practice. I am called Morlenden Tlanh Deren."

"I am Sanjirmil Srith Terklaren. I, too, respond to other addresses."

Morlenden thought, hearing the form of her name, *Aha! An adolescent after all, however scruffy and abrasive.*

She added, "What do you here in Lamkleth?"

"Going home," he said, trying to ignore her, hoping she would receive his intent and depart. A brat.

* Secondary sexual characteristics in the ler were subtle where they existed at all. Sometimes it could be difficult even for a ler to determine the apparent gender of another.

"Can I have some of that Bel-lamosi?"

"Are you old enough to drink fermented spirits?" he asked, aggressively.

"Fourteen less one and *didhosi*? Of course! Old enough for other *didhosi* things, too."

"I can imagine . . . well, here. Drink the wine." He offered her the jug, which she took, shyly for all her previous belligerence, and turned up, drinking deeply. He looked closely at the girl, Sanjirmil. On a second inspection, perhaps she didn't appear quite so childish as he first thought. Her shape, under the ill-fitting overshirt she wore, was already full and ripe; no, not childish at all. She was dark of complexion, olive skin and coarse black tousled hair which fell carelessly about a face of planes and angles, a face that could be harsh and peremptory, yet a face of a certain beauty as well. The strange eyes were of an indeterminate color, dark and brooding, and her nose was delicate and fine. The mouth was thin-lipped and determined, the chin set, but there was also an intriguing pouty set to her lips as well. In the poor lighting of the pavilion, her skin seemed dark enough so that there was little contrast between lips and face; it gave her face an odd expressiveness. You had to watch the shadows. This Sanjirmil could very well be just the unwashed and underage brat she seemed. But there was also about her an unknown quantity of something more.

He asked, as she set the jug back on the table, "Have you eaten?"

"No."

"The cookhouse is closed now."

"I know."

"My serving was overlarge. They were cleaning up for the night. You may have what you wish of it. And what would one be doing out adventuring without money, begging for a supper? Or do you sing as well?"

Sanjirmil took the proffered food shyly, but she could not conceal her hunger and ate quickly in swift, catlike bites. In between mouthfuls, she haltingly said, "No sing, no dance. Had some money, but it ran out. Was going to go home tomorrow . . . maybe tonight, if I had felt like it. You know of the Terklarens?"

"The Second-players? Of course I know of them. But I had never met one."

"Northwest. Day and a half."

"A long walk. You're a young one to be so far out in the forest."

"No, not us. We're adventurous . . . besides, we never take the *vayyon* as you are doing."

"How would you know what I might be doing?"

"Watched you, I did. *Mavayyonamoni*, they're always the same, looking for something and not finding it. I guessed; and I was right. I come here a lot, at least this year."

"Meet a lot of friends?"

"Some. Not always the ones I want. When do you weave?"

"Soon, this year. I think sometime around the winter solsticeday. My own *Toorh* has already done hers and returned. We have felt the tension at home."

"Hm. And I am free for a time yet . . . as little good as it will do me. So: if you are on-*vayyon*, then you are *Toorh* also."

"Just so; Fire aspect. And you, Sanjirmil?"

"I also—both, just as you. That is very good."

"Not so necessarily for you. You're too young."

"Indeed? For what? What did you have in mind?"

Morlenden looked away from the intense, eager face for a moment. All the time he had been on his pilgrimage, he had turned every possibility, looking for the flow, the current, the onrush of the one single magic meeting. Now he felt the undertow, the pull of a powerful current indeed; and both of them of Fire aspect, strong in will. He could interpret this drift and flow only one way: that they both were working powerfully for what was to come, whether they would admit it to themselves or not. He glanced at her again, out of the corner of his eye, seeing the warm honey color of her skin, the streaks and shadows where her muscles ran under it. She was thin, but wiry, angular and strong; he could not deny her beauty, her sense of earthy, pungent sexuality; there was something wild in her, something desperate. The rumpled, unrepaired overshirt. Contrary to this, he also thought that this Sanjirmil was not exactly what he had walked all over half the reservation for. He wryly added to himself that if it had come to molesting thirteen-year-olds, there were several much closer to home he perhaps would have preferred. Those were second-thoughts. There were third-thoughts as well. Morlenden told himself that she wasn't really his type, that he preferred amorous adventures with girls who wove flowers in their hair for their meetings, who were softer and rounder . . . and he didn't really know how he could tactfully disengage himself from the piquant, earnest face before him.

"No," he said, "I didn't have anything in particular in mind; except going home tomorrow myself. As you have doubtless guessed, the *vayyon* leads us to few of the great adventures it seems to promise. You may see that later; or perhaps you are precocious there as well."

Now she looked away, sadly, he thought, as if she were reviewing some painful interior knowledge. Then she turned back to him, fixing him once again with that odd, sightless yet penetrating gaze. She said, "No . . . it's not precocious. But I do know it. That's why we don't go on it; none of the Players. There are things we have to give up. The *vayyon* is one of them. So we get our little dash of freedom earlier, Morlenden."

"And later?"

"We are the Players of the Great Life Game; we do things that others do not even dream of . . . even now, I can already do some of them. . . ." She trailed off, making odd fingering motions with her hands. She grew self-conscious, rubbing her hands nervously, almost as if she were on the verge of saying too much.

Morlenden knew well enough that there were two Braids of the famous Gameplayers in the ler world, and that their line had been maintained from the beginning with a focused sense of purpose which defied all reason, for the Players did nothing to integrate themselves into the elaborate structured relationships of ler society, except barter some occasional garden produce. All they did was play the Game with their rival Braid. They were curious and secretive, and did not answer questions. Most put them out of their minds, for the Game was cerebral and difficult and had few partisans. Suddenly he felt very much out of his depth.

Sanjirmil continued, "Yes, and we . . ." She stopped, biting her lower lip. "Yes, just so. Indeed we do. But I may not speak of them with you. Please understand, it is not you yourself; you are not one of the elect, and you are not of the Shadow. I may not speak of it with you. But personally . . . I think I like you. For instance," she added cheerfully and matter-of-factly, with disarming candor, "I should rather sleep with you tonight than spend the darkness in the freehouse."

Morlenden looked at the harsh, determined face, the thin mouth with the faintest trembling hint of a smile trying to form on it. After a time, he said, "I hadn't really thought so far ahead. . . ."

"I know."

"Very well, then. As you have seen, I am free and without commitment. I shall invite you to repair to my cabin, which I have taken yonder in the grove." Having taken the step, he suddenly felt awkward, uncertain as to how brash he could be. He added, "I hardly know you, no more than just now, and I wouldn't have you take offense."

"I saw, before, and I knew it would be so. I watched you; that is why I came to you."

Morlenden pushed his chair back. "You will come with me, then?"

"I will, later. I have to go wash first. I have been running a lot and should not come to you as I am."

"Never mind that. I took a special place, one with a fine bath. You can wash there." He paused, and then added impulsively, now swimming full in the current he had released himself into, "As a fact, if you will, I'll wash you myself."

"Oh, very good! What girl could resist such an invitation in the least. Indeed so I will come."

"Do you need to gather your things?"

She gestured at herself. She said, "These are my things." The gesture took in a rather bedraggled, rumpled girl, barefoot, whose sole visible possession seemed to be a smallish waist-pouch slung carelessly over one hip.

All the time they had been talking, the girl had remained standing; now Morlenden arose from his chair uncertainly. He hesitated, then offered his hand to her shyly. She took it into hers with an exaggerated gesture of gallantry, almost as if she were playacting. Morlenden looked about to see if anyone might be watching. But there was no one; the pavilion was now deserted. Far down the lakefront, one of the elders was blowing lamps out, carefully tending the colored paper lanterns that hung along the beach and cast their reflections out into the lake surface and the night. One by one, the lanterns were going out, and the dying sense of summer gaiety as well. Soon there would be nothing save some boarded-up sheds and cabins, and the winter darkness. He listened, and heard a wind rising back in the pines and arborvitae, rushing along the sharp needles and sprays of delicately scaled branchlets. There was a sudden spatter of cold rain, gone in an instant. He turned and set out in the direction of the cabin, the girl following, grasping his hand tightly.

Along the way, they kept silent, saying nothing more to each other. Morlenden listened to the wind, now alive all around them up in the trees; there was a chill in the pungent, resinous air. Impulsively, he placed his arm about Sanjirmil's shoulders. She was shivering, ever so slightly.

Once inside the rented cabin, Morlenden set about getting a fire started in both fireplace and water-heater, while Sanjirmil brought in armfuls of wood. They did not talk, waiting for the water to heat, but sat quietly looking into the fire. Once, perhaps twice, Sanjirmil looked at him shyly from under her eyebrows, a faint, tentative smile forming in her face in the moving, dancing firelight. This touched Morlenden; for he had expected once that his great adventure would be with a brilliant conversationalist, one who would engage him completely, as they savored the last fling to the very end; but here they sat, and said nothing, save what their eyes said in quick little glances. That was everything. Yes. He was beginning to enjoy the idea.

The water began to groan in its tank, and testing it, Morlenden pronounced it hot enough and began filling the tub, a huge round wooden tub on a low stand. Sanjirmil stood, stretched, removed her waist-pouch and carefully laid it on the rough platform where the sleeping-bags were. Then she slipped her pleth upward, over her shoulders; her motion was graceful, but fatigued as well. She tossed it into the water, and feeling as she went, followed it into the tub.

The only light in the cabin came from the fire in the stove, and in this weak light, even weaker to his eyes, Morlenden looked at the body of the girl who was going to spend the night with him. Her body was muscular and hard, but thin, a little paler than the sun-browned face, but still a deep olive color, streaked and shadowed in the firelight, where the muscles and tendons showed; Sanjirmil was thin and wiry, yet she was also smooth and supple and utterly feminine. She sat slowly, gingerly into the hot water, wincing from the heat of it. As she finally settled completely into the water, Morlenden pushed his sleeves back, soaped his hands, and began scrubbing her back. Sanjirmil leaned back against the pressure of his hands and turned her face to the dark ceiling, her eyes closed.

And after a longer time, and many scrubbings, when her skin had become rosy, she finally said, very softly, "You should know that I told you a little lie back there at the pavilion; I did not want you to think I was such a little beggar. The truth is that my little bit of adventuring-money ran out several days ago. But I kept on staying, as long as I could, longer, grubbing, borrowing, stealing a little . . . because . . . because when I go back there, there will be no more holidays for me, no more adventuring. I'm almost fourteen, and that is when the insiblings of the Terklarens are initiated. This autumn. I know some things already; you can imagine it if you watch closely . . . there really isn't any other way it could be, or so I think. But after initiation, the real work starts and one must learn, learn, learn, master it, control it, impose oneself upon it. One fourteen and two years to become a master of the Game, and a fourteen more before the next crop of brats. And then you teach and guide and end up in the Shadow, a Past Master. People think we are idle, that we do nothing, but it isn't like that. It is the hardest Braid-role of all. Already I can feel it drawing me to it. And so our time for adventuring is very short and we usually do not get so very much of it. And I want it all, both the Game and the Life; yes, the power but also the lovers and the dreams that all the others I see have. I hoped you would want me."

"I didn't, at first. I thought you were just another of the urchins; but there is a likeness between us now, and I see through the years that separate us."

"Say no more of separating; I would have you speak of joinings and meetings."

"So then I will: ours now-tonight." He stood up from his place by the washtub and offered Sanjirmil his hand.

She stood, wet and dripping, now soft and flowing curves and firelight shining along planes of wet skin. She said, almost in a whisper, "You are more loving-kind and giving than you know; I hope that you have fortified yourself for a long night."

"Indeed I have done marvels in the way of abstinence in the last few weeks." While he searched for a towel, Sanjirmil retrieved the much-abused overshirt, and wrung it out. Morlenden brought her the towel, and she dabbled absentmindedly at her body with it. She swayed a little, balancing on one foot, and Morlenden reached to steady her.

Sanjirmil laughed, turning to him. "You should remove that fine heirloom of the Derens that you wear, for I shall surely dampen it if you leave it on."

He slipped his overshirt off over his head and laid it aside, and stood bare in the firelight and resin-scented air just as she had before; she looked at him as he had looked at her. Morlenden felt a curious distortion of time from the intensity of their upwelling emotions, as if the whole of his past, or most of it, had occurred within this cabin, the water and the tub and Sanjirmil's bare, wiry body before him, and his future only extended as far as the next few moments. This sense of distortion was not static, fixed, but a growing, dynamic process, happening now, still working its alchemy upon his perception; there was a tense silence in which he could hear his own heartbeats. He reached forward, palms out, and stroked Sanjirmil's shoulders softly, following along the angular line of her collarbone to her neck, following with his eyes the soft shine of her skin in the dim light. She stepped out of the tub unsteadily and to him, touching him all at once, lips, limbs, body. Morlenden felt the bath-hot, strong, vital body touching him, the smooth skin, and knew madness in his heart, wildfire, and time collapsed into a dimensionless present moving forward at the speed of light. The salty taste of her mouth, the childlike, musky scent of her person close about him. She moved her body, pressing hard against him. Her legs moved.

Her mouth moved to his ear, and she said, almost so softly that he missed it under the roaring in his ears, "Now."

"Yes, Sanjir, now," he said, brushing his face in her coarse, dark hair, moving, half carrying the girl to the sleeping-bag, half falling to the platform, never quite disengaging themselves enough to retrieve the covers, while they performed that which made one where two had been before. The fire sank and the air in the little cabin cooled before they became aware of it. . . .

And some time later, with the fire now diminished to a bed of glowing coals, they moved under the covers for warmth, side by side, yet engaged still, touching their noses. Morlenden felt completed, perfected, arrived at last; but in this completion and ending he sensed beginnings, too. Many beginnings. He sensed above all that he and Sanjirmil were not finished with each other, and would not be when their time in the now ran out. By him, she breathed deeply, evenly, seemingly relaxed, yet he also knew that she was not asleep.

He said, "Truly, you are Sanjir to me now."

She answered, "Would that we were Ajimi and Olede, if you will. We are something more than casual lovers coupling on the path."

Morlenden lay quietly, feeling their legs rub together, a distant warmth, a rustling sound in the quiet dimness, a hard foot. He tested the feel of the girl's body-name in his mind, projecting, wondering if it had gone that far. He could not say; at once, he felt that they had not come to that, and that they had gone far beyond it. Yes, that was the great secret here—they had gone beyond it and were in a region of desire where there were no guides and no landmarks save those monuments they chose to erect.

"Ajimi . . ." he mused aloud, "and yet we have known each other but hours, and we are being taken away by currents in time that cannot be denied."

"And gathered by the same," Sanjirmil added. "I know. And consider—are we not both Fire aspect? Were we not here for the same thing? And are we both not soon to change?"

"My life passes through its progressions more or less in the traditional manner, prescribed by the rote of orthodox ways. My individual variations are my own, but no one else will do them, I think . . . you know that well enough, well enough to know me. But I know nothing of what you will do."

"It is simple enough, as much as I can say here to you: we got to the Magic Mountain and master the subtleties of the Game, expand its scope, delve deeper into it. It has no end, no limits, you know."

"No. I know nothing of it."

"It is something I would have us share besides what we already have, but even what little I know I cannot give you, even though I shall call you Olede and always think of you so. At initiation, I know that I will not be able to face the foremother of my foremother if I do, when she will ask me if I have spoken of the Game to others who are not of the Shadow."

Morlenden chuckled at her sudden seriousness. "You could lie."

She put her fingers over his lips, abruptly. "No, no, we must not even talk about such a thing! She will be able to read that in my face, my every move. She is the great Past Master: she reads truth from the traces and ripples that acts leave behind them. You and I, even such as we, we can read the guilty face immediately after the sin, the worry after the crime, can we not? But she can read faces and see—literally see, with the eye of projection, things as they happened long ago. And so tonight by love I shall tell you what I know to keep you, and sixteen years hence I will stand before her in the smoky lodge of the elders of the Game and hear her denounce me and describe how we lay together."

"What would be so vile about that, Ajimi? This is sweet beyond my wildest dreams."

"You do not understand. There are others there, too, who have power over the non-Game parts of our lives. Not only do I lose the Game; I lose place, Braid. As strangers are made honorary insiblings, *shartoorh*, by arbitration, so are made *sharhifzeron*, 'those to be designated out-Braid bastards.' I could, if so judged, lose my life. We Players know well the saying, 'and Tarneysmith spoke aloud of the Game in the market, and what person now remembers Tarneysmith? It* did that which caused its* name to be stricken from the lineages and records and totems. Where one smile was of opened knowledge, now there are two."

"Ajimi, you lose me. I don't understand."

Sanjirmil took a deep breath, and shuddered. "In plain *perdeskrist*†, so I am led to believe, one called Tarneysmith, whom no one knows now as Tlanh or Srith, spoke of the Game openly, or carelessly perhaps, or displayed knowledge to impress others—who knows? They cut its

* Singlespeech also uses an asexual, genderless personal pronoun.
† "Singlespeech" itself.

throat. Then they expunged all the records and made everyone forget. There is left only the name as a reminder. To die is bad, but to be erased is a horror."

"And your fear is real."

"My fear is real."

"Then I am endangered as well. I have bedded down . . ."

She interrupted him. "No, say it not! Not true! For I have not told you secrets. The danger is to me and all the others of the Players. What we have is a thing to be desired over all things, even love. But we see others as yourself and envy your lives, you who have all your *didhosi* years to have lovers and dreams, to make liaisons, to absorb the ordinary things of life. But for us the fun ends at fourteen. And I want something sweet to remember."

Morlenden felt a warm arm laid over his, pressing his back. He searched for Sanjirmil's thin mouth, kissed her lightly. "Yes, and I, too."

Sanjirmil moved her body, her limbs, pressing herself closer still. Muscles moved invisibly beneath warm skin. Morlenden, who had been lazing in post-love contentment, suddenly felt something awaken in him, deep down, illogical, apersonal, animal. And she felt it as well. He felt sharp white teeth along his neck, shoulders, and heard her whisper, "Again, yes?"

They moved slowly, deliberately, again knowing the rushing surge of anticipation. He whispered back, "Slowly, slowly. We have time. And what we have not we can make, for a little."

She replied, distantly, as if from miles away: "You do not know how much we have to make in what little time."

"But we do not have to go our ways tomorrow, either, Ajimi."

And Sanjirmil did not answer him immediately, but moved closer to Morlenden, if that were possible, embracing him yet more tightly. And she said, "No, Olede. But someday soon."

"And until then . . ."

Then their senses were fully awake, and for that night at least they talked no more. At any rate, they said little more of explanations and histories and legend.

They stayed on at Lamkleth a few days, sleeping, eating, dashing into the cooling lake water for quick wild splashing dips, and making love when the mood fell upon them, sometimes lazily and contemplatively, students of an art each would shortly lose in one fashion or another; at other times they would suddenly fall upon one another in wild bursts of passion and desire, as if each moment were to be their last. Until the little store of money which Morlenden had laboriously built up during his travels had begun to come to its end.

In the meantime, Morlenden, one not given over to fits of brooding self-inspection, mused over the odd circumstances of his meeting with the younger girl. He had soon lost sight of their differences, as had she, and both of them had begun to see each other as contemporaries, at least in the days of their futures to come. True to her age, Sanjirmil was somewhat abrupt, erratic, and irresponsible; but she also carried in her head a whole cargo of insights far in advance of her years, and he learned to feel at ease with her peculiarities. It even came to seem as if most of her odd behavior came not from her youth, relative to him, but from an innate nature common to all the Players. At any rate, there was less a gulf between them than the years might have suggested, for after all they were both still adolescents, and in the highly structured environment they lived in their behavior was more similar than different.

They decided to remain together for a time longer, and left Lamkleth, to wander from one Braid holding to another, from village to village, from elder lodge to elder lodge, helping with odd jobs and the harvest, which was just now beginning. They walked along paths in the forest, along the edges of fields, cultivated and fallow alike; and when the weather permitted, slept outside, wrapped tightly together for warmth. After the first night together in the cabin, they talked little, and when they did, their words were only of little things, insignificant things, things which they could see immediately in front of them. As long as it was possible for them to do so, they set aside time and lived in the present, from moment to moment, making love when they found the time and place and ambience right, sitting quietly together when they did not.

But all things end which have a beginning, some sooner than others; and after some time, Morlenden and Sanjirmil became aware, as if they had been bemused, of the passage of weeks into months. The nights grew steadily cooler, and then cold, and then some days did not really warm up, even in the sun. The canopies of the forest began to open up, and washes of bright color flowed over the face of the mornings. They spent fewer nights in the open. And gradually they began to admit time between them once again; they spoke of the lives behind them and before them, of changes; Morlenden of the role coming to him of parent, of holdingsman. Sanjirmil spoke of the Players and their insular, abstracted yet passionate lives. She spoke no more of the Game itself. He did not ask. They did not really listen to the words, though they listened close enough, for it wasn't what they said in words, in Singlespeech or Multispeech, but rather what the unspoken words under the spoken words said of their inner uneasiness, and their knowledge of ends. For now Morlenden was beginning to feel change stirring within himself, an odd set of unfamiliar new sensations, as if the prolonged liaison with Sanjirmil had stimulated the onset of his fertility. He knew it was not yet. But it would be soon. Very soon. The ancient, cultured pair-bond of the Braid between himself and Fellirian began to reassert itself, driving his orientation toward the odd, wiry hoydenish Sanjirmil away from the flesh and more into the heart.

And she, in her turn, began to grow apprehensive about her return, which was now long overdue. The Players, so it seemed, did not care so much for long visits out of their own environment. Certain elders, whom she would not name, would be angry with her for staying so long. There were punishments, of which she would not speak.

They allowed their wanderings to carry them around, drifting to the northwest again, more in the direction of Sanjirmil's home territories, by unspoken agreement. And they spent their last night together in the ruins of an ancient, pre-ler water-powered gristmill somewhere deep in the upper waters of the River Hvar, in a place where the old stone and brick buildings were overgrown with creepervine, trumpetflower, and kudzu, and where enormous aged beech trees hung over the mirrored surface of the millpond behind the piled-stone dam and shed their yellow leaves into the muddy water. It was rainy and miserable on the night they found the mill, but the morning was bright and clear, cold and windy.

A variable, willful breeze played in the leaves and ruffled wavelets over the shallow pond. They did not speak of it, of ends and departures, but stood by the dam for a long time, standing close together, hands interlocked. Sanjirmil looked at Morlenden once, with the disturbing blind, fixed gaze of hers, the scanning motion of her eyes readily apparent from so close. And after that, she turned abruptly and walked swiftly away across the dam, deftly skipping over driftwood which had piled up over the years along the upstream side of it. It was only when she was completely across, off the stonework dam, on the far side under the trees, that she looked back. Morlenden watched her for a moment, seeing the wind teasing her short, coarse black hair, ruffling her overshirt, the same much-mended one she had met him in, and he waved, as casually as possible. Sanjirmil waved back. Morlenden looked away; and when he could look back, Sanjirmil was gone. The woods on the farther shore were empty.

He returned homeward directly, seeking no further adventures or idle wanderings, taking shortcuts, wasting no time. It took all of that day until far after dark, but he made it all in one day. And when he had at last come into his own *yos*, the old, homey, weather-stained ellipsoids of the Derens, after a long, thoughtful soak in the icy water of the wash-trough outside, he found Fellirian waiting for him in the hearthroom.

She looked questioningly at him for a moment, but said nothing be-yond an offhand greeting, as if he had just now stepped outside to fetch a pail of water from the creek. And although he found that he was actu-ally deeply happy to see his insibling again, he said no more than as if he actually had done just that: gone outside for water an instant ago. He found that his earlier desire to make a clever allusion to his great adven-ture had vanished completely; what had happened to him could not be told. And he knew a deeper secret about the *vayyon:* that below the level of the first revelation, that there was no great adventure, was a second, more cryptic level of the heart—that it was perhaps better not to find that for which one searched. He wondered if she had seen that as well.

They did not speak of such things. But that night, sitting together, sharing a bowl of stew, they made the small talk of members of the family, neighborhood gossip. Who had done what, with which, and to whom. Births. Deaths. It was only as they were banking the hearthfire for the night and blowing out the lamps that Fellirian told him that she had become fertile in the last few days.

"I'm not surprised, Eliya," Morlenden answered from across the hearthroom, not looking at her. "I've felt some twinges myself. I don't think I am right now, but it will be soon, now that you've come in."

"Kadh'Elagi and Madh'Abedra have set a date for the weaving."

"When?"

"Winter Solsticeday. And they've already made arrangements with a lodge."

"So soon?"

"Yes. We wondered what had become of you, if you would be back in time . . ."

"I was unavoidably detained, ah, by the harvest."

"Indeed. They do say that it has been a good one this year. Did you work hard?"

"Yes. It was good for me."

"So it appears . . . you look somewhat the better for it. And more, too: from the look of you, you'll be fertile yourself by Solsticeday."

"Such are my suspicions as well." Morlenden and Fellirian paused by the curtained port into the children's sleeper, sharing an odd conspiratorial look. "Well, Eliya, after you."

"All right, I'll go first. But we won't be in here much longer, you know."

Fellirian climbed into the sleeper. As she disappeared behind the curtain, Morlenden reached up and patted her rump affectionately. When he had himself pushed the curtain aside, Fellirian met him, whispering fiercely "You randy *hifzer* buck! You know you shouldn't touch me now. You don't know what it's like yet." She quieted a little. "Really, it's no fun. Not like wanting *dhainaz* at all. I fear it. And I fear even more going long without doing what we must."

"I'll stay away, if you want."

"No, I don't want that either. . . . Did you have a good time, Olede?"

"I learned a great deal—the last few weeks, months . . . has it been months? Someday I'll tell you some of it."

Fellirian was spreading out one large double comforter on the soft floor of the sleeper. Morlenden was folding his kif, feeling around for the proper shelf. He asked, "And where's mine?"

Fellirian slid her kif off her shoulders and let it fall to the floor. She gestured to the comforter she had spread. Morlenden nodded. She was fertile, and nothing mattered now. He could not refuse her, even had he wanted to refuse.

She said softly, "It has to be us now . . . I have laid aside all mine of the past. You must do likewise, and comfort me."

The light in the sleeper was dim, but there was enough to make out the smooth shape across the comforter from him. Familiar, as everyday as an arm or a leg. Fellirian . . . she was smooth and subtle of shape, inviting. He bent over her, touched her face, lightly. Her scent had changed, was no longer the tart, flowery, slightly pungent scent of an adolescent girl, but something warmer, richer, riper. It had an odd and immediate effect on him, and the speed of it surprised Morlenden greatly. He began to learn about the compulsions of fertility.

At last the sequence ended and Morlenden returned to the present, now sleepy. Beside him, he heard Fellirian's deep, even breathing, felt the familiar warmth of her body. *All those years,* he thought. *And us with a girl-child a year or more older than Sanjir was then . . . amazing!*

He had not spoken to Fellirian about his adventure, just as she had never spoken of hers. And in the intervening years, he had not been able to follow Sanjirmil very well; the Derens had led a busy life, and Morlenden had been doing most of the field work, and of course all the Players, of both Braids, kept very much to themselves. Rarely, he and Sanjirmil had passed on some errand, but they had said nothing. He had once heard a distant tale, distortedly repeated by the tenth bearer of the tale, that something had happened to her, some drastic accident which she had survived somehow . . . here the tale had been unclear. And at any rate, he had seen her at a distance not long after that, a few weeks, and she had looked no different. There had been no injuries, no disfigurements.

But the disturbing tales continued, and they told that Sanjirmil had been changed in a way no bearer of tales could tell. But here again, he had never seen any evidence of change.

So now he lay awake in the dark, remembering, reliving it all again, his inner mind returning with abrasive insistence, to the same questions he had asked before and found no answer to. Why was it that the Perwathwiy Srith, an elder, should walk in haste to the holding of the Derens; and why bring with her Sanjirmil, her own insibling descendant, two generations removed? And the Perwathwiy had been, of course, a Terklaren herself, the *Klandorh* of the Terklarens, just as would be Sanjirmil in her turn. Next year. Maybe sooner.

Sanjirmil. Morlenden had enjoyed recalling the affair they had shared, with its strong sense of poignant emotions and extravagant eroticism; indeed, a piece of him was tied into that time forever, even though he had grown used to the knowledge over the years that their liaison was doomed from the start, made hopeless by the years that separated them. So one went one way, one another. A little ripple passed through him, something not quite laughter; soon she would look upon her own children with the same sense of astonishment that he did. It seemed to be forever coming, and then it was over. Yes, there were some regrets. But now . . . he did not care so much for the speculations, unanswered, that the visit suggested.

FIVE

*The Game visually generates certain patterns which remain in
one location and pervolve; others move over the playing field at
various speeds, retaining various degrees of internal identity and
coherence. Here, we have no difficulty whatsoever understanding
that it is the Game and the parameters of a specific Game set
which make such figures move. In the physical universe, however,
we see similar motions and various conditions of identity and
stability; and have thereon erected an incredible and erroneous
set of "laws" to explain such conditions. When the laws fail to
predict, add complications and subtleties, precisely as the Ptole-
maic astronomers added epicycle after epicycle to their basically
wrong model of planetary motion. So a better theory was devised. We speak of Copernicus, of Newton, of Kepler, of conic sections and conservations of angular momentum. Seen from the
perspective of the Game, these things are hardly less wrong than
Ptolemaics. We shall now discuss these things under their true
names, understanding, of course, that they are expressions of a
much better model.*

—The Game Texts

IN THE EARLIEST societies, the symbol of force replaces the force itself,
and then symbols replace symbols, each becoming progressively more
subtle: club, spear, knife, sword, pistol. They evolve to bearers of such
things, mere suggestions to be sure, but not less in the importance put
upon them by the observer. Or the owner. In the settled, civilized,
mostly nonviolent bureaucratic state, these symbols become even more
abstract: counters, desks, offices. The more massive the desk and the
more empty the office, the greater the authority. The more insulated
and invisible the office, the greater still. Klaneth Parleau, Chairman of
the Board of Governors of Seaboard South Region, had such a desk,

such an office. The office was excessively large, and would have been in any age, but in an age in which volume and space were at a premium and all buildings were designed with function and efficiency first in mind, it was particularly impressive. There were no windows; windows were conducive to distraction and daydreaming, and there was little time for that. Parleau, for one, could not imagine an age when there could have been time for it.

One who came into Parleau's office would first have to traverse the apparent vastness of the length of the room, and then face Parleau's desk, which was a massive cruciform shape made of a single casting of titanium, brushed and anodized to a dull, almost black finish. To increase the illusion of distance, the base of the T-shape of the desk was slightly narrower than the part nearest its occupant, which had the dual effect of making the occupant seem both farther away and at the same time larger than life. This neck of the T was used occasionally as a conference desk, and chairs were stored under it. They, too, were part of the effect, for as they increased their distance from the head of the desk, they grew smaller and more uncomfortable to sit in. And the occupant of the head of the desk could select, from a console blended into the working surface, which chair would be slid out for the visitor, varying status with circumstance. There wasn't a weapon within miles of this office, and it was doubtful if the chairman himself could have done violence to a starving orphan; yet within his office full in the powers of his position, he could reduce grown men to worms and they themselves would admit it first.

Seaboard South was not particularly more powerful than other, similar administrative units into which the whole habitable Earth was divided, save in one area: it possessed the Charter of Overmanagement for both the Institute, which was the interface between the humans of Earth and their artificially mutated step-cousins, the ler, and the reservation in which the ler lived. This made it, in effect, the broker for the vast amounts of data which flowed into and out of the Institute, detailing every art and science of the planet.

In similar fashion, Chairman Parleau was not especially different from his theoretical equals, the chairmen of other regions near and far, except for this one area, and the Regional Chairman's consciousness of that fact. Parleau personally had as yet done very little in the way of direct manipulation of those powers. Yet. But the very idea that he could, should he choose, kept chairmen of the neighboring Regions closely attentive to events in Seaboard South.

Parleau himself was a large and heavy-boned but generally trim, balding individual of apparent early middle age: mature, securely settled in high office. No single facet of Klaneth Parleau would have distinguished him from a thousand other career administrative executives—other than a rather aggressive manner and a more closely cropped than normal hair-style (of what hair remained to him). When he moved he exhibited a crispness and a dynamism which somehow most of the others lacked.

In fact, Parleau was somewhat younger in years than his appearance suggested, and far from reaching a pinnacle, he was in fact being groomed carefully for higher advancement still; some thought to Codirectorate Staff, an anonymous coordination position. Others, no less well-informed, felt that it would be at the least to a post on Continental Secretariat, with a leg up to the Planetary Presidium somewhat later. Seaboard South had been his first regional chairmanship, and with its long association with the ler and the Institute, it was a key posting, selected by his peers. Historically, it had always been a make-or-break assignment, and the odds had been against most past chairmen. The majority, upon completion or replacement, had elected to move to positions of lesser ranking. But a few had made it into the rarefied upper levels, where they generally prospered.

The problem, as Parleau formulated it, was not that the New People were troublesome or unruly, but to the contrary. In fact, they were generally better behaved than their human neighbors. It was a fact that they seemed to react with less stress to crowding and personal restriction, but, he thought wryly, with the population density they had, they could hardly complain about a behavioral sink, however restricted they were to their reservation. More, the reservation did not impose a drain upon the resources of Seaboard South, as such a project might have been expected to do. No; together, the reservation and the Institute were both self-supporting, and their gross output net was larger than any conceivable alternate use to which the land could have been put.

No. The problem underlying everything seemed to be that humans knew no better now than in the beginning how do deal with the New People. In developing them out of their own mixed stock, the men of 2000 had been reaching for the goal long dreamed of—controlled mutation, and the transformation of man into superman. This would be the last victory of the flower of the old science, actually greater in significance then the as-yet-undiscovered faster-than-light drive. For they had cast aside the old myths about a mere physical specimen, a superman of body; they were reaching for the mind. And then they would have planned programmed men who would, under careful supervision, carry them to heights unreachable in the random, recursive, agonizingly slow processes of nature. They would, in short, not wait to grow into the garden of Earthly delights, nor would they countenance stumbling into it by accident, but would storm it by force, the force of the mind. But the program, starting innocently enough with experiments with lower lifeforms, had progressed steadily through ever more complex forms; and when at last they had performed the final, half-magical reading and attempted programming of human DNA, they found that they had not constructed an avenue into the future but instead constructed a strange and mysterious door into an unknown and unknowable future. A door which only worked one way, and one that only the key of DNA would unlock. After a hundred years of "production," the door was finally sealed; and then destroyed.

Nothing was ever forgotten; it was rather that the whole discipline became discredited, then unprofitable, then unfunded. One thing technology never solved: it was frightfully expensive to alter DNA under controlled conditions in which results could be expected. And, paradoxically, unlike every other essentially technological process, the cost did not go down as it was repeated. The last ler brought into being artificially cost virtually the same as the first. In a time when a thousand projects were worthy of more attention, they beggared the planet to make something they couldn't use for themselves. Mankind wisely concluded, reinforcing the judgments of the theologians, that however thrilling it might have been to play God, it was also damned expensive. To do as well as the original might well be feasible, but it could not be paid for.

Physiologically, humans knew the ler easily enough, although the number who made such an area their interest steadily declined with time. But physiognomy was only the smallest part of reality, and the cultural gap widened yearly. Man opted for efficiency, the ler for harmony. Everyone had, rich and educated, ignorant and poor alike, anticipated the supermen: they would be large in size, strong, dominant of disposition, possessed of keen analytical minds, masters of technology at last, knowing all consequences in advance. There would be no haven for superstition and vanity.

But the New People—or ler as they decided to call themselves in their own developed language, meaning "new" but also "innocent"— were determinedly unheroic. On the average, they were smaller in overall size, lighter in weight, and slimmer in build than the average human. Moreover, they retained into adulthood what seemed to humans as an excess of human adolescent features. That this was the natural result of forced evolution, a process called neoteny, in which youthful stages were expanded at the expense of older mature stages, did not reassure those who insisted upon viewing them as children, something their adult members were not. And by the time a truly ler culture had begun to develop and take root, the specimens were increasingly wrapped in impenetrable veils of language, ritual, mysticism, and an eclectic, bucolic philosophy that seemed to deny every common-sense notion of progress. "How quaint," cried the harsh voices of the cult of expediency, entirely missing sight of the fact that ethic and ritual protect us from one another. . . .

And so Parleau spent each day in his office, hoping over the distraction of the other sides of Seaboard South, that there would never be a problem, which his contemporaries and peers might have referred to as "an opportunity to excel." And after dayshifter hours, which were his permanently by virtue of his high position, he would return to his set of cubicles alone* and hope, all the more fervently, that the next day would be quiet as well.

The quiet had come to an end. Parleau knew and faced it matter-of-factly. It had been coming, of course. He could see as well as the next with hindsight, but he could also see, even without the Situational Analysis training the controllers got, that this situation could not remain stable and peaceful forever. Why should it? Nothing else in the known universe did. So at some point, the hostility would have to take an overt form. Then what? It appeared that the humans still held all the cards. But that was the weakness. It was a dependent and vulnerable command position. The Old People were in fact completely vulnerable to the output of the Institute, so much so that now, in this century, continued stability (they had long since ceased calling it progress) was tied directly into its steadily increasing output. There was no way out of it: the Institute tinkered with basic efficiencies, the very stuff of which a million lives a day hung in the balance, hung upon five hundredths of a percentage point of difference. Yes. Things were that tight. Had it been something so simple as some material shortage, Parleau felt that they could have coped, some way. Done without, maybe. Invented substitutes. But all those avenues had been explored already. The time had

---

* Members of the high executive class did not have families.

passed, several hundred years ago, when they could deal with simple shortages. The very idea. It was the hardest problem civilized man had ever faced, and Parleau did not expect to solve it himself in the course of an afternoon.

Consider mathematics and the classical three-body problem: even with computers to speed up the process of computation a millionfold, they still couldn't conceptualize it as it was, three-simultaneously, but ran it as a series of twos. Now blow that up, enlarge it, complicate it to a billion-body problem, crank in several theories of economics, five major schools of politics, including anarchy, add the now-semicontrolled ecology of the entire planet, and muddy it with an unconnected human population which had continued unreduced, if slowed to virtual zero growth, at the unimaginable level of twenty billion. Yet, in a limited way, this was just what the Institute attempted to do, one question at a time. The human members posed narrow and specific questions, and the researchers designed alternatives they called parametered solutions, series of *iffy* courses of actions whose basic trade-offs were known or strongly suspected. The questioners debated and made the value judgments.

It was painfully clear from this that the ler and their Institute had become indispensable, which was the utter horror of every leader and bureaucrat since Hammurabi. Indispensable man has a handle on you. Only when you can make all men and indeed all creatures immanently dispensable and interchangeable can this threat to the superstition of executive omnipotence be made to fade into insignificance. And the solution that came most often to mind—simply eliminate them and rationalize it afterward for the muddy thinkers—was in this case both ethically repugnant and obviously disastrous. They had long since assumed that to go it alone now without the ler partnership was possible, but all things considered, it wasn't desirable at all. There was a most delicate balance of tomorrows.

Now this thing, Parleau thought, suddenly too agitated to sit still behind his desk, the symbol for which he had worked so hard, and made so many resentful enemies along the way to it. A girl about whom almost nothing was known, save that she appeared to be circumstantially connected with some minor and unimportant vandalism. A simple incident, surely, but somehow along the way she managed to lose her bloody mind. Then responsible parties discovered that she was a ler adolescent. That they could see for themselves. Parleau stood by the corner of his desk, shuffling through the morning reports from the previous eve and mid-shifts; the quality control data, the indexes, the graphs. He was not interested in them, but only in the answer to the question, *Why me?*

The administrator in the outer office signaled that the visitors Parleau had called earlier were now assembled and waiting there. The time had come. Parleau cleared his throat, sighed deeply, and recomposed his expression from one of worry and concern to one of stern action. And they would not have to worry about interruptions, either. All other business save natural disasters and civil unrests had been tabled for the day. They had to know, here, now; that was for sure. This could prove to be either a nothing incident, forgettable and forgotten, or an invitation to conspicuous failure.

He depressed a button on the desk, signaling assent, and soon his visitors began to enter. They were all well-known figures, key personnel of the local regional upper administration, but at the same time Parleau recognized that he knew none of them well. They were all either holdovers from the previous regime or imports like himself, brought in from other parts of the world.

Edner Eykor entered first. He was one of those who had come from somewhere else. Parleau had looked in the records, but had not assigned the facts any importance, and had consequently forgotten them. Like the other users of programmed names, Eykor's surname lent no clue as to place or origin. Where had it been? Europe, somewhere, Parleau thought. Eykor was a thin, nervous man who always seemed to be in a hurry, always on the verge of missing some item, at least in appearance. A bad sign, Parleau had thought more than once. Nervousness in an intelligence man. Not good at all. His opinion was that an intelligence man at the staff level should be as impassive as an idol. Eykor had sandy, nondescript thinning hair and a long, horselike countenance, upon which a set of rubbery lips ruminated aimlessly.

The second was Mandor Klyten, the Regional ler Expert. He was a curious one, for his post was almost totally unconnected with the Institute. Until Klyten had filled it, it had been little more than an academic post, a sinecure. Give Klyten credit: at least he had done much of his own field work, a notion unheard of for years, indeed if not generations. He studied and worked hard, and his advice regarding ler matters, while curiously unspecific, was always worth listening to. Outside the reservation, he was as well-informed as it was possible to be. Klyten was a short, plump, rather disorganized man of middle age; Parleau was not confused by the absentminded appearance. Under that thinning gray hair lurked a formidable and keen intelligence. Parleau did wonder at the turn of preferences that led such a one to scholasticism.

Aseph Plattsman was the last to enter. The analyst and Controller. In an earlier day, Plattsman might, from his general appearance, have been a musician, an artist. Today, a Controller. One who watched and monitored, who supervised, who managed. Who controlled. Odd, that, but again, not so odd. Parleau had heard more than once that the discipline of the Controllers, Situational Analysis, had become the last art form. And equally often, Parleau had also heard that the majority of Regional Chairmen were former Controllers. Not vast majority. Just majority. Plattsman was long and aesthetic, dark of complexion, having black, unruly hair and deep chocolate eyes that expressed little but observed everything. He moved without obvious gesture or mannerism, but with an effortless exactitude, as if every motion were exactly what he had intended it to be. Youngest by far on the staff, Plattsman could easily move to some Region as chairman someday. Slow and deliberate, when the pressure was on he could change into one of the most serious and stern of taskmasters. Parleau felt no particular threat from Plattsman, knowing it would be years yet; Plattsman had not been sent to replace him, but to learn. Parleau understood these things, and the loneliness of this path; after a time, nothing was worth any effort but the work and the power. Still, he felt the most empathy here, to Plattsman, and wished him continued success.

The three visitors waited by their accustomed places until Parleau gestured to them that they should be seated, lowering himself into his own chair as he did. He waved at them impatiently. "Good day, good day, daymen. Shall we leave the pleasantries and go to the matter at hand?"

They nodded, and began unpacking briefcases and untidy portfolios. Eykor, so it appeared, had the smallest pile, so by common consent he would be the first to speak.

He began "Why we are here relates to security, so I propose that we . . ."

Parleau interrupted. "Wait. I have read the résumés. Who reported the information and how far upchannel did it go?"

Plattsman answered, "CenRegCon did, Chairman. The original B-twenty-seven report was on late mids. I have the pertinent duty logs. The first, capture, was routine and normal, so it went, eventually, all the way up. ConSec. No further, though. Not to my knowledge. The second one, of last night, was stopped here for comment or amendment before going on."

Parleau breathed deeply. Shorted out by the wily Controllers, just on suspicion, until it could be checked against the files. And it matched. And they held it. They could have let it go, and who could have taken clear reprisals against them? The Controllers were notoriously independent-minded; so they were saving him, but for what reasons? He would have to run that one later.

Plattsman produced several sheets of electroprint and read, from the forms; "Thirty-one Tenmonth two-three-four-five local hour . . . Item forty-six incident of suspected terrorism, Regional Museum of Technology and applications. Watchman reports certain instruments in the Petro section dismantled, destroyed by acid. . . . The next entry is . . . yes, Item sixty-two. A member, female, reported apprehended without papers or reasonable explanation near Museum, attempting to cross River Five on a methane pipeline from the composting dumps. Remanded to Interrogation."

He paused, shuffling the papers some more. "Then here's a follow-up, 'subject member refused to give name of number. Remanded back to Interrogation.' "

"And here . . . the last report, a follow-up, which we stopped. It looked wrong. By this time there's a case number on it. We were going to have a look into it anyway, but then this Medic Venle reports that Interro had somehow put a live female ler into a sensory deprivation chamber. While inside, something so far undetermined occurred to the subject, who we may now refer to as 'Item forty-six,' and Item forty-six upon recovery was observed to have no measurable mental processes beyond infant state; some kind of regression had taken place. One of the things that stood out was that this report was made in B format, but of course a B is not appropriate because as a ler, she never had an A submitted on her. It was kicked out of process control. When we cross checked, we found the references. That's all, Chairman."

Parleau said, "We will have to follow it up and finalize, because at Continental there's an open case file. Understand? But careful, now. Nothing on this goes out without my initials." He tamed to Eykor. "Now. What's gone on there?"

"Chairman, it's all pretty much as in the reports. I was present part of the time, because the interrogators said that they could not crack her. We tried, but nothing. It was minor, of course, but the more we said, the tighter she became. We did not try drugs or stimuli, but total isolation seemed to be a good idea. At the time—we had no idea. . . ."

Klyten asked, "And what was her age?"

"She never said. We took tissue samples, along with the other routine identification procedures, but they read out too young using human data base. We didn't have the ler data and didn't want to ask for it, you understand, but fifteen certainly seemed too low."

Klyten commented, "You're right, there. It is too low. I might say a better guess would put her, say, about twenty. Yes, twenty, plus or minus a year. How long did you give her in the box?"

"Well, at the time she was taken out, about twenty-five days."

"Twenty-five days? I've heard that hard human cases break in ten!"

"Well, now, Klyten, that's more or less true, but we just assumed she'd react similarly."

"Judging from events, a poor assumption, something even a student adviser would have advised against. Or did you know then that they have the ability to autoforget, dump all the mnemonic data they have collected since birth?"

"No, we . . . well, hell, so we made an error. But all the same, we had enough evidence to connect her to the Museum job, and terrorism is a capital offense anyway, so . . ."

Parleau interrupted Eykor again. "Wait. Terrorism, is it? You must have a live victim to have terrorism."

"Chairman, we interpreted the destruction of valuable instruments and artifacts as a distinct crime against society, harming the people in general. After all, there were persons on duty about the Museum also."

Parleau looked off into space for a moment, then turned back to Eykor. "Eykor, all sorts of deeds, good and bad, have been done in human history, and they all carry the same reason: that they were done for the good of the people. Now I'm no moralist or ethicist, nor squeamish when it comes down to what must be done. Let it roll! But whatever we do here, please let us all use more rigor in our definitions that 'it's for the people.' That's just bullshit, and you and I alike know it. Now what were these valuable instruments?"

"Some ancient devices used in geodesy and petroleum exploration, to search out likely sites."

"Specifically, what?"

"A highly miniaturized Magnetic Anomaly Detector, apparently originally towed behind an aircraft. The other was a Gravity Field Sensor, likewise miniature. That was why the acid. This last measured the local field strength of gravity. The custodian informed us that both instruments were reputed to be very sensitive and capable of precise resolutions, say, on the order of a handsbreadth across."

Parleau said, "Curious, curious. What could possibly have been her motive?"

Eykor answered, "We have no idea."

Parleau looked at Klyten, who shrugged. Then at Plattsman. At first he shook his head, but began tapping on the metal desk surface with his long fingers. After a time, he said, hesitating, ". . . The instruments were used to find subsurface oil sites, you say?"

Parleau saw immediately. He exclaimed, "To prevent the discovery of something, some mineral or petroleum on Reservation land!"

Plattsman stood. "Perhaps, Chairman. But I want to use your assistant's terminal. I need access to the Archives."

"Go ahead." Plattsman left, briskly. Parleau turned to Eykor. "Only one thing wrong, there. Oil has been out of use for several centuries. There's still some of it around, but just small pools, not exploited. Not worth it. Residuals, curiosities. Besides. I don't think the reservation area ever had a reputation for natural oils anyway."

"I could not comment on that one, Chairman."

Klyten asked, "Has anyone inquired why no mention was made that Item forty-six was a New People adolescent?"

Eykor replied, "No. It was unimportant. Is. We were interested in the crime itself."

"Unimportant? By Darwin's organs, that's the central fact of it, not what she wrecked. Why she wrecked it. If we worry about what she did, and forget who she was, or why she was there, we're chasing the bird with the broken wing. It's who she is, what she is. I agree with the medic, what's his name. This is serious. We are dealing here with large unknowns, perhaps dangerous for our welfare. We need to solve it."

Eykor, rebuked once again and told his own business, opened his mouth to put Klyten in his place, but at that moment, Plattsman chose to make his return.

Parleau asked, "Well?"

"There is no evidence of either oil or ore deposits about the whole region on either side of River Nine. In or near the reservation. No inquiries were underway, nor were any being considered. I also queried the use of instruments, the Magnetic Anomaly Detector was used in several ways, militarily, to detect undersea craft, and mines, and also, later, to locate high-density ferrous bodies, mascons. Meteorites, buried in the drift. The other was used to determine the exact shape of the Earth, and also in the search for mascons. But the recorded data indicates that there were no such anomalies in the reservation area."

"So we're no better off than before. Unless they were to hide something they found themselves. . . ."

Klyten observed, "We should not be so hasty there. We are reasonably sure that they are not, except in very specific and limited fields, technologists. So what could they discover and hide that our finest instruments could not perceive? I add to counter my own argument that we also know that their area was never exploited. It was given to them because of that—there seemed to be nothing worth while in the area."

Parleau mused aloud, "But even if they had oil, what would they use it for? We have better and cheaper fuel and the material stuff we get from synthetics the same. They have no need for it, and they couldn't give it to us. . . ."

Eykor asked, "What about metals?"

Klyten said, "A better case, there, perhaps, but still tentative."

Eykor asked further, "But if so, why hide it? They know the reservation's sovereign ground. There hasn't been a human actually inside it on the ground for a good two hundred years, and I don't know of any case . . ."

Plattsman commented, "The previous government had in its time also displaced aboriginal tribes and set aside inviolate reservations. But for a long time, as soon as anything of value was found or suspected on such lands, ways were devised to circumvent or disregard such pacts. The ler are aware of these facts, perhaps better than we. All they would have to do would be to compare their own population density against anywhere outside it. There, are, for example, more humans living in Tierra Del Fuego. There is pressure from that alone, and only by surplus production do they buy that appetite off. Never mind any resource."

Eykor shrugged. "I know that as well. And I, for one, would have to assign a lower probability to some resource. But there are other possibilities; something hidden, something made or built. The first thing to mind would be a weapon of some sort."

Parleau exclaimed, "It's my turn to assign probabilities, and that one is low indeed. Why, if they had a weapon to hide that would do them any good, why haven't they used it?"

Klyten shook his head, agitatedly. "No, no, no. Anything they could use would have to be powerful or of widespread impact, which starts by violating their most cherished beliefs. And it would have to be an artifact, probably quite large. There are delivery systems to consider, aim, use, range."

"Wait, there," Parleau said thoughtfully. "Mind, I don't actually think it might be that, but . . . Eykor, did you run any cross checks on this Item forty-six? Does she have a record?"

"No, we didn't. She seemed such an amateur. . . ."

Plattsman asked, "Can we run one now? I mean, not a full scan, which would take days, but just a quick collation from the Comparator. That will give us a quick glance over the continent. The matches, if any, should be along shortly."

"I have no objection."

Plattsman left, and returned shortly. "I referred to the record holos you took off her in Security Records. The Comparator will review all the Current Operations records of the stress checkpoints and see if there's a match."

Parleau asked Eykor, skeptically. "Are you sure you have gathered any evidence at all on this case?"

"Chairman, we had just started when this last event occurred. We were moving discreetly because of the sensitivity of the issue. There is another aspect to this, and we were trying to integrate the two. From our overflight series . . ."

"Overflights? Were they not prohibited?"

"We have been using gliders, launched across the reservation. Battery powered, inertial guided. Flown at night in the proper weather conditions, they are undetectable. They couldn't see one if they had radar."

"Go on."

"It's an old program. I didn't initiate it. And who will complain, when they can't see it, don't know it's there? At least, we assume they have never seen it, for there have been no complaints."

Parleau said, "Poor assumption. The one does not necessarily follow."

"Do you want it stopped?"

"Stopped . . . ? No. Continue it, of course, but supervise it closely. I realize many of us are new to these people, if they are that."

"Of course, and also we can . . ." And here Eykor launched into a detailed account of delaying, frustrating, obfuscative and annoying practices and examples of the same, which the Regional Government might have occasion to use. He continued at some length, until stopped by a signal from the outer office. Plattsman excused himself and left.

The group waited, expectantly. Plattsman was gone for longer than they thought, and they all began to grow restive. Presently he returned, animated.

"Incredible, actually incredible. Why we overlooked it is beyond me—more of these assumptions, in my branch as well as the next. There is simply no substitute for thoroughness, is there?"

Parleau said, "Well, on with it."

"The tentative match list was too large, and had to be narrowed. I had to cross-refer it with the chemosensors. When I did, I got this list." And Plattsman read: "Orlando, New Orleans, Huntsville; five discrete locations in Seaboard South; three more in the Oak Ridge area; once, Dayton; and twice on the West Coast, once in Sur and once in Bayarea. I requested pictures. And this is only in the last year!"

Klyten was first to speak. "She can't have walked to all those places clambering along methane pipes!"

Parleau said, "No, indeed not. She has moved freely among us, and for what purposes? I was not aware they could do this."

Eykor said. "They're not supposed to be able to. . . ."

Plattsman laughed. "And now it gets interesting. Not a vandal, but a spy. A real one! We haven't had one for centuries!"

And Parleau said, "Yes, very funny; one who risks her life to destroy instruments, and who faces the box and oblivion to conceal why. Plattsman! Have your people see if they can find some more of these instruments, somewhere, in working condition. And continue your check of the Comparator network. I want to know exactly where she's been, when. Stay out of the Institute until I say—she's probably left a dozen spider webs to trip over. Check her identity discreetly, open source stuff, for the present. We must know more. You, too, Eykor. And you were saying something about overflights . . . ?"

"Yes, I was, and this fits perfectly. There seems to be a pattern of activity that defies analysis, almost as if it were being purposely randomized, but we can draw conclusions from its growth and spread. We had made these tentative guesses—that there is a secret somewhere in the reservation, apparently unknown by most of the inhabitants, and that Game theory suggests a definite break with past patterns, in the near-future time-frame."

"What kind of time-frame?"

"Five to ten years."

"That's no better than an entrail-reader of ancient Rome could do. I could do as much with common sense."

Plattsman interjected, "Chairman, begging your pardon, but reading entrails is precisely what we do. We've substituted Data Terminal Printouts for the original bloody guts, but otherwise it's all the same—a little guessing, a little larceny, a little luck, and damn good observation of the present."

Parleau smiled. "And so, Eykor, that was why your people were so anxious to get something out of her?"

"That is correct, Chairman. We needed a key, a tool to get at the larger problem. She offered a perfect chance. Unfortunately, we got nothing out of her directly."

"But the second chance, man! Now we can."

Klyten said mildly, "Maybe not. I must advise you that she would not do these things—if indeed it is her and not the error of an overzealous machine or that of a careless programmer somewhere along the line—completely on her own. They are a communal people and act together in all things and enterprises. The few who live alone become sedentary, fixed in place."

Eykor exclaimed, "As I suspected all along! A plot!"

"Yes," Klyten continued. "And they are most fond of subtle ones. There are many possibilities here, and not the least of them is that she may have been dragged under our noses to prevent us from smelling something else, as the saying goes. I don't think they would sacrifice her willingly, that's not their way, but her capture could have been accidental. Or she could have been designed to cause us to precipitate certain events. I have long suspected forms of this type of manipulation—control by negative aversion. You see obvious forms of this in some of our own less sophisticated child-rearing practices, but as a management technique, it is capable of great refinement and control. There is the well-known study by Klei that shows grounds for suspecting that they encouraged and fomented the immanent racialism which suddenly terminated with their move into the reservation and their consolidation."

Eykor observed, "I see. Had they gathered themselves together of their own accord, it would have generated great suspicion, even in an environment of basically neutral feelings, but with a slight degree of encouraged race-fear, and proper stimuli . . . but that's social control on a very large scale. Do they have that kind of control, and what are the margins for error?"

Klyten had their attention. He continued, "There is where we have not been able to reach the bottom of it. After all, as Controller Plattsman will doubtless agree, we have some fairly subtle methods ourselves, but there are operations we prefer to stay away from. So much so that there isn't enough data even to estimate how much control they have. We do note with relief that this sort of thing seems to have died out after the consolidation. I know this is rather far afield, but it supports the idea that we must consider this in our range of possibilities."

Parleau remained silent still, thinking hard, letting the others do the talking. But he knew Klyten's argument to be a valid one, and that they had many more options than simply the first one that had occurred to them. One simply could not know, now. There was need for more data, more caution. He had always figured in fudge factors throughout his career, and with the instinct of the careerist, he sensed the need for them now—large ones, in fact. To be caught off guard by them would be unfortunate, but not fatal. However, to make the wrong interpretation and then take the wrong course of action and precipitate undesirable events . . . unthinkable. More was at stake here than his own merit report file at Continental.

He said, "Klyten, is part of our difficulty here the result of the way we perceive them? Or, I should ask, the way we respond?"

"I think so. The whole culture goes to great length to rationalize their apparent voluntary primitivism . . . I think that many of them themselves are not aware of the dichotomy. I mean, you look at some of the solutions coming out of the Institute, and there's evidence of fine, educated technological minds at work, and then around seventeen-hundred or eighteen-hundred hours, the owners of these fine minds go home and chop wood, or draw water from a stream. We also see evidence in other ways that they are in fact not primitive at all . . . their houses reflect chemical engineering and knowledge of geodesies, blended together, a field so far ahead of us that even with a sample of the material in front of us, we can't describe how it sets up and works. This branch of specialized technology is the monopoly of a single Braid, which cooks over a charcoal fire and bathes in an unheated stream. If this were occurring in the wilder sections of New Guinea or Borneo I could cite rapid change and incomplete assimilations, but here this is not the case; they turn away from the technology of personal convenience and then manage to master highly subtle alternates of essentially the same basic areas of knowledge."

Plattsman said, "Not necessarily suspicious in itself. Many of our people would do likewise if they had a reservation to live in and the low population density to get away with it."

Klyten concurred amiably, "True enough, I suppose. Still, we must consider all possibilities, and in the light of other knowns, weigh it."

Parleau asked, "Then what is our best course here? Continue the investigation and try to get a vector downstream?" His use of the jargon of the Controllers and their pet discipline caused a faint smile to flow across Plattsman's face.

Plattsman provided the answer. "Yes, certainly. We do not have enough data even to identify the problem, much less work on alternates for solving it."

"Eykor, if we did actopt*, what kind of options do we have?"

"There's the graduated response system. For this, I should imagine Conops-two-twelve† would elaborate on the theme of trade-off and provide great flexibility. At the ultimate expression, where they were completely uncooperative and immovable, we could occupy the reservation complex, annex it, and remove the denizens to someplace like Sonora Region. Perhaps Low Baja, Mojave Inner. And we could segregate fertile populations."

"How far does that go?"

"As far as we have to, to get the idea across. I imagine that if two-twelve was implemented, it would come to that."

"It would," commented Klyten. "They have been known to take a drop in population in order to segregate obvious defectives. But there are serious objections to that, ethically. We are really dealing in unknowns, there. They would, of course, have become overtly hostile long before that, if we followed two-twelve to the letter."

Parleau said, "No worry about that. We haven't yet reached the point of two-twelve and as far as I'm concerned, it may not be used."

Eykor agreed, "Completely. More investigation is in order."

Plattsman offered, "You can have complete cooperation from Control."

Parleau now asked, "Will someone come for her? Or should we dispose the item . . . ?"

Klyten responded immediately. "No. Assume that someone will eventually come for her." He tried to ignore the knowing looks Eykor was displaying to all. "Somebody wants to know what has happened to their favorite, and eventually they will come looking. Even though they will get nothing out of her, now, she is still worth saving, because with loving care and patience, a new personality can be grafted onto what is left. The end result is very similar to severe retardation, but it is functional."

"Very good! We will dig further. Route everything through me and keep Denver off distribution for the time being. Stall."

Parleau stopped for a minute, thinking private thoughts and appre-

---

* Bureaucratic jargon: means "to decide upon an active course."
† More jargon: Conops means "Concept of Operations. An arbitrary definition of projected reality in which to act."

hensions. He said, "And, Eykor, send me up a copy of two-twelve. I'll want to be looking over it, just for information, you understand."

Eykor agreed. "And anything else, Chairman?"

"Yes. Find out, working with Control, who that girl is. Or as Klyten might have us put it, *was.*"

Parleau stood, indicating to the others that, at least for the time, a solution had been started. That was something; still, he had to admit that there were far too many unresolved factors here. He had left out the issue of the propriety of Eykor's actions deliberately, and instead let random remarks carry the meaning of his displeasure. He wanted to see how far Eykor would go, and in which direction.

The members of this meeting departed without ceremony. Parleau watched them go, trying to resettle his mind to the other matters at hand, the thousand things he needed to look at. That long-overdue Letter of Agreement with Appalachian Region, for instance. He had hoped this latest proposal would keep them quiet for a while, but apparently the letter hadn't yet come up through channels. He sighed. Just impossible. He ran his hand through the thinning stubble of his hair, a gesture of impatience left over from the old days, when he had been a junior executive in Sonora Region. He was just getting into position to resume his seat behind the desk when the door to the office opened. It was Plattsman.

Parleau looked up, curious. "Yes?"

"Chairman, I was on my way over to Eykor's with something new and interesting. It occurred to me that you might also like to see it. It's just a suspicion, but . . ."

Parleau looked closely at the younger man. He could not be absolutely certain, but the Controller seemed a little worried, concerned. "Yes, I would be. Continue."

Plattsman came to the edge of the desk, producing from a portfolio a sheaf of photoprints. One he set aside, and the others he carefully held, indicating that Parleau should look for himself. Parleau bent closer.

Indicating the single print, Plattsman said, "Observe this print: this is the file image of the girl, as she appears now." He paused to let the image set in the chairman's mind. "Now this one," he said, adding one more from the pile, "was taken before she was put in the box. Standard surveillance stuff through one-way glass. Can you recognize her?"

Parleau nodded. "Yes. There are more differences than I would have imagined."

"Correct. This apparently is an effect of her regression. I should imagine from these alone that whatever happened to her, she lost everything, even the little quirks of personality that really lend us all identity. But the point is that you, not a trained observer, could still recognize her. Now let me show you these." With that, Plattsman spread out the remaining prints over the dull surface of the desk. He stood back.

Parleau looked at the prints, then to Plattsman. Plattsman pointed to the prints. Parleau looked again.

And again. He saw typical point-surveillance crowd images, much enlarged to center and to expand upon single persons, the pictures somewhat fuzzy along the edges from enlargement. At first he failed to see what Plattsman was obviously leading him to. He saw pictures of a girl, mostly dressed after the styles of the day, more rarely in ler clothing, the overshirt, short hair, dark complexion, although not as swarthy as Plattsman, intent expression which could have meant anything . . . in some of the images, he could make out the shape of clean, strong limbs impressing their shape on the garments. He looked again. He had almost given up when something nagged at his mind's eye, caught it. And again. And then Parleau saw what had captured Plattsman's attention. The chairman made a choice, reached for two of the prints, removed them and set them aside.

He turned to the Controller and said, "Those two are not our girl, Item forty-six."

"No, Chairman, they are not. You and I have a greater depth of discrimination than the machine, no matter how sophisticated it gets. Especially where faces are concerned. Faces are more complex than retina patterns or fingerprints, but we are tuned to them by our own heritage of natural programming. You are correct. There are a couple more in question. We are analyzing the events."

"You didn't come back here to tell me your machine made a mistake."

Right, What we can tentatively project from the data we have— sensors, time of day matching, and the like—is that the second girl, whose face we can't make out so well, was involved in some way with the first one, Item forty-six. Same place, virtually same time, with the second passing the sensor after the first."

"Shadowing?"

"Seems so, although why is a mystery. Also, from the chemonitors, we know that both are ler, female, contemporary in age, more or less, and that the stress level of the second was always lower than the first, Moreover, Physiology informs me, again tentatively, that the kind of stress is different in the two. The first, Item forty-six, always has a fear-component. It may be with other emotional sets, or pure, but it is always one or another variety of fear."

"The second?"

"The second's emotions equate to nothing we can identify by analogy with humans. But whatever internal state it reveals in her, it is always seen pure, absolutely alone."

"I've heard something about the way you use those tracers. Something about mixed and pure sets . . . refresh my flagging memory."

"A pure chemtrace in a human almost invariably indicates a psychotic condition, usually a psychopath, I believe the ler system is similar enough for us to draw the same conclusion. I am presently having the idea verified."

"But think of it! Two of them! What is the connection?"

"We're going after it, Chairman. But it looks like nothing simple, that's a fact."

"Well, by all means pass that stuff on to Eykor. It will not make him feel any better, but he needs it all the same."

Plattsman nodded, gathered the prints, and left. And Parleau sat back in his chair and stared at a blank, random spot on the wall opposite him. He did not pick up his routine paperwork for a long time.

SIX

What, they ask, is the Game? Most simply put, it is a recursive sequence of changes in state, which are varied by the Players according to rules. It can be as simple as a sequence of digital data, or numbers; it can take more complex forms in arrays of repeating cells deployed over a two-dimensional surface; it can occur in three-dimensional matrices, yea and more. It can be played with blocks, on a checkerboard, inside frameworks; it can be played on paper, or with a computer, or, best of all, totally inside the mind. Now they ask, what good is it? And we say that through it we learn to understand consequences and the recursive patterns of Life and the Universe. And through it we learn how much we do not know.

—The Game Texts

MORLENDEN AWOKE, MAKING the transition from dead sleep to awareness with no apparent symptom of change. Beside him, he felt the warmth of Fellirian's body, and along his neck the contrast of the night-chilled air of the *yos* in winter. There was light showing on the translucent ground-rock panes of the narrow windows, a soft dawn peach light, but also a light with a hard steel-blue undertone to it, a sense of the clean air of winter, morning and clear sky. He moved slowly, cautiously and experimentally feeling the air, testing it, as it were, before committing himself to it. He stretched, hearing soft creaks and pops, slowly and gently disentangling himself from Fellirian without waking her. She moved, shifting position, but the rhythm of her breathing never varied.

Morlenden slid free of the comforter, listened: all he could hear were the sounds of the forest in the beginning of whiter. Outside, the animals were already up and about in their pens and barns, complaining, as usual, that no one had come out to see them. On the other side of the *yos*, beyond the children's sleeper, the creek gurgled and bubbled contentedly . . . there was no rain-sound, not even a hint of a rain-drip from the trees overhead.

Now he was beginning to feel the bite of the cold; he took a deep breath, shivered violently, stood and began rummaging along the wall shelf for a fresh winter overshirt, estimating the cold. Not so bad, today, he thought, selecting a pleth of medium weight, slipping it over his head, and then retrieving his long single braid out of the back of it.

Rubbing his eyes, Morlenden climbed down out of the sleeper into the hearthroom, listening carefully to see if anyone besides himself was awake yet. There was no sound, save Kaldherman's light snoring from the sleeper. He must have moved, he thought. He wanted to knock over a pan, or something, so someone would wake up. He restrained himself: he did not wish to awaken Sanjirmil . . . but as much as he hated bad news, he wanted to get on with it and speak with the Perwathwiy. But no, there was no one up besides himself, not even the youngest, their little addition, Stheflannai, who was always the first to hear anything. Morlenden shrugged, and began rekindling the cookfire in the hearth; after a time, when he could see that something was coming back to life from the ashes and coals of the night before, he continued his way to the entryway to collect his boots, noting as he pulled them on that they were stiff and cold.

Stepping out on the platform, he paused to test the air, reading the morning, as they said. The sky was indeed clear, an astonishing clear, deep blue; in the east, the sun was rising out of the remnants of a shredded fogbank, shining through the spidery network of bare trunks and branches, starting to put some life back in the cold. It would be crisp, all day. Very fresh, as he was fond of saying, a phrase Fellirian always twitted him about when the weather was behaving at its worst. He went down the stairs, feeling better already, taking the turn in the paths across the yard leading toward the outhouse, reflecting upon the things that needed doing, as he always did. First would be the recording and cross-referencing of all the material he had gathered on his last field trip; then properly entering it in the record ledgers, indexing, tagging. They would need to start a new batch of paper, too. Stock had been getting somewhat low, he recalled, and that was one of their Braid obligations—the paper concession. What a pain! Probably would need at least two weights unless Kal had done up a batch of Number Three ordinary while he had been out in the field. And, of course, meeting with the Perwathwiy, whatever it was she wanted. Perhaps that wouldn't take so long, and they could get on with matters at hand.

He remembered to watch for the root, which he had tripped over for several years on the way to the outhouse, climbing the ridgelet behind the *yos*. He was barely in time; he saw it, on the verge of tripping over it once more.

Damned thing! I've tripped over that one root since I was five years old, and, total recall or not, I still trip over it! And every time, I threaten to cut it off, root and branch, the whole damned tree. But I never have, he thought reflectively. *It's a sourwood, and they're rare . . . and what is it that Perwathwiy wants? Damn elders anyway! She could have sent Sanjir down anyway, by herself; probably wants us to start keeping all the records of membership of the lodges as well. They've been after us for years to do it for them, as if we weren't busy enough just keeping up with the Braids.* Now he'd have to repeat the whole tiresome argument all over again from the very beginnings. Yes, the whole argument. Perwathwiy wouldn't sit still for a simple negative. And even if it was only her own lodge, Dragonfly, that wouldn't change it: start keeping *their* records, and all of them would want the same thing. Service. Balls on a goose! Let them keep their own records! He reached the outhouse, a rustic little shanty carefully hidden in the midst of overage Lilac bushes. . . .

Walking slowly back to the *yos*, coming over the ridgeline, Morlenden could see now that a fine plume of smoke was rising from the largest ellipsoid, the one of the hearthroom. Nobody was visible, but the smoke was evidence enough someone was up and about now; he guessed one of the children had got up and was tending the fire, putting on a pot for an infusion of root-tea, a pan of meal to boil, a couple of the fine sausages from the locker that he and Kal had put up earlier this fall.

Higher up the hollow, toward the watershed, he saw the elder, Perwathwiy, approaching him on the path, negotiating the way in a measured, careful manner, but at the same time not betraying any hindrance arising from her age. He had not seen her the night before, or in years, nor ever well. But he knew Perwathwiy well enough; she never changed. He couldn't recall ever seeing her any different than she was now, a stern, agile ancient with iron-gray hair and the sourest disposition this side of the Green Sea, at the least. She was known never to smile, and little children repeated the doggerel that she had been born just as she was now.

The *starsrith* approached, stopped, nodded politely. Morlenden returned the gesture, acknowledging her respect for the holding. So this was the Perwathwiy, "First Spirit of the Eagle-cry," as the name went in

Fire aspect. Morlenden knew the data without having consciously to re-call it. A lifetime of recordkeeping, ordinary full-memory (or was it the elder's overbearing sense of presence? A Fire trait to be sure), but there had always been something more than simply aspect to the Perwathwiy. Sanjirmil also seemed to have that trait. Perwathwiy was and had been for years the elected chief hetman of Dragonfly Lodge, certainly the most powerful of the elder lodges. There were rumors, too, of secret in-fluences, but Morlenden had never given such theories much thought; Dragonfly was quite powerful enough in his mind without the addi-tional reinforcements of sinister conspiracies conducted in stealth. But they were secretive, and also the most conscious of themselves: power-ful, sure, almost arrogant people who veiled their comings and goings in mystery and arcane mannerisms.

The Perwathwiy was small in stature, thin, her skin wrinkled and darkened from decades of exposure and weathering. As befitted an elder, her hair was arrayed in two long braids that hung down neatly in front. The hair was absolutely gray, not a hint of color in it. Gray, not white. He could not recall ever hearing what color her hair had been. There were deep crow's-feet around the eyes, but the eyes themselves were bright, clear, birdlike, and of no particular color. Save perhaps rain-wet rock. Morlenden knew her age, and was surprised that the old woman was still in such good shape.

She spoke first, "I have been at my meditations. The letters are always clearer at dawn, as they say, but one must arise to see them, eh? You do not know the letters? The Godwrite of the ancient Hebrews, the cabal-ists: Hm. It is a defect you should remedy. I should have preferred to speak with all of you last night, Morlenden Deren, but savoring as I do the subtle essence of second-thoughts, I think the better of the morn-ing. I might have said more than I intended. Yes. I was in haste, tired. One makes mistakes then, and in this matter there must be no more."

"The matter is . . . ?"

"To be revealed to you all. It is no light thing, but something all the adults among you must decide. It will seem like nothing at first, but I fear it will become a burden beyond bearing before you are done with it, if you agree to it. There are unsuspected depths in it, and once com-mitted, your silence must be absolute. But for the now, let us return to the *yos* of the Derens and gather a good meal. I am hungry, and can lay to rest the horrid legend that elders subsist upon nothing more than a diet of boiled clabber, lentils, groats, and spurge."

Morlenden redundantly indicated the way she should go, and they went down the path to the *yos*. As they neared the stairwell on the downhill side of it, Kaldherman emerged, rubbing his eyes.

He looked at them sleepily and said, between yawns, "I see that you two are the early birds. The girls are, however, yet abed. Ayali is now snoring in a most girlish manner, but you don't have to say that I was the one who told you. They proved impossible to awaken. Peth and Sanjirmil have temporarily buried the knife and are busy at the hearth. I imagine we shall prove the poorer for it, but at the least we shall be well-fed."

From within the *yos*, they could hear a voice floating bodilessly, saying, "I'm coming, I'm coming, just this minute!"

Morlenden asked the Perwathwiy, "Where will you take yours?"

"You require an answer? On the stairs, here, of course. Finish yours and join me here, in the yard, without the children. Only Sanjirmil will witness for the *Zanklaron**."

Morlenden reflected a moment, then asked, "Then you didn't come all the way down here to remonstrate with me about the Derens keeping elder records of enlistments and transitions."

"Hardly. On that I should approach Fellirian anyway. She is *Klandorh*, is she not? But on that subject, yes, I know I have hectored you for years, and I will doubtless continue. All of you Derens are stubborn, whether born to the role or woven to it. It is a most important matter, ever on our minds, but rest assured that I would not walk leagues in the rain to hector you some more. This, in fact, may change the requirements . . . but never mind. Go and see that all are fed. I have far yet to go, and one among you may indeed have to go farther."

And not long afterward, with everyone up and about and fed (as Kaldherman had predicted, with a stock of the sausages he and Morlenden had put up), the four Deren adults joined the elder Perwathwiy and Sanjirmil, who were waiting silently by the creek a little below the *yos*, out of earshot, so they hoped, of the curious adolescents required to stay behind.

As the Derens approached, the Perwathwiy continued to keep her silence, appearing to listen to the creek, as if meditating, choosing her words. The sound of the rushing water filled the cool air. Then Perwathwiy turned and stared at them pointedly, finally speaking.

* "Players of the Life Game," the manner in which both Player Braids were referred collectively.

"Dragonfly Lodge, with the cooperation and encouragement of Braids Reven, Perklaren, and Terklaren, has empowered me to request of our community registrars the finding of a person. This is to be regarded as a most important *thaydh** for which Klanderen will be compensated. *Mielhaltalon†* to determine the whereabouts, fate thereof, or confirmation of transition of this person, restoring aforementioned person to us, specifically Dragonfly Lodge, if alive. I may say no more than this. We are on very dangerous ground here, and since we have no police as such, decision was made and implemented to come to you. You know everyone, you trace relationships, and in addition are known to be adventurous and resourceful."

At this last remark, a fine description to be sure, everyone save Cannialin raised their eyebrows. Yes, save Cannialin. She lived entirely in the present, never anticipating, and thus was almost never surprised, neither at the things people said, nor what they did. It was all one.

Perwathwiy paused. Then she said, "Upon your concurrence, you will receive from myself a packet containing a name on a slip of paper. What say you?"

They did not answer. The hint of danger, the secrecy, all put them off; but the amount offered for the service was even more astounding than all of these, for nothing any of them could imagine could cost hardly more than a *tal* of gold, and here were offered, in decimals, 2,744 of them. Of the Derens, Fellirian was the most shocked, for she was accustomed in part to the standing-wave inflation of the human world and its corresponding devaluation of currency. In 2550, with such an amount in pure gold, Fellirian could have bought outright title to every building in Seaboard South Region. Even having so much to offer was unimaginable.

But she was first to find her voice. "And why us? Or perhaps I should ask, why not you yourself or the parties you represent?"

The Perwathwiy answered forthrightly: "Eventually, someone will have to trace these things out. You have all the records and, moreover, you are all used to meeting people, going among them, ferreting out relationships. You are known everywhere, trusted, and hence will be able to make discreet inquiries. Most importantly, you are now and initially

* Literally, a quest.
† Fourteen to the third power grams of gold. Approximately 2.75 kilos. Considering that most transactions were valued in fourteenths of a *tal*, such a sum was beyond counting.

ignorant of certain aspects of this affair, aspects which may well turn out
to be matters of survival. Our survival. We think that eventually you
will have to go outside, which Fellirian does weekly, and it will arouse
no particular suspicion. And why not one of us? We do not wish it
known that it is we who are interested in this person. We suspect foul
play."

Kaldherman said, "Dangerous then, is it? To you, but not so to us?"

The Perwathwiy looked away, to the sun, now clearing the branches
of the trees and casting a golden morning light into the yard below the
yos. Then she looked back. "Of course there can be danger to you. Possible. But certain if, for example, I walk through the Institute gate into
the outside. But then, there is danger in all things; even an innocent trip
to the outhouse can be full of perils: witness the uncut root in the pathway of the Derens."

Fellirian said, "Come now. We ask specifics, and in return receive the
parables of a hermetic philosopher, which in this case we all know as
well as you. Especially the famous root, which is not the peril of the
Derens so much as a pet of Morlenden's. Speak straightly or not at all:
danger or not?"

She answered, "Yes." But her answer was framed in a quiet and suddenly respectful voice. Fellirian was a person of regard even in the circles in which the Perwathwiy moved, both for reasons widely known
and for some not so well-known, and she well knew them both. "Yes, it
is so. Very likely. The one whom you will seek was an adept, one of us.
You will have to be discreet . . . indeed, secretive would not be the
wrong wordings-way of it. And of what you uncover, you will speak of
it to none, save in whispers among yourselves. And you will make your
report to the Reven, who will correct you if you have gone astray too
far. And you must start soon, for yesterday is almost too late. We have
tarried overlong, and I admit the responsibility."

Morlenden sensed a sudden weakness, but he did not let her off, but
pursued her, his hard, angular face becoming harsh, his voice keen and
peremptory. "We are not armored knights as the humans of old, to set
out on fearsome horses to the ends of the Earth. We know this little
reservation to be a large place when one must cover it on foot, and look
under every sparkleberry bush. And the outside?"

"Say I that the ends of the Earth may well not be limit enough. If we
are too late, it could be to the ends of the universe. . . . But say it so now:
will you do this thing? The price alone should convince you of our seriousness. It is the largest sum in our history ever paid for anything."

Fellirian asked shrewdly, "Will we be here to collect it? And having collected it, can we survive it?"

The Perwathwiy looked at her directly. "To the first, yes. To the second . . . only you know the answer to that."

She said no more, and to emphasize the point, withdrew a little from the group, and turned away to contemplate the waters of the creek. Sanjirmil also turned away. The message of these gestures was not lost on them. As poor as the data was, now they had to decide based upon it. They moved back, instinctively, closer to the *yos*, and spoke in whispers among themselves.

At first, they defined basic positions each of them held, to begin the discussion. Cannialin was against it, calmly but openly apprehensive. Kaldherman was mocking and skeptical, openly hostile. They could refuse it, and he knew it. His vote was for sending the old woman back with a head ringing with vulgar instructions, most of which would be impossible for her to assume anyway. Fellirian was suspicious, but also carrying the reverse of the coin of suspicion, the obverse of curiosity. She sensed what difficulty it had been for one of the proud and distant Dragonfly Lodge to walk in humility halfway across the reservation, and start a sequence in motion which would certainly lead to the Derens being included in one of the arcane secrets of the Gameplayers. She did not know if she really wanted to know. But there was no denying the old woman's desperation. Nor the importance of the matter. One could not imagine what would bring them to offer so much—for the finding of a person. What had this person done? What had happened?

Morlenden, at first against it, shifted to favoring the proposal, and even argued for it. But he remained almost as hostile as Kaldherman, mentioning many reservations, so that they could all evaluate and decide cleanly. While they talked, he glanced in the direction of Sanjirmil and the Perwathwiy, trying to read something in their faces, derive some little hint of it. But the faces were blank and empty. Once Morlenden had seen pictures in a book, statues carved by humans on some empty and faraway isle. Easter Island. Their faces looked like that. Empty, fixed on the level horizon of the endless sea, terrifying in their impassivity. Rather, the Perwathwiy's. Sanjirmil showed the same, but it was only a veneer, and underneath there was too much. Panic, desperation, fear? He could not guess. She would not meet his eyes, would give no sign, not even of recognition.

He knew that they knew. The Derens could refuse this, even though the Revens were involved, because in the language of the proposal, the word had been *thaydh* . . . a quest, not a mission. A hope, not a command. But even if they had commanded, they had little enough power to enforce it without the support of the Derens, for outside pure physical punishments, the main penalty was disenfranchisement, and one could not disenfranchise the franchisers themselves. . . . He looked back to Sanjirmil. He saw only the haughty, arrogant face, with its sharp angles and thin lines. Strong and predatory. The dark olive of her skin, her deep eyes, framed in deep black hair, long for an adolescent, now considerably below ear level, with its bluish highlights in the sun. He turned his attention back to the group, where the tide had turned in favor of the proposal of Perwathwiy. They did not accept it gladly, or enthusiastically. But they agreed in the end to do it.

Fellirian left the group and walked to where the Perwathwiy was standing, apart, by the creek, formally, as befitted the head of Braid, speaking for the Braid. She said, "We will do it. *Rathaydhoya.* We will go questing." She had deliberately configured her assent as a verb of motion, transforming the noun *thaydh* thus so there would be no mistaking what she thought of it. Perwathwiy nodded, agreeing with Fellirian's selection of words. Verb of motion, indeed, it would be, before they were through with it.

There were no formalities, no speeches, and there was no particular change in the face of the elder. Indeed, if anything, there seemed to be regrets on the face of the Perwathwiy. Upon Sanjirmil's face, there appeared most briefly something too swift, a grimace, a shiver of revulsion, perhaps, but it was too swift to be sure. It was gone before any of them could read it. Morlenden, who had seen that face better and closer than any of them, saw nothing familiar in it, but something alien for a moment, then taken away.

Perwathwiy spoke. "Then, good, although it pains me. You will be paid in full upon completion. Delivery or report. Now I must return to Dragonfly and report to the Gathering, the Dark Council. Here is the packet. Good hunting."

She turned and began walking briskly toward the shed where she had left her meager parcel of worldly traveling goods. Sanjirmil broke and ran, suddenly, like a frightened animal, to the *yos* to gather her own things, racing up the stairs. Almost immediately she reappeared, ran breathlessly down the stairs, and took off after the Perwathwiy, who had already started out along the path upward. Catching up with the elder, the younger girl turned back only once, and fixed Morlenden with another odd expression on her face, an intent stare, blended with the odd scanning visage of her eyes, which the older Players seemed to lose. But whether it was an expression of sorrow, regret, or perhaps anger, he could not tell. They walked over the top of the path and behind the ridge, and then they were gone. . . .

Fellirian held the packet—containing what? She said thoughtfully, "You know, I got the idea they personally did not want us to take this. Especially that Sanjirmil."

Morlenden agreed. "I as well. All the more reason why we should take it," he added gruffly.

Fellirian said, "I think Mor and I should look at this and decide some things now, at least start the work. Do you all agree?"

Kaldherman said, "Fine with me." Cannialin nodded assent. And added mischievously, "Call me when Perwathwiy's danger shows up. I'll bring my chicken-splitting knife." This was not completely in jest, for she was fearsomely handy with the narrow blade with which she dispatched the Braid fowls. The two of them climbed the stairs and went into the *yos*.

Fellirian exhaled deeply, and opened the packet. Inside there was a slip of paper, bearing one word. A name; in childish, almost rude capital letters: *MAELLENKLETH*. That was all. Nothing else. No honorific, to determine sex; no Braid name to determine family line. Fellirian muttered to herself and handed the slip to Morlenden.

He took the slip from her and squinted at it owlishly for a moment, as if expecting it to talk to him. He looked at Fellirian, then said, "Female, insibling, Braid Perklaren. Right, *Klandorh?*" She nodded. "We'll check, of course. I want to review everything about this one, but I believe that's the one. Adolescent, as I recall."

Fellirian agreed. "About twenty. I know her, but not well. She spent some time at the Institute, same as I. Somewhere down in Research. I have no idea what she did. But we should look up all the facts, make sure. I want to see if we can . . . see what we're getting into."

"Agreed. Shall we start today?"

"You heard the Perwathwiy even as I. Are you up to it?"

"You bet. She was agitated enough. Let's see what we have here."

The recordium was in a third sleeper built into the *yos* of the Derens, being added on between the children's sleeper and the one of the parent generation. It was not on a higher level than the hearthroom, as were the real sleepers, but lower, in fact mostly underground, reached

by a short companionway delving downward. It was also the only place
in the *yos* where there was a door. A locked one. Inside, there were
standing shelves of small and large ledgers, roll-racks containing various
scrolls, charts of Braidholds, flowery family trees, all recorded more or
less alike, according to what was being recorded, but embellished by the
individualisms of three hundred years and more of Derens, each with
different talents and desires to apply to the problem. There Morlenden
rummaged absentmindedly among the shelves and racks, humming an
aimless song to himself, while Fellirian held the lantern. There was a
musty odor of old paper and dust in the air.

"Hm . . . dum de dum de dum . . . m-hm! Yes. Here it is! I think,"
he said, pulling out a large, rather new volume, opening it, and leafing
through the pages, stopping at last, following down the page with his
middle finger, still half talking to himself, which was a habit of his that
infuriated Fellirian. He ruminated. ". . . May, Maen . . . yes, Mael. Mael
Len-Kleth, 'Apple-skin scent,' aspect *Sanh*, Water. Born in the summer, yes, here it is, Human Calendar, 2530, July fifth. Let's see, the
generation-totem is . . . right, here it is, way over here." He looked
aside at Fellirian. "Who did this record? Everything's out of place, all
strewn over the page. Never mind, I can find it. Generation-totem is
Muth, Condor. They all use birds for totems, eh? That is the last one
shown."

Fellirian said, "Yes, that's the last one. And what's to prevent them
from using birds for generation-totems? We use the names of the trees
for the Derens and no one questions it."

"Nothing, nothing. But it just seems odd, that's all, especially since
they stick to it so rigidly. Does that go all the way back?"

"I believe it does. The Terklarens, too. There is a letter of agreement
in there somewhere, where they agree to use different sequences, so
they won't have the same totem in use at the same time in both Braids."

"What I mean is why the symbolism of birds? We use the symbolism
of trees because that's where we get paper from, from the plantation
back over the hill. But what the hell do birds have to do with Game-
playing?"

"Well, how should I know, Morlenden? We don't have any say in it.
They choose what they wish."

"I was just asking, was all. You said, 'last one.' What was that?"

"I remember now, there was something out of sorts with that generation. Like two female insiblings. The other one's name was Mev-
something. It will be in the Braidbook. MevLarnan, perhaps. I'm not

sure. I didn't make the entry. I heard Kadh'Elagi talking about it once, but I really wasn't listening to him."

Morenden replaced the ledger on its shelf, carefully. Then he turned to another shelf, bearing others, rummaged again for a time, but now not absentminded, instead rather more intent. He found the volume quickly. On the spine, the name *PERKLAREN* was labeled neatly. Per Klarh (Gh)en. Earth aspect, he assumed—thinking of the popular association of the name: the Gameplayers.

Of course, any root word in Singlespeech had at least four meanings, mostly according to aspect, and many had more than that. Something tugged at Morlenden's mind, the totem of birds that had bothered him a moment ago. The root *klarh-* was no different. "Play," as with some game, was only one of its meanings. Earth aspect. In Fire aspect, the root meant "Fly," whence the association of birds. . . . Nothing connected. Insects also flew, and bats as well, and, for the matter, airships and the like, and they could have used those as well. Odd people, those Players, all of them. Secretive and eccentric. He let the speculation go. There was certainly more to the Player Braids than wordplay on the meaning of names, which few took seriously anymore, even those professionally interested in it. And what did they do, anyway? They alone had no functional relationship with anybody else—just with each other, although they did some barter for various things. All they had to do was play their Game in public, several times a year, and contribute to an elaborate discipline called Gamethink, which no one outside their environment knew or cared anything about.

Morlenden supposed some took an interest in it, but he never had. It was interesting enough, the Game, if somewhat too abstract for Morlenden's tastes, and Fellirian's as well. Cannialin he knew to be totally ignorant of it; on the other hand, Kaldherman had been known to cast wagers upon Game outcomes. But since weaving into the Deren household, he had kept his vice at bay, or concealed. And he was sure that Kal knew no more about it than he did, however well he had followed it in the past. That was just it—even those who followed it knew little about it. They saw patterns developing, upon a screen, controlled by some, while others tried to disrupt the emerging pattern and its stable afterimages.

It was also generally known that at most times the Perklarens were favored to win, save in unusually bad years, but the Terklarens seemed to collect the most spectator support. They drew their strengths from the crowd, as it were, while the Perklarens played from some unknown interior élan. Humans from outside sometimes attended the major tourneys, but Morlenden suspected that they followed it no better than the ler spectators.

He returned to the ledger he held in his hands. In the Perklaren Braidbook, he quickly located the most recent generation page, the last entries. The position of *Nerh*, elder outsibling, of the adolescent generation, was filled by a Klervondaf, Tlanh. The *Thes* was also Tlanh, listed as one Taskellan. The insiblings were both Srith, so listed as Maellenkleth Srith and Mevlannen Srith. A large asterisk was scrawled alongside their names in the margins, along with note, apparently in Berlargir's hand, to the effect that special attention should be paid here, as if nothing intervened, these girls would be the last bearers of the Perklaren name.

Morlenden looked at the entry again, then turned and showed it to Fellirian. He said, "Now wait. This Maellenkleth we have to locate: She is a First-player insibling, but her Braid is terminating. And she also goes down to the Institute? How much of this does Vance know?"

"Hardly anything, I imagine. She only substituted for me once or twice. He would know that she worked in Research, when she came at all. She was never a regular. Remember, Vance is one of their pure management types: prefers not to get involved with the technicians, as they say. Now, Morlenden, don't look at me like I wasn't all here; that's the way they do things down there."

Morlenden's mind suddenly went off along another tangent, the manner of human management theory suddenly laid aside. "What was it she did in Research?"

"Its full name is Research and Development. Something to do with space flight, I think."

"What interest could she have in that? Unless it's all more of this traditional Player eccentricity. Or terminal generation lunacy. Now there is truly erratic behavior."

He placed the Perklaren ledger back on its shelf, abstracted and thoughtful. For a long time he remained in that position, one hand on the shelf, the other reflectively scratching his chin, his eyes focused off somewhere in empty space.

Finally he said, "I don't think we're going to find much of her inside. She's got to be outside somewhere. It makes it a lot harder: that's a big world out there if we have to do the looking. Do those folk have some sort of tracing system?"

"Well, yes, they do. A fearsome great thing, too. But it can be beaten, if one is willing to go to some trouble, and do without. I could beat it easily."

"You know it well. But how much could she know?"

"Why do you think outside?"

"If she was an everyday sort of a person, very much like you and I, she would remain inside, like the rest of us. What reason do we have? But she's missing, and for some time. Remember the Perwathwiy—'Yesterday may have been too late to start.' And they can't find her—which means they've looked inside, themselves, in the places where she might be expected to be. And they wasted a lot of time doing it, too, yes? But she's missing, and obviously important for such a price."

"Very well, I follow and agree so far. But someone still has to start inside."

"Oh, yes. If for nothing else than to find out something about her. I don't even know what she looks like."

"I can give you a Multispeech image of her, but it's not a good one, because as you know I am not that good at Multispeech, and also because I never saw her closely, or paid much attention to her. You have to get a good image. I suppose what I could transmit to you wouldn't distinguish her from Sanjirmil."

"Why Sanjirmil?"

"They don't really resemble one another, but there are enough basic similarities that in a vague-image it would confuse them in your mind."

"Hm. No, thank you, Fel, no Multispeech, if you please. If I have to put up with that, I want something good for the indignity. We'll want a good one, from someone who knew her well. Recently. We should start, I suppose, with the Perklarens, and then go on to her friends, lovers, and the like. . . . Fellir, I really do smell something unsavory here, and I want to talk to some of them first, to see if I can feel out what we are getting into. Danger, the Perwathwiy said, and hedged when it was referred to us."

"Indeed. I feel similarly. This could be a sticky business, one you and I really have no business in. And . . ."

"And?"

"I don't know why it should all be so mysterious. I mean, from Perwathwiy. And why not her own Braid, Morlenden?"

"Yes, go on."

"It's . . . deceptive. We haven't been told everything."

"We've been told damn near nothing."

"What's the word I'm looking for? It's something that draws attention, but it's not the real thing."

"Decoys," he said, after a pause. "So how do you call it?"

"I say start inside, soon, today, if you feel up to it. Tomorrow, for certain, no later. I'll await you and return to the Institute and see what I can find."

Morlenden groaned aloud. "Back on the road! What a beast you've become!"

"Don't complain so. I've got to go back, too, and but for the walking, you have the easy part."

"You always say that, Fel, but the mono never seems to go to the places I have to visit. At the least, you get to ride."

"You wouldn't like the environment. I've been outside, and I know. *I* don't like it."

"All right, then, settled." He paused for a moment, motioning to her to start leaving the recordium. As she turned and opened the door, he said, half to himself, "And if I get started, I can get there tonight."

Fellirian turned around. "Where?"

"The Perklarens, of course."

The two of them left the recordium and closed the door securely. Then, with the help of Kaldherman and Cannialin, they began to assemble the things Morlenden would need for a short-notice trip upcountry. Some food, extra clothing, an undershift for winter. His worn rucksack. Kaldherman accompanied him out into the yard, where the morning was wearing on into midday.

"You sure you don't need some help?"

"Not now, anyway. This shouldn't be anything but a brisk walk, some talk, some more walking. But never fear, Kal. Later on, this may require all of us."

"Strokes and blows, perhaps?"

"Eyes and ears and sharp wits, which you've as much of as fists and truncheons. Be ready! and I'll be back in a day or so."

"It will be as you say . . . keep your eyes open, yourself, Mor. It would appear there's something afoot. There may be those who don't care for your questions."

"I'll do that." He waved at Kaldherman and set off.

SEVEN

The Game requires for definition five parameters that describe any conceivable individually specified game. These are: Dimension, Tesselation, States, Surround, and Transition-processes. There are two more supplementary parameters, nondefining, which are necessary to operate a given game. These two are Symbolism and Analysis.

Dimension sets the dimensional matrix in which a Game occurs—within a linear sequence, upon a surface, throughout a solid, in and about an n-dimensional matrix. Tesselation defines how the dimension is subdivided. Linear sequences subdivide into bauds, which are the cellular units. Surfaces subdivide into familiar plane geometric figures, such as triangles, tetragons, pentagons, (never regular) and hexagons; but one should bear in mind that there can be many surfaces that are still two-dimensional. There are Euclidean surfaces, and also hyperbolic, parabolic, ellipsoidal, and spherical. Similar breakdowns also occur in volumes and n-dimensional matrices.

We have spoken of things that have either theoretical or practical limits. Now come parameters that have no limits of either kind. State refers to the number of conditions possible to a cell; it can be the most simple—as binary, on and off—or each cell can assume more states. In certain Games, different cells may even have differing states. Surround is that number of surrounding cells that influence and cause changes of state in a given reference cell. A Surround might be immediately adjacent to the reference cell; likewise, it also might be deployed some distance from the reference cell. It could also be asymmetrical, or changing.

Transition-processes are the rules that determine change. They may be as simple or as complex as one desires: simple summations with distributions of actions determined by decision-points on a probability curve of distributions. Or they might be instructional programs with hundreds of steps and subprocesses. Interweaving both summation of conditions in the surrounding cells with consideration of the position of these conditions.

Symbolism pertains to the system by which one orders one's perception of these parameters. Analysis is the study, comprehension, and prediction of whole-conditions within a Game. Symbolism and Analysis, considered in the abstract, define nothing; but without them, nothing can become, in our minds, which is the only theater of action.

—Elementary Definitions

MORLENDEN SET OUT walking in the ground-covering stride he used for distance walks to the more remote portions of the reservation, reviewing in his mind as he went the things he wanted to determine or, at the least, build a handle on. When he had a complex problem to consider, he could become quite oblivious to his surroundings, and this time was such an occasion; he disregarded, and then ignored, all of the things he usually looked for along his trips in the field: certain angles of view across fields, patterns of sunlight into groves of trees, hills and knolls of unique shape whose aspect had not been noticed before. This was a common diversion among the ler of all ages, and indeed, an elaborately structured art form was built upon this Aspectualism, as they sometimes referred to it. Morlenden was no dedicated savant of the art, nor of its near relative, the Practice of Subtle Bowering; nevertheless he was fond of dabbling in Aspectualism, and always recalled especially fine places he had discovered along his many travels within the reservation.

He became so absorbed in the problem at hand that he quite forgot in what direction he was heading, and the rate of his progression, and before he could notice it, he had progressed quite far northward and westward along the Main Central Longitudinal Path, and had, in fact, began to angle downward into the valley of the Hvar. Long, open vistas across open fields began to replace the hill-and-dale views that had been passing by him unnoticed. While this progress pleased him greatly, as it was cutting down the time he would have to be on the road, he recalled with a jerk, stopping suddenly in the middle of the path, that the Perwathwiy and Sanjirmil had also departed northward along the same pathway, and had only about two hours' start on him. The Perwathwiy was a hardy old goat, he thought, but not all that fast on the road. And he did not wish to meet either of them again today, especially Sanjirmil. True, many years had passed, and little contact had occurred between them, yet Morlenden also remembered vividly. And just as vividly remembered the Sanjirmil of the last twenty-four hours, with her dour, pinched, unreadable expression, and her brooding, withdrawn silences . . . not the best of circumstances in which to sit together in a sunny glade along the path and reminisce about the sweaty pleasures of the past, the soaring flights of emotion they had known for the short time allotted to them, the dreams and fantasies they had whiled away the days with. He had always wanted to see her again; but today did not seem appropriate. There had fallen an opaque screen between them, and through it he could glimpse her shadow only dimly. She had seemed to have the same problem seeing him. . . .

Morlenden looked ahead, and across the lower country immediately to the west, falling away to the line of trees that hid the watercourse of the Hvar. Today, now, everything seemed empty and peaceful, devoid of throngs, bands, and solitaries. The only sign of life he could see was some faint smoke far to the west, a bluish, smudgy haze, as if someone had a late smokehouse going. He reflected, looking about for cues from the landscape. *Yes,* he thought, orienting himself effortlessly out of the detailed mnemonic landscape built upon total recall of thousands of trips. *This would be the country of Velsozlun, where conjoined the Hvar and the Garvey. Just ahead. And the smoke would be most likely of the forge of Braid Sidhen, the ironworkers, or the Kvemen, the charcoaleers. Fine people, salt of the Earth. Ought to drop in on the way back, just to say hello.*

But not today. He had a long way to go yet. Morlenden started off, resuming his long stride, picking up speed slowly, feeling the right pace set in, at last swiftly moving down toward the joining of the rivers.

For a time some new-growth trees and the turnings of the pathway obscured his distant view, but it was no matter; the air was fine and crisp, the sky was clear, and the afternoon slants of sunlight across the valley of the Hvar lent a subtle, old-gold patina across the aspects of bare trunks and branches, drifts of fallen leaves, quick flashes of hints of openness, and a deepening of tone in the shadows and tree-crowded forest, as if the whole were under water of the most crystalline clarity. He began to feel expansive and energetic, and confidently strode forward.

Ahead, the path lowered, curved, straightened for its plunge across the Terbruz, the double bridges across the Hvar and the Garvey, just above their confluence. Beyond, the pathway turned to the left, changing its direction more to the west. Morlenden stopped abruptly, peering ahead, all enjoyment suddenly set aside. On the point between the rivers a figure was standing, as if in contemplation, the recognition patterns of its stance and clothing broken up by a spattering of shadows from the liriodendrons across the Hvar, and the leaves on the ground, dropped by the winds. The person was not turned so that he or she could see him. Morlenden walked very slowly, as silently as he could, letting his drift take him toward cover as he moved closer to the Terbruz. Time began to slow, and his sense of progress with it. Sun, so still and fixed, began to crawl across the sky. The shadows lengthened. Morlenden crept as close as he dared. The still figure remained as if carved from an old deodar stump.

The afternoon wore on fractionally. Without anticipation, the person ahead suddenly moved, as if unfreezing, flexed itself, and looked about. Perwathwiy! The old woman looked about, as if reassuring herself that she had not been observed. What had she been doing? Meditating? Morlenden did not know. She set out confidently, if somewhat slowly and carefully, not across the bridges, but northward along a barely visible pathlet running between the rivers. Morlenden remained where he was, sure that she had not seen him, for her glance had been cursory, a quick scan across the directions, nothing more. He felt embarrassed, hiding from an old woman. He watched the Perwathwiy fading into the distant jumble of undergrowth and tangled hillside, finally disappearing. He straightened. Not once had she looked back. He began moving forward, watching cautiously, listening. No. She was gone, out of sight. He resumed his walk, his gestalt perceptions shouting a fact at him. Sanjirmil had not been with the old woman.

Something about this nagged at his mind. He dismissed it. Why should she remain with the Perwathwiy? Her business was done—she had witnessed for the active Players, Perklaren and Terklaren alike, although Morlenden felt uncomfortable with that as well. Why should a rival witness for another Braid? For the moment, he dismissed this as another odd quirk of the eccentric Player Braids, and continued along his way into the golden light of the late afternoon west, passing under the great, tall boles of the riverside liriodendrons. True, this dismissal, he realized, was but provisional, but so was so much else in life, and he had miles yet to walk. He emerged into the open and increased his pace.

Perhaps, he thought, with a sly little chuckle, *Sanjir has found someone else who will whisper "Ajimi" softly in her caramel-colored ear.*

The sun drifted, settled, waddled along the horizon bristling with tree branches, reddened in the industrial haze out of the far west, and faded as one looked at it. Morlenden did not stop for supper, preferring to continue and go as far as he could. Twilight lingered, deepened. Night came and the stars came out. All vestiges of afterglow vanished from the west and north. It grew colder. The air, mostly calm all day, grew utterly still. Morlenden's hearing expanded in the crystalline darkness, reaching out into the passing country, evolving from fields and alternating forests to a country even more sparsely habited and partially returned to the wild. He thought he could glimpse, under the stars and the sky-glow along the horizon, the bulking of the ridgeline that terminated in the fabled Mountain of Madness, Grozgor. Morlenden shivered, not entirely from the cold, for he was walking along at a hard, driving pace, now. No, not the cold. They didn't venture along the slopes of Grozgor, none of them. There were tales, superstitions, legends. The whole reservation was riddled with ancient ghost stories learned from the last of the humans who had lived in the area, and passed on unforgotten and embellished for several hundred years. Of course he did not believe all of them. But neither did he care to cross Grozgor at night. It was reputed to be the haunt of Players taken by strange and fey moods—they came at night to restore their vision, whatever one could make of that.

The *yos* of the Braid Perklaren was located in the northwest of the reservation, close under the southern slope of Grozgor. Across the mountain, the ridgeline, lay the holding of the Terklarens. Not far away, north and east somewhere, was Dragonfly Lodge. More to the east was the holding of the Reven, the ruling Braid. Morlenden had never been to any of them before. This was called the lake country, although the arm of the lake that had once extended eastward from the Yadh to the west had long since silted up and been allowed to lower and dry out, forming a rich, though narrow plain, interrupted by ponds. Here the country was given over to pine cover, much of it of a variety of pine that formed, at maturity, dense, umbrellalike canopies high up at the top of the trunks. This cover lent the land a hushed, covered quality, deep in shade, the dense canopy overhead seldom permitting much light to enter. At night, the high fronds shut out all light, making a dense and impenetrable darkness in which Morlenden found some difficulty navigating.

Here, as in the rest of the reservation, they did not form towns, for at the heart of the ler way of life lay the canons of agricultural self-sufficiency. No matter what their role in the extended, low-density city that encompassed the entire society, each Braid and elder commune was expected to be in part a farmer, The solitaries became hunters and gatherers. Nevertheless, in certain areas, increases of density did occur. The lake country was one such area, as was Morlenden's own neighborhood, the Flint Mountain area.

Under the trees, then, he could catch an occasional flash of light, broken up by the habit of the locals of situating their dwellings in the middle of the densest groves of the oldest pines. But no more than those narrow, fleeting glimpses. Earlier, he had stopped and inquired of the location of the Perklarens, but now, in the dark, with landmarks gone, he wasn't so sure. And the still air was getting noticeably colder; there would be frost-heaves in the ground tomorrow. He passed a junction of the innumerable subtle pathways under the trees, an odd angle that seemed familiar, turned in the recommended direction. After an interminable stumbling walk, at last he arrived in the dooryard of someone's *yos;* whose, it would remain to be seen.

Morlenden stared ahead in the gloom under the trees; here the meshed umbrellalike canopy overhead was so dense he could see virtually nothing, save the rounded shapes of the *yos* directly ahead. According to his directions, the Perklarens had cultivated a privet-ligustrum as their ornamental yard-tree. If he could find that . . . yes, there was the pot. He moved closer, trying to make out the shape of it, looking for clues. And yes, sure enough, that was what it was, an ancient privet-ligustrum so large it could not be taken in at a glance, its semievergreen canopy spreading overhead and blending invisibly with the dark canopy. He turned toward the *yos* somewhat more confidently. Dark or not, he would go up and bang on the door-gong. Dense under here, he thought. Morlenden was as fond of his shade as the next during the hot, bright days of summer, but he also liked to have a window open on the sky; he sensed something oppressive and closed in, dark and brooding, here under the pines. He also reflected that the wind would sound much differently here. And in the *yos?* There were lights in the back, not so many in the front. Missing was that sense of suppertime business, coming and going, the sounds of voices; the *yos* seemed enveloped in an air of half-abandonment, despite the lights. In fact, it seemed almost as if no one were at home.

Morlenden climbed the stairs to the entryway and pulled upon the thong of the guest-bell, this one being a weighty and impressive terracotta affair suspended from a bracket that could have held up the whole *yos.* The bell rang with a deep, hollow, plangent reverberation that seemed to spread and die away, a soft, yet penetrating pulse of sound. The after-vibrations in the bell could not be heard, but they could be felt, and they continued, long after the original sound had faded away. He was about to ring it again, receiving no answer to the first, when at last a face appeared at the door-flap. It was a plain, very pale, rather awkwardly square face, framed in tousled, curly brown hair. The face peeped out farther. It was a girl, he thought.

"Yes?" she asked.

"Is this the *yos* of *Klanh* Perklaren?"

"Yes, it is," she admitted blandly. No more information was offered. The girl seemed to be slightly irritated with him for being there. In a similar fashion, Morlenden likewise began to feel a slight irritation beginning to rise in himself. Here, of all places, what should he meet but the most bland and literal-minded of evasiveness. This infuriating oblique girl could keep him standing outside in the night forever while he asked question after question.

He observed, "It is chilly tonight, is it not?"

"Oh, indeed it is."

"The traveler looks upon the house of a friend after a long journey as his own, and dreams of food, beds, and talk among those who would share experiences."

The girl nodded, agreeing most pleasantly.

"So now. Were you a Perklaren, I would ask to be admitted within."

At this, the girl seemed to lose the air of bland bemusement, and brightened a little. It was, Morlenden thought, an excellent transformation, for once animated, the girl's plain face became extraordinarily pretty. She exclaimed. "Me? A Perklaren? Oh, no. Not by a long way and a half. Did you think I was Mael? No? She doesn't live here anymore, I mean, she doesn't stay around here much. . . ." She stopped, as if she had perhaps said more than she had intended to. She continued, "But do come in. I think it would be all right." With that last remark, she vanished back into the *yos*, behind the door-flap.

Morlenden could hear her moving back into the other parts of the *yos*, calling to someone she named "Kler." Yes. This was the right place. That would be the *Nerh*, Klervondaf Tlanh Perklaren.

Morlenden pushed the door-flap aside and entered, pausing in the entryway to remove his boots. By the time he had finished taking off his outer walking clothes and entered the hearthroom proper, another person was climbing out of the children's compartment to meet him. Out of the children's compartment, that is, if they followed the same notions of left and right as did the Derens. The girl was peering around the edge of the compartment entryway, looking at him with undisguised curiosity.

Morlenden imagined the newcomer to be Klervondaf, the Perklaren elder outsibling; Klervondaf was a late adolescent of slender build, rather dark complexion, and a long, mobile face that suggested considerable flexibility of expression. Morlenden knew him to be approximately twenty-five or so, but in some ways he looked much older. He carried himself with a weary diffidence that suggested many things. This one, he thought, knows much, or has had to do much, a long way beyond what he expected. Klervondaf turned to face Morlenden, rearranging the front of his overshirt, looking at the visitor out of muddy brown eyes, a rarity among the ler.

He said, in a measured, careful manner, "I am Klervondaf Tlanh Perklaren, *Nerh*, and, for the moment, within the *yos*, responsible for Braid affairs. What was the matter you wished to discuss? If you are looking for the public house, you missed the turn back down on the main pathway; it is back down by the old dock."

Morlenden answered, "I am Morlenden Deren, Kadh and *Toorh*."

"Aha! Of the Derens! I know of your Braid, sir. Have you come," Klervondaf asked saturninely, "with weaving offers for what remains of us?" In itself, the question was a curious one, certainly made not less so by the trace of sarcasm underlying the boy's voice.

Morlenden answered diplomatically, "No, it is hardly that. At any rate, we are not weaving-brokers, but rather registrars. I am aware, though, in general, of the plight of your in-siblings, and have been on the lookout for suitable young men who are to be available. But for the moment, let us disregard that problem, for it is not for that I have come. I have something more immediate: Maellenkleth and Mevlannen."

"Mael and Mev? Oh?" His guard, invisible before, immediately became apparent. The boy added, "And what is it that a registrar would wish to know?"

Morlenden decided to proceed honestly. "In a word, everything you can offer me that would assist me in locating them, in particular Maellenkleth. She is now believed to be missing, and we Derens have been given a commission to find her. I do not think it possible unless I have some idea of her life."

For some reason, this seemed to allay Klervondaf's suspicions, and he relaxed somewhat. But not completely. "That will take some time, yes, some time. Maellenkleth . . ." He stopped abruptly and made a nervous little motion. "You must excuse my impoliteness. You must be tired, if you walked all the way up here, and hungry as well. Please sit, make this dwelling your own, to enjoy at your pleasure. I will fix some things."

The boy turned from Morlenden and said, over his shoulder, "Plindes, I hate to ask, but can you leave for a little while? I need someone to go down to the Rhalens and tell them to send Tas home."

A voice, belonging to the girl, answered from deeper within the *yos*. "Oh, I suppose so." After a time, the pale-faced girl Morlenden had seen earlier behind the door-flap reappeared, dressed now in an outer over-shirt as well. What he could sense of the concealed body beneath the heavy winter garment would have been pale-skinned and slender, some-what like Peth, but older and a little more rounded, fractionally closer to adulthood. Her hair was indeed a muddy, rich brown, still tousled, full of undisciplined curls. She hurried by, unspeaking, pausing only briefly by Klervondaf to brush his hand with hers. He returned the gesture shyly, and the girl departed the *yos*, pulling up the hood of her overshirt as she slipped through the inner curtain of the entryway. For another few moments, Morlenden could hear her rummaging about in the dark, finding her cloak and boots, but finally he heard her clatter down the stairs, and there was silence.

The boy waited, listening. Then he walked quietly to the entryway inner flap, looked sidelong through it, and then also outside, peering carefully through the outer flap. He returned momentarily and ex-plained, "Plindestier and I are close enough, as doubtless you may see for yourself. But she is a most curious one and in this *yos* we do not speak overly loud of the doings of the Perklaren insiblings. I would not put it past her to eavesdrop."

Morlenden asked, to pass some small talk and set the boy more at ease, "Have you been lovers long?"

"Off and on," he said, noncommittally, and busied himself with the task of adding some more wood to the hearth fire. After a bit, he added, almost disarmingly and candidly, "Plindestier is excessively shy and I ef-fectively have no Braid. We console one another." He checked the teapot to ensure there was enough water within to prepare an infusion, then turned back to Morlenden, who was sitting on a hassock, idly looking about the hearthroom.

Hearthrooms were, as a rule, laid out in much the same fashion no matter whose *yos*. But as Morlenden looked about this one, he could not escape the impression that there was something about this one that set it off. For instance, the decorations around the walls. It was considered traditional to clothe the bare walls of the hearthroom with antique geo-metric patterns, or at the least deviation from this, simple woven tapes-tries illustrating stereotyped religious images. Where this one differed was in two striking aspects. The first was that the walls displayed several excellent photographs, startlingly clear and beautifully mounted, of objects in the night sky. Morlenden knew that they were images of stars or starlike objects, but he recognized none of them; they were obviously greatly magnified. One appeared to depict a violent explosion somewhere in deep space, the tangled streamers of its detonation writhing outward into space, glowing with blues and violets. Others seemed to be large and small groups of stars, some of the assemblies globular in shape, others of loose, random associations, with tantalizing suggestions of an order that was, or might be yet to come.

The other difference was more subtle, for after all these were indeed woven wall-hangings. But unlike all others he had seen, these seemed to be representations of Game patterns. They were, one and all, strikingly suggestive, but Morlenden couldn't quite see through the symbolism into exactly what it was they suggested. Some were of a single color; others showed wild variation of hue and texture.

Klervondaf waited politely for Morlenden to finish looking. Finally, sensing an appropriate moment, he asked, "You wished to become knowledgeable about Maellenkleth and Mevlannen?"

"Yes, I did. Excuse my inattention. I was admiring the fine pictures."

"The photographs are the work of Mevlannen; she is a photographer of some note as well as other things. On the other hand, the Game tapestries are Maellenkleth's."

"It is in both cases admirable work, I agree. But with the girls, where is it that we begin?"

"Best at the beginning, less some minor things you would not wish to burden yourself with. So, then. As you know as well as I, at the *vrento-ordesh**, both insiblings turned out to be female. Had conditions been as in the expected norm, of course the insiblings would have commenced instruction in earnest at fifteen and would by now be deep in the Game, playing at least in the novice class in exhibitions and tournaments. But for many reasons, it was decided not to go this way with Mael and Mev."

"Curious, that. I am no enthusiast, I confess, but I have seen Games in which both centers were female. They could have played . . ."

"True, but only until weaving-time. And consider," he added with a minatory gesture of the hand, waving it didactically, "it surely would have done no one any good to become tournament level Players and then find themselves in, say, Braid Susen."

* Literally, "Season of Insibling-birth." A time of great stress.

"I understand that a hog-farmer would probably have little use for the esoterica of Game enigmas."

"Exactly. And concurrently, decision was made to allow future Games to be conducted under the aegis of Klanh Terklaren, which will be re-named simply Klaren, as soon as Taskellan can be woven. After that, the Game is intended to come to an end, which will necessitate the reori-entation of the Terklaren-Klarens. But that will be later; there are some final actions to be taken before termination of the program."

"Ended? Just like that?"

"The utility of it has, I understand, come to an end; perhaps more properly, I should say, will come to an end." Klervondaf stopped mo-mentarily. "Understand, I am not the originator of these plans, nor was I included in any discussion of them. I relate to you such as I have been told."

Morlenden mused, "Since this will involve considerable manipula-tions of Braid-lines and -roles, I would imagine at that the Revens are deeply involved and fully knowledgeable."

After some hesitation, Klervondaf concurred. "Yes, of course. So in our case, the Perklarens, the parents picked up certain terminal com-mitments, and began spending most of their time with the Past Masters, developing the Game further. So they seldom sojourn here, but are busy with affairs. As you can imagine, as the carriers of the Perklaren tradi-tions, they possess considerable lore, most of it carried solely in the minds of insiblings, to be passed on verbally and secretly in the initia-tion and weaving ceremonies. Much of this must be recorded, tran-scribed, analyzed, recorded for posterity."

"Strategy and tactics . . ."

"That which enabled us to keep the Terklarens in their place during most of the history of the Game."

"They are zealous and dedicated indeed, to so cleave to a dying Game and leave the four of you children to fend for yourselves."

"Zeal and dedication? Indeed. So are we all." He added the last vig-orously, as if now expressing his own feelings. "And speaking for myself and Mael, I should wish it no other way, given what has been. Consid-ering circumstances and plans, the configuration of eventing, what we have done has been generally for the best. Of course, they spent much more time with us all when we were younger; we were not abandoned, nor are we *hifzer* waifs, by any means. For the past several years, I have been in charge of Braid affairs outside-Game, and nominally over the two girls. And I have raised Taskellan."

"You said, 'nominally.' "

"Yes . . . Mevlannen is perhaps the easiest to explain. And if you require, easiest to find. Now let me explain: the Game is a game, true enough, but it is rather intricate and multiplex, and capable of truly bottomless subtleties. Therefore each who enters it comes to see different things in it. Some see music; others, language. Still others, life processes; and others, chemistry and the like. Mevlannen saw science and technology. And gradually, she drifted that way, into the life of a researcher, a technician, an engineer. We ler do not develop those modes save in certain elder lodges, so for fulfillment she would have had a long wait, and Mevlannen is not, may I say, particularly patient of nature. She made contacts through the Institute, entered, became knowledgeable in astrophysics and optics; other things, too. Two years ago she joined the human Trojan Project in those capacities, and so went to space. We hear from her still, occasionally, but ever more rarely. I do not know her intentions for weaving, which would occur in ten years, more or less; she has lived in the human world for some time and has naturally acquired some of their values."

"What is the Trojan Project?"

"As I understand it, the humans are building a large telescope system, multiband, in the trailing Trojan position, equidistant from Earth and the moon. They are not finished with it yet. It is, just the telescope proper, so large that it had to be sent up piecemeal and assembled in place. Mev was in charge of the optical systems . . . in fact she developed the mirror material that would make such a large structure possible in the first place."

Morlenden expressed astonishment. "Mevlannen? An astronaut? Working in space?" He was truly incredulous.

"Indeed just so. Rest assured, we are not less astounded. She spends little enough time on the ground anymore . . . her base is on the West Coast somewhere, close by the launch site and the fabricating works, and of course she spends most of her time there now."

"And what about Maellenkleth? Did she go also to the humans to learn the mongering of strange metals?"

"Into space? No, unless you could call where she went a kind of inner space, a truly unexplored region. Here I am facetious, for which I apologize. Mael, as a fact, despite all, stayed with the Game. She showed an unusual affinity for it at an early age, and was, well, something of a prodigy. We tried to discourage her, but of course she was never expressly forbidden, for we hated to lose such talent, you understand. We had hoped that when she was old enough to understand what had happened to us, she would abandon it on her own resolve as a lost cause. This was not the case. Maellenkleth is intensely competitive; she does not, in her own words, acknowledge the existence of odds. Her idea, which became over the years something of an obsession, was to become so good at the Game on her own that the Revens would be forced to weave her in-Game to retain the lore."

Morlenden interrupted Klervondaf here, saying, "Weave in-Game, you say? But since you and the Terklarens are out of phase in time, that could only mean that an outsider would have had to be brought into it. Or am I astray?"

"No. Distasteful as is this to speak of, that is exactly how matters were going. In the Game, she was considerably ahead of her plan, and had already won back much influence in support of her larger plan. But the choice she made for outsider. Many spoke openly against her, saying they'd rather have a human than whom she wanted to bring."

Morlenden laughed aloud. "Now there's a one, for sure. Sounds just like my own *Toorh*, Fellirian. Really, I intend no offense; but I would have supposed that if he was acceptable to her, it wouldn't matter what his Braid."

Klervondaf spoke back proudly. "Had he but a Braid! But alas, he did not, but was a half-wild *hifzer* from the Eastwoods, scion of a defunct Braid line that went astray. Oh, it was a scandal, never fear. The shame of it stung us all to the core. They were deeply emotionally involved as well. Just imagine—Dirklarens, whose *shartoorh* was a *hifzer*."

Morlenden said mildly, "Well, I understand the objection, but of course we all were just such in the beginnings. All the original Braids had members whom now would be called *hifzer*."

Klervondaf obviously found the subject distasteful, and Morlenden's bland acceptance of it even more so. But he held whatever comments were in his mind, and proceeded with his story. "It was considered hopeless, and most wrote Mael off as simply gone mad. But things began to change; there were rumors, whisperings, shocked expressions. And I myself, as far from the Game as I am, have heard that there were some in the Council of the Past Masters who were now supporting her. And that the Reven, too . . ."

"Pellandrey Reven, himself?"

"Indeed. He implied he was like the rest, but took no action to stop it. And he had never approved it, either, but when the Terklarens formally petitioned him, neither would he forbid it, either. The Perwathwiy examined Mael for truth and testified that Mael had not revealed the Inner Game to the *hifzer*."

Morlenden thought a moment, then said, "It would seem that she was slowly succeeding, against the odds, just as she felt she could. It would seem, then, to ignore odds would be the good course."

"You can ignore odds only if you are supremely good at what you do. I would not dream of doing such a thing. Even if I could stifle my repugnance at touching a *hifzer*."

"So, then, she was successful?"

"Who can measure success? But she had now made the possibility of Third-players real. And I do know that Maellenkleth was immeasurably better in the Game than Sanjirmil of the Terklarens, our rivals. But Sanjir is older—she and her *Toorh* are within a year of weaving, something very close to that. I have heard some of the old Past Masters say that as a mature Player, Mael would have been the best in the history of the Game. Without question. Not even close to anyone of the Greats. I am not deep in the Game myself—no outsibling can be. But I have heard Mael explain aspects of it with insights I have not heard elsewhere, and of the living Greats, even the Perwathwiy deigned to ask her opinion from time to time."

"Tell me more about this *hifzer*. Who is he?"

"He styles himself Krisshantem. He is a bit younger than Mael, but well within the tolerances. And recently, she never stayed here at home, but away with him. They were together all the time. They had built themselves a place to live together and work. A treehouse, not a *yos*. It is far east of here, in the forest. And besides the practical aspects of such a venture, them using one another to mutual advantage, they were deeplovers, and since meeting him, Mael did become somewhat more restrained. He is reputed to be something of a mystic; fey, strange, full of all sorts of knowledge of wild things."

"Did Maellenkleth sojourn here much before Krisshantem?"

Klervondaf paused before answering. He looked into the hearth fire for a long, reflective moment, and then back to Morlenden. "Maellenkleth was beautiful of face, graceful and desirable of body, passionate of disposition. She was one not greatly given over to excessive self-restraint. She was of the Water aspect, *Sanh:* she had in her life many lovers, many friends, many in-betweens . . . here, she was in and out, more or less, according to the season. But until she moved in with Krisshantem, she remained here."

"She was gone a lot."

"Yes, that. Gone. Rather more often than not, even before Kris-shantem, and not always in the expected places, either. I know, because I had to go look for her. Then she'd show up. No one seemed to mind. Where was she? She would say, with so-and-so, or with the Past Masters. And other times she said nothing."

Klervondaf stopped now, as if he had said what must be said. He would offer no more for the time. Morlenden now reflected upon what he had heard; there was, concealed within the easy answers, almost glibly given, almost a kind of distraction from something else. There was something deeper here. This Klervondaf spoke, but he knew more, and suspected even more yet. But the answers helped to conceal, mislead, trap. Nevertheless there was truth in it, Morlenden could see. It hung together well enough, in loose fashion. He felt like the fox watching the bird with the obvious broken wing.

But it could have been just like that; the unweavable insiblings because of the same-sex rule, and then one of the girls turns out to be a prodigy for exactly the Game. One misfortune after another—it would disorient anyone. In a society that made the family more than a genetic unit, strengthened by the resonant occupation and interrelatiorial ties to the rest, this ending of the Braid line would be catastrophic, especially to the younger members, within any Braid. But here, in the intense competitive atmosphere between the Player Braids, and in the elitism of their social status, it would have been more. Yet they acted strangely—rationally in one way, inexplicably in the other. They just give up and get irritated with the errant insibling who wants to keep going. The parents give up and apparently move out early, turning everything over to, of all people, the outsibling. Morlenden never credited himself with the penetrating powers of a *mnathman*, but he could see that here were many contradictions, many mysteries; whole areas opened up to question. But he was equally sure that they would not be answered here.

He could not let the whole of the idea go: considering that one would expect them all to be close and submissive. But not so—to the contrary. One even goes out and competes with the humans in their own pet project, and gets herself made a minor chief of it. And the other insibling, now missing, takes on the whole of ler society and its ostensible rulers, and her own *Klanh* chiefs, and with a *hifzer*, starts building a new Braid from scratch, counting on her verve and aggressiveness to carry it over. And seemed to be getting away with it. And the outsiblings cope. The enemies Maellenkleth must have made! Think of it—Sanjirmil's Braid petitioned! And we're denied, what's the more.

His musings were interrupted by a noise in the entryway; Morlenden suspected that it would be the *Thes*, Taskellan. And it was; in a moment, a barely adolescent lad brushed aside the door curtain and entered. This one was small, full of swift, sharp movements, possessed of a deft, foxy face. Wary as a young squirrel; not gone bad yet, but definitely one to watch, Morlenden thought. So were they all, these Perklarens.

The younger boy glanced sidelong at Morlenden, a piercing, knife-stroke look, then said to his elder outsibling, "Kler, Plin said that you wanted me to come home. What do you want?"

Klervondaf looked up from his silence by the hearth, where he had been fiddling with the meal, and answered, "I wanted you home that you could get to bed and get an early start tomorrow morning. You will need to take this Ser Morlenden Deren down to the place where Kris and Mael built the treehouse."

Morlenden interjected, "Why can't we go tonight?"

Klervondaf answered, as if explaining to a child younger than Taskellan, "For one, it's a long walk, and so I hear, hard to find in the best daylight. But Tas knows the area—not so well he could find it in the dark, mind—and he can take you there. I hardly think you have such haste you would be willing to wander all over the old forest through most of a winter night."

Taskellan added, "Is that all? I could do it blind. We were just getting started down there. Let me go back!"

"Will you promise to be home early?"

"No later than the sun, Kler," said the boy, smirking.

Klervondaf ignored the provocation. "Oh, go ahead, go ahead. But be here and ready to go."

"Right!" he cried, and was halfway through the curtain.

"Hey!" Klervondaf called after him.

Taskellan stopped. A small, nagging voice said around the curtain, "Yes?"

"Where did Plindestier go?"

"She went home. Said she'd be along tomorrow."

"Very well, go!"

The younger boy clattered about the entryway and was gone. For a time they could hear his footfalls in the clear, cold air outside. Then it was silent. Klervondaf retrieved the pot from the fire, poured off a mug of tea, and handed it to Morlenden. He shook his head slowly.

"It's been a job, I will tell you that; raising Tas has been a piece of work for an elder outsibling . . . mostly it has been just myself and Plindestier, although Maellenkleth helped. And it was easier when she was around; she had a way with Tas. He looked up to her. Then, too, when she was here, there seemed to be more people around, in and out, then. Tas is half wild, I don't know what will become of him."

"How many years has he? Fifteen? One and a fourteen?"

"Yes, that."

"How long ago did the older Perklarens leave . . . or begin staying away most of the time? A year, two?"

"Ah, long before that . . . although leaving is perhaps not the most proper word. They were just absent more and more. It was about the time Tas was born that things changed, I think. Yes, it's been a long time like this."

"It wasn't when Mevlannen and Maellenkleth were born?"

"Well, now that you mention it, I don't think so, no." The boy's voice faltered, as if he agreed with Morlenden, but at the same time he realized he had admitted the fact that the absence of the parent Perklarens—their strange, intermittent, almost permanent absence—had nothing to do with the same-sexing of the insiblings. And also, their absence could have little or nothing to do with Taskellan. That simply wouldn't fit. No. Something had happened about fifteen years ago, something out-Braid, perhaps even unrelated to it. Morlenden suddenly felt the boy's resistance go weak and soft; he thrust.

"Then there was an exterior event, eh?" The expression on Klervondaf's face told Morlenden that he had indeed got inside the boy's guard and was closing on it rapidly. He could sense it, something concealed, something hidden, coming into shape, almost tangible. . . . He reached, blindly, gambling. "And when Maellenkleth was known, known, I say, to be missing, why didn't her own Braid go looking for her—or at the least come direct to us, the Derens—instead of it being done by the Perwathwiy, a former Terklaren?"

It was the wrong stroke, and the missed target and the delay allowed Klervondaf to recover his composure by a supreme act of will. He breathed deeply, and answered, "So how should we know she was missing? She came and went as she pleased, and since she's been living off in the woods with this *hifzer*, she's hardly been home at all. Is that all so strange? All of us run off for a while, if nowhere but inside our heads! You, you are now Ser and Kadh so you had to be insibling when you were adolescent. Did you not walk away and have an adventure as well?"

Morlenden reflected an instant, and the earnest, strong, hard-defined face of Sanjirmil flashed across the window of his mind. He said, "I must admit that things have been much as you describe them." He felt the surety of the moment ago slipping away. And now again it was truce. Standoff. The two of them looked at one another, slightly belligerently, for a moment. Morlenden added, "You haven't been completely open with me, have you?"

"No," said Klervondaf, directing his glance downward to the floor. "No, not completely, even though I believe you and know you to be just what you say you are. And as much of what I've said, that's truth. There are just some things of which I am not permitted to speak, things that no nonplayer may have the enlightenment of. No matter what." At last, he looked up again directly into Morlenden's face with an expression of tentative, if unmistakable, defiance.

Morlenden tested his resolve. "What, then, was Maellenkleth really doing?"

"She was living with an adolescent *hifzer* calling himself Krisshantem and planning to reconstitute another Player Braid with the connivance of the *hifzer*."

"That's all you'll say?"

"That's all I can say. Maellenkleth herself would tell you no more. And besides what I won't tell you, there is much that I would be unable to, if for no other reason than that I only suspect, I do not *know*. I have been admitted to a level of secrets appropriate to my position as *Nerh*. Of a matter of course, Mael was much deeper in, parent-level or perhaps deeper. She spent much time with Kris, and much time at the Holy Mountain, or with the Past Masters. . . ."

"The Holy Mountain?"

"That which the nonplayers call Grozgor, the Mountain of Madness. . . . But I also know that sometimes she was not in any of those places. Where was she? No one has told me."

Morlenden slanted off, leaving the boy with his perilous integrity intact. He said, "I would know Maellenkleth's appearance, her *vidh*. My *Toorh* Fellirian said that she had seen her and could do me a Multispeech visual, but I wanted a good one, one from those who knew her well. Her own Braid."

Klervondaf smiled. "You should have taken it when it was offered. I am unschooled in Multispeech, other than the pure speech modes. I can't do visuals. Only in words, in *perdeskris*."

"Tell me."

"She is small, but not tiny. A little under average, but more muscular than most girls, most adolescents. Humans, they'd say 'athletic.' She is dark-skinned, like myself, but not so streaky-swarthy as Sanjirmil. Do you know that one?"

"Yes, I know her. Tell me more."

"Maellenkleth has heavy eyebrows, a triangular-oval face, a little cheekbone show, hardly at all, a delicate and slender neck. Her lips are pursed full, as if she were on the verge of thinking of kissing someone. But her mouth is small. She's quite pretty, gentle-looking, abstracted, elsewhere: do you know? You don't see the determination and the fierceness until you get to know her better. She has dark eyes, deep-set, shaded. Intense. She and I share a Madh, but really, we don't look much alike, as much as Tas and Mevlannen. Tomorrow, ask the *hifzer.* Kris-shantem can give you a visual. He's reputed to be good at it."

"What might a *hifzer* know about visual modes of Multispeech?"

"I know not, but as a *hifzer* did he learn it. And Maellenkleth taught much more of it to him, the whole range, all modes, even Command. That was part of the training she was giving him. She could handle all modes, easily. Especially Command. All the Inner Game Players have to know it."

"Anything else?"

"She's very lean and spare. There's no extra on her—it's all muscle. Lean, but not thin. Her hands give her away; they're very long. And if she's not doing anything with them, they almost seem clumsy, bony, awkward. But when she uses them, they are strong and perfect."

Morlenden was going to follow some more of the intangible leads and half-starts about the person of Maellenkleth, when he was interrupted by another rustling at the door curtain. Both Morlenden and Klervondaf looked up, not expecting anyone. The entryway curtain parted before either of them could rise to meet it, to reveal Taskellan and the girl, Plindestier. Both were ruddy-faced and rosy-cheeked from the cold outside, which was, at this late hour, growing intense.

The girl said, "Klervon, by the time Tas got back to the Rhalens, they had all turned in for the night, so he came over to my *yos* and got me. I brought him back here, for he shouldn't be out and wandering in the cold."

The younger boy came into the hearthroom shyly, heading for the children's sleeper, but as he passed his elder outsibling, the older boy cuffed him affectionately across the back of his shoulders. Taskellan rolled with the mock punch and continued on toward the children's sleeper, slyly digging out of his overshirt part of a fresh loaf of bread.

Klervondaf said, "Well, Tas, you little thief, don't eat it all! Give some of it to Ser Morlenden. He's a guest, you little pig."

Taskellan turned back and began carefully dividing the loaf. The girl had remained by the entryway curtain. Klervondaf asked her, after Taskellan had shared the loaf and climbed into the sleeper, "Can you stay, Plindes?" His voice was hesitant, tentative.

She removed her heavy winter outercloak, sighing with visible relief. "I can always stay here, you know that." She turned to Morlenden. "Here, Ser and Kadh," she said, and handed him a small wedge of cheese. "I brought this from home. You may have part of it."

Morlenden took the cheese, broke off a piece, very informally, and passed the remainder to Klervondaf. The girl continued, as if musing aloud to herself, "I don't know what these two would do if I didn't look in on them every few days. Two outsiblings with a whole *yos* to themselves."

Morlenden watched Plindestier for a moment, until she grew self-conscious under his scrutiny. He thought that here was a fine situation indeed. More than a simple love affair was passing between these two adolescents; from her secure position in her own Braid, she was supporting these two. And why not? *We make no provisions for orphans; everyone has a Braid. Except Klervondaf and Taskellan.* He turned his attention back to the older boy.

"You are to weave in about five years; what will happen to Taskellan then? Is there a place for him around here?"

"I'll keep him with me until time comes to weave him."

"That's a hard job, maybe harder a one than the raising of him. You're talking about ten years yet after your weaving. And now, apparently, there's little enough you can offer in the way of weaving-price to an insibling, even if Taskellan were to become civilized enough to become interesting to one. I know the way of these things. You need influence. Now listen: would he come with me, come and live with the Derens? I have a *srithnerh*, his own age, and with the contacts we have it wouldn't be difficult at all for us to see he gets a good Braid to weave into somewhere. He needs the environment, the sense of Braidness, and we have room enough."

Klervondaf paused. "What would I do with the *yos?*"

"Close it up and turn it over to the Revens for transferal. Take what you wish and move in with someone else. You need it, too. Five years with someone is better than going it alone. You seem to have had to be too much the parent ahead of your time. I assume that wherever your elder Perklarens are, they won't come back for any length of time. . . ."

". . . They can't. You don't understand. I can reach them if I need, but they feel they cannot. We agreed."

"Surely someone in the community here . . ."

Plindestier offered, "Why not, Klervon? You could move in with us; we have the room, and it wouldn't make any difference to the rest. You and I are about the same age, and the *Toorh* are going to weave soon, so the elders of us will be gone." She added, turning to Morlenden, "I'm *Thessrith*."

The boy replied hesitantly, "I don't know, I'd have to talk to Taskellan, think it over, get permission from Kreszerdar. . . ."

Morlenden said, "Not to hurry it. Take your time. If and when you are ready, send him along downcountry to my place. We are easy enough to find; people come to us. I know not why this has gone on as it has, but I could not meet it and not make this offer, for it needs fixing. Your people have their reasons; even so think upon what I have said."

Morlenden finished and returned to his bread and cheese, withdrawing from the two adolescents, allowing them space to settle whatever uneasinesses lay between them. He refrained from asking any more questions about Maellenkleth, for the time being. He knew more now than he had when he had started out this morning, but he also realized that what he had learned was not yet to the degree at which he could begin to solve anything . . . perhaps even frame an intelligent question. He felt confusion, subtle, complex disorientations; the basic assumptions about his own people were that they had chosen simplicity, directness, orthodox transitions, and left subtlety and multiplexity to religion, language, philosophy, and art form. People themselves, so the proverb went, were plain as planks. Not so, not so . . . multiplex beyond belief. This Maellenkleth . . . A weak smile flickered across his face, as he recalled some inner vision. *And so are we all, in our own dirty little ways.*

Later, alone in the parent sleeper, settled in the heavy winter comforters, with an additional blanket wrapped around himself for double warmth, Morlenden lay, isolated in the silent *yos*, listening into the spare density of the night sounds of winter, which were even fewer here: somewhere off in the distance, he thought he could hear a dog barking, rather disinterestedly. The nearby creek whispered, almost silently, below the threshold. One had to listen hard for it, and even then, one could not be sure. Was it really the creek, or was that sound simply what one wished to hear? And the trees were silent—there was no wind to move among those overhanging pines and make the susurrous whispering. Whispering? Yes. There was whispering, and it was originating from inside the *yos*, not outside it, where there was no wind.

It was coming from the other sleeper, and judging from their timbre, the voices belonged to Plindestier and Klervondaf. He could not make out the words. It sounded like an argument, but with no words to hang the thread of it on, he could be wrong. He was not, suddenly, sleepy, even after the long walk upcountry; something would not settle. He began trying to relax himself, finding sets of tense muscles and loosening them, one at a time, He had never known this method to fail to put him to sleep. It always worked before you could finish. And while doing so, he tried to review the suspicions he had gained in the *yos* of the Perklarens.

Not very much, he had to conclude. A lot wrong, but they accepted it as right and due, some obligation. . . . And he thought again. Anomalies and enigmas casually strewn about as if their very multiplicity were intended to confuse, ensnare the mind, waylay. You could become so absorbed in figuring out *what* was wrong that you could walk right by the *why* of it. First there was this *hifzer* Krisshantem, influencing her as he was being influenced. And an insibling off working with the humans, a telescope builder, an astronaut, a photographer. Parents gone more or less for fifteen years. But at the least, he had the poor words of a verbal description to go on, although he could project several possible images of girls who could fit that description. And with Kris, at least he'd get a real image.

He was relaxing now. It would be soon. But his musings were interrupted by a soft whisper from the curtain leading down into the hearthroom. There was a movement. He looked, but could not distinguish who was there.

"Whoever is there, come along, if you've a mind."

A softer voice answered him. "It is I, Plindestier." The girl climbed into the compartment with Morlenden. He watched the shadow-on-shadow shape as it climbed in, bent, stooped, settled smoothly on its haunches. He could tell by the flowing of the motions and a soft, insistent fragrance of girl in the compartment, that Plindestier was quite naked. She bent close by his ear, to whisper.

"Klervon and I talked. We decided that you should know as well."

"Know what?"

"When I left, the first time, I felt as if someone were watching me, from nearby. He or she followed a little, then left me. Nothing I could see. That was why I hurried home; I was afraid. And when Tas and I came back, we were very quiet, like a couple of little sneaks, and we came back a different way. Tas has good wood-sense. And we saw someone by the entryway, someone who sensed us, and slipped away before we could get closer."

"Who was it?"

"Who? *What* as well, for I know neither. Not Tas, not I. It was formless and quick. It faded into the shadows. . . . We looked all about before we came in, but there were no traces."

"Then someone was outside listening to us. . . ."

"It must be so. I know that you were talking of Maellenkleth. Klervondaf will not discuss her around me; he says that we will all know about Mael someday, that she will be great among us, but he does not say how this will be. And around here, near the mountain, it's always a little wilder than in other places. There are lights, sometimes, and funny noises. Tremblings in the air. There are tales . . . well, people just don't stay out so much at night. But I had never seen anything until tonight. We agreed that I should tell you to be very careful and watch your back-trail as you go with Tas and from there."

"Be careful? Am I in danger?"

"Just take care, he said. Be alert. He will tell you no more than he already has, and that is too much. But despite that, he wishes you well on your quest. He thinks that something bad has happened to Maellenkleth, and that it could affect all our lives, if it has gone too far. Does that mean anything to you?"

"No. But I will keep my eyes open."

The girl rose from her haunches and flowed ghostlike out of the sleeper. For a moment, Morlenden could hear her moving through the *yos*, but then it became quiet. Her scent remained in the sleeper also for a time, about as long as the faint rustlings far off in the *yos*, and then it, too, faded, leaving behind it bittersweet afterimages in Morlenden's mind of things that had been once, long ago, now irretrievable forever. He felt a curious light-headedness; someone hiding under the curve of the *yos*, listening to their conversation in the middle of the night! What a thing to happen! But he now knew the questions: *Who was Maellenkleth? What was Maellenkleth?* They were the things in his mind that made him light-headed, for simple as they were, they demanded answers filled with voids and shifting, indeterminate vistas. Morlenden recalled his primary schooling, sitting in the yard at the feet of his own

Kadh, Berlargir, and hearing about the human philosopher, Godel, and Godel's stunning discovery—that, ultimately, nothing was provable. Nothing was knowable.

Morlenden recalled that vividly and chuckled to himself in the darkness and silence of the *yos* of the Perklarens: Godel, indeed! And, Godel or not, he set it firmly in the innermost part of his resolve that he'd get to the bottom of it all and root it all up. That if he could even make an approximate answer to the two questions, the slippery *tervathon*, then he'd know where she was and what happened to her. And more yet, most likely. She would be illuminated, as would he. He was sure. He sighed, and fell into sleep without further thought.

BOOK TWO

Vicus Lusorum

EIGHT

You need some square-ruled graph paper, some tracing paper, a pencil. Make a Surround-template by cutting out a three-by-three square from a strip of the graph paper, and set it aside.

Now memorize these symbols: each square on the graph paper is a cell. An empty cell is symbolized by nothing inscribed in the cell, while a full cell is symbolized by an inscribed circle. These are the only conditions that exist. Just two. Binary. Now there are two operations: empty-becoming-full and full-becoming-empty. The first is symbolized by a dot in the center of the cell. The second becoming is symbolized by an X over the cell.

Lay out a pattern of filled cells of your choice on the graph paper, leaving plenty of empty cells around the outside of the pattern. Anything you want; but for beginners, keep it simple: you'll see why. Now you have a playing field. There are within it filled and empty cells.

Apply your Surround-template to every cell in your pattern, ensuring you work all the way to the outside of it on all sides, according to these rules:

• If the center cell (of the three-by-three) is empty-state, and exactly three of its eight adjacent cells are filled-state, mark this center cell with a dot. This cell will be filled-state upon the next move. Any other number of filled-state neighbor cells will cause this cell to remain empty. Mark this condition with an X across the cell.

• If the center cell is filled-state, and two or three of its eight adjacent cells are filled-state, mark this cell with a dot inside the circle. This cell will remain filled on the next move. Any other number zero, one, four, or more, will cause this cell to become an

empty on the next move. Mark this condition by crossing out the cell.

Copy the pattern of dots and transfer the pattern to a fresh section of grid paper. Move one is over and repeat over again for move two, the neighbor rules. You should continue this procedure until your playing field either becomes empty of filled cells or attains a stable or cycling condition.

The first thing you will notice is that your initial pattern will immediately undergo startling transformations. No doubt some of you will see your pattern vanish without a trace. Others will learn secrets.

Oh, yes. Don't use a computer. You miss the best parts of it. You are now a Gameplayer.
          —Apologies of the Author to Martin Gardner

There are simple games and complex ones, but the only ones worth playing are the multiplex ones in which all parameters are in a constant state of flux and change.
          —The Game Texts

VANCE SAT BACK in his office chair, picking a sheaf of papers from the desk as he settled; he wasn't interested in their contents. It was simply and purely a gesture of defense. Vance wanted to put some distance between himself and the visitor his administrative assistant had announced. This Errat, whoever he was. A Controller. Vance did not wish this morning to talk to a Controller about anything, face to face, or via any alternate mode of communication one would care to imagine. He pretended to be vastly absorbed in the papers before his face, squinting owlishly at them and frowning. When he looked up again, he hoped that he would see this alleged Nightsider* just coming through the door. It was not to be so: Vance was surprised to see the man already in the room, standing before his desk in a posture suggesting painstaking neutrality. He had come into the office unnoticed in absolute silence.

Vance saw before himself a man of about his own age, late forties, perhaps early fifties, dressed in Nightsider navy blue pants and tunic and wearing on his right breast a Master Controller's Badge. Vance also observed that the badge was an old one, with decorative fringes and flour-

---

* In Shifter jargon, one who worked straight midnight shifts.

ishes done in the style of roundels and curlettes in vogue some thirty years ago. Vance nudged his estimate of his visitor's age upward. After another reflection, he recalled that even a Nightsider was of higher status than any shiftworker, and that the badge was so obviously dated. Vance thought that in the condition Errat appeared to be, he must have been on gerries* for the past twenty years at least.

Now this Errat. Who was he? Vance had never heard of him. He may very well have been a Controller once, but he certainly had to be more than that now. Staff? Vance doubted that as far as Region Central went, even considering the newcomers who had come in with the investiture of Parleau. Continental Secretariat? Who could tell? Those people never went out in the field. In appearance, the visitor was tall, loose-limbed, erect, and alert; he managed to cast an impression of both great dignity and sinister decisiveness. Errat was dark enough of skin and curly enough of hair to have had more than a trace of black ancestry, although considering the intermingling that had gone on over the years, Vance knew instinctively that Errat was as far from a hypothetical ancestral African as Vance was from an equally hypothetical ancestral northeastern European. There were no more pure types left. Errat had a peppering of gray in his hair, and had over the years overlain the full, sensual mouth with a hard, compressed line of determination.

Vance also considered the name: Hando Errat. Programmed name. Those had arrived with the establishment of Shifter Society, and were simply no more than pattern-generated assemblies of phonemes and vocables, internationally acceptable to all, with all traditional or meaningful or even suggestive contracts deleted from the list. The original intent of programmed names had been to offer persons an opportunity to style themselves without reference to any known national, ethnic, linguistic, or religious point of origin. One had to have a name, but the name didn't have to mean anything, other than a simple personal label. Name-changing was nothing new; waves of it had often swept through new movements, signaling new allegiances and new bindings. But programmed names had come, and not gone. They had endured. And even now, if anything at all, they signaled allegiance only to cold efficiency, expediency, and the unifying power of IPG, the Ideal of Planetary Government, which was sought daily, but, according to releases, never quite attained. Vance knew better. It may have been patchwork; but of one piece it was now.

* Geriatric treatments, primarily but not exclusively drugs.

But now? For a long time, the bearers of programmed names had seemed to have an edge on those who retained their old names, with their taint of residues of older loyalties, and virtually all of the key positions were held by such persons. But some decay had entered the system as well, for Vance was sure that there were many careerist coat-riders who took them merely to gain points in the Shifter Society establishment

Vance acknowledged his visitor. "Yes, Citizen Errat."

Errat responded politely. "Citizen Vance; I see that you are at your work early in the day. Or is it late, as in my own time-reference?" Errat's voice was deep and resonant, but carefully neutral in tonation. And highly controlled; nothing showing save that which Errat wished to be seen. Vance felt some apprehensions—this one would be to no good for someone.

Vance replied, "It is early. As you see, I'm a Daysider." Vance hoped his voice had come off as level as Errat's. Errat was obviously playing with him, because he knew damn well that Vance was a Daysider, from Vance's tan clothing. It was nothing more than a status-game. Vance chose to ignore the bait and engage in emotional arm-wrestling with Errat, to demonstrate that even with a career going nowhere in particular, a traditionalist name, he was yet somebody to be reckoned with in the affairs of Seaboard South. A provocateur, this Errat. That would have been exactly the reaction Errat wanted, to provide the key into whatever he wished of Vance. Vance knew field Controllers well enough. They were the same breed who had run the surveillance program against Fellirian. Or had that been a decoy for a target program upon himself? He would never know.

"Aha! Well, we Nightsiders are a misunderstood lot. Here I am finishing my duty day, just as you commence yours."

"Do you really like Nightsiding?"

"Never knew anything else; it would now be difficult for me to change. Circadian rhythms, you know. But regretfully, as I must say, to the matter at hand." Errat reached within the front of his tunic and extracted a thin, pliable envelope, from which in turn he produced a single, flexible transparency. He handed this across the desk to Vance. Vance took the proffered document, and looked at it.

While Vance was studying the flex, Errat commented, "The person in the flex is a New Human. She had been detained outside for questioning under, ah, I believe the word would be 'suspicious circumstances.' There has been some justification for the belief that some sort of shabby plot is afoot, within the reservation, possibly here at the Institute as well. The subject you see in the flex appeared to be useful for these inquiries, but she was . . . uncooperative. Now we poor Controllers must not only pursue our normal onerous investigations and establish vectors of probability and consequence, but we must also turn aside and determine why she has been so reticent. I wish to ask your assistance in this, to help us to identify her and tie her to something."

"She looks familiar, like someone I've seen here. Why not ask the ler about the Institute?"

"We would not have them alerted. After all, the girl was outside, and seemed to know her way well. She had, we reasoned, to have left some traces in our world. Those are the threads we must pick up first."

"I have heard talk from others about suspicions about a plot. Is there anything to it?"

"The situation is by no means clear, and at the present it is a matter I would rather not comment upon, lest I express points which may prove to be wrong. We are also interested in any New Human attention to this girl, attempts to locate her, and the like. Naturally one observing such an interest would be motivated to report such persons."

Vance nodded. "Of course . . . it will be as you say. Complete cooperation."

"You mentioned a familiarity . . . do you know her?"

Vance glanced at the flex again. He looked back at Errat, levelly, wondering what he was giving away. He said, "Well, yes, I do know her face, now that I look at it closely, but not very well at all. Her name slips me right now. I had used her once to do the visitors' information-releases, as a replacement. I can tell you no more at this moment than the fact that I remember her as cooperative and competent."

"I see. Could you recall more after some refreshing of your memory?"

"Yes. It will be a moment. Can you wait?"

"It should not be required. . . . Take your time. We would like to know everything you can find out about her, her activities. You will be contacted later. You may retain the flex."

"Thank you."

"Should you wish to make a report prior to contact, you can reach me via ASTRA line, code BD, extension eight-four-eight. Any time." Vance listened closely. There was absolutely no clue. An ASTRA line could be anywhere.

Vance asked, "I shall do so." He noted the reference on his pad. "What's she done?"

"All in all, rather a small matter. But there live those who wish to know why such a small offense should warrant such a strong defense, or as much fear as there reportedly was in the subject. We wish to know more about this curious person and the even more curious circumstances surrounding her . . . transition into her present status."

"Will you stay for some coffee?"

"No, no, I must be off, now; there are many minor affairs to be concluded before shift-end. So, then, good day."

Errat turned and departed in the same silent and fluid manner with which he had come.

Vance placed a call for Doctor Harkle to call him when she came in, and sat back again, reflecting. What had been the name of the girl in the flex? He couldn't remember. Had it been Malverdedh? No, it wasn't that. But they wanted more than a name, they wanted to see who came for her. That sounded simple and effective, but erroneous as well. Suppose the real conspirators sent someone who knew nothing. Send innocents after the girl. They could lose nothing. Vance found himself wishing that Fellirian was here; she would be able to make more sense out of this . . . or perhaps not, for he could hardly tell her everything. But if there was a trap here, she could spot it, he felt sure. *But who was the trap for?* With Controllers you never could be sure. Was this another setup for Parleau's house-cleaning, setting himself, Vance, up for the emeritus executive treatment? Damn.

Vance would have worried more about it, but at that moment Doctor Harkle arrived, as usual, without announcement. She habitually forbade the clerks to say she was coming. She simply would not allow them to put her off. She was a severely dressed, somewhat portly woman of definite middle age, who retained, for those who in her estimation deserved it, great humor and warmth. With her she had brought two great steaming mugs of coffee.

She began, "Here, have some of this, Walter. We brew it up down in my shop, and it's a damn sight better than the stuff you have served up here, or in the buttery. That stuff is industrial strength cheese-dip."

Vance accepted the mug gratefully, for there was more than a grain of truth in the statement. He said, "I will take it; please take a chair, if you will. I asked them outside to call you because I needed my mind jogged." He handed her the flex.

Doctor Harkle looked at it momentarily, then back to Vance. He asked, "Isn't that one of the girls who works down in your place?"

"Yes. I remember her well, although my recollection of her is not the same as this image. What's the matter with her? She looks lifeless in this; perhaps catto, except that you can be sure that a catto is hiding something, and this one seems to have nothing to hide. Relaxed. Wait, I know a better word. Uninhibited. As if there's no personality here, not even a distorted one."

"I do not know the circumstances. What is her name?"

"Maellenkleth, I recall. Yes, Maellenkleth. Srith Perklaren."

"That's right! I remember. A First-player. What does she do for your people?"

"Primarily math, tensors, astrogation. She's quite gifted in the area, the whole thing, when you can get her attention. She goes at mathematics in an unorthodox way, but one can't argue with the results she obtains . . . she seems to run everything through an odd sort of iterative internal program; I should call it a topology filter, the best I can visualize."

"Get her attention? Was she absentminded? I have never seen one of them so."

"Well, yes, in a way, I would say absentminded. Or preoccupied. I have no idea what her people would call it, if they even noticed it. This, by the way, had been on the increase in the last year. She appeared to be working under some kind of pressure. When she worked, that is. Toward the last, her visits began dropping off. As a fact, I don't think I've seen her but once since we took the new kids up to the Museum on the field trip."

"Museum? Field trip? What is this?"

"Every so often I round up the newcomers, the ados who are drifting into the Institute, and take them on several side trips out into the big, wide world. Actually, hardly farther than Region Central."

"Oh, a routine sort of thing."

"Well, not exactly routine, you know, but certainly recurring. I mean, when they do come down here to work steady, they will be dealing with essentially human problems, and I like them to get a look at the people they intend to go problem-solving for. . . . It was last spring. I had taken a group up to see the old Tech Museum at the old Research Triangle. They were all very excited, you know. I'm sure you recall the place—it's where they keep all those old worthless artifacts, in the old Tech Center. There was a university there in the old days. But they see so little of a genuine technological civilization that these old things are wonders to them—real eye-openers. Puts things in proper perspective. But this girl, Maellenkleth, reacted oddly. She was skeptical or contemptuous to begin with—I could not say which. But when we returned, she was morose and moody, much more than usual. As if something she'd seen had really shaken her somehow. I thought it might have been more of the usual stuff, intrinsically hers, but the more I thought on it, the more I was sure that it was something she saw or realized in the Museum. Then she got fidgety, couldn't wait to be gone. After that, I saw her only once, and then she wasn't working, but was visiting some friends down here."

"It certainly sounds odd, not at all like the usual ado we get down here." Vance was remembering Fellirian when he thought of the stereotype ler adolescent.

"Definitely, Director. No doubt of it at all. Now let me ask you one or two: why the sudden interest in Maellenkleth?"

"It would seem she's got into some kind of trouble and has been detained. One of these Controllers was here this morning asking about her. And of course, there are some other things, too, that I know. They seem to think there's some kind of plotting, conspiracy."

"Who suspects? Continental? Or Region? There's a difference in methodology you can measure."

"There's nothing I could pick that would tie him to Denver; on the other hand, he didn't resemble any of the Regionals I've dealt with in the past, either. There was definitely something high-level about him."

"Hm." Harkle snorted. Then she said, more reflectively, "You hardly ever see the Continentals stir themselves about anything, but just the same they seem to catch it all sooner or later. One thing for sure: if they're on to something, it could well get brisk. Very brisk."

"That's the trouble. I have no idea who he is after, beyond the girl herself."

"Worried? . . . Oh, I understand. Well, if the fellow who came to you is a Continental, you needn't worry about double-blind setups and entrapments. They work direct. They suspect you, they call you in, ask you a few questions, and post you off to Rehab." Here Harkle looked about, conspiratorially. "Or they Adminterm*, They don't have to justify things the way the Regions do. They just do it."

---

* "Terminate via administrative procedures." In 2550, there was no legal death penalty. Nevertheless, certain people did disappear from time to time. Nobody asked where they went.

"As a fact, Hark, now that you mention it, I would have to say he didn't seem like the Regionals at all."

"Fine, then, You have nothing to worry about. We can tell them what we know. It's little enough."

"Yes. Well, thank you for the information and the coffee. They were both welcome."

"And to you, Director. Call me any time. Now," and here she arose, straightened her clothing, "back to the cobalt mines."

Vance nodded absentmindedly, reaching again for his paperwork. Doctor Harkle left the office, leaving Vance alone for his next appointments. Eventually, he did get back to work, but it was not immediately. For a long time after the conversation with the Chief of Research and Development, Vance did exactly what she had told him he had no need of doing—worrying. Because even if what she had said were true, he couldn't avoid the feeling that a trap was closing slowly . . . and that its jaws were going to close on innocents as well. He knew from Fellirian and his conversation with the Regional Controller that essentially there was no plot, no conspiracy. Then he thought again: or was there?

Simultaneously, some distance away, a person who had been passive up to this point moved from reflection into the domain of action, exemplifying, as the ler might have said, had they been aware of his presence or functions, the trait of Fire. He had been sitting in a smallish darkened room filled almost to the exclusion of everything else with racks of electronic devices, instruments, rows and banks of switches, indicator light panels, illuminated and darkened buttons (marked "press to test"). The only noticeable sound in the room was the whisper of cooling fluids through miles of heat sinks and the quiet movement of air through the ventilators. There were others in the room as well, seated in reclining chairs before the racks, all seriously intent upon matters at hand, oblivious to all the others.

The person arose from his position at one of the consoles, stood up attentively, and paused. He seemed to be listening to a headset he was wearing, a light arc of silver metal terminating in a tiny plastic earpiece. Then he removed the appliance. After consulting some notes he had made on a plain ruled pad at the console, he walked a short distance to another panel, set high up in one of the racks. Thereon were two matrices, one 3 x 3, the other 5 x 5. One contained numbers, the other letters. A set of zeros of various denominations bridged the two. Machine functions were displayed to the sides. The person played over the numbers and letters, both matrices, with one hand, deftly, occasionally manipulating the machine functions with his free hand. Almost instantly, dim letters began forming on an electroluminescent panel directly above the buttons. The letters said:

#330-12239 ANSWREP TO SUBKWERTASK A10/BT
GINIA SENDS/BT
SUB APPEL MAELLENKLETH SRITH PERKLAREN
RMK 1 ARRANG NAMEWAY INDIC ADOLESCENT
RMK 2 SURNAME NAMEWAY INDIC NH FAM GP
& OCCUPT/VOCAT EXHIB OF RITUAL GAME
& CF SUBJ/ACAD MATHEMATICS
& HUMAN REF FOLLOW:
1. VON NEUMANN
2. CONWAY, J. H.
3. GARDNER, M.
! 1950-2550 PERIOD/BT/BT

The person read the message, then depressed a button marked "INTCL," and returned to his position at the consoles. He replaced his headset, adjusted his larynx pickup, and began speaking quietly as if musing aloud into thin air. The persons at the other consoles paid no attention to him. They never did.

He said, "For Plattsman, Ginia sends. Vance uncovered the name for us. Got a little more from Archives. Awaiting further query instructions. Taping relevants and forwarding. Acknowledge, now!"

He depressed a small extended button on his own console. Above it a small light lit red, changed to green, flashed red again and went out. He smiled. He waited a moment.

He pushed some more buttons, paused, said, "Operator, there was a break during the last transmission. Can you rebroadcast while I manual address?"

The operator apparently answered yes, for the person then set some switches on his panel. He also depressed some additional buttons, apparently another address group. These were not the same letters as the first. The acknowledge-light went red, then green, then a quick flicker of red again, and out. The person said, "Thank you. Seems to be working properly now. There will not be a requirement for further service or write-up of discrepancy."

Then, and only then, did the person settle back deeply in his chair, releasing a long, controlled sigh. He looked about quietly, but nobody was observing him. He sighed again. And after a moment he returned to his work, consulting some other logs. These were routine matters, for he went at their accomplishment with none of the vigor or decisiveness he had displayed earlier.

Plattsman was not in his office to receive this message. He was instead in the office of the chairman, Klaneth Parleau. Several subjects of general interest had already been discussed, and after those Parleau asked, "Well, what about those Comparator studies? Did they ever lead anywhere?"

"I have been waiting for you to ask! Indeed they did—to more of the same. Finally we were able to program the damn machine to discriminate, but the chemtrace of the emotion-sets still have us baffled. According to the medicos, that second girl shouldn't be able to walk about rationally, much less organize herself enough to carry out any program, but Klyten says to disregard that. Apparently they have an internal system for overriding chemical insanity, whatever the original cause. Very little is known about it, except that some selected higher functions of discrimination are temporarily lost, while the subject experiences the effect of heightened perceptions. I am told it is rather like alcohol intoxication minus the visual effects and the loss of motor coordination. Klyten is researching it now, and at our next meeting hopes to explore this further. This stuff is all buried, lost, mislaid. We know the original data exists, but it's hard to find."

"The second one is insane, then?"

"From the readings we have, yes. No other condition is possible. It's just too far out of balance with the rest. But we have to understand that ler insanity is unlike human . . . you know that it's said that if you think you're going crazy, it's the surest sign you aren't."

"I don't get it."

"Chairman, it's this way: if humans go crazy, they don't know it. Crazy people think they are sane. And contrarily, if you're sure you're going over the edge, that's the peak of your rationality. But with ler, it's the other way around: they know when they're insane, and they can compensate for it until someone else can effect a cure."

"In other words, functionally, insanity doesn't exist."

"Correct."

"So why is this one walking around loose unchanged? How long have we traced her now?"

"There are indications that some of the traces are four years old. We're digging."

"Four years?"

"Right. At about the same level, too. But mind, we still see much less of the second one than we do the first. But there's yet more, and the best yet."

Parleau groaned aloud, "Oh, no! Tell me no tales of a third!"

"There's a third, it's a fact, but the third one is a human, leaves no traces whatsoever on the chems, and in fact was only caught by accident. All the images are bad and we can't identify."

"Who is he following?"

"Crowd-scans so far have associated 'Human X' only with the first girl, but we are suspicious about some incidents . . . the trouble is that the only way we see the third man, so to speak, is through criteria that are worthless for addressing the crowd-scans for him alone. The data don't discriminate enough to pick him out alone."

"So, Plattsman, what you're telling me is that we have two ler girls who are agents and a human who is in league with them?"

"Such was my first impression, Chairman. We Controllers are prone to assemble things that way. But evidence suggests that is a wrongful vector; we are now exploring the possibility that we may be dealing with a whole family of plots, which may or may not be connected. But one thing we know for sure."

"And that is?"

"We ran some tests on the enlarged faces from the crowd-scans. To volunteers over at the medical school. Now you know that facial expressions are part of our infant programming and that we retain these residues all our lives, adding layers of subtlety as we go. So when we ran these images, with suitable controls, against the volunteers, we were able to statistically match the facial expressions on the three against known categories. . . . The first one is afraid and worried. The second is blank, and the third . . ."

"Yes?"

". . . is violently hostile."

"You can do this, and not identify them?"

"Recognition is one thing, of basic emotional sets. Picking individuals out of a hat quite another."

"Good work, Plattsman. Good work, indeed! This is better than I expected."

"I'm not so sure, Chairman."

"How so?"

"We are very uneasy about these multiplying coincidences. They are drawing our attention away from the original question. And as you may recall from the Control Functional briefing we give to all chairmen, the more diffused the question, the more useless the answer. None of these programs seem to be leading us to the questions we originally asked. We are not getting our vector of Karma."

"I understand muddy water hides many things. Still, you Controllers have information theory to help you extract data from noise."

"True, Chairman. But these things take time to run properly, and after that come the interpretations and the decisions. I want to return to the original penetration; pursue the first girl. We propose bringing Klyten more into it."

"Very well. Until the next meeting, then?"

"Yes. And I hope we shall all have more to say than we did the last time. All we did there was allow ourselves to recognize that we had a problem."

"True enough . . . and so far we don't know yet exactly what that problem is, do we?"

"I am happy that you agree with our interpretation!"

Plattsman turned and departed Parleau's office.

NINE

The finest tragedies are always on the story of some few houses that may have been involved as either agents or sufferers in some deed of horror.

—Aristotle, *Poetics*

THE PLACE WHERE Maellenkleth and Krisshantem had established their workroom and ad hoc dwelling remained to Morlenden curiously vague in specific location, even though the boy Taskellan hardly talked of anything else during their long walk eastward through the naked winter forests of the wild northern provinces of the reservation. And during their walk together, Morlenden also learned the boy was something more than the simple rowdy he had first appeared. While it could not be denied that Taskellan was deficient in most of the approved social graces, it was also apparent that he held his two insiblings in almost worshipful regard, sharing, as it seemed, most of Maellenkleth's likes and dislikes. There were many: Maellenkleth was perilously decisive in her opinions. But it was through such second-order reflections that Morlenden was able to begin to get to know the girl he was searching for. What impressed him far more, however, was the even greater regard the younger boy held for the *hifzer* Krisshantem. Morlenden half expected any minute to be informed that this Krisshantem was also proficient in faith-healing and dead-raising, among his other skills.

Morlenden was neither surprised nor amazed, even considering the exaggeration which Tas would have to be adding; a *hifzer* would learn fast to be quick or he would simply not survive. And this one did, apparently, survive rather well. He lived alone in the woods, far from any habitation, and seemingly prospered. But beyond the location of the treehouse, there seemed to be no way to determine in advance exactly where Kris was likely to be. It was as if the *hifzer* boy obeyed some internal variant of Heisenberg's principle—that one simply could not predict where he would be.

Krisshantem, so the story went, unraveling as they walked, was and had been a nomadic sort of hunter and gatherer, tied loosely by association to Braid Hulen, the potters. Kris ranged far and wide, uncovering various small deposits of clay and trading these locations with the Hulens for the few things he could not make for himself. By and large, the kinds of clays the Hulens used were few to begin with, spread all over in tiny nodes. But even they could not cover them all, and so Kris had moved in on the periphery. And there he remained, silent as the shadows of a wintered branch upon the new fallen snow. He wandered, seeking just the right beds of clay and mineral colorings, meeting rarely with one or another of the Hulens to exchange information.

Taskellan said, "The Hulens themselves are closemouthed, secretive. They are something of wanderers, themselves, and they drift in and out, saying very little. They go off in the woods to their special places and bring back loads of clays. They all might get together once a week, and they don't say much even then, or not so I could tell. They're all deep in Multispeech and use it among themselves more than anyone I ever saw, except perhaps the elders of Dragonfly Lodge. That is, when they talk at all. Mael got to know them well, through Kris, and came to like them after a bit. She was put off at first by their silences; she always did like to talk, argue, expound. But she told me that they listened a lot. Like this: that Kris could locate a good creek-bed for clay just by listening to the water flowing and tinkling, the way it sounded, the way the sound filled the places around its origin. 'Clay comes from peace in the water,' he said. 'Rest-peace, not stagnation. Once you learn to listen, water-wording is just like Multispeech.' "

Morlenden commented, "We Derens are not such masters of Multispeech. We keep the records and Singlespeech will do for that. I can listen to it, but I don't like to give up to it and to its speaker* and I've never had what I'd call a successful transmission."

Tas disregarded Morlenden's disclaimer. "Mael knows it real good. I mean, she was good before, but since she met Kris, she's been able to do really wild things."

---

* The reception of Multispeech demanded that the receiver allow his will to become passive. This relationship of individual submission to another's will had traditionally limited the use of this linguistic ability to certain Braids and elder communes, who included in their traditional regimens compensatory disciplines to handle this problem.

"For instance?"

"You know visual-mode? How you can send holistic pictures with it? These pictures seem like life, but aren't, because they're not movable. Or is that just stuff the elders tell the children?"

"As far as I know, it's true."

"Mael could make them move. Not so fast as real, slower, but they moved. I let her in once and she showed me."

"I had heard once that two or more elders who had worked long at it could do movers. I never saw one."

"I heard that your mind isn't ready for it until you can control auto-forgetting." Morlenden winced at the boy's remark. Autoforgetting was a phenomenon they did not mention openly. Taskellan, for his part, caught a trace of Morlenden's discomfort and lapsed into silence, mumbling monotones when spoken to, or more rarely, subvocalizing, as if talking to himself. Morlenden followed behind, walking on through the frosted morning of the cold winter day.

Along the way from Yos-Perklaren, Morlenden had not once seen anything remotely resembling a *yos* or a dooryard, a bower, or even a widened place at the junction of paths where strangers might meet and speak without omen. They walked, seemingly, through a trackless, leaf-strewn hardwood forest, illuminated by a pearly, translucent sunlight filtering through a high deck or finely detailed altocumulus. Morlenden could remember hearing Fellirian call such a sky in some old human terms she had heard from an antiquarian. Mackerel sky, they called it, or sometimes buttermilk sky if the cloudlets were larger. They themselves in Singlespeech said *Palosi Pisklendir.* Pearl fish-scale sky. And the other they designated *Hlavdir*—curd-sky. After all, they were much the same in either method of speech.

When they had started, the forest had been the artificially cultivated parasol pines, but out of the lake country, it soon reverted to nature and became a forest of oak and hickory, gallbarks, shagworts, mossycups with cupleaves, on the poorer soils and rocky outcrops. As the sun neared, attained, and began to pass the zenith, there was further change, and the trees appearing were beeches and ironwoods, wild-privets and planetree, sure signs they were in stream-dominated country. Not bottom-land. There were still no paths. They walked on, in silence now, saving their breath, making only the small forest noises of rumpled leaves underfoot as they went. Shortly after what Morlenden thought was noon, they stopped, their breath steaming lightly in cold air as limpid and trembling-clear as spring water. Morlenden thought on it a moment, and realized with a start that he was hungry. He slid out from under his pack and retrieved the fine wayfood Plindestier and Klervondaf had thoughtfully provided—a small mesh bag of apples, sausages and bread.

Their lunching-place seemed little different from most of the lands they had been walking through all day, since firstlight. Save that here, of course, the forest was predominantly beech, and that they were in the shallow valley of a small stream, surrounded by the silvery naked trunks with their suggestions of the ropy strandings of muscles, broken only by the darker, more somber boles of ironwood, with its bluish bark color, or the deep, vibrant green of aborvitae. More rarely, there were scraggly junipers.

Despite the cold of the day, Morlenden was relaxing, wrapped well in his hard-winter pleth and traveling cloak, and full of a fine sausage as well. But Taskellen broke into his meditations. "We're likely to find Kris somewhere around here, if we find him at all." The boy waved his arm about freely, indicating the general area one could see through the network of smooth trunks and bare branches, some still holding a cluster of this year's browned leaves. "The treehouse is a lot farther, but it's on this creek, and the last time I saw him, he was working this area. We passed the way Kris usually goes over to the Hulens, but I saw no sign he'd been there."

"We could miss him easily in these pathless woods. Are you certain that this is the area?"

"No doubts, no doubts at all, Ser Deren. We would find him somewhere around here if for no other reason, than that he'd wait for Maellenkleth. She wouldn't wander all over the place with him. No! Not at all! She sat him down and told him to light in one place and stay there—and he did. After all, it was Kris who was being wooed, not the other way around. He was the one who had to learn the new role, not her! Ha! As if she would!"

Taskellan looked about, as if to reassure himself. He saw a forest floor covered with beech leaves, tree trunks, their numbers growing with distance until they formed a solid barrier and blocked out all sense of horizon. Tas looked back at Morlenden, not quite so sure. "This is where he'd be . . . but even if he was here, we could miss him if he didn't want us to see him . . . they say that he can disappear, just like that. Zip! He's there; and then he isn't. I came with Mael once and he showed me. He just got still, a minute, and then he was gone. No noise, no nothing."

"People can't just vanish. How does he do it? What's the trick?"

The boy shrugged. "Just his way . . . I don't know. Kris is strange. He and the Hulens alike are hunters and they eat a lot of meat, so they need to be sneaks, wood-crafters. They wander around in all kinds of weather and can't be bothered with carrying around a lot of provisions with them on their treks to the clay-pots."

Morlenden nodded, acknowledging what Tas said, but nevertheless, he was surprised. True hunters were rare in ler society, for several contributory reasons, not the least of which was their basic orientation toward farming, with its commitment to a fixed plot of land. They had long ago chosen this life. More, the restriction against the use of any weapon which left the hand weighed heavily against those who might have been so inclined. "Kill not with that which leaves the hand," went the stern injunction, reaffirmed by generations of Revens and their interpretations of the basic tradition. And so far as Morlenden knew, it was always obeyed, never broken. It was their most serious individual act of crime. To break it in any fashion made one outcast; against a person called for death by any means, fair or foul. . . . No doubt this made a hunting existence extremely difficult, or an interesting problem of discipline. He observed, after thinking it over for a moment, to Tas, "Then they and Kris must be very good at their hunting."

"You bet they are! Quick. They use hands and knives and *tengvaron**. *Graigvaron*, too, though I've never seen one. All kinds of animals, small and large, although they don't hunt the larger ones so much, unless they have time and feel like smoking it. But if Kris is anywhere around here, he knows we're here, probably what we came for as well. He's spooky; I think he can read minds."

"Road apples!" said Morlenden.

"That's what I heard!"

"So is Kris like the Hulens?"

"No. Much more so. I don't know what he was before he came here and started bartering with them, but he learned from them. And became something more than them . . . they're afraid of him now and

---

* *Tengvar*, a light, elegant, half-meter machete. *Graigvar*, a delicate thrusting-spear. These were rare artifacts as they were weapons and used for nothing else. Since they were uncommon, considerable mythology was woven about them. For instance, each one possessed a name of its own, generated in the same three-root fashion as were the names of persons; each one possessed a complex, highly detailed history, which was learned rote by each bearer in turn and never committed to writing. "Gvarh" means weapon (and has no other meaning, being one of the few trans-aspectual roots).

avoid him, not for what he does, because he's very quiet and restrained, but for what he now knows. That's like him all over; I mean, I know Mael deep, a lot better than Kler, and I knew that he would have to be something special of himself for her to have anything to do with him, much less have *dhainaz* with him, even less integrate as they have done. . . . I don't think you'll get much out of him; he knows more than Kler and is a lot more secretive."

Morlenden asked casually, "Do you know what Maellenkleth was doing?"

"No. I don't *know*. I heard some stuff, but I always thought that it was all made-up, legends and fairy tales. It doesn't fit together so well and as for its *zvonh** . . . it's just not."

"Sometimes it's hard to separate lack of *zvonh* from a lack of more facts, or perhaps degree of subtlety."

"It's as you say, I know . . . but I never worried about it. Mael knew what she was doing and Mael trusted him and that was enough for me. And I know she took her oaths as a *Zanklar* seriously. She was a Player of the great Life Game, and would not betray guild secrets. But she had taken him far into it. They were in it deep."

Morlenden had been sitting with his legs folded under his body. He now unfolded and arose, stretching. "Well," he said, "we should go on a little farther, shouldn't we? At least to the treehouse. It's past noon already, and I don't care to sleep in the open in this wild country and the cold."

Stretching more, brushing leaves off his cloak, Morlenden bent over to pick up his traveling-bag, feeling different parts of his body readjusting to the new repose of his clothing, new patterns of warmth and cold. The day was cold, indeed. Cold and still and beginning to be damp, and though it was yet not far from midday, a bite lingered in the air of the beech forest. He looked along the shallow valley, upstream, trying to make some estimate of how far yet they had to walk to the treehouse. He could not. All he knew was that they had covered an impressive distance on foot in half a day, and that much more remained, in an empty forest without trail or path or blazon. He looked again, trying to get

---

* *Zvonh*: resonance. Ler set an extraordinary, in some cases, excessive valuation upon a logical concept called resonance or harmony. This was also called self-consistency. Nothing was unique or independent, but a part of some larger unit, which possessed purpose and meaning. To lack *zvonh* was to have contradictions, inequalities. Although a valuable logical tool, it was often popularly misused.

some better feel for the distances of the forests . . . and saw, standing not ten feet away, a person who very definitely had not been there before. It was not the exact way he had been facing, but likewise it had not been behind him either. Yet there he was. Morlenden stared at the silent figure, feeling an odd prickling along his backbone, and in the center of his fundament, a hollow tickling sensation. The person returned his gaze without expression or apparent comment, with all the impersonality of some natural object, a stone, a leaf, a tree trunk. The person appeared to be an adolescent, one of the people, a boy, very fair-haired, although not so pale of skin nor so gold of hair as Cannialin, he caught himself thinking. He was dressed in a patched and well-worn winter overcloak and felt boots, although the clothing was very clean and well cared for. He was hardly different from any other mop-head adolescent; slender and wiry, an angular, stony, serious face, muscular and hardened from years of exposure to the weather and the uncaring that had driven him here to the edge.

Morlenden spoke quietly, so as not to disturb the apparition. "Taskellan?"

The boy looked in the direction Morlenden was looking. He also got to his feet, and said, "I see. That's Kris. Come on, I'll acquaint you. And then I have to go back. Long way homeward, you know."

They gathered their things and moved slowly, cautiously, to the place where the other boy was standing, waiting for them; the still, silent figure nodded, virtually imperceptibly, now acknowledging their interest.

Taskellen said, "I present the worthy Krisshantem to a Ser and Kadh of the Braid of Counters, Morlenden Deren." All in the proper order. And as soon as he could estimate that the two strangers were measuring one another, he turned, abruptly, as if afraid this fragile meeting were going to suddenly evaporate, that one or both might bolt and run and return back the way they had come. The younger boy waved to Morlenden. In a moment, he was gone. In a few more moments, his scuffles in the winter-fallen leaves could be heard fading away. Then there was silence, at least to Morlenden's ear.

The two stood and watched one another. In the light falling through the clouds and branches, the impression was of being under water, a very cold and clear water. Morlenden watched the still, angular face before him with its sharp definitions, planes, and angles, and felt a tension, a wariness. Not danger. He was being weighed to an exquisite level of discrimination, and it was disturbing. He broke the silence of the forest. "And you, then, are indeed Krisshantem, who was the lover of the girl Maellenkleth Srith Perklaren?"

"Dhofter," the boy corrected. The correction was offered in a self-confident clear pleasant alto voice. The term *dhofter* surprised Morlenden somewhat, for the *dhof* was a specific category of personal relationship among lovers which went rather further than the usual pledges of undying desire that such persons were prone to utter in the salad days of their affairs. Far beyond the casual meetings, affairs, sharings, puppy-loves, however intense the sexual desire that went with them was. *Dhof* was a serious thing, neither done nor said lightly. There were obligations. . . .

Krisshantem asked, "Who sent you to me here?"

"The Perwathwiy Srith, hetman of Dragonfly Lodge, presented us with a commission to locate Maellenkleth or determine her fate. I went to her *yos*. Klervondaf recommended me to you." Morlenden added as tactfully as he could, "Although he was not overly fond of so doing."

The words seemed to make no impression on the stony face before him. "She is not here," Krisshantem said after a long pause.

Morlenden also paused, trying to synchronize somehow with the boy. He said, after a time, "Where is she?"

"Outside. Had you not guessed by now?"

"I suspected. Do you speak from knowledge?"

"Just so, no more."

"Will she return?"

"I think not . . . no."

Morlenden persisted. The replies were coming a little faster, now, reluctantly to be sure, but faster, as if the act of conversing were warming up some little-used mechanism somewhere deep within the boy. "Could you find her?"

". . . No. I do not know where to go, outside, in the human world. I do not know the texture of it. If I went, I would enmesh myself more deeply than was Maellenkleth. I do not think I could bring her back."

Morlenden breathed deeply. *What a mess to stumble through! The hetman says nothing. The outsibling evades. The younger outsibling worships. And the lover is stunned and withdrawn, waiting here in the deep forest for that which he knows will never come back. . . . Nothing.* Outside! The whole planet Earth, Manhome, teeming with billions, miles and miles of cities, labyrinths, procedural jungles of the mind of which they collectively knew nothing. She could be anywhere, and the closer he came to the flesh-and-blood body of the girl he sought, the more invisible she became. And the more crucial she seemed, but to what? *What was this*

thing, and why was everyone associated with her so much . . . such a . . .
Morlenden searched frantically for a word. *Yes. Basket-case.*

Krisshantem sensed some of Morlenden's exasperation, and volunteered, carefully neutral, "You intend to go out, then? For her?"

Morlenden felt some tentative stirrings of hope. He said, carefully,
"Yes. We hold just such a commission. We will honor it. My word as
Toorh, with that of my insibling and co-spouse Fellirian. But it is not an
easy thing, and it promises to get harder, Krisshantem, for I have found
so far in my studies that this simple girl, this didh-Srith, hardly older
than the *Nerh* of my own children's Braid, is an enigma greater than the
Braid of the Hulens or the passings of a certain outcast boy."

Krisshantem smiled faintly, but unmistakably. "I agree, Ser and Kadh
Deren. Aelekle was full of destiny, as we have said, she and I. And others. Fate walked arm and arm with her and conversed with her daily. I
do not know the substance of these conversations. But the Hulens? Myself? I am no mystery; I am as plain and obvious as weather. I live deep
in the woods and partake of its essences."

"You are quieter in the day than a good thief in the night." Morlenden
recalled the tale of Plindestier, of followers and silent listeners under the
curve of the *yos* . . . someone woodswise and crafty. The thought submerged before it could emerge clearly. Morlenden thought, *No, not this
one. He'd not sneak and lurk under* yos-*curves, listening at the doorway,
and slipping off. No This one Plindestier would never have seen.*

"I can teach you tree-ness in a day; it is nothing."

"But the girl; I cannot know where to pick up her trail outside until
I discover what she was. And no one will tell me."

The boy looked sharply away from Morlenden, now attending to the
distances, into the background of naked beech-limbs, the tracery of
branches and twigs, of curdling buttermilk skies, as if weighing, calculating something obtuse and difficult, amorphic and ineluctable. A
truth, they might say, that could be approached only along a ladder of
parables and enigmas and silent little explosions of enlightenments. He
turned back and fixed Morlenden with a burning gaze that made Morlenden acutely uncomfortable. Something had shifted.

"What is it you wish to know, Ser Deren?"

"Everything you can tell me, will tell me. We must know what we are
going into."

"Of course. Everything I can. And there is much. Some things I know,
others . . . I know not. But all of them alike, one and all, you and I will
explore and project from. We will listen to the voices of the night. Will

you do thus with me in a treehouse far in the forest? Otherwise we shall have to seek shelter for you with the Hulen guesthouse, and it is far."

"I would not wish to walk so far, but I will sleep in a treehouse. I have not done so since I was a buck."

Krisshantem nodded, vigorously now. "Come along, then. Follow me as you may." And Krisshantem turned and began walking up the stream-valley, silently, not looking back to see if Morlenden was coming along. They did not speak again until they had reached, much later, their destination.

TEN

Tragedy is intimately associated with freedom; we only find its depiction in art by people who experience it. Collectivists, when moved to emotion at all, prefer to substitute disasters and calamities, which invariably and inexorably "happen" to masses, multitudes, and other assemblies of crowds. Tragedies, on the other hand, are just as invariably caused by individuals, and so felt by other individuals.

Freedom is a most interesting subject; it must, in the bizarre systematology of basic ideas stretched to the breaking point, include the freedom to choose to be free of freedom.

To avoid the responsibility for complete study at the initiation of a plan guarantees that blame must be found for its unavoidable failure in the end.

—M. A. F., Atropine

IT WAS considerably farther than Morlenden had anticipated to the treehouse; he walked, or trudged, now, along behind Krisshantem, growing weary as the distances unreeled behind them. The boy did not seem to hurry, but his progress was steady and covered ground at a rate Morlenden found somewhat exerting. He himself was no slouch at walking, and had made many a distance run himself, but here the effort was beginning to tell on him; he was, in a word, tired. And Krisshantem moved on through the seemingly endless forest of beech and ironwood silently and unhurrying, while the shadows softened and lengthened, and what blue remained in the sky deepened in color; the western sky, which was behind them, grew pastel bright and full of colored veils. The boy made no sound in the fallen leaves, crackled no twigs, left no mark at all of his passage. Morlenden was embarrassed, knowing that to Krisshantem's acute hearing, his own passage must sound like that of a wild bull, breaking through the leaves behind the boy. No wonder Kris never looked back—he could follow Morlenden's passage easily enough just by listening.

At last, they reached the treehouse, with evening close upon them, full night only moments away. Krisshantem did not hesitate, but went straight to the rope ladder extending out of the house and climbed within. Morlenden had been expecting something rude and unsubstantial, a shanty stuck willy-nilly in the crotch of a tree—but it was, as he watched Kris climb, an impressive, solid structure, built with an eye for endurance and resistance to stresses, carefully braced in an ancient, stolid beech. Far from appearing tacked on, it seemed to be so much an integral part of the tree and the surrounding forest that one could easily overlook it. He was sure that it was nearly invisible in the summer with the leaves to shield it and break its outlines.

They reached the inside by means of a crude rope ladder, which Morlenden found exacting and difficult to climb, something he had not the practice for. But once inside, any suspicion that the treehouse could have been crude vanished entirely. It was sparse inside, but comfortable and roomy. Rather like a combined hearthroom and sleeper, but instead of a hearth, there was an ancient iron stove, a wood-burner. A human artifact, from the days long ago. He assumed that they had found it nearby, for it seemed so heavy and massive that they couldn't have dragged it very far on muscle alone.

After lighting several lamps, Krisshantem reached into a locker and produced a couple of freshly killed squirrels, already gutted, dressed, ready for cooking. These he put into a pot, along with some potatoes and onions from another pantry, and threw in a couple of suspicious red peppers for good measure. Then he went to work on a fire, and within a short time, had a fire going, the stew cooking, and some of the edge began to come off the cold.

Now warming, they both removed their heavy winter overcloaks and sat on the floor silently, relaxing. Morlenden offered no words. The boy seemed tired and drawn as well, as if he had come a great distance, for the coldness of the treehouse suggested that it had been untenanted for something more than a day. Krisshantem offered nothing, apparently deeply immersed in some private inner reverie whose boundaries only he knew. Morlenden did not interrupt him, and so they sat for a considerable time, in silence. But at last Krisshantem looked up, directly at Morlenden, with that same disturbingly intent gaze he had seen before.

This time, the glance did not waver, but stayed; Morlenden found the sudden intense attention disconcerting.

"Ser Deren, you will wonder the reasons for my silence?"

"Yes."

The boy looked out the window, a real glass window, not one of the travertine panes they favored for *yos* windows, deep into the north and west. Only a hint of color remained in those skies, a deep far-violet; otherwise, it was night. "I was setting an image straight," he began, "making it just right in my mind, for a Multispeech transferal to you. Can you read such an image if I send in the visual-mode?"

"Indeed I can receive, and have the readiness for it. But tell me, where does one such as yourself learn the fine arts of Multispeech?" Morlenden felt apprehension over the voluntary submission in the will during reception of Multispeech, and wished to make the boy a little defensive before he gave up to him.

A light flared in the boy's eyes, then dimmed. But did not go out. "I learn well. Many things, from such as will instruct me. But it is good that you elect to receive and I to send, for thereby you will at least be able to say then that you know more than just a name."

Morlenden said, "Before I set out on this journey, my insibling said that she could send an image, but that it would be one weak and blurred. I had hoped to find a good one, with those who knew Maellenkleth well."

"And so it shall be, Ser Deren! You will see, as I did, with the eyes of my mind . . . are you indeed prepared to see-in-*perdeskris*?"

Morlenden felt the intimidation behind the words, but nodded, tense, apprehensive, yet nonetheless determined to go ahead with this . . . not without misgivings. Multispeech had many modes, many aspects. One was the direct transmission of an image direct from one mind to another, in which the medium of transmission was a kind of speech, voice, sound. But it was speech that far transcended the normal linear coding and sorting aspects of traditional language, language as the humans had known it, language as the simpler Singlespeech was structured.

In single-channel language, the signal was broad-band, a fingerprint pattern of bands of harmonic tones, shifting frequency slightly, the whole pattern being broken from time to time by sharp clicks, drops, and hisses and combinations thereof: vowels and consonants, former and latter. But in Multispeech, the harmonic bands were individually controlled, and the breaks in tone came separately in each separate band; only with intense concentration would it normally work at all, for there was no instinct for it: it was all learned. And on the part of the receiver, total submission. This was the part of it Morlenden liked least, this sense of losing control, of giving in to another's will. In the past, he and Fellirian had played with it, experimented, but they were both unskilled, and in any event, uninterested in it. It was nice that the people had this ability, he had thought many times; still, they didn't need it in their *klanrolh* . . . or did they? Well, in any event, there was as yet no suitable method of writing it. Or were they truly primitive . . . and was Multispeech their true communicative way? And this one, this *hifzer* Krisshantem, was reputedly a master of it.

The boy sat across the room from Morlenden, hidden a bit in the patterns of shadow and lamplight, wrapped in his long overshirt, a plain but much-mended *pleth* without decoration. In his hand he held a small, pale stick or wand, and with this he began tapping regularly, slowly, on the platted flooring before himself; simultaneously beginning a slow rocking motion with his body. Morlenden shut his eyes, instinctively, to concentrate on the sound, even though he knew well enough that if they did establish contact, he would be blind while he was receiving; Multispeech in certain modes overrode and cut out the visual centers, programming routing from the ears into the visual cortex instead.

. . . he heard the night sounds of the forest and a nearby creek; he heard the rustling, blurry noises of a hardwood fire, the hiss and bubble of the pot. He heard the musing of a weak breeze outside which had come up, microturbulences as it flowed through the limbs and branches and branchlets and terminal twigs . . . each tree had its own sound in the wind. Each individual tree as well . . . there were those who had made an art of tree-listening and claimed to recognize individuals blindfolded. He heard the creaks and stress-shifts of the treehouse, as it moved in tune with the tree of which it had become a part. And he heard tapping, tapping, some where far off, somewhere near.

He heard the tapping of the wand, and under it, a monotonous, repetitive humming, a droning, like the melody of a song such as a forgetty might make up, simplistic, iterative, recurved inward upon itself, simple, over and over again; yet when one tried to listen to it . . . Morlenden found it full of sudden shifts and changes, permutations which had not been there before; unseen, unheard. Shifts in key, subtle changes in rhythm, damned subtle when he first noticed, and then getting harder to hear; he had to concentrate deeper on it, trying to anticipate, to find the key to the order of the changes. That was the way of it. Now listening very closely, Morlenden observed, half aware of it, that he thought he could perceive not a tone, but a harmony now opening up; two melodies, perhaps more—yes, there were three, four, five and

THERE he had it, grasped it an instant, lost in as fast, but now he knew it was easier to pick up the thread, follow the changes, feel the coming shifts, and he always had more than one thread of it. The first step, the first linking between himself and the boy Krisshantem. Odd, odd, it was like monocular vision, or an ear blocked; something was trying to form in his visual center, vague, shapeless, a lump, a nothing, a blur, not-yet-ness. Morlenden began to hum the aimless tune along with the boy, tapping with his fingers, picking up the melody, the rhythm, the changes, the shifts, hoping the feedbacks would let Kris know he really was trying, despite his distaste of it, really trying to reach for it, and

NOW NOW NOW and the sensation of sound blew out like an impossible implosion and Morlenden felt himself grasped, in utter silence, by a monster raw will-force, pure aspect stripped of its vehicle, the body-person, an enormity, a formless pulsing power that was reaching deeply into his innermost mind, imposing, dominating. He felt sudden panic, raw fear, madness, lust to break this web of Multispeech and run screaming out into the night. But it was too late. He had achieved empathy and synchronization with Krisshantem, via the aimless little forgetty song, and there was no escaping, no running, no avoiding. They were not completely separated in their minds, now.

Morlenden's memory flickered out, was gone, never had been. In its place was nothing. Immediately the vision started. At first it was dim and vague, but also somehow definite. In one moment, it had not been there; and the next it was there, as if it had always been there, clear as his own memory, and oddly offset. He could see it taking shape out of blurred nothingness, but as yet he could not "look" directly at it or any of its parts. Swiftly, now, the image, blurred and vague, began to brighten, to sharpen, to become detailed. Contrast improved. Blurs and shadows shaped themselves. The resolution improved. The holistic pattern of a Multispeech visual was working, forming like a hologram, the process making an image whole in two dimensions with the suggested dimensionality of parallax, just as Kris had seen originally, and remembered. The image was not built up of lines and dots; the time factor controlled how clear it became, as area worked in a hologram. The more Morlenden received, the clearer it became, and the more directly he could see it. The pressure increased from the will outside himself.

Now she was clear enough to see . . . it was a girl, here, in this place, this treehouse, sitting in a beam of sunlight that had passed through the window . . . smiling warmly, and almost nude, her legs folded to one side under her hips, toward him. She was wearing the dhwef, a long-tailed, embroidered loinclothlike strip, held on her narrow hips by a belt of wooden beads. She was turned slightly, her left side toward him. It had been summer; something of the flat tone to the light falling on her body, the warm, tanned tone of her skin. The image brightened and clarified. So this was Maellenkleth, the First-player who was lost. She matched very well the words he had heard to describe her, but in this case, as with all the rest, the words had not matched the reality very well. She was lovely—Morlenden, now seeing with his own memory-eyes, felt his heartbeat speed a little, recalling the days of his own adolescence, how she would have seemed to him *then*, when he was a buck, how he would have responded to her. She was rare and exquisite, half of the perfect, taut body, lean and muscular, and half of the imperious will that animated it, filled those comely limbs with life and will.

Now Morlenden had a living memory of the girl, in this image of her identical with Krisshantem's own memory of her. It was so detailed, he could see-remember a tiny mole under her left breast, see-remember a light sheen of perspiration on her forehead, her collarbone, see-remember a soft youthful bloom along the skin of her ankles, a healed scratch on her knee. Her face narrowed down to a finely structured, delicate chin. Her nose was small, narrow, her lips soft, not quite full, slightly pursed. Her eyes were clear, not deep-set, open in their expression. There was determination and innocence in her every gesture, arrested here in midflight, but there was also a sweet, open smile forming on her mouth, too. Enchanting . . . Morlenden felt himself both voyeur and burglar, despite that he was being given this, for he would always now carry the memory of that smile, its slight adolescent awkwardness and shy offering, and know that it had not been directed at him, though it seemed so. . . . Visuals were a cheat.

The image had long since ceased to become clearer, and now Morlenden felt at last that it was over. He relaxed, anticipating the moment when Krisshantem would release him and he would fall out of this reception-self. The pressure increased, became greater, painful, excruciating, making him wince, feel fear now, and the image faded, faded, became gray, blurred, indistinct, even though he could remember it well enough. It was what was being sent. That image faded, vanished. Nothing replaced it. There was darkness and void. Suddenly a series of ideas flashed directly across his imagination: *So you woven scum think a* hifzer *shouldn't learn your precious multispeech, do you? Then watch this elder-to-be, and learn how well one such as I learned his lessons.* The concepts were as if shouted by many Krisshantems, all at once, echoing and bouncing and multiplying, feeding back and forth across one another, feeding back upon themselves until Morlenden's whole mind reverberated with them. Then he went totally blank, aware only that something was being put into him, bypassing his conscious mind altogether—he would know-remember it later, but not now. Instruction-mode. Raw data. He knew something was happening to him, but he couldn't reach it.

Then he was aware that he was not receiving anymore, that time was passing again, that the presence had withdrawn, that the will which had gripped him with a force he could not have broken had faded away without notice. He was himself, sitting in a treehouse, now warm, smelling squirrel stew. He opened his eyes; Krisshantem was no longer sitting, tapping, humming the monotonous melody, but instead was casually stirring the stew with the wand. Morlenden did not know how much time had passed, nor how long the process had been stopped. He felt shaken, light-headed. Afraid to move. He remembered Maellen-kleth, as if she had been his own then; yet it was not then, in that summer, but was here, moments ago . . . and something else; he remembered the Game. Morlenden touched the memory of the data, stuffed into his mind raw, without referent. Yes, it was all there, the Outer Game, what Krisshantem knew of it, stripped to essentials, his mind filled with strategy and tactics, millions of rules and configurations; one could wander there forever, bemused. He put it away. He wanted to inspect this curious new learning another time. He cleared his throat. Kris looked up at him, blandly, matter-of-factly, as if nothing at all had happened.

Kris asked casually, "Did you get it all?"

"Indeed I did; completely. . . ."

"I thought as much. I stopped augmenting the image of Maellenkleth when I sensed from your feedback that you had most of it. First it's slow, then it comes fast, then slow again . . . it never quite reaches an exact copy. Not much good going on indefinitely, although I suppose one could. Pardon the intrusion, but I sensed doubt. You have doubtless realized that you are now as I in knowledge of the Game. That will save us much talk."

"I had no idea you would be able . . . How much of that did Maellen teach you?"

"I knew some before. Not very much. Most of it came from her. I would have to know all modes to sit with her in the citadel of the Inner

Game, which at present I know not. Nor you. I have some ideas on it, for one can always project from the data at hand, but, frankly, some of the conjectures I have imagined are so odd or perhaps outrageous that I have not pursued it far, thinking it had to be wrong."

"I remember it now, but I have not thought on what I have newly learned, whether I wished to know or not. How long was I under that?"

"There is, they say, no time in Multispeech . . . I have no idea, but the stew is done. I have heard some elders say that the universe waits until one is finished. However, I remain skeptical there, for to the stew you may add the datum that there is no more light yonder westward. Perhaps the stars have more imagination than the average elder. Those are her words as well."

"You are too good at it. I think I shall not allow that again," Morlenden said without heat, stating a fact.

"I will not try again, although I must tell you that there is a variant of Command-mode which insibling Players must learn, Command-override, which does not require permission, or even knowledge of it on the part of the receiver. . . . Mael taught it to me, and it is a fearsome thing I will not use. But you may meet others not so restrained as I in your travels."

Morlenden was aghast. "But how can I protect myself?"

"No way. If you are of the people, you are susceptible. You can't even autoforget out of it, that is why they restrict its teaching . . . it's very hard to do right. I can't teach it to you. As I said, it's difficult. Mael taught me only part of it. I didn't use override on you. I am sorry I was angry; you chose not your position, as neither did I. But I suggest you get someone to teach it to you—you can at least strive with one who would use it."

"Who would try?"

"I don't know. But you get it all only in the Inner Game. But I am but a novice, one who sits at the feet of the great who deign to lend their arcane skills. I am not so good as you may think; instruction I can do; Maellen who was Aelekle to me and me alone I can easily do. . . . Obviously, for I knew her many ways. I knew her as a lover, and as a student of her wisdom. Random images are harder, abstract ones still more so. But should you wish another demonstration, I can now send you a picture of yourself, as I have seen you. . . ."

"Myself through another's eyes? Thank you, no. I must refuse. Please leave me my illusions and memories of the way things were. I should then no longer be able to imagine myself a buck like yourself. I know very well that I-now-Morlenden possess a potbelly from overindulgence at too many weaving-parties. Nevertheless I prefer to imagine myself a svelte youngster, lean and mean."

"Ha!" Krisshantem smiled at that. It was the first time Morlenden had seen him do so. And inside himself, he forgave the intrusion. He had in part asked for it. He was thankful this wild boy knew no more than he did.

During the meal—the stew turned out well despite Kris's heavy hand with the red pepper—they did not speak, but ate in silence, Morlenden was hungry, for he had walked far in two days and had eaten little, save pathway-food, cold meals packed to be eaten along the way. This was the first real honest meal he'd had since leaving home. Krisshantem, too, ate quietly, with a self-possession and attention to the present that surprised Morlenden. After all, it was beginning to be more than merely apparent that Kris had lost Maellen, to accident, not the usual cause of such separations, and he was only barely older than Morlenden and Fellirian's own Pethmirvin. But where Peth was still very much a child at fifteen, for all her busy sexuality, this boy was something more than the usual adult.

Finishing, Kris went to the pantry, returning by way of the stove, pausing, and producing along the way an infusion of the ubiquitous root-tea, then returning and settling back in his place, folding his legs under himself after the mannerism of a tailor, or perhaps a rug-maker.

Morlenden cleaned the remainder in his bowl with the last crust of bread, observing, "You cook well, indeed. I would become the fatted calf in your house."

Kris answered pleasantly, "Not so. When the cook is good, one uses him less . . . once a day or less."

Morlenden sipped his tea, looking at the boy from over the edge of his mug. The pleasantries were now over, and the introductions finished, the measures taken. He began, reaching with the words, "You are, so I have observed, a cool one for one who has been along the ways of *dhofterie*. . . . I should have thought you more, well, apprehensive about the whereabouts of Maellenkleth."

"My apprehensions are real enough, for all that I refrain from displaying them publicly like yesterday's unwashed laundry. They are, of course, much as you might suspect, perhaps more. But they do not, translated into the here and now, have much of an effect upon the na-

ture and course of things. However strong they are." He looked away
and did not meet Morlenden's glance.

"Have you thought of going after her yourself?" Gently, here.

"No. She told me specifically that not under any circumstance should
I come after her should she fail to appear. She felt about her little expeditions that if she ever got herself into something that she couldn't
handle, no one else would be able to do it for her, and it would be just
throwing good people to waste after bad."

"We are edging into it. Shouldn't we start at the beginning?"

Kris answered, "Start at the beginning, start at the end, or in the middle; in a well-lived story it makes no difference. Does not everything
lead to something else?"

Morlenden replied, "True, but for all the sophistry, the accipter flies
not backward to present life put of its beak and talons to the Lago-
morph."

"Hawk and hare . . . you are correct. I have been rude. You know that
I do not wish to face this; that is the way of the words."

"I know these things and walk with you, though I may not now face
them myself, in my own life. Once I had a lover. . . ."

Kris mused, "We never know what we will face and what we will
not . . . let me caution you of that at least."

The remark rang oddly in Morlenden's mind. Not that its truth was
in question, but that it sounded oddly prophetic after the manner of oracles; ambiguous, indefinable, unknowable as the dream-that-predicts.
Until the moment came. What did this woodsman know?

Kris continued, "But, still, I would tell it my own way. Time clouds
things, masks significances. You will want what I have, to add to what
you already know or suspect."

Morlenden laughed. "Then say on as you will, for what I have is precious little enough." He sipped at the tea again. It was still almost too
hot to drink properly.

"This time," he began hesitantly, "was to be her last venture outside.
Yes, there were other ventures. Many of them. I do not know where she
went, or what she did. But they were all short, never more than a few
days. But she said that before we met there had been some longer
ones . . . months, seasons."

"Maellenkleth was outside for a season? Three months?"

"Yes, among the forerunners the whole time, and they knew it not."

"Clandestinely? Where could she go for so long?"

"She would not speak of it any more than the others. Save once . . .

she said in a mood of reminiscence, 'The humans said long ago that God created the universe in seven days, yet just now have I been to a place where the creation is still going on. And if that be true, perhaps their god still lives and works in that place.' I know not where it was, nor would she say, in the sense of how to get there. I saw, in *deskris*, as she sent, and she said that there would be a place like that for us someday. I said, 'Would we go there and live, us, out of our little land?' and she became suddenly sad and said no, not there, never. I saw it, but never *where* in relation to anywhere else: there was a dark sea, salt water, there were rocky beaches, cliffs, brown mountains, that ran in rippling waves above the waters and plunged into them at their northern ends. The sun set into the sea. No one lives there. It is free and open, but now empty. She said that once, long ago, they came there to be cured, to be healed, but that now no one will even walk in it, or pass near it."

"A human *sfanian*, a place of healing?"

"I would not have thought it, but I am blind to many of their ways."

"Just so am I. . . . But the last time she went outside: it was important?"

"Yes, very much so. She could refuse, but she would not. She could not let it go."

"Did she say what she was to do?"

"She was to break two machines no longer in use."

"Absurd! Perhaps if they were in use, but otherwise . . ."

"They—those with whom Mael spoke—were worried that if these things, still operable, were used, then the Forerunners would be able to see something they must not know before their time. That none of us could know until we were prepared. They could make more of these machines, but they wouldn't be so good, and by then it wouldn't make any difference."

"Did she not realize that destroying them would point a finger at the very thing she wished hidden?"

"I asked her the same question. She shook her head, saying that she knew. That all that had been considered, but she still had to go."

"I cannot imagine it. What was the secret?"

"Believe me when I say that I never learned it. I know the ways of trees, I listen to the speech of the waters, I have learned to watch the clouds move and permutate, I can slow time for myself until the sun whirls across the sky. I have mastered the silences. But I could neither get it from her, however else she gave freely, nor see it in her. Maellenkleth was indeed of the aspect of *Sanh*, the Water, but something in her was harder than the finest steel, and her mind was a mirror, as are those of all *Sanmanon*. She received instructions, and she obeyed them, whatever distaste she herself felt."

"The faithful soldier."

"I think that she liked some of it."

"Hm!" Morlenden snorted. "Instructions from whom? The Perwathwiy and her elders of Dragonfly Lodge?"

"Oh, no. Not from those, or perhaps not directly. Mael worked not for the elders, and in fact she held them in some contempt, for they were so willing to let the Perklarens go without a ripple. She took her instruction from Sanjirmil. Do you know such a one?"

Morlenden's mind stopped short, as if he had suddenly walked into a wall. "Sanjirmil? The Terklaren?"

"There can only be one, as custom allows." It was a pointed reproof. Morlenden of all people should know there could only be one living Sanjirmil. He looked away for a time, and said quietly, "I know her. Or thought I did." Morlenden thought deeply, unable to complete the import of it. Sanjirmil, who came in the night with the Perwathwiy. Sanjirmil who kept secrets at thirteen. Sanjirmil who was an arch-rival, and a co-plotter in something . . . and they were all operating something under the Game called the Inner Game. What had he walked or stumbled into? What devil's work were he and Fellirian doing, and in reality, for whom? And what cause was he taking up almost by accident, as he followed Maellenkleth's path, finishing her business? He left it. There was not enough yet.

He said, "Tell me about your weaving with her. How was that to be arranged?"

Kris answered, "We met and became lovers by accident. Indeed. I am Air aspect. It became more than casual, and she found that I could do certain things, things she gave value to. She offered to me, and I accepted. That is not so hard. Imagine, me becoming a *shartoorhosi* player of the great Game! But once I learned it, I felt it odd and . . . unfinished, and I thought of the flow of the life I have learned in the forest and visions of the sky. Very odd, those two."

"Odd? Why?"

"Because at first the two seem so different, but from a certain level of awareness they are much the same thing."

"I know. The wise say that there is only one reality, and that we catch only glimpses of it. The mad are so because they cannot turn away from it; but they also cannot live in it. They are pulled apart. And that categories are errors caused by the degree of imperfection; the more highly categorized, the greater the degree of imperfection. But the universe is one."

"Spoken like a Gameplayer, Ser Deren!" Krisshantem exclaimed. "But for all that," he continued soberly, "we imperfections must live on a workaday world, where there are, after all, categories, divisions, classifications."

"There is always, in any good list, a sort called 'other.' "

"Thus the Game as well. I had always thought of it, when I reflected on it, as a kind of manipulation, but as I learned more from Maellen-Aelekle, I saw that it was also a very curious way of looking at a process of perception, to perceive small detail and large overview simultaneously. Perception!"

"All games are that in part."

"But this one more so."

"I know that Maellen was a player of the First-players. A good one, indeed. Which came first—was it that she was to rebuild because she found you, or were you the last part of a larger plan?"

Kris answered without heat or offense, "We came first. She had thought of it before, but never seriously. She went for it long after we met. She did not use me, nor was there trade—legitimacy for becoming a Noble Player. In fact, she thought of taking the Inner Game by storm. It was rather impractical . . . the one we could have done in time, but the other would have been death for both of us; Maellen had many enemies."

"To start a new Braid would require the permission of the Revens. And I know that they do not grant that lightly, even to the simplest of farmer Braids. And to Gameplayers? When the community of the Players, past, present, and future, was allowing the Perklarens to end, just like that, without a whimper of protest—including the Perklaren parents themselves?"

"It sounded fantastic to me as well, when we talked and plotted of it, here, in this very place where sit you and I. But not impossible. I said she had enemies; she also had powerful friends. There was something about a check upon Sanjirmil, which both Pellandrey Reven and the Perwathwiy had come to. I think that they came to regret the decision to let the Perklarens go, after it was too late and they were committed. The others had a stake in it, and wanted things left as they had been committed to. Still, one must train for the real Game. That which I gave you in instruction-mode is nothing, just the basic foundation. It is not something most have any talent for. In fact, Maellenkleth was the only one anyone ever heard of who had a real talent for it. And, of course, the Terklarens were rather violently against it. They said that the work of two Player Braids was done," He paused, and then added cryptically, "Whatever that work really was."

"So, then; attend. You are now, for all intents, a Player, if somewhat unauthorized and unpermitted. Why would Pellandrey wish Sanjirmil counterweighted?"

"Hard to explain, Ser Deren. As a Player, now, I see things I could not realize before. There are many revelations therein. Now Sanjirmil, she's competent enough in the Game, I suppose, but there's no style to her. It's like swimming or dancing or making love or just good old *dhainaz* . . . there's a sense of flow, motion, style. Dynamics. Maellenkleth's Inner Game names among the masters were Korh, crow, and Brodh, otter. But Sanjirmil has no grace, no style. After all, she knows well enough that at fertility she'll be the Terklaren. Perhaps I should say the Klaren."

"I know. She is very strong-willed."

"I know not how you know her, but I know her in the Game; strong-willed is not the word. She is fierce and dominant. The masters call her Slansovh, Tiger-owl, and Hifshah, the Werewolf. She is Fire aspect. Her Braidmates, co-spouses, follow her implicitly. They are already woven."

"Woven?" Morlenden exclaimed. "Why, they aren't fertile yet, none of them!"

"None the less, it is so. She already has them trained. All four of them. The Revens know, the Perwathwiy knows. And had things gone as Maellen and I had hoped and dreamed, so would it have been with her and me and two others I do not know."

Morlenden sighed. "And we, the poor Derens who must register such things, are the last to be informed. I have never heard of such a thing, even among the Revens. Do they live together?"

"Indeed. The old Terklarens have already left, and joined Dragonfly Lodge; with the Perklarens. Once enemies, now uneasy allies."

Morlenden interjected, "Against two romantics."

Krisshantem said, with great dignity, "I assure you there was nothing of the sort in it. There I know Maellen well. There was more than desperation in her plan; rather, an urgent sense of necessity." He paused momentarily. "Maellen was very concerned about this preweaving of the younger Terklarens; for, despite the radical air which she may have projected, she was in fact very traditionalist-minded, very conservative. Her view of this was that is was stealing what you already possess, in the person of Sanjirmil, which is as you may know one of the omens not desirable to be seen. And so her idea was that with practice, and constant pressure on them, we could eventually win it all back and recover the rightful order of things. But however much she showed me of the Game, she always left something out; I sensed deeper purpose in it, but it remained behind the veil—within an inner adytum into which I was not yet permitted. And she did obey the Law of the Game, thus. I put together that there was to be an initiation in a cave somewhere near or on the Mountain of Madness, but only Pellandrey could permit it—or, in my case, perform it. And she said, 'not for love, not for *dhof*, not for all the sweetness we have shared, will I initiate you until they say I can. It is something more than I can give of my own desire.' "

"Even in *dhof*? She spoke exactly thus?"

"Aye, even in *dhof*, just so, Ser Deren."

"So now—what could it have been?"

"There I am lost, blind. Yes, with all that I can do of my own added to all that she gave me, it is still *ankavemosi*, that which is concealed. 'You cannot get there from here.' It is unprojectable; the knowledge of the Outer Game is both insufficient data and a program of misdirection as well. But now you are a Player just as I . . . everything varies in it, even the dimensional matrix. Those were the kind of games that Maellenkleth liked best. Because Sanjirmil falls upon her fundament within the higher-order Games. And Mael said, 'Present Sanjir-Dear with a matrix higher than four-dimensional and she can't tell her own arse from a knot-hole in a plank.' As unskilled as I was, I could see that from the plays I saw her make. But the lower-order Games she could handle well enough: crude, but very effective—her Game plans are heavy-handed, brute-force assaults. There is a feeling of destruction about her maneuvering."

"I believe," said Morlenden.

"When she faces a problem, she burns her way out. Power, raw imposition of order. Maellen, of the other thumb, plays a delicate, laughing Game . . . artful, skillful, balanced. To follow her Games is to experience the wind and the water, to know sailing and flight and the surge and rush of the mounting wave of the sea."

"I have the idea," said Morlenden, "that much seems to be focused in these two . . . Braid traditions as well as what they may differ among themselves."

"Indeed, indeed, both. Their natures, their talents and abilities, the force of the traditions of both Braids. That was why two Player Braids were established in the beginning—that each should explore different aspects of approach to the Game, substance and style. Another battle in the eternal war between harmony and invention. We must have both elements. And you must not think that Sanjirmil was of necessity at a disadvantage for her lesser talent in the Game. She had other abilities . . . the majority would follow her, within the Game, and she has power under those closest to her; lust, hope, and fear. She is dangerous."

"But they work together!"

"They have no choice. Sanjirmil is forbidden to leave the reservation as the Master-Player-to-be; yet there is much, so they say, to do outside. Sanjir is responsible for the work outside, and has only Maellen to send. And before Mael and I met, she had little else to do, anyway. And in that aspect, they do treat one another correctly, if somewhat coldly. Sanjir has now the power, the authority, Maellen has much valor. It has been so since Mevlannen determined to go out."

"Nevertheless, Maellenkleth sounds determined herself, to go so far against the will of so many."

"Determined? Yes, she was so. But she was also gentle of speech and manner in all things, save the subject of Sanjirmil, about which she could surpass a bargeman in vulgarity. . . ." And here Krisshantem looked abstracted a moment, as if recalling something, setting a tangled web of data straight, things he had assembled piecemeal over the months. "They made the decision to let the Perklarens terminate and unravel when Mevlannen was born. She is younger-insibling. Sanjir was about ten, then. And later, something like five years, I don't know exactly, something happened to Sanjirmil . . . something of the Inner Game that none will speak of save in whispers. Not an accident, but as if something happened too soon . . . there is something about timing of certain events in the Inner Game. At any rate, from then Sanjir became ever more ungovernable and wild. Fey, arrogant. And she became conscious of what she had won, and that she had won it not by valor or skill but default. The Terklarens had always been the underlings. Now time was helping her, and all she had to do was wait and her traditional enemies would be gone. But it wasn't enough—she wanted to win it. She was hungry. Some of the elders became regretful of their earlier decision, but by the time enough had spoken for action, the years had passed and Mevlannen had determined to go out. And when Mael and I had become lovers, she was spending most of her time inside in meditation, trying to free herself of the hold of it . . . because once you play the Game, there is nothing else that will satisfy you. Truly it is a most dangerous and addictive poison, even though it illuminates."

Kris continued and Morlenden listened to every word now, trying to pick up the threads of this tale. "We toyed with it, and I surprised her with my response to it; we traded. I taught her how I learn in the forest, from weather-watching, from trying to see the wind . . . you can, you know. It is hard, but one can. It flowed both ways. And she began to have hope again, and began to act again. We met Pellandrey once in the woods north of the Mountain of Madness and she spoke plainly of what she was doing. Then came interminable interrogations by the Past Masters. They called Mael names, they insulted her. Never mind what they said to me. But some were intrigued, captivated by this new situation, Pellandrey, Perwathwiy, even though she is of Sanjirmil's own line of the Terklaren Braid. Make no mistake: they are all afraid of Sanjirmil, even her supporters. Again the Inner Game and her strength and position in it."

For a moment, an inner fire, an enthusiasm, had risen in the boy's eyes and voice. Now it wavered, at the last, flickered, and went out. He resumed his demeanor of quiet resignation. He sighed deeply, and said, "But we knew however much help we had, it was a lost cause. Less than a year, and Sanjir has everything."

"Aside from her approaching fertility and investiture as senior Player, how so? I don't understand. Could Mael not challenge her later at her own fertility, with you as her *shartoorh* co-spouse."

"No. They let the Perklarens unravel—some say it was caused—because the Inner Game conceals something, and in the middle of Sanjirmil's generation, they will no longer need to conceal it. Whatever the Inner Game is, Sanjirmil will manifest it openly, to the astonishment of all, ler and human alike, and there will be no more Game."

"No more Game, but one Braid of Players remains!"

"Thus. And so that was why Maellen was desperate. It was her whole life, her special talent, and she could not bear to part with it; she would go against them all to keep it, even to seek"—here Kris paused delicately—*sharhifzergan.** She would declare herself so and stay here. We would rebuild it from scratch. Think: the only Player ever born with the inborn gift for it, and by long love of it, she is far and above any Player, living

---

* Perhaps, "honorary bastardhood." In the context of ler society, such an event was considered impossible, the ultimate in undesirability. Maellenkleth would be untouchable to untouchables.

or dead, in skill, in knowledge of its range of subtleties. All that, then, to waste, perhaps spent in the pursuit of excellence in turnips. A Perklaren, who only held the Revens above them."

Morlenden asked, "The other, Mevlannen. What is she to this?"

"They were insiblings without the sexual bond; yet they have always been close, deep into one another. They always met whenever they could, even after Mevlan's work took her to the far places, space itself. There was more to it than two standing together in the storm of troubles; Mevlan was a part of it as well, what they were all doing, in the Inner Game, and in the outside operation."

"I thought Mevlannen was with the humans, working on a telescope in space."

"True. But she also spends a lot of time on the ground. Now when Maellenkleth went out this last time, it was to be her last trip out; and after it there was to be a trip to meet with Mevlan openly, to get something from her. They were all elated, anticipating . . . things were to change. That is all I know of it. I asked, and they all said, *Hvaszan*, Inner Game. I had hoped to learn more. . . ."

Morlenden interrupted. "And so you may yet. Now listen and attend: if Maellen is yet alive, we can get her back. Fellirian is working that end of it. But if she was as deep in secrets as you say she was, and it is as touchy as her own Braid acts, then there must be the possibility that what we will find, if we find her, isn't Maellenkleth anymore."

"You suggest she autoforgot? *Sharhifzergan* she considered, but autoforgetting . . .'"

"I consider it possible, on the basis of what you have told me, and what else I have seen with my own eyes. This last errand outside—if she was taken alive, she would have to protect what she knew . . . and if she would not tell it to you who were her only hope of getting back, then autoforgetting cannot be ruled out. It is distinct."

"Then it would be a task indeed to bring her back, and in the end, nothing in it for me . . . for if she autoforgot, then she is a stranger, an alien. Not Maellenkleth. Her body was sweet and full of life, but that which I loved has gone forever."

"Painful as that is, so it is truth. And now I must ask, who can do a reconstruction in Multispeech, if we bring her? Neither Fellirian nor I have the skill."

Kris mused over the question, pondering imponderables. "A reconstruction? I don't know who does them . . . I can do it, although I never did it before. You can't practice it, you know—it's too dangerous. But I do know how, if only now in theory; it's rather like the Game, in fact it's related. But it's tricky . . . you need two others at minimum to do it. Mael told me how before she left. It was her last gift to me."

"As if she knew she might need it. But why that? She would have known if she autoforgot she wouldn't return. Just the body."

"I don't know."

"But you agree that we have to try to look, and if we find her, bring her back and try to reconstruct something; we owe that to her."

"I owe her more than that."

"So then, the reconstructors you need. How skilled must they be?"

"Only one need be skilled, and the other two only obey . . . are you volunteering?"

"Fellirian and I, yes. She will agree to it. And perhaps she can devise some way that we do it there, so we don't have to carry her back, if we find her. It will solve many problems if she can walk back under her own power. And you have invaded my mind once already; I suppose I can live with it again."

Krisshantem asked, tentatively, "Do you think there is a chance we could regain her?"

"I think that we must be prepared for that, so that we shall if we can. And there is no other place to look. Fellirian is looking into this, even now as we talk, perhaps walking into a trap now set for whoever comes looking for Maellenkleth. But it's worth trying—at least talking with Fellirian."

"Of course, yes."

"Can you come now?"

"Yes. I will. Not with you, but I can meet you at your *yos* on the next day. I had contracted with the Hulens and I must tell them I am not going to deliver."

"And afterward you will meet with us there."

"Yes, I will come. And along the way I will practice, as I walk alone in the forest where no one will hear the spells I cast in Multispeech."

"Are you sure the very rocks will not respond?"

"No, they will not."

"Good!" Morlenden reached across the low table and patted Krisshantem's suddenly tensed hand. "And perhaps we can find out what was going to or coming from Mevlannen Srith Perklaren. But first we find Mael; then bring her back. Then we find out."

"But from whom, Ser Deren? The Perwathwiy?"

"I doubt from her," said Morlenden.

"From the Revens?" asked Kris hopefully.

"Perhaps yet from Maellenkleth herself." And Morlenden added, "She may have left something for us after all. I refuse to believe that a plot so intricate and impervious as this one seems to be would end in a nothing forgetty, a blank tablet."

ELEVEN

The things that really stand out in your memory of the past were, at the time you recorded them, so ordinary and unprepossessing that they were truly unmemorable. Yet the things which you imagined to be stunning and ever-memorable cannot be recalled save as vague blurs, phantoms, mergings, and rubbings. We admit to a problem here: we fail to learn what is significant until its significance and immanence serves no purpose save to haunt us.

—The Game Texts

MORLENDEN AWOKE AS the sunlight was streaming in the window on the east-facing side of the treehouse, into an alcove in which a large and roomy bed-shelf had been fitted into the erratic, form-following structure. A patchwork counterpane, a soft and downy bottom bag. Him between them. Coherence returned slowly. This was the treehouse in the woods, of two adolescents, Krisshantem and Maellenkleth, who had been lovers. And something more . . . allies in a war against an opponent who shifted from day to day and seemed to refuse to be defined. Morlenden blinked and rubbed his eyes, as if that would clear the fog in the inside. Perhaps the lack of definition was in him, not in the boy and girl. Better, perhaps they were all suffering from perceptual problems. The human of Chinese military history, a man whom the people studied often, Sun-tzu, had averred that if one knew his enemy and knew himself, he could not lose. Maellenkleth appeared to have lost; therefore . . . the ler mind, strong in intuition, made the jump for him: she had not known her enemy. And this made his scalp prickle, for he did not know her enemy either, and he himself seemed to be well-committed to a course of making that enemy his enemy.

Their house, their bed. Not like a *yos* at all, with its sense of being above the individual. The *yos* belonged to the standing wave of the

Braid, belonged to time. When their time came, they left it, never to set foot in it, or any other, again. Objects were the artifacts left behind by forms of life. This treehouse was another life-form's artifact . . . something powerful and vital. Different. Alien. It gave him an eerie feeling, like wearing someone else's clothing: they were clean and of the proper size, more or less, but somehow they weren't *right*, they weren't of a piece with one's self.

He and Kris had continued talking long into the night, long past the time either of them usually went to bed. But what they had said between them had added little to what he had already discovered, reasoned, put together. Just details, color, the living texture of two lives which had somehow been tangled together, and which had come undone, for reasons neither of them knew. Details. Morlenden knew that he was the only person Kris had spoken with about Maellenkleth, since she had departed on her last errand, two months ago now. His deep *hifzer* self-sufficiency had not served him well in this at all; his silence and reticence had salved not at all the loss of that which he prized above all things.

Morlenden pushed the counterpane down, stretched, groaning, and allowed the chill air to bite at him, nudging him more awake, his hands behind his head, collecting thoughts. Somewhere outside was a thirsty evil that drank the lives of innocents whose only crime was an excess of zeal. Something outside, in the human world of 2550, which had roots everywhere, within, around them. *She was a natural Player,* he thought, *and their only genuine prodigy born to it, reputed the best they had ever seen in the history of the Game. But she was also playing in another Game, several games, and in those she was just a novice, an amateur, a loser from the start. A Water-aspectual playing in the area of will and discipline. Playing in an area in which unknown persons bent others to their wills.* She went out, she was a spy for someone, perhaps an operative, for Sanjirmil surely, but for who else behind that one? But she didn't like it, she was terrified of it, and on this last mission she even suspected trouble, judging from the preparations she had made, the things she had told Kris. And still she went! *Fools!* Morlenden rolled over to one side, leaning on his elbow disgustedly, pondering innocence. Their innocence, his innocence.

That's the problem with her, me, Kris, he thought, *with us all; we lermen have not known evil. We have always had the luxury of attributing that to the humans. Aye, evil, vice, stupidity. Not for us! We were the New People, the mutants, the ler, we were as innocent as newly fallen snow, trackless and blameless. And what were your sins, Morlenden Deren? That once in your adolescence you refused a plain or homely girl's desire and injured her sensibilities? That you sometimes overcharged for your services as clerk and registrar? That you were sometimes overly fond of your tipple? You are stupid and know almost nothing of that which you have fallen into; into which you will assuredly fall more deeply if you pursue this Maellenkleth to the end.*

He felt apprehensions; yet he also was aware of a powerful current of wrongness, injustice, malice, something even more strange to him—that a person could be brought to nothing, by something no more involved than an idle procedure, or perhaps the blind machinations of a plot that didn't concern her at all. She was just in the way of others, who would not see what she was offering them. No, not that, either. There was malice in it. But from where? Whom? Morlenden looked for the manifestation of a power, an elemental, deep in his intuitive sense, but down there, there was only a sense of shimmering contradiction, a dichotomy. Wrong, wrong. He lacked data. He sat up on the bed-shelf. He had decided something. He felt uneasy about it, for an instant dizzy with fear, but he stuck to it, and presently the queasy feeling faded. It did not vanish, and he suspected that it would be with him for the rest of his life, but still it had subsided to a bearable level of intensity.

Kris had slept on the floor by the stove, offering Morlenden the bed-shelf. Obviously the boy could not have slept very soundly under that counterpane, full-remembering the emotions that had motivated the acts and encounters performed there, himself and Maellenkleth. Morlenden got up, pulling on his overshirt, and climbed down to the lower level of the treehouse where were the stove and the hearthroom, the room they had talked in. The treehouse was silent, empty. There was no sense of presence. Morlenden knew well enough that Krisshantem was a silent one, but not that silent. He looked about. Kris was gone. By the stove there were some hard-boiled eggs, some bread and cheese, and a note. He picked up the note and read what was written therein, lettered in a neat and precise hand.

> *Ser Deren, I kept you up far too late last night, still I had to be on my way. There are provisions for your return trip home. I will be there to meet you in a day or so. I did not tell you this last night, for I would not speak aloud of it, but be warned and full of care. Someone has been about, shadowing us, more likely you, although I do not know why this should be as it seems. I thought to hear traces of them in the night, but they know me, whoever*

*they are, and they know my range and will not approach close
enough for me to identify. At dawn I found a partial trace in the
forest. But I still do not know who. I sense danger here, and know
you have not the wood-sense of those of us who live here. So go
straight to your own holding and do not tarry. I will catch you
as fast as I can. Guard yourself as best as you are able.*

Morlenden read it through, and read it through again, wondering at
the message and pondering over the odd, abrupt choppiness of style, so
unlike the speech of Kris in person. Perhaps he really was apprehensive.
So there were eavesdroppers in the night by the Perklarens, or rather
what was left of them; and a watcher out of range by the treehouse in
the woods, someone who by Kris's own admission was able to move
with skill enough to neutralize his formidable perceptions. Indeed, it did
appear as if someone were following him, watching him. Morlenden did
not seriously consider that the two events were unconnected. Such skill
was rare. He went to the window and looked through it into the forest,
not really knowing what he expected to see. He saw nothing but the
trees, the leaf-strewn forest floor, the bare boles and branches, the shadows of the morning, the sky filming over, hazy, vague. The light held a
pearly, graying, fading quality.

He turned to the food, and, gathering it up into a bundle, arranged
his clothing for the outside air and began to leave the treehouse, opening the trapdoor to let in the air. The air had warmed during the night;
it was not nearly so cold as the day before. Rain coming, the kind that
would go on for days—start as drizzle and end in a mud sticky from the
slow soaking. He thought that he could make it back to the Deren *yos*
before the rain started in earnest, though. He thought, somewhat ominously, that such would be the case, assuming that he didn't meet anyone along the way. On an impulse, he looked about for a weapon,
something he could use, a knife, a bludgeon. There was nothing visible;
and Morlenden had at this point much too great a respect for the inhabitants of this house to rifle through it, looking for a weapon. Which
probably didn't exist in here anyway.

A weapon! Morlenden had walked alone all over the reservation,
sleeping in the open when the weather permitted, and sometimes when
it didn't, working with the rowdiest and the roughest, and unlike Fellirian, had never carried a weapon in his life. Fellirian did. But not him.
He had never thought to need one. Nor for the matter, did Fellirian. But
who could imagine him needing one? Fights he had had, in no shortage,

knee and fist, foot and elbow, lost and won alike in equal measure. Still he carried no weapon. And now there wasn't anything. Morlenden turned to go, feeling uneasy, apprehensive. But also defiant: *So if my enemy is one of us, then let him close with me, face to face, blows on the front! I may be done with love but I can still fight, and I'll thrash his arse!* Morlenden knew that it was poor weaponry, those brash words, but all the same they made him feel better.

Before he left, out the trapdoor and down the ladder, he stepped out on a narrow landing, not large enough to be properly called a porch; just a place to recline on. At the far end, the corner, it widened into a shelf, a little balcony, a place on the west side to catch the setting sun; something he had seen before—but not before . . . he felt an odd sense of déjà vu. He remembered.

The image of Maellenkleth. There had been a pattern of light and shadow about her, and he had assumed it had been from the window, but of course it hadn't been; it had been sunlight falling through the summer foliage. Of course. The image now returned as clear as when Kris had sent it and he saw *her*, as alive as if he had seen her himself. And there was something about her he had not noticed before, dazzled by her youth and beauty.

Not the body or the pose, relaxed, at her ease, the lover's tentative smile-of-invitation playing along the planes of her face, welling out of her eyes; what was it about her eyes? The skin was a warm sun-browned tan-olive, the limbs still slightly awkward, unfinished, adolescent, the hands long and bony, just as Klervondaf had suggested. She had a high forehead, childishly hidden under the bangs she wore her dark hair in, in the front. And the eyes . . . the eyes! That was it! It had been in the eyes! Although the image had not moved, but had been a single instant's slice, still something about the eyes had been disturbingly familiar, and now he could see and integrate it. Morlenden had seen that same abstracted and vacant gaze long ago, in one who spent much of her time and life training herself to see primarily with peripheral vision, the eyes tracking in a pattern to be read out in the visual center, rather than concentrating upon and following a single object. Like Sanjirmil of sixteen years before, only here rather more pronounced. But it had not seemed a handicap at the time to Sanjirmil, nor did it seem so now to Maellenkleth. Of course, they were both Players of the Game *Zan*, and something they did in the Game gave them that peculiar gaze, that fixed, staring abstracted look. Morlenden reflected again: But Kris, taught as a Player, did not have it at all, and in his own inserted memories, he could not find anything that would give rise to it, that it would be so pronounced. It could be only a behavioral artifact of the Inner Game, something neither he nor Krisshantem had ever seen or known!

He turned into the treehouse, climbed through the trapdoor, and descended the ladder to the ground. Morlenden looked about, as best he could, and then set off southwestward, through the empty woods, guessing direction in the frosted, translucent shadowless gray light, carefully watching for signs of company along his trail as he went. That he saw no sign reassured him not at all. For when he and Taskellan had found Krisshantem (or had it been the other way?), Kris had materialized, so it seemed, out of nothing. Perhaps there were others similarly skilled. At least enough to follow him unawares, and stay away from Kris so that the follower could not be identified.

By the afternoon, with the air turned cold again from a wind out of the north with more than a hint of dampness in it, Morlenden faced the conclusion that he was not going to arrive at his own *yos*, or anywhere near it, on this day. By his own internal system of dead reckoning, which he admitted to be in error more often than not, total recall notwithstanding, he thought he was located southeast of the lake district and the Perklarens, and about a day's walk northeast of his home. The area he was now traversing was nowhere as wild as the far northeast, the country of the Hulens, Krisshantem, and apparently few others, but it had still only recently begun to be integrated into the holdings of the reservation Braids and was rather underpopulated. Morlenden knew of few holds in this part, and those which he could remember were nowhere near here, wherever *here* was; he was not exactly sure. He knew only that if he continued in the direction he had been faring, he would eventually strike an area he was familiar with.

The afternoon wore on, after the manner of land under the influence of diffuse and slow-moving weather systems; soon one could expect the rain to start, perhaps snow, and it would continue for days. Now the light was failing, a late cloudy-day light, weak and blue in overtones; the ler eye, with its larger proportion of retinal cone cells, progressively lost discriminatory ability at lower light levels, and in gray light became particularly poor. Morlenden resigned himself to being cold, and began casting about for suitable shelter for the night. Unthinkable to walk on blind through the woods and tangled new ground, cluttered with raw second-growth: eventually, he would trip and fall over something.

It was while he was looking for some suitable natural shelter, an out-crop, a fallen tree, some ruins from the period when this land had been under the humans, a barn or shed, that he became gradually aware he was in a place showing subtle signs of use: a fresh path, one used fairly recently by travelers. An odd clearing in the half-grown woodland, where a tree had been artfully removed. Rather unlike the work of a Braid, working the land for some product. They would be more careless, and also more specialized. So there was probably an elder lodge some-where in the vicinity, most likely recently established. That could be anything: Morlenden had never concerned himself with the organiza-tions of the elder class and in fact knew only of the more famous ones, where they were and how they lived. He listened carefully, unable to determine anything visually with any certainty in the distances, in the overcast pre-rain murk, shades of gray and violet. Nothing. A sluggish creek nearby. A dripping sound, very slow, somewhere off in the oppo-site direction. An expectancy, a waiting for rain. Yes, for sure there would be rain. He could feel it. No snow.

From far off, muffled by distance and the weather, and by the half-overgrown lands, Morlenden thought he heard the tolling of a bell, from across the overgrown fields. He listened again. Silence, for a long time. Then the sound: a bell's tolling, slowly, single deep pulses spreading like the slow ripples across a stagnant pond, tangled and choked with weeds and debris . . . again, pulse, followed by silence. Assuming that the first one he had heard had actually been the first, he counted them, as the almost inaudible pulses flowed deliberately through the wet air. The eighteenth hour. He did not know who might be ringing the evening in, but he turned in the direction the tolling had come from.

It was almost completely dark by the time he was sure, after much stumbling, that he was in fact coming to something; there was evidence of cultivated fields, cut-over brush, and an impression of neatness and order, almost parklike as he drew nearer. A light mist had begun to fall. Morlenden followed what seemed to be a well-used path. Something was ahead.

Walking along, half stumbling in the poor light, he almost walked into a figure standing in the pathway in an attitude of silent waiting. It wore a cowled winter pleth, dark in color, and stood, head bowed, even when Morlenden approached. Morlenden went around to the front of the figure, and peered within the dark hood. Within, a pair of calm eyes slowly moved their focus from the ground to Morlenden's face, fixing him with a steady, expressionless gaze.

Morlenden said, "I am a wayfarer, Morlenden Deren by name, home-ward bound, caught out in the rain and the fall of night. Is there shelter nearby?"

The figure did not speak, but raised its arm and pointed along the path in the same direction Morlenden had been walking, inclining its head in that direction, once. Then the figure returned to its meditations, looking back to the earth as if it had been Morlenden who had been the apparition.

Morlenden inquired politely, "Do you not speak?"

The silent figure made no reply, and indeed made no further ac-knowledgment of Morlenden's presence.

Morlenden did not press the matter, concluding that perhaps he was already disturbing some delicate equilibrium; he turned from the figure and proceeded in the indicated direction. After passing through a few bends in the path, now bordered by tall and dense hedges of privet and pyracantha, he came upon a rustic wooden gate, and within that, a ram-bling compound of buildings, rough stone and half-timber stucco, some obviously pens for livestock, others worksheds. A few were larger, of two stories, apparently the living quarters. More of the cowled figures were about, proceeding on their errands with exaggerated slowness. One passed by Morlenden, paused, and pointed to one of the large buildings. Then it turned and continued on its progression, all in the profoundest of silences. One thing he knew now: this had to be an elder lodge. Which one?

Continuing to the indicated building, Morlenden found a door and entered. Inside there was a low counter, and behind that, a smallish and rather austere refectory. The counter was covered by a massive slab of blue glass, with a legend etched into its bottom in reversed letters, which read: *Granite Lodge.* In smaller letters, it was stated: CONTEMPLA-TION AND THE SILENCE. Morlenden found a neat little sign on a post which advised: *Distinguished visitors will share in our meditations. The buttery serves from the fifth hour until the eighteenth. Suitable accommoda-tions in the floor above. The discerning guest will find the enumeration of specific tariffs unnecessary.* Morlenden understood; he dug into his waist-pouch and retrieved several small coins, which he placed in a conven-ient depressed place in the glass surface. He looked about uncertainly. There seemed to be no one in the refectory. He sought stairs or a hall-way to another part of the building; far to the right, a darkened hallway terminated in narrow stairs. Morlenden set off in that direction, and began laboriously climbing to the upper floors.

On the second floor, there was a narrow hallway, illuminated by fat, slow-burning candles mounted in sconces of black iron. Inside, the half-timber construction of the outside walls continued, broken by heavily timbered doors, which apparently led to sleeping-apartments throughout the floor. Morlenden went to the first door, tried it. It was locked. The second—located at an angle across the hallway, and a little farther on—was not; he entered.

Within, there were two beds, rather after the human mode, but very simple, mere frames for padded platforms. But they were piled high with plenty of coverlets and counterpanes. Morlenden opened his outer cloak and tested the air. Cold; he would need all those coverlets in this damp pile. At the far end of the room, a table and chair rested under a tiny window, which was set high up on the wall. There was a single large candle on the table, now unlit. Morlenden removed the candle and took it outside, where he presented it to one of the candles alight in their sconces, lit it, and returned to the room. Now illuminated with the warm yellow light from the candle, it did not seem quite so bare and stark. The woodwork was of the finest hand-craftsmanship, although with that suggestion of raw patina that signified new material, not yet seasoned by time. On the table was a large, heavy tome, accompanied by a sheaf of paper, a pen, and an inkstand. He looked more closely; the legend on the front of the book read: *Knun Vrazus**—*The Doctrine of Opposites.* Morlenden smiled faintly and leafed idly through the book. Hand-inscribed, beautifully illuminated and lavishly illustrated with quaint drawings of mythological beasts and figures, demons, angels, metamorphs. He understood very well: one was intended to meditate here, in this little cell, and pass on one's thoughts and ruminations to the future inhabitants, as well as the denizens of Granite Lodge. He sighed dispiritedly: Morlenden would have preferred to visit the taproom for a dram or two, perhaps a draft, and a bit of conversation. He dug the remaining boiled egg out of his traveling-pack, and cracking it, ate it, sitting gingerly on the hard edge of the bed. As he ate, he listened to the noises

---

* A collection of anecdotes, told by obscure, unknown, or imaginary ler over the years. These always culminated in a dense parable, which might take the form of being too obvious, or else totally incomprehensible, at least until the reader realized the point. The work was considered open-ended and unfinished, and there was a large commentary and criticism attached to it. Humans of the era, where they were aware of it at all, considered it gross cynicism pushed to levels of perversity. It may be interesting to note here that Morlenden considered it boring.

of the place, noting nothing save the dripping of rainwater off the roof into puddles outside, and a light, sweet gurgling farther away, the running of water in a gutter or downspout. There was no sound of people at all.

Finishing his egg, and drinking water from a small pitcher that he uncovered in a tiny wall-cabinet, he looked about the small, bare room once more, shook his head, and began to undress, hanging his outer clothing on a peg on the wall. The rest he folded and placed on the desk, leaving on only his undershift. Morlenden set about making up the bed, grumbling to himself, chiefly about the nature of cold boiled eggs before bed. He was just about to blow out the candle when he heard footfalls on the stairs, then coming into the hall outside. *Another guest*, he thought. *May they attend the same party I did.* He listened. There was a faint rattle at the first door; just as he had done. Then the visitor tried his own door, which was now latched but not locked. It rattled once. There was a pause, and then the visitor knocked on the door. Raising his eyebrows, Morlenden took the candle and went to the door, and opened it: and found himself looking into the rain-wet face of Sanjirmil Srith Terklaren.

She was still dressed in a heavy winter overcloak with a hood that fell far over her forehead, the overcloak was turned water-repellent side out, and in the wavering candlelight, hundreds of sparkling points shimmered all over it, and along Sanjirmil herself where she was uncovered, her face and hands. Her dusky eyelashes; deep black with the same bluish overtones as her hair.

She spoke first, either recovering her composure or never having lost it, saying, "And you, here? May I join you?"

"Yes, yes, of course you may," he stumbled, waving the candle. "Yours is the first voice I have heard here; you will be welcome."

Sanjirmil entered the room shyly, avoided facing Morlenden directly, speaking as if to herself. "You have not visited here before? They are silent, these ones, true enough. Never have I heard them utter a single word." In the center of the room, she removed the outer overcloak, shook the rain off, and cast about for a peg on which to hang it. Finding it, the empty peg on the opposite side of the room, she hung the cloak, followed by a large bag that she had worn slung over one shoulder, which clanked dully as she let it rest against the wall.

Morlenden could see that the overcloak had not kept out all the rain, for there were damp patches along the shoulders and hem of her pleth.

This she also removed unselfconsciously, draping it over the end of the unoccupied bed. All that was left was her undershift, which she left on. Morlenden noticed many things about her now, but the first thing that caught his eye was an embroidered design worked into the right shoulder of the undershift, similar to the patterns he had observed earlier in the *yos* of the Perklarens, but different in shape. Where the others had been simple geometric patterns, more or less symmetrical, the one on Sanjirmil's undershift had no obvious cellular reference and was asymmetrical—a line of blue dots, arranged in a curve at either end, the right end being larger than the left. He recalled the basic Player information Krisshantem had forced into him, looking into his new memories for the figure, and found it. It was one of the moving patterns from the beginner's Game, a figure that moved orthogonally along its base across the field in the direction of the larger curl. Like all persistent figures in the Game, this one had a name: *Prosianlodh,* which was to be rendered by an enigmatic idea—ship of the empty place. The name was not explained. Inner Game.

But he saw other things as well, things he had not troubled to see, or avoided, when the girl had accompanied the Perwathwiy Srith to the *yos* of the Derens before his trip upcountry. Sanjirmil was now hesitating on the edge of her own fertility, at the summit of adolescence, the end of it, trembling on that edge. He remembered in his mind's eye the hoyden, the ragamuffin of sixteen years before. Seen closely, as she was to him now, there were still large amounts of those same qualities present—the gestures, the hesitant impatience, the thin, pouty, determined mouth, the half-frown of concentration along the lines and planes of her face. But more, indeed, was there. Her hair was as dark and coarse and tousled as it had always been, but it was longer and fuller now, falling carelessly about her shoulders, almost ready to be braided into the single woven strand that was the mark of parent phase. Her body was fuller, also, mostly adult, but possessing something not quite lermanish in its rounder curvings, yet not human either, still subtle and muscular after their fashion. She took the candle from him and placed it upon the desk, moving with measured grace, as a young girl might before her lover, a flowing, dancing motional set, allowing the undershift to swirl about her, and standing afterward so that the light from the candle would shine through the undershift, suggesting much and revealing nothing. It was a classical move, only slightly less direct than a spoken invitation. Morlenden saw and appreciated all that she was displaying here for him, understanding the message completely. *She knows no less than I that my time for that is gone, past,* he thought. *So it is not so blatant as it appears. It is not invitation, but reminder. As if either of us could ever forget.*

He had not forgotten: Sanjir-Ajimi had been hot and sweaty, pungent as the scent of burning leaves, wet wood, and her skin had retained, even after washing, the faint taste of salt. He had caught her scent here as she had passed him: sharp and imperative, smoky as ever, more so. For the first time in his life he caught himself admitting to some regrets upon the course of things. Morlenden looked back over his life for a moment, quickly, and recognized Sanjirmil for what she had been to him: an ultimate, certainly of the domain of the body, of *dhainaz*. And of how many other things that he had missed? *What was it she was offering?*

Sanjirmil seated herself gently on the edge of what would be her bed, a little tiredly, stiff as if from a long walk. She asked, half-mockingly, "And what do you here, Ser Deren?" She leaned back on her elbows, allowing her undershift to fall more open about her throat, another classic ploy that Morlenden could not miss; and in the candlelight the yellow light fell along her dusky-olive skin, the shadows in the hollows of her collarbones, a place for kisses.

He answered cautiously, trying to maintain some semblance of neutrality, some little vestige of secrecy, a futile task, he knew, in the face of this arch-keeper of secrets. He said, "Little enough. I have been searching for an image of her who we must find, so that we would know the better to look and where. I was on my way home, caught in the rain, and happened on this lodge."

"You did not find her for whom you search."

"Hardly. We did not expect to. Just understand who she is, what she is. Or rather, *was*. Fellirian is exploring down the other way, about the Institute with her friends there. We think she is still alive. At the least, we are proceeding as if she were."

"You will go out for her?"

"Of course."

"Why? When you find where she is, you can report to the Perwathwiy and that will be the end of that."

"Why? An honor thing, I suppose. We said that if we could, we would find her and return her. There is much, though, which we do not know yet. If she lives, her condition." He changed the subject, feeling an oppressive weight about the subject of Maellenkleth. "And you, Sanjir, what do you here, in this place of silences? Are you perhaps out of the rain, as I?"

She did not answer immediately, but looked off into space with the old blank gaze of hers, gradually turning it toward Morlenden. Yes, the eyes, dark, heavy-lashed, wine-dark; they still had that eerie scanning quality, but there was a controlled directness in them as well now, flashing with lightning and fire when she concentrated upon something. But for now, they were faraway, seeing something Morlenden did not know. She said, after a time, "We met here, often, our group. It is an excellent place to discuss secret plans, for they who lodge here will not speak of what they hear or see. . . . Over the years, I have grown fond of it, of this place, and come alone betimes. And I was troubled, and so I came to seek solitude, peace. To learn peace, Morlen. I know I do not have it in me, but would like to see it once, if but to refuse it."

She fell silent again, chewing the inside of her lower lip. Tonight her lips were pale and colorless, lighter than her face, which lent her an odd, ghostly quality. The lighter pink of her mouth against the dark olive of her face. Then suddenly she turned to him and fixed him with an intense and uncomfortable regard, saying, "You are thorough in this, indeed. And why so? I know you well enough and know that you never cared a whit for the Game or its Players. You have been no Gamefollower, always at the exhibitions. . . . You have no side, no color, no pennant to wave, neither a red nor a blue."

"It is as you say . . . I am no Gamefollower, nor have I supported one against another."

"But you must know of the rivalry between our Braids, and that Maellenkleth and I were exemplars of that traditional rivalry?"

"Indeed. I knew that before you spoke of it."

"So why pursue this girl to the very end? You need only determine it and report."

"It would appear," he said after a moment's reflection, "that there are many intrigues about the house of Perklaren, some of which I must needs unravel as I go along. It appears extremely complex, just as does Maellenkleth."

"Maellenkleth was to the contrary; she was simple-minded and one-sided. I know her well, saw her often."

"So much have I learned. And that also she was reputed to be an excellent Player." Morlenden felt the necessity to be on his guard here, but he felt a greater need to needle Sanjirmil into revealing something more. He was right: she reacted immediately, although she covered it well.

She said, her voice unsteady, "Ah, who was it told you that? They also said, most likely, that she was a better Player than I. Well, I think not better—merely different. For my view Maellenkleth was overly concerned for matters of style, elegance, finesse, little internal codes. But I believe in results, that they tell the true story. And I get them, too." She added, "As a Player."

Morlenden felt reckless, and pursued the topic. "And I had also heard that she was possibly to be allowed to reenter the Game—the Inner Game, whatever it is—again as a *shartoorh* Dirklaren, of the first generation of Dirklarens."

Sanjirmil's face became darker, flushed, stormy. She responded immediately. "That was foolishness, stupidity, a nuisance! She—they, that out-Braid *hifzer*—hoped to change the inevitable by little hearthroom children's games and plots and scheming. But I tell you that it could not and did not have any effect upon me. For the law of the Game, arbitrated by Pellandrey himself, says that only a woven *Toorh* may be *Huszan*, master of the Game: I am woven, a *Toorh* and *Klandorh* to add to it, and the present parent Terklarens have already retired in my favor, voluntarily. Therefore by the law I am the master of the Game, to say who may and who nay. The Perwathwiy and the others, they may advise, but likewise, the responsibility is mine and I may ignore. And I will be *Huszan* and *Klandorh* until our *Toorh* children weave in their turn. Now we are talking, Morlen, about another thirty years, more than a span." She repeated the number, emphasizing it: "Two fourteens and two! And the Revens may manufacture all the Braids they wish; in the end only I can admit her into it, her and her outsider. So what should I care about Dirklarens, Beshklarens, Nanklarens*?"

"Technically, you are not woven until, for example, I say that you are. I, or Fellirian, or Kaldherman, or Cannialin."

"But of course I am! I am fully initiated! Oh, yes, indeed, am I ever initiated!" And here, Sanjirmil laughed, involuntarily, as if at some irrepressible private joke.

"And you quote the law to keep Maellenkleth out of the Game, but you do not wish to hear the same law applied to you yourself." Morlenden allowed an edge to come into his voice, as if correcting a child. "There is no record; no Deren witnessed."

"Oh, but there was a ceremony. Even Mael attended. . . ."

"And carried flowers as well, I suppose?"

He did not wait to hear her answer, but continued, "And there was no

* Third-players, Fifth-players, Nth-players.

notification to those who would legitimize your place and position. Not even a courtesy call, a letter by messenger." Here he also reminded her of their past, for it had been Sanjirmil who had so often insisted upon writing, but after the promises, had never done so. "But in the scale of all things, rights and wrongs, I suppose after all it doesn't really make any difference, either way. You need our approval: you have it, now, this minute. Write down the full-names of your Braid members, and I will enter them in the records. Done. I would not, in any event, obstruct what is obviously already accomplished. . . . I could only go to the Revens for arbitration, but I can gather from all that I have seen that they already know about it."

"Morlenden, you do not know all the reasons. . . ."

"Reasons, are they? The tyranny of reasons, so it is said; we can always find a *zhan* of them to explain things we shouldn't have done in the first place. And of course we can reasonably project that Maellenkleth is done for anyway."

"She was told of the danger long ago! Clearly, no tricks and nothing hidden! Still, she elected to soldier for us, we did not make her. She was of a valiant heart and could not be denied, but allowed to the very front of the battle, as it were. She pushed it that way . . . thus she gained obligations from those of us who could not go out, as I, even as I. That was not my issue to judge."

"And you say that you are *Huszan*, master of the Game, but *chlenzan*, too, prisoner of the Game."

"Prisoner, yes! So it is with all mastery! I am not so unique! And I do not regret what I have given up to get it, the trade of the one for the other. Any other. If you knew as I did, you would take it thus as well, and if it were within your grasp, you too would reach for it."

"I cannot speak of temptations I have not faced."

"But you could face them and gain thereby if you would but listen to me."

"How is it that I reach for that which has not been offered?"

"I have always offered it, just as long ago."

"To cleave to you as an elder when we could not otherwise? To make with our minds in the future that which we made with our bodies in the past?"

"Why not, then? I say of it that it was the best and sweetest of my life; and for one time, one only, I was free, just myself, and I forgot my name. I know it would be the same; you have reserves and perceptions you do not know. . . ."

"Even were I to agree to such a thing, so I would have to wait for you. . . ."

"As I have waited. But it is as nothing; something we of the longer sight see over, beyond. I never forget those days of the autumn. It is true that we all carry the obligation to the people, to the body, to bring forth and ever keep the line that was given us. Nevertheless the heart and mind know their needs as well."

"Neither have I forgotten. But we were skin-drunken, kiss-drugged, and it was done and left behind ages ago. You must have thought along the way that we were badly unsynchronized in time: we had our moment, but both of us have had to walk along unique ways."

"But I have heard that you do wish for something more to be in your free years. And they are free, yours to ask for. And have; that I can offer, that, and more."

"I remain skeptical. From what I have learned of the Game I am not so sure I would wish such an adventure. We are simple folk of field and forest, remember; accordingly we have essentially modest ambitions. Because I have spoken unguardedly of learning new things—for example, to swim—should not be taken to mean that I wish to swim the Green Sea all the way to the land Yevrofian. Do you offer the Game, or will you accept what elderhood I offer?"

"I am not offering the Game; for the one, I cannot. Maellenkleth did thus, for Krisshantem, but they were children. It is too late for that. Too much to learn, reflexes, Morlenden, reflexes. Knowledge of that is not enough. It's the speed you use them with, and it takes almost a full span to get them right. Action, decision, foresight, and the sense of timing. Too late, I must say."

"Then what is it you wish me to take?"

"Just myself. What more can I offer you?"

"I know only one part of you . . . and even now, I cannot know how well I know even that part. Things change, and I know even less of what things have passed in your life."

Sanjirmil shook her head. "Little of that, to be sure. I have not known another with whom I would have my elderness. Could I speak plainer? You shame my essence evading me thus."

"It cannot be a thing I would say easily, or on the moment. At the least, I would like some time."

"Time, is it? The fifteen years until Pethmirvin weaves? The twenty until Pentandrun and Kevlendos are invested with the records of the Derens? We do not have twenty years! We do not have fifteen years!"

She had allowed her voice to gain in volume and presence, but now it dropped abruptly to almost a whisper, as she added, "We do not have even five."

"Of course we do. We have until the end of time."

"We do not! Within the . . ." Sanjirmil stopped. "I say we do not, and there I speak as *Huszan*, because I know it as *Huszan* of the Inner Game. Believe me."

"With no reasons for this unseemly haste, save 'believe me'?"

"You are as bullheaded as you ever were!"

"It is not bullheaded to ask why. You must tell me how it is you can be so sure of the time—so sure that you almost gave me a date. What is it and what is to happen?"

"I cannot. . . . It is true that I read the law lightly, as you say, when it comes to my own actions, but even so, I could not initiate you until I was sure you were committed. To me."

"Those kinds of assurances do not come easy; the requirement is as difficult to satisfy as to fill a bottomless pit with stones. So, after all, this is just another case of Maellenkleth and Krisshantem? She would not initiate him either."

"So much you have heard of Kris? But he did not know Mael as well as he thought: so she told him she would not do it. But she told me that she would initiate him anyway, permitted or not! She promised, she did, although I should prefer the word 'threaten.' "

"Had she actually done that?"

"So she said. But we were at least spared that embarrassment by her departure on this last mission instead." (How convenient, Morlenden thought, if any of what she was saying was even half-true.) "It would have come, though, never fear."

Morlenden observed, coolly, "This Game and its Players grow more interesting with every Player I meet."

Her reply came in a low tone, and she peered at him from under her heavy eyebrows, so that the lower whites of her eyes showed. Although the words were mild, the effect was menacing, and Morlenden felt it was intended to be. "Be careful that you do not gain too great an interest before your time."

"I do only what we have been paid to do by the Perwathwiy, and Pellandrey Reven as well. Go to them for comfort; I will even go with you. But as soon as we are a little more knowledgeable, we are going for Maellenkleth, and whatever it takes to do it, knowledge or arts, rest assured we will attain it. Understand me: I would not pay so much as a thimbleful of the yield of our outhouse for one word of the Game or its Players, *in themselves*. But it is a matter of a missing girl who departed under the oddest of circumstances, and it needs uncovering. And to determine where she might be, we must learn what she was."

"If you find her, what will you do with what you find?"

"Bring her back, if she lives."

"And if she lives disminded?"

"As you know, she can be restored, slowly over the years, or quickly via Multispeech, each as circumstances warrant. She has intrinsic value in several ways, not the least of which is that she is a person. And as one of us who I think was caught in something quite beyond her; and as a future parent, who will have to bear the future with the rest of us. And the beauty and the spirit I have heard so much of? Surely it would be a waste to let it all go so casually, lose it without further thought. Not all of it was memory—some of it must reside at the cellular level, and thence to us through the children."

"But she has no family that can take care of her, that can take the time and trouble to rebuild her. You know that rebuilding a forgetty is much harder than raising the original child, for with a forgetty the instinctual cues and programming for learning readiness are gone."

"She is of such an age that if all else failed we Derens would take her in. Or perhaps the Hulens. I am not so sure that would be to Kris's liking, for he would still lose her, but even so . . ."

"Hulens? Ragamuffins, hooligans, wanderers, tramps, nomads!"

"I cannot speak of their methodology, but as much of it as they passed to Kris seemed to be effective enough. True, he is withdrawn and solitary, but he is competent and practiced in the basic social graces. He had to learn from someone, and with his tenuous contact with the Hulens, their way must have some values."

"Morlen, what have we lost that I cannot reach you now?"

"Now? We cannot lose what we never had, Sanjir. As for the rest, we lose no more than others have done, gracefully and tactfully, in somewhat similar circumstances. Do not misunderstand: I cherish the time when we were together. I can in truth compare that with no one else. But time has passed and conditions changed. You and I alike are *Toorh*, and we have debt to others, no matter what we feel. Not to mention other emotions that may have become operative in us. You for yours and likewise I for mine. Would you have me run off willy-nilly into the forest as some moon-child?"

"Then you will persist in this folly?"

"Even if I were disinterested and wholly mercenary I would proceed. Word is word. But there is far more. This Maellenkleth has obviously been ill-used by the very people who should have shielded her from the terrors of the wider world, whether she desired it or not. She was a child—she had no business being a spy. That is not the business of the young and zealous, but of the seasoned and calm. I know there are high stakes outside, worlds won and lost. Perhaps inside as well. But I have my own values, my own interests. And there seems to be much too much afoot to allow it to remain hidden for no other reason than that it may be sensitive cult-dogma! I owe the truth at least to myself, since now I apparently risk that person. And of course the Perwathwiy deserves what she paid for. So I would learn how Maellenkleth came to be where she is."

"Even though you *know* you are on the edge of things you may not be a witness to yet?"

"Indeed, there. Just so. But have no fears; I am discreet by nature and will retain any secrets I uncover."

"You expect to find them along the way, like stones in a path?"

"Of course! An excellent choice of words! I could not have put it better. For I have already, hardly looking, turned over several interesting stones of such a nature, things I imagine people would not have left casually strewn about."

"Morlenden, Morlenden, I urge restraint, I caution you! We are not a riddle to be solved, a puzzle for the curious to decipher . . ."

". . . but a mystery cult of which to stand in awe? While you stand serene and secure above the rest of us? Then explain it!"

"I cannot, I simply cannot. I would lose much, starting with you. You may see that in time, and why, although I wish with all my heart that you do not."

"Well enough," he said, almost grimly. "Well taken, all your warnings. But I continue."

"How far?"

"Until the end."

"I cannot be responsible, then. Not in your debt."

"For what?"

"For what may happen . . . it is suspected that Maellenkleth fell into a clever trap, the like of which has not been set before. It may be set even now for you, should you go to it."

"I will take that chance and rely upon ingenuity. She had hers and went, clean-eyed; I can do no less, with the less that I have to lose."

To this last, Sanjirmil had nothing to add, and so she sat, for a long time, saying nothing, her eyes totally reverted to the blind scanning, devoid of expression. At last she got up from the bed, wearily, as if she had been through some great internal struggle. She moved to the place where Morlenden was sitting on the edge of the bed, leaning forward. She took his face in her hands, which were hot and dry, and pressed his face to her abdomen, the muscles within taut as wires. She was trembling slightly, in the grip of some strong emotion.

She moved his face upward, pressing it to her breasts, then looking him directly in the eyes with a burning regard Morlenden did not know he could hold indefinitely, so intense was it. She said slowly, "I will not ask that you sleep with me; I still want you, the past is too well-remembered, and I know that you are beyond me now. But I will ask a last kiss."

"A last kiss?"

"A kiss before sleeping, that we may remember each other as once we were."

She bent farther and pressed her lips to his, childishly, her lips relaxed, making no attempt to shape them. As they touched, Morlenden felt the image of the past within his memory emerge, take over, become as one with the present. For all her aggressiveness and belligerence, he remembered vividly that Sanjirmil had been from the first a shy kisser, not teasingly falsely shy, but truly so, as if she were afraid to really give of herself, afraid to abandon herself even to a kiss, and much less what would come after. It was the same, exactly the same, the soft, relaxed mouth, barely parting the lips and not offering her tongue until he touched it with his. Morlenden remembered the past, their past, too well. But for the present, he felt nothing save some subtle, ephemeral emotions that had no form and no name, except in that they were related to a form of sadness, a form of regret. She breathed once, deeply, through her narrow nostrils, then broke, turned abruptly, and blew out the candle. Morlenden felt moisture on his cheeks; he did not need to taste its salt to know that it was tears, notwithstanding that he had neither felt nor heard a sob from her. It was blind-dark in the room now, and he could follow her only through the sound of her movements, the rustles of her undershift, the scuffling of her bare feet along the rough wooden floor, the touches and taps of her hands, and he heard the bed creak as it took her weight. Then silence matched the darkness, Morlenden turned under his own covers and began sinking into sleep almost immediately, one last thought surfacing in his mind like some great bulkhead behind the dam: *Yes, the bed creaked, but just this little once. We creaked, too, Sanjir and I, when we took the weight of each other's bodies; we still creak from it.*

In the morning, in the gray light of a rainy-day morning, Morlenden awoke and saw that Sanjirmil was still sleeping, breathing slowly and deeply. He slipped out of his bed carefully and quietly, gathering his things and dressing so as not to wake her. He wished no more of the laden conversation they had made the night before.

Taking one last look about to be sure he had left nothing, he paused, wishing to take one last look at Sanjirmil, Sanjir whom he had met in the forest long ago, Ajimi with whom he had been a lover, and also the new and disturbing Sanjirmil . . . Terklaren, yes, adult, who spoke of traps and threats and still more enigmas. Sanjirmil was on her side, lightly and carelessly half covered, half curled, her lips slightly parted, still deeply sleeping. He looked closer, remembering. Asleep, her now-face lost much of its new harshness and seemed soft and childish again, a ragamuffin, yes, but also a ragamuffin who was very alone, very frightened of the uniqueness being pressed upon her. The aquiline nose lost much of its predatory curve. Relaxed, it was a face of desires and passions and something close to loveliness, ever so slightly slanted in the angles of the eyes, this face delicate and strong-lined at once, smooth and sleek as the face of some wild animal at peace. He saw there was no mystery of how they had come to be together when they had met; Sanjir was indeed in a class all by herself. Striking, commanding, she would have been exceptional even in the midst of girls of great beauty.

He moved yet closer, cautiously, so as not to awaken her, peering closely at her eyes, which were still closed. He thought to detect some movement under the lids, as if she were having a dream. He wondered idly what such a one would dream about. Closer. Behind the closed eyelids, there was movement, but as he watched her, Morlenden could see that under the soft black lustrous lashes the movement was not the erratic, looping motion of a normal person's dream, but a version of the same scanning pattern he had seen in her before. The eyes scanned, rather than tracked, in a raster pattern: a line across, then repeated, a little lower, until the bottom of the field of vision, then repeating the cycle. It was slowed now, and he could see the component motions he could not see before. Odd, indeed, to be so impressed upon her that she would even dream it that way. What was she dreaming? The Inner

Game? At the same time, he saw that her lips were also moving, as if sleep-speaking, but he heard no sound. He leaned closer, trying to hear, identify the mode, listening closely, knowing that even if she were speaking Multispeech he would be in little danger because there was no synchronization and no submission on his part. He could not be caught in it.

It was there, and he caught a fragment of it, an odd form, an unusual mode he couldn't quite identify, something similar to the mode of one-to-many, but with an odd lilt, a catch, a syncopation in the rhythms, almost as if she were somehow controlling actions in another, others, three people. He began getting quick visuals. Visuals caught. And now receiving the full blast of what she was sending in her sleep, Morlenden was pinned in an iron net of command-override Multispeech, and he saw and performed, and did not understand what he was seeing and doing, but he did with great urgency, the persona being projected by Sanjirmil, because he could not help doing exactly as the instructions were passed to him. He did not have the option to disobey or reflect; and he did not hear, for through sound and modulation and the heritage of the people, Sanjirmil had somehow inserted her own persona directly into his mind and was manipulating Game skills he didn't know he had. A single will permeated everything, a force filled him with energy, with verve, with skill and power: hell and death flowed along his arms into his hands as they flew like manic butterflies along the controls of a Game keyboard that seemed to surround him, all around the domains of his reach. It was the Game, of course, and he could see it all above him; he was reclining, looking upward, scanning a ceiling the whole of which was a subtly curved Game display panel alive with patterns of light, color and darkness, the shapes and patterns permutating, evolving, shifting with terrible urgency, immediacy. Something was coming and they blanked it with some motion that caused the rest to tremble and shift and emit pieces of themselves. Waves of change, of destruction, and of reordering flowed across the field. There was more, and it continued, the intensity growing, but all he felt was confidence, exultation, the semblance of something coming into reality at last, of being victorious, of imposing some concept upon something else, and then there was a terrible stroke they all did together that made the multiple personality wince, flinch, shrink back with horror, but they could not reflect; they must move on. He felt and rejoiced in the exultation emanating from she-who-controlled: triumph, vindication, the utter joy of performing the ultimate crimes and atrocities upon one's most hated enemy, something hated and feared and not long ago hidden from. As stability returned slowly something was now being done that was incomprehensible to him. Energy long-stored, locked up in the prisons of cold matter, rigid, now leaped into freedom and fled shrieking at the skies; there was fire and carnage.

Morlenden knew he was feeding something back to the Control, the Will, but until now he had not attempted to insert himself. Now he did. It had gone on long enough. And he saw himself now as a sage, a governor, a steadying influence against excess, a stay against impulses even more wild than those he had glimpsed. Like oil on the waters he tried to steady what they were all doing, through feedback; after all, was he not Fire aspect, did he not have the Will also? There was conflict, here there could be only one Fire and *out*.

Shaken, he drew back from the sleeping girl, and he was now back in the real world. Or was it? He saw and did not understand. Now he remembered, and still he did not comprehend. He looked at Sanjirmil again. She was moving restlessly in her sleep, now muttering something unintelligible, the scanning in her eyes stopped. She had been acting out some dream only she knew, and Morlenden's hands trembled and tingled as if he had received some electric shock. It had been the Game, sure enough, but it had been in a form he had never seen, in a place he could not imagine. He tried to remember: the image was furred and distorted by being someone else's dream, but he could see it, crudely—he had been within a reclining couch, contoured to his body, slightly tilted, his hands at the ready arrayed along massive keyboard controls that lay all about him. But he had been scarcely conscious of all that, immersed in concentration upon the huge Game screen that curved all over him, over them all, dwarfing the tiny beings who manipulated the flying shapes that fled and changed over its surface. Morlenden could not imagine what it was he had seen, been within. The environment was abstract and alien. But there could be no mistaking the confidence, the arrogance, of the sender, the girl who lay before him, now relaxing again, drifting back into deeper sleep, almost pretty, exotic in coloring and shape, innocently dreaming in the gray early hours of a rainy winter morning. She moved slightly, adjusting her position, disturbing the covers, causing them to emit her scent, still that tart and sweet maddening odor of warm adolescent girl, gamy, all body. Morlenden shivered violently, shaken by the contrasts his senses and memories were making in him. He hurriedly fastened his overcloak, and slipped from the room as quickly and as quietly as he could. And as he carefully pulled the door to behind him, out in the cold and drafty corridor, he knew that how-ever brave the words he had used, he was in fact very much afraid of this unknown, this incomprehensible being concentrated in the sleek tawny body of Sanjirmil, who had been, upon a time, Ajimi.

He hurried down the corridor and then the stairs, empty as the night before, half-dark, feeling a pressing danger, a peril, a murderous threat, a panicky urge that inspired him to get out right now. The alternative to the search for Maellenkleth was to get out of it as fast as he could ex-tricate himself and Fellirian. He suddenly did not wish to know how Maellenkleth got wherever she was; he wished to forget the whole thing, and return all the money to the Perwathwiy and all her henchmen.

But by the time he had reached the ground floor, he felt reason com-ing back to him, the old sense, familiar resolves and character, and the old curiosity and self-confidence. He entered the refectory and saw peo-ple again, and even if they were unspeaking, takers of vows of silence, it reassured him. He thought of Fellirian and her calmness, her steady pace, her quiet resolve to undergo this, she having many of the same misgivings as had he. The thought of his partner, insibling, co-spouse, mate, and rarely, lover, all sobered him. He suddenly found himself wishing to be free of the past, of memory. And of this suddenly uncer-tain future; to be resolved. He looked around and saw a few guests at their tables, all caught up in the rituals of silence in respect to the mem-bers of Granite Lodge, as well as the members themselves, a few of whom were present. One was the cook, standing nonchalantly behind the serving counter and methodically frying sausages as if that were the most important task in the whole world. At that moment, Morlenden understood that it was just that, exactly and precisely.

He walked across the refectory and took up a position by the serving counter, holding a simple wooden bowl, wide and shallow. He also un-derstood now that much speech was unnecessary; for to stand behind a counter with bowl in hand was as clear as speech; perhaps talk was what was unneeded, the idle rattling of acorns in a jar.

The cook piled his plate with a generous helping of sausages and flat-cakes, nodding at the butter-jar close to hand, and proceeded on with his tasks. Morlenden helped himself, chose a table, and filled himself, knowing that he would have to walk all day on what he ate here. He re-flected, as he sat and ate, that perhaps all the talk Sanjirmil had made about the members of Granite Lodge keeping secrets was indeed but an excuse, for the food was unsurpassingly excellent. That was a secret worth keeping. He looked again, and saw that all within sight were well-fed, no doubt about it. He had visions of great platters of roast dripping with gravy, tankards of ale, and laughed inwardly to himself, thinking also of what was expected of one in way of payment: meditation upon the curious strictures of the Doctrine of Opposite. *Just imagine*, he thought, *do that which you fear most; therein lies freedom.* And then he thought again, and it did not seem so curious after all. Perhaps he might yet have an entry to make in the tomes of Granite Lodge. But however it went, he resolved to bring the rest of them back here. At least for the food. As for the rest, he was sure that only Cannialin would actually like it. She loved quiet. Fellirian liked talk too much, and Kal was hopeless.

Refreshed and mind more at ease, he left the table, setting his bowl in a place set aside for them, and departed the refectory and the common-house, leaving behind some more coins from his pouch on the way out. Yes, indeed, he thought. A fine place to visit. And perhaps to live? He would have to think on that. He loved talk no less than Fellirian.

Outside, the day was cold, overcast, and still drizzly. A vile day for a long Walk through the woods. But soon, he was on his way again, covering the ground with his practiced pace learned along many a path across the reservation. He followed paths now pressed into the fabric of the rainy damp forest, the trees covered with a sparkling film of clear water, dripping clear sweet droplets, the pines covered with silvery luminescence.

He headed southwestward, and after not too long a time, began to recognize familiar landmarks. Now, knowing a bit better where he was, and being closer to home than he thought he had been, he increased his pace as much as he could, considering the slipperiness of the path, now well-worn down to bare earth. But throughout the gray day's passage, as he walked through the empty woodlands and fields, the temporary sense of well-being he had gained gradually left him, to be replaced by some of the uneasiness he had felt the night before when he had been with Sanjirmil. Not the morning's panic. No, not that. An uneasiness, and growing. But he began to have some sense of apprehension, and by early afternoon he was watching his back trail carefully, recalling the incidents of the *yos* of the Perklarens and at the treehouse of Maellenkleth and Krisshantem. He saw nothing, heard nothing that he could actually identify, detected no hard evidence whatsoever of any follower lurking behind him or to the side, but he never lost the feeling that he was being shadowed by someone expert at it, perhaps rivaling Kris in ability to track at a distance and still keep contact. Kris would not have exploited that talent; he would always approach directly, silently, but directly.

As he thought of it now, he realized that this intuition of being followed had begun not long after he had left Granite Lodge, and had continued, strengthening during the day. He began to keep closer to cover, attempting to conceal his location, trying to walk ever more silently. At first, these intentions had no measurable effect, but after a time the sensation of being followed did begin to decline a little. It neither eliminated it nor cured it, but merely reduced it; as if by being evasive he had broadened the area of probability about himself, and his shadow had withdrawn a bit, uncertain exactly where he was. Still, he felt followed.

The primary result of his efforts was direct and immediate; it made a long walk longer; and by the time he was truly back into what he considered his own territory, near the holding of the Derens, it was beginning to shade off toward darkness again. Late afternoon. The only consolation to him was that the rain and the intermittent drizzle had stopped. The ground was extremely slippery, here in the clay-and-hill flint country; red clay that stuck to one's boots when it was not threatening to trip one into a nasty fall. But the air was clear as spring water, washed, clean, sweet-smelling, and the overcast was breaking up. There were patches of luminous blue showing, and there was a lightening along the borders of the west, behind the Flint Mountains. It would be clear again by morning. And suddenly he noted that the sense of being followed had vanished as subtly as it had come, that it was gone, and had been for a considerable time. Fine, that. Perhaps it had been imagination after all, easily spooked by the incident of Sanjirmil's dream-speaking. Or perhaps he had lost his follower through all the detours he had taken. Ahead he saw—through the leatherleaf oaks, some still bearing browned leaves along their dark and twisted branches—his own outhouse, and beyond was the rise that hid the Deren *yos* from view from this direction. It made him feel a great deal more secure, although the logical part of his mind still persisted in reminding him that he was in reality no more secure here than he was anywhere else.

Morlenden detoured by the outhouse before turning down the hill to the *yos*, and, finished with his detour, was proceeding slowly down the slippery path, ruefully considering that after all he should indeed take the ritual wash down in the trough, and most assuredly it would be cold. He shivered at the thought of it. Perhaps he could lie to Fellirian, who would insist. No, that wouldn't work either; she'd spot that fast enough, call Kaldherman for help, and they'd pitch him in while Cannialin would stand to the side and laugh her laugh. But it was cold now. A freeze tonight for sure. Below, in the dooryard, beyond the pot holding the *yos*-tree, an overage blackwillow, he caught sight of Fellirian and Pethmirvin walking slowly up to the *yos*, their breath steaming in the cold, damp air. Fellirian saw him, nudged Peth, and they both waved. Morlenden returned the wave, remembering to watch for his ancient enemy the root at the same time. There it was, and for once he had missed it, but in watching Fellirian and Pethmirvin, waving, and avoiding the root, he had misjudged his footing on the rain-slick path and the red clay, and began a ludicrous slip, now waving both arms wildly for balance. He thought in the midst of a most undignified escapade that he heard a sudden, sharp, woody noise close by, like a chop of an ax, but it was indeed a busy moment and he could not be sure. What was much more curious was the fact that he did not fall, but hung suspended, a strange happening indeed until he realized with a chill that he had been pinned to an oak by a large metal arrow, dully anodized into a vague greenish-brown color to make it blend into the background. Morlenden felt ice in his veins, for the arrow had passed through his clothing under one armpit and driven into the tree with such force that when Pethmirvin and Fellirian arrived, all three of them together could not pull it out. Morlenden worked free of it, and shortly afterward Kaldherman arrived. He returned to the shed behind the *yos*, retrieved a large machete they used against the always-encroaching brush about the *yos*, and immediately charged off into the brushy woods in the direction from which the arrow had come, following back along the shaft. That he found nothing, save some vague and scuffed tracks that shortly disappeared in the undergrowth, surprised no one.

TWELVE

. . . is there no place left for repentance, none for pardon left?
None left but by submission; and that word disdain forbids me,
and my dread of shame among the spirits beneath, whom I se-
duced with other promises and other vaunts than to submit,
boasting I could subdue the omnipotent. Aye me! They little
know how dearly I abide that boast so vain, under what tor-
ments inwardly I groan.

—Milton, *Paradise Lost*

THEY WERE ALL in Chairman Parleau's intimidating office, making small talk before the meeting got under way; Eykor was having one of his interminable low-grade arguments with Plattsman over the differences in functions between Security and Control, as well as the historical reasons for the rise of the latter at much of the expense of the former. Parleau took no active part in the argument, although from time to time he would goad one to make some audacious sally, which was immediately pounced upon by the other.

The heart of the discussion at this point lay in Eykor's accusation that over the years Control had actually usurped much of the best part of Security, namely, the prediction and anticipation of events warranting the use of deadly force. Plattsman was following the counterargument that the aim of Control, with its sophisticated statistical analyses, monitor stations, and status-reporting networks, was in fact to make the predictions so good and so accurate that corrective action was backed up from corrective, but coercive, force, to a "best trade-off" action taken this side of force. It might have been moot to say that the original object of the whole system of Control was to illuminate problems and cure them, a true bridge between managerial government and naked power politics.

Plattsman was saying, "Ultimately, we could not usurp Security, for we have, in plain fact, no troops."

"We are your troops, most of the time," replied Eykor.

"Symbiosis, then. Hands and eyes that work together. The ability of the hand to sense its field of action is limited to close field work—touch, heat detection. On the other hand, the eye sees and integrates, but can of itself take no action to implement its evaluations. It can't even evade a threat."

They could have continued much longer, and would have, but Parleau grew restive and waved them to a halt. He knew, of course, that Plattsman was basically correct in his analogy of hand and eye, but that he had left out several factors. One of these was that once Control had become firmly established, it began to evolve from an initial position of rather altruistic professionalism toward the self-perpetuations of the classical bureaucracy, thus lessening its true functional growth. Secondly, Control over the years had become vastly entangled in the manipulation of information for its own sake, and had, on several occasions, come perilously close to strangling itself on its own internal flow problems and turbulences. They had weathered these crises remarkably well, and their integrity was a watchword within the various regional departments. But Parleau was of the opinion that too much reliance was placed upon them; there had always been a requirement for "wetwork," as the jargon of the day put it. Parleau's own phrasing of it might have been, as he sometimes observed to his most trusted associates from the old days, "At the bottom line, you're always going to need some hard-faced bastard to kick the arses and take the names. There is simply no substitute for a good truncheon, a rubber hose, or perhaps a coat hanger, applied with a will and decided upon unhesitatingly." Security filled that requirement commendably, although it could often be denounced for excesses of zeal. And its requests for manpower were simply not to be believed!

Parleau motioned for them to begin. All those present shuffled papers, rearranged their notes, made their positions ready, moved restlessly in their seats, then fell quiet. Plattsman would be first, of course. He had the data they had been waiting for, or so they hoped and had been led to believe. Plattsman had sheaves and sheaves of machine-print reports and summaries, analyses and conclusions.

Plattsman began, "Well. Monitors in the office of one W. Vance, Institute Director, recorded a conversation between Vance and a Hando Errat, apparently of Continental, their subject being a representation of the girl who was picked up in the vandalism case."

Something stirred in Parleau's mind then, about Errat. He had heard that name before, but he couldn't place it. Had it been at Continental? He tried to remember, but the expression on Eykor's face distracted him, and he lost it. No matter, they could follow it later. What interest did Continental have in this?

Plattsman paused slightly, to be sure he had their attention with his use of the word "vandalism" when Eykor had called it "terrorism" from the beginning. Then he continued, "Shortly thereafter, Vance solicited assistance from one Doctor Harkle, head of Research and Development. She recalled the girl immediately, and this data was reported up-channel. We also were able to capture a disprint of the repro, and it matches the girl."

Parleau interjected, "Was this recorded? Did you run a check on this Errat?"

Plattsman hesitated, then replied, "No, Chairman, no record was made. We had been overseeing Vance somewhat earlier, and the tap had been taken off. There was still sampling being conducted, but it was being run on a priority-five basis, which is 'no recorders.' We were extremely lucky to get this, as it was. Indeed, were it not for some quick thinking, with the disprint equipment, we wouldn't have been able to match the girl up. It was only uncovered for a few minutes."

"Naturally, no disprint of Errat."

"We didn't get one. By the time our monitor realized what was happening, Errat was gone. We did check with Continental Control, but they could not discuss the matter over an open line. Referred us to Section Q, Denver. We did not press the matter."

"I understand." Indeed Parleau did understand. People who asked questions of Section Q were asked questions by "the Q" and then faded away from sight.

Something was still nagging at Parleau's mind, but now Plattsman continued, "Pertinent data follows: the subject is one Maellenkleth Srith Perklaren, age twenty; sex, female. She was a part-time research assistant in the Math Department, then R and D. She was, according to evaluations we have been able to obtain, of a tendency to be somewhat abstracted and distant, but competent. She appears to have been shy and retiring, but withal, cooperative and pleasant. There was one uncorroborated entry about family problems, but we were unable to determine their nature. She is listed in the Institute personnel records as being an insibling in their family reference."

Plattsman stopped, and Parleau looked up, expecting more. This was what Plattsman called a meeting for? He asked Eykor, "Is that all? What does Security have?"

Eykor said, "We didn't think we'd find anything, because we don't get into reservation business. I would like to have chased down her family relationship, and all that crap, but we ran a routine check of our own stuff to see *if* there was any correlation. We found nothing on this one, but we did find in the records a reference, indeed a file, on another, who was listed only initially as Perklaren, M.S., in the space program, if you can believe that. We went further into it, actually physically dug out the fiche files. This one was called Mevlannen Srith Perklaren, and from the photo we determined that they are not the same person. The Perklaren that Security found is also a ler female, now has a security clearance of Level Four, Access type B, ratings excellent. Performance has been rated as 'outstanding and innovative.' Assigned to Team Trojan Eye. She is normally located about the West Coast Test Range, or actually in space. I cross-referred with Control and we were able to pinpoint her location as on the ground at present. Additionally, we were able to insert a request to keep her there for the time being. Distraction and excuses. We could bring her in easily enough."

"What does this Perklaren do?"

"Apprentice free-fall structural technician, and optics specialist."

Klyten laughed. "Now there's one for you! A ler in optics. Might as well find an amputee employed as a pavement-breaker, handling a chipper-stripper!"

Everyone turned and stared at Klyten. He recovered his academic composure and explained, "They are rather notorious for having what we consider to be poor eyesight. The ler retina is almost totally comprised of cone cells. They have an extreme degree of color acuity, but less capability of resolution; and of course they are severely handicapped in light levels of semidarkness, where a human would see quite well, if primarily in monotone. They compensate for this by having more kinds of cone cells, and a broadened spectrum that includes, so I understand, two distinct 'colors' below what we call red and one in the near ultraviolet, but it doesn't help them much. So one working as an optician, building a telescope, is really something. You know, on the ground, here on Earth, they are reputed to have great difficulty seeing anything in the night sky below Magnitude three, rarely four. That's why I laughed: she's working under a severe handicap."

Parleau observed, "She must also be very good at what she does to work under it and still produce results. Is there any connection between her and the girl we caught?"

Klyten answered, "The custom in naming is that the names don't repeat. Each person carries a name that is unique and meaningful, if somewhat fanciful and exotic for my taste. They try to run seven generations before repeating a proper name. As for the surnames, they don't repeat either. Each surname of a family group relates to an occupation, and if they have more than one such group in an activity, they prefix a number to the name root. According to what I have in my files, the names 'Klaren' would equate to, well, 'Player.' But they have two such family groups, so the older is called Perklaren, 'First-player,' and the second, Terklaren, 'Second-player.' Now since neither name repeats, and we have two who are the same, then they are in the same group. Properly speaking, they don't use surnames once they graduate to elder status, so these would have to be in the same generation. Eykor, what was your girl's age?"

"Twenty."

"Then they are insiblings to one another. Hm. . . . But that would mean that their family group, or Braid, as they call it, has two insiblings of the same sex, unless there was a twinning we don't know about. This could be the source of the family problems."

Parleau said, "How so? I don't understand."

Klyten replied, "The tradition is that the insiblings marry, or weave, if you'd rather, each other."

"That would be incest," observed Parleau.

"Perhaps. Depends on your definitions. But it's not, genetically; the insiblings have different parents, completely, and are not related at all, as we would call it, even though they are raised together, if anything, more closely than the usual brother-sister relationship. But now, in this case, it would appear to follow the condition they call *Polhovemosi*: 'sexed-out.' If the insiblings are of the same sex, then the Braid ends and all must weave into other Braids in the outsibling position. They lose a lot: status, continuity with the past, tradition. These things are highly valued among them. To lose one's family-group role is one of the unkindest blows."

Eykor observed, "Well, I suppose that's interesting enough, but not of very much use to us, here. Is there anything worth digging into in their surname?"

And Parleau added, as an afterthought, "And how about the connection between Maellenkleth the Player and Maellenkleth the vandal? If she resented her situation, as well it appears she might from what you say, then why didn't she vandalize something of her own people's? After all, we didn't make up their cultural structures for them."

Eykor said, "It would appear that at least one of them harbored no resentments, at least visibly. Her ratings were impressive, and doubly so, when you consider Klyten's dissertation on her eyesight."

Klyten answered, "It is true what you guess by instinct, that their family groups tend to be very homogenous in their value systems; that the one is an achiever probably doesn't mean that the other would be, but it does argue against her being a vandal. . . . But these are only probabilities, not oracles or predictions. What say you, Plattsman, for Control?"

"As always, that we need more data. Basically, I agree, but vandalism is an intricate structure, and I should like to know more about the girl, her matrix, internal values of the class of which she belongs. I don't know if we can project the human family structure or sexual values onto them with any accuracy either. Need some work, there, back in the vaults."

Klyten nodded, as if his suspicions had been confirmed, and began to feel his way into Eykor's question, which had almost been forgotten. What, indeed, was in the surname? He said, "I said that every Braid has a role or profession, which is indicated by the name. In the case of the two Player groups, that is what they do—play a Game. It is a very curious matter, just another of their oddities."

Up until this time, Parleau had been somewhat disengaged, aloof from the flow of the remarks, but now his interest deepened. "They play a Game?"

"Well, yes, it is peculiar, full of all kinds of anomalies; it seems that they have, included in their social order, two families whose role is exactly that, to play a Game in public exhibitions. But as we understand the term, professional sportsmen somehow seems inappropriate to this. You see, it happens to be the only organized sport they have, played with formal rules and organized teams. Without exception, all of the rest of their games are informal and very unstructured, more like traditional children's games than anything else. What's more, it, this Game, is not played on a field or a court, but on a portable electronic display panel. This, mind, in a culture that almost never uses electric power or electronics."

Parleau raised his eyebrows, and opened his mouth to speak, but

Plattsman contributed before he could, "We have also studied this game, in Control, and what Klyten says is true. Their board is both portable and durable, apparently has an independent power supply, and is extremely reliable. At the least, they have never had a breakdown during a public Game. We can deduce that a computer has been integrated into its structure, although we cannot as yet specifically locate its position within the machine."

Parleau leaned back in his chair, reflectively. He mused, aloud, "No breakdowns in public is not so hard to attain with good mechanics, engineers, and tight scheduling. And as for where the switching and logic and memory units would be—good, tight design could work it into almost any volume you could care to mention."

Plattsman replied, looking at the chairman's shiny forehead. "I understand, Chairman. That's all true. What Klyten is trying to point out, and I as well, is that this is occurring, over a period of generations, within a culture that suppresses technology, particularly electronic technology, as we know it."

Klyten put in, before Parleau could think of some rationalization, "*And* a formal Game with elaborate rules and rigid operations in a culture that plays unstructured children's games that occur spontaneously. Now consider this, too: this inside a conceptual Surround in which every family group has a functional occupation, a necessity to society. The Players do nothing, aside from some low-level self-support, except play the Game."

Parleau returned to a normal position, then leaned forward, his heavy arms and hands pressed flat on the surface on his desk. He said, "Every Braid supports and contributes to the whole, but the Players are, in effect, subsidized?"

"Exactly," said Klyten.

Plattsman added, "We don't have access to their macroeconomics, but by the models in the studies that have been done using offset simulations, it would appear that considerable cost is involved."

Klyten added more. "And that is verified by their whole value system. Marginal activities—for example, arts—exist in quantity, but only as sidelines. In fact, there is an extremely sophisticated management system integrated at the popular culture level that simply eliminates occupations that don't contribute, no matter how attractive they might be. And this management system is as hard to pin down as the location of the computer in their Game display board. We know that the function must exist, but no one yet has located it. There is also some consideration of the idea that the vast majority of the ler people themselves are unaware of this system. They fit into it so harmoniously. . . ."

Parleau knotted his brows. "This is hard for me to say, because I never believed that I'd ever find myself saying it. What you are saying by all your remarks, is that in fact these woods-bound rustics actually operate a . . . nation, with almost no visible government, at a greater efficiency and with less friction than we do."

Klyten answered, "So it appears. These facts have been known for years, of course, but it is so low-key that nobody ever assembled it before. This explains much—how they can operate the reservation at a profit, not counting what the Institute brings in, and it also explains the true source of the product of the Institute, and the data they feed us."

Parleau reflected, and said, "So they are, in effect, feeding us off the top of their system?"

Eykor interjected angrily, "Programming us, I'd call it!"

Parleau looked blandly and without rancor at the chief of Security. "There's no denying that if they are, it's been to the general welfare. I say, if it works, then let it be. Unless Control can project some nefarious purpose in these manipulations."

Plattsman said, "Control until this minute was unaware that we were being manipulated. And I hardly see evidence of detail work, the kind that would be necessary to bring us to some point desirable to them. But I'll certainly send this through Research, to see if we can prove it, and if so, find out where it's going." He spoke slowly, as if unwilling to believe the implications of what they had uncovered here: Control was totally unaware that a more subtle system was probably being applied to them all, a macrosystem involving—and here Plattsman's mind took a giant, risk-filled leap across normal deductive logic—yes, very likely the large-scale nudging and controlling of the whole damn planet! And for what purpose? As Parleau had most accurately put it, "to the general welfare." That could not be denied. He added, as an afterthought, "Yes, I'll have those crazies down in Games-Theory Branch get cracking on it right away."

Parleau nodded approval, and said, "I want to hear about that girl and this Game they play. How old is it?"

Klyten answered, "According to the annals, the Game appeared coincident with the move into the reservation. It seems to be tied up deeply in the popular religion, a kind of movable morality play. They have factions, rivalries, the whole thing. It is very Byzantine, and the fine points are shrouded in layers of allegorical nonsense."

Parleau observed, "So they sublimate aggression into sports? That's nothing new. We've done that, ourselves, for aeons."

Klyten persisted, "No, no, it's that there is an aggression present within the Game that isn't present anywhere else. Literally. And by no means does it reach all the people. In fact, on the whole, the people are rather uninterested in it. Less than half even bother with it in any degree and the number of real fans is probably less than ten percent, counting the Players themselves."

The data made no more sense to Parleau than it did to anyone else. He pondered on that for a moment, then asked, "Well, what in hell is this Game? We're talking about another of these things we can't see, or are we fishing in the dark there, too?" A sudden light had been illuminated in Parleau's mind. If he could but penetrate into this system, which he sensed was part of a larger, elaborate plan, then by opening it up, he would pave his way, beyond Denver. If he could only prod these blockheads to find the answers. Yes. Suddenly merely surviving his assignment to Seaboard South seemed petty, unvisioned, lacking scope.

Plattsman said, "It's a recursive system. . . ."

Klyten added, interrupting the Controller, "Yes, recursive. The Game itself, as we see it, appears to be very distantly related to chess, or checkers, but of course it is almost inconceivably more complex than either of those examples. It is manifestly difficult even to try to describe it. . . . They normally play on a two-dimensional field, which can be divided at will into one of several tiling arrays: triangles, squares, and hexagons, those being equilateral and regular, and also quite a number of irregular pentagons and hexagons. These divide the field up into cells. Inside the cell, one can have a number of conditions, ranging from binary on-off two-state on up. I don't think there is a limit to the number of states a cell can have, although obviously there are some practical limits. The Game begins with some simple, and I use this word guardedly in this context, patterns of states in cells . . . a move in the Game, or a time-component unit, is the sum of all the changes produced by considering each cell, serially, in relation to a surrounding number of cells, sometimes by raw sum, and sometimes by position of cells of different state arrayed about the referent cell. This neighborhood can also be varied, from close in to far away. Then they apply transition rules, some statistical, some arbitrary, and make the changes. When all the cells have been processed according to the program, then the whole changes and they start over again. The object of the Game appears to attain certain desirable configurations in shape and color and dynamics, while the opposing team tries to manipulate certain parts of the rules and other factors to prevent it; but they, too, operate under elaborate rules covering what they can do."

Plattsman contributed, "You have to understand recursive math to comprehend the Game."

Klyten added one more thought, "We think that this is why they evolved their cumbersome number system of variable-numbers with no permanent fixed base, as our decimal system. It makes it easier to understand the Game, when you have to or want to, in the case of the spectators."

Plattsman continued, "We in Control have tried to explore recursive systems also, because the concept is deeply tied up with decision-making, controlling functions, and programming. The concept was first worked out in the twentieth century, about the middle, if I have my history straight. There was an extensive literature on the subject well into the twenty-first century."

Klyten said, "They were playing random-start Games even then: just fill it up, more or less randomly, and watch it evolve."

Plattsman counterpointed, "But simple Games with unchanging rules and neighborhoods. Most people played on computers when they could get access, but a few fanatics were known to play it on graph paper, some of which they had to have specially printed for the purpose. Absolute maniacs!"

Parleau asked, "Why the difference?"

Plattsman answered, "The computer-players could see the motion and the patterns of change, and spot productive patterns faster, but the graph-paper players, while vastly slowed down by the need to run every single step in the program manually, were able to see farther into the scope of it, and the things it could lead to. Eventually, however, they were also forced into computers by the sheer volume of transactions, but they used the computers only as working aids. All ongoing work in the Game tended to originate from the minority Graphists, and what we know from the Archives indicates that the ler built upon one particularly active Graphist faction—one could almost call it a cult—that was active in the latter third of the twentieth century."

Parleau shook his head exaggeratedly from side to side. He sighed, looked at the ceiling, scratched his neck, and returned his attention to the group. "Tell me no more! I do not wish to become one of these Players— just relate this unknown girl to what she was doing and why, and why she insisted upon withdrawing into herself rather than answer a few simple questions. I will accept your description of things as provision-ally accurate in substance, although I admit to incomprehension. By what means do they control the display?"

Klyten said, "By a keyboard, something rather like an organ of the old days."

"I fail to see why they would devote so much energy to something that demonstrably produces no results. What *is* the use of it?"

Klyten observed, "We have been unable to determine that. Obviously it is of great importance to them, and nobody thinks that its sole pur-pose is entertainment. I mean, after all, the Players have a certain re-gard, an exclusiveness, but hardly are they lionized as popular figures."

Plattsman offered, "Chairman, we have some tapes of some Games material, if you would like to see them. It makes more sense if you can see it in action, perceive the motion in it."

"Yes, by all means," said Parleau. "I would like very much to see this Game. Perhaps we can all learn something from it. You have prepared recordings?"

Plattsman replied, "We have an extensive file of them, Chairman. Control has been studying the Game for many years. From that, we have selected what appears to be a typical, although short, round of a Game."

Klyten added, "This recording was made a few years ago, at their Sol-stice Tournaments. I have it on the good word of those who claim to be authoritative on such matters that this particular Game is a classic of its type, but is rather short in duration. The curtuosity here is after the manner of chamber music, rather than oratorios, symphonies, and grand operas. We mutually apologize, Plattsman and I, for the lack of sound, but none had been thought necessary, since the play is almost exclu-sively visual as medium."

Plattsman motioned to an unseen operator. The office dimmed, a sec-tion of the far wall opened, and the panels slid back into cleverly hid-den recesses in the walls, revealing a softly glowing screen occupying most of the space between floor and ceiling. After an uncertain pause, the screen flickered, flashed bright momentarily, then went completely dark. Then gradually a moving series of images began to fade in, grow-ing in brightness and contrast until it seemed natural to the viewers' dark-adapting eyesight.

The screen showed an open space in the forest, a pleasantly bucolic environment, a natural depression that had been subtly modified into an amphitheater. The show was in color, and though it appeared from the light within to be evening, there was no fading or overexposure; they saw as if they were there. They watched and became absorbed in it. It was a summer evening, deep evening shades and shadows in the small gathering-place of the Players and their audience; they sensed, rather than saw, that somewhere offscreen the sun was yet in the sky; nevertheless it was evening, not merely late afternoon. A subdued, middling crowd was present, all ler, at least as far as could be seen. Some wore summer clothing, light overshirts, loose robelike affairs, which were the everyday, general-purpose ler garment; others wore a garment suggesting a kimono, but with the belt or sash looped and hung loosely over one hip or the other. Many of the younger ones present wore only a saronglike wraparound about their lower bodies, leaving their chests and abdomens bare, while the ends of it fell to their ankles. Even then, with the identical haircuts, it was difficult at first glance to tell boy from girl, to Parleau's eye. You simply could not differentiate. . . . Only if he picked one and watched it for some time could he determine which sex it belonged to. It was as if the whole secret of defining lay in dynamics and motions, rather than in states-of-being, a disturbing notion indeed. He watched what he believed to be a boy, who was engaged in teasing, very subtly, what appeared to be a girl. What was it, the difference? She seemed softer, more delicate, smoother perhaps. He couldn't say just what it was. The way she moved, smiled? They were both trying to appear most serious and attentive, but of course it was a summer evening, warm and scented, and their minds were elsewhere, as well they might have been, with the soft shadows falling across the leafy little glade. The one who had recorded this little drama unawares had not even been observing the boy and the girl, for in the image they both were far off-center, and as Game time came closer, he lost them entirely, expanding the image and zooming closer to take in the display board and the Players.

The board itself was a large, square unit, supported on a simple, broad base, completely unadorned. It looked simple, but in no way did this display board suggest primitiveness, or crudity; to the contrary, it seemed the product of a highly professional technological civilization. Before it was a small, desklike console, furnished with several rows of buttons, while to either side were two larger consoles with imposing multiplex keyboards, which resembled organ consoles more than they did anything else. The Players were already in place, the Reds to the right and the Blues to the left, two Players by each console, and two more behind them. An announcer, was addressing the crowd, apparently in a most relaxed, easygoing manner, as if he (or she—Parleau could not tell) were among friends and acquaintances.

The announcer finished whatever remarks were required, and then retired offstage with a fluty little flourish, to be replaced by a stern and imposing couple, elders by the look of them and the twin long pigtails of iron-gray hair that hung down the fronts of their garments. Their color was dark; Parleau thought black, although he could not be sure . . . the light of day was slowly fading in the recording. These would be the referees. They made no speeches or gestures to the spectators, but turned to the center console and one of them made a chopping motion with his hand. And on the board, immediately appeared a preliminary figure, a mildly complex geometrical figure in five colors. It stayed in place a moment, winked out, and then reappeared.

The whole board shimmered, came alive, changed to a hexagonal cellular array, retaining the figure as well as it could be accommodated into the new matrix; a series of indecipherable symbols began flowing across the top of the screen, and the figure began changing rapidly, evolving into different shapes and densities as the initial moves of the Game proceeded. Parleau watched in attentive astonishment, riveted to his plush chair, as the figure first lost all its color, becoming black against the illuminated background, and then abruptly began to change shape, colors flowing over it like firelight flickering over a wall, or perhaps summer lightning. The most basic color appeared to be green, and it seemed that the Reds were trying to control the figure and manipulate it into other shapes, desired configurations, while at the same time, the Blues, just as tenaciously, attempted to hinder this operation and tried to arrange things so that the developing figure would fly apart and dismember itself. The symbols flowing across the top of the screen changed constantly, scoring? A running commentary while the game was in progress?

At first, despite the interference of the Blues, the Reds seemed to be having the better of it; they manipulated the vibrating figure into a larger shape that seemed more impervious to attack, but this lasted only minutes. Soon, Blue attacked with increased zeal and dedication, their centers laboring mightily over the keyboards, arms and heads blurred in motion, moving faster than the scan rate of the recording device. Soon, the advances of the Reds were blunted, dissipated, brought to a halt. Parleau looked back to the Reds: they were playing, if anything, with even more vigor than the Blues, and as they occasionally turned, he could see that the expressions of intense concentration, indeed, they grimaced with effort.

Suddenly, a foul was called on Blue, and the referees engaged their controls; the Blues were forced to sit helpless for a measured time, their keyboard locked out, while the Reds advanced and rebuilt their figure into an impressively complex configuration. But when they returned, they reentered the Game furious with zeal, and by dint of extreme effort and a brilliant, virtuoso attack, forced the Reds to give up much they had gained, and in fact, as Parleau remembered, forced them to return to an earlier configuration. A foul was now called on Red, and now they also had to sit helplessly aside while Blue, with glee, dismembered the complex figure. But returning, they did not give up, were not routed, and hung on gamely. The Reds began to advance again, slower now than before, but inexorable, like the tide coming in. Blue sensed that there was nothing to be gained by further delay, and they changed the array to square cells, and after a moment, to the triangular lattice, all apparently in an effort to disorient Red and keep them off balance. At first, it seemed to succeed. Red seemed to lose momentum and drift, uncertain of what to do next. Parleau, now indeed caught up in the swirling patterns of the Game, sensed that this had been a reasonable course on the part of Blue, for Red had, he sensed, been gaining, if slowly. Perhaps this could lead to a stalemate, which would of course favor the defending Blues. But soon it became apparent that the maneuver was to be unsuccessful, for Red was still gaming. They had ridden with the attack, drifted with the changing current, and were now fully in possession of the field again. Blue riposted by a move of desperation, changing the field to a beautifully weird pentagonal tessalation, the cells irregular polygons, and after a moment, back to the square grid. But it appeared to be too late, this rearguard action; the audience was waving little red pennants, while partisans of the Blues stood about glumly, their heads lowered, expecting the worst.

It was not long in coming: in an amazing tour de force, Red finally manipulated the figure somehow into an astonishing and enigmatic shape, one which hung on the display board screen for a long time, emitting coherent sparks and particles that fled to the edges and vanished. Across the top of the board, the cryptic symbols flowed on for a moment, as if they had fallen behind the action, and then they stopped, abruptly, and without warning the board went blank, dimmed, and went out. Red partisans and their friends waved their pennants and applauded, rather restrainedly, while Blue fans began to walk away, dejected and expressionless. Some, however, despite their loss, also joined in the subdued approval, showing that they could appreciate a good Game, even if their team had lost. One of the centers of the Red team turned from the console and made a short speech. The view expanded, as if the operator had wished to take in more of the crowd; Parleau looked for the boy and girl he had noticed earlier, but they were almost conspicuously absent. The screen went blank. . . .

Parleau breathed deeply, once. The rest said and did nothing.

After a time, he asked, "Control, what can you tell us about that particular Game?"

"We can set up simplex sequences back in the labs; that is, Games with unchanging parameters. Now, this one you just saw," said Plattsman, "escapes detailed analysis. We think that this one was held to a minimum deliberately, probably varying between three-state and, say, fifteen-to-twenty-state for an upper limit. They use color to symbolize states; in some of the higher-order games, this can get serious, because they have greater color-discrimination than we do. The grid changes you saw yourself. By and large, most cellular arrays are pretty straightforward—equilateral triangles, squares, hexagons. But the pentagonal arrays are all irregular and have some tricky rules; the neighborhood can vary, even when it's at minimum closest to the reference cell. And the rules! Here is where we really are at sea! We think that none of those remained stable for more than a few moves, two to three. We have to deduce it by effect. They used to say, back in the old days, that one insurgent could tie down ten regulars; it's the same ratio here: to compute backward takes about ten times the number of computations, and without long time-strings of steady states of rules, that does us no good. The rules are never symmetrical with respect to time—they only work as rules one way. When you try to work them backward and figure back, you get an uncertainty factor. . . ."

Parleau exclaimed, "Jesus!" He reverted to ancient oaths, and they came easily, even though most people had forgotten the reason why they had been originally said. "Why hasn't someone been working on this longer, brought it up at Staff? All you have to do is look at that equipment and look at what they do with it. Those people are about as primitive as Buckminster Fuller!"

Plattsman said, "We had been trying to come to some conclusion about where the activity was leading . . . so far, it has defied all attempts to vector it."

"How long?" Parleau insisted.

"About . . . ah, since the Game appeared, Chairman."

"And nothing?"

"Nothing. It doesn't change in any manner we can measure. It appeared, and we took sample recordings, and attempted to analyze them. Inasmuch as we have been able to determine, the sole difference between a Game of say, last summer, and one of a hundred years ago, is the same as between any two Games out of the same cycle: individual variation and style of the moment, you know, personal variations."

"And you can't conclude from that?"

Plattsman answered shamefully, "No, sir, we haven't to date."

Parleau leaned forward, and added projection to his voice: "Well, I'm no Controller, but I can see of that remark that, if it is true, what you are seeing is a finished product, an artifact! Sports as we know them continuously evolve and shift, because they are responding to changing needs of the people who play and watch them. But your people, who are the masters of the science of change, can see no change in this Game, and you're stymied! That's the great secret! The Game doesn't change! You idiots, what does it conceal?"

Plattsman hesitated. "I don't understand. . . ."

"That's why I'm chairman and you're a Controller! An artifact doesn't change—*it's the end of the process!* They do something with it that has nothing to do with sports or entertainment or bleeding off aggression. Now what is it?"

Plattsman said, "We pursued that angle early, Chairman. That was the first thing we thought of, just as you did. Now this Game does have fine possibilities for a system of processing information, but it seems like an awful lot of elaboration, and a lot of calling attention to themselves when they could certainly be more secretive about it. I mean, it's like using a code—in some circumstances, that just alerts people to the fact that you have something to hide. Now a code can give you security, but you want the parameter of speed and reliability also in any information-flow system, and the use of codes lowers both, in some cases appreciably."

Klyten helped Plattsman. "The speed of the responses of the Players, and the actions they take, indicate that whatever messages are concealed in it apply to them. The crowds apparently see no more than we did, that one side or the other gains or loses control of the shape of the figure they are working."

Plattsman agreed, nodding his head vigorously, and Klyten continued, "And you have to remember that those Players are raised on a diet of that practically from birth. They get serious about it at around age fourteen, as I understand. By the time they are playing in tournaments, they've all had at least twenty years of it, more. Plus a lot of theory that we don't ever see; they release nothing about the Game or recursive mathematics through the Institute . . . they won't even acknowledge its existence."

Parleau's earlier attack seemed to lose direction now. He seemed stopped in his tracks by the fact that the Controllers had asked the same question he had, years before, and had seen nothing in it but an unchanging Game. . . . He said, "That's another aspect of this that bothers me; exactly that. The long time they spend learning it. How do they maintain motivation? Say what you will about training, about ability, about privilege, I can still see that that stuff doesn't come easy for them, no more than it would be for us. Those Players in the recording were working hard! How much exposure do they get?"

Klyten answered, "They have the great tournaments at the Summer Solstices. Lesser Games are played throughout the warm months. Technically, the Game runs from spring equinox to autumnal."

"And that's all they have to do?"

"That's correct, Chairman."

"Then they are only employed six months of the year? That's the damndest thing I ever heard!"

Klyten said, "Well, it's not entirely without precedent: their ruling Braid, the Revens, does almost nothing. Their role is to arbitrate disputes, but very little ever gets taken to them, so they *do* almost nothing. . . ."

"But they symbolize authority, nationhood, and all that, like the hereditary kings of old."

"Yes, Chairman, that's true, but you have to bear in mind that if they are following the royal-dynasty model, they are doing so without any of the traditional symbols of royalty; they have no ceremony, no 'court,' no deference. When he is not 'in his role,' as they say, the High Reven is a dirt farmer, just like the lowest."

Parleau said, "So this Mallenkleth . . ."

"*Mael*lenkleth," Klyten corrected, changing the broad, open *ah*-sound Parleau had used to a shorter, flatter sound, something intermediate between an "A" and an "E," but without the nasal quality of the North American Modanglic "ae."

"What's the difference?"

" 'Mai' means 'bad,' 'Mael' means 'Apple.' There's a difference."

"You're the expert. So, then, this insibling of a Braid of Gameplayers."

Plattsman and Eykor answered together, "Right!"

Parleau continued, "And a mathematician with the Department of Research and Development at the Institute, and a captured 'vandal' who elects somehow to disappear inside herself rather than reveal one single word? And now she's gone and we can't ask her anything? Damn! I'd really like to know if there is any connection. So now we all know some things, but not which is relevant among them."

Klyten said, "We had hoped that these recordings of Game phenomena would suggest something to you that none of us had seen before. We have all tried, in our way, beforetimes, but there was nothing. . . . No one ever paid much attention to the Game before, other than cursorily. And here, we got the criminal, as they say, red-handed at the scene of the crime. But no motive. A great anomaly. It's obvious that . . ."

Eykor interjected, "Obvious that they're up to something. Otherwise, all that we've heard still adds up to nothing. No other way! And now I must needs ask the learned doctor of the mysteries of the New Humans another question: what exactly is this stuff they call 'Multispeech,' anyway?"

Klyten looked about, sharply. "Why do you ask?"

"Our monitor facilities seem to be picking up a lot more of it now. Significant statistically."

Klyten said, "Little enough is known of it. They talk freely enough in their everyday language. Singlespeech. It's just another language, far as I know, if it is a bit more regular than most, and of course it has its difficult parts for one to learn. But now Multispeech. . . . perhaps multichannel language would be a better term. It is something different, a new concept. Now we express ourselves multiplexually, too, but the media are different; ordinary voice, a broad, harmonic system. Then there is body-language. And there is the frequency-modulated fail-alarm system present in our voices all the time. It's just a tone that's always present in your voice, you never *hear* it. Nervous system to nervous system, direct. Until you have anxiety. Then the tone drops out and your voice flattens a bit to the ear. When you hear loss of safe-tone, you also lose safe-tone until you discover the source of the anxiety. Even infants respond to it. It has uses in verification interviews. Now, what has apparently happened in the ler brain is that they combine all three systems into one channel of communication, via sound waves modulated by the larynx, and their resonances are so arranged that they can control the individual harmonic bands of the sound, modulate them individually. We know they can communicate with it, but we don't know all that much of what they can do with it . . . we have some studies indicating that in Multispeech the data-rate drops. In other words, it takes longer to say the same thing. Quite a bit longer. So we can deduce that speed is not one of the reasons for using it."

Plattsman commented, "Wrong, there, Klyten, though I hate to say it. Communications systems are the heart of Controlling, and we know very well that we will gladly sacrifice speed for accuracy, because in a system that programs noise and semantic distortions out, the resultant lack of misunderstanding and the increase in clarity means an ultimate increase of speed in the end."

"That's no news! We already know that the principle applies to Singlespeech, which has a rather slower data rate than any modern, historic language. It's slower than Modanglic by far."

"Then why have they exploited the ability? It must be that much more accurate. And it may have other uses. Communications systems do more than pass words, you know."

"We know little about it. They tell us nothing more than that they can talk to three people at once, saying different things . . . we don't even know how different the texts are."

"Have you correlated Multispeech to specific activities?"

Klyten replied, "It is used extensively in playing the Games, but precisely what part it plays, we cannot determine."

Parleau snorted, "Hmpf! The further we go, the more we find that someone ought to have been looking into. What *have* you people been doing all these years? Writing evaluations of evaluations?"

Klyten said, thoughtfully, after a longish pause, "Perhaps, Chairman, these things we are just now turning up fit somehow into a picture that we were never supposed to see, and that this is the reason why the girl allowed herself to reach the condition she was found in, in the box."

Parleau answered, "That's possible. But in essence, we observe what people do and predict therefrom; not why they do it. After all, once you start asking why, all kinds of speculative Pandoras open up. . . . But if we assume that there was a plot, it can only be that others were in it; and if the girl allowed herself to be reduced to gibbering, slobbering idiocy to prevent us from making certain associations . . . then those associations must exist. I think we have parts of a picture now."

Plattsman interjected, "Or an unfinished map."

"Very perceptive, that difference," agreed Parleau. "But we are also in a bit of a bind ourselves in this. We cannot act precipitately. They keep a much closer rein on this Region than I ever saw at Mojave. We could move first, of course. I mean, execute a Two-twelve, full occupation, tomorrow. But we do not at this point know what we are looking for, or where to look for it. Hell, it could be nothing more tangible than an idea; and an ignorant execution of the occupation would in those circumstances amount to destruction or removal of any evidence or artifacts. For the labor we'd get nothing, and we'd spend the rest of our days explaining why we took the action to Section Q. So we can't act now, however attractive it might seem, working on no more than we have. Disconnected anomalies that's paranoia."

Eykor added, saturninely, "Sometimes even paranoids have flesh-and-blood enemies." He paused a moment, then said, "We in Security know that there is something to hide. Give me a little time, and I can document it, and possibly locate it."

Parleau stared at Eykor, as if he had not heard him. "So granted."

Plattsman interrupted. "Pardon me, but I am receiving a signal. May I retire for a moment?"

"Certainly," said Parleau.

He left the office hurriedly, but he was not gone from it for long. Plattsman returned, saying, "Well, news, of a sort. Not what we might have expected, but something."

"Go ahead."

"Our monitors report that Vance just entertained a group in his office. There was a reference there to an earlier conversation, which we must have missed; they could find no record of it. Probably was in a desensitized area. Anyway, this group claims to have taken a commission to locate a girl. Maellenkleth by name, and they asked for an introduction to Region Security, for assistance. Vance has forwarded them here, per request."

Eykor asked, "According to instructions?"

"Oh, indeed. Vance has become docile enough, and cooperates freely now."

Eykor chortled, "Wonderful, wonderful! A nibble at the bait, so it is, and soon, too. Great concern, within the plot. And who are our nibblers?"

"In the course of the conversation with Vance, they were identified, apparently he knew some of them personally. There are three: a Fellirian Deren, a Morlenden Deren, and the third was identified only as a Krisshantem. No surname. Vance did not know him."

Klyten said, "He gave no surname? None at all?"

Plattsman answered, "Well, I have only the report to go on, but none was listed. They are pretty thorough and if he had given one, it would have been forwarded."

"A curious matter, no surname. Everyone uses one, even elders, who style themselves with the surnames Tlanh or Srith as befits their gender, or rather former gender. We usually translate it 'lord' or 'lady,' as fits, but I suspect we miss something of the flavor. . . . Could be he didn't want anyone to know what it was."

Eykor said, "As if he were a Player. . . ."

Parleau asked, "What is the probability of Vance being in a plot with them, here?"

Plattsman replied, "Low. Lower than twenty percent correlation. As for the others, we are not so sure. The female Fellirian Deren was cleared previously; she is a long associate of Vance's in the Institute."

Klyten added, "By the names, the one called Morlenden is the familial co-spouse of Fellirian, although we can't see the exact relationship. If she is clear, he probably is also. But the other one, this Krisshantem. He could be anything. It certainly is possible that he could be, as Eykor suggests, a Player, or one of the plot, but it is also true that he could be in another relationship, either with the girl, or with the Derens, or something else, a specialist of some sort. We have no way of knowing, short of interrogation."

Parleau said, "I cannot permit that at this time, not after our loss of the girl."

Eykor commented, "Loss, perhaps, but look at what that loss has led us to."

Parleau answered, "Yes, I see what it has led us to: anomalies and more questions than we were asking at the start! So I direct that they be given the girl without obstruction. But not without the closest of observation. Have the medics state that we found her that way and have been conducting an investigation."

Eykor asked, "Is that entirely prudent, Chairman? After all, they may be able to learn something from her. And here we have three more . . ."

"No, no, no, don't take them. Unless they themselves show cause, and then handle subtly—we don't want three more of these basket-cases on our hands. However it occurs. Plattsman, can your people follow them?"

"Not easily, Chairman, but I believe we can work out something."

"Well, do your best. I want every move recorded and analyzed. As much as possible, Klyten, you go down to Control and work with them, interpret. And we will also want some reserves close to hand."

"No problem, there, Chairman. I can have a Tacsquad in parallel all the time."

"All right! So get to it and keep me informed."

Parleau waved them off, naggingly, hurriedly, as if he were shooing a group of schoolboys away from some valuable statue, or out of a tree they were not supposed to climb. The rest collected their portfolios and departed, leaving Parleau alone in the now silent office. He leaned back deeply in his chair, sighed thoughtfully, and at last, put his heavy feet upon the desk. At first, he placed his hands across his belly, but later, he folded them behind his head, thinking. He tried to fit the pieces together, but there were too many other pieces missing, and he could not make them fit. He reflected that Eykor had had the first crack at the girl, and had failed to extract anything; likewise, in turn, Control. Klyten admitted ignorance of reasons, but supplied considerable data, much of which disturbed him more than the original incident, the destruction of the instruments. That seemed very far away now, a niggling little problem not worthy of solution by him. Yes. There was much there, strands of coincidences . . . something was nagging, nibbling at the back of his mind. What was it? He tried to relax and free-associate. Yes, something to do with families. They certainly were strongly oriented to the family, maintaining their line with what seemed to Parleau to be a most artificial system, and keeping it going. Families. And those aristocratic Players, two family groups of them since the dawn of their time, doing something that had no function.

An alarm went off, silently, in his mind. Yes, he was on the track of it now. Yes, the Player families. And he sat back, mentally, as it occurred to him what they all had missed. It all fit, beautifully. They had control, they had management, even if no one could describe it and locate it. And they had an electronic Game in an anti-tech culture, a competition in a cooperative, primitive communist society. And a family, no, two, who were subsidized to do something that had no function but to entertain, in an economic environment that saw itself as severely practical. It all smelled. But not half so bad as the idea that was arriving sideways, as it were, deep in the recesses of Parleau's mind: that one of these Players was given away to the humans, and that the other was a spy, obviously out of the Game, and that the Braid, the family group, was being allowed to end. And Klyten hadn't even seen it. Parleau felt a rush of pride: he had seen something their ler expert hadn't, even as he had been commenting on it. Sexed-out, he had said; they had to seek new identities. But the Game as he had seen it required two sides, and very soon, in a few years, there would be only one. They were going to let something go that they had carefully nurtured for three hundred years or more, without a comment! Parleau sat up abruptly, all semblance of relaxation gone. And from a recess in the desk, he retrieved a vocoder and began transcribing some ideas and instructions, as fast as he could consider them. Yes. It was all tied together somehow, and he was going to derive the answer, if he had to run all of them right into the ground.

THIRTEEN

In the Game, it is arbitrarily considered that the total number of operations on every cell in the pattern-area constitutes one unit of Gametime. How we do it is unimportant, serially or by parallel computation, or by scalar patterning; that is our limitation as finite creatures—but in reality it all occurs simultaneously, instantly, for that is the smallest unit into which time can be divided, an absolute. . . . And so across Gametime, we observe motion, as moving particles with varying degrees of coherence and self-identity; as ripples of unique wavelike patterns of presence and absence; as "invisible waves" that seem to transit empty cellular space and cause reactions in target portions of the developing pattern. There is no motion and there are no waves. Period. That is illusion. There is only the sequential and recursive interaction of the defined Surround with the associated Transition-rules and Paradigms. It is necessary to order our perceptions from the cellular unit outward, that we may fully comprehend higher-order phenomena of appearances, and thereby not be deceived, as one might easily be working from the macrocosm to the microcosm.

—The Game Texts

TO BE ATTACKED with malice in mind was, while relatively rare enough, at the least understandable under certain conditions, Morlenden and Fellirian alike could vividly recall the heyday of the Mask-Factory highwaymen of a span ago; likewise they could also recall several inter-Braid feuds and vendettas of greater or lesser importance. In particular, the Khlefen—Termazen—Trithen triangular vendetta of the generation past could come to mind, even though in the present it had been reduced in scale and severity to minor incidents of mild disrespect, or perhaps contemptible behavior within the precincts of neighborhood markets.

At any rate, they, the Derens, had no feuds at present with anyone, and it was obvious that robbery was not the motive for the attack on Morlenden. But whatever the intent, it had come by arrow, certainly a weapon which could only be used leaving the hand. On this basis, and after studying the arrow itself, a deadly metal construction, they all reasoned that the assailant had to have been human. But this raised more questions than it answered, for who could it be among the forerunners who moved silently through the forest and brush, in the middle of the reservation, and then vanished without a trace? And then, more importantly, what human would wish to injure Morlenden? Only a handful even knew of his existence.

Kaldherman, who was prone to eccentric ideas, had voiced a suspicion that the assassin had been one of the people, a concept which had disturbing overtones indeed. And to add influence to this position, Morlenden had commented that Sanjirmil had indeed expressed apprehension about his possible uncovering of Game secrets. But he did not tell all the reasons why he could not bring himself to accuse her, and the rest could see no reason why one elder Player would hire them, and another try to prevent them.

Krisshantem was also suspected, if for no other reason than his uncanny silence in the woods. And his status as *hifzer*, who might be capable of anything; once the one set of traditions went, who could say what others might follow? But he had the least motive of all, and in fact later arrived to dispel the notion in person, a day behind Morlenden, and in the company of one Halyandhin, one of the elder Hulens, who completely verified his story and whereabouts. And the issue remained where it had been—unsolved. Krisshantem examined the place where the attack had come from, but he would say nothing of what he saw therein, if indeed anything. When pressed on the matter by Kaldherman to the edge of insult, he admitted ruefully that it seemed to him to be the work of a human of superior knowledge as a tracker, a notion he considered outrageous. There simply were none in the reservation at all.

So it was that with great apprehensions the party had departed the Deren *yos* and journeyed down to the Institute on the mono, and spoken with Director Vance; Morlenden, Fellirian, and Krisshantem. These were the ones Vance gave directions to. There were two more whom Vance did not see, and whose directions came from Fellirian: Kaldherman and Cannialin, who were to travel with them, but keeping a discreet distance, as if unconnected. Tourists, a young couple, out on a holiday.

Departing the tube-train at Region Central, the three ler appeared at some distinction from the humans who were using the underground terminal at that time of day. It was somewhat after the noon hour, so the terminal was relatively empty of the ebb and flow of shift changes; yet there was considerable traffic, incidental people on errands of unknown significance. Smaller in stature and lighter in build than the humans, they were also recognizable immediately by their clothing; the simple fall of overshirts, even heavy winter ones, was greatly different from the heavy folds, tucks, pleats, and stiff fabrics of their human co-travelers. They had thrown their hoods back; two had the long, single braid of hair that marked the adult and parent phase ler, while the third wore his in the anonymous bowl cut of the adolescent. To the casual eye, they suggested a family group on an outing, an air Fellirian had suggested that they cultivate, for the farther they were from the reservation, the less people would actually recall about ler Braid ordering, and would project their own images upon them. Kaldherman and Cannialin maintained contact, but also distance. They seemed to be only country yokels who gaped in astonishment at almost everything they saw. At least in part, for Kaldherman, this was not entirely playacting, for it was his first trip outside. He was astonished, in fact.

Standing in the station, pausing before further onward motion, the tube-train waited, making soft mechanical noises, while along its length, doors opened and closed, and in the terminal itself, along the platform, echoes moved in the air, up and down, seeking a quiet corner among the dull concrete facings in which to spin out and die. The underground terminal was a broad hall of indeterminate length—a smoky bluish haze obscured the distant ends where the tunnel dipped down into the earth again. One could sense that the end walls were there, not so very far away, but still vague and unmarked; there was nothing for the eye to fasten to, and the prevailing dimness, lit by weak lamps spotted along the low ceilings, stretched the capacity of their eyes to the utmost.

By the stairwell leading upward, a sweeperman absentmindedly poked with his pushbroom at an insignificant pile of trash, coughing randomly with no great urgency. At dimly lighted kiosks along the stained walls, patrons discussed apparently the prices of fares and the configurations of schedules. The answers, like the questions, were tentative, hedged, rationalized, qualified to a degree no ler could hope to understand, holding a melancholy air of perpetual indecision. As if, having nowhere to go, the indefinite wranglings over schedules and fares had become a peculiar free entertainment, a substitute for more meaningful communication and relationships. Over all hung an odor, extremely peculiar and noticeable to the ler sense of smell. It filled the clotted damp air: ozone, lubricating oils and greases, metals and metallic compounds, metalloceramic and plastic hybrids, stale clothing, cigarette smoke, humans of several degrees of hygiene.

Climbing the stairwell to the surface, Morlenden asked Fellirian if the humans, with all their vast technology, could not perhaps have installed a moving stairway, better lighting, as they were reputed to have done in some of their great cities.

Fellirian answered, smiling faintly as she climbed the stairwell to the upper world, "They have a phrase that describes that perfectly: they call it somewhere-else-ism. If you ask why anything isn't as it should be— social inequities, shift disparities, mechanical malfunctions, nonexistent conveniences, and loaded benefits—the responsible parties always cite some location, preferably rather far away, where things are just right. To your question about slideways, the local engineer would most likely say, 'Oh, they have just installed that system this very week in Tashkent Center.' And in Tashkent, or Zinder, or Coquilhatville, they are saying at the same time to *their* complainants, 'In Old North America they have all that stuff, and low taxes* as well.' And there's a time variation of it, too, not just of place: either they had it, and it broke, or it's coming next summer. And they repair the hot-water pipes in, you guessed it, the dead of winter, too. No, Olede, I fear that very little of the technology leaks down to the street level. In fact, these,"—and here Fellirian gestured at random passersby with a slight motion of her head—"have rather less, on the whole, than their foreparents did. Thus is the way of all things like this, and why we pursue them with greater caution."

They reached the top of the stairwell and emerged into the more open air of a plaza, about which low, subtly-colored buildings clustered. Before the stairwell opening, a painted sign mounted on posts listed significantly organizations nearby, presumably of interest to the arriving traveler, identifying their locations according to building numbers of the structures in which they were housed. Morlenden, not as familiar with

---

* To the ler, all permanent taxes, or standing taxes, were conceptually a horror; taxes were intended to be specific and unique. Since Braid Deren collected such taxes as required, Fellirian could speak with wry authority on the subject.

Modanglic as Fellirian, thought there was something odd about the sign, something he couldn't exactly place, until he realized that several of the words on it were apparently misspelled, or so it seemed. One word was misspelled twice, in two different ways. The errors cast a singular air of bland incompetence about the sign, and by inference, those who had erected it, an impression reinforced by the shoddy repainting the sign had received many times.

The air of the city was translucent, an effect compounded of a light fog, overcast, steam from underground vents, and various fumes; and as in the station platform belowground, there was a similar vagueness, an indeterminacy, to the distances. A few forlorn trees filled elevated planters of concrete sited at random intervals along the main plaza walkway, the inhabitants now mostly bare of leaves and foliage and dripping with condensate.

Of the buildings they could see, as they paused to allow Fellirian to orient herself, none appeared to be larger than three or four stories, and none bore any indication relating to their occupants or their functions; but they did, each building, bear enormous placards at their corners, which in turn displayed numbers, none of which seemed to have any relationship to any other displayed number. One announced, "3754." Another, immediately adjacent, said, just as definitively, "2071." The streets moved off in a square grid pattern, with regular ninety-degree corners, but it was the pattern of a maze, rather than thoroughfares; none of the streets appeared to go through to anywhere. Morlenden vulgarly observed aside to Krisshantem that it seemed the humans laid out their streets after the tile-joints on the floors of the public toilets at the Institute: the neat, ninety-degree lines went nowhere.

They knew where they needed to go—to Building 8905, as Vance had told them—but this building was not listed on the directory sign, nor could any of them locate it from their viewpoint on the plaza. Fellirian, more at home with humans than either Morlenden or Krisshantem, accosted a passerby and asked the location of Building 8905.

The man responded somewhat furtively, and hurried on his way, into the terminal, down the steps. Fellirian returned, and said, "That one said that eight-nine-oh-five is to our left, a few blocks over. Head left from the plaza, right at the first street beyond the end of three-seven-five-four over there, skip an alley, and then left and left at the very next streets. Left, right, skip, left and left."

Kris exclaimed under his breath, "Insane! None of these blocks is numbered in any order. Why number them in the first place?"

"I know," she answered. "It's an awful system. The original intent was a good one, I suppose; then there was order. But with rebuilding and changes, it got all mixed up. Now and again, some administrator tries to reorder his district, but when you change the number of a building, you also have to change all of the references to it, all of the records. All the directories. And people get confused. You should try to make a call through the public commnet as it is! Much worse! It takes, on the average, five or six calls to get the office or the person you need. Why, I know of one case where I called one number, and a person answered. It was not the man I was calling, so he gave me another number. I called it, and it rang; the same man answered the same instrument, and told me my party wasn't in! And the directory entries make no sense at all: supplies are carried under the section 'Logistics,' while the Logistics-Plans Offices are listed under 'Plans.' At first I thought that it was just me, that I was at fault for not learning the key to it all, but Vance told me it was the same with everybody; all of them carry around little personal directories, compiled over the years, listing the real numbers and offices and people. Some people actually have a side job on the sly as professional listers. Others sell personal directories for astounding sums."

Morlenden shook his head. "It certainly would seem that these numbers lend the appearance of greater order."

Krisshantem added, "I am surprised that they can have a working society at all on such a basis."

She answered, "Vance has a theory, to which I also subscribe, that there is a good reason for such tangles and why society chooses to work through them. He thinks that bureaucratic systems and number messes like this arise, not through carelessness, but through specific, if half-conscious, attempts to put distance between people, because the civilization has somehow compressed them closer to one another than they are capable of being naturally. They build a time delay into all their transactions, because, crowded in personal space, they must expand into time."

"They have traded frustration for satisfaction, no doubt," finished Morlenden as they started off to the left across the plaza toward 8905.

She said, "True! But that frustration with the time delay is a forebrain problem: one can rationalize it, which adds to its effectiveness. But body-space contact aggression is at a deeper level, more instinctual, and thus more difficult to control. No, trading time for space works."

He laughed. "And so we're building the very same thing! Look at us,

you and I, Eliya; with all our records of births and deaths and transfers to elder lodges. Braid-line diagrams, Braidbooks, collations of
names. Aren't we now preparing the groundbreaking for the same
thing to come? I mean, in *miel* years, we could all come back and visit
and see scores of little Perderens, Terderens, Zhanderens, all busy,
scribbling away in their little offices, just like this, and instead of us
visiting them, they will all be required to call us upon every minor little event."

Fellirian did not answer him, Krisshantem added, most cryptically,
"Too, it is a way to slow or stop time. All events leave ripples, and these
methods are sad attempts to make standing waves of those ripples. It
gives the illusion of permanence and eminence to those who feel swept
along in the general rate. But the events themselves are never prolonged
beyond their time; they aren't even touched, for these things avoid
them."

For some unaccountable reason, this remark left Morlenden with a
dire sense of moody foreboding, some unspecified menace. Krisshantem
was prone on occasion to utter oracular parables, statements whose true
import even he did not understand completely on the conscious level.
Nor did Morlenden. . . .

Now off the plaza, they had made their first turn and were proceeding along a narrow street between two buildings which seemed smaller
than the general rule. The pastel, stained, or unpainted surfaces, the low
cloud cover, the suggestion of winter fog, the pervasive mechanical
smells, odors, tinctures, distillations, all combined in an alien gestalt to
lend a sly, just-out-of-range-of-recognition melancholy to their journey.
There was danger in this, indeed, so they all knew, great danger. But
however near it might very well be, it also seemed remote, miniature,
disinterested, accidental or blind policy if at all. All that remained was
not excitement, but an odd sadness, a peculiar emotion they could not
recall feeling before, though they had all known painful circumstances
in their lives. It impelled one to lassitude and blind, wheel-spinning action for the sake of action at the same time. And passing humans
seemed also to share it.

To ease the tension rising among them, they began to talk among
themselves. The basic gray, the basic color behind the overcast gray day,
changed and shifted, clotting suddenly, and then clearing again, only to
close in again. Now it was yellowish, now blue and violet, and now
again, pinkish. The cloud deck was thin, and as the clouds moved overhead in the spaces of sky between the buildings, above the faceless and

nameless buildings, they changed the quality of light passing through their vague, unformed layers.

Krisshantem was the first to speak openly of it. "Why do we feel as we do? Is this city so alien to us?"

This time it was Morlenden who did not speak. Fellirian glanced about her once, muttering something uncatchable under her breath, adding, "They used to call it *sienon* . . . the blues. But few know the term anymore. They feel it, all the same. There is no natural law that says that men can't live in cities, or us, either. It's just that this kind of city isn't right for them. Or us. We feel the wrongness."

Krisshantem digested this in silence. Then he asked, "And so you are sure that we will find Maellen here, in this pile, in this eight-nine-oh-five?"

She said, "So much Vance averred. But he also added that according to his informants there was something wrong with her. I have adjudged it was a good thing that we spent those extra days practicing recovering and reprogramming a forgetty."

"Now that we are here," Kris said, "I like that not at all. We should not even discuss such a thing in this place, much less assay to perform it here."

Morlenden agreed in part. "I'd also prefer to do it in a safer environment, but then there's the problem of carrying her back. . . . I also didn't want Kal to see us do it; he'll probably think it the vilest sort of black magic." Then he added, "But *rathers* don't count so much, do they?"

Fellirian laughed, deep down in her throat. "True, what you say . . . but I have a trick in mind, and for it to work, she will have to be self-propelled and ambulatory."

Morlenden continued, to Krisshantem, "So, then. You who have instructed us in the way of restoring forgetties; are you sure we won't get back any of the original Maellenkleth?"

Kris looked idly about himself, at the chipped and cracked facades, the blind windows, which were few enough, and those filmed over with dust and grime and the streaking added by the rain. He said, coldly, impersonally, "Completely sure. Nothing. Well, there may be fragments left, indeed, we can expect to see some, observing her over a few months, until the new persona digests and integrates them. Little odd pieces, flashes of partial mnemons, but the memory and the old persona? It's all gone. I have heard that forgetties say odd things, hints of the old, but they themselves don't know why they say them, and in time they stop."

Fellirian reached to the boy as they walked, touching him with an affectionate gesture, half a mother's reassurance, and half the consolation of one who has shared as co-equal. Krisshantem was a bit in both worlds. She said, "So this is doubly cruel, that she will most surely be a forgetty. You lose her, even as we are engaged in recovering her. What we will get back will be a stranger."

Kris responded, "That is how it will be, how it must be."

"I am sorry, sincerely sorry that we had to drag you into this. There were others, after all. . . ."

"It is no matter to regret, Fellirian Deren. I would not have it otherwise; it repays much of what she gave freely to me. Have no fears: I will do it right, lead you well. That sorrow has already been struck, and I do not moon over echoes."

And now they had made their last left turn, and stopped, looking about uncertainly. At last they discovered a small, grimy sign affixed to the side of an inconspicuous building, which read, *8905*. After further searching about for a few more moments, they located the small and insignificant entry, passed through it, not without some misgivings, and were inside. And what had Vance told them? *In eight-nine-oh-five, do not sightsee or evidence any idle curiosity; ignore that which you see that is not specifically shown to you. Eight-nine-oh-five can be a house of lamentations for those who look too closely into it.* Inside, all seemed innocuous. A preoccupied, diffident reception clerk at a disorderly desk piled high with forms and worksheets directed them to a small anteroom, where they waited, sitting in plastic chairs that someone had, some time in a remote past, mistakenly assumed would be form-fitting.

After a wait of unknown duration, for it seemed that time was curiously exempted inside this building, a single human appeared, dressed in a plain, very dark blue tunic and pants, unadorned except for an odd heraldic device affixed to the upper left chest. This one was very dark in complexion, imposing and dignified, reticent yet vital, all at the same time. His face was immobile, but of a certainty not vacant. Fellirian, as she saw him, made an involuntary gesture, nervously brushing back her fine brown hair at her right temple; a nervous gesture. Morlenden had seen her make that gesture only rarely, and only when she met someone of considerably more *takh** than herself. He became very alert. This was the one.

---

* Best translated, "force of personality," although a full explanation involves considerably more than just personality, delving far into concepts of aggression and projection.

The man spoke. "I am Hando Errat. I have been assigned to assist you, expedite any forms that may have to be completed. You are the persons assigned to take custody of the girl?"

Fellirian answered, rising to her feet, "Yes. We hold such a commission from her family. We are the keepers of the census records, the nearest thing we have to a civil service." Morlenden saw, as she stood to address Errat, how large the human really was: he topped Fellirian by almost two heads.

The immobile face did not change expression, but intoned solemnly, "There will be a small difficulty. She was apparently responsible for the destruction of some valuable instruments."

"We were not aware of this," she answered, carefully neutral.

"There will be no requirement for punishment. Compensation will be required for the value of the items. She has also received some custodial care in the interim since that time."

Fellirian said, "We have brought no currency for such a contingency. But in any matter concerning fees, I am certain that any agreement I sign will be honored in full by our sponsors. My word as head of Braid."

Morlenden asked, "What were the instruments?"

"Implements of no great account. A curious case; we have been unable to comprehend exactly why she did that. I believe the charges and surcharges will come to something near a thousand valuta," said Errat, disappointment showing subtly in the set of his face, his posture, the tone of his deep voice. Fellirian read him, and saw, relaxing herself, that he had weighed them and found them innocent. Controller-Interrogator, she thought, finally deciphering the badge. He would obviously have been box-trained to read minutiae, derive volumes from the most careful evasions. And he paused, as if weighing imponderables, unseen quantities.

Then, "What will you do with the girl? She is now in a condition that I would term inoperable. I have been advised that it occurred under unknown causes."

Fellirian answered, "It is one of our liabilities. We were aware of the possibility of such an occurrence. We intend to return her to the community of the people, where there are methods available to restore her . . . although not as before. She can never be as before; she has lost her entire memory."

"Amnesia?"

"No, something more. It's gone, that's all. We will rebuild a new personality in her, enough for her to function."

"You have such abilities?"

"She will relearn, after the manner of a newborn. All we do in accelerate the process somewhat. Personality and memory are timeless, dimensionless, a wave front. We will start another wave."

"You will reprogram her?" Errat was dangerously perceptive.

"In a word."

"We were not aware of this quality in the people."

"It is neither short nor easy—not on her, not on they who will build the new one."

"How is this done, may I ask?"

"By a process that has no analog in your people, and is useless to you; and of course, I would demean my honor by divulging what is in essence a highly religious ceremony."

There was an uncanny silence while Errat digested the import of what Fellirian had said. He felt that the small, diminutive New Human female was telling the truth, or at least most of it. Now, reprogramming! That was news! But it was also a distraction, for they would not offer it so readily otherwise. And it was a tacit admission that whatever the girl had been, whatever she had known, it was gone, for them as well. They wanted her back for religious reasons! Culture! What rubbish! But in the heart of Errat's certainty, he felt a tiny quiver of apprehension. There was perhaps a clever illusion here, but he couldn't quite grasp it; something just beyond. Well, she had said it would be so, but even so, instructions were clear enough, as was his own plan. *Let them have the room and see what they do with it. They are but simpletons pretending to be sophisticated, knowledgeable. But under it all, still just that: simpletons.* And another voice said, *Wrong, wrong. What was it about this?*

And he said, "Certainly, indeed. I would not dream of violating a trust. We have such as well as you. But, of course, any insights you could pass along, through the Institute, would be most gratefully appreciated by us all. Do you have contacts there? No doubt they would like to apply this kind of thinking to some of the problems we are facing. We have a considerable problem in this area . . . people mislay and forget things, drift off into irresponsible reveries, start spending time daydreaming."

Fellirian shook her head. "Speaking with due attention to your goal, I see little we could add to help you. What we do does not aid memory, increase the span of attention, or energize people whose wits are slipping. But I will mention your needs to my friends in their departments; I am sure that they will be able to offer you some insights which will be useful to you." Standoff! Errat had been trying to lead Fellirian by negatives; let her deny enough areas of applicability, and he could find the area and fill it in himself, with a little cleverness. But she had simply fed back his own categories to him, and then shut down the conversation.

Errat nodded. He understood what had been said, as well as that which had been implied. He stood back a bit and motioned to them to follow. "Well, come along, then. We can release the girl if you're ready for her."

They followed Errat out of the anteroom, and Morlenden watched closely, direct vision averted, warily, as they proceeded by a most roundabout way through the viscera of Building 8905; there were corridors with poor lighting and many abrupt turns; short, dingy stairwells, lifts, walkways, ramps. To his eye, 8905 was fey, alien, a structure embodying concepts they hardly knew, much less cultivated. Its strangeness, he felt instinctively, possessed a complexity that concealed its essence from even its regular users. And he could not escape the suspicion, arising just as instinctively, that the way they were going was not the main route through the building, but was a back way, a janitor's route, or a watchman's patrolway. Or perhaps a secret route, known only to initiates. Errat did not hesitate: he seemed to know exactly where he was going. Along the way they met few people; all, to a person, minded their own business and did not look, beyond a cursory inspection. And on they walked. Sometimes up, sometimes down. The light from the frosted windows remained exactly the same, no matter how they found the windows, and the light did not change in quality. Morlenden knew that they had walked farther than the outside of the building could have contained. That, and the unchanging light, convinced him that wherever they were, it was not inside the building they had seen from the outside. A cold chill passed rapidly through him. *This whole neighborhood must be eight-nine-oh-five, passaged like an anthill with connecting tunnels and over-walks, and every single one of the windows is blind to the outside, its lighting controlled artificially. What shows on the outside is just a front, and located on a side alley as well.*

He glanced covertly at the others who had come with him; Fellirian, his insibling and co-spouse. She was not such a stranger to the ways of the forerunners, and in this place, seemed to be only slightly more alert than usual. It was obvious they were going to give them the girl and let them go. What else they might have in mind, she felt they could handle. But along her face, around her large, expressive eyes, around the corners of her broad, full mouth, there were also infinitesimal little lines and tics revealing her concern for the condition in which they could expect to find Maellenkleth. Or, rather, she who had once been Maellenkleth. No more. She who was yet to be in this body they would call Schaeszendur, for though the body be the same, the persona would be different.

On the other hand, Krisshantem was tense and wary as a wild animal confronting the zoo for the first time. Every sense was alert, every perception was peaked at maximum receptivity. Morlenden had learned to trust the boy's perceptions, and he recalled that during their journey to this place, this anthill warren, he had not been so nervous, but moody and belligerent. Therefore he sensed something about this Building 8905. What was it he had seen, sensed, or inferred in these bland, sometimes cracked and stained walls, the substantial, heavy doors, the rare figures they passed who averted their eyes, and the silences? The silences? These, Morlenden knew, were not the quiet of absences, but a pressure of closeness, things carefully hidden.

At last they came to a section that revealed, in its better lighting, and a sharp, astringent scent in the air, it was devoted to medical purposes. In the odor-complex, there were also undertones of many other substances, mostly organic, some natural, some highly artificial. He could identify none of them. They passed through a brightly lit area that seemed to be the source of most of the odors, a laboratory, and onward into a suite of wards and rooms. Errat spoke briefly to an attendant who seemingly materialized out of thin air, and they entered one of the rooms. There was an inhabitant, tied lightly in a hospital bed. It was Maellenkleth.

To Morlenden, who could remember the mnemo-holistic image impressed into him by Krisshantem, the girl looked much the same in overall configuration and shape, although she was a bit thinner than he recalled in the image. But the expression in her face was neither that of a living adolescent, nor of a person who had withdrawn within, but rather like an abandoned newborn: vacant, blank, uncoordinated. It was easy to see, but that difference said everything, even as one almost overlooked it and its simplicity. The personality, the persona, the undefinable, unboundable person that inhabited this body and acted in it was now gone, as if it had never been. This was not, strictly speaking, Maellenkleth, but an empty shell that had once responded to that name.

Morlenden had never seen a forgetty close before in his life; and if it had not occurred to him before, it was brought home now to him with redoubled force that something had indeed been very, very wrong, to lead to this result. He did not know yet the secret Maellenkleth had been protecting with her life, but knowing as much as he did, he was sure that this was no accident. Intuition: this did not happen. It was caused.

He watched Krisshantem closely. This time, above all others, must not be the one ruled by the power of Water. The emotions. Kris must not reveal to any watcher that he had any relationship with her whatsoever. What would he do? The boy did nothing. Krisshantem looked closely at the girl, dispassionately examining her as if she were just another specimen of these labs, and then turned back to Morlenden. The expression on the boy's face told Morlenden what he wanted to see: *This person is not the girl I knew, loved, slept with, made* dhainaz *with, uncounted sweet moments we hoped would never end. Yes, it was she, once, but this one is a stranger. It deserves care and respect, this strange* ksensrithman *girl, but little more than that. And of revenges we shall speak later, when we know more. Much more.* It was a look of logic and duty. No more, save deep down under it there simmered fire.

Both Fellirian and Morlenden suddenly felt all their careful plans empty into a stagnant sump, dissipating. What could they do with her? She was helpless, and they could not in any way recover her here. Madness! They were at a loss for the proper action. Should they just go to the bed, and unceremoniously pick her up and cart her off, like a sack of potatoes? What could she do, or not do?

Errat, sensing their quandary, politely suggested, "To us, she appears to have no more responses than the average newborn, in fact, somewhat less than the human standard we have compared her with. She doesn't seem to learn as fast. At the first, it was necessary to restrain her, as she thrashed about uncontrollably; later she did gain enough control to avoid abrupt movements. Now she is generally quiet. She cannot turn herself over, nor sit up, nor care for herself in any way. It is a most odd condition. Is this a peculiar ler form of psychosis?"

Fellirian answered, "Most definitely not a psychosis."

"We have even had to exercise her, but I am sure there has been considerable muscular atrophy. . . . What will you do with her?"

Morlenden volunteered, "We'll have to carry her back to our home. We'll need something to carry her in. I suppose a . . . stretcher. Excuse me, but my Modanglic is strictly school level, and I don't know the exact terms."

Errat answered smoothly, "Yes. Of course. One can be obtained." He turned to an orderly, who exchanged words with him and then vanished. Errat made an impatient gesture. "Yes, easily. My man has gone for it even now. But even with the three of you, you'll need help."

Fellirian said, "We can manage."

Errat seemed to become fractionally more insistent. "It will be no trouble at all. In fact, the two who would accompany you are the very ones who have been working with her in therapy. They are both strong of arm and knowledgeable of mind."

"Oh, very well. We can certainly use the help," she said. As she spoke, Morlenden had the thought that he could indeed be certain that the orderlies would be strong and knowledgeable. Indeed. And a more accurate description of their role would be "agents."

Errat left the room for a moment. Fellirian started to speak, but Kris motioned her to silence. And shortly afterward, he returned with two large, muscular men, dressed in white uniforms, and they were pushing a low, wheeled stretcher. The two went to work immediately, gathering Maellenkleth and placing her into the apparatus. They did not appear all that expert in their work.

Errat said, as the attendants were completing their preparations, "We assumed that you would wish to return her to your own environment without further delay; the trip already has been a long one. So arrangements have been made; we have procured tickets on the southbound evening tube. If you leave now you can make it." He added, as an afterthought. "We had to settle for a local, so there will be more stops, but at the least, there will be private compartments."

Fellirian watched the two men bundling Maellenkleth clumsily onto the stretcher, and said, "Very well. We accept." She watched the two orderlies closely. "And what about the forms you mentioned earlier, the damage claims, the surcharges?"

Oddly, the question seemed to bother Errat no little bit. He looked about, almost apprehensively, saying quickly, "No problem there, at all. We can paperwhip it here and send the rest to the Institute later, through Vance. Yes, the forms will be routed through the Office of the Director. You may sign them at your leisure."

Fellirian nodded agreement, otherwise making no motion, no sign, but Morlenden saw a quick flicker in her gray eyes, a tiny brightening of expression, and then it was gone. Errat had not seen it, he had been turned away. And how would Errat have known to send it to Vance? He should know that paperwork routing and deliveries were the bane of civilization, and that one did not send valuable papers blind. Had they been followed all the way from the reservation, from before, even? How much did these people see?

The orderlies, having arranged the girl for transport, now began to wheel her off. They were fussy about their work, however inexpert they were at it. They did not, so it appeared, want any of the ler party to touch Maellenkleth in any way.

They indeed did depart 8905 through a different way than they had entered. Looking back once, Morlenden thought that the place where they left had the unmistakable look of a warehouse loading dock to it, rather than a regular door; and at that, one in not too much use. He also worried lest Cannialin and Kaldherman lose them through this labyrinthine game of evasion, but after a few turns, they were back on one of the main avenues debouching on the plaza, which the younger Derens had remained close to. Morlenden saw them pretending to admire a statuary group, all the time scanning the plaza entrances for them. They saw them, and across the distance, Morlenden could make out Cannialin whispering to Kal. And now they began moving off, as if to enter the terminal station from the other side.

The party escorting Maellenkleth boarded the tube without incident, although Morlenden, now carefully watching every move the orderlies made, observed that the orderlies were most careful to retain the tickets. Fortunately, they were separated into two compartments. He saw that Kaldherman and Cannialin also boarded the tube-train, taking a coach just ahead of them. And oddly enough, Fellirian had little trouble, once aboard, in convincing the orderlies that Maellenkleth would be better off in their compartment, with her people. It was as if the orderlies—agents—felt the train more secure. From what? Where could they go in the endless alternating urban centers and industrial suburbs of manworld? Escape was remote until they were at the Institute stop. Or was it secure from interference? Morlenden thought that if Fellirian had a plan, she had better use it fast. All had been smooth up to this point. Too smooth by far. It was not to have been so easy. That was the reason for including the others in it. And now?

Morlenden and Krisshantem moved into the compartment with the girl, while Fellirian remained behind momentarily, conversing confidentially with one of the agents, the one who seemed to be in charge. After a moment, she joined them also, closing the compartment door.

Motioning them to silence, she paused, and then began to speak in Multispeech, using the one-to-many speech-mode, but with the side channels suppressed. Morlenden was impressed; he would not have thought that she had learned the skill.

To any human that might have been listening, it sounded rather like nonsensical music, wordless, and with an odd, ringing purity of tone. Fellirian had told the agents that they would now perform a rite over the girl and that they would hear chanting. But to the ler ear, there was no music in it at all, indeed, as in most forms of Multispeech, there was no consciousness of *sound or ears* at all. It was just ideas, stripped to simplicity, somehow whispered directly into their minds.

She said, "Spy.two.they.now.here.speak.past.Eliya.tell.Godseek.for. her&thisspeak.noread.they@&! do.it.now.quick.yes??"

And Krisshantem answered in the same mode. "Two.here.know. parts.&&.same.now.Stop. + Two.here.make.base.line&three.make.her &lose.them(!)(!)."

Keeping the chant up, but now not sending anything in it, they moved quickly, carefully placing Maellenkleth on the floor between Morlenden and Fellirian. She was awake, but passive and unresisting. They arranged her as Krisshantem directed, and settled into position themselves, assuming a studied, rigorous posture with their legs folded under them, and sitting back on their turned heels. Krisshantem took up his position at the head of the girl, in the same posture. The process began.

Now Morlenden and Fellirian took up the chant, immediately shifting the mode, making it even more submelodic, exactly as Krisshantem had instructed them. Morlenden now felt his vision dim and fade, as the new mode took hold and blanked out his visual center, readying it for another purpose.

"Remember," Kris had admonished them with adolescent severity, "you must, you two, make the base line. The persona is four-dimensional, and the maker will erect the restored one upon that line. You must keep it steady; that is the hardest part of the whole thing—the steadying of the reference line. When I get fully into the rebuild pattern, if I get that far and residuals in her mind do not resist me, I can compensate for some dislocation, but if I get tied up in that follower sub-routine I will lose the growth pattern, and we all may be in danger of getting sucked into that forgetty program stored in her. Remember, no one ever shut it off. It is still the paramount instruction in her mind. That is why they couldn't do anything with her. Most of what she learns she erases immediately. And in the net, she can do it to us. Never forget this: this is dangerous to us. Also remember that I am no expert at this. I have never done it live before; only received instruction from Mael. So you *must be steady!*"

The theory, he had explained, was that the persona was a four-dimensional figure, a tessaract in space, the elementals Fire, Earth, Air, and Water permutating and pervolving upon themselves, making a cruciform (in three-space projection) figure of equal lines and ninety degree angles. For their part, Morlenden and Fellirian would make the reference line, which set orientation in space and the length determined how much would go into it. There was one such line, uniquely placed, for everyone, if one could but find it; here, they were making one from scratch. In Maellenkleth's case, they could, within limits, select any line they wished, for they were starting anew.

Holding the developing subject rigidly in the growing pattern, the maker reprogrammed the subject, nonverbally, inserting concepts directly into the appropriate parts of the brain. And to her, there was further risk: do it right, and they would end up with a retarded but functional Schaeszendur. And do it wrong, and a thousand disasters awaited them. They could kill her, for one choice. In another, she could become a dangerous maniac, beyond their abilities to subdue her, physically or multispecifically.

The Deren insiblings reached deep within themselves for calmness and strength, striving to make the base line, bring it into being, and hold it just so, at such a position in space. That was near what she had been before, Kris had advised, suggesting that orientation because she would be less likely to fight them. Yes, he had said. They had told each other what their lines had been. They had been *dhofters*, had they not?

At first the effort was just a song, but before long, Morlenden could see it in his mind's eye, slowly coming into being in the web of Multispeech, a bright, hard, sodium-yellow line, piercingly narrow, now varying in length and waving about in a rubbery, unstable, nonoriented manner, then slowing, stiffening, stabilizing in length, feeling the right angle of orientation, coming to rest now, but still as unstable as the opposing poles of two magnets, slippery, elsewhere wanting. And it came into hard focus, and all vagueness vanished. There was nothing else, a universe of utter black night. Night and darkness and the hard, burning yellow line. Morlenden, seeing it, tried to see through the vision and pick up something of the coach-sleeper, some outside sight. It was no use; he was completely blind, save to the vision being generated by Multispeech. He knew that Fellirian must also be equally blind now, completely into it.

The line steadied, and now, delicately touched and nudged by a third power in the net! Krisshantem. It drifted slowly, still moving in orientation, becoming steady. He let Morlenden and Fellirian hold it thus for a moment, to get the feel of it, measuring the chant he was entering and increasingly controlling. Holding the line was hard, hard. He heard, somewhere very far away, a subvocal moan from her who had been Maellenkleth and was about to be Schaeszendur. The line wavered with his attention, and he returned to it, increased the power, and nailed it down. And on the other end, he could feel the feedback from Fellirian, also clamping down, mastering the unstable yellow line. He remembered to take a deep breath, and concentrated, and

Now a third point in the furry darkness appeared from nowhere, and the line was a square, empty, hanging alone in space, still oddly and rigidly oriented. It hung a moment, a little uncertain. The Derens applied more pressure, more inner strength. It steadied. Morlenden could not now sense Krisshantem as a person, but as an intense force, somewhere offstage, who was manipulating their visions, their work. That was what it was. He could not imagine what Kris was seeing now. The same as they? And now Fellirian was fading as a person also, becoming the anchor at the far end of the line, holding it in space. He could not sense Maellenkleth-Schaeszendur at all: she was in the figure only. That was she, and they were making her now. But there were four here in the unity that three were controlling. They held the chant, held down the square in a vise of Will, and

Now the figure trembled off-center, making odd little perturbations, paused, and sprang into three dimensions, a stick-figure empty cube, now beginning to fight them, to resist, to know Will. It seemed to want to go back into its old square shape, but the Krisshantem would not allow it to, and in a sudden moment of weakness he had it and

Now it leaped into the shape of the tessaract and they saw it not as a projection in three dimensions, a cruciform shape with an extra cubical arm in the front and the back, but there was no time to contemplate it; the outlined, stick-figure tessaract suddenly became solid, instantly, without sense of transition, opaque, solid, tangible, hanging in the empty space of their minds, and the whole surface was covered, a living, scintillating mosaic of changing black and yellow tiny squares all over the surface, cells flickering, changing; patterns washed over the now solid surface in their minds, patterns that moved and lunged like the reflected light of flame along a wall, more so, the yellow *burned*, the bumblebee patterns reminding them too closely of the striking visual display one saw in a migraine attack. Like that, yes, and it went on and on, the deeper rhythms washing over the surfaces like the play of summer lightning. Morlenden grunted with effort. And at the far end of the now submerged base line, he could also feel Fellirian straining as well. And something was now actively resisting them, something inside the crawling figure in their minds. It took all their effort to hold it still, for now all of Krisshantem's attention was devoted to controlling the wild patterns flying over the surface of the tessaract.

The process continued, seemingly endless, inexorable, and they could see no apparent change in the patterns. They could not determine how long it was taking, for there was no subjective sense of time when that time had been integrated as a spatial dimension. To Morlenden, it seemed to go on and on beyond levels of endurance he thought he might have had; days, weeks, a whole span devoted to a sustained effort of raw Will, Fire-Elemental, *Panrus*. He ached in odd places in his body, places which in his mind's eye did not correspond to any known locations in his old familiar physical body.

Then there was change. The pattern on the surface of the enigmatic tessaract slowed, slowed, slowed some more, and changed to a regular, surging motion, rather like the slow and rhythmic beating of waves onto some low shore, calm, reflective, steady. The figure also relaxed something of its taut straining, and became easier to hold. A sense of time came back, into them from the edge of the universe, intruding a little, and they were able to hear, as from some immense distance, faint sounds from the everyday world. Everyday world; not the real world. This was the real world, and they were making it. The everyday world was now, seemed disheartening, disappointing; after all, the perceptual surround of a Multispeech reprogram was seductive and addictive. It was naked Power. And along the intruding edges they heard the voice of Krisshantem, speaking ordinary words, inserted into the stream of Multispeech, as if he could retain the present pattern by nudging it now and again.

The voice said hoarsely, "Worst over, the longest part. . . . Motor coordination, control, body . . . all in place, calibrated and tested. . . . Next will be verbals and pseudomemory, the repersona, Schaeszendur. Different . . . she'll fight us now . . . hold it down like never before . . . now, now, now," and

Now the voice vanished, blown out like a candle flame, as if it had never been, never could be. Darkness and the tessaract. The tiny cellular units seemed to randomize slightly, lose coherence momentarily, but in the cellular units, a new coherence was building, surging, coming in like the tide, like an approaching storm, powerful and inescapable. The sensation of waves rather than firelight became very pronounced, and Morlenden tasted a brassy, metallic flavor in his mouth, smelled an unknown, spicy and rotten odor; gone instantly. And this one was becoming much harder to hold. There was definitely another force now, opposing them, something whose location they could not determine, but which seemed to be emanating from deep within (?) the projected figure in their minds. It tried to move away, escape them, distort the shape of the tessaract. Morlenden reached deep, for reserves he was not sure existed; and there he found something that allowed him to hang on, clamp down some more, for a little longer. But the figure's resistance was also increasing. Yet now it was not so steady; it waxed and waned, now fighting them, now withdrawing, and oddly, sometimes catching the sense and rhythm of what they were doing and in quick flashes surging ahead of them, anticipating almost, very nearly helping.

Yes, it was harder than the first part, but it was not as long in duration. Already they could sense a weakening in the resistance, and as the resistance slackened, it became passive, submissive, waiting. It was now much easier to hold, almost no effort at all; and with the easing of their common tension, now Morlenden began to feel fatigue for the first time, much deeper than mere tiredness as he had felt before. He was weary; releasing the figure felt like sinking into an ocean of warm syrup. And the resistance faded even more, and now they could definitely feel for the first time the actual presence of a fourth in the web of Multispeech that had bound them all together. This fourth was warm, engaging, friendly, like a small child, of no great mind, but pleasant and without any force whatsoever. They . . . he was on the verge of welcoming her and

Now with no warning or anticipation the tessaract in their minds everted, collapsed, and with it went the universal night: and they were sitting on the floor in a compartment on a tube-train, lit by ceiling fixtures that seemed too bright, and they were back in the old, shabby world of reality, yes, as shabby and subtle as it was. And in their midst, a girl named Schaeszendur was sitting up, leaning on one arm, looking idly and vacantly about, gazing passively over the compartment with a dazed, uncomprehending expression on her pretty face, the soft, pursed mouth.

Morlenden looked long at the girl, now-Schaeszendur, comparing the image of her with the memory of then-Maellenkleth, which he would never forget no matter what happened to him. There was no doubt of it; there was a noticeable difference. This Schaeszendur was as pretty as the old Maellenkleth, perhaps more so, but there were lacks. This one lacked the drive, the ambition, and the prodigy intelligence of the old; she now was relaxed, at her ease, submissive and passive. This was only a gentle, retarded creature who wanted but to please, and to be happy and free of pain and sorrow. She would be functional, she could look after herself. And if cared for lovingly by people who knew what they were about, in time, she would grow to be almost a full-person again. But never the Maellenkleth who challenged the Gameplayers and three hundred and more years of tradition, of course.

Morlenden tried to move out of the position he had been holding himself in, but his muscles would not obey him, and he more or less half fell over on one side, supported by one arm. As he had fallen closer to Krisshantem, the boy felt the motion and turned to him. Kris spoke slowly, as if recounting a dream, as if trying to recapture the exact flavor it had. "You felt her in the end, how first she fought us, and then helped? There was a lot left of the original in her after she had disminded; also many of the mnemonic fragments did not subfractionate completely. She fought us, but she wanted to come back purified, too . . . that was not your imagination, for she really was there in the net with us. She was, unconsciously. Beforetimes, when she was Maellenkleth and whole, when we were together, we would speak Multispeech while we made *dhainaz*, the whole time, however long we took. That is like projecting mentally . . . mentally, that which your bodies do with muscle and flesh. There were echoes of that in this Schaeszendur."

Morlenden tried to speak, but his voice came out a croak. "Is . . . everything all right with her?"

"Yes. She is whole. It worked better than I imagined it would. We did a better job than I had hoped for, even better than she who taught me could imagine. But all the same, this Schaeszendur is a stranger. . . . And I know a secret, that the maker must want the new persona to come terribly. That would be common sense; but also the holders must want it almost as much. My motivations are clear enough, but what of yours and your insibling co-spouse's? How is it that you, a stranger to Maellenkleth-who-was, want this as I?"

Morlenden answered wearily: "I have not known a forgetty before. Had we done this as strangers who had just met for the purpose, upon an utter nobody, perhaps things would have been different. I . . . just felt that she needed this restoration to balance justice, that she had not, whatever she did, deserved to come to the forgetty fate. I learned to care very much about Maellenkleth, just as I suppose we should about everyone. . . . Fellirian told me it was the same with her, as she pursued memories and reflections and echoes down in the Institute. And neither of us would see anyone ill-used, no matter by whom."

Now Morlenden felt more control returning to his limbs; he got to his feet with effort, still somewhat dazed, and went to the girl, helping her to her feet. She stood unsteadily, blinking in the harsh artificial light. Morlenden hoped that the pseudomemories Kris had programmed into her mind were pleasant ones, of cool nights and warm hearthfires, of kindness and body-friends, and of love affairs that did not end out of phase with their owners' times. He took her hand and gently led her to one of the sleeping-bunks, and she came with him, unquestioning, trusting, accepting without doubt. Morlenden was of course now long past the days of his fertility, the springing erect seasons of desire, the sudden emotions, the tidelike urgings as it had been with Fellirian. But he had not forgotten the embraces of the girls he had known, nor the soft sounds they made in his ear, the unspeakable words they had said to one another, the sleek strong bodies; nor would he forget, let go the various thrills, anticipations, satisfactions, and, yes, dissatisfactions of which he had measured his portion. Even so, as he led the girl Schaeszendur to the small bunk, as he undressed her out of the voluminous palliatory coverall, as he laid her down, he felt something like an echo of what had been but was no more. And Schaeszendur who was Maellenkleth was slender, gracefully muscular without seeming angular or stringy, her skin a rich soft olive color with darker shades along the accent lines and creases; the tendons of her neck, the insides of her elbows; honey and olive and sandalwood. Similar to Sanjirmil, perhaps, but richer, more range, more degrees of contrast. Morlenden smiled at her, knowing what little else to do, hoping it would reassure her, tucking her in under the covers and kissing her forehead chastely, as if she were a very young child, which of course she now was, whatever the lovely, lean body shouted at one. And like a child, she fell asleep instantly, effortlessly, not fidgeting, playing, daydreaming or twisting and searching for just that right position to enter the Dark World. Her eyelids simply fell shut, and she was breathing deeply, her rosy mouth opened very slightly. . . .

He returned to Fellirian, who had not moved. She was still sitting on the floor, head bowed, breathing in lengthy deep sighs. Morlenden knelt behind her and began kneading the muscles of her back, neck, shoulders. He felt a shiver ripple across the spare, graceful frame he knew so well, better than anyone else, better almost than he knew himself. She sank forward to the floor and lay, facedown, groaning.

After a while, she turned her face to the side and said, "Once of that in a lifetime is enough. I feel as if I'd been beaten."

Morlenden lay down alongside her, turning his head to face her. "And I also."

"It's too close to childbirth to suit me. It's not fair, me going through that: my time was over long ago. Done. Even if this was all in the mind, not in the body."

"It is a birth, that's a fact."

"Except this is all at once, you don't have that year and a half to get ready for it*. . . . What does she seem like to you? You put her to bed."

"Mixed, Eliya. Some ways, like a very young child. Other ways, like an adolescent, but with odd pieces left out."

Then they no longer spoke. They lay side by side for a long time, in a halfway state between sleep and wakefulness, conscious enough to be aware of the deep, regular breathing of the girl, and also to hear the faint but undeniable snoring of Krisshantem. They felt the motion of the vehicle carrying them at what unknown velocity through the bowels of the earth, through rock and dirt, far from the sky, the tube-train adjusting magnetically to tiny irregularities in its roadbed, a motion curiously alive and animal-like, more like careful walking than anything else.

After a time, Fellirian moved closer to Morlenden, whispering, "I hate to speak of it, but I think we should depart this machine at the stop before the Institute terminal."

"Why so? Errat seemed manifestly uninterested in Mael. . . ."

"Only *seemed*. I am certain that we have been monitored in various ways since we left Vance's office; it's their way, but they're sloppy about it, so I doubt we've given anything away. They don't watch the tubes, they think they're secure enough if they control the entries. But I sensed planning in the way they tossed her off onto us; they expect us to make certain moves. It is my intent to confuse and muddy those predictions. But there's a problem."

Morlenden asked, "Which is?"

"The tickets they use are always coded magnetically for a specific destination. The numbers are integrated into the material; you can't see them. So if we just try to get off on our own at another stop, we'll set off an alarm and they'll spot us for sure."

---

* The ler period of gestation was eighteen months.

"We're stuck with them, then."

"No, there may be a way . . . yes. The ones who came with us, the agents. They would have to have some way to override the destination register."

"If they are in fact agents."

"They're agents, all right. Trust me in this."

"Do you know how they override it?"

"Yes, I remember. I heard Vance talking about it once, long ago, to someone else. I was very young. Before we wove."

"So somehow we must get them to open the doors."

"Yes, exactly. And the stop before the Institute is a busy one. Not for us, but for them. Big factory town. I know this local will stop there, never fear."

"But they'll soon find out we're not where we are supposed to be."

"So let them. All we need is a little head start. I know the way. We can cross into the reservation by climbing the fence, in the northeast provinces. We'll have a hard walk, perhaps a run, ahead of us, and what's more, after what we have just done. And Schaeszendur out of condition as well, but there's no cure for it. I know ever more surely that if we stay with these two primates we'll never see the inside again. It's been too easy. And I don't want them to see what we've done for her, either, even if I did insist on building her as we rode. Do you see why, now? She must be able to walk on her own. We could not carry her all that way. And she would also have to respond to simple instructions."

"Eliya, have you been planning it this way all the way along?"

"Not completely. . . . It really didn't dawn on me completely until after we built her back up, since we received her from that Errat . . . the whole situation smells like a trap set to catch more victims, some who might talk, in place of one who didn't."

"You think she did that on her own?"

"Absolutely. They don't have the facilities to cause it. She was facing something she couldn't handle, and she made sure the secret of the Inner Game never got out from her. Or that no association be made between those instruments and any living Gameplayer."

"So you say. But even now, you and I, we know in fact very little."

"They don't know that. And we have suspicions, too."

"How much time do we have to get ready?"

"Not very much, dear. I lost track of time while we were deep in it back there, and afterward . . . wait a moment." Very quietly, Fellirian got to her feet, opened the compartment door, looked out, adjusting her overshirt. She left for a moment, and did not return for some time.

But she did return, slipping into the compartment as quietly as she had left it. She bent close to Morlenden, whispering softly, "Not so much time as I thought we'd have. We'll have to wake Kris and Maellenkleth-Schaeszendur, get them ready. While I do that, you go up into the next car and collect Kaldherman and Cannialin; bring them here, quietly, quietly. Be a sneak for once. And you and I, too; you'll like this, Mor."

FOURTEEN

Everything you have ever done is training or the next moment.
—M.A.F., *Atropine*

OUTSIDE IN THE corridor, Morlenden and Fellirian waited and watched through the single window for the appearance of the next underground station platform; they saw unrelieved darkness passing, a blurred blank wall, illuminated only by the dim running-light glow of the tube-train corridor, light leaking out through the few windows. There was not enough light to distinguish any details, and what few were there were blurred by the terrific speed with which they were hurtled through the tunnels in the earth.

They could not sense any change in elevation in the train, or increase or reduction of its unknown speed; if there was any it was too gradual to be distinguished. But apparently change was coming, for without warning, a series of bright lights flashed by the window, too fast for more than a glance. Whatever message the lights conveyed, it was not verbal, as the patterns did not form any letters Fellirian could recognize. And shortly after the lights, they began to feel the train slowing, as simultaneously a slight pressure told them that they were rising. The train slowed more, obvious now, and then the walls nearby fell away from the window, first into an empty blank void of darkness, and then into a more open space, dimly illuminated by fixtures set at intervals along the ceiling. The chamber was low-ceilinged, the fixtures long out of repair; many of them did not work at all. The train slowed now to a walking pace, and they could make out a large, dingy sign painted on the concrete underground wall, which red *CPX010*. And the tube-train stopped.

As Fellirian had anticipated, there was considerable coming and going all along the length of the train, in fact more than they had seen earlier in the day at Region Central. The activity suggested an air of busyness and relaxed conventions, but after a moment, this early impression corrected itself under closer observation; the procedure was formal, deliberately interrupted, highly formatted all around. Patrons who wished to depart the train walked up to the sliding doors, inserted their tickets in a convenient slot beside the doors, and waited for the doors to open. And when they did, and the waiting patron departed, they hurried over the doorsill, and the door closed smartly behind them, with enough force to injure one who was unlucky enough to be laggard in his motions. So one lurched through, a jerky, graceless motion, which they nevertheless performed with the expertise of those who made such motions through similar doorways often, daily.

Fellirian watched carefully, until most of the traffic in the underground terminal had died down. There were yet some people scattered along the platform, but they seemed either to be idlers, or else deeply engrossed in their own affairs. They were completely uninterested in the train, or any of its passengers. At a signal from Fellirian, all the members of the party assumed their positions: all save Morlenden and Fellirian hid themselves carefully in the compartment. They all paused, took deep breaths. Morlenden rapped loudly on the door of the agents' compartment. And, oddly, it took some time to get a response out of them; apparently both of their guards either had gone to sleep or had been dozing.

The older agent, most probably the senior man, appeared at the door, bearing an attitude composed of nine-tenths irritation and one-tenth suspicion. "Yes, yes, what is it, what is the problem?"

Morlenden hoped that he sounded panicky. He cried out, blurting, "It's the girl! She's gone! We finished with our rite and slept—everything seemed to be in order. But when the motion of the train at the stop here woke us, we saw that she was gone! Fellirian thought she heard the compartment door closing, but we had just awakened and could not be sure. It could have been some other noise."

"Gone? Where the hell could she go?" The irritation slid into apprehension, and the apprehension glissaded into stark panic. "Gone?" he repeated idiotically, as if she would reappear by magic and prove him wrong. "Gone? That's impossible! Someone would have had to . . . Shit! They did! Well, she can't get very far by herself, nor can anyone else carrying her." He turned aside, back to his own compartment, saying to his partner, "Bill! Here, get it up now!" A moan rewarded his efforts. He reiterated, "Come on, bones! The girl's gone and you know what that'll mean. Go and check it out, starting with their compartment, then we'll do the rest of the tram. She may not be off it yet."

The second agent appeared, dull with rudely interrupted sleep. And Morlenden and Fellirian watched the pair very closely, while they let their plans mature.

The older one commanded, "You go to their compartment, I'll hold the tram. Quick, they can't have got far, her and whoever's helping her. She'll have to have help. Look for at least two, most likely three!"

Now he turned to Morlenden. "There were three of you besides the girl; you two and the boy. Where's he now?"

Morlenden shrunk, diminishing his smaller stature even further, hoping to appear embarrassed. He said slowly, as if he hated or feared to admit it, "Well, I don't exactly know that. We haven't been able to find him either. I thought he might have wandered off down the way, looking for the public convenience, but he's not in this section, and I . . ."

The senior agent suddenly looked ugly. A flash of desperation rebounded across his already homely countenance.

Fellirian added, "They were lovers, beforetimes. He *has* been a bit unstable."

The agent interrupted her. "Where would they go?"

"I don't know. None of us know Complex Ten at all, and I know for a fact that those two don't."

Now the second agent appeared, arranging his clothing, and ill-concealing a yawn, still addled with heavy sleep. The senior agent hurried to the exit doors, removing a red ticket from within a little wallet inside his coat and inserting it in the slot. The doors opened, remained open, as he muttered to himself, "Damn it all, anyway! My last override spent on this goddamn wild-goose chase, and they're harder to get every day. Have to sign your life away now just for one, the chintzy bastards."

Meanwhile, the junior agent had pushed the door of the other compartment open and looked within, carefully enough for the brief time he had spent in looking. But he saw nothing. He turned to the senior, still standing in the doorway, and said, "Nobody here."

"All right. You stay here and watch this car." He looked menacingly at Morlenden and Fellirian, towering over them. "And you two also. I'll check outside, just to be sure. They won't get far in Ten, and that's a fact!"

He turned abruptly and hurried through the opened door. The second agent looked on for a moment uneasily and uncertainly, as if something were escaping him as he stood there, something nagging at his mind which he should have noticed, but had not. Fellirian made nervous little motions with her hands, breaking her tension, hoping that she looked worried and afraid enough to convince this one. The junior agent looked from one to the other, at Fellirian, at Morlenden, who was nervously watching the terminal outside the car; and back, tentatively, at the compartment. And at the compartment again. He turned suddenly and returned for one more look, this time actually walking into the compartment, the one vacated by the ler. They heard him start to say something, but what he might have said was never finished. "Oh, yeah, there's a b—!" There was a sudden silence, followed by faint rustling sounds, and presently the four from inside appeared: Kaldherman, Cannialin, Schaeszendur, Krisshantem. Kris was last, and he carefully locked the compartment door as he left, but retaining the key in his hand. He said, "How much time now?"

"No time!" she hissed. "Quick, now! Into the terminal!"

They all filed out into the terminal, quietly and sedately, into the concrete caverns. Sounds echoed along the concrete, faded into the dimmed distances. This place was smokier than Region Central. Fighting the urge to run, they walked almost disinterestedly to an empty kiosk along the wall, half in shadows, its own lighting disconnected. They could not all hide in it, but they concealed themselves as best they could, standing very still, just as Kris had showed them, still and silent as stones. And almost before they had had time to assume their positions, the senior agent returned, blundering down the grimy stairwell, leaving a trail of noisy footfalls they could all follow with their ears. He wore tiny metal taps on his shoes. He appeared, breathing hard, still in a half-run, and without looking either to the right or the left, still muttering to himself, he boarded the tube-train, flipped open the wallet containing the tickets, and inserted a green ticket into the door-slot. The door closed, and almost immediately, the train started moving, softly and slowly at first, but all the time accelerating rapidly. They could see him easily through the moving windows: he went into his own compartment without looking, slamming the door, making the plastic of the window bulge. The train began moving off into its tunneled darkness under the earth, at the end of the terminal platform. Outside, in the kiosk, they stood absolutely still. As the section in which they had been riding began to approach the tunnel mouth, far down the platform, they observed through another window how a figure suddenly burst out of a compartment, frantically looking up and down the corridor. He vanished, apparently into their compartment. As he went past the window, he looked out, sweeping the platform with his practiced agent's eye, a well-trained glance, yet his glance had been trained to record motion against a stilled background, contrast. And for human subjects, the stained gray concrete walls made a fine background against which to pick up nervous, jerky motions, people wearing dark clothing. That was exactly the intent ingrained into people, and the dark clothing the only kind available. But the six ler were still and quiet, although standing openly visible; but their winter overshirts and cloaks were gray, and to him they were virtually invisible, and would have been even if the train had been standing still in the station. He had not seen them, and it was apparent from his panic that he had found nothing in the upper world of Complex Ten, either.

The train glided onward, supported on magnetic fields, increasing its speed, sliding, and suddenly the last coach was disappearing into the dark mouth of the tunnel entrance. And it was gone. The tunnel gaped, empty. A butterfly valve doorway closed silently on the tunnel portal. Above the portal, an orange light remained illuminated a moment, then turned green, and then went out.

Morlenden, not yet daring to move, said, out of the side of his mouth to Fellirian, "As you said, a good trick. Yes, I liked it. Now how much time?"

"More. Maybe an hour. With some luck, which means mistakes on someone else's part, still more. These agents are now normally issued only one override ticket at a time. They were abusing the privilege, so they were made to sign for it; it was an awful issue a few years ago. But now that the train is moving, it must go on to the next local stop; it can't stop in closed sections of the tunnels, and it can't back up. Of course he can communicate, through his comment interconnect, but before he makes his report, he'll have to figure out what happened. By the way, the other one: you didn't kill him, did you?"

Kris answered, "No, although your Braid afterfather was frowning like a cat licking gravy off a hot basting brush, and your aftermother was fingering her chicken-slitting knife and leering. No, he'll sleep, with bad dreams, and feel the worse for it. And they may have a problem communicating, for I palmed the unit you are talking about, I think. The second one was carrying it."

Fellirian looked at Kris blankly, saying nothing. After a time, she said, "Well, I suppose we can make some use of it. We can listen to it, and it may give us some warning; then we are that much more ahead of them. So keep it, although I wish you hadn't taken it. And keep it out of sight, and whatever you do, whatever it does, don't touch anything on it."

Again she paused, as if she were thinking out something that was easy to conceive, but difficult to say properly. Fellirian had always been diplomatic and polite, sometimes even to a fault. At last she added, "And now let me offer some advice: were I to go adventuring in the deep forest in your company, Krisshantem, I would adhere to your guidance, obey your lead, for that is most properly your world. Just so, thus. And this world that we walk in now is, as much as it can be for one of us, mine. And this world is much more perilous than any of our reservation forests, our wild lands. This is for you *Beth Mershonnekh*, the house of the devil. If we meet any more forerunners, take nothing from them. Nothing. This is not the time for explanations, and I accept the error of faulty instruction. For the time."

Kris nodded.

"Now," she continued. "We must move. Walk briskly, as if you had somewhere to go, somewhere near, an affair to see to. No nonsense and no trotting or running. Schaeszendur, do you understand me?"

The girl answered distantly, passively, "Yes, fast enough."

Then, Fellirian leading the way, they emerged from the kiosk and climbed the grimy, littered dim stairwell to the open-air street level of the terminal.

Complex Ten was one of the more industrialized places in the Region; and whatever products were manufactured in this concentration, it required a lot of lighting in the streets, and produced considerable dust. It was much dirtier, by and large, than had been Region Central. There were other differences: most of the structures here were clearly devoted to industry, not administration, as had been the case in Central. More, the atmosphere, the ambience, was suggestive of a cruder, more expedient system of order than had seemed to prevail in the almost overfastidious Central. Here there were no plazas, no intersections with planters, no streets that artfully went nowhere. Here, the streets were broad, straight, and long, and the building numbers followed one another in careful order, sometimes affixing additive letters to signify relationships; 242 was succeeded by 243, and immediately adjacent lay 243a.

Fellirian, who seemed to have some basic familiarity with the layout of this strange and seemingly now empty city, led them along a swift path through streets and lanes and freight alleys, dodging drains and gutter-runs brimming with black water floating an iridescent scum on its surface. Nowhere did they see heavy traffic, although there was plenty of evidence that everywhere the trafficways knew heavy and prolonged use; the main routes were generally free of trash and dust, blown clean by the fans of hovercraft and burnished to a dull sheen by thousands of rollers, bladders, and pounding wheels. Only rarely did they see any sort of vehicle at all, and even less frequently passersby.

They passed through empty streets flanked by large, flattened buildings whose purpose could not be determined from their shapes. All were illuminated within in various degrees, and as they passed each one, they sensed different orders of additional evidence: heavy thudding pounding, or grating, rattling sounds. Odors of hot metal, plastic reek, burning rubber, ozone, and hot grease. Smaller buildings were arrayed at random among the larger edifices, some housing units, barracks, small retail outlets, kiosks, stands. An occasional store; more rarely, offices. In the damp, smoky air, there was in the heart of the city a sense of desolation, abandonment, which sat squarely at variance with the obvious busyness of the place. They crossed canals, where drains trickled limply, dark water steamed, and lusterless surfaces eddied flaccidly.

Walking briskly, they soon crossed the more industrialized area and moved into another—this one devoted to dwelling-blocks, barracks, dormitories, flats—beginning to alternate with open, vacant lots and small fields. Near one such unit, apparently a housing unit, they passed a straggling group of people who were standing by a vendor's kiosk, drinking steaming cups of some heated beverage. The patrons' faces were lit by the brighter lights of the stand, and there was a certain sense of reserved camaraderie among them. Two older men made earnest conversation with three women, while a younger man stood aloofly to one side, making a small contribution from time to time, largely ignored. Mostly he seemed to brood upon affairs known only to himself, keeping his nose in his cup. The patrons took little, if any, notice of the ler as they passed across the street. Morlenden tried to imagine the whole of the scene before him; conjectures rose easily in his mind, but none of them were of any impressive degree of verity. It was a static scene, extracted out of time and life, held poised in a moment of cryptic significance.

After they had gone well past the group, he asked Fellirian, "They didn't notice us?"

"No, not in Ten. Those are Midnighters, about to go to work, so I should guess; they are half asleep. If they thought anything at all, it would be that we are Midnighters just like themselves, going to work somewhere. And if they bothered to recognize us for what we are, the people, it probably would not bother them greatly. Some of the Institute ler sojourn here at times."

Farther back in line, shepherding Schaeszendur, Krisshantem could be heard, muttering, "A vile place, this! Worse than the other. What business could our people have here?"

Fellirian said, back over her shoulder, "A lot. Ten is a kind of test site, where things are tried out; that's why it looks so . . . transient, impermanent."

"Still, vile," Kris added, his distaste not to be denied, "You would not see many of us living in a place like this."

Fellirian agreed, "Not now, no. But when Earth held only a few millions of forerunners I doubt if they would have lived so by choice, either. . . . And I am not so sure that in the end we would arrive in any more style, even though we say now that we'd choose a different destination. . . ." For the moment, she fell silent.

Morlenden said, "I'll credit you with knowing them better than I, than most of us, their nature and history. You work with them. But we are conjecturing a very distant future."

She looked back, saying, "Yes, a far future. And you know the legend as well as I, that someday the people will leave Earth, crossing the oceans of space to make our own world somewhere. . . . I wonder about that future, though I will not see it; if we would be exiles there, too, though we were lords there, when here we were only poor relatives, cast-off and restricted. Here, at least, artifacts though we may be to some, we still share chemistry with the other creatures of Earth. I often try to imagine those strange skies, the different odors on the wind. Would the skies be blue? How will we react to that? Not us, Olede, of course."

Morlenden said nothing, preferring to let her mood take her where it would. She would return presently and become the practical Fellirian, Madheliya, once again, leading them as befitted head of Braid through a strange and dangerous world. A deep and brooding one, that Eliya, he thought. Always conjecturing serious things that at least for the moment were manifestly improbable, if not damned impossible. Ler living in factory towns! Crossing space to another planet in a spaceship! All that was legendary, true, but he had never pondered deeply upon it. Children's tales, they were . . . tales to tell children under the stars of summer nights. But when he had looked back at the girl Schaeszendur when Fellirian had been talking about ships and journeys and futures, he had seen, just for a second, a trace, a print, an echo of an expression on her face which he could not identify, even as he had seen it. The remains of an odd little half-smile, and a lambent flicker in the dark eyes, a subtle tensing of that soft, full, pursed mouth, sweet as a ripe persimmon.

They walked on and on, now passing sections of cultivated fields, interspersed with fewer of the low, flat enigmatic buildings. The fields were empty, their crops harvested. And the air was changing, too; it was still every bit as heavy with the tinctures and essences of the city, but now there was also a fresher undertone in it. They approached and passed what seemed to be a warehouse, or processing depot, now vacant. Morlenden looked back at Schaeszendur again; she had begun to trail them a little.

They stopped and waited for her to catch up; when she had caught up with all of them, he asked her, affectionately, "How do you feel, Schaeszen?"

"Tired," she answered in a dull voice. "I hurt."

Fellirian went to her and began to stroke the girl's arms and shoulders, gently but firmly. She said, "I know. You haven't walked so far in a long time. You have been very ill."

"I have? Was I in the house of a healer?"

"You have been ill and those who looked after you acted as best they could according to their lights. Don't worry now. I don't want to force you to do more than you can, but we do have to go on as fast as we are able. I promise that when we get home, you can sleep as long as you want. We'll take care of you. Rest now, here, this little bit. Then we'll go on some more."

The girl said softly, "I'm cold, too."

Fellirian said, "Kris, warm her."

Krisshantem, who had been standing alongside uncertainly, sat down on the roadside on the curb beside Schaeszendur and put his arm around her shoulders, tentatively, shyly. She adjusted to his contours, fitting herself to him, smiling and glancing at the boy from under her eyebrows, half-expectantly. There was also, in her face, something of a flickering smile, very like the one Morlenden could still see vividly in the image he had of Maellenkleth. Krisshantem looked back at her, smiling also, but weakly, and then looked away, blank.

Damn, thought Morlenden to himself. *He's the first male this Schaeszendur has ever seen in her real life, save me, when I put her to bed, and of course she wants him already for a little casual flower-fight. And her body needs it. What an irony! Or could there be something left over from before, from Maellenkleth; could she be remembering flashes of that which she had done before with this one?* He moved close beside Fellirian, sitting, feeling the familiar contours and warmth of flank and thigh, buttock and shoulder, contours so ingrained in his own mind that he knew he could survive autoforgetting with them intact.

He whispered, so the younger couple would not hear, "Eliya, is there any way she could remember him from before?"

"I don't think so. . . . Here, put your arm around me as well; I'm cold, too . . . there. And Schaes, remember? No, no way, according to all that I've heard. To autoforget is final. And even if there were mnemons left, pieces, the rebuilding would obliterate many of them, substituting things in their places. I suppose that she would catch some glimpses, but they would be meaningless to her; she might feel some familiarity, as with certain dreams, but she wouldn't know why. Don't trouble her, you'll only disturb her. Poor thing, this Schaeszendur was only just born a couple of hours ago."

"I've heard much the same about this as have you, Eliya, but I've been watching her: there's something there."

"Perhaps. Remember, neither you nor I have known a forgetty before. You could be mistaking what you see."

Morlenden suddenly felt mulish, obstinate. He started to say, "True, true, but nevertheless I . . . ." He had intended to continue in the infuriating manner he had often used to good purpose with Fellirian in their long days together, but he was interrupted by a sudden noise from Krisshantem's waist-pouch.

The boy hurriedly dug out the tiny electronic unit, small enough to fit comfortably in his hand. Commnet Interconnect, Fellirian had called it. Krisshantem looked dumbly at the unit, while a speaker somewhere in it made an eerie wailing noise, not particularly loud, but a sound that carried, a repeating sliding tone that shivered up and down a short scale, rapidly, oscillating.

Fellirian started violently, tensing her whole body. "Kris, give it to me!"

Staring at the wailing unit, he handed it over to her carefully, as if it were about to explode. As he did, the wailing stopped, replaced immediately by a tired, bored voice, male from the sound of it, speaking Modanglic.

"Green system test call, green system test call, test call in the green system, system green, I say again. All operatives initiate roll on my mark . . . mark!" A tiny red light illuminated at the top of the unit Fellirian was holding in her hand, both near and far thumbs gripping it so her knuckles were white.

She looked frantically over the unit, trying to see if she could discover the correct button to press. But nothing on the Commnet Interconnect was lettered or numbered. She looked at it again in the poor light. Even if she could press the right one, what if anything, was she supposed to say? Again she went over the unit carefully. Then she laid it carefully on the ground, getting to her feet. The red light began winking on and off, on and off.

The speaker said, still in the same, bored voice, "B-fifteen, depress your acknowledge button."

There was a long pause. Following Fellirian's example, all of them arose, anticipating.

The speaker now said, "B-fifteen, procedure two." This time an edge had crept into the voice.

There was another pause. Then the red light went out, to be replaced by two orange lights that flickered on and off, alternating in a hypnotic rhythm. The speaker said, with finality, "B-fifteen, ninety-eight. Alpha Alpha, break, out." There was a pulse of static, a click, and the speaker went dead. The orange lights continued to alternate.

Fellirian began dusting herself off, scuffling the area where she and Morlenden had been sitting. "Get going, all of you. We have to move now, run if necessary. I don't know how to operate that model, but I can guess what it is doing: it's sending out a signal so they can locate it. So scuff your places well before we leave here; they'll bring infrared trackers and in this cold weather our body heat will leave ground-glow like hot irons. And come on, move! We've got to get away from here, now!"

Krisshantem helped Schaeszendur to her feet, with some difficulty, and even after that she stood unsteadily, swaying and shivering while the rest of the party scuffed up their places, and hers. As if by an afterthought, Fellirian picked up the Commnet Interconnect, looked at it stupidly for a moment, and then turned, and in one flowing movement threw it into a nearby field as far as she could. Then they began their journey anew; Fellirian leading, Morlenden helping the girl along, followed by Cannialin and Kaldherman, with Kris guarding their rear, alert and awake. They immediately left the road and began an erratic, zigzag course among the accessways in the fields, always trying to keep a shed, or a clump of brush, between themselves and the place where they had stopped and rested. Whenever she could do so without delaying them too much, Fellirian led them through brush, and close by sheds and warehouses. At first, she paced them at a brisk walk, but after they had warmed up to that pace, she increased their speed to almost a half-trot, something more than a fast walk.

Morlenden, and especially Krisshantem, had no difficulty at all keeping the pace that Fellirian set, nor did the others, but they could tell easily that Schaeszendur was tiring fast now; she had used up almost all her reserves just to get as far as they had come already. Still, she was trying mightily to keep up and not slow them all, neither crying nor complaining. But as Morlenden helped her along from time to time, he could see her mouth moving, as if she were talking to herself. He could not hear words, nor make out what it might have been, but all in all, he knew that she would not make much more distance on her own.

They made better progress toward their unknown destination than would have seemed possible on foot. Moving in and out of shadows, brushlicks, odd little copses, groves, clusters of sheds; they were now moving through land almost completely given over to agriculture, and were beginning to hit patches and plots not completely recovered from the wild, or else perhaps returning to it again. The sky-glow from the lighting of Complex Ten was growing fractionally dimmer, to something nearer the light level one could see at night inside the reservation. And with their gray winter overshirts and hoods and cloaks, they were close to being practically invisible, if their motion did not give them away.

And now that they were spread out somewhat, Krisshantem seemed at times to disappear, and reappear again, unless one watched him constantly, and with an effort of will. Morlenden looked back at the boy often, marveling at his facility; and also at the way Kaldherman and Cannialin were following his example; Krisshantem's motions were almost the exact opposite of that of the humans they had seen earlier in the terminals—the jerky, learned, deliberately difficult motions, deliberately designed to make the user stand out against a background, and become obvious to a trained observer, deep in the secrets of the perception of motion. Kris, on the other hand, moved in a manner that could only be called transinstinctual, the sinuous weaving, looping, graceful, sine-curve motions, half random, the minimum energy curve, the motions of a feral creature who had carefully cultivated the little bit of natural wildness remaining to him. To glance at him casually, one would have seen only a person walking, but on the second scan across the target, Kris would not break the background, by pattern or motion. He was grass in the wind, a tree, a leaf, a branch, a bird. And Cannialin and Kaldherman were imitating him, following his example.

After a hard, fast walk, they reached at last the edges of the cultivated areas and entered the boundary woods, which in this place were composed of young pine trees, more or less regularly spaced. They all stopped as soon as they had attained the dense, furry growth, now on rising ground, and looked back over the fields in the direction from which they had come. It was a good distance; they had done very well, all things considered. And there across the fields was the suggestion of activity, blurred by the distance and the darkness: movement and lights. Distant hummings and fainter throbbing sounds. For the moment, the activity seemed rather random, purposeless, and undirected, but it was nevertheless in the exact spot where they had stopped to rest. Morlenden watched and felt a curious duality of emotions: complete disassociation from the meaningless motion and activity in the far distance, and simultaneously a personal feeling of dread, a definite suspicion that the activity was, under the muddled surface, very purposeful and highly intelligent. A semiliving gestalt organism whose entire consciousness was becoming focused upon their group, its prey. Yes, it was a predator taking shape back there.

Fellirian stopped and let the rest gather to her side as they caught up, one by one; Morlenden shepherding Schaeszendur, Cannialin and Kaldherman, Krisshantem bringing up the rear. Schaeszendur they brought into their midst, closing their bodies tightly about the girl, shielding her from the sudden chill of their stopping in the cold air. They were all breathing hard, and Morlenden could see, in the sky-scatter from the city lights, that there was a fine sheen of sweat glazed over Fellirian's face. Her eyes were alert, but heavy-lidded and tired; she had been in no better shape for this than he.

She said, between breaths, "Now we can assume . . . that the agents have made . . . their reports . . . and that they have located . . . the Commnet Interconnect. Probably . . . seen some . . . witnesses in the city."

Morlenden suggested, "The group at the hot-drink kiosk."

"There, yes. Maybe others; we did walk openly. With what they know, they can easily anticipate that we will be coming this way, to the reservation boundary. And they will certainly be bringing tracking equipment."

Krisshantem asked, "Could we not now take another course, to throw them off?"

Fellirian, recovering her breath, answered kindly, "No, that would not work except to our disadvantage. Attend: we cannot push Schaeszen, which we must if we turn now. And we would lengthen our exposure in the forerunner world; it is not like your woods out here, Kris—away from this area, close upon the reservation fence, there is nowhere we could survive for very long. None of us, not me, not you, know their ways well enough to pass unseen and uncaught in their midst for long. No, no, we cannot; we must go as straight as we can and hope that they have difficulty in picking up our trail."

She stopped, suddenly attentive, listening. In the far distance, a change had come in the humming sound, and the throbbing increased; they looked back, to see a group of lights detach itself from the others and move upward, slowly. It continued to move about, without apparent purpose or goal, but they could also see that it was quartering over the fields about the place where they had rested.

Krisshantem observed, "That, at least, is no mystery. I know that: it is an aircraft, looking for tracks."

Fellirian said, "Yes, so it must be. We'll soon know whether to rest a bit more, or make the last run to the fence."

The random, quartering motion of the lights continued for a time, but apparently the aircraft did not sense any obvious tracks within its sensor search pattern, for after several sweeps over the search area, it returned to the cluster of lights on the ground, merged with them, and as it did, the humming noise faded. The sense of activity around the cluster of lights in the distance continued, and if anything, increased in motion.

Fellirian watched the activity closely, and when the aircraft had landed, she did not seem any more optimistic by that which she had seen. She sighed deeply, and said, "For now they have missed us on the first cast. From the sound and movement of it, it's a hovercraft, a platform on ducted fans. . . . They know the general direction we must come, though, so they will try again. And once they pick up a good trail, they'll let shock troops down on ropes. . . . We had better move on now. We have much less of a lead on them."

Fellirian now turned away from the group, facing the direction they must go; she saw only pine trees, densely packed together, an uphill slope, a suggestion of higher forest farther up the slope, a darker sky that had no lights under it. It was not physically far as distances went: no more than the same distance back to the place where they had rested. But the aircraft was very close now; on a good trail, the troops could be upon them in minutes, and they were all past their best now.

Krisshantem laid his hand on Fellirian's arm. "Wait. I have an idea; you say that I am not wise in the way of cities, and that is so . . . but are they not equally unwise in the open country? And you say that they track by body-heat? So would not a brighter target capture their attention better than a muted one?"

They had no flares with them, and it was too damp for fire . . . Fellirian's mind leaped ahead. "Krisshantem, I forbid . . .".

"Now let us not speak of forbiddings and permissions. Were I blind and deaf, I could evade such as those; I have watched the clouds change, measured the color of the sky, seen the green of the winter sky. I have watched day-shadow move. And they will see where I have been, they will hear echoes, but where they look, there I will not be."

The humming in the background increased again, as if to emphasize Kris's point. He also listened, and then continued, "Now, listen. You start—you, Morlenden, Schaeszendur, Kaldherman and Cannialin will come with me. When you get to the fence, you will be near my old territory, and I can catch you there, never fear. But you are better at this than I would have imagined most townsmen to be, so you may get a bit ahead . . . but you cannot lose me. I will always know where you are. And we will lead them on a merry chase."

Fellirian stood still, saying nothing. Morlenden thought on it, considered. It would have to be that way. They could not now hope to get Schaeszendur across the fence to safety, back inside, unless someone decoyed the forces now arraying themselves against them, and distracted them away from the one moment they needed. He moved the girl, nudging her gently, to let her know that the rest was at an end. She moved sluggishly, as if under water, turning her face to Morlenden's, a blank, blind gaze of exhaustion.

Morlenden said, "Schaeszen can't run any more. I'll have to carry her. I agree with Kris's proposal." Close by, Kaldherman set his face into a grim expression and nodded assent. Cannialin looked upward, at the sky-glow, and let her mouth fall into a weird, beatific smile.

Morlenden thought, *Just such an abstracted smile I have seen on her pretty face when she was slaughtering a chicken, slitting its throat with that long knife of hers.* . . .

Reluctantly, Fellirian agreed. "Yes, I see. Very well, Mor, I'll find the best way for you; follow my sound, and I'll help you at the fence." She listened to the sound. Then she turned to look at the wood once more, and back for a moment, calculating, indecisive . . . then started off at a lope into the piny brushwood, resolutely negotiating a passage. Morlenden, helping the girl along, half carrying her, set out behind. Kris and the others remained where they were, staring after them.

Kris called out, as they disappeared into the dense and prickly underbrush, "Don't crash so, you dray-horse! They will hear you even over the motor noises!"

Deep in the brush, Morlenden paused and looked back. Through a small gap he could see the boy removing his felt boots, while Kal and Cannialin did the same: to leave heated footprints in the cold ground, while he and Fellirian and Schaeszen left less obvious marks. And farther back, behind them all, on the edge of the city, a cluster of lights was moving, not exactly toward them, but close enough. Then the lights went out, but the humming and throbbing did not change. And after a moment, Morlenden thought he could sense, at the edge of perception, a darker spot, vague in shape, moving against the background sky-scatter. He turned and looked back up the hill: there the sky was darker, and there was no sound, save the passing of Fellirian through the pines, making as much noise as she could now. In that direction, there were no moving shapes in the sky.

Now he started out, helping the girl along as best he could, partially supporting her, as she walked now only a little under her own power. He discovered that he could keep up with Fellirian, ahead, as she moved back and forth, searching out the easiest way for them. He hardly ever had sight of her, but he could follow her by sound almost as easily, listening carefully. And behind them, the humming grew louder. Morlenden looked back, over his shoulder, and saw the dark patch moving, against the sky again, more clearly now, but still not distinctly enough to make its shape truly. It had covered most of the distance to the beginning of the woods, but seemed to be drifting a bit to the south of his present position. There was no indication that they who flew in the craft had actually seen anything, not yet. Morlenden increased his pace, moving deeper into the woods.

Schaeszendur sobbed, and Morlenden felt her full weight sag against his left arm; further progress had become impossible for her, even with assistance. She had reached the end of her physical resources. Morlenden bent, and let her fall across his shoulders, taking her full weight. She was lighter than he expected her to be . . . Maellenkleth had been well-formed, comely and strong, but this Schaeszendur was made of fluff and bubbles, her flesh soft and stringy. She had, after her long confinement, retained her basic build, but much reduced . . . and despite her weight, he made better progress, because he did not have to half-drag her along.

Now he did not turn to watch the aircraft; he listened. He heard the hum and throb of the motors change tone abruptly. He tried to ignore it, but could not; swinging the load of the girl slowly around on his shoulders, Morlenden turned clumsily about, to see. The darkness in the sky was almost abreast of them now to the south, and it was falling, as an autumn leaf might glide downward, but without the sudden turns and swoops of the leaf. Lower, it stopped as if running into a wall of feathers, the motors surging mightily, then falling in tone again. The craft hovered, now stopped dead-still in the air, and the lights came on again. Other lights came on with them, searchlights directed against the ground. In their glare he could see rope ladders falling, unrolling out of the craft, and immediately, on them, figures climbing down, many with bulky backpacks. Morlenden struggled with his burden and lurched off in the direction he imagined Fellirian to be, trying to move faster and more quietly. And behind him, he now heard voices, faintly, muffled by the trees and the air, ghostly, unsubstantial. The hovercraft powered up, rose sharply, turning as it did and withdrawing a little back toward the city. He stopped, listening for Fellirian. Over the pounding of his heart and the throb of the hovercraft motors, he could not hear her. Morlenden listened again, carefully, all senses tense and strained. The motor noise was fading. Otherwise, nothing.

And the voices faded also, fell silent. He now began to feel a touch of fear . . . he half expected to hear, as he continued slogging up the hill along what seemed to be the best way, a sharp, peremptory command. Or perhaps nothing, a sudden pain. His skin crawled. Where the hell was Fellirian?

There was no actual sign that he was being pursued. Everything seemed quiet nearby. Morlenden continued walking, and noticed that the upward slope was beginning to level off a little, and that the trees were larger, more mature; he knew instinctively that they had to be near the fence, but as yet he could not see it.

Behind him, now far down the gentle slope, Morlenden heard a curious, half-muffled sound, more a prolonged puff or whooshing than a report, of gunshot. He had never heard anything like it before. After the sound died away, he also heard calls, cries, hoarse exhortations, also distorted by distance and the intervening trees. Kris, Kal, Ayali. . . . He heard more sounds, faraway crashing and tearing in the brush, more calls, so it seemed, all in Modanglic. How many? Three? Four? He had seen five or six men climb down from the hovercraft. But from the noise they made, it sounded like a small army. All the same, the continuing racket reassured him; they would not be so loud, if they had caught any of the decoy party. No, Kris would be teasing them, drawing them off. That would be Kris's way; and then he'd just vanish among the trees. The crashing and shouting moved farther off, more southerly, became fainter.

Morlenden stopped now, his head reeling, feeling the full weight of fatigue. He stooped over, and, as gently as he could, laid Schaeszendur down, resting her head on a pile of pine needles he had hastily scraped together. Kneeling beside her, he examined her closely; she seemed conscious, but she made no attempt to speak. Her eyes remained, open, but the expression in them was glassy, unfocused. Morlenden looked around himself. He saw nothing save darkness, the ever-present sky-scatter, the shapes of trees, black trunks looming. It was dense here, like the forests inside. He knew they were close, they had to be, but now the ground was level and he could not determine in which direction the fence lay. He could guess one way, for there was some thinning in the trees, a sense of openness. From that direction he heard faint scuffling in the carpet of fallen needles underfoot, glimpsed a suggestion of movement, a dark shape, becoming a gray whiter overcloak; it was Fellirian. She was coming at a half-run.

Fellirian saw him, the girl on the ground, and called out, "It's not far now, just over there, where I came from. It's more open near the fence. Can you make it?"

Morlenden was still short of breath. "Have to. They drew them off to the south, I think. It's quiet again. But there are too many ifs. They know there is more than one of us, so they might catch on to the trick. And we are more visible here." He looked upward as he spoke, nodding toward the throbbing that now never faded entirely from hearing.

Fellirian reached them, knelt beside the girl, held the girl's eye open and looked closely. Then she looked in the same direction he had indicated, and nodded. Breath-steam wreathed her face and the overhanging cowl of her overshirt. She said, "I'll help you with her. Come on."

Together, they lifted the girl between them, and began moving forward again, supporting, half dragging Schaeszen between them, dodging around tree trunks, stumbling over fallen branches in their way, abandoning the pretense of stealth and quiet. They crossed a low rise, a swell in the ground, and stopped. Just ahead of them, Morlenden could see an old-fashioned chain-link fence, about twice his height. They stumbled forward to it in a last rush, reaching the fence and stopping, leaning against the links and mesh of cold metal. There were thin flakes of ice on some of the links.

Fellirian asked, "How do we get her over? I was counting on her climbing herself. Now, I don't know; I don't think she can climb it on her own."

"I don't know. Let her rest a bit more; let me think." They tenderly laid the girl down again, propped against the fence, Morlenden kneeling partially supporting her. Fellirian stood over them, legs slightly apart, panting. Suddenly she turned her head, back, the way they had come up the hill.

She said urgently, softly, "Olede! Voices, there, speaking Modanglic! They're coming!"

"Sh! I hear them. Lights, too; see them? It has to be now, doesn't it, Eliya? Give me a hand with her, here."

Morlenden now leaned over Schaeszendur, shook her roughly, sharply, "Schaeszendur!" There was no response. She looked at him, but did nothing else. Her eyes were dull, lifeless. He shook her again. "Schaeszendur! Maellenkleth!" Some luster reappeared in her eyes. "Aezedu! Aelekle! Wake up! Listen to me!" The girl seemed to listen to him now. "Can you hold to me if I carry your weight?"

"Yes." The voice was flat and unaccented, but it was clear, steady.

"Then you must do this: hold to me, no matter what. Rest, and sleep are not far now. Just one more effort and you're safe. Use all your strength and hold to me! We have to climb a fence!"

The same calm, distant measured voice answered him. "Yes, I under-stand, I must hold to you. I can. I will do it."

He stood and helped the girl to her feet, while Fellirian steadied her. She was very shaky on her feet, although she did now stand on her own. Her eyes were clear also, but somehow she did not seem to be aware of her surroundings. Morlenden turned to the fence, getting into position, reaching for and feeling the cold metal strands, experimentally feeling with his toe for a foothold. Fellirian helped the girl onto Morlenden's back, arranging her arms about his neck, placing the girl's hands so she would be steady, locked in position however Morlenden had to move on the fence.

She whispered in Shaeszendur-Maellenkleth's ear, "That's a good girl. Yes, just like this now, hold on, whatever happens; hold on to Morlenden."

Then to Morlenden, "We'll have to hurry, Olede, the lights are close now. I'll try to get them away from you." Her presence suddenly withdrew.

It was true. He could clearly hear the sounds of crashing in the brush back in the woods, not so far at all now. He took a deep breath, looked at the fence, tensed his muscles. *One more obstacle, and we're over. They won't dare touch us inside the fence.* He drew another deep breath, tight-ened his grasp on the cold metal, thrust. He could not look upward without moving the girl. He took his first step up, feeling the full weight of the girl settling on his back, shifting through his arms down to his hands, his fingers, pressing on the wire strands.

And behind him he heard footfalls in the ground-cover, sharp scufflings off to the left, in the direction Fellirian had taken. Then there were more from the same direction, but farther off. And now directly behind him, sudden crashing of brush, footfalls on the hard ground pounding, and an actinic light cast its glare upon his hands on the fence.

He heard a voice shouting in Modanglic, "There they are, two, on the fence!"

Another shouted hoarsely, "You! You, stop! Get down from there, *now!*"

Morlenden shook his head slightly, to himself, and took another step up. There was more commotion behind him, scuffling, hoarse exclamations, oaths, curses, and as someone cried out some unintelligible word, he heard at close hand the same odd sound he had heard earlier. A whooshing, a hiss, very close, especially loud. He felt Schaeszendur tense her whole supple body, sharply, heard her emit a short grunt, as with great effort. Her grip around his neck tightened convulsively, strongly, and she was choking him. She coughed, wetly, and the intense grip began to weaken. She was going to let go, she would fall; Morlenden let himself back down, and as he felt solid ground under his boots and bent to cushion her fall, she let go, relaxing completely, sliding off and slumping against the fence in much the same posture she had rested in only moments before. Morlenden turned around.

He felt a black, consuming rage rising, suffusing him, distorting his vision, altering his perceptions. He felt enlarged, he felt time slow, he expanded into something strange, fey, an evil released, clenching his hands convulsively, breathing in deep, steady breaths. Morlenden turned around, withdrawing his fish-knife from its baldric. He saw a confused blur of action.

They were all there—Fellirian, Krisshantem, Cannialin, Kaldherman— moving about a perimeter enclosing a small group of five humans, one of whom was struggling with an unwieldy piece of elongated equipment, gunlike in shape, but not exactly a gun, either, in the traditional sense. The remaining four seemed to be protecting that one. It seemed that none of them noticed Morlenden, so intent were they on the flashing, whirling figures approaching from outside their group. Morlenden tightened his grip on the long, thin knife, walking like an invulnerable sleepwalker. They did not see him, the invisible one, and he would deal among them like the angel of death. He felt like Kris, more so, invulnerable and invisible, charmed. The rest skirmished to the rear, opening up the gunner for him. The one with the odd, bulky gun was open, in front of him, still struggling with some adjustment; perhaps the weapon was jammed, broken. Morlenden walked calmly, quietly to him, almost reaching him before the man became aware of him. The man looked up, startled, raising the weapon, and as he did, Morlenden casually stepped inside the reach of the gun and calmly, still calmly, pushed the knife into the man's chest. There was a resistance, and blood flowed around the wound. He pushed harder, looking directly into the man's shocked eyes with a lover's intimacy. The weapon dropped from his hands and the man looked at Morlenden accusingly, incredulously, as if this could not be happening to him, him the weaponeer. And a darkness greater than the night passed over his vision, as he slumped to the cold ground.

The others now saw that their weaponeer was down, and they menaced the five ler with hand-pistols, while one among them struggled, panic-stricken, with a small device, something similar to the communications unit Krisshantem had taken off the agent. They seemed confident now, slowed, sure that none of the group facing them would use any kind of released weapon. They had been briefed. Before he could set the controls the way he intended to, Fellirian menaced him, her own knife drawn, before any of the others could bring a weapon to bear. The man danced backward, holding it high, out of reach, as the others tried to get into position for a shot. One went down immediately, as he suddenly met a Kris who wasn't supposed to be where he was, throat-chopped. Morlenden sliced at the hand holding the communicator, heard, as if under water, a harsh cry, and the communicator was on the ground. He stepped on it, breaking its delicate inner structure into a jumble of metal, now smoking and sparking as its power-pack shorted out. Cannialin dispatched that one, while he was trying to avoid Morlenden, with the crazed look in his eyes of a berserker, and Fellirian, who steadily advanced upon him, uttering terrible words in a language he did not understand. The last saw his position, and tried to run, but he met Kaldherman and Krisshantem and his journey, even in flight, was a short one.

And there was silence in the forest, marked only by hard breathing, and a distant hum and throb of motors from the hovercraft, quartering the distance, far away. Morlenden felt the rage abating, saw what they had done, saw that the others saw it, too. They did not speak, but dumbly walked about the scene of the battle, numb, astonished. Morlenden could see clearly again, and looking at Fellirian, saw streams of tears down her cheeks, although there was no change in the expression on her face. They all knew they had avenged something here, they had defeated armed men, with no more than their hand weapons. But something had snapped, and would never be the same again. There was blood on the ground, that had not been spilled in such a way before.

Krisshantem was the first to find his voice. He said slowly, "After a time, they began to realize what we were doing. They had tried a shot at us, to no good. While they shot at where they thought I was, Kal and Cannialin got one of them. But the rest saw, and knew we were not the ones they sought. So they retreated, turned back. They found your trail with that weapon, and followed it. They would not be diverted. We tried to intercept them, but they were then between us, and running hard. It was no good, no good, we couldn't prevent it. . . ."

Time was resuming its normal flow. Morlenden asked, distantly, "Eliya, what did they shoot her with?"

Her voice was flat, overcontrolled. "A filthy thing, a wire-guide. It launches a tiny rocket with an explosive head containing barbs. It's connected by a wire to the gun itself, which follows the flight with a computer, guides it. All you have to do is keep the target in the sights. They like to use it against fugitives. . . . Do you see? Once hit with that thing, the target cannot escape, even if it didn't have a mortal wound."

Morlenden said dryly, "Now I understand the weapon prohibition better. . . ."

"Yes," Fellirian said. "So do we all who were here. A weapon that leaves the hand magnifies the user too much, so much that often the original will that guided it is lost, expanded, diluted. Washed out. And that is why we fear much technology, why we labor to retain our innocence; other things magnify, too, just the same way, and we are not wise enough yet to know if we really do want to see that magnified image of ourselves . . . until we have a better control of ourselves. We are not restrained enough yet by half. Were it so with them, too."

Morlenden said, "Innocence . . . I do not feel so innocent. There is blood."

Cannialin interrupted. "Sh! Listen!"

At her command, they all stopped, in a circle, facing each other, the five of them, and listened. Schaeszendur. The girl was not yet dead. They could hear her in the silence after the violence, by the fence, where she had fallen. She was talking aimlessly, now protected by shock from the pain that would have come. She was talking, but most of it was just babbling, nonsense, not even words. The mortal wound she had received, the fatigue, the unstable implant persona, they were all coming together now. They listened to the soft, hoarse voice, childishly high in tone. Just babbling. Morlenden felt a vast dull pain in his heart. And they turned from the place where they had made murder, where they had fought in heat with the men, the forerunners, and walked slowly to the fence, to her.

They all knelt close around her. She was lying, partly propped against the fence, as they had left her. Morlenden cradled her head, feeling the soft, dark hair, the heated skin along the back of her neck. He wiped her mouth; there had been blood at one corner of it. And brushed the adolescent hair off her forehead, out of her eyes. An odd frown creased her forehead momentarily.

Her eyes had been open, but had been moving aimlessly, sometimes independently of one another. She did not see, except some artificial ulterior scene Krisshantem had implanted in her . . . some memory. But without warning, the expression of dull shock and confusion in her face faded away quickly, changing radically into something else. The contours of her face began to shift, as if obeying instructions from a different set of muscles, a different personality. The childlike roundness of face faded, vanished, and was replaced by a harder, more adult set along the jaw, tense and concentrated around the eyes. The eyes cleared, became focused, calm, then intense. Without moving her head, she looked hard at them all, from face to face, pausing especially long when she came to Kris. Morlenden recognized that look in her eyes at once: it was the look of one who saw strangers and knew not how they came there. Only Kris was familiar. He knew. Maellenkleth knew only Kris among them, while Schaeszendur had known them all alike. This was Maellenkleth, how, he didn't know, but Maellenkleth it undeniably was.

She took a deep breath, breaking something deep inside. They heard a rattling in her throat. She grasped Morlenden, who was closest to her, and with a capable, terrifyingly strong grip, pulled him down close to her, so that his face was by hers. All of Morlenden's senses were alive, tensed to ultimate receptivity, alert: he sensed all of her, how short her time-line was. She had only seconds to live. He smelled sweat, fearscent, the reek of adrenaline, blood, musky, salty, all overlying the sweet fragrance of a young girl.

And he heard the harsh voice in his ear, ragged with shock and the leading edge of the wedge of pain. It was not the simplistic child's voice he had heard before, when it was Schaeszendur; this was different. Hoarse and wounded and dying it may have been, but it was also the voice of one almost adult, filled with knowledge and desires and incredible will for one born in the sign of the Water elemental. The grip tightened. And the voice rasped, "Mevlannen . . . Mevlannen . . . to Sanjirmil."

"What?" he asked.

The rasping whisper repeated again, ". . . Matrix . . . from Mev . . . from Elane . . . get the matrix from Mev-Elane . . . take to Sanjirmil. . . ."

"What matrix, what for?"

"Get the matrix from Mevlannen . . ." and then the voice trailed off into another series of nonsense words, drifting back into the childish intonations of the forgetty, Schaeszendur. Or was it? The face did not change, though the grip was now relaxing. The voice trailed off. She was yet breathing, but it was obvious that she had but a few instants left to live. Krisshantem stepped forward, and it was as if she was seeing him for the first time. Morlenden felt the hand holding his over-shirt clench hard, almost as if she were going to try to rise to her feet. Then he saw her lips moving, trying to form words, and she found her voice, her eyes cleared completely, and she spoke, and

Now an immense Will suddenly grasped their minds and clamped down, hard, so intense it was painful. All five of them immediately lost the sensory input of the world around them. This was Maellenkleth, Maellenkleth the master Player, and she was sending an image in Multispeech. In visual Command-override, so powerful they could not move, or block it out of their minds. They all saw the same thing, and it would remain impressed on their minds, reverberating, forever. It was not a message, an instruction, a command, but a picture. A picture of Maellenkleth, not quite as any of them had ever seen her before, her face shining with rapture, turning slightly to her right side, turned a little away from the viewer, her arms outstretched from her torso. All around her, surrounding her, outlined in faint, glowing blue, were the outlines of a tessaract, encompassing her, protecting her. It was clear that here, in the vision, she had truly come into her own. She floated in space, inside a translucent tessaract, wearing the ritual robes of a high Perklaren contestant of the Game, the Inner Game, intricate and arcane Game patterns and emblems embroidered vertically down a panel of linen on the front of her robe, and also along the hem of the robe about her pretty, delicate feet, and on the borders of the wide sleeves of the garment. Behind her, almost in the direction she was facing, as if looking over her shoulder, was a background of the patterns of some Game projected upward onto a spherical ceiling and part of a wall, an immense multicolored Game diagram, stopped in mid-flight.

They felt the Will fading, the image fading with it, not changing, but dimming, losing color contrast, becoming pastelled, becoming empty outlines, fading, fading, graying, darkening, and out. Their optic nerves resumed transmitting the images of a nighttime forest, by a fence, to their visual centers. And Maellenkleth lay relaxed against the fence, as if asleep, the face relaxed, peaceful. Morlenden, his hand still under her slender neck, could feel her cooling. Life had departed this body.

Fellirian hiccupped nervously. "What was she sending?"

Kris answered, "Something about a matrix Mevlannen has. Take it to Sanjirmil. . . . She's dead now."

"I know," said Morlenden. "Had you ever seen her send an image like that before?" He knew very well that somehow she had imposed an image of herself upon a background of the Inner Game. He also knew that none of the rest of the Derens had seen that before.

Krisshantem answered, "No, nothing like that. I could recognize a Game display, but it is in a strange form. Was that Inner Game?"

"Yes. And I don't know what the significance of it is."

The boy said, "I never saw her do anything like that before. I didn't realize she could override like that, even though she taught me override. . . . That pattern on the display she did show me once, but plain and flat, not like that curved screen-ceiling. . . . It is something very special, I know that, something very secret." He sat back on his heels, shaking his head. "That was the old Maellen, there, in the end, the old Maellen and something more. She was sending Truth, then, not playing or concealing, though she had not the time to tell us what it means. I know it not. But it must have been a powerful thing, to have endured through autoforgetting and restructuring; she believed something powerfully."

Fellirian said slowly, 'Truth is what we believe; and of course we become what we believe ourselves to be. Unlimited things. Only the lesser are provable. She sent to us what she was to herself."

Morlenden asked, "Do you know what she meant?"

"No."

"Must we, then, do as she asked?"

"I still shake from the force of it; of course we must, we cannot choose at this point, but follow it through to the very end. That is why she sent that image in the end, the very end. She said, there, 'Do this for me, it is my very life.' To have retained it through all she endured, it must have been the central immanent fact of her life, something she lived with daily, ingrained in her at the cellular level, beyond the reach of even autoforgetting. It was that which lent meaning to her life."

Kris added, "It was truly her, this I know. There was much that she did not tell me, but I could sense that we were close to it; she took me as far as she could. And if you will not pursue this, Morlenden, then I will."

"Rest in ease, Krisshantem. I will take it. I think not to the ends of the Earth, either, for Mevlannen I can find."

Fellirian added, "And it must be quickly, too, Olede. There was an urgency in her, something that must be done quickly. And we should do this without informing the Perwathwiy or Sanjirmil. It will be difficult and perilous, a risk, that trip all the way across the continent. They will be watchful, wary, after what was done here tonight. I know some tricks yet, though, and with the watchfulness there may also be much confusion, enough to slip through. . . ." She stopped now, thinking. "And now let us act in reverence toward this poor body that has endured so much, and for what? Yes, let us do it, for they will come, looking for their shock troops."

Kris said, as Fellirian got to her feet, "She said once to me that she did that which she performed outside because she enjoyed it, the shadow-play, the feints, the skill of passing unseen on many errands; but that overriding all personal likes and dislikes was a higher reason, that we would all know of it, within her lifetime. She thought, before fertility, which was why she was working so hard to instruct me in the Game basics, and gather support for her proposal to have us declared *shartoorh* Dirklarens. I do not know why, but I know the meaning of her words and her deeds: this was for us. The people."

Morlenden said, also getting to his feet, "Then may it have been a worthy price, for she paid with two lives for it: not many would go so far as to risk even one."

Kaldherman had been silent through the whole adventure. Now he spoke. "I have an unraveled thread of my own, you thinkers and worriers and ponderers; I wish to know how it is the five of us, with no more than knives, best armed and trained forerunners?"

Cannialin also asked, "Indeed. Where are the wild-eyed, merciless humans, who are reputed to shoot and burn without stint? These were willing enough to shoot one in the back, but when the scars would be in the front side, they milled about like geese in the slaughteryard. I admit to no cowardice, but I had not thought myself so fearsome before. Kalder, perhaps: he had a look about him just now that would have wormed a dog, but me?"

Fellirian said, "Ayali, you do not know how strange you look with knife in hand . . . indeed, I fear you myself sometimes at home, when you are slicing a fowl's throat. The only thing I can say is that they must not be accustomed to resistance, much less attack upon themselves; but that raises many questions in my mind, and an answer that makes questions isn't such a good one, is it?"

Morlenden said, "You mean they just have to threaten, not actually do anything?"

"So it seems. They respond quickly enough. That I have seen with my own eyes, and the targets always run, and are gathered. No one resists."

"And what if someone did?"

"Unthinkable."

"Do they have any idea what a foundation they have built upon, that a dozen determined men could take over the whole planet?"

No one answered Morlenden's question. And now they all stood about Maellenkleth, and bent to pick her up. In the background they could still hear the humming and throbbing of the hovercraft, now somewhat nearer. Morlenden was still somewhat stunned, and he felt light-headed, still not quite himself. It had been unthinkable that he had been shot at by an unknown assassin; but to do as he had done here, this night: that was an even more remote conception. Yet he had done it, and as he thought back on it, he felt convinced that it was right, proper. Revenge, and self-survival. And something, some unknown quantity in the unseen underworld, had shifted, changed, and now he was being borne along on the main current of an uncharted stream, flowing to an unknown destination. He shrugged, a gesture that the others missed.

And he said, half to himself, which they also did not notice, lifting the girl up to Kaldherman and Krisshantem, who had climbed the fence, "Watching? Confused? Yes, they will be all those things . . . and maybe they will not be watching half so well as they imagine they do. This one moved among them unseen. Now I . . . ?"

And they began the painful process of lifting Maellen's body over the fence. She was of the Water elemental, and would have to be returned to the waters; they would have to carry her a long way.

FIFTEEN

When I write, betimes, in my Journal, I always feel supremely
confident I solve all problems, not only with ease, but with style
as well, seasoned with considerable wit. . . . We also may note
the same condition in men who have been deprived of Oxygen.
This is enough to make one wonder.
      —The Vaseline Dreams of Hundifer Soames

THAT WHICH HAD gathered in the office of Klaneth Parleau, Chairman of Seaboard South Region, could only be called a mob, and at the moment, all of its constituent parts were trying to talk at once, to each other, to nobody, to anybody, perhaps even to themselves, all utilizing the maximum in volume to make themselves heard. Nobody managed to hear anything but din and confusion. It was, in a word, chaos. Parleau watched in astounded consternation, striving mightily to capture their attention, but his efforts, normally successful, were useless. In fact, they added measurably to the reigning confusion. The members just talked louder and heard less. At last, in total exasperation, Parleau picked up a heavy paperweight, a large stainless steel cube a handsbreadth on a side, and pounded his appointment book until the noise at least died down enough for him to be heard.

"Damn it to hell!" roared the chairman, uncharacteristically in the full grip of his temper. "Is this a Regional Board of Inquiry, or a panel discussion among anarchists?" The noise level dropped some more. They were offended that the chairman should call them anarchists. It became almost quiet. Parleau did not intend to let them rest there. He roared on, "Is this the office of a Regional Chairman, or is it a bandits' den?"

And at last, true, blessed silence fell. Parleau commanded, "Blantine, read the names of those present!"

A voice, hoarse from bawling at the others, started, from somewhere near the far end of the table, "But, Chairman, we . . ."

"Shut the hell up, Gerlin! Recorder, read the names as instructed—
programmed, unprogrammed, and soon to be deprogrammed."

Blantine, the recorder, a junior administrative apprentice, hastily borrowed from the shift currently working days, began in a voice full of uneasiness. "Doctor Mandor Klyten, Department of Alien Affairs; Edner
Eykor, S-eighteen, Security; Aseph Plattsman, S-twelve, Control; Thoro
Gerlin, M-six, Tactical Units . . ." And continuing through several others, at last finishing and sitting down, trying his best to appear inconspicuous. He had not listed himself as a member. He did not intend to
add anything or contribute, save record what they said.

Parleau was still standing. He added, not willing to let the apprentice
clerk off the hook, either, "And Cretus Blantine, Recorder." He noted
that the reading of names had its desired effect: they were now all quiet
and attentive.

Parleau began, "We are here to determine the causes and consequences of a series of incidents that occurred two days ago in this Region, in or near Complex Ten." Parleau observed some fidgeting out of
the corner of his eye, and added, "This board is hereby convened by instruction of Continental Secretariat, Denver, Central High Plains Region." Here he paused to let it sink in, with the implications. A Regional
Chairman held power in his own region, of course, but impelled by
ConSec, he could bring forces to bear from outside the region. He
thought, *Argue, would they? We'll see what kind of song they sing for Section Q when they go to explain this.* He said, "Plattsman, review events."

Plattsman, after consulting some logs, began, "At about the sixteenth
hour, the girl we had been holding, the vandal identified as one Maellenkleth Srith Perklaren, was released in the custody and responsibility
of a party of New Humans who had previously been identified. And immediately the problem commences. Somehow, the transaction, though
handled according to instructions and regulational data, was actually
performed by a Hando Errat, accompanied by agents under his personal
control. We conjecture that there was a plan to abduct the whole party
at some other point, before they could return the girl to the reservation.
However, at Complex Ten, the New Human party somehow evaded
Errat's men and escaped into the Urblex. I may add here that none of
this was reported until much later, owing to the substitution of agents.
Also, reporting and monitoring was further delayed because somehow
the New Humans removed the Commnet Interconnect from the agent
who had been carrying it, abandoning it several miles to the west. This
unit had not responded to a routine maintenance call-up, so autolocation

was initiated. At the same time, our own monitor at the Institute stop reported no contact, and Complex Seven picked up the false agents in the tube terminal, failing exit procedure. Regional Control called for a Tactical Team, but too much time had elapsed, and detailed tracking with chemsensors was deemed unlikely. The TacTeam was deployed into the woods adjacent to the reservation boundary, reporting a live track. They descended, grounded, the carryall standing by. After some time elapsed, the carryall reported no contact, although it observed some action. It returned for reinforcements, onloaded, and returned to the site. The team on the ground did not respond, so a thorough search was made of the area. One member was found near the grounding site, and the rest were located near the fence, in deceased condition."

Parleau said, "Continue."

"Subsequent investigation, necessarily hasty, has established that six New Humans were observed transiting Complex Ten. Of the weapons possessed by the TacTeam, only the wire-guide had been discharged. One dart was not located, the other was still attached to the guide. That dart retained blood, which lab has identified as identical with the blood of the girl we were detaining. Nothing else was found. All members were terminated either by knife wounds, or by blows of a blunt instrument, skillfully applied. From appearances, the investigation team concluded that the party crossed the fence into the reservation, taking the girl with them. Her condition is unknown, but from the amount of blood on the scene, her survival is doubtful."

Parleau said, "I wish to emphasize several interesting points about this preliminary report. One, of most pressing interest, is that there was a mix of agents. What was to be a routine exercise went to hell in a handbasket, and fast. We, in short, have been penetrated, but by whom and for what purpose? Item two: all witnesses in Ten say that there were six New Humans. I repeat. Six. How so six? We knew of three, plus one basket-case. But there were six, self-propelled. Item three: the call for TacTeam was requested under signal forty—operative in the field needs assistance, fugitives to be remanded for interrogation—but no description was given, and when Control tried to recontact, the line was dead. Four: six members of a TacTeam, and the best systems money and mind can make, were defeated and heinously slain by unarmed farmers, who disappeared. If you do not have questions out of all this, I certainly do."

Eykor responded, "We have the junior agent. It appears that he knew little of what was going on, being kept deliberately in the dark, by Errat and the other agent. I am ashamed to say that he was one of our own men, recruited under some peculiar circumstances. He was low, and had no access, and so could not verify or disprove what Errat told him. I have recommended retraining and reconditioning, and tentative reestablishment, pending good behavior, of course."

"How did Errat get on that detail? Why weren't your own men on it?"

"They say they were properly relieved by Errat."

"Who the hell is this Errat?"

Plattsman answered, "Both Errat and the other agent have vanished into thin air. All routes have been closed, but I think that will prove nothing. Errat identified himself as an operative out of Secretariat. This was formerly true, as we have uncovered. He was assigned to Section Q, Overseas Branch, but at present had been in retired status. I might add, that was Retired Status After Cause. He was last reported residing in Appalachian Region. That was from Section Q. Appalachian officially denied ever having known such a person. We believe that Errat was the one who called the request for TacTeam. He had all the correct codes and authenticators, and the call was made, so we have traced, from Building eight-nine-oh-five. He had never left it, at least until then."

Parleau asked, "Are you sure he isn't there yet?"

Eykor affirmed, "We have screened everybody, body-search. The building has been scoured. He isn't there."

Plattsman continued, "Control Staff, in conjunction with some friends we have at ConSec-Q, think that Errat had two purposes, not one. The first was to prevent at all cost the girl from returning; she would there be turned over to others in the plot with him for unknown uses. The second was more interesting: you see, there is a faction in A.R. that would like very much to gain control of the Institute for their own purposes. As you know, the Region is historically poor. Errat has been identified as a sympathizer with this group by an informant we have planted. The secondary purpose of this mission for him was apparently to embarrass us. He did so, but by then the rest had started to add to it, so it was completely out of control. We think he wanted us to recapture the New Human party. The resulting uproar would make us look bad. . . ."

Parleau asked, sitting down at last, "Could Errat have been working with them, the ler? They did have a supremacist organization way back in the old days. . . ." Parleau had been reading his history.

"We have not found any evidence whatsoever that Errat was working with *any* group of New Humans, present or past. His dossier lists him as being violently anti-ler. Our implant in A.R. confirms his association with like-minded groups in the Region, and elsewhere."

Parleau sighed deeply. "Well, whoever he was with, had his plan worked, the girl would have been taken and we'd be in the thick of it for sure. We were saved that, at least. But what we're in isn't a whole lot better. . . . And Errat's gone, you say?"

Eykor answered, "Not out of Seaboard South, unless he got out almost immediately, and there is low probability there. We sealed all crossings, everywhere. Nobody in or out without authenticated identification. There is no way he can get out, unless he walks through the reservation, which I doubt. It will take time, but we'll get him."

Plattsman commented, "You may not, so plan for the contingency. What we have been able to get out of Q suggests that he was formerly engaged in some pretty slippery wet-work for ConSec, working Incontinent and Africa-Sud for them. God only knows what he was doing for them; those people are tough and they play the game hard. I think that if he could survive that as a career, he could probably come and go here pretty much as he pleases."

Eykor exclaimed, "But he was a Controller!"

"Ostensibly, a Controller. In fact, he was the worst sort of spy, and I suspect an assassin. Don't flinch; we still have them, and have good use of them. The Federated Earth Government hasn't been able to eliminate local interests, and right now they're not likely to. As a fact, we encourage it as general policy; the war of spies prevents a war of men, of armies."

Parleau said, "Perhaps, but that's a dangerous game, that substitute. It could lead to worse than skirmishes and riots. And to think that someone turned a wild man like Errat loose among us. . . ."

Plattsman countered, "No, Chairman, they did not turn him loose. He was acting on his own, or with at best a small group. Certain other bodies found it convenient to look the other way. Apparently his friends in A.R. hoped that if the cards fell out right they could make their move. But as things go, they are stumbling more than we are—you'd think it happened there, to hear them deny any connection with Errat."

Parleau exclaimed, "Acted on his own! Nobody acts on his own!"

"Errat did, apparently," Plattsman said blandly.

"No, no, I refuse to believe that, in this day and age. Could he in turn have been manipulated . . . ?"

"Manipulate a manipulator? Now, there's an art form indeed!"

"I'm serious. Klyten, had this worked as planned, could this have benefited anyone in the reservation?"

"Chairman, there was a supremacist faction long ago, but it was largely discredited by the separationists and has not been very noticeable since. The separationists were the ones responsible for helping to consolidate the people and for setting up the reservation. It was heading for a showdown, but segregating the populations cooled things off, and the extremists were replaced by more flexible groups. But back at the height of it, the supremacist faction was in contact with some humans, the most extreme. Were there any left, I suppose that Errat could have made contact."

"Too many loose ends . . . this gets worse and worse, doesn't it? Well, now: what about the six ler? What happened to the girl? We know she had to be one of the six."

Klyten answered, "All we can say is that she recovered. How, in so short a time, is beyond me."

"Recovered! Is that possible?"

"As fast as it must have happened? I have no idea. It must be, but the method is unknown. Also the reason why they would risk an obviously secret method to recover her. I thought that she might have been faking, but no, it couldn't be. I *know* what an autoforgetter looks like, and she was one for sure. This condition has no analog in humans—it is not amnesia. It is in fact a form of bodiless death. The persona ends. Of course, it isn't perfect, but for practical purposes it works as advertised. Now, supposedly, such a person can be retrained, but the result is something similar to severe retardation . . . but what she knew and was protecting, she took with her. They did not retrieve her to interrogate her. Nor did they make her functional by an unknown methodology to do that, either."

"What could Errat have wanted with her?"

"Unknown. I personally think he wanted an incident."

"That's even worse."

"Yes, Chairman, that is so. Oh, and by the way, speaking of things worse, and no human analogs, my research people found out. What is wrong with the second girl. You know, the one Plattsman found in the photographs."

"Tell us that one, Klyten; there's no shortage of bad news here, so you may as well add your share."

Klyten ignored the remark, and continued, "They have a psychotic condition, which in the literature is called, for want of a better term, 'Serial Obsession.' "

Plattsman asked, "What is the effect of it?"

"Apparently it is occasioned by extreme mental stress, and involves a severe breakdown in the seat of consciousness. It renders the victim incapable of handling reality in a multiplex, simultaneous manner; they then address each simplex component serially, one at a time. Because the rest drift and go astray, they try to compensate by extreme attention to the problem, and then the next one as it comes up. Because they are behind, and know it, they have to be more attentive as they handle the next problem."

Parleau commented, "That certainly doesn't sound like a psychosis to me. It doesn't even sound like a problem."

"Well, Chairman, they say that every psychosis has an analog in a political theory. They also say that psychoses are remnants of earlier attempts at consciousness. According to what I have read, Serial Obsession is a normal condition for humans—it isn't a problem to us, true. But it is a severe one to them. The corrective oscillations become progressively deeper and more violent with time. Very gradually, but certainly. The end-product is continual manic violence applied to everything, rather like a standing temper tantrum."

He paused. "And two things apply here: the first is that it's like other ler psychoses in that the victim knows he's insane, and can compensate for it and seek a cure; the other is that the by-product of the compensation is a state of vigorous well-being that increases with time . . . the victim just can't understand why things keep getting worse despite his best attempts. They tend not to seek a cure, and have to be overpowered eventually. Thankfully, this extremely dangerous condition is very rare. We found only enough cases in the records to substantiate an analysis of the condition. But in regard to the second girl, I can imagine no more dangerous an adversary."

Parleau asked, "Why is that important, here?"

"Because, Chairman, this so-called plan of Errat's shows many of the hallmarks of the influence of such a person; the apparent indecision upon a concrete goal, the ambivalence, the confusion. We were confused because, in essence, Errat and his plan were confused. I agree with you in that something as audacious as this would be doubtful, energized by Errat alone. And if he were acting with a group, this aspect of it would have been suppressed by the combined minds of the group—that is how we humans handle the problem. We dampen it by the views of others—we discuss and argue and mutually agree, and then act. Yes, now that I think of it, I am sure of it," Klyten said.

Plattsman said, "Possible, possible. Fits Control Theory well enough. The planner influences the plan. Plain, straightforward. That's how we trace plans back to their source, no matter how obvious the first reading of the source is."

Parleau said, "So it is possible, then, that Errat was working for a ler? That's unreal! What could they gain from it?"

"Rationally, it would seem little. But we are conjecturing a possibly dangerous, shrewd psychotic, too."

Plattsman exclaimed, "The third man in the crowd-scans! Damn! Why didn't we think of it before? I didn't even think to try to match them with the file images of Errat. I'll bet they match."

Klyten said, "Probably will. But it doesn't help us anymore. We still don't know what he wanted, ultimately. Or his contact, if there was one."

Parleau said, "Wait, wait a minute. We are drifting farther and farther away from the central issue. In fact that seems to characterize this whole proceeding, from the time the girl was discovered in Isolation."

Eykor brightened. "A plot, Chairman?"

"No, inattention to the main issue. The committee system doesn't seem to save us from serial obsessions of our own, for which I thank Klyten for reminding me. We have been reacting to the wrong stimuli all along. We may be seeing too much, and becoming bemused with the process. We're looking at details, trying to run an investigation . . . and the real events are flowing along and jumping up and biting us on the asses, now almost daily. We are looking bad, may I remind you. We simply have to get on top of this thing, and quickly, too."

Parleau stopped, and looked up at the distant ceiling. He mused, "Now here we have a girl who most probably has something to hide." He shot a quick glare at Eykor, then at Plattsman. "And don't try now to figure what. And by contrast, we have a group of ler who ostensibly have nothing to hide, in fact, one is certified clean by our own Control. But the first, the girl goes passive and loses her mind, and the latter fight like a regiment of devils. Now what in hell are we dealing with? Answer me that."

Klyten said, "The girl knew escape was improbable. The group was close to the fence."

"Hmph. That tells the obvious. It doesn't explain the severity of the response."

Eykor said, "There was a man-loss in that."

Parleau responded, "I hardly need reminders of that, either. What I am after is *why* they were so aggressive."

Klyten said, "Defense, revenge, who knows. We can't even determine who made the first move."

Eykor interrupted, "They made the first move! They fled, they evaded, they . . ."

"They would possibly have done neither had not Errat set a goon-squad on them," commented Parleau. "So now let me summarize where we are. All this time we've been playing it close to find out, to see, to know. And with this we get behind. And so we now find ourselves being put in an increasingly defensive position in regard to Appalachian and ConSec. I can well imagine what will be next: Piedmont will start agitating for a piece of the action, on some shabby pretext—they always wait for someone else to stir up the muck, and then they try to scoop up whatever they can."

Eykor asked, "Then what are we to do, different than we've been doing?"

"I have the plan, suggested by this very meeting. First: Control and Security, get Errat, and I don't care how you do it. Alive. I want him interrogated, no restraints, and I want everything out of him. But especially what in the hell was he trying to do and for whom. Second, I want to go back to the original incident, the girl. The instruments. Make up some working models. Eykor and Security do both; the rest of you do what he asks. I'm beginning to think we were right in the beginning. That's what comes of second-thoughts. And now," he said, wagging his index finger pedantically, "I have to leave, for a conference call with ConSec. I hope what I have to say will satisfy them for the moment, buy time, until we can get a basic handle on this. I hope that we all have this reasonably straight. And if you have any further business, feel free to continue. I'm off to the Communications Center."

Parleau stood, as did the others in deference to him. He gathered some notes from his desk, and left the office without ceremony.

The others who were left were silent for a time, but that was only for the moment, and shortly the old free-for-all resumed. The clerk, who had sincerely been trying to keep up with the discussion, now gave up in consternation and elected to sit back and wait until his services were called for. They were not. After an hour, he discreetly left the table, and then the office, and returned to his shift assignment. They didn't even know he was gone.

The members of the Regional Board of Inquiry, occasional though the Board was, were creatures of ingrained habit and products of a unique environment. That this environment included in its capabilities the ability to monitor and observe distant events through electronic relay systems and Controllers was taken for granted by all of them. But the very ease with which they monitored distant events and made decision upon that which they saw, tended to build in them a habit of overconfident insularity, of projecting pseudorealities that possessed the disturbing habit of coming unglued, without existential reference and constant updating.

Thus, in their analysis of the event that occurred near Complex Ten, they were basically correctly oriented to the most pressing problem: Errat. But lacking data, they all too hastily were willing to accept the assumption that he was running. He was not. Or that he knew a lot about what the planner behind him was after. He did not. Errat was content to act, as if alone, on a set of internal directions. He was, in essence, inertially guided, rather than controlled, by Command or exterior reference.

Errat knew these things both from his long association with Controllers and his experiences as an agent for Continental Secretariat; especially that the key personnel of Seaboard South Region would make those assumptions, or something very close to them. He also knew that the successful undergrounder did not so much physically hide or run, as he relied upon flaws in the perceptual field of his opposition. He had not been in the field for some time, but the old skills did not die out, being founded upon universals about behavior, and he found them coming back easily. And his feedback told him that, at least to date, he had been completely correct.

Nor did Errat trouble himself overly with deep self-analysis. He was in the field primarily because he enjoyed his work in that environment. Perhaps it would have been more correct to venture that he was addicted to it, and had been away from it so long now that he had been playing a very minor game in his own right, just to keep the hand fresh, so to speak. Then this had come along and offered a fine opportunity to work on a project, and, as a fine, artistic flourish, betray them all, and vanish, letting both parties go down locked in a death-grip; he felt only contempt for both parties, the secretive contact who had intercepted him, and the Region authorities alike. He thought of an aphorism to cover the situation, as he often did: the conspirator(s) were secretive because they were weak and ineffective; the Region authorities were weak and ineffective because they were secretive.

Hando Errat was not under any illusion that he was secure, however much contempt he had for Seaboard South Region. Indeed, the greater part of his camouflage was based upon constant mobility, lack of fixture and base. This, admittedly, was somewhat a challenge in a society that placed a premium on lack of movement, but that only added spice to it. And wasn't particularly difficult. He had been prepared for it. That, indeed, had been one of his first lessons, one that had enabled him to survive—that a good agent is not necessarily the one who gets quick results and promotions, but the one who survives to come another day. He had reflected on that lesson often, since this contingency had begun. Perhaps they would be interested to learn just how easily one could move around, when one could anticipate. After all—after Al Qahira, Esh-Sham, El Kuds the Holy, Jidda, Aden—Seaboard South had been a piece of cake to penetrate.

Errat had affected the appearance of a maintenance man in this phase of his movements, and it had been a good disguise. He would hate to give it up. The fastidious avoided his grimy coveralls, and the local precinct Controllers and Security men never looked twice; maint-techs were considered the most conservative and habit-bound members of society, stable and fixed, beginning one day, ending it, always in standard time.

He was engaged in moving his location again, but still within Region Central. He had never left it; indeed, he had not properly even left the sight of an observer perched atop 8905 . . . had there been such an observer knowing what to look for. They would expect him to make for the northern border of the Region, toward his ostensible home. But there was only a cubicle in the public dormitory there, and he could give that away without a thought. No, he had remained in Region Central. Later, he would drift to the south. They expected him to run, and he was standing still. And why chase him at all? He had left deliberate traces of himself at the last, so they would; he had even used his own programmed name, rather than an alias.

Of course there was real danger; but for now he discounted the possibility that Seaboard South would call in operatives from ConSec, some of whom Errat had first trained himself. No, they wouldn't do that; they were too tied up in their own embarrassment to call them in, and by the time they came in on their own, he would be long gone. Let them look for him! But of all things, he was not worried about what Eykor might think of doing; the man had the imagination of an earwig, and in that hadn't changed since Errat had first seen him as a Security man, way back when, in Alexandria, posted there from somewhere in Europe. His handling of that mutant girl had been typical: doing a halfway job, depending on machines, and then half-covering it up, protecting department hands. Contemptible all across the board! He knew that if he had got hold of her, she would have spoken, indeed would have begged to sing. And when they had got what they wanted out of her, it would have been worth sweeping it under the rug and to hell with the protected people, the Muties and their fine little country farm. What did they have to enforce it with? A pack was only as good as the arms that backed it . . .

Errat walked through the rainy streets of the night, all in all, not too apprehensive. Alert, but by no means paranoid. Nobody seemed to be following him that he could detect, although a couple of incidents had cast some suspicions that way and sharpened his senses. Nothing he could put his finger on, though, and there were none of the follow-on betrayals of presence. He had highly sophisticated means to spot trackers. No, he had written it off as a symptom of his being out of practice. He felt completely in control of the situation, and being out in the open, on the street, actually gave him a feeling of exhilaration.

In the quarter in which he was now walking, there were fewer lights and less traffic. He could see very well, however, by the sky-glow, the city light reflected from the low clouds. December, Twelvemonth. In this part of Central, the buildings were still the pastel-stained blocks of the newer parts of the city, but this was not a part of the city devoted to plazas and terminals. Rather more like the warehouse quarter, local supply depots and the like, mixed with shabby rooming houses, trans-dorms, workers' godowns. He listened to the sounds of the city at night: distant machinery sounds, relaxed and unhurried, muted. Water gurgling in drains, splashing from vehicles. The humming of a hovercraft. There would be few out on a wet night like this. He listened carefully, for this was his environment, as some ancient predator might have listened to the sounds of the jungle. The predators were gone, but their example remained for the last predator, Man. The world was City, denser or less dense. The pattern of sounds now completely reassured him; things were normal, and exactly as they should be.

Errat reached his destination, a down-at-the-heels roomer, used mostly by assistance-recips, itennies, retired laborers, and taxmen, all of whom had never made it to secure a family license. He looked it over carefully with his practiced eye, verifying what he had thought of the place earlier. A safe place for a couple of days, from which to put out his sensitive antennae into the grapevines of the neighborhood, time to watch the vidcasts and read between the lines. Then, thus reoriented, to move from once more.

There was a doorman, as he expected, but this one did not seem either alert or zealous in his duties. In fact, he seemed half asleep; perhaps more than half.

Errat approached the doorway, feigning a slight confusion, a hesitation, all the time watching the doorman for signs of betrayal. There were none. The man was becoming aware of him, but there was no alarm in his manner, just a slight annoyance, countered by a desire to interact with someone while at his post. And a sense of superiority, out of the position of doorman, while the stranger in the street, in the rain, had nothing, no place, no peers. He could afford to be haughty, but not so much that the stranger would become angry. A delicate balance of pecking orders. The doorman thought he knew his game well. Errat was a player of the same game who was leagues ahead of him.

Errat greeted him, "Evening."

"Yourself," answered the doorman. "Need in, or just visiting?"

"Like in if I can." Errat set down his duffel, which looked as if it contained tools, but which in reality contained clothing and makeup.

"Bag?"

"Corrosion-controlman, me. Hell of a job."

"Looks like. Where ya been? In the sewers?"

" 'Bout. Workin' the cableways. You'd think they'd make 'em so's a body cud stand, but no, ya haf'ta crawl." As Errat registered the doorman's speech patterns, he swiftly and subtly aligned his own speech patterns to fit them. Nothing worked so well as a properly reproduced local accent.

" 'Ja see any?"

"See any what?"

"C'rosyun."

"Shee-yit."

"Looks like. Well, what's yur name and number?"

"Tanner, twenty-four-A— Wait a min't, I'll dig those papers out, they're aright here. . . ." Errat fumbled for something in the deep pockets of the coverall, a prolonged process.

The doorman, convinced of his sincerity, watched him fumble for a time, and then said, "Man, there's no need, there. Bugger it! Hold on, the nightmon's out, but I'll get you something. We got empties."

"No, no. I'll need 'um for the ledge."

"Na, na, bugger the ledge, the ledgerkeep, and the 'orse 'e sat 'is arse on. We'll get to it, by and by. How long ya be?"

"Semipermer, me. Working this sector."

"Well, then, all right! No prob, come on." And he lurched off his stool, opening the outer gate for Errat to enter. Now together, they walked down a drafty, damp, poorly lit hallway, arriving at a board beside a small window in the wall. The window was closed. From the board, the night watchman now removed a key, fumbling and deciding, handing it to Errat. There was a tag attached to the key, with a piece of dirty and frayed string.

"Here y'are, two-oh-one. Up the stairs and to the right; ya can't miss it. It's the only one to the right, har, har. Say, want a sip a' caffers?"

"I'd like, but I gotta bag. I mean, the sheets are really barkin'. Been a long un. How 'bout tomorra?"

"Ya off?"

"Can take it."

"Well, all right! Say then, see ya then, um?"

"Will do, there. What was your name?"

"Bork, me. Paulie Bork."

"See ya then, Paulie."

Errat turned to the stairwell and started up, feigning tiredness and an older, hard-worked body. He reflected as he did so that he didn't have to fake too much; he actually was tired. Letdown. He was past the last event of the day. This place was going to be perfect, perfect. Shabby and forgotten, except in the mind of some renewal planner, who would replace it with something no less trashy. How else keep the proles busy? But it was no matter tha'. He found himself slipping unconsciously into the gutter idiom as he climbed the narrow stairs, unable to resist the temptation to fall completely into the character of it. No doubt about it, he was tired, but it was also good to be out in the field once again, out on the killing floor, on the line.

Errat found the room, unlocked the door, and entered, relocking it as he closed it. He let his bag settle to the floor, quietly. In the dimness he could make out a bed, a wash-stand. The bed was small, probably too soft and too lumpy. Where was the chair and desk? There was usually one. Yes, there it was; by the window he saw an outline of a chair, his eyes adjusting. He smelled deeply, sifting the odors of the room, waiting for the expected odor of transient old rooms, of musty sheets and smoke-abused curtains. Yes, just like he expected. And Errat's skin crawled.

There was something else in the odors of the room. He reached for the light switch on the wall behind him by the door, felt for it, fumbled, fighting panic generated by something he could smell but not see, found it, flipped it. Nothing happened. He tried to recover quickly, get control of the situation. He admitted to a moment of fear. He cursed the slowness of night-vision, trying to see into the furry shadows, backlighted by the window. Yes, the desk. On the desk. It was between two windows, and the backlighting had obscured it. Something bulky and body-sized on the desk. He inhaled deeply and slowly, trying to catch the elusive scent, muttering under his breath about faulty lights, emitting minor obscenities, reaching for his throw-knife at the same time. A heavy plastic, it could not be detected by the finest weapon-detector, and could even be bent, slowly, to fit. He also had a gun, made of similar material, but he knew he'd never reach it. But he knew one thing; he had time. If it was here to kill and ask no questions, they would have already tried.

He felt the reassuring warm solidity of the throw-knife. What was that scent? Wet clothing. Somebody had been out in the light rain, with him, for the rain had only started less than an hour ago. Ergo, following him. Hmph. Damn skillful job, that. ConSec, already? No, darkened rooms weren't their game. And under the wet clothing, a warm body, also damp, a little sweaty, a little nervous. Still. There was another scent, an adrenaline odor, and something else, something tense that made him tense in turn. And there was more, too, female, perhaps, and something more.

Errat took a chance. "Zandro? Zandro Milar?" That had been the name of his elusive contact through this whole thing, the contact who had sought him out, found him. The one who made payments, advised, called, always by maddeningly indirect methods. All Errat had managed to discover about this contact was that the owner of the name was probably female, and younger than himself. He had further suspicions, but they made no immediate sense, and he needed additional data. He breathed again, trying to get a bearing on the source of the odor-presence. No luck. Whoever had come in had been in long enough to muddy the air. He watched the bulk on the desk intently, watching for movement. He could not tell. His eyes were still adjusting.

A voice emanated from the desk, much like the one he had heard before. Female, throaty, almost hoarse, but with the betrayals of youth in it, too. "Indeed. Speak quietly, there may be monitors." Yes, the same. And what an odd accent. Errat plumbed his encyclopedic memory, trying to place the accent. He couldn't. It didn't register at all. It continued, "Yes, you were correct. I am Milar. And you certainly have stirred up the anthill."

Errat listened carefully, finding direction. Smell wasn't good enough to find, in a situation like this, or in wind. But sound was, almost as good as seeing. He moved his head slightly from side to side as the figure spoke, getting the range. Yes, he had it. He could do it. Just like the time in Zinder, when he had got his man in total darkness. The fool! He had stopped to gloat, and had paid. This one was the same. They all were. The source of the voice seemed a little off, little low, as if the owner were half reclining. Odd pose for a threat. She probably had a needler on him. No problem, there! Needlers were invariably low-velocity. He could do it, and move, playing the slowness of her reactions and the slowness of the weapon against her. Yes, there. He thought he saw the suggestion of movement, a slight shift. Or had it been?

He said, buying time, "You said that I was to kill the girl and those who came for her, or salt them away, and keep them confused. I did not get the girl, it is true, but much confusion resulted. Seaboard South," he hazarded, "is now discredited."

"You hired reptiles to do primate work." Errat heard, and thought that an odd turn of phrase.

"Couldn't get anyone else." He was stalling now. He edged imperceptibly closer to the figure on the desk. God, but she was careless, talking while he closed in. Send babes to do grown-up's work was just not the word. But he could hear the threat in the voice, accent or not. Yes, this one would be easy.

The voice said, "We are dissatisfied, unfulfilled in our most fervent hopings."

Errat listened, still weight-shifting, creeping immeasurably forward, slowly, closer, closer. Shooting in the dark like this, you had to get as close as possible, reduce the CEP* of a quick-thrown knife. Yes, it was Milar. The odd speech patterns, the accent, the Modanglic of an edu-

* Circular Error Probable.

cated foreigner, one who didn't speak Modanglic as a native. Where could that be? There were few places left where it wasn't spoken, and he thought he knew all those accents. Errat felt some regrets. He would hate to kill this Milar before he found out who she was and who she represented. All the same . . .

He said, "They may have set hopes too high for realization. And the direction I received was not a model of clarity."

"Those are insignificant. Our affair here is with the failure of the prime operative."

Errat now had his knife straightened, in pre-throw position, his muscles relaxed, but set and ready to obey for the one swift stroke. He said, taunting, "Not the operative, but the purveyor of instructions!" On the last word he threw the knife at the target he had picked. It would be the throat. He could not risk the blade being turned by the ribs. The throat. Disable now, and polish off in a moment, after some tactical repair and a quick interrogation. He was expert at that. But even as he released the knife he had the smallest hesitation, as if something weren't right. The feeling had been nagging him all afternoon. Even as it left his hand, he knew there was something wrong, all wrong, and he had made the wrong move. What was it? The knife struck, that he heard, but the sound was not that of a knife penetrating flesh. Instantly, as the fact registered in his mind, he felt a sudden sharp pressure at his back, up and to the left side between the ribs, like a rough shove in a crowd, in a queue, followed by heat and pressure at his heart. Incredible heat! He tried to move, to take a breath. He couldn't. His feet seemed nailed to the floor, his chest bound with iron. The universe contracted to a node of pain, his chest, his back. *So this is what it feels like to be knifed*, the rational part of his mind thought, coolly and idly.

He did manage to start a turn before he completely lost control of his legs. Yes, his assassin had been behind him all the while, waiting by the door, absolutely quiet. He must have almost touched her. How had she projected her voice, been so quiet? These things disturbed Errat greatly, and he thought upon them, as he collapsed to the floor, his consciousness fading. And the last thing he saw was the figure of a woman bending over him, her heavy clothing rustling loudly. And then there was nothing.

The person who had claimed to be the bearer of the programmed name Zandro Milar slipped quietly out of the shadows, the deeper shadows by the door, moving stiffly, awkwardly, to stifle the rustling of clothing. The figure bent over Errat, as if listening, or casting for a scent, a gesture curiously animal-like. It did not touch the body. Apparently satisfied, it straightened and stepped over the body to the desk. There, it removed an object from the bundle on the desk, inserted it in a small carrybag it was carrying. Then it stopped, pausing, not so much looking, as it did not move its head, but reminding itself, reviewing circumstances. It recalled something, and went back to one of the windows, carefully opening it a crack. There was a slight draft, and then the night air started seeping into the room. Then it stepped over the body, reaching the door, where again it paused, an interminable moment, listening. There was no presence in the hall outside. It opened the door a crack. There was a stronger draft. Setting the lock, Zandro Milar stepped outside and closed the door, listening for the click of the lock.

In the hallway, had anyone been there to see, the harsh light would have revealed a slender, smallish woman, dark of complexion, a swarthy olive that suggested a Mediterranean type, sharp-featured, perhaps an Iberian, or an Arab, who might have been attractive had it not been for a predatory cast to her facial structure. She wore the awkward clothing of the day with singular gracelessness.

Milar walked quietly down the hallway to a room at the far end, entered, carefully closing the door behind her. Inside, she seemed to slump, relaxing, and sat on the bed, removing her shoes, which seemed to bother her more than all the rest of the clothing. She leaned back and wriggled her toes, relaxing at last. After a moment, she got up again, and removed all the clothing she had been wearing, and adding the carrybag, placed all of it in a small suitcase. She finished, straightened, and walked across the room to a closet. Passing before the single mirror in the room, she glanced at the reflection, seeing it only very dimly, even in the city light coming in the windows from outside. She smiled. Out of her clothes, her motions were no longer lumpish and crude, but fluid and graceful. She flexed her hands, stretched until joints cracked. She checked the closet, verifying that another set of clothing was there, a man's coverall. Satisfied, she returned to the lumpy bed, lay on it, naked, pulling the covers around her, and fell instantly asleep.

After a time, her breathing became deep and regular, and then she revealed, unknown to her, her only flaw as an operative. She began to mutter, almost inaudibly, in her sleep. Even then, some part of her remembered who and where she was, so that the muttering was very quiet, indeed. It was doubtful if it could have been heard outside the room. Even inside the room, one would have to listen closely to hear it at all. And it would have been valueless to hear it, for the muttering was not in Modanglic. More specifically and strictly, it really wasn't in a language, at least not in the sense of anyone who might have been there to hear it.

When the light from the window had brightened to a certain degree, Milar awoke, as if on some internal timer. She dressed, first donning a tight undergarment that smoothed and obscured the shape of her body, which although undeniably female, was also subtle of curve, wiry, and muscular. Then, over that, the coverall of a hard-laborer. Her hair was short, a deep dull black, gunmetal blue in the highlights. This she tucked into a tattered flat cap affected by most heavy workmen. She checked a cheap pocket chronometer, nodded to herself. Then, carefully inspecting the room one last time, picked up the suitcase, left the room, and headed down the hallway.

Last night's rain had blown off toward the east, toward the Green Sea; now it was whiter-bright outside, and the light was full of blue overtones, which she saw and appreciated. In the building, she could hear others getting up and being about, getting ready for the events of the day. More significantly, which brought her back to reality, the doorman would have been relieved now by a Daysider, or perhaps no relief at all. She looked, as she entered the lower hall. Correct. No one was there. She walked calmly out of the building, fighting an intense urge to run. She fought with herself, knowing she had to get control of herself. It began to pass. The adrenaline she might release could trip stress-monitors all up and down the street. She forced herself to be calm, repeating certain formulas to herself. She paused by the corner, looked back. Good. Nothing. Now she relaxed in truth, feeling it flood into her.

Not for nothing had she followed Errat carefully, at great risk to herself from him and from others. She had studied him before she had picked him to do the task for her, and now that it had been bungled, she had used that information to predict his movements. It had been interesting, but also too easy. Not half as hard as the one she had him set up. That one had escaped for almost a year before she finally nailed her down. And of course Errat had to be eliminated, for in him was a trace to her. Unlike Errat, she did not enjoy wetwork, as she had heard him call it. But there had been no cure for it; she had to do it herself. And by the time they discovered Errat, she would be long safe. Yes, and maybe more. . . . Perhaps then she would have the hammer in her hand, the power, and then there would be a reordering, a replacing, indeed. But back to affairs. There was one more tiresome loop to close, a painful one, but one that had to be.

She placed the suitcase in a public locker, designed to foil the most determined thief, paying the fee into the credit-box, extracting the identification slip, with its magnetic numbers. This she took to the tube-train terminal and threw in a collecting trashpile, wadded up and unrecognizable. After that, she purchased a ticket for the Institute Halt, and settled in the waiting room, smiling an odd little half-smile to herself. She had taken some extra days, it was true, to do this job herself, but it had been good work. Now, if she could only catch the other in time, she would have all the loose ends tied off for good.

BOOK THREE

Navis et Arx

SIXTEEN

When one extracts all the irrational elements from love, that which is left is a thing unendurable, unreasonable, and it is most irrational that one should care to pursue it.

—*Ibid*

WITH ASSITANCE AND advice from Kaldherman, the aid of a rascally, squint-eyed elder known as Jaskovbey the Smuggler, who lived on the banks of the River Yadh, and an attitude of bored disinterest on the part of officials of Piedmont Region, across the river to the west, Morlenden—using nothing more elaborate than Manthevdam, an assumed name—openly boarded a tube in Piedmont Central, and with one change in Oconee Region, and another on the West Coast, reached a point close by the reputed location of the house of Mevlannen Srith Perklaren. In three days.

Morlenden had his directions to get there, gained from Klervondaf as they walked home from the northeast: west from the old settlement of Santa Barbara, continuing on the local transport, now aboveground to Jalama, where the route turned north, and follow the coast. It was not entirely without hazard; he was walking in the back door of the main continental spaceflight center, but it was not, by and large, guarded, reflecting the widespread belief that the main concern of Man lay not in ways to depart the Earth, but in ensuring more ways to survive upon it. In fact, the space program had rather languished for the past two centuries, and aside from timid, careful forays around the inner Solar System, and rarer probes into the outer portions, there was little activity. Even the telescope project, which to Morlenden's ears had sounded amazing, was half asleep. Work progressed at a measured pace. A slow one. And there were no enemies to guard against. . . .

Morlenden left the transport early in the morning, and aside from a glance around to get his bearings, did not look back. He spent the morning negotiating country given over to pasturage, some desultory farming; but soon the land became too isolated, too precipitous for even that, and even that shred of civilization fell behind him. Now he walked along above the empty cliffs, above a most strange sea in the waning light of afternoon, plodding on toward a holding hidden away in one of the last pockets of wilderness on the coasts of old North America.

Morlenden was not well-traveled, and had never seen salt water before (Fellirian had seen the Green Sea once, before their weaving. He had asked, "What did it look like?" And she had answered, "Just like a big lake; you can't see the other side. Oh, yes, it smelled funny, and there were waves.") and now he was walking along the edge of the largest ocean in the season of storms. He found it fascinating, full of novelty and endless mystery, but also alien and disturbing; this was the Pacific, and the season was winter. A cold wind blew off the sea, and though he could remember seeing palm trees farther back, it was a cold wind that chilled him to the bone. The sky seemed clear, but there was a milky film in it, an unsettled unsteadiness, as if, at any moment, a storm might blow up, or fog, or rain. He had heard as much about the region. And along the way he had walked, he had seen the ruined remains of buildings and posts, eroded and abraded by the constant salt-laden wind.

Mevlannen reportedly spent her days on Earth, when she was not working, in a cabin perched atop one of the local mountains. Pico Tranquillon it was named in the older human language of the area. Morlenden thought, looking about himself as he walked, that the name was most curious: a tranquil peak above a quiet sea. That was what the name meant. But the sea was not quiet; the surf grumbled away, sometimes roared, sometimes growled, and constantly ground away at shells and rocklings in the shallows. It heaved and crawled, that quiet sea, like some live thing. Morlenden avoided looking into the shimmering, pearl-horizoned distances overly long; he sensed some weakness in himself for this empty place.

And the tranquil peak? The wind whipped at his cloak, and now it was rising, fretting and fraying the wild grasses, hissing at the windblown trees, dark cypresses. The sky watched, unstable, ready now to permutate and change on the instant. In the place of the peak of tranquility, there was nothing tranquil at all, unless it was the wavelike repose of the land and its life, its sense of steady enduring, in the midst of flux.

He walked on in the fading afternoon, becoming uncomfortable in the bite of the relentless wind off the cold ocean. He had seen colder weather, even slept out of doors in some of it, back in the reservation.

He had seen snow, often, and he knew it was rare here, yet it was still uncomfortable. There was a feeling of unwelcome to it. The wind, the unimaginable sea full of mysteries, the merciless alien surf and its constant grumblings, the iodine reek of the sea close to hand, unescapable. And he was uncomfortable with his role as well—the bearer of bad tidings. And no doubt she would be expecting a younger Tlanhman; she would get a parent phase half-elder long past the change, who moreover was beginning to feel fatigued, snared in cobwebs, enmeshed in a labyrinth of plot within plot. It could be unpleasant. And he could not imagine how the girl lived out here alone.

The path—once upon a time, long ago, a road—had led him inward from the beach cliffs and across some deserted flats where yellow wild grain glistened and rippled in the afternoon light. There were remnants of buildings, sheds; this had been a prosperous farm once. Long ago. They were all gone now. Out on the point, on a headland, west and to his left, he could make out the shapes of another ruin, some building long since fallen in upon itself. There were pilings in the water. Hawks patrolled the air, rattlesnakes guarded the ground. There was something lonely and beautiful beyond bearing directly here; he could see clearly, although he could not frame it in words. Descriptions wouldn't do; what it needed was a legendman to set a terrible drama in these lands, for only in lines of action could the true shape of the place be drawn. Now there was a pervasive melancholy in the air, something in the light. One was impelled to heroic deeds, but also to much brooding. Yes, perhaps the light, an odd, porcelain light, half filtered by the sea air. Or the wind, which was definitely rising, now roaring on its own account from time to time. Morlenden pulled his cloak tighter, raised and fastened the hood, and followed the path upward, stopping occasionally to catch his breath.

He had worked a good part of the way up to the peak when the light began failing, a thickening in the air. The shadows deepened, spread, grew. Clouds began to appear overhead, subtle, close to the earth, vague in exact shape, salmon and rose-colored, tints of an impossible fleeting yellow. He felt more uneasy, although in his life he had walked many a lonely mile; and from somewhere far below him now, he heard, from far away, carried by the wind, a strange howling. Like a dog, but unlike, too, full of idiotic laughter. He shivered, and not from the wind; he had walked there not long before. An eerie place for the girl, full of ghosts and spirits.

He almost walked into the place before he realized that he had attained it. Morlenden had been following switchbacks, one after another, walking up the unending mountain trail, and suddenly there were no more, and he was in a shallow saddle between the peak itself and a lower western shoulder. He could see into the north, across a tumbled, shadowy land of valley and uplands beyond, now filling like a bowl with darkness. The clouds were closer overhead, moving swiftly, rippling and leaping with eagerness.

And before him, sheltered under the shoulder of Pico Tranquillon, was a tiny stone cabin, the yellow light inside it spilling out into the darkening evening and the night. A thin streamer of smoke was being torn from the stone chimney. An odd little place, not at all like anyplace a ler would live in, but for the moment, he thought it was the cheeriest thing he had ever seen. And above, on the peak itself, were more ruins: shells of concrete, the twisted frameworks of some metal apparatus tangled above them. The wind hissed in the metal, hating it, wearing it down only slightly slower than it wore at the rocks. Morlenden hurried to the door, knocked.

He hadn't expected Mevlannen, the insibling of Maellenkleth, to resemble the latter. After all, it had been the *Nerh*, Klervondaf, who had shared an insibling parent with Maellen. This one would be a stranger; they had different parents in the flesh. The person he saw in the opened doorway was a ler girl of the appropriate age, about twenty, but she looked older. She was dark-haired, as much as he could see of her, but pale-skinned and rather light-eyed. She had a sharp, foxy quality of face that contrasted sharply with the rounded softness of Maellen. But none of the predatory in it, as Sanjirmil, either. The sharpness here was one of fineness and delicacy, not of muscles held tensed in opposition.

Her hair was straight, dark brown, very fine in texture, worn longer than was seemly for a girl her age. . . . Then he recalled where she had been the last five years or so. Her skin was a pale snow-creamy color, lightly spotted with tiny freckles. The nose was straight and narrow, this reminding him most of Taskellan. The winter overshirt she wore concealed most of her body, but from the long, slender neck and the fine, delicate collarbone, he could see that she was thinner than the average, who tended toward a slightly more strong frame.

Behind the girl was a fireplace, and in it a fire was built and brightly burning; not a traditional hearth, but a heavy stonework fireplace, presumably of human style, although Morlenden had never seen one. The fireplace, and a couple of oil lamps, seemed to be the only light. The girl, backlit by the warm glow, looked at him with unconcealed curiosity.

She began, tentatively, as if describing a phenomenon, rather than speaking directly. "I was told by the public message service that a visitor was coming . . . and one stands in my door, in the evening, after the fashion of a traveler, almost as one who would go on the Salt Pilgrimage. Yet there is not salt here."

He answered, "I am Morlenden Deren, and I am your visitor. The name I have used to travel under, and the clothing, only suggest a poor enough disguise."

"I am Mevlannen Srith Perklaren." The voice was, for all its indirection, even and plain, cool and reserved. It was the voice of one who had learned privacy, and who did not offer invitations casually. "Am I the one you seek?"

"You are. May I come into your house? There is much we must say."

She stepped back from the doorway, making a motion with her right hand for him to enter. The motion was in the same underlanguage as had been her words, reserve, skepticism. Yet also within was hunger and loneliness as well. Morlenden saw, and deeply regretted the news that he was to bring. More yet he regretted that he had been born too soon: he deeply appreciated what the graceful, reserved motions offered. What was being displayed here. All for nothing. He stepped inside the door, over the threshold, hearing the door latch behind him.

She held out her hands to him to take his cloak, and he slipped out of it and handed it to her. He proceeded forward bluntly. "The reason I have come is twofold: one, to bring you bad tidings; and the other, to be told something by you, if you will believe that I am indeed the one to carry it."

She hung the cloak on a peg in the wall by the fireplace. "I had thought when the word came it might be something bad," she said quietly, turning back to him. "You know that no one ever comes here. Ever. At first, I would journey home, but as things went forward, lately . . ."

"I understand some of it. I have been to the *yos* of the Perklarens. And I see that you are now a stranger in your own *yos*."

"True. But are we not all thus, one time or another? But never mind that. I have a nice supper. Will you eat here with me, sleep with me tonight?"

"I had hoped to. I have never come so far before."

She turned from her place by the fire. "This is one of the few places where the world as it was of old has been kept. It used to be said, of the lands along this coast, and another place farther north, that here creation still continued. Mael was here . . . and loved it. My fellow workers think it peculiar that I should live alone on top of Pico Tranquillon, but it suits me. They are terrified by the loneliness, but those are my needs. Solitude. I am not bothered here; when I am down, I am free to sit by the window, watch the sea and the sky, and dream. . . . You know that I am an engineer, but were I that and nothing more, I would be a poor one, I think."

Morlenden looked about the tiny cabin. He nodded approvingly. "Yes, I understand. It is a cozy home here. I did not know that it could be thus, here, outside."

"I tried to get a *yos* cast here, but the Revens would not hear of it. . . . So I built this place myself. It is a copy of a human cabin; I learned from places I have seen along this coast. Odd, that, for in the older times, this country, here, was the place where all the newest things were tried. . . . And now it is the only place on the continent where even a trace of the old ways remain."

Morlenden agreed, noting her hands as he did. Built it herself? With those delicate, needleworker hands, pale and slim fingers? There was more to her than met the eye. But he knew that would be the case. Too much ocean, too much deep space, too much an alien society, the society of humans. Mevlannen had undergone a sea-change.

She said, "So. We will have all night to talk about things. And I read from your face, Morlenden Deren, that I will be unhappy by that which I will hear. So let us eat. Come, sit." She faced him with an arch, coy expression, yet with something wistful in it as well. And as if she sensed his appraisal of her, she said, "I know well enough we could not be even casual lovers, even for a night; but you can, if you will, lend me for a time some small part of that which I have given up. Lost, now. I need talk, the warmth of my own . . . too much have I seen of silence and conspiracy." She finished and moved around the table with a curious floating grace, a slow, flowing, dancelike motion that caused her overskirt to flow, and eddy about her slender body.

Morlenden sat at a rude table that incorporated benches into its form. It looked hand-planed, rough-finished. She had said that she had made this cabin herself. The table too, obviously. She was a capable one, this Mevlannen, for all her delicacy and slenderness of figure. . . .

After supper, which they partook in silence, they sat by the fire on cushions, cross-legged like tailors, and drank steaming cups of coffee, to Morlenden's taste a harsh, bitter drink. Mevlannen had also laced it heavily with brandy. The girl seemed used to it, and as he drank, Morlenden found that it did banish the fatigue and apprehensions he felt.

Mevlannen looked blankly into the fire. She said, suddenly, "Bring me your bad tidings, now."

He began hesitantly, "It is Maellenkleth . . . she had an accident." He stopped. This would lead nowhere. He could circle it all night and never tell her. She needed to know. Bluntness would be best. The cuts of it were deep, but they would heal faster.

"Some months back, Maellenkleth was captured outside by humans. After that, something they did apparently frightened her, and she auto-forgot."

Mevlannen continued looking into the fire, giving no sign. She nodded, once, curtly, to acknowledge that she had heard him.

He continued, "We, the Derens, were commissioned by the Perwathwiy Srith to locate her, determine what had happened to her. But they would tell us nothing, none of them. . . . We went to Krisshantem, a *hifzer*, who was her last lover, and with him, we retrieved her from the place where they had kept her. And with Krisshantem leading, performed a restoration. On the way back to the reservation, some agents tried to prevent us from reaching our destination. In escaping them, they pressed the hunt, and on the fence she was shot by a wire-guide. She died soon after that, after we made revenge upon those who would use a proscribed weapon."

Mevlannen nodded again. "Who performed the rites? She was of the Water elemental."

"We knew, and we did it. The Derens. Taskellan witnessed for the Perklarens, or rather for so much as is left of them."

"What has happened to Kler and Tas? Tell me."

"Klervondaf is living with the Braid of Plindestier. We have taken in Taskellan. He was too young; he needed a Braid, a home. Why were your parents not at home? Why did they not come? Your Braid is full of mysteries, but that one is most far from me."

"Didn't they tell you anything? The Perwathwiy? Sanjirmil?"

"They would say nothing. I wormed out some information about Mael from them, as I went, but it was not much, and concerned only her. I have talked with Sanjirmil, but she was more opaque in her words than the others were in their silences."

"I see. Yes, I can imagine that—that they would not have told you. They couldn't. Yes, it is true . . . the parents Perklaren were not at home as they should have been, and they could not do right for Mael. I know why; I understand. They would do it that way . . . there was no choice."

"So you know."

"Yes. All too much. That is why I do not travel. I am, I suppose, in it even thicker than was poor Mael. She was our valiant soldier, she was, all the while we stayed in the back, working, working. . . ."

"I was told, in her last words, by Maellenkleth, to get from you a matrix, to return and transmit it to Sanjirmil. Do you also know the significance of this?"

She started, an abrupt movement, alarm on her face. "The matrix? Now? Are you sure of this thing?"

"Certain as I am of little else. She was dying, and a part of the old persona emerged, just enough to get that out. Will you give it to me, and will you tell me what is so important that a girl should die twice before her time to protect it?"

"Yes . . . I will tell you. Everything. They should have, themselves, from the beginning. You could stumble, and undo the work of generations. You should have known. They should have done it all, initiated you. . . ."

"Krisshantem taught me the Outer Game."

"Not good enough by far, but it will help you understand."

"Then why not more?"

"They probably feared that outside you would trip stressies."

"Stressies?"

"Chemical stress-monitors. They detect anxiety chemically. In your scent, your breath. They are everywhere, but of course more so in the East. They work on us, too. In fact, we usually give stronger readings through them. That is why they would not tell you. You must take oath to autoforget to protect it."

"I would not reveal a secret, no more than Maellen."

"Just so, just so. I do not doubt you. But we simply could not risk sending many into oblivion. And if a centipede loses enough legs, even it will stop walking. And of course, things can be traced."

The girl arose now, refilled the cups, and returned to the place before the fire. She did not evidence any emotion Morlenden could identify, but her eyes were moist, reflecting brightly the light of the fire. She blinked rapidly. A log in the fire collapsed, sending a whirl of sparks up the chimney. Outside, the wind took up a constant moan, and Morlenden could hear rain pelting on the windowpane.

Mevlannen looked up. "I will tell you what I know. Then the matrix. You will understand it then. I will not have you stumbling in the dark anymore. You are far too dangerous that way. But you must oathmake to me, on your name, that you will autoforget to protect it."

Morlenden hesitated, drawn by the mystery, but also repelled by the idea of autoforgetting. He said, "Then so be it. On my name, which no one else has ever carried."

She looked deeply at him, into him, with eyes as bright and piercing as needles of fire. They were a soft, pale-blue color, almost gray, but in the firelight and the intensity of the moment, he did not see the color, so much as he felt that he was being weighed and measured as he had never been before. Apparently she saw what she wished to see. She took a deep breath.

"Very well . . . now I don't know how to tell this to you properly, for I am not a tale-teller. I know not where to start it; I have lived with it, as did Mael, all my life. And for some of the recent parts, since I came out here, there will be guessing. They will be accurate enough. You see, Mael was to come here in person, when the time was ripe, for the matrix. No other way; her, alone, when the time came. And so by what you have said, and its truth, I know it is time, but faster than was expected. After this, you may tell me why this is so."

Morlenden settled back. "I will do what I can. And now, I am ready."

SEVENTEEN

Every word that we utter must decrease the ignorance and increase the mystery.

—*Ibid*

The real beginnings of a journey occur long before the act of physical departure.

—*Enosis ton Barbaron*

MEVLANNON BEGAN, "AND now will I give you blunt stroke for blunt stroke, Morlenden Deren. It is thus: we who are the pampered and protected curios, we who live lives characterized by the forerunners as all too agricultural and oversexed, we who supposedly fear technology . . . *we* possess a true ship of the deep spaces, ship and ark, ark and weapon, which was to have carried all of us to a new world beyond the stars, our own place, our world."

Morlenden listened to her, heard her words clearly, with no misunderstanding of them, but all the same he wondered if the news of the death of Maellenkleth had not undermined her sanity; that perhaps she was now reliving a vague legend that had circulated about the reservation for several hundreds of years. She had taken the news calmly, too calmly, and now her words were those of romantic bravado. . . . Or was it true? He asked, not concealing his disbelief, "You mean a machine, like the humans build and use to take you to the telescope? And this would take . . . *all of us* to some other world? Aside from being preposterous, where is such a large and weighty device located, that no one has seen it all these years?"

"I will answer your objections, one by one. Our starship is like the forerunner craft only in that it moves in the same medium, it moves living creatures across the void. But end-functions do not determine things, only the manner of their use. The means, not the ends. And the means determine the shape of the tool. But yes, originally, it was for all of us, and yes, it will go to the stars, as far as we have to. And above all, yes, it is hidden now, but soon it will be revealed. And it was to protect that secret that Maellen paid the price, her price, her value. And why you have been told nothing up to now, why you never suspected. It has been a secret since before there was a reservation, indeed it is the *sole reason* that there is such a thing as the reservation, quiet and isolated from the struggles of this world. And there has never been a leak, not when this was just a dream, a theory, nor when it was building, nor when it is almost ready."

"Not completely leak-free. There are legends, common knowledge among the children, though we all called them nonsense sooner or later. Who could imagine such a thing?"

"Legends? *We* nurtured the legend. We, Morlenden; the Perklarens, the Terklarens, the Revens, Dragonfly Lodge, we who are *Kai Hrunon*, the Shadow that Governs. We kept it alive, so that when all was in readiness, need, we would send word in a truth-speaker, and the people would come."

And now Mevlannen stopped, thinking, reaching for some graceful entry into the story she had longed all her life to tell someone, a stranger, but never had. But all her life she had lived in the community of those who knew those whose whole lives consisted of an intricate dance about a point that all acknowledged, an understood, unspoken, implied but invisible keystone of their lives.

She began again, "It was in the beginning, when they started the Braids, the Law, the Way. Before the reservation. You must understand that. The whole thing with us, the entire culture, the way we perceived, everything was engineered to convince all outside observers that there never could be such a thing of the people. A vast prestidigitation that also had to fool the magician as well, or at any rate most of him. And of course it was successful, as you will be the first to admit. So successful that even our own imagine it to be no more than a child's fable; so successful that the disguise has taken root on its own, and now guides the inner long-range plan as well. The values of the disguise have now permeated the real plan. And when we leave Earth, the concepts and the way of life that we take with us to transplant on strange soil are not the values of the originators of the plan, but those of the shadow-play that protected them all these centuries.

". . . But in the beginning, we were not sure it could be done; it was a hope, a theory, a gamble. But the suspicion was so strong we could not ignore it; so it was started at the mountain called Madness. Inside, it was hollowed out, a little at a time, a handful, a pocket-load, to make a place for the ark that was to be. And just as gradually, in the smoky meditation halls of Dragonfly Lodge, one pocketful of principle at a time, it began to come into view, to manifest itself. It was then we learned that the whole concept of ideas about space travel we had been laboring under was wrong, full of limits we would *never* transcend . . . like powering aircraft with coal-fired steam engines. It would never fly, and should it, by accident, it would never take us anywhere, or anyone else for that matter.

"Now spaceflight had been approached by the forerunners, and some good work they did, work we are still using in the very program in which I am involved. But it has limits that any child can see; and to escape them, a whole series of fantasies was concocted, leading nowhere in hard science. What was the concept? That one moves in space according to Newton and his bloody laws of motion: forced-power, imposition of will, the Fire elemental, chemical rockets, ion-drives, solar-wind sails. All wrong. It was exactly like when the forerunners in prehistory first sailed upon seas; they could only use natural forces—buoyancy, floating ships with sails to catch the wind, launched by the tides. And we, standing on the shore of a new and terrible sea, would do the same; we, too, would tap tides and winds and currents. Only all those would be analogs, stranger forms of energy-flow in a larger and more multiplex universe."

Morlenden said, "I have world-knowledge; you mean that you tap directly into things like gravity, solar wind, things like that?"

"No." Her sharp, delicate face became focused, intense. "No. Those things you speak of, the principles, they are nth-order derivatives of the basic underlying forces we tap. In the things you know, there are no words for the currents, the flows, the forces, the concepts. And we have taken care to ensure that this remains so, forever, until we are ready to give up the secret.

"Now we saw that space was sea, the great sea. And we saw the analogy of ships of one kind of sea comparing to ships of the other sea. Just so, so that even in Singlespeech we still call a container of people that moves according to control in that medium a *ship*. But the flaw in the old concept was that we tried to leapfrog to powered ships, fueled ships, before we even knew the nature of that new sea. Or about the kinds of power we could use. Then we *saw*. And understood. And when we did, we also understood why we could not test it with a model. You will see also. So we pushed the thinkers, the theoreticians; some collapsed from the effort, others retired in disgust and discouragement. But always some stayed, and at last we knew enough to begin. Then the Player Braids were formed: first were the Klarens, who were to become the *Per-klarens* when the second Player Braid was added, the *Ter-Klarens*. And thus we have been, until this last generation."

"Thus you have been. To do what?" asked Morlenden, with a hint of sarcasm in his voice. "Indeed do *what*? Play a distracting Game for three hundred years?"

She laughed, a light, playful silvery laugh. "No, no. You all have been carefully led to assume that the root *klarh-* was Earth aspect, 'to play.' Hence, in turn, the *Players*. . . . It is not Earth aspect: it is Fire, and that means . . ."

". . . to fly! Not Players, but Flyers!"

"Indeed, to fly, to soar, to float upon the currents. We are not idle, privileged entertainers, Morlenden Deren; we are the pilot-astrogators of the Great Ark, the One Ship. There was no other way to keep the skill and the knowledge alive, save in a public Game that everyone could see and think he knew."

"Very well. What does the Game have to do with piloting? I know the Game, thanks to Krisshantem, but I fail to see . . ."

"The hard question; thus the hard answer. Let me build a dynamic identification-series for you: consider vehicles. You make a cart, a wagon, hitch it to a pony, and off you go. Its purpose is to go, but it can be stopped, and it doesn't change, or stop being a cart. Yes? Now consider a bicycle, which must be in balance to go. Yes? Now an aircraft; it can only be stopped when it is finished being a functional airplane, yes? You can't stop it just anywhere, and never in the air, unless you have rotary wings, which is just cheating the system. Yes? Just so the leap to the Ship. It is a quantum leap into a new concept in machines, if indeed that is the proper word. Before, we had machines that could be turned off. The more complex they became, the harder to turn off. With the ship, we enter the concept-world of machines that can't be turned off—at all. They must be *on* to exist. Once you reach a certain stage in the assembly of it, it's *on* and that's all there is to it. And when you build it, you are building something very specific; that is the Law of Multiplexity. The more developed the machine, the more unique it becomes.

"So, then," she continued, "this machine can only operate, be *on*, exist—in one mode only. A spaceship, which can't be turned off. Now, in the true-mode of that existence the laws we limited living creatures perceive about the universe are so distorted that they may as well not apply. One doesn't look out a window to see where one is going! The kind of space that the ship perceives, operates in, is to creatures such as you and I, chaotic, meaningless, and *dangerous*, when perceived directly, if we can at all. To confront it directly is destructive to the primate mind, indeed the whole vertebrate nervous system. At present, Dragonfly Lodge thinks that this underlying reality-universe is destructive to all minds, whatever their configuration, life-form or robotic. Basic to the universe: that its inmost reality *cannot* be perceived. A limit. So we interpose a symbolizer, and that translates the view into something we can perceive, and control. And we must control it, for like the sailing ship our Ship emulates, it cannot exist uncontrolled, and there can be no automaton to do it for us. It is flown *manually*, all the time; even to hold it in place relative to our perceptual field. For at the level of reality we are operating at here, to perceive *is* to manipulate. As you go further down into mystery, they become more and more similar; even the forerunners know that. But at the Ship they converge."

Morlenden thought a moment, then said, "And I see; the symoblizer portrays a Game."

"Just so. That is the Inner Game. And the Outer Game we have played in public is a much simplified form of the kind of thing we see in the Sensorium, which is display screen and control system all in one. Not combined; it *is* both. That we see the functions as separate is a measure of our distance from the Eternal. It is accurate enough, but of course certain configurations cannot be attained in the Outer Game, since they would lead to flight, too, and an open gameboard is no ship to fly in, but only an unmounted sail."

"It . . . flaps away?"

"About that. Yes, very good. And in two-dimensional display, we have the tesselations: triangular, quadrangular, pentagonal, hexagonal, octagonal, although this last leaves holes in the continuum and therein uncontrolled things happen. These symbolize the different kinds of space we can use . . . space-three, space-four, space-five, space-six, and space-eight. Each one has a different range and kind of thing it can perceive and control. *Pertrol* equals both. Within limits, we can set distances as we will."

"I see; when one flies the Ship, one actually is playing a more difficult Game, in which space itself plays the role of antagonist."

"Yes. And there is no way we could practice using the Ship's display. There, to simulate is to replace. So we invented the Outer, public Game, to keep us trained in the basics so we would always be ready when the time came."

"You are one of the pilot-astrogators?"

"No. I would have been, had either Maellen or I been born male. It takes four, and no less, to face that which the symbolizer depicts . . . this is why Braids were invented. The real reason. Not the genetic reason we use—that it keeps us all mixed and gene-pooled. That is excuse. You see? There must be four, and the only bond that will hold is the sexual-emotional one. You will not understand now, but I will say and you must believe that the Game in the Ship cannot be approached as a job, a vocation, a career, or recreation. To the contrary, it is Life and Death itself at work there. In the Inner Game, we call the Game *Dhum Welur*, the Mind of God. And that Mind is a terrible mind, that one may not face directly and remain whole. Some of the forerunners guessed it long ago—first the Hebrews far back in time, others along the way, and they wisely left it alone, left the Arcana alone. That is why those who studied the occult arts were either fools or doomed. Fools if they were wrong, and most were; doomed if right. The forerunners *know*, and stay away."

"It's that alien?"

"Yes. More than you can imagine. . . . Consider now, here in this cabin atop this mountain. We will go outside and look at, into the sky. We will see clouds, storm, and through rents in the clouds, stars. Ordinary enough, you can say; yet I have seen the same sky and the same clouds-of-the-world in space-three . . . it is different, full of terrors, of things we cannot understand, save to avoid, other things. . . ."

She stopped for a moment, apparently looking into some interior memory.

Then she continued, "So I suppose that things would have continued thus indefinitely. But the Ship was nearing completion, and it was estimated that the need for two Player Braids and the deception of the public Game were at an end. Thus the Perklaren insiblings, who were yet to weave at that time, and because they were the higher Braid, took a drug that disrupted the normal sexual-selection process of the insiblings* for that generation. They knew that it would make the *Toorhon* turn out to be the same sex, but they did not know which sex it would be."

---

* The first offspring was randomly selected, but thereafter the sex of the children was controlled pheronomically to maintain the fifty-fifty sexual ratio required by the insibling mating pattern.

"They did this by intent?"

"Yes. And it would have been . . . was to be . . . of no great effect. But that is one of the ironies of the Game, I think. It does not let you go so easily. The Ship can't be turned off; the Game can't be left, just like that. It will have its price. And so here is the essence of it: Sanjirmil was the inheritor of the Game, by the actions taken by the Perklaren insiblings before the birth of my generation. But in the province of the Game, Sanjirmil is actually not suited to it at all. Relative to the Game, and only to the Game, she is uninspired and . . . well, stupid. She hasn't the mind for it, although she is capable in other areas. Maellen, on the other hand, had a natural-born talent for it, the best we ever had. She was, by irony or accident, a natural prodigy for the Game, the only one ever so born. A genius. But it was too late, things had gone too far, the momentum was carrying us, perhaps the Game now controlling us and wished to teach us a lesson. I don't know. But as it stood, it would have been cruel enough. But this ties into another problem. . . ."

"Which is?"

"I said that the Ship was a machine that could not be turned off. That there was no way; that at a certain point in its construction it becomes *on*, activated, and assumes some of the responsibility for constructing itself, growing itself, while being guided. And so at that point, it turns itself on; *and flight begins, ready for it or not.* We knew it would be that way—thus the theorists had predicted. After all, it's not a hard prediction—you or I could do as well. But they could not tell the time when the event would occur. That is why we had the two Player Braids—to keep us all sharp and prepared for it by means of the artificial rivalry between us. And well it was, too, that the Terklarens had done so well by this generation; but evil, too. An evil star was after our fate. For the event occurred about fifteen years ago."

"About the time of the birth of Taskellan?"

"Yes. Just after. Maellen and I were just five, little children, *hazhon-hazhoun*, children's children. So the Flyers all had to go to work, alternating in the Sensorium, all the hours of the day, the days of the week . . . for fifteen years."

"I don't understand. . . ."

"It must be manually flown to hold it in place!" she exclaimed. "Its position at a specific place upon the Earth is not held there by gravity and momentum, as are the other things; that it stays in that place, it must be flown *there*. As we sit here, we move in many ways, but are held fast in a matrix of local forces. The Earth rotates, revolves in the Earth-moon system, revolves about the sun, follows an orbit about the galaxy, moves with the galaxy in the local galactic group, and participates in the steady-state expansion of the universe . . . those motions and their multiplex sum must be reversed and fed into the Ship so that it stays in its cave. Those motions, and many others that we do not see . . . some of these countermotions are those which may not be seen. There are terrors in the universe, and they are not the ones we imagined. And if we do not compensate, then the Ship would drift off on its own, following the currents as it feels them. . . . Perhaps the word *drift* is inappropriate, for seen by an outsider on the surface, this drift would seem like an explosion; the Ship would explosively depart the immediate area at something close to *c*, the velocity of light, a significant fraction of it, interacting violently with matter in its path and around it. At the value of *c* it possessed, it would have enough mass, once it moved, to disrupt the balance of the whole solar system. It would, of course, be destroyed in the first moment of unguided flight, but no matter; it would destroy everything else."

"I don't understand . . . why doesn't it disrupt things now, if it has that much mass?"

"Speed alone. Relativity. The mass approaches infinity as the speed approaches unity-*c*. Held at rest, it has its own material mass, a few thousand tons. This is damped by the control field, so that it appears massless. Makes it easy to move, short-field. But turned loose, it takes off at almost a full light; so that the mass is approximately equal to two-point-five *suns*. This is above limits within a given volume of space, so the result is a linear supernova as long as it lasts. Those are the limits . . . say, from the mass of Jupiter to two-point-five suns. There is some inexactitude in our calculations, but at any rate, at either extreme, the result is doom; so what does it matter? And as if it made any difference, we cannot determine the vector either. It is a heavy responsibility, flying."

"Indeed, to know the Flyers have been sitting on a bomb for fifteen years. They have been flying it *manually?*"

"Manually. While the rest of the Ship was being grown and built. Finished, the life-support systems completed. There have never been enough people to do it, the work that isn't done by the Ship. And by the Canon of the Law of the Flyers, only a formed Braid can fly. That means that only two crews are available, although exceptions are made by executive order of the High Reven, to allow relief so the outside Game can go on, and continue its deception. . . . The last time I was home, I was told that an exemption would be made for Sanjirmil and her Braid, if she could assemble one."

"So that is why the parent Perklarens were never home."

"Yes. And why I am here. But their story first. They were at a holy mountain, the Mountain of Madness, inside the Ship, flying alone in the darkness, in space-three, triangular tesselation, hardest of all. Matrix twelve; fine detail work deep inside a gravity well, the solar gravity well. The Ship is spherical in shape and sits in a cradle in the rock, in the cavern; it has only moved about an inch in all that time. You could sit on that very hill and not know it was there, a few score feet under your very fundament."

She said, after a moment, "Klervondaf was initiated but not trained. Taskellan was not initiated. Both Maellen and I were, of course. We did not stop being insiblings. The Inner Game was our heritage and our right. But instead of Player-Flyers, we were to take different roles, so that the last step might be implemented; I would come here, to the Trojan Project, and Maellen would secretly soldier for us in the outer world. I chose loneliness, and Maellenkleth chose danger, and ultimately, death."

"Who decided? How?"

"The Shadow, as in all things. We divided it up, Maellen and I, with no more thought than we would share a piece of cake. There was no particular reason. We were so very young . . . and she was good at the Game, and wanted to remain where she could at least study it, pass on her insights. I am only average, like anyone else. Better than Sanjirmil, but nothing like Maellen. And so I am here . . . but in many ways I like my work, both the outer and inner portions of it. I like to make things work, and so have done well by my employers, even as I used their instrument to do other things. . . ."

She shook her head, as if still unbelieving. "So I am an astronaut, an engineer. When I would prefer a *yos*, and now, until I weave, an eager circle of lovers."

Morlenden interrupted her musing. "I see that Maellenkleth was to run destructive interference for the rest of you."

"Yes. One last trick."

"And you?"

"Mine was the last part, a small one, but important. I was to see that the telescope was built, and help build it, so I could have a good reason for using it without arousing suspicion."

"And what were you to use it for?"

"You know we have poor night-vision; that is why the telescope. Not for magnification, but for the gathering of light. Otherwise one of us could have done this from the ground. So, then, I was to obtain views, visually, polychromatically, of the space all around Earth, in all directions, and memorize. Then, using all those views from different points along the Earth's orbit about the sun, combine the views together, to make up in my mind a three-dimensional map of interstellar space from eidetic memory. I would have an excellent dimensional view, because I would have a parallax baseline one hundred and eighty-five miles long, the diameter of the orbit. After I had the image, I could convert that into a three-dimensional grid map, using Multispeech space-matrix coordinates, which would then be used in the comparison astrogation base."

"How so?"

"On a clear night, you look at the stars. Can you see any order in their arrangement?"

Morlenden hesitated. ". . . No. I see the brighter constellations, but they are somewhat arbitrary. I cannot tell what is near or far, or in relation to what. Lights in the sky. Jupiter and Mars seem as far, or as near, as Sirius, Vega, Deneb." For the names of the stars and planets he had used, Morlenden had unconsciously used the words as he had heard them from Fellirian; the old Modanglic names. It was only after he had spoken the words that he realized how alien and strange they sounded. Mevlannen noticed as well. A light smile danced across her face.

"You do not know the names of the stars, for those who name are also those who seek order. It was a slow process, for we had to work in part from ancient maps. We do not see them all from the ground. Painstaking research, thousands of nights of careful watching, care and secrecy lest it be known that we even look at the stars. But we have our own names for the stars, the near ones that we know and feel, and the far ones that we use as reference points. You know the Canon of Names: one syllable for things, two for places, three for people, four for stars, and five for the 'Attributes of God*.' So that Borlinmeldreth is that which the forerunners call Sirius; Kathiarvashien, Sigma Doradus; Skarmethseldir, Deneb. There are many names we have had to learn, recite by rote."

* Theological terminology. But in this convention was also a tradition that a person's name, proper plus surname, also equated to five syllables, by dropping all numerical prefixes to the surname. (The last syllable of the surname, -en, was a short form of the syllable *ghenh*-, a root meaning "family." By and large, the ler found the guttural—*gh*—distasteful and would drop it whenever they could get away with it.) In this view, then, all persons were theologically considered to be "Attributes of God."

Morlenden said, "Names, yes, but it is still without order."

"So it seems. But there is a great and mighty system of order in space, although it cannot be seen by a creature on the surface, without a matrix in the imagination. It is on too vast a scale for us. And we are talking about visuals, that which we see with our eyes; you cannot begin to imagine what the same volume looks like when seen through the symbolizer in space-four. Or any other. More than chaotic, it is alive with forces and unknown objects whose nature we cannot determine. Eddies and currents are there, and waves and winds and storms whose source and sink we do not know. And as the ancient forerunner Polynesian navigators saw lights in the sea that indicated land over the horizon, the glory of the sea, so do we also see glory in the sea of space, but it is a glory that makes us very afraid as well; it crawls like the Pacific Ocean down there below Pico Tranquillon. And for such a Ship, there can be no anchorage anywhere; for the pilot, no landfall, though a planet be found, and the passengers, the people, disembark. For us, a planetfall is just more work in space-three. . . . And there are other things, too, things we can only dimly perceive in the Game, things which have no visual analog at all. They move, they appear to have volition. Are they forms of life? Perhaps. So however well we think we see space in the display, we have to have a reference set of coordinates from the visual perception. Because some things show in the Game that cannot be seen and we must know where these are. And we must know arbitrary things, too—like which way is Galactic North, G-South, Solar North, S-South. The reference for Galactic Meridian. Translating. Our eyes see geodesic lines to the stars, but in the Ship there is no such thing, and the two must be integrated. That integration has been my real mission, and it is this for which I have been trained."

She paused, then continued, "It is a problem in synesthesia as well; we always assumed sight was sight, period. But it was not to be so: what the symbolizer depicts would be best described as being most like a sense of smell, whose operation we then see through the symbolizer. That is not good, but it will have to do."

Morlenden at first suppressed a smile, but then he laughed aloud. "So you sniff your way along, blind but for the memorized view, eh?" But he laughed uneasily, for he did not like the image that came to his mind— that of a hound blinded, nose to the earth, questing in the air, cautiously sniffing out a trail to a place he never knew before, but which had to smell right. And avoid a universe full of things, whose perceptions he could not verify by sight. Morlenden added, "That is the damndest thing I ever heard in my life."

Mevlannen smiled with him. "I laughed, too, Morlenden, when I was initiated, and so have we all. Except Sanjirmil. She never laughed. But the dangers are real, and there is much confusion. Naturally we do not desire to get lost—only to leave Earth and make planetfall on a world upon which we can live. And so thus was my part in it: to reconcile what we see with our eyes and what we perceive in the symbolizer. This I have done, and my task is finished."

She stopped speaking, her voice at the last becoming hoarse. Now she looked, and she saw that her cup was empty. Morlenden's was as well. Adding his cup to hers in her hand, she arose, refilled them both, and returned to her place by the fire. She seemed dazed, abstracted.

Morlenden also was abstracted, trying to integrate what he had heard here with what else he heard. Mevlannen had explained a lot, the whole background. But, astounding though it was, it did not explain what had happened to Maellenkleth. Or to him. He thought again; he thought he could see the answer on the horizon, but he did not care for the shape of it. There was much yet to comprehend.

He began, "I have many questions, Mevlannen. The Shadow, Maellenkleth, Sanjirmil . . . I hardly know where to begin."

She answered tentatively, "I know the basics; I also know what I have done. But recently, I am out of touch. Remember, I have been out here five years; there is much you will know better than I."

"Well, then. The first part. I understand secrecy. But I feel cheated that a whole way of life was engineered as a deception, rather than a reality, however good it was for us all. . . . There are things we do out of that which do not come easy, after all. I know these things well. What will it all have been for?" he asked.

"That we will be free, to have a world of our own. Is that not enough? And remember the means defining the tool . . . it was thus we were defined."

"Have you considered, you of the Shadow, that the people will become cynical?"

"That was considered in the beginning, but it was hoped that they wouldn't be, that they would graft on those values; 'the grafted tree bears the sweetest fruit,' say the Pomen Braidsmen. And it has been good for us, we have thrived under our increased family structure as we would have under no other model we had at the time. And now we are used to it; I should not wish any other way."

"So we say, here . . . but there is also the idea of the government. Ostensibly there were the Revens and the Derens, and that was it—cheerful, law-abiding light anarchy. But now you tell me that this has not been so, that we were ruled in reality all these years in secret by a government we didn't even know existed, a council calling itself *Kai Hrunon*, 'The Very Shadow.' Was the Reven Braid the real ruler?"

"In a word, yes. In another, no. You would, for example, never have been permitted to challenge an arbitration by Pellandrey or his insibling Devlathdar; that it was never done in the past is a measure of our tact, which is what civilization *is*."

"But it was always otherwise."

"Mostly. Outer: a Braid to settle disputes, and another to confer familial legitimacy; but inside, in the Shadow, it was a majority of elders, and at that, primarily of the Flyer Braid background. And there one rules. The Perwathwiy Srith. And the traditional rote is that the Reven arbitrates only aground. In space, the senior Flyer rules. In the name of the Shadow and the Plan."

"I see a danger here: if the Ship cannot be turned off and is always flying, then what now prevents the most ambitious Flyer from taking power and keeping it, using the argument that since the Ship is flying, his is the power. What prevents this?"

"Necessity for discretion. Tradition. And the fact that as of now, most of the people are still outside the Ship, and would probably ignore orders from within it. Also there is always violence; we are not forbidden it."

"Who is senior Flyer now?"

"When my Perklaren parents took the step to end Perklaren continuity, leadership automatically went to the Braid with continuity. That would of course be the Terklarens."

"Sanjirmil!"

"No, at least, not when I left. She is not yet of age. Her parent generation, the Terklaren insiblings Daeliarnan and Monvargos; such were affairs when I left."

"But it would go to Sanjirmil?"

"Yes, that is so."

"And you said that Maellenkleth was your soldier, your valiant one?"

"Aye, just so. She always demanded to be in the front of everything, since she could not have the Game. She was brave, even foolhardy."

"Did she act alone, by her own will, or was she directed?"

"In matters outside the reservation, Sanjirmil spoke for the Shadow, when she was not flying. A lot of exemptions were made for her. She was to be allowed to make up her Braid co-spouses early. They needed that, for the work of flying is too demanding for just two crews, and each crew must be four."

"This deception and its effects; one of them may have been the unnecessary death of your insibling. Do you understand this from what I have said?"

She looked away from Morlenden, uneasily, her eyes fixed elsewhere, on nothing, anything. After a time she spoke, but it was with a voice quiet and subdued. "We always knew that there was peril in the way we had chosen. Risk and reward, you know. They who risk not, receive not. But we always had to balance those dangers against what would happen if the humans derived the secret of the Ship. We knew that we could not build such a Ship openly, for they would simply take it. How could they not want it? Starships? And once we considered sharing it with them, but that was voted down. Studies and tests indicated that if they ever discovered the Inner Game, the matrix overdrive, they would integrate autopilot devices into it; and therein is horror. What we deal with in the Game no machine can handle, because what we do, every second, is *decide*, and no machine can do that for us. And we use hunch to make those guesses and decisions. We are using resources we do not entirely understand. But under an autopilot, things would start to slip and the corrections would pile up and the machine would just lock up. It is extremely dangerous to manipulate underlying forces in the universe, and one must always do it consciously, never automatically. . . . To observe is to manipulate and once you start you must continue or destroy the device that allows you to do it. But you can't play span-of-attention with it, play with it and then forget it. And robots would get tied up in the nature of transcendental numbers and become bemused by the algorithm, which is endless."

She added, "We were all told, in the most graphic terms imaginable, what the risks were at each stage of the Game, both to the people, and the ones in individual situations. I know Maellenkleth knew the risks, and she took them freely; I cannot question that further. That she paid it is to the honor of her memory."

Morlenden answered, "I cannot find fault with your loyalty, nor with Maellenkleth's. She stood up to the heaviest of responsibilities, and performed as she said she would; she was no oath-breaker. But there has been the suspicion in my mind that such a sacrifice need not have been made, and that there was more to her capture and death than meets the eye. That there are forces at work, right now, in your carefully cultured system that could be destructive to the people and the Ship as well."

"But I cannot imagine . . ."

"Of course you cannot. You have been out of touch for five years. But there is evil afoot in out garden, and I am now trying to find the source of it. What you have told me is valuable, but it does not yet bridge the gap. So let me ask you: *why* was Maellen sent out to destroy instruments?"

"It must be that she was sent, Morlenden. She was not willful in that way. Only in regard to the Game. But destroy instruments? Unusual, that. The outriders were supposed only to observe. What instruments?"

"As I was told, a device to measure magnetism, feel the field strength of the area in which it was. Another measured the field strength of gravity from point to point. Small, portable things, but accurate and discriminatory. Also not presently in use, which we all found curious."

"As I do also. . . . You could detect the Ship with those instruments, but since they were not in use . . ."

"You could detect it? How?"

"If you have a large mass of ferric ore or metal, it distorts the local magnetic field, concentrates the lines, makes the field more intense. The Ship, operating, causes the reverse of this—it weakens the local magnetic field. As for the other, the gravity meter, that could also be used in similar fashion: in essence, the mass of the Ship shows much less than you would expect. This is because the inertia is constantly damped by the matrix overdrive. Surveying a mountain with such an instrument, one would expect a higher reading due to the increased mass, but instead, what you see when the Ship is inside is as if there were a massless hole in the mountain. If the instrument was tuned for fine-detail resolution, you could see that the 'hole' was spherical. . . . If they were going to use them, or could conceivably be expected to, then I could understand destroying them. But of that I cannot speak; I know nothing."

"So we cannot determine if they were to be used or not, here."

"No. Like so much of the wide world, Morlenden, you and I can talk all night, share what we imagine, what we know, but all the same there is much else which we cannot know, of what we share and meld together. Truth takes many, and even then we err. Both true things and provable things as well."

Morlenden said, "Well, then, true or not, I will have to return much as I came . . . but at the least you can return with me, rejoin your family and friends."

"No. I can never come back. That was one of the prices for this. I have a short tether. I will continue my work."

"We may have taken on the values of the macrodeception, but that does not mean that you have to do the same in your part of it. And we need your skill, Engineer. And if nothing else, we still require the services of a resident star-gazer, if only to remember the lore of the skies of Old Earth for those who will have left it forever, and to search out the skies of the new world, wherever it will be, though I find it strange and awesome even to speak of it. Or is it that you fear to return?"

"Perceptive and cruel you are, even as you extend your hand. It is true I fear it. I have lived here long. . . . We here have become accustomed to one another's strangeness. But after the manner of the people, I have been contaminated by many of the concepts I have worked with."

She stopped, fatigue showing along the lines of her face, her straight, delicate jawline. Fatigue and repressed grief were beginning to penetrate her defenses, break down the fortress of her solitude. The pale eyes softened, looked inward. Morlenden could not read the sense of her thoughts: perhaps she was thinking about space; or of past childhood days with her insibling, now vanished into the dust and the past. He could imagine her as a child of the people, but harder it was to picture her in his mind in a spacesuit, the tender, pale adolescent body encased, indistinguishable from the others, forerunners one and all. It disturbed him, following the idea to its hermetic conclusion, that only in gentler environments did creatures allow themselves the differentiation in form between male and female. The harsher the environment, the less difference showed. Space . . . even that was not the ultimate yet. There were worse things, he sensed.

Mevlannen began speaking again, now reflective rather than assertive. It was gentle speech, and her eyes were unfocused, undirected. She spoke of the stars; and Morlenden let her go uninterruptedly, for she needed this.

As she spoke of the stars and her work, a gentle glow animated her face, a something-inside which had not shown before. Morlenden thought that he knew the stars well enough; he could see the brighter ones as well as any ler*, but the night sky was no spangled glory to him—it was a furry black emptiness, broken by a number of scattered points. How could he comprehend what Mevlannen Srith Perklaren saw in space, sidereal day after sidereal day in the endless lidless night of space, perched like a bird in her instrument's prime focus, struck dumb, he was sure, by the incredible, unimaginable sight before her, and awed into insignificance by the three-dimensional image she was building up, line by painful line, position by position, via eidetic recall comparison. And she pronounced the resounding four-syllable names of the stars, in itself a wild, haunting poetry of unknown places and distant journeys, that curdled unknown longings in himself as he heard the names for the first time.

Thondalrhenvir, Alpha Crucis; Lothpaellufkresh, Betelgeuse; Norrimveldrith, Great Rigel. On and on went the multisyllabic list, mixed with ancient Latin and Greek and Arabic names and numbers and letters, the recitation, points of light in a sky of darkness, reference points and possible future havens for astrogators and pilots who were going to step off the fixed and safe shore and swim in that ever-moving stream. There were names of distant galaxies, which Morlenden did not know at all: Lethlinverdaerlan, M31 in Andromeda; Vardaindralmerran, Maffei I; Klaflanpurliendor, the Greater Magellanic Cloud. Some equated only to numbers on obscure surveys, most by human sky-watchers, a few numbered by Mevlannen and her predecessor, Thalvillai, a Perklaren of another generation: Avila 3125, Elane 10110. Morlenden wished to be able to visualize it, desperately, but he felt that he was falling short of that inner image that illuminated the eyes and face of the girl, places she would never be closer to than right now, no matter she stayed on Earth or left it. And there were the nearer stars, the neighbor-lights that Man and ler alike had looked at with longing and burning curiosity: Yallov-yardir, Tau Ceti, twelve lights; Diylarmendar, Epsilon Eridani; Thifserminlen, Epsilon Indi; Holdurfarlof, 61 Cygni A; Dharhamnerlaz, Lalande 21185; Melforshamdan, Proxima Centauri;

---

* On the whole, from the surface of the Earth, considering also the generally dusty air of the times, the average ler could, on a clear night, perhaps see down to the fourth magnitude. Norm most of the time was only third-magnitude objects.

Tandelkvanlin, Barnard's Star; Partherlondrin and Khaliannindos, Alpha Centauri A and B.

And Morlenden thought of his own life, the routines of it, of log-books and Braid diagrams, of visits and ceremonies and parties, of the security of position and identity in a stable and fixed hereditary society. He thought of foot journeys in the changing forest, all the familiar things he and Fellirian knew. And however restricted the reservation had been, he knew that it had been a good life there and he did not wish to leave it. And which now to lose—the place or the role? He was sure it would be place-lost, for one could always change role; the outsiblings did it every year.

When she stopped for a moment, he gently interrupted her. "Mevlannen? There is another thing I should have told you. Do you know anything about a boy named Krisshantem?"

She looked at him blankly. "Nothing."

"He was Maellen's last lover. I understand that she was planning and working toward petitioning the Revens to allow her, with this Krisshantem, to form a Third-player Braid. They would be *shartoorh*. She taught him the Outer Game, and in fact was apparently receiving some covert support for her plan from Pellandrey Reven, and I think, the Perwathwiy also. Was it possible that this would have any effect on the Ship?"

"I don't know. We could not predict when the Ship would activate, so we could not better predict when it would be ready for flight. When I left, it was felt that the Ship would fly before Mael and I would come of age. Just before. That would have been ten years from now. But as you have doubtless found out, Maellenkleth was always dissatisfied with her change of role, and who could blame her? She was an authentic genius in the Game, and therefore also in the Ship. But of course that plan of hers would be against the decision of the Shadow and the beneficiaries of that decision, the Terklarens, and of course Sanjirmil. Against Maellenkleth at the height of her powers in the Game, Sanjirmil would have been ridiculous as master of the Game, and could not have survived open competition for it. And fear not, Maellenkleth would have forced it. No doubt the intent was resented, especially her bringing an outsider into the Game. The Shadow always carefully selected the outsiblings we wove with."

"So it would have hurt Sanjirmil."

"Indeed, oh, without doubt. Oh, and I see what you think! Hm . . . no, she is capable of it. They feared each other greatly, Mael and Sanjir.

And we all knew that the way things turned out was largely a matter of accidental timing. But when you are dealing with generational turnover periods of two fourteens and seven years, you have to have the bearing that considers a lot can happen in those years. So it fell to Sanjir, and many of us did not like it, but what could we replace her with? When I left home, nothing. Any way we moved, we were distorting our own canon, which we had always obeyed in our advantage. It would have been cynical indeed to go against it because things did not turn out as some of us might have wanted."

She looked away a moment. Then, "You must understand that in one way, the way most of the Shadow would have seen it, Maellenkleth was wrong. They would say that since the Braid in agenetic, talent doesn't matter when it's low, so it shouldn't when it's high. We all loved her dearly, but almost from the very beginning she read herself out of it. There was no accident with the Players; they took deliberate action. The accident was with Maellenkleth; she was too good, and what an irony that was, how cruel! And she never understood why she had to give up that which she did best of all things. You know she was a prodigy, but what does that mean? I will tell you: she was a full-Player, rated at level fourteen, when she was ten years old. The best we ever had prior to her was the Perwathwiy, and she only attained level eleven at her peak, and by the kind of discipline that breaks minds and bodies before their time. The average is around seven, and you must be a five to be admitted to the Inner Game."

"What is Sanjirmil?"

"Her norm, which is set when one is a child, was always subentry, a three or four. But somehow she made it with a five when she had to. How, I don't know. The numbers are not additive but exponential; there is no way a three could become a five and stay sane; it takes too much."

She stopped, then said, "Now come close to me, for I will give you the numbers. I have not made up my mind yet, and would sleep on it; yet I will give them to you so they will not be lost if I decide to stay here. . . . Now listen close, for these are matrix numbers and they are hard to catch just right."

Morlenden assented and moved closer to the girl, very close, so that their faces were almost touching. He became still, opening his mind and will to Mevlannen. All he could see of her were her eyes, whose exact color was now elusive in the firelight. The eyes were expressionless, but they were reddened in the whites and glittered with moisture. Her breath was heavily scented with the brandy she had been dosing the coffee with, and he could also detect the scent of the oil of her face. There was no preliminary warning, as there had been with Krisshantem, but rather like Sanjirmil, it started immediately, seizing his mind, blanking his vision, and inserting the coordinate matrix at once, easily. He did not understand what he was receiving, but he had no time to think of it, just retain the matrix the way he got it. It came at lightning speed, but, for all its speed, it seemed to go on for a long time, and soon Morlenden became aware of nothing but spatial numbers, sometimes broken into shorter or longer strings. Holistic, like a visual, but also something different. This did not build a picture that he could see. By the time it came to the end, which came without notice or warning, save a little twist that he did not catch, the fire was much dimmer, and he saw again, the sad eyes close before him.

He said, "I have it. Are you sure Sanjir will understand?"

Mevlannen unfolded her legs from beneath her and stood, stretching like a cat. She looked closely at Morlenden, as if seeking some reassurance, or looking for a sign, of something. What? She said, "Yes. She will understand, all that I gave, and more. . . . I add a caution; never speak of what you have from me to anyone, never recite it to anyone but Sanjirmil, even to yourself. You must do neither, or you will fail us all. Only Sanjirmil!"

"Why can't you tell her yourself?"

"Because I was not to come back!" She almost wailed. And after a moment, added, "And anyway, knowing what I do now, I will not be permitted to get close to Sanjir. They will think of me, rightly or wrongly, that I carry a vendetta against her."

"I know. I see it, too. I do not know how it came to be, but she is my suspect."

An unpleasant grimace flashed across Mevlannen's face. It creased her mouth upward at the corners for that moment, but it could not be called a smile. She said, "Indeed . . . so remember your oath, and my instructions. Only to her! Do you feel arightly? You look peculiar."

Morlenden did feel odd, and he could not locate the source, which seemed to be fading even as he tried to find the cause of the feeling. There was something . . . no, nothing seemed out of place. "Yes, of course, I'm fine. Very tired."

"Do not feel bad over that; you now have much of what we have carried all our lives. It is a weight. And for you, now, it is fresh. . . . You will pass through the stressies unmarked."

She turned away from him, allowing the loose overshirt to flow around the contours of her slender, almost fragile body after the manner of all ler girls since the beginning of their time, walking slowly around the room, putting out the lamps and candles that were still burning. She stooped and shook down the fire, at the last, covering the fireplace with a metal screen. The room sank into a deeper darkness, and in the soft, dimensionless dimness, Mevlannen took on an air of expectation, of longing. Morlenden remembered how it had been, and in his mind kicked himself for the circumstances that were. This was indeed a priceless gift, and he was powerless to do more with it than appreciate deeply.

She picked up the last candle, and said softly, "Now you must sleep with me, for there is but one bed."

He started to protest, but she came quietly to him and laid a finger gently over his mouth. The hand was uncharacteristically hard and cool, for all its delicacy a hand of great strength. She said, "I understand all too well what you will say. I know its truth as I know my own. But though I would have that, I wish more. . . . We are sharers now of a great secret, and are comrades endangered by the world, more than you know. That makes us close, as close as poor Mael and I. The last of our kind who slept with me was her, Maellen who gave up nights with someone much more exciting, to come here and be with me. It was just like when we were little children and all we had to do was play games with what we thought was life, and when we were tired we would tumble into bed and sleep in a pile like cats around the hearthfire, making each other secure against the unknown we had both seen. I have never slept so soundly since."

Morlenden said, "I understand. I will hold you, too."

She said, "There is one thing more . . . I should have thought of it."

"What is it?"

"That in the Outer Game, we always allowed the Terklarens a certain latitude for cheating when they were in the adversary role, the role that equates to the real universe in the Inner Game."

"Cheating? What for?"

"So we prepare for the real thing. That is what the real universe seems to do: cheat. Perhaps it does cheat, although that is a conscious process and that leads to speculations I do not care to make about the nature of things. . . . But it has its own rules and our job as Players is to understand those rules as best we can. We can manipulate the microcosm and the macrocosm through the Game, but we cannot impose our conception of order upon it; we have to play its way. So there are degrees of subtlety, and then further subtleties, and just when we think we've got it fixed and secure for all time, it makes a change on us, some little change, some exception. . . . We all know that this means we must learn more, but it feels like cheating. Not fair! So we had allowed the adversary Player team to cheat a little in the Outer Game, to prepare us for those little shifts in the Inner, which is not a Game at all, but basic life and death."

Morlenden asked, "Wouldn't this tend to make the adversary Players a little dishonest?"

"There is no doubt of this side effect. All things have consequences, paraconsequences. Sometimes we look too hard at the effect we want, and forget that there are others, some of which may be of greater strength."

"Why do you tell me this?"

"So that you may know what you have walked into. We know it and compensate for it. It is so automatic that we do not even think of it, normally. They did not tell you, and I did not until this moment. An oversight. But one that could have crucial ends."

"All of you?"

"Around other Players, we allow for it, but around others we sometimes lose sight of the fact that others do not play by our rules."

"So now that I have at last contacted the Players, I risk being tricked and gulled at every stage of the Game."

There was only a little light by which to see, but in that light he could see that at his last question Mevlannen had turned away from him slightly, an expression of pain on her face. "No," she said. "Not so much that. Or perhaps yes, you may." She straightened. "Be on your guard now, even with me. But especially with Sanjirmil."

Morlenden was tempted, but he did not speak of what else he knew and suspected. "Sanjirmil?"

"Yes. Because she never learned the counterprogram to the cheating. It is an ethical exercise. Somehow, she never got it. They tried to catch up, but you know how those things are. Once out of sequence, and it's gone forever. They tried, but no one knows if it took. . . . She can be dangerous."

Morlenden nodded, an idea forming in his mind. He saw that it was not lack of data which had prevented it from coming earlier, but that he had been suppressing the obvious conclusion all the time. And the knowledge did not cheer him; it told him of a blind side he had carried unknowing, a dirty little secret about almost-forbidden fruits, of sweaty, hard supple bodies and salty kisses, and an image which would never have mattered save for intervening circumstances and an accident. Yes. Now he knew. It remained only to verify it.

He followed Mevlannen into the rear of the cabin. There, in a separate little room, was a hard, Spartan bed, after the human style, piled high with crude but homey quilts.

She blew out the candle she had been carrying to light the way, making a fragile little puff of breath as she did so. Afterward, in the darkness, over the sounds of wind and rain and storm fretting at the cabin walls, and the stunted, slanting jumpers sliding against it, he heard the silky sounds of her overshirt, slipping off her body over her head, and falling to the floor. He sensed, rather than seeing or hearing directly, the girl Mevlannen moving across the floor, and then heard the quilts rustling as she slipped her bare body into the bed.

He removed his own overshirt, not without hesitation, and then, feeling the chill of the room, slid into bed beside her, feeling first the hard, rough fabrics against him; she moved close, flowing into a space he had made with his arm, stretching full length against him. Although the intent she had was not particularly erotic, nevertheless it was, and as such was maddening. The change in Morlenden had been years ago; he and Fellirian had lost both the will and the way after Fellirian had completed and delivered her third pregnancy. But they still retained their memories and they never forgot, and the senses still performed their functions. So he knew fully the desirability of this smooth, supple young girl, eager for love; yet at the same time the thing he felt would not proceed further than a thought, a memory. If it had any body-response at all, he felt it only vaguely somewhere in the vicinity of the heart, perhaps the diaphragm, where it diffused into a something for which there was no word Morlenden knew: something ludicrous and incapable of response, feeling like some unnamed intermediate sensation, between extreme tenderness and indigestion.

She lay quietly, breathing evenly, deeply. After a time, the breathing became softer, shallower, and once or twice, her body trembled slightly. Now the combination of fatigue and Mevlannen's amazing revelation began to tell on him, and the warmth of the body next to him relaxed him further, into semiconsciousness. It was in this half-sleep that he thought he heard her say something, but he could not be sure she had said anything at all. It had sounded like, "Forgive me for that which I have done." But when he listened again, there was nothing, and she never repeated it. And so, with a head full of rushing visions and dire suspicions, Morlenden dropped into sleep like a round pebble falling into a quiet pond.

When he awoke in the morning, the rosy light from the east was pressing at the curtains of the tiny window, which he had not seen the night before; he noted immediately that the warm presence that had been next to him was not there, that she was gone, and that the cabin now carried the silence of emptiness. He arose, donned his old clothes. There was no note, nothing. He rummaged around, and eventually found some biscuits in the cupboard which apparently had been left for him to find. He slipped his cloak over the overshirt and left, trying to find a way to lock the door behind him. There was none. Apparently, it could only be barred from inside. He gave up, and started down the path, back the way he had come, along the saddle which would take him down to the cliffs above the blue sea, now smooth and glassy, except for perfect swells breaking in precise patterns along the shore, rippling their crests from left to right, leaving a faint rooster's-tail trailing above and behind them. Old Sun painted a clear, golden light over the ocean, the grassy clifftops.

He negotiated the saddle, and turned through two sharp switchbacks to a lower level, where he found Mevlannen sitting on an ancient jumper stump, dressed in a heavy winter overshirt and cloak that looked as if they had not been worn for some time. She was looking silently down at the sea; now and again a stray puff of breeze would ripple a loose strand of hair that had escaped the hood of the cloak.

He greeted the girl, "Daystar light your way as mine! Are you waiting to say farewell?"

She turned and looked at him blandly, as if he should have already known what her answer would be. "Here is a place I love dearly, and here I gave my part to the plan; but here I will not stay and offer a barren fertility to the forerunners while my kin journey to the stars. I will come with you if you offer me the new family of Taskellan."

Morlenden nodded. "Just so and no more; but you will have to call me now Kadh'olede, not Ser Deren."

"So much will I do gladly. It has been a long time. Will your own Braidschildren not resent us?"

"No. I think not, although our *Nerh*, Pethmirvin, will not approve of your stealing boyfriends from her."

"Oh. I don't know yet if I can."

"Never mind. I have something in mind to keep you busy for a time."

"You will keep secrets?"

"Indeed I will."

"Very well." She stood, shaking herself off. "Can we get back, do you think?"

"I had no difficulty coming here. Their attention seems elsewhere, now. We will ride, and then we will walk a space; what can we do but try? Tell them you have been on the Salt Pilgrimage, if they ask. And of course, use a name other than your own, just as I will do."

Mevlannen nodded. She looked back, up the mountain, just once, at the summit of Pico Tranquillon. She could not see the cabin from where she stood. Then she turned and started down the narrow path to the sea, rippling far below them in the morning light. Morlenden joined her and together they walked down to the sea, and back into the world.

EIGHTEEN

The pathology of the poet says that the undevout astronomer is mad.

—A.E. Waite

EYKOR, CARRYING A sheaf of papers, untidily arranged into a cumbersome bundle, greeted Parleau in the hallway outside the chairman's office. "Chairman, a moment; may I have a word?"

"Certainly, Eykor. It's free, now. Come along." Parleau led the way past the shiftsman administrator who sat impassively and said nothing.

Eykor followed, carrying the unwieldy sheaf of paperwork as if it concealed a very touchy bomb. Once inside the private office, he carefully placed the bundle on the conference end of Parleau's desk, and turned to the chairman. He began, excitedly, "Chairman, over in the department we have been pursuing several aspects of this series of incidents centered on the girl-vandal. We have found more loose ends. Too many. We are now in the embarrassing position of having more clues than crimes or criminals."

"Go on." Parleau knew very well that to one such as Eykor crime flourished everywhere, even in the mind. He would never root them all out, but all the same he would never stop trying, either, heedless of the misery he caused along the way, and the mistakes he made. It was not hatred of crime that made him that way, but rather an excess of zeal to duty, and too narrow a view. Such types were ultimately dangerous to all unless kept under strict supervision; and of course, well-supplied with a variety of real criminal activities to keep them to task, preoccupy their attention; everything was evidence, otherwise.

Eykor said, "We found Errat."

"More specifically, please."

"Errat was discovered in a terminated condition, in a rundown rooming house near the warehouse quarter. Here, in Region Central. It was handled routinely by neighborhood Security, until an alert watchman noted the reports. Then we got the department into it."

"Aha. Continue."

"By the time we got there, of course the body had been removed, but the room had not been too disturbed, so we were able to have the forensic pathologist go over the room microscopically. We did the same with Errat, when we caught up with the body. Errat had been dispatched with a single penetration of a sharp, pointed object in the upper left back; he terminated virtually instantly; there was not a sign of struggle, anywhere. We believe he was taken by surprise."

"Knifing's a common enough cause of murder."

"This was different; it was done without slashing, no side movement at all. We were able to reconstruct the shape of the weapon."

"Errat seemed to be a free agent for persons unknown. This would indicate that one of them got close to him and had time to aim carefully."

"Exactly. And it was an unusual weapon; it was straight, two-edged, about two hands long, but rather thick, for the kinds of knife we are familiar with. It was not metal, but wood, a very hard wood sealed with a coating that was once volatile and which contained many impurities."

"I know of no tool like that."

"Neither did we. At least not in our own community. But with the New Humans, such knives are commonplace. They are used for dress and for the settling of feuds. Moreover, this suggested deduction was confirmed by other traces we were able to derive from objects in the room. You see, the fractions are different, between us and them, the chemical traces. The detector-men went crazy until it occurred to them that their machine was actually correct. I got into the Archives with Klyten and we reconstructed a basic outline to describe the person who was in the room with Errat: it was a ler female, probably adolescent, although there are conflicting indications. Also, the traces were distorted by a very high reading for adrenaline fractions and residuals, and another family of residual fractions that doesn't equate to anything. Whoever was in there was very tense, more or less permanently. And we also checked with Control. The traces we found, the unknown ones, are the same as the unidentified female in the crowd-scans."

"Good God, man! What else could you get on whoever it is?"

"Very little else, Chairman. But at least we were able to make that correlation. Of course we checked out all the inhabitants of the building very carefully. Nothing. And of course no one could recall any ler being in the neighborhood for any period. Never had seen one. But female, allegedly from Inspection Bureau, had been there, but was no longer. The name she used is unimportant; it didn't check anywhere. The stress-monitors in the area were tripped, but they had been that way for years—nobody had checked them, so it would seem. I am sad to say we lost the trail there."

"Nothing? No trace, no track, no description?"

"Nothing that would do us any good. We think that whoever she was, she was also using multiple identities and disguises; it is a ler, all right, but she knows procedures well and moves with impunity."

"A sobering thought, Eykor. The other one, the one we caught, also moved freely among us for years. I wonder how many others are doing the same."

"Plattsman is running a close-order check of all the stress-monitor reports now. Of necessity this degrades current operations, but we have to know."

"Agreed. That we must. And how about travel permits?"

"All accounted for. Nothing this side of the reservation. There is another thing about this . . . we don't know the motive for Errat's murder. We think he was silenced. His usefulness was done. He seemed to think he was more important than he was; but he was just a screening pawn, and when his part was over, he was dispensed with."

"Ugh. Cold-blooded, that one. Well, I agree, this largely negates the earlier possibility that he could have been a free agent. He was tied to someone. But who, and for what purpose? There is someone inside. . . ."

"Yes. The operation was professional. Every person either knew nothing and dead-ended there, or was eliminated. We think Errat seriously underestimated his contact. Why, with his noted experience in wet-work, we can't tell."

"That is odd."

"He was known to be violently anti-ler and we do not believe he would have willingly allied himself with them. But this raises more questions, too; what kind of group or organ of the ler would wish such an incident precipitated? Or, perhaps, what was intended to happen failed. That was why they got Errat."

"This sounds worse and worse. Will we ever get to the bottom of it?"

"Perhaps we can find one answer, Chairman. Recall the original incident? Well, we wouldn't have caught her, but for the fact that the patrols in that area had been put on increased alert. Why were they? Who put them on it? Their chief got a call purporting to be from Security Central, but there are no records of the call anywhere, and nobody can make any connection at all. We think the call was made by Errat; we have tentative vocal identification with the man who received the call. Again, how would he know to do that? He must have been instructed to. But why?"

"Eykor, have you considered the possibility that this entire sequence of events has nothing to do per se with us? That would explain why it seems to go nowhere. We are seeing it from the wrong angle, as it were."

"I thought that, too . . . but why go to all the trouble, Chairman? We checked with Klyten. The ler can have a feud any time they want. They have no prohibition against murder. Only against certain kinds of weapons."

"Someone wants a vendetta, but doesn't want it known."

"May be that, Chairman. But I have something more, which you should also integrate."

"More? By all means go on."

"The instruments the girl destroyed. We persuaded Research Section to try to rebuild them. They were not able on short notice to reconstruct the originals, but they did something almost as good: they built up replicas. Breadboard jobs, to be sure, but they work. They are crude and delicate and they lack the fine discrimination of the originals, but they tell an interesting story. We tested them out and used them in the gliders."

"What did you get?"

"It's all in the report and the attachments. But here's what is significant: we uncovered a most singular feature." Eykor turned from the chairman to the pile of papers and leafed through them until he located a large semitransparency covered with contour lines. This he displayed to Parleau. "This is the averaged collation from all the runs we made. It depicts the field strength of gravity in the general area of the reservation. And here," he said, withdrawing another sheet of similar size from the pile, "is a carto of the reservation, in the same scale, for comparison; what we should expect to see is a general correlation and co-location of regions of higher density of gravitational strength with areas of hills, ridgelines, and the like. And low-density areas with depressions, valleys."

Parleau looked at the unlabeled masses of contour lines. He said, "I see . . . but what am I supposed to see?"

"The expected correlation is true everywhere on the reservation grounds and surrounding area, except for this one unique area, here." He pointed out a location on the density chart. "In the northwest we found an area that shows a definite negative correlation."

"You are certain it was not instrument error."

"Absolutely. That is why it took so long, so many days, to get this to you. We wanted it to be complete. There were some anomalies, but they occur everywhere, and they shift in time and location, as one would expect in transient malfunctions. But not this place. This one shows perfectly circular every time. And when we tried the Magnetic Anomaly Detector, we got the same thing, in exactly the same place; a circular area of greatly reduced field strength."

"You are certain there is no doubt of these readings?"

"Absolutely none. It's all there in the report. A fine piece of work by the junior Security men, I must say."

"What do you attribute this to?"

"Unknown. We sent the phenomenological description around, but nobody could come up with any probable cause. We thought a hollowed-out cavern, but the readings we have are much too deep for that, on the gravity scans, and a cave would hardly affect the magnetic field at all; if it did, it would be very slight. Also, a cave would have to have an entry, of which photo recon did not find any trace whatsoever. In other words, simple absence of matter isn't enough."

Eykor wasn't finished. He turned again and withdrew still another chart from the pile, which was now becoming scattered and untidy. "There's some more, here. This chart, on the same scale as the other two, is a replica of a sociological chart that was prepared for Vance and Klyten, twenty years ago. What it shows is the location of each family group and elder commune, and their interconnections. Like a market diagram of a primitive society. The colors, if you study it for a while, reveal a certain hierarchy. Now, up to the present, this has lain in the files, collecting dust, an academic curio, nothing more. But transposed in the proper scale, and overlaid on the other charts we already have . . ."

Eykor spread the charts out, and aligned them according to little tick-marks on the sides, so that they were in exact relationship to one another. He said, pointing with his free hand, "Now here is the mountain where we located the anomaly; here, in this ridgeline running north-eastward from the river. And here, on the north side, is the home of the Second-player family group, while just opposite, on the south of the ridge, is the home of the First-players. Now east and north—and here, again in the north—is the elder commune, Dragonfly Lodge, and opposite that on the south is the house of the ruling dynasty, the Revens or judges. The locations form a perfect square, with the anomaly at its exact center. The locations are also at the four major points of the compass with regard to the anomaly. We had them run a Fourier analysis of this last chart, using the most elaborate program we could devise, plus trained recon interpreters, and we can say that nowhere else does a configuration like this exist in regard to any feature, natural or otherwise. All the rest are either randomly placed, or located in relation to obvious economic nodes and crossings. There is only one interpretation: that those four groups have access to the anomaly!"

Parleau stood back from the desk, scratching his chin, staring down at the charts. "Plausible, plausible, indeed."

"We cannot dismiss this as not being a weapon. It is assuredly not a natural object; natural objects are neither massless, nor do they usually depress a magnetic field."

Parleau mused, "Agreed. We can't assume that it's neutral or benign. . . . It has been there for some time, obviously; and were it for the general welfare, I should imagine they would not have hidden it so well. And of course, we see that those groups have been mixed up with it from the beginning."

Eykor continued, "Yes. And this at last explains why the girl, a First-player by family, chose to lose her mind rather than take the chance she might reveal even an innocent association that could lead eventually to this. But we still don't know why she did it; I mean, it's stupid, after all; it just called our attention to it."

"Maybe she was preventing an ongoing project from seeing that by accident."

"We thought of it; and checked the records. There was no such project in view. The instruments would have lain there another thousand years for all I know."

"Come on! Are you certain, Eykor?"

"Absolutely, Chairman. Control ran their collator through it; Research Center also. There was *no plan* to use the instruments in any manner."

"Then she did her work for nothing. Or did she? Is this like the Errat thing, where we can't see the true intent because it isn't aimed at us? But if we hadn't caught her, we'd never have made the connection."

"We might have thought to make up breadboards and use them."

"But against whom? We'd have the whole world as suspect, then."

"Chairman, I believe we agree that Errat was working for someone, on instructions. Someone he didn't know. He called the patrol out, and she was captured . . . what if she was supposed to be captured?"

"God, you're a worse speculator than Plattsman. What would be the purpose of that?"

"I can think of innumerable possibilities. It's expensive, but you've heard of agents provocateurs. We use them. This could be the same thing, only with an event as bait. To get us to do something precipitately. Also, Errat was at the root of the incident in which the girl was wounded or killed."

"Aha! The first time wasn't enough, so they trailed the bait in front of us again, eh?"

"Something like that . . . they seem to be trying to provoke a first strike. But people who invite first strikes usually do so secure in the knowledge that they can weather it and use something worse in return. They want justification to use it. What? Whatever is located in the anomaly!"

"Hm. An exercise in subtle moralities. . . . But all this does not match well with their high regard for life, nor with their ideals of lack of interaction with us."

"Someone wasn't nonviolent with Errat. Someone precipitated some very un-nonviolent behavior to the girl, probably intended. There's no high regard for life, ours or theirs, in that. But they're uninvolved, I should say . . . so uninvolved they don't care how they get our attention."

"There is something in what you say. . . . Does Klyten know these conclusions?"

"No. He saw the questions we had, not the end result."

Parleau depressed a call-button and requested that the administrator call on Mandor Klyten. After a short wait, for Klyten spent considerable time in that very building, and happened to be in, the academician appeared in Parleau's office, arriving slightly flushed. Parleau quickly made a résumé of the case so far as Eykor had presented it, summarizing their opinions. Then he asked, "We've gone so far, but we lack a certain expertise to analyze intentions. I'd like to hear your view of these developments."

Klyten hesitated, looking about randomly, as if trying to build an image in his mind's eye to match that which he had heard. He shook his head.

"I agree completely with Eykor that something is there and that it can't be natural . . . but we can't say what it is, based solely upon what it is *not*. We can prove negatives, until doomsday and we'd still be no closer to it than when we started; the range of negatives is infinite. But I'm hesitant to leap to the conclusion that it is a weapon, just because it isn't natural. They do in fact have an elaborate ethical system that does invite the aggressor to make the first move, and their culture has elaborate structures built into it to reduce and displace the already low level of aggression which is in them. Yet, they know as well as we the kind of things we can bring to bear on them. We still have the old nuclear warheads stashed away, and we have no shortage of people, too. Hell, we could send a million-man army in there, each man armed with a switch, for that matter. And I don't understand the kind of logic that would invite that kind of risk at all. That's too much. So I'll say this: if there is a weapon involved, that's not all it is."

"Not only a weapon . . ." Parleau mused, "then a principle, an invention . . . an artifact, a thing which could have many uses. What might be some of the possibilities?"

"Damnation! Wide open, there. Be imaginative. People don't hide things, or their containers, for generations, unless the thing is very special, a breakthrough in concept. So we can disregard little piddling things like a new aircraft, a new gun-sight, a more efficient power source. They do that stuff in the Institute every day and don't care who knows it. Think wildly: matter transmission. A faster-than-light drive-system. Force Fields. Hell's bells, why not a time machine? Who knows?"

"So . . . it's an *it*, truly. Do we want it?"

"Want it? Chairman, of course we want it! We want it all, as the saying goes, and the horse it came on. The question is—can we use it and will it do us any good?"

"Hmph. We get it and then we worry about that."

"No, no. All technology is not an unlimited blessing. Everything has consequences. We pick for the consequence we want, and to hell with the rest; we'll adjust after the fact. But we usually don't stop to ask if the particular consequence we are seeking is even major or minor, and what are *all* the others. For drugs, we do this, and take risks accordingly, giving a man a poison for the chance it will cure before it kills. Consider the bad old days, when we had the old sovereign nations. Some were well-off, some were very badly off. So one chooses, say, to spend money on the ability to build a nuclear weapon, when one should be investing in the most carefully structured management system. Now one has a bomb. Not only does this piss away money for nothing, but it prevents its being spent on something useful. And not only that; now the influence of it allows this state to influence the spread of its incompetence into neighboring areas, eventually blighting the entire region. There was exactly such a case. The entire area just collapsed, taking with it into oblivion a billion lives, half a dozen cultures, and about ten major languages. There's a consequence we don't want," Klyten said.

"It's not the technology—it's the use they put it to," Parleau said.

"Yes. But in their case at least they knew what they were buying. We don't even know that. We might even have to invent a need for it. Remember lasers? History? They invented them, and then worked like dogs to find a use for them. Or noble-gas chemistry; the same. There wasn't any use for stuff like xenon tetrafluoride; still isn't. It could be very dangerous for us even to try to use it."

"We've been dealing with them through the Institute for three hundred years, applying Institute solutions to just about everything that's come along. So far it's helped us greatly—helped us survive, as a fact."

"That's true, Chairman. But you miss one facet of this relationship: the Institute always operates on the basis of strict question-and-answer. Problem-solution thinking. Very specific."

"Explain, please."

"They don't accept a problem to work on unless we ask the question."

"What's so difficult about that?"

"The Institute does not do open-ended research for any group of humans on the planet, or anyone else, for that matter. The Institute works only on conceptual problems that have cleared the Priorities Board; limited stuff, that's all. Ask the question first. Like Columbus—he would ask, 'Which way to America?' They would answer, 'We'll tell you where it is.' But he didn't know it existed. Now he says, 'Is there an America?' and they tell him that it isn't part of the Indies. Not the right question. Now in some of the communes they do pure research, you know, really open-ended speculation, just to see where those roots lead. But the by-products of that are never made available, even for their own people. As for us, those people won't even pass the time of day with us."

Parleau exclaimed, "Well, then, we've been fooled the whole time!"

"No, no, I couldn't say that; they have applied themselves down there, and they've done good work. They produce solutions, tools, programs, plans, and it has always been a high-quality, first-class product. Why, the kind of loosely federated planetary government we have today was invented there. I can name a lot of other things we take for granted, too. Shifter Society is another. They have always given their best."

Parleau was following another track, and did not pursue the values of the Institute, but soundlessly shifted gears into something else that was bothering him. "You say the elders do some pure research?"

"Some elders; some communes. The ones that do so tend to specialize in one degree or another. One, for example, does genetics, another natural science, another higher mathematics. And of course certain Braids prefer to wind up in certain lodges that are somewhat restricted, while other lodges are no more than what they seem to be—simple communes, resembling the monastic communities of our own history. There is even, so I hear, an analog of the Trappists: silence, meditation, devotion, poverty, humility. Their product is an illuminated devotional text; that, and paintings. From what I have seen, they seem fond of the Dutch Panoramists—Holbein, Bosch, those."

"Do you know Dragonfly Lodge?"

"Only slightly, mostly by reputation. They do Game work; and they are by far the most secretive. . . . Oh, I see. Yes, of course. The girl was a Player."

"Klyten, you haven't seen the half of it; I should well agree they are secretive, since it appears that they have something to hide. Eykor has associated that lodge with the Players Braids and the ruling Braid as well, and tied that to the original incident with the girl. And, in addition, an unusual anomaly that ties in also . . . and most probably to Errat."

Klyten, taken somewhat aback, maintained his composure. When Parleau had summarized before, he had done so lightly, without attributing significances. Now it all came together. He replied, noncommittally, "I know them by reputation only, so to speak."

Eykor saw his opportunity to press a point. He asked, pointedly, "Is it true that when they turn the house over to the next generation, the ex-parents then move into various elder lodges?"

Klyten answered absently, "Well, that's not strictly true. Just generally. Some go off alone, others . . ."

"But most go to the lodges?"

"Yes, you could say that, but . . ."

"And do Braids go where they please, or are there trends and standing associations?"

"Oh, definitely, trends and associations. Braids tend to be associated with lodges as a matter of tradition. Not exactly on a one-for-one basis, you understand. There is some mixing. Here you must understand that they don't ever see choice as an Aristotelian dilemma of two options; I should use the word *quadrilemma*, if anything. They would call such a choice situation the consideration of the Fire Path, the Air Path, the Earth Path, the Water Path. Tradition and habit and precedent also play their parts; what one is expected to do by one's peers, for instance. . . ."

Eykor interrupted the dissertation. "For instance, where do members of the Player Braids go when they reach elder status?"

Klyten knew he was being led, but he seemed powerless to stop it. "Wait a moment, there, let me think. I study the ler, not emulate their mental processes, particularly the one of total recall. . . . It would seem that I've seen something on that; yes, of course. They go to Dragonfly Lodge. Yes, I recall it now. They have the highest correlation of any occupational group with an elder lodge."

Parleau asked, "Correlation?"

"Yes. That's where I saw it. A sociological report written some years ago. The Perklarens have a correlation with Dragonfly Lodge of something near ninety-five percent. The Terklarens are even higher; in some periods they have maintained one hundred percent for several generations running. The next association with that lodge was much lower, less than fifty percent, and all the other elder lodges show even lower correlations, down in the twenties, usually."

"Who else joins Dragonfly Lodge?" asked Parleau.

"Only one other Braid: the Revens. Almost all the insiblings, none of the outsiblings. Or the afterparents. Yes, now that I recall it, I wondered about it at the time, that association of the Revens with Dragonfly. I could see no purpose in it. . . ."

Parleau said quietly, glancing at Eykor, "Then it would be reasonably accurate to aver that, for the most part, Dragonfly Lodge is composed in the main of ex-Players and ex-judges."

"I believe that is accurate. There are some scattered few other individuals, but they are rare . . . something less than five percent of membership. It's a restricted lodge."

"Restricted? How so?"

"There are four kinds of lodges: open, closed, male, female. The male and female lodges are obvious in their member selection; they recruit. The open lodges take in anyone. They welcome all. Closed lodges take in only those they want; word gets around, and few apply who are not wanted."

"Four elementals, again?"

"Exactly. Opens are Water aspect. Male and female are, respectively, Air and Earth aspects. The closed lodges are Fire aspect."

"What does Fire aspect connote to you?"

"Decision, order, organization, will, discipline. Willpower, planning, that sort of thing."

Parleau asked, following another tangent, "And in what aspect does the root *revh-* mean 'judge'?"

"Fire."

Eykor began pacing back and forth rapidly, saying, "We've got it now, for sure."

Parleau asked, "What do we have? We have little more than what we had from the beginning. Just putting it together better, confirming the connections. We still don't know what the artifact does."

"But, Chairman, we can now confirm that this is no yesterday's plot; it's been going on for generations! Those Braids got together, they made a perfect disguise and refuge, an elder lodge, and set up . . ."

Klyten interrupted, "No, no. Not that way! You've got it ass-backwards. The Braids didn't invent the lodges; it was the other way: the lodges invented the Braids!"

Parleau asked, "What?"

Klyten continued, "That's basic ler history, Chairman. I hadn't brought it up before because I assumed that it was common knowledge. The institution of the lodges predates the first generation of the earliest Braids by about a hundred years."

"Who made the decisions, then? Who was boss?"

"Of the organized lodges in existence today, less than a third can trace their roots to the pre-Braid, pre-reservation period. At first they were mixed all over with us. At that time, I believe the DNA conversions were still going on. The organization now known as Dragonfly Lodge was simply the best-organized group of them. They set the whole thing in motion."

"You say, 'now known as.' What were they then?"

"Hm. I believe they were then working on large-scale synthesis of all that was known in certain areas, you know, catching up and integrating. Mathematics, space flight, power-source technology, nuclear engineering, quantum mechanics. They especially revere Max Planck."

"Planck?"

"Planck, Dirac, Einstein, Fermi. A few others. Also Von Neumann, Conway. They were early games theorists."

Parleau withdrew a little, as if he were studying some deep interior panorama. At last he said, "I had a suspicion about this, always did, about those little bastards. Especially after Eykor showed me the maps and cartos of the area of the anomaly. We always feared that they would turn around on us and produce an advanced human type completely off the scale as far as mind and ability went. And that's what I almost thought it might have been. But now, I think we can narrow it down more than that, for they would fear that more than we would. So,

Eykor, I want Plan Two-twelve implemented quietly, no fuss. As soon as we can get it going gracefully."

Eykor was not prepared for what he had won. "Implement it, Chairman?"

"Yes, implement it. Mobilize the assault forces and as soon as we reach readiness phase, go in there and take that hill and whatever is in it. It cannot be ready to use, or else they would already be using it, on us, doubtless. Never mind the occupation of the reservation, that part of the plan. We don't need the whole thing, just that hill. Get us there, and in."

"Chairman, it'll be hard to get it started. It's Twelvemonth, near New Year's. A lot of the troops we could call up are off on otpusk*."

"Well, get them back as best you can and get to it. Don't wait for me, build it up to readiness and go on in. And have your people ready for anything. Anything. They would be fools not to try to defend it, perhaps destroy it. Let's have no more of the business of the TacTeam that went after the girl. They must be ruthless and grab, and shoot. After we get it, we won't need to make apologies for what we did, to them, or to anyone else."

Eykor was still a little behind Parleau. He asked, "But what's in the mountain, Chairman?" He now saw something growing in Parleau's expression, something whose traces had always been there, but which had been subtle, camouflaged, blended, hidden. But with the ultimate before him, in his mind's eye, Parleau was matching those ultimates with some ultimates of his own. He answered Eykor, smiling once again, satisfied that he now knew all he needed to know: "It is either the damndest weapon you ever saw, the key to supreme power, or it's a starship. Nothing else would be worth so much trouble to them. Perhaps both. Either way, it has power. And whatever people say, we were here first, it's our planet. And I think the time has come to terminate the reservation, the Institute, and all the rubbish that goes with it. Their useful life is over, and they've delivered it. Klyten, could you operate what they find in that cavern?"

"You jest, Chairman. Of course I couldn't. And I doubt seriously that if what you say is true, we'd find anyone to operate it, either. Willingly."

"We'll get someone, Klyten. Be assured of that. We will find an operator, one way or another."

Klyten looked away, and pretended to become interested in the un-

---

* Otpusk. A Russianism that had replaced such terms as furlough, leave, vacation.

tidy pile of documentation brought in by Eykor, turning and hiding his face so that neither Eykor nor Parleau, now earnestly engaged in a discussion of plans, programs, options, could see him clearly and read on his face what was thereon plain. He saw Parleau more clearly than usual, now that Parleau thought he knew what was hidden in the anomaly in the hill. He had always kept his vice in check, playing the system and abiding by its rules, but with even the hopeful hint of raw power close to his hands, he was now throwing off all restraint and betting everything on what he thought he could capture and use. This last made Klyten apprehensive; for while his loyalties were not in question, he too had followed the argument from its inception with the capture of the girl. And from his own knowledge of the ler he felt the leading edge of fear: for if there was anything at all to the conjectures of the chairman, there would be defense for it, even for probing directly at it. And Klyten could not say with assurance that his own people had the resources to pay that price, and all its unforeseen billings. Best to have let this all alone, yet none of them could stop the procedure that was gaining momentum here, leading them here, to this choice-point, this nexus, with all the consequences it could have. They didn't even see them. They didn't even know such things existed. And of course he could see that they were in the act of rendering his own position obsolete; he would end his days in Inventory Management, yet.

It was in that state of mind that he caught a fragment of Parleau's speech, not said in anger, or even excitement, but calmly, as if one would ask an associate to pick up some article of commerce for him. Parleau said, ". . . And while you're at it, pick up that Vance and bring him up here. He's had far too close an association with those people. His hour's passed."

NINETEEN

The Times we know are pregnant with the seeds
of Change, that mighty idol of the race
of youth, which seeks in each and every place
to lend new hope to oft-recurring deeds;
we say, the future holds our dearest needs,
but Present holds for us the barest trace
of those who were, with sometime-tortured grace,
the builders of our world, who built with deeds.

But now—they've come and gone, and what they made
now fades before our very eyes; and when
it's gone, we'll sing of this—our Golden Age,
forgetting that each age is purest Jade,
while Time, that Eiron to the hearts of men,
will smile at us, and turn another page.
—Time the Eiron, 1964

THERE WERE FOUR: Fellirian, Morlenden, Krisshantem, and Mevlannen, all alike now standing on the northern slope of Grozgor, the Mountain of Madness. So it had been, that in the last clear light by which to see, they had reached the end of the narrow pathing under the trees, among the weathered rocks of a dry streambed, and now they stood waiting, listening. Their directions would take them only so far and no farther. They listened for what they might have expected to hear; perhaps the sound of muffled machinery from that which was inside the mountain. But there was nothing; no sign, no presence, no trace. The mountain was silent. Far to the west, near the horizon, the sky was red, while higher up, it was the color of winter, a pale aqua. Overhead it was a hard ultramarine. The shortest day, Winter Solstice; it was a holiday in the calendar of the New People, and they would now all have been home in the *yos*, partying and cooking, singing and drinking homemade beer, while in the yard, the heavy baking oven would have contained a large goose, stuffed with a bread-and-sage pudding. The children would have been into everything, Peth fidgeting to get away to the woods and her latest boy, winter or not. . . . Solsticeday was older than the ler.

They stood in the cold, shuffling about nervously, cold and acutely uncomfortable. Here was Grozgor, and here came the elders of the house of Dragonfly, as it was said, "to restore their flagging vision." For them, a holy place. For the rest, a place of unknown damnations. Morlenden wondered about the wisdom of coming here, now, when back in the security of their own *yos*, it had seemed straightforward and easy: they would come here and ask for judgment of the Reven. Now . . .

Fellirian shyly asked Mevlannen, "Have you ever been inside it?"

She answered, "Many times. But long ago, to be sure. Much will have changed since then. They will be finishing what they have of it."

Fellirian touched the girl's arm lightly. "Sh, now. Someone comes."

They looked in the direction Fellirian had turned; there, in the weak light, was one where none had been before, a pale, still figure, in the place where the dry wash had deeply undercut the banks. The figure, dressed in a simple, light overshirt without decoration or herald, seemed to ignore the cold, which had become intense. They could see that it was probably parent phase, but they could not make out enough of the face under the raised hood to tell who it was.

The figure came a little closer, hesitating, then speaking softly, gravely, as if in reverence of the place in which he stood. "I am Pellandrey Reven. What will you require here?"

Fellirian felt rooted to the cold, stony ground. She said, "Some who have come to seek justice: Fellirian, whom you know, and Morlenden, of the Derens. Also Krisshantem, one who has none to sponsor him, and Mevlannen Srith Perklaren. Those also are known to you."

Pellandrey stepped closer, saying, "Yes, I see. Forgive me for not recognizing you. I came here from bright light." Pellandrey was slightly built, almost thin, with fine, smooth, classical features on a long, well-defined face. Still, with an inner calm, Morlenden had never seen before. Pellandrey added, "Are you well, all of you?"

Fellirian answered quietly, "We are well."

Pellandrey said, "You speak of justice?"

"Yes. And of a message which Morlenden must bear to Sanjirmil. She is in this place?"

The answer was guarded, cautious. "She is here."

Morlenden said, "And we must speak of things within the mountain, and of things between exemplars of your Game."

"Is that the issue of judgment?"

"No, there are others."

"So, then. I, Pellandrey, am your servant and your guide here." He seemed to sense a measure of how much they knew, and it did not seem to bother him greatly. "But inside?" He continued, "Ah, now, there is a thing . . . you understand that it is not permitted to speak out in the world of that which is within Grozgor? If it is that you are knowledgeable and have kept the faith, then you may enter within and become illuminated in truth. And if not, then I cannot permit you to leave."

Morlenden answered, "There is much that we do not know, but of what we know we have spoken to no one."

It was dark now, dark enough so that they could not make out the features of the face of Pellandrey, but they could sense movement, a gesture—a smile? Morlenden thought not; such a face as one that went with the words would not smile . . . and if it did, it would be a smile he did not wish to see. The Reven said, "Who was told? By whom?"

Morlenden said, "Mostly, by Mevlannen. Much I have suspected from what was told to me by others. I have spoken of these things only with Fellirian; there are few secrets between us. Only that which we each did during the *vayyon* remains private. Krisshantem does not know, save what he has assayed on his own. And no one else."

"Only the *vayyon*, eh? A good thing, that. It is the only secret an insibling should have. And this other, it is almost the same, the kind one should keep above all. So it must be; you will see another sunrise." They all felt a withdrawing, a fading of an icy regard. Pellandrey turned from them, saying, "Follow me." He assumed obedience without comment. As the High Reven, the Arbitrator of the People, he had but one commandment: preserve the people. He completed the motion and began walking back up the streambed, never looking back, or even seeming to notice them. The four who waited followed.

The entrance, if that was truly what it was, appeared to be a simple cleft in the rock face, set in an odd little corner where at some time in the past the intermittent stream had undercut the rock in its passage down the mountain. It was not apparent as an opening into anything conceivable from any angle, appearing only as some blind pocket whose deepest corners were filled with shadows, even in the brightness of day.

Here, Pellandrey stopped and again turned to them. He said, "There is not time for proper instruction in the form of the motions, so perform as best you are able according to your lights. Watch the motions I make and perform them exactly the same. Otherwise there is danger. Do you understand? Let Mevlannen go first; she knows. There is an interface at this point between two universes, and great energies are involved. Do this seriously. On your own. No one can do it for you."

He turned back to the cleft in the rock, and stood quietly, facing the darkness. Taking a deep breath, and holding it, he then raised his arms to the side, as if for balance, then bringing them around to the front, as if he were intending to dive into a pool of water. Then he stepped off, a half-stride, half-dance, two steps, and made a short, easy jump, as if leaping gracefully over some unseen obstacle. He moved straight ahead, but as his figure merged with the darkness of the shadowed cleft, it seemed as if he had somehow turned a corner, for they could no longer see him, or even sense his presence. It was as if Pellandrey had never been. No sound accompanied this act, and no sense whatsoever of anything having happened at all. But Pellandrey was gone.

Mevlannen stepped forward, moved to the place where Pellandrey had stood. She looked back once, nodding, adding in a voice that was now very small, "Yes, this is the way of it." She made the motions, took the two steps, and, just as Pellandrey had before her, vanished as soon as her shape merged with the cleft in the rock face.

Morlenden, Fellirian, and Krisshantem looked at one another tentatively, unbelieving. Krisshantem shrugged. "One must believe," he said, and without further words, went to the place, faced the rock, made the motions. And was not there.

Fellirian looked closely at the place, as if not believing her eyes. She slid closer to the cleft, tried to peer inside. She saw nothing. A darkness, an emptiness within a shadow. She listened, cocking her head; there was no sound. In its place there was a stuffy deadness, as if something were absorbing sound. No. No one was there. It was absurd. She shook her head, once, and then went to the place from which the others had already started. From there, she too took the deep breath, made the motions, took the two steps and the little leaping glide, and went straight into the corner that one could not see. There was silence. Fellirian was not there anymore.

Morlenden listened. There was nothing but the silences of the rocks, the out-of-doors. There was no wind in the bare trees over his head. Now he, too, walked to the cleft, peered inside. He thought he could make out the end of it. It was shallow, after all, not a cave. But when he tried to focus on the end he thought was there, his eyes refused to form an image. Too dark, he thought. Although it didn't feel quite like darkness, absence of light, something below a threshold. There was something else. Something he could not see. He shrugged, straightened, looked all around himself, as if for the last time: at the streambed, the mountain, the sky, the trees. Then he, too, went to the place, made the motions—the indrawn breath, the arms, the steps, the leap; he expected to land in a dark cave and stub his toe, but as he left the ground and the darkness met him, he felt an instant of weightless vertigo, a picoinstant of formless churning chaos and blinding energy, a roaring in his ears of disorganized, torn sound, a brightness and a body-wrenching that made his stomach churn. And he was standing.

Morlenden had shut his eyes at the lights, as if from reflex. Now he opened them. He was in a plain, dim chamber, apparently brown in color. The light came from every place, no place. There was no opening anywhere: it was a perfect cube. Sealed. The others were waiting for him. The chamber gave back no sound whatsoever; the silence was the deepest he had ever heard. Yet there was, under the stillness, some subliminal perception of energy, tremendous energies, carefully balanced and held in check. He said, "Where are we?"

Pellandrey said, reluctantly, as if he did not wish to, "No place. Keep as still as you can and make no attempt to touch the walls. Watch me and do as I do again. This is the difficult part; yet, if you make the transition successfully, you will be in the Ship. Feel the resistance and pass through it into reality again. Now attend!"

Pellandrey moved to the exact center of the chamber, stood quietly. With a minimum of preparatory actions, he suddenly jumped straight up; about at the exact spatial center of the cube, he vanished. Silently. Morlenden had tried to see exactly what had happened to him, but it eluded him conceptually; it seemed that the figure *receded*, too fast to follow, yet stayed where it was.

Now Mevlannen followed, now Krisshantem, now Fellirian; all moved, one by one, to the center, leaped upward, vanished. Morlenden stood alone. He looked carefully about the small, bare chamber. There was little enough to see. There was air, but it seemed stale, like cave air. The sound was dead. He had to listen carefully to hear himself breathe. He looked more closely at the walls, which were no more than a bodylength away. He could easily step forward and touch them. He approached the nearer wall, looked closely, tried to find a point on it, focus on it. He could not. What he thought was surface was only an illusion of a surface; when he tried to see it directly, he felt disoriented instead. He was unable to define the depth of what he saw. There was no reference point upon which to focus. Morlenden strained, again trying to force an order onto it. And at the furthest extreme of his efforts, he sensed, rather than saw, motion, perhaps the suggestion of motion; a slow boiling or churning, immensely powerful, a Brownian motion that concealed a subtle sense of underlying order beneath the random movements. He looked down at the floor; there, he now saw, at the extremes of vision, the same effect as in the walls, which were all alike of a dull, rich brown that remained a surface only as long as one did not look at it too closely.

Again, he shrugged. They had had faith and made the absurd motions; he would also. From the center, Morlenden also jumped up, straight up, flexing his knees as little as possible.

His first thought was that there was something wrong with the force of gravity, because instead of slowing down as he rose, somehow he was accelerating, and the chamber faded, and in its place there was nothing, no sensation of anything. Where he was, was an imaginary number, a software program with nothing to manipulate, pure abstract process. He hung sensationless, divorced even from feedback from his own body. He did not know if he was breathing or not. He tried to move, but felt nothing. He tried imagining that he moved. He felt a resistance. It gave him an eerie feeling in the pit of his mind. The more he imagined, the more concrete feeling became. Gradually, he felt an opening, but it seemed too small. He embraced it, pulled. He was moving rapidly above a plain, conveyed by forces but not in any vehicle. It was lighted from an unknown source, an absolutely flat surface, littered with shapeless lumps that were the same brownish color as the plain, the same color as the walls of the chamber. He was passing by the lumps, but there were more . . . there was a suggestion of shape to them, but he couldn't quite see it. He was moving to an abstract perspective horizon, a child's drawing, the imagination of a madman. He made an effort, the lunge of panic, trying to free himself, and the plain vanished.

Spatial orientation and normal sensation returned. He was alone in a small, bare room, but at least a room made of things he could understand, touch: it was basically metal, but was overlaid mostly with beautiful dark wooden paneling, dark wood and handwoven cloth, familiar as the product of his own people. This air had odor, temperature. It was cool, almost cold. Yes, it was chilly. He shivered. There were odors of machinery, material, distant people. The floor was reassuringly solid and in the right place. He moved from the center, to touch the walls, make sure . . . as he did, in quick succession, the rest materialized into the room, displacing air with little puffs as they materialized. Pellandrey came last. When he saw Morlenden to the side, his face took on an expression of amused consternation. Fellirian had come with her eyes tightly closed, standing in a semicrouch, a wrestling posture. She bore on her face an expression of strain, grimacing with effort.

Morlenden reached for Fellirian, touched her shoulder. She opened her eyes, looking quickly around her, straightening. There was a sense of Machine all around them, a presence of controlled, bound energy, of vital, surging power. Faint noises came now to their ears from other parts of the Ship: metallic sounds; muffled voices; something that sounded like very ordinary hammering.

Fellirian asked, "Where are we?"

Pellandrey answered, "On the Ship, of course. You will note that Morlenden arrived before us, although he was last to depart the staging chamber. That is an effect we get sometimes when we go through the gate more than one at a time. Sequence reversal. We do not understand the continuum through which we just passed very well at all. The entry was not a product of design. We would prefer the door-flap of a *yos*, to be frank. But in part, it . . . ah, happened. After we found it, we were able to modify it somewhat. Now we can control it a little, and come and go."

Morlenden said, "I saw a plain, with odd lumps scattered over it. I was moving, flying; there was no end to it."

"The plain? You saw it?"

"Indeed I did, and I did not like what I saw."

Pellandrey shook his head. "We do not know where that place is . . . attempts to explore it, examine it, more closely, have failed, mostly. Most do not experience it at all, and most who do, do not live to tell tales of it. The lumps are, we believe, the remains of those who have failed, over the years. I have been there once, and I will not speak of what I did there, nor what I learned." Here he stopped, as if recalling something distasteful. "I will not return, willingly. There is one among us who does, though."

Morlenden asked, "Who?" But he thought he would know the answer.

Pellandrey said, "Sanjirmil." He would say no more, not of her. He added, "You are lucky to have seen it and lived."

He turned now, and brushed aside an ordinary doorway curtain, as if doing no more than escorting visitors into a *yos* somewhere, motioning them to follow him along a dim hallway that was revealed. "Come along," he said. "We'll go now into the Prime Sensorium; there we may speak of what you will."

He set off along the corridor, making no further remarks. The four followed, equally silently, struck dumb by the contrast between the unreality of the entry and the plain homeliness of the interior furnishings. They moved steadily through a maze; all save Mevlannen. She knew where she was.

They came to an intersecting corridor, turned into it, and immediately began walking down a steep incline. Other corridors ran into it from both sides, leading off into other sections of the Ship. From one they heard the hammering noises they had heard earlier. There was also the odor of sawdust, of iron.

They switched corridors many times, sometimes walking on the level, sometimes down inclines. Some passages were narrow, connecting hallways; others were broad thoroughfares. No section was straight for long, but would jog off, and then back again. Fellirian followed politely, but after a long time of this she could not contain her curiosity any longer, and asked, "And where are the engines, the fuel, the bunkers?"

"None," answered Pellandrey. "This is not a powered ship, a fueled ship, but the analog of a sailing ship; we only take enough power to run life-support, operate the synthesizer. That power comes from batteries which are energized by the flux around the Ship." He added, as an afterthought, "The problem is not that we don't have enough, but that we have too much."

"Then what do you do with it?"

"It must be used within the system from which it was derived; we have been using the excess to regularize the orbit of Pluto, the outermost. It is small in mass as planetary bodies go, but it is sufficient. Understand we do not do anything radical to it. And what we do is not very obvious. Mevlannen can tell you that, I believe."

Mevlannen agreed. "For a year I watched, compared, made calculations; the change we have put into it will not be sensible enough to read for thirty years."

Morlenden started to speak, but the moment passed, and Pellandrey turned again to lead them through the maze of corridors. They went through another series of junctions, nodes, at last a dim nexus of five passages. Pellandrey stopped before a large, metal hatch set into the bulkhead, secured with threaded T-handles about the perimeter. There was no legend on the hatch, but in a place of curtains and easily sliding panels, such a doorway could only have one meaning: *Keep out*. Pellandrey bent and began to unfasten the handles, methodically, one at a time. When he finished, he turned back to them, hand on the hatch, poised to push it inward.

Mevlannen said, "I cannot pass within, if Sanjirmil is now there."

Pellandrey asked, "And why so?"

"We are enemies; long ago we made a pact. I thought that it would not come to a meeting again, so I agreed. Outside, in the forest, alone, one on one, I would take my chances, but here, in the seat of her power, I would fear. I cannot enter; I will be attacked on sight."

"Just so. She is there. But you came for a judgment, so you must enter, else we hear and decide in the place where we stand. To judge is most serious; would you have us settle the matter like conspirators behind the warehouse, skulkers in the alley?"

Morlenden said, "I ask that it be here, if Mevlannen so wishes. I am her sponsor in any event—it is my argument."

Pellandrey shrugged. "Very well. Speak."

Morlenden did not waste time with formalities, saying, "You know the history of the Perklarens, so we need not recite it; you also know whence came Krisshantem, here, and what his course had been, and your own part in it. Thus, and thus. These two are of suitable age, and both possess valuable knowledge that must not perish. I ask that they be declared *shartoorh* here and designated to weave upon maturity in their own Braid."

Pellandrey turned a cold, steady gaze on Morlenden. "You already know too much, Morlenden Deren. And what will be their role? What will they do?"

Morlenden pressed on, not turning at all from what he came for. "I confess that my original intent had been to resurrect the thrust of the course Maellenkleth had been on, but I see now that such would be folly. Therefore I ask that they be called Skazen, lore-masters, those who know and those who remember. Too long have we left that function to elders who will answer to none."

Pellandrey turned a little, avoiding them all with his expressionless eyes. He seemed to look into a distance, weighing imponderables. After a time, he said, "There is much consequence to this. I see, I know; ripples in time across the centuries; there will be the usual objections."

"It is against just such that I strive here, Pellandrey Reven. These two have earned what I ask."

"I know, I know; just as had Maellenkleth. Even as I steered her for my own reasons, I recited arguments to myself upon why I could not do what she asked in the end. And had it come to a Dirklaren Braid . . . I do not know. We cannot spend much time on would-have-been's."

"Very well. This petition, then, on its own weight."

The Reven looked now intently at both, Mevlannen and Krisshantem. He asked, "You two are known to one another? And do you agree to this?" They both nodded agreement, moving closer together instinctively.

"Whose idea was this? Let it speak now."

Morlenden said, "Mine, but only of late."

"There will be a price. Will you two agree to pay it?"

Again they nodded. Pellandrey said, "The ritual is inappropriate for the circumstances. Therefore I do exercise that right which is mine by inheritance. So be the request of Morlenden Deren, let none here forget it until the end of time."

Mevlannen and Krisshantem looked at each other with shining faces. Pellandrey added, grimly, "Do not forget the price among the rejoicing of new-lovers, as I see you have become." They turned back to him. "And my price is thus. Mevlannen, I lay a prohibition upon you for the peace of the people: you and all your descendants hereafter will be forbidden the Game, Outer and Inner. Krisshantem, you and all your descendants hereafter will make your dwelling place in the heart of the most dense habitation among us. When we build cities, there you shall go. And last I invoke a tradition, which may not be contravened, upon both of you. It has been the practice of the past that *shartoorh* do not know one another, or at the least, as little as possible. Thus henceforth you shall live separately until your fertility commences. This means one of you must leave the *yos* of the Derens. Now you know the weight of it. Decide."

Mevlannen spoke before any of them. "It will be me."

"Very well. . . . You were to give the matrix to Maellenkleth. Who has it?"

"Morlenden Deren carries the matrix to Sanjirmil."

"So, then. You two will depart from this place to the common room. Never stand before this door again."

They lingered for a moment, as if trying to think of something to say, but nothing came; and at last they turned together, and, Mevlannen leading the way, made their way into one of the ascending corridors, fading into the dimness.

Again the sound of the Ship returned to them. An odd silence, broken at intervals by distant, faint sounds of continuing construction;

faint, unintelligible voices, hammering. Pellandrey waited, until he was sure that Mevlannen and Krisshantem had passed from hearing. Then he turned back to the massive hatch, saying to those remaining, "This is Prime. You might wish to say control room, or bridge, or perhaps quarterdeck, recalling the sailing ships of old. Within here is the Inner Game. Follow me."

He ducked and stepped over the high sill into it; Morlenden and Fellirian followed. Pellandrey closed and dogged down the hatch behind them.

Morlenden and Fellirian stood quite still for a time, trying to relate what they saw to something they knew. They could see immediately that they were in a circular room, roofed by a low, broadly domed ceiling about two hundred feet across. The floor was an inverted, shallow truncated cone, descending to a central pit. They were on a wide ledge that circled the chamber.

Morlenden saw, but he could not assemble it into a meaningful picture. It was too alien. Nothing in the room related to anything he had seen before.

If Morlenden had not known what to expect, Fellirian's problem was that she knew too much. More used to human ways of doing things, she expected a control room to contain dials, screens, banks of instruments, lights, indicators, windows, portholes, levers, knobs. Considered in that light, it was an austere, bare, and enigmatic room.

Above the platform, there was only the ceiling dome, a Game display, made of some dull translucent material that did not reflect any of the light from the floor. And at odd intervals around the sloping walls of the cone leading to the pit, there were small recesses spotted here and there, each fitted with comfortable reclining chairs. Beside each were small panels, containing a few indicator lights, some empty receptacles, a button board. Steps recessed into the material of the sloping sides led to these from the pit floor. There was the actual control; there were four identical consoles, with their operators' chairs, also recliners, tilted back, so the occupants could see the ceiling at all times. The chairs were actually luxurious cradles, surrounded on both sides by massed banks of keyboards, very much like the Game control keyboards of the Outer Game except that there were many more of them, enormous curved banks of keyboard strips and panels of tiny buttons, arranged on both sides of the recliners within arm's reach, not in front or behind.

Above, the dome was dimly lit; only the central portion seemed to be active, about a fifth of its entire area. The only other lighting in the room came from small lamps over each keyboard bank, and panels in the narrow strip between domed ceiling and conical pit. The recesses were all empty; the operators' positions were filled. They did not seem to be overly exerting themselves.

The four in the pit appeared to be late adolescents by appearance, reclining in their operators' cradles, all with both hands moving steadily over the banks of keyboard controls, not hurriedly, but steadily and deliberately, touching here, gliding, pausing there, always moving on; and they never took their eyes off the ceiling for an instant, always keeping the living, changing, ceaselessly permutating display above their heads in sight. At the same time, though serious at their work, there was also a casual air to it as well, a watchful casualness, as if they were doing something easy and long-practiced. Each wore about their heads a light, lacy framework, which supported tiny earplugs and a microphone before their lips. And if the visitors on the deck above them watched very closely, they could see, from time to time, their lips moving ever so slightly; and when one spoke, the others' eyes would follow to a particular spot in the display above. The movements of their hands would change in rhythm, in scale, and somehow, something would change in the display. Neither Morlenden nor Fellirian could spot what changes took place—the Inner Game was simply too fast-moving. Morlenden found his inadvertent indoctrination as an Outer Player to be of no help at all.

One below nodded, spoke into the microphone. The others nodded, too, and it seemed that a moment of watchfulness had passed.

Morlenden whispered to Fellirian, "Yonder lies Sanjirmil. On the right hand, to the rear. I would recognize her anywhere; her hair has a dusty blue sheen that even this half-light cannot obscure."

"Indeed. And that must be her Braid, with her."

Pellandrey, overhearing them, agreed. "Yes. The Terklarens-to-be. Tundarstven, her *Toorh*, to her left; in front, Sunderlai and Leffandel, Srith and Tlanh. Both were *Thes*."

Sanjirmil's *Toorh* wore a gray homespun overshirt, plain and austere, with light woolen cloak against the chill air of the Ship. Sunderlai, a rounded, soft girl with a childish face, wore one in pale blues, shadings in shadowed snow. Leffandel wore brighter colors, with a brown cloak. Sanjirmil wore black; her overshirt was of the color of night, broken by short, vertical strokes in curvings of stark white. Her cloak was of leather, lined inside in dark gray, of a lusterless black.

Pellandrey said softly, "Morlenden, you spoke of judgment; say what you must now."

"Little more than a month ago," he began, "the Perwathwiy Srith came with an offer of gold, that we would find Maellenkleth, determining along the way what became of her. We have done so, as far as we have been able." And he began to tell what he had laboriously put together, the whole tale, how there had been enmity and rivalry between Maellenkleth and Sanjirmil, how the younger girl, disenfranchised by the onrushing weight of consequences, had been driven from the one thing she did best of all, and how Sanjirmil, a poor Player at best, had by the same consequences inherited the Inner Game. He told how Maellenkleth had planned to challenge her rival, and how an already poor relationship had deteriorated into open hostility, and how Sanjirmil had intentionally sent Maellenkleth on a fool's errand, knowing she would be captured. He told Pellandrey how Maellenkleth died, and what she told him as she did. And he spoke of other things as well, of veiled threats, of an arrow, of a creature of the forest who haunted his steps. And at last he said, "And now I am come to this place for judgment against her for all that I have said. I will stand for the truth of what I have alleged."

Pellandrey looked at the ceiling dome for a long time, saying nothing. His hands gripped the rail tightly, as he leaned his weight upon it for support.

At last he turned to Morlenden and Fellirian, saying, "We already know of the uproar over the instruments. Sanjirmil herself told us that much after her visit, with Perwathwiy, to your *yos*. So much we could verify ourselves, and so we made appropriate plans. I suppose as she knew we would."

"Then you agree that I must have this judgment?"

Pellandrey glanced wearily to the place where lay Sanjirmil, controlling the Inner Game, the Zan. "In principle, I agree, concur, all the way. But I am not free to act in this, and I cannot render judgment to you."

"Why not?"

"Because I myself am not entirely without blame in all this; and as you have accused Sanjirmil, then so must you accuse me, for much of this would have been prevented. Could have been. It is a most long story; will you stay a while to hear it?"

"We will," they said.

"Very well. In your tale, you said what Mevlannen told you, and what you had put together. So you will remember that the Ship activated on its own fifteen—a fourteen and one—years ago? Very good. What you do not know and have not known until now is what happened on that day. Now I will tell you and you will see."

"The Ship was not active then, so we only maintained a watch here, not a flying crew. But there were hours in the day when we used the display, which was completed, for the training of the novices. That it was complete should have warned us, but it did not. We kept our eyes too close to the old plan. And so on that day, there was a student at the controls, with two elders giving her additional instruction; she needed all the extra she could get, for she wasn't good at the Game at all; in fact, we were despairing of ever getting her up even to novice level. But she was a fighter, and she persisted, where others would have given up and accepted their true role. Where others *had* given up in the past history of the Game. So there was an extra session. Perwathwiy and Trethyankov were making her pretend she was flying solo, one of the emergency procedures. She had just taken the controls, was not even properly prepared to control, and the activation commenced. There was no warning, no symptom, nothing. One minute a working board seemingly connected to nothing, the next live. She, the poor girl, thought it was an exercise Perwathwiy had dreamed up, and she was determined not to fail, even though she knew that she would. She could never catch on to the way of it. So she took command and ordered Perwathwiy and Trethyankov to their places. But they knew, already. The ship was starting to move. By a supreme effort of will, the elders managed to get her steered in the right direction. Then Trethyankov died. Of shock, of strain, of fear . . . who knows? Then Perwathwiy collapsed of the strain of it, passing out completely. The girl flew on, now much too busy even to notice. She knew she was alone, solo, in the real thing, at last; she knew she couldn't do it, but she had to, for there was no one to call. All she could do was hold on until the changing of the watch, on the hope that some Player would happen by the sensor control and relieve her. She had no hope . . . but she had nerve and a fierce will to survive, to win, to prove to the people that she could, when they needed her. And so she did. Alone. Trethyankov, of course, did not revive. Perwathwiy would come back to consciousness, but would be beaten down each time, over and over again, by the combined assault of the living display and the voice of the girl-student, which was by now full Command-override Multispeech.

"And so it continued. We knew what had happened, for when the Ship activated, it sealed itself. Those who were in were in to stay. As it was, it was a full day before anyone thought to look in here. They were immediately struck down, just as had been Perwathwiy. She had built a wall about herself, and no one could enter here to relieve her. At last, a combination of earplugs and iron discipline allowed an emergency crew of four to take it from her, remove her, and start flying properly.

"She had to be physically overpowered with great violence, and after it was done, she, too, collapsed. Three days she had flown solo in a task that takes four people, without food or water. She was raving, hysterical, and quite mad. Utterly insane. For a year she lay as one dead. Perwathwiy took nearly as long to recover. We cared for the girl, for we all were deep in her debt; she had done the impossible. But we could not effect a cure. The wall still stood. Not even a battery of Speakers could break her. She was impervious. And after a long time, a year, she came out of it, of her own, seeming normal, and possessed a great skill in the Game, albeit a heavy-handed skill that none of us liked. And so with care we brought her back to this room in short stages, gradually letting her fly again, with a crew of elders who had been most carefully selected. During that time we also tried, from time to time, to get into her mind by Multispeech, to see if she was sane again. But she would never allow it. In fact, some of those who tried did not return from the attempt."

Morlenden shuddered. "And so the girl was Sanjirmil. . . ."

"Exactly. And we were all wrong to let her back into it, in this place, for we came to depend on her. This, here, is not a thing you can get a replacement for off the path outside. Even among the theorists. And so I was wrong, too, for having been a part of allowing it to happen. When Maellenkleth came along, I sought to bend Sanjirmil to my way by the threat of the return of Maellenkleth. Yes, of course it was Sanjirmil who sent her to capture, disminding, death. I would even suspect her of leaving none of it to chance. She doesn't in anything else."

Fellirian said, "But you cannot let her go unpunished!"

Pellandrey answered. "It is not me who lets her go in any condition. She has solidified her position, of course, and in matters of flying is the sole arbiter, not I. My charter has diminished greatly. And even if I had the power to do as you wish, I would likely not, for she cannot now be replaced. And still there is no one who can use Command-override on her. She has built a defense against it. There are few who could dare her physically, and none who could do both at once and neutralize her. . . . You have only confirmed what our worst fears were, laid on the last line."

Morlenden said, heatedly, "No one will dirty their hands, is that it? Then I will. I'll go down there now and give it to her with a bark still on it."

Pellandrey said, "I would have you do it, but you do not realize what you face. Others have done the very acts you say you will do. They are not among us now; do you understand that? You saw the amber plain. You saw what was on it. That is what happens to those who have tried: cast into limbo. Down deep in her mind she is still reliving the three days when it was Sanjirmil against the living, ongoing pattern of the universe. And won. But the price was her sanity, and unlike all others, she will not permit a cure. If she did, it would be to return to the old self, and the pride that drove her to survive is too fierce for that. Believe me. I know these things. I am a fourteenth-degree master of Multispeech, and of single violence. I tried. Command-override Multispeech with the most skillful assault I could muster. For my pains, I, too, was cast forth like a leaf in the wind. And there I remained for a long time, or so it seemed to me. There I wandered in the silences of a dead place out of space and out of time, still defending myself against an enemy who was not even interested enough to appear. At last I was permitted to return. I knew then what we had on our hands."

Morlenden said, "I saw that place. Why couldn't you just use the Game controls when she is off-shift and block it, or move it away?"

"Because it is not under the control of the Game; out of space and out of time. When you go there, you may exit, if you do at all, before you entered it. Or perhaps the same instant. Or perhaps centuries later. It is not a place in the universe, speaking analytically and strictly; it is a place built by the part of her mind that never sleeps and never stops playing. It is, in short, a place which is under her absolute control. You have the visual reference matrix in your memory; give it to her and make no attempt on her. I have warned you of the consequences."

Fellirian said, "It would seem to me that you have put yourself in a most unpleasant dilemma: you cannot keep her for the poison that is in her, and you cannot throw her away because she has become *Huszan*, the master of the Game. If you persist in this she will undoubtedly lead you into courses not foreseen by those who planned this venture. She will take a vehicle of life and make of it an instrument of death, of conquest. I have seen much of the forerunner world beyond the reservation; I do not care for the way they run it. But even less would I care to see Sanjirmil in her present condition made ruler of it all."

"At present, she remains true to the original program. Part of her is still with us. We use that part to guide the rest of her. But all this has complicated our task immeasurably. For instance, there is the matter of takeoff time. When we found out about the instruments, and saw the increase in investigative activity, we knew we would have to move things up."

Morlenden interjected, "And she told me there was no time to wait, when I said we had the rest of our lives!"

"Exactly. We did not know the cause of the event then, but our response to its consequences was plain enough: takeoff day had to be moved back, or else the confrontation would come here. As it is, we will just make it barely in time, and for that we have paid a terrible price. . . ."

He was interrupted by the hatch, in which fastening bolts were now unscrewing. Presently the hatch swung inward, and four elders, led by Perwathwiy, stepped over the sealing edge and into Control. Pellandrey turned to her and said, "It was as we feared. I was telling them about takeoff day being moved back."

Perwathwiy answered, "Yes, just so. We will all pay for what we allowed to happen. We spent Maellenkleth badly, and for it will receive sorrow. But it goes far beyond us, and into the wider world of the humans."

Fellirian asked, "How so, that?"

"When the plan to leave Earth was devised, it was debated then whether to attempt to rule men by force, or slowly, over the years, build within them, of their own selves, a way that would save them from themselves. It was the latter; after all, we owed our existence to them. This plan, which was to bring their world under control and let it down to a more reasonable level, was to have been complete at about the same time that the Ship was completed. Because, after it activated, the Ship grows itself, and for the estimated population we would have then we would need so much space. Then we would leave and we would have also paid our debt."

Fellirian said, "You say would . . ."

"Just so. Would have been. Not to be, now. We have had to cut it off, to ensure the survival of the people and the values we have nourished."

"But it should be almost complete!" Fellirian said. "Surely they will have the benefit of that part of it which has been finished!"

"No. Not to be. It was a holistic plan, the only one we could use; they could not be aware of it until it was complete. Absolutely complete, the last step done, in exact sequence. By aborting it as we have done, we have only postponed the reckoning, not put it away. At first nothing will seem amiss. Ten years, fifty, a hundred. More. But from the first, because the weave of the seamless garment was not completed, it will begin to unravel. First a little, then more, then a lot."

Morlenden said, "The result?"

"Ten thousand years of barbarism. Those who come to follow us to space after that, when civilization rises again, will have little, if any, knowledge of these years. They will see the ruins, but they will not understand them."

Morlenden said, haltingly, "Srith Perwathwiy, I am sorry for the news I have brought."

"I knew all along . . . I and the others, we only wished that we might have it proved otherwise. . . . Now you are illuminated, just as we are. And you have come with no better cure than the ones we have already tried and failed. And so now I leave you, to relieve the Terklarens of their shift. I hear that you bring the matrix of Mevlannen. Go ahead and pass it on to her, that we may be the more swiftly on our way." And she turned from them and walked along the ledge until she came to a passage down into the pit, the others silently following her in the dim half-light, like phantoms on a phantom errand. Elders, in overshirts, their hoods pulled up over the heads like cowls . . . they descended into the pit with the motions of familiarity, but with reluctance, too, dragging their steps. They were trapped into an iron sequence of events and were blindly following that track now, though it might lead them all to something unimaginable—doom, unknowable change.

They reached the floor of the pit, joined the Flyers at their keyboards. There was no ceremony, no camaraderie; Perwathwiy went to the main console and spoke briefly with Sanjirmil. Then, taking the headset from her, she slid into the reclining cradle as Sanjirmil slid out of it, both without any wasted motions. It looked easy. But in Morlenden's mind was the knowledge of how many years had gone into those motions.

Now standing, Sanjirmil waited patiently, her head thrown back, still attentive to the small active section of the Game display being shown in the dome overhead. Perwathwiy from her master's chair now directed the changeover of the rest, minding things carefully while they exchanged places, one at a time. Each slid into place and took up the motions of his predecessor, eyes on the ceiling. Those relieved moved away from their cradles, staring blindly after hours at it. None looked up. And when the new crew was in place and now in control, Perwathwiy's bony, ribbed hands flickered over the master keyboards to either side of her, and in the ceiling over their heads, the full display came on.

A muted white light immediately flooded the entire room, and the ceiling came alive, the whole surface of it, down to the coping along the vertical wall bordering the observation ledge; and the domed ceiling was covered with the same flickering, roiling, permutating endless recursive pattern of a complex and large-scale Game in progress, but moving so fast the untrained eye could not follow it for more than an instant. This array used tiny cells of the triangular tesselation, demarcated by fine black lines, fine as a spider's web. The activity was dense and *busy:* currents of motion flowed through it, forms appeared, coalescing out of others, then dissolving. Others held their existence and their position, but changed in shape constantly. To Fellirian it was a stunning window into hell and chaos, the primal chaos that underlies all appearances of the outer world of trees and rocks and stones and creatures, buildings and power and abstract reasonings. Here was displayed in graphic, visual form, the way things were, at some unknowable and unimaginable microlevel, and there was, to the eye, no meaning to it at all, much less the thought of controlling and manipulating that mighty flow over their heads: it was madness to look at it for more than a second.

Fellirian dropped her head, breathing hard, her breath coming in long sobs that shook her whole body. After a time, she said, simply, "My mind is too small." Morlenden had been staring at it, awestruck, dumb, his mouth hanging open in astonishment, for nothing he had seen during his partial indoctrination into the Game had prepared him for this. At last, he too dropped his head, a dazed expression on his face.

Pellandrey said, "This is the array Mevlannen spoke of, space-three; fine detail-work inside a planetary system. I know you are not Players, so I will not try to point out bodies in the solar system in the display. This display in full is part of changeover; the smaller partial unit is enough to keep the Ship moored, but we must take the larger view every eight hours, just to keep an eye on things."

Morlenden said, "I don't see how you could show me any particular body in that welter—it all looks the same, the same density everywhere."

"It always looks thus. The great Game we tap into in the universe goes on everywhere, source and sink and flow; it is different kinds, different patterns, rather than different densities that determines, in the macrocosm you and I inhabit, just what an object becomes—here, a planet; and there, an unseen flux of energy from a distant galaxy."

"How far can you see in these various display patterns?"

"There is no limit save that which we bring to it—the finite limits of ourselves, imperfect creatures just as all the rest. The greater the area of the display, the more you can do with it. The small partial is sufficient to hold the Ship; we need full to move it out of the planetary system.

And of course there are limits to what even a trained mind can handle—it gets too dense. Space-three is only good out to about, say, a parsec. In deep space, with virtual velocities in whole-number multiples of c, we use the higher-order tesselations; space-four, the several fives, the three sixes. Those we use for the most distant viewing."

Fellirian was regaining control of herself once again; she looked to the ceiling display once, then away. The Perwathwiy, down in the pit, sensing that they had seen as much as they could understand at that time, abruptly returned the display program to the reduced section they had first seen when they had come into this place. The light in the control room died back to its previous dimness.

Fellirian said, "And what of time delay? When you look into the distance, do you also see into the far past, as they do with the telescopes?"

"No. The Game has the same time everywhere; everything that we see and everything that we see happening is happening at that instant. That which is here displayed is an absolute universe, not a relativistic one; this is how things are, right now. No matter how far we have pushed it."

She said, "And what of us? What are we to do when Mor's transmission of the matrix to Sanjirmil is complete?"

"We had all hoped that you would rest from your journey here, in the Ship, until the morning. Then we have a decision to make."

"Is time really different in here?"

"Sometimes . . . but mostly it's just a manner of speaking. Stay here tonight; there will be time tomorrow."

"Will there be, Pellandrey?"

He hesitated. "Time enough," he said laboriously, "for that which we all must do, painful though it will be. I should have you fresh for that."

TWENTY

In the Game, Symmetry, however and whenever attained, is not lost, nor can it be.

—The Game Texts

AND SO THEY all waited along the encircling ledge for the relieved Braid to come up out of the pit to meet them. For a time, Sanjirmil stood close beside the Perwathwiy Srith, by the main console keyboard, apparently answering questions, adding small operator observations. The visitors could not catch the words, nor discern their meaning; the words were inaudible, and accompanied by an odd, but total, lack of bodily gestures; Fellirian inferred from this that Perwathwiy and Sanjirmil were speaking in one or another mode of Multispeech.

And while the leaders conversed, the others began drifting up out of the pit, picking their way along carefully, as if dazed, now that they were free of the strain of flying. They were all visibly fatigued. The younger girl, Sunderlai, in particular, seemed dazed and disoriented by the weight of her past shift at the controls: her attention seemed distracted, her motions as she climbed the stairs almost clumsy. A shame; Sunderlai was a small, delicate girl, of soft, rounded contours, whose skin was the color of whipped honey. The girl was yet just a child, round-faced, pleasant, pretty although not a beauty. But all in all, a healthy, lively young girl. Or would have been. Fellirian could imagine it well enough: selection, unbeknown to the girl herself, then early uprooting from *yos* and homelands, and placement into hard training so that she could fly under the hardest taskmaster of all—Sanjirmil.

The others were not so different. They were all fatigued and distracted. Numb from the long hours at the consoles. In Sanjirmil's insibling, Tundarstven, the effect seemed less pronounced, replaced by something more like a deep indifference. And Sanjirmil turned from her conversation with the Perwathwiy, said something to her insibling that Fellirian did not catch completely, something about the session they had just finished, deep in Inner Game terminology. And the habit of the flying shift was still deep in him, for he turned to her immediately, but his reply, which came after a little pause, was consciously himself and nothing else, accompanied by a little gesture of the hand, signifying indifference. By that little exchange, Fellirian could see the influence Sanjirmil wielded over them; some Daimons could be exorcised only by indifference.

The three others of Sanjirmil's Braid climbed out of the pit, and departed the room immediately through the main hatch. Sanjirmil, last to leave, was now apparently finished with her remarks with the Perwathwiy, and she, too, left the console area, turning away from it, so it seemed, with reluctance and dragging step. She began climbing up to the railed ledge about the pit, shedding as she climbed some but not all of that steely air of control she carried with her when she had been controlling. She, too, was visibly fatigued, but she did not seem disoriented as the others had. Sanjirmil had reserves they had not begun to learn of yet. And as she approached closer, Fellirian noticed the younger girl's eyes in particular; they held a peculiar expression, an almost glassy cast, which upon closer inspection seemed not so much inattention or unfocusing, but an unconscious scanning habit, an almost total reliance on peripheral vision. Of course; she understood: only with trained peripheral vision could they see and respond to the visual field shimmering above them, especially when the full display was on.

Sanjirmil reached the landing, opposite Fellirian. The eerie scanning gaze turned in their direction, took in Pellandrey, Fellirian, Morlenden. She read all their faces instantly, selecting that which she would fix her real attention upon. She knew Pellandrey had nothing new for her. Fellirian she dismissed from the first. A traditional rival Fellirian had been, the loyal insibling, but no more than that.

In the timeless way of all creatures that move about freely, as they faced each other, they took the measure of one another's worth and weight. For her own part, Fellirian felt the confidence her maturity and parenthood had brought to her—through the hundreds of decisions she had made therefrom, the problems solved. She also had her place at the Institute to support her as well. She knew herself to be a person of consequence. But Sanjirmil possessed an enormously strong will, a ferocious directional vector, and of course the deception of her insanity; she was convinced she was right. And here, in this place, she had the power of her position behind her, for in effect the Ship was hers. But there was more: Sanjirmil possessed an almost terrifying power of sexuality. Fellirian could sense it, could almost feel the waves of it buffeting her, waves of pure body. Extreme, perverse. Fellirian had never met a girl before possessed of such a raw force, such a strength of it

Sanjirmil approached her slowly. Fellirian watched her come, powerless to run, or to turn her aside. Seen from the ledge, when she had been reclining in her control cradle, the dark clothing Sanjirmil wore had been hardly more than a distraction, but here, close, on equal level, Fellirian saw the figure coming toward her, impressively dressed in stone black, broken only by thin lines of white. Their eyes met, focused, locked on; the glassy, unfocused look in Sanjirmil's eyes faded, being replaced by a disturbingly direct gaze of naked will, corrosive ability, unlimited malice. It was a gaze that burned. Fellirian instinctively looked away, breaking first, protecting herself from something she sensed was far beyond her abilities to subdue.

She spoke, almost involuntarily. "Morlenden has the matrix from Mevlannen."

Sanjirmil nodded, shifting her gaze back to the scanning mode, as if it had been no more than what she had been expecting to hear. And now she faced Morlenden, fixing him with that same disturbing gaze. He saw her much as had Fellirian, but deeper, too, for this fey, dangerous creature, almost out of control of all of them together, this girl in black, had once been known to him; and had sat not an arm's length away in a silent room, with him. But now she was at her time, at her full maturity, at the summit of her powers, secure in her own place, and he felt the strength of her rather more acutely than had Fellirian.

Sanjirmil's working overshirt was limp from the hours she had spent at the console-keyboard in the pit, and through it, the angular, primitive contours of her body showed easily. Along her face and neck and forearms, the only exposed parts, the warm streaky tone was more obvious; a hard, burnished olive along the lines of bone and tendon; soft, dull rose in the softer hollows. Wiry and yet ripe, too, erotic without comment, where others of this color were only lovely, or attractive. He thought that perhaps this effect was due to the shape; for Sanjirmil did not follow the rather undifferentiated unisex shape of the typical ler girl, flat-chested and narrow-hipped, but was closer to the ancient human shape, with its curves, hollows, fullnesses, increased sexual differentiation. And Morlenden was aware that even tired from a full shift at the master console, her body could still evoke responses in himself, even after the great change. He felt intimidated, demanded upon.

He sensed hostility in her, not well concealed, under the drive and power she projected. It was not a hostility of envy now, however it might have been in the beginning; now it was a hostility of arrogance, contempt, hubris, nurtured, for all too long, by too much responsibility piled on by accident, in one by nature not prepared for it. There was no cure for it, he saw as had Pellandrey; circumstances had worked their evil magic upon them all, just as they had with others and their plans, dreams. Morlenden did not doubt whatsoever that whatever strange creatures shared the universe with human and ler, they also had faced the same dilemmas; indeed, just now, somewhere else, some *thing* was facing the problems they faced, or something similar. Morlenden felt a sudden surge of sympathy for the unknown beings; for he did not like the weight of it. He felt it acutely; too acutely. There was something lurking in the back of his mind, something just out of sight, something enlarging this meeting with Sanjirmil into something more than what it was. . . . And what could he say to her in reproof that Pellandrey had already not tried? He searched; there was nothing he thought he could add; yet there was this anticipation growing in him. It was most curious, as an emotion; for he now had no real desire to see Sanjirmil again, certainly not with a lover's zest and zeal; but it felt something like that. But alien, too, as if there were more components to it.

She was before him now; and he could see her as through an enlarging glass, with an immanence and a terror. As with all strong-natured ones, she possessed a roiled, complex, turbulent persona, further stirred by a stormy, disturbed sequence of memories. She might well be insane; Morlenden was certain that her memory would be all the clearer for it. Empathetic, he reached with his instincts, a gestalt perception of her, projected outward and continually verified by the reality of the ever-present *now*. Yes, he could see it, in the larger-than-life figure before him, coming closer, closer, close enough to reach out and touch, although he knew not if he dared, now. Yes, he could see it: Sanjirmil had been a tomboy, *Dantlanosi*, wiry, strong, aggressive; she had preferred to do it standing up, under a cool bridge in the rain, quick and hard, no quarter asked, none given, a hot and sweaty, piercingly sweet embrace and coupling.

That was her nature; but it has all been taken from her by the accident that had made her a Player, but also a monster. What was left was the intense inwardness of the insibling, but now, of course, greatly magnified out of proportion. Once she had had the same chance at the rude freedoms of the adolescent as the rest of them, the easy and casual promiscuity, the relaxed and lazy affairs that came with time and the twenties. But she had not had them; instead, Sanjirmil had known a terrible stress, and won; but at what price? And somewhere in her was the knowledge, carefully hidden from obvious surfacing, that as with all insanities, the price for return did not stay fixed but slowly and inexorably grew ever larger. He knew that she would not return normally, of her own will, now. Now? Now there remained only the matrix to pass to her, and perhaps a few words, now that he knew. Yes, perhaps that was the sense of apprehension he felt. He would have Sanjirmil in a position of weakness when she was receiving; perhaps then he could . . . deflect her from her course, nudge her aside by a reference to their shared memories, their past?

He spoke first. "I have brought the matrix from Mevlannen, to you as directed. Are you ready to receive?" And as he spoke to her, he felt a wild surge of anticipation, quite out of character, and he did not understand why he should feel so exultant, so . . . wild. What the hell was happening to him? The room began to shrink, to converge, to focus on himself, Sanjirmil. *What was happening?* Whatever it was, he felt increasingly powerless to change the course of things. A wild abandon took him, whispering in his inner ear, *Let it be! Let what will come to pass, so come to pass. You will like it and ride willingly with it into the future!*

Sanjirmil answered simply, softly, with a voice betraying deep fatigue: "So I have waited, knowing the time to have come for the integration of Game and matrix. Speak on, then, messenger. *Deskris* . . . I await you."

Her eyes ceased scanning, found Morlenden's, locked on them. Morlenden began, and it was easy, for all he had to do was remember the sequence Mevlannen had inserted in him, recall it and let it go. There was no composition on his part at all; just remember and release. Easy. And the wild anticipation in his heart leaped up like a wildfire, exulting. *Almost there*, it seemed to say, *almost there, and the moment will be within this scene.* He sang the sequence softly to her, slowly feeling, inexpertly, how she as receiver was leaning slowly into his influence, becoming a part of him, an extension of himself. All the result of Multispeech, of course; but also a lot of the relationship went into it, too. She was letting Morlenden take over part of her because she trusted Morlenden as she trusted no one else in the world. And he saw on the edge of his perceptions that somehow the feral glow was fading out of her eyes, the tense set of her harsh, angular face, once loved violently and intensely. There were other, familiar emotions beginning to show upon it, and something she heard and recognized, something she could say she truly knew as no one else did. These new emotions flickered over the harsh but softening face, like firelight over a raw, new stone wall. Her thin lips were tensed and white with concentration, as she reached for the more subtle nuances of the matrix, integrating it as she went.

And the string of matrix numbers suddenly ended, ran out; there had been no warning, no anticipation, nor was there for what replaced them: Morlenden found himself speaking, quite involuntarily, in the strongest Command-override he had ever heard. Sanjirmil's ego defenses, her will defenses, against outside control by Multispeech Command-mode were not down, but they had been relaxed to the point where they might as well have been. The sudden assault, which took Morlenden by as much surprise as it did Sanjirmil, battered down her will, hammered it flat, beat it down, and began reaching for the central node inside her mind that would make her sane; yes, sane, as it also killed her from inside. His voice echoed and boomed in his head like the voice of a god, probing, tearing, reaching. And an image of Mevlannen, who was saying, *Sorry about the compulsion, Morlenden. I warned you that we'd cheat you. I knew who sent Mael to her death, but I would never get close enough to do it myself. But you would, and here you are now. And now extract our revenge! Destroy this thing before you. It can't be cured, it can only be killed, and from the inside. NOW!*

So here was the source of the anticipation, the exultation, that he had been feeling as the moment approached; not himself at all, but a compulsion Mevlannen had set into him as she had herself passed the matrix to him. Morlenden hesitated, for as much as he wished to avenge Maellenkleth, he had never attained malice toward Sanjirmil. Only anger. And now, that hesitation almost became the end of him, for although Morlenden still had inhibitions, even to the resistance of Mevlannen's compulsion, Sanjirmil had no such inhibitions whatsoever. And he was about to find that where survival was at stake, she could shed fatigue like a pine tree shedding raindrops in a sudden wind.

In the instant he had argued with himself, hesitated, fought the compulsion, his attention had dropped off Sanjirmil. And now she recovered from the Multispeech assault upon her. And he lost belief in the program Mevlannen had set into him, and now the words became just words, falling off Sanjirmil harmlessly. The room winked out in his perceptions, and was replaced with a boundless darkness. He could imagine, but not see, Sanjirmil, gathering herself, recovering, now rising to strike back. He moved hesitantly. He was in great danger, he knew, and began looking for a way he could defend himself against the approaching counterattack.

And a voice shouted at him from all sides: *So it was to be you after all, was it? It was just as I feared the day I came with Perwathwiy: you would unravel the long string and turn against me, too, as have all the rest. Well, then, you have come so far; so witness what others who have tried came to see. Some are there yet. You will join them.*

And instantly the furry darkness was replaced with the abstract plain he had glimpsed before. Only now he was standing on the surface, dazed, disoriented, looking about. There was no one there but him. A brown, flat plain, illuminated by a wan, amber, sourceless light, arrowed off into infinity, a horizon that seemed staggeringly far away. Sanjirmil had dropped Morlenden into her own private limbo.

He forced himself to think, not to panic and run, which he was sure the others had done. Run wildly, as they had done, and he knew death would come from a thousand directions, in unknowable ways. He had to think. Morlenden looked at the "ground." It seemed faintly etched with parallel lines, which he could follow, now that he saw them, off to the horizon. Then there was something regular about this place, after all. And he knew that this limbo was Game-generated, by Sanjirmil, but part of some Game program still. He forced himself to remember all that he had learned from Krisshantem, to try to find a way out. He began, hesitantly, vocalizing short bursts of Game language, in Command-mode. At first, nothing happened, but with one segment there was a sudden wavering of the brown horizon. Yes. His heart leaped. Yes! He could pull this limbo down and walk out of the ruins. He probed at it again.

Now a spot developed, just off-center in his field of vision, like a migraine spot, a pulsing, wavering blot of black and bumblebee-yellow, pulsing, growing, writhing into his field of vision, taking his attention. He increased his efforts. The patch of yellow and black increased in intensity, and he began to hear a humming in his ears, becoming louder, and at the same time he began to feel a will pressing hard against him, harder, harder. . . . The patch of writhing color grew, becoming immense, covering a third of the scene, and then suddenly shrank, taking on form, someone . . . and Sanjirmil materialized out of the patch, with no warning, with a curious, dancelike motion, her leather cloak swirling about her and settling as she materialized into this strange world with a faint *pop* of displaced air. And now she stood only feet away, dressed in black, her figure set in a posture of dire menace, slowly approaching him, slightly circling.

"Ho, Morlenden!" she challenged him. "You are more resourceful than I thought. A Player, no less! How did you come by it?"

He faced her, ceasing for the moment his efforts to break the walls of limbo. "The same way I came to attack you, Sanjir. Things have been put into me that I did not ask for."

"I know Mevlannen set a compulsion in you; things like that leave traces, like the scent of the hunter on his traps."

"Krisshantem set a program of an Outer Player into me. And I see the light, with it. I'm going to pull down this hell you've made."

"I don't doubt for a minute you would, if I let you. You are the first to realize it could be done, although far better Players have come here . . . and failed. That is why I come in person. What must be done . . . but you know that. Can you dissuade me before I . . . ?"

"Dissuade you? I don't intend to. Keep your distance, or I will reactivate the destruction program of Mevlannen. I know you are powerful, Sanjir, but you cannot cover both ends." And without warning, he slipped into Command-override, trying the instructions of Mevlannen again, but this time with belief and a deep sense of self-preservation behind them as well. Sanjirmil was unprepared for the second attack; she had apparently thought that all she would have to do was enter limbo and dispose of this troublesome stranger. . . . Now she staggered back, her image wavering, the horizon suddenly gone unsteady. She had never caught one like this! He was fighting back! Unthinkable! She exerted a mighty effort that made veins emerge into sharp relief around her forehead, countering in Command-override of her own; and Morlenden again felt himself gripped in the clutches of a monster will. The strange world steadied, as well as her image. And she began circling him, like a wolf, closing slowly. Morlenden also began moving, circling her, keeping up his own song as he went, for he knew that to waver now would be instant termination; he would never return from this place, wherever it was.

He called to her, "Ho, Sanjirmil! I can stalemate you indefinitely! Attack me and I unravel your limbo. Patch up your world-lines and I'll attack *you.*"

She replied through a grimace of effort, "Stalemate, you think. There is no time here save my time. I'll wear you down. But know that this is not my heart's desire, Morlen. . . ."

"Speak of heart's desire, then. We have little else to say to one another, it would seem, here, save malice."

"If you will cease fighting me, and join me in my crusade against stupidity, I will share it with you, thus and thus. Share and share alike. You are too good to waste in absurd combat like this."

"Why did you send Maellenkleth out to certain capture?"

"You have said it, therefore you know why. I read the old human story of *Damvidhlan and Baethshevban** and saw my way clear. Maellen fell, of course, to the role of the Great Hurthayyan, or as the forerunners call him, Uriah-the-Hittite. Like him, she was fond, overly fond, of the front of the battle, and like him, she was espoused to a being I coveted, the regard of the rest of the Game community. So I, like Damvidhlan, sent her to the place where it was hottest."

Morlenden interrupted. "It would not be like you to leave a thing like that to chance."

"No," she said sadly. "No chance. I had been cultivating a vile agent of the humans, holding him for some extraordinary deed. And there it was. Through him I made sure she was captured. A man named Errat. In the end he became too slippery, and I had to dispose of him. Too dangerous. It is a fearsome thing to deal with humans; they are dangerous . . . full of a thousand enmities. Their thoughts subvert one's own, take over, and you become like them. That is why I went out to finish Errat; he was corrupting me."

"Hah!" Morlenden barked. "You corrupted by Errat? I should think it the other way. If you did eliminate him, you did him a favor."

"I shot the arrow at you, to warn you. Do not make me wish to be sorry I missed."

"Not much of a miss, was it? Or do you claim it after the fact? That is the score I must even with you myself: you loosed upon me a weapon that leaves the hand."

"I saw you were coming to it, and would not be deceived by hope. Perwathwiy and the rest I could keep off, for they wanted to believe . . . but I saw the way you were going would lead you to me in the end. I agree it was unwise . . . but you cannot obtain judgment upon me for it, for I have narrowed the field of Players. They need me now, notwithstanding the fact that I am master of the Ship."

"Then you do not need my help." Morlenden turned from her and began unraveling the ends of the strange half-world Sanjirmil had made. She abruptly countered, stabilizing it again, a flush of anger radiating from her.

"Stop that! You know not what forces you will release!"

---

* David and Bathsheba

"Since you were caught by the Ship, Sanjir, you have lived by playing upon the unthinkable, that there were things others would not do. I see that. But I will do them, won't I? You have gone too far, and I will stop you."

"Regardless of the cost to the people?"

"Look at what you have cost them already! We were innocent, but evil has entered us, wearing your overshirt, your boots, your leather cape. I do not wish to see this evil carried to the stars, however you will have it."

"Join me, come with me, be my love again as you once were. We fly soon to the new worlds, and I will set you above me when we land, above Pellandrey."

"No."

"You owe him nothing. He stole the heart of your insibling in her *vayyon*, long ago. Yes, I know, though you do not. It was Pellandrey and Fellirian, and it has remained so all these years."

"No. The *vayyon* is the *vayyon*. One can do that. I hold no grudge. Will have none of it. Is it now that you cannot overcome me, so you bring forth these cheap arguments? Indeed you are wavering."

"I do not waver in what must be done. See!" And again Morlenden felt the pressure of her will, beating upon him, relentless as the tide. He felt himself being forced, step by step, move by move, into a crouching posture, an ancient posture of defense. And now she advanced on him, pressing close. Morlenden fought back with all the powers he could muster, defending, picking at the wall that was closing around him, compressing him, closing him in. She stood before him, a figure in dark clothing in the eerie half-light of the amber plain, her hands flexing. "See!" she cried. "It would be so easy to snuff you out. But I am merciful, and something of me still loves you. Desist, O Morlenden, from your resistance against me; join me. You are worth far more to me as a willing friend than as a vanquished enemy. Anyone can vanquish enemies. It is easy."

In her gloating over her Multispeech powers, and her immense powers as a Player, she had come too close, closed her web of power too closely about Morlenden. He looked at it closely, feeling along its boundaries with his mind, feeling for a line of weakness. She had to have one, somewhere.

She was saying, "My last offer: you have the basic skills, I see. I offer you one half of everything that is mine, the power and the glory. Only say that you will accept me for what I am; for I cannot help that."

"No." Morlenden grimaced, still feeling along her will for a weak point. And he found it. A minuscule crack: her memory of him. It was the one thing that someone else would have easily missed; for she had told no one of their dalliance long ago. Into this crack Morlenden flowed, working his way along the weakened lines of will-force in the web of Multispeech Command-override. And then he was inside her defenses, no longer outside, and he did not hesitate now, for to falter here would mean the end. She wailed, "Nooooo . . ." and he found the node in her mind he was looking for, and turned loose, in all its horrors, the destructive program of Mevlannen, but now under his control. She fought him like a wild beast, and the plain vanished utterly, and he was filled with vertigo, but he did not let go for an instant. She turned and fled, but Morlenden pursued her like an avenging angel. He was now pulling himself laboriously through a labyrinth of insanity, of the whole elaborate network she had built up over the years. But at last he came to the center, to the central node, the event in her memory that had started it all, the memory of that time in the Ship, when it had activated and she had had to face the awful cosmos alone. And Morlenden saw the basic flaw, reached into it, and repaired it, and watched the rest, now falling into line after it, readjusting. It was over. The process was now fixed, unstoppable, and in the end she would be different. He was sure she would be diminished, though it pained him to reduce her thus.

And they were back in the master Control room, with no warning, seemingly at the same instant they had left it, only now he was holding Sanjirmil in his arms, supporting her as she sank against him, her body heaving with dry sobs that shook her whole body. Her eyes were closed tightly, and between sobs, she was moving her lips soundlessly, muttering something. Pellandrey and Fellirian looked at the two of them, amazed at the change in Sanjirmil, which had seemingly come instantly; one moment she had been master of the Control room; the next, collapsed in Morlenden's arms.

Pellandrey stepped forward, eyes blazing. "What have you done to her?"

Morlenden spoke over his shoulder, never taking his eyes off the girl. "Cured her, that's what. She'll probably never fly again, but she can remember the basic integration, the matrix plus the Game-view of the stars, and she can guide you. But she's disarmed now. I've clipped her wings."

"You fool, do you know what you've done? You've condemned us to wait until we can replace her. And we don't have that much time; the forces she stirred in the human world will be reaching here within the week, according to our computations."

Morlenden said, over his shoulder, "If you let this one as she was lead you to that pass, then you're a fool and deserve the blame yourself for what happened. She was insane, you dodo, and she was poisoning all of you, one by one. You let her get this far; all along the way there were actions you would not take, and she knew it, read you all perfectly. Until she had you locked into total dependence on her. God only knows what she would have done once she lifted the ship off, in the condition she was in. She'd probably have turned the whole range of weaponry you have aboard here on Earth and blighted it. All we want to do is get away clean, not leave a legacy of revenge behind us."

Fellirian agreed with Morlenden. "I follow his argument; if we allowed that to happen, they would never forgive and they would never let it leave their minds. They would reinvent the starship just to hunt us down. I will not have that Daimon pursuing us across space to the ends of the universe."

Morlenden added, "If worse comes, sit in for her yourself. I know she was systematically eliminating potential replacements; but there have to be some left who can take her place. Use them. And make her work for you as an astrogator. You have the leverage now."

Pellandrey answered, after a time, "You are right, of course. I admit the flaw; we have all here been living with it too long, and the rationalizations always come too easy. And so what did you learn from her? What are the crimes of Sanjirmil, in specific?"

Morlenden said, "To punish her further is meaningless. She will flog herself to a shred, now that she has her whole mind back. What more could we do to her that would bring her victims back? What can we add that will strike down other Sanjirmils to come? We can do no more than be ready for them when they come, and stop them then. I will not say what I learned of this one. Let it rest there: you would not judge her and act, because of her position as master of the Game. So I took my case to the Game master, disagreed with her arbitration, and settled the matter with her alone. Proceed with your plan, Pellandrey."

"When I finish telling you what I started to a moment ago, you will not be so kindhearted."

"Pah. I have never been kind in my life. I am being practical."

"Very well, practical. But you will recall that we sensed increased human interest in this site as a result of Sanjirmil's manipulations? That this had interrupted and aborted one timetable, the program we were putting into human society?"

"Yes."

"It interrupted more than that; it also interrupted the orderly growth of the Ship. . . ."

Fellirian put her hands to her mouth, and said, simply, "Oh."

"And the Ship grows only at a certain rate, controlled by the Game. This gives us our basic ulterior space, which we must then render habitable. We had things tied into our racial birthrate, so that at a certain time, the available space in the Ship would be exactly that required for the whole of the people."

Morlenden said, slowly, "So if the Ship can fly now, it would do so with less room. . . ."

"Exactly. According to what Maellenkleth knew from her own capture, the time was then near. We are actually overdue a departure even now. We must fly next week at the latest, or risk, according to our studies, having to fight our way out. It may be so already, now. And there isn't room for everyone. Do you understand? There isn't room."

"So someone must stay behind?"

"Yes."

"Who?"

"All children and adolescents will go. All elders, except for a handful designated as absolutely essential, will stay behind."

Fellirian said, in a very small voice, "You left out the parent phase."

Pellandrey said, "Some Braids will have to leave two of the parents behind, with the elders."

Morlenden laid Sanjirmil down, very gently, along the floor of the ledge. He straightened, and said, "And who are these Braids? Are they known to you? Better yet, are they known to themselves?"

"Tomorrow we send the runners out, to bring the gathering of the people. We have worked it this way, so the knowledge of role will not be lost: All Braids that carry a number in their surname must cast lots among themselves, or somehow make a decision. And of course, what little government we have will set the example and bite this most bitter bullet."

Fellirian said, "There are only two Braids in the so-called government . . . you and us."

"Yes. Correct. Us, and you. And so now you know, Fellirian Deren; and you are *Klandorh*, so you must decide how you will levy it among yourselves. The Revens have already made their decision. I should have waited until morning to reveal this to you, for morning is a better time for bad news."

Morlenden said, "There is no time for bad news. And you say this will bring the numbers down to what the Ship can carry?"

"Yes. With a little space left over to cover pregnancies that occur along the way. Right now, we do not know how long we will be in space."

Morlenden said, "And what is the decision of the Revens?"

Pellandrey answered, "You do not reveal the crimes of Sanjirmil; neither do I reveal what is already set. You will see which of us leaves the ship grounds, when the Ship leaves. I would have none copy our example, for the sake of copying it; it *is* a hard way, but I have decreed that each so affected must face it themselves. And so you as well."

Fellirian shook her head, as if clearing cobwebs from her eyes. "Then we shall have to return to our *yos*, and there take counsel."

Pellandrey placed his hand on her shoulder. "That is why we asked that you spend the night here, think, and return fresh. It is the kind of thing that we would have none do in a hasty way, for the results will be forever."

Fellirian looked at Pellandrey blankly. "No," she said. And to Morlenden, "I don't know how long, subjectively, you were locked in with Sanjirmil. Can you brave the cold, insibling?"

Morlenden placed his hands together, locked them, and pulled hard on them until his shoulders creaked. Then he straightened, and said, "Tonight it is. Let us return now." And to Pellandrey he said, "When must we be here, and what must we bring?"

"The runners leave tomorrow, and decision must be taken upon the news. Bring your most precious goods, what each can carry with his own hands. And what you can remember, for we will build this world again. That is what will go out with the runners."

She said, "Then we must leave. We will be our own runners. Although I may have to call for help to convince Kaldherman. He will doubtless think it absurd." And she smiled, but it was a weak smile.

Morlenden said, "You may escort us out of this labyrinth, Pellandrey. Although I am sure it will be easier to come and go, now that Sanjirmil's tumor on the body of space-time has vanished back into the noplace from whence she built it."

Pellandrey turned back to the hatch, with heavy step. "Very well. It shall be as you will. Make the choice wisely. There can be no regrets."

And so they left the master Control room. Along the way, Pellandrey met some elders, whom he directed to go to the Control room and care for Sanjirmil. And seemingly in a shorter time than it took them to enter the Ship, they were at the portals of the great Ship, which were now standing open, as Morlenden had suspected. They walked forth, into the night, and Fellirian did not look back.

For a time, Pellandrey stood outside, in the cold, clear night, the stars shining brightly overhead, clear for once through the haze of the sky of Old Earth.

But when they reached the last point on the trail that they could look back from, and Morlenden and Fellirian stopped, to look back just once, there was no one to be seen. And they turned homeward, and began the long walk back, in the dark and the still cold, breath-steam clouds wreathing their faces. They were not entirely certain of exactly when the moment occurred, but after a certain time, they noticed they were clasping one another's hands tightly as they walked. Morlenden grinned sheepishly at his insibling, and Fellirian looked back quickly at him, but the expression on her face was not one which could easily have been read in the chilly darkness.

TWENTY-ONE

SPRING, 2610

IT WAS THE end of a day that had promised rain, the skies being filled with ragged, wet-looking clouds, rag-ends of clouds, all moving by overhead at a fast pace through the branches which were just now beginning to green out. But not yet. Not a drop had fallen. The air was heavy, oppressive, but at the same time filled with promise, for it had been a dry spring, a late one, too.

Morlenden leaned on his shovel beside a long mound of fresh earth, and looked off into the distance, as if looking for a sign. It was darker over in the west than it had been, and it seemed there was the distant rumble of thunder there, although he couldn't be quite sure; his hearing wasn't quite what it had been.

For a long time, his thoughts had been quite blank, devoid of any particular sense of direction; now he let it come again, reminding him of what else had to be done. Here was Fellirian. Earth aspect; now returned to it, in the spring, under a hawthorn tree they themselves had planted, how many years ago. Before Pethmirvin. It didn't matter when, exactly—for the tree had grown to some size, and the branches were drooping with age.

They had not been morbid about the end, when they had talked of it at all; yet under their hopes and fears, somehow they had always assumed that they would be part of some family group, some lodge, when one or the other came to the end. But it was not to have been—in the end, it was just them, living in the same *yos* they had been born in, still marveling they had not tired of each other's company after so many years; she had complained of feeling tired, and had lain down for a nap. And like that, so easily, had sighed, smiled once at Morlenden, and breathed no more. Somehow, he had managed to do what had to be done. There was no one else nearby to help him with it.

.   *   *   *

Now he remembered it all. How they had returned home, and argued violently through the day, deciding who would go with the children, in the Ship. But there had been no wavering on Fellirian's part, for she had made up her mind on the way home, and would not be budged from it, no matter how Kaldherman had argued, fumed, and stormed about. And so they had agreed that Kaldherman and Cannialin would take the children to the Ship and go with them, and that they would remain behind. And then they had left, and the *yos* had fallen silent.

The insiblings did not go with them, nor did they journey to Grozgor, to see the Ship depart, for it was too painful for them. But they heard it emerge from the hollow place in the mountain, and there were lights in the sky in the northwest, and a distant murmur of sound, and then all was quiet again. The Ship was a full day ahead of the finally mobilized occupation forces, which arrived at the mountain and found only a smoking crater. They had been met there by a small delegation of elders, who politely explained that they were late, and they could do as they liked. Another group had emerged at the Institute, there using what communication facilities were available to spread the word into the forerunner government, explaining exactly, painfully exactly, what had happened. And what must then be done.

It had been a trying period. There had been much change in Seaboard South Region; but there had also been turbulence in other places as well, as the impact of the departure of the Ship and the people had permeated through the levels and bureaus. There had been a great unwillingness to believe that there had been a holistic plan, to pay off the debt to Man for having brought the ler into existence in the beginning. But in the end it had quieted, and the remaining ler and the humans had set out to work together and salvage as much as they could of the original. This had been Fellirian's aim. Vance also returned from the sanctum of 8905, to the Institute, and played a major part as long as he had been able.

Had they been successful? No one could tell, for the momentum of the plan intended for humanity had been so slow and long-ranging that even in a span of sixty years, they could not yet see any sign of change, though they looked constantly. The world had not yet changed in any way they could see. Even those elders most familiar with it could make no predictions, no forecasts. Earth went on much as it had before, only now more cautiously.

Morlenden tried to project in his mind how it must have gone for the children in the sixty-odd intervening years. He could not. Sixty years. In the last meeting with Pellandrey, they had been told that the Ship was expected to be in space less than a year, before they stopped it and began settling a new planet. And then, the resumption of their lives, under strange skies. Or perhaps they might not be so strange. Sixty years. Peth would have woven into another Braid, lived her entire woven period out, and become an elder, living somewhere else. He found it hard to imagine. For him, things remained as they had been in 2550. Morlenden shook his head. He knew these things to be true, but all the same he could not see them.

At last, he straightened, plucking his shovel out of the ground, and started back to the *yos*. Yes, he thought he could hear the mumbling of distant thunder off in the west, which had grown very dark now. He stored the shovel in the tool closet, under the overhang of the back of the *yos*, and made his way around to the front. He climbed the stairs to the entry, pausing to remove his boots before entering the *yos*, an action he had performed so many times it was almost automatic now. He moved slowly. Age was beginning to catch up with him. It was hard to bend over. And as he finished, and was just straightening back to a standing position, one hand on the wooden railing, he felt a very cold and very fat raindrop impact on the back of his neck, sending a little shock wave of shivers through his body. Morlenden smiled in spite of himself. Yes. She'd be pleased. He looked out over the yard. The wind was up, whispering in the trees. There was an odor of ozone in the air, a promise of another season of growth. He understood the symbol: life goes on. Yes. He understood completely. He turned and went into the *yos*, and began laying out a fire for supper.

The Warriors
of Dawn

For Matthew

PART 1

Chalcedon

1

"A ler called Maidenjir, of the period when they were still on Earth, is reputed to have said, 'Fools think that everything must have a name and so apply themselves, forgetting that at the completion of their activity, the Universe will end. Now shall we speak of last words?' This has its roots in the curious ler doctrine of ignorance (facts are finite, but ignorance is as boundless as the Universe) and in their concepts of person and number theory. But more than one human scholar has seen in this an interesting parallel to the ancient Hindu belief that if one repeated the name of Shiva, Lord of Destruction, often enough, He would open His eye and destroy the world."

—*Roderigo's Apocrypha*

IN THE EARLY history of one particular planet, Seabright, human colonists came and broke the ground for a new world's development, and built a port town of tarpaper shacks, warehouses, dumps and shabby repair depots. Likewise, they thoughtfully installed brothels, gambling dens, beer halls, and filled the city up with a raw new world's drunks, entrepreneurs, derelicts and whores. It was a vast running sore, and they named it "Boomtown," taking precedent from many hasty towns which had sprung up before on other worlds.

But Boomtown, of course, like all things, changed with time; it was renewed, urban and otherwise, rebuilt, scraped over, moved several miles down the coast, moved back, burned, and built again after being shaken into ruins by earthquakes. Now, Han reflected, enjoying the bright morning light playing among the apartment balconies, it was perhaps more resort than anything else, with "minor government center" trailing in second place. Tourists swam in the clear water of the bay around which the city curved in a sophisticated embrace, hoping to find artifacts and old coins. The Boomtowners made it beautiful and they moved part of the government to it, but they retained the awful name out of a bizarre sense of humor and a sense of the power of habit: the name was several thousand years old and every attempt to change it had ended in failure.

As with every city worth the name, yokels arrived daily out of the hinterlands seeking adventure and fame. They found neither. Boomtown was now lazy, bright, lovely, seductive . . . and people woke late of mornings, as Han Keeling ruefully thought in reference to himself as well. He finished his bun and coffee, paid the waiter, and departed the half-empty sidewalk café, knowing well enough that he was already late.

As he walked towards the top of Middlehill, in the direction of an unpretentious residence and office building, he reviewed what he knew about his appointment, which was little enough.

He was an apprentice Trader, almost finished with the trade guild's finishing school. He was in his mid-twenties, sound of mind and body, and a moderate success with the lazy, teasing secretaries of Boomtown. And he had been told by the Master Trader that if he wanted an interesting and undescribed assignment, he could report to a certain building on Middlehill and once there, go to room 900 at a certain time, and press on from there. Press on! That was the guild's overworked motto. Press on; in the face of dire calamities, fires, cannibals, slavers, economic "readjustments" and accidents. Indeed. But in this case, if he took the job and completed it successfully, he would get his Trader's papers, and his license.

And of course, he was late. Han quickened his step, and so doing, caught a glance from a passing, brightly dressed girl, apparently on her way to work. She wore a flowerprint gauzy dress that floated around her, suggesting curves as it swirled from her motions in the clear morning air. He surreptitiously checked his reflection in a shop window: slim, elegant, knowledgeable, competent, relaxed. So he thought. The figure that covertly glanced back at him in the reflection was dark of hair, smooth of face, with features which a more critical observer might have described as being slightly too sharp, too well defined. But he was not a critical observer; he saw the reflection as being somewhat taller than average, and dressed fashionably enough after the tastes of the times.

He arrived at the building and went in, without passing any checkpoints or observers he could see. At the door of room 900, he paused before entering and reviewed his excuses for being late. He was sure, however, that little would be made of it, if anything, for everyone in Boomtown was always late; to be early or precisely on time was considered slightly vulgar, in bad taste. He knocked, and entered, through an old-fashioned door which swung open rather than sliding.

The room inside was brightly lit by the morning light streaming in over the terrace; there was no other illumination. Beyond, the blue sea. Steelsheen Ocean, rolled and played, throwing quick flashes of sparkling light and sudden glimpses of whitecaps. The room itself was a large one, floored with natural stone. Instead of the expected furniture, there were planters scattered about, some containing miniature trees which, by their gnarled appearance, were very old and carefully tended. But the decor of the room went far beyond mere mannerism; there was something delicate and natural about it, a difference one could sense below the level of direct perception. It was a ler room.

There were nine people in the room, obviously waiting for him, because as he entered, they began settling themselves at a low table on the terrace proper. Four were humans, which Han could distinguish by their colorful Boomtown clothes and gestures of impatience. The remaining five were ler, which he could distinguish by their slightly smaller stature and homespun robes. There was an almost total absence of decoration on any of the robes, which Han recognized as an indication of high status.

A florid, heavy-set human approached Han and introduced himself as one Yekeb Hetrus, regional coordinator. The other humans introduced themselves in turn; Darius Villacampo, Nuri Ormancioglu, and Thaddeusz Marebus. No other titles or positions were referenced; this caused Han to become more attentive. That they would not mention titles indicated that they were either very high or very low. He decided that they were high. Most likely Union Security people, who were reputed to be a closemouthed lot in any circumstances.

The ler were more interesting, if for no other reason than that they were rare and strange in this part of space. And as he had often heard, he could not distinguish at first sight whether they were male or female. In a certain way, they looked disturbingly like slender, graceful children with slight signs of age and maturity beginning to show on some of their faces. They were all rather uniform in height; Han guessed they would all be around just over five feet.

Han knew very well that ler were human-derived, the result of an early atomic-era program to accelerate human evolution. The theory had entailed DNA manipulation and a reliance on a magic-number hypothesis analogous to the early approaches to quantum mechanics; to continue the analogy, they had been reaching for the next stable junction on the "magic number" grid. The project had no sooner reached its goal than it was attacked from without, by humans who felt genetics was oriented to the environment, and by the specimens themselves, who had stabilized and formed a culture of their own. After several hundred years of uneasy relations between ten billion humans and several thousand ler, the ler had discovered a faster-than-light drive, built a spaceship in secret, and departed. Before they left, however, the world government of the day had become dependent on them to supply the necessary technological input to keep an overconsumptive culture afloat far beyond its years. Naturally, when the ler left Earth, there was a "readjustment." Humans had called them ungrateful, and were terrified of the implications of an advanced human type in their midst. The ler were not competitive, were terrified of human numbers, and wanted to be left alone. That was ancient history. Since that period, they had mutually colonized a large volume of space, the humans expanding spin wards along the galactic disc, and the ler antispinwards.

Still, Han experienced something akin to awe, as they introduced themselves. Neither race had ever found any other intelligent life in the worlds they had discovered, by now, some forty worlds. There were traces here and there, an occasional undecipherable artifact, but no aliens. So, in the popular mind, they had become, to each other, the alien race.

The first introduced itself as Defterdhar Srith. Han knew enough basics from school days to recognize the last "name" as not a surname, but an honorific that indicated that the individual concerned was a female past the age of fertility. She was as quiet and self-possessed as one of the large stones that stood here and there about the terrace. The second and third were, respectively Yalvarkoy and Lenkurian Haoren, insiblings to each other. Han looked closer. Male and female. The fourth was dark, rather saturnine and quiet, but with bright, animated eyes. He did not speak, but instead stood quietly with his hands in his sleeves.

The fifth, and closest to Han of the group around the table, was at second glance a female, and a young one at that. In fact, she was, as he looked and listened more closely, much younger than the other ler present. She gave her name as Liszendir, Srith-Karen. Han's suspicions were confirmed: the ler girl was young, in their terms still an adolescent, although he could not guess her age at all. She might have been sixteen standard or twenty-eight. Their adolescence went up to thirty standard. Somehow, subtly, he became aware of her not as a member of a race near man and derived from them, but as a young girl. She had plain, clear features of no particular distinction; her hair was short and pale brown, almost uncolored in its neutral tone, cropped off artlessly neat about ear level. It was straight and extremely fine in texture.

Her manner suggested something unfathomable and contradictory; an apprentice sage; a tomboy. She had a small, delicate nose and a broad, generous mouth. She was not a beauty in human terms of reference, but at the same time, she was attractive in a clean and direct way. Her eyes, however, were the most noticeable feature of her face; they were large and gray, and the pupil almost filled up the whole eye, except for corners of white. A faint yellow ring exactly divided the inner and outer iris. Han looked away from them. They were intense, knowing eyes. He looked at Lenkurian, the other young ler female present. Yes. There was some difference. Han could catch a hint of it; Liszendir was much better-looking than the other.

At this point, Hetrus made some introductory remarks, and then indicated that they were to listen to a recording, which he initiated by pressing a concealed switch. The recording started, identifying itself as a Union Security tape, subject, an interrogation, and circumstance, the statement of one Trader Edo Efrem, Master Trader. Han did not recognize the name at all, and assumed that Efrem was probably not of the Seabright system, but from some planet further out.

The interrogation recorded by the tape went as follows:

—Proceed, Trader Efrem.

—Very well. As I said before, I had headed outwards towards Chalcedon to do a little trading and see how things were. None of us get out that far on the edge very often, so I was sure I could sell a load of primitive toolstuff I had picked up deep inside as a . . . ah . . . a speculation, so to speak. I arrived at night, so of course one couldn't see very much. We set the bazaar up and waited for morning. But nobody came. I sent my Crew Chief into the local area to see if he could stir anyone up. Much later, he returned with a handful of people. To my surprise, of both kinds. In fact, I hadn't made a voyage to Chalcedon before, and I didn't know . . .

—Yes. We know about that aspect of Chalcedon. Go on.

—Well, to make a longer story shorter, they had been raided. Now, we all hear tales, of course, but we rarely ever see any hard and fast evidence. But they had gotten it there, all right. Later, I flew around the planet, and it was all over. Destruction everywhere. Some of the craters were still hot. Apparently, they came in, shot the place up, looted and took captives. They stayed about a month, and then abruptly left. Incredible damage. I unloaded as much as I could afford and beat it back here as fast as possible.

—*Did you hear a description of the raiders?*

—*Yes, and that was what bothered me. It didn't make good sense. Both kinds of people on the planet described them as "ler barbarians." They all had their hair either shaven off, or done up in plumes and crests. They wore loincloths and many had tattoos. And they were definitely ler.*

—*They were sure?*

—*Absolutely. Both kinds said so.*

—*What about captives?*

—*From what we could make out, only a few ler were taken, but quite a few humans. At first, the locals thought that the purpose in mind was ransom, but when more time passed and nothing was heard, slave-taking seemed the more probable. It was pretty strange, though; the raiders only appeared to take certain types of people. Perhaps "types" isn't the right word. They used a ler word which means something like "subrace" or "one who has a tribal characteristic." They did not seem to pick according to any known standard of beauty or utility. Now that's what bothered me. You hear tales, of course, but slavers and raiders? Besides, as far as I know, nobody has ever known ler to do anything even remotely like that. They fight well enough when the occasion demands, but they aren't aggressive.*

—*Did anyone know what kind of weapons the raiders used? Or what their ship looked like?*

—*No, to both. Nobody saw what caused the craters. And nobody saw the ship close. Some saw it above, at night, but all they could see were some lights. It was a terror raid, simple. There isn't anything on Chalcedon except a few mines and farms. There are no defended places or anything like that. No concentration of wealth.*

—*Any indications of where they came from?*

—*The survivors said that the raiders called themselves "The Warriors of Dawn." But that could mean anything. Every planet has dawns; plenty of them, too. No. Nobody knew. But I would guess, as did everyone else on the planet, that they came from somewhere further out.*

—*What language did they speak?*

—*The ler on Chalcedon said that it was a very distorted form of their "Singlespeech," barely understandable. There were words mixed in that no one could identify.*

Hetrus turned the reproducer off. After a moment, he spoke, slowly and at length.

"This tape has been primarily for the benefit of you two young people, Han and Liszendir. The rest of us have already heard it. Likewise, the history you are about to hear. It is well known to some of us, but probably not to you.

"You already know that the ler originated as an experiment in forced human evolution on Earth. After they fled Earth, many years later, they founded a world they called Kenten—'firsthome.' No contact was made for many more years, partly out of inability and partly out of mistrust. When contact was made, it began an unpleasant period, which was a shame to both our peoples. The Great Compromise ended all that, with humans expanding spin wards and ler antispinwards. New worlds would be, as discovered, for one or the other. Disagreements would be kept local. This worked for more years.

"No provision was made in the cases of inwards and outwards. Inwards, there has been some rare skirmishing, but nothing of any great importance. Outwards, however, it has been completely peaceful. Towards the edge, at the farthest known habitable world, the guiding councils of both decided to dual-colonize one world; to see if perhaps the rent in our fabric could be mended. To date, we have been successful—on Chalcedon."

As Hetrus paused, Lenkurian broke in. She seemed impatient, and spoke in a whispering, breathless voice which seemed so quiet it hardly sounded at all; yet curiously, it carried effortlessly to all parts of the terrace.

"When we heard this report, naturally we were interested. Note that the raiders were apparently ler, but of no origin anyone could determine, and of decidedly abnormal behavior. This caused some strain among our senior governing bodies. So we urgently wish to look further into this matter."

Hetrus continued, "Naturally, we wish it to appear innocent. We know in fact almost nothing, and we do not know if the area is under observation. That is why you two were suggested. Han is waiting for an assignment; Liszendir is likewise unoccupied at this time, and can be considered to be making her journeying for her skill, "her *'tranzhidh.'*"

The girl nodded approval at the alien use of a ler word.

Hetrus said, "You need not feel particularly gifted. Others would have perhaps been better; but you two were readily available. Neither of you has family responsibilities at this time, and you are not likely to develop any attachment to each other beyond the business at hand. We have provided a ship, an armed cutter, and some goods to suggest traders. You will voyage to Chalcedon and pursue the matter further. Efrem was in a hurry to leave; you need not, and may follow it as far as it leads. Your skills complement one another's admirably."

Han and Liszendir looked at each other. As if she anticipated the question in his mind, she said quietly, with a subtle undertone of belligerence, "I am Liszendir, an adolescent of Karen Braid, infertile, *Nerh* or elder outsibling, unwoven. You would say unpromised and unattached, I believe. My age in standard is twenty-six."

Han felt immediately put on guard by the frankness, which, he reminded himself, was not so much a personality trait of the girl herself, but a cultural trait they all shared in various degree. Still, it seemed that as she spoke, she had deliberately dropped the little femininity he could perceive, and become something different. Something fey, wild, tomboy. Aggressive. He wondered just what her skill was. And if she could turn on her femininity as easily as she turned it off.

Han asked her, "I am Han Keeling, male, unattached, Srith-Karen Liszendir. May I ask what your skill is?"

"You may. I am a violet adept of the Karen school of infighting."

Han nodded politely. He felt misgivings by the score creep up the back of his neck. Consider: a girl alone on a long voyage. A ler adolescent, no less, and hence, by human standards, highly sexual in her behavior, which in her society was normal and expected. All that was pleasant enough. But a trained killer of a discipline that was feared even on ler worlds. He looked at her again; she appeared relaxed, feminine, tender. Her skin was pale and very smooth. Yet he knew very well that she could probably take on every person in the room and leave them, at her choice, submissive, maimed or mangled beyond recognition. She would be the human equivalent of a perfect gymnast, trained in something like karate and kung-fu, and expert in the use of all weapons "which do not leave the hand," as the ler put it. They had moral objections to that, at least.

Han had heard tales. They were not for him to verify. Alone, he realized, he could probably not overpower her even with a beam rifle: she would be too fast. He resolved to leave her strictly alone. She noted his appraisal through his facial movements.

"That is good, Han. You know what I am. So there will be no problem. I accept."

One of the continuing reasons why humans and ler avoid each other revolved around the sexual issue. One concept intimate with revolution was neoteny, an extended immaturity. The ler had gotten a heavy dose of it, and so to human eyes retained the beauty of youth well into middle age. But of course the attraction did not flow both ways. They saw humans as "ancestral primitives" and wanted nothing to do with them in any way that even suggested a sexual relationship. There were other strains as well. Ler were infertile until their adolescence ended around age thirty, but their sex drive started at the beginning of adolescence, around age ten. They were encouraged to enjoy their bodies without restraint, and since they were infertile, even incest was permitted. Humans, on the other hand, were more restrained by necessity. Lastly, even if there had ever been love between two of different kinds, it would have had no yield: the cross between ler and human would not even produce offspring. The original project had gone that far.

Cultural differences had grown alongside physical ones. To humans, ler society seemed too agricultural, static, and oversexed to the point of madness. To ler, human society seemed mechanistic and overhurried. Methods of aggression differed, also. A ler dealt with his or her fellows directly, or ignored them. If the issue came to a fight, then so be it. But they regarded any weapon which left the hand with horror, and by extension, any practice that avoided direct involvement. Lastly, the ler birthrate was low, and so all adults were expected to share childbearing to their limit. Humans used every form of birth control known and it still wasn't enough to keep overcrowding at bay on some worlds.

So Han knew without thinking about it very deeply that he would not be able to play sex-games with the girl, Liszendir. Very well. He could match her in his skill, which was in bargaining, piloting, machinery. He thought, with rueful complacence, that she did not know anything there. They did not train their children for general purposes, but to a particular role, which went with the family, the "braid" willy-nilly.

"I accept also," Han added.

Hetrus nodded, in conformity with the others. "Fine, fine, sure you'll work well together. Now. You can leave at your convenience, although we would prefer it to be as soon as possible. The ship is ready at the spaceport, already cleared. It is set up to be human-financed and ler-registered. It is called by a ler name, *Pallenber*, which means, I am told, 'pearly bow wave.' Just notify the departure controller when you are ready."

Liszendir arose with no ceremony. "I am prepared now. Let it be done and finished."

Han also got to his feet. He thought on the name. Yes, that sounded nice, poetic, bringing visions to mind of sailing ships on a blue sea, with brightly colored sails. Yes, indeed. But it didn't take a linguist to devise, out of those same roots, a name somewhat like "Bone in his teeth," which referred to warships bent on destruction. But he said, "I will need to get some things, make some arrangements."

Hetrus interposed, "No need, my boy, no need at all. You have every-thing you need already aboard the ship. The Master Trader of Boom-town will take care of all arrangements, your papers, your affairs. We advise discretion and deliberation in most things, and they are good practices. However, in this case I am sure you will understand . . ."

"In other words, get going," Han interrupted.

"In a hasty word, which implies no diminution of good will, yes."

"Well, then. I suppose that since this is the case, then I can go now, too. I would as well see it finished." He directed the last at Liszendir, who either failed to notice, or pretended not to.

Preparing to leave, the ler group arose quietly and began their depar-tures with no ceremony whatsoever. Hetrus and the remainder of the humans, Ormancioglu, Marebus and Villacampo, paused by the terrace rail to speak privately about some matter which seemed to occupy their full attentions. Han and Liszendir looked at each other coolly and crit-ically for a moment, then started for the door. Liszendir went through the door first, apparently within her own frame of reference already broken with the group and its business in the room. However, by the door Han turned to the quiet ler who had not given his name.

"I beg your pardon, sir," he began quietly, although no one was near them within earshot, "what ever became of the trader Efrem? And what was your name? I don't believe I caught it . . ."

"Efrem is here in Boomtown, Han Keeling." From the timbre of the voice, Han guessed that the creature was male, although from appear-ance alone, it was even more ambiguous than the normal ler. The voice also seemed curiously resonated and accented, although he thought no more of this than considering the possibility that the ler could have come from some very remote world. The creature continued, "Efrem feared murder, and decided to retire on a generous pension. You may well guess that his cooperation came at a price. But what he had, he sold. You need not worry that he left something out. There would be no point at all in your seeing him. None at all."

"Well, fine enough. Am I being impolite in asking the name, commit-ting some breach of etiquette?"

"No, no. Not at all. Pantankan Tlanh at your service. And may I be fit to assist you in any way that you require."

He had answered in a soft fashion which left Han with the impres-sion that he was being played with. There was something hidden and devious in the expressionless face, some quality which was not present, say, on Liszendir's, however haughty she might have been. Something he wanted to probe. But there was no time for it. Pantankan was headed for the stairwell, now retained only for emergencies. Liszendir was waiting in the lift with an expression of utter boredom on her face.

Han walked to the lift, and joined the girl. The sliding doors closed and they were alone. They avoided looking directly at one another. Yet something was gnawing deeply at Han, and it was something which wouldn't keep quiet long. They reached the ground floor and started out of the building. Liszendir started out confidently in the general direction of the underground tube to the spaceport.

Han looked about in the midmorning crowd to see if they were being noticed, which would be only relative since the ler girl would stand out in her self-conscious plainness here in Boomtown greatly; the ler came here only rarely. He slowed, stopped, and motioned to her to come closer. She did, but with some impatience and annoyance.

He said to her, "I think before we leave, we should stop off and have a little chat with Efrem. We've got time, and it may give us some ideas on what exactly we're looking for."

"I see no need of it," she replied. "We were told the essence of the facts. Besides that, we hardly know where to look for him."

"I can't believe you see it as all that simple," Han said, with some of his own annoyance. "But however it seems to you, I'm going. The dark ler who didn't speak during the meeting said Efrem was here. In Boomtown. I suspect you can't fly the ship by yourself, so I ask you to accompany me to his quarters. You will prefer it to a boring wait at the ship."

"Really? You think I could not force you here on the street? You are very foolish, or dangerously brave. It is true that I could not fly it, nor do I wish to learn. But you would be happy, perhaps overjoyed, to do it for me, should I exert a minor effort which would surely go unnoticed by these barbarians."

Han looked about helplessly. He had not intended to goad her, or excite her temper. But he believed what she said. Perhaps guarded by a platoon of snipers concealed on the roofs and balconies at all points of the compass, he might have had a chance. But they were not present. Therefore he decided to try to reason with her. Ler were reputedly logical folk.

"As you say. But there is a thing I am uncertain on, which I must know before we go on. Will you allow this?"

"Go on. But we waste time."

"All of your names mean something, yes? They are not just meaning-less sounds, a label? And you recognize the significance of each name?"

"It is so. We do not call ourselves by numbers, or by letters that ful-fill the same purpose."

"What does Pantankan mean?"

"That is foolish. It is not a name. It can't be. As a symbol, it means, I think, what you would call an alphabet. You say the old names of your first two letters. We say the first three. Panh. Tanh. Kanh. P.T.K."

"That's all it means?"

"All and only. To my knowledge, that trisyllable is not to be used for a name."

"Well, that is what the dark ler told me his name was. Could he have been joking?"

"No. Names are not joking matters."

"He made it a point to say that Efrem was here, but that we would learn no more by seeing him."

"Did he say this before any of us?"

"No. We were alone, by the door. You were waiting in the lift. Did he give his name to your people, before I got there?"

"No. He did not. We would not ask, if he preferred silence. A name, in some ways, in our system, is . . . private. But. Never mind. I agree. I see the rat in the grain. Yes, we shall go and see this Efrem. But by my lead. There is a trap here, I think." She said the last with something al-most approaching friendliness, or camaraderie.

" 'Alphabet' wants us to go there."

"I think not. It seems baited for you. I should not have been inter-ested, and you should have been ignorant enough to fail to tell me, or if you had, fail to convince me. No. I am sure now; the trap is for you. Good work! You are sharper than I would have given you credit for!"

"Thanks." Han added, "Just what I needed." He hoped this shallow foray into sarcasm would not set her off again; but she only gave him a cool glance in return.

The public telescanner catalogue, to their surprise, indeed listed one such Edo Efrem; and the address was not far away. Han at first wanted to call him, but Liszendir urged caution and deviousness. He agreed, and so they set out by roundabout ways which he knew. Along the way, Liszendir made a running commentary on the disadvantages of human cities, but as she did, she also pointed out strategic locations should street fighting ever be required. It was a subject she seemed ferociously knowledgeable in. Han felt he was no sissy, but all the same, he shuddered, invisibly, he hoped, at some of the things she calmly suggested.

When they arrived at the building where Efrem was reputed to live, she paused thoughtfully. She asked, after a moment, "If you were going to visit someone in one of these hives, how would you go about it?"

"Through the front door and to the lift. Then to the apartment and stand before the door and state who you are. If anyone answers, you go in."

"Are there stairs?"

"Yes."

"Then we will use them."

Inside the building, at the floor they wanted, the third, she cautioned Han, "Ring the bell from the side, from as far as you can reach. Then step back. I will hold you."

Han did as she asked, extending his hand to hers. She grasped it, firmly and directly. He felt a sudden shock: it was a soft, cool, feminine hand of no apparent great strength. The double thumbs, one of each side of her rather narrow hand, locked around his wrist in a peculiar grip. There seemed to be no real restraint in the grip, but he knew instinctively that he could not be pulled free of her.

Han rang the bell. A pleasant voice from within said, "Please enter," and the door slid open noiselessly. Han leaned further forward, but Liszendir pulled him back, none too gently. He looked at her; she was making a gesture with her hand and her face . . . she put her finger to her lips, pointed to both eyes, then to her forehead, and then made a rotary motion with the finger. Han recognized the crude sign language. She was saying, "Be silent, watch, and learn."

Liszendir moved around Han to come nearer the door, carefully lay flat on the floor, and *undulated*—there was no other word to describe the motion she made—into the doorway. Then she half raised, and made a peculiar motion upwards with her free hand. Immediately, from within the room, there sounded a faint hiss, which ended virtually instantly with a low *thunk* in the corridor wall behind her. Han started forward, but she said, in a low voice, "No. Stay where you are!" Some long minutes passed. Liszendir lay very still, as flat as a rug. Then there was another *hiss-thunk*. The girl gained her feet in one flowing, smooth motion, and darted into the room. A moment later Han heard her voice from within, "It's fixed now. You can come in."

He went into the room cautiously. Liszendir was standing opposite the door, holding a pistol of unfamiliar type. It looked like a pistol, but like no one Han had ever seen before. It was molded in one piece, of some dark and apparently heavy metal, and as he approached, could be heard to be hissing quietly to itself. The barrel was long and very slender, while the handle or butt flared into a bulge shaped somewhat like a shoe. To the side of the room lay a corpse.

Liszendir said, "This is a devilish thing. The gun was set in a triggering mechanism keyed by the door. There was a timer; there was no radar or sonics I could find." She indicated the muzzle. There was a tiny hole in it. "I have disarmed it. It uses highly compressed gas to fire rifled slivers, probably made of a material which will dissolve in the body. The slivers would also contain poison and a coagulant for the wound. They are terrible things, but luckily for both you and me, weapons like this do not have a great range."

She opened the magazine expertly, and removed gingerly a tiny, glistening needle of some transparent material. She handled it carefully, putting the needle down on a shelf to look at it. Han reached for it, but she stopped him.

"Some things like this are hollow. This one does not seem so. If that is true, the whole needle is poison and may be activated by handling."

He nodded agreement, then turned to the body.

"No," she said. "It may be trapped. We can learn nothing from it. We can call the police from the ship, although we should call Hetrus. But let us leave here, quickly. I have danger-sense. This room is loaded with traps."

They left the room cautiously. Han picked up the strange little pistol where Liszendir had dropped it.

"Can this thing be recharged?"

"Oh, yes. The reservoir I bled off is the secondary one, the one that powers the firing chamber. The main reservoir is still almost full."

"I thought I'd take it with us. We may have need for it."

"You may. Do not ask me to touch it again. I will explain after we have boarded the ship. But not now! We must move fast. Someone wanted at least for you to come to this room, perhaps to be killed, perhaps to be caught and accused."

Han agreed, and pocketing the deadly little gun, hurriedly left the apartment.

2

---

*"The sage knows more than four seasons; the Fool says that the
four of which his calendar speaks are of no importance."*
                    —Ler saying, attr. to Garlendadh Tlanh.

LISENDIR WAS TENSE during their trip to the spaceport, and did not
fully relax, or reach a state which appeared to be relaxation, until
they were actually on the ship, *Pallenber*, and well into space. Indeed, she
had gone over the ship with extreme care, looking carefully for snares,
traps and miscellaneous tracers, bugs and the like. After a few days, she
pronounced the *Pallenber* free of all such devices. Han agreed, although
privately, he reflected that such an absence might in itself be curious in
the light of the events which had occurred just before they left.

In the meantime, he had also been busy, counting and checking their
provisions, the ostensible trade goods, the state of the weapons carried
aboard the ship. He had also been engaged in several commnet conversations with Hetrus over the matter of the body in the apartment
(which had indeed proved to be that of Efrem), the possible trap and
the identity of the unknown fifth ler. Hetrus was definitely interested,
and was pursuing matters with a great amount of bureaucratic zeal, but
at least up to this point, he had uncovered nothing. The ler he had contacted knew no more than he did.

Among these jobs, they entered matrix overspace, set the course and
settled down to routine. They set up shifts, so that one of them would
always be awake. Liszendir did not enjoy being responsible for the ship
while Han was asleep, but she accepted the training he gave her stoically
and agreed to awaken him immediately should an emergency occur. He
didn't expect one, but at the same time he saw no lack of virtue in a little caution.

He wondered what it would be like if she should have to wake him
up in an emergency. Would she pitch him out of his hammock in some

artful way, so that he would perform some odd pervulsion of motion before he hit the deck? No, he thought. To imagine that was silly. More soberly, he suspected that she would not use her "skill" without good reason or provocation, in line with other, similar disciplines which had appeared from time to time among humans. No. She would be completely inhibited during normal situations by a complex code, or if one preferred, a set of rules of engagement. Such creatures would be incredibly dangerous turned loose in society without some inhibitions of that nature.

After several days, however, he found out. He had fallen out of sleep early, for some reason, and was just lying in his hammock, drifting, imagining, half-asleep. Then he became aware that without his noticing it, a presence had entered his cabin and was watching him, silently. He lay quietly, waiting. After what seemed to him as an almost eternal passage of time, she leaned forward and touched him gently on the shoulder. As she did, he caught the tiniest shred of her scent, which was her own and not perfume; it was heady, rather grassy, with some sharp, but very faint, undertones.

He nodded, pretending that he had been asleep, and got up, hoping that she would not see that he was pretending.

"Is it time already?"

"No. I woke you early. After a few days of this, I am bored and lonely and need some talk, some interaction. We are not used to solitude. Do you mind?"

"No, no; not at all. I feel much the same way. But I did not wish to offend you by forcing anything you did not want." The last was a barb at her early haughtiness. If she noticed it, she gave no sign.

"I understand. We are not all that different. Good, then. I will wait for you in the control room."

She turned and departed, as silently as she had come. Han wondered at that. At first, during the busy first days, he had not noticed, but as the time they had been alone together on the ship increased, he began to notice, more and more, the silence and grace with which she moved. It looked effortless, flowing like water in a stream, but he knew with the logical part of his mind that a thousand years or more of tradition and training went into that uncanny movement.

His thoughts strayed further. She was in no way he could identify like the girls he had known, chased, loved in short and desultory affairs which were the norm for Boomtown society. She was curved and feminine, true enough, now that he had time to notice, but the shape was all subtlety, suggestion, hint. He thought, almost like a riddle, whose question was at too fine a focus to be put exactly into words he knew. The shapeless robe she wore, a standard ler garment, was a concealer which revealed, and contributed in no small way to the growing sense of eroticism that he felt. He was sure that to ler eyes, she was young, agile, pretty and extremely desirable. And of course, easily attainable, with no qualms on either side. But to him, it was a different matter.

That, he shut off, abruptly. He strongly suspected that he would be able to cherish no hopes in that area. He didn't even know if anything would be possible between them, emotionally or physically. Ler adolescent eroticism was well known among humans, yet at the same time, there were few tales of any adventures between the two. And such tales as were, were invariably structured like the vulgar stories of little boys, whose imaginations so easily outstripped reality, and even probability.

Still, even after thousands of years, the ler were remarkably casual about dalliance; or for that matter, about refusals. Oddly enough, all their myths seemed to revolve around the efforts of individuals; nowhere was love or passion about it featured in even a major role.

So Han dressed, depilated his beard, and went to the control room. The forward part of the room, which was the largest on the ship, was not a window, but a converter screen which passed a real-space view even when the ship was in any one of the matrix overspaces. Moreover, it was tunable over a wide range of frequencies. It was now fully open, tuned to the slightly broader response characteristics of the ler eye. The only light in the control room came from this screen and from the instruments; outside, with no apparent barrier between them, lay the deeps of starry darkness, drifting visibly at the corners of the screen. Liszendir sat quietly in the pilot's chair and looked out on the spectacle. If she noticed Han enter, she gave no sign.

"Have you traveled space before?" he asked, trying to start a conversation. He knew very well that she had, because there were no ler anywhere near Seabright.

"Oh, yes, many times. But never with such a view as this," she replied, almost cheerfully. After a short pause, she continued.

"This is not new, it is just the endlessness of it which both attracts me and disturbs me at the same time. There is more here than all of us together can ever know. Here, I become receptive to the reality of my own insignificance."

Han agreed, but only in part. He did not understand why she should become so pensive over the immensity, and implied infinitude, of space.

It really didn't matter whether you were on a planetary surface or not, you were still a finite creature working and striving, or just coasting with the current, in infinite systems. But he replied, "Yes, it does prompt that feeling. I know it well. Still, we must do what we will measured by what we are able to do."

"Yes, like the sea. At my home, on Kenten, our *yos*, where the braid lives, is beside a body of salt water, a narrow bay of the sea that connects up in the west with the ocean. All around are mountains, some wild and rugged, some terraced with gardens and orchards, other *yosas*, towns, towers. I used to watch the sea before the garden for hours. The waves, the play of light, the changeable winds and that timelessness which is great time, *kfandrir*, passing, greater than our lives. The sea said to me, 'I was here, reposed, filling the basins of my will, gathered, caressed by the wind, before ler came to this planet; and when they have gone, I will still be here.' The waves, such little things, mock us in their infinitude; I look here outwards in my shift and I see the same words."

Again she became silent, and resumed looking at the darkness immense and the spotted glory of the far stars. Han tried to imagine the depth of the picture of her home she had painted. He could not. He knew about ler "family" structure and how it dominated their society, but he had no insight into it, *how* it was.

The ler "family" structure, the so-called "braid," was dictated by their low birthrate, which rarely produced more than two offspring per bred female during the fertile period, which ran roughly from age thirty to forty. But other elements played important roles: the long, infertile adolescence with its high sex-drive tended to make individuals independent and solitary by nature. The short, fertile period with its long gestation periods, eighteen months. And their original low numbers, with the associated small gene pool. On Earth they had had several family models to emulate in their early period, but they had liked none of them. So they invented a structure which would widen the gene pool, use the birthrate to the fullest, and provide an organism for raising children. But it was not, like human models, a heriditary chain, a bloodline, but a social procedure which wove their society together in a complex fashion.

Basically, the braid originated with a male and female of the same ages, at fertility. They would mate, hopefully producing a child, who would be the *nerh* or elder outsibling. At age thirty-five standard, the two would select and recruit second mates for each other, and remate. Each pair would produce a child, who would be called *toorh*, insiblings.

After that, the inductees would mate and produce a last child, called *thes*, or younger outsibling. All lived under one roof, together.

At *their* fertility, the insiblings, who were not blood-related to each other, having separate parents, would weave and become the nucleus of the next braid generation. The *nerh* and the *thes* would weave into other braids as afterparents. So each child-generation would be distributed into three braids. This process kept the genetic pool wide and actually prevented inbreeding and the establishment of racial traits.

As soon as the insiblings had woven, the parents of the old braid would leave and go their own way, leaving the house and everything that went with it in the hands of the new generation. They were then considered free of all responsibility and could do as they would. Some stayed together, some went off on their own.

That was *what* it was, but few humans, if any, had any feel for *how* it was, as it was completely at variance with the way humans, with variations, structured their families. At times, on various planets, some enterprising humans would set up analogues of the ler braids. But they never lasted very long. The strains were too great, emotionally, sexually, and particularly in the matter of property. And in the fact that, after all, the braid was a mechanism for making full use of fertility. Used with humans, it was like throwing gasoline on a fire.

Han said, "Tell me about your family, your braid. Your friends. What you did at the school. I suspect that you know more of the way I live than I of your way."

She turned back to him. "Not necessarily so. You know I am *Nerh*. I am now at a point in my life when for all practical purposes school is over, but I am not quite old enough to be invited to weave as aftermother with another braid. I was head of house, with the other children of my generation, probably much like an older sister in your terms, but with more authority. Still, it was a waning authority. My insiblings were Dherlinjan and Follirian. They pay attention to me, but they know very well that all they have to do is wait. In your society, eldest gets all. In ours, the insiblings get everything—house, title, braid name. Even the parents leave when the insiblings become fertile."

"Where do you go? Do they put you out in the cold?"

"Oh, no." She laughed in a low tone, quietly. It was the first time he had heard her laugh. It was a relaxed, pleasant sound. "As for me, or like me, by then I would already have woven. The *thes* stays at home until they are chosen. But the parents—they are elders, then. They are free; they can do anything they want. They have gender, but no sex. So they are completely free. Some go off in small groups, you would say communes, although it is not exactly like that. Others go into government or business. Still others become *mnath*, the wise. They live alone, rarely in pairs, in the hills and forests."

"Don't the adults of the old generation stay together?"

"Yes, sometimes, they do. But as often as not they don't. There is no rule and people do as they please. With the Karen, it is tradition that the insiblings stay and teach at the school, which belongs to the braid. Sometimes the afterparents, who were outsiblings before weaving, stay as well. But our braid is an old one and such traditions are meaningful to us. But the elders do not live in the *Yos*. That is forbidden. This way, a *yos* need only be of such a size, so everyone has much of the same size of house. That discourages vanity."

Han was surprised at the insights he gained from her. He had always thought of ler weaving as something either akin to marriage, or sanctioned cohabitation. It was neither, and apparently was regulated more strictly than either. He was, however, still dissatisfied. "Well, that sounds nice, but what about rich and poor? Don't the rich have bigger houses? Or don't you have rich and poor? And who runs the government?"

She answered easily. Liszendir either ignored sarcasm, or did not recognize it. "Oh, yes, we have rich and poor. But you think in terms of family, and inheritance. With us, it is the braid that is rich or poor. For the rest, all you take when you leave, outsibling or elder, are some personal things, clothes and the like. We know that possessions enslave. And it is the same with land. The property one owns is where one works or lives. No more. Nothing less. Some elders become very rich and powerful. But when they terminate, all that they have made goes back into the common treasury. All of it.

"And as for the government, you know that braids are set for certain roles. One bakes bread, another builds houses, another performs still another function in the community. So it is with the government; a certain braid runs it, others perform supporting roles within it. You met Yalvarkoy and Lenkurian Haoren? They are also from Kenten, and they are what you might call 'a braid which is responsible for the ministry of the interior.' But our governments are small. We restrain ourselves, so that we do not have to call on someone else to do it for us. And the way to outlaw complex, weighty governments, is to outlaw preconditions which lead to complex problems."

"That doesn't sound very free."

"Well, in the matter of running the government, no. But our government leaves us alone."

"You said self-restraint. I must ask if some are not so restrained?"

"Yes. Some are. And that is where the school comes in. We Karens are something like what you would call police and judges at the same time. Our law is equivalence. We are as prone to dishonesty as any folk, I suppose, so I am trained in ler law and in many degrees of violence. And in philosophy, for only the wise may judge, and only the gentle command violence." At the last, Liszendir slipped into a peculiar kind of measured speech, almost as if she were chanting.

"Or, 'An eye for an eye, a tooth for a tooth'?"

"Or in some cases, the money equivalent."

"Then you know a lot about ler society."

"Yes. Would you like a recitation?" She laughed. "I can recite the *Book of the Law*, the *Way of the Wise*, the *Fourteen Sages' Commentaries*, and if you desire, all the names of my insibling chain back *zhan* generations. That number is the second power of fourteen to you, and has the same significance as your one hundred."

Han laughed back at her. "Anything else?"

Liszendir sat pensively for a moment. Then she brightened and said, "If we had a very long voyage, I could also teach you Singlespeech, which is our everyday language. You could not learn Multispeech, but I am a master of both modes, *one to many and many to one*, and could at least tell you about it. I could also teach you sliding numbers, which you would find useful."

"Sliding numbers?"

"We do not have a fixed number base, like your tenbase or the one your machines use, two-base. We use many, as fits the situation. We are non-Aristotelians: hence to us, reality cannot be categorized into any fixed number of states. So we use many bases; theoretically, we could use any number as a base, but we restrict ourselves to bases which are twice a prime number, such as, in decimals, base of six, which we call childsway, or base ten, which we discourage, or base fourteen. There are many others. Base ninety-four, or another which uses most of the wordroots of Singlespeech for numbers in its unity sequence."

"Why not ten and two, like us?"

"Two reasons. To program non-Aristotelianism into all, and to prevent children from counting on their fingers. We have five digits, just like you; but we make them go abstract from the first—it makes things easier later on."

She held her hand out for him to see. It was a graceful, strong hand, smooth and finely shaped. It was very similar to a normal human hand, except that the palm was narrower, and the little finger had separated and moved back, like a smaller thumb. It was opposable, just like a thumb, and in the matter of writing, ler were not "handed," but wrote with either hand, holding the pen with either thumb. She wore no rings of any kind. The nails were pink, plain, and clipped off short and neat. The only distinguishing mark of any kind was a small tattoo at the base of the inner thumb, suggestive of the ancient Chinese symbol of Yang and Yin.

Han asked, "What is that mark?"

"That is the badge of my skill."

"That is very similar to an ancient symbol of old Earth. Chinese. Did your firstfolk model on them?"

"Yes. Some things. The best example is language. Our Singlespeech was modeled on theirs, but in phonetic root building only. We did not imitate their grammar or sounds. Each Singlespeech root has three parts—leading consonant, middle vowel, and final consonant. Within the rules, every combination has four meanings. But only that far. We used old English for the phonetics, for we lived in a country where it was spoken. And we did not like using tones. In that way, we modeled much on their ideas, but we used different materials. It is that way in other areas."

Han started to interrupt, but Liszendir went on. "And especially we borrowed from them the lesson of change. They knew change and permutation well, and that all things end. All that begins must end, and all that is, must be something else. They were called backward, yet their society lasted on Earth much longer than the ones of those who trusted in stone and metal and illusions of changelessness. The ones who hoped they would live forever."

Han arose from his chair, went to the kitchen unit and programmed it, and then returned. Then they talked about humans. Han felt at a disadvantage here, since he lacked the continunity with his ancestors which Liszendir seemed to have. Here was a puzzle: ler society seemed static, old-fashioned, primitive, tribal. Yet they assimilated some forms of technology with no apparent effort and seemed to suffer no cultural shock from those newer ingredients. And as a group, they showed little change in time or space. They were remarkably homogeneous; ler from different planets spoke the same language and held the same social structures in common. Humans were changeable, divergent.

Of his own forebears, Han only knew back to his father's grandfather, who had come to Boomtown from somewhere else and become a trader. Beyond that, he only knew that the great-grandfather had supposedly come from Thersing V. What had members of the family been before that? What difference did it make?

He saw, in Liszendir, a girl of such basic culture, that, having learned basics from her, he could reasonably expect to find the same motivations in another ler from any place. The individual would be different, just like humans, but there seemed to be much less of a range. One human was easy and tolerant; the next might be a bigot of the most intolerant sort. But to her, she could not hope to have the same assurances: every human she met would be different.

Religion was another area where there was a deep rift between their mutual comprehensions. He described human practices in this area in great detail, hoping by conversational trade to elicit some description of ler practices out of her. As always, the ruling classes of human society were more or less agnostic, paying lip service to whatever cult happened to be active in their area at the time. This was one human constant that ran unbroken all the way back to Gilgamesh. The deeds remained the same, and only the excuses were changed to protect the innocent. And as in all other areas, human society varied in religion in both time and space.

But of ler religion or lack thereof, men knew little or nothing. Some savants averred that there was indirect evidence of this or that structure; but upon more sober examination, these theories seemed to revolve more upon the prejudices of the author than on the practices of the subject. Nor could Han get any information out of Liszendir: she was curiously reticent to discuss the subject, and avoided questions with great dexterity. The only positive statement he could get out of her was in reference to the projectile weapon they had found set for them in Efrem's apartment. She was definitive in her distaste for it; apparently projectile weapons of any kind were ritually unclean to her. He remembered that she had handled it with the greatest reluctance, and when he asked her now further about this, she said little. She had shuddered, and said sadly, "No ler would touch the filthy thing. And especially no Karen." She made a curious gesture with her left hand, the one that bore the yang-and-yin mark. That was all he could get out of her.

As they ate, the talk drifted towards sexual topics. It was an area Han did not really want to come up, but he felt it was almost inevitable; a certain tension was rising between them, and here was its obvious source. Han was no beginner, and was not particularly bashful, or ashamed of the things he had done. Yet he was reticent to talk at length about his past adventures. However, the girl was not restrained in the least, and became more animated as she discussed this aspect of their lives in detail. The kitchen delivered its work, and they sat down to eat together.

For a time, they traded some relatively innocent stories back and forth. But it became clear that here was a very great difference between them.

She said, "I am surprised at only one thing about your way—that you wait so long. You are concerned first about your identity, then later, sometimes after you have become parents, with sex. It is just the reverse with us. We do not worry so much about our identity until after we have become parents.

"I will tell you how it was with me, not to satisfy your curiosity so much as to work something out in my own mind. You see, for us, I was somewhat late in getting the idea. As children, we are very free—we can do as we want, and curiosity about the body is not discouraged. And in good weather, we do not wear clothes. So as a child, a *hazh*, that is a pre-adolescent child, you see young people, adolescents, *did-has*, playing body-games with each other all the time; no one goes to a great deal of trouble to hide. But you do not have any interest in it— it's silly, you know? But one day it isn't silly any more and you want to do it."

She stopped for a moment, as if she were reaching for a memory, savoring it, weighing it to determine its exact substance. She smiled weakly. "As I said, I was late. All of my friends the same age were all crazy about this new thing they had discovered they could do with each other. But I didn't seem to understand why it was so important. So one day we were swimming, not far from my *yos*. It was very warm. And a boy I knew, Fithgwinjir, very pretty, took me to the beach, holding my hand. I felt very strange. I saw he was different, ready. But all I felt was expectation. He said, 'Liszen, let's do it together, now.' That was the first time anyone had ever called me a love name. We only use the first syllable of our names when we are children. Two when you are adolescent. And later, three. I told him I didn't know how. He told me he would show me. We kissed, and then we lay down together in the warm sand. The others, some looked, and some didn't. It wasn't important to them.

Just *madhainimoni*, 'they who are making love to each other.' But it was very important to me. I felt turned inside out. And I loved Fithgwin, of course.

"Afterwards, I wanted to talk to someone, but I knew the other children would laugh; they were way ahead of me. It wasn't new to them. I was ten. They had been at it for months, some a year. My insiblings were about five, so they knew nothing, and my *thes*, Vindhermaz, he was just a baby. So I told my foremother, my *madh*. She was very happy— she was worried I would be retarded.

"But I learned fast. At first it's like that. Play. Fun. Something to do. Then you fall in love, over and over again. You begin spending nights with your love at each other's houses. Then you have group parties together. But by your late teens you are settling down, playing at more adult games, hoping you will be chosen to start a new braid as *shartoorh*, honorary insiblings. That is very wonderful, because that is the only time you can pick who your mate will be. That is what we all dream about before we are woven.

"So. Now. The present. Wendyorlei was my last lover. We were living together, schoolmates, in a *yos* which was not presently being used. We felt the same way: we hoped we could stay together and be chosen. But we did not have a great love. Yes, we cared, we were loving-kind to each other, but we still wandered, too. We had other lovers, and as is custom, we did not hide them from each other. That is training for when you are woven—there can be no jealousy in the *yos*. None. You learn to erase it before you weave.

"School finished. Wendyor was needed at his home, which was across the mountains. We were waiting for something. And I heard of this, and so came. I harbor no illusions. I will never see him again close within my arms." She took a very deep breath.

Han told her a parallel tale, the story of his adventures in love, the ones he had felt like they were the last thing in the world. And the others, which had been just fun. But he admitted that he had started much later, and couldn't come near her in quantity.

She said, "Well, I approve, of course. And I understand why you are so cautious. We are not fertile—it is just fun, with no price except the one you pay with your heart. But you do not have that room to move about in. A mistake, and your life is out of control, yes?"

"Yes," was all Han could say.

"Now. Your name is very close to the form of a ler name. It is easy for me to call you 'Han,' but hard in another. The single syllable reminds me of a child, but there is nothing childish about you. Also, the child name ends. And I do not know how to handle that."

"I would be less than honest if I said that I had not found you desirable, even with our differences," Han said, after some hesitation.

Liszendir had finished eating. She leaned back in the chair, stretched gracefully, and her face took on a coyness, an arch flirtatious look which Han found unbearable. She had, in an instant, become beautiful in the soft light of the instruments and the stars. He could not turn away the thoughts he had of that smooth, completely hairless body under the homespun robe.

She said, in a soft voice he had never before heard her use, and which matched perfectly a face which had become mysteriously lovely, the broad mouth soft and generous, "Yes. I see, and I have felt some of the same with you. It frightens me, for I know very well that physically we are compatible; yet it is said that such things are not to be done, and with wisdom, for our endurance is different from yours. We can do it many times. So it is not to be done: but you are male and not unattractive, even if you are too hairy." She laughed shortly, and then became pensive and sober again.

After a long, silent moment, she said, quietly, "You must not touch me when we are in this mood. The urge to couple in ler is very strong, more intense than to you, until we are no longer fertile. I have not made love for some time and my need is great. And you and I should not to do this thing, Han."

As she finished, she rose and turned away. "It is now your turn at the watch. I will do my exercises and sleep." She started towards the passageway door.

Han said, just as she paused at the door to go through it, "By the way, you never told me the meaning of your name."

She looked back, startled. "You do not know what you ask. But it is no secret. It means, literally, 'velvet-brushed-night.' A 'liszendir' is a special kind of sky . . . it is when the night sky is very clear, like there was no air in it, but streaked with very fine, high cirrus clouds, filmy, lit only by starlight. It is normally a winter sky, although we rarely see it in summer."

Han, mystified, shrugged. "Well that's progress, at least. Now we know each other better."

Liszendir looked unfathomable. She made a gesture of negation. "There is no progress. There is only change." She vanished through the door.

3

"There is no such thing as a doctrine, a theory, or an idea which lacks the capacity and the ability to imprison the mind.
—*The Fourteen Sages' Commentaries,* v 1, ch 3, Suntrev 15

THE REMAINDER OF their journey to Chalcedon passed in what Han would later think of as courteous silence. Yet, there was something unfinished between them, something unresolved, which in other circumstances might have posed no problem at all.

Han, amused and bemused by his own reactions to his growing appreciation of Liszendir's intense sexuality, consoled himself and, so he thought, made things easier for her, by growing a fine full beard. Beards were not, as a general rule, very common in more settled areas, but it was a habit indulged in occasionally by most traders. At first, it grew slowly, but soon it was coming in with fine speed, and an increasingly silky texture. It grew in dark, darker than his dark-brown hair, and he was pleased with it, and spent considerable time training it.

Liszendir disapproved, as he had hoped; her race grew no beards. In fact, they had no body hair whatsoever below the eyebrows, a fact which disturbed him somewhat whenever he let his thoughts stray in the direction of a possible liaison with the ler girl. Would it be like making love to a child? No, on second thought, he doubted that very much, watching her wise and knowing eyes, the way she walked.

In turn, she made all attempts to be businesslike and completely unsexual. It did not work, completely, for as she observed, such a thing was like a rabbit pretending that he did not really like greens. She had never had to repress it before, and admitted that indeed it was a fine exercise in the art of self-control. Han agreed. Self-control, indeed.

To pass the time, he taught her how to fly the ship. He argued the necessity of this through the logic that there could be an occasion when they would need someone to fly the *Pallenber* while the other operated the weapons, of which they had a considerable variety. And he knew very well that she would not use those weapons unless at the utmost extremity. According to the ship's papers they carried, the *Pallenber* was listed as an armed merchantman; Han knew this as a euphemism for "privateer." He knew well enough that such things were done, but they had been unheard-of in his portion of space for many a year.

As they worked—which went slowly, for she seemed to have a rather low degree of mechanical competence—he asked her how the ler fought wars, if they had any among themselves. He could not see how they could fight a war, without using weapons that leave the hand.

She answered, "We have wars, enough for anyone's taste. 'Once through a ler war and you become a pacifist,' so the saying goes. But we have our disagreements, and if it comes to a resolution by force, then so be it. All participate. But we fight over issues which can be seen in front of you. Immediate things. I suppose you would call them light-infantry actions. But for all that, they are rare. Another difference from humans is the fact that our sense of territoriality is much weaker than yours. It was considered a disadvantage to those who were trying to breed us at the first. And we do not fight over things like politics and religion. Those kinds of things mean that the fighting goes far beyond the battlefield, where such things should be settled."

So when there was a war to be fought, they took up knives and swords, shields, bludgeons, hammers and morningstars, and set upon one another with all the skill they could muster. After the issue had been settled, the combatants retired from the field, the winners took what they had been fighting for, or against, and the losers consoled them-selves. After all, in losing, they did not lose everything.

But they were not pacifists, and it was true that ler were not partic-ularly unaggressive. Fights between two were not uncommon, and brawls in taverns or on the street were known. But they did not resort to weapons which left the hand, whatever the level of conflict, however many pursued it. A ler who did that would be instantly lynched, then and there, by his fellows. It was the only unappealable death penalty they had.

And for all that they were opposed to their use, they were not blind to the uses of projectile weapons. They extended their penalty to any-one who used them; and since the penalty was eradication without quarter, few ever considered it. They had developed the perfect defense against interplanetary war: try to bomb a ler planet, and they activated a device which caused your sun to go nova. Then they went after your ships and tore them apart with grapples. If anyone should survive to the surface, they were met in turn by a horde which had removed all restraints. They would not give up, and they would not stop until the entire invasion force was in shreds, literally torn apart.

In trade for teaching her how to fly the ship, Liszendir offered to teach Han a few basic moves and falls, so he would, as she put it, "be able to look after yourself in close quarters." The instruction went smoothly, but it developed that Han had the same lacks in motor coordination that she had in mechanics. He appreciated what she taught him, but he ached for days afterwards with sore muscles. And the body contact disturbed them both more than either of them would openly admit.

"Liszendir, do boys and girls train together in your school?"

"Indeed. Together. We make few distinctions according to gender or sex," she said with some amusement.

"Well, aren't they stimulated by the close physical contact?"

"Certainly. They train in the elementary part, the first six years, nude. They have to learn basics by seeing muscles. Feeling them. And if they have a problem, why they just go off to a corner, or to the bushes, and satisfy themselves. Why not? You humans allow your students breaks for needs they have. So do we. But in the more advanced parts of training, they learn self-control."

But after a few attempts to instruct Han in some of the finer points, she pronounced him, for the time being, a hopeless case. But when she said it, she was smiling. And Han had done better than either he or Liszendir had imagined he would have.

In the meantime, Han consulted the instruments and announced the end of their journey to be near. The star which was primary to Chalcedon was drawing near. Soon, they would be back on the ground again, to see first-hand the evidence of the "Warriors of Dawn."

They made a festive occasion of their last meal together while the *Pallenber* remained in matrix overspace, decorating the control room, and setting what pretended to be an elegant service for two at the control panels below the view of space transmitted into the ship by the huge screen. They sat, and ate, in relative quiet, each savoring the better parts of what had happened since they set out on this trip to the edge of known space.

As they finished, Liszendir asked, "Can we see Chalcedon's star in this?"

"Of course. It's been aimed at that point since we started. Here. I'll show you." He depressed a small button on the panel: immediately two lines, finer than the thinnest hair, appeared on the view, one horizontal, the other vertical. The screen display suggested the illusion that the fine silver lines had been impressed upon space itself. At the point where they intersected, a single star waited, seemingly nearer than the millions of other points.

"It's still too far away from us to show a disc, just yet. And we'll drop out of overspace before it gets an appreciable one. But there it is, nonetheless."

"Could we see Chalcedon with this?"

"Not as it's set now. It will only process objects of a certain angular diameter when it's set in this mode; that's why the background looks black. We have to get closer and be in our normal space."

Liszendir became quiet again and resumed staring at the screen. Ler ships, for all their sophistication of drive systems, were worse than primitive when it came to sensory receptors. In the particular matrix they used, there was nothing to see; in normal space, the crew and passengers looked out on the universe through nothing more exotic than quartz panes, heavy and ground optically flat. Their pilots sat way up on top of the great round bells they called ships, in a little cupola, and flew the huge things *manually*.

So this view was particularly impressive to her. She had spent most of her waking hours here in the control room, looking through the viewscreen that looked like a huge picture window.

Something was nagging Han from the screen; a suggestion of movement. But as he looked, he could see nothing more than the drifting points of the stars. Then he would look away, and his peripheral vision would start acting up again. The more he thought about it, the longer he recalled having noticed it. Still, try as he would, he could actually see nothing. Trying to catch it by watching along the edges of his peripheral vision, at last he became sure. There was a motion. But what?

"Liszendir, do you see anything moving in the screen?"

"Moving? No. But the image has been disturbed all along. Could you not see it? I thought it was something in the equipment, and that you knew about it. It looks to me as if I was seeing this image under water, and I was directly above the surface, looking down into it. Ripples move across the surface from a point, but nothing I can see is making them."

"Hm." Han, muttering to himself, blanked out the screen, and put its computer through a self-check routine. In a few minutes the screen came back on, no different than before. He asked her, "Is it still there?"

"Yes."

"Where is the point the ripples seem to be coming from?"

"At the crosshairs. The star of Chalcedon."

Han reached into the console and produced a great heavy manual, which listed characteristics of known stars. He thumbed through the manual for a time, and then spoke. "According to this, Chalcedon's star is A VILA 1381 indexed, a normal GO yellow star of median age, securely on the main sequence, no abnormalities whatsoever. If that ripple is a real effect, and not an error in the display, I would expect some kind of gravity abnormality in the system, there. Like a very sick star, or perhaps a neutron star that had wandered into the area. But the star is listed here as a perfect example of a star that's right, not wrong, and wandering neutron stars have a very low probability of being captured by such a system. They almost always move across a system in hyperbolic orbits. Granted, if it was a wide pass and a shallow hyperbola, we might see some effect as long as this trip—even longer, if we had the really fancy instruments the colonial survey uses. But that's just guessing. Besides, A VILA 1381 is not so massive it couldn't be moved about by a neutron star in orbit. We've got detectors for that kind of wobbles, and ours hasn't uttered a peep the whole trip. It's not impossible, of course. Any event always has a probability of plus zero—that's old science. And it's been months since anyone's been out this way from the interior. But . . ."

Liszendir interrupted him, "It's stopped!"

"Just like that?"

"Yes. Quick. While you were talking. In the center, and the last ripples fled to the edge. The image is quiet now."

Han got up, and consulted several instruments. He also ran the computer through some computations. He looked up. "Whatever was causing it is not in the star."

They both became quiet and thoughtful. During the entire trip, they both had been guilty of thinking of the trip as nothing more than a quick flight to the edge to gather a few facts; an excursion, as it were. Now the possibility had loomed that there was more here than met the eye. The tape Hetrus had played had not mentioned any such ripple effect, or any effect that could stop suddenly. Of course, there were reasonable explanations—Efrem's ship didn't have modern detection, and coming back he would have been aimed away from Chalcedon and its star. Ships had rearward screens, but it was a universal superstition among traders to the effect that it was bad luck to look back. Etc. Etc. But where Han and Liszendir had felt on sure ground, well within the known, before, they now felt the touch of the unknown. Han retained his apprehensions within himself. In civilization, the universe was tame and well-behaved. Here . . .

Liszendir was not so quiet. After a moment, she said, "When we were at that meeting, back at Boomtown, before you came, I had a few words with Lenkurian, in Multispeech. She told me then that she thought that however it seemed to Efrem, here was no simple raid for loot or slaves. It smelled of deliberate provocation from an unknown source. That and more. There is darkness and evil off Chalcedon, and a mind that has weighed things to a nicety. And the Warriors? If the worst of our suspicions are true . . ."

"What?"

"We *know* nothing. Only suspect. But if half of it is true, I shudder to face the Warriors. But let me tell you a story. When the first ler ship left old Earth, it was many stops before they found a suitable world. But they did eventually find one. That was Kenten. It wasn't long after they landed that two factions developed. One desired to stay and build our culture like we wanted it to be on the new world. And later, others. We knew so little about ourselves then—for hundreds of years we had been buried in an established human culture. And like all buried minorities, we defined much of our own natures in reference to human terms. But there were others, of different opinions. The main other faction, led by a female named Sanjirmil, wished to go on, and more . . ."

"I have heard of Sanjirmil. In your histories, or at least the ones I have heard, she winds up being something like a cross between Lucretia Borgia, Lilith, and perhaps Rosa Luxemborg thrown in for good measure."

"So it was. I have seen holograms of her. She had a beauty that was terrible, like a wild animal. But there was a great disagreement. It almost broke us. We thought that the two factions would lock each other in a death-grip, and in a couple of generations, along would come the earthmen to gather up the ruins. But in the end, when the elders thought the matter was settled, Sanjirmil and her braid, the Klaren, or 'flyers,' and their adherents stole our one spaceship and departed. In those days whole braids flew the ship. We thought it would work better. The Klaren had been woven years before any of them were fertile, just for our flight from Earth, and they were more disciplined in working together than any ler should ever be. And Sanjirmil, while not actually the pilot herself, but the navigator or astrogator, was also f—" Liszendir cut herself off in mid word, before anything recognizable got out.

Han caught it. "F—"? He said, "What were you going to say she was?"

"Nothing." Liszendir answered sullenly. "It is," she added, apparently deciding to brazen it out, "something I cannot tell you. You are not ler. You would not understand. You must forget that I ever started to say anything else." She waited a moment, to see if Han was going to pursue the topic. He didn't.

"So. On that ship were incredible weapons. Things we would see today with horror. And projectile weapons were just the beginning of it. Vile things! And they were never heard from again. We have always assumed, perhaps you might say, 'hoped,' that they crashed somewhere. Or went to another galaxy, as they had said that they wanted to do. That would have been almost as welcome. But nobody knows. There is a whole cycle of legends about them."

"So since the Warriors of Dawn seemed to be ler . . ."

"Ler they are, make no mistake. Your people suppose as mine, that the general hominid shape goes with intelligence as fangs go with carnivores and horns with grazers. But look at you and me, Han. We are ultimately of the same soil, the same planet. Ler and human, for all the obvious differences you and I know so well now, we are perilously close. You and I were picked for this trip because we have the same blood type—we can give each other transfusions! Did you know that?"

"May I use the term 'Kfandrir' as an oath?"

"It is impertinent and irreverent, but I understand."

"I had no idea . . ."

"Neither did I. But it is true. One of your four types and one of our two are compatible. Even so, we could couple if we were very foolish, but nothing would come of it, even if I were as fertile as you are now. But you know the shape is different for us in details. So aliens would be upright, have a head, arms, legs, and all that goes with those things. But they could also be very different. But the witnesses Efrem talked with described precise details."

"But that was some time ago, wasn't it? The original crew would have been dead for years . . ."

"Yes. Thousands of years, many thousands. Sanjirmil and the rest are of the fourth century, atomic. And their children's children."

"Even if this is true, which I don't believe—it isn't any more probable than . . . Oh. I see. Exact details. It would be difficult to arrange those kinds of coincidence, wouldn't it?"

"Especially for ler. We are *artificially* bred in the first generation. I do not know if we could even occur in a completely unguided sequence. But as we say, 'Never mind where I came from, I'm here now, for love or hate.' We're organic enough now. But we control our race! Who knows what they have done! On Earth before we left, they were restless and impatient with braids. And they wanted to stay and fight. On Kenten, they wanted to go further and conquer the galaxy. No, I do not know, and neither does anyone else, if the Warriors are the descendants of Sanjirmil. But I hope they are not. You have your race-fears, Han; and I have mine. The *klarkinnen* are one of them: the 'children of the flyers.' "

"And we are approaching Chalcedon," he reminded her after a moment. "How are they living there, humans and ler? Together, or in separate communities, or countries, or what?"

"I cannot imagine such a thing." It was her only answer. Nor would she say any more about her suspicions during the short remainder of the voyage to Chalcedon. Only hours remained.

Han expected to be met off Chalcedon with suspicion and requests for detailed identifications, what with the recent raid; they were bound to be suspicious. But as they approached the planet, there was no response on any frequency. Nor were they being tracked by any detection system which used electromagnetic waves. Liszendir was unconcerned. She thought that if you came to someone's house, and there were no lights, you could at least knock on the door. They couldn't see you otherwise in the deeps of night.

Han, however, was inclined to look at things in detail before doing anything rash. So they let the preliminary orbit they had established carry them around to the night side. There, it was more informative, but only slightly more active. With the screen at full magnification, and the instruments at maximum gain, they could see and hear the signs of a civilization in its early technological stages: illuminated towns below on the surface; some light radio traffic, most of it point-to-point, for Chalcedon didn't have much of an ionosphere; and also in the radio bands, faint popping or tapping sounds which indicated internal-combustion engines.

But after several passes around the planet, which was about ten thousand miles in diameter, they believed what the ship's senses told them: Chalcedon was early in the colonization stage, and only one continent was inhabited to any degree. And not being near any known line of commerce, the locals below were proceeding at their own rate, which was the slow-time of almost complete isolation. They decided to land at what their charts indicated to be the capital city.

As they settled to their landing site, which was an open field some distance from the capital, they were neither hailed nor intercepted. It gave Han an eerie feeling; they had flown over the city, which was not large, so he knew whoever lived in it could see him, but they didn't seem to care. He had been trained for space flight in an area where ships were monitored every instant. But with no one to tell him not to, he hovered momentarily, then settled and grounded the ship. They shut it down, and debarked to an empty field. Apparently there were no customs procedures either. So they locked the ship and started walking in the direction of the capital, which could be easily found by noting a plume of dust above the trees.

As they walked down a dusty road which did not seem to be heavily traveled, he said, "It gives me a strange feeling to come as far as we have, all to walk down a country road at noon, as if we'd never even seen a spaceship. And so unprotected! You'd think they would be alert as bees after someone robbed the hive."

Liszendir answered by flinging off her soft boots and turning a cart-wheel in the road. Then she dusted herself off, retrieved her boots, but did not put them on, and said, "I care only now that I have honest earth under my feet again."

As she walked on, barefoot, Han noticed her feet; like the hands, here also was a divergence from the human original. There were four toes, instead of five, and they were short. The ball of the foot was wider, in proportion, but back toward the heel, it was more slender. It was a foot that was a degree more adapted to walking rather than holding. Her footprints in the dust of the road showed that she put little weight on the heel.

They walked for some distance before they saw anyone, although there were signs of settled life all around them—cultivated fields, some grazing animals of recognizable shape but curious detail, an occasional house in the distance. In fact, they were almost to the capital itself when they saw, coming down the road towards them, two persons who waved from the distance. On closer sight, the two resolved into a human and ler, both male, and seemingly overworked to the point of exhaustion. The human, tall and gaunt, introduced himself as Ardemor Hilf, the mayor of the Capital. He apologized for the name—they never had taken the trouble to name it, so it was called simply "the Capital." The ler with him appeared to be a somewhat overweight elder with long hair woven into a single braid. He called himself Hath'ingar.

Hath'ingar was not bashful. Immediately he said, "And never mind all that *tlanh* and *srith* crap. We scarcely have the time here, especially now, to be civil enough to shout 'Hey, you' at one another."

Hilf stayed only long enough to find out who they were and what they had in mind. Then he took his leave, asking Hath'ingar to see after them. The shorter ler patted Hilf familiarly on the shoulder and told him to be off. Then he turned to Han and Liszendir.

"I'm the deputy mayor, here and now. Before that, I was an honest farmer north of here, growing radishes." He displayed strong, callused hands. "When we were raided, the Capital was struck quite bad; so I wanted to come down here to see what I could do. I was drafted. But what we have done is not enough." He gestured at the roiling dust clouds. "Not enough."

Liszendir waited quietly, somewhat startled by Hath'ingar's brusque manners coupled with some startlingly human habits. He, in turn, favored her with an evil leer almost as obvious as an expression on a stage performer. "Ah, were I thirty years younger! A young civilized ler adolescent girl, ripe as a berry and body-knowledgeable as a professor of erotic arts! And all-atravel with this young primate, eh?" He dug her rudely in the ribs. But immediately he returned, mercurially, to his previous mood, a blend of fatigue, melancholy and overwork. There was a large amount of meaning in these gestures, but neither Han nor Liszendir could determine if it, any of it, was the meaning they were looking for.

"Well. The unwoven rascals, the shaven-headed apes, at the least left us with a tavern." And motioning them to follow, he led the way towards a shabby wooden hut which apparently served the neighborhood as a beer hall. At this hour, most of the patrons were away, as he explained, stepping down into cool darkness. The floor of the establishment was of packed earth and gave off an aroma redolent of wet ground and old beer. Liszendir fastidiously put her boots back on before venturing completely into the dive. After securing a single pot of ale from behind the bar, where a human woman slept soundly, snoring faintly, Hath'ingar led them to one of the cleaner tables and invited them to be seated. He took a healthy swig of the brew, wiped his lips, sat the pot down, and waited.

Han began, "We are traders, financed by a group on Kenten. I heard of your plight, here on Chalcedon, and so set out as soon as Liszendir and I could get free of Trader Efrem. Do you remember him?"

"Ah, yes. Efrem. The rascal, a first-class robber and for all I know, a bugger as well. Such was his disposition towards money, at any rate. He was almost as hard to endure as the robbers, but by some shrewd trading we did manage to get some good stuff out of him before he headed back to civilization."

"Why did he leave, then? For money? He told us he wanted to get off Chalcedon to get some credits for some things he dropped off for free." Han fabricated as he went along.

"I'd expect such a tale of Efrem. No, we paid hard cash for the goods we bought, platinum, thorium and gold bullion, if you please, and a hard bargain it was, too. No, indeed. He left because we were going to put him to work here. I'll wager he's swanking it now at some human-planet resort town, right in the very jaws of civilization."

"No. He's dead. Somebody murdered him the day we left."

Hath'ingar raised an eyebrow, which, as Han observed, was singed. "Murder, now, was it? Hm. I'm sorry to hear it. He robbed us, Efrem did, true enough, but I would not have deemed it a life's-worth, even before the Kenten judicistrators." Here, he turned to Liszendir. "And you, my lady, do you not speak as well?"

She answered, seemingly in a retort, but the language was not anything Han had ever heard before. It seemed to be a singsong clipped dialect. One of the Multispeech modes, he thought. But before she could get very far, the deputy spread his hands, palm outwards, in a gesture of negation.

"None of that, here. We all speak Common alike, here on Chalcedon, or do now, at any rate." He looked oddly disturbed by the incident. "We have all had to pitch in here. There was a lot of mistrust. And the Warriors were ler." He made a small pause, and added, as an afterthought, "And may they couple with scavengers."

Liszendir said, "I came to see. I heard of this voyage, and being *nerh*, I was superfluous to both parents and insiblings. I am to learn trade, and could not have a better opportunity. We suspected that Efrem had been murdered for his money, which was never found, and that being so considerable and a probable motive, another could be made. We," she gestured at Han, "are temporary partners. I own half, and answer for the registry of our ship." Han was astounded. A liar as well. But he watched her closely. He did not know if she was suspicious of this strange creature before them, or was merely being cautious.

Hath'ingar quaffed another mouthful of the sour ale and passed the jug to Liszendir. She sniffed at it, dubiously, then sipped daintily. She turned aside, sneezed quickly like a cat, and made a wry face. Then she passed the jug to Han, who was thirsty and accepted it with relish, guzzling gratefully.

"Well, well," said the deputy mayor. "What won't we have next, out here on the frontier? But I suppose we'll see more of this as time goes on. But it was not so when I was a young buck." He became serious. "But I understand all too well about your outsiblingdom, your *nergan*. In my own braid I was *thes*. Here on Chalcedon. And a fine lot I got. 'Hewer of Wood and Drawer of Water,' so I believe the ancient human tale has it. So I ran away from the *yos* and found some boon comrades of these parts, and we started up our own braid. I was forefather, and those were certainly the days. Myself, and Kadhrilnan, Jovdanshir and Merdulian, so we were; tried and true! But I digress. You must tell me more."

They replied that the first thing they needed was a place to stay while they were arranging for sales. It had been a long voyage out to Chalcedon, and they were tired of the ship. They realized that housing was probably scarce because of the raid, so they would take anything reasonable. After that, the local merchants could come and they could start trading in earnest. Hath'ingar agreed, and arose to leave, saying he was off to see what could be found. Then they were alone in the beer hall.

Han and Liszendir sat alone, except for the snoring woman, who was still behind the bar, and said nothing to disturb the cool darkness or their thoughts. They were also thinking about disposing of the ostensible trade goods, for they certainly would have to keep up a front here.

He asked her, half joking, half serious, "What's the matter with the ale? Don't you drink?"

She made another wry face. "We are as fond of our tipple as the next, although we fear spirit greatly. Our tolerance to it is lower than yours. But this stuff! It is terrible! It is stumpwater! Ugh." She returned to her musing, and Han did not disturb her again.

Presently Hath'ingar returned, bearing a key ostentatiously, which seemed to be of dubious appearance for locking doors. Still, a room was a room, and they followed him out of the beer hall without protest or comment.

Outside, the light of day had mutated somewhat to an air of afternoon; shadows were lengthening. For the first time, Han began to look around him at the world on which they had landed. Notwithstanding the considerable destruction caused by the raid, Chalcedon, or at least this part of it, appeared to be a relaxed and lovely place. It seemed to be a rather flat world, with clear air which faded gradually into the blues of distance, marked with no hills or mountains, but with gently rolling ridges. He observed as much to Liszendir, who agreed. Her own world, Kenten, had no really high mountains, but it was hilly and precipitous all over. Hath'ingar, hearing the remark, spoke somewhat boastingly on the charms of Chalcedon.

"Ah, yes. You notice the fine afternoon sun slants, the openness, the quiet, the grace of the feather-trees." He pointed towards an exquisitely tall tree nearby of great charm. It had a smooth, off-white bark, hanging boughs, and long drooping cascades of shiny, scimitar-shaped leaves. A pungent, aromatic odor wafted from it, which teased the sense of smell rather than offending it. Han looked again; it was tall, over three hundred feet. As his eye became more accustomed to the background, he saw more of the feather-trees, scattered here and there. Some of them appeared to be even taller.

"You marvel? But Chalcedon is a quiet world. No great winds, storms, earthquakes. And we have no seasons as we have a regular orbit and virtually no axial tilt. So the trees grow tall. Of course. I find it too quiet, too orderly, if you know what I mean; but never mind that. A mild climate, and plenty of wealth, all for a little harmless grubbing. But how I ramble on! Here we are!"

They rounded the tall feather-tree, under which huddled a small wooden house of dilapidated rustic appeal. It looked abandoned and rather dusty, but at the same time sturdy and solid. Liszendir observed quietly to Han that it was not to her taste, but that it would do if that was all there was. There was no ceremony: Hath'ingar, on hearing her comment, handed her the key, announced he was off to gather in the local merchants, and departed.

As he left, from the distance, his voice drifted to them; "I will bring them here at dark, on the very instant." He gave a great flourish, and faded into the dusts of the road.

The little house was very dirty, so they were first occupied with cleaning it up so they could bear to stay in it. It seemed to have stood empty for years. Thus they spent the long Chalcedon afternoon. When Liszendir asked Han how long the day was in standard hours, he was forced to admit that he had neglected to look it up, or reset his variable-rate watch to conform to the rate of local time, but he could recall something like thirty standard hours. Towards evening, after they had finished as much as they were going to do, Liszendir went out for food to last them at least a few days.

After a while, she returned, waking Han up from the nap he was taking on the front porch. She had bread, sausages, cheeses and smoked meats, plus a few fruits. She brought the provisions in the house, and as soon as it was laid out, they both fell to it. It had been a long day and they were both starved, Liszendir especially. Her metabolism ran at a higher rate than Han's. Soon after they had satisfied the most immediate part of their appetite, she began talking again, in a low voice.

"While I was out, I rummaged around to see what I could find out. Believe me, I have been cautious! There is something going on here I cannot measure; and the ler here are very strange—like none I have ever seen before. It is a beautiful and prosperous world, all over very much like this around here, so they say, but it abounds with the oddest rumors."

She reflected on something for a moment, and then continued, "I was unable to ever get any kind of description of the weapons used by the Warriors. Nobody seems to know. They always used the same pattern—bombardment from the air, then they would come in. But the explosions! All people knew was there would be a tremendous explosion, followed by a crater. You are deep in these things; what kind of device could do that with no warning? Others spoke of streaks in the sky afterwards, and fireballs. It is all very confusing to me."

Han thought for a moment. "I don't know. Except for the craters, it sounds like coherent-radiation beams, lasers, or masers, at any rate outside the frequency response of either ler or human eyes. On the other hand, beams don't leave impact craters. And they start fires. We detected no gross radioactivity when we landed, I checked it for that reason. If we had some reading, there, it would tell us something, too. Total conversion at distance? I doubt it. TCD has been demonstrated theoretically, but it's the devil to control in the real world. And I rule TCD out for the same reason I rule out nuclear weapons—we'd see evidence of fallout, which you always get with the kind of ground burst that leaves a crater. And we'd also, see flash burns on the buildings and a lot of people. None of that. It completely baffles me. But whatever it is, they must have a lot of control over it."

"It is true that very few were killed. They avoided the residential areas entirely."

"So they were not strategically destroying supplies, or killing people, but making an impression."

"I agree, Han. But for what?"

"For the captives."

"Yes. Efrem said, only humans of a certain kind, and a few ler as well. But those were at random, or so it seemed."

"So we don't know any more?"

"Not really. But I know what I heard at the market: they think the Warriors haven't left, that they're lying off-planet somewhere, perhaps hoping to ambush a battlecraft when it comes in."

"Did they cite any evidence to support that?"

"No. But they all seemed sure. And they were scared."

But however, it was, they were given no more time to speculate on the problem that evening, for the sun had finally set, A VILA 1381 moving infinitely slow across the wavy horizon in a slow demonstration of old gold. And Hath'ingar was in the yard under the feather-tree with an unruly crowd of local merchants, just as he had promised earlier.

During the remainder of the long night, until quite late, past midnight, they argued and haggled, made proposals and counterproposals, some of which were met with derisive laughter, some with hoots of scorn. And they wheedled, extolled, told various atrocity stories, and rarely made a deal. It seemed to Han that if Efrem had had to put up with much of this, he got out well. The merchants of Chalcedon were hard-nosed, unyielding, and taletellers of incredible abilities. He used all the tricks he had learned and practiced at the Traders' Academy in Boomtown; he sulked, he threatened, he made allusions to parents, he looked disdainfully over his nose, hoping he had the professional sneer just right, and he seemingly ignored the horrendous fates of, so it appeared, thousands of women and children who were simultaneously ravished, singly and multiply, violated, buggered and burned many times over. Liszendir said nothing, beyond the disclaimer of looking after her interests. But Han could tell now that he could read some of her facial expressions that his performance must be having some effect—she winced from time to time.

One thing became clear, as they digested the meat out of all the stories they heard. The people on Chalcedon had indeed had their wits scared out of them, but all things considered, they had gotten off remarkably well. Very few had actually been killed or injured. And the stories confirmed that the Warriors took only certain types of humans with them, and they were not picking at random; they knew their business well, and knew exactly what they were looking for. After several sessions of small talk during impasses in the haggling, Han was able to determine that, for instance, the Warriors had cleaned the Capital district completely out of redheads of any shape below a certain age; also, those with the odd combination of blond hair and dark complexions. In other groups or classifications they had been more selective, seemingly picking by individuals.

One of the merchants said, "Oh, absolutely, absolutely." He waved his hand around in an ostentatious maneuver which Han, despite a great deal of tolerance, found personally disturbing. "The Warriors would arrange the people in a line, and then groups of threes of them would come along, prodding and poking, for all the world as if they were at a livestock auction. But you could see some order in it; they—that is, the threes—were each looking for a certain type. By type, I mean the degree of likeness that you see among people in a large crowd, or when you see a stranger and he reminds you of someone you knew before. Someone has said that basically there are only about a hundred kinds of combinations of face and build, you know. They were not interested in sex, nor in beauty, but in youth; they assembled great wads of uglies as readily as any other standard, or so it seemed to me. Then they would visit each other's groups of prisoners and crow over the size of the take. The ler folk here said they were speaking Singlespeech, but it was very distorted, and with a lot of special terminology thrown in. *We* couldn't understand a word of it. And of course they were proud as peacocks over what they had gotten, every one of them."

Another merchant, this one dour, short, fat and more to the point, said, "They all went around in threes. Some of these groups had all male members, some all female, some both. And each threesome acted as if they thought their fellow triples were clods of the worst sort. The local ler they took were also arranged into threes as they herded them off. After that, which they encouraged us all to come to, they climbed in several bulky personnel carriers and departed for their ship; I hear they ransacked other parts as well. After they were done, they threw around a few bombards for good measure, and left Chalcedon."

But no one had any idea as to the nature of the "bombards." The one which had struck the Capital had arrived with no warning at all: a bright explosion, a loud noise, and the ground rang like a gong. Afterwards, some held that they had seen a vapor trail to the zenith, and they heard thunder in the air. But even these were unsure. Whatever it was, it did something to iron and steel. No compass had worked right in the area since the attack. And the effect was strongest near the crater. Magnetic bombs to disrupt computers? Such things were known; yet use of such an expensive weapon was unlikely in a place that didn't have a single computer more elaborate than an abacus. Chalcedon was a frontier planet: they didn't have an excess of data to worry about.

Other than that, they learned no more during the night of haggling and trading. And finally, everybody began to run down, so Han and Liszendir closed the trading off, tallied up the deals which had already been made, and promised to deliver on the morrow, should trucks or wagons arrive at the ship to carry it off. The arrangements were made, and the locals left. And Han and Liszendir collapsed into the nearest thing resembling a bed and slept immediately.

The morning came, clear and limpid as water from an ancient village well. The feather-tree was on the east side of the house, but the sudden light woke them up, and after a quick breakfast, they walked back to the field where they had landed the ship. There, a great disorderly crowd had already gathered. During the remainder of the long morning of Chalcedon, Han and the girl supervised unloading and loading of the goods they had taken in exchange.

By noon the greater part of the work had been done, and they were left in the midst of a colossal mess. Piles of boxes, crates and trash. The field had been rutted and gouged by wheel, track and hoof. The *Pallenber* was coated with a fine patina of dust.

Hath'ingar now approached from the last truckload to depart. He was as grimy as the rest of them had been, but he seemed indefatigable and curious.

"Ah, now, all done, a profit made, and so you leave our stricken parts. What's this? Weapons bays?" he added in surprise, pointing at some suspicious protuberances in the smooth line of the hull.

"Yes, weapons," Han answered. "We thought it best to come prepared for the worst—for all we knew, we very well could have met the Warriors coming out here. Or even more ordinary raiders. Such things are not unlikely even in this age. It had been said back there that this was why Efrem left in such a rush—he feared for his life."

"Well, so be it," Hath'ingar replied evenly. "Still, it did him no good, did it? Everyone goes at his time and to music, some to gay lover's tunes, some to heroic marches and flourishes, and others to dirges. But all go!"

It sounded strange and alien in Han's ears. Even stranger was Liszendir's reply, which she made shyly in her own tongue: *"Si-tasi ma-*

haralo al-tenzhidh." Then she translated for Han's benefit: "Thus endures the way of the world." There was no response from Hath'ingar.

There was a pause, as if no one knew quite what to say. Then Hath'ingar spoke, "Now where will you be off to?"

Han answered, "We thought that we would fly over to the west coast of this continent. Our maps are probably very much out of date, but they show a large city there. It seemed to be large, so was probably hit; they will be needing some goods as well."

"Yes. That would be Libreville. So they are in need. In fact, I have heard that they were bombed out pretty badly and have left the city. But I know of other settled places all over which do have needs. I assure you I'll be no trouble, but I could show you where the places are. You can conclude your affairs sooner and be on your way."

Liszendir had already entered the ship. Han looked long at the ler elder below, on the ground. After a time, he said, somewhat against his nagging better judgment, "Good enough. Come on up."

Han stayed on the ladder to see if Hath'ingar needed any help climbing up the high ladder to the entry port. He didn't; in fact, Han was surprised to note that Hath'ingar climbed the ladder with a great deal more agility and style than he had himself. He credited it to good physical conditioning and forgot it. The two of them entered the ship.

Once aboard the ship and in the control room, Hath'ingar wandered around, looking at everything, seemingly amazed and very appreciative. "An absolute paragon," he enthused. "Indeed, superior workmanship, fine stuff! Is this ship a ler or a human work?"

"Human," Han answered, as he was settling down in the pilot's chair. Liszendir sat down beside him, as he observed, with an odd motion that suggested uneasiness. Han felt it, too, but he couldn't pinpoint the source.

They lifted off and retracted the landing legs. Han thought that they would not be going very far, so he did not set a course for an orbit, but selected a lower altitude for a powered cruise. After he had done so, he turned around. "Now where to, Hath'ingar?" There was no answer. The overweight elder had disappeared. "Well," he said in Liszendir's general direction, "He's probably gone looking for the convenience."

At that moment Hath'ingar reappeared, but this time, he was not dressed in the traditional ler overrobe; he was naked except for a loincloth with long, brightly decorated ends, and in place of the gray, long braided hair of an elder was a glossy, shaven pate. On his bare, hairless chest was an elaborate tattoo illustrating a titanic battle between two peculiar beasts, neither of which Han had ever heard of before. Nor was he as old as Han had previously thought. Han groaned aloud; Hath'ingar held a gun exactly like the one which Liszendir had disarmed in Efrem's room back in Boomtown. Where was that one? Han groaned again. If it was not the one in Hath'ingar's hand, it was secured in a locker, which was directly behind Hath'ingar. It might as well have been back in Efrem's room, for all the good it could do them now. And the figure across the room: he was still overweight, but the fat was the dynamic fat of great strength. The erstwhile deputy mayor waited poised, standing expectantly on the balls of his feet.

"Yes. Tricked," he said. Liszendir moved to regain her feet. Hath'ingar continued, "Now without delay and no tricks, set a course for the two gas giants of this system. They are in conjunction, now, opposite the main fields of the galaxy. There we will rendezvous with my warriors."

"Your warriors?" Han wished to stall for time, although he did not honestly know what he would do with any gained. Below, Chalcedon was receding slowly, turning beneath them to the east as they flew north and west. If one looked well, one could already see a slight curve to the horizon, barely perceptible.

"Yes. I am hetman of the outer horde. Now move slowly. This gun fires slivers of a most unpleasant substance. And though its effects are swift, it takes consciousness last. I am expert with it as well as with other arts. Do not, either of you, think you can outmove me."

Han glanced out of the corner of his eye at Liszendir. It was hardly visible, but it seemed as if every muscle in her body was working invisibly under the robe, warming up for use. Her jaw muscles clenched and flexed slightly, an eerie sight on the face which Han had seen once or twice in its full beauty of amorous interest, or perhaps recollection. Who could know? Ler had fully eidetic memories.

As Hath'ingar took a preparatory step towards them, she shouted one word, "Move!" and performed an incredible maneuver. Han let himself fall to the deck, rolling, just as she had shown him. Effortlessly she leaped straight up, apparently without flexing her knees, leaving the soft boots behind as she rose. At the overhead, she was upside down and leaving the robe behind; using her legs to carom herself, she left the robe behind and sailed across the control room to Hath'ingar, or whoever, or *whatever* he was. Han gaped in astonishment at the naked white form: she had done that in a full 1G field. He was still rolling when he heard the puff of the gun. He felt nothing.

Hath'ingar could not bring the gun up to bear on her and avoid her at the same time. He elected to avoid, diving forward in a motion which looked clumsy, but which Han knew wasn't. But he retained the gun.

There commenced a scene Han could not follow. Afterwards, all he would be able to remember was the blurred speed of fast motion, move and countermove. The two of them moved with blinding speed. Occasionally the forms would meet, and there would be a quick flurry of activity, sharp grapples and attempted holds. Neither succeeded. And Hath'ingar still retained the gun. Liszendir moved back and forth across the control room in a dizzy white loom of motion. Han saw that she was deliberately preventing Hath'ingar from taking aim at her or even tracking her motion; and with an extra person in the room, it was for the time threat enough to keep things at a stalemate. Then they came together again. This time something happened, and then Hath'ingar bolted out of the control room. Han caught a glimpse of him as he left; he had been trying to fire off one more shot, which went wild. His right ear had been pulped.

She locked the door and stood before him, naked, shiny with sweat and panting heavily. "Got him one good lick, but he's tough! And the shave-topped ape got away from me! Damn it! Damn him!" It was the first time Han had seen her angry. She was angry with herself.

She asked, peremptorily, "Do you have a way out of the ship?"

"Yes. Life rafts. In the locker behind the pilot's chair. Should be five or six."

"Then get into one and get off!"

"Liszendir, I . . ."

"No! Do as I tell you! Against him alone, I have an even chance, and I can fly the ship if I have to. I learned. I remember. He is too much for you with what you know now. You only have hostage value. If he gets you we are beaten. I am not degrading you—I am trying to save you. I must kill him. He used a projectile weapon against us. I can only succeed alone: he is extremely dangerous—you do not know how much."

"He's got that gun, Liszendir . . ."

"Never mind that. I can beat that as long as there is only one of him. So if I win, I will fly the ship back. If he wins there will be no back—for either of us. I am doing this for you for my own bad reasons. It is wrong, it is forbidden, it is not for us ever—but I care and you must not be caught by him. Now go! I must get him, soon. I am in *bandastash*—high anger flow. It gives me speed and strength, but I cannot keep it long: it costs terribly." She pressed her cheek against his, briefly. It was burning hot.

Han saw she was right, but to give up the ship? No. It was the only way, bad as it seemed. He remembered a thing she had said when she had been teaching him simple holds: *If you cannot give up the ground upon which you fight, in order to win, then you have lost already.* He opened the locker and climbed into one of the rafts, ready for launching. As he pulled the airshield over himself, she reached in and touched his face, very tenderly. She said, "If I am successful, I will come to you in the mountains north of the capital, near the ridge with two pinnacles we could see from there. If not, farewell and remember me. Your name means 'last.' " She slammed the lid violently and ejected him.

There was a moment of vertigo, as he felt the switch from the artificial gravity of the *Pallenber* to the real gravity of the planet Chalcedon. Then he could see the ship, falling upwards away from him. Suddenly, it jerked off westwards at tremendous speed. The sled functioned automatically, and began its descent. It seemed slow, but Han knew that was only an illusion of the distance he was above the planetary surface. He looked down to the surface below, blue-green and brown, mottled with puffs of clouds which did not tear into streaks. Chalcedon did not have rapidly moving major weather systems. It was the last he saw. The automatics took over, and he lost his consciousness to G-forces and a special gas, released just to keep the passenger quiet; it had been assumed by the builders of this kind of raft that for a person to witness his own fall from orbit or suborbital distance would itself be fatal in the absence of injury. They were, of course, right. Han knew nothing.

"Once upon a time, on Chalcedon where men and ler both lived in relative peace, a certain human rushed to the hut in the crags of Klislangir Tlanh, a very old and wise ler, who was considered by many to be a holy man. The human, a mere boy, bore a message that said Klislangir's insibling Werverthin Srith had just died, wishing him well. The sage continued to study the sunset clouds. Finally, he said, 'I am also grieved to see these lovely clouds that will be no more with the night and its clearing.' The human, one Roderigo, ejaculated, 'What? How can you be so callous as to talk about clouds at a time like this? The lady, alsrith, had lived with you from birth, almost, and for years after the next generation were home in the yos.' The sage answered, 'It is exactly for those realizations into the meaning of sorrow that I am called wise.' He turned away and did not speak again that day. In that instant, Roderigo looked at the clouds also and was illuminated. He returned to his home, disposed of all his goods, and became a disciple of Klislangir Tlanh. In later years he was accounted wise as any ler holy man."
    —*The Chalcedon Apocrypha*

"One alone in the wilderness is never bored, nor does he feel the despair of a meaningless job—to the contrary, everything is invested with meaning, some of it dire, indeed; but in the heart of a great city that tramples the stars themselves underfoot, one needs ceaseless entertainment to distract him from the knowledge of his vileness, which lies about him, everywhere. The herb of our cure is a bitter one, but gnaw it we will."
    —*Roderigo*

STANDARD LIFE RAFTS were required on all spaceships, and few flouted this regulation. They were intended to be used near a planetary body, or as a refuge in deep space until such time as one could be rescued. Near a body of certain mass, they worked automatically. All during space flight, men of both kinds had compared space to the sea, and indeed the comparison was valid in all ways except in the scale: space dwarfed all the water seas that ever had been, were, would be, could be. And its shores were infinitely more perilous than the shores of the wildest seas. Therefore, the standard life raft. It was designed first to get its passenger through that surf and those perilous reefs of an un-powered landing from orbit. They were neither kind, nor comfortable; but they worked.

Han awoke, knowing nothing, and aching at every point he could imagine as belonging to him; and some whose ownership could have been debated. He tried to move, but immediately felt his motion arrested. He felt a quick flash of panic, but then he remembered. He stopped, and rested for a moment, thinking. Through the transparent shield, he could see that he had landed in a wooded area, and it was deep dusk, almost dark. Vents in the raft were bleeding in fresh air. He slept. Sometime later he awoke, and it was completely dark; stars were shining through the branches. Now he remembered the opening sequence, and after a few fumbles, was able to stagger away from the coffinlike life raft. The air was cool with night, and the forest was silent.

Traders, like everyone else, were schooled for a variety of reasons: tradition, someone having excess money and wishing to keep it, whatever came out of the hands of functionaries, or society wanting to have an excuse to civilize its children. But perhaps best of all was the reason that traders had to be both shrewd and prepared for anything. And Han had, on the whole, been a good student at the Traders' Academy, although he had played their mercantile trading game with a vigor that earned disapproval. Also, he reflected, he had been evaluated as having "spent too much time with the girls." But he remembered well.

Paraleimon Kardikas in *The Survivor's Manual: If you ever crash, no matter if it's in your own yard, STOP. DO NOTHING. Remember first who you are. How you got there. Trust no impression, make no identifications. The survivor is Adam, but he is an Adam who does not know if he has fallen into Eden or Hell.*

Han sat to the side of the raft on a fallen tree in the dark, remembering. The flight, the ship, Liszendir. And so, here he was, somewhere on Chalcedon. That was excellent—at least he knew which planet he was on. And with no food, no money and no equipment. No, that wasn't true. He had some basics in the raft, and some survival tools—wire, saw-blades, a knife. A water distillery, for drink and for the basic food con-centrate. He got up, went to the raft, and removed the survival pack. Now what?

Kardikas: *Travel at night wherever possible, for lights are visible. But greet strangers by day. Get the lay of the land.*

Han could not see very well or very far in the dense woods. He knew he was on a slight slope, so, leaving the raft, he walked quietly through the darkness until he found the top of the low hill he was on. Through gaps in the trees he could see stars, outlines of more distant hills, darker places where valleys were. He performed several turns about the hill; he could see nothing—no lights, no smoke, no indication anyone but he walked the surface of Chalcedon. He didn't even know directions. But he waited. He could find out. It would take time, but he had plenty of that.

He marked groups of bright stars near the horizon, making a game of naming new constellations, which also helped cheer him up. He gave them fanciful names, some obscene, but he also noted very carefully both the shapes of the groups, and where they were in relation to his subjective landmarks, and their shadows—tree-shapes, rocks, peculiar horizon lines. He did not wait for a moon—Chalcedon didn't have a moon either.

Time passed slowly on Chalcedon, but after a time, what his watch said was several standard hours, he looked at the sky around the hori-zon again. Some of his constellations had sunk below the edge of the ground. Others had risen high in the night sky. Still others had moved more to one side or another. From his efforts and waiting, now he could determine the position of celestial north: it was higher towards the zenith than he had thought it would be. He was far to the north of the Capital, which was closer to the equator. And he knew which way was east, west, and south, even if he did not know how far their flight had offset them. He suspected he was somewhat to the west, also.

There was no way to go, then, but south westwards. Han gathered up the pack, put it on, and set out, picking his way cautiously through the quiet darkness. He kept his knife out, at the ready; he did not know much about the native animal life of the planet, which was an object lesson he would never forget. If he ever got the chance to use such knowledge again.

*   *   *

He walked through an empty land for days, until he lost count of them. Chalcedon was not a flat planet; it had a surface which undulated gently, sometimes more hilly, sometimes more flat, but never quite attaining real hills, or a plain. He crossed rivers, was rained upon, and walked, in a routine which soon evolved into two sessions each day: predawn to forenoon, rest, late afternoon to early night, rest. He found that walking as he was doing, he could not accommodate himself to the long day-cycle of Chalcedon. He was able to refine his measurement of the day; it was almost thirty-two standard hours long. And it did not vary. He could not estimate how far he walked, either; there were no landmarks visible for more than a few miles in any direction. One of the hills or ridges looked very much like another.

He saw no animals, although rarely, at night, he heard cries from far away. He was not being tracked—the cries were never the same, except in their suggestion of endless emptiness. Nor did he see birds; apparently there were none on the planet, a fact which disappointed him. He knew the fruits were edible, that was one fact about Chalcedon which helped him along: it was one of the kindest worlds in the universe, without poison plants of any kind. Those he ate, adding his food concentrate, which he ate stoically, because it tasted terrible, and he purified water by the side of streams. And walked on, avoiding the thoughts he might have had about what he would do when he got somewhere.

Han had stopped for the night, more tired than usual from climbing among rocky terrain all day. His place this night was in a dense grove of fragrant trees down in a narrow valley. So for a long time he did not notice that one part of the sky on the horizon was ever so slightly glowing. Much later, taking a turn around the patch of woods as he always did, just as a precaution, he noticed the glow. It had been too many days, and he was too tired to feel any excitement; besides he did not believe it was anything more than some natural phenomenon. He retrieved his pack, and wearily climbed to the top of the ridge.

At the top, he looked down into a broad, flat valley, so wide he could not make out the far side, even with his newly used and practiced night vision. But that was not really what he was looking at. There were lights in the valley—weak, to be sure, but lights, like windows shining into the darkness. Not just one, either—many, as if of a small community. It was the most beautiful sight he could ever remember seeing. Forgetting his fatigue, he started out down the slope towards the lights, practicing the story he would tell, with all parts clear except how many days he had walked.

As he drew nearer to the lights, a process that seemed interminable, probably since the clear air distorted distances for him, he first grew suspicious, and then disappointed. One by one, the lights went out, except one group which seemed to belong to a house. Han had hoped for a human settlement, but apparently this was going to be a ler village; he could catch an occasional glimpse of the suggestion of shape of the houses—and humans did not live in low, rambling ellipsoids. The braid houses they called the *yos*. As he drew nearer, he could see that it was a thriving little community—there were well-tilled fields on all sides, barns, sheds, houses, now mostly dark. But it was isolated—there were no power lines, no beam towers, and beyond the narrow paths beside the fields, no roads. The paths were marked only by hoofprints and footprints, footprints that showed, even in the dark, four toe marks and hardly any weight on the narrow heel.

Han guessed that just about everyone would be asleep by now. Ler liked sleep, and normally went to bed soon after dark, even in their civilized places. Here, they probably worked hard during the long day and would never stay up late. Still, though, it was late, yet the lights were just going off. Only one *yos* was still well lit, and it seemed to be making up for all the rest of the village. He was close enough now to hear voices in the dark. Voices! They were faint, and what he could hear of them was in a strange and alien language—ler Singlespeech—but they filled him with joy. He suppressed an urge to shout, and continued on.

Presently he stood before the well-lit house, or *yos*. Han knew about their peculiar custom of living in a dwelling without angles—but he didn't know why they preferred them. The barns and sheds seemed angular enough. He had never seen a *yos* except in pictures. It looked just like descriptions he had heard—a random collection of flattened ellipsoids, following the contour of the ground, each "room" mounted on its own pedestal, a foot or so off the ground. He wondered, how did one announce oneself? Did one step up to the door and knock? There was no door on this particular *yos*, but a woven curtain. Perhaps one stood in the yard and crowed like a rooster. He felt giddy, drunk with fatigue and a longing to be with people again.

The problem solved itself. Out of the *yos* came an oldster, with long, white hair. The person stopped, looked incredulously at Han for a moment, and then, quite coolly, considering the circumstances, spoke to him. Han didn't understand a word of it. It was indeed ler Singlespeech. He shook his head in what he hoped the creature—he couldn't tell if it was a man or a woman, the usual ler apparent sexlessness becoming even more ambiguous from aging, as was also the case with humans—would understand him to mean that he couldn't understand what he or she or it was saying. He started to speak, but the oldster interrupted him, saying something and pointing at the ground. It seemed to mean, "Wait here." Then it darted back into the *yos*. Han waited.

Presently a younger one appeared at the door, cast a quick look about the yard, and disappeared. In a moment, it returned. Han identified it as a young girl, mature, fertile, for she was carrying an infant which she nursed. Then the creature spoke.

"Yes? What will you do here?" Han felt a certain sense of unreality. The voice was unmistakably male. He felt an edge of something like lunacy, remembering, idiotically, the words of a character in a written novel of the classical period: *If you think you're going crazy, it means you aren't*. He decided to answer anyway.

"I am Han Keeling. Trader and spaceman. There was an accident and I was ejected from the ship. I landed north of here, many days, I don't know how many. I would ask your hospitality and assistance if you have any to give." It was the longest speech he had made in many days. His voice sounded strange to his ears.

"I am Dardenglir. You must excuse us for acting so odd, but we are very far out here and we see few humans. Hardly any of us even know Common: this is an old village and most of us have been here several generations. I am not from here by birth, but my own village is hardly less isolated. But of course we will help. What do you need?"

"Food. A few days' rest. And directions. I am trying to get back to the general area of the Capital."

"I understand. It will be easy. Will you accept our, house, here?" The words sounded peculiar. "We are crowded now, for there was a birth tonight, and we have stayed up overlate, celebrating. But we have room, and there is food, warmth, people. We can find a place."

"I accept gratefully, Dardenglir."

"Then come in." He did not wait, but turned and vanished back into the house. Han could hear him speaking inside. He followed, climbed the stairs, and went in, through the curtain, which in Chalcedon's mild climate seemed to be all the protection they needed from the elements.

Inside, the room was circular in plan, and a wide shelf went all around it, except where round holes interrupted the curve, and except for an area to his left, where a raised platform served as a hearth, smoking outwards through a hooded vent into the ceiling. There were candles, lanterns, and people. They were strange to him, but he felt the same as all survivors—they were people. He blinked in the light.

While one of them gathered up some food, apparently from the party which had been going on, Dardenglir introduced them all. There were two infants, one small girl-child, four adults, and four older ones. It was the whole braid—past, present, and future. And there was no mistake, Dardenglir was male. But Han kept quiet.

Indeed it was a birth celebration. One of the females had apparently given birth this night, for she lay back on some cushions, bare, and her face was flushed and happy, while the infant nuzzled at her breast. Han noticed the cord was still attached. They looked at Han with more curiosity than he felt to them, while Dardenglir spoke rapidly, in Multispeech. Then they all smiled. They waved at the hearth.

"Eat, drink. Be happy with us. There is a trough in the yard for washing and you can sleep in there, to your right."

Han nodded with what he hoped was a polite gesture, and gratefully did as he had been asked. He ate, went out and washed in icy water, returned, and with a gesture, crawled into a dark, smaller space; there he found, eventually, something soft, like a blanket, and pulling it over himself, he slept, deeply.

He awoke. Alone. There was light in the room, another smaller ellipsoid; the light came through translucent windows which had the appearance of cloudy stained glass. Han reached over and touched one: it felt rougher than glass—it was rock, ground down to translucency and polished, travertine or alabaster, he thought. The effect was one of warmth and beauty, even though he could see no way to open them. How did they get circulation? He looked around, and finally saw that there was a vent in the domed ceiling very much like the one over the hearth, only smaller. The whole "room" was a bed, apparently. All around were quilts and cushions, neatly folded, seemingly placed at random. No one was in the room except Han. The surface underfoot was yielding, but not soft. Like everything else he had seen since he had entered, everything seemed to be handmade. He wondered about the unopenable windows, as they obviously did not have, and would not want, any kind of air-conditioning equipment. But perhaps they looked at houses, especially in this mild climate, as being more shelter than fortress or castle; if you wanted to see outside, why you could go outside and perceive it totally.

He crawled out into the larger room, which served as entry, common room, and kitchen all in one. It was also empty, but cleaned and straightened from the night before. He listened, trying to determine if anyone was in the house. There was no sense of presence in the house at all, although he was aware of voices outside. He hesitated. Han felt his beard, which had become unkempt during the long walk. And they would not have anything to trim it with, probably. He wondered how he looked to them, if Liszendir had thought him "too angular, too hairy." Proportions all different. Still, they had been both generous and kind.

He went to the front and pushed the curtain-flap aside. The *yos* was, he now saw in daylight, situated on a low hill. Not far away, a clear stream made water noises with restraint and probity, commenting on the site, the village, the clear air. A wooden trough conducted water to a point near the house, where it collected in a large wooden tub. The overflow was led back to the stream by a similar wooden trough. At the place where the used water rejoined the stream, he could see a small naked girl-child, about four years old in human terms, playing, making little dams, which she would then subtly damage and watch the penned water flow out and overcome the dam. She looked up and saw Han. She looked at him directly, unafraid, but with a certain amount of wide-eyed wonder. She stopped playing, and shyly approached the steps, coming up to Han to touch his beard. Then she laughed, and abruptly ran off, calling to someone in a gay, musical voice.

Presently Dardenglir, the ler Han had met the night before, arrived, still with the infant slung under his arm. Yes, he had been right: it was definitely a male person. Now that he had been around Liszendir for a while, he could sense differences—the walk, the hips, the general carriage. Dardenglir greeted Han courteously.

"The sun is up, friend, and now so are you. That is a good thing."

"I don't know how to begin to thank you . . ."

"Not at all. We have very few visitors here. The last human visitor we had built a large edifice on yon hill." Han turned to look. There was no edifice, nor were there signs one had ever been there. He looked back to Dardenglir, smiling. "So you see it as it is. Even ler do not come so far often. And we are easy—all we ask in return are a few tales, and a hand in the fields."

"The fields part I can do, but what kind of tales?"

"Events. What occurs in the wide world."

"Oh, those kinds of tales. Well, I can tell a few, but I doubt if many will understand my words."

"No matter there. I will translate. And if you stay long enough, I will

teach you Singlespeech and you can tell it yourself. But right now, you
and I are the only speakers of Common in the village. I am grateful for
the practice—it has been a long time. I grow rusty, here in Ghazh'in."

Han came down from the steps into the yard. "Where are the rest?"

"Here, there. Tanzernan, she who gave birth last evening, is today visiting with the insiblings of her old braid. She was *thes*, there. Today she
has something special for them. She and I are *korh* and *dazh*, you would
say 'aftermother and afterfather.' I wove with Pethmirian, who was
madh, foremother. This is ours. She is out in the field today. Bazh'ingil
repairs a cart yonder, by the barn. Do you know much about us?"

"Only basics. I know no ler well, except . . . but never mind."

"You saw you came in the midst of a party. It was not only a birth we
were celebrating, but the continuation of this *Klanh*, this braid. We now
have our next insibling generation, boy and girl. The little one who likes
your beard is Himverlin, of Bazh'ingil and Pethmirian. She is *nerh*, but
for all that, she is a shy one."

"I understand. What happens if both are of the same sex?"

"With the *nerh*, it is pure chance, but from then on, it is partly determined. By our interactions. I don't know the word . . ."

"Pheronomes? Chemical traces, like hormones that carry messages
among individuals?"

"That is how it works, but it is not perfect. If the *toorh* are both of the
same sex, then the braid ends. They have to weave with others, like outsiblings. Even if we can find another braid in the same straits, with insiblings of opposite sex, ours and theirs both end. The four start new
braids, with new names. But not so for us, now."

"So I see."

"It is good, then. Now, what of you?"

Han did not answer immediately. And of him, what indeed? What of
the ship, the mission, Liszendir? A sudden pang passed through him.

"Well, I have a long tale to tell, indeed. I may ask more than I answer."

"Aha!" exclaimed Dardenglir. "I see you are an apprentice *mnathman*
of the ler."

Sage or *wise man*. "No, certainly not. Why would you think that?"

"Because it is always the part of the wise to ask, not to answer; is that
not why they are wise?" He smiled. Han felt like an idiot. Here he was,
a cultured and educated member of a technological culture, a civilization which stretched across twenty-five planets or so, human worlds. Yet
this farmer with an infant in his arms could disarm him in an instant.
He realized better now why humans avoided ler, even though they were

graceful, even beautiful creatures, man's own kind, and peaceable in addition. It was disturbing. So, he thought, might have felt some poor Neanderthaler who had wandered into a Cro-Magnon tribe's camp, in the Ice Ages of prehistoric Europe.

"No. I am not a sage, of the ler or anybody else. As a fact, I feel somewhat like a fool. But never mind; you will hear all, when all of you are gathered together. And for the answers, and the help, I will freely offer what work I can do and what I can learn."

"Gladly, with the answers, such as we have. And work? There is plenty of that."

So in the morning of the long Chalcedon day, Han went to work at simple agricultural tasks. He spent the day with Pethmirian out in the field, picking beans and filling a small cart, which they pulled along the rows behind them. She showed him how to do it, shaking her head sadly when he displayed his one-thumbed hand. Her hands flew among the vines like small birds. But he learned.

Towards evening, a shower blew up, moving lazily and deliberately after the manner of all Chalcedon weather, so Han and Pethmirian repaired to a shed, joining Bazh'ingil, where they spent the remainder of the day shelling the beans they had picked. Occasionally Dardenglir would drop in and talk for a while; then he would be gone again. As the afternoon rain slowly evolved into the deep blues of night, gradually everyone drifted to the water trough, where, with a great deal of splashing and whooping, everyone stripped to the skin and washed, bodies, clothes, everything. Han joined in; he was not bashful, but he was slightly embarrassed because nude, the differences between the two peoples became the most noticeable.

Dardenglir had presided over the preparation and serving of supper, a performance which bothered Han a little until he recalled that they carried sexual equality to what even the most rabid partisans of equality of the human sexes would call extremes. And in direct reverse from human models, ler became more equal in sexual roles as they became more primitive. They believed it with conviction; Han already knew that one of their most solid beliefs was in the convergence of function through evolution. Not ler, nor their successors in a million years, but perhaps after three or four more evolutionary generations, it would arrive where both sexes would be completely undifferentiated, even as far as bearing children. Sex would then be a function purely of individualism, and not of gender.

After everyone had eaten, they began talking. Dardenglir told Han a few anecdotes about ler. With his eye for minute expressional details, he had noted Han's surprise at his nursing of the infant. His explanation was that from the appearance of mammals, males had carried vestigial nipples and glands to go with them. It had been suspected that adding function to those glands had been a subroutine of the basic DNA developmental program which occurred very late in the sequence, and that their structure worked very well for them because it shared the work of caring for the young child.

From the far corner, Tanzernan, the girl who had given birth the night before, said something and giggled. Dardenglir translated it into "Man-milk makes the children mean!" From the opposite side came a taciturn remark from Bazh'ingil. It was translated, "But it makes the boys better lovers later on." All of them, including Han, laughed at this exchange.

Han began to notice another facet of them, besides their sense of humor; there was considerable difference between individuals, even though there was a great deal of cultural conformity. Bazh'ingil and Pethmirian were more alike, as might be expected, as they were the in-sibilings of the old braid. But even there there was difference: both were quiet and reserved, but Bazh'ingil kept just below the surface a rude sense of humor which Pethmirian lacked. She was small, dark, and hardly ever spoke. But for all that there was a lot of thought behind her eyes. Dardenglir was smooth as warm oil, crafty as a snake. Wise and alert. Back in civilization, Han could easily visualize him as a diplomat, and one to watch constantly. Tanzernan was bright and pretty, a kind of sprite, who was always, it seemed, laughing about something. During the day, he had discovered that she was something of a practical joker as well.

So he told them his story, leaving nothing out, including the development of an odd attachment between himself and Liszendir. As they listened, they asked question after question, curious as children. When they had asked him everything they could think of, and resumed gazing at the fire with their large-pupiled eyes, then he began asking his questions. About the raids, the Warriors, and which was the best way to get to the mountain with two pinnacles north of the Capital.

They knew nothing new. The raids had been nowhere near the remote community of Ghazh'in. They had heard tales, seen lights in the sky, noticed more meteors than was usual during the raids. But that was all they knew.

They knew about the pinnacles Han had mentioned; indeed, it was a major landmark on a planet which had little variation of local relief from place to place. It was about two weeks, in their computation, to the southeast, which meant in his reference twenty-eight days. Han explained why he felt he needed to go there. They all scoffed it off, and Dardenglir explained why.

"There is nothing there, no habited place, no town, no village. Nobody lives in those hills. How would you eat? And if the girl Liszendir succeeds, she will come in the ship—and not finding you will begin looking. She will eventually hear of the visitor at Ghazh'in; wanderers will have spread the tale. So she will come here for you. So you should stay here with us until she comes. At any rate it would be dangerous for you to return to the Capital."

Han did not like to admit the possibility, but nevertheless he asked the question anyway, feeling deep misgivings as he did. "And what if she failed?"

Bazh'ingil answered, and it was translated. He spoke seriously and earnestly. "If she fails then you are no more than a colonist, like us. Ships call at Chalcedon"—which he pronounced as *Chal-sedh-donn*—"but seldom. Face truth and grow strong from it; you are stranded on the beach. If this is so, then we will go over to the nearest human village and find you a nice girl of weaving age, of your own sort, and you can move out here. There is plenty of room—raise children and beans! There are worse things."

Han could not answer him. It was a future he had neither considered nor had he wanted to consider. Now it was late, and there was quiet throughout the *yos*. One by one, they drifted off to sleep, cleaning up after supper as they went, casually but thoroughly. There seemed to be great liberty about who slept with whom, and they appeared to be unconcerned. Bed had no sexual connotation to them, not when lovemaking was condoned even in public. And here in the *yos*, they certainly knew who could mate with whom. It would be Dardenglir's and Tanzernan's turn next. Han wound up with the little girl, Himverlin, curled up in his arms. She liked his beard, and was soft and warm, but she kicked and poked mercilessly in her sleep.

So Han entered the cycle of daily life among an isolated farm community of ler. Remote, steeped in what they called wise ignorance, they gently but firmly taught him, unceasingly and patiently. The days went slow and hard at first, but then one began to merge into another. The umbilical cord which still bound Tanzernan and her child finally became nonfunctional and separated; that was one of their peculiar adaptations, too. And Han waited for the coming of Liszendir and the ship, but with each day, it receded a little further off, like a lake drying up, desiccating in a desert.

They were especially insistent on his learning ler Singlespeech, and constantly worked on him. Han found that very hard at first, but it soon began to start coming through for him, in short bursts and flashes. It was a strange language; it was completely regular, without any form of special expressions, but that was not so surprising, considering that it was, in origin, an artificial language.

The grammar was complex—involving a case declension system for nouns and adjectives, and a highly elaborate system of interacting voices, moods and tenses in the verbs, but its regularity helped greatly. But something else about it troubled Han as he was learning it, and continued to for a long time thereafter. Each word root had one syllable, and was composed of one or two consonants, plus a vowel, plus an end-consonant. There were about fourteen thousand of these roots, each pronounceable combination being used. But each root carried at least four meanings, and there was no way to distinguish which of the four was being used—it all depended on context, which was maddening until you could follow the context. That gave them a one-syllable basic vocabulary of somewhere in the vicinity of 55,000 *basic* words. When you started figuring in two-syllable and three-syllable words, the numbers of possible words became astronomical in a hurry. He could sense a system behind the allocation of meanings, how each of the four was related to the others and the root itself, but he could not grasp the concept, and they seemed curiously reticent to explain that. They told him he didn't need to know that.

All he could figure out of this hidden order was that Liszendir's name, as she had translated it when he had asked, was related to fire in some curious way, and *hanh*, meaning "last," was related somehow to water. He told them of this conversation, and they called him, from then on, *Sanhan*, like a nickname. Water-last. And there were four words which did not have four meanings, but only one each, about which there seemed to revolve some deep secret which they would not share: *Panh*, fire; *Tanh*, earth; *Kahn*, air; and *Sanh*, water. It sounded vaguely like some type of alchemy, but Han knew little enough about that, so he did not pursue it further.

In Ghazh'in, there was little need for written material, so Han saw little of the way Singlespeech was written. After one glance at a book Dardenglir had brought with him, he wanted nothing to do with it; it seemed each root was written with only one basic character, to which were attached diacritical marks above, for the vowel, and below, for the end-consonant. Han had seen samples of ancient Chinese—it looked like a simplified form of that, even though it was not ideograms, but a true spelling script.

As he learned, he worked with them, doing the thousand chores and tasks that life on a farm required. And except for his concern for Liszendir, he found that he rather liked the life: it was natural, spontaneous, unhurried and unconcerned. But with all the good points it had, he knew very well that he was an alien among them and could not stay forever. And he missed his own kind. And love and sex. Each night, the flashing bare bodies at the water trough did not help.

He did not know how many days had passed, but it was a large number. He had reached the point where he needed almost no help from Dardenglir to talk with them. But Liszendir had not appeared. So he told them that he felt that it was time to leave, much as he hated it. He would go with Dardenglir and Bazh'ingil to the regional market and there try to make his way back to his own world and time. Despite what they had said earlier about finding him a "nice girl for weaving," they were honest. They congratulated him for a wise decision, good for him and themselves as well. But they offered him a share of the profits from the sale of their produce, in which he had helped greatly. At first he refused, but after a time, he gave in, and they began making preparations to leave.

Not so many days later, at sunrise, Han, Dardenglir and Bazh'ingil loaded and boarded a long, heavy wagon, and after many goodbyes, departed the village of Ghazh'in. The wagon was hitched to a team of four animals who resembled overweight alpacas. They called them *drif,* but Han understood that this was a purely local name—the beasts were common on most agricultural worlds and had been spread because of their adaptability. They followed a narrow, pale road winding over the rolling landscape. It was the only road into or out of Ghazh'in.

The three of them took turns driving, while one slept, and one kept the watch as a lookout. This perplexed Han until Bazh'ingil told him stories about miscellaneous ghosts, bandits and ravenous predators which could be encountered. But during the trip, they saw no more than Han had seen on his walk to Ghazh'in from the place where his life raft had landed. Furtive suggestions of movement in the dark—an occasional wailing cry. Nothing more. The land was empty. Whatever one could say about Chalcedon, it certainly had plenty of room, room enough for many people.

Finally, on the fifth day, they arrived at the market town, a place which the ler of Ghazh'in called Hovzhar, but which Dardenglir told Han was actually an old human town which had been called Hobb's Bazaar. It was now mostly ler. They named places with two syllables with the same persistence they named themselves with three. He asked if it had ever had a ler name. It had not. They were content to call it by a worn-down form of the old human name, which they had all along.

Hobb's Bazaar was a sizable community of both peoples, now mostly ler, which served an extensive hinterland as a trade center and depot for farm produce. Dardenglir was animated and excited. "Back to civilization," he cried, pounding the plank seat of the wagon with the palm of his hand. Bazh'ingil, taciturn as ever, expected to be cheated and pronounced anathemas on all, indiscriminately, of the region. "A vile lot of rascals and thieves," was all Han could get out of him. Bazh'ingil, rather short and stocky for a ler, contrived to look as short and belligerent and uncouth as he could as they were driving through the streets of the town.

To Han's eyes, Hobb's Bazaar was quaint and old-fashioned. It was a wooden town with high, angular buildings, most of which had high, peaked roofs, apparently for decoration, since the region had no snow or heavy rains. The streets were made of cobblestones, mostly poorly laid, and everything was painted in bright and clashing colors.

But inhabited by thieves or not, they were able to dispose of their goods with a tidy profit, Han helping, haggling in his new found gift of Singlespeech, even if it was still shaky and accented. He had made mincemeat of a couple of merchants, who were very uncomfortable, being accustomed to fleecing the farmers of the local area. By the evening, they had cleared out the wagon and partially filled it again with supplies to go back, and all three of them were feeling expansive and generous.

Dividing up the profits, of which there was a considerable sum left over, they offered Han half, to his surprise. At first he refused, arguing in fairness for fifths, but they reminded him that in ler usage, the braid was a single entity, a "person," and its share could not be divided. More-over, their half was much larger than they had expected to get. So, in the end, Han agreed, and they repaired to an outdoor restaurant where something was being roasted whole over a sumptuous smoky wood fire, which filled the whole town with the odor of woodsmoke and roast mingled. Meat! Han could not remember the last time he had eaten a nice greasy roast. Ler farmers did not eat much meat, not because they were vegetarians, but because square foot for square foot, they could develop and raise vegetable protein more efficiently. But it seemed years, although a logical part of his mind said that he had been on Chalcedon only a few months, perhaps half a standard year.

The three of them loaded up plates, took tankards of fresh ale, and sat down at a rickety table to eat and enlarge upon the day's profits. The evening went through its slow blue and purple evolutions, at the measured pace of Chalcedon, and they ate on, refilling their tankards from time to time. They were in the latter stages of the last bits of roast when Han noticed a motion, a figure, out of the corner of his eye. He looked, through the dust and gathering darkness. It was Liszendir.

He got up quickly, and excusing himself, walked quickly towards her. She seemed disoriented, and as he came closer to her he could see that she was bedraggled, dusty and thin. She also carried her arms in a peculiar way, gingerly, as if she were carrying hot coals, or hot potatoes, or perhaps very delicate flowers. She did not see Han at all until he was almost upon her. Ignoring the stares of the crowd and the amazement on the faces of Dardenglir and Bazh'ingil, he touched her shoulder and opened his arms to her. She fell into them, grasping Han with a strong, steady grip which did not relax for a long time. She buried her face in his chest and clung to him like a child. After a long time, she released her grip and stood back. Her eyes were red, but there were no tears in them. They did not speak.

Han led her to the table, where they immediately made a place for her, sending the potboy off for another platter of roast. While she ate, Han performed the introductions; she started slow, as if she had never seen food before, but as the long evening wore into night, she progressed slowly but steadily through three servings of roast, two plates of vegetables, and three tankards of ale. She did not talk, but only nodded politely at an occasional remark, and now and then raised an eyebrow at Han's use of her language.

At last she finished. The four of them made some small talk for a little while, but not too long thereafter the two from Ghazh'in admitted that they had to leave for bed, so they could get an early start back tomorrow. After all, with only two driving, it was a longer way back. So in the end, Han and Liszendir were alone again. She sat very still, staring into nothing, immersed deep within her own thoughts. Her eyes drooped, and finally closed; she relaxed in the crude chair. Han paid the bill, picked her up, and carried her to the inn. She was as light as a feather.

Liszendir slept for three days, in a deep sleep which displayed no hint at all of any struggles or remembrances she might be replaying. While she slept, Han cleaned her up and doctored her scratches and bruises as well as he was able, with the advice and guidance of a cranky herbalist who operated a nostrum shop next to the inn. Slowly, the color came back to her skin, and the tone to her muscles. On the evening of the third day she woke up. She said nothing for a long time, staring out the window which ran narrowly from floor to ceiling, watching the square below under an overcast sky, where human and ler haggled and strove for advantage just as they had days, years before. It was a scene ten thousand years old. Finally she spoke.

"You can see for yourself that I failed, and cost us the ship."

"To tell the truth, I was more concerned with you than I was with the ship. I had given up hope."

"You are kind. But it is so, nevertheless. And he will be back. If so, then we are captured; if not, we remain stranded. And I have lost some of myself, as well."

She held her hands up. The wrists were still swollen, out of alignment. Han felt something bitter worming its corrosive way through his emotions; both wrists had been broken.

"Yes. As you see."

She was silent again for a time. But she began to talk, slowly, hesitantly, and so gradually the tale unfolded. She was reluctant to tell it all, but it all came out anyway. After she had ejected Han, she had gone hunting for Hath'ingar; he had been elusive, and had kept his distance well, apparently trying to set up an ambush. But she had caught him, and for a time gotten the gun away from him, but in doing so, she would not use it, and it was then that he had caught her and broken her wrists. By superhuman effort, she had gotten away from him, but she knew she was as good as finished. With all her abilities, she had just barely had the edge on Hath'ingar—now the advantage had fallen to him. The first chance she got, she made her escape the same way Han had left, using the life raft. He let her get away. He didn't care. He knew she could not survive.

But she did survive. She had landed somewhere far to the west, in completely uninhabited lands, wide prairies. The food concentrate in the raft made her ill, from some trace element present or not present.

So she started hunting. It had been a problem at first, with two useless hands, but somehow she managed. Worms. Grubs. Small animals. Berries. Leaves. Finally, she had come to an isolated settlement, where, surprisingly enough, word had drifted in that a spaceman had crashed and taken up living in a tiny village called Ghazh'in. She had not waited, but started out immediately, moving cross-country to cut time down to size. By the time she had gotten as far as Hobb's Bazaar, she had just about reached the end of her endurance. She estimated that she had walked sixteen hundred miles across the planet. The wild food had made her sick, too, but she had kept it down. She had to.

Finally she said, "I don't know any more. I learned no more from Hath'ingar, if that is indeed his real name. He sneered at mine, so I think the name he gave us is false. But for now we have failed. And if it is at all possible, we must get off this planet; people know you and I live. He will come back, he said so, and he will hunt us to the ends of the universe." It was the first time Han had seen her admit defeat, or fear.

She lifted the bedcovers gingerly and looked down at her bare body. She was scrubbed clean, and the scratches and scrapes she had come to know so well had been started on the way to being healed. Some were already disappearing, although she would bear some of those fine scars to the end of her days.

"You did this? You?"

"Yes. You had a much harder time of it than I did. And you needed care. Better by me, strange as I am to you, than with strangers, or so I thought you might think. There is much I don't understand about the way your people think, but I know much more now than I did when I saw you last." He spoke now in her language, and then, halting and stumbling over the odd and cabalistic way the four meanings lay within the single roots, he told her his story, all he had done and learned at Ghazh'in. At last, he finished.

"You have seen much, learned much, penetrated far into us, here. That, at least, is not for nothing. And though your accent is barbarous, worse than Hath'ingar's when his mask was off, it sounds sweet to my ear." She reached to him and embraced him, holding him tightly to her for a long time. Han felt embarrassed, confused by this sudden display of emotion, so uncharacteristic of her. She had apparently become completely unhinged during her long walk.

She sensed his thoughts. "I was alone, absolutely alone. I have never been alone in my life before. I saw visions sometimes, I could not tell if I were remembering or seeing something new. Old lovers, friends. You.

I was confused. And so I finally find you, here, and you are not the proper human any more, but you speak to me in Singlespeech, *poor kenjureith*, and heal me as would the most intimate body friend. Only one more event between us and I will have to tell you my body-name, something I have never told anyone outside my braid."

He let her run out of steam, and she gradually fell into a pensive silence once again. Han got up from his place beside her where he had been sitting, and after a quick rummaging through an ancient and much-used wardrobe, produced a new overrobe he had bought for her, which was embroidered with designs in vines and flowers according to the bucolic tastes of the region.

"I know it's not your style, Liszendir, but I thought something like this might attract less attention, as we traveled. People would probably take you for a native. As if a pair like us could not but attract attention, even if we were dressed in grain sacks.

She threw her head back and laughed aloud. Then she shut it off, abruptly. She was herself again, certain, brash. "So now what of us?"

"I'm not sure at all. I do know there is little likelihood we will get off Chalcedon in the near future, possibly in the conceivable future. The *Pallenber* was the first ship since Efrem's, and his was the first in ten years. Chalcedon is very far off the normal lanes. And if the Warriors don't come back, we can count on being stuck here. Until you are fertile."

"Like that?"

"Yes. I had thought to head for the hill of the two pinnacles, where we were to meet. We could try to get some money and wait for the first ship. But we could not go to the Capital for any period of time . . ."

"No. 'One rat, another,' goes the proverb. And so it is. We can't wait for a ship in the Capital. But why not the hills. There is no better way, at least until we feel the pressure of time on me."

"And if nothing comes, Liszendir?" He did not finish. He knew very well what would happen. They would have to go their own ways, the ways of their people; and something undefined was taking shape between them.

"I know." It was all she said.

5

"Events follow definite trends each according to its nature. Things are distinguished from one another in definite classes. In this way change and transformation become manifest."
                    —Hsi Tz'u Chuan, *I Ching*, Introduction.

HAN AND LISZENDIR stayed in the inn at Hobb's Bazaar for only a few more days, until she had begun to recover her strength, at least enough to travel. During the long walk, her wrists had started healing, but they had not been reset properly, and so, although they were regaining their function again, especially with the enforced rest Han was insisting on, she would bear the mark of their disalignment the rest of her life. Liszendir offered no more intimacies, and Han cautiously avoided any situations likely to produce them.

When she announced she was ready, together they took the money Han had made and bought up a store of provisions and a pack beast, a *drif,* similar to the ones of the team which had pulled the wagon to Hobb's Bazaar. This one was slightly smaller, however, and it definitely possessed a livelier personality than either of those in the team.

Neither Liszendir nor Han were particularly knowledgeable with animals; but with much trying, they eventually got it to behave more or less as they wanted, all to the general entertainment of the stablemaster and his louts and hangers-on. After the initial trying session, they led it through the streets with a light bit and halter. Liszendir favored the *drif* with an evil leer, then turned to Han in resigned disgust.

"One thing is certain: if all else fails, we can at least eat the intractable beast!" At the tone of her remarks, which he sensed was not completely to his advantage, the *drif* raised a ragged eyebrow, lowered an ear, and thereupon seemed to behave with slightly more decorum. Liszendir was unimpressed; she continued to glare at it from time to time. She was still hungry. Han grimaced and added, for emphasis, a few remarks of his own.

"And on the hoof might even be more effective. Then it can serve both ways!" He also leered at it meaningfully. "If we can find any meat at all under this fluff." He poked experimentally in the general area of the ribs. The creature was covered with a fine rich pelt of light tan-brown color.

Despite Han's suspicions, however, the *drif* did have meat under the soft fur, and for all its seeming fragility, would carry a huge load without complaint. In fact, it misbehaved only when it had no load.

Thus they set out for the hills to the southeast, where they had originally intended to meet. Curiously, Liszendir was reluctant, when it came to it, to leave Hobb's Bazaar; but she admitted readily the wisdom of it. The two of them together attracted too much attention, too much curiosity. It was true that ler and human both lived in peace on Chalcedon; but they did not yet cohabit. Han and Liszendir were not intimate, but they had been together, and he noted that a new side of her personality had appeared since they had gotten back together, after she had wandered, dazed, into the market. She was more relaxed, less peremptory, less standoffish. Sometimes she could be as charming as a child, innocently affectionate, and full of unexpected turns of thought and word. She was not the only one changing; he was noticing changes in himself as well.

Along the empty road to the south and east, they passed few travelers. An occasional wagon, a herd of *drif* being driven by country louts who gaped in astonishment at them, and at anything else which happened to pass. As they walked, Han outlined his plan.

"We cannot live in the Capital. We both agree there is a high probability of spies. Yet we must live somewhere within reach until a ship comes in. We could farm, I suppose, but I know neither you nor I are knowledgeable. I have thought that if we can find a deposit in the hills, we could pan for gold or other stuff. It has no great value here, but it could support us—we could make short trips to the edge of the city for food supplies."

"And what if no ship ever comes?" she asked, looking intently at Han.

He did not answer her for a long time, even though he knew the answer well enough. Finally he spoke.

"If all else fails, then I suppose you will have to weave here, within a few years." They did not speak again for some time.

*   *   *

At last the ground began to rise above the gentle ups and downs of the Chalcedon landscape. After that, which had taken many days of travel to reach, it was not long before they sighted the two pinnacles they were looking for. The last time they had seen them, it had been from the city; that now seemed years ago; time was distorted on this world of long days and no seasons. Long ago, Han had disposed of his chronometer, which was set to standard time. The one with a variable rate setting for spacefarers who might land on many different worlds was far behind, somewhere with the *Pallenber,* wherever it was.

They turned off the road and climbed the hill towards the outcrops, looking for a suitable site. To their surprise, they found soon a small abandoned cabin, human in style, but sturdy and comfortable. Nearby was a shallow stream of clear sweet water tumbling over a sandy bed in which gleamed specks of gold. Nearby were remains of industry—rotted chutes and spillways, pans and shovels; the owner was long gone.

Han speculated that the owner had been one of the original settlers, a fellow who had come up to the pinnacles alone to pan for gold. He had hit upon a rich field. But gold was common on the planet, and so had no real value anywhere except at the port, and even then only when ships came in. So what would, anywhere else, have been instant riches, became only a source of isolation. And eventually, perhaps many years later, he became sick, and with no one near, died. Liszendir agreed with the scenario, but added another thought.

"I do not worry he will return. These tools, structures, and so forth show evidence of long time upon them. He left or died long ago. It only underlines how little we know—that we do not know how long Chalcedon has been settled. I have been guilty of making the assumption that it was only in the last few years, but it appears roots here go deeper than we thought."

"Yes. And as you see that, I see that it may have been long enough for the ler settlers at the isolated village of Ghazh'in to abandon Common as a working language. That would mean that they did not teach it to the children, not that they forgot, because I know your memories work differently from ours. They would not forget, but they might not pass it on."

"You open doors of speculations into which I do not care to look, less walk through."

"But I do not, having the disregard for personal welfare which characterizes us ancestral primates. No, I am not aiming that at you. But consider: Chalcedon has been kept a secret. And we were sent out here, untold, as if it was just next door. I know technology shrinks distances, but this is too far. Now: Hetrus was chief, for the humans, at that meeting. Who was boss for the ler? Not you, you are an adolescent, you have no standing or status to speak for society until you have been woven and given birth. Not Yalvarkoy or Lenkurian Haoren, either, although they may have known. That other one we can discount as a spy from somewhere else, who wanted us killed. So who is left? Defterdhar Srith the elder. Who is she and what does she know?"

"Defterdhar Srith is very old and wise, but more than that I know little of her. She is not of the braid of those who assume responsibility for Kenten. She has a reputation of being one who will ultimately be called among the wise. Some call her *diskenosi mnathman*—the fifteenth sage. There are only fourteen."

"But as you suggest, we can open the door, but we cannot go into it very far."

"No. Possibilities, possibilities."

They spent the next few days in making the little cabin habitable. The cleaning was easy. Repair they managed by cannibalizing superfluous parts of the cabin and the sheds attached to it. For recreation, they made little side trips, exploring the area around the cabin. It was during one of these explorations that Liszendir found a skeleton, far up the stream, near its source, which was a tiny spring trickling water out of a cleft in the rock. She examined the bones carefully, and pronounced the skeleton a human one, from the structure of the hands and jaw. Ler did not have wisdom teeth. Han was not superstitious, but he felt uncomfortable in the presence of this reminder of mortality. But to the contrary, Liszendir called it a good omen, and immediately became noticeably more animated and personable. Han was mystified at her behavior.

She said, "No, no, this is not bad! This is a good sign, a good omen. I have been looking for something to lend depth to this place. Tone. This is very good! I will explain."

He agreed to listen, suspecting that he was in for another long explanation. Han was beginning to suspect that the reason why ler society was so static was that all their energy went into producing the next generation and keeping it stable for the future.

She continued, "You know about us now, that when you have woven, had your children, and raised them, you are free and often go off on

your own. Many become solitaries. So the person, alone, feels this end
near—then he goes out, alone, doing what we call *tsanziraf,* cure-
seeking. Sometimes it heals and you know you were wrong—it was not
yet time. Other times it brings the end. At any rate, it solves the problem. There is much wild land on ler worlds, and *tsanziraf* must be in the
wild. So when you terminate on one, you lie where you fall. We do not
dispose of the dead—they dispose of themselves. Perhaps I should not
tell you so much—this is high religion. But it is so; just so. The body returns to the earth. To find skeletons in the wild is a good omen because
it means that someone was there, fulfilled."

"But that's a human skeleton, not ler. For all we know he wasn't at
peace, or even satisfied; hell, he was probably scared half out of his
wits."

She dismissed his objections with an airy wave. "No matter, no matter. So it was human, the prospector? Think—such a one would have to
be at some peace with himself to travel space and then walk out here
all alone. I know gold lures, but it does not change nature, however
much we might wish it so. Could you do this? You will say no and give
me a thousand rationalizations; you are young, you wish company,
mates, lovers, make a living after the lights of your own kind. I know because I feel exactly the same way. I would not come out here. I cannot
live alone." For a moment she stopped, and became pensive, abstracted.
Then she continued again. "Even now, I should be making the first tentative steps toward seeking insiblings. And at fertility, weave and bear
children. But him, now. So he was probably greedy. So he was disappointed. But if he stayed, I know he would have eventually seen
within—humans can do it too, the only difference between us there is
that you have to want it more than we do. Otherwise he would not have
stayed, and ended his days in the city yonder, hiding from himself with
other old people."

But they had to admit that, omen or not, the place possessed a wild
beauty all its own. The cabin was situated about two-thirds of the way,
up a rocky defile which ran parallel with the line of the ridge. At the top
were the two pinnacles which could be seen on the horizon from the
Capital. There were trees all around, in some places becoming thickets,
and the stream wound through the defile, saying the things streams felt
important to say—comments about humus and rock, rain and long days
of sun and shadow. The sunlights played among the heights, and down
in the plains below, cloud shadows prowled over the land in the slow
and measured way of Chalcedon weather. In the defile, there was a

breeze most of the time. And from the pinnacles, the view was uncommonly magnificent for a planet with such generally low relief. True, it was a lonely, isolated place, but it was quiet, conducive to thought, and the morning light slanting into it from the east was lovely.

After a few days of living and working together, things slowed down to the point where they realized that they had now a certain problem between them: they were now too close to each other, both in physical proximity, due to the close confines of the cabin and their common fate since arriving on Chalcedon, and in a certain emotional sense, which both of them felt apprehension about exploring. One night, after supper, the day they had finished arranging the cabin to suit them, they fell into a discussion about this.

Han started it by admitting that he found their closeness more disturbing now than when they had been together on the ship. She only laughed, teasing and provoking him.

"How so? In Ghazh'in you lived for months with ler, *fertile* ler. But they neither molested you nor buggered you in your sleep!"

"You know it's not the same with us."

"Ah, now. That I know. All too well." After that, she lapsed into a serious, brooding silence. But he wanted her to talk, and seriously. Something had been bothering her since he had known her, something about ler which she could not or would not express. So he tried to steer her to more openness by asking about herself, her people. He had learned much at Ghazh'in, but not so much he could do without her insights. She cooperated, and opened up as he had never seen before.

He began, "I have always thought of ler as just something like another race or culture of men; distant enough so that we could not crossbreed, of course, but like that, nothing more."

"No. It is not like that at all. We are different in more ways than you know. You see it as a cultural difference—and that it is, but there is much more underlying it. Your people have forgotten how it began, but we never do."

She continued, "Look at your own kind. You have the comfort of ignorance about your origins. You have the option of following evolution, and the unknowable part of science, or otherwise believing in creation myths that aren't scientific, but at least they cover everything. The first is a process only, in which no instant of time is more significant than the other, the latter significance without process. Either way, you arise of primal chaos. Ah, but we cannot delude ourselves with either. We were *made*. A product, like a new kind of screwdriver. To bring a race into the universe with no more thought than designing bathroom fixtures! Your scientists were playing with truly cosmic laws, more lunatic than a child playing with a nuclear weapon trigger. Pragmatism! Experimentation! And in almost total ignorance!" She grew agitated, angry.

"So, Han, we know they wanted to see if they could breed the supermen they had always dreamed of. So they played with human DNA, they arranged matings. They raised whole generations in laboratories under accelerated growth, creatures who never saw consciousness, may the *One* blight them with eternal senility. Now I tell you that evolution is both multiplex and multifarious. Common is awkward here, but I know an ancient Russian word that fits perfectly: *raznoöbrazny*— of various features. But nobody knows all its laws, all its realities. Not humans, not ler. So when finally the coherent form appeared, it was just like magic to them—actions and incantations. They had reached the next stage of self-resonance. Like music. The next halftone. Without knowing anything about chromatic scales. Better, the next chord. Or like physics—the next stable element. Magic, magic. I shudder at what they played with in their arrogance. But they were happy and so made many. They knew how. And they raised us in little camps. But the Firstborn knew what was going on—they could see with intuition better, so they knew. So they isolated themselves in tribalism, studied primitivity. They *were* primitive. You had ten thousand years to design a culture to fit you—we had to leap from creation into the second century atomic without so much as a wiggle. Out of nothing, they made a culture for us.

"Then humans found out that they could not crossbreed with us. They had attained the superman very well, but it could never do them any good! Supreme irony! They reached for the impossible, and got it— but they couldn't use it! And they realized one truth, that it was like *Homo sapiens* and its relatives in the far past. Different. Maybe not higher or better. Just different. Six thousand of us, with a low birthrate, so low that if we weeded ourselves in the interest of stability of our genetic line, it took us generations to recover our numbers. And on a planet of fifteen billion humans. So they used us, until many years later we escaped.

"So it is true we have abilities you do not: you make much of eidetic memory, but with retaining everything comes the problem of what to do with it—so we also have the ability to forget. And it is not like what you call forgetting. With you it is misplacement, not loss. With us, it is loss, completely. And when we edit, we have to be so careful, because one slip and you have lost everything. Of course, there can be no torture—because you cannot scare a secret out of someone who can forget everything, even that he exists. We have better vision, because light has the broadest bandwidth of all natural sensors; two extra colors at each end of your spectum and eight wavelength receivers instead of three.

"But liabilities, Han. We have no special night vision. That is why we turn in with the end of day—we have only color vision at night, and it's less sensitive at low levels. And what about the low birthrate and short fertility, timed like one of the animals in the field? It is said that this is one of the laws of evolution—that the higher the form, the more consciousness it has and the less instinct, the lower the birthrate . . . and everything else, too, our size, our hands. Or the appearance of youth you envy us for. Yes, we know about that. It is only neoteny, the retention and expansion of youthful characteristics, supplanting more mature ones. And the sex of adolescence. They gave it to us on purpose and not for our pleasure—it was so we would be so obsessed with it that we would have little time for anything else. And so it is sweet, body-love, but we never can confuse it with anything else, anything more than that. It is casual, everyday, mildly affectionate. Love is rare.

"You want to know how it is? I will tell you: it is twenty years of fun, pleasure, intense feelings, but fruitless, fruitless. But we fear fertility, because it is more than fun then, we almost have no choice. That is why all the elaboration with structure—it is too powerful to be treated any other way. Why do you think we would make something as complicated as a braid if we did not have good reason? It is to retain some vestige of control over who shall be born and what we shall look like after instinct has run its course. And that is why it does not last for life, too. We would not design such a thing for the exercise of curiosity.

"You did not see this with the ones you visited with. The insiblings of that braid, Bazh'ingil and Pethmirian, were already becoming infertile. For the others, they were waiting for it to start up again—it would be a year or two before Tanzernan becomes fertile again. She and Dardenglir—they may like each other, as *people*, they may hate each other; it will make no difference, none whatsoever. The desire overcomes everything. The insiblings will not envy them, they will pity them, for they had all their lives to get used to one another; those outsiblings are relative strangers, and what they will do is beyond their control. Have you not wondered that our elders live alone, when they can? They do so out of choice, not necessity, and they are *grateful* for it."

"But, Liszendir, what about one's loves before weaving? Why not weave with them? And what happens after the weaving is done? What then? Glad to be alone or not, do they wander in the woods and wrestle with desires like fasting anchorites?"

She laughed, shortly, an unpleasant sound. It was a laugh, but there no humor in it. "Were it so. But it is not. Each step forward in evolution, however halting, however sidewards, means that each process becomes fractionally more finished. For us this means that when fertility is over, all of us undergo something related to menopause, like human females. But all of us. Males alike. And ours is more finished: when it is done, we do not want sex, nor do we have the ability to have it."

She was near tears, as close as he had ever seen her. Not anger, not hurt, but realizations of finality. "We call it the sadness. Why? Because we can remember so well, the exact degree. Eidetic memory can also be a curse. We have no subconscious. So we remember it all, not impressions and composites and special significances. Exact scenes, just as they occurred. This is how I have kept myself from you. I simply remember others. You see only the sex. The fun. The irresponsibility. But how we pay later. Think of how it must be: you have a lover, with whom you have shared body-love for many years, you feel the deep kindness for each other. Then you are woven and you are separated. Insiblings pick you—you do not say no to them without good reason. And when you see your lover again, years after, you are free but the two of you can do nothing except remember how it was. It is painful.

"But for insiblings it is worse. *Nerh* and *thes* are encouraged to roam, to wander, to sleep around. After all, they have to weave with strangers. But insiblings cannot; they grow into one another. We do not forbid sex at home, no taboos, but come what may, they have to stay together. And since they are the same age, they compete and fight constantly."

"You didn't answer why not just do like we do, two by two?"

"Because our genes are unstable. We cannot risk ever developing even a recognizable family trait. It could lead to races, subraces, special populations. Each species has a unique rate of mutation. Artificially developed breeds have very high rates. And we have such a one."

"I didn't know . . ."

"It is a marvel that all do not autoforget into oblivion. Some do. But it is rare. But not unknown."

She fell into silence. Outside, it had become quite dark, and Han could see her face dimly lit, in the darkness. He knew, now, he could see more of her than she could of him, although she could probably track him accurately enough by scent and sound. Far away, in the trees and rocks, some unknown animal bayed at the stars. Liszendir sighed, once, very deeply.

"And so we come to us. You have spoken of desire to me but your acts have spoken deeper. And I am adolescent, hungry for love. In my eyes you are too close to the wild, too angular, but not unlovely. And you have been kind, knowing. All that has passed makes me feel something deep I know I cannot handle so easily. But nothing can come of it. We have no future. Do you not see it?"

He could not answer, immediately. It was far too close to his very thoughts at that moment. He knew a deep secret about himself—he had changed from the "easy come, easy go" attitude he had held about love. Fun, play. Not so. It was deadly serious. And for them, there was another difficulty.

He said, "Is it also true that your love-acts last longer than ours?"

"You needn't be tactful. It is true. Longer and more often. Both ler sexes have multiple capacity. So it is cruel for you and me to be around each other. What could we do, save that you burn out my heart, and I burn out your interest in love-play."

It expressed what he felt perfectly. And it was a dilemma he could not answer. He felt a tension in the small cabin, a need for some kind of action; it was as close as they had ever come to what had always lain between them, so close that it fit the old saying perfectly: "If it had been a snake it would have bitten them." Both. But he got up, and began to gather the pots and bowls up from supper. As he busied himself around the cabin, Liszendir vanished outside; shortly, he could hear her splashing in the stream.

By the time he had finished, she was returning, wearing a fresh robe, to hang the old one out to dry on the porch. Han left then to go to the stream and wash. There, the icy water chilled him, but only the skin. The old wives' tales were no more true here than they were about anything else. It did nothing to a deeper fire that was burning inside him. The night was unusually cool. Scrubbed, Han climbed to the top of the broken rock of the nearer pinnacle and looked out on the plains to the south. Far in the distance, a thunderstorm was being born, moving invisibly, already rivaling the weak lights of the Capital, glory without effort, rearing above the dark, silent, enduring plains. In the low winds of Chalcedon it might stay in that place for hours. Han watched it flicker for a while, too far away for the thunder to reach him, and then, with a deep sigh, climbed down and returned to the cabin.

He entered the cabin, catching a trace of the odor of clean female, a warm, grassy scent that was intoxicating. He did not hesitate nor edit what he felt.

"Liszendir? . . ." He waited a moment, then asked, softly, "Liszen . . ." Her love name sounded strange as he said it.

A bundle of quilts in the corner opened itself, to reveal a pale form in the darkness.

She said only, "I have been waiting for you to say that." There was a softness in the voice he had never heard before.

"Liszen, let us take what happiness we can as we have it."

He touched the still form, the smooth pale skin. It was cool, like the night air, but underneath there was fire. She said something softly, breathing the words; they were words he did not understand at all: Multispeech. He didn't understand the words, as he knelt beside her, his knee touching her thigh, but he knew their message; they were sad, tender, loving, passionate—all at once.

He felt the desire take him, loosing his grips on reality. Her face, close and pale, gleamed in the dark like a lantern, all afire. How could he ever have seen her as plain, tomboyish? She was lovely, utterly feminine. Before he went completely under, he had time for one last sane question, which he remembered asking, idiotically, like the popular song tunes you can't get out of your head, for the rest of his life.

"Do you kiss?" He still wondered if they had taboos.

She answered with a sudden fluid movement. Han was unable to speak coherently for a very long time. Darkness closed over him, removing every reality except one. Darkness and fire.

From that night on, they entered a totally new dimension in their relationship. Within their new framework, they had no guideposts, no knowledge of how to act with one another. Only emotion and appetites; so they pursued the deep needs they felt, mingling them well with a growing deeper emotion. Time ceased. Han saw the sun of Chalcedon, AVILA 1381, rise and set. It meant nothing. They ate. They slept. They made love. Liszendir was inexhaustible. Han was not; he kept going as long as he could, but at last, he could do no more. He collapsed in a state of complete exhaustion.

He did not know how long his final sleep was; he only knew that it was morning when he awoke. Or was it? Perhaps it was evening. Han had heard of people who could tell the difference in a strange place just by the tone of the air, but he had never been able to do it. Dazed, he tried to remember which side of the cabin got the morning sunlight. He couldn't. After a time that seemed like centuries, the shadows fractionally lengthened. The light dimmed ever so slightly. He felt warmth beside him. Liszendir was curled in his arms, breathing deeply. Sensing his movements, she awoke also. Her eyes were clear and bright. She stretched, smiling; Han ached, feeling her muscles move under her skin. It seemed she had voluntary control of muscles he didn't even know people had. They did not speak: what was there that could be said now between them in words?

So it endured for a time that never seemed to have an end. They spoke little, they explained no more, they recited no histories, they explored no speculations. They lost count of the days. They dismissed them with a laugh. They were, as Liszendir put it, "locked into the present. There is no more past, no more future; no more *me* and *thee*." They took a full measure of delight in the smallest, most ordinary things they did, and she took to going about during the warmth of the day completely bare. Han grew to appreciate deeply the firm, compact, pale body; everything about her was subtle, economical, graceful. To his eyes, she resembled in build more a human of oriental race, but the face and hair were different, and in the cool air of early morning, her skin was pale ivory, shadowed and flushed with pink.

She did not demand. They both knew she could easily outendure Han in what they were doing; so she conserved him, saved him. And teased, provoked, and tormented him.

They ran out of food. Han collected a few things together, loaded the *drif,* and journeyed over the plains to the outskirts of the city and traded what in Boomtown would have been a fortune in gold dust for a few more weeks. He returned to the pinnacles without learning any more about the Warriors, and he and Liszendir resumed again where they left off.

Very gradually, they began to talk again; at first it was just short anecdotes out of the past, shallow remembrances, but soon they began to flesh out the problem they shared again.

It was a warm night, with a thinning overcast which had served to keep the heat of the day in longer than usual. They sat by the stream, close together, arms around each other, and talked. Liszendir spoke first.

"Now it is different with us, you call me by my love-name, Liszen, or by my body-name, Izedi. That is good: it is your right and my pleasure. This has been a lovely time in my life. But there is no sign that any ship will ever come, so you know that this must end as we have foretold."

"I had hoped to forget, Izedi." He used the body-name more and more, now. It was a special thing, certain letters extracted in order out of her full-name, which could only be used according to ler custom by someone who had deep body-ties to the one so named.

"And I also, dear Han. But my body does not. Will not. With it I cannot pretend. Already I can sense the beginning of some changes; small things, true, but changes. Now time remains to us, good years, if we wish. And I do wish it—with all my heart."

"I know nothing else we can do but stay here and pass the days as we have done, as long as we can."

She spoke hesitantly, shyly. "The closer in time we come to my fertility, the less I will want you—what we do will not be enough to fill the emptiness, do you know that? But never mind. Listen: sometimes in late adolescence this very thing that we know happens to ler couples, too. So they make a vow, a promise, to return to each other, after weaving, bearing and raising, knowing that when it does come, it will be unlike it was before to them. Some promise, many fail. But will you consider this thing?"

"What?"

"That wherever you are, I will come to you again after everything is done. Would you accept me then as I will be? We will not be able to do it, then. No more *dhainaz*."

"What about your people, your ways, your own plans? You would give all that up for the hope of something forty years away?"

"Indeed I would. What is our living for except to be happy? Only fools think life is all duty. For the body, I can do nothing about that, but all the rest, the culture, the special things . . . they are just mannerisms. I can learn more." She took a deep breath, looked at Han closely. "There is much you do not know yet, much I want to tell you, but I can't, yet. But I can tell you this, now. Each of us has a sign. Mine is Fire, and and it is associated with the will. With will comes the ease to make mistakes, to go against. I do it, thus."

He thought long about this. It was one thing to promise for a love that could be fulfilled now; another to say, one part now, another part in forty years. Who could know what the future could bring? But he remembered the things they had said and done, the still white form in the dark of the cabin, the graceful figure walking bare in the stream, shining with water, the soft, short, silky hair.

"Yes. It is strange to me, stranger than all we have done. But I will see it in the end, if I can."

"Good. Then I will come to you. You will be traveling among the stars, trading, but I will know when it is finished for me, on whatever planet I live on then, Kenten or Chalcedon." The stream before them rambled on in its unending discourse, as they fell into silence again.

After a time, Han arose and went up to the pinnacles, to look out over the land and think about how it would be then, when they were much older. As he came to the top of the ridge by the broken rocks, he looked to the south, and felt ice in his heart. There were lights over the area of the city, lights which moved together, slowly. A bulk darker than darkness lay behind them; and Han knew that it could be only one thing.

He stood for a long time, looking at the lights of a huge ship, one in the darkness whose true size could not be guessed. Liszendir, noticing his long absence, joined him quietly, so that he did not know she was there until he felt her warm hip pressed against his. She said nothing, but she looked at the lights for as long as he had.

Finally she spoke, bitterly. "There is a ship."

"I don't believe it will be going the way we want, Liszen."

"No. But we may yet ride it."

"Do you think they will hunt for us?"

"I know it with the same certainty that I know we cannot escape them. And even if I were whole in my wrists again, and you were armed to the teeth, it would be nothing against the numbers they must have in that thing."

As if in answer to what Liszendir had said, the cluster of lights began to move, slowly gaining altitude, moving north, towards them. Han saw the movement, and started violently. Liszendir watched for a moment, and then laid her hand on his arm.

"Not tonight. They can't see us from that thing. They will come later." The dark mass and lights moved into the clouds overhead. But they could still see some of the lights. It moved majestically northwards, and then disappeared.

She motioned to him. "Run the *drif* off; he will be all right. And come inside with me. We will have one more night, at least."

*   *   *

Han half expected not to wake up again. Thinking it very well might prove to be their last time together, they had outdone themselves; she had been exquisite, delicious. He yearned to take her again, but he knew as he awoke that he could not. He left her, warm and half-sleeping, and started out of the house to the stream. He was only a few feet from the cabin when he became aware of an incongruity in the now-familiar landscape. He looked again. It was Hath'ingar. And many more. The *Pallenber*, unmarked and undamaged, had been grounded and sat placidly, somewhat down the defile, shining in the early morning sunlight. He looked back to the cabin, hesitantly. Liszendir stood in the doorway, looking quietly out on the scene in the dooryard.

Hath'ingar broke the silence. "Bravo, bravo! You see the wisdom of inaction! You cannot run, you cannot fight. There is hope in no direction. And of course no one else will come. You must wish to know how I came here so easily. It is simple. No magic, no powerful instruments. Just good ears. I heard her say to you on the ship that she would meet you here. So I came here also. I agree with you—you have excellent taste: this is indeed a fine place."

Han was steady. "What do you want of us?"

"Really, little enough to fear. I am revenged for my ear, as you and she doubtless know by now. In other circumstances I would be tempted to seek more, but she is a highly trained fighter and much more valuable than the petty satisfactions of personal pique. We have many uses for such as her on Dawn."

Liszendir said plainly, "I will not aid you. I will autoforget before then, and you can treat the remainder as you will." It was a good threat. Total autoforgetting would erase her personality. The body would respond, but Liszendir would no longer be in it. Han felt a deadness inside. Yes—she would be beyond the reach of pain. And pleasure.

"I think not. Your pet, here. You would not see him treated unkindly? So none of us would. You can escape inwards, but he can't. So by certain arts, if it came to that, he would remember you forever, and us, of course. And little else. But let us not descend to such a level. Besides, I wish you no bizarrity. You, Liszendir, will breed and teach the Warriors. No indignity. Share and share alike. Leave these four-bred weaklings. The Warriors will engulf them all in time."

Han asked, "What about me, Hath'ingar?"

"You have a certain value. You appear to be close to the, let me see, ah, yes, the Mnar-geseniz type, and doubtless capable mechanically. I have no interest myself in that breed, you understand this is nothing personal, but I can sell or trade you on Dawn. Who knows? If you two conduct yourselves respectfully, I may even sell you to her," he said, gesturing at Liszendir. "If she can afford my price. You, Han, are a trader. So am I, in my very own small way."

Han saw motion out of the corner of his eye: the ship of the Warriors was returning from the north, bulking over the horizon. As it came closer, Han realized that its size was far beyond any artifact he had ever seen before. It was truly colossal, a great fat rounded shape, somewhat conical. He could not accurately guess its real size; it distorted scale and measure in its immensity. Accompanying it was an orbiting swarm of irregular blocks, each one following its own circular path generally in the horizontal plane. Han looked again. The blocks were apparently meteorites. One passed under the approaching ship, passing near the ground and a landmark Han had become familiar with. He was impressed. That one appeared to be a good half-mile in diameter.

Hath'ingar said, "You marvel at our ship and its toys? That is good! Those are our weapons. They need no fuses, no tricky timers, no magic juggling of atoms. Just good old iron, the warrior's tool. When we need persuasion, one goes out, to gain momentum, and back, using planetary gravity in part. If we shoot from high over the planet, it is even better: then we can speed them up so that they act like real meteors when they impact. One of those beauties, so employed, will leave a beautiful clean crater, about a hundred miles across and several miles deep, say, a score or so. No escape, no hiding, no fortifying. And no defense.

"We expect," he continued, "to move inwards shortly and indulge ourselves to the great disadvantage of so-called civilized humankind and four-by ler. The latter we will liberate from their effeminate enervating philosophy, and the former we will own. We need more ships, but I am sure you can see we could do the task with just one."

Liszendir said calmly, "The ler will not cooperate with such a scheme."

"Then we will obliterate them. They will cease to be. And as for your nova-detonator, we know about it and fear it not. How shall you aim at a star whose location is unknown, and whose inhabitants have already left?"

From the bulk of the Warrior's ship looming nearby, as if to lend weight to Hath'ingar's words, a shuttlecraft emerged, at first looking tiny against the enormous, pitted mass. But as it approached, Han could see it was almost as large as his own ship. His and Liszendir's, the one they had lost.

Without further expostulation, Hath'ingar herded them into the shuttle as soon as it landed. Inside, they lost all view of the outside, for there were no windows or screens in the section in which they were housed. After a short, rough flight, they stopped. Then Han was herded off to one part of the large ship, while Liszendir, well guarded, was marched off another way.

He eventually found himself in a small, padded cell, which was, though secure enough, not especially harsh. It was fully equipped. The door closed. Han was immediately knocked off of his feet by a whole series of tremendous lurches. After some minutes, the violent motion stopped, or rather, subsided to the point where he could sit or stand upright. He guessed they were on their way.

PART II

Dawn

"Desire arises of the face and not of the body or any of its parts."
—Fellirian Deren

"Love is a thing whose degree of intensity is directly proportional to the degree of strangeness of the partners."
—Leskormai Srith *(The Tenth Sage)*

"We all interpret the new in terms of the old and are thus comforted or terrified, as the case may be. But the error to which we are prey does not lie in the area of misidentification, so much as it does in the area of scale. One may identify essentially correctly, say, for example, that an object is a mountain, and yet get the scale so wrong that the identity must be questioned. It is true that a ripple is in fact a wave, but very small ones are not of importance except to a weather-seer, medium-size ones a type of beauty, and large ones a great danger."
—*The Survivor's Manual*

FOR A CERTAIN time, Han knew nothing. The food was insipid, but self-dispensing at regular intervals from a slot in the wall, and it kept him alive and well without apparent ill effect. There seemed to be a bit more than he needed or could stomach; Han suspected that the rate of dispensing had been designed for creatures with a higher caloric requirement than humans. Namely, ler. It made sense to him; they were slightly smaller than humans, and seemed to eat more, or so he had noticed from observing Liszendir. He remembered achingly the heat of her body. He suspected their normal temperature was higher, also. But he ate the pellets, stuffing the remainder in his pockets in case he should get hungry, which seemed remote.

Days passed, or perhaps it was weeks. Han had no way to mark time, and all attempts he made to gather an idea by timing his own body functions, breathing and heartbeat, seemed to make the time stretch alarmingly long. So he stopped that. The cell was lit, and the light stayed on, without relief. He knew very well the danger to his mind in such an environment, but he did not think they had intended it that way. Now and then, at irregular intervals, groups of Warriors would come by to look in on him; they always came in threes, and like all ler Han had met so far, minimized sex differences as far as was possible. But Efrem had heard correctly—they were a barbaric-looking lot. Some were tattooed, males and females alike, and all wore their hair in various odd configurations, plumes, queues, bristles, fuzzes and indescribable concoctions. None of them spoke.

Han began playing a game with himself, to retain his sanity. He called it, "See how much you can learn about a ship from the sounds you can hear from its brig." It wasn't particularly long before a definite idea began to creep into, and then dominate, his mind. But when it came fully out in the open, he was astounded. It came in a flood: this ship, this colossal fortress that hurled meteors for weapons, and was certainly capable of wrecking an entire planet, was old and in an advanced state of decay and disrepair. Only extreme and clever maintenance had kept it alive as long as it had. How old was it? He had no idea; hundreds of years, perhaps thousands. He half-recalled Liszendir's tale about that ler rebel, Sanjirmil. The Klarkinnen. Yes. He stopped pondering and listened.

The ship groaned and vibrated constantly, and occasionally lurched uncontrollably. Han fingered the padding material; it was new stuff, of course. This whole section seemed new, or recently rebuilt and refurbished; and any ship would show some modifications across time. But the material, rather crudely woven, did not make him feel any better about the ship. The creaking and groaning went on, and increased ominously.

He had also noted another distressing symptom: the air vent system only worked sometimes. Now and then the air in the cell would become stale, and at other times, it would develop peculiar odors. And these symptoms also seemed to become worse as time passed at its unknowable pace. Han began to grow apprehensive. Finally the lurching, shuddering and discoordinations reached a climax. Then silence.

Not too long after the silence came, to Han's surprise, Liszendir appeared at the cell-door window, looked in, and opened the door. She had a large bag slung over her shoulder, he guessed, filled with food concentrate pellets, and in addition had brought with her an ancient cross-bow and a quiver of darts. It had to be for him. A crossbow? In a space-ship? But he took it, gratefully. The first time he did was to cock the weapon, using an obvious foot-strap, and load it with one of the crude but deadly-looking iron darts. Liszendir was smiling, unhurt, and not even busy-looking.

"Come on! No talk, now. You won't believe it, but I really think that we can get out of this thing. We're on Dawn."

A single guard appeared in a corner of the corridor, looking confused and harried. As he or she—Han couldn't tell—caught sight of them, he shot it deftly without hesitation. The plumed Warrior sank to the floor, and the only sound it made in dying was a small groan, which appar-ently went unnoticed. Liszendir gave Han a look which he could not quite interpret—as if she approved of the action, but not the method-ology. But she had brought him the weapon, so she intended that he use it, even though she wouldn't.

Han recocked and reloaded the arbalest, thinking dire thoughts about men who designed single-shot weapons of any sort, and hurried off down the corridor with Liszendir. She led the way through a series of tubes and halls until they were at a shuttle craft, either the one which had brought them to the ship, or one just like it.

She asked, "Can you fly it?"

"I don't know. Damn! All the controls are for hands with two thumbs, and the labels are in their characters."

"That is old writing. We used to use that system long ago. I can read it. Let's see . . . ah, this one, it says *hovgoroz*. Even the right verb form. Do you remember *hovgoroz* from your language lessons?"

"To go out. Verb of motion. Easy." He pushed the button, having an afterthought that the word could also mean escape, and in that case, how did the mechanism work? He did not want to be pitched into space again. But no, it was the right interpretation. Before them, a sec-tion of the wall opened, as a section of the shuttlecraft wall suddenly became transparent before them.

Liszendir was still puzzling out the indicators and controls. Finally she pointed to some levers and knurled wheels, half-sunk in the console. "This one for speed. This one, this stick, for altitude. This one controls vector. And this, this silly little furry button, is what activates it." She pushed that one herself.

"Hang on," said Han. There was no sound, but the shuttle craft rose smoothly, hovering. Han pressed the levers in combination. The craft gave a great bound for the portal opening, slewing sideways as it did. They barely missed colliding with the portal edge. Finally, Han got it figured out which motions he had to make for pitch, roll and yaw, synchronized with velocity. Liszendir was busy holding on, and Han was busy with controlling the craft. By the time they had time to look out at the world, they were well outside the warship, falling out and away from its bulky mass. The controls were impossible to handle correctly; they were tiny, but their effects were great. The craft responded immediately, as if it had no inertia of its own. Han reasoned that this was a power effect, not one of the unified field, as if they had had that, they would have not felt their own inertia in the cabin.

They had fallen into a world of harsh, piercing bright light. The shuttlecraft was flying above a great plain, flat as a table top. Han got a quick glimpse of the ground. To one side a sandy riverbed meandered, bordered by a darker growth, which appeared to be trees. He couldn't tell. The distance was too great. The sky was cloudless, and a brilliant, electric blue, almost violet color he had never seen before. The sun was stark white with a tinge of blue, powerfully and painfully bright, and objects cast razor shadows, so sharp they seemed dangerous, as if they would have cut one if one had fallen on them. It was impossible to tell what time of day it was, morning or afternoon. Behind them bulked the ship, its orbiting meteors grounded on the plain below, still and unmoving. In the distance, seemingly not so far, jagged mountains reared. Near? He looked again. The lowest peaks in front of the range, and the lower saddles between them, were streaked with cirrus. Near? They were a great distance away. He revised his estimates of their size; they must be enormous.

Liszendir said, gloating. "We had to land for repairs. The ship is falling apart. They couldn't even make it to their own country after we made planetfall—that is several thousand miles away, on the other side. We had to land, to adjust the drivers. No sooner had they stopped, than these people came rushing over the plain and attacked the ship. They are using chemical rockets and cannon, and the like. And they have done some damage! It seemed to be light, just chips off this hulk, but it made the Warriors *mad!* You should have seen them! They all sallied out to fight like a crowd of maniacs. They were actually worried about their monster. Look below!"

Han looked below to the plains. There was fighting there, and figures rushed madly about, smiting and being smitten. He could not distinguish figures into factions from altitude, but the action seemed lively and vicious. Groups on foot strove against groups mounted on animals of some indeterminate sort.

As they increased the distance between the warship and themselves, Han asked, "So we're on Dawn?"

"Yes. I think their country is behind the ship relative to us. This area is considered no man's land, under partial control. They either can't subdue it, or they think it isn't worth the trouble. Those are humans down there attacking, not ler. The Warriors used some term for them—it was *klesh*. Part of it—I didn't understand the adjective. *Klesh* is what we call a domesticated animal."

Han looked again. There was a puff of black smoke perhaps from a cart or carriage. Seconds later he could see a small explosion on the underside of the warship, now well behind them. This was answered by green flares from the upper part of the large ship.

"That's the recall signal!" Liszendir exclaimed. Below the groups began to disengage, some of the tiny figures scurrying back to assembly points, where shuttles from the warship were already arriving. And farther out, the meteors began to stir in their landing spots, at first rocking back and forth, wobbling unsteadily. Then, one by one, the smaller ones first, they began lurching off, rolling and bouncing as they went, leaving huge gouges on the plain and shedding chunks of themselves as they attained flight. Short bursts of dazzling light came from the ship; if the bursts were from weapons, they were singularly ineffective.

Liszendir said, "For sure, we've got to hurry, now. They don't know you and I are gone. They left me in the control room with three guards. A mistake. Now they are reduced by three." She chuckled to herself and smiled, baring her teeth in a gesture of hostility. "One person can't fly that monster by himself; it takes a whole crew, all over the ship. Otherwise I would have stolen it while they were out and dropped some of their own eggs on them."

"I thought your wrists couldn't take stress. And I thought you wouldn't use anything that left the hand for a weapon."

"Well, for the first, I still have elbows, knees, feet and heels. And forearms are almost as good. And as for the other when that beast Hath'ingar shot at me and you, he removed any restraint I might have. It is open season on them now for me. I can commit atrocities if required." She smiled with evident satisfaction. Han found it chilling.

Their speed increased. Han was gradually descending in altitude as they drew away. Liszendir was watching the warship in the rear screen.

Han asked her, "Can you find any thing on this shuttle that looks like it might be a power source?"

"No. Nor have I felt any since we started. Do they have stuff that good, and they can't fix that ship?"

"I doubt it. I think these shuttles run off beamed power from the big ship. Probably a high-power microwave, using part of the echo from the shuttle to align itself. If this is true, we are going to run out of power in a few minutes, when the big one gets going."

"Ah! You may be right. The big one is moving now, off the ground and away, towards their own country. And one of their rocks . . . Han, it spiraled upwards right out of sight!"

"Well, we can't go any faster; I've got it on full power, now. If the ship is moving, we won't get far away."

"They're going to drop one of those rocks. Yes, the attackers are scattering, too. They know!"

But their speed did not increase; on the contrary, it slowed appreciably and steadily, as the big ship drew away from them. Han said, over his shoulder, "Speed dropping now, and the controls feel mushy. Inverse square rule, power drops off. And the atmosphere may attenuate the beam signal strength, too." He brought the shuttle lower as fast as he could, now. He didn't know what would happen when the power went off for good. They seemed to crawl over the plains, now visible as being covered with a kind of grassy plant cover, golden in the harsh bright light. Time crawled, became infinitesimal in its pace.

He looked around at the rear screen Liszendir was watching. The big ship was still visible, but it was now far away and at some altitude, receding fast. But it was still good; as long as it was in sight they still had a chance. Ahead of them, in their path, rose a grassy rise, a ridge line. The plains were not absolutely flat. They would probably make it.

"I'm going to drop us behind those hills in front. If their aim is good with those meteors, we should be fairly safe there."

"They claimed to me that it was quite good, decreasing with speed, of course. Within ten miles of the target point for this kind of shot."

"Good. Now be ready. We may crash, after we drop behind the hills. It will cut off the signal."

In the rear screen, the ground rose as they put the ridge line between themselves and the big warship, now almost out of sight, fading in the very distant haze, not in apparent size. The warship dropped below the apparent horizon. Instantly, the control panel in the front went completely dead, and the shuttle dropped sickeningly in free fall, then braked, none too gently. They felt themselves gripped by a sudden force field, that faded even as they noticed it. Automatics. Then they fell free another few feet, and impacted. Han and Liszendir were shaken up and dazed, but there seemed to be no injuries.

Liszendir looked up, glassy-eyed, from the floor. "What now? Can we run?"

"Won't do us any good. Just get free of the shuttle. It may roll about. Lie on the ground. Roll into a ball."

They helped each other up, and climbed out of the shuttle. It did not seem to be damaged in any way, other than some dents, which might have been there before. They ran a short distance, threw themselves on the ground, rolled up into balls, and waited. They didn't wait long. There was a single bright flash from the zenith, followed instantly by a lurid quick glare near the point over the hill where the warship had been. Then they heard the shriek of rending air, and then a titanic sound that could not be described. The earth shook violently, opening small cracks all around them. Dust rose and hung in the air, close to the ground.

Han looked up. "Now we wait for debris to fall. Keep an eye out. Chunks could come this far."

Liszendir got to her feet, looking into the sky, with an expression of disgust on her face. "That was truly obscene."

"I know. It's a projectile weapon. I feel horror, too, even though I have no prohibitions such as yours."

"It is ultimate sin. I have seen evil."

Han got to his feet, and started for the hill. "Come on. I want to see what it did. Maybe someone made it."

She was obstinate. "No. I will not look. Go. I will wait. After all, where do I have to go?"

Han started out for the top of the hill they had sheltered behind. It took a good half-run to get there. The clear air distorted distances even more than on Chalcedon. At the top of the rise, he stood panting and out of breath, gazing out on a scene of utter destruction. He felt dizzy. The air was very thin, he thought, too thin. He sat down, laboring for breath.

Below, where the plains had stretched unmarked, yellow and clean, there was a crater. A large one. A huge cloud of dust and dirt obscured the impact zone and the crater, so he could not see fine details. Streaks radiated away from the crater, for several miles. The grass was on fire in places. He tried to guess the distance. He could not. The thin air gave no hint of depth. There were no marks by which he could judge. Guessing, he estimated about fifty miles. They were lucky. The projectile had probably been solid nickel-iron, a third of a cubic mile perhaps in volume, moving at higher than orbital speeds. They were indeed fortunate. Nothing moved, back on the plains.

He returned to where Liszendir sat, with a puzzled look on her face, mingled with a trace of pain and fear. She had rifled the shuttle while he had been gone, and had the food bag with her. And the crossbow. And some blankets from one of the shuttle lockers. For the time, they would have some shelter and food.

She spoke, as he came up, in a whisper. "Han, what are our chances now? You are the survivor, not me. I did it once, but it was by guess and I almost died of it. What is this place like? Where do we go?"

He answered, "I don't know." Then he took a long look around them. The land was nearly featureless and flat, except toward the hill that had saved them, and in the direction of the mountains. The distant mountains stood quietly as Han inspected their outlines. Distant, deep blue with distance. They were high, high, even if they were only ten miles away. And he knew they were farther. He tested the air, glanced sideways towards the sun.

"Without instruments, an atlas, knowledge? I know now only what my senses tell me. That is little enough." He jumped up and down experimentally. "The gravity feels about right—about a little higher than a standard G, maybe 1.1 G. But the air is very thin."

"Yes. I noticed. I am not breathing well at all."

"This seems like a high plateau. Feels like around thirteen thousand to fifteen thousand feet, but with a higher oxygen content. Altiplano. *Kadhyal* to you, if you have any on Kenten. It will get cold at night. We can also expect altitude sickness, headaches, earaches, maybe vomiting. Respiratory bleeding. We will have to get off this plain to survive. I can see no way out, but towards the mountains. There may be a gap, or a canyon. But notice the snow on them. It only goes up so far. Above that, it's naked rock. Those clouds you see on the lowest peaks and saddles are cirrus. They are high-altitude clouds—35,000 feet, in a gravity and an atmosphere near standard. Here, higher gravity, thicker atmosphere. I don't have any idea. But they are very far away, and they are much higher than us. Miles higher. They may go up to sixty, seventy thousand feet equivalent. Higher. I know we cannot cross them on foot. But that way is our only chance. Mountains that high and that rough more often than not have a trough behind them, if they have a plain high up in

front, like this. Continental edge. There should be a sea behind them."
He finished. He wanted to say more, but he couldn't. He was out of breath.

Liszendir gazed at the mountains for a long time. She shaded her eyes, peering intently. "Yes, you are right. They are far away—many days for us. But I agree—it is the most reasonable way to start. I do not fancy walking out on that plain, not after the meteor. But notice how the sun moves. Already it is getting on into afternoon, and when we landed it seemed near noon. The day here must be very short. You can almost see the sun move."

"Don't look at it! That blue tinge means ultraviolet. We can get a vicious sunburn, especially you. And it will burn your eyes out."

Resignedly, they covered themselves as well as they could, and, gathering up their few possessions, they started walking.

"Walk slowly, Liszendir. Breathe deeply. We can't hurry."

She smiled back at him. "Who's hurrying?" She spoke cheerily, defiantly, but it was with effort. Han began to worry, it might be hard on her. He did not know how tolerant ler were to altitude. But he knew one thing about them. They never lived in extremely high places. Yes. It could be very hard on her.

Nightfall was as abrupt as a door slamming, and they had not gotten very far by the time that it happened. And Liszendir had developed a headache. In the mountain wall ahead, Han had picked out a saddle, a notch in the gargantuan wall, which had a peculiar, easily recognizable shape, for reference. He wanted to see what kind of progress they were making, if any.

They found some water. It was a murky trickling spring, with no apparent source, and the water sank back into the ground no great distance away. Han, smelled it, tasted it gingerly, and looked all around the area for slimes and iridescent deposits. There were none. They drank at its meager output for hours.

The light behind the mountain wall across the world went to an indescribable color, a burning pearl-blue that hurt the eyes, then dimmed, darkened; and went out. After eating the food-concentrate pellets without enthusiasm, and without conversation, they made a shallow pit in the ground, and in it, partially covered and wrapped around each other for warmth and comfort, they settled in for the night. Liszendir was suffering. She gasped for air in deep breaths which were constant effort.

Han enclosed her in his arms. He was feeling bad himself, extraordinarily tired, for no more than they had done; but it was not as bad as he had expected. The oxygen content must be high.

The stars came out, shining with unusual brilliance and clarity, although even at the zenith, they sparkled and flickered like stars close to the horizon on more normal planets. Yes. A heavy, thick atmosphere, low in water vapor, high in oxygen. But they were utterly strange, and after the gentle, kindly nights of Chalcedon, hostile in their strangeness. And it was cold. He had been right—the temperature did indeed drop fast.

They did not sleep well; nobody does with altitude sickness. The cold and the discomfort. Han was almost glad to see the sky brighten in the east after a short, seemingly too short, night. The sky first turned, without warning, so it seemed, a hot pearl color, then burning, then the piercing sun again. It was quick, brutal. He now understood why they called this planet "Dawn." It *was* beautiful, in a hard way, like the glint of fire on blued steel. The temperature began warming up before the sun had completely cleared the flat horizon in the east. The foot of the mountains was masked in darkness.

Liszendir was awake. She looked feverish and bedraggled, and admitted to little sleep either. The thin air was a slow torment. But stoically and quietly, they picked up their things and pressed on through the short day, west, straight for the mountains.

Several times during the day they felt earthquakes; not severe ones, but large enough to notice. Liszendir noticed them, but said nothing. Han told her, "These mountains ahead, the high plateau, the earthquakes. We must be near the continental edge. If we can make it to the mountains, there must be a way through them, a gorge or canyon. On the other side, the altitude will drop down to something nearer sea level. There will be lower country on the other side, and maybe an ocean. All worlds have drifting continents—that's what piles mountains up like those, it's the only thing that could pile them up that high and that regularly north to south. The only thing that differs on various worlds is the rate at which they move around."

She nodded. She had heard and understood. They walked on.

The mountains grew no bigger, not even by a little bit, and Han revised upwards his estimates of their altitudes, and the distances he and Liszendir would have yet to walk. They stopped early, too tired to continue until actual darkness. There was no water at this place; they ate listlessly and curled up together against the coming cold. Han took one last look around the featureless plains, and at the mountains. The sun was just dropping behind them.

To the right, or north, of the notch he had marked the day before. Not a lot, not a great distance, but enough to be noticeable, and he knew that they could not have moved so far to the side of their route, north or south, to make that much of a difference. It was disturbing, but the answer was not apparent, so he filed the fact away, and lapsed into fitful sleep.

Then there was the short night; which was followed by another day, which was very much like the one previous, clear and unmarked by weather of any sort. And another. And another. At first, it only became important whether they had water when they stopped for the night, but even this faded. They stopped talking. They ceased to notice any differences at all.

But there was a difference, as the days passed endlessly and monotonously. The mountains were coming closer, and the plains were beginning to undulate in rolling hills; it was hard for them to go up the gentle slopes, but pure pleasure going down the western slopes, even though there was one more just like it just ahead, and just a little higher.

They rationed the tasteless pellets as well as they could, for neither of them could visualize even the hungriest man bolting them down in an abandon of hunger. Yet, as well as they stretched them out, they knew they were drawing on their reserves, and Liszendir was showing severe weight loss; her face was becoming drawn and haggard, and Han thought she looked more worn than when she had stumbled into the market at Hobb's Bazaar. Hobb's Bazaar. It seemed years, ages in the past, in another time, remote as childhood, meaningless. The numbers of the days were meaningless as well—and the only realities were the amount of food concentrate remaining in the bag, and the distance to the mountains, which was now growing less, at last. Each evening, the violet shadows rising from the bases reached them sooner, earlier. And the sun was moving daily to the right, the north. Han's mind was fogged. He knew that movement was significant, but somehow the connection always seemed just out of reach. The significance grew into suspicion, still unformed. He could not put it into words, but something deeper knew and told him that they must get off that plain and down;

they were casting shadows at noon, shadows that fell to the south, and every day, they were a little longer, at noon. The earthquakes grew stronger and more frequent. And the mountains gleamed above them, now dominating the western half of the horizon, giant fangs raised skywards in a terrible rictus of defiance.

At the end of the next day, they came, quietly and undramatically, to an enormous gash in the earth, which they did not see until they were almost upon it. The other side faded away into the violet haze of the evening shadows of the mountains, and could not clearly be made out. The far side merged into the tumbles of the foothills, imperceptibly. And below them it went down and down from the gentle break at the rim, the air growing misty toward the bottom, where they thought they could see the suggestion of a silver river, wearing away at the stone. They stood in the short twilight on the rim, looking down into the depths; the river, if there was one, seemed to flow to the south and the gorge seemed to trend back toward the mountains, although they could see no hint of break in the wall above them. Like everything else on Dawn, the gorge exceeded anything in their experience in sheer size. It matched the mountains well in scale.

Liszendir looked downwards with shining eyes. "Air, that's what I need. If I could just breathe again, I could go down there and die in peace." Her voice was a croak.

Han added, "And I as well. It will be enough, if we can just get down there." His voice sounded even stranger to him.

They started down immediately, not willing to spend even another night on the terrible high, cold plains. But despite the apparent gentleness of the upper slopes, the going down was not easy, for the distances were deceiving; and the slope soon became steeper. In the dark, under the stars, and for the first time with a restricted horizon, they stopped.

Their distance per day dropped to almost nothing, but they moved steadily downwards. Each day the rim to the east rose higher, and the air grew fractionally denser and warmer, easier to breathe, and each night the shadows came earlier. And still they crawled down, down, making slow progress. But one thing had improved—they had water all the time, fresh water dripping from springs in the rocks. With water they could stretch the food concentrate even further. But it was showing on them. Han was gaunt and skeletal, but Liszendir was worse; and what bothered Han even more, now that he could think better in the denser air, was something he had noticed the last day, although he had dim recollections of it starting back on the high plains: Liszendir was starting to hallucinate and talk to herself.

They ate the last of the Warrior's food concentrate. There was enough for both of them to stretch two days, or eat it all and go as far as they could. They ate it all and threw the bag away, laughing. And far from being sad, they felt, as they ate, the closest thing to joy they had known since Chalcedon. And after they had eaten, Liszendir seemed to return to her senses. It was good—she had been babbling most of the afternoon about castles and the thirsty eye.

"So, Han, here we eat our last. Now how far can we go?"

"If we were in good shape, about three days' worth, but as we are. I'd guess no more than two, to amount to anything."

She looked around. "So here is where it will end, our most amazing thing, something no others know. I do not fear it. Look around us, look at this."

Han did as she asked, and in the swift evening fading light, the buttes and buttresses of the gorge reared above them, sizable mountains in their own rights. Now the high range was out of sight behind the western rim. Han was thankful for that, for he had felt daunted and humbled in the sight of those naked, high rocks. No human, nor any other conceivable creature, would ever walk those passes, climb those peaks, "because they were there" or for any other reason. There was no air. They towered miles above the high plains, higher than any mountains Han had ever seen or viewed pictures of.

Liszendir began again, not waiting for him to reply. "You cannot see it, but I can. There is far-violet in the deep shadows, *nefalo perhos 'em spanhrun*. The rocks, the river below. This is a place of giants in the earth, heroes, *reison*, cold, relentless, cruel beauty. I have journeyed far to see this." She seemed entranced by the spectacle, like a child again, he thought. She looks death and termination in the face and says, "How lovely. Look at the view." Han saw only oblivion and darkness forever. Pain and cold and the big sleep.

Night fell and they slept. In the morning, which was coming later and later, they picked up what they had left, the blankets and the crossbow, and continued on their way down. They saw nothing to give them hope. There were plants, now, fairly common, but they looked suspicious, and neither one of them wanted to eat them. And they were wrong about two days' travel. He knew that they could not go any farther than they got this night. And as the night closed about them, she went far ahead of him, pushing what was left of her strength to the uttermost. In the last light, he saw her far below, her face shining with joy. Joy? It was probably, he thought, a combination of fear and hysteria, which he was feeling himself. And exhaustion and starvation. Yes, perhaps she was right—it was better to face it this way, than to meet it cringing.

She was waiting for him by a large boulder, her face full of happiness. Han hesitated to join her, fearing her insanity, if that was what it was. But she did nothing more irrational than falling into his arms and pulling him down in the shelter of the rock. Not for love, for they were long past the strength to accomplish it, even a part, but for comfort against the night they knew was coming for them. She cuddled against him like a small child, and later, semi-conscious, she began talking in her sleep. It was Multispeech again, and went on at a steady pace for a long time, the voice, now soft, whispering next to him, saying many things simultaneously that he would never know. She would not stop for long. He looked at her face before he went to sleep; it was very thin, drawn and worn, but she was smiling as she talked, happy, even rapturous. She probably did not expect to wake up. Neither did Han. He stroked her hair, and went to sleep.

But they did wake up the next morning, early, with the first light. They arose listlessly, silently. This would be the last day, absolutely. He felt he could not walk another step. Once more they gathered up their blankets, more for the reassurance of ritual than for any other reason, and automatically started around the boulder.

Before them spread not another interminable slope down, but a large, level terrace stretching parallel to the river, still far below. And not fifty paces from them was a house. A rude stone house, with thin blue smoke rising slowly out of the chimney. Lights within the house glowed yellow in the deep blues and violets, overlain by the nude pearly sky overhead, of the morning of the planet Dawn. A chill was in the air.

He looked at Liszendir. Tears were streaming down her thin cheeks, and as he watched, she slowly folded up and sank to the ground. He picked her up; she was light, hardly a burden at all, a mere collection of bones. He knew. She had been starving, so he could get the lesser amount he needed. And he knew why she had been so carefree the last day. Carrying the small load, Han started for the house, but he only made it as far as the gate of the dooryard before he, too, sank down. The owner, much to his surprise, found them there about an hour later, as he was making his morning rounds.

* * *

The farmer was human, and had a wife and two daughters, big strapping homely girls, all of which Han noticed very little. He ate, and he slept. And ate and slept some more. He heard voices speaking ler Singlespeech, or a version of it. It was far away, and it meant nothing. He slept deeply.

He finally awoke, clearheaded, to find Liszendir, thin but recovering, sitting on the floor beside his pallet. It seemed to be noon of some day, a day he didn't know, but he knew one thing. He was recovered. He looked at her, seeing that she had been waiting for him to wake up.

She asked, "Are you feeling better now? I can tell you that I am."

He nodded. She was fleshing out again, but the experience they had been through had molded and eroded and rebuilt in her a new, sober and more thoughtful beauty. Whatever her age-status was in ler glandular terms, she was now neither adolescent nor tomboy, the intriguing ambisexual creature he had met in Boomtown, and loved on Chalcedon. Her eyes reflected the electric blue of the light of the sky.

"I think you will have trouble talking to them for a while. They speak only Singlespeech, but it has changed even more than the version the Warriors use, and at first, even I had trouble with it. But humans! That is what amazes me, Han, I really must admit to prejudice and wonder why your people persist in speaking such irregular and redundant languages. Even when given a regular language, they contrive to make it irregular."

"Are they friendly?"

"Yes, friendly enough, although you will possibly think them rather close-mouthed. I have told them that we escaped the Warriors and walked here from a great battle scene miles to the east, up on the plateau. Better that than the truth. It is all they can handle, and even what I gave them is a lot. They distrust me some, because I am ler, they can see that. But my hair and the way I let it fall straight has convinced them at least that I am not a Warrior. We are heroes, to have walked so far."

"You look beautiful."

She looked away sharply for a moment, as if the remark pained her. Then she turned back. "We can also get down the gorge, on the river. It gets low in this season, and they say that they raft down after the harvest. And if we will stay and help them, they will take us when they go to market. Guess where it is? On the other side of the mountains! The gorge does go through."

She looked back outside again, as if searching for a reminder of some knotty problem. "There is something very strange, here," she said at last.

"I hear echoes of the proper words for seasons in his speech, but they have additives which distort them terribly, more than any other part of the language. If my ears do not lie to me, I understand from him that there are eight seasons on this planet. Two winters every year. I have never heard of the like. How could that be? Would the high mountains cause it?"

Han suddenly sat upright. It was what he had been waiting to hear, the missing pieces that fit the puzzle of the swift sun drifting to the north so fast. "What season is it now?"

"North, or short winter is coming. This is little autumn."

"What happens in short winter?"

"It will get dark, but not as long as long winter, which they fear."

"Now I know. I suspected when we were up on the plateau, walking, but it didn't make sense to me then. I have heard of planets like this one, but all the known ones are out of the habitable zone for our kind of life forms. They are called uranoid planets, after the first one discovered, back in the old Earth system. Remember Chalcedon? It had no seasons because it had a regular orbit and no axial tilt. This planet has an extreme tilt; its plane of rotation is closer to perpendicular to the plane of orbit. It means that from the ground, the sun will be over the poles once during the year for each pole. The polar regions overlap the tropics. It will be a strange place with a stranger climate. Probably the only thing that makes it livable is the presence of high mountains, high enough to block mass circulation of the atmosphere with the rotational direction."

"The days are already shorter, and the sun is more to the north than when we were walking."

"Right. Here, they have eight seasons, four when the sun is to the north, four when it goes to the south. At the poles, it would be even stranger; if we were there, we would see the sun rise, spiraling around the horizon, and then it would climb to the zenith, or near it, still spiraling. It would wiggle around overhead for a while, and then start spiraling back down. Then it would get dark for a long time, three-quarters of the year. And cold. It must be hellish at the poles."

"How?"

"Temperature. At the poles, once the sun rises, it stays risen and in a day, illuminates every object from all sides. It probably gets hot enough on the surface to melt lead in the polar summer, and in the long dark winter, cold enough to freeze some gases out of the air."

"Yes! He said that. I did not understand; I thought it was the language. He said that the air freezes in places and falls to the ground."

Han thought some more, then asked, "And how far is it to the ocean?"

"More problems for you to figure out. He said that there wasn't such a thing anywhere near here. He didn't even know the word. He used the old word for pond or lake, or so I thought. I corrected him, and he said not that, but a lake, and he waved his arms around to show me how big. Not very big at all. A salt lake, very far down and very hot in the summer. There are salt deposits all around, and it sometimes boils. They go there and get salt in other seasons. But he had never heard of an ocean."

"That is curious."

"However it is, over the mountains are people. Plenty of them, too many for him. Human and ler, both. But while he was telling me all about the region, thinking I'm from a far country, the whole time he was talking about the ler, not once did he mention the four parents, the four children. They marry by twos, human style. Except for the Warriors, whom he fears greatly. They do something else, and it isn't by fours. He didn't know what. The word for 'braid' does not even exist on this planet."

Han didn't know what to make of that, either. He got up from the pallet, dressed, and started out to meet the farmer. As he did, he looked down at his body, now still thin from their hard trek across the high plateau. He was clean. He looked at Liszendir. She smiled.

"I pay my debts." It was the only thing she said, all she ever said about it.

The farmer and his family were indeed friendly, if somewhat reserved, but they balanced their suspicions of Han and Liszendir with their admiration and awe of their exploit of walking across the bare high plains. He himself had heard that people lived up on the plateau, but he had never seen any direct evidence of it; as far as he knew, the air was too thin for people to live in it. Han and Liszendir agreed with him. The farmer also thought that perhaps the plains were the abode of ghosts and various dire spirits, although Han could not be sure just what he meant; his language was sketchy to begin with, and Han's command of it was none too good. So, after the local accent, the peculiar usages, the irregularized grammar and the changed phonemes, the ambiguity of the resultant idea in Han's mind was indeed high.

But he had been right about the course of the sun of Dawn through the heavens; it did go to the very pole, or very close to it. Of course, no one had actually seen the polar summer—only from the edges, where some mining was done. And in the winters the poles were far worse. The farmer said that once, during south-winter, on a trip north, he had actually seen a fall of dry snow, luckily from the inside of a snug cabin. He was terrified of it, and Han did not blame him; those temperatures were nothing to face with bravado and a hairy chest. A space suit would be more appropriate.

There were small freeholds all along the gorge, usually in places where large natural terraces had been formed, and they were all completely independent, free of tax and overlord alike. No flags flew in the gorge, no armies marched. Only scattered farm families, making a precarious living between the dangers of wandering nomads, who infested the lower gorge, the cold of the winter, which was more severe on this side of the mountains, and the unknown of the high plains. On the other side, however, the density of population went up; there was even a city, Leilas, which the farmer regarded as the very nadir of corruption. There was another range west of the large mountains, separated from them by a trough, which was extensively cultivated. The river had cut a low point through the trough as well as the rocks, and the trough actually had two arms, south and north, which rose gradually away from the great river. The lower parts were generally human, and were ruled from Leilas, while the upper parts were mostly ler, and were ruled from, it was reputed, castles perched high up in the farthest reaches of the troughs.

As the description of Dawn went on, Han was disappointed by the news. It was a primitive society, more feudal than anything else. And in addition, the natives had to put up with an impossible climate which kept them constantly at bay, and an incredible geography, which kept them isolated and ignorant. To the farmer's knowledge, there were no oceans or seas—just lakes. Dawn consisted of vast, rearing mountain ranges, which were separated by huge sinks, or high plateaus. Earthquakes were common, in fact, so common that Han could feel very slight tremors almost constantly. The difference was not between earthquake and no-earthquake; it was between a greater intensity or a lesser. He tried to visualize the kind of imbalances in the crust which would produce mountains like these. He couldn't. And besides all that, the specter of the Warriors hung over everything.

Years would pass with no incidents, and the memory of the Warriors would be forgotten. Then they would come again, to sift the people. They never took many, but they always took some. Naturally, they were never seen again. They generally left the ler of the higher troughs alone. He knew them well, and called them by a curious name: firstfolk. Even Liszendir derived a wry amusement from that.

No one had any idea about the size of the planet, or anything in the area of astrophysics. They thought the world was flat. Han did not question him too deeply on this subject, knowing that sometimes questions revealed more about the questioner than answers about the answerer, and he did not want to get involved in any kind of religious dispute. A flat world! Archeoforteans! He thought wryly that the theologians of Dawn would have evolved an interesting cosmology to explain the erratic path, or even surrealistic path, their sun followed through the heavens.

Han and Liszendir, for their part, agreed to stay and help with the harvest, and further, help him dispose of it for the best price in Leilas. Han identified himself as a merchant by trade, and vowed to obtain the best possible price. The farmer, in turn, agreed to transport them downriver in several tendays, depending upon the harvest and the weather.

Liszendir asked him how they returned from Leilas. He told her that they took their pack animals with them, loaded them in Leilas with the things they needed, and walked back, up the gorge. By the time they got back, it would be in the first half of north-winter, but it was not so bad, and gave them time to prepare for the rigors of the half-year darkness of south-winter. From the times he mentioned, Han hazarded a guess, in Common, to Liszendir, that they were somewhere around thirty degrees north in latitude. The information was not particularly important. They had nowhere to go.

"This is not the real world. The real world is Yar, a great place of bright cities, towers, magic, fertile ground and gentle rains. For our sins, we were banished and cast forth to Limbo, which is here, by Hoth the Sun-God, and here we expiate the sins of our ancestors. We do not know today what those sins were; they must have been terrible, however, for such a punishment to come to an entire people. It is said that they cannot be described with words. So, we are here. The dual hells are nearby and convenient. One is located in Uttermost North, the other in Uttermost South. Those of excessive passions are cast into the North, where Hoth visits them with fire. The cold-blooded go to the South, where Hoth visits them with cold unimaginable. The Firstfolk maintain the purity of the Word, and the Warriors dispose of the impure in thought and heretics, chiefly from among the young, who are prone to harbor resentments. Those are judged, and sent to the appropriate destination. The Warriors live in the lower heavens, but they follow the orders of Hoth, who goes to all parts of the rocky world, who sees all and judges that we may be deemed fit to return someday to Yar the Beautiful, Yar the Kind."
—The story of creation, as told to Liszendir Srith-Karen by
Narman Daskin, the farmer of the gorge.

"It is only when one has somewhere to go that it becomes manifestly important to know precisely where one is."
—Cannialin Srith-Moren, woven Deren

THE RAFT, MADE from boles of light, spongy timbers from the slopes of the gorge, made its clumsy way down the great river, piled high with bales of produce, grains, legumes, and tubers of several sorts. Besides them, there were others on the river as well; Han had seen them pass, just as heavily loaded, poled and steered by crews of dour men who spoke little greeting as they passed me shoals below the farmer's house. Mostly, they spoke no greeting at all.

Narman Daskin, the farmer, stood lookout at whichever end happened to be the front at that time. His two daughters, Uzar Rahintira and Pelki Rahintira, worked broad sweeps at the end which happened to be facing rearwards, back upstream. Han and Liszendir wielded poles in the middle. The way was surprisingly smooth, free for the most part of rocks and rapids.

Pelki had explained why. "The south-spring flood-thaw sweeps the lower gorge clean of rocks and gravels; they all flow down with the great waters and collect in a great wad below Leilas, down on the salt flats by the bitter lake." So had spoken the younger daughter, the more personable one. The older one, Uzar, was a heavy-set, brooding girl who was no beauty and who said little, even in the way of routine pleasantries. Pelki was no less homely, but she evidenced considerably more animation, and at times almost approached plainness. Han was not deceived. Neither was a prize.

Liszendir had thought that Pelki's half-hopeful flirting at Han had been interesting and had so informed him, to his general discomfort. As for him and Liszendir, he felt a certain confusion about their relationship, as it seemed to be for the present; their intimacy had been dormant, secondary for a time. She, for her part, was not avoiding him, but on the contrary, had become closer, more confiding, more affectionate, relaxed. The haughty Liszendir he had met at Boomtown had entirely vanished, but the replacement Liszendir was still full of unknowns, perhaps more than before. All this was true, yet it was also true that she had withdrawn into herself in an odd way Han could not quite discern.

From the other side of the raft, she observed, in Common, "If all else fails, at the least you could probably marry Pelki."

Han replied in the same tongue, "Well, I don't want to, not now nor any other time I can imagine. Not that I would care to choose if driven to begging, but she can't be the most exciting woman on Dawn, in looks, and besides that, she's dumb."

Liszendir laughed. "So I thought it would be. Really, Han, I agree also. I was just teasing you." She shifted the subject. "You know they have a strange custom in these parts, for all I know, all over Dawn with the humans here: they do not have family names—just proper names and a patronymic for boys or a matronymic for girls. Boys are regarded as the yield of the father, girls of the mother."

Han stayed on the subject of Pelki. "Why would you wish such a thing of me? If that is all the choice I have I may not want a mate."

"No reason. You may as well have one, for if I stay here very long, I won't be able to have one."

"Well, do without, then," he said, half-irritably.

"Oh, it's not so simple as that," she replied, rather impishly. "Besides the strength of the drive, unless I conceive within a certain time after the onset of fertility, which means even if you and I stay together, I have another problem. If I don't conceive, my reproductive system will shut itself down."

"You mean you will become sexless."

"Yes. Permanently. Just like after-fertility. It is a modification performed upon us by the firstborn, before they destroyed all the means of how to engineer such genetic changes, and the records. Its purpose has been to prevent obvious failures and grotesques from passing bad genes on. Use it or lose it, you know? All it takes is about half a year."

"Well, that shouldn't worry you now. If I understood your standard age correctly at Boomtown, we've got years yet before we have to worry about that. I hope we can either get off this planet, or find you a partner of the ler, before then."

"In normal circumstances that would be so. But here, the short day-cycle has been acting to speed me up, to fit its cycle. You, too. You and I have started sleeping Dawn hours the last few days. It doesn't seem to have any effect on you, but it could very well bring my fertility sooner."

Han looked away, at the dark water. He could not answer her unspoken question.

Now on the great river they slept and poled, poled and slept. There was, according to Narman, need for haste.

"Notice the sun! It is well to the north, now. Darkness incarnate rises out of the south. The days are short; soon will come the cold. The upper waters freeze, the lower ones dry up. Then the river is not passable. It is only now that it is in the whole year."

The whole family agreed that there was more to it than simple failure to reach Leilas. The lower gorge, particularly where it had dug across the mountains, was infested with bandits and vagabonds of dubious origin. These feared the river and all moving water, so as long as the travelers were securely on the river and moving, all would be well. It was if they were to become stranded that they would have cause to worry. It had happened before. The goods were stolen, and the passengers eaten, so tales had it.

Han looked about suspiciously. He could see no evidence of habitation of any kind. The river whispered quietly with chilling power, moving swiftly through a vertical trench cut into solid rock, tormented layer upon layer of deeply metamorphosed basement rock. Distorted and tormented, crushed, folded and fused.

Pelki said, from the back of the raft, "They live high up. Above the cliffs. They lower themselves down on ropes, after the lookouts tell them someone is stranded."

"Well, why don't they bother you on the way back? Isn't that just as dangerous?"

"They are inexplicable people. They disappear after the last boat."

Han asked, "Where do they go?"

"Who knows? Never in memory have they molested a homeward trek. Perhaps they have taboos. Perhaps they are demons who fear the dark."

The raft grated ominously along its bottom, lurching slightly, pausing, then freeing itself. Pelki's eyes rolled in a sudden spasm of fear. She pointed ahead. Sure enough, there was a figure hanging down into the deep vertical part of the gorge in a flimsy contraption of ropes and slings. Han could not tell if it were human or ler, at the distance. Han drew his crossbow, cocked it, and waited as they drifted closer to the figure. As they came within range, he aimed carefully and shot at the figure. The first bolt missed, and the creature began screaming imprecations downwards to the raft, and instructions upwards to comrades out of sight behind the rim. The sling-and-rope contraption moved upwards fractionally. Han cocked and fired again. This time he hit the creature in the back, and he released his grip and fell backwards into the river with a wailing cry of despair. Faintly, from above, invisible, they heard answering calls of woe, hoots of disappointment. The echoes rang eerily down on the hard rocks and smooth river surfaces, bounding and rebounding. They saw them no more. The creature who had fallen had apparently vanished below the surface instantly.

For the rest of the journey, there was no more trouble. Han and Liszendir spent the days, when they were not poling, leaning against a bale, napping, watching scenery. There was not much to see; the gorge cut off all sight of the uplands whatsoever, as it wound through the complex, meandering trench it had cut through the mountains. All they could see were the various textures and colors of rocks, and patches of blue sky above, now flecked with clouds increasingly often. Sometimes it grew darker, independently of the time of day or apparent weather they suspected then they were passing through a particularly deep part. But down at the bottom of the gorge, on the great river the air was humid and mild. When they crossed infrequent patches of sunlight, it felt almost hot. And so the days passed.

Finally they emerged from the deep defile and floated on stiller waters. They still were in a deep canyon, but they inferred from the lightening of the air and the sky that they were on the lake above Leilas. The sky above their heads was no longer oppressed by deep blue shadows, except in morning. They were on the west side of the mountain barrier. The lake was shallow and very muddy, its bottom vague and sticky when found. They poled and rowed westwards, seemingly getting nowhere.

On the fourth day on the lake, with the air very light and noticeably cooler, they sighted an elaborate dock area on the water, slightly to the right of their course. Behind it, bare bluffs rose, capped by the rosy, smoky haze. Han asked Narrhan if that was Leilas.

"No. Leilas is up on the bluffs, out of sight. The fume exudes from their kitchens and shops. What you see below, here, on the water, are only the docks. We will sell everything there, on the water. Porterage costs too much! Let them haul it up the slope! That which you see is smoke from the great city—they cannot move it down on the water because of the floods when the sun comes back from his visit to the hell of the south."

They began to pole towards the floating docks with more energy. Han watched Liszendir as she worked at her pole, setting it from the fore part of the raft, walking with it, leaning into it all the way to the back, and then deftly snatching it back out of the lake-bottom muck. He looked at the daughters, Uzar and Pelki. All three were female, yet there was some quality about Liszendir not shared by the other two. For the moment, it escaped him. Then, suddenly, he had it. The image came into sharp focus. The difference was that Liszendir seemed, somehow, "more finished" than the other two. He blanked the image of the ler girl from his mind, and strained to see the other two girls as he might have seen them in a situation with only humans. Yes. Uzar became just plain, and Pelki became, with some work, almost attractive in a heavy, rawboned way. Capable and competent. That fit very well with talk he had heard. More finished.

As he watched Liszendir, he saw something else as well he had suspected, but had half-feared to let surface. Now she was allowing her hair to grow longer, as the short style was a mark of adolescence. But he remembered how it had been a straight fall, parted in the middle, to the ears, styleless and sexless, just like any other adolescent. But he could not confuse her with a male figure by any stretch of the imagination. It was as if as the cultural differences between the sexes fell away, the innate differences that had been there all along came into full play; as if clothes and hair style keyed to sexes obscured the issue, rather than dramatizing it as he had always thought, as all of the humans he knew thought. People said that if boys and girls wore their hair alike and wore the same clothes, how could you tell them apart? But the boys and girls never seemed to have any trouble; they knew. And now Han knew, too. The quaint culturalisms of the ler now glared with harsh realities humans feared, knowing themselves almost as well as the ler knew themselves, but not quite as ready to admit it, or what they saw, within.

Liszendir now caught her hair up at the neck, with her characteristic nonchalance, with a piece of string borrowed from one of the bales, but it hung down her back with a grace that could not have been attained with the finest silk. She noticed he was watching her, and turned to him, easing off on the pole.

"I have a riddle for you, since you seem so thoughtful today. Are you ready? I want to know how running water of no greater depth than we have seen can cut a gorge across a range of mountains miles high."

Han laughed. "You, a philosopher, ask me? Does not water conquer all by its humility that seeks out the low places, and does not elevate itself?"

"A *mnathman*, indeed! Dardenglir was right about you Han! You must cast off these delusions about riches and become a holy man. We cannot make you ler, but you are ready to learn secrets. Where did you find that?"

He laughed again. "I retire to certain caves in the required season, and by sheer mental effort, deduce the secrets of earth and water, of red and black, of man and woman."

She laughed and corrected him. "*Tlanman* and *srithman*, do you not mean? Male-person and female-person?"

"No. Man and woman. I have to confine my efforts to us *hyunmanon*, the old people, lest I suffer a spasm, as if from eating too much roast *drif*. Ah, me! How I wish we had eaten the rascal before Hath'ingar caught up with us and carted us off to this vegetarian place. No, I will answer, Liszendir. I think the reason for the river cutting through the mountains lies in the floods they mentioned in the summer, when the sun returns from the south. When the sun is at the one pole, at the other pole an icecap develops, which melts all at once. The water has to go somewhere, and if the pole is high ground . . . I think the river is older than the mountains, and kept cutting down as they were raised up, slicing each summer through what had been built up the year before. All their water here comes at once. And as it ebbs, the smaller particles and silt get dropped here in the lake, renewed every year; that is why the lake is so muddy."

Narman had been following this closely, despite the language barrier, which was as hard for him as for Han and Liszendir. But he caught the particulars, and nodded enthusiastically. "Yes. The river scours out the gorge every year, just like that. But the mountains are cut by it for punishment, because they aspired to be sky, therefore they are cut and tormented by water, which multiplies into a terrible force. It is like women."

Han and Liszendir respectfully agreed. They had accepted Narman's orthodoxy without comment.

They were appreciably closer to the docks, now, and were able to ease up on the poling somewhat. Han found himself anticipating the city, however it was. He had not seen one since they had departed Boomtown. He did not count Hobb's Bazaar as a city by any stretch of the imagination. To hear Narman describe Leilas, it must be the veritable navel of the world, a wonder to equal the storied ancient cities of old Earth. Cosmopolitan, fleshpot, center of commerce and culture; he waited for the experience. But Liszendir only looked suspiciously at the haze above the bluffs, and an occasional visible chimney-pot, or tower, and shook her head. She had been skeptical all along about Leilas, and the few remarks she had made were not enthusiastic.

They moored the raft to a floating pier, and immediately were set upon, boarded, hounded and invaded, by as rascally a gang of hagglers and potential cutthroats as Han had ever set eyes on. The selling of the crop commenced immediately, with no introductions or formalities; and no quarter asked—or given. He was hard put even to keep the shirt on his back, and in fact got a substantial offer for Liszendir's shift, if she would be so good as to step behind yon bale and remove it. It ended late at night, and began again the next day, before the east had become decently light. By the end of the second day, everything was sold, a few items stolen, and they had a bit of money to split up between them. If you could call it money; it was currency only in Leilas.

They went up the bluffs to the town, with only the pack animals left, and some clothes. There, before the walls of Leilas, they made their farewells, and they were short ones. Narman was in a hurry, and they had caught sight of some other gorge farmers getting ready to be outfitted for the trip back upriver. The long walk. It was all understandable, since they saw each other once a year. Han and Liszendir took their share, and after watching the group for a moment, entered the city.

In its own terms, Leilas probably was a very great city, with no rivals within traveling distance. And to the locals, it very likely seemed to be the very center of the planet Dawn. They knew of no other city at all. But to Han it was a living text out of the far past, long before space-flight. As they wandered through the narrow, dusty streets, they saw no weapons more advanced than crossbows, and at that inferior to the one he carried, now disassembled. The sewage disposal system was nothing more than a series of noisome ditches and stone channels, some covered with boards which might be rotten or not, as determined by whether they would support weight or not, which ran through the streets in the general direction of the lake. This was fairly intelligent, as the lake got flushed out yearly, but if it ever missed a year, this city on the north shore would change, or move. It would have to, for even in its prosperity, it was a place of incredible density of smells, odors, gusts, and miscellaneous stenches.

No street was straight, nor long, nor did there seem to be any organization to it at all. Houses, inns, shops, villas behind walls, and slums all lay tooth and jowl together. But it did seem to be the center of a flourishing trade, which was natural enough, considering the size of the hinterland it must serve. The river upstream, the broad trough valleys north and south, and some large territory westwards, down on the flats, around the salt pits. But however prosperous it was, it was not the metropolis Han had expected; rather, he guessed that Leilas had a population of perhaps thirty thousand, if that many.

Liszendir's only comment during their first day was, "They have fallen far, here." And she said it with genuine sadness in her voice. They saw a few ler about, on the streets, in shops, but they did not attempt to contact them. Han saw that Liszendir did not want to, and even he could detect some difference, but exactly what it was could not be discerned. He only knew that they were not the same as Liszendir. To her, the difference must be glaring, especially since ler were not, as a rule, strange no matter where they came from. For the first time in her life, she was seeing strangers, citizens of another country, and it disturbed her.

After much looking, inspection, and searches which ended, as often as not, in some blind alley, they finally located an inn, which was surprisingly comfortable inside, in contrast with its outside, which resembled a dungeon, complete with stained and streaked walls, and heavy bars on the windows, "For security from burglars and footpads!" exclaimed the owner. The inn was called the Haze of the West, and was an eccentric, stucco, blocky, rambling structure which seemed to have grown together out of several buildings over the course of many years. Han and Liszendir secured a set of small rooms overlooking a pleasant courtyard, with balcony, for which they paid extra, and, wonder of wonders, not running water but a wood-fired bath, which cost nothing. The rooms were plain, but late in the day, the evening lights and shadows played along the undecorated whitewashed walls with great charm.

Liszendir was most excited about a real bath, so they arranged to have water put in the tank on the roof by the potboy, and a load of firewood brought up. While she busied herself with making the fire up, Han told her to take her time and use all the water, and he would go out to the public baths down the alley. He wanted to look around some, anyway, he said. Then they could go out and try to find something decent to eat.

When he returned a few hours later, he found Liszendir fast asleep on the small bed, a fresh shift on, her face scrubbed and rosy. The only light in the room came from a candle, still burning beside the window. Outside, it was quiet. Leilas went to bed early, however its reputation was. If they went to fleshpots, they did not go late at night. She woke up as he came in, awake instantly.

"Did you enjoy yourself while I was out?"

"You will never know! I have not had a hot bath, a real bath, in years, so it seemed. I went to sleep in the tub. But now I am ready for whatever Dawn can hand out. Bring it on! We have outraged probability on all sides." Then, "So here we are in great Leilas! Leilas, the pearl of Dawn. Now, what?"

She sat up on her elbows, a motion which tensed her collarbones, and cast shadows on her skin in the soft light.

"I went around, trying to get an idea of what we can do here. It isn't much. About all we can hope to do in Leilas is find out more about Dawn, and then we should try to get up to the ler communities in the upper trough. North is as good as any other. Reputedly, higher up, there are ler countries. I don't know what we will find there. Maybe nothing."

"Maybe nothing. I agree, but it is still better than sitting still here in Leilas. The ler I have seen do not look like much, and they may be no better high up. But there is nothing here—this city is tenth-century preatomic, at least."

"Yes. Maybe worse. And it looks old, you know, like it's been this way, just like we see it, for a long time. They aren't going to build a space-ship tomorrow in the next alley."

She shook her head. "I see. Now tell me, Han. What you want to do. Yourself, not us. Really."

He sat on the edge of the bed, and reflected quietly for a long time, looking at the candle. Finally, he said, "I want to try to get back, of course. But if I can't do that, then I suppose live as good a life as I can, here, if nowhere else. I want to return to my own world, my own peo-ple. I want to try to steal our ship back from them; but they are all the way around the planet, and for all we know, by the time we could get there, they could just as well be off somewhere. But I have no other."

"What did you find out about Dawn?"

"Not much. There are geographers and astrologers, which is what passes for erudition and enlightenment. We will have to find out where we are in relation to where the country of the Warriors is, and then see if we can get there from here. And as for the upland ler . . . I don't know. All we can do is go and ask."

"Ah. So then, we should begin tomorrow. Our money is short."

She arose from the bed, walked around it quietly, and stood by the window for a while. Han blew the candle out, and joined her there.

"There is another matter, Liszen . . ." he said, expectantly.

She shrugged her shoulders and let the shift fall to the floor, her eyes shining. "I thought you would never ask again," she said softly. "Tell me, body-love, what is your wish?"

He slipped out of his clothes as well. "That I could, this night, go all over your body, like a man with no teeth or arms or spoon eating a bowl of warm applesauce." It sounded odd in his ears, but he knew by now from her that it was what she would have expected to hear from a lover of her own kind. She smiled at him, and shivered, deliciously. He moved closer to the girl, smelling her hair, filling himself with the scent as if he would never know it again, touching her cool skin. They turned, as one, and lay down on the small bed together, every sense wide open, even conscious of the rough blanket. They did not sleep for a long time, but neither did they bother to go out for supper. Supper could wait. This couldn't.

The next day they slept late, but as soon as they were up and around they set out through the streets of Leilas to see what hard information they could find out about Dawn. If it was anywhere to be had, it would be here.

There were no books, they soon found out, except in the lockers of collectors and certain religious establishments; the printing press hadn't been invented on Dawn, or had been forgotten, much the same thing. Nor were there anything like schools, where you could go and ask a ridiculous question like, what is the geography of this planet? Nor were there maps; the general outlines of the areas around Leilas were known to all, the gorge, the troughs, the mountains, and the flats west of the lake. All areas beyond that would have been marked "unexplored," and left conspicuously blank. So in the end, they were reduced to visiting astrologers and soothsayers, prophets and religious savants, adding together what information they each contributed, and sorting out the suggestions of fact later on, back in the inn.

Han was particularly frustrated with the lack of knowledge about Dawn, evident on the streets of Leilas. Sorting out their information, which Liszendir had memorized as she heard it, he complained in some heat about the general ignorance of the area. Liszendir was unconcerned, which made Han all the more agitated and impatient.

"I want to know, how are these people ever going to do anything without schools, knowledge?"

"Those things don't really matter. People always learn what they have to, what is appropriate to their environment. Han, you grew up in a culture which has schools for general purpose and schools for every conceivable subclassification of data, but they do not as a rule spread knowledge or wisdom—just assemblies of data. As you have them, schools work on your society just like the differentiating fashions in clothes your sexes use, and hair styles as well—they obscure the innate differences, muddy them, make everyone equal, but it is the equality of a facade. People really are different from one another. And schools obscure the only kinds of knowledge worth knowing."

Han remained unconvinced. "Well, how do people learn to do anything unless they get some instruction? And what about your school, the one your braid operates—isn't that a school?"

"I have two examples for you. One, human and ler children learn to speak whatever language is native to their area, without school, at home, with playmates, with other adults in the area. At first their phonemes are unclear, their grammar is primitive, but they learn because they must communicate, and by the time they are adults, they do passing well enough. Sending them to school has only one effect—it makes them dishonest, for at school, they say what the instructor wants them to say, and when they leave, they go on talking the way they always did. Second, recall your own world, Seabright. It is a world of small continents and extensive seas and oceans. Winds blow over the water, and so sailing is still common there, even though you have powered ships for work. What is the difference between those sailing ships and ones which preatomic men sailed upon the salt seas of old Earth ten thousand standard years ago? And what did those sailors know about the physics of gases and liquids, principles of flow, drag, lift, coefficients of friction? Nothing. But they could see a smooth object moves easier than a rough one, and an elongated shape better than a blocky one. So they made boats, and held up sheets to catch the wind."

He retorted, heatedly, "Yes, and they lived with ignorance and superstition for thousands of years as well."

"Every age is superstitious, no more, no less, than any other, your and my age, as well as in the ancient histories of old Earth." She answered back amicably, as if speaking to an errant child. "Han, knowledge is just like a mathematical notation of a number and a part, what do you call them?"

"Decimals? Where you symbolize the fraction by successive repetitions of the number base, after a point which cuts off the whole number?"

"Yes. We have the same thing in our numbers. Very well, let me use your system, ten base. You have a number, yes, which is not divisible by whole numbers evenly—it has a part left over. So you keep after it, you say, 'I've got to know exactly what this quantity is,' and so keep dividing, dividing. But it doesn't end, it just keeps on going, and each new digit is unexpected. You discover, but for every one you derive, you know there is another one waiting for the operation in the next place."

"You mean irrational numbers?"

"Yes. And what do you call things like this? Irrational! Yet they are the very symbols of the universe, the very heart of what rationality it has. So, knowledge is just like that—you can drive as many places as you please, the next one is just as unknown as was the first, and there is no end to it. Do you understand me? There is no such thing as exact knowledge."

She waited a moment to see if he was following her. "And so we do not have what you would call public schools which teach things the child can and should learn on his own. The only people who learn in schools are the dumb. But we do have other things, where you learn a particular discipline, an art. Do you know that? Ler do not have science, we have arts only. We have physicists, chemists, mathematicians, as many as humans, but they practice *arts*, they learn discipline, and they do not play with abstractions. It is things like that which brought the ler into being in the first place.

"In my school, the place of the Karens, we take the child only when it becomes adolescent, sexed. What do we teach? We teach philosophy, knowledge of the body. How do we start? We make them sit down and learn about themselves, about nature. The first year, all they do is look, at waves in the sea, streams, leaves, small animals. We have a saying: 'To learn calligraphy, leave pen and ink at home, for calligraphy does not consist of pen, brush, and ink, but of what is within the calligrapher.' Or you will say, 'I wish to learn how to paint pictures of nude humans,' and ler as well, for all I know. So you gather up all kinds of surfaces upon which you will paint, you arm yourself with brushes, knives, various sorts of paints, you spend years learning about these things, and all this time you have not learned anything about the body, that irrational surface which you will represent, or how you may feel about it. And to treat it well, you will have to love it and be at peace with yourself. So you come to a ler school for painting pictures, and the teacher will say, 'Now, you take all those brushes and things and we will go and have a nice bonfire with them, perhaps cook something over them, because what I will teach you is not of brushes and techniques, but of the subject, for if you do not know it, you will never represent it.' You say, 'Oh, but I want to paint!' He will reply, 'We can get to that later, perhaps.' So I know how to fight, hand-to-hand, I am trained, I am an adept. I did not get this way by learning about tensile strengths of bone, compressibilities of skin and tissue, about weights and forces. I learned by thinking, exercising, making love with my fellow students, dancing, and other things. You look to the side of a star when you wish to see it, yes?"

"Does that help us, here?"

"Yes. We do what we can, with such style as we can muster."

But they discovered there wasn't very much they could do, alone on a strange and primitive world. The locals of Leilas knew very little about conditions elsewhere on the planet—they thought that the world was flat, and that the sun moved, and that earthquakes were caused by the carrier of the world, a primitive reptile called a *khashet*, which occasionally stumbled or itched. The poles were hells for sinners, unknowable and unapproachable, and the middle latitudes scourged by two winters a year. West of Leilas the desert started, and as far as they knew, it was endless. The mountains marched far to the north and south, and the only break in their great ramparts was the gorge, cut by the great river, which led to the "freecountries."

Geography was against them. The country of the Warriors was somewhere around the curve of the planet, probably at least 12,000 miles away, and to get there, they would have to walk, braving the winters, short but hard, and physical conditions which had brought civilization on Dawn to a standstill, to its knees. Who could cross mountains on foot whose *passes* were at the pressure equivalent of 20,000 feet altitude; who could cross high plains such as they had landed on the edge of when they escaped the Warriors; or cross desert sinks where water boiled when the sun was overhead?

Nor could they join trade expeditions, pilgrimages, or the like. Outside local areas, there was no travel on Dawn. It was rumored that there were other settled places, lands, cities. The Warriors, for example, were reputed to live in a very large country. But nobody went there, unless the Warriors came to get him in their ship. So people were stagnant on Dawn, barely holding their own, ever so slowly becoming steadily more crude as the years marched on.

And from what they could determine, Dawn as a planet was in an early phase of the evolution of life; there was no animal life native to the planet more complex than things intermediate between reptiles and amphibians, and the plants, save some things which were obviously imported, were no better. It was a world, young and raw, on which its own mammalian life forms were somewhere three hundred million years in the future. If the primary didn't go nova first.

And the Warriors had Han and Liszendir's ship, and their own. These were the only two spacefaring craft on the whole planet, and in fact were the only long-distance craft of any kind on the whole world. Thousands of leagues lay between them and the ship. They could do little. Before they went to sleep, they slid into each other's arms, and made a slow, exploratory kind of love, again. And then slept, daring to hope for no more than that, for the present.

*   *   *

On the morning, they bought a small pack animal similar to a burro, and loaded it down with food and provisions, on which they spent most of their money. Han suspected that the ancestors of the little animal had arrived with the people. They left the inn, the Haze of the West, with sadness, for if what they had learned had been hard to bear, the peace and rest they had known within its walls had been welcome to them, a quiet time they had enjoyed deeply. The last of the money went for a short sword for Han and a dainty, but effective-looking, knife with a leaf-shaped blade for Liszendir. With all of their things stowed on the pack animal, they departed Leilas through the north gate for the country of the upper trough.

As they left the city and began climbing up the gentle but steady slope, they looked back briefly at the great city, or what passed for one on Dawn. The wall around it was neither high, well fortified, nor continuous, being broken in places by time in two winters a year. They may have needed it once; that was many years ago, judging from the condition of the wall. Behind the wall, the irregular, rambling city spread itself out in the harsh sunlight, and as they got farther away from it, blended into the background of rock, mud, and sparse vegetation like some natural growth of dun-colored moss, or perhaps an odd type of lichen.

They faced to the north and began walking in earnest. On their right, they could see full on the harrowing mountains which rimmed the high plateau to the east; they went up, up, first snow-covered on the lower slopes and peaks, then naked rock, and still higher, the terrible broken summits whose highest points stood glaring over the planet from a height above ninety per cent of Dawn's atmosphere. To the west, their left, there was another range, lower, and from all appearances, mostly volcanic. No vent was erupting at present, although several peaks trailed thin streamers of smoke from their summits. And although the west range was lower, it still was too high to be passable. Once away from the city, they looked out on a bleak, harsh landscape, lit by a piercing sun, that was not a lot better than the view they had seen from the high plains.

In Leilas, Han and Liszendir had been in a relatively warm climate, low down close to the river. During the day it was decently warm, cooling off only at night. But as they gained altitude walking up the north trough, the air cooled noticeably, and began taking on the unmistakable colors of autumn. They were not walking fast enough to keep up with the sun of Dawn on its journey north to the pole. A steady wind began blowing from behind them up the trough, whose end lay over the horizon, out of sight. As each day passed, the sun made smaller circles in the northern sky, and in the south the darkness grew. It became colder.

Human forms of buildings, particular styles of houses and outbuildings, ways of cultivating land, began to give way to ler forms, gradually, then predominantly, then finally completely. The houses were not the ellipsoids of the ler familiar now to both Han and Liszendir alike, but smallish stone houses of two stories, each with what appeared to be a watchtower attached to it. By the time they had reached ler country, the weather had finally turned sour, and rain and cold were common. They met fewer and fewer travelers on the road, which grew more and more narrow. They were both beginning to feel like fools. The few ler who would talk to them were worthless for their purposes—and they seemed even more ignorant and benighted than the humans of Leilas and its outlying areas. Liszendir pronounced them hopeless, fidgeting with frustration. They were not the people she was looking for.

On a night of a wild storm of either very wet snow, or half-congealed rain, they could not be sure which, they reached the top of the trough. In the darkness and wind, they would not have noticed, except for the fact that as they were looking for a place to shelter, Han saw that the sluggish creek they had been partially following no longer flowed south, but northwards. North, there was a hint of greater darkness than there had been before. They had no idea how far they had walked; only many days, perhaps twenty, in the worsening weather. In the dark and storm, they finally managed to discover an abandoned shed, and just as they were moving into it, it started snowing. Inside the shed, they were protected only from the wind, not the cold. They looked outside several times, but it grew no better. Without any comment, they resigned themselves, and curled up together in their blankets, unspeaking and unmoving. They were beaten, most of the food was gone, and there was nothing left to do but start back for Leilas.

In the morning, Han went out to see to their few remaining packs of food. Inside, it had been cold, but as he stepped through the door of the shed, the air bit at his face with a new vigor he had not felt yet on Dawn. It was a portent of what would come with colder weather. He looked about in the dim, north-autumnal light leaking over the mountains. There had been a fair amount of snowfall during the night, and most of it had drifted in the winds; but for the while, it was all they were going to get. The sky was absolutely clear, deep violet-blue, through which an occasional star could still be seen. Eastwards, the mountains reared high above them, casting deep shadows. The south lay in a hazy darkness, and to the west, the other range looked hardly less forbidding, though at the least the west range had snow on its summits. It was unhuman, wild, fierce beauty. He stood in the cold morning air for a moment and looked out over the rocky, desolate scene. They were at the high point of the trough, and there was nothing there, absolutely nothing.

Something far away, on the edge of the west-range, caught his eye; something moving. He looked closer. He couldn't make it out. He looked away from it, then back. Yes, now he could, but just barely. It was a building, the same color as the dark, andesitic rock of the volcanic mountains to the west, now not yet out of the shadow of the higher mountains eastwards. The moving part which had caught his eye seemed to be smoke, a thin wisp of smoke which dissipated quickly. It was too far to tell what it was. But there was smoke! Somebody did live here, high up on the hard crest of the world Dawn.

Han went back into the shed, hurriedly, and woke Liszendir. As he gathered their things together, she went outside to look at it herself, the dark, smoking building. She came back in, shivering. But she agreed. They set out for it immediately.

The distance was greater than they might have guessed, for neither Han nor Liszendir had learned to guess distances accurately, either on Chalcedon or on Dawn, but there was another element—the drifted snow, which had fallen the night before. It slowed their pace from a walk to a crawl, and for hours they seemingly made no progress at all. But they did close some of the distance, and as they drew closer, they could see the smoke more definitely, and they could also see the shape of the building better. They were not particularly encouraged by what they saw: it was apparently a castle or fortress, of grim black rock. The sun finally cleared the mountains and shone on it from the northeast, illuminating it with a stab of harsh light. They could see it clearly, although it was still miles away: a castle, with pennants or flags visible above the higher parts. Whatever it represented, someone lived there, and they were home.

It took the greater part of the short day for them to reach it through the snowdrifts, but at twilight, with the light fading swiftly, they stood before its gates. The gates were closed. Nor did it appear to either of them that they had been opened for a long time. Another dead end. Small, stunted trees grew in patches of windblown dirt which had collected in the lintels. In exasperation, Han walked up to the gates and pounded on them with the hilt of his sword. Liszendir watched for a moment, then raised her voice, calling out loudly. They expected no answer; to pound on the door and shout was better than nothing. But in a few moments, lights and faces appeared at the top of the walls. The light failed, and all that was left of the daylight was a hesitant, trembling pearly color in the northwest. In a few moments they were directed around to the other side, and there, through a small door in the walls, which would have been near-invisible even in full daylight, they were let in, pack animal and all, and shown to a room for the night.

Inside, it was very much as Han had expected it to be; he had been a reader of medieval romances as a young child. A nobleman's castle was exactly what it was, but one without the splendor of the ones in ancient tales. It was run-down and dirty, and fading hangings of no distinction, past or present, many frayed and tattered, covered the bleak stone of the inner walls. Shabby watchmen and servants passed on errands of seeming urgency, as shoddily decorated as the walls. It was a cheerless, ugly place, cold and damp.

"I can't believe ler would live up here to begin with, but if they were crazy enough to, they surely would not live in a pile like this." Han observed to Liszendir, as they washed in the cold room one of the servants, a human, had set aside for them.

"It is certainly beyond me, but after talking to some of those we met along the way up here, I should not be too surprised at anything we'd see. Brr!" She shivered, goose-pimples popping out all over her skin, which Han was scrubbing at that moment vigorously. Then she continued, "But why a fortress? People build fortresses when they expect attack, but from whom? This would not even be worthy of the notice of the Warriors, either for its strength, or how many could hide in it, for it is too small." Han could not answer her question.

They were even colder after washing. Han searched the small room, which was filled with shelves and closets along the walls, until he found some rough blankets. Then they lay down together on the small, hard bed, which creaked ominously as they both put their weight on it, and curled closely around each other, primarily for warmth. Soon, the fatigue of the day and the warmth of their bodies began acting on them, and they drifted off, asleep without realizing it.

They were woken sometime later, they did not know how long, by a majordomo with a leer, who announced through the opened door that the lord of Aving Hold would be pleased to have their company at dinner. He spoke with a cynical air which chilled Han to the bone.

Without speaking, they got up, dressed, and began following the major-domo, who had respectfully waited outside. He conducted them through a bewildering array of portals, drafty hallways, junctions, nodes, nexi. Sometimes they passed rooms and halls where there were lights, voices, the sense of the presence of many people. Other times they seemed to go through parts of the castle which had been abandoned; doors stood ajar on darkened rooms whose only inhabitants were piles of trash, stacks of wooden fagots, dust, as glimpsed in the quick light of a sputtering oil lantern borne by the servant. It was to Han an eerie, fey, dangerous place, perhaps the most perilous they had entered yet on their journey. If Liszendir felt any of the same apprehensions, she gave no sign, spoke no word; she was totally absorbed in gathering sensory impressions of the castle. After what seemed to be an interminable walk, they finally arrived at a grand hall, or what would pass for one in this hulk. It was decorated and lighted in a semblance of gaiety, of celebration, but Han mentioned to Liszendir that it was generally as shabby as the rest of the castle, and that he hoped at least the food might be a little better. She smiled weakly back at him and nodded.

Once inside, they were seated before ornate place settings at a large octagonal table. There was a fire in the fireplace to one side, candles and lamps all around, and to the other side, what appeared to be a platform, as if for musicians, or entertainers, a stage. Some of the servants were busy there at this very moment, arranging chairs, moving other articles, cleaning and dusting, all with great haste and urgency. They were soon interrupted, to their general annoyance, by the arrival of a troupe of musicians, who carried instruments the likes of which were completely foreign to Han. The instruments were all of the stringed-instrument family, handmade in fine style, but their bows were complex mechanical devices, which used battery power, apparently, to drive belts of bowstrings or little pluckers. The musicians settled themselves into an order of seating known to them, activated their electric bows, and commenced playing, without introduction or hesitation. There was no conductor. They all seemed to play together without effort. The motors concealed in the handles of the bows made a very fine whirring noise, which, oddly enough, seemed to fit into the music very well, particularly when certain of them varied its speed for a particular passage.

Something jarred Han's perceptions about the musicians. They all seemed to be humans, well enough, he could see that from the configuration of the hands, if by nothing else, yet they themselves bore a striking resemblance to one another, almost as if they were members of a family. He watched them closely. No. Not a family, something else. He had seen shows put on by families of entertainers before. Family members had features which differed a certain amount, but their expressions were similar. These resembled one another rather more closely, but the effect of likeness was distorted, broken up, by a great variance in expressions and mannerisms among the individual members. This latter impression was very strong, so that they did not appear to be a family group at all.

But however much the performers looked like one another, their instruments varied greatly, almost impossibly, in an astonishing array of shapes and materials, woods and metals and hides and other unrecognizable materials, and they produced an even more astonishing variety of sounds, seemingly every possible vibration, harmony, squeak, overtone, resonance, microtone, slide, drone and gasp. There were no drums; the rhythm seemed to be implied, rather than directly stated. Liszendir listened intently to the music, and after a moment, pronounced it to be of ler origin in musical structure, but highly mannered and in her opinion, far gone into artistic decadence.

Han laughed to himself and said to her, "You have been many things to me since Boomtown, but I hardly suspected you were an art critic, too."

She looked at him incredulously for a moment, then laughed herself. "Of course you wouldn't know. But I am, indeed. You see, for us it is the reverse of your human way of doing things. We have a word in Singlespeech which means a person who does nothing but make art of one medium or another. This word is also a slang or popular word for what you would probably call a freeloader, if my Common is correct. We regard art as the province of all, and the profession of none. And as for myself, a special curriculum of art was included in my training as an integral part. Performance and criticism, both. I am trained in many media, senses and limbs. You know that there is an art for each sense. So then: I know symbols and visual methodology, music, poetry, as well as dance, mime, and other forms which have no parallel with humans. My degree of accomplishment varies somewhat, for we all are not equally competent in all ways of expressing ourselves, which is a truism with which you are doubtless familiar. I do three things: ler poetry, in which

I am known in a minor way on Kenten; in painting, which I do well enough, but am not known, and do not wish to be, being one of the leaf-painters . . ."

"Do you mean painting on leaves?"

"No. Pictures of leaves and branches. It is an ancient discipline of concentration and form. And the other is music. I play an instrument which makes sound with a reed and you control the pitch with fingerholes and pads. You would say woodwind, although the *tsonh* has no exact parallel to anything you would know. It is double-reed, like the bassoon, only higher in pitch, like a female voice, alto. Yes. An alto bassoon. It is about so big . . ." And she made a gesture with her hands. "I have been in some public concerts, although none of them have brought me fame as the world's greatest *tsonh*-player. Still, I was neither booed nor hissed. Sometimes I play alone, sometimes with backgrounds, and with groups which play all together and then apart."

Han sat back in his chair, dumbfounded. He tried to imagine Liszendir playing her instrument, the soft, full mouth, which kissed so well, intent, drawn, tightly gripping a double reed, concentration on her face. He gave up. It could not be visualized.

She watched his face, carefully reading expressions. An impish, fey look flashed across her face. "Aha! You think I work hard at it, that I make wrinkles in my face. Not so. I like to play very much, it is very relaxing, transporting, I do not live in this world then. It feels *good*, it is not work. But I have to admit to you that however much I like it, the *tsonh*, I do not play it so well as I write poetry, or so is the opinion of those on Kenten who have seen me do both. So, for art, I shall be a poet, I suppose. But I do know music, too. That is why I say what I do about these."

She would have said more, and Han would have let her. It was completely incongruous, that they should have had the escapes and adventures they had had, and be sitting in the hall of some unknown character, with the future, even as close as the next minute, being completely blank, blurred, unknown, and be calmly discussing music; amazing. But that added spice to it. But they were interrupted, not by an addition of something, but by a deletion. The music had stopped. The silence was dead and empty after the rich texture of sound that had filled the background of their perceptions. It was broken now only by the whirring of a few electric bows, as apparently some of the musicians had forgotten to deactivate them when they stopped playing. The others glared at the clumsy offenders, obviously novices, and the tardy musicians silenced their bows. The whisper of hair on little pulley wheels stopped.

The cynical majordomo they had met before marched into the room with an odd attitude which suggested equal measures of insubordination and abasement, coming to a halt at the head of the table, where he announced in a stentorian, grating voice. "The Lord of Aving Hold and his honored guests!" Then he departed. Han stood up, as did Liszendir.

Two figures emerged from behind a curtain and strolled up to the table, smiling and very obviously pleased with themselves. They were both ler, where the servants had all been human, and Han and Liszendir knew them both. The short, bald one was Hath'ingar. The taller one was the very same elder ler who had told Han in Boomtown that his name was "alphabet." He wore a black overrobe trimmed with silver, and underneath a simple shirt laced up at the neck, tightly. But when they spoke, it was Hath'ingar who spoke first, while the other waited, respectfully. He was, whatever he was here, as "Lord of Aving Hold," subordinate to Hath'ingar, completely. It was a very bad development, and all they could do for the present was to look at one another in astonishment, just as they had been doing since they recognized the identity of their hosts.

8

"The direction of the aim of evolution is toward the production, or creation, of autonomous creatures who will be able to alter their structure to fit the environment, and pass that structure on, by conscious choice: Homometamorphosis. 'People,' as we define them, human and ler, are as yet intermediary in this matter of relationship with the environment. We are not even wise enough to visualize how such a creature might make such a decision, or what it would seem like in our evaluation of decisions."
—Al Tvanskorosi Ktav, *The Doomsday Book*, Pendermnav Tlanh

"WELL MET, WELL met again, and the third time pays for all!" Hath'ingar exclaimed with great cordiality. "Be seated, eat, indulge and enjoy yourselves! Aving's cooks are the best on this side of Dawn, or so travelers and other rogues tell me. Well? Go on, fall to it! There is no trap and no trick." He sat himself down and began to eat, with great gusto and an air of appreciation and satisfaction. The tall one, Aving, signaled to the musicians to play, and they began, immediately commencing a relaxed air.

Han and Liszendir sat down, stupefied. Han looked at the ler girl. She sat still, as if paralyzed, staring at the pair across the table. He leaned toward her and said, "Eat, Liszen. We have endured enough of that clabber he calls food concentrate on the ship, and because of him we have both starved, more than once. So take it." She looked down at her plate as if it were some strange implement about which she knew nothing, could know nothing. Then she blinked, and began to eat.

"Excellent, excellent advice. After all, why face the future hungry, whatever it may become? We all need well-padded bellies against the cold and circumstances, and besides, we have much to say to one another, and what better time than over a friendly meal?" Hath'ingar was completely at ease, the very image of a perfect, jovial host.

Liszendir looked up, sharply, eyes flashing. "I cannot imagine what we could ever have to say to each other."

"No?" His amazement seemed sincere, a genuine expression of puzzlement. "Ah, but there is much indeed. Indeed and indeed! But I have been remiss in my duties as host. Let me introduce my friend here. Aving. And my real name, which you may use, no titles, please, is Hatha." Han caught a flicker of motion out of the corner of his eye, from Liszendir, at the mention of the stranger's real name, Aving. Something about a name, about words, about Singlespeech, which was the universal language of Dawn, which was phonetically completely regular, even as used by the Warriors or the humans on Dawn. Aving! Of course! No word or name in Singlespeech ended in two consonants, even "ng." It was a trait they had noticed in the speech of the family they had known in the gorge, and in the people of Leilas. Now he had it, and he could see Liszendir had it, too. But what was the reason? In a language which allowed no exceptions, the one exception they had seen flared like a beacon, but its brightness obscured the reason behind it. But Hatha-Hath'ingar was continuing. He had not noticed. ". . . Aving is here to keep an eye on things in this district, this area around and about Leilas. The castle deters the locals from prying into affairs which are beyond their scope, and which will not only remain so, but withdraw to increasing distances. When you arrived, here of all places, Aving remembered, and so notified me. I came from the home countries of the Warriors, flying your ship, if you please, and may I say that it is as fine and responsive as a passionate adolescent girl. Why you would come here is beyond me, but now that you are here . . ."

Han tried to betray no confidences at the remark about adolescent girls, but some movement, some grimace, gave him away. Of course. The remark had been designed to do just that.

"Ah, yes. So I see. Yes, I am aware of the interesting liaison you two have formed along the way, have been for some time. How do I know? By reading body language. Han, yours shouts to one who is an adept in such reading, but I hardly need to turn to shouts, when even Liszendir, with her training, which appears to be extensive, cannot silence her own. And it tells me far more, and in greater detail, even though it is muted." Han turned to look at her. He knew the gestures, the ways people acted to one another, but he was no reader of the language of gesture, except in a very primitive way. And what did Liszendir really feel?

She answered Hatha, calmly, coldly, "So much I admit, which is my problem alone, and which I shall solve under the law in the proper season for such things."

"Poof and pah. We are not concerned in the least degree with the strictures of the fours. We have overthrown such bucolic botchery, and have substituted in its place a truly noble concept—one which recognizes the true evolutionary status and duties of our people. So, Liszendir, do you wish toys for the body? Then take them. It is your right. And when you are finished, then cast them out in the trash, or if you feel charitable, give them to the poor in used condition. I care not. I am elder phase, and do not envy or resent your simple gratifications, when I have a greater one, the itch for power."

Han interrupted, "We can discuss toys another time, but you live under a misconception if you still believe that nonsense about supermen. Hatha, it has long been proved that the ler are not *hyperanthropoi*, but *alloanthropoi*, not supermen but other-men."

"So we shall see in time, shall we not."

Liszendir, always to the point, asked, "So what are your plans for us, now that you have us again?"

"A good question—a good answer. First: you both are now beyond punishment, and I have absolutely none in mind. For you, Liszendir, an honored place with the horde. And for you, Han, also honor. You will teach us about your drive system. As you now know, we do have problems with our drive, with the great ship, now called *Hammerhand*. It is old, but it has also been rebuilt, in a hurry, and there are other technical problems as well. I know you are not a technician, but you know enough to be of great use. Both of you have shown extraordinary skill in escaping me twice, and we can certainly use the mental workings behind such exploits. Also observe: you have survived to walk to Aving's castle, which is a feat no native could imagine, and one no Warrior, unfortunately, would attempt. And not only survived, but prospered, as you wished. Ah, yes, we need that greatly, more than little revenges."

Aving added, "It will not be all work, of course—there is conpensation, according to the degree of service you are able to perform. Both of you will have choice of mates as well. For you, girl, the meaning must be clear—you will be fertile soon. There are Warriors in plenty, as many as you want. And for you, Han, you do not have the faintest idea of what we have to buy your cooperation. None whatsoever. But I will hint. You see, we are engaged in a great program for humankind, one which you would never have been able to do for yourself. We are domesticating humans, cultivating them for their potentialities as the farmer grows and selects his varieties of grains. For all the long generational times, humans are as plastic as wax, as changeable as weather. Some will be livestock, others for creatures of burden, others for technicians, still others for amusing pets, just for the exercise in control of shape and color. I know humans keep pets, but ler never have. So we remedy still another lack. And like the small carnivores humans are so fond of, we shall also take our pets with us to hitherto unknown heights of luxury, and shape them into forms, sizes and colors never imagined by them, just like humans have done with their animals and pets."

Han asked, "Is this a new idea, or is it an old one?"

Hatha answered, "It is as old as time, and actually can be traced back to human beginnings."

Liszendir commented, "I am surprised you go on this path, so easily. You violate many wise principles, many things which are not opinions, but insights into reality. I am well grounded in these. People, and I include ler in that term, are low in efficiency as loadbearers, and as food they are hopelessly inefficient. Because a creature is high in evolutionary position does not mean it falls in a usable position in the chain of ecology. We have found many planets, and on every one where there was indigenous mammalian life, in its seas there were whales. Whales do not eat other whales—they live on the simplest foods available. Whalebone whales, the majority, live on beds of floating plankton, the simplest sea life. We take this lesson of success for our own."

"It is not a course I, Hatha, chose, but one chosen by the firstborn, many years ago. Besides, the lesson is meaningless for us: there are no seas on Dawn, and certainly no whales."

"So the person of the city, lacking words in his language for natural forms of terrain, imagines that such things do not exist, and that he can imagine glaciers in the equatorial deserts, or put horns on a tiger. Are you of the blood of Sanjirmil?"

"We are indeed descended of the line of the great foremother. The humans we took later. We intercepted, by accident, a colonial ship. Some we began domesticating immediately, others were strewn over the face of Dawn, to grow wild. They could endure greater extremes than we could. This was long ago, and is counted matter of legend. Myth has it, it was done in the time of Sanjirmil, although there are those among us who reason that it was several generations later, on the basis of old tales. What difference does it make?"

"Only that these people survive in an environment beyond you."

Han asked, "What becomes of us if we refuse your offer?"

"I will personally give you a sack of grain and escort you to the door, from which you may fare as you will. Yes, both of you—the girl alike. I wish to woo you, not dispose of you. Disposal is easy, and an easy thing is a cheap thing. Is it not so, trader? Who will work for a cup of sand, and who will buy it with hard-earned coin? So refuse and go your way: I can afford to be generous. But consider—you cannot leave Dawn, for I have the only two spaceships within many a year of space. You cannot stir the locals up, human or ler of these parts. They do not care. They will kill you for heretics if you persist with your wild tales. Survival here is enough: and without our assistance, they would soon be back to grubbing roots on the plains and living in caves. And for yourselves; you know very well what is going to happen to Liszendir. Now she will cohabit with you, you will be lovers, you will do all the things to each other that such do. But once her fertility commences, she will either leave you, or come to hate you. It is a cruel time. So you will spend your lives for nothing. Do so. I will, as I said, show you to the door with a sack of grain. Walk back to Leilas and squat in the streets and void like the beasts."

He paused, to let it sink in, and went on further. "And as for the ship which was yours . . . in time we will puzzle it out. We have other resources, and some fine domesticated minds we can direct to it. We are not in a hurry."

"At least you do no discredit to the firstborn by annulling that principle." Liszendir spoke with some heat.

Han felt a chill of despair and disgust pass over him. Hatha had drawn a cruelly accurate picture, one which was not attractive in any aspect of it. They had a choice, but it was no choice at all.

Liszendir said, "All this sounds very well, of course; very well thought out. Crude, but possibly workable. But I have many questions to ask."

"And answers you shall have!"

Han could not mistake the gloating in Hatha's voice. That he expected. But Liszendir, fishing for something with this monster? There was no mistake, he had heard a distinct element of curiosity in her voice, of interest. Could she actually be interested in working for him? He looked over to her, watching her face intently, carefully. He could not read her face. Han felt another chill, a sinking sensation, a vertigo. What of her loyalties? Han felt all of the certainties he had known in the past, their past, turn into mud, hot wax, to slump and run, permutate into new shapes, shapes of disturbing outline. He looked at her again. The face he knew well now was no longer lovely, child-plain, charming, promising adventure. It was blank, vacant, the face of a statue, despite the movement that was in it; her thoughts were elsewhere. He saw no longer the lover, but an alien female of completely incomprehensible motivations, and possibilities.

There was a lull in the conversation, during which Han kept glancing at Liszendir, trying to read some intent, or pattern, in her face. There was none visible to him. The face was stony, distant, abstract, where before, even when it had been disagreeable, it had been involved, concerned. She blankly watched the musicians, the guards, Aving and Hatha, the table setting. Aving and Hatha were now in the process of having a polite but intricate argument. Aving might very well be the subordinate, but he clearly considered himself knowledgeable in some area over and beyond any knowledge Hatha might have. Han could not follow it: they were using an arcane technical language, more involuted than the hairsplitting of theologians, and even if he had known the subject, the language alone would have been enough to bog him down. Liszendir appeared not to be interested.

The argument concluded, or so it seemed. The results seemed as inconclusive as the subject had been incomprehensible. Aving signaled to the musicians. Some, according to no order Han could discern, stopped playing, deactivated their instruments, and departed, as the others continued playing, without pause or hesitation. From a side hall behind Aving, others appeared, bearing even stranger musical artifacts. These new instruments were powered, as had been the first ones, but these had small compressors driving air into a bladder, whose pressure was valved out through tubes of various configurations, some controlling pitch through finger-holes, others by pads and levers, others by slides and still others by valves. Some appeared to utilize bizarre combinations of all four controls. The new arrivals, who had the same general appearance as the first group, family yet not-family, settled in their places and began playing their ornate, overdecorated instruments, entering the stream of sound effortlessly. Han listened to it for a minute, but gave it up—it gave him a headache to try to sense order in the alien music, although he could, by straining, catch evanescent hints suggestions, outlines which faded as swiftly in his perceptions as they had come. He stopped trying; its seeming simplicity concealed an underlying order which stupefied the mind.

Aving noticed that he was trying to listen to it. He said, conversationally, "I see you appreciate the music. This type they are playing now is very special—it has been patterned so that it avoids the persistence of memory of melody, which is a special feature of the human-type brain. Oddly enough, the musicians cannot learn it as you might learn some tune—they have to memorize the parts and play by rote, which detracts from the flavor of the performance, don't you think?"

Han politely agreed. Hatha took notice of them again. When he spoke, it was with an air of great confidence.

"I did not mean to imply earlier that you two had an unlimited sphere of decision and freedom of action. Ah, to choose, to steer one's own course: that is a privilege given to few, the high and the mighty. As we proceed down through the lower strata of society, naturally we find that such moments of choice become fewer and fewer. Now you, Han, have no class at the moment and hence no span of choice at all, as an integral part of your person. But I have much choice-span, and will, as we say, lend you a bit of mine, temporarily, for this issue. So: join the horde or go to Leilas, or at any rate, outwards out the out-gate, as we say. Binary, the very system you humans have tied yourself up in such knots over. The choice does not extend beyond that point of time, although in theory, you will doubtless accrue some choice of your own in either case, more perhaps in Leilas. Liszendir inherently has a bit more, because she is of the people and has reproductive potential; but in essence it is so little more than yours that the distinction is academic. However, I wish to make the distinction that hers is partially an inherent part of her potential class, even though at this time, it is of necessity rather low."

So they attached importance to the degree of choice one had, rather than material things, or money, as an indicator, or was it result, of class. Perhaps that had been the substance of that argument they had been having—Hatha's speech suggested quasi-religious overtones as he had been outlining the matter. Han said to Hatha, after this reflection, "I see what you mean, and cannot question your framework, because I do not entirely understand it. Yet, such as I see of this thing about choice, I do not agree entirely, because studies have shown that in human society the head of the organization most often has the least freedom, that freedom decreases as one moves upwards. But we see the ultimate in freedom as absence of responsibility, the vagabond who has only the primal concerns of his body to worry about—sleep, food, warmth. Apparently, you see ultimate freedom residing in the top, in something like an autocrat."

"An interesting point you bring up. I had not thought you quite so perceptive. And I should like to pursue this, as well as any other insights you may have. Yet, regretfully, I must use persuasion here, and remind you that you are embedded in my system, like it or not, be it intrinsically right or wrong. As matters stand, if I averred that the sky was made of stone, and had the power to treat with it as if it were so, you would be compelled by reason to agree, at least provisionally, would you not? So then! Make your choice! Choose carefully. You will have no further opportunity such as this."

Han looked away from Hatha, considering. As he did, he noticed something very peculiar: Aving, who had been ignoring them, was listening to the music with rapt attention, as if he were following it, note for note, melodic line for line. Han looked at the musicians. They were concentrating, deep in thought as they played. They could not play it by ear, but Aving could, apparently, follow it. He put his attention back to the matter at hand—go with Hatha or back to Leilas. He looked at each path carefully. Leilas was tempting because it was away from the horde, the Warriors. And it was free, or at least so it seemed. But the freedom was meaningless. He would stay in Leilas forever. The other was repugnant, but in it was the hope that he could somehow get close to the ship, the *Pallenber*, once again. And to the little deadly gun which hopefully was still located in the locker at the back of the control room. And if he could learn how to activate it. . . .

"I have decided, Hatha. I will go with you, although for what it is worth, I am not overjoyed at it."

Liszendir said, tonelessly, "And myself as well." It was short, decisive, with no hints of feelings, hopes, plans.

The music played on. The new instruments produced sounds of great complexity and perhaps even charm, full of harmonics, overtones, resonances. They seemed to be more like woodwinds than anything else with which Han was familiar, which might go far to explain why Liszendir seemed so interested in the music. But there were disturbing suggestions of other kinds of instruments as well, and many things unknown to Han.

Liszendir asked, "I'm interested in one thing: why did you first try to capture us on Chalcedon? I mean, you yourself. Why not just send a crew of subordinates?"

"For one, there was no one else there. A spy needs to operate effectively, a great deal of choice, so of necessity he must be high in class. For what we were doing on Chalcedon, and why, the class level required was approximately that of myself. I was there to observe, and if possible, guide the reaction, if any, into proper courses. Efrem, you know? He did not come. We caught him lurking off-planet, the dirty little profiteer, waiting until we were done with the place. He planned to do some ravaging on his own. So we took him on a little tour, gave him a bag of money, and sent him on his way, to spread tales back in your Union area."

Han exclaimed, "So you had Efrem murdered, so he couldn't tell the truth!"

Hatha answered, thoughtfully, "No, in fact I had nothing to do with that. You surprised me with the news, if it was true."

"It was true enough. I saw the body, and there was . . ." Han was interrupted by a powerful kick under the table, of which above its surface there had been no indication. It was from Liszendir. He stopped. He had intended to say that Aving had been on Seabright, at the time, but she did not want him to say it. Aving noticed nothing. He was caught up entirely in the flow of the music.

Hatha noticed the pause, but apparently gave no thought to it. He continued, "So I was there, waiting for the reaction. You two took me by surprise, but the size of your expedition convinced me that we were either dealing with timidity, or subtlety so vast that it could not be distinguished from the former. A bully attacks two cowards; one cringes, and says, 'I am a coward!' The other cringes just the same, but he says, 'I am only waiting for time to strike.' But both cringe, you know? So subtlety dissolves into just another tawdry excuse. I thought first to catch you because I assumed high class, by a system of reckoning similar to mine. You were alone, you had choice, thus you were important, key people. Later events convinced me of my error. I saw that you two were most expendable, low pieces of no value at all, except as sensors for a greater, more cautious organism, whose real strength I had no idea of, even after I had seen you. I do not know, even now, and will have to make some more exploratory moves. Do not be so swift to take offense, for that was not my final evaluation. So I then thought, 'Capable, resourceful, but cheaply spent, withal.' Not so. In resource and adaptability alone, you both are more than a match for any of my line Warriors—were they of like disposition and patterns of thought, we could have had the Union long ago. So now, after many corrections of course, I feel I am arriving at last closer to the course that is true, the one which will lead me to the answers I want."

She answered back. "There are indeed answers which we ourselves do not know. But since we join you, rest assured there are some areas we are only too anxious to communicate—when we find the answers, ourselves. Now. What do you do in place of weaving, the four-by-four way? That has bothered me since I have been on this terrible planet."

"You are wise, Liszendir, but not so wise that convention blocks the view of the horizon for you just as it does for others. But that is an interesting question, which I shall answer. We have several systems. When we first came here, there was great dissatisfaction with weaving in fours. It was held to be reactionary, antiprogressive, stultifying. Many held the four-by-four weaving responsible for the lack of enthusiasm of the old majority for the dreams of Sanjirmil. They refused adventure. So we applied ourselves to the problem, and devised a most interesting system. But first we went back to the old way and married, human-style."

"You should have known that that would produce subracial traits shortly."

"So it did, and rather more quickly than we had anticipated, a curious fact, a difference in rate which we have not yet explained. You can turn your efforts to that one, in addition to other things I will have you do. But soon a dominant tribe established itself, and established the new order. Now, we regarded couples as low-class, a human thing, and the weaving of fours as wrong. So we made up the triad system, which has parts of both in it, and which, being more complex, fits our view of ourselves."

Han interjected, "May I not appear so argumentative, but my people think that higher-order forms do not necessarily exhibit more complex features in all things."

Liszendir said quickly, before Hatha could answer, "I don't understand. Triads?"

"Thus. On Dawn, all society is divided into classes. The several types of humans, wild and otherwise, occupy the lower order. For the ler, there is a further division. The lower ler who are not Warriors continue to arrange their families in human fashion. The upper classes, in adolescent years, arrange themselves into threes, more or less randomly, although we ensure that all types of triads have equal numbers according to whom they will mate with. We call the threesomes oversexes."

"Oversexes?"

"There are three persons in each triad-oversex. They may not have sex with each other. Only with an oversex group of opposite gender. With three individuals, and two base sexes, there are eight possible arrangements of order, which divide into four types—three of one, three of the other, or two which are two-thirds male or female. Of course, the pure triads form the highest classes."

"I see. *Khmadh!*" The word Liszendir used appeared to be an obscenity, but if it was, it had no effect on either Hatha or Aving. It was equally meaningless to Han, who had no idea what it referred to. He had never heard it before. But he could see one effect of the triads right away: it would reintroduce and keep reinforced sex-specific behavior. He could also make a reasonable guess that the predominantly female oversexes would be the ones which would raise the children. Probably in isolation from the adults, in a subculture world of their own. But it made a sort of sense: a punished child grows up into a punisher, and one who is pushed into seeing his own age group as a special category of people will be a separator as an adult. With the main population of ler, of which Liszendir was a part, they obliterated cultural differences between the sexes to bring each sex up to its full contribution; they would apply similar processes to the difference between child and adult, with the seemingly contradictory result that the child would be more child, the adult more truly adult, than if imposed differences, with commercial origins, were grafted on them. But the Warriors had carried the other extreme further than anyone else. They probably would show a corresponding degree of aberrations. Han did not reason this out in linear fashion; it came to him all at once, as he thought of it, "sideways." He felt proud of it—he had learned more than just language, or even the expressions of love, from Liszendir.

Hatha added, "Such oversexes, once formed, last until the members die. For example, I now stand alone because the other two members of my triad have been killed in battles."

"Let me guess," she said. "Your triad was all male."

"Indeed."

"It figures." She looked at Aving. "And him?"

Aving replied, "Of the highest of the lower ler. But have no fears—our order is flexible. My offspring have joined the Warriors as good triadists."

"Please tell me no more. I must digest this new order, to see what sort of place I might have in it."

Hatha said, "Good enough. You will see more on the morrow."

Han felt impatient, anxious to get going. "Why tomorrow? Why not now?"

"Nothing mysterious. It simply is late and I have been flying all day. I will need to be alert, with both of you aboard tomorrow. So, then. Liszendir's choice: do you desire to be apart this night, or together?"

"Together." Again Han thought; the old decisiveness. No hesitation, no second thoughts.

"So be it, then," said Aving, and made a gesture to the musicians, who stopped abruptly, in midstatement, as it were. The majordomo came forward, from an alcove to the rear of the hall, waited respectfully. Aving and Hatha arose and departed immediately. The servant motioned to Han and Liszendir. Without words, they followed him back through the winding, confused halls, back to the room where they had rested before. The only change was a welcome one; the room was warm and comfortable, where before it had been cold. The door closed behind them, clicked shut, snapped locked with a heavy, definitive sound. They were locked in.

Han realized as he became acclimated to the warm room that he was tired. He began undressing as Liszendir was turning out the lights, small lamps that used some aromatic oil. With darkness in the room, they could see a high, tiny window they had not noticed before; through it, dim, frosty starlight came into the room. His eyes recovered before hers, but not before he heard a rustling sound, and then felt the warm, smooth body beside him on the small bed.

He half-turned away from her, and asked, "Can you really see anything we can do? Or do you hope to join these creatures? I can't bring myself to call them people."

She did not answer immediately, but to his surprise, curled around him, over his body, sensuously, erotically, with a sinuous motion he knew well now. Only this time there was something extra in it, an extra component. It definitely had an effect, and it was more unbearable, feeling her so close, smelling the scent of her hair. She brushed her face close to Han's ear, began murmuring something in a soft, lascivious voice he could hardly make out; who ever listened to those exact words, anyway. But then he did listen.

"Listen to me closely. We can talk no other way now, and I must be sure you know what I do, now. So listen. I am sure, by instinct, that we will be watched as long as we are together." It was clashing, discord; the tone of the words, their rhythm, volume, all carried the timeless messages of lovers since the beginning of time. But the words themselves, they came across to him like spears of ice out of a warm, wet fog. They glittered like diamonds. He couldn't tell if this effect was subjective, imagined, or an intended one. But it confused and chilled him. The soft voice with the hard words continued, ignoring his vague motions of escape.

"Do not suspect me now of race loyalty! I owe you more, body-love, than to any of these apes, despite any likeness which may be in reality or illusion between our hands. A hand is only as good as what it holds, and the use to which it is put, two thumbs or one. Or none, if there are such. But there is no other way—we must go with him! You acted perfectly, there. In Leilas there is only futility, filth and superstition. I will tell you about us, first. So you will understand all that I do. Completely. Consider that in Common your people still have only two words to cover what happened to us—love and sex. And the word 'love' only rhymes with two or three other words, neither of which can be a noun. In Singlespeech, we have almost four hundred words to cover various kinds of love and desire. And every word in Singlespeech has over a hundred rhymes! Love, hate—they are of no more significance than white and black, and the universe is filled with shades of grey and a full spectrum of color. So. Somehow, we have made between us, for my part, what we call *hodh*. It does not translate. But of it come deep emotions, and choices far beyond sex and loneliness. I did not give you my body out of weakness or lust. Fool! I am trained to deny the first, and the second I can banish by nothing more complex than full-remembering. It is just like before."

The tone of voice was amorous, hypnotic, lascivious. But the words! Han felt as if he was in the grip of some master witch, who could distort reality at will, with just words! They were savage, burning like fire, like swords and daggers. He groaned.

"I understand. Your percepive field will not take the contradiction, the strain; you hear what my skin says, the tone of voice, and the words. You cannot take much of it, for it will tear your mind apart. You are fortunate I do not use Multispeech on you, it would be faster, if you could under stand it. Even for us, this is hard, and this is where multi channel speech had its roots. This is *perdeskris*, Doublespeech. Now listen.

"I suspected that Hatha from the beginning, but I hesitated, did not act, and so much of all this is my fault. You already know why we keep a wide gene pool through the *klanh*, the braid. To abandon that system is to open the door to chaos. Mutations, freaks, who knows—all of which much faster than with you. Remember, we were made. So that beast in there will finish by destroying both humans and ler—the former through conquest, the latter by accident and negligence. We have to stop him. Quarantine Dawn. And to do that we have to act loyal, get close.

"There is more. Hatha did not know Aving had been off-planet. Keep that to ourselves; he already has an excuse ready, and Hatha will believe Aving, for the present. And you know as well as I do that Aving is not ler. He only looks like one. That may be cosmetics. He was listening, most carelessly, to the music he said neither human nor ler could follow. You saw too! And he has been careless with his name—it is probably his real one. It ends in -ing, like no word of anybody's Singlespeech. And we must look into this higher-than-expected rate of race-forming he spoke about. If it was enough to pass into folklore, then there is something here on Dawn causing it. Something perilous to ler, perhaps to humans.

"I have guessed what is coming for you and me when we get to the place where the country of the Warriors lies. Now I must ask you: if what has passed between us had happened back in civilization, with ler planets close by, or we had stayed on Chalcedon, at my fertility, would you have helped me to weave into a nice braid? Would you?" He nodded. "And so would I for you. So will we both, if we get the chance. But from now on it will be hard for us, for there are things I must do, and things you must do as well if we are to survive. This is more dangerous than when we were up on the plains. So perhaps tomorrow, perhaps even tonight, I will do and say cruel things. You must act and commit yourself as if I were no more. And soon it will be so anyway, because of fertility. So. You must do as I tell you. A test is coming. And tonight, you must reject me. Yes! You will do it! Now!"

He felt numbed, befogged, incapable of action. How long had she had him in that net of words? He looked to the small window. The same stars were visible in it, he remembered them well. Not more than a few minutes. But he remembered her instructions. Resisting her was hard at first, but slowly, he began to master, to override what his emotions and body were telling him. He pushed Liszendir away.

"No."

"But this is the last night for us."

"No. Do your worst. But I will not be a toy for you, while I see my own kind sold into slavery or worse."

Liszendir moved away, a motion of rejection, but in the faint starlight leaking into the room through the high, tiny window, he could see that she was winking at him. He ached. In the weak light he could also see her shoulders gleaming in the starlight. She pushed him over to one side.

"Very well. But I will sleep here. I am cold. Move over."

Han moved over and made room for her, and she settled into the small bed beside him. They did not speak again.

Han could not sleep, although soon he noticed that Liszendir's breathing had become deep and regular. He had not had time to reflect, time to foresee, since before Chalcedon; actions had been required, and actions were taken. Decisions had been necessary, and were made, to the best which could be expected under the circumstances. The method she had used to pass on this last bit of mutual planning had stirred all that up, brought it all to the surface, and moreover brought their relationship into sharp focus. Sleep was impossible; his mind was humming, busy, remembering, projecting.

All that she had said since they had been together had been so close to what he had been thinking himself that he had accepted it as they went along, putting the categorizations she outlined into the framework about such relations as he knew, his past. Now he saw that such a system had been totally inadequate to the task. Perhaps if he had been more experienced in affairs, instead of occasional encounters, which, for all their fun and sensual enjoyment, did not involve the participants very deeply, it might have worked, with some adjustments. But it was not so. Liszendir had been a completely new level of experience for him, and it would have been so even if she had been a human girl, and utterly conventional. But of course the first did not apply, and hence the second also went out the window, however conventional she might have been strictly within her own ler reference. But even after allowing all that, and recognizing the change in attitudes within himself, he could see still another problem area, and its secondary position in time could not obscure its primal position in importance. For a long time, he had been immersed in an alien surround, notwithstanding the fact that so much of ler ideas was seemingly familiar, as if the shapes were the same, but the colors different. That was not so, either. They had been in a survival relationship, in which they had had to learn to support and depend upon each other; they had become lovers. Was that because of the needs of their survival, or was it additional to it? He could not resolve that one, lying here in a strange room of an alien castle on the planet Dawn.

He felt deeply towards Liszendir still, undiminished. But at this point, the human and the ler view were coming into contradiction. His basic ideas told him that he should stick with her, whatever happened. Semper fidelis! But hers told her, and he was becoming increasingly aware of the ler idea that what they had made had reached a level from which there could be no denial. Circumstances might require other commitments, other liaisons, perhaps forever, but those things could not change the uniqueness they had known. As she saw it, then, necessity was necessity, and one had to weave. Liszendir would not take on the human outlook here, so hers would have to apply to him as well: because of what she had called their *hodh*, they would now make the supreme effort, the final gift, and find weaving partners for each other. If they could get back to civilization, even Chalcedon, then she would expect him to assume this role, which in other circumstances would be done partly by her, partly by the old braid generation. And what was more significant, she would take it on herself to do the same for him. It was a difficult attitude to accept, but it was clearly coming, at the greatest time they could hope for, within a few years, two or three, perhaps four. He had seen this coming, for Liszendir, since Chalcedon; what was difficult for him to absorb was that she saw the same thing clearly on the way ahead for him as well. The import of Aving's remarks, added to her words of a few moments ago, now became clearer; he would be exposed to human girls again, of unknown shapes and sizes, and there was a high probability that he would be offered one, to keep, as an enticement. If he could think like Hatha and the Warriors, that would be easy—take it, and use it. But through his deep experience with Liszendir, such an act would be untenable—he would assume even more responsibility for the enticement than he had for Liszendir.

He thought, for a moment, about something she had said to him, on Chalcedon, as they were having a mild argument about comparative philosophy: "Han, you humans build your systems of categorization of reality, your sand-sifters, as we call them, *praldwar*, upon assumptions which you provisionally say are rock-hard, and then you stagger up onto them, blinking and gasping, like some lungfish on a flat rock. But in the ways of looking at reality, we are chaoticists, we return to the water. There is nothing stable, except the striving of life to impress its will upon the universe contrary to the direction of the flow of entropy."

To her, all living things, and many nonliving things, were individuals and deserving of respect. This was revealed by the language; symbols had one or two syllables, but *names* had three or four. She had said, "It is not practical, of course, to name them all, but when we are learning this principle, we are always instructed to look out upon the waves of the sea. 'See those waves?' says the teacher. 'Every one of them has a name, all that you can see, and all of them, all the way around the world, that you cannot see, will never see, *can* never see. We lump them all together, we say these are waves, but you should never let the convenience of that act of categorization blind you to the greater fact of the individuality of each one of them.'" So, he thought of girls' bodies—sweet

things, delightful. But there was nothing casual, nothing light whatsoever, in the things that passed between male and female, and that was
the reality of it—not the excuses one told oneself to hide the early blunders one made upon others.

He saw the result of all these things coming. And, oddly enough, his
new appreciation of how they fit together gave him a sense of complete
relaxation, and he went to sleep immediately. His last thought was not
verbal, but imagic: he felt an odd sense of accomplishment, but whether
it was from a long-term change in himself, or what he had seen this
night, he could not tell. It wasn't important, anyway.

They were awakened before dawn the next morning by the same
leering head servant, who escorted them back to the large hall where
they had dined the night before. There Hatha met them in great
good humor, speaking in a most friendly manner, especially to
Liszendir, and even offering her a place at the table. Han watched his
actions closely, and after a few moments, was sure that she had been
basically right; by some method, they had indeed been observed last
night. There was subtle knowledge showing in Hatha's behavior.
That was good for them, for it meant that he was starting to read
things wrong. For a very short moment it flashed through Han's
mind that perhaps it was he who was reading Liszendir wrong, that
here was subtle double game-playing. But no, it blew away, vanished.
She was not that subtle, but rather the opposite, direct and uncom-
plicated; and if she had wanted to dispense with Han, she could do
it easily enough by a virtually unlimited number of methods. Now,
if only Hatha would continue to read things wrongly, and if he and
Liszendir could continue to play the charade out until they got close
enough to move. If. If.

For his part, Han did not join in the breakfast discussion, but attempted to appear sullen, uncooperative, broken and resigned. Hatha
spent scant attention on him, and apparently satisfied any suspicions he
might have had early; thereafter he paid only cursory attention, if any
at all. Hatha and Liszendir made a lot of inconsequential small talk,
which underneath its bland exterior was really quite transparently interrogation. And of a high order, as well, skillfully professional. Hatha
seemed to be trying to gather information primarily about Union ler attitudes and weapons, using a peculiar indirect approach as subtle as the
music had been the night before. But she gave nothing away, avoiding

the interrogation easily enough, sidestepping the cautious, fencing approaches. Liszendir was a slippery fish who could make herself smaller than the meshes of the net being used to catch her. As he watched this performance, Han could not avoid evaluating the girl in a new light, much as he had been doing since they had met; a continuous process of re-evaluation. Hatha was obviously capable and alert, sharpened by decades of experience gained in the exercise of power, and in the effort to climb to those heights; Liszendir was, in her terms, not yet adult, but through an accumulated and passed-on store of wisdom, and training, she was, on the whole, almost a match for the leader of the Dawn expeditionary forces, by herself.

Everyone seemed to be finished with breakfast. Hatha looked around impatiently, then gestured peremptorily, which caused the immediate appearance of three of the triads, nine warriors in all. They were all young, younger than either Han or Liszendir, but they seemed confident and dangerous, fanatics accustomed to instant obedience. Moreover, they were armed with several kinds of weapons, some of which Han recognized, and some he did not.

"Naturally," Hatha mentioned with a very courteous manner, "to the intelligent, the obvious never need be explained. Why explain such things—it is like explaining a good poem, or perhaps a well-constructed joke; the explanation takes the impact of recognition away." It would have been a good allusion if addressed solely to humans; but to Liszendir, and Han as well, now that he was also a speaker of Singlespeech, it was doubly pointed. Because every word-root had four meanings, and because the basic roots were "saturated," every pronounceable combination within the rules *was* a true root, with the resultant possibilities of confusion and misidentification, Singlespeech abounded with puns, "jokes," double and triple entendre, and from what Han had gleaned from Liszendir, the poetry was even worse, with severe syntactical compression and odd literary references to add to the confusion. Get the point, indeed. He thought Hatha might be overobvious. To the girl, the attempt at "subtlety" would be as brazen as a raucous shout in a quiet and secluded grove deep in the forest.

Hatha continued, "I do not wish to be troubled or disturbed by further futile attempts or false bravado. So. Han, you will fly the little ship. Now that I know something of how to operate it, doubtless primitive in technique by your standards, I can observe you to judge if you are performing correctly. I am sure you are able to cause the ship to perform some pervulsion detrimental to us all, but hardly one which will incapacitate ten of us, and yet leave you and Liszendir standing, or should I say, operable."

"I understand very well. It shall proceed as you wish."

They left the hall with no further ceremony, and went to the place where the ship had been grounded through another winding and dark passageway. After the close, dense darkness, their sudden emergence into the stark, clear openness of Dawn was something of a shock. It was early morning, and the north-autumn light was all around them. The sun was now low in the northeast, just clearing the far ramparts of the high and naked summits of the large eastern range. The air was still, transparent as spring water, full of blues and violets. For Dawn, it was cloudy, with planes and swathes of layered clouds all over the sky, lightening toward steely grey and hints of pearl in the north, darkening into rich, deep blues and violet and darker tones in the south, which now was severely darkened. Han tried to imagine what the extreme of winter would look like from this point; the sun would describe shorter arcs across the northern sky, would move closer to the northern horizon, and would finally disappear, leaving behind only a vague northern glow which would dim and brighten daily. An eerie blue twilight, lit from the north, not the west, and overhead, the stars would shine. The South would be almost completely dark. He looked around, to remember the impression; it was unspeakably beautiful, the shifting planes of the sky, the piercing bright sun, the shadows and tones of the mountains, the spatters of snow left from the storm of two days ago. And the ship was there, too, grounded on a spur of rock. It, too, was beautiful. As they walked toward it, the ground underfoot crunched with frost. Before they entered the *Pallenber*, Han paused by the foot of the ladder, gazing out at the colossal mountains to the east one more time.

Hatha noticed. "You approve, you appreciate! That is good, very good! As for the natives of this Leilas district, they haven't the wit; they are terrified of them. They imagine them the abode of demons." Han could well believe the tale. Who else could live among those torn and rended surfaces than demons and malevolent spirits. Dawn had its beauty, but is was a terrible beauty which daunted and humbled and cast fears, rather than a beauty which reassured, comforted. Hatha went on, "We call those mountains the Wall Around the World. Technically, it is a misnomer, for they reach north and south only about two-thirds of the half-circumference. As far as I know, there is nothing like them anywhere else, on Dawn or on any other planet. They are so high that they break up the circulation of air, which is actually a help, for if they, and others similar to them, did not break it up, Dawn would be quite uninhabitable. I assure you it would not be so lovely here if the winds followed their natural bent—they would blow with truly hellish velocity. And they tell me that the mountains are still growing!"

They climbed up the ladder, and entered the *Pallenber.* As they filed into the control room, Han expected to feel at home, reassured. But he didn't; he felt profoundly strange, like some wild tribesman out of the bush, suddenly thrown into a room full of incomprehensible machines. The triad guarding him was watching him very closely. He did not think now was the best time; if they were expecting anything, it would be now. Later was better, if he could get the chance again. But he knew it would be better to wait for a better opportunity than act in a situation where there was little or no hope.

Han went through the sequence of activating the ship, slowly, carefully. When it was fully operable, he turned to Hatha and said, "We're ready."

"Good. Go simply—straight across. I had thought that perhaps we might take a grand tour, but on reconsideration, I think it might be better if we waited for that. Call it a reward, if you will, for good behavior. So, now; proceed!" He turned to the guards, who crowded the control room, and said something to them which Han did not exactly follow. He didn't need to; the meaning was transparently clear from the situational context. It most likely had been something like "Kill them at the slightest pretext." Han turned to the controls, but then turned back to Hatha.

"Wait. You can fly this kind of ship manually, if you want, but the most common practice is to set it up for automatics. It requires less energy of the ship, and definitely less of the pilot. But I can't insert a course until I know data about the planet—size, mass, reference points for arbitrary latitudes and longitudes."

"I don't have any of that information. We don't use those . . . what you called them. And size is of no matter. When we want to go anywhere, we just get up high enough to clear obstacles, and go there." For the first time, Hatha seemed genuinely perplexed.

"I can rise vertically, calibrate my altitude, and determine the size and mass from measured G force and angular diameter. Then if you tell me which direction you want to go, I can put it in. By your leave?"

"Of course, of course. Up, then down again. Fly the course in the fringes of the atmosphere; just enough to clear the peaks. There are no other mountains between us and the homeland of the Warriors." He now seemed not only uncomfortable, but actually embarrassed. Why?

"Done."

Han enabled the drive, and the ship rose vertically until the planet lay below them, mostly dark and shaded, the terminator curiously slewed in respect to the rotation. In the far south, the land was covered by a mist or fog, which grew steadily denser and thicker in the direction of the pole. At the northern edges, nearer the equator, the cover graduated into ragged pieces, shreds and tatters of clouds moving up out of the cold parts of Dawn. Han steadied the ship, and began taking his measurements. Dawn was, as it turned out, quite large, even larger than Chalcedon, which was oversized, as habitable planets went. There was something else notable on all the instrument readings, but it was ambiguous in one sense, so for the time he kept it to himself. Finished, he informed Hatha that he was ready to take the course he indicated, which Hatha gave him, in vague terms. Han thought he knew what Hatha meant, and inserted the course.

The ship then dropped back down to approximately the level of the highest peaks. Han stared at the maser altimeter: it was indicating 75,000 feet above the top of the trough! He put the course into activate, and sat back, work done until it would be time to pick a landing site. Hatha looked impressed, and Han told him, "There is no need to fly it yourself, manually, in a gravity well. Besides, it wastes energy. You just set up a suborbital path and the ship flies itself along the minimum energy curve. Energy is low for lift, so all you get is thrust."

Hatha looked even more impressed. It occurred to Han that the reason for this must lie in the fact that he had flown the *Pallenber* from the land of the Warriors to Aving's castle manually, not even knowing about orbits, or the ability of the ship to follow them automatically, once commanded. But he had already flown space, in a ship of his own! What kind of energy were these idiots playing with? But he did not follow these speculations very far, for they were moving slowly now, crossing the high mountains, the Wall Around the World. The screen was showing titan naked summits so close it seemed that they could reach out and touch them. The effect was deceptive: the peaks they were looking at were miles away, and it was only their size and, at this altitude, the lack of atmosphere which lent them the impression of nearness. Han looked again; they had the same general appearance as free-floating asteroids he had seen. Over them, on the far side of the range, was the sun. Above them, the sky showed totally black, except for a pearly-blue band close to the horizon in the north. Below, the land on the far side of the mountains was a dull gold-brown color.

The high plains rolled beneath them, as their speed increased. They moved, and pushed the mountains back into the west. Han looked down onto the bare, apparently featureless surface. He supposed that he was looking at the same general area over which he and Liszendir had walked with such difficulty only a few months ago. But he could not make out any feature. Even the crater was invisible, at least so far as they had seen. The altimeter showed a decrease in altitude from the reading they had taken over Aving's castle. But this was apparent altitude, distance to the ship, not reference altitude above an oceanic level. It was higher than Aving's castle, as he already suspected very well. And they had walked over that surface. A blemish, a mark, drifted into view from his right, somewhat more to the south than he had expected. It was the crater, and there was the line of brush they had seen from the grounded warship. He could not see anything else.

"Hatha, when did you notice we were gone from your ship, when we first landed here?"

"Actually, quite soon. I suspected something when I came into the control room on my ship and found the young lady, here, gone, and the guards, ah, incapacitated. Permanently. I fear that out of gun range, I shall have to keep her under guard by many. She is more docile now, but for a while I thought that it would come to removing all her extremities, in order to keep her safe without doubt, and even with that drastic step, one might not be completely sure." He nodded politely towards Liszendir. "Correct, dear?" She smiled sweetly in reply, a facial gesture which really did not resemble a smile at all. Under the circumstances, it was thoroughly unpleasant.

Han turned back to the main screen. Ahead was new country. Below the ship, the land grew hazy, masked by a layer of thicker air, to which the altimeter agreed that the land was indeed lowering slowly in altitude. Some geography began to be visible on the face of the barren plains, and cloud formations could be seen. Ancient traces, mere rock colorings now, showed where mountains had been once, and sluggish lakes and rivers crawled over the surface. The lakes resembled nothing so much as the roots of tuberous plants, or perhaps curious organisms which might have anchored themselves to a sea-bottom, and fed in the upper waters.

After a time, Han saw, slightly to the right and south of their course, the object he had been looking for. It was near the terminator of approaching night. The trip had indeed taken only about an hour, but now they were on the other side of the world, and winter night was coming. The object was visible, even from suborbital distances, or perhaps it disturbed the weather enough so that was the visible part of it. But whichever it was, there was the ship of the Warriors, a visible bump on the surface of Dawn. As they drew closer to it, they could see that what they had first sighted was the weather it produced, for they could see it more clearly, and observed that it trailed streamers of cloud downstream of its bulk, the shreds and tatters blown away from the cloud masses by the prevailing winds out of the south. A lenticular formation with at least ten layers they could see domed over it, and the overcloud picked up fragments of the pearly light out of the north and spread the iridescent second light all over the area where the warship had been grounded. Han revised his estimates of the size of the warship upwards. He turned to Hatha.

"How do you ground that monster, and keep it in one piece in a gravity well?"

"Easy, easy. We simply never turn it off!"

"Never?"

"Never. At least not since the great ship was rebuilt and refitted, altered from its old role to fit its new one."

Liszendir had been silent the whole trip. But now, as they approached closer to the dreaded oversize warship, she became attentive and alert. She interrupted, "Is that the ler starship, the first one ever built, which left old Earth so many years ago?"

"Yes. The same. Although it is much changed; the old interior is completely gutted and filled with machinery. It takes a lot of it to be able to move those rocks and control their motion at a distance. The exterior you see is not the old shell, either; the outside part had to be enlarged as well. I must admit that its size is somewhat a problem to us, for as Han has probably guessed already, if we deactivated it while it was grounded, it would collapse under its own weight. Perhaps we could turn it off in space, above the surface, but there, we need its stress-field, because it will not hold air without it. It leaks."

"Hatha, we are finally being detected. When we land, may my first task be the chastising of your detection operators? We've come well within striking distance, and before they even knew we were coming. I hate to embarrass them, but don't you think you need some cover?"

"No. There is no one to watch for. Look at the sky! When you are on the other side of Dawn, by Aving's castle, that part of the planet is pointed to the main part of the galaxy. But over here, we look out, in winter, on the utter void. Look!"

Han looked in the upper part of the screen. The stars were indeed few, and the few which were in the field were generally rather bright, as if they were all nearer stars.

"You look, you see, and perhaps therefrom understand; there is no one to be looking for. You people back in regions where the stars cluster thick as mudsprouts after a rain could have no idea. Out here on the edge there is nothing. It is farther than you think from here to Chalcedon, and even Chalcedon is considered far out towards the void."

"Well, I'm no militarist, by any means, and don't intend to be; what I say is just opinion, unexpert, subjective. I do know that we haven't found intelligent alien life forms yet. Yet. But the people occupy a very small part of the galaxy, even considering exploration efforts. And were there anyone about in these parts, they could certainly come and go unnoticed, doing as they pleased. And your ship, from space, is a sitting duck. A fish in a barrel. Wide open to attack. Anyone coming in here with half-good detection, or better kinds of gear, such as we have on here, would have you before you ever knew they were in the system. At the least, you need an off-planet watch. And if you can rebuild that warship, surely it's within your resources to build a couple of orbital forts—have them up, on watch, from alternating polar orbits."

"Our capabilities are not for your speculation."

"No?" Han felt a slight prickle of the sense of danger, but it was not particularly strong. He could go on a little further. "Well, I assumed that I was now, per our decision, working for you, and my contribution was to be knowledge. That goes further than just building and operating weapon systems. I know that one does not build ballistic missiles and use them for crop-dusting! And there is more about this system you should know. For instance, when I raised the ship to take the measurements, back at the castle, I got a very curious reading—as if I were picking up traces of an anomaly somewhere in this system, like another spaceship, but with its drives masked or in some kind of standby condition. And it was so well shielded that I couldn't get a location on it. The energy flux was too low to be resolved from one detection position. To find it accurately, I'd have to take readings from several positions. You can increase the effective resolution power of any sensor system, mechanical, electronic, or logical, if you move it around; it acts as if it were the same size as the area you move it around in, if you synchronize all your readings. But I had time for only one scan of the system, so all I can tell you now is that there is an anomalous, unexplained neutrino source in your system."

Hatha said lamely, "That must be the *Hammerhand* you are picking up."

"No. Your warship isn't an anomaly, it's a beacon! Now, this ship has good instruments, but not the best there are. But even on this ship, with some looking, I alone could pick up your warship from as far away as the far side of Chalcedon. With both Dawn and Chalcedon between us and shielding you. A trained operator, which I am not, and good detection, really good equipment—why, your ship leaks so bad, they could probably pick you up and track your movements from old Earth. And that's with the drives shut down! Just sitting there. I can imagine what kind of emissions that thing puts out under battle speeds. You're lucky all of you haven't been fried by now, if not sterilized."

Hatha was not to be daunted by suspicions. He asked, "Well, what about a hot gas giant? We have one in this system, a huge gas planet, with an unusually high temperature, much higher than others in other systems we have visited. It presently is on the other side of the sun, but most of the time it is very visible."

"No. Gas giants, even hot ones, don't emit radiation like that. If you get anything out of them, it's infrared, and nothing any more involved than that. What I'm talking about is stellar interior stuff, or spaceship drives and power sources. That star out there puts out more than its share to suit me. And your ship is sitting there, blazing like a bonfire to the right kind of instruments. Unless the high-pressure dual source is causing a malfunction in the detection gear itself, I would have to say there is still another source here, hiding under the output of the other two sources. I am not sure we could locate it, even using spread detection."

"Land there. Before the *Hammerhand*. We will discuss this later."

Han did as Hatha had directed, moving the *Pallenber* down, settling close to the *Hammerhand*. Indeed they had not turned it off! It sat there, happily emitting across the whole spectrum, drowning out half his detection instruments from anything else. No, you certainly could not ignore it. But he kept his other thoughts about the ship to himself. The first time Hatha tried to run that thing up against a proper defense system, or went into battle with real armed ships, they'd carve him up like steaks at a banquet! Worse. At the first direct hit, it would probably explode, and, overpowered as it was, would probably blight a whole system before it was through. The Warriors were wild and brave, he granted them that, like so many peoples of the past who thought that they had the ultimate weapon. But there was no ultimate in weapons, ever, and when you matched power for power, the superiority vanished like a candle flame in a high wind. A man with a knife could terrorize a man without one, but what if the one threatened suddenly revealed a pistol, even one of the old projectile-hurlers? Or revealed himself to be a master swordsman? Or was a Liszendir—a master of hand combat? She wouldn't even blink at a knife.

As they landed, Han could see an emblem painted on the side of the ship, in a place set aside just for that. It showed a pictorial image of a giant mailed fist smashing a proud tower, while all about played lightnings, and over all a huge red eye glared. Below the tower, its inhabitants leaping out or falling, waited a horrible fanged mouth, the very jaws of hell. It reminded him of something, he could not remember . . . wait, yes he could, too. Tarot cards! The ancient divination still hung on, on the fringes, for science had no such hope of explaining the whole. They considered science a success when it worked well on one of the parts. Han had seen them, the cards, once, and had felt disturbed, threatened by those emblems out of the far past. They mocked the familiar things he knew, they suggested, "all this grubbing after facts means nothing! We knew in the dawn of history, and we know now." The image on the warship was very similar to the trump card of "The Tower." And that was a card of singularly bad import. To carry it as emblem was even worse. Han looked over to Liszendir, for he knew that most ler dabbled in their own form of Tarot, one with a different underlying numerical base, but a Tarot just the same. She did not notice his glance: she was too busy looking at the insignia herself, and the look on her face was not one to reassure the superstitious, or even mildly questioning.

Still, as he settled the ship on its extended landing legs, he looked at the warship next to them and marveled. There it sat, a flying wreck, yet it towered over the world, even the world of Dawn, from the ground view. Void of space! It must have been several miles tall, close to seven or eight, and something near the same dimension in diameter at its widest part, closer to the ground. And according to Hatha, most of it was machinery!

Liszendir was pursuing another angle. "Hatha, you say that you used the old shell to build upon. Do you still use the old drive system that was originally built into the ship?"

"I have no idea. I suppose so. I do not trouble myself with mere mechanics. I command troops, forces—for that one needs to know how to command."

The fatal error so many would-be overlords made, Han thought. By denying that they had to know anything except leadership and command, they made themselves prey to kingmakers who had spent their lives learning the specialty of command and influence. And so fell into the sordid tangles of palace intrigues and political maneuvering, wasting time, wasting their underlings, wasting themselves and in the end doing nothing except becoming addicted to luxuries, which were fed them by the kingmakers, gladly. Pomp distracts from the matters at hand. And that which distracts is a drug, regardless of the container in which it is packaged.

Liszendir was continuing, "I was just thinking. We abandoned that drive system long ago. We sold it to the humans, but they found something in it which we had missed. Say what you will about the old people! They are persistent, and they fill in outlines. The old drive system, the way it was, used a dimensional lattice which was strange and very dangerous to use. That was why we abandoned it. And why the humans changed it. I am not technical, I do not understand such things. It worked fine for us, so history says, from old Earth to Kenten. They knew no problem or danger."

Hatha reflected a moment, then said, "There has been no danger or odd problems I know of. None has been spoken of, outside of certain legends, which I discount. We are as prey to fancies as anyone else, I suppose."

Han was thinking about the ancient conquerors out of history. Mostly of the period when people, human and ler, were planetbound to one world; conquerors were few in space, because even with matrix overspace drive, the distances were just too large, the communications stretched too far, the material tonnages too great. So what could this situation here on Dawn be compared to? Tamerlane with nuclear weapons? Hitler with spaceships? Or Darius the Usurper with those odd machines which used fluid dynamic lift, Bernoulli's principle, to support them as they moved through the atmosphere, what was the word—yes, airplanes. Yes. But give them only the devices, vastly oversimplifying them so the users would never be able to build more on their own, or repair the ones they had. When they were used up, there would be no more, and any reaction generated by the mixing-up of cultures would be self-limiting. Teach them only the rudiments, and make sure they wouldn't theorize. But these people on Dawn were ler! They should have been hunch-theorists of great power. What had been happening here? Whatever it was, it was neither simple nor completely recent, but a vast enigma which had deep roots in the past, perhaps all the way back to the half-legendary Sanjirmil.

But he was allowed no more time to speculate. Hatha motioned to him. "Shut it down, now. We will leave."

Han ran through the shutdown sequence with ill-concealed reluctance. Then he got out of the pilot's chair, and went with the party out into the evening.

Outside, in the open, the bulk of the *Hammerhand* was even more impressive, especially standing comparatively next to it. Or perhaps one might better say "oppressive." It towered over them, a vast, pitted, sculptured mass wreathed in clouds; and doubtless crowned with lightning in the proper season. The shuttles lay on the ground before it, arranged in a neat row. And the meteors with which it fought lay all about in careless profusion, quarter-mile blocks of nickel-iron, streaked with heavy rust from long immersion in a corrosive, oxygen-rich atmosphere. Han hoped that nobody on Dawn relied upon compasses, because they would clearly be useless—all that iron would disrupt compasses for a thousand miles around. But of course they wouldn't—only oceanic or sea peoples used magnetic iron. On Dawn, they navigated from one landmark to the next. But they could have. When he had taken his measurements, he had seen that Dawn had an enormous magnetic field, the highest level he had ever seen. It would have to; otherwise, that hot star which was the primary would fry them with charged particles. That would indeed play hob with the unstable ler genes. Yes, and . . . he choked it off for now. He had to see more.

Han turned from his observation of the warship to lower levels, around the ground level. Of course, they were farther south, and therefore winter was somewhat more advanced. It was cold. All around in the gathering darkness, the low sun in the north flashed its slanting, pearly light over tents, sheds, and miscellaneous buildings scattered all over the plains, as far as Han could see, without limit. There seemed no end to it. It was a city, but it was not a city. Rather, it was a large and unorganized assembly of people, in a place, for no other apparent reason than that they had to have a place, and this one seemed as good as any other. An unurban city in which one could virtually disappear overnight, if one were ler. He didn't know about how humans might fare.

Hatha echoed his thoughts somewhat. "We sojourn here on the Pannona Plains. When we tire of a site, we move on, sometimes a great distance, sometimes only a few miles. Some go with the ship, while the less favored walk. And of course, we have permanent settlements all around this part of Dawn. There is a lake on the other side of the warship, and we like it here. This area is where our heart is."

"I cannot fail to be moved by the sight of all this," Han commented, genuinely impressed.

Few people of either sort were about, visible in the evening dusks and glooms and blue and purple shadows cast every where by the slanting sunlight, waning fast, and the building, scattered randomly all over. Han thought it was probably because of the cold, and the fact that they had arrived somewhere near local suppertime, although for him it was only an hour or two downstream from breakfast, and still morning. As he looked, he could make out a few figures, seemingly Warriors, but none of them were close enough for it to make any real difference. They walked through the cold over to the rather nondescript front of an unimpressive building, whose size and extent was masked by the front surface and the dark. Inside, it turned out to be a sort of combination state residence, guardhouse and administrative center, and seemed to have no limits towards the rear of it that Han could determine. It was surprisingly comfortable, if rather spartan in decor and furnishings.

"These," Hatha said, with a sweeping motion of one arm, "are my personal quarters. We will settle you two temporarily in the vicinity, and later, see to something more permanent."

"Do you rule all this camp?" asked Liszendir.

"No. By no means. I fall under the high triad. I am . . . what you might call something comparable to a minister of foreign affairs. Ha! That has been my role all along, but in fact, until a few years ago, I didn't have much of a job."

Hatha led the way into a small parlor, or sitting room, and, making a motion, signaled the guards to depart, which they did, silently. Han suspected that wherever they went, it was not far, and that should Hatha want them back, the slightest sound would bring the same bunch back, erupting out of the very doorjambs. Hatha settled himself down in an armchair. Han and Liszendir remained standing.

"Now, we shall, as you say, get down to business. Sit. Be comfortable, relaxed, and at your ease. I am aware that the overall circumstances of your . . . ah, service, are perhaps not to your highest expectations and ambitions. But then, what circumstances are, for any of us in this troubled universe of chagrin and tears? We do what we can, myself no less than you, despite appearances that deceive us one and all. So then! To work! We have arrangements to make, tasks to be determined."

Liszendir sat down in another overstuffed chair. "I see one thing. If you expect me to teach infighting of any degree to all these people, I will be a very ancient elder when I am finished."

"Ah, not so at all! Not all, but only an elite. I should hope that you can complete most of your work within a year."

"Even so, I hope not all by myself. I should think the best way would be to train trainers first, and then set them to work on the others. It would proceed faster."

"You have no idea how small the group is. It is very well within your scope. And what you have is a very dangerous weapon, do you know? So we do not want such secrets widespread. No, no. A small group. I will bring them to you, and I will respect any evaluations of them you care to pass on. If they are not suitable, then so state! I am most definitely a believer in the privileges of rank, but then who, having rank, says otherwise? Only those who lack it despise it! But I also believe strongly in the recommendations of experts and professionals. Friendship and personal favors—now, they are fine things in small scale, in the home, in the small business, in the lower administrations; but where things are really at stake, we have to look to capability and knowledge, not ambition and alliances. I assure you, Liszendir, you should be all done by the time of your fertility. The reward for successful accomplishment will be, of course, your choice of mates from the whole horde. Do you understand? Choice comes out of position, and position out of deeds."

Liszendir looked puzzled at the short time Hatha was talking about, and in regards to her future degree of choice, she indicated nothing. But Han reflected on that for a long time. Choice, indeed. In her system, the one she had grown up with, such choice was deadly to the race, it held the potential of disaster for them. But more importantly, he saw something else, which he was sure Liszendir did not see, for she was no politician: Hatha was after far more than just the conquest of the inner worlds, all for the glory of the high triad, whatever that was. He was, first and foremost, after power within the Warriors, and what he had in mind for Liszendir was the training of a corps of shock troops to be used against his own people. And more flowed out of that realization: the factions surrounding the central authority must be very strong in their own right, or Hatha, the wily old beast, would have moved already. Han felt mixed emotions. It had been easy to hate Hatha-Hath'ingar, back on

Chalcedon, at Aving's castle, where he could be cast in the role of a personal devil to himself and Liszendir. But on closer inspection, Han saw that the evil in Hatha was mostly an evil as defined by Han in personal terms. He could never like the hetman, or follow his goals voluntarily. But he could not help admiring, cautiously, his capability and wit. He was sharp.

Excerpts from *'L Knun al-Vrazuus, The Doctrine of Opposites:*

> *"The reasons for change, the true reasons and not the illusory ones, and the direction of events in a given system are, to the novice, the uninitiated, paradoxical and multifaceted beyond enumeration. Moreover, the following course of events is most often exactly the reverse of what the untrained expect. Thus we observe the phenomena that, (1) the amount of administrative effort increases as the function becomes defunct; and (2) that the severity of military training increases as the possibility of war becomes more remote. It follows that the first level of adepthood will be to see beneath the illusion, which is generated by poor approximations of theory; the second is to learn to conduct oneself as if one did not see these contradictions, while all the while unraveling them so that others, not so perceptive, will not become meshed in their tangles."*
>
> —Borzalhai, Rithosi *mnathman*

> *"The only constant aspect of change is the fluctuation of its rate."*
> —Weldyanzhoi the Great

> *"Water is soft and has no will save that to be low and level. Yet, given time, water levels the high and distinctively individual mountains and disperses their substance to the winds and the bottoms of the seas. Space is of similar nature, even more devoid of will, yet it absorbs everything and manipulates it so perfectly."*
>
> —Jwinverlis the Blind

"Humans invariably elaborate upon that which they lack, in their myths. Ler do not, as a rule, but the reason lies not in substance, but in culture and certain disciplines arising out of it."
                    —Shennanskoth *(Kadhos Liszendiruus)*

O N THE NEXT day, Hatha disappeared, which left Han with nothing to do, except sit and think, or wander around the place where Hatha made his headquarters. He tried to visit other parts of the building, but guards and locked doorways limited the room he had to move around in to only a few chambers. They were all singularly bare. He was definitely a prisoner, even if he was not having his face rubbed in the fact any more by more obvious methods. Nor did he see any sign of Liszendir, either. She was either in another part of the building, or gone with Hatha, wherever he was. This all left Han with considerable time to think things over, resort and reclassify facts in his mind, and neither the facts, nor the conclusions they led to, were very comfortable to live with. They suggested a certain direction to the flow of events which had definitely disturbing aspects, far beyond considerations of personal safety.

Han considered the threat of the Warriors and their massive warship. It was true it was a monstrous war machine, which now effectively cowed and dominated two planets, Dawn and Chalcedon alike. But Chalcedon had no ships of its own, and on Dawn, nobody outside the Warriors had anything more destructive than a crossbow. Under those conditions, he reflected, he himself could probably rule the two worlds with no more than the weaponry installed on the *Pallenber*, which was, after all, a rather small ship. So, too, with surprise, the Warriors could very easily make a further early conquest or two, but once the mercenary men-of-war located them by the pattern of their raids, and the leaky emissions of their warship, it would be settled in a hurry—that much was obvious even to someone who had neither military training nor interest in it in particular. Hatha didn't see the obvious, which meant he knew nothing about civilized worlds, except by hearsay or deliberate misinformation. So, after discovery, then what?

There was another aspect as well: all the technology represented by the warship strongly smelled of cultural grafting, the imposition of high-level machinery upon a relatively low-level culture, and recently, too. The warship was a powered ship, so it had to be refueled eventually. Who would do that? Han had seen no evidence whatsoever of facilities which could either fuel or repair a craft like that. Or perhaps that was intentional—no repair facilities, and just enough fuel to get them into trouble. And he considered the fact that Hatha had a spaceship which could cross space and devastate a whole planet, but he knew nothing about orbits, minimum-energy curves and geodesies, and sat grounded on a plain, visible from orbit, and had not a care about defense or detection. And the ship was in such shaky condition that it could not land unpowered, nor could it be fixed. And it was deteriorating fast, judging from what he had seen. All these things hinted strongly at some unknown and unseen agency highly skilled in the manipulations of primitives, and skilled at hiding as well, at least from the primitives themselves.

That thought led Han onwards to the anomaly his instruments had suggested in the Dawn system. That, too, smelled. But it had been a subtle indication, possibly questionable, unlocatable. And the instruments could have been decalibrated by some inadvertent act of Hatha's when he was flying the *Pallenber* manually. But for a moment, he could have been almost sure that there was something. It was true—it would take years of measurements to pinpoint the location, and actually find out what was causing it. By then, it would be too late, of course. Hatha now had two ships, and two ships was a fleet, in these parts. It was very slick, if the anomaly was, as Han suspected, another ship, hiding in the Dawn system somewhere with drives on standby and highly shielded. Han saw it as a problem in cryptology, with which he as a trader was familiar, at least with commercial applications of the arcane science. And he knew very well that the first principle of cryptology was that no system is secure perfectly, nor is it intended to be; the purpose of a system of concealment is to slow detection down until the moment of exposure is well after the actions concealed by the system. So cryptosystems slowed eavesdropping down, and then you could run an operation, capture a market, get in and get out before anyone else knew about it, or could take advantage of it. And the same principle applied here. It was hidden, well enough, and by the time anyone could read the truth in it, it would be much too late.

There were more mysteries. Dawn had a powerful magnetic field, which was good in view of the radiation being put out by the hot star that was Dawn's primary. Otherwise, Dawn, even with a mild climate and normal rotation, would be quite uninhabitable. But planets with measurable magnetic fields switched polarity periodically, and by Kahn's Law, the stronger the field, the greater the rate of change of polarity. Neither the ler nor the humans on Dawn would ever be aware of it, because they did not have compasses. And he didn't know if they understood electricity or not. He suspected not. But the rate for Dawn! It must switch poles on the order of every few thousand years, or possibly even on the order of every few hundred. Han saw what had been happening on Dawn, from that.

It went approximately like this: Sanjirmil's followers stole the ship, and fled to the edge, looking for a planet where they would not be located for many years, years beyond counting. They happened on the world Dawn, and settled on it. Some years later, cruising about, probably on the lookout for other planets, they detected a human colony ship bound somewhere. This they captured, probably with the motive of slave-taking in mind, and nothing more than that. It would not have attracted much notice—many of the early ships were lost, and never seen again; a certain attrition rate was part of the risk. They returned to Dawn, to institute their new slave-based society. Then perhaps the original ship malfunctioned, or they forgot how to fly it. Individual ler would probably not forget, but the society could over a few negligent generations. So the ship became a holy relic, and a period of long quiet ensued. The humans were either enslaved and domesticated, or turned loose on Dawn to fare as they could. Who would care? They couldn't get off the planet, even if they thought such a thing were possible. And every few generations, the human and ler populations of Dawn would get a massive dose of radiation from their primary, when the planet's magnetic field was switching, and all barriers were down to charged particles. Effects of this would show in the humans, but the ler would begin to show effects immediately. It would probably run their already-high mutation rate completely off the scale. And long before, they had abandoned the wide-pool braid system, which would certainly have delayed any change, and might have saved them. So instead of advancing, or maintaining certain superior traits, they were devolving, and as far as Han could tell, were actually below the human norm in abilities. That, of course, would make no difference to the slaves—they had been conditioned to believe in ler superiority for thousands of years, and would have never had the opportunity to see anything different. But for the ler, they were back to city-states and bands of nomads, and they had apparently lost the ability for Multispeech. A few more thousand years and they would be back to body language, grunts and squeals, and would lose what little civilization they had. That would have been bad enough on a planet which had run its own evolutionary sequence through time to the point where complex organisms like man could survive, even in the wild state, but this was not possible on Dawn—the ecology was simply too primitive, and very likely wouldn't improve much, even in the very long run. There was potential for a circular, man-only system, but that wasn't a very pretty one any way you figured it. And what was happening to the humans, while the Dawn ler were devolving?

But now there was a kink in the program: the ler on Dawn, a culture hardly above the ability to forge spears, were operating a monster war-ship which dropped meteors as weapons. All this very definitely pointed to an agency or persons standing behind the Warriors and using them as a screen. But who were they, if it was indeed a "they." and what was the underlying purpose, the one which was being screened, not the screener? Han, since Chalcedon, had wanted to hurry back to Seabright, and tell Hetrus that his suspicions were wrong. Now he felt an even more urgent need to hurry back and tell him that he had been, in essence, right. But, as it appeared, there was for the present little chance of telling Hetrus anything.

In the afternoon, Hatha and Liszendir arrived from wherever they had been, and both of them seemed pleased with themselves. Hatha disap-peared again, almost immediately, but Liszendir hurried over to Han. She spoke in a low tone, very fast.

"I can't say this except quickly, nor can I explain much. You will have to take it on faith. He will be back—he is not gone for long. Three things: one, this triad-oversex thing is a nightmare. They have no sex as adolescents, and in fertility, the offspring are raised by the predomi-nantly female triads. They think no sex increases your strength. Vital-fluids doctrine, if you can believe it. Even the worst humans have given that cult up in disgust. Second: if Hatha offers you a female human, or offers you a choice of one, take what choice you can. He thinks that what we did was mere hunger, sensual gratification. He must not sus-pect anything more than that. Act like some barbarian lord: he will ap-prove. And you must not think in reference to me or what we have done. Think of it as if I were helping you become woven, as you will do for me someday, I hope. You must remember that she will, however strange, be of your own kind, and I wish it of you. Understood? Good. Third: there is something very wrong here. What is the word you use? Synchronization? They do not have it here. Things are badly distorted somehow. I do not understand what I have seen, but it is coming. And I do not like the outline that is taking shape."

Han knew he had to make his decision with her now, no second thoughts, no turning back. And what they had done, what they had been, would never be again. It was like the conditions which set up a total eclipse: they approached maximum, they culminated, the bright spot of the returning sun appeared, and the eclipse was over. They had, now, only the residue to live with: memories and commitments, to be discharged in ways outside the body and beyond the heart. He answered, "One—it figures. Two—I will do what I can, but if I have changed you, you have changed me, too. Three: I know." They had no more time: Hatha could be heard approaching around the corner. He came into the room.

"We have had a most interesting tour. I must say that this girl is flexible and alert far beyond her years and sex. I will be overlooking much for her services. And you have a part in this as well—do not dissemble! I can detect your influence, and much to my surprise, I find it generally beneficial."

Han answered, neutrally, "That sounds wonderful."

"Now, Han, you and I," Hatha said, waving Liszendir off, "have an area to explore. Have you thought of some way you might be of service to us, while you have been waiting?" Liszendir left the room through a door to the rear.

"Well, in fact, something has been on my mind, since we came to your camp, here. I think, if I may speak freely, that your defense system could stand some improvement, otherwise when your conquest starts, you're going to be wide open. Those meteors may be fine against a planetary population but against armed ships who can see you before you see them . . . Do you see? I'd like to see your ship, your equipment how your people operate it. Perhaps I can suggest some ideas. You are going to have to keep your hindside covered." He thought if what he suspected was true, that that small action would change little.

"There is warrior's wisdom in what you say. I, too, have thought on this, since you brought it up yesterday. So then. Matters shall proceed! We will go to the ship!"

"Now?"

"On the very instant. Come along. We will gather some rations along the way."

Hatha turned and barked an order to a subordinate who apparently had been waiting just behind the main door. There were sounds of departure, and only minutes later, returning. The functionary reappeared, saluted, and left. Hatha montioned to Han, and marched off through the door. Han followed and outside, saw Hatha disappearing into one of the shuttle from the warship. He caught up with him, the door closed, and with no preliminaries, Hatha activated the shuttle, and began flying a course towards the warship.

They arrived in a reception bay similar to the one through which Han remembered himself and Liszendir marching. How long ago had that been? It seemed like a very long time, but he could not scale it to any time frame with which he was familiar. Six months? A year? It was much like before, but this time they began to follow the maze of corridors, upwards, and the surroundings began to take on a more operational look. Finally, they arrived at a large room with a low ceiling, curiously low, which had the distinctive aspect of a command center. It was almost completely filled with panels and light displays, now mostly deactivated. A few screens, apparently cathode-ray and not micro vision, were mounted on some panels. There was only a handful of people in the room. These were all seated before—Han could not believe his eyes—what appeared to be radar scopes. It looked crude.

The operation came to attention as Hatha entered the room. Commanded, they explained their equipment and duties, and as they became more involved in so doing, warmed up, and spoke freely, and with considerable pride. Han paid close attention to them as they discussed their detection system, of which they were knowledgeable, at least in how it worked. They thought it was the best in the universe. Han thought otherwise, but he kept his thoughts to himself. Range-azimuth radar scopes, coupled through receivers and amplifiers directly to steerable mechanical antennas mounted atop the warship. Incredible! It was like a class in ancient history, with a neolithic farmer explaining how a broken branch could be used as a plow. Yes, the women went in front. They could pull, but steering was a finer art.

After a time, Han was able to understand enough of their system to make some suggestions for some slight improvements, which would not, considering their equipment limitations, materially increase their capabilities, but it would seem to. He also busied himself jotting down some notes for a set of operating instructions, since the operators were, for all their pride, manifestly too ignorant to make them for themselves. Han also agreed to train additional triads, who would be required either for use or backup duties, when the new system was implemented.

"Now," he said. "How about communications? Delegation of authority? Identification? Rules of engagement?" The answers he got stupefied him. They had electrical communications within the ship, but outside, on the plains, they used couriers and heliographs, whose light source could be supplanted with lanterns when the light level was low. These last used a complex, highly redundant code which the Warriors considered a paragon of secrecy. Han suggested some improvements, but for the present, no really radical changes. A simplified code. Better heliographs with a narrower beam. And a powered light line direct from the ship to Hatha's tent complex. And yes, a duty officer with some authority.

To Han's surprise, Hatha readily agreed, vastly impressed and not at all discomfited by Han's suggestions and evaluations, which Han himself thought were all rather overly obvious. As they toured the rest of the command room, Han found another piece of the puzzle he was working on. They had only simple detection; nothing that could even be called modern, by the remotest stretch of the imagination. And the command room had the same air of hasty improvisation and newness as the part he had seen earlier. That was interesting indeed. When the ship was rebuilt, whoever did the work left out—was it on purpose?—the very thing they could have used right here on their own planet. But he kept those speculations to himself. And he was not quite up to pressing too closely into origins, not unless he had some further sign from Hatha. He pronounced himself satisfied with his tour, and began outlining projects which Hatha would need to oversee or at least approve.

Hatha appeared to be both astounded and grateful. As they returned to the shuttle, he fairly bubbled with enthusiasm.

"Ah, yes, cooperation and progress! My boy, if all took your attitude we would be spared the onerous and time-consuming tasks of bombardment, siege, reduction. You are a very storehouse of valuables, which you volunteer. Rewards and honor! I hope we will see more of this. As you see, things are in need of improvement. True, work has been done, but it always seemed, somehow, unfinished, do you know? I am no technician, I do not know these things personally, but I have always felt that somehow, some quality was . . . not right."

"I thought you were going to sell me."

"That was a hasty remark engendered by the events on Chalcedon. Actually, aside from your knowledge, you have no great value in particular. No offense intended, but you are too close to the wild stock to be of any value to those who make a specialty of refining pure strains. Our domestic varieties are highly refined."

Han thought ruefully that here, in Hatha's remarks, was part of the reason why they were going downhill steadily on Dawn. The ler were

devolving on Dawn, and the humans, whatever they were after an unknown number of years of selective domestication, were, if Han knew
anything about slaves, probably glad enough to get the next meal. Hatha
interrupted his train of thought.

"Understand, I am no breeder myself. I consider it all a waste of time,
to labor over an essentially alien species while one's own seems to get
nowhere, no matter what we do. And matters have not improved with
the ship, either."

"How long has this domestication been going on?"

"Since the first, when the humans were captured. At first, with the
raids on Chalcedon, we thought the new blood would build up the stock
types we had; but most knowledgeable breeders now hold that the new
acquisitions will only lead to new types. When they got the captives
back here, they were definitely different, compared with the old types,
even where there was a superficial resemblance. And of course, none of
them have been as flexible as you."

Han bit his tongue again. More flexible, indeed! A batch of farmers
and small tradesmen and children, sifted for their physical characteristics; they would be both ignorant and terrified. How could they be expected to know anything about spaceships, and even if they had, who
could have been expected to volunteer anything? But something else
was apparent here, something that measured how far down the ler on
Dawn had gone: they would not have made the mistake of thinking the
new captives looked like the old if they had retained the eidetic memory which was characteristic of mainstream ler. Indeed, it was one of the
main reasons why ler navigators flew space manually—they could compare two views of the sky from different points and make up a mental
stereo image in their minds. Given two positions in space, the ler pilot
"saw" space in three dimensions in a plane at right angles to the line of
movement. But neither Hatha nor any of the Warriors, apparently, realized this. Nor did Hatha realize how much he had given Han. The Warriors could be outwitted.

"Well, I promised you reward, and reward you shall have, if you will."
A calculating gleam came into Hatha's eyes. "I will set aside some quarters for you, a place to work, and assign a clerk or two. But, best of all,
you may, at my expense, select a female of your choice. You see! Already
you rise in status! I grant you choices even many of us do not have."

"How shall I exercise this choice? I have seen few humans, the old
people, in this camp."

"There will be no problem at all. Because you have not seen the *klesh* does not mean that they do not exist. Ah, humans. If you lived in a cave, you would deny that stars existed. But more seriously, during normal times, there would be few, at least so that you could see them. But it happens that now, this season, we hold a winter exhibition of our art— our only art form, by the way. Would you say sub-racial types, or breeds? Or perhaps tribes. But at any rate, come along! Exert choice! Be discriminatory!"

Han entered the shuttle with Hatha. He suddenly felt uneasy, apprehensive; he did not think that he really wanted to see the product of several thousand years of forced breeding. What would *klesh* look like? Would the Warriors have aimed for beauty or function? And, more importantly, in whose terms? Han expected to see, at least in part, freaks, mutants, deformities, teratological amazements. But he went. They flew to an area north of the ship, quite far from Hatha's own place. Night was already falling in the short day cycle of the winter of Dawn; below, as they flew, Han could see a large complex, partly by its shape, partly by scattered lights around it. It seemed rather better lit than most of the camp. Hatha waxed proud.

"Here you are lucky indeed. This is a yearly spectacle of interest, education and enlightenment to us all. It goes on for many days. I suppose that for us the timing is fortuitous. If we had come here days earlier, all we would have had to pick from would have been agricultural specialties; good enough for work and production, but surely nothing there for the man of discriminating tastes. But now; now we arrive just past the peak of the exhibition. On display now are examples of *klesh* bred purely for purity of bloodline and beauty. Control of genetics. Marvels. True wonders!"

They landed. An attendant triad bowed respectfully to Hatha as they emerged from the shuttle and started toward the complex. It seemed to be a kind of tented structure, but as they went inside, it did not resemble a circus or carnival at all, as its outside might have suggested. It seemed plush, neat, even luxurious. Hatha was expansive.

"These on display now are, ah, ornamentals. They generally have no duties, no responsibilities, except to be cooperative and well behaved. Of course, some have functions—but now these are but shadows of the original purposes. Most are quiet, although some types tend to unruliness. You will doubtless find this entertaining, pure edification."

They went into the first section. What Han saw there completely dislocated his sense of reality. The displays were open cubicles with a portion in the rear closed off. They were furnished with rugs and cassocks, and those inside were prevented from wandering by a mesh of fine wires in the front. The specimens were labeled, on boards at the front of the cubicles, in an arcane terminology Han could not decipher. Also, attached to the boards were elaborate knotted designs, which Han presumed were symbols for various prizes and awards. Inside the cubicles sat or paced males or females, naked but neat, clean, and seemingly unconcerned, either with their situation or their nudity. The faces exhibited curiosity or animation, but in them there was no resistance, no calculation or hatred. In this particular section, all appeared to be redheads who bore an astonishing resemblance to one another. It was much closer than tribal, at least in the sense Han understood the term, and indeed, the individuals looked more like each other than members of most families. He had to look closely to see differences. But they were there. To the creatures themselves, they probably saw the differences as glaring, obvious, and certainly, the personalities would vary wildly— seen from inside the breed, as it were. These had dense, deep-coppery hair which fell free and more or less straight to their shoulders. Their skins were creamy and light in tone, smooth and hairless except for the pubic region and, oddly enough, the lower legs, which were, from the knees down, heavily furred with the same coppery red hair, males and females alike. They were, as a group, rather small-boned and delicate in appearance, and they all had deep sea-green eyes, of an intensity of color Han had never seen before. Hatha commented knowledgeably, while Han stared.

"Here you see the best examples of the *Zlat Klesh*. It is an old breed. I am told it was difficult to establish, and is still difficult to maintain according to breed standards, which exclude blemishes and freckles, as well as a certain heavier bone structure. These things tend to recur in Zlats. But as a group, these are generally fine examples. Zlats are not to my taste, of course, but everyone has his own preferences."

Han felt a hundred emotions boiling within himself. Impossible not to feel rage at this slow atrocity generations long. He looked at the smooth faces, the small, delicate nostrils. The males were bearded in pleasing patterns. The females looked pampered and untroubled. Most were young adults, approximately Han's age, or comparable with it, but a few were older. One distinguished-looking male in particular was middle-aged, but in perfect physical condition. His mustache dropped with flair and charm; patterns of iron gray streaked his hair and beard.

"I confess, Hatha, that it shocks me to see my own kind here. It would shock me to see ler displayed like this."

"So, indeed. But by expressing it as you do, you pass another test. Not many of your kind can see this, and fail to run crazy. But to what end? These imagine no rescue. They lead lives of pampered boredom. It is also so with the others." The voice was coldly rational.

Han stifled an urge to attempt to strangle Hatha. He had seen him in action, against Liszendir, and he knew that he could not hope to best him barehanded. Futility. Frustration.

"I can't read the signs. Who has won what?"

"Ah . . . Let me see. This one, here, for example, is unbred, a young female, as you can doubtless observe for yourself, and in late adolescence. Fourth place in her class—unbred females. Not so good, for a first show. The fault is delicacy—she is just a bit too fine-boned, I think. Now this one over here is a first. You will notice that she differs chiefly in . . ."

As Hatha went on, describing the virtues of another Zlat female, Han looked at the girl who had placed fourth. She was sitting relaxed on a cassock to one side, looking at nothing; she seemed to be dozing. As he watched, she became more alert, possibly sensing that she was being watched, not just idly glanced at. She arose, moved gracefully over to another cassock, which served as a storage area, opened it and removed a complicated object which she began to handle deftly, manipulating it into another configuration, which required considerable effort and concentration, but whose results seemed to please her. He looked closer at her.

Her face had an oval shape, with the slightest hint of cheekbone showing below her eyes, which were deep and thoughtful. They slanted slightly, which accented her face beautifully and subtly. Her mouth was finely formed, small, with rather full lips, slightly pursed. The upper lip was fractionally more full than the lower. He looked again. She had a beauty that was mind-wrenching. Han let his eyes fall downwards, to the body. Like her face, it was small, delicate, finely formed and outlined. Her breasts were small, round, accented with delicate brown nipples. She looked back at him and smiled vacantly. Then, recognizing him as a human like herself, although very different in appearance, she looked curious, friendly. Han turned away, entranced and sickened at the same time.

Hatha had turned back from his explanation of Zlat virtues. He had been saying that Zlats had been originally bred to perform fine-detail electronic assemblies. Han heard, and noted the fact, but it was just another piece of data.

* * *

Hatha was inexhaustible. He walked Han for miles, or so it seemed, through exhibits of every type Han could have imagined. There was more variety here than one could find in a hundred years on any one planet; sifted, classified, bred, rebred, inbred, to produce pure specimens, far beyond any concept of race. That staggered Han; back in the normal world, one hardly ever saw any person near a pure type, so mixed had people become in the course of long years and many migrations. But these were races, which, strictly speaking, had never existed. Only here. Han recalled his first sight of the warship; this was a sight which paled that into utter insignificance. Finally, mercifully, Hatha reached the end of his travels. There was more, but there was only so much one could take in at one time. The variety was staggering.

Hatha announced, "This is by no means all. We have only seen slightly more than half. But it may serve. Did you see anything that caught your fancy?"

"Oh, many, many. It is hard to choose."

"Indeed it is. That is why only the high have it. Strength and fortitude! But was there anything in particular?"

"Only one?" He had a rash thought of asking for all of them. But that would solve nothing. They wouldn't understand what he expected of them, would probably resent it, and certainly would not be able to get along with all the other breeds. The race issue had caused humans problems since the dawn of civilization, and that had risen from racial differences which were, in some cases, subtle, accidental, or even imaginary. Han could easily imagine, from that, the kinds of prejudice which one might find in artificially bred populations of pure types. But he could not know how they would act together.

"Only one."

"Well, if I must . . ." He thought back, verifying an earlier impulse. Yes. It was still true. He had seen here girls more sexually attractive, more lovely, more than almost anything. But one had possessed a quality that combined them all, and yet under the blend remained visible as a person, something more than just a body, or a face. "Of all we have seen here today, I think the one that enchanted me the most was the first one we looked at, the young female of the Zlats. The fourth class."

"Indeed? A Zlat? A fourth? You disappoint me in some ways; but in others you exhibit a refinement in taste, in which I will admit to a certain deficiency. Now, then, so be it. We shall go and conclude the arrangements. But as we go, let me tell you what I know of the breed, which I suppose is little enough. They are generally intelligent and quick, and are still occasionally used practically, for performing fine-detail work, at which they excel. The only fault here is perhaps lack of persistence, which I suppose arises from lack of practice. Also, they are affectionate and dependent, becoming tense only in situations of sexual rivalry, at which the females are as belligerent and demonstrative as the males. They are known to require considerable care, grooming, and so forth. Fourth class! You must see something I miss. But well enough—Zlats are all supple and responsive. And a fourth will lower the cost as well, for which I, with limited resources, thank you. Your taste may very well carry a component of tact, eh? Also, you will not have to compete with other prospective breeders, as a fourth would not be in great demand for breeding stock, even as a speculation."

"Does she know the nature of her award?"

"No. She does not read or write. But that will be no problem; she will be very adaptable, if what I have heard about Zlats is true. By the way, do you plan to keep her as a brood female—for breeding? Do you intend to become a Zlat fancier? If so, I would advise a better specimen, even though such advice will cost me dearly. Thus I demonstrate my altruism and camaraderie."

"Well, no . . . I was thinking of perhaps a more selfish approach . . ."

"Never mind, never mind, my young buck! No confidences! I understand perfectly. Ah, were I a youth again! How the juices flow! Well, then: matters shall proceed as you have chosen. Come along, now."

They went back to the area where the Zlats were displayed. Han looked for the girl again, but most of the specimens had retired for the night, apparently, to the closed-off portion in the rear of the stalls. It seemed that a very long time had passed—Han became conscious of the passage of time again; he realized that he had completely lost track of time while they had been in the exhibition. After a lengthy search, Hatha was able to locate the manager-keeper, who was well into his years. He wrote out a note with a great flourish, and in return, the manager-keeper gave Han a folder, inside which were printed lengthy instructions regarding the care of Zlats, all written in an elaborate script and arcane breeder terminology which was far beyond Han's current level of comprehension. Then there was another form, in several copies, which the keeper-manager filled out, retaining one copy for himself; it was apparently a kind of registration. Still other paperwork appeared, which listed in considerable detail the girl's ancestry backwards for twenty or more generations, with amplified and expanded sections dealing with champions in her line of particularly high honors, and fortuitous crosses between specific lines. No doubt about it—the girl might very well have only earned a fourth place herself, but she was certainly a Zlat beyond any shadow of doubt. Han looked through the wild squiggles of the letters, and finally pointed to one.

"Is this her name?" Transliterated, it probably would have taken forty characters to spell out.

"Only in a sense," answered Hatha. "That is a registration name. We would not use that in speaking with the girl herself; she wouldn't recognize it as having any connection with her. She wouldn't respond. Now, what do they call her, colloquially? Let me see . . . Ah! Here it is. Usteyin. That's her name."

"Does she talk?" Han felt completely insane as he asked the question.

"Oh, yes, indeed. Speak slowly, clearly, as with a child."

The party returned to the area where the Zlats were on exhibition, finding the girl's cubicle without difficulty. The keeper-manager, Han could see, was concerned for, and even fond of, his charges, and would brook no mistreatment. As they went, the ancient ler admonished Han vigorously and definitely as to care, exercise, diet and kindness.

"These Zlats are a sensitive lot! But treat them right, and they are wonders, absolute paragons. They can do almost anything, except, of course, feats involving gross strength. I myself prefer the Haydars. Noble beasts, indeed!" Han remembered the Haydars well. They had been striking people. They were a lean, tall, attenuated people with olive skins, long, powerful limbs and great, bladelike noses. Their hair was oily black, dense and curly. Deeply set under heavy foreheads were sad, sad eyes whose pupils were almost completely black. Hatha had told him that they were hunters and trackers. It was only later that Han began to wonder what it was the Haydars had tracked and hunted, on this planet with no native animal more highly evolved than oversized toads. Of course . . .

The girl Usteyin was indeed asleep. Han watched her for a moment, repressing an urge to gather her up, embrace her on the spot. But she was a stranger, completely, more of a stranger than Liszendir. Her form was girly, attractive, familiar. But she was a highly cultured product of a society more alien than anything of either Han's or Liszendir's societies. She lay in a small bed in the back of the enclosure, wrapped up in a soft, light blanket. It looked hand-woven. Her mouth was slightly open; she was breathing deeply, slowly, and apparently was dreaming of some pleasant circumstance, for a soft smile was drifting across the oval, exquisite face, the rosy, pursed mouth. Something tugged at his mind, something about the face. He couldn't place it. Han signaled the keeper to wait to awaken her until the dream was over. Presently she shifted position. An idle thought flashed through his mind, a remark of the classical writer, Durrell—"unfair to watch a sleeping woman."

The keeper woke her up, gently. At first, she seemed frightened, as Han expected she would, by the numbers of people in her cubicle, but the keeper patiently explained what had transpired, and as he did, she relaxed, brightened up, and even became excited and animated. Han resisted an impulse to go completely mad; this lovely creature was actually happy to be sold. She asked, timidly, of him, if she could take her few little things with her. He agreed, heart pounding.

While she gathered her few belongings up, the complicated gadget or thingamabob, a small pillow, the blanket, a small bag, presumably of toilet articles, the keeper divulged some more information about the breed.

"Now, these Zlats: records only go so far back, but with these we have accurate records farther back than most. They are one of the oldest types, and their roots go back almost to the beginning, the first humans on Dawn. They, like us all, have had their ups and downs. But for the most part, they are rather docile—she will not try to escape. You must treat her with care: her bones are fragile and will break, if she is handled too roughly. She will also need some protection from the worst airs, and considerable grooming. There is a good description in the papers I gave you, but they do not ever capture the dimension of one's responsibilities."

Han thought about the remark about not trying to escape. No, he could see that easily enough. Escapees would have been hunted, and he did not care to speculate upon their fate. So they would learn, over the years and generations, that escape was not an option for them. No out. They would develop a peculiar outlook, a psychology, which no other creature would have: they could not escape—but would have to face things as they came. He looked back to the girl, who was happy, excited. She had rolled her possessions into a neat ball, and stood quietly, waiting. Han reached to her, took her hand, the first female human hand he had touched, it seemed, in years, centuries. It was soft, delicate, warm; the nails were exquisitely manicured. She followed them quietly back to the shuttle.

Outside, it was completely dark, for night had fallen. Han again thought of the passage of time: they had been in the exhibition a long time—it must be very late. A snowstorm was trying to start up, blowing gusts of fitful, dry, gritty snow. As they walked to the shuttlecraft, he noticed that her teeth were chattering. He took her blanket, a soft, delicate thing much larger than it seemed, unrolled it, and wrapped her in it, while she looked at him with wide-eyed wonderment. He looked down at her bare feet, as finely formed as the rest of her, leaving footprints in the new snow. Her toes were red with the raw cold. She did not complain.

In the shuttle, Han suddenly felt the weight of fatigue begin to fall on him, a heavy curtain, a fog. Through this fog, he heard Hatha, vaguely. Hatha was telling him that he should busy himself with his new pet and get to work on the procedures to be followed by the watch aboard the *Hammerhand*. At the hetman's headquarters, Hatha conducted them to a set of rooms, comfortably furnished, and departed.

10

"Civilization is a thing which man does not really want; it is also a thing for which he can demonstrate no clear-cut requirement. Therefore, by the most simple and innocent probings, we are brought to those disturbing and terrible questions which always seem to begin with 'why . . .' "

—Roderigo's Apocrypha

"You may expect everything or nothing, as it suits you, but both are equally false. Only one thing true—something will happen to you; events are imperishable.

—'l Knun i Slam (The Doctrine of Submission)

SEVERAL OF THE short and dark days of the winter of Dawn passed, while Han tired to accommodate himself to his new reality; a task which was complicated greatly by the fact that he did not know very well what reality he should try to adhere to. He tried to examine his present context in the light of past experiences and found that impossible—the past would not fit the present, and neither would engage with any future he could imagine. Most of this was engendered by the quiet and almost unnoticeable presence of the girl, Usteyin, for she, as nothing else, reminded him of how far his adventure had diverged from his original position.

What had started as a relatively simple journey had become impossibly complex, a total wilderness in which issues of morality, emotion, loyalty and the very personality were all blown this way and that. So long as the flow of events had been simplex and serial, as he and Liszendir became drawn deeper and deeper, farther and farther out, he had maintained some balance. But now, it all returned. His system, he realized, had been jury-rigged and jerry-built. Or was it jury-built and jerry-rigged? He knew the ancient formula, but he could not get it straight. He suspected that it did not really make any difference. So, with the undeniably human girl, he came back to the roots of things. To a reality. But it was a reality that made no sense.

As for Usteyin, she had installed herself with a minimum of fuss and was indeed as advertised, docile, quiet and neat. Han was mystified by her in several ways—for although a young girl, barely adult, if that, she was completely self-sufficient. She had a sense of self-possession that was beyond anything he had ever seen or heard of. He thought that if by some chance he could maroon Usteyin on some obscure asteroid, she would continue her routine until her supplies gave out, and face the void calmly, as if it were nothing more remarkable than awaking from a nap. He had watched her as she slept; she slept like an animal, lightly, with little movement. She dreamed, for he could watch the changes of expression moving over the exquisite face, but they moved with a slow, steady rhythm that resembled no one he had known. She had a reserve and a sense of self-discipline that made Liszendir look like a wild barbarian by comparison. She responded to Han directly, without artifice or mannerism, speaking in simple, short sentences, in a girl's clear voice, but one which was absolutely steady. Whatever she thought she was, she was absolutely sure of it. Perhaps she really did think of herself as nothing more than an animal, a pet, a breed. But he could not tell—she was completely opaque and revealed nothing. Han could thank Liszendir for teaching him that such behavior was indicative of depth, just as overly demonstrative behavior was indicative of great shallowness. If this was true, the girl Usteyin was an ocean.

As he saw more and more of her, he became more convinced of his original impression of her—she did have a mind-wrenching beauty, and was as different from Liszendir as any living person could be, and still remain a person. He visualized Liszendir as a picture in monotone. A picture in great detail, a picture filled with a thousand details, highly erotic and suggestive in the mind of even more than the body could accomplish. But Usteyin was something done in full, broadband color, a dazzling figure whose brightness concealed—something, everything. He viewed the prospect of any further relationship with her with misgivings. So, indeed, had he been advised to take his choice, and so he had done. He could not see any materially different result; and the few days only served to allow him to realize the depth of the problem. And he did have a problem. Owning her had been as simple as just asking. But in reverse proportion to what he really wanted of her, he felt as if he had set an impossible task upon himself—for to truly possess her as he wished, now, he would have to know her, and she would have to know him.

Han considered cultural shock, but as a meaningful symbol it fell far short of the reality. Already, there were subtle hints that within her, a delicate balance was being upset, slowly, to be true, but nevertheless, upset, completely. He had come to want her more than any other girl or woman he had known, but he did not want it at the price of ruining her forever, by destroying the very basis of her intangible appeal.

He considered that a person who had never had any money could suddenly become rich, through a lottery, or some similar circumstance. Likewise, a farmer could move to the city; a person from a backward and rude planet could arrive on a developed and sophisticated one. But all those were of one range. The next level down was that of a slave become a freedman, or perhaps a responsible member of society. Then, below that, was Usteyin, who did not even think of herself, as well as Han could determine, as a person.

This was doubly ironic, he realized, because as a result of the heavy bombardment of charged particles Dawn received periodically, when the planet's magnetic field reversed polarity, the renegade ler who ruled most of Dawn were sinking, losing abilities, and some of the humans were undoubtedly advancing, or at least holding their own. Han strongly suspected that given equal conditions, Usteyin was probably vastly more capable and intelligent than even the better Warriors. He could pursue more paradoxes—for in comparing Usteyin with Liszendir, he could see that Liszender, while denouncing civilization, was completely civilized, and Usteyin not. Yet in another sense, if civilization was an exercise in self-control, then it was Usteyin who was the furthest along of all of them.

A pet. But a highly refined pet. One did not hitch a thoroughbred horse to a plow, nor did the lapdogs of a previous age pull carts and sleds. She was not a drudge, a scullery maid, or a concubine. It had been the most quixotic of hopes to take her at all. And to maintain such a self-view required a balance equal to that of the finest chronometer. He feared damages to his own ego, if he treated her in error; but he feared even more for her, if he tried, too abruptly or too coarsely, to turn her into a human being, a person, overnight. And he found that the longer he had her in his presence, the more he wanted just that: she would do something to his life forever.

He was suspicious of the word "love." So he had been, long before, and since Liszendir, doubly so. She had been right, of course—there were an unnumbered quantity of things, states, relationships that all fell, in human society, within the large expanse covered by the symbol. It was as if someone asked if the city Boomtown were located in the universe! But he saw in himself a continuum here, beginning with a native selfishness and an idle concern for sensual pleasures, which had been fun, never regret it. But he had reached a deeper level with Liszendir, a mutuality that was far different. And with Usteyin, he could sense, somewhere out of sight, a deeper sense of commitment, in the same degree of logarithmic scale. It did not change or degrade anything which had passed between himself and Liszendir. He realized with a sudden pang that it indeed was past-tense, now. Rather, it brought it into more meaning.

His mind went off on another tangent: what about the other *klesh*, any of them, the Zlats, the Haydars, and the Marenij, who resembled the Zlats in build, but who were slightly taller and who had gold-olive skins and fine, silky, pale-blond hair. The girls had been breathtaking, simply unbelievable. He had read the material in the folder, eventually deciphering it out: the Warriors who were fanciers of *klesh* thought that they were, by breeding, working back to the original human types. But you could not work backwards this way, and they had instead created, unwittingly, several hundred types of races, each with its own strengths and shortcomings. Han had no doubts that immeasurable harm had been done in the weeding process over thousands of years. But it had also brought some qualities into piercing, burning focus; all the *klesh* would have to have something to survive. And from what he had seen, the Zlats were the furthest along of all. If they all could only be brought back into the common stream of humanity . . .

As for Usteyin herself, she seemed content in her new home. He had no idea what her old one had been like. She gave no indication of sadness at leaving her past, whatever it had been. She was clean, fastidious, neat, and took care of herself with the seriousness of some ancient courtesan, although much of the effort she expended was, at second glance, completely asexual in nature, and very probably served to pass time. She had a small bag of toilet articles, a comb, a simple brush, a miniature file, a crude toothbrush. She spent the days grooming herself, sleeping, or occasionally manipulating the gadget that looked like a tangle of fine silver wires. More rarely, she sang quietly to herself, aimless and endless songs in a dialect Han could not follow. In these times she seemed to be oblivious to everything, withdrawn into some private universe whose dimensions only the Zlats knew, and perhaps only she knew them accurately. Han let her sleep and make herself comfortable when and where she would; at night, she curled up in the corner by his bed. And slept lightly, for many times he was awakened by a sudden noise, or a shout from outside, and looking about in the darkness to locate the source of whatever woke him up, he would glimpse in the corner, the sheen of her eyes, wide open. But in a moment, the sound of her breathing would become audible and regular again. As soon as he realized what he wanted with her, he wanted to begin immediately, but thought it best, for the present, to let her establish a routine comfortable to her before he started trying to unravel the fabric of probably six thousand standard years of intensive breeding and an ingrown, introspective culture; and a score of years on her own.

He had not been able to locate Liszendir, or find out anything about her, during the days in which he and Usteyin were left to themselves, and he had begun to worry about her. But finally she appeared. His feelings were mixed—relief that she was present and in seemingly good shape, and acute embarrassment over the presence of Usteyin. But he could sense in her eyes as she came in that whatever had been between them, it had now evolved into something different, and there was no jealousy in it. Rather, something comradely responsible. Han followed the hint closely, for he felt the same way.

"I have come because we can meet and talk more freely now. I have some interesting information. Apparently, we are now to be trusted somewhat by these clods; I am doing what I can. They think I am teaching them great secrets, but in reality, I am only giving them beginner's-level exercises. I feel guilty, because they will be deadly enough here, but it will be child's play if they try to use it back in a ler civilized place. Some of them, it is true, have a high degree of native skill, but it seems to be caught by accident and personality and circumstance. Hatha, for example, is not a member of a class, but an individual in his skill, which by the way increases my professional regard for him, though I detest him and everything he stands for, just as before.

"Also, Han, your behavior at the *klesh* exhibit was a factor in this. Hatha was astonished! He actually respects you! It is the talk of the camp. So here I am. I came to tell you to stay on the course you have chosen. And to see the girl."

Han called Usteyin. She appeared shortly, and stood quietly, obediently, while Liszendir looked her over carefully. Now that he could see the two of them together, it reinforced his impression about Liszendir being monotone, monochromatic, while Usteyin was something in color. But there were other differences now apparent. Usteyin was slightly smaller in size than the ler girl, and considerably more delicate in structure, yet through some process Han could not fathom, she seemed to be the stronger of the two. It was Liszendir who had to exert some effort to keep her face expressionless.

Finally, she spoke. "I understand completely. In a house full of everything you could desire, you chose better than you know. She is far more than a pretty face, a young body, even though even to my eyes she is lovely. And you and I know how it must be with us. No bitterness. No recriminations. You must do this thing, for it has been set long before you ever saw me at Boomtown."

"It is a thing I have wrestled with deeply, Liszendir," he said, avoiding her eyes, still as full and liquid gray as they had been in the bright sunlit room where he had first seen Liszendir Srith-Karen.

"I know what you feel. But you must not project traditional human emotions, out of what one of your Boomtown secretaries might think, seeing you with some new lover, onto me. I feel no jealousy or envy. I wanted you to do this, and I know that were things reversed, I could not have done so well. Indeed, I feel as Hatha; in Boomtown, my first impression was of a lazy human fool, I see deeper now. Our peoples misunderstand much about one another; we should get back together somehow. It has been too long."

Han did not say anything. She went on, "You will save this one, she will be your life, and you will come back, or send back for the others. I see this. I visited the *klesh* exhibition also. It was disgusting—not the people themselves, but in how they came to be where they are, and what they are. But every human on Dawn is worth it. As for me, I have not found one ler on the whole planet I would lift a finger for. They are both inferior and evil—let them devolve back into the chaos and bestiality they deserve."

"I did as you suggested, and as I felt the pressure to act. It was like feeling the cleavage in a piece of wood. I knew which way lay the grain, and which way lay the knots. I must have learned how to think that way from you."

"You did well, completely. You know that you were not being rewarded; you were being tested. And in passing it as you did, you have astounded Hatha so much that we now have room to move about."

"Liszen, I have not forgotten . . ." At the use of her lovename, he thought he saw a quick shadow flit across her face.

"Nor have I. Nor will I ever. But you know we could not spend our lives together, that I must someday weave with others. I want to; even when you were within me, I knew what I would have to do. Even your name was an omen. It means 'last,' in the mode of the power of the water, which governs the emotions. I can tell you that, now. You know ler too well to have anything like that concealed any longer. And she? She should be obvious to you, even if you are not trained in such things. Look at her color: red hair. She is powerful in the air elemental, she radiates it, she is a living spirit of the power of events, the onrush of things. I am Liszendir-the-fire, a creature of the will, but it is so strong in her that she would blow me out like a candle. She is small and fragile, but she bears the weight of the universe behind her.

"So, now, Han. You know what must be, with me. You knew long before you asked me if ler kissed. So would you stand outside the *yos* of my braid and bay at the moon? No. And I would not stand outside yours either. And if I can help with what will be your most difficult task. I will. Ask it of me, for what we made between us with our bodies was *hodh*, and afterwards we are closer than parent and child. Will you have enemies? Let them tremble in the night, for I will lay hands of fire upon them. And wilt thou lovers? Then I will warm them with my heart as I once warmed you. It is all now far beyond what you call love and sex."

She turned and left.

Han turned to Usteyin and looked at her for a long time. He regarded elementals as rank superstition, but there was an undercurrent of sense in what Liszendir had been saying, something which could not be denied, however rationally one pursued it. Usteyin finally spoke. It was the first time he had heard her speak directly to him, in confidence. Her voice was lower, and had a slightly throaty quality.

"Who is that lady?"

"She came here with me. From another world."

"Did she own you?"

"No. We were both wild." He had to use the word. There was no word for "free" in the distorted ler Singlespeech of Dawn.

"I fear her greatly. Females as cruel. She is warm one way, I see that, she has known love, but in another, she is cold, like ice, like the wind of the south, now. Like the darkness out of the south. She came before you, to the place of show. I thought then she must be from some far place. She looked at me with hardness, with eyes of wands."

"Usteyin, what do you want?"

"Want? I do not understand."

"Desire. Ambition. Need. Before you were in the show." He paused. "Plans. Hopes."

"I . . . want to have some honor, that I may mate. If not that, a kind home, where there are people who will treat me well, even feel warmth, protection." She paused, thinking. "But I know from the way the people acted when they were deciding who was best that I did not fare well."

"Is that all?"

"All? Is there more? To have hope, an alien thing, one must be either of the people or the wild. I am neither. I would see that my life is good as it unfolds, but I am prepared that it be otherwise. There is no past, no future. Those are things-not-real which unwild creatures tangle themselves into."

"They told me you were not high, this show, but of what I saw, I wanted you more than anything else. Above all."

"Above females nearer to yourself?"

"Yes."

"Then I am happy. It is good to be wanted, even more to want, and find that which is yours."

"What do I look like to you?"

"When I saw you first, I was very surprised; wild *klesh* never come. I thought you were a person from far away. But I saw your hands, your face, the fear on it. What was that from? You are *klesh*, even as I, yet you must be a great one, just so, to walk with the people as one. *Mnar*, I thought, but I saw then that it could not be so. You look like them a little, but only at first."

He could not explain everything. Not yet. She waited a moment, then continued.

"Sometimes we see wild ones. There were many, not so long ago. I did not meet any myself, but I heard tales. It was very hard on them; they pined, they languished, they refused to eat. Many fought constantly, and some were killed. What do the people wish of you? Will they mate you?"

"No, I don't think so, at least not the way you mean. They wanted to, at first, I think, the fat one who was with me. But later he changed his mind. He said I was too close to the wild to be of any value to any breeder. No demand. They can get all the wild ones they want, here. I work for him. He was pleased, and so gave you to me as a present."

"Me?"

"Yes."

"Will you let me mate? I desire it very much." She said the last with a coy glance from under her eyelashes in a mannerism that was something more than a flat statement. To be sure, he wanted her—but he had hoped to put the issue off for some time, start changing her first. He realized that he should have known better. She had seen through all that with insight, and had gone directly to the point. He decided to be honest, and step ahead.

"I had hoped to win you for myself. Perhaps not immediately, but when you wanted, later. For a long time."

She did not answer him, but instead looked downwards to the floor, shyly. He looked at her eyelashes: they were long, feathery, the same deep coppery color as her hair. Suddenly she became, without doing anything, very desirable. Her posture relaxed imperceptibly, suggesting confidence, submission. Han felt his hold on his old resolves growing slippery, hard to hold. The moment was now, approaching like a thunderbolt.

Han said, softly, "I wanted to wait, because I didn't know if you would want me, or one of your own kind more."

She looked up, demurely, her eyes moist and shining under her lashes, her mouth soft. "Another Zlat would have been fine. But you are beautiful to me, because of your strangeness, because of something I saw in you when you looked at me there, the first time. Something I have known only in stories, not something I would expect to see. Why did you not speak of this earlier?"

She stood quietly, looking into nothing, expectant. Han could see the pulse in her fine, slim neck. It was racing. He turned and locked the door. When he turned back to Usteyin, she reached up, hesitantly, and stroked his beard, softly, tenderly, her eyes glassy. Han felt fire. He could not speak now, and he knew that he could not even begin to say, "No, later." Whatever was coming, let it come, he thought, feeling his own pulse going up, feeling the light-headedness, the sense of falling without vertigo. He touched the clear, creamy skin, brushed against her dense, fragrant hair. Time changed to Usteyin's concept of itself: it ceased to exist.

Usteyin was a complete beginner in lovemaking, knowing almost nothing. She was artless and seemed to be guided only by the things she felt, and tales she had heard. It was, in fact, difficult for them at the first, for as Han recalled, she was "unbred," to use the phrase of the *klesh*-breeders of Dawn. But she made up the lack of knowledge and experience with a naive enthusiasm, and an ability to learn, which Han found to be both disarming and disturbing. He treated her with tenderness and patience, and she responded with a fierceness and an immediacy; Usteyin could not live for maybes or laters. She lived now, and it was reach it now first. Other times would be other times. Foreplay, apparently, was another of the things she knew nothing of. That, for her, now consisted, so it seemed, of a few fleeting gestures. Then to work. The spirit of it was not one of selfish gratification, but one of the fear that it would never be again, and so it was to be experienced to the fullest. He thought afterwards, as they lay close together, that she had volumes to learn, and that he would enjoy being the instructor.

She made a motion to return to the corner where she made her bed, but Han stopped her gently, asking her to stay where she was, close to him. Wordless, she curled close beside him, seeming almost to glow in the dark from some inner sense of happiness. It was something beyond her wildest dreams. As he moved his shoulder to make room for her, he winced. However delicate and fragile she looked, it was not apparent within an intimate embrace; she was both violent and strong. At the height of her own feelings, her muscles had rippled like hot wires. And she bit. He gingerly felt new tender spots along his neck and shoulders. He winced again. Yes, that had been in the sheaf of instructions, too. Zlats were passionate.

When he awoke, it had become dark, and was late at night, the long night of the Dawn Winter. The lamp was on, and under it, Usteyin was combing out her hair. She sat in her corner, her blanket draped over her legs. The lamplight cast golden planes on her skin, rippling fiery highlights in her hair. She noticed immediately that Han was awake, and looked to him expectantly, then away, in the shy, submissive gesture he had seen her make before. But now he knew what it meant.

She said, her voice soft, "You and I, we must do that often, as much as we can. I am afraid they will take us apart. I expect it. But I would have this last forever."

Han watched the girl, and did not speak, for some time. He found himself feeling much the same, and he could not explain it to himself; but however it was, this girl had become priceless, the end of all searching. There was no reason for it—it simply was, and he knew, from long before Liszendir, that a love (however broad and meaningless the word was in general usage) which could be explained wasn't much of a love at all. If you could say "Because . . ." then it was already over, a thing of the past. He said to her, "So I would have it too. What do they normally do when it is just two Zlats, your own kind?"

"We stay together only long enough for the girl to conceive. Sometimes days, sometimes weeks. But not long. But with you and me, I don't know . . . they did not put us together to breed more Zlats, so it could be shorter or longer. Who knows what they want of us?"

Han felt icy. The Zlats, and all the rest, were pets! They would be very fertile, bred for it. And no contraceptives; they would be light years away. He had forgotten, in his long time with Liszendir, when they didn't have that problem. He looked closely at Usteyin again, sitting quietly under the lamp; the exquisite figure, the deep, thoughtful sea-green eyes, the spirit, the strong emotions . . . no. He was sure. He would see this thing through to its ultimate end, whatever came. He felt a sudden surge of possessiveness, something alien to him. Yes, he thought. To the end. In civilization, on Dawn, or in Hell.

"Usteyin, we have much to do."

"I know."

"Not only more than you know, but more than you can know, right now," he said, paraphrasing Haldane's law. "But aren't you hungry? Come on. I will find something for us."

Her reaction was not what he expected. "You would share your sleep with me? Your food?" she asked suddenly, and began crying. He went over to her and put his arms around her, saying nothing, letting her calm down of her own accord and at her own pace. Even such simple things as that were more alien to her than she could be to him. Or so he thought, at least for the present. Again, he reflected that he had a lot to learn, as well. She calmed down quickly, showing the same speed of realization and readjustment that she had displayed before.

"Now I understand more. We are people, you and I, in the place where you are from. Not them. You see me that way, not as an unwilling Zlat, or any kind of Zlat. Do you want that? They will probably kill us when they find out." She said the last bluntly, unemotionally.

"Yes, just that. We are people. Back in my place, the world is filled with people, just like us. There are no *klesh* there. We are the people."

"I . . . I fear that greatly. I cannot see it. I am afraid of the wild."

"It is not all that wild. Better than the people here have."

"Then you must tell me, and I will understand. About a place where the *klesh* are people. I have heard this tale before, in parts, but I did not believe. That is the kind of thing that we tell ourselves in our stories. Thus, have some of the wild females talked, sometimes in words I did not understand at all."

"That is *klesh* speech from the other place. Our speech. There are many different ways of speech."

She laughed. "So you think. Many, all different, like the *klesh* here, but I know that we are all the same under the skin, and so I know that however we wish to say our needs, so it can be understood by all, with a little trying." Then she suddenly became serious again. "But you must return me, send me back. I do not think I can do this thing. I will fail you. Send me back, now, while the desire is still deep in your eyes. I do not wish to see the other."

"The other?"

"The anger you will feel when you discover that I cannot follow you, that I will be too weak."

"Oh, no. You will do well." He was not saying it to calm her fears, her sudden loss of confidence. It was true. Han had never met any creature that learned as fast, adjusted as fast. It was almost as if she had nothing to reject, which was probably quite close to the truth, at least as much of it as he could see, as much as anyone could see. "Come, now. Share food. We will talk. You first. Tell me everything."

"Everything?"

"All of it. I want to know."

"And you will give me your everything in return?"

"As much as you can take."

"There is darkness and the night in your words, behind your eyes. But I will come, and I will take it, gladly, for this is a thing far beyond even the make-believe stories of the Zlats."

Somehow, he had imagined that she might eat with her fingers, but she did not, using the utensils with deft accuracy. Familiarly. But she ate fast. She said, "Food is a serious thing. That is why I was surprised you would share, even after what we had done. It would not be thus with a Zlat male. We are always hungry."

"You must keep a little of that. If you eat too much you won't be pretty any more."

"Ugh. Yes, I have seen a few fat *klesh*. They are not so pretty."

After they finished, Han gave her a cup of hot beer, which she sniffed at suspiciously. She said, "There is people magic in this. It is forbidden."

"I know. It is good, and it is not forbidden any more, to us. Not to you, now."

"Do you really mean to keep me, yourself, always?"

"Yes, I do, if you will stay."

"You would let me choose?"

"Yes. Not here, but in my own land, my country. You will be free there, even of me, if you wish it, though it pains me to offer it to you."

"It is no matter. I will not exercise such a choice, either here or there. I have only one life to live, I only want one such a love as this. It is so much more . . ." She stopped and thought for a moment. "Besides," she said, with a flash of sudden shrewdness, "we are not there yet."

"That is so. Now we wait. Tell me now of the Zlats. Everything. Come, let us sit together."

She joined him, sitting closely beside him. At first she began hesitantly, as if she were revealing deep secrets, but gradually the hot beer worked on her inhibitions, and the tale began to unfold.

It was a simple story, really, and they had forgotten much. The way Usteyin told it, before there had been chaos, in which humans were as wild as any other creature. The people, the ler, came, and set things in order, then producing the breeds. It was a narrow, narrow world, but within its limits it was relatively secure. She knew that there were still wild humans, but she did not envy them. She had never even thought deeply about it before.

The Zlats, of course, were the only breed she knew well. They seemed, to Han's ears, somewhat more advanced and sophisticated than most of the others, but even then, they had so little of what might have been called culture that he could not compare them to any society he knew. They were something even below slaves, and were not used to any practical purpose. They did not have religion, nor did they have any sort of underground. Keeping them separated for most of their lives, over thousands of years, had ensured that there would be none of that. They bred only when allowed to have a few days together, and the rest of the time they were carefully segregated. Children were raised by their mothers, and after a certain age the boys were raised by the males. Usteyin knew about sex, about the love of the parent for the child; and

she knew many stories about men and women, but they were not real—
they were for the quiet times only.

That was what the tangle of wire was for: it was actually a mechanism which could be put into an almost infinite number of possible
arrangements and configurations. Those, and the way light fell on it, and
the motions she used to set it, were all elements of a symbolic system,
probably closer to an abacus than anything else, but it was a system that
coded relationships, emotions, events and desires, whole realities. She
could tell to herself an infinite number of stories on it, learning the
proper motions and settings from others, when they had their rare personal contacts. She was proud of the one she had, for she had made it
herself, when she had been young. The word she used, however, was
"grown." She had grown it. But she was afraid of it, too. "You use it too
much, the story-block, and it catches your mind. You stay down there,
in the wires and the beads; no one can get you out of a story-block, except yourself."

The only other thing she did was a hand-weaving, by an unusual
method which did not use a loom. Her blanket was as fine a thing as
Han had ever seen. It was her only item of property, so to speak, and
was both cover, house or place, and clothes, when the weather required them.

She knew about the other kinds of *klesh*, but in an odd and abstract
way. She would have said more, but she began to grow sleepy, and like
most of her kind, when she reached a certain degree of drowsiness, she
simply went under, like a lamp being blown out. Han carried her to the
small bed, placed her in it, and covered her up with her own blanket.
As she settled into her new position, a soft smile grew on the delicately
formed face, and she murmured something in her sleep, too quietly for
Han to hear. He was not sleepy, not just then, and turned away to think.

Han reflected on Usteyin. She lived, exactly in the present. She did not
measure herself, as did Liszendir, by a set of traditions, or like a civilized
human, by an unconscious set of cultural values, but solely by an unknown sense of interior balance. Han could see that she did this: he
could not see how that interior balance was structured, and he imagined
that he would never be able to glimpse it, even for a moment. To grasp
it, one would have to strip off all civilized values, then program oneself
to think of a personal image something more than a wild animal, but

less than a slave, for at least slaves had functions, duties, and contributed something, even if that something was unwilling support of the rest of the society.

But she was fully human, not ler, and not an animal. And as such, she had vast reserves of curiosity, of mind, which would be used for something. So far, all he had seen was her incredible flexibility. Liszendir had made Han partly ler as far as she could, to make herself comprehensible to him. Usteyin simply absorbed everything, integrated it, and pressed on in her eternal present.

Abandoning that train of thought, he picked up the folder concerning the care of the Zlats, and read the crabbed characters until his eyes burned. After a bout of struggling with the boring expostulations, the overaccurate language, the many injunctions, he finally felt sleepy, and turned out the lamp, getting into bed beside the sleeping girl, warm and soft in complete trust and relaxation. He thought about her in relation to all others he had known. He was no stranger to girls, not at all. But there was something different here, some inner essence that the others had simply not had. Her beauty was manifested in body, face, skin, carriage. Yet for all of that, it was not a mask to hide something less inside, but something which escaped from the inside despite all the limitations the physical body placed on such expressions. There was something sweeter just out of reach. Was it her scent, disturbingly like a child's? No, something abstract. Something about time. Time. Wife? Lover? Family. Children. Red hair and furred lower legs . . . almost under. Time. Sense of time. Children.

Then his eyes opened wide. He had it. The answer. He knew who was manipulating the Warriors. And why. And all the proof required would be a few answers from Hatha. Simple questions. It was all so clear. And for an instant, invisibly tiny, unmeasurable in time, he glimpsed a fraction of the reality that was Usteyin. He slept.

We have learned one thing about nature: that it is a great generalizer—it forces its component parts to be multiplex or perish, all in degrees commensurate to their ability to influence other parts around them. Artificial things do not show this trait; and this applies to the living as well as to the nonliving, if you prefer that level of distinction. So it is that within a narrow range of specifications, we ler are indeed superior to the old people, the humans. Yet one cannot escape the weight of evidence—whole for whole, ler and human are approximately equal—different, not better or worse in either case. No ler surprises a human, after the initial shock of acquaintance, but humans continually surprise ler, just as they do each other. We prefer our own carefully structured society. But we, I assure you, stand in considerable awe of people who live closer to chaos than do we, and do not fear it, as we do very much.

—Klislangir Tlanh

HAN SOON BEGAN to be worried about Usteyin, and Liszendir as well. If his guess was anywhere near correct, even partially correct, they were all in great danger, much greater than anything Hatha could do to them. In fact, he was beginning to feel a certain pity for Hatha and the whole crew of the Warriors. They, in fact, were being used, and much of their potential for future evil was reduced by the same amount. And, to continue, if the suspicion was right, then they were a disposable tool as well.

He countered these thoughts with reminders of the miseries. Hatha had caused with his vainglorious raids—the broken families, the sundered friends, the deaths, the appalling view one had to take, to survive at all, once on Dawn. And the meteoric bombardment was a horror beyond most weapons, for realistically, it could be used only against populations. A terror weapon, solely. Aving's cold remarks about livestock, and of course the history of the Zlats, and all the other *klesh*. If by magic he could forget the rest of the universe, judging solely from Dawn, he would have to agree with Liszendir's fierce condemnation of the Warriors—let them fall to their fates, except that he would attempt to get the humans off the planet first. But conditions were not like that, and there was the issue of the real villains, who would have to be neutralized before they could do anything, because he was sure that whoever and whatever they were, they had the means to eliminate any threat from the Warriors, should one appear. One did not, however advanced, work on nuclear weapons without fail-safes, and to manipulate a whole culture was potentially even more dangerous. To do what must be done here, he would need both ships and Hatha's cooperation. And he would have to do it without Liszendir. And he would have to get it quickly, for he had heard rumors among the guard staff to the effect that recruiting was now going on for a new and more extensive adventure than any they had previously had.

Again, he set out, looking for Hatha throughout as much of the rambling quarters as he could move around in; but he looked in vain, and found no trace of him. Hatha was gone, and apparently so was Liszendir. After wasting the greater part of the day with guards and clerks who either knew nothing or would admit to nothing, Han finally located a subordinate of the hetman's who still possessed a little initiative, who agreed after considerable persuasion to send a recall out by heliograph. But he could not promise that it would be answered. "The hetman," he said, "comes and goes as he chooses." Han gritted his teeth with impatience; it might take days to find him, and what he had to do could not be done with anyone else. The rest of the ler Warriors around Hatha neither trusted Han nor would they pay any attention to him whatsoever. Why should they, he reflected. Han, like Usteyin, was not a person. He was, in fact, now no less a pet than the girl.

He returned, enthusiasm blunted, to the little quarters where Usteyin waited. As Han came into the room, he saw her sitting quietly in her corner, as he had come to think of it, going through her morning routine: a thorough combing-out of the fine, copper-colored hair, to be followed by a short nap. He went over to her and settled down beside her. We will, he thought, still have some days left together; and then, either many more, or none at all. He touched the girl's hair lightly.

"Show me how to do this, with that." He pointed to the little comb, seemingly undersize, which she used so expertly. Usteyin slowly handed it to him, a wondering expression on her face. He continued, "And I will show you some other things, which I hope will make you happy. Others . . ."

Hatha did not appear that day, nor the following one: So, having caught a moment of time, they had time to consider, to decide, and to try the feel of it on for size. It fitted them both better than either would have hoped.

As he spent more time with her, he learned something else about the girl Usteyin: she learned fast, blindingly fast, much faster even than he had suspected at first. He had a lot to expose her to, and he went slowly at first. At times she balked, or would cry in frustration, but she would recover, immediately, and they would go on. Gradually, Usteyin learned all about a world she had suddenly been born into. But if Han had worried at the first about turning the universe loose on her, it was now the other way around—he worried about turning her loose on the universe. And once it was brought out of her, into the open, she had a matter-of-factness that was even more abrupt than Liszendir's.

"So if you catch the fat one again, then we may go back to your home, to the wild-ones-who-are-people? And you want me, a Zlat, for all time you can see? Do you not have others whom you would want more?"

"Indeed I do not."

"It is a hard thing to see, for me. Your world. I will not know how to behave with decorum."

"I will show you, and you will act as you wish. Do you want this thing?"

"If you were offering to send me there alone, I would say no. But I will go with you, and I will stay. Do not fear! I have made my mind the same way you have made yours. I feel something with you I did not know even existed for creatures of the world. Only in story-blocks. But I ask one thing of you."

"Ask, Usteyin."

"Please do not make me take the hair off my legs. That is the most prized Zlat trait. I will cover myself, if that is your way, curious though it seems. Do your women not think they are beautiful, that they have to hide what they are, and then show only certain parts? Would you cut off the hair on your head?"

"No. And you can keep it. I have grown to like it, too." He stroked the fine, silky hair which covered her lower legs to the ankles. He had, he admitted to himself, indeed grown very fond of it. As he sat, absent-minded, he noticed her looking at him, expectantly, shyly.

"Now come closer to me, here. I wish to nibble on you some more," she said softly. "Of all the things we have done together, that is the sweetest."

So the days and nights passed. And he did not grow tired of her. She had aspects, sides, angles which he had not been aware of at first, but which unfolded, like some vastly accelerated recording of a plant, developing. But the day came when Hatha returned, and their time was over. Han was notified as soon as he had come back into the compound. It was suppertime, and Hatha summoned him. Han asked to take Usteyin, and to his surprise, Hatha agreed, although with a cynical leer Han found disturbing, and dangerous.

Liszendir was waiting for them, in the hall where they were to gather. Han looked at her closely: she appeared to be tired, drawn, overworked. Whatever had been happening, she was being pushed close to her limits, somehow. He did not think it was physical, but something deeper. The strain of cooperating with the Warriors was beginning to tell on her. And as far as he could see, she did not know what he thought he knew, which made this temporary cooperation much easier. And she did not have an Usteyin.

Hatha would not hear any talk until the meal was over. He was, he announced, a bit worn himself. Han restrained himself, with difficulty; but at last, the moment came. Hatha spoke.

"I see that you have done wonders with your new friend. I, too, can no longer bring myself to refer to her as a mere possession, a pet, a breed. You have undone in a few days what it took us thousands of years to do. She is now human. You will realize what this accomplishment means. She can never go back to the Zlats, or even be allowed near one again. She knows entirely too much for her scope. Yours I overlook, for it arose in an erroneous society; but hers is new, special. So if she went back, I think she would very likely become, ah, fatally unhappy with her place." It was a reminder and a threat. He was in very ill-temper, tonight.

But Han went ahead anyway. "There are many things which have been bothering me, since I came to this planet Dawn."

"Some valuable, some inconsequential rubbish." Hath scoffed.

"May I ask you some questions? I suspect something. And if I am wrong, then I will keep silent forever; but if I am right, even partly right, then you yourself will not wait for me to ask for action. You will demand it!"

"Indeed? Well, then—proceed!"

"How long ago was the *Hammerhand* built?"

"Not so very long ago. That is no secret. About twenty of your so-called standard years ago." A relay closed in Han's mental picture. Step one, verified. The rest grew brighter and clearer by a degree.

"How did this happen? Did you just think it up, or did someone suggest it?"

"It was acted upon in the great council. Some of us, who were junior at the time, thought to enlarge our scope, to assume our rightful place in the universe."

"Who brought it up?"

"As a fact, I did."

"Where did you get the idea?"

"To be more truthful than I prefer, it came from a valued associate. But it was I who acted decisively."

"And you did well. Who was the valued associate?"

"Aving, in company with his three sons." Relay two closed. The image was coming into shape fast now.

"Did you know Aving before this?"

"Ahh, this is nonsense. I grow tired. I have not been so shabbily interrogated since I was a buck."

"If you will grant me the liberty of asking a few more questions, I will do you and the Warriors a service that you will judge to be greater than Aving's."

"How could that be? You are nothing but a wild *klesh* and a prisoner. But go on a little more. A little. Only a little. Now, Aving. No, I did not know Aving, then. The position he held had been vacant, defunct. He took it over. I assumed he came up from the ler folk of the upper troughs. They are, by and large, an unassuming folk, and such ambition would be rare, but valuable. He came here."

"Did you check his origins? Do you know, personally, where he came from?"

"No. I would have no reason to. He was ler, he came to the Warriors."

"Has anyone ever seen him or his so-called sons unclothed?"

"Ridiculous and impertinent! No. Their Triad . . . No. I do not know."

"If you look as you may, you will not find one who has mated with any of them."

"That would take days. And for what? We are a restrained folk, compared to you, or to these overcivilized ler of which this girl, Liszendir, is a specimen."

"This is my suspicion: Aving is not a native of Dawn. He, if you can call him that, if his people even have sex as we know it, and gender, is very likely neither human nor ler. Check with your oversexes. They will have had no contact. Aving has set up a vile thing here; he is a spy, and worse. He is using the Warriors, your culture, to perform his own ends."

Hatha was on his feet instantly. Mad, raging. This was perilous, now, if he had not planted the tiniest seed of doubt. Usteyin already had heard his suspicions, and agreed. In fact, she had been able to fill in considerable detail. He glanced at her: she was rigid, tense, waiting. But Liszendir was just catching on. Yes! She saw it, too.

"What is it you say? Do you seek to sow dissent? I will put you in a cage! I will . . ."

"Wait! Who rebuilt the ship?"

"Guards! Guards! Here! . . . Who built the ship? That makes no difference! I will . . . Aving and his sons built it." He paused, reflecting, suddenly sober. The guards rushed in. He waved them to a halt.

"And they took it off-planet, didn't they?"

"Well, yes, after some local repairs. They said they needed weightlessness, to make the changes."

"Could you ever see the ship from the surface of Dawn?"

"No. They said they were to fly to the gas giant—the one we call Pesha. For certain tests."

"How did you explain their knowledge?"

"We accepted their word, their Warriors' words, after they had been initiated. They said that the family had been studying the holy books, the old manuals, and that they had discovered a new way out of the old. Well? We could not use it for much as it was. They seemed . . . But they were gone for a year. A Dawn year. I had not looked at this in this way before. But I fail to see, even if what you say is true, how this affects things. It makes no difference. We have the weapon, we have used it, and we can use it in the future against whomever we choose."

"Hatha, a weapon is only as powerful as the uses to which it is put, and the defenses used against it. Arrows daunt those who have none, but those with armor and shields merely laugh as they cut the archers down. Liszendir tells me that your ship once had extensive detection equipment on it. What happened to it all? I saw none, on that tour you took me on."

"They said that it was not necessary." He was still not convinced. But he was wavering.

"Listen. I will tell you something you do not know. In mine and Liszendir's ship, a little ship, which you fly manually, knowing nothing of what it can do, I could detect you long before you even were aware of my existence; and then I could inflict enough damage on yours to immobilize that monster out there. Mine and hers! And ours is the smallest one made with arms! Do you know what would happen if you took the *Hammerhand* into a real battle? They would carve you up like meat! Conquest! You fool, you'd stir up a war for someone else's profit, and pay all the costs yourself. Oh, sure, the first planet you hit, you'd probably win. But then the armed ships would come, from the other worlds, and ler ships, too, filled with warriors who give no quarter, once you use a projectile weapon against people, a planetary population. Who was it that told you to capture wild humans?"

"It was Aving . . ."

"Of course. He wanted the Warriors to be seen. Identified. Reported. As they were. Otherwise, how would anyone know the Warriors were ler? Did you know that while you were lurking around Chalcedon that Aving was back in *our* civilization, visiting?"

"When?"

"Before Liszendir and I came to Chalcedon. He made sure that the news got back, and then he killed him, Efrem."

"That's impossible. I don't understand. How could he get there? He was here, in the camp, when we left on the raid. And I commanded the only spaceship on Dawn."

"Crap. *Khashet* manure. He waited until you left, then went to his own ship, shadowed you. While you were playing around Chalcedon, he was waiting somewhere nearby, waiting for a response. Then, before you left, he returned here. He left Seabright after us. But we detected his ship decelerating for Chalcedon, so he had passed us in midflight."

Liszendir broke in wildly. "Yes! Yes! It was he who we ler did not know, who wanted only two of us to journey to Chalcedon, not a fleet!"

"We shall see if Aving will admit to this."

"No. I have a better idea. Take your guards with you, and go to my ship. We will fly, and find the anomaly I saw as we flew here. Then you will see, and then you can come back here, get the big ship, and treat it to the sting of its own lash. Only let us all stay together, now."

"And if you are wrong . . . ?"

"No, I am not! And there is more. They would incite a war, identify the tool, and afterwards see all the evidence destroyed. Do your people know how stars evolve?"

"Evolve? No. Are they not eternal?"

"Great gods of history, Hatha! Your star out there is too big. It's going to explode, and I'll bet within a few years. Before anyone could work back to this isolated planet, and uncover the truth. That would seal up the evidence for sure. Aving would know; that is why he chose this planet as a base of operations. It had everything he needed—a steerable, primitive culture, complete ignorance of the inner civilized parts of this part of the galaxy, and something which would eradicate all the evidence that anything had ever been done here. And you had a spaceship you couldn't, or wouldn't, fly. A little cosmetic surgery, small price to pay, and he was in. What he couldn't know was that the ler here were devolving into a more primitive form, from the repeated bursts of hard radiation that gets in when your planet, Dawn, reverses polarity of its magnetic field. They might have known a few things, but not that kind of detailed information, to compare, which Liszendir would see instantly, and even I caught after a little time. You talk about superior types, Hatha, but I'd be willing to bet that the Warriors are no better on the whole than the wild humans of the Leilas area, and your pets may very well be superior to you. The only thing that would keep them from taking over is the ingrained belief that they themselves are not people, but animals. How could they think otherwise? They have no native primates, or even mammals, on Dawn with which to compare themselves."

Liszendir said sadly, "It is true, every word of it. I see its sense, now. You have lost Multispeech, this I know, not just forgotten it, or let it fall into misuse. Your people are indeed devolving; you don't even know what standards are except for the physical ones you impose on your pets, like this girl, Usteyin."

Hatha's face was blank, and his only response to this sudden revelation was to turn and gaze at Usteyin. When he did speak, it was towards her, but the tone was abstracted and distant, as if he were ruminating to himself.

"I have not believed them until now, of course, but we have several legends which speak to that effect—that the people of the past were somehow greater than we are today. This is the root of our desire to annex the older worlds and bring them to the realization of the great truth. And we have other legends, too. About the Zlats, in particular. It has been said that the Zlats have supernatural powers, that they are waiting, biding their time, until the day when they shall all speak a great spell in unison and in an instant they, not the Warriors, will be the masters of Dawn. When did it arise? I cannot say. I have heard that they know something which cannot be realized until they are all together; hence comes the prohibitions about gathering more than a few together."

Usteyin looked directly at Hatha. "So I have also heard. But I can give you no knowledge of how it would be done, for I do not know myself. That has never been said. Only that we would know when the moment had come, and we would know what to do. Then. I have always felt it just a story, that we would never do it. Just a story. And win or lose here, in this, I foresee that it will not come to pass. You will escape us. But we would have treated you with some honor, for though we hated you deep inside, we were also grateful, for without the Warriors, there would have been no Zlats, no what-we-are."

Han said, "I have nothing from you to be grateful for. You have favored me, but you have brought misery to uncounted millions, and ruined your own people as well. I would wish my own revenge, therefore, but I will not have it, because there is a greater danger, and I would not see any people be used as you have here."

Hatha asked, "Everything but reason. Motivation. Why would they— if there is a they—do such a thing as this, a task which at best would take years?"

Liszendir answered, "They are probably an old race, and are now declining in numbers. They will have exhausted the energy potential of the worlds they control, and would seek others. Only they know that now they cannot conquer by force. But we both are still expanding, full of low-energy demands, since the first runaway days. They will take us who have saved, and live like lords after we have worn ourselves out fighting each other. It will be like nothing you can imagine."

"One more thing, Hatha." Han said, getting to his feet. "The gun."

"Gun?"

"The one you had on Chalcedon. Where did you get it?"

He looked like a bear at bay. He moved from one foot to the other, uncertainly, vaguely. "The air gun came with the ship!" he blurted out.

"There is one on my ship as well. Liszendir and I took it from a murdered man's room, in Boomtown, on Seabright, which you have never seen. Who put it there?" At the last, Han was shouting; the guards looked nervous, jumpy, hairtrigger. Never before had they seen Hatha, the great warlord, the hetman, addressed in such a manner. Han continued, "Go to the *Pallenber* and look in the locker in the rear of the control room."

During the last exchange, Han had been slowly moving, almost unnoticeably, imperceptibly, closer to the guards, away from Hatha. No one had noticed, except the glittering bright eyes of Usteyin. Even Liszendir was fooled.

Han asked, softly, "Can you trust these guards, who have heard what we know? How do you know who is a creature of Aving's, and who is one of yours?"

"I will have them strip, now; then . . ."

But Hatha was unable to finish what he had intended to say, just then, for one of the guards had dropped his ornamental sword and his crossbow, and was displaying one of the deadly little gas guns. Two others followed suit, almost in unison with the first. They immediately shot the other guards in the room, who were presumably real ler. As soon as they had done this, they turned to the others in the room, but it was too late, for Liszendir and Hatha had overturned some tables, and ducked behind them, knowing that however deadly the little darts might be, they had no real penetrating power. And Han had been close enough to one of the phony guards to strike him with an elbow chop, which, to Han's surprise, doubled the creature over. It appeared to have died instantly from the blow, which Han had not thought deadly. Using the fallen one as a shield, and grabbing the fallen gas gun, he shot the other before it could get a shot off. It fell, grimacing horribly and convulsing. Whatever was in those poison darts, it worked as well on the guards as it was intended to on humans and ler. From his position, he could see Liszendir's pale face, grimacing with distaste at his use of a projectile weapon. But this was no time for her mannered niceties!

By this time, which seemed to Han to have taken an eternity, but which was quite short, all of them had gotten under cover, except Usteyin, who had vanished. Where was she? Han could not go looking for her, for the remaining phony guard was hiding in the doorway, and he had them pinned down. He was screeching in a loud, piercing cry, in a language none of them had heard before, presumably calling for assistance. It was liquid, trilling, suggestive of birdsong, but in a much lower register. But it carried well. Han called out to Liszendir.

"I was right! They are not ler. They do not have a rib cage, but something like a cartilage tube. Hit them in the middle! They break there."

The remaining phony guard was still in the doorway, still screeching. Han thought desperately. That one must not get away, and we must get him, somehow, before he can get reinforcements in here. Hatha added to the din by bellowing like a bull, calling for his own reinforcements, if any of them could hear him. It probably did no good, but it added to the confusion, and lent Han some spirit. Suddenly, the trilling, liquid screeching stopped abruptly, as if cut off. Hatha continued for a breath or two, then he, too, fell silent. Han looked around, cautiously. Where the hell was Usteyin? The one guard seemed to have also disappeared. Han took a chance, and ran to the doorway. The guard was slumped backwards, behind the edge, and standing over him was Usteyin, holding one of the ornamental swords, which was dripping with a brownish fluid, rather watery, which was not blood, even though it obviously served the same function. She had wormed along the wall, gotten out of the room somehow, and stabbed the creature from behind.

Han looked at her for a moment, amazed. She looked back, and there was a feral, wild light in her eyes he had not seen before. It faded, even as he watched. He turned from her, and called to Hatha.

"Hatha, what did you do with that crossbow? The one Liszendir and I had when we came to Aving's castle. Where is it?"

"In another room, here. Three doors down, on the right. I kept it. I was going to send it back to the warship, but never got around to it."

"I'll get it. It is better than the ones your guards carried. Stay here. Strip these bodies. We will need the gas guns. Yours, too."

Motioning Usteyin back into the relative security of the room, Han made his way down the corridor to the room Hatha had indicated. His skin began to crawl. Damn! It was dark in here! How many more of them were there? He began to feel along the back of his neck the aim of a sniper. But the dart did not come. He made it to the room. There, on a table, was the crossbow, still disassembled. He picked it up, and ducking beneath the table, assembled it, cocked it, and loaded it. The quiver of iron darts was still with it. Then, hurrying back up the hall, he joined the others, who were waiting in the doorway. Together, they made their way towards the outer exit from the building. Nothing happened, until they reached the door to the outside, suspiciously standing wide open. Hatha started into the opening, but Han pulled him back. Just as he did, a sliver pinned one edge of Hatha's cloak to the frame. He returned to a hiding place, pasty-faced.

Han wriggled to the opening, lying on the floor. Outside, the winter darkness was complete, as he had expected. He could see nothing from where he was without exposing himself further. But the angle at which the dart had struck suggested a direction, just out of sight. Han motioned to Liszendir; she came up to kneel beside him.

"Can you get across this doorway, very quickly, too fast for whoever that is out there to get a good shot at you?"

She nodded assent, tensed her muscles. Han got ready. "Go!" he whispered. Liszendir flipped across the opening. A sliver of something struck the wall behind her, with plenty of room to spare. Their reactions were slow. Han thought that he could have beat their aim himself. But he saw the sniper. He took careful aim and fired. There was a howl, and a figure burst out of concealment, staggering, making a weird howling noise. Before it became completely still, another came running from the right, to help. Han recocked the crossbow he had just used, and shot the second one. This one fell silently and lay still. The other was still as well. It seemed odd. They were killers, but they died at the slightest blow, the lightest wound. He could have sworn that the wound would not have been mortal. Curious . . . He got up and ran recklessly out into the night, looking around, followed by Liszendir.

It was a clear, very cold night, without fresh snow or cloud cover; frosty starlight spattered the Pannona Plain with weak light, bluish in tone. Han caught a hurried movement out of the corner of his eye. He turned, and saw still another one of the phony guards drawing an aim on him. He bent over, falling, knowing it was his only chance. The first shot missed, and Han kept moving, trying to recock the crossbow as he went, knowing that he would probably not complete the act. No thoughts at all passed through his mind; just a sudden sharp pang. But the figure did not take advantage of this, but instead burst out of hiding, running, trying to get away. Of course! He was the last. Before Han could load and fire, the figure suddenly performed a wild somersault and sprawled on the cold ground, biting the icy dirt and convulsing into impossible, topological shapes in his frenzy. Then it gave a tremendous heave, and became still. Han looked around. Liszendir was standing, slightly behind him, with a gas gun in her hand, and in the weak, faint light, a wry expression on her face.

They looked at each other, and she said, in a low voice, "I menaced him with this, to give you time to reload. You would have gotten him, too, had he tried to shoot, because he would have had to choose between us. But instead, he tried to run. He would have gotten out of range for you. So I did the deed. All laws must be broken, at least once. There is not a single one that does not have an exception, in some circumstance. Remember what I told you about your irrational decimals being the only rational parts of the universe? Well—I have met one face to face." But however casually she uttered the words, there was a price, within her, to be paid. Now she, the cold one who had avoided passions in her youth, had broken two prohibitions. Han touched Liszendir affectionately on the shoulder. She had turned away, but she looked back. "And now I shall be known as Liszendir Oathbreaker, for all time. No one else has gone so far." Han could not answer her. Suddenly the illusion of closeness between them, which had been growing since they had boarded the ship, together at Boomtown, vanished. This was something she could not share. An edifice in Han's mind, which had seemed as solid as the mountains far to the west, turned to fog, dimmed, and vanished. Illusions, that was what they had been to each other. Phantoms. But that was what defined the deepest feelings, loyalties. Then it stablized. Liszendir receded with the speed of light, in his mind, shifting all the frequencies to the red. Then became still. She was now of the past.

Han left her, and went over to the last guard. He removed the cloak it wore; felt the body, which seemed to be losing heat more rapidly than it should, even in this cold air. He could sense some difference in the creature, but exactly what he could not determine. It looked ler-like enough, but that was probably cosmetic surgery. He pushed, experimentally at the area where the ribs would have been. It gave oddly, as if it were not bone, but a tube of cartilage, flattish, of one piece. Odd . . .

He rejoined the others, who were coming out into the open. He said, "To our ship, quickly. We can fly it over to Hatha's. We need to get both of them off-planet into space right now, before we run into any more of these."

But apparently there were no more of the creatures in the immediate area, for they had no further incidents. They made their way to the *Pallenber* without seeing any further evidence of them. Still, with as much hanging in the balance as was here now, they could not waste time, nor take any more chances. Hatha had recovered, and was in his characteristic temper, fuming and enraged. While Han was sealing and activating the *Pallenber*, Usteyin came to Han, where he was working in the control room. She was still carrying her small roll of possessions with her, and she had also kept the ornamental sword.

"I have never done such a thing, never dreamed of it, never tried to set it in the story-block. But he—that thing was trying to kill you, you more than all the rest of us, for you had found it out, and it knew that only you could find its masters. Myself—so what is termination but the end? Our regrets and pain are short; but to lose you is a price I will not pay." She was shaking and her eyes were overflowing. But she gained control of herself, and placed the sword to the side, repeating, "I have never dreamed of such a thing," half to Han, and half to herself.

Han lifted the *Pallenber* off, hoping they were making as little noise as possible, and flew rapidly over the short distance to where the *Hammerhand* sat in the frosty starlight and the silences of the winter night, grounded. Han found one of the shuttle bays open, yawning, and without hesitating, flew carefully into it and landed. Hatha was waiting at the outer lock, and they had hardly stopped when he had bolted out, running with an agility that none of them would have credited to his bulk, until they might have recalled his abilities during the first fight Han and Liszendir had had with him. It seemed that he was there, and back, before they had finished recollecting that first scene. He returned to the control room, breathing hard.

"There is only a small crew aboard, a duty watch, but it will be enough. I told them everything, and to go as it is, now." Even as he was speaking, the warship began the rumbling, rocking motion Han remembered. Hatha watched for a moment in evident satisfaction, and added, "A runner is already on the way to the rest of the senior Warriors with this tale. We must alert the camp."

Han turned to him. "Go back. Have them leave the meteors here. It will speed takeoff. Go to the place where you get more, and gather some large ones. Bigger than these. I think that these may be too small for what we will have to do."

Hatha sprang for the lock again, shouting over his shoulder, "So it is! I will tell them. We will meet them there!" Then he disappeared, reappearing after a short interval. He locked down the outer door, and said, "All is ready. They will be awaiting us. Now let us go!"

Han had the *Pallenber* ready, and without effort, they lifted off the floor of the bay, glided outside, and took to the air. Han switched the screen to ventral view, and they watched the huge bulk dwindling on the darkened plains below, until it was at the edge of visibility. Before it merged into the dark background, they could see that it was moving, hovering uncertainly, finally moving off at right angles to their course.

Once they had risen out of the steeper gradient of Dawn's gravity well, Han set an automatic course in to bring them up out of the orbital plane. Usteyin stood close by him, her eyes wide, entranced, staring at the instruments, the controls, the screen, now switched back to look into the endless night of space. Han watched her closely; what could she be thinking, how would all of this seem to her? She moved closer to him, touched her arm against his.

Hatha watched the screen for a time, also. Then he turned to Liszendir. "What he says fits together well enough. But I am still not satisfied with the reasons why these creatures from the void chose Dawn as the place to begin their aggression. You tell me why. You have odd insights into things."

Liszendir was standing towards the rear of the room. She answered, absent-mindedly at first, "Oh, I suppose they thought to start at the weakest point. You know, no one ever attacks anyone else for a reason, but because they think they can get away with it. They have reasons enough, but they are only for questioners among their own, and others. They are most assuredly not the real reasons. This is true on the individual level, on the level of tribes and nations, and between planets. True of ler, too, and I would project all sentient life forms. They doubtless think all of us primitives, but the problem in dealing with primitives is that on the average, the individuals of a primitive culture are more capable than those of the superior culture, culture differences, notwithstanding. Aving only saw mine and Han's problems, our blunders, our stumblings. He was perceptive, there, and saw far into me, and my own thoughts of lacks in my life. He thought we would bumble it up good! But the further in we got, the more we learned. You played a part, too, Hatha. We are all in a chain of causality that has not yet ended, nor whose end I can see."

Han and Usteyin were not listening too intently to the conversation. Han was, now that they were out into deep space, programming and running the detection sequence, hoping to get a more accurate position on the anomalous emissions he had seen when they were flying from Aving's castle to Hatha's camp. Usteyin watched with great attention, as the panel lights flickered on and off, many colors; while on the various screens to the side, numbers and letters appeared briefly, vanishing seemingly as fast as they appeared. Other screens displayed possible configurations, arrangements of points. Nothing seemed stable for any length of time. Occasionally, there would be a hint of a promise of something definite coming into view, surfacing out of mountains of meaningless data—facts; but nothing of any definite shape would hold, longer than a few seconds. Han explained as he went to the girl, knowing that it could not be making very much sense to her. After all, the symbols and numbers could mean nothing to a person who couldn't read and write, or count past five. After a frustrating period of time, he stood back from the panels in resignation.

"It's the same problem as before. I can definitely tell now that there is something here," he said, pointing at various indicators, meters, data, "but I can't pin it down. We'll have to keep taking readings from different positions until we get a better fix. This could take years."

Usteyin looked at the ship's detection equipment and computation panels with something between curiosity and, impossibly, recognition. She watched it closely, as if she were working some puzzle out in her mind. Then she abruptly turned and grabbed Han.

"Why didn't you tell me before you had a story-block? You kept a secret, you pretended you didn't know what mine was. Why did you do this?"

Han looked back at her, understanding nothing. "What are you talking about, Usteyin? What story-block? I have nothing like that tangle of wire you use. I don't understand what you mean." He felt completely blank.

She darted to her blanket roll, dug out the small bag in which she kept all her small things. She reached within, deftly, and brought out the complicated tangle of wire Han had seen her use before, as she said, to tell stories on. She unfolded it to full expansion. Han peered at it closely, trying to make something coherent out of its randomness. It was still a seemingly random tangle of hair-fine wires, silver or platinum, tied at the junctions of the wires, and strung with hundreds of infinitesimally small beads. She held it up to him proudly, but she would not let him touch it, when he reached for it, to bring it closer.

"This," she said, as if explaining something very obvious to a child who was refusing to cooperate. "I told you before. I tell stories on it, to myself. We Zlats all have them. But this one of yours—I know it is a story-block, too, but it is so big. You cannot carry it around with you. And what is wrong with it? Why won't it read back? Can't it tell you the things you wish to see?" Concern replaced the tone of mild irritation which had slipped into her voice.

"Tell me again, Usteyin. Slowly. I am just beginning to see what that is."

She shook her head, as if clearing cobwebs, a gesture of impatience. How could he fail to see this, he who had seen so much, of herself, and of other creatures. "This is mine. I made it, grew it, when I was very young, a tiny girl, with my mother. We all have them. Zlats. No one else.

I know. When I wish time to pass, when I need to know a story, I take it like this." She held it in a peculiar gesture with her left hand. "And I make it tell me stories. Like this." She made a quick series of flickering motions with her right hand, hardly touching the tangle. Some of the beads moved, changing position. The deft, sure finger motions were almost too swift to follow. She did something else to it, tensing it with her left hand, and it responded, very subtly, shifting in some way, becoming . . . another random tangle of wires with beads strung along them. "Can't you see it?" she asked. "That was the tale of Koren and Jolise; they are Zlats who have a great love story, they stole the jewels and ran away to . . ." She trailed off, watching Han's face, closely. "No, you don't see, do you?" Her enthusiasm turned to disappointment.

Han stared at the tangle, dumbfounded. "No. I can't see it. I don't know how. How many stories does that thing have stored in it?" Han began to imagine that it was a symbolic kind of memory bank.

He was wrong. Usteyin said, "There is no end to stories you can tell on a story-block. I made it well. I know. I may be only a fourth, in my first show, but my story-block is the best one the Zlats have ever made. You see wires, beads, how they are in relation to one another. There are the motions, the way you hold it, the way light strikes it. I can always invent more motions. No end. It is all me when it speaks, hands, motions, eyes, me, the story-block. I see in it, all at once, when it does the change." Usteyin stumbled for words, hesitating, growing suddenly shy again. They obviously did not understand story-blocks. She took a deep breath and began again. "All at once, no-time. Then I remember it as it happens, afterwards. In there, there is no time, so I have to put that in myself, afterwards. After it changes. It comes . . . sideways. I string it out in my head, put the story in the way that we see things as we live. Time is an illusion to us, not real. Everything is instant. But we do not live instantly, so I make it fit my rate, how I move. Do you see, now?"

They did. All of them stared at the shining tangle in Usteyin's left hand. Han felt superstitions crawling about the control room, ghosts out of the far past, oracles, magi, bearded gurus walking out of the forest, yogin who could move from one place to another. Milarepa, on old earth, the Tarot, the Cabala, the I Ching. Witches. This copper-haired girl who had no clothes, who could not read and write, who had not known how to make love, who did not even consider herself a *person*. Liszendir's matter-of-factness broke the spell.

"What can you put into it to make a story?" Liszendir understood what a story-block was.

Usteyin saw the expression on the other girl's face and recognized understanding. "Anything. I make up stories, I retell the old ones I know. There are many-many. I do not know them all. The Zlats have more stories than one can know in one's whole life. They are about love, excitement, lands, people, heroes. Things-that-are-not. But we cannot use it so often. It is dangerous, perilous. Too much story-telling, and reaching too far, and it catches your mind, it captures your spirit, and you are trapped there, in the wires."

She paused, looking at all of them, seeing more comprehension now on their faces. And Han, too. Now he saw. That was good, she wanted him to see it, desperately. He had to. She continued, "Now, Han, love, why won't yours work? It is broken? Has he," she gestured with her bright eyes at Hatha, "tried to use it?" Hatha was lost. He saw, but it was far beyond him.

Han answered her, "No, it works well enough, but it can't tell me what I want to know." How could he tell her that the threshold level was too low, and that the detection equipment could not locate it out of the noise of the background? Or that the data was insufficient? He said, "I can't get the settings just right. It is too subtle for the equipment."

"I will fix it later," she said, pleased that she could see what the problem was. "I am a Zlat. I can do such things. Yours is strange, but a story-block is a story-block. I will move some time, and you will be able to do with yours as I do with mine, although I wish there was some way I could make yours easy to carry around, like mine. But why is this story so important? I could see part of it; I watched, I knew. But it was about . . . things, where they are. Rocks or things in different places."

"Can you run that story on your story-block?"

"Oh, yes. That is an easy one. Wait." She took it up again, shaking it. Han winced; he knew what she was doing: clearing the memory. "One more thing," she added. "Show me your starts again."

"The whats?"

"Starts. The things you begin with. The pretty lights, and the pictures."

Han silently complied, running through the detection sequence again for her. As he saw it, the results were neither different nor better than the first time he had run through it. Usteyin watched the instruments intently, singlemindedly, ignoring everything else in the control room. He stood back. Finally, she looked back to him.

"Is that all? What a curious story. I could almost do it without this.

Now . . ." She paused, looked deeply *into* the glittering tangle of wires, and made a few quick adjustments. It moved, sprung, a few wires shifted position. She manipulated it again, and it responded again for her. She looked off into the viewscreen, into space, reflecting. Then back at the story-block. Then she looked up, and laughed, lightly. "How strange! You are a very curious person, Han. You must teach me these stories you know. They are like nothing I ever knew from the Zlats. They are short and easy to set, but they are full of odd jumps and shifts. And I do not understand all that I see, there . . ."

"Tell me what you see, just as you see it."

"There are three things, they have light of their own. One is that." She pointed at the star, filtered by the compensations of the screen. She apparently did not recognize it as the swift sun of the planet Dawn. "That one. It is very bright. Then there is another. We can't see it now. It was where we were, but it has moved, far away. It starts and stops. And there is one more. It is . . . ahh, what? Wait. It is big, but not big. I see it both ways. Hazy. I can see through it. It looks big one way, small the other."

"That is the one I want. Where is it?"

"Show me the world. I will show you where it is."

Han moved some switches, changed the display to read out a map of the planet Dawn. A globe appeared, then a picture of a map projection, then stabilized. It was Dawn. She pointed to the south pole, after looking at the map for a second. She said, "You want to find this one very much. Go to this place." She suddenly giggled, a very little-girl sound. Then she recovered. "I am sorry. But it is a very silly story."

Hatha interrupted, "What is this mad *klesh* saying?"

Han answered, "She's telling you where Aving's ship is. At the south pole."

Hatha looked at them as if they were all insane.

Usteyin was excited. She had pleased them! She looked sidelong at Hatha. "He wants to go to it, to break it. But he must not go! There is more!"

Liszendir was staring at the story-block, and Usteyin, open-mouthed. "Can you see the now with that thing?"

"Oh, yes. No story has end or beginning, like the all. We just start and end where it suits us; after all, we do not want to see everything—our minds are too small. I stopped it, but wait: I will finish the sequence." She had not yet cleared it. She turned her attention to the story-block, tensed it once more, and looked at it for a long time. She stopped, then looked back, as if she had made an error. Then she exclaimed, "Oh!" and hastily cleared it.

She started speaking, rapidly, shaken by what she had seen within the tangles of wires. "There is evil there. Bad things. I stopped it. I do not want to see them. They are like worms in a manure pile. Moving. Angry. They are watching . . . us. They can see us in some way I do not know. If we go near them they will hurt us, with white fire. It is very strange. They look like people but they are not people. Not any kind of people; they are something else. They can see me and my story-block, but they cannot reach me." She looked around, wide-eyed. She moved close to Han, huddling against him.

"Do not let them take me to that place!" She began babbling uncontrollably. But Han noticed that whatever was the degree of fear, or even mild hysteria, that she felt, it did not break the grip with which she held the device, nor the angle at which she held it. She grasped him tightly with her free hand.

Han stroked her hair, comforting her, calming her down. Reassuring her. Then, as she subsided, he turned to Hatha.

"They have weapons, Hatha. Beam radiation weapons. They'll fire on us, if we get within range."

Hatha said back, "I care not. Let us go to my ship, where it gathers meteors. I will go back and punish them with something even their fire cannot stop."

Liszendir came closer, watching Usteyin, the story-block. She sighed, in resignation. She said, slowly and sadly, "I finally see what she is and what she can do. But I cannot do it myself; no ler would ever be able to use that thing. There is no mystery to it, no occultism. She has a feedback loop in that tangle. Human minds are structured to use it. It multiplies your consciousness through an odd sort of motional symbolism."

Han looked at Liszendir as if she had suddenly become a stranger, a most completely alien being. "What do you mean, Liszendir?" He had never seen such an expression of sadness in her face.

"Can't you see it? That thing, plus hand, eye, mind, and probably different kinds of light as well." Usteyin nodded, agreeing. "It's not electronic, it's not magic. It isn't even mechanical in the strictest sense. It's like the thing you count with; primitive people use them. Beads on rods. An abacus. But that thing doesn't stop with numbers: it symbolizes whole realities. It's a macroscope and a computer all in one. Don't you see what you have brought to yourself, what you have loved and won, at my insistence? You can hide nothing from her, in time or space."

Usteyin collapsed the story-block. She released her grip on Han, and moved close to Liszendir, looking into the other girl's eyes deeply. "You know, so then you know that I have seen the thing that you and my Han made together, before-time." Liszendir flinched, but Usteyin was not angry with her. She put her free arm around the ler girl, spoke in an affectionate tone. "But you are a good person, you are innocent. You thought that your life had not been passionate enough, that you had not had a great love. Yes, I looked. All the way back, you and Han alike. I know. But we do not do that often. It is not good to look at your own life from outside. But I had to know."

Liszendir asked her, in a tiny voice, "Did you see this, before?"

"No. How could I know? We do not look at our own futures, for we do not want to know. It is the only story we have. And one must have the starts. But then he came, he bought me, he made me his own. It was so strange that I had to look. I did not dare for a long time. But yesterday I did. Your life is so different from mine. To me, we are none of us yet the real people, we are just all poor creatures acting out what has been preplanned for us, flowing in current, but to you, you are a kind of ultimate. I see that I was wrong, you too. Creatures fade into the other, and there is no ultimate. We are all related. And you have known many loves, many ways, your body is a fine instrument to you. And you will mate with two more, in an odd ritual I do not understand. But I have only one. And I will have an even stranger life than yours, and now I understand it less than I do yours. But it will be far more than the Zlats could imagine—maybe not so adventuresome, but much sweeter. There is much peace there, and I fall into it, pretending I am flying. You will not change, but I will. This is fixed, like rocks, like the old stories of the Zlats. But you should not fear me, Liszendir Srith-Karen of a many-many generations of Karens. You prepared him for me, and it is a gift for which I will be forever in your debt."

"All religions originate in discredited sciences."
—Holden Czepelewski, *Cahiers*

"Truth, such as we find it, appears in mythic stories, while recited facts fall into mere opinions. And the more facts are enumerated, the more opinionated and erroneous the matter becomes. At the level of pure facts, there is nothing but chaos. Ah, to be sure, facts are real, one should respect them, but one should beware of them greatly, for it is the feel of the flow that makes the dancer beautiful.

—*Brunsimber Frazhen*

HAN TURNED AWAY for a moment, and began programming a course that would bring them to a rendezvous with the larger ship. When he turned back, one of them was smiling affectionately, and the other was still staring off into some personal noplace, blankly. He wanted to break the stasis of this scene, somehow get things back into some framework of motion, at least of the illusion that they were moving, but he could not bring himself to it; he sensed that the slightest tap from him might prove to be a blow which shattered.

Hatha broke the silence by asking, "If what my eyes and ears tell me is true, then I take it that she, or any Zlat for the matter, or even any human, if trained, can see through that tangle, that wad, into anywhere?" He stopped, searching for a word which didn't exist. "Anywhen? And how did they get them?"

Usteyin answered, "It is just as you say—anywhere and anywhen. But where we were, on the plain, as what I was, I did not know many things, and those things of the outer world I knew, I did not care about. If I do not know you because you live in some far place, I would not ever have a reason to see to that place, to see you, how you are. No. We did not use them for that; we used them to tell stories on, to make us proud, to give us identity. We made them ourselves, from the first. That is one of the stories—how the Zlats made story-blocks. It was our specialty—in the old days—but the things we made fell into disuse and we had no work, no place. So we made something for ourselves—I call them story-blocks to you, but to another Zlat I should say 'the last gift.' We used to make big ones—like this one on this ship. We had no power, no machines—so we made one that needed no power but that of the spirit, and no machine but the hand."

She smiled, as if to herself. "I used to think that all these things were just make-believe. But now? Perhaps all the time we were looking across time, across distance—to the long ago or to the yet-to-be. That the story of Koren and Jolise, remember that?—is perhaps real, somewhere, some when. I do not know that. I do not want to know whether it is real or not, for just as this can show beautiful things, it can show things of terror and evil."

Han asked, "Could I learn to use one?"

She reflected for a moment, then said, "No. I do not think so. Not because of what you are, but because you are too old, you know words too well. You have to start before you become too tied up in words. Very young. Not yet walking well, that young. And them, the ler? Not at all, never. They do not have the mind for it—they cannot let go. Now you are changing me to your life, you have told me, shown me, and so as I learn, then I lose this. After a few years I will no longer be able to use it at all, it will be just a tangle of wire. Do not be sad! I want this or I would not have come with you. Since I am with you I no longer need stories, I live one, ever so much more than what you see in here."

She looked at Hatha. "So under them, we just had time, time, which we called an illusion. It had to be so, to use the story-blocks. No time or it won't work. That is another reason why you can't use one—you see too much time, and *they* see nothing but time. You, Han, see that everything has a connection, one thing makes another. She, Liszendir, thinks that things happen on their own. Both are wrong."

Han felt out of his depth. This girl who had been a pet a few weeks ago was calmly discussing the dimensional continuum of time and space—and dismissing it, in the speech of an eight-year-old.

Liszendir said, "I don't agree, and I will not change, but she means that 'causality is an illusion of time, chance is an illusion of ignorance, and time itself is an illusion of . . . ah . . . length, perhaps, is the best word.' "

"Yes, yes, you see it!" she exclaimed. "That is how it is. It does not move. I lack the words. We move, in here, in our minds."

Hatha scoffed, "You may believe in fortunetellers all you wish, but I have always run them off whenever I found them skulking about the camp. This is nonsense! She is a *klesh*. She knows nothing."

The girl turned on him with a voice that carried venom. "It is because I know what you call nothing in your vanity that I can use this and see through all your schemes. A higher people keeping pets. What foolishness! Your pets are higher than you, keeper. And what you think you know is less than nothing. Trash in a pit. Broken bits, shards of a jar you will never see as a whole nor use for water. This is not magic, fortunes, divinations. This is a tool which helps me to see—what is, what was—and what is to be. Do you wish to know what else I have seen in here? That you will never see the sun rise over Dawn again, that is what I have seen."

Hatha retreated from her, illogically, in view of what he had said before. "Stay away from me, Zlat witch!"

"I do nothing to you! You will do it to yourself!" She was angry now, and despite her small size, and lack of obvious weapons, she had suddenly become a figure of danger and malice, something not entirely controlled. Han reached for her, touched the soft girl skin of her shoulder. At his touch, she began calming, returning to her earlier state.

He said, "Wait. Do not waste this on him. Let him go his way. If you must use it again, then use it to tell me one more story. He will want to see it, too."

She turned, calmed. "What is it?"

"The bright one, the star. Tell me its story, and where we are in it. I will show you the starts."

"Once more, no more. I cannot use it again, after this. I have already used it too much this day. I fear it now. Let me tell you something about it, how it is used. Now if I wish to make a story about just such a place, exactly such a person, at a special time, it takes many starts, many motions, many settings before I move it. The more detail, the more I have to put in, and the less it gives me back. To watch one grain of sand fall, in one place, at one time, it would take me a year to set it just right, maybe longer. And who would wish to see it? But at the other end, if I wish to ask it, 'What is the meaning of life?' then there are no starts. Just tense it and look. Many starts, short story; few starts, long story. And the last one is the longest of all: it never ends, it lasts forever. And since there is no time, that means you are trapped in that, where the illusion won't work. So we never ask that; that is the one answer that traps you for ever. Your spirit is lost. You can't get back yourself, and no one can get you out of it."

Liszendir added, "Irrational numbers, again. The realities that device symbolizes are all irrational numbers, nonrepeating decimals. But in her system, she has a way to cut them off at any point, except in certain questions. Without the cutoff, you have to keep considering the operation. I see why it is deadly. Never mind that I can't use one—I wouldn't think of even trying."

"Yes. And it jumps at the first, the first part sets everything up, even the end, of each story. You need do nothing at the end. But I know that is because it was there all along, the jumps because in reality it was smooth, but all that went before has to be compressed at the first."

She finished, and turned to the panels, expectantly. Han began the sequence, a complete data acquisition sequence for the primary of Dawn, all-instruments mode, all-sensor. He did not understand how she could derive any meaningful ideas from what she saw, for much of it was being displayed in a set of symbols which were strange and unknown to her; but on the other hand, perhaps Usteyin, as she had suggested had been the case for the story-block, didn't see data at all in any kind of symbols, but gestalt patterns of flow, vectors, directions, intersections, and could insert her own symbols for specific items. It did not seem to make a great deal of difference to her.

"Again, please."

He started the sequence over again. Yes. Now he was more sure; that was the way she saw things, probably the best possible way, except for the fact that it must be nonverbal, nonsymbolic as he understood symbols, and being thus, could not be explained by her, any more than a two-year-old could explain how he walked.

"Enough. I can do it. Now I need light, strong light. Can you make the window brighter, give me daylight? This is a hard pattern, I will need hard light for this; light is a thing in this, too. It controls accuracy and the rate of movement." Han adjusted the viewscreen, keeping the bandwidth constant, but lowering the filtration, as he turned the ship so the star came to rest at the center of the screen. Usteyin was already at work. She said, absent-mindedly, to Han, "Yes, that's right, just right . . ." and trailed off, muttering to herself, absorbed in putting the settings into the story-block.

The glare of the star flooded the control room, erasing color and making contrasts strong, glaring black and whites: in this light a petite witch

with burning white skin and hair of space-darkness held up a glittering
miniature silver galaxy, her body oriented exactly ninety degrees to the
light source, eyes focused intently, mouth slightly open. She made the
setting motions for a long time with her free hand, occasionally moving
her lips silently, as if subvocalizing something; Han could not read her
lips. Then, without waiting, she tensed it: he could sense movement,
within it, something shifting, moving, falling into a new configuration.
Beads moved, a wire shifted its orientation. Usteyin gasped once,
cleared it with a sharp motion that implied pain, and looked away
quickly. Han darkened the screen, and Usteyin, moving like a zombie,
carefully collapsed the story-block and stowed it away in its place in the
small bag. She stood up, but did not say anything. She looked dazed.
Han touched her. She did not respond. He took her with both hands,
shook her.

"Usteyin! Are you all right?"

The voice seemed to bring her back. She looked at him nodded. "Yes.
But almost not. I had to make myself get out. I have used it too much,
tried to see too much, too far. No more."

"What did you see? What about the bright one?"

She hesitated for a moment before answering, as if trying to recall the
exact flavor of the experience. Then she began "It was long ago, very
long ago. There was darkness. Stars. All far away. Emptiness, loneliness,
the void felt tension. There was something there, but it was weak,
spread, all over. Then it came together; it looked like smoke, boiling,
moving upwards, like for smoke, but inwards, to a point. Knot formed
in it, things that glowed, lit up, caught on fire. Many of them. Then the
air cleared, the lights became bright, hard fires, and then they began to
move apart. This one I saw. It was larger than the others, and it had little cold knots all around it, which did not glow. It took longer . . . but
then it grew quiet. I came closer to it. The rate of allmotion that you call
time speeded up, raced, slowed down. I was to understand by this that
many-many years passed. The thing grew slowly, it stayed much the
same outside, but inside it was a sick, heavy, toppling, like when you
stack rocks to see how high you can get the pile. Then it became bright,
and time slowed greatly, so I could see it, but even with that it was too
fast. It became large, bright like this." She made a ball of her hands, and
then opened them rapidly, spreading her fingers and moving her hands
apart. "There was only a little thing left of it, but it was very strong. I
could feel it, pulling at me."

"Where are we in that story?" Hatha asked.

"Near the end. I saw us, we will be gone, then. You want time, how-long. Go to the land where we were before. The sun will make the full circle of the two winters five times. No more. They will see it, too. It will be morning, the late spring of the north-winter. Early in the morning. There will be no clouds, they will see . . . and . . ." She stopped. "What does it mean?"

Liszendir said, "You see and you do not know?"

"I see many things I do not know. That is how you get trapped in a story-block: you keep saying, 'What is this, and this, and this?' This last time, I saw others like the bright one, like, and not like. How they become, what they become, what all of them mean . . ." She trailed off, became still, glassy-eyed, staring into some interior noplace.

Han took her again, shook her roughly. At first, it seemed to have no effect, but by the second or third, she was out of the trance, returning to reality. As she recovered, she quickly touched Han on the face, chest, shoulders, then turned to Liszendir and touched her, also. She sighed, deeply.

"Yes, here. Back where I am, where I belong. Do not ask me to look into it again, in these stories you have. Please."

Han turned to Hatha. "She has seen the future and the past. Your star. She has seen it explode. It will supernova in five of your years. You will have time to get the people off Dawn and get away, but no more. And far away. That thing will poison everything within many years' travel of Dawn, moving outwards almost at the speed of light itself. And we will have to come back and get the humans, too."

They made their rendezvous with the *Hammerhand* on the other side of the Dawn system. And its new weapon, a huge clod of nickel-iron almost as large as the warship itself. At first, the scrub crew operating the warship had been reluctant, even hesitant, to make contact; but, thankfully, they had been finally convinced by the sight of the smaller *Pallenber*. Somebody aboard that monster evidently remembered. They landed in one of the bays, which was opened for them, and then closed over them. The outside sensors reported normal air pressure was returning to the bay. Hatha prepared to return to his ship. At the outer lock, Han and he had a few last words.

Hatha spoke first. "Well, now! All ends here, so it does. It would seem that you have managed to elude me at every turn, so after so many times, I finally admit to a bit of learning. Usually, with a captive, particularly a captive spy, I have found that the value of the individual decreases with time, from the capture. But you and Liszendir fared just the reverse. I had to conclude that I was wrong earlier, or that you two were not spies, but something else entirely."

"We were not spies, at least as I would think of them. We were not sent out to penetrate anyone's realm and send back secrets, but rather just go and have a look at what had happened. Hetrus, the human who seemed to be in charge of this, apparently smelled a rat, either in the planted trader Efrem, or in the reported circumstances, or perhaps both. But however it was, you would have done better to let us alone on Chalcedon. Why meddle? Nobody there knew anything; I found that out, after you took the ship away from Liszendir. Things would probably have gone much as Aving had hoped."

The reminder of Hatha and the Warriors having been used as a disposable tool stung, and Han intended it to. That would not repay any of the Warriors for the generations of *klesh*, but it would be a gesture.

But if Hatha felt any direct resentment, he kept it to himself. "Possible, possible," he said, noncommittally. "But now we must go our ways, I to smite the aliens, and you back to your own planet, with two girls."

"Yes, back. But were it not for the fact that you will have to get your own people off Dawn before your star blows, I would fire on your ship myself, for what you tried to do regardless of the source of that motivation. But I will not. Your ship has its uses. And when you have done it, then save your people. But time is precious. And be warned. Liszendir and Usteyin and I go, but we will all be back, within a Dawn year, and this time at the head of a fleet. We humans will take our own back, all of them, and I swear that if one Warrior so much as raises one spear against us, I will polish Dawn as smooth as a steel ball. And they are not to be harmed or carted off to another Dawn."

"All? Even the pets? Some have treated them kindly, and feel affection for their own."

"Every single one. Leave them and go your way, follow the teachings of Sanjirmil or the devil. But take one, and we will hunt you to the ends of the universe, for we have Usteyin-who-sees. She can find you, even if you hide in the core of a dark star."

Hatha looked around, idly, a gesture of resignation. "Very well. I suppose I would feel the same, were things reversed. So it will be! I will do as you ask. And have no fears, if I do not return from this expedition, now, for it is a possibility. When I sent the messenger off, I told him

what might be. And without a ship, they can of course go nowhere."
Here, he brightened. "But now, we have a mutual enemy."

"I will follow you down. Come onto Dawn from its north, out of the
sun; follow the curve of the planet around, and drop your meteor as you
move away. You should have a chance, because they will have to shoot
at it first—I don't think even the weapons they have will deflect a mass
like that. We will make sure nothing is left, and then go get Aving's castle. And Aving, hopefully. And so, good fortune."

"I will say one more thing: you have garnered more choice and kept
it, than I would have reached for. And you have done much, with very
little. I know you are no spy, no militarist. Such a one would have spent
his energy on resisting. But I see much, at this late hour, and even a little bit of what that Zlat girl sees, and why. Go! I will await you on
Dawn, a year hence, in a ship without weapons." He turned and left,
with neither further word nor gesture. As Han was closing the outer
lock, he caught a glimpse of Hatha, hurrying through his own lock, in
the cavernous bay.

He returned to the control room, where Liszendir and Usteyin
waited, Liszendir looking for him, and Usteyin gazing at the screen,
which was once again displaying a view of the stars. Hatha had opened
the bay, released the *Pallenber*, and they were drifting free. She turned
to Han as he came to the panels.

"Now what will we do? Go to your place, your world?"

"No. We must finish a thing here, complete the affair with Aving.
Then we will go, but we will come back, to take all of them on Dawn
to a place where they can be people again."

The *Hammerhand* had already started moving, heedless of energy, on
a manual course straight for Dawn. The large meteor, or small asteroid,
however one wished to look at such an ambiguous object, trailed behind, sluggishly, reluctantly, as if it did not wish to leave its old comfortable place in the void. Han watched for a moment, then set in a
course and let the *Pallenber* fall towards Dawn on a geodesic, down an
invisible curve no one of them could see, except the ship's computer, or
perhaps Usteyin, and she would not look. As they began their fall, Han
showed Usteyin how to use the screen and make the adjustments. As
with everything else, he didn't have to repeat anything he showed her.

Then they were over Dawn, catching up with the warship, which was
close to the surface, near the upper atmosphere, skimming, accelerating,
the meteor still trailing behind, but beginning to show some motion of
its own. Then, as they watched, under magnification, the *Hammerhand*

began a long, shallow tangental curve outwards, away from the planet. The meteor dipped briefly into the atmosphere, flaring greenish fire, and curved back into space, and then down, on a course which would intersect the south pole, now covered in complete darkness and ice. Nothing showed at the pole except the unrelieved blankness of the ice cap, lit only by the weak light of the stars. Han knew only that they were down there. What they had or how they managed was beyond him.

Seemingly from nowhere, a pale bluish beam appeared from the polar area, waving around uncertainly, seeking. It played briefly upon both objects, one moving away, accelerating, and the other incoming with unmistakable intent. It hesitated, flicked back and forth, and selected the incoming meteor, becoming a narrow lance of burning white light that set off alarms all over the *Pallenber*, a searing, purple-white dazzle that left painful afterimages. The meteor simply vanished. It was gone, as if it never had been. The light became the pale, broader beam again, almost invisible until their vision returned. They could see a fine cloud, looking like dust at this distance. That was all.

Han began activating defense screens, fields, sealing off sections of the ship. He also opened the weapons bays, although he suspected, with a certain, sinking feeling, that nothing he had could match that terrible beam. But Hatha had also seen what had happened to his meteor, and had taken an action of his own. By the time the pale guide beam had found him again, he had reversed courses in a hairpin maneuver and was falling directly onto the pole, apparently under full normal-space drives. The warship was completely dark, and it seemed to be flickering.

Han said, "Suicide dive. He's got all his power off except the parts powering the drives and the defensive fields. He wants that ship badly!"

The aliens recognized what was happening too late. Again the full power of the beam flashed out, to skewer the oncoming ship and blast it into a cloud of dust. It had no effect. It glanced off the blurred warship without visible effect, showering the darkness with glittering points and streaks of light. Suddenly the screen began an odd, pulsing motion, like ripples spreading on the surface of a pond, the same motion Han and Liszendir had seen when approaching Chalcedon. Both of them recognized it simultaneously. They knew what the aliens, Aving's people, were doing. They had turned the full drive on and were readying their ship for flight, with a peculiar drive that distorted his screens. Then that was why they had seen this near Chalcedon—Aving had stopped off to see how things were going, in secret, before returning to Dawn. At the pole, something was moving, the ice cap was breaking up, something was coming upwards, out of the ice. Still firing—although they could not do both well, for every time they fired with the intense beam, the disturbance in their screen gave off extra pulses, as if operating both the drive and the weapon made them interfere with each other. With all shields down, detection gave him an honest reading now, pinpointing the source. The power plant was like the one on Hatha's rebuilt ship, but much more powerful, not even reasonably comparable in relative strengths. Han expected that. Give the natives rifles, but keep the Catling guns for yourself. And it was large, as large as Hatha's ship, perhaps larger; something as yet invisible, down there in the ice, struggling like some insect to get out of the way.

But it was too late. Before the alien ship, still unseen, only a suggestive motion below the surface, could emerge, the two objects merged. Han seemed to be seeing it in slow-time, the action fantastically slowed so he could see every detail. They moved together, embraced, intertwined; the mass did not explode, but simply glowed redly, and sank from sight, one undistinguishable, unrecognizable mass. The glow disappeared in a huge gout of steam, fog and cloud, and the pulsating disturbance on the screen faded away to nothing, was gone. Detection showed one remaining source of drive energy in the Dawn system—the star of Dawn, now invisible behind the bulk of the planet, only showing shreds of its swollen corona behind the curve.

Liszendir had watched the entire event without comment or reaction. After a long silence, she finally said, in a calm voice, "You may think I might see this as only evidence of further dishonor and perfidy on the part of Hatha. Not so, not so at all. The law says, 'Use no weapon that leaves the hand.' So in the end he did not; it did not leave his hand. Nor does suicide distress me, for it is only an act, and the value of an act lies solely in its purpose in the present and immediate future."

Han looked at her from the instruments, slowly. He said, "I see that. I also see that in his system, a noble had choice—the higher the noble, the greater the degree of choice. This was an article of faith, so that when he arrived by his own acts into a situation which left one no choices, then one was no longer noble, could not be. He also faced some interesting explanations upon his return, for in the same system, the free chooser does not allow himself to be used as an expendable tool."

Usteyin added, somberly, "So it is done. They hurt him, just as I said they would. As I saw."

"He hurt them far worse," Han answered. "Now the master plotter is found out, and he is trapped, with no place to run. Look at what he faces: he cannot stay on Dawn. The Warriors will be hunting for him, even now, and even if he escapes them, he has the nova to worry about. And of course, the only ship that would take him anywhere is disposed of, gone, ruined, destroyed."

"No. Not that way of hurt, not the body. I mean they hurt him when he finally realized what they had done to him first, and then to his people. You told him before we came onto this ship, but he did not really examine it in his heart until he was back on his own ship, off this one. For us, he kept a front. A story, if you like. Then he thought. And what he did was planned, not an anger-thing. Those things could deal with the weapons they themselves gave him, those rocks, but they were paralyzed when he used the ship as a weapon, a simple thrust. He knew they would be, that they would think he would save the warship at all costs."

Liszendir said, "And so I have lived to see the end of a legend, the end of the tale of Sanjirmil. Somehow, I wish I hadn't, that something better, or the unknown, could have been for them. . . . But now it is over, and we can go home. We are free."

"We are free, and now we have choice," said Han quietly.

"What choice?" Both girls spoke almost in unison.

"We can go back now, or attend to some other unfinished business."

"What could we have that is unfinished, here?"

"Aving. Have you forgotten? I know Aving was not on that ship below the pole. He could not be—he would not be able, even on a place like Dawn, to go and come unnoticed in such a ship; it was as big or bigger than Hatha's. No. The only time he could board it was when Hatha was away, and the season kept everyone else indoors, at night, so they would not see. And he couldn't live at the pole, either. So Aving has not yet been caught up in the ruin of his adventure. He will have had communications with his ship, and now he knows it is gone. They cannot answer his calls, the equipment will be silent, and so he will have guessed something. If we can bring him back, dead or alive, we can prove what we say, for however much he may look like a ler, I will bet everything I now have that he will be different inside. And more: we do not know that he can't communicate with his homeworld. He may even now be calling for help. We don't know where it is, or how far. It could be hundreds of lights away, or over in the next system."

Liszendir looked grave, thoughtful. "Yes. It would almost have to be as you say. But what you are thinking, Han, that is more dangerous than anything we have done yet. Think: we came to look, and we were dragged off to the ends of the universe, hunted, beaten. If we go looking for trouble, to seek one out like that, ah, now, that is a fine peril. And I do not wish to be hauled off to any more planets, save my own, which I will allow you to do."

Usteyin was equally concerned. "I agree with what Liszendir says. And more. Who will do this thing, capture or kill this creature? There are only three of us; you two are fighters, that I see, but I am not, even if I have ended one of those things."

"I do not mean that we should go back there blind. But we should at least go and have a look at the castle. We know he has no ship, and we can reason that he has no weapons heavy enough to do us damage at the castle. We would be able to detect the power source, if one were there. And if he has gone, then we can't spend the rest of our lives looking for him. But I do not want to leave him here."

Liszendir moved around Han, and set the course in herself. "All right. I see it. You are right. I do not want him loose either."

Usteyin looked at both of them. "I do not like this at all, but I have no way to stop you, and I see there is no way to get off this machine. I am not brave. I have fear of beings who could use the people so."

"Not brave? I don't think that's true, Usteyin. And if you lack it, you are going to have to learn it soon. Because if any of us have to go into the castle, it will have to be you and I. Somebody who can fly the ship has to stay in it, and that is Liszendir."

In a short time, they were approaching Aving's castle from the south, flying the *Pallenber* down in the upper atmosphere. As they passed over the location of the city Leilas, Han and Liszendir looked below through the ventral pickups for signs of life. There were none. Leilas was buried under snow. All they could see, even with low-level augmentation, were patterns of different tints of snow and rocks, the random traceries of hard winter and night. Soon after, they were over the top of the northern trough, dropping lower and lower, decreasing their speed as they came closer. They passed the castle, carefully watching for any sign of life about it, but there was nothing. In the twilight of the north-winter, the castle sat on its outcrop, dark and empty. It had been abandoned.

While Han and Liszendir were looking at the castle and the lands around it, Usteyin was looking ahead, northwards, on the main viewscreen. It was not long before her sharp eyes saw something far ahead on the gently dipping slope of the northern end of the trough: small knots of people, fleeing north, to the polar summer, and perhaps another way out, or back, or into obscurity. Or just away. She called to Han and Liszendir.

Han flew closer to the straggling knots, to get a better view of them. Yes; they were fleeing, all walking away from the castle. He could not make out any features on any of them, but something of the way they hurried, the way they scattered as they heard the approach of the ship; those ways were not the way of an Aving. Liar and deceiver he could be, but he would neither scuttle nor cower, even in defeat. He also felt with all the strength of a hunch that Aving would not be one to run, if he ran at all, into isolation—that would make him all the easier to spot, to hunt down. No—he was not with these. He would be back at the castle, hiding, or perhaps in Leilas. He turned the ship around and headed back to the castle.

The strength of the hunch waned as he came closer to the castle. It had been a foolish idea to come back here at all. They would never find Aving. The sly fox had too much of a head start on them—even if it were only an hour, it was enough. They could not expect to locate one creature from a spaceship—this was one time when machinery and technology could not help them, and they did not have time to go down and search the whole planet on foot. But a trip into the castle might be worthwhile, for artifacts, if nothing else. Proof. They flew around the dark hulk several times, but they saw no sign of life on it, not even smoke. On an impulse, he flew right up to the castle and grounded the ship inside the courtyard, although there was barely room for it. It was a small ship, yet inside the walls, it seemed improbably large. The *Pallenber* settled into the snow, gingerly, tentatively, protesting the soft, yielding surface under its landing legs.

The ship quieted, became silent. Han set the controls on standby, and began getting ready to go out. "Liszendir, you stay here. If anything goes wrong, if we don't come back, you will have to get the information back into the Union. Take off and fly it—you know how. And burn this place to a cinder before you leave, if it comes to that. Forget your inhibitions once. You can go straight through on Matrix-12. I've already set it up. Just punch it in."

She became obstinate. "This is not right! You and I should be going in there. If you must."

Usteyin began wrapping her blanket around herself. "I fear this place, and I fear to leave the ship, for it is the only place, save our little room in the camp on the plains, where I have felt my reality so strongly. But I must go with you, even if all I do is carry things. You understand me, Liszendir, and you will not be offended, but my life with you would not be so much as with him."

"I am not. Now go! Let it be done and let us leave this place."

Han gave Usteyin one of the gas guns, showed her how to use it. She listened patiently, grimly serious. For himself, he went to the locker and removed two weapons, just in case. One was a flash gun, which generated a narrow beam whose wavelength was in the near infrared. The other was a devilish reactionless pistol that fired tiny rocket-powered projectiles guided by a fine attached wire. The projectiles were also explosive. He found also some extra clothing, and offered the things to Usteyin, for it was cold outside. She refused them.

They left the ship, climbed down the ladder, and stood for a time in the courtyard. They could not see the sun; it was now below the horizon, below the walls, and behind the mountains. But its glow spread a diffuse, weak light all over the northern sky, fading overhead into an overlay on the darkness, of a color suggesting blue flame. The stars shone brightly, what few there were. The courtyard was all shadows, suggestions of shape, in the strange twilight, made by the erratic sun of Dawn, halting, standing still in its yearly spiral sunset.

Overhead, in the depths of the eerie, darkened sky, a faint, almost invisible, flickering began. Both Han and Usteyin stopped and looked up: it was an aurora starting up, now too weak, too undefined for them to be able to make out any details or colors of it. Standing barefoot in the fine, powdery snow, her blanket wrapped around her, Usteyin tilted her head and smelled the icy air, her delicate nostrils flaring; in a situation of both suspicion and possible danger, she had reverted to patterns of behavior that stretched across time and space to the dark glacial forests of precivilization old Earth. Then they walked through the snow, hearing only the whisper of it underfoot, to the great hall entrance, which hung open, ajar. Waiting another moment, like burglars, they stepped cautiously into Aving's castle.

Inside it was as cold as the outside. Usteyin whispered to Han, "They are all gone. There is no presence here. The people left before the ship was destroyed—they have been gone for hours. This place is cold, dead."

"How could that be? They should be only about an hour ahead of us. This place should still be warm."

"Remember? When I used the story-block, on our ship? I told you that they could *see* me, with some sense I do not understand, not-sight, but something that acts like it. Perhaps they gave the alarm then."

But as they passed through the darkened castle, Han could see that she was right—there was no one in it, and it had been empty for hours, much longer than from the time the alien ship had fallen to Hatha's dive on it. But all through the castle there were signs of recent and hasty abandonment: an astonishing variety of junk and trash was strewn all over, and some ways into the castle, they found some bodies. Some were ler, some human. None were of the aliens. There had been fighting, but over what they could not see—perhaps over the spoils, or something else.

As they made their way to the central hall, and found the corridor Aving had used to come into it, Han told Usteyin, "When Liszendir and I came here before, they had a musical troupe here, in this hall, playing for dinner. At the time, I knew nothing about *klesh*, I thought the players were all members of a family, or something like that—a caste or tribe. But they all resembled one another about to the same degree that you Zlats look like each other."

"Music? They were actually doing something? You know that most of the *klesh* have long since lost their old functions; they no longer do the things they were specialized for. I do not know which those you saw would be."

"I don't think there have been any of them among the bodies we have found. They were light in complexion, not especially pretty in the faces, and stocky. They had brown hair, with some curl in it, and big noses—not as large as on the Haydars, but large just the same. Larger in size than you, but shorter than me."

"Ah, ha! Those would be Peynir. I did not know there were any left. We all know, in a general way, about each other; the Peynir are supposed to be almost as old as the Zlats. There are *klesh* and then there are others."

Farther up the corridor, they had better luck. In a room at the top of a flight of stairs, narrow and littered with papers, they found a communications device, or at least what appeared to be a communications device. There were several meters and light indicators on it, but what gave it away was a small, oddly designed microphone and earset, still plugged into it. The rest of the box, or console, made little sense, and they did not touch it or attempt to manipulate it. There were various knobs, push-places, transparent windows which must have been indicators of some type, but which now were indicating nothing. They could not even find the power pack for it. There was some writing, but neither of them could understand it; it seemed to be made up of narrow lines with infinitesimal, subtle variations in thickness.

Han said, half to himself, "The Warriors had radar, of all things, the oldest kind, with steerable antennas, physical things, but they had no radio. That is like us having voices, but only using them to find out where things are around us by listening for the echo. So Aving could use any number of ways to transmit to his ship, any wavelength: no one on this planet would hear him. But the best way would be the longer wavelengths, very long waves. That way, he could bury the antenna underground, and they would be able to send back and forth even under the magnetic storms."

Usteyin whispered, her breath steaming in the cold, "I do not know what you are saying. It appears that this Aving was a wizard, and you are one too. A greater one, for was it not you who saw through his deceptions? But wait! Look out the window."

Han went to the narrow window, the only one in the room, and looked out, around, upwards. This room faced somewhat to the north, and on the horizon, he could see the sunset unmoving northern sun, in one corner. It was on the horizon, just below it, but there the sky was tinged with pale rose, lemon, wild blues that carried strong greenish overtones. What caught his attention more was the strong flickering that came from overhead. He looked up. Yes. It was a strong aurora.

Usteyin came to the window and joined Han there, looking upwards, momentarily entranced. It was the strongest aurora Han had ever seen, vast curtains converging on a point in the zenith which seemed an infinite distance away, vast curtains that moved and rippled along their lower skirts, and which were lit up, from within, from the sides, from below, by particolored beams of colored searchlights, or bonfires. The outside had become lighter, noticeably. Usteyin stood, face upturned, beautiful in the flickering light, unreal, twin plumes of breath-steam flowing out of her delicate nostrils, the light painting wild iridescences in her hair.

She came down from the window. "That I have seen before, many times, but never so bright or so easy to see! Nor so wild. Now let us leave this place! There is no one here."

Han reluctantly came away from the window also, and scooped up some things that appeared to be books or manuals. He had no idea what they were, but he thought, irreverently, that if he were going to be a burglar, then he had to burgle something, anything, and they had seen nothing else. Usteyin picked up nothing; she had seen nothing she wanted, even for burgling. It was clear to Han that she did not like this place, nor her being in it, not in the least.

They made their way back to the *Pallenber,* through the empty and silent cold halls and corridors, seeing no more than they did when they had first entered the castle—bodies, rubbish, abandoned rags, dropped weapons. All the way back, they went quietly, moving from shadow to shadow, feeling as if any moment there would come a sudden shock, a cry, the bite of steel, a sudden stab of bright pain, then darkness. But there was nothing in the still darkness except the pounding of their pulses. In the courtyard at last, the ship still bulked over them. All appeared secure. The lights were still on, the port was still open. There was no change, except in the sky above, where the aurora still held court, playing, dancing. Han looked at Usteyin. There was no more awe on her pretty, serious face; just apprehension. He sighed in a minor kind of defeat and resignation; Aving had indeed escaped them, probably for good, for they could not very well sift the whole planet to find him. He could be anywhere. ·

They climbed the ladder, Han first, Usteyin waiting below, gas gun at the ready, in case. She was jumpy, suspicious, although Han could see no reason why. She kept looking around, as if there was something wrong somewhere in the scene around them. Something out of place. But it might take weeks to find that as well. Han made it to the lock, and covered Usteyin while she climbed. They were on the point of going within when she suddenly stopped, taking a deep breath of the icy air.

"Wait. Just one minute, for me. I want to take one last look out on my world, for I will never see it again."

"All right. But hurry—it's cold. When you pass the second door, press the black button; that will close the lock port doors and retract the ladder."

"I'll just be a minute."

Han went ahead. Usteyin might not mind the cold, but it was beginning to bite into him. He didn't know how she stood it, and walking around in that place barefooted, too! And that had been odd, what she had said about not coming back to Dawn. Of course she would come back—they would have to, to see to everything, when they came back for the humans, and the *klesh,* to take them to a place of their own. That was a shame, in a way—that Dawn would end in five of its years, burnt to a cinder, scattered over the void, later to be incorporated in some other star, some other planet, recycled. He had been himself appalled by the visage of the planet, its terrible weather and seasons, its impossible geography, but there was something there—in a universe of marvels, Dawn was something special, one of a kind. A place of terror and isolation and ignorance, but a place of heroic beauty as well. The Warriors were not all to blame themselves, nor could it all be laid to Aving's manipulations—the place itself acted in an underground way in the mind, conjuring up visions of heroism, of greatness.

Han went ahead, entered the corridor, and started to enter the control room. Just as he opened the door, he heard a squeal from Usteyin. He stopped in the doorway, holding the panel half open and looking back to the lock, and called to her.

"What is it?"

"Han! The snow! That is wrong. I knew something wasn't right! You and I, we came and went: four tracks of footprints, yours with shoes, mine without. Four! But there are five. Did Liszendir leave the ship? No! Somebody came here. To the ladder."

Han knew, before he heard the voice from the control room, the voice he had heard before, the voice which did not belong, by any stretch of the imagination, to Liszendir. It was not a human voice, not even ler-human.

The speaker said, "I hold a flash gun on your ex-lover. Bid the *klesh* girl come in, and enter yourself, leaving your weapons by the door. And do it quickly, for we have far to go and little time remaining to do it in."

He turned and called to Usteyin. "Come in. Cycle the door." He was thinking as fast as he could, for some way. There was none. Better to follow this line, inside the ship, a little longer, than face a certain end, freezing in the castle—if any of them lived beyond the threat. With three of us, there may just be a chance, he thought. He did not see one at that moment, however hard he tried.

13

"Characters in a story or tale are, in four dimensions, equivalent to, in two dimensions, the waves on the sea, the ripples on the pond, the waving fields of grass, the snowdrifts, by whose motion and shaping we become able to discern the shape of the wind. It is hard to make up that shape in our minds, just so, but even harder to see the shape of the winds of our own lives, which are displayed by type in the various tales.

—*Zermanshan Tlanh*

USTEYIN CAME INTO the control room, both excited and apprehensive at the same time, saying, "Han, there are extra footprints out there in the snow, not ours, I think . . . Oh!" She entered the room quietly, closed the door, and stood beside Han, slipping the blanket off herself.

Aving said, "This is a flash gun. It is very good for close work, such as we have here. I have it set on maximum dispersion. It does not completely kill humans or ler at the first shot, but it does incapacitate with severe burns, which produce fatality, later. I know that this one, this girl, is trained for combat, so that by neutralizing her I can easily keep you two in check. Unlike Hatha, I waste no time on tribal-level status-measuring mannerisms and appreciations. She is completely expendable, as are the *klesh*. I know that you will not sacrifice both."

He paused briefly, letting that sink in. They did not doubt him for a minute. Liszendir sat quietly in the pilot's chair, saying, doing nothing. But the expression on her face would have curdled fresh milk in the next town, as Han had heard said. The next town? The next planet.

Aving, seeing that they understood, continued, "So, then. The program is simplicity itself. You will fly us to my homeworld, where you will remain, in one mode or another, as circumstances dictate, while the overcouncil approaches this problem from another angle, to see if anything can be salvaged from this wreckage. And I do not sleep. So, then. To work!"

Han desperately wanted time to think. He asked, "So we were right about the situation here on Dawn?"

"Yes. The Warrior-ler did not see it at all. Whatever abilities they may still have, they are not devious, like all primitives. But we had not reckoned on the abilities of some of the old people—yourself, for example, or that Hetrus on Seabright. He saw far into it, at least by suspicion. I was able to influence events there so that two relative incompetents would be sent. Naturally, you would either see nothing and report the same—or find out something, and vanish without a trace. But you, like Hetrus, have proved to be resourceful, and the ler girl has contributed all out of proportion to our perspective on the ler. You do not see well ahead, but you find ways out. That kind of thinking has managed to create complete disruption of the plan here, and in fact has nullified the future uses of Dawn as a staging base for further operations. You have guessed, I suspect, from your instruments, that that star out there is very sick. By the time we could recover momentum here, a factor in events as well as bodies, there would be no time left to establish an orderly progression of happenings. We do not salvage lost causes."

"What was that progression?"

"That is no interest to you, now."

"Satisfy my idle curiosity, if you will."

Well, there is no harm, I suppose. That, too, was much as you have probably suspected. We hoped to instigate a war between the humans and the ler—you know, 'no fight half so vicious as between members of the family,' I believe you say. We hoped that such a conflict would weaken both to the point where we could move into the area and take each world, one at a time, until the strength of the remaining would not matter. We are on the rim and must needs expand inwards. We prefer our worlds already civilized for us—we do not imagine ourselves a race of pioneers, living among the beasts of the wild and hewing forests."

"Is your appearance a true one, or is it disguised?"

"The basics are as you see. Only certain details have been altered to fit into the Warriors' surround. But during this project, which has already occupied several lifetimes, we discovered that we look rather more like ler, so it is easier to masquerade as one; but in patterns of thought, we resemble humans, the old people, more, if you can sense the difference between the two types. Except more so! Much more so. But all this wastes time. We can talk on the way, if you like, but be seated and let us be on the way. Or stand, if you prefer. Only remember that she will be the price for creating any suspicion in my mind!"

"I will stand. I will tell Liszendir what settings to insert, and she will do it." More like humans in the way they thought. . . . That keyed something. Yes. Han did have one idea. It might work, yes indeed. In fact, the more he thought on it, the more sure he became that it would work, or at least cause enough distraction for him to get the flash gun. Then Aving would see who would burn. They could not afford to take any more chances. If they got any more of their own. But this . . .

Aving said, as Han moved closer to the panels, "Don't you want the course?"

"Not now. Have you ever flown on a human ship before?"

"No, Nor ler. I used my own craft to make the voyage to Seabright, and other places."

"Let me explain, then. I do not want you getting suspicious over any act that I might perform. When we traverse space, we use a set of preset points in space whose locations are known in the ship's memory. I did not know of the location of your planet, so I shall have to set the course manually. Both end-points of the transferral coordinate, because Hatha brought this ship here in the hold of his warship. This process will require a calibration routine, for I shall have to determine my location exactly, bearing Heisenberg's theorem respectfully in mind. This will require some time and work."

"Very well. But perform it with dispatch and use no tricks. You know the penalty. First this one, then the fire-haired klesh girl. You do not wish them to suffer? Then haste. I feel the pressure of time."

Han nodded, grimacing inwardly to himself. If he was wrong . . . "Just so. Now we will enter space." And as he set the course in for the point he wanted, he glanced covertly at Liszendir, and then Usteyin. Not a flicker of recognition was stirring in either of their faces; both were passive, resigned, apprehensive. But nothing else. What he had in his mind depended on that—they must not recognize what he was going to do until he did it; otherwise. Aving might suspect something was coming that was more than it seemed.

The ship reached the point Han had programmed in, and the drives shut down. There remained a minor manual correction, which Liszendir did herself, bringing the Pallenber exactly into position, between the planet and its primary. The star glared whitely through the main screen, an obsession, a fire that drowned out all the rest of the stars in the darks of space.

Now. He turned to Aving, saying, "The girl will now have to hand me a certain object, which I will use to make an exact calculation. It is there, in the small bag. May she get it out and give it to me?"

"What does it look like?"

"To you, a tangle of wire."

"Are you sure . . . ?"

"Do you know anything about navigation, astrogation?"

"No. This is for the crew. Mere mechanics."

"Yes, then. I am sure."

Han turned back to Usteyin. Now she would have to be completely straight. One slip . . . Usteyin still had not caught on. Only concern showed on her face.

"Are you sure you want it, Han? It is dangerous, and I don't understand . . ."

"Never mind, never mind. I need the block, Usteyin. Please give it to me. I know what I'm doing." Han felt a slight sense of irritation, of anxiety; this was tense. If she said one word about the story-block's real purpose . . .

She didn't. Usteyin moved to the bag, reached within, very carefully withdrew the story-block, opened it to its full size, and handed it to Han, with a reluctance that could not be hidden. "Here, But you must be careful. When somebody else uses one . . ."

Han cut her off. "No matter. I know the cautions." He took the device, risking a quick glance at Liszendir. Something was in her eyes; yes! she knew. And at Aving. Suddenly, he was very interested in the story-block, watching it with eerie intensity. Han ignored the alien, held the story-block up to the star, so it would catch the light, looked into it, hoping his pretending would seem reasonably enough like some astrogator taking a measurement.

Curious, he thought, as he held it in his hand, watching the play of light among the wires, the junctions, the positions of the beads. Odd, that you could use a thing like this to symbolize anything. What was it Usteyin had said? Nonverbal. Yes. No words. He wondered how her perception of it was; he stared into it, looking for something suggestive, a symbol, an inkblot, an optical illusion. Nothing. It was just a tangle of wire, just a tangle of wire, but you could follow the lines of it indefinitely, it was hypnotic, relaxing, he felt muscles in the back of his neck relaxing, tiny strain lines in his face loosening. Yes, it could at least put you to sleep, if you weren't careful; must speak to Usteyin about that part of it. What time was it? Time felt odd, like it was not passing right.

He looked away, feeling a reluctance to take his eyes out of it. He looked back. He had not registered the time on the panel chronometer, except the second hand. That had stood out, starkly: it was ten seconds past. Ten seconds past what? Nothing. It didn't matter. There was no time, time was an illusion, he would see that here, just a little more, the effort that was not effort, the unpremeditated act, the sudden sneaking up upon reality, reality.

There was motion, movement, the control room, the ship was shifting, flowing melting, no not doing anything, he was moving, evolving, changing, the streaks of light were forming themselves into shapes, suggestions, fast, fast, he knew his mind was doing it; slow it down, timeless, timeless, bring the rate down, untryingly trying, effortlessly efforting. Efforting. Not-word. Ha ha. Funny, words. He had no need of them, it was so easy, just beneath the surface, reaching for it, the water changed the apparent angle, things were offset, groping in the water . . . water, silvery wires, swift flowing water, water falling to the bottom of the sink, the well, the pit, water seeking its level, water wetting, soaking, sea-changes, there was a sea on Seabright, something was urgent, he had to do something. Water, that was it. He was water, flowing, penetrating, moving into every space, every void, space had taken the place of water in the old symbolisms, he was water, he was space he could seestars, allonething seerseen seerseen-mediumoftransmission light-wavescrawlinglike worms starsstars and therewassomething more reaching reaching.

STOP. nondeceleration. Juststopinstant. Alone. No. Notalone. Others. Nearfar/herethere. No, he said, trying to find some numbers for this, mask it with symbols, break the chain, why heHan was here in the controlroomnow, there was Aving, and Liszendir and Usteyin and himself himselfselflff. No, must get out of it, goddam deadly thing, got to get out, turn around easy and *move*. He turned around. There was no around. He looked up. There was no up. The referent universe had vanished. It was gone. How could you get out when you didn't know how you got in, how could you reach a place if you didn't know where you were. What difference-diditmakemakemake? A vast joke, and that it was onhim was onlyfunny. Unimportant. Here were them all, Hatha, Dardenglir, Liszendir, Hetrus, a child with red hair, whothehellwasthat? Others. He could blank them, one by one. There was no time. Child-out. Hatha-out. some more anuncountablenumber-out. Gone. Aving, too, he wasn't anyway. Out. Now him, Liszendir, Usteyin, but not in the right positions. They were all moving around, Liszendir behind him, but he could still see herherher Usteyin in front, the stars came back into view, notstarshere, starssomewhere-else, thick, dewyspiderwebs, clouds, seas, water. He was water, yes! Usteyin was looking toward him, reaching her face. Liszendir was pushing him, notrejecting, moving him, she had sadness on hers, but on Usteyin's there was more, he was not getting closer, she was expanding, enlarging, beckoning to him with her sea-green eyes from the edge of the universe. No. Outside it, they were expanding, filling it, filling everything, the stars became galaxies, the galaxies shrunk, diminished, faded, went out. Blackness. Then stars again, a few, then many, then repeating cycle again. Stars, galaxies, the night, starsgalaxiesnight. Flashing, flickering, then merginginto continuoussmoothgrey, The Aleph, and Usteyin was now enormous, she filled his vision, she surrounded him, he felt no fear, no apprehension, there was no danger, it was preplanned, programmed into the steady state universe, right-correctproper like falling, falling Liszendir was a point, a one-dimensional object of singular purpose tremendous power, the will, fire, the magicians wand, green sprouting branch, lifegiving, Usteyin was event, air, swords, that the three of them would fall together was a property of the universe, the universe, he could go forwardsbackwards, tofro, sideside, updown the meaning was just out of reach, one more effortlesseffort nownownow its in my hand slippery slippery can't hold it the more i catch the less i have got to get it all usteyin back into being reaching she has a story block in her other hand other hand, which is the other hand from the other hand/ like a box on both ends it says open other end endless spiral, doctor, which sex is the opposite, i know i no negate gate / usteyin how her body felt when they had been one creature reaching reaching slippery a soundless flash.

He heard the air moving through the ventilators into the control room, he saw the instruments on the panel, he felt time passing at its own rate again, and he held a story-block in his hand, at which he must not look. He felt purged, cleansed, washed out, but he had seen a story, if he could just sort it out, something warm, close, he and Usteyin, and there was Liszendir too, in the future, or was it the past? No. The future. She had long, long, hair, it was iron-gray, she had lines in her face. But stop. Han looked at the chronometer. That was absurd. No time at all had passed. But the second hand had moved, to the 15 mark. Five seconds? Or had he gone all the way around the clock? No. It was now. Han felt himself beginning to shake, to sweat, instantly clammy. That thing was dangerous. Perilous. He looked over to Usteyin, looked at her directly, as if he were seeing her for the first time. She looked back at him, seeing that he was out of the story-block, free, unharmed.

She spoke, and broke the silence. "Did you make your measurement?" Now she knew.

"Yes, I did. It is very simple."

He looked over to Aving. "Ah, that was a hard one. These outer regions are the very devil to astrogate in. I think we should invent a better way to do it. Don't you have a better way, Aving?"

Aving said, "What is that thing you were just using?"

"It is a calibration device. We use it only at times when we have to make a transition with both end-points open. Machines are good, machines are fast, but they are more limited than we are. With this, we can see directly, then translate the vision into numbers for the ship."

"Are you finished? Let me see that thing! I have never seen such a device . . ."

"Well, I do have to make some more measurements, but . . ."

"Give it to me! I wish to examine it. I cannot determine how it works, there is no structure . . ." He trailed off, unfinishing what he might have said. He was staring *into* the story-block, becoming glassy-eyed. Rather more like humans, not so much like ler, Han reminded himself, still remembering echoes from his own vision, still feeling bits and pieces.

He told Aving, "It is electroptical. Look into it, watch the wires. Hold it at right angles to the star, you'll see better."

Aving took the story-block, and held it as Han showed him, never taking his eyes off it. He still held the gun close to Liszendir, but he was becoming oblivious. Han felt sorry for him, just for an instant; what was going to happen to him either way wasn't going to be pleasant, not at all. . . .

Aving muttered, almost inaudibly, "I can't quite see it . . ."

Liszendir, listening to the voice, was starting to move. Han checked her with a motion. She must not interrupt this. Aving was a fish, and he must take the hook himself.

Han said, "You need more light, Aving," and Han turned the dial controlling the filter circuits of the viewscreen, simultaneously pulling Usteyin and Liszendir down to the floor as he did. The filter circuits opened and the screen passed all of the energy in the visible band into the control room, all the output of the star within the range of visible light. The glaring, stark, white light filled the room, and in that light Aving was visible, standing quite still, holding a tangle of wire in his free hand, gazing into it with eyes gone completely vacant. The flash gun dropped from his relaxed grip, to dangle on the trigger guard from a finger. Liszendir reached up from the floor beside him, and carefully took the gun from his hand. Han reached over the lip of the main panel, and returned the filter circuits of the viewscreen to a lower setting. The screen darkened, dimmed the glare of the star, and the cabin returned to semidarkness again.

Aving stood in exactly the same position, holding the story-block, still gazing vacantly into the depths of glittering wire. The three of them, Han, Liszendir, and Usteyin, all got to their feet. Aving did not react, nor did he give any sign that he was even aware of them.

Liszendir asked, with awe shading the edges of her voice, "Is he disarmed, now?"

Usteyin answered, "Oh, yes. Forever. I did not see what Han was trying to do at first, but then I saw it. A good trick, one I would not have thought of myself. Look, I will show you." And she walked over to the silent staring figure, and disengaged the wire tangle from his fingers, pulling it out of his hand with some effort. He did not want to let it go. As she did so, the figure shuddered, as if with a sudden chill, but made no other motions, and continued to stare at the place where the story-block had been.

"Good. Just right," she said, with a soft voice that revealed satisfaction, and some light anger as well. Then she went behind Aving, kicked the backs of his knees, and caught him a he fell to the floor, breaking his fall. Then she turned to Han.

"A good trick, the best I have ever seen. But you have cost me my story-block to do it—a little high for the likes of Aving." Here was the source of her anger, now fading.

"How so? Why?"

"I told you before—you go too far and it traps your spirit. That is what happened to Aving, you tricked him into it. But now the story-block has his spirit, and the next person to use it will get it back, part of Aving impressed into his selfness, his mind. Maybe a lot, maybe even Aving's self will be strong enough to trade with yours, if you look again."

"How can that be? That is just hypnosis."

"No, it is more than that, what-you-say, the way you hold it, the tension, everything is input. Ask Han. He knows now, he got a taste of it. When you do not put any starts into it at the first you are asking for the meaning of everything, you have put no limtis whatsoever on it. And you go within, with your mind. Are you really inside it? I do not know, except what I learned when I was young, beginning to use one. The

Zlats say you go within. And when you look into one, you get out what has been stored; and if it is someone who has been careless, who looked too far . . . Aving was an evil man, even in the little part of him that we knew; I do not know what other evils he may have been prey to. But we will not have the problem of letting Aving out into one of us. I will destroy it." And before either Han or Liszendir could stop her, she took the story-block, carefully avoiding looking at it directly, and crumpled it up into a wadded tangle, a crushed mass. Then she placed it on the floor, and stamped on it until it was completely unrecognizable.

"Liszendir, you have the flash gun. Make it narrow, strong! Burn this, melt it, now!" Her voice was sharp, peremptory. "Do not worry about that body there on the floor! It still functions, but it has no mind: and I know no way to get it back. Now, the gun! Quick! You must do this now or my resolve will not last!"

Liszendir adjusted the flash gun, pointed it at the crumpled object on the floor, matted and wadded as far as hands could make it, and fired, playing the beam over the story-block until nothing remained of it but a charred lump of melted silver, unrecognizable, smoking.

Usteyin looked at the lump for a long moment, sighed deeply, and relaxed, becoming herself again. The change in her had been so gradual that Han had not noticed it, until she returned to her normal self. "So now it is done. The body is of no more use to us, so we can eject it into the night."

"But he's still alive. Shouldn't we try to take it back?"

"No. He will die soon. The story-block got a lot of him, even things like breathing. He was more susceptible to it than either Han or myself, and he had less defense against it—none, in fact. It was catching him before he even took it from Han. The body will go bad. So we will tell them, back in your place, and they will believe."

"Couldn't we bring him back to his senses, interrogate him somehow?"

"No. Nothing is kept. I know of no one who has ever recovered from an event like that. They die sooner or later. Yes. Look at Aving. He is dead, now. I can't tell you hows—I only know whats. Just like I said. It traps the spirit. And once that has happened to a story-block, it is no good any more and the metal must be purified by fire. It is unclean. This normally happens with one's own, you know, from looking too far. But for mine, it was a stranger who was caught. If we had not destroyed it, then the next time I looked into it, I would get Aving's spirit impressed onto mine. And my self would go inside. Then you would have Aving back, but in my body. I do not think you would want that."

"Can you get another one, from the Zlats, or can you make another one?"

"No—neither. I cannot make another one. Period. As for anyone else's, they are individual. If I tried to use another's, I might see the same stories, but they would go all wrong, and if I tried to *see* with it, it would show lies. I might try to rerun the story of Koren and Jolise, remember? But in someone else's, Jolise might try to kill Koren, in some terrible way. The pattern of strong emotion would be there, but it would have been shifted into a different particular expression. Do you see? In a story-block, there are no whats, only hows. I supply the whats."

Usteyin bent to the body of the alien, began trying to drag it to a place where they could jettison it into space. Liszendir moved to help her. It was not heavy, and they dragged it with little effort. Han showed them where the disposal bay was, and Aving vanished into space.

At last, they returned to the cabin, to the panel, where Han inserted the course, a matrix-12 course which would route them directly through to Seabright. As the *Pallenber* began to move in normal space, orienting itself, Han showed the initiate handle to Usteyin, a rough-finish simple gray lever-type device, offered it to her.

"You turn it. Just hold it firmly, turn it by rotating your hand, as if you were bringing your thumb up."

She looked shyly at Han, and then at Liszendir; reached for the handle, hesitantly, then grasped it firmly, and turned it. Normal space in the vicinity of the planet Dawn vanished, and they were on their way back. Usteyin still, for a time, tightly held the gray handle, as if she feared that if she let it go, the magic would end. Finally, convinced that it would not, she released it and stood back, smiling an odd half-smile to herself.

14

EPILOGUE

"Ends? What ends? I know only beginnings!"
—*Valdollin Tlanh*

ON THE PLANET Kenten, the first home of the ler after they had left Earth, it was spring, early spring, the particular time of the year when things are just starting to become tinged with green, and some days may be balmy, pleasant, but in the dregs of the day, the old winter is still hanging on, hoping against time that it still can make its presence known.

In spring, then, in a small town located on the shore of a small sea that connected two larger seas, Han walked back to the teahouse where Usteyin awaited him, savoring the wet rain, the damp air, the suggestion of sea-odors, feeling the cold, and reflecting on all that had been said in the final report on Dawn, which Hetrus had arranged to have forwarded to him there, through the local post. This town was called Plenkhander, in accordance with the ler custom which decreed that the smaller the town, the longer the name.

But he was not so concerned with the report, which at any rate was no more than a courtesy; Han's part in the events on Dawn had ended, by his own wish, and Usteyin's, and instead of going back, they had all three come to Kenten, to Yalven province, to Plenkhander, to see Liszendir woven, and to fit themselves into a more normal life again. He reflected, as he passed rainstreaked shop windows, that adventuring was all right, all well and good, for those who sought it out, but he had not, however it had come off, and for the moment, he did not want any more adventures of the sort that saw one carried further into the unknown with every minute of time. He realized that this was, of course, just an extreme parable of life itself, always into the unknown, no matter if you spent your days in a shop, selling cookies, but he had wanted time; and they had given it to him. They had come to Kenten, left the *Pallenber* at the main spaceport, and journeyed here.

As Han had expected, Hetrus had wanted them all to go back to Dawn, and lead the operations there. But he had refused, and he was glad he had done so, for not only did Liszendir have her problem, compounded by the fact that her age group had already made most of their arrangements, but she also had Usteyin's problem: she had a whole world-idea to learn. So Hetrus had paid them all, handsomely, for all they had done, given them the ship (they had earned it, he said), and left them alone.

He had heard that ler planets were, as the phrase was politely put, backward, but that one word missed much of the charm and sense of relaxed living which flowed all through them. Time was here, one was conscious of it constantly, one never forgot it, particularly on Kenten. He had expected something—either vast technological progress, or at least great intellectual subtlety, but he had seen neither. Just people, and the basic realities of life, as might be seen at any place and any time. It was much of what he and Usteyin had needed.

Plenkhander was named for an ancient stone bridge which still stood, relaying light traffic over a sluggish creek which met the sea here, a bridge which had been standing, mortarless, from a time before Han's own planet had been settled. The shore here was straight, without points or embayments, so in a later period, they had added a jetty, and a small dock, to facilitate trade with the interior, which loomed behind the town, tumbling hills rising into the middle distances, culminating in a sawtooth ridgeline not so very high, no more than a few thousand feet, tree-covered to the very summits. Farther down the coast, to the east, the mountains came closer in to the shore, and that was where Liszendir had grown up, in a place near a town called as the remembered it, "mill-wheel-stream."

Usteyin had been enchanted at the site of the house, and a larger building nearby which served as the school, and he himself had not wanted to leave, such was the peace and timelessness of it. It was just as she had described it—the house, or *yos*, the orchards, the farms along the slopes, the narrow beach and the sea before the house. In the fore-yard of the *yos*, there had been a dwarf tree in a huge stone pot. But dwarf was only a relative term, for the tree had overspread much of the yard. It was, apparently, a giant sequoia from Earth, lovingly cultivated in miniature, forced to concentrate on bulk and spread instead of height as it would have done on its own. Injhe space behind the *yos*, where the structure had sprouted two wings that flowed up the hill, there was another, nestled in the comer. It was a local tree, called grayflank, which had a trunk that was veined and corded like the arm of a wrestler. It spread its branches over the *yos*, shading it in the summer with its foliage of small, rough leaves which Liszendir said turned bright yellow in the autumn. The *yos* itself was no longer the beige, off-white, parchment color of newer material, but a soft brownish-gray, streaked and stained and mossy with age. It looked as if it were part of the landscape.

The parent generation was still around, as they said it, but none of them seemed very interested in staying at home, and save for a few chance meetings, they saw little of them. As for Liszendir's insiblings, they were not yet fertile, but after the older girl had left, they had gradually taken over the *yos* themselves, and now were fully settled in their new role, painfully shy, serious, and busy as newly weds in a new house, even though they had lived in it all their lives. They, too, spent much of their time up at the school, for they would be the ones to carry its ownership on. Which left the *thes*, the younger outsibling, Vindhermaz. Liszendir called him Vin, which embarrassed the boy terribly, but he bore up under her ribbing gracefully, smiling knowingly whenever they would hear a soft, feminine voice call for him from outside, using his love-name of two syllables.

They had visited just long enough to become acquainted, and then set out for the larger town several miles west down the coast, from which they could obtain a wider view of available insiblings. Liszendir had taken little from her home, save a few clothes, her musical instrument, the *tsonh*, made of fine, dark wood, finished in natural colors, and accented by silver keys and pad-covers. And a string of wooden beads, simple, unornamented, made of a dark, reddish wood. They were made of the wood of the tree before the *yos*, and were several generations old. These she gave to Han, saying only that by them he should remember her. For Usteyin, a soft summer wrap she had worn earlier. They were both touched deeply by these gifts, which were not either things which could be bought anywhere.

So they returned to Plenkhander. At first, Liszendir had disclaimed the two of them, saying that she could look after herself well enough, but she did not resist when both Han and Usteyin insisted, and Han chartered a room in an obscure but comfortable hotel, for several months, with an option to renew the lease. Since then she had become gentle, even wistful, when she was not traveling all over the local area, following up leads, which were, still, turning out to be either dead ends, or past-tense, by the time she found the insiblings in question. This problem was not only one of availability, but was further compounded by a factor she told Han about only after they were safely on Kenten: her attribute being "fire," she could only weave into a braid which lacked a "fire," completing the square of Fire-Air-Earth-Water. And neither Han or Usteyin could help her in this, for no ler would speak openly about the matter, even among themselves, and to talk about this with humans, the old people, was completely out of the question.

So they waited, in Plenkhander, and felt time passing in its measureless way. Here, the rain fell and blackened the trees, still bare from winter, and the wind in the night made the trees creak, and the air smelled in the soft blue twilights of sea and salt and woodsmoke; wagons and hooves rattled in the cobblestone streets, and small children on their way home played small flutes, and carried warm loaves of fresh bread flavored with onions back to clusters of ellipsoids nestling under trees that resembled plane trees or poplars. They ate their fill, slept deeply, and spent the days walking in the rich, rain-wet air, and visiting whatever struck their fancy. Usteyin did not want to leave, even after Liszendir became be woven.

The braid-houses were, here as on Chalcedon, the low ellipsoids, loosely joined together, usually surrounded by low walls and spread gracefully under the trees, while buildings devoted to public use or commerce seemed to follow a more human shape—one- or two-story square buildings as often as not topped with low domes. The streets wound around without seeming purpose, wandering, random, as if they had followed paths before they were streets. The ler were not obvious, this Han knew well, but even more, neither were they ever in a hurry, even to get home. Rarely, a few braids lived in their shops, overhead, but this was considered low-class and on the verge of poverty, so there were few.

And back to reality, to the present. Han was nearing the teahouse, which was a low building, open, glassed in, with a low dome, which squatted or floated according to the mood of the observer, beside a ferry landing. Today, in the afternoon light, the sky was leaden and the rain pelted in Han's face, and the slate-colored sea heaved and tossed as if in some mild agitation; yet it was not dreary, apprehensive, or moody. On the contrary, Han had never felt so full of life, so involved. He looked ahead to see if he could pick Usteyin out of the crowd in the teahouse. Yes. Even from a distance he could distinguish her red hair, for, dark as it was, it was of a color no ler would ever have, and she wore it falling in cascades over her shoulders. She sat quietly unmoving in the tea-house, features rippled by the hand-poured glass panes and the streaks of rain on them, and sipped tea daintily, her full upper lip marking her face, looking out on the sea with the patience and inward calm reflections of the ler, who Han had observed watching the sea for hours if so disposed.

Han entered the tea house, shaking the rain off his cloak, and then hanging it on a peg set in the wall, secured another pot of tea from the counterman, and joined Usteyin. As he sat down at the small table with her, she turned and smiled to him with an expression at once so peaceful and at the same time so intimate and warm that he felt a sudden pang.

He said, "Have you been bored waiting? It was a very long business, picking up that message."

"No, no, I am learning to like this very much, this ler place, the way they live, not at all like the Warriors were. I fit it well. And more than once, I have caught myself wishing that you and I, we could live here. It is so . . . what? You are the one who knows words. No, I was not bored. You know that I watch the sea and spell stories in it, stories without end. We did not have seas on Dawn; only some salt lakes where nothing lived and the smell was bad. But not anything like this; this is more a wonder than the view from space. But I know there is much more to see and I want to see it all." Han looked mock-scandalized. She looked at his serious face, and then continued, "Well, the boy said they had a long message for you at the post. What do the others say?"

"That there is a planet for the *klesh*, all to itself, far away from Dawn. They had been keeping it in reserve, but this is a good purpose, and they at least will need a place of their own. After knowing you for a while, I do not worry about the Zlats adjusting. Oh, no. We are the ones who would have trouble adjusting to them! But the wild humans will come back, to backwater places, and later, they can come into the mainstream worlds, if they feel up to it. As for the ler on Dawn, I don't know. Factionalism has at last entered ler politics. One faction wants to leave them where they are and let Dawn's star take care of the problem. The other faction wants to get them off. And neither wants them integrated into mainstream ler culture. That's funny, if you think of it—I mean, they had no races as we humans do, but all the time, despite all their strictures about a wide gene pool, they were really extremely racist. Now they have a race problem as well."

"They are strange people, very strange. More so than I thought. Those on Dawn were . . . very ordinary, I suppose. Here, in their old place, this Kenten, they are deep in the way of . . . nature, but not wildness. They are warm, and treat one another well, according to their lights; yet they can be hard and cruel, too, to each other. But I am trying to imagine what a whole world of *klesh*, and wild, too, would be like. What will happen to them after they are moved?"

"I don't have any idea at all. I have never seen or heard anything like this. I suspect they will form tribes, first, oppress and exploit one another. You are a Zlat. How would you act?"

"I wouldn't know how to act on my own, in a society, at first." She said the word "society" as if it were some strange pungent herb. "We would have to, or run wild in the forest. I shouldn't want that—I would be cold, running about bare. You know that we were in some ways very primitive. I have been studying, Han, so I know what I was. But I am not ashamed. But more, we were not wild, but really a kind of privileged class, protected by a kind of civilization. On Dawn, many would have died. I know about winter." She made a motion as if she were shivering in bitter-cold airs.

Back in civilization, Usteyin had finally taken to wearing clothes, and although she was not entirely satisfied with them, and appalled at underwear, she had been dressing ler-style, in long, rather plain homespuns that covered all of her. But she had once, back in their rooms, exposed one creamy delicate shoulder and exclaimed, "A hundred and twenty generations to produce that tone of skin!" She raised the bottom of the robe as if she expected to be surprised by what she would find there, displaying her lower legs, and the fine, copper-colored hair that covered them, furlike. "And that! And now all covered up, for custom and for weather!" But at the same time she had discovered clothes with all the innocent joy of a child in a palace of toys, and however much she said that she would prefer to go about bare, she still wore them with considerable flair and pride. Liszendir had not completely approved of the styles she chose, but she had had to admit the Usteyin fitted well, and quickly. The only noticeable difference in her was her hair color and slighter build. By human standards, she was almost petite.

Han said, still thinking about the *klesh* and the new life that was approaching for them, "I'd guess they would form tribes at first, like kinds, but there would be some mixing, even at first, and more later on. There will be suffering and fighting and injustice. But Hetrus says that they are going to send some outside people there to keep a reasonable sort of order, at least within a certain area, and let them go into the wild as they will."

"Yes, they will fight. The males will fight over the females, and vice-versa. I would have, in my old life. In some events, I would even now." She raised an eyebrow archly.

Then they both, as if by mutual unspoken consent, fell to looking at the sea again. The subtle colors of the rainy afternoon flowed over it, changing even as they watched, but so gradually that they were not aware that a change was taking place, until it was over, and had evolved to something new. The rain stopped, and over the west a pale patch, a glowing warm tan, told of cloud decks breaking up, clearing. The sea took on a silvery surface gloss and lost much of its chop, and on the landing, a tied rowboat stopped its wild tethered leaping and began moving more sedately. The effect was hypnotic.

They began talking about Liszendir; she was, in fact, having considerable difficulty finding exactly the right braid, and was now spending most of her time traveling around to the many small villages in the area, searching. The situation was somewhat similar to an analogous predicament for a human in a society of arranged marriages; in her own village, she would have been known and it would have been fairly easy for an insibling pair to find her, go through the delicate maneuvers of determining one another's aspect, begin serious negotiations. But on her own, she had to resort to the town bulletin-board, where strangers usually advertised. Han thought the custom a curious one, even verging on degrading in a way, but Liszendir didn't see it that way at all. Besides, she had to spend most of her time, now, traveling.

They had a saying—one of many, in fact, for ler culture seemed permeated with sayings. This one went: "Harder to please than an insibling." No wonder, there: they were the keepers of the nongenetic family line, the braid continuity, the continuation of the weave. The insibling females picked outsibling females for their insiblings and the males picked males, each one balancing jealousy and fear of strangers with an accurate appraisal of the needs of the braid-identity and the matching of personalities within the group. It was often a hard task, indeed, for no matter that the insiblings were not blood-related to each other, nevertheless they had grown up together in a fashion much like brother and sister, and there was considerable tension between them. So the preweaving arrangements were somewhat of a strain for all parties, and during the period, most were touchy and irritable.

Usteyin was even more astounded at the weaving customs than was

Han. She observed, "I see not so much difference between how we did it on Dawn, and how humans back here in civilized parts order their lives. There is a relation, a bridge between us, however strange things seem at first. But in their thing, Liszendir's people, they went further and made the family a purely social thing, not part social, part genetics; so for them, the difference between family and society has never arisen. But myself? Oh, no! I couldn't do that, no matter how well it works for them. I couldn't share you with anybody now."

Han agreed. "It's been tried in a couple of places by humans. It looks good, but it only works if you have a low birthrate and have been raised on a steady diet of sex from about age nine on. It takes a special kind of personality, too, to make it work right. They have a lot of sex, and a lot of fun, but there isn't much passion in it. That's the key. I think only one group survived any time at all, and actually made it a generation. Then that fell apart. A lot of people have to participate in the system or you get ferocious inbreeding. The ler keep elaborate genealogies, but they are designed to prevent that kind of thing."

Usteyin finished her tea, arose quietly and gracefully from her seat, and stretched like some exotic, piquant feline. "Well, I'm sleepy now, and I should have a nap. Shall we go home?"

"A good idea. I was watching the waves while we talked, and it was making me sleepy, too. And more . . ."

"Oh, indeed! I would like that very much, too."

They put their cloaks on, and left the teahouse, to walk back to the hotel through the winding streets that still shone with rainwater. Afternoon was drawing to an end, and there was a tang, a scent, in the air, which promised clearer weather on the morrow. They were almost alone in the narrow lanes, for it was the end of the day, shops were closing, and the quiet of evening was settling over Plenkhander.

When they had climbed the stairs to their room, which they had shared with Liszendir when she had been in town, they found her gathering up the last of her few belongings. She looked tired, worn-down, but underneath that, there was a glow that told them what they had all been waiting for.

She smiled weakly and said, "You must wish me luck, now."

Han asked, "So you have found a braid?"

"Yes. It was ironic, that. All day, I have been across the mountains, at a place called Thursan's Landing, a fishing village. A vile place. I did not want to be a fisherwoman! But when I came back here, just now, there was a letter for me, downstairs, and so I went to see her. Imagine! After all this work, this traveling around, their *yos* is just down the beach road, hardly across the bridge. And so we made our arrangements."

Usteyin asked, "Liszendir, when you weave, do you have to do any ceremony, any special kind of act, before someone?"

She paused a moment. Then said, "If I may ask such a thing of you."

"It is no secret. For the insiblings, there is something they do some-thing with the parent generation, the old insiblings, but I may not speak of that. It would not be for me, anyway. But for the outsiblings who are to be afterparents, there is nothing, either in religion or in law. You are accepted and you move in with your braid. They have accepted you, and that is authority enough for any hierarchy. When we are all formed, all woven, then there will be a party, friends and relations will visit, and there will be talk, singing, dancing, all night." Then she became serious. "But you know that I have never seen him, whom I will weave with. Nor do they have an afterfather yet, either, and he will be my second. But this is all I need. I was worried, deeply. I was beginning to think that no one wanted me. That is very frightening to us."

Han thought for a minute, then asked, "Do you like the girl you met? Do you think you will be happy there?"

"After adventuring, the strange things I have done, the oaths I have broken? Nothing can ever be the same for me again. But they are good people, very deep, as we say. That will be good for me; I need that deep-ness. I am pleased with them, at least such as I know of them. But I am finished, here. Come along. You shall see, too!"

Han and Usteyin each took a parcel for her, and together they left the room, went down the stairs, and came out onto the street.

Liszendir said, "It's not far. Practically under our noses." She was be-ginning to relax, visibly, yet at the same time she seemed anxious, anx-ious to go home. The three of them stood under the soft lights of the doorway lamp of the hotel and looked at one another. Liszendir guessed from Han's and Usteyin's faces that they were reading her with accuracy.

She said, warmly, "Yes, that is true, too. It is my home now. For forty standard years; until the insiblings weave in their turn. Here, right here, in Plenkhander." She looked around in the dim light at the trees with their sparkling drops of cold rainwater. The odors of the sea filled the air and from the beach, only a row of houses away, the sound of the surf could be heard, a light regular stroking that worked at the brown sand gently with the calming of the sea.

Han said, "It's hard to picture."

"To you, perhaps. But not to me."

They walked eastwards, crossed the ancient stone bridge, and within a few hundred yards came to a low stone wall, overgrown with vines. The *yos* lay deep in a grove of huge trees, trees with heavy mottled boles that resembled planetrees, still bare, and was brightly lit by the door with hanging lanterns. Liszendir rang the bell, a huge pottery bell that rang with a mellow deep sound, as they entered the garden. After a moment, out of the *yos* ran a young child, obviously the elder outsibling, the *nerh*, but what sex it was could not be determined. All Han and Usteyin could see was that it was about three or four years old. It was followed by a ler female, who stood in the light of the lanterns, waiting for them. She was small and dark, pretty-pleasant but not beautiful. She looked busy, and wore her hair, considerably longer than Liszendir's, tied up in a sort of kerchief. As they came closer, Han noticed that her hands were reddened from washing apparently, but they were strong, capable, busy hands. She would be about five years older than Liszendir.

While the child ran around them, staring shyly when it thought no one was watching at Usteyin's hair, the girl came up to them, embraced Liszendir, pressing her cheeks to the new girl's quickly, and turned to them, smiling shyly. Han repressed an urge to laugh: she had a missing tooth. But he didn't, for it added a certain charm to her face, which was painfully earnest. Her face was plain, like Liszendir's, but different, narrower, more oval, and her hair was darker. She had a soft, generous mouth and clear, direct eyes, eyes that were the color of rainwater, or the color of the sheen on the sea after a storm.

She spoke. "I am Hvethmerleyn. I am sorry you cannot meet the *kadh*, the forefather, for he is still up in the vineyards and will probably be out for several more days." Her voice was clear, a pure tone. She pronounced the "hv-" of her name with a breathy inflection that added some essence, some indecipherable attractiveness to her manner. "Will you join us tonight? Please stay for a while, for this is special, and we have few visitors. I would be very happy."

So they all went into the *yos* under the trees and spent the evening eating, drinking, telling part of their story over again to Hvethmerleyn, who listened to what she heard with hardly concealed amazement. If Han left some parts out, neither Liszendir nor Usteyin corrected him. And as the night went onwards, he noticed that the two females seemed to be warming up to each other well, becoming confidential, intimate. He wondered not so much how it would be for Liszendir: that he already knew, at least part of it; but rather for Hvethmerleyn. To spend your whole life with one male, more or less, and then pick yourself a second mate for him, bring her into your house, the house of your own family group . . . He tried to imagine it. He could not.

They learned that the braid-name was Ludhen. Ludh meant "wine" in Singlespeech! They were vintners! Hvethmerieyn laughed her warm laugh, and Han, now wise to some ler ways, saw, just for a moment, that Hvethmerleyn was, in ler reference, very warm, very sexy. That would be exactly what Liszendir needed, for he had begun to suspect something about her, something about a thing missing in Liszendir's life. She was pleased that Han recognized the Singlespeech word-root, and insisted that he and Usteyin take a bottle of wine to remember them by. And she talked about the forefather, her insibling, who was called Thoriandas.

It seemed that Hvethmerleyn suspected that his remark about being up in the vineyards was just an excuse to go out and look for a suitable male outsibling for her. Thoriandas, apparently, had a robust sense of humor, and had promised that he would dig up the worst sort of riffraff, a drunkard and a reprobate, and probably a thief to boot. Usteyin laughed out loud.

"And what will you do with such a one?"

"Oh, I'll reform him," she answered, suddenly coy, arch, demure. "Or," she added, "I'll wear him out in the process!"

The child, Tavrenian, had proved to be a boy, and had tumbled off to bed earlier. As they talked on, Han saw that Hvethmerleyn was also getting sleepy, and he knew that Liszendir would be about run down herself. Ler went to bed early, and got up early. So they made their goodbyes, in short form, without ceremony, and made ready to leave the *yos*. Liszendir came with them to the door, while Hvethmerleyn stayed behind, sensing that they had one more thing to say that was private, part of Liszendir's old life. In the yard, it was dark and quiet, save for the remains of the dripping of rainwater, now almost stopped, and the mutter and gentle splashing of the surf behind the *yos*. Somewhere hidden by the trees and houses, a wagon was slowly rattling along the cobblestones, blending into the water sounds in a stream of sound that fitted together perfectly.

Usteyin broke the silence, saying, "Liszendir Now-Ludhen, you have a piece of loveliness here I wish deeply we could share. But I wish you, in your life to come, the same of what we have found in ours and hope to keep for the time that will fall to us."

"Yes, it is so. This is a good place; I think I will grow into it. And it is as you say. So I will not say goodbye to you, nor will I forget. I have seen your lives, and you have seen mine, and we have all walked in one another's shoes for a time. And it ends, well, more than what I once thought would never be." She stopped, biting her lower lip indecisively. Then she impulsively embraced them both, briefly, and ran back into the *yos*, stopping only in the doorway to say to them, "Many children! And many years!" She quickly disappeared within.

Outside, in the dampness of the night air and deep in the sounds of raindrip and surf, Han and Usteyin turned and walked up the path to the gate, and from there, back over the stone bridge, back to their room, through the wet streets alone, silent, deep in thoughts, occasionally touching one another as they walked.

AN EXPLANATORY AFTERWORD
ON LER NAMES

A S IN MOST speculative stories, some of the names of beings, particularly the alien or the strange, may strike one as hard, odd, or impossible to pronounce. This is not the case, at least by intent, as far as the ler names used in this tale are concerned. After a moment's investigation, they should be both possible and easy to sub vocalize.

All ler personal names were composed of three Singlespeech basic root-words or syllables, coupled directly together and pronounced as one word. Each root-word in Singlespeech ends in, and only in, a vowel-consonant pair. In the English spelling convention we use here, this may appear at times to be more extensive, but the units are always single phonemes. Knowing this, we may break up the name into its three parts, correctly, by finding the vowel-consonant ends of each root. An example of this is the name "Liszendir," which breaks "Lis-Zen-Dir."

Now while the generation principle behind the structure of the root words of Singlespeech was modeled on the Chinese example (i.e., few patterns of basic words, using all possible combinations), the phonetic values used to fill in the blanks were equivalent to those values in use at the time of the origin of the ler in the country where they happened to be, which was an English-speaking country. Modern English of the standard American variety is close enough. Only two consonants out of the whole thirty-six-character alphabet were not natural to that context, and they were *kh* and *gh*, added to the system to make it regular, both in a phonetic sense and a ler-qabaslistic one.

Ler personal names had, for the ler, a curious duality in regard to meaning which is difficult for us to understand fully. For us, civilized men, personal names have largely lost their function of totem and meaning;

Georges do not, as a rule, imagine themselves to be workers of earth, nor do Leos emulate lions, nor Leroys imagine themselves kings, no matter how much self-esteem they may have. Our names are derivative, meant to honor a family namesake, a famous person, or—even sound pretty. (The girl-name Pamela is reputed to have no denotative meaning whatsoever!) So when we think of names having literal meaning, we think, perhaps, about more primitive kinds of men, American Indians of the Southwest, or of Africans of the equatorial forests.

For the ler, however, names could be, according to circumstance, very meaningful, as for the tribesman, or completely meaningless, far more so than for us, since it was the ler custom that no child could be named for anybody. The names were supposed to be as original as possible. If one by chance repeated, it was strictly by chance. Ler would not knowingly repeat a name, certainly not one used within their local area. Because of the secret nature of the "aspect" (Lssp: *plozos*) of the individual, a ritual part of ler culture, and the relation of the "aspect" to the particular meaning out of four possible meanings for each root, a person's name-meaning could not be determined unless one knew the aspect. Within the braid, of course, such things were known, if not discussed, and one's name tended to form a basic guide to character. A ler whose name happened to mean "fire-eating devil" *(Pangurton*)* would in fact be prone to a certain amount of belligerence and irrationality, and others would also be guided by the meaning attributed to their names, in like manner.

*Fire *(Panh)* aspect.

Outside the braid, however, it was another matter; one's "aspect" was not told to anyone, except for weaving-custom, and without the context of discourse-speech to aid meaning, a translation could not be determined. In the case of the ler girl Liszendir, no ler outside her birth-braid knew her aspect, or the meaning of her name, until she was accepted by Hvethmerleyn into Ludhen Braid (Klanludhen). That she told the human Han first what it meant, and later that she was fire in aspect, can be viewed as a measure of her feelings, as it was a major sacrifice on her part.

As syllables were not repeated within names, and all three parts had to be of the same aspect, the number of possible interpretations is fortunately limited; however, it is still too high to guess and beat the laws of probability, even for ler. Consequently, considerable time was devoted among the ler, socially, to determining the aspect of one's associates and friends (not to mention lovers), a practice which was countered by equally strenuous attempts to keep it concealed. Perhaps by this, some of Liszendir's actions may appear more explicable.

Liszendir's name, "(fire) velvet brushed night," carried overtones of abstraction and distance in interpersonal relations, and in fact she was rather cool and aloof, intellectual rather than intimate. While she had known lovers much the same, and to the same degree, as any other average ler girl her age, she had not had what she might have called a great love affair of passion, and felt thereupon a certain lack. She knew well enough that humans did not follow ler custom in personal names, but out of habit and to pass the time, she was not above playing a minor little fortunetelling game with Han's name, much as she might have done back in her own environment. This became more than just interesting when one considered that Han's full name was Han Keeling; by altering the -ng at the end of his last name to an -n, would produce, by accident or design by persons unknown, an acceptable Singlespeech ler name, Hankiellin. Liszendir already suspected Han of being strong in the sphere of emotions which would fall to the water aspect (see further Taro symbolism, the suit of Cups). That, if it were true, would make the string of roots mean, more or less, "last-passion-meeting." All things considered, it was a dire message indeed to derive from a minor session of the fortunetelling game.

M.A.F.

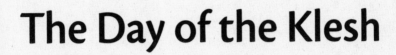

The Day of the Klesh

For Eugene

1

"Anyone who reaches a new world must conform with all the conditions of it."

—A.C.

THE SUMMER LABOR fair on the outskirts of Kundre, on Tancred, had been an established feature of the country for years past counting, reaching far back into the days of ancient tradition when Men alone ruled the world Tancred. The coming of Ler-folk in the latter days had, in its due course, changed much, as always, slowly and subtly, but not Kundre, and not the fair. It persisted. It grew, for nothing remains the same: and the fair, which had begun as a hiring place for harvest helpers, had slipped back into summer, then early in the season, almost into spring, encompassing more trades, jobs, specialties, finally virtually everything. Most importantly, it had become a place where young people seeking change might choose and hope to be chosen for many tasks, long and short, near and far, on-planet—or off it.

The cities of Tancred were uniform and uncosmopolitan: Kundre, by the fair, was not appreciably different from its sisters, Bohemundo, Isticho, Athalf, Ricimer and Amand. The fair, on the other hand, evidenced diversity and difference; there were star-captains, laborers, entrepreneurs, hiring-bosses and foremen, all of several kinds of creature: Humans, in egg- or teardrop-shaped craft; Ler, in windowless, featureless spheres; and, typical of this sector of space, Spsomi, foxy, sharptoothed humanoid beings who resembled lemurs or galagos, but who were not, technically, primates at all, being descended from an unspecialized carnivore closest in form to the raccoons and pandas of old Earth. Spsomi took to space in asymmetrical slipperships whose shapes were never repeated and remained difficult to describe for they most resembled doodlings in three dimensions, smoothly finished and gracefully curved, broken by exterior piping and conduits, as eccentric as the ler ships were featureless.

Odor, sound, sight; contrast and difference filled the region of the fair. Cooking proceeded in booths scattered over the fair grounds. There were also dust, odors of beasts, chemicals, scents to repel and allure. Prospective employers set up their placards and tables and glowered at one another—Humans in all-purpose coveralls or spacesuits, or pajama-like utility garments: Ler in *pleths*, like nightshirts, or in loose tunics and pantaloons; Spsomi in vests and loincloths, which were patterned in ornate designs and worked in colors of jarring disharmonies. There were sounds of motors, the wheels of carts and barrows, cries in several languages, fragments of incomprehensible words, and music—accented, rhythmic human forms, accentless, formalistic Ler music, erratic, syncopated Spsomi tunes and jangles.

The place of the fair was an open, spacious plain set among distant, low hills. To the west, opposite Kundre, a river made a broad sweep, enclosing the field within a long curve of tall trees. There, along the river, the ships grounded.

From those hills, by way of Kundre, had come four young men, all of an age alike to wander and explore, to see new things, new lands, or to sight the invitation and return, sobered by a secret self-knowledge: Ilver Quisinart, Grale Cervitan, Dreve Halander, Meure Schasny. Their distinguishing characteristics could be noted at a glance: Quisinart was lanky of build, long-nosed and querulous. Cervitan was long of trunk and short of leg, thick and stocky, with smooth contours in the heavy bones of his face. Halander was unremarkable in any degree, unmemorable, bland and neutral as a store manikin. Schasny was wiry and delicate, small-featured. Otherwise, they were similar in skin tone, eye color, hair texture and color, and general shape. Humans were now as uniform as Ler; there was only one race of man, with only minor planetary variations.

All were acquaintances, loosely friends, but of somewhat differing origins. Quisinart was from an experimental commune; Cervitan the sole child of a herdsman; Halander the middle child of a merchant family; Schasny the youngest of a family of landtenders. None had futures that were both desirable and assured. And it was for such as these that the fair by Kundre had existed since time immemorial.

The four passed a Spsomi booth, surrounded by a half dozen of the slender, foxy creatures, who were at that moment all talking at once in their sputtering language with its accompanying gestures, slow-

motioned as the deliberations of sloths, but also frantic; measured nervousness. The Spsomi looked their way, and foxy, delicate muzzles bared
needle teeth in the Spsom version of a smile. Drooping feeler-whiskers
waved, preposterous curved ear-trumpets waggled, opened and closed,
swivelled independently. Behind was a sign, crudely lettered, which pro-
claimed, "Fame—its fortune, in employ the Great Capitan Iachm
Vlumdz Shtsh. Sojourn Pstungdz, Whulge, Tmargu, SfaDdze—bonded
pipemen: 9 their-places." While they watched, one of the Spsom bent to
a communications device set out on the table, listened, raged back at the
device as if the voice in it came from there, not somewhere else in the
field of the fair, and then peacefully walked to the sign and changed the
number 9 to a 6.

Quisinart gaped in open wonder; Cervitan stared. Halander frowned.
Meure Schasny looked at the four-digit hands, which waved, gestured to
them, motioned, beckoned. Each digit was tipped with a ridged nail,
which in the course of normal wear shaped itself to a needle-sharp
point. He made a polite sign to the Spsomi, continuing past the booth.

As they passed on beyond the booth, hopefully out of earshot or notice of the furred Spsomi, Cervitan remarked, "No fame there—all one
sees on a Spsom ship are the interiors of conduits."

Quisinart asked, "What are the pipes for? They don't seem to discharge anywhere." Quisinart greatly admired the man-of-the-world air
possessed by Grale Cervitan.

Cervitan answered, "No one knows, that I've heard. The Spsom don't
tell—all they want to do is hire someone else to clean them—it's considered to be a job suitable only for convicts, outcastes, and offworlders.
All I know is that they have to be kept spotless. Some are dusty by nature, others get greasy. All smell funny, or bad. They are cleaned both in
flight, and on the ground. There you have the extent of my knowledge
concerning Spsom pipe and conduit."

Halander interjected, "No fortune, either. Pay is computed on the
basis of 'lays,' which is a fraction of the net profit of the voyage. The rub
comes when the lay gets 'adjusted.' They add a lot on; food, taxes,
bonuses, antibonuses, ship stores, stipends, garnishments. One is indeed
fortunate to arrive ahead at all, that is, owing the furry devils nothing."

"What, no money for liberty?" asked Meure, in tones of mock
outrage.

"Absolutely none," answered Cervitan. "Fardus shipped with them
two years ago, and had to swab conduit the whole trip. Never saw a
thing. And they put him out on Lickrepent for debt and he had to

work his way back here, almost begging. As it was, there was fuss enough; the Spsom captain threatened to fricassee him, but the Lerfolk on Lickrepent would have none of that. At the least, they paid him out."

Quisinart asked, incredulously, "Would they really have eaten him?"

"Never a doubt." Cervitan said the last with all seriousness, but he also flashed a quick glance at Halander, which Meure saw. The true answer was that they probably wouldn't have, although there were enough stories going around about the Spsomi to that effect that Quisinart would believe it.

Here they passed by a small, semipermanent office, with a signboard in the window listing inbounds, outbounds, and ships currently grounded on the field. There were three rows, showing status, and three columns, showing race of the crew. The four strolled over to examine the listings. The first column listed human ships, the second, Ler, and the third, Spsomi.

Halander read aloud, "*Zahed* and *Zain* are departed, as are *Assiah* and *Sadran*, which left yesterday. *Baal Chalal* and *Aur Chasdim* are yonder in the field. *Nistar* is also down, here, but is awaiting parts and is not in commission. *Tiferet* and *Merkava* are known inbound, with *Zemindar* and *Kavannah* reported."

Cervitan commented, "Little enough there to work with. *Baal Chalal* is a scow, and *Aur Chasdim* is worse, according to rumor. *Nistar* is an excellent ship; well-run. That's why her Captain took her out of commission. Most would order the part and fly on. *Tiferet* I've heard mentioned, but the others I don't know. *Zemindar* . . . Hm . . . probably not so good, either."

Halander squinted at the listing for the Ler ships, and continued reading, "Let's see what the Lerfolk offer spacewise . . . Ah. *Dilberler* is gone. A shame. That's a good ship. *Forfirion* departed day before yesterday, in the company of *Gennadhlin Srith*. *Tantarrum* and *Holyastrin* are still here, *Murkhandin* and *Volyasmus* are reported. And the Spsom? Let's see. . . . None have left recently. *Thlecsne Ishcht* is down, as are *Vstrandtz*, *Warquandr* and *Ffstretsha*. *Mstritl* is due in next week."

Cervitan commented, "*Vstrandtz*. That'll be the ship of Iachm Vlumdz."

Halander asked, "Do you know the other three?"

"*Thlecsne* is reportedly a privateer. There's a war going on, the far side of Spsom space, so they say, so it could be on this side, doing some trading of raid-booty. *Warquandr* is a scheduled liner, and I think *Ffstretsha* is a tramp for hire. Watch that one! There's no telling what kind of work they'd get into."

They passed onward, aimlessly drifting in the fine warm afternoon from place to place, passing booth, stand, field-table and outdoor restaurant alike. At the hiring booths, some advertised tasks which were elaborately specified, listing duties, responsibilities, hours of employ. Some went further, and added elaborate pay scales and types of promotion ladders, as well as pension plans. These were also equally exact in their requirements for prospective candidates. Others advertised more simply, even to the point of deliberate obscuration. These simply promised "good money" for "hard work," specifying neither the task to be performed, nor the employer for whom it was being performed. These they sensibly avoided; the conventional wisdom held that employment so advertised would, of necessity, be either illegal, dangerous, risky, underpaid, or any combination, possibly all four simultaneously.

They visited a small emporium specializing in roasted sausages and foamy, pale beer, settled themselves in a convenient booth, and took a relaxed lunch, each sitting quietly to himself and savoring whatever revelations the day at the fair had brought them.

Meure Schasny was, in a word, bored. Aside from sightseeing, they had accomplished little this day, and the next ones promised more of the same. He knew that as long as they contented themselves with sightseeing and sign-reading, they were unlikely to go anywhere in any employ, dangerous or not. Finally, seeing the bland expression of Cervitan, the blank face of Halander, and the gullibility of Quisinart, he said, "And so? After the sausages, what do we plan to do?"

Halander ventured, not even surprised, nor bothering to reflect upon his answer, said, easily, "No problem there; Kundre is within walking distance, and there are always a number of footloose girls there. I move that we address ourselves to the town and avail ourselves upon them, of course allowing nature to dictate the turn of events."

Cervitan agreed, finishing the last of his beer. "I would have said as much. I agree. Let us proceed with all dispatch."

Quisinart pulled his nose and asked, "Could we not go down by the river and look at the ships? I never saw one closely before. Perhaps we might get some ideas there as well."

Halander and Cervitan glanced at Quisinart with expressions of disdain, but Meure agreed. "Indeed! A good idea. I agree with Iliver, for once. We two will stroll along the riverbank and interview crewmembers, if they will talk with us, and you two can return to Kundre and satiny flesh."

Cervitan lowered his heavy brows and glowered. "One moment. The satiny flesh is by no means certain; and anyway, how will you two know what to ask? You are babes in the woods."

Quisinart ventured, "I can tell a regular fellow from a rogue, and I intend to sign on with no Spsom, whatever their promises."

Schasny agreed, "And I will do likewise. We will have to start somewhere, and," here he hesitated, ". . . prosper or suffer as circumstances will come to dictate." It was brave, nevertheless, he regretted saying it immediately, for it had established a certain relationship with Cervitan that could not end but in one of them losing face.

Halander tossed down the remainder of his beer and said, agreeably, "Well, that settles it. We shall go look at ships and converse with crews. And afterwards, if nothing has come of it, can we take ourselves to the city?"

"Agreed," said Meure, and with that, the four of them arose, settled their bills with the cook, and set out in the direction of the place nearer the river where the spaceships were grounded.

The fair proper had always oriented itself on the side of the field nearest to Kundre. But as one proceeded westward through the temporary structures of the fair, the fair soon fell away and the grounds were merely open field, fading away to the riverbanks. From Kundre, the ships were hardly noticeable, abstract artifacts by, or under the distant row of riverside trees. From the fair, they were little more, but out in the open of the fair grounds, they began to assume shapes of a greater distinction. Schasny found himself glancing upward, now and again, so as not to be surprised by another ship settling in.

Nine spaceships were arrayed, following the broad curve of the river; from the far distance, they had seemed small and insignificant, but as the four walked across the open, the ships grew in size and importance. The nearest ship was the Human spacecraft, *Nistar,* awaiting parts. No point in going there. They were obviously not going to sign on anyone for a while. Although deactivated, the scene was far from being over-relaxed. A pavilion had been erected before the entry-port, and members of the crew were engaging in an afternoon buffet with some ladies of Kundre. It was all very sedate, orderly, and impressive; the green of the branches and overhanging fronds of the riverside trees, the gold-brown color of the dry summer grass, and the deep green with which the ship *Nistar* had been painted. They were close enough to read the name and origin placards attached over the entryport: *Nistar,* and below, *Port Callet, Samphire.* The crewmembers they could see were suave and polished, making elegant gestures effortlessly, and in full-dress uniform. The four walked past, trying to appear inconspicuous. Surely such a craft did not recruit actively on a back-country world like Tancred. They would want able spacemen, merchant officers, pursers. It was, as such craft went, rather small. Schasny suspected that *Nistar's* cargo was usually valuables, money, jewels, wealthy people who could go visiting. He sighed, hoping the others would not hear him. That was something like what he wanted, but which seemed, here and now, light-years away.

The next ship was a large Spsom ship, without a nameplate. From its naked armament-blisters, however, they could deduce that it was most probably the *Thlecsne Ishcht.* This one was shaped in an asymptotic curve, the pointed ends elevated. It also carried noticeably more than the usual number of exterior pipes and conduits, and was colored a sooty brown. The pipes had probably once had color of their own, as was the custom with the Spsom, but the paint appeared to be either burned off or worn off. They kept a certain distance from it, not wanting to be suspected as spies; but they saw no activity. Nevertheless, *Thlecsne* conveyed an impression of wary activity; a faint hum could be heard from somewhere underneath, and none of them doubted for an instant that it could spring into furious life then and there. They passed on, hoping they had not been noticed, but sure that they had been.

Somewhat farther down the irregular line of ships was a smaller Spsomi spacecraft, considerably smaller than the *Thlecsne Ishcht,* but considerably more open. This one seemed to be shaped into a rough crescent, although one end was higher, shorter, and more sharply curved than the other. It was a dull coppery color, but it seemed clean and well-cared for, the exterior piping was maintained after the full rigor of the Spsom custom—each pipe was garishly painted in bright, prismatic colors, so far as any of them could tell, each differently. As they drew nearer, they could make out, under the tangle of piping, an open entry port. Over the port, with its attached stairwell, several ideograms in the Spsom manner were painted. To the side, another legend they could read: *Ffstretsha, Imber, SfaDdze.* By the stair, a single Spsom had opened an inspection plate in the hull and was taking readings on a portable device which he would attach at different points inside. Satisfied, so it appeared, with the measurements, the Spsom disconnected the device and turned to re-enter the ship. An ear swivelled around, followed by the foxy head. The creature stopped, halfway up the stairs, as the four approached.

The Spsom spoke first, distorting the language in the peculiar way Spsomi did when speaking a human language.*

"Yis, yis—y'r wis'n watt?"

Cervitan, who seemed to have a little knowledge of the odd creatures, repeated the question for the rest, " 'Yes,' he says. 'What do we wish?' "

"To look at the ships," volunteered Quisinart.

The crewmember seemed pleased, for both ear-shells now rolled around to point at them. It said, "Vv'ri gidd, yis, v'ryvry gidd. Pit wvi nid nnu ppeypmnneuw. (h)'eff gidd ppeypm'n frr'm Vfzyekhr; sle-vess, yis."

Cervitan repeated, "He says that's very good, but they already have pipe-men, slaves from a world he calls 'Viz-yekher.' I don't know where that is. Probably a long way from here."

Meure Schasny said, glancing upward and around at the exterior piping which encompassed the Spsom ship, most of which seemed large enough for a person to slither through, "We are sorry to hear that. We are still looking for work, though. We won't touch anything. We had never seen one of your ships close before. Thank you."

The Spsom wrinkled its brow in concentration, and answered, making a serious effort to speak correctly. "Wirk yi went, yis? Fff . . . gu erundt thirr, bbehend ddhi sh'p. Lirmin thirr, nid two merr. Inskild, yis? Go-u see Lir-men, bey dhii rrver. New m'st gou. Ness t'telik 'f yu. Gid dey, yis?"

The Spsom turned and sprung upward into the ship, through the hatchway and out of sight. They hoped, out of hearing.

Schasny shook his head. He said, "That's our speech?"

Cervitan answered, "That's nothing! That one spoke it very well, indeed. The last was the most important. It said, 'Work you want? Go around behind the ship and talk to Ler. They need two more, unskilled.' "

---

*Spsom distorted non-Spsom speech in numerous ways, not limited to grammar and phonetics. The least of these effects was due to Spsomi mouth structure—which forced most of the formants of speech to occur forward of the palate. This, in turn, lent a whistling, spitting quality to Human or Ler speech. Further, Spsomi had few resonance cavities, so their speech sounded timbreless and flat.

Schasny said, "That's what it sounded like, all right."

Then the four looked for a long time at each other. Halander finally broke the silence. "Ler, behind a Spsom ship. Grale, what do you make of that?"

"Charter, likely, if they're really with this ship."

Schasny added, "Can't hurt to ask. All they can say is no."

They stood for a moment, irresolutely, looking at the Spsom ship, the late afternoon shadows now gathering around the curves of the hull, and farther, over by the riverbanks under the trees. And at each other all over again. Then they set out in the direction the Spsom had indicated, being careful to keep a distance from the hull of the ship and the fantastic network of piping that surrounded it.

Beyond the ship, the dry-grass meadow sloped gently to the banks of the river. Overhead, tall Aoe-trees formed an overarching, lacy canopy, which was just beginning to stir with the evening breezes, for which Kundre was justly famous. Beyond the tree trunks was the river, the water slow and opaque. And on the riverbank was a small group of Ler, sitting quietly and talking among themselves. Two Spsom were also with the group.

As they drew closer, they saw subtle differences between these Spsom and the one they had talked with at the ship's entry way; these were more reserved, moving about very little. They also seemed to be outfitted more completely—the open vests the Spsom seemed always to wear were carefully ornamented with little strips and tags of gray hide, and the more imposing of the pair wore also a design in wire on one shoulder that suggested the piping encompassing a Spsom ship. That one also wore a gold armband on its upper arm.

Spsom, no matter how much one saw them, were a form of life that men never became accustomed to. It never had been that they had been incomprehensible culturally, but that their physical proportions sat wrongly on the human conceptual framework; they simply didn't look *right*. To start with, the limbs were two-jointed in the middle of the limb, so that there were three sections, rather than two. This was accomplished by an elongation of what would have been ankle or wrist bones. The feet were digitigrade, with a short, bony spur projecting backwards for stability. The hands were four-digited, but arranged two by two, permanently opposed. However long the evolutionary path had taken them, Spsom were a very long way from their natural origins. Legs completely adapted for running and leaping, and arms and hands modified into highly specialized organs of grasping.

The body trunk was short, and the limbs were long; an overall impression of them would bring to mind such terms as delicate, wiry; sometimes, gangling or awkward. More, they had retained their fur, from their days as pure animal; a short, dense pelt of a neutral, slightly ruddy, brown, with darker accent lines along the face and shoulders, and a lighter stippling along the flanks and thighs.

The hand was quite different; it was virtually palmless, and consisted chiefly of the four digits, normally carried two-by-two, opposed. And last, the head. Spsom faces were narrow, triangular, slimming down to a narrow muzzle, incorporating nose and upper jaw. It seemed almost foxlike, until one considered the large eyes, the swell of the skull, and the highly mobile ears near the top of the head, constantly in nervous, yet measured motion. Spsom looked more like animals than some animals did, yet they always conducted themselves in what could only be called a civilized manner; i.e., they spoke, they read and wrote, they flew spaceships and lived in cities, and also made a low-key form of war upon one another. More rarely, upon other races.

As for their relations with Humans and Ler, there was a difference. Where Humans and Ler saw similarities in each other, Spsom saw the differences. Ler they treated respectfully, carefully neutral, at a distance. Humans they liked and lost no opportunity to associate with them, circumstances allowing.

Besides the two Spsom associated with the group, there appeared to be three Ler, two Elders, judging by their long hair, and an adolescent, dressed in loose tunic and pantaloons. The Elders wore the traditional *pleth*, or overshirt.

The four young men approached the group cautiously, not knowing which person to address; the adolescent, the Elders, or even the Spsom. Grale went first, followed by Meure and Halander, with Quisinart bringing up the rear. When they had effectively joined the group, Cervitan stopped, looking about a little uncertainly, trying to select the best one to begin with.

The Elders solved the problem for him. Of the two, one was fuller-figured, more round. The other was thin and saturnine. The round one said, "You are here for work? To sign on with us?"

Cervitan answered, "Yes. We heard there were some places left, and would like to look into it."

The Elder said, "Straight enough. So attend: we lack two places yet, and will depart when we have them, at that moment. I will describe the offer of employ, thus: *Daorman,** that is to say, general porterage and housekeeping assistance, serving, cooking. Pay is the customary rate for unskilled *daormen*, and the term is for the duration of a voyage to a certain planet, and the completion of our duties there. You may select return to Tancred, or as customary, first-port-of-call. We do not go to make war, nor settle vendetta, therefore hazard rates are inappropriate. We intend to exhibit prudence in danger, as applicable. It will be about a year, local, more or less. Do you have your cert?"†

Cervitan answered for the group, "Yes, we all have them."

At this point, the smaller, and less-dressed of the two Spsom said something in his own speech, a sibilant whispering, broken by labial stops and dental aspirates, uttered in general, as if addressed to no one in particular.

The adolescent Ler now stepped forward, between the two Elders, and indicated Cervitan and Quisinart. Closer now, it seemed to be a girl. She said, "These two, the one who speaks, and the one in the back, will not be suitable, according to Adjutant Iflssh."

The Elder nodded, and added, "Therefore I withdraw my offer to the two individuals indicated." He turned to the girl. "The others?"

"Acceptable."

Meure now spoke, "Why are they not acceptable?"

The girl said, "Scent. Spsom have sensitive noses and can predict general demeanor. We want no one that is too bold, nor one who is not bold enough. These two are thus; no dishonor intended, but we cannot use you. You two remaining are fine, if you find the conditions correct and in order."

Meure said, "They are correct as far as they go, but much remains to be seen. We know nothing of your project or mission, nor how it is organized. Can we not hear more?"

The girl glanced once at the first Elder, then turned back to Meure. It was a girl all right, very slight in build, almost weak. Nor was she pretty, or full of the robust tomboyness of the average Ler girl. She said, "We have chartered this available ship, the *Ffstretsha*, of the Spsom owners, to transport us to a certain world, and there, to various points on its sur-

---

*A temporary servant, hired for completion of a specific task or mission. No status change is implied. General work to the task at hand is suggested, but sometimes clerical duties were also performed by "temporaries," on a renewable contract basis. In this case, "Porters" might be the best translation.

†Cert: A document issued by the local prefect, stating that the bearer may act responsibly in his own behalf.

face as required. And then back to the nearest Ler world, where your
group and mine will part company. We intend to return to our proper
places by scheduled liner. The *daormen* we hire from this world will be
expected to perform odd jobs aboard ship, primarily porterage on the
planetary surface. One among you will operate communications equipment. This is, you may say, a scientific expedition to gather facts. That is
all. You may consider our group a fact-finding organ, one that would settle a long-standing question among my people."

Halander asked of her an odd question. He said, "Why Tancred? I
mean, why hire here, and not someplace else?"

"Why Tancred? Because it happens to be along the way there, that's
all," she replied, as if surprised.

Halander said, "Oh," and was apparently satisfied with the answer,
but Meure thought, *They could charter a Spsom ship anywhere at all.*
They go everywhere. But Tancred is the last of the settled worlds, I know
that. Beyond us lie only the colonial worlds, and the wild ones. And the
Spsom don't voyage outside much, at least, not in this part of space. They
come from inside ordered space, and if Tancred is on the way there, then
there is outside.

Meure asked, "Does this world have a name?"

The girl answered, "It is called Monsalvat."

The name meant nothing to Meure, nor to any of the rest of them. It
sounded like a corruption of a Ler name. The four looked at one another, missing the girl's attention, which was on them intently. The
name didn't register. Meure turned back to the girl and the Elder.

"Very well. I apply for the position of Daorman."

Halander added, "And I also."

The Elder paused a moment, glanced at the two Spsom. The smaller
one nodded, quite humanly. The larger one, with the fine shoulder decoration, said nothing, made no gesture. He seemed oblivious to all of
them. The elder now turned to a small valise on the ground bent,
opened it, and retrieved two sheafs of paper. "These are your contracts.
Thumbprint, please." Meure placed his thumb at the place indicated.
Halander, after a moment's hesitation, did likewise. The Elder then separated the sheaves, handing one set to Meure and Halander, one set to
the girl, and one set the last, to the smaller Spsom, who turned and
sprung off in the direction of Kundre.

The Elder now said, "You are signed on. You may enter the *Ffstretsha*
immediately, if you have no further errands to run."

The remaining Spsom also turned and departed, without a word, striding off around a projecting corner of the *Thlecsne* and disappearing. Meure Schasny and Dreve Halander looked at Cervitan and Quisinart. All this had happened too fast, and there seemed nothing adequate to say to fill the silence. Cervitan managed, "Good luck, you two! We'll be on the next one!"

They finished their short goodbyes, and Cervitan and Quisinart started off back in the direction of Kundre. Meure and Halander started uncertainly for the entryport of the ship.

The Elder who had talked before now walked straight for the ship. The remaining one stepped forward and said, "Come along, now. All are aboard, save us. The *Liy* Flerdista* can be explaining your duties while the Spsom crew is securing the port. We are ready to leave. Surely . . . Is there something else?"

Meure answered, "No, no we are ready, as well. Let us be off." But as he walked toward the *Ffstretsha*, he looked back, more than once, at the receding figures of Cervitan and Quisinart. They did not look back.

Meure reached the outthrust entry-ladder and saw that he was indeed the last one to enter the asymmetrical Spsom ship, the *Ffstretsha*. He could see inside; only the Spsom crew-member, apparently the same one they had talked with earlier, was there, waiting in the passage beyond the port for him to enter. Meure climbed the unfamiliar, wide-spaced treads, grasped a projecting lip of the port, swung into the alien ship, and stood aside.

He was in a short passageway which joined another not far ahead. He felt a sense of vertigo, a strangeness; this, already, was an alien world, of course. Impressions crowded his perceptions: the light in the ship was soft and indirect, with a yellowish tinge. There were various odors and scents—the acrid flavor of the tanned leather the Spsom habitually wore, and the scent of the creatures themselves, ever so slightly sweet, like bread, or perhaps cookies. And sounds: there was a faint hum that told the ship was already energized, and over that, a mindless little tune hummed by the Spsom as he went about his task of closing and sealing the port. He realized that he did not know which way to go in the corridor ahead.

---

*Liy is a title-of-reference used where an order of nobility is implied. In this case, for an Elder to so refer to an adolescent, it could only mean that the girl, Flerdistar, was of a Braid of very exalted status on her home world, the Ler equivalent of near-royalty. *Liy* should thus be rendered as Demoiselle.

The Spsom crewman spoke into an intercom in his hissing, sputtering language, and then turned to Meure.

It spoke slowly and deliberately, knowing that Meure found it hard to understand. "B'spoke yu b'fore, eotside. So yu came wif us, efter all. Virry gid ey thingk, yis, virry gid indid." The Spsom indicated itself. "Vd-hitz. Ey. Mesellf."

Meure looked closely at the Spsom called Vdhitz, trying not to stare. He saw bony, strong hands, wiry, lean limbs covered in dense, short fur; a figure larger than himself, and definitely more sure of himself. Where skin was exposed, it was a dark color, not black, but a very dark brown, dry and dull. The pointed muzzle, the sharp, white teeth, the ridiculous mobile ears, the fine whiskers which he could now see, all those things shouted "animal" to him, but the gesture of the hands and the intelligence of the expression said "person" more persuasively. Meure pointed at himself. "Meure," he said. "Meure Schasny."

"Myershtshesny," Vdhitz repeated, pleased with his success in communication. He pointed at the corridor ahead, and then to the right. "New yu go therr. Yu wirk fir the Lirmen, net thee Spsm. Shee will tell yu whet yu hef tu doo." He stopped, then added, "Kell un me. Ey kenn hhelp."

Meure started off toward the corridor, and turned to the right as he had been told when he got there. He looked back. Vdhitz was busy at some task, manipulating controls on a panel which he had opened. Meure turned and walked ahead.

The main corridor had a flat floor, of some dark, resilient material, like rubber, but not rubber. The walls and ceiling merged into one, smoothly curving. The corridor itself veered to the right, then curved around sharply to the left, as if detouring around an obstacle. In the middle of the detouring curve back to the right was a door, and voices. He went in.

The room was a spacious compartment, with curved walls and ceiling like the corridor, and lit by the same type of indirect lighting, soft, shadowless, yellowish. Meure thought of a day when the sky was covered by a fine, high overcast. Yes. The Spsom homeworld must be cloudy, cool. Perhaps the dominant race of Spsom originally came from a region of rounded, eroded rocky defiles and canyons. Perhaps. He did not know. 'Rrtz, the world of the Spsom, was incalculably far away.

Here, there was a table, integral with the material of the floor, translucent, moulded, obviously manufactured, yet with an air of nature to it, as if it were a form of peculiar rock which had just happened to be formed to that shape and size to fit in this room, now.

There were already seven people present, seated or standing according to disposition, for Meure could sense no order in their placement. There were four Ler: the Liy Flerdistar, who reminded him ever so slightly of poor Quisinart, but with infinitely more reserve behind the thin, bony face, the two Elders he had met outside, and another adolescent, with still, perfectly regular features. There were three Humans as well: Halander and two girls. One of the girls was strongly built, but smoothly contoured, with a reddish tint in her brown hair, cut short almost after the manner of the Ler adolescents, and with a warm, tanned tone to her skin. The other was slender and delicate, pale-white. She had large eyes, dark hair, a full mouth. The first girl seemed bored; the second, apprehensive and nervous. And Halander obviously was pleased with circumstances. *So*, reflected Meure, *am I*. Both girls were attractive, after their own fashion.

Flerdistar noted Meure's arrival and waited for him to find a place, patiently. There was absolutely no sense of time in her manner whatsoever. Meure, nevertheless, felt an embarrassment for being the last and hurriedly found a seat by the table.

The Liy Flerdistar began, "Good. We are all present. I will make the introductions and we may then go about our tasks, which for the moment are simple enough." She indicated the Ler Elders. "These respected Elders are Rescharten Tlanh, whom you may regard as the leader of this, ah, expedition." She nodded toward the heavier Elder, the one who had spoken first outside the ship. "And Lurtshertan Tlanh." That was the thin one. "The *Didh* to my right in Clellendol Tlanh Narbelen, and I am Flerdistar Srith Perklonen.* The Forerunners are Meure Schasny, who just entered our common room. The other young man is Dreve Halander. The girls are Audiart Jendure," here she indicated the strapping girl with the reddish tint in her hair, "and Ingraine Deffy." The thinner girl shook her head, briefly, nervously, a motion that made her loose, cascading hair ripple.

Flerdistar continued, "The Spsom you will see little enough of. Shchifr is Captain. He wears an iron medallion on a chain around his

*Ler surnames reveal occupation, or profession. *Narbelen* is a contraction of the phrase *Narosi Bel Ghenaos*, "ninth thief its-family (Braid). Similarly, *Perklonen* indicates "first historian family."

neck. Mrikhn is Astrogator. That one is small and dark. Vdhitz, who was by the port as we entered, is First Officer—Technician. Zdrist is Second Officer—Overseer. There are two natives of the world the Spsom call 'Vfzyekhr.' They are in the ducting and I know not if they have names, or what the custom of their world is.

"Your term begins now and will continue until such time as we are successfully off the planet to which we are going. Some of you will doubtless wish to continue your employment and provision will be made then. The rest will become passengers and must pay, just as we. You can elect to return to Tancred, or first port of call otherwise, which I do not know now. Until we land, your duties will be simple: rationing and housekeeping. There is concentrated foodstuff and facilities for preparation in your compartment, which is to the left. We occupy the cabins to the left. Audiart Jendure, whom we have appointed head *Daorman* until planetfall, has our schedule. Otherwise, you are free to do as you feel inclined, in the time remaining. Do you have questions?"

The girl, Ingraine, said softly, "We are to go to a world called 'Monsalvat'; how long will we be on the ship?"

Flerdistar answered, "It is a long voyage, but we go straight, with no stops. The Spsom tell me six weeks, perhaps eight, depending on currents. Yes, it is long, this way. Spend your time well. The *Ffstretsha* is a small ship and there is little room for us to impose upon the other. Now let me tell you a thing about Spsom and their ships. It will be true on this one, and on any other you may ever ride: outside this cabin, you may go anywhere freely where you see an open door, or open passageway. You may not pass a closed door. Custom varies as you must know. Do not pass through a closed door. Do not knock on it for entry. If you must pass, you must wait. This is the only prohibition I lay on you."

Halander asked, "Is there anywhere we can see out?"

"Only from the cockpit and the wardroom. You will see very little of either, if anything. What would you expect to see? It is only space. The Spsom instruments transmit a coherent image, but the view is not different at night. For the most part, the Spsom areas will stay closed-door. Remember what I said. There are serious consequences to you first if you disregard this. Is that all? Good. I believe Miss Jendure has the schedule. After the supper hour there will be tonight a short honorary visitation with Captain Shchifr. The Elder Rescharten and I will attend. Schasny, you stand by for service there if required."

The Ler girl turned and quickly left the room, followed by the rest. Clellendol was last. He arose from his seat with measured, careful movement, taking a look about the whole room, noting each of the four remaining, making some unknown assessment of each of them. They each felt slightly uncomfortable under that reading glance; a scion of the Ninth House of Thieves*, indeed. And then he, too, slipped into the quarters Flerdistar had indicated were the cabins of the Lerfolk.

It could have been an uncomfortable moment for them, when they were left alone, but Audiart did not permit them time to think about possibilities; she immediately began explaining what they had to do, in a quiet, sure voice. Her manner was carefully respectful, distant. Meure kept sneaking glances at the other girl, the slender one, Ingraine, and as he noticed also, so did Halander, but at the same time he appreciated Audiart's taking charge, and risked more than another look at her.

Then she took them into their own quarters, of which there was little enough to see; a narrow corridor, an odd sleeping room of six enclosed bunks, three on one side, three on the other, stacked atop one another. There was a tiny, but complete, even luxurious bathroom at the end, and the kitchen and locker were next to the door into the common room.

Audiart indicated the bunks. "I suppose we can pick as we will. I claim no authority, but there appears to be room for all. The two extra we can use for storage. We all have little enough."

Meure looked closer at the stacked bunks. There seemed to be enough room within for a person to sit up without bumping his head. Access was gained by a narrow ladder, and a sliding opening presumably at the head of the bunk.

Halander ventured, "Are we to follow the custom of the Spsom in the matter of open doors here as well?"

Audiart started to say something, stopped, began again. "The practice seems understandable enough," she said, carefully neutral, and not at all warmly. For the time being, there was no open invitation here offered to Dreve.

She indicated a small locker. "Liy Flerdistar has provided us with a generous stock of clothing. I fear it is after the Ler fashion, but there is

---

*Ler, with the thoroughness typical of their kind, had instituted Braids to perform what might have been left to accident on Human worlds. The various Belen Braids did actually steal, as their hereditary occupation. Of course, under elaborate and traditional restrictions. Members of the so-called "dark Braids" were often called upon by others for their unusual skills, so it is not particularly unusual, in the Ler context, that such a person as Clellendol would be included on an extraordinary undertaking.

quite a bit of it on the shelves therein. Take what you desire—it is all plain and discreet and should fit us all reasonably well. Go ahead and use it; it comes with the job. Now—we should get things ready for the supper hour. Them first, and then us. Come along now, we can settle dividing up the clothes and selecting the bunks afterward. Schasny, you may have to pick a bunk, at least. I don't know how long you'll be up in the wardroom."

Meure said, "I'll take top right."

The rest agreed. Then they set to the work of getting everything in order. In the small space, everything seemed to fall into place quite smoothly. The supplies were all where they were supposed to be, the equipment was in working order. In fact, they were well into the work, and starting to work efficiently together, before Meure thought to ask something that had just popped into his head.

He was standing by the door, getting ready to take the bowls into the common room, when he turned to Audiart, who was then making some adjustment to the cooker. There was only a small lamp over the counter, so the entryway was quite dim. He looked at her, the light outlining her short, straight hair. He said, "When do we leave, Audiart?"

She made the adjustment, turned away, to the counter. She answered, "Didn't you know? We left when you came aboard. We've been in space for several hours, I should guess. We're well away from Tancred by now."

After supper, Meure left for the wardroom. Audiart had told him what to do there, and how to get to it. It was simple; a short way along the main corridor, up a ladder, down another short corridor, and up a short stair. The door was open.

It was a common room similar to the one below, only somewhat smaller, and different. The walls were interrupted by screens giving views into space. Between the screens were shelves of drinking bowls with elaborate handles, ornamented plaques, framed mottoes or certificates written in the Spsom ideograms. There was room for four or six, and that was all.

Meure recognized the Spsom Captain from the description Flerdistar had given: the medallion. The Astrogator was not present. Presumably he was flying the ship. Vdhitz was the other Spsom. Meure entered without knocking, as he had been told, and stood by the doorway, his hands behind his back.

They were talking, Rescharten Tlanh and the Spsom Captain,

Shchifr, with Flerdistar and Vdhitz translating by joint effort. Sometimes they would discuss a point at some length before rendering the offered statement, going either way.

Meure did not understand much of the discussion, and the Spsom end was incomprehensible, so he did not listen very closely. They seemed to care not at all what he overheard or didn't. So he took the opportunity to look at the screens showing the view outside the ship. The stars moved. First, the fields of stars shown in the viewscreens drifted slowly past, the obvious effect of their motion through space. They also moved slightly along the other axes, as if the ship itself were changing its orientation in space. It was a motion not unlike that of the sea upon a boat, save that it was slower, a different rhythm. Meure watched one screen in particular, until something intruded on his field of vision from another. He looked. There, to all appearance off on the rear quarter of the ship, was another ship visible in the screen, flying formation with the *Ffstretsha* across the oceans of space: he recognized it. The accompanying ship was the *Thlecsne Ishcht*.

"Imagine, then, how I gloried in the flow of the silken waters about the ship, in the fantastically immaterial outlines of the hills, in the gloom of the frondage of the forests, in the curves of the cobra coast, in the sinister stories of wreak and piracy which haunt that desolate abyss through which we were steaming, where for nine months of the year one can scarce distinguish between sky and sea, so dark and damp is the air, so subtly steaming the swell; while beyond, as in a hashish dream, arose the highlands, provinces all but unknown even to the civilized inhabitants themselves. There, primrose to purple, was the promise of undreamed-of tribes of men, strangely tattooed and dressed, with awful customs and mysterious rites, beyond imagination and yet brutally actual, folk with sublimity carven of simplicity and depravity woven of the most complex madness."

—A.C.

THE REMAINDER OF what passed for conversation between Rescharten Tlanh the Elder and Shchifr the Spsom Captain passed by Meure unheard and the proceedings unseen. He kept watch, as unobtrusively as possible, on that rear quarter viewscreen, watching as the erratic motion of the *Ffstretsha* would, from time to time, bring the ominous outlines of the *Thlecsne* into view. The privateer neither advanced nor dropped back, but maintained its position carefully. The Spsom Captain, Vdhitz, Rescharten, Flerdistar, all must be aware of it. They could not but see it, just as he; yet they were totally unconcerned, therefore they knew it to be an expected condition. Meure then wondered indeed about their destination, that they should be accompanied by an armed warship in order to go there.

Shortly after, he sensed that the momentum of the meeting had been lost and that affairs had been completed. The two Ler arose from their places and bid the Spsom goodbye, for the moment, and left. After a moment's hesitation, Meure followed them.

The girl seemed preoccupied with something, perhaps fatigued; Meure did not think it best to ask her overmuch now. And Rescharten? He thought even less of asking the Elder. They returned to their quarters, through the ladders and corridors, in silence. At the common room, they found the other Ler adolescent up, studiously reading from the leaves of a reproduced text. Rescharten ignored the boy and passed directly into his own area, closing the door. Flerdistar paused for a moment, as if she had intended to say something, but Clellendol ignored her presence entirely, and after a moment, she, too, passed through the doorway into the Ler living quarters, not without a glance back, an unfathomable expression on her face.

Meure now felt the events of the day pressing time upon him. He was tired. He also saw no reason to remain, and reached for the handle of his own compartment door.

On a second thought, he turned and said, "You know that we are accompanied."

Clellendol looked from the book and turned a disturbing, direct glance onto Meure. "The *Thlecsne*? Yes, I know." The boy pushed his chair back and stood slowly, laying the sheaf of reproduced pages on the table.

Meure asked, "Why should a privateer fly formation with a small chartered liner?"

The boy smiled, not unfriendly. "A privateer? Yes, so it was told. Actually, it's something rather more than that; *Thlecsne Ishcht* is a commissioned warship of the Spsom Federal Naval Force, and a very special class at that. It has, so they tell me, the general plan and size of a frigate-class vessel, but more the armament of a cruiser."

Meure felt a sudden spasm of awe. That these people were wealthy enough to charter an entire Spsom ship, and a battleship as well . . . He said, "Your party hired both ships?"

Clellendol shook his head. "Hired them both? No. Not even Flerdistar could arrange that. The *Thlecsne* is the request of Shchifr . . . No. Say no more. There is more to this than a night's talk will cover. I dare say the Spsom first Officer may already have warned one of you. Aha, it was you. Well, there's no cure for it, Schasny. Let it soak in—we've the time for it, and I want no panics."

Clellendol indicated the sheaf on the table. "Here. This will tell some truths about where we are going. You will need to know something. And stay away from the *Liy* Flerdistar. Ask her nothing."

Meure ventured, "She is yours?"

Clellendol yawned, stretched like a cat. "Quite to the contrary . . . I mean in quite another sense."

"Why me, of the four of us?"

"You seem to have your head screwed on right, that's all." The adolescent Ler spoke with a certain impatience, as if Meure were deliberately avoiding what he had been trying to suggest all along. He added, "I have made contact with a certain Spsom, who shares my apprehensions. I see from your expression that he has also approached you. Read what I have left you and, in your leisure time, speak with Vdhitz, however difficult it is to listen to Spsom speech. Become aware. There is need for it."

Clellendol turned and went to the door of his quarters. He glanced at the papers, once, to be sure Meure did not miss his intent, but he did not wait to see if Meure picked them up. Meure had not missed the pointed invitation, although he seemed sure that he was not overtly being asked to join a conspiracy as such. He gathered the papers and took them with him.

Inside, all were asleep already, or so it seemed. There was only a weak glow of a night-light by the cooker. He looked at the bunks. All were dark, the sliding doors closed. All was quiet. He felt a small moment of relief. It seemed that Halander had not yet succeeded. Meure looked again. All the sliding panels were closed, save the one he had picked. He had no idea whatsoever what lay behind them, nor the number of occupants therein.

Meure climbed the narrow ladder to his bunk, leaned over into the opening, climbed within. Inside, it was surprisingly roomy and comfortable, furnished in considerable detail and evident quality. Immediately inside the sliding panel door, there was an upholstered shelf; the bed proper lay at a slightly lower level. Along the walls were cabinets and shelves. The light came from a ceiling panel, but there were other lamps as well, cleverly recessed into the walls. Looking about, he found a panel of switches that controlled the lights; he also noted that there was another panel on the wall, with odd receptacles, for which there were no instruments in evidence. Spsom entertainment devices? Communication system plug-ins? He did not know. The switches did not feel right to his hands, and from that he knew it to be a standard Spsom compartment; but other than the odd feel and action of the switches, there was no alien feel to the compartment whatsoever. He felt perfectly at ease, completely at home.

After some experimentation, he found the switch that controlled the ceiling panel, and when he had found what was ostensibly a reading lamp, he turned the ceiling panel off. Inside the shelves, he found blankets, but no pillows. He then undressed, wrapped himself up in the blanket, and rolled another up for a pillow. And remembered a sheaf of papers. He was tired, and hesitated for a moment, wondering if he shouldn't just go to sleep and forget about the article Clellendol had given him. He yawned, sighed, and picked the sheaf up resignedly. He thought he would look it over before he turned the light out.

The first section was a dry text about the known features of the system of which the world Monsalvat was a part. Meure read through it quickly; it appeared there was nothing notable about the system at all. Nothing? He read through the section again. Nothing of particular interest. There were six planets, one habitable, one other technically habitable but not exploited. Monsalvat was the Third from its primary. The other world was called Catharge, the second planet, and was hot and dry and rocky. There was no gas giant in the system, a fact that struck Meure as a little out of the ordinary, and the primary was a close double of K6 stars, again, rather odd, but nothing to cause alarm. The system was both exceptionally stable and apparently very old, judging by the metals percentage in the spectra of the two suns, which were as close to being identical as would seem possible.

There was no evidence of intelligent life forms in the past of Monsalvat. There was native life, sure enough, but the Human discoverers of the system had found no trace, no artifacts, no ruins. It was a fact that had given them much pause, and Monsalvat was set aside for further study. And before final conclusions could be drawn, there had arisen an unexpected need for a whole world, off by itself, and the planet had been colonized in an odd and rushed manner.

There was a break in the text. Then the description started again, rather more now in earnest and less in the abstract.

". . . (It read) . . . Monsalvat, a rather watery world, has four land masses of near-continental extent: Kepture, Cantou, Glordune and Chengurune. The last is the largest, and Cantou is the smallest. The total land area, including known offshore islands, represents nineteen percent of the planetary surface. This land mass has, to all evidence, been insufficient to close both poles off simultaneously to free circulation, so Monsalvat lacks evidence of planetary or even hemispheric glaciation, even though all continents, save Cantou, show evidence of light glaciation in their geologic layer systems, but therein was found no synchrony.

"The climate, therefore, is rather even for the degree of axial tilt to the plane of the ecliptic (twenty-eight degrees), this being due to the moderating effect of the large amounts of water in both liquid and gaseous form. . . .

". . . If the climate could be said to be even, the weather is a different matter altogether; Monsalvat has a day of twenty-two standard hours and a small satellite that exercises little tidal influence; therefore the weather is strongly variable, if one may speak conservatively. In the equatorial and sub-polar regions, it is violent, characterized by high winds on the surface and rapid change. In the South Polar part of the world-ocean, with no land masses or major undersea rises, waves and individual storms can sweep completely around the planet. In temperate regions, storms are much less frequent, but change is more manifest. In a deep atmosphere, with a high content of water vapor, there is considerable activity of cloud formations as a result. Curious though it may be, Monsalvat is not a rainy world. Little precipitation falls, considering the water vapor content. This has been attributed to the general freedom from atmospheric dust which is characteristic of the planet. Consequently, from the surface the sky, when clear, assumes a deep blue-violet color. Clouds can range from white and gray, with a yellowish tinge, to orange, depending upon the angle of light from the double primary.

"As one researcher subjectively described it, the light of Monsalvat possessed a most peculiar quality—piercingly clear, yet also possessed of a sense of fluidity apparent to the eye, the presence of a medium, something more than just air. Rays and beams slanted through the layers of sky, with its stirred curds and streamers of clouds, and always there was subliminally the sense of constant change, ferment, activity, that eventually began to wear upon the nerves. 'One was always looking around, over one's shoulder, behind. The background was never still long enough for one to be sure there was not some activity transpiring against it.' "

Meure yawned and turned the page. There was more, a section delving into planetary features at a highly technical level. Meure found most of it indigestible. He glanced through the data, nodded to himself. Nothing about Monsalvat was extraordinary at all; he could summarize it easily; a little larger than average, a bit lighter in mass. Monsalvat was a watery world of stormy oceans and a planet of pedestrian proportions. There were no great ranges of high mountains, although lower ranges

were common. The oceans were deep, but not abysmally so. So far, it
sounded pleasant, perhaps a resort world. A place of relaxation, retreat
from more pressing affairs. He turned the page.

Here was a section, extracted from some other tome, on the history
of the planet and this he read more closely.

"... in 9223, the Klesh People, who were Humans who had been ar-
tifically racialized into a number of pure strains by a long-degenerate
splinter faction of Ler, were removed from the planet Dawn and trans-
ported to Monsalvat, which had been reserved for them alone. At the
time, they were considered too divergent culturally from the common
Human institutions to mix freely, and were to be segregated in the system of Monsalvat to allow them time to adjust. Since no one could be
considered wise enough to select among the various breeds and races of
Klesh, they were left to fend for themselves, under a planetary governorship which was to maintain order and encourage peaceful habits.

"... The history of the settlement on Monsalvat can only, in retro-
spect, be regarded as one of the great failures of mankind. Nothing in
human or Ler history compares to it. Governor after Governor, administration after administration, all were posted to Monsalvat, with the
same result: while learning the rudiments of survival, the Klesh also
grew ever more recalcitrant and barbaric with the years. In time, they
came to regard themselves as a destiny-blighted race, fit for nothing save
the endless skirmishes, enslavements, crudities, and general barbarisms
upon the surface of a planet far removed from their origins.

"... All Klesh, whatever their type, possessed a curious view which
they never gave up; none ever longed for the planet Dawn. Moreover,
there was no memory whatsoever of their condition before Dawn. No
folktales, no legends, nothing. The Warriors of Dawn had utterly erased
their connections to the past. The result was a ferocious longing for the
future, a detestation of all Ler, and a contempt for the rest of humanity.
Aside from these qualities, the average Klesh may also be distinguished
by his dislike (at best) of all other Klesh breeds not his own.

"... It had been assumed that the isolation of Monsalvat would keep
cultural shock to a minimum, and that general regulations would prohibit unscrupulous traders from capitalizing on their needs for the artifacts of civilized society. After a time, however, the regulations fell into
disuse; Monsalvat was too far out, and the (here the text had not reproduced correctly, and a section was blotted out) ... approaches too
dangerous, and the Klesh themselves remained too faction-ridden to assemble the organization necessary for their own move into space.

"In the meanwhile, the various Klesh types flourished and declined, intermingled and crossbred, died out and were reconstituted in the eternal ferment of the planet. The number of surviving Original Breeds (the Klesh word is *Radah*), of course, declined exponentially through time, but new breeds were constantly arising in the flux, to produce in turn even more varieties than there were in the beginning (it was said that there were over 500 types of Klesh when the ships were loaded on Dawn). All, of course, claim equal merit. This process has continued to the present time. Curiously, little, if any, homogenization has occurred on Monsalvat. The culture—if it can be called that—of Monsalvat at the least agrees upon one point: that racial purity is the utmost aim, and that mixed men are to be avoided as pariahs.

". . . In 9403, the Arbitrator's post fell vacant and was not filled. Within the year, the tiny enclave of civilized society was inside an armed perimeter, and the Governorship was effectively at an end. By 9405, all remaining Humans were off Monsalvat. It may be added here that the surviving members of the mission were rescued by armed warship, an astounding turn of events not seen since the Tau Ceti Crisis of 5225.

". . . Traders, explorers, various academic bodies continued to make sporadic visits from time to time, but, over the years, these contacts became even more hazardous, and in consequence, the visits declined. Monsalvat is no longer a port of call. Now and again some ship passes by, perhaps a rare landing is attempted; the results of these brief visits tell the same tale—the Klesh seem to have stabilized as to number of types, but the life there is as hazardous as it ever was. Conditions remain chaotic, if not anarchic."

There was a simple map, followed by another section discussing the various Klesh types, their numbers, locations, habits. This information was wryly preceded by a caveat that it was sadly outdated and would probably no longer be true, for anyone foolish enough to attempt a landing on Monsalvat. Meure read the descriptions with amazement and wonder, made fearful by the range of variation among creatures very like himself, ultimately sprung from the same soil. Humans, he reminded himself, now showed little more variation than the Ler. But there, he read of races on Monsalvat whose members were well over two meters in height; others were hardly more than a meter. Some were so pale and unpigmented that their veins lent a bluish tinge to the skin: others were colored a dull carbon-black. Some were hairy enough to be considered furred; others were totally hairless. Every conceivable variation occurred on Monsalvat. Some persisted, none seemed to gain any permanent advantage, and none seemed able to dominate any major section of either of the four continents.

Meure placed the papers on a nearby shelf and turned out the light, pulling the covers up. Monsalvat! He had forgotten it, of course. It had been a tiny datum in the history courses in school, something to forget. The place where men still had races, a concept so savage and barbaric he found he could not imagine it. And they were going there, directly there, not just visiting, but for a purpose. Meure felt sleep coming, and did not resist, despite the feeling of apprehension that had entered his mind.

Sleep was not peaceful. He tossed and turned in the compartment, certain he was disturbing the others. But all remained quiet and dark, and each time he went back to the uneasy sleep. Finally, he began to dream. At the first, there were merely disconnected fragments, symbols, images. They would flit into view, and then vanish, permutating into something, someone else.

Then, quite easily and unexpectedly, the transformation took place and his dream became coherent, as vivid as reality. He was in a palace. That was clear. Not very luxurious, he thought curiously, but he knew that to be a subconscious comment. It was a palace, all right. A place of stone, great dark stones, heavy and massive, cut and dressed and fitted together without mortar. It was a palace, and it was his. He could move at will. But he also knew it to be a prison in some subtle sense. There was one of whom he was aware who served, but who was to be feared. Meure knew this, but did not comprehend. He was pacing back and forth in an anteroom. Then, shifting, he was in a deep vault under the palace, or fortress. There was light from pitch torches set in crude metal sockets bolted to the stone walls. He paused uncertainly . . . he was about to do something. Something he feared, something . . . dishonorable, so it seemed. Something his mind would not form an image of. He feared unknowns, and alternatives surrounded him. But there was a horrible bright emotion of triumph mixed with the fear and the horror, a feeling of a revenge to come, an emotion so raw and direct that Meure almost woke up. He returned to the dream, sensing that he was losing it. He held something in his hand, something cold and metallic and sharp, almost cutting his hand, so tightly did he grip it. He set a deadfall in a doorway, then stepped within. Inside was an ornate mirror, and he turned and looked in the mirror, as if for a last look. A block of stone was poised to fall over the doorway. He looked, and the image would not form. He tried harder, he had to see, in the dim red light, what he looked like. And at last, something cleared, and Meure felt himself floating upward into wakefulness. But he could see the face in the mirror, he could see: it was the face of a stranger, an utter stranger. It was a sharp, harsh face, full of lines around the eyes and mouth, framed in curly red hair and marked by a neatly trimmed full beard and mustache, the same wild red color as the hair. A hard face, angular and bony, but small, too. The eyes were squinting to see in the light, but there was a leer of triumph, too, an evil smile. Clenched teeth gleamed.

Meure Schasny awoke in a clammy sweat, eyes staring. Something with the eyes! He had looked from the mirror, downward . . . he could not remember. The thread had broken. For an instant, fully awake, he felt an odd paradox often noted by persons who have had an especially vivid, enigmatic dream, an oracular dream: that the memory upon awakening was stronger than the dream-experience itself. The redhaired man, the harsh, sharp face of a roughneck, a brawler. Familiarity hovered close, immanent. Meure almost knew the man. A shivering sense of unreality passed over him, as a chill: he knew the man—he *was* the man. And yet at the same time, he wasn't. He was also himself. He felt as if he could almost remember a name . . . Meure Schasny had never personally known a red-haired man in his entire life. The sense of immediacy began to fade. Meure heard small noises from the other parts of the communal cabin. The others, they were now rising, up and about.

Meure did not think of himself as overly introspective, and he filled his time with things to do, reasoning that the curious dream was no more than that; a curious dream, and that his attention to it would wane after a time. He did not speak of it to anyone. Not Halander: he would think Meure a mooncalf. Not Ingraine Deffy, who had already put on one of the overshirts in the locker. Not Audiart . . . not yet, at any rate. Certainly not to any of the Ler present. They were polite enough, but also very distant; Flerdistar and Clellandol were also occupied with one another in a way Meure did not understand, as if they were studiously avoiding one another. In any event, neither seemed interested in anything deeper than the most superficial contact with him.

Day-cycles passed aboard the *Ffstretsha*. Audiart donned the Ler clothing, as being more comfortable. Halander followed, and then Meure, too. He visited the wardroom on the upper deck several times, once just wandering around. The view through the vision screens remained the same in general features as the first time he had seen through them: blackness, distant points of stars, slowly moving past, and in the rear screen, the ominous bulk of the cruiser *Thlecsne*, although at the last viewing it seemed that there was more of the rolling and pitching motion visible in the screens, and that the *Thlecsne* in particular seemed to be rolling rather heavily, almost laboring. . . . Meure did not understand how Spsom ships operated, so he admitted that he could not interpret the rolling motion as anything relevant to himself. But he kept thinking of the image in his mind of a ship, rolling and pitching on the heaving surface of a very rough sea.

A change began to be visible among the Spsom as well. Meure's first impression of them all alike had been one of relaxed competence, knowledgeable professionalism; they seemingly ran the smallish ship *Ffstretsha* without visible effort or interpersonal friction. The Captain reigned; the Astrogator flew; the Overseer kept the unseen slaves busy, and Vdhitz saw to the general functioning of the ship. To be sure, the change was subtle. But it did seem as if the crew were now in a hurry more than at first, that they were going to additional effort. The doorway into the bridge stayed closed more often, and then all the time. Then the wardroom was closed off. Vdhitz, when seen, seemed to be slightly in a hurry.

And the dream remained in the back of Meure's mind. After some time, several day cycles, he sought out Vdhitz in the Spsom's usual location in the after part of the ship. No closed doors stopped him; he went farther and farther back. The curving passageway hid the view ahead, and grew narrower. At last, it opened up into a cramped circular chamber. There, Meure met a most curious scene.

Vdhitz was bending over a still form lying on the floor, an odd shapeless form which Meure's mind at first refused to resolve. Behind Vdhitz stood another similar creature, looking down, unmoving. Beside the creature was Zdrist the Overseer, bearing in one hand an odd device, part handle, part glove, open at irregular intervals, a handle for a thin rod; presumably a Spsom weapon, although Meure could not see what its function was. There were no openings, nor anything appearing to be a projecting device.

The two creatures were apparently the natives of Vfzyekhr. The one standing was about half the height of a Spsom, completely covered with a deep pile of off-white, colorless dull fur. It had two legs, two arms, both short. It seemed to possess a head and neck, but he could make out no other features; the fur covered everything. After a moment, Meure could not be certain the creature was even facing him.

He waited. Vdhitz stood, spoke quietly with Zdrist, who answered. Then, both spoke in an undertone with the remaining Vfzyekhr, who made only a slight rocking motion from side to side. Then the two Spsom conversed again. Vdhitz reached to the side, to a wall panel high up, touched a lighted button. At the back of the compartment, where Meure had not seen a door or any suggestion of one, an iris formed, and then opened to full dilation. The Vfzyekhr turned about and scampered up into the revealed silvery passageway beyond, apparently crossing the axis of the opening at a right angle, where it turned and waited. Zdrist manipulated the device on his hand, and removed it, handing it to the other Spsom. Vdhitz took the device, and Zdrist climbed into the opening with the Vfzyekhr. Vdhitz closed the opening; then caused another opening to form off to the left and low. Into this he thrust the still form lying on the floor. It was only when he had completely finished his task, including stowing the antennalike device, that he turned to face Meure.

He said, "Eh hef been brectising specking. Yur speetsh. Eh hhowp it iss bbeter now, yis?"

Meure unconsciously fell into the Spsom frontalized accent, "Oh yis, much better."

Vdhitz motioned with an ear-trumpet to the back of the compartment. "We lusst one of our Vfzyekhr now. Very bed, thet. Zdrist will now hef to hellip, in the tubes. If we lose the other one, Eh will hef to sweb them."

"What did the . . . ah, Vfzyekhr die of?"

"It was hurrt, frem the worrk."

"Injured?"

"Yis, yis, the word. Eendzhur'red. It is verry rough now, bed spess here, *verry* rough. Denjurous! End there iss a sterm now too."

Meure ventured, "I see motion in the screens in the wardroom; it seems rougher now than when we started. Is that what you mean? We can't feel it in the ship."

"You will, soon. If it gets stronger. But wee egsbected something lek this. But not so rough."

"What do we do then? Turn back?"

"The Kepiten will hef to speek with the Lirmeń. Eh don't know; they hef alreddy ped, end, eh, eh," he laughed a short, barking chuckle. "Shchifr hess alreddy spendt dit. A SSpsomspi shipp iss elweys in debbit." He reflected for a moment, then added, "Et's thet Demm plenet Minsilvet, ef kurs. Thiss iss a pert of spess we evade, ehh, how you seyyit . . . lek the plegg!"

The large, expressive eyes tracked off Meure for a moment, moved randomly, unfocused, as if Vdhitz were reflecting on some internal vision. At last the attention returned, and he added, "Spess iss net emmpity, end ets different from one pless to another; one pert iss smooth, enother reff, still enother full of udd mutions, whish we learn . . . Thiss pert sims to heff the werst of ehf'rrything."

After a time Meure asked, tentatively, "I wanted to ask you if Spsom ever had dreams."

"What iss 'drim' word signify?"

"Visions when you sleep; you see them and live them, but it is all in your mind."

"Aha—sa. *Mstli*. Yis." The Spsom said no more, and Meure could sense a subtle disapproval, as if dreams were an area Spsom did not discuss. Vdhitz added, almost off-hand, "You hedd one you den't enderstend, eh?"

Meure nodded. Vdhitz said, "Heppenz ell the temm in these parts. Ell peeples err trubbled by semething eround here, sem mere, sem less."

Meure started to speak, but Vdhitz motioned him to silence. "Tell me net of it. It iss fery bedd ferm among erselfs. You can tell it to the Liy, perhepps she will see into it end tell you whet she sees."

"The Liy Flerdistar?"

"The semm. She does something lekk thet, su eh hear."

Then he turned away and became busy with indeterminate tasks, as if he found the subject distasteful and wished no more with it. He had recommended Meure to Flerdistar in the same way one would suggest a purveyor of a vice which one found distasteful. Meure, in his turn, did not wish to make the Spsom angry at him, and so turned and left, without pushing Vdhitz further on the subject.

That evening, after the hour of supper, and after all his chores had been finished, Meure put on the cleanest overshirt he could find in the clothes locker and sought out the Liy Flerdistar. She was not within the suite; neither was Clellandol. He went out into the hallway; *Ffstretsha* was a small ship. There were only so many places where she could be.

Up to now, the ship had been quiet. There were, however the Spsom ship propelled itself through space, no sound effects attendant to the process. Once out in the empty corridor, away from the rest of the people, though, he became conscious of a sound, a series of sounds, a family of sounds, he had not heard before. They were faint, hardly discernible; mostly unrecognizable, and coming, so it seemed, from the ship itself. Meure listened. He could not identify the sounds.

He passed along the passageway toward the front of the ship, climbed the ladder to the second deck. The door to the control room was closed tight, and a dull red light shone above the doorframe. The wardroom door was open, though, and a light was coming out of it. As Meure moved toward it, Clellandol stepped out, looking back into the wardroom. When he saw Meure, he said something unintelligible back into the room, a phrase with the trilling, buzzy quality of Ler Multispeech. There was no answer from within. Clellandol passed along the passageway and disappeared down the ladder, saying nothing more.

Inside the wardroom, the room was empty, save for one occupant: Flerdistar. There were two mugs on the center table, both still steaming.

Meure had not thought the Ler girl attractive since he had seen her, and aboard the ship, she had not grown any more so. She was thin, almost bony, and unlike the slender human girl Ingraine, moved with no grace at all. Further, Meure had been put off by her imperious manners, and had avoided her as much as possible. Now, close, across the table, he could see her directly; her skin lacked tone, her mouth was thin and colorless, the eyes dull gray and slightly watery. What made the physical impression of her even stronger was the fact that she was wearing an unusual garment, such as he could see of it; it was a loose diaphanous blouse, open-necked and translucent, so that the body underneath was suggested. She sat with her elbows on the table, her body leant forward, as if weary. There was none of the usual precocious belligerence in her now.

Meure asked, "Am I intruding . . . ?"

Flerdistar answered, voice soft, controlled, but tired. Meure felt fatigued himself, just hearing the overtones in it. "No. Ask what you will of me."

Meure looked again. He could see through the cloth quite easily. There was little to see. Ler girls were nearly flat-chested as a rule, and Flerdistar was more so than most. The figure he saw was slight and boyish. Or rather childish. He began, "I do not know the forms to say this . . ."

She waved one hand, without removing it from the table, signifying that forms were inapplicable now, for some reason.

"... One of the Spsom crewmen told me you could interpret dreams. I had one, on this ship, that lacks all meaning, and I wondered if you could help."

She smiled. "Interpreting dreams, now. There's what we need ... No. As such, that is not what I do. I am a pastreader. I listen to the present, which is full of the ringing echoes of the past. I sift words, tales, things which literalists say are distorted, not true, but which have once been true. And gradually, line by line, I can reach out ... and touch it. See it, very much as it was in reality. I can, if given long enough to work on it, reconstruct things people think they have forgotten."

"Why are you here, bound for Monsalvat?" Meure asked of her.

"There has always been a great mystery among my people. To you it may not have any meaning at all. Many Ler feel similarly. It is simple enough: once there was a Ler rebel. It had been assumed that she remained one, judging by subsequent events, but there was always the disturbing tale that she wasn't. There is more to it than that, of course. If she wasn't, why then did the rebellion occur, in her name. The rebel's name was Sanjirmil, which in your speech signifies natural spontaneous combustion—will-o' the wisp. Foxfire. But those Ler who were with her descended into the Warriors of Dawn, who later dwindled, and vanished. There were Humans, whom the Warriors captured, mistreated, enslaved, and bred into many pure types, and who lost. We are going to Monsalvat to talk with some Klesh, who are the only link with that past."

Meure objected, "Well enough. Everyone has heard of the Warriors, and their Klesh. But time! There is a long time between the Klesh brought to Monsalvat and the time of Sanjirmil. They would not remember her; she was gone, having lived her life probably before the Klesh-breeding started. And by all accounts, even more has happened since they have been on Monsalvat. Ferocious events, to them, at any rate. You may be fortunate to get anything coherent out of them at all, much less a memory thousands of years old."

She looked blankly back at Meure. "No, it's not like that. What I weave into a coherent whole seems to the untrained to be random noise. But we know two things: we *know* them. Not speculation. Sanjirmil set forces in motion that made the Warriors and the Klesh, and separated them both from both of us. And the other is that all of the counterstories—that Sanjirmil was victim, not perpetrator, have been traced back to one common source—Monsalvat and the Klesh. I have tried to pastread elsewhere, and all I have gotten, I and all the other pastreaders that have gone before me of the House of Historians, is a radiant point from Monsalvat. Beyond that is a curtain we cannot pierce. So the answer is there, buried in the collective memory of the legends of the people."

Maure looked askance at her. "Why not ask Ler who were the wardens of the Warriors after their resettlement? After all, you do have a recall we do not."

Flerdistar shook her head. "Not so easy. We did that first. All we got from that was that there was a secret about the origin of the Warriors which was known only to certain of their number. This cult was never divulged to any Ler who guarded the remainder of the Warriors. We are prone to keep secrets. It is our nature, and I can tell you that there were Warriors who autoforgot to preserve their secret, even though by then, it was largely gibberish to them. Another problem was the Warriors themselves; they were not really Ler any more, but something else. Not Human, either. The radiation of Dawn was slowly loading them with lethal mutations. We are rather sensitive to that, you know. So that much of what we could get to by relay-memory was lost, even more so than among Humans, who would at least retain traces of the events, built into the fabric of their legends, unknown to them. No. The Warriors were a dead end. And they never revealed their cult internals. So we switched to Humans. And there, it is as I have said—either we get the official account, which we suspect, or we get Monsalvat."

"Why is it important, after all these years, centuries?" Meure asked, genuinely perplexed. "What difference does it make whether she was really a rebel or not? It was done, that's all."

Flerdistar looked directly at Meure. "It involves a very basic question about the nature of . . . being itself. Something more than Humanity, than Lerdom, than intelligence. Something Basic. Long, long ago, in your own history, a struggle to define it took place. You have forgotten it, so I will not burden you with it. But therein was no victory, for one side apparently was uninterested in defining the issue, and let the others have their say. Everything we are, you and I, goes back to that. Everything. And yet every time anyone even tentatively feels around this, there is a nagging suspicion that the other side was right."

Meure said, "What difference does it make? So they were right: then we'll change."

"It goes beyond that. If they who lost were really correct, and theirs was the more accurate view of reality, then all of us, in their terms, are insane, and have been, and will always be. But I have said much here that is far beyond you; indeed, most of it is beyond me, too. I am only repeating much of what I have heard. I am an investigative vehicle who searches for one kind of truth. And I will try to read your dream if I may. Speak of it."

Meure felt off balance, distracted by the abrupt turns of mind; he had felt a trace of the same feeling when talking with Clellandol. Almost as if, in the cases of both, their, attention was . . . somewhere else. But where? He decided it didn't really make too much difference. He almost was glad her attention was divided; that he was not getting the full benefit of her attention. He began, "Everyone has dreams, but most are nothing out of the ordinary; an occasional nightmare, and we are purged. But this was . . . clear, like it was really me, but at the same time, not me, either. Someone else; I was in a castle, or a fortress—it was all made of dark stone. It was very confusing—I was the master of that place, but I feared it, or someone in it. Almost as if it had become my master. Then there was a shift, and I was in a deeper chamber, underground. It was damp, in the air, but the stone was dry. I was going to do something I feared very much, but that I knew was necessary. There was something in my hand but I can't tell you what it was; it . . . it was sharp, but it was not a knife. I don't think it was solid. I saw myself in a mirror, and I wasn't me, I mean not the real me in front of you now. The person I saw was red-haired and had a beard. He was like the laborers who drift in and out of the Fair at Kundre. A rowdy, a roustabout, a roughneck. I was in great fear and a sense of wrong, but what dread thing we would do was to be anyway. Then I woke up."

Flerdistar looked away from Meure, her eyes focused on something very distant, something probably beyond the walls and doors of the wardroom. She said, without shifting her attention, "Understanding proceeds fastest when phenomena are sorted into related groupings; even if one's initial array is partially incorrect, the order inherent in the system suggests corrections until an approximation is reached. Dreams are also phenomena, and can be grouped. If you are not a student of this branch of knowledge, I will not bore you with the classification system currently in use; it will be sufficient to say that your dream does not arise from unsatisfied yearnings, unresolved conflicts in you; nor can it be deja-vu: the anticipation of the future, for you are obviously not red-haired and show no inclination toward that coloration."

"How do you know . . . ?"

"A rather simple deduction: I am a stranger, of an alien race, female—if your dream were wish, you would already have forgotten it—you would certainly not tell it to me, nor would you seek interpretation, for you know the meaning already."

"True, I suppose . . . but when I say the 'I' of the dream was red-haired, I do not mean of the red hair of the Humans of today, but of old: Bright red, not the auburn-brown, say, of Audiart. That was significant to me, why I could remember it."

Flerdistar turned her full attention onto Meure now. If there had ever been any distractions in her mind's eye, they were wiped away without effort. Meure felt exposed and naked, because of the sudden attention, the full weight of it, made even more noticeable by the childishness of the girl, the watery eyes, the thin figure. Many of the old terrors of the strangeness of the Ler returned to haunt Meure then; they were adults who grew old and gray and seemed to retain the values and appearance of children; and they were also apparent children who possessed an eerie adulthood far beyond real adults.

She said, carefully, "It's that it's you, not that it has red hair."

Meure said, "But that's what I'm trying to tell you: it's not me. I didn't think anything was wrong with the dream until I saw the mirror—and I knew it wasn't me."

She replied, still focusing her full attention on him, "But you didn't know it until you looked in the mirror, eh?"

"Well, yes . . . it was—wait—too clear for a dream, like any I've had before. It was as if I were remembering it. Yes. A memory."

"What was your name?" she asked without warning.

"I can't remember it. It's just on the tip of my tongue, I know it, but I don't. I ought to know it, because I can feel it even now, hanging over me, like a threat. . . . It's a simple name, with one meaning. I can sense that. I just don't understand it; we never had barbarians on Tancred. . . ."

Flerdistar interrupted Meure, "It didn't come from Tancred, your dream. I know Tancred's history probably better than you. In fact, it was because of that history that we recruited there, rather than, say, on Lick-repent, or Ocalinda." She sighed, and some, not all, of the intense regard departed. She reflected, "Humans have become bland and normal in the last few thousand yearlings; I mean that you seem to have become as immune to history as we are. People lead ordinary lives, accomplish their ends without causing vast miseries, griefs. Gone are the great wars, the mass movements, the prophets. Tancred happens to be a product of this period, and is blander than most worlds."

Meure said, "Well, isn't that what people have been striving for all these centuries? Ler used to complain that Humans were too erratic; now that we're orderly, is that a fault, too?"

He expected a hot retort, perhaps a reprimand. Instead, Flerdistar said gently, more than he imagined she had in her, "I meant no offense . . . Ler history, such as there is of it, is smoothly contoured largely because we wish it that way. We are a cautious people. History less history is our nature; it is manifestly not yours, and when Human history becomes as smooth and uneventful as ours, then we expect to see other things in connection with it. You are . . . unbalanced, somehow. Peace and contentment you have attained and kept; but your total population is declining, and you are no longer opening colonial space."

"I know these things; it's no secret, either. But no one would trade his heart's-desire for a maybe-glory . . . particularly on someone else's concern."

"Well, enough, then."

"What can you tell me about the dream?"

"As I told you, this is not my specialty. I know about some of it, as one might say, by fortuitous accident. There are certain parallels . . . let me say that if I were a witch of the ancient times, and you were of my tribe, I should tell you that you had been possessed, that you should perform the appropriate rites in the secret places known to the wise men of the tribe. But of course I am not a witch, and you and I are not Stone-age tribesmen squatting before the fire."

"I don't understand what you are trying to say."

"I don't know, myself. I can put it in one context, and it comes out coherent, but when I try to put it into contemporary reference, I see a recursive pattern of contradictions."

"Explain, Liy Flerdistar; I am completely lost."

"Just so: possession. To the savage, that covers a lot of things which we classify another way and come up with a family of ills, we civilized creatures. But even if we admit such a thing, after all our civilizing, we now have to admit that we no longer have the mechanisms to cope with the .001 percent real thing. I read your event as contact with someone else, and that you should protect yourself from that influence; contact increases susceptibility."

Meure thought a moment, and said, "It would seem there is little enough I can do; as you say, I no longer have the refuges of the savage, and in addition, I am on a spacecraft bound for a destination I did not choose. Shall I apply to Shchifr to turn about and avoid Monsalvat?"

The glittering attention returned, burning. "Why do you say that?"

"It's where we're bound."

"You should hope it's not from there."

"I was reading about Monsalvat, before I had the dream. Are there red-haired Klesh?"

"There once were, long ago . . . There is much here that I like not . . ." She broke off, suddenly, as if she wished to say no more.

Meure pressed the Ler girl, daring just once. "What else?"

"Monsalvat is a planet of chaos, compared with the rest of inhabited worlds. Little better than anarchy reigns there. But other than its unusual history, there is much more—the whole region of space about it has a bad name: communications devices, fool-proof, don't work there, or rather *here*. Ships are stressed, broken up, never seen again. We fly aboard a Spsom ship because no Ler ship can approach it—here is one of several places where our Matrix Drive doesn't work."

"Somebody got in, once. They brought the Klesh to Monsalvat."

"We don't know about that period. Only since. What we know now is that it's a region of unusual turbulence, unusually strong. Like a region of storms on a planet's ocean. We are in such a storm now, and we are in great danger. The only reason we have survived so long is that *Ffstretsha* is small. *Thlecsne* had to break off days ago; it was being severely overstressed, and was near being disabled. Their Captain disengaged."

"Ours didn't?"

"Not that Shchifr wouldn't, if he could. No. It's that he can't. Spsom ships, of course, use a different system from Ler ships', but they are like ours in that they have no contained power source, but rather tap forces of space to generate momentum. Like sailing ships."

Meure said, "Like sailing ships . . . No power?"

"They have drive systems to land and take off in a planetary system. Nothing more. For distance work, they tap outside forces, just as a sailing ship uses its sails. And we are now in a situation analogous to a sailing ship in a great storm: we cannot turn, and we cannot stop. To turn would stress the sails, dismast us, and roll us out under the waves. To take in sail will allow the following seas to catch us and swamp us from behind."

"But you said *Thlecsne* disengaged . . ."

"Our last communication with *Thlecsne* was to the effect that soon after she disengaged and hove-to, the storm driving us abated in their region and they were able to proceed normally. They were damaged and had to turn to the nearest port. Believe me! Shchifr has tried. In fact, they have worked at nothing else."

"Do you know where we are headed?"

"Where else? Monsalvat, more or less, the last fix we got, at about twice the normal top speed of a Spsom ship. Can you not hear the ship groan with the stress? Can you not see in the screens the tossing and rolling? Look! Listen!"

Meure turned from the Ler girl and looked into the viewscreens; now the stars, the starry background, which had once swung to and fro, back and forth, with an easy motion, as if from a ship on a sea, moved jerkily, erratically, with sudden unpredictable lunges, after which the motion of the ship seemed in the screens to be uncharacteristically mushy, as if it were not answering its controls properly. Another thing impressed itself upon him; no longer was the medium of space empty, a mere vehicle for impulses. To the contrary, space itself seemed muddy and roiled; disorganized violent rippling motions were passing across the field of view of the viewscreens. Simultaneously, Meure listened to the ship, and the odd sounds he had heard earlier. The sounds were still muted and subtle, but now he could hear them for what they really were—the sounds of Spsom alloys in protest. He looked back to Flerdistar.

She said, "We don't yet feel them inside the ship; the system that generates the sensation of gravity negates that motion of the outside and we do not feel it. But we will, soon enough. By my reckoning, sometime tonight. Things are wearing out, being carried away by wavelike surges outside."

Meure heard the words, and digested their dire import, but somehow he failed to derive any emotional sensation from them. They were in great danger, trapped in some kind of storm, a violent cyclic alternation of the stuff of space itself, they could not apparently get free of it, and the ship was slowly being torn apart, being driven down upon Monsalvat . . . He saw that it was true, but he did not fear it; He said, "Then they, the Spsom, are all in there." He gestured toward the bridge, where the door was closed.

"Yes. I know no more than that. Shchifr is reckoned extraordinarily skilled in ship handling, and *Ffstretsha* is built for strength according to the Spsom Canon, however odd it seems to you and me, in appearance."

At that moment, although neither one of them had heard any sound, Vdhitz appeared in the doorway to the wardroom. The Spsom was a different creature now; the fine, short fur was streaked with damp marks—perspiration, and the Spsom's eyes did not seem to track completely together. Its ears were drooped and dispirited. Nonetheless he motioned to Flerdistar.

When she responded, Vdhitz immediately began in his own language—a seemingly endless series of hisses, clicks, dental stops and spittings. Without waiting for a reply, he slid back toward the bridge and vanished.

Flerdistar sat quite still for a moment, staring off into space, as if ruminating. Translating? She pushed her chair back from the table, and it slid, not along the floor, but according to some positioning mechanism. She stood, and said, distantly, abstractly, as if discussing some far-off exercise, "The situation is thus: *Ffstretsha* is finished. All the directional control projections are gone, blown out, torn away. Space-anchors are deployed stern wards and a single surface remains forward to stabilize us. The conditions outside have at the least stopped worsening; we have held together thus far—we should continue in one piece. We are approaching the system of Monsalvat at great speed, but fortunately, the planet is on the far side of the system primary, and the turbulence of the planetary system added to normal forces should slow us to a manageable approach. Shchifr believes he can make a clean planetfall, but that is all he can do. The ship is . . . broken, somehow. There was a lot in the other's speech I did not understand. We will have one shot at it, straight in and land. Once we go sublight, we'll start losing air. They got off a distress signal, which was heard and relayed by the *Thlecsne;* and answered by a Spsom craft called the *Illini Visk*, which will attempt to approach Monsalvat after discharging cargo and rerigging for extreme duty . . . The *Illini Visk* is a smaller vessel, but very spaceworthy. At the least, they will make the effort."

"How long will it take . . . the rescue?"

"We will see Monsalvat sometime tomorrow; it could be as much as a year until we see *Illini Visk*."

"I don't understand. If they could answer a distress call, how could they be so far away?"

"Spsom communications systems have great range; the *Illini Visk* is a great distance from us. There are a few others nearer, but none sufficient for Monsalvat. So, now!" Her manner shifted without warning, became peremptory. "Below, and make ready! Gather all we can carry. We shall have to survive there until rescue can be effected."

She made to depart the wardroom, and Meure did not hinder her. As she cleared the table, he could see the remainder of her clothing, which had been concealed below the table. Flerdistar had been dressed in *Dhwef-Meth-Stel** fashion, a mode of dress not ordinarily displayed, by custom, before Humans. The long lines of the *Dhwef* swirled about the girl's narrow hips, and then she was gone.

Meure slowly made his way out of the wardroom, down the ladder, back down the passageway to the suite of rooms. In his mind he heard the words of the girl about the fate of the *Ffstretsha*, and in his ears he listened to the now-audible creaking and groaning of the ship. He felt a slight vertigo from time to time, as if in a light earthquake; the motion was beginning to be felt. And at a deeper level, he remembered what he had gone to seek out Flerdistar for: the dream, and what she had told him about it. Possession. He snorted to himself. No, not quite that, she had said. Something like that, but conceptually more subtle. The ship gave a sudden zany lurch sideways, which could definitely be felt, and Meure occupied his attention with holding on.

In the common room, there was no one. Seemingly, Flerdistar had already passed this way. She had not stopped. The lights were turned down to minimum, and the doorpanels were secure. Meure turned into the right side, the compartment for the four Humans, entered, closed the panel behind him. All seemed quiet, at least for the moment.

Meure climbed the narrow ladder to his own bunk, slid within. He wondered if Flerdistar had intended for him to awaken them all immediately. He thought not, listening. Here, the noises of the ship were somewhat less than outside, in the corridor. He could hear no motion from the other side, no sounds here, either. He reflected, somberly; surely a ship as well-finished as the *Ffstretsha* had alarm bells, or horns, or klaxons, or buzzers of some kind to alert passengers. After all, Spsom

---

*Basic forms of Ler clothing remained static, and were oriented toward one or another of the four elementals: Fire, Air, Earth, Water. *Stel* was a gauzy, translucent, loose blouse, tied with ribbons at the top, which was a loose, open neck; below, it fell about to the hips, where it was tied with another ribbon. *Dhwef* was a long, wide, trailing loincloth, the ends falling to the feet. The upper end was usually held in place by a string of beads, or in extreme cases, by a chain of flowers. The mode most common to wearing of the *Dhwef* could be politely described as the "mood conducive to amorous dalliance." It could also be construed as an invitation to the same. Needless to say, after the Ler manner this was behavior governed by the Water Elemental.

had ears, too. Tomorrow, she had said. It seemed time enough. Meure removed his clothing and turned out the light.

He turned to the wall as he pulled the covers over him, settling into what promised to be an uneasy sleep. Then Meure remembered that he had left the sliding panel to the bunk open. The ship made a motion. He thought of closing the panel, for he did not wish to be pitched onto the deck; it was a good drop to the floor below. So he turned to close the panel, and saw, silhouetted in the glow of the standby lights from the kitchen unit, a dark, rounded shape filling the opening. The visitor slid into the bunk-compartment, and closed the panel. Meure started to say something, but he felt a finger placed over his lips. He could still see a little, for the compartment retained tiny indicator-lamps recessed into the walls. Enough to recognize the shape as that of Audiart. He half-rose, on one elbow, to sit up, but she pulled the covers back and slid in beside him, almost before he could make the motion. Meure covered the girl, finishing the motion by embracing her with his free arm. Her nose brushed across his, and the soft, fragrant hair trailed across his face. She said, below the level of a whisper, "No words, is all I ask." Meure nodded that he understood, feeling cool bare skin against his own; warmth beneath. He knew what to do; now there were no doubts. None whatsoever.

3

ACELDAMA

"This question 'who art thou?' is the first which is put to any candidate for initiation. Also, it is the last. What so-and-so is, did, and suffered: these are merely clues to that great problem."
—A. C.

NIGHT IT WAS: the terminator had long since passed its westerly way across the high plains of the land Ombur, which was an antique central portion of the continent Kepture. In the western sky, a first-quarter Moon could be seen, dim and small, casting hardly more light than that of the stars.

To the east, the roll and whoop of the prairies increased their pitch, culminating in a low, undistinguished range of hillocks, which fell away on their farther sides, down through broad swales and gullies, to the vast delta of the river Yast, the far side of which could not be seen even in the light of day. But down there was a great darkness, and the pin-pricking of a multitude of tiny lights. The lights shimmered and flickered in the nighted gulfs, as if ripples were passing before the points of light; but overhead the light of the stars was steady and flickered very little at all.

The dim starlight resolved, at distance, few details of the plains of Ombur. Little distinctive could be made out, save a faint trace, a bare track, winding eccentrically from west-southwest to the east, where it wound between two knolls and vanished. North was an emptiness, where the plains stretched to meet the Yast as it curved to the west, unseen. In the south, a gradual rising of the land led to a series of hogbacks which obscured the view. Beyond were more of the rolling prairie uplands, more of Ombur, which extended far to the west and the south.

Those-who-used-Names recalled the name Ombur with fondness,

for Ombur had once echoed from horizon to horizon with the name of one lord; perhaps Ombur had possessed one lord before that, or many times: Time was long, in Ombur, just as it was in the other named lands of Kepture, which in their times had also known one lord of their own, once, twice. In the West of Kepture were Ombur, Warvard, Seagove. Across the North, facing the Polar parts of World-Ocean, were ranged Boigne, Yerra, and tiny Urige; the East was Intance and Nasp. In the center were Incana, encompassing most of the highlands, and Yastian. Kepture bore the outline of two potatoes grown together, the western part being the larger, but the eastern extended somewhat more to the North, whereupon Urige was cold, and Cape Hogue at the southernmost tip of the western parts was tropical.

Ombur was neither lifeless nor empty, nor even free of movement across its broad swathes and textures. One such motion now was proceeding out onto the plains from the line of hills to the East, a motion which was that of a small cart, unpainted and weathered quite gray, moving along slowly and with deliberation, almost with leisure, pulled in no great haste by two gaunt creatures of anthropoid shape, heavy-framed and large, walking steadily, methodically. The cart rolled on two immense solid wheels, and featured a small roofed cupola at the front for the driver; the whole followed the irregularities of the track with a patient, rolling motion, swaying from side to side.

On a shelf attached to the rear of the cart sat a hulking, lumpy shape, motionless save for that imparted by the rolling of the cart; inanimate, or asleep. Or merely still. Inside the cupola at the front sat the driver, who now bestirred himself, looking carefully about the landscape, as if looking for landmarks. He paid little attention to the creatures pulling the cart. The driver appeared to be well-furnished about the midsection, fleshy but just shy of fat, a balding man approaching middle age.

The driver, by name Seuthe-the-Bagman Jemasmy, now nodded to the draybeasts, the Sumpters, whispering in a low tone to them, "Dur, Dur." The Sumpters paced on for a time, glanced at one another out of the corners of their heavy-browed eyes, and let the cart slow itself to a stop. The creaking and rattling of the springless vehicle continued, then it too stopped, and now only the breathless silences of the night could be heard. The figure at the back of the cart looked awkwardly over one shoulder, leering madly, teeth gleaming in the starlight. Jemasmy turned and leaned over, to speak into a compartment inside the cart, saying softly, "Morgin. Are you awake?"

A grunt answered him. Presently a stiff and slow-moving figure, a spindly man of no easily discernible age, phyle or sept, topped by a bushy, iron-gray stubble on his head, emerged and climbed into the vacant seat to the right of the driver. There was yet silence among the rolls and plunges of the land Ombur. Little wind could be sensed. All that could be heard was the deep breathing of the Sumpters, the gaunt, heavy creatures who pulled the cart.

Jemasmy volunteered, "Your wish was to be awakened when Sovin Hogback obscured Vatz Pinnacle, on the plain. We are here."

"What now the track, Seuthe?" queried Morgin-the-Embasse Balebaster, in a hoarse voice.

"The Lambascada Swathe, of course."

Morgin mused for a moment over the empty plains, at last getting to his feet, and leaning out and holding a roof-brace precariously, looked about, as if to reassure himself that he was where he wished to be. He stood thus for a long time, sometimes smelling the air, and also pausing to listen carefully. Morgin looked long into the empty, rolling distances; then he slowly and stiffly climbed down from the cart to stand thoughtfully in the track, alongside the Sumpters, who towered over him, longlegged, short-armed. The Sumpters stood quietly, shifting their weight from one splayed foot to the other in an unvarying, monotonous rhythm. Morgin patted the nearer one affectionately on the rump.

He said, "All seems proper for the moment. Very good. Have Benne feed and water the Sumpters." At this, the dray beasts blew air through their cheeks, making a flapping, blowing sound. Morgin continued, "Here we shall pause; there is time to read the signs before we leave the swath and sojourn to the west."

Jemasmy queried, "Not indeed to Lambascade?"

"No. Not directly, although it was my intention that *they* so imagine." Morgin gestured with his head in the direction from which they had come. "First," he said portentously, "on to Medlight. Then, in turn, to Utter Semerend. We can turn south to Lambascade after that; I would speak with Ruggou first."

Jemasmy chuckled, "And not let the others know, eh? Ayoo! Good old Gutsnapper! He may not rule over as much of Old Ombur as he'd like, may St. Zermille continue to thwart his plans, but you still have to account for him firstly. Rightly so, Master Morgin. To Medlight, then, and Utter Semerend."

Morgin winced at Jemasmy's use of the vulgar cognomen of Incantor* Ivak Ruggou, leader and chief of Sept Aurisman. He hoped that Jemasmy would not forget and blurt that out in the hearing of Ruggou, or one of his favorite henchmen. There were not many to call Ruggou Gutsnapper to his face, and remain ignorant of the procedures by which he had gained that name.

Jemasmy hung the reins upon a peg and also dismounted, making a sign to the hulking figure at the rear of the cart. Benne-the-Clone dismounted the cart awkwardly, as if it were the first time he had ever done it, and began to rummage under the rear quarter of the cart for barrels of water and bags of mash for the Sumpters. Standing back from the cart with a load under each arm, Benne displayed a short, bowlegged figure with excessively long arms corded with ridged muscles.

As Benne carried his load to the Sumpters, Jemasmy, now by the massive axle, could be seen to be carrying a large pouch slung over one shoulder, with something weighty in it. Jemasmy inspected the wheel-mountings of the cart, while Morgin walked about, apparently at random, an abstracted expression on his face. Finally Jemasmy straightened from the wheel, and rounded the cart to join Morgin in his perambulations.

Jemasmy waited a little for Morgin to notice him, and said, "By the Lady, let be a pest upon the Delta and all its ratfolk! I do believe that the bearing is going bad!"

Morgin appeared not to have heard the remark. He asked, still looking into the distances, "Were we followed?"

Jemasmy answered, "No. At the very least, not from the Delta itself. Up the swale, I saw nothing. All was innocent. But once on the plains, the Sumpters have been somewhat uneasy. Not from something close; perhaps a band of distant hunters, watching for a straggler from the Delta."

"One never knows," somberly reflected Morgin. "Perhaps you are correct; in any event, let us continue to hope. On the other hand . . . could

---

*Incantor: a middle-ranking title-of-nobility from the Phanetical system, which included, from the highest, Phanet, Feodar, Incantor, Deodactor, and Sphodic. The suggestion was that the office was elective, despite the fact that it usually was not. Titles in the Phanetical system were not usually associated with dynasties, which were covered by the Phyacic system, listing from the highest, Phyacor, Erchon, Hospod, Peshe and Phreme. Both these were the ancient orders of nobility of Kepture and the other continents as well. An Incantor would equate somewhat to a Baron, or perhaps Warlord.

be Haydars, or Meor. I should not care to meet either in the darkness of Nightside, although were the band small enough, we could probably stand off Meors."

"Three of us . . . Hm. We do have a ballista in the cart, and Benne is good with one."

Morgin reflected, "There is an immanence in the air which I sense with the Sumpters. As much as I would regret it under other circumstances, perhaps we should consult the Prote. Yes, have it decyst."

Jemasmy advised, "Morgin, you know it will be ill of temper. You did keep it decysted during the whole meet."

"Yes, yes, of course. There was little enough choice there. Yet here, too. I am uneasy, apprehensive. Something stirs in the nighted gulfs about us; there is motion, fear, and . . . hope. I know; I feel it. But not from whence it comes. Most certainly we must have a reading of the locus . . . I could not place it above Hospod Alor of the Lagostomes that he pay a Meor formation to harry us."

"Alor? But what could he pay?"

Morgin made an airy gesture. "What else? The usual, of the course: girls. Or a brace of gelded bucks for meat." He shrugged. "It's all they have."

Jemasmy said resignedly, "Very well. Now, I tell you, thusly never went events in Cantou when I was Bagman to Thrincule." He reached gingerly into the pouch, as if half expecting to find a live coal there. He felt along a cold, hard shell, feeling for a certain node. Jemasmy located the node, pressed, felt something gelid give a little. He withdrew his hand fastidiously, adding, "In Cantou, one could always trust the Cantureans to treat an Embasse and his Bagman rightly. No treachery."

Morgin agreed. "Kepture seethes with it, rightly enough. Just so came I from great Chengurune and the Dawnlands of the east; and there, too, we had Embasses in plenty. Here; there are never enough."

"Or in Glordune," added Jemasmy.

"Glordune," said Morgin, "will have to wait. It is not for me."

Jemasmy commented. "Nor for me. They still adhere to the old ways, so it's said."

Benne growled, from the general area of the Sumpters. "The old way, yes. 'Yoo, they keep it good, too, they do, the Glorionts, but they call on the Lady no less than we." Benne-the-Clone had once been a sailor on the wide bent seas of Monsalvat, and had set port in Glordune, wildest of four continents."

Morgin said, half-irritably, "Respect to St. Zermille none the lesser, but the Embasses were not her doing, nor the folding of the tribes*. Those are of Cretus the Scribe."

Jemasmy added, ritually, completing the formula, "Before the treachery out of Incana that brought the Empire to nothing; that kept the Kleshmen from their natural home the stars."

Morgin mused, "Such a strange old dream, that . . . Is the Prote decysted yet?"

"Not yet, Morgin." Jemasmy felt inside the shoulder bag, experimentally, gingerly. "Softening, but not open yet."

Morgin nodded, acknowledging. He expected no better, for back down in the Delta, he had pushed the Prote to what he had thought were its usual limits—and beyond. But it had not once broken cooperation. Curious.

One of the native life-forms of the planet, a prote was a creature of curious abilities and even more curious limitations. No one was quite certain exactly what a prote really was, nor had anyone stepped forward with knowledge of how it fed, lived, excreted or reproduced. If indeed it performed any of the acts which fell under those headings. Generally sessile, a prote could exude pseudopodia and move, very slowly, on occasion. It rarely did.

But while having no identifiable traits common to most life-forms, a prote did have two abilities recognized as uncommonly useful by all: The first was speech, via sound waves to Humans, and by some unknown method among each other, apparently with little or no limitation of distance.†

The second ability was, in the end, even more valuable, and even less understood; a prote perceived. With no identifiable sensory organs, and having no permanent characteristics save its own protean flesh, a prote

---

*An event in the far past of Monsalvat. It was said that Cretus spoke to all septs, tribes, phyles, directing them to be complementary to one another, rather than maniacally competitive. That this ideal failed was unimportant. Cretus was remembered for that he was the first of Monsalvat, which is of the Klesh, to say so and try to implement it.

†Not via electromagnetic radiation. The first explorers had confirmed intercommunication among protes, firstly by observing one prote act upon information only another had known. Later, when they could speak with protes, they had testimonial evidence. But they did not uncover how the intercommunication took place. The electromagnetic spectrum was searched, without success. The problem had not yet been solved when organized society abandoned the planet.

was capable of perceiving the disposition and condition of everything about itself, on occasion to considerable distance. That was their inimitable key to survival. A wild prote simply watched its surround, and, at a certain threshold of danger, encysted, becoming impervious to any method of attack yet discovered on Monsalvat. Fire, sword, projectile: all were alike in their uselessness. Thrown into bonfires, they vanished. Thrown off cliffs, they were not found. Taken into space, the containers arrived empty.

There were no young protes, nor had ever one been seen to bud, spore, mate or perform any known category of reproductive act. And the communication that passed from one prote to another, while seemingly unlimited in space, was curiously circumscribed in content: descriptions of conditions passed effortlessly, but complex ideas, or rational discourse was blocked.

Protes were somewhat rare; and they were the jealously guarded possessions of the Embasses* of Monsalvat. Or, perhaps the Embasses were the property of the protes. Klesh did not trouble themselves with distinctions that made no difference to the order of things. And the protes? They found the Embasses to their liking, or tolerance, or to an emotion known only to protes. If they possessed any. Embasses who stepped beyond their function were quickly humbled, for their prote would leave them, or contrive to be lost, and found again by another mixed-blood. A prote could not be coerced.

Morgin had now been in Kepture for about twenty of the years of Monsalvat, and for the whole of that time, with the services of several Bagmen, he had carried his prote. In the course of that association, never entirely pleasant, Morgin had learned much he could not always put accurately into words. But he had also become sensitized to unusual

---

*An Embasse was a person, usually of dubious origin and questionable race, who performed communicative functions between the various tribes, and other social organisms of the Klesh on Monsalvat. They could not be called peacemakers, for they arranged conflicts as often as they negotiated to prevent them. Rather, they functioned as leavening, controlling agents in the eternal racial ferment of Monsalvat. "Civilization," denoting desirable conditions of order, was related solely to the effectiveness of the Embasses of a given area, not to any arbitrary concept of order held by any tribe or group. In this context it may be noted that the continent Glordune was considered "wild" solely in that there were no openly-practicing Embasses there. The kinds of barbarisms practiced in Glordune were not more in kind or number than on other continents—just more disorderly.

conditions, and had learned when to call upon the powers of the prote. An act he never did casually, for protes were both ill-tempered and rather oracular in their utterances.

Now in the soft plains night, in the silence under the stars, Morgin began to walk about restlessly, casting short, sharp glances at the horizons, the empty prairie distances, not so much looking for a sign as casting for some subtle something out of place. The sense of Immanence was becoming stronger; from its rate of onset, and the strength of the growing hunch, he could almost read it. Almost. *Haydars*, he thought. A Meor band would leave more obvious traces, hang back, probe, feel them out, and take days to make up their minds. Morgin could recall travellers who had been trailed by Meors for ten days before being attacked. Haydars, on the other hand . . . They would vanish, leaving a sense of terror behind, or suddenly come straight in without warning.

Jemasmy broke into his searching, "You suspect treachery of the Lagostomes? I shouldn't think they'd have it in them to dare to."

Morgin looked back, from the deep-blue darkness of the horizons, curiously, as if he were seeing Jemasmy for the first time. He answered, after a moment, "Lagos? What? Oh, that; yes, of course, of a matter of course, Seuthe. Of a certainty I suspect them. They are more desperate than most—driven into the Delta by pressure from surrounding tribes and Phyles, and now stuck there. Floods, and then storms from the Inner Water, nothing to trade and never enough food, and the highest birth rate in the whole world. And all around them the predatory races of Kepture, and an ancient compact which says that where a lance in the ground does not bring water, so there does the Lago become prey. And nothing to make a ship of, and no land to receive them, if they had, Inner Water or Outer*. So now they seek to buy a stone's throw at a time, slipping back up the Yast and trying to confound both Ombur and Incana. This, Ruggou suspected. And so likewise thinks Molio Azendarach of the Kurbish Windfowlers. A pact with the Meors to the south. The Lagos know that we must return to Ruggou, to the Ombur. If Ruggou knows, then so will Azendarach. And then all these careful moves for nothing, once more exporting slaves to Azendarach, while Ruggou combs their western bluffs and encourages the Haydars. Then the Meors will tire of them, too."

---

*The Four Continents enclosed the world-ocean into an Inner Sea and a much greater Outer Ocean, which in turn covered more than half the planetary surface.

Jemasmy ventured, "Is it not the Embasse's part to be neutral?"

"Yes, yes, of course, but not to blindness. The Lagos are a plague. Unchecked, they would engulf all Kepture, and no less than Azendarach and Ruggou, I also desire to see them kept in the Delta, in their land Yastian. So have all the other Embasses." Morgin paused. "And the Prote?"

A flat, timbreless voice issued forth from the bag, sounding clearly, close at hand, but also as if the speaker were a vast distance away: "To the disturbance of One-Organ Morgin is this instrument come; speak, then, O singlet."

Morgin cast down an evil glance to the bag. "Address me not with such endearments; perform function, encyst again—this is all that I ask, not these repeated abuses." Morgin's vulgar cognomen arose from a fact pertaining to his anatomy, a lacking occasioned by an injury sustained in his more ribald youth. It was said that Morgin had engaged the attentions of a young lady whom, it would seem, had already been spoken for. Morgin never appreciated being reminded of this. Jemasmy looked away, concealing a ribald smirk. Benne-the-Clone stood by the feeding Sumpters and chuckled to himself, adding an insane giggle now and again.

Benne said, at last, calling across the Sumpters, "Give up the one, Morgin! It is only a goad! Emulate your loyal servant, disciple and retainer, and be liberated from the gusts of hot temperaments!"

Morgin ruminated to himself. "While I try to steer a course through storm and reef, one asks why, one calls names, and the last urges castratodom." He sighed deeply. He would never be free of the abuse of the Prote, nor the ignorance of Jemasmy, nor the inappropriate advisements of Benne. He spoke, now clearly, to the Prote, "East Ombur. Danger I query. Read place and tell."

There was no immediate reply, nor was one expected. The Prote said nothing, but after a moment, there began a slow stirring in the bag. Jemasmy removed the bag from his shoulders and carefully laid it on the ground. The shape-changing of the Prote was disquieting to him, an event he had never learned to like, or even tolerate. He walked away from the bag, which continued to shift slowly, fluidly. There was motion on the ground beside the bag, a darker shadow.

After a time had passed, and the circling stars moved a little way across the skies of Monsalvat, and clouds moved over the face of the darkness, the voice spoke again in its flattened, measured cadences, "The suspicions of Morgin the Embasse transpose into the farsight of a prote."

Morgin now approached the bag on the ground, circumspectly; neither he nor any of the rest said anything, but rather remained silent, to allow the prote to develop its oracular remark after its own fashion.

The Prote continued, "Darkness and light are one, but for the shadowcaster; Ombur teems with movement, fierce life, men, near-men, not-men. Korsors and Eratzenasters,* Haydars and Meor and Lagostome. To certain of these, such as this band do not exist; to others, interest. To others, central attentiveness. Lagostomes observe your movements from the eastern swale, awaiting a small band of Meors arriving along the hogback. All are persuaded by reasonable doubt: ahead are Haydars. Their presence disturbs, makes resolve hesitant."

Morgin asked quietly, "Where are Haydars? How far? How many? Why are they here?"

The Prote answered, "They see you in the present; you will see them in the future. Afoot in their custom, they could speak with you within minutes. A moment: sensing . . . there are . . . fifteen. One is a girl, the omenreader. Another is an Embasse."

Morgin paused, then asked, "The Embasse. Captive?"

"Negation. They seek new lands. This is a vanguard party, who came by air to seek an omen. The Embasse is for order as they pass through lands."

Morgin thought swiftly, trying to foresee consequences, considering factors which would cause a band of Haydars to come to the East of Ombur, far from their more usual haunts. They preferred the west and north. Their presence would certainly disturb things. . . . Ruggou might become more demonstrative, but the Meor would certainly withdraw farther south. He asked, "Is their prote decysted? Can you read names?"

The prote answered, "They are . . . Talras Em Margaria, Rhardous N'Hodos, Kori D'Indouane, Zermo Lafma the Garrotist, Segedine Dao Timni . . ."

Morgin cried out, "Stop, stop! May the Lady prevent me from asking who might be found in the Delta! We would spend the next ten years listening to a recitation of all the full names of all the Lagos that are, plus all the little splitlips begotten while the first list was being delivered! Three I need, and of what clan. Phreme, Embasse, Omenreader."

---

*Native life-forms of Monsalvat, both predatory. The Korsor was somewhat bearlike in size and general shape, but much swifter and more graceful. The Eratzenaster was a nightmare resembling nothing known on any other world. They were large flying predators of the upper air. Both forms were occasionally tamed and put to odd uses.

The Prote answered in the same toneless voice, "In that order, *S'fou* Ringuid Goam Mallam, *Cland* Joame Afanasy, *Lami* Tenguft Ouarde. Dagazaram Clan."

Morgin straightened. There was no danger to them from this group of Haydars, and their presence might be an asset. Indeed. He reflected that neutral Haydars were the best protection available. And that to read names, their prote had to be decysted. He stepped back, so he could see better around him, and said, "Let them approach. If they haven't attacked by now, they've no intent of it."

The Prote said, "They come already . . ."

Morgin asked, "Are the Lagostomes and Meor the sole danger? If so read, then you may encyst. These will cover most contingencies."

The prote did not immediately respond, and the slow, fluid movements in and around the bag continued. The voice said, now as if from a great distance, "A moment, One-Organ. The currents are roiled and turbulent. Time is required for deeper reading. . . . There is an immanence somewhere . . ."

And the bag made further motions, as the prote made adjustments to its form to enable it to read more fully the surround. Morgin was used to this pause, and expected no more from the prote. Presently it would return to its normal encysted condition. Protes always read as far as they reasonably could; they were professional worriers. But a deeper reading did require time. Morgin walked away from the bag by the side of the cart, preparing to meet the Haydars.

In the front of the cart, the Sumpters began to move nervously, stamping their feet, wagging their ponderous shoulders from side to side, causing their harness to rattle and slap against the heavy drawbar. Benne spoke softly to them, trying to calm the dray beasts. Morgin and Jemasmy both looked about apprehensively, trying to see, to hear something, but whatever it was disturbing the Sumpters, it was more subtle than their perceptions could detect. The Sumpters became even more agitated, almost as if they were in fear of their lives. Minutes passed slowly, as hours. And then, without any anticipation, the Sumpters became still, so abruptly that their harness continued to rattle momentarily after they had stopped. Morgin and Jemasmy looked closely about, trying to penetrate into the darkness, the limpid and deceiving distances. On a low rise no more than a few meters away was a small group of deeply hooded and cloaked shadows of the night; the two groups nervously watched one another, neither making a move.

Four of the tall, thin shadows detached themselves from the distant group and began to approach the cart in a measured, deliberate manner. Jemasmy shivered suddenly, as in the grip of a violent ague, but Morgin, sensing the motion out of the corner of his eye, smiled to himself. The motion of the approaching Haydars reassured him; he knew something of the Haydar way, and it was in just such a manner that one suggested benignly neutral, if not peaceful, intent.

They came closer: now Morgin could discern differences among the shadows, differences of outline, gait, tallness, posture. He glanced behind the approaching tetrad; the remainder of the band had vanished. Of those approaching—now Morgin could resolve a pouch such as a Bagman might carry, after the manner of Jemasmy. A Bagman. Another walked directly, with businesslike stride, with his cloak flapping about his shanks. Afanasy, the Embasse. One other was proud of bearing, but deliberate and aloof: most likely Mallam, the leader. And the last moved as any Haydar did, flowing, striding, using its incredible height to maximum advantage, but at the same time, with a more fluid, more graceful series of motions. The girl? Morgin strove to recall Haydar lore. Yes. Only one unwed could serve as tribal wise woman. So: Tenguft Ouarde.

Now they were near, glancing over Benne and the Sumpters, passing them by. Jemasmy they ignored, and Seuthe the Bagman was grateful for their inattention. Before Morgin they separated a little, each facing him equally. The girl, if Morgin's suspicions were true, bent, stooped, lowering herself, and laid a spear on the ground. It was only slightly longer than her height, which was well over two meters. The others were taller still.

Morgin reached within his caftan, removing a poinard-like knife-sword, with a wavy edge; by all accounts, a vicious weapon. This he laid on the ground before himself.

One of the group spoke, a deep, hollow, mournful voice. "I am Afanasy. You would know me as Embasse."

Morgin replied, "I am Morgin Balebaster, Embasse of the Ombur. You surprise me. I ask without intent of offense; are you truly Haydarrada?" The allusion was to Afanasy's lineage; it was the force of tradition that an Embasse be mixed-blood.

Afanasy answered, the cavernous tone of his voice changing not at all, "Not Vere-Dagazaram Haydar, as are my associates. I am of the Techiascos. Mixed enough to take the prote of my predecessor, but somewhat true in form. How may we assist you in serving order, Master Embasse of the Ombur?"

Morgin said, "Lagostomes dog our trail from the Delta, and our prote reads Meors in collusion. I think dispersed along yon hogback. I bear reports, and desire only to pass unmolested into the west to the waterplaces Medlight, and then Utter Semerend."

"Are you not under warrant?"

"Only within the Delta country."

"Fear them not. We met a band of Meors at dusk when we landed. Those are not worthy of the name 'enemy.' Those who survived fled east. They were unworthy of running to earth. These will do nothing. We are here to feel out new lands. No Haydar range the East Ombur, save in rare hunts."

"You will settle here?"

"The Dagazaram will divide; Ullahi will remain in the ancestral huntlands. The Iasamed will range East Ombur. Who will oppose, Embasse?"

Morgin reflected, then spoke. "I understand that Incantor Ivak Ruggou of Sept Aurisman desires that his people extend somewhat to the east."

Afanasy replied, "Aurismen? We know Aurismen. They will stay in their little walled towns and break the sod around them. So long as they content themselves with their gardens, they will know no Haydar. We do not contest territory with men of the soil."

True enough, thought Morgin. *But hardly know them? Haydars were the legendary ogres of the night, on every continent. No place was free of them, entirely, for only the Haydar were fierce enough to break and ride, in the air, the gruesome Eratzenaster. Yet it might not be such a bad idea to have a small band settled permanently in East Ombur; Haydars reproduced slowly, and they would of a certainty dilute the ambitions of Ruggou. Brave or not, only fools willingly moved into an area known to be Haydar Huntland. They ate trespassers.* He added, aloud, "Molio Azendarach, across the Great River, has thwarted the expansions of the Lagostomes; since they cannot walk on water, Ombur becomes worthy of their notice; the more so since the Meor can only be pushed so far southwards down the coast. I may not speak for the Meor, being out of their favor in the present—yet I could tell them that Ruggou has plainly stated he intends to occupy the uplands if he senses any movement west by Lagos. This issue is a perpetual one in these parts, usually resolved by the Lagos remaining in the Delta. My reading is that they are to the point of defying Ruggou—he is farther away than Molio Azendarach and has notable supply-line problems for an investiture of the East Ombur."

Afanasy reflected, not speaking, while Mallam stood back. The girl, Tenguft Ouarde, stepped closer to Morgin, close enough for him to make out individual features, instead of a gaunt Haydar wrapped in a shapeless cloak and robe, further covered by the soft night darkness: she was tall, indeed, tall enough that Morgin had to look up to see her face. Under the hood were bottomless, hollow eyes, a great blade of a nose, a small mouth. Yet in her own way she was also smooth and young, and full of the confidence of bearing that only beauty brings. The beauty was not in gross shapes, in structures, but in something deeper that animated those shapes.

She spoke, a tracery of youthful boastfulness counterpointing the husky adolescent voice, a girl's voice, even in the deep resonances of the Haydar throat, "Lagostome peoples are only fit for the casting of omens; they are soft and weak and have no sinew in their souls. I read your brow! You do not know the Haydarada: *game* is that which fulfills us, not those who spend their lives in breeding. You may rest easily now, Master Morgin the Embasse of the Ombur and the Incana, and say the same to Ruggou and his Aurismen. Upon the Sun's coming, I will walk along the ridgeline there in the east in my hunt clothing, as I came into the world and time, with spear and knife my only companion. And not one will cross the river."

Mallam rumbled, "*Lami* Tenguft suggests a solution to affairs of these parts."

Morgin commented politely, "It is as you expound, Ringuid Goam Mallam. I shall say as much to Ruggou; it would appear to be to his advantage, indeed. And so the lands of the Aurismen will not change, nor those of the Lagostome. Upon what or whom will you hunt, may I ask?"

Afanasy said, "The outcast, those who have done great wrong in their own lands; the outlaw bands, robbers and murderers; and of course those who come to hunt Haydar . . . what should they expect."

Morgin reflected and was content. Yes, just so were things resolved, usually. Be patient and an answer would come. The Haydar band would bring stability, a continuance of the state of things. And Ruggou would not be brought into contact with the realm of Molio Azendarach, which would have the effect of keeping Molio on his side of the river, and would save Sept Aurisman for a more temperate leader to succeed Ruggou, one with more pedestrian dreams. Yes. He said, "I see no impediment to your coming here."

Mallam nodded, smiled, flashing white teeth. "A-ha! That is good. So, then, here we are, all of us." He signalled with one arm to the remainder of the band, and in response several dark shapes materialized, seemingly out of the very earth, out of shadows. Mallam called to them, "Talras,

Segedine! Make the signs to free the beasts! We stay! Rhardous N'Hodos and Tesselade! To the south, for a fete, one Meor. One will be sufficient for us, for the stranger-Embasse is not of the blood!" He turned to Morgin. "I may proceed assuming you do not share our custom?"

"Without offense. I hope I give none in turn."

"It is as you say . . . there are few like us in the wideness of the world. But will you rest a while? Lafma has his tamgar, for the song, and the *Lami* carries in her mind the visions of the people. She will sing of our great hunts, that our young men may on the morrow feel the wind and see far, and make the motions by the firelight that they may have before their spirits the image of the perfect woman of the people."

Morgin answered diplomatically, "When I spoke with *Lami* Tenguft Ouarde, I could see with all my senses that she was indeed a worthy vessel of your dreams. Would that I could see and hear it all, that I, an unworthy Embasse of unknown lineage, might glimpse that which your people know in full. But yet I have affairs of my own, as well, which call. I would speak with Ruggou, that his mind be correct in the way of things."

"Just so . . ." He was interrupted. One of the Haydars who had remained behind now approached, quickly, and spoke to Mallam. The hoarse whispers said, "My S'fou Mallam: I made the signs in their proper order, but they who fly do not depart. They continue to circle, and have been joined by wild 'Natzers as well!"

Mallam responded, "Into hunt-dispersal, then! Call in the hunt! Embasse! What of the Prote?"

Tenguft, having heard, had been craning her head back, hood falling off and back, looking at the sky and the stars. Morgin looked at the girl, then at the sky. He saw nothing, but a suggestion of motion nagged at the edge of perception. Something was up there, that was sure. Tenguft said, "When they circle and are joined by the wild, there will be blood. There are almost fifty 'Natzers now waiting."

Morgin turned to Seuthe-the-Bagman, but it was not necessary, for now the Prote of Morgin the Embasse had chosen to speak. The voice of the Prote was strained, full of wavers, and hesitations. It said, "The reading is complete, near and far. Danger! Encystment has commenced. Do not move, especially to the north or east. A star is falling, and one may not run from it. Impact by the breaks, east. Something burning, from the other side of the world, from deep in the night, from far away, around the horizon. There is energy! Something is interfering with placeread!"

Morgin started. "A falling star? Here?"

The Prote continued for a little, its voice now much weakened, "Not stone, One-Organ. Something that slows, that moves against the stream, that moves of itself. I fear." At the end, the voice was highly distorted. The Prote spoke no more.

Morgin said to Afanasy, "And yours?"

"Encysted already."

Morgin said, "That which moves against the stream is a ship! The true men are returning! The men return!"

Tenguft retrieved her spear. "Or the warriors, may they eat grass, such as shall lead them to." She lifted the blade to her lips, kissed it quickly, thrust the long spear upward against the night sky of the east. She repeated fervently, "Let the Warriors return and meet their creations!"

Morgin turned with the rest and looked now to the east: at first, they saw nothing—there was the night and the darkness; the lights of the Delta could not be seen from the plains of Ombur, where they stood. And down from the starry zenith, the near stars shone clearly, without flickering, but near the horizon, close to the planet, through the dense atmosphere, they winked and trembled as if ripples were passing before them. They marked out the familiar constellations of the proper season: The Reaper, The Crown, The Netsman flinging his sparkling cluster into the South. Close to the horizon, they seemed to go on and off, some winking out for moments at a time. But there was another star there, in the East, that did not go out, red-orange and burning in the night, rising from the east, a baleful star that neither wavered nor flickered out of sight. It cleared the horizon and vaulted into the sky, growing as they watched.

4

"I once examined the horoscopes of a number of murderers in order to find out what planetary dispositions were responsible for the temperament. To my amazement, it was not the secret and explosive energy of Uranus, not the sinister and malignant self-ishness of Saturn, not the ungoverned fury of Mars, which formed the background for the crime, but the callous intellectual ism of Mercury. Then comes a most extraordinary discovery. The horoscopes of the murdered are almost identical with those of the assassins. They asked for it!"

—A. C.

FOR A LONG time, in the warm darkness of the compartment, they did not say anything; no words seemed necessary. But after an un-measured time, Meure could no longer contain some of that which was in him, and he said, simply, "There are words that I wanted to say be-fore, then, now, for I came to remember."

It was quiet again for another time, marked only by breathing, by heartbeats, by a small, rare rustling of the coverlet. But in the end, Au-diart spoke also; she said, as simply, "And I came to forget." And then, "To cast away, be rid of, be unencumbered of . . . but I see that even as I wipe away that which has passed, the marks of my wiping make a new record, and nothing will come of what I wished but more change."

"I am changed."

"And I, by no less." But she rolled away from him and curled her body a little, as if she wished to sleep now.

Meure remained still, listening, waiting, remembering. He let his senses return him to his surroundings, to collect the feel of the ship *Ffstretsha*. There was yet a dim light in the compartment, splayed along the ceil-ing, coming from the kitchen lights down in the space below. He re-membered: he had intended to shut the compartment door, but that had been interrupted, and it was still open. His body was damp with sweat, and there was a warm, bare body next to his. And now he felt again the motions of the ship: rockings from side to side, damped, gentle, but reduced greatly from the true motion which must be outside. The ship moved on all three axes, sometimes simultaneously, sometimes by two axes, sometimes along one axis alone. The motions were random, unpredictable, now seemingly less severe, but broader in scope. The ship calmed, and almost became still, and then without anticipation began a surging motion ahead. To Meure, his inner ear system suggested a mushy acceleration ahead, as if pushed from behind, while the ship pitched upwards, nose-high; this was followed by an indescribable slewing, which rapidly altered into an angry shaking, a series of jerkings. He heard, from below, a hissing sound from the direction of the kitchen unit, and the lights went out. Not at once: they faded out. A red light illuminated in the ceiling of the compartment, and from a concealed speaker, a beeping tone began, interrupted at regular intervals by the breathy lisping of a recorded Spsom announcement. The compartment door began sliding shut. Meure half-rose to reach to stop it, rising at last out of the passive waiting, suddenly realizing; he reached across Audiart, who was also trying to move, but he felt a prickling along his fingertips, a numbing. He reached closer, and there was a bright flash of energy discharge. He drew back, rubbing his fingers, against the back wall. Audiart pressed her body back from the doorway, now fully closed. From somewhere in the framework of the ship, several metallic sounds occurred, strongly suggesting the operation of a locking mechanism. They were locked in.

They pressed close together; there was a sensation of pressure, of numbness in their limbs, and then there was no motion sensible at all, and in one more instant, nothing at all. There was no fading, no drifting, as in sleep, or unconsciousness. Time just ended. Meure had only time to start to say, "I th-

STOP

-ink it is some kind of protective field." Time began again, the door snapped open, and from speakers all over the ship, a gong began tolling, punctuated by a Spsom voice enunciating at regular intervals, a single word that sounded like 'Vv-h't.' The outer door of their shared quarters burst open to the noise of much confusion without, and at last the voice of Clellendol broke clear through it: "Up! Up! All out of the ship!"

Meure and Audiart hurriedly retrieved their hastily-discarded clothing from the places where it had fallen and struggled to put it on, while below, in the compartment there was the sound of doors and cabinets opening and closing, and then quiet. Now they could hear the sounds of the ship.

The sounds were not so much in the air, as in the very fabric of the ship itself; there were long, sustained groans, punctuated by ominous pops, cracks; in the background, the hissing of escaping gas could also be heard from time to time. They took no time to gather anything, but dodged through the kitchen into the common-room, where the lighting was still working, but was flickering. The ship settled to a new center of gravity with an easy, floating motion, which seemed to start up a new series of creaks and groans. They balanced carefully across the shifting compartment and attained the hallway, where the lights were definitely out.

At the curving of the bulkhead, Clellendol waited for them, looking nervously about. "Come on, come on," he fidgeted. "They are waiting for us at the port. We're down successfully on Monsalvat, whatever luck that is, but *Ffstretsha* is breaking up and we must get out of it. That Vdhitz tried to explain it, but I couldn't make sense of it."

The three of them hurried through the swaying central corridor to the entry port, where the remainder of the crew and passengers was awaiting them: three Lerfolk; Dreve Halander and the slender girl, Ingraine Deffy; two Spsom, Captain Shchifr and Vdhitz; and the single remaining slave, the diminutive furry creature from Vfzyekhr. Vdhitz was anxiously looking outside, half-hanging out the port. Without looking back, he made a motion with his free hand to the rest, and swung through the port onto the ground. Shchifr glanced quickly over the survivors, and gestured at the port. Then he stood aside to let them pass.

Meure was at the end of the line and could see little enough of the view outside the ship; he had an impression that the ship was somewhat tilted over on its side, so that the port was looking downward, rather than directly out, as would be the normal case. There was a peculiar reddish light, but he could not imagine the source, and he asked Audiart, "What time is it?"

She looked back over her shoulder, her face blank. "Time? It's the middle of the night, of course! When else shipwreck? Come on! We're here, that's what!"

Audiart reached the port behind Clellendol, grasped the edge-handles awkwardly, and swung through. And with Shchifr urging him from behind, Meure followed her onto the soil of Monsalvat.

Meure felt dazed and disoriented. He wanted to stop where he was, in the now comforting shadow of the bulk of the *Ffstretsha*, under the tangle of the absurd Spsom conduit system, but Shchifr had now dropped out of the ship, and was hurriedly removing devices from his vest and tossing them back into the open port. Inside, all was dark. Here, there was a faint light, but the source was out of sight. There seemed to be vegetation underfoot, wiry and stringy, matted down by the ship when it had landed. He heard voices, sensed motion ahead, under the piping, and Clellendol's voice urging him to run. He ran ahead, ducked under a sagging conduit, whose paint was burned entirely off, and whose broken end waved loosely about like some live thing, and at last saw the group ahead of him, running from the ship. Meure followed, trying to catch up; Shchifr easily ran past him with the half-bound, half-leaping motion of a Spsom running.

Shchifr waved them on, and together they ran another distance, slightly uphill, not looking back. Meure sensed motions around them, in the air, along the ground, a great confusion somehow, but he could not stop to look.

Finally they attained a rocky knoll, where they stopped. Meure found Audiart, sitting on the rocks, knees clasped closely to her chest, looking, staring back, in the direction of the ship. No. Past the ship. At the morning.

He cast himself down beside her, looked back. In the east, the star of Monsalvat was rising into a new day. A double star called Bitirme.

The star rising out of the eastern horizon was a close double, the two component stars being of apparently the same size, both of a rusty-orange color. They were separated by what appeared to be something a little more than a diameter, and their position seemed to change slightly with respect to one another as he watched. The sun (*or was it suns*, he thought) was filling the dawn sky with color, bringing the day out of night with an impossible indigo color, while clouds tinted in oranges and reds floated in impossibly clear air; around both stars was an envelope of pearly radiance which was fading with the daylight even as they watched.

The ship lay partly on one side in a little hollow in what Meure saw to be rolling plains that fell away eastward; there were still lights showing in parts of it, but it also seemed to be settling into the ground, as if it no longer had some structural integrity necessary to conform its odd shape. Yes, that was it: it was relaxing, like some exotic, overripe fruit.

And Meure looked upward and saw now the source of the motion he had sensed, perhaps. There were shapes in the morning light, darting, gliding, impossible shapes his mind at first refused to resolve; and from behind the ship people were running, running madly for the ship. People! Humans, judging by the shape of them in the distance, and their gait. They ran like people across the bristly, grasslike vegetation, which Meure now saw to have a distinct blue tint.

The people surrounded the ship. Meure could see that most of them were smallish, slight of build, but most were carrying long knives, or short spears. They seemed to act like savages, capering and gesticulating madly, some rushing up to touch the ship, while others tried to wrench off a piece of dangling piping; it looked ridiculous, like ants attacking a ground-car. Meure felt a motion beside him, smelled a warm-cookie odor.

Vdhitz said, half-whispering, "Semtheng neuw to sirprese dem volk den dere; Tshchiff'r set the Pile to iverlode biffor hee kem den. Blew soon, heh, heh, heh."

Audiart heard the Spsom and started forward to her knees, half to her feet. Meure grasped one arm, and from behind a rock, the Ler girl Flerdistar stepped in front of her. Flerdistar said quietly, "Do not oppose this; you will only die without changing the result. Spsom do not permit aliens to capture a disabled ship, and of a certainty not on Monsalvat; those will be Shchifr's instructions, and he must carry them out. It is his last act as captain of a vessel, forever."

Audiart settled back, but she said, "Those are people down there."

The morning was now coming to light rapidly, the color coming up through various blues into a rosy color. And by the ship, the crowd had become large indeed; but some, at least, were suspicious, and urged the others to withdraw. Their prudence was soon rewarded when one end of the Spsom ship suddenly glowed, sagged, and began to melt, sinking to the ground. The throng outside drew back, and Meure could hear their voices, calling angrily, hissing their displeasure. They left a respectful distance between themselves and the ship, but continued to watch attentively, milling about, brandishing their weapons at the ship.

Flerdistar looked, and said, "There is no answer to that. We think those are people, but we do not know. This is Monsalvat, and the word has strange meanings here." And she looked away from Audiart, and did not meet her returning gaze.

Now some of the crowd about the ship were regaining their boldness, and were leaving their compatriots to make little forays to the ship, as if it were some live thing they could daunt with their boldness. Or perhaps they knew their gestures made no impression on the *Ffstretsha*, no longer a live thing to dance and flow in the currents of the oceans of space, and their demonstrations were for the benefit of their associates, more of whom seemed to be arriving every minute, so it appeared, from the east, from behind a low rise.

Some became bolder, after some moments passed with no further events aboard the ship, although the melted end continued to glow redly with no visible change; one especially bold darted quickly to the entry port, hesitated, looked back once, and swung upward and inside. Another followed closely behind, not wanting to be thought less bold or resolute, but the second one did not enter. The crowd edged closer, throwing rocks at the ship.

From the relatively undamaged end of the ship, a fluting whistle began sounding in short bursts, each of the same duration, equally spaced, an unchanging rhythm. Now, there was a pause, and then the fluted tones began again. Broken by another pause, then starting over again. Something was changing . . . each time, after the pause, there was one less whistled tone. Meure counted as soon as he realized what was happening: seven, *pause*, six, *pause*, five, *pause*, four, *didn't the fools see what was happening inside the ship? It was counting down a warning. Pause*, three, *now the crowd sensed something was astray, and many of them drew back*, pause, two, and the one by the entryport was shouting something into the ship, *pause*, one, the one inside appeared at the port, waving his arms wildly, and then there was light shining behind him, the figure was a dark blot silhouetted in a doorway losing its shape, the crowd was running away, then the *Ffstretsha* became an instant, rigid, white, spiky flower, a hemisphere of thousands of white streamers that *came*, and hung poised, even as the punctuation of the explosion rent the air with a sound never before heard on Monsalvat, and then the magnesium whiteness left the streamers, and the rising suns lit them from behind, suffusing the dust with lights of rose and old peach. Pea gravel rattled among the rocks. In the morning light, Meure could see that most of the former crowd were prone, all laid neatly and radially away from the place where the *Ffstretsha* had been, but that farther away from the ground zero, many were beginning to stir, to pick themselves up, to feel their bodies carefully, and to call to others.

As explosions went, it was not worldshaking; neither was it extremely destructive. It did erase the ship completely. Where the ship had been was now a small crater, littered with small miscellaneous unidentifiable debris. Some were glowing, but their glow was fading even as they watched. The explosion cloud was now almost completely faded and dissipated.

As the crowd below revived the merely injured, Meure now looked upward, again, to try to see the shapes flitting overhead, a motion which had ceased just before the explosion, as he recalled. He saw creatures flying through the air in swift, uneven courses that did not seem to be under too much control: the things zoomed and careened madly, sometimes barely avoiding collision with another by desperate, lurching maneuvers. Their speed and darting courses across his field of vision made details hard to make out.

Meure looked away from the east and tried to follow one of the creatures; found one in a labored turn back into the scene of the action, followed it carefully now seeing it in all its improbability: size was difficult to judge, for he did not know the altitude of the flying creatures, but they seemed large, much larger than a person, all leathery wings. The creature he was following with his eyes was long and narrow, with two sets of narrow wings, one very close to the front of the beast, and a larger set, about twice as large, far to the rear. Each wing was narrow, tapering and tipped with a knobby cluster; the wings seemed to be partially rigid, partially stretched along bony frameworks. The front pair were swept forward, while the rear pair were radically swept backward, beating slightly out of time with one another, the front pair downstroking first, the motion rippling to the back pair. Between the wings, the body was narrow, compressed. A third set of the knobby clusters was located at the narrowest part, about two-thirds to the rear, just before the broad rear wings. The fore end of the creature seemed to lack what could properly be called a head: the body, or central spine of the creature merely tapered down rakishly to a depressed point. There were features along that tapering, drooping prow, but Meure could not make them out. Sensory organs?

Out of its beating turn now, the creature pitched up a little, and smoothly halted its fore wings in their downstroke, locking them together under the projecting fore part. The rear wings increased their stroke, in amplitude and rate, and the speed of the flying thing accelerated. It passed overhead, a little to the north, and Meure could see that the rear wings were curved a little behind, joining at the very end in a smooth parabolic curve. There was a tail, but it was very small. From the front point to the wings in the rear, the curved outline of the shape was smoothly concave, exponential in shape. Aft of the rear wingtips, the curve was shallowly parabolic and convex. It seemed impossible and improbable, but there was no quality about it suggesting humor, or decoration. To the contrary, it moved through the limpid air of Monsalvat with strong, confident strokes, powerful and purposeful, alert and probably dangerous. It paused, gliding over the scene of the action, rocking slightly from side to side, making microcorrections in course with the huge rudder in front formed by the down-folded wings and narrow headless neck. Gliding away, it lost altitude, then opened its fore wings to help support it, and began another hundred-and-eighty degree turn, both wings beating again.

Now the folk who had survived the explosion seemed to notice the creatures flying overhead; indeed, some of them were making passes over the site where the ship had grounded, at quite low altitude. Meure could not tell if their behavior was caused by fear of the flying things, or rage at their losses to the explosion. But they seemed to go completely crazy, running madly back and forth, gesturing at the sky, looking about for something with lunatic energy. Clellendol whispered, "They are looking for us, I'll wager!"

Flerdistar said, from the side, "I'd not care to face that mob. But you're correct: They know the ship was essentially intact, and that it was open, and there were no bodies."

Clellendol added, "And that someone set a bomb and left it running. No, indeed; this is not to my liking at all!"

Meure volunteered, "The flying things distract them; perhaps they will overlook us."

Almost as if Meure's voiced hope had been a cue, the large beast he had followed overhead, which had circled around from the east to the south, now approached the shallow depression where the strange folk were gathered. Meure and the others, from their elevation, could see the flying creatures circling back, but those below apparently could not; they were oblivious to the creatures save those they could see overhead. It barely cleared a low ridge, both sets of wings beating madly, as if for speed, not altitude. Now they were looking down on one of the creatures as it set its wings to glide, its speed much too fast for conscious reaction by the people who had come to the ship. The flying beast had already calculated its trajectory. They could only glimpse parts of features along the narrow forward end: several paired spots that seemed to be eyes, and something else that emitted a deep red light in pulses . . .

one of the people was running, and some sound, some feel, some perhaps sixth sense warned him. A single glance back over the shoulder, and he made his decision: run faster, turn to the left, there were some rocks not far away.

Meure watched helplessly; to run upright was clearly useless, as the flying creature was closing on the intended victim at a velocity easily ten times the man's top running speed, probably more. At the last moment, the man also recognized this and dove for the ground, almost under the forward-swept fore wings. The creature made a last microcorrection, dipped, covered the spot where the man would have been; something talonlike reached from the narrowest section of the creature, and it pulled up into a steep climb and began beating its wings again. No man was on the ground.

Audiart made a choking sound, turned away. The two remaining Spsom looked on stonily, saying nothing. Clellendol muttered something under his breath. Then he said, more clearly, "We needn't worry about any suffering of that thing's prey: acceleration alone would break every major bone in its body, never mind any other trauma the creatures might inflict upon contact."

Meure paused, and wondered what kind of structure the flying creature had that was resistant enough to take those impacts itself.

Now the creature was climbing to the north. Some of the other creatures, mostly smaller, made half-hearted attempts to pursue it, but soon returned to their circling overhead.

Below, the people now became wary and cautious. But they retained their older sense of urgency and mad activity as well. Now taking cover wherever it could be found, they gathered in little knots, now and then shouting from one group to another. These groups now began to spread away from the spot where the ship grounded, some members watching the morning sky, while others carefully looked over the ground. None of the groups headed back to the east.

Flerdistar observed, "Now they are looking for the survivors. They already know we are not to the east, for they came from that direction. Their activity has obscured any track we might have made near the ship, but they will find it farther out, soon enough."

At the onset, the cautious searching by the little people in the depression, watching as they also were for attacks by the flying creatures, seemed to gain them nothing. Others among them began to see to the injured, helping some to their feet, calling for assistance with others. Some were examined, and left behind. But after a time, the results began to bear fruit. The depression was examined carefully, and one by one, very systematically, the possible hiding places began to be eliminated. Various groups called back and forth across the natural amphitheater in harsh, nasal voices, coordinating their efforts.

One industrious individual found something on the ground that interested him greatly: others he called to his aid and concurrence. Several more joined him, and a discussion ensued, accompanied by extravagant gestures and much waving of the arms. They started out carefully in the direction of the rocky eminence in which the survivors of the shipwreck were hiding, occasionally looking up to the rockpile to verify their progress. In the rest of the depression, others began drifting over to join the group, while still others started back to the east.

Meure said quietly, "I think they know we're here."

Halander added, "Fight or run, and I don't see how we can fight a crowd of that size; besides, the action would bring reinforcements."

Audiart asked quietly, "Where can we run to? Do we even know what continent we landed on?"

Vdhitz held a brief discussion with Shchifr, and then said something more toward Flerdistar, still in his own speech. The girl reflected a moment, nodded, and said, "We're on the northwest continent, Kepture, somewhere in the middle of it. Neither Spsom got to see too much, coming in; Vdhitz thinks he saw a large body of water extending to the south, and it seemed too large for a lake. If that's true, then we're in the west of Kepture . . . I suppose it doesn't really make any difference which way we go. No native can be assumed to be friendly, so there's no reason to go in any direction save to retain our lives. They agree: we should leave this place immediately." Suiting action to words, she stood up to begin climbing through the rocks to the west.

The motion was noted by sharp eyes below, and an immediate outcry was raised. Clellendol roughly jerked the girl to her feet, but it was, of course, too late. Meure could see them clearly now: the people below were now converging in their direction. Meure looked around, and saw Vdhitz bare his muzzle, exposing fine, needle-sharp teeth; he also drew a slender, dully finished knife. Audiart looked at Meure, her eyes blank, staring. Meure searched through the rubble, grasping, measuring, finally settling on a wicked, flinty shard of rock.

The vanguard of the mob drew closer, now rather silent. They no longer shouted back and forth, but said small phrases to one another, making gestures of anger. Now Meure could make out their features better; no longer were the people abstract and generalized human shapes, but identifiable, with perceptible characteristics. They were smallish in stature, rather ler-sized, but more angular. Their skins were light brown to pale, with an unhealthy pallor that seemed at some variance with the clear air and bright, ruddy sunlight. Their hair was lank and stringy, off-brown or dirty blond. But their faces arrested his attention the most, for in every face he could see the upper lip was cleft in two; more in some than in others, but never absent. The appearance of the people was dichotomous and contradictory; the cleft lip lent their faces an engaging, rabbity look, but the obvious expressions on those faces were, to a one, those of rage and hatred. They moved up the slope with maniacal, detached deliberation, always talking back and forth, watching each other carefully. They were a people used to joint activity, and to large crowds.

Their clothing seemed to be whatever scrap each one could have found, arising in a hurry; some wore patched, loose robes, hardly more than a sheet with holes poked in it, or perhaps unfair advantage had been taken of holes already in place. Others wore shabby leather breeks, made of some limp hide and held in place with rope belts. There seemed to be no leader, no order, no sense of formation. But they were approaching now quite close, only meters away. Meure was certain they could see them all.

Clellendol now stood, facing the group climbing up the scree, holding a slender rope in his hands. Meure also stood, holding his rock flake at the ready, thinking no thoughts at all. And the two Spsom now stood as well, stretching to their full height, both holding knives. No words were spoken, no gestures were offered.

The foremost of the crowd climbing the rockpile now stopped, carefully considering that which lay ahead. He could almost hear their thoughts, considerations of how many lay ahead, in the rocks. Perhaps a bad place to attack, with three aliens of unknown powers. Who among them knew what a Spsom could do? The front of the group crept slightly forward. Though now still, they emitted a palpable emotion of crazy ferocity, an utter disregard for personal safety. Short, rippling glances whipped back and forth across the faces of the crowd. Meure thought it would be any minute, now.

At the rear of the vanguard, they were beginning to crowd and jostle, their numbers being ever increased by those arriving from behind. But the ones in the forefront, who had been looking from figure to figure calculating, now looked as if through the survivors, and at one another again, and the feral light in their eyes began to fade, translating into apprehension, doubt, then badly-concealed expressions of fear and loathing. Some comments were passed up and down the line, quietly now, as if the members of the crowd wished not to disturb something. The crowd stopped piling on at the bottom of the slope. The members of the vanguard began backing down the slope, always keeping their attention on the rocky outcrop. Slowly and cautiously, the people began to retreat back down the hill. Meure looked out over the depression and now saw the others leaving, moving off in the direction of the east, not hurriedly, or in panic, but with many a backward glance.

Meure relaxed, breathed deeply, realizing that he could not remember the last time he had breathed: Something had changed their minds, but he hardly thought it would have been the Spsom. Alien they were, but there were, after all, only two of them, and armed with no more than knives at that. He looked down the slope now at a retreating mob, fading away as fast as they could in good order. He risked a glance at Audiart; she was still sitting, completely still, her face an expressionless mask. She sensed his gaze, turned to meet his eyes. They both wanted to see what it was that had turned the crowd, if they could. Together they met each other's eyes, and turned to see.

Meure felt ice in his veins. In the rocks behind the Spsom were standing, absolutely still, three elongated figures in hooded robes that swathed them from head to foot. He could see little of the shape of what lay within the robes, but the figures were Human, judging by what suggestion of facial outlines he could make out, and they were holding long spears tipped with leaf-shaped blades whose edges gleamed silvery in the morning sun. Their hoods shadowed most of their faces, but what Meure could see was no less frightening than the faces of those he had seen on the slope; save that these faces were thin and gaunt, and focused on large, bladelike noses. Above the ridge of the nose, heavy, hairy brows shaded deepset eyes that seemed to have no color at all—merely pools of darkness.

Two remained in the same unmoving posture, gazing eastward rather into the unfocused distance instead of directly at any particular object. The third, ignoring the mixed group in the rocks, moved fluidly and quickly around them to a better vantage point, the better to oversee the people now departing the depression. This third newcomer stepped out onto the slope and again became still for a moment, looking.

Meure watched intently. There was nothing about the figure he could identify as male or female, but he found himself thinking unconsciously, "she." Something about the effortless, flowing movement; or the appearance of slighter stature. He didn't know. The creature now lifted its free arm, shaking folds of the sleeve of the voluminous robe to reveal a slender and shapely hand of long, tapering fingers. This it lifted to its face, and emitted a long, piercing cry, an almost-soprano howl that set Meure's nerves on edge and struck fear into him.

Down in the depression, those departing heard, and looked back, over their shoulders, not turning full around. As they heard the sound dying, most immediately broke into a quick-time trot; some began running hard at once. Atop the slope, the creature shrugged, made an indescribable wriggling motion, and the robe simply fell away, revealing a naked, slender girl of long limbs and wiry, taut muscles, whose long, black hair was tied tightly at the neck in a folded braid. Her skin was a rich olive brown. The girl tossed the spear she held to free the robe, recatching it, and stepped off onto the slope, letting gravity accelerate her, now guiding and controlling the motion, flowing down the slope in lengthening, beautifully exact, flowing paces. And below, in the depression, the entire field broke into a dead hard run, as if they were to a man stricken with the utmost in stark terror. The girl reached the flat ground and lengthened her stride into a ground-covering run, easily moving more than twice as fast as those who were now bent solely upon escape. Meure, watching, did not know what the girl was doing, but it certainly seemed as if she were hunting the rabbit-faced people, that they were prey.

He looked at the rest of the group, who had also watched the scene in the depression, and were now looking away, as if not to see the logical conclusion, turning also to look at one another and to the two remaining newcomers. Now there were five, the three additional newcomers indistinguishable from the first. For a long moment, each group looked at the other, making no moves. Then one of the hooded figures made a gesture with the hand, motioning toward itself and half-turning to the west, from whence it had come, seemingly. The meaning seemed clear enough. They were being invited somewhere. The gesture was made without motion of the weapons the creatures carried; indeed, it seemed that the leader went to some pains to avoid attention to his spear.

Vdhitz made an almost-Human Spsom version of a shrug, and sheathed his knife, followed by Shchifr. Clellendol coiled his rope, and said, half under his breath, "Does anyone imagine that we have much choice, here?" There was no answer, but the rest reluctantly got to their feet. He continued, "These are dangerous, as you see . . . but I prefer these and the unknown west to those who came from the east."

The one who had motioned did not understand Clellendol's words, but he seemed to comprehend the motion of the group easily enough. Without further word, he nodded, and turned back to the west, moving along an almost-invisible path with effortless, graceful motion. His compatriots stood aside to let the group pass. And one by one, they followed the gaunt newcomer down the rocks, and onto a rolling plain spreading before them into the west, seemingly without limit.

---

*"It is not enough to dip the Magus in the Styx; he must be thrown
in and left to sink or swim."*

—A.C.

NOW IT WAS getting on into the afternoon; Meure awoke with a
sudden jerk of his head. He was sitting in the shade cast by an eccentric, two-wheeled wagon which was apparently pulled by two of
what appeared to be very large and very stupid men. The others were
still about him nearby, in similar positions; Halander was curled protec-
tively about Ingraine Deffy, more under the wagon, in the shade. It was
warmish. The rest were nearby, and Audiart was closer to the front of
the wagon, half in the sunlight, the orange cast to the sunlight copper-
ing her hair. She was awake, staring out into empty prairies, her face expressionless, her thoughts manifestly elsewhere.

Meure shaded his eyes against the brightness of the sky, which was a
deeper blue than seemed natural to him; deeper blue, but also curiously
opaque, instead of transparent like an evening sky might have been on
Tancred. . . . It was only then that he began to understand that he was
now in a different circumstance, truly on a new world, in a new world,
a different universe. In the ship, they could pretend that they had retained the old with them, but without it, things were different.

The land rolled away to the distances, covered with a wiry, bluish
vegetation that suggested grass, but wasn't. Here and there, small, meaningless features broke the open spaces; a dwarfed and stunted tree, a
rockpile. Clouds drifted across the sky, the kind he had always associated with summer and fair weather; well-defined puffs, whose edges
were as solid in appearance as the land beneath. Many were darkish
along their lower edges, and one, far to the north, seemed to be trailing
a veil of rain, which trailed out into nothing high above the ground.

One of the tall creatures they had accompanied was visible far to the rear of the wagon, squatting motionless and impassive in the sunlight, its hood completely shadowing its face. Meure thought it was not the girl he had seen in the morning, although he could not say precisely how he thought he knew this. He could not see the creature's face, nor its eyes, but he was sure it was watching them. Where was Flerdistar? He looked about in apprehension: where were the two Spsom? The furry slave?

Meure stood up awkwardly, stiff in all his joints from the hard ground, and the wheel he had been leaning on. If the guard cared, he evidenced no sign. Meure looked about; some distance to the front of the wagon, a frail sunshade had been erected, slung between poles driven into the ground at outward-leaning angles. Perhaps the spears he had seen the tall ones carrying. There were the rest; he could make them out clearly, and some others he had not seen before, different from the tall hunters. If he listened carefully, he could make out the distant hum of their voices, although of the hum he made no words. But the tone of their voices reassured him; they were neither hasty nor angry. Each seemed to speak in turn, carefully and slowly.

For an instant, the idea of escape crossed his mind; of just walking away, then perhaps running. . . . He did not know where he would run to, and he was certain that he would not get very far, should the hunters decide to follow him. Meure remembered how the people with the cleft upper lips seemed to fear even one of the hunters; perhaps this was justified by past experiences. He decided that he did not wish to test how tight were their invisible bonds.

He glanced toward the tent, and saw that the meeting seemed to be breaking up, casually enough; the tall hunters withdrew to confer among themselves. Meure could make out the angular shapes of the two Spsom, still engaged with a group of three of the tall ones, apparently communicating mostly through sign language. One of the hunters handed Shchifr his spear, which the Spsom captain hefted experimentally, then demonstrated his style of throwing it. The hunters seemed to think the style as odd as the alien shape of their visitor, but they could find no fault with Shchifr's accuracy, for he had hit the little bush he had aimed for exactly, the spear now standing, rigidly vibrating, driven into the wood. After a moment, more sign language ensued, which seemed to be an earnest discussion about hunting, or some similar activity. Meure had not known the Spsom hunted; indeed, he could think of very little that he did know about them, of themselves.

Flerdistar and Clellendol returned to the wagon, accompanied by one of the hunters, and two of the strangers, one stocky and beefy-faced, the other thin and rather stern in appearance, bearing a shock of disorderly iron-gray hair; both were dressed in well-worn garments resembling undecorated bathrobes—simple wraparounds with a cloth sash to hold the front closed, which fell to the knee. Both wore what seemed to be crude, but serviceable stockings and heavy sandals. Unlike the hunters, neither seemed to be a figure of fear or awe, although judging by the expressions and gestures of the hunters, and the Ler young people, they were certainly figures of respect, men of influence, at least locally.

Flerdistar excused herself from the group and joined those waiting at the wagon. She saw they were indeed attentive, so she began at once, "For the moment, we can relax somewhat, if any of you are inclined to harbor morbid thoughts. We are in no immediate danger from these, so long as none of us makes a rash move, such as an escape attempt. These people are nomads who call themselves the Haydar. The best I can tell, they are one of the original Klesh stocks, and their folklore is extensive and elaborate. They have maintained their way of life with little change since the beginning here; with them alone I should spend the remainder of my life. But that is neither here nor there. They bear us no hostility, but as nomads, they cannot keep us, and only the Spsom are capable of joining the hunt with them, so we will . . . not remain here."

Audiart asked, "Where are we?"

"On Monsalvat, on the continent Kepture, as we suspected. We are in a portion of Kepture, somewhat to the west and south, which is called Ombur. North and east is another land called Incana. It is there that we will go, I think. The names do not refer to countries, or governmental organizations, or anything like that. Time is long, here, and the various lands have collected names through the years. We await now the return of the girl from the hunt; she is, in effect, the Shaman of this particular group. She is the one who memorizes the epics of the Haydar and reads the omens. The leader of this band wishes to remove us from this area, but he must allow her to cast the omen and ratify his decision."

Flerdistar paused, then began again, "They seem amazed that we do not fear them. Even explained as simple ignorance, they still regard us as people of extreme self-control. By all means, do nothing to suggest otherwise. That way lies safety. And you may be sorely tempted to break, for these are an abrupt people who make hard decisions."

She continued, "These other two belong to a class of wandering intermediaries, whose function it apparently is to communicate between groups who detest one another. The general rule is that they may not be harmed, robbed, detained or made hostage except in very specific circumstances, upon which I would not now care to speculate.

"The speech here was Singlespeech at one time, but with the changefulness of Humans, it has undergone much development. I urge you to learn it as fast as you can assimilate it. There are also many other variants, which I would class as cult jargon, tribal lore-speech, and functional languages. Most of the people here will be fluent in at least three or four basic patterns appropriate to their station, and the intermediaries will of course be conversant in more."

Meure ventured, "Are there cities, towns? Or is the whole planet wild?"

"There are . . . cities, although when we see one, I think we will not call it so. Places where men gather. Communities, places of safety, of defense. No land is under the control of any one ruler, but is divided many ways. There are no borders here, no frontiers, no lines of demarcation, no customs-collectors. Things change on Monsalvat, which by the way, they call 'Aceldama.' They know the name 'Monsalvat,' but they prefer the other." She sighed deeply. "We have, indeed, much to learn, much to take with us."

Halander added, "If we survive to greet the *Ilini Visk*, a year from now."

Flerdistar looked away, and said, "We have to learn that, too; and it may be a hard lesson. Be perceptive. And flexible. It will be as hard on you as on us! Never have I met so much diversity suggested in their speech: each tribe here is as different from another as we are from the Spsom, and they know even more aberrant groups in lands farther away. But for the present, be as comfortable as possible. Rest. Events will permutate tonight, and we will see . . ."

Meure was not thinking anything specific, just listening to Flerdistar, but a sudden flash idea flickered across his mind, so rapidly he almost missed it; even so, having caught the fugitive thread, he struggled with it for a time to put it into speakable order.

"*Liy* Flerdistar, do you have any idea what we can do until the *Ilini Visk* comes for us?"

He knew as he said it that he had made it too general, too comprehensible. Thus she had missed it. What he wanted to say, his mind was screaming, and which he did not dare speak aloud for fear of alarming the hunters, was more. It was, *if the sample we see before us is accurate, there is not place for us here. Here, on Monsalvat-Aceldama,—whichever it was, there are the various tribes, none of which we resemble, who heartily despise one another at the best, and eat one another at worst. Or perhaps that is not the worst. At any rate, we must survive. To survive, we must find matching tribes, and be scattered to the four winds. Rescue! The terrifying thing was that Flerdistar, now the ostensible leader of the group, did not even see that there was a problem. She was totally wrapped in what she was reading in these people.*

She answered casually, "In the land Incana is an historic strongpoint. We must get off these empty plains. Empty lands on Monsalvat are lands in contention. For the moment, we have powerful protectors, and we must contrive to keep them until we can reach a place of greater security. One step at a time."

Meure nodded, then looked away from her. It was reasonable enough, on the surface. Problem: get out of Ombur. Solution: get these natives to take them to another place. Then we figure where to go from there. Meure could not imagine it: He looked out again over the empty plains, the rolls, the bareness, the sky. He couldn't bring himself to say he liked it, but he was sure he wanted to live, and he understood something about Monsalvat immediately, without being told it: that whatever any of them did *here*, in this place and time, it would initiate consequences immediately. He knew nothing of what lay west and south; he feared the rabbit-faced people of the East. Wrong, wrong, to go north, into this Incana. And even as he became sure of the wrongness of it, he knew that they would go there.

Flerdistar gathered them all together, save the Spsom, and the little creature who had been a Spsom slave, and commended them to the care of a third member of the negotiators, a misshapen, troll-like man with enormous arms and a broad, evil grin, who appeared from the rear portion of the wagon at a motion from the gray-haired man, bearing a basket loaded with flat biscuits and slivers of some cured meat, which he began passing out, naming each item as he passed it. This was to be their instructor. Meure turned his attention to the newcomer, began to listen with growing interest. He did not care so much for the mission of the Ler, who had hired them, nor the concerns of the Spsom, who had flown and lost the ship. Here was survival. Meure saw in this troll, not a freak, but a halfbreed, or even misbreed, who had survived. He would be worth listening to.

Now the day was softening into twilight; at first the shadows had lengthened, but as they grew longer, they softened and merged. Meure had been, for a reason obscure to himself, avoiding the direct light of the star-pair Bitirme. Somehow, he didn't want to see the close binary. Now he thought he could, with a head full of Aceldaman lore, as much as he could digest. He reflected on that, too. Of them all, he seemed to pay the closest attention to the manservant, Benne. The rest, Audiart, Halander, Ingraine, all seemed repulsed by the troll-like figure and crude mannerisms, but Meure had sat and listened and repeated the strange words, many with disturbing hints of the familiar in them, and listened closely to the meaning of what Benne was teaching them. Eunuch and misbred he might be, but there was a fine, honed mind behind that lowering forehead, and many years of survival behind him. More, he was a natural teacher, starting with the immediate and practical and expanding spirally into steadily more complex ideas. Meure knew his new vocabulary was insufficient, that his grasp of the structure of the language was equal now only to the most primitive needs, but he had a little base he could now expand himself. The others?

Meure stood, stretched deeply in the cooling air, and stepped out, away from the wagon, more properly, he thought, into the environment of Monsalvat itself. The Haydar watching them turned its head to observe him, briefly, then turned back to its original position.

Far off in the west, Bitirme was sinking into veils of high cirrus clouds, spreading its orange-tinted light across a violet sky. The star now appeared to be distinctly ovoid. Before him ranged the seemingly endless plains of Ombur, rolling gently away into the uttermost west. The plains were still and quiet, supernaturally so; Meure could hear tiny sounds he would not normally be aware of. He thought he could hear the grass that was not grass growing. The strange men who had been hitched to the clumsy wagon had been sitting awkwardly, still in the traces of the wagon, but now they were beginning to stir, to make little grunting noises to one another. They were the most curious of all he had seen so far: giants in stature, with heavy-boned, gross features, pale waxy skin, stringy, limp blond hair, and expressions of blankness on their homely faces. *Sumpters,* Benne had called them, enumerating various creatures native to this part of Kepture, or domesticated here. Odd, that: Benne had not referred to them as a tribe, but had listed them with the animals. But then he had not included the rabbit-faced people, the Lagostomes, in his list of Humans, either.

Meure looked about, more widely—Flerdistar and Clellendol and the two intermediaries, and the Ler elders were still holding an earnest converse behind the wagon, while over by the sunshade, Spsom, Vzyekhr, and Haydar were carefully taking down the covering which had shaded them in the day. Audiart and the other two were still by the wagon.

Far off, from the southeast, he heard a series of howls, first one alone, then that echoed by an irregular chorus. The Haydar remaining in the vicinity of the wagon immediately stopped what they were doing and turned their heads to listen to the howls. Meure could hear no words in the far-off faint sounds, but he could hear a difference from the chilling call he had heard the girl use this morning. Whatever information the howls carried, it seemed to please the Haydar hunters, for they returned to their task with seeming enjoyment, their dour watchfulness changing into an odd joyousness. Some gathered, and produced firemaking tools from their voluminous robes, and began kindling a fire. On this they laid longish chunks of some dark substance. Meure searched the horizon in the direction of the howls, but he saw nothing. The darkness was falling fast, now. Bitirme was below the horizon.

He looked to the sky in the east, sensing some movement there, he thought. The first stars were beginning to shine there. But he saw nothing. All was quiet. The distant howling stopped. Now he turned back to the wagon and started toward it, to rejoin the others. There was something he had to tell Audiart, something she seemed to need, although it was obvious to him that she was older and more experienced than he.

It was still evening quiet, each sound magnified; in this quiet he heard a rushing noise high up, faint, rhythmic. Looking up, he caught sight of a group of the odd two-winged creatures he had seen this morning: about ten or so, in cruise configuration, with forward wings partially folded, heading westward. A sudden fear crossed him; but when he looked back down to the Haydars, they seemed unconcerned, looking up, then returning to the matter at hand, as if they had expected them. *Eratzenasters*, Benne had called them. Meure looked back. The eratzenasters were slowing, descending, and one of the larger ones seemed to be carrying something on its dorsal surface. The light was uncertain now, and he couldn't be sure.

The creatures expanded their forward wings now, and continued to descend, turning southerly, and then circling back, approaching the ground reluctantly, steepening their angle of attack, the lead wings beginning to flap at the air in anticipation of a stall. The smaller ones were now close to the ground, and settled onto it with an awkward motion, part fall, part glide, part stall. They seemed to kill their forward motion by running along the ground on unseen limbs beneath the stiff wings. The larger ones took longer, made more shallow approaches, landed with more skill. The largest one landed most delicately, as if it did not wish to dislodge that which was aboard it. The payload moved, sat upright, legs straddling the narrow midsection of the eratzenaster. There was no mistaking who it was: it was the girl who had hunted the Lagostomes, still as nude as she had been when she had begun the hunt.

The eratzenasters moved about beyond the perimeter of the temporary camp, looking for suitable places to settle, and folded to the ground, one by one, resembling irregular, long rocky outcrops. The large beast Tenguft rode continued to walk on its unseen limbs, slowly and carefully, into the camp. As it came closer, Meure began to see just how large a large one might be, and what an odd form it had; it was about thirty meters long, with the larger rear pair of wings extending outwards less than half that, although they were not fully extended now for flight. As it moved on the ground, the whole body flexed somewhat, as if the whole of the creature were partially rigid. At the ends of the wings, at the points, were stubby, clawed appendages, whose function Meure could not fathom. On its walking legs the spine rode higher than the height of a man, even a Haydar, and the wings drooped almost to the ground.

Meure felt lightheaded, but he felt no fear. This one was obviously under control. He approached it, while the others stood respectfully back; save one Haydar, who came carrying a long robe for the rider of the eratzenaster.

It was almost complete night; details were difficult to make out. Meure looked closely, eyes straining; the front of the eratzenaster was just a front. It narrowed down to a bony point. No mouth, nose, nothing. Farther back, there were eyes, four of them that he could see, gleaming an oil black. Set in the middle of what he would have called a forehead was another eye, this one dull and with a suggestion of insect-like faceting. The creature now towered over him, turning slightly to perceive him; Meure felt an odd prickling on his skin, a vibration, and the faceted eye began pulsing, glowing with a deep red light from within. Meure felt heat on his face. The light faded, and facing him, the creature stopped. He was close enough to hear its breathing, a sighing, rushing noise emanating from somewhere under the wings; he could also smell its odor, an odd compound of something pungent, and also musty, like old fur. He felt the prickling on his skin again, and the eratzenaster folded itself to the ground, forward end first, followed by the rear. Settling, it arranged its wings as the others had done. Tenguft swung a long, slender leg over the spine of the beast and slid to the ground, where the hunter awaited her with her robe. This she tossed overhead with the minimum possible movement, and strode off to meet the other Haydars.

There was a stir beside him: Clellendol. The Ler youth said, softly, "A fearsome beast, that one."

Meure thought a moment, and questioned, "Which?"

"A-ha. Very good, very sharp. And you are to be the innocent one, yet you ask me which . . . well, I answer, *both, or either.*"

Meure said, "I fear both, this horrible flying nightmare with my instincts, and she with my mind."

"The former—that can be overcome, overridden, or utilized as a goad unto excellence; but the latter . . . we have spent much time overcoming instinctual fears, so much so that we have neglected the latter."

"Yet what I fear about her is that she's probably not the worse I will meet, here, on . . . Aceldama."

"Do you know the word?"

"No. I am no student of arcana, ancient or modern."

"It is from very ancient times. It means, so Morgin the Embasse tells me, 'A place to bury strangers.' Its usage is traditional; as are the words used to signify humans, or rather, beings of human origin." The difference in Clellendol's phrasing did not escape Meure. Clellendol continued, "They call all menlike creatures by the old word, *'Klesh'*; and humans that have managed to retain human ways they call *'Ksenosi.'* Strangers. An ancient discipline is operative here, one both your and my people have sidestepped, avoided, not resolved."

"Say on."

"In the ancient times, humans, *Starmanosi*, the old people, entered an ecological niche on the homeworld in which they effectively had no competition. Therefore they competed among themselves at a certain critical population level. This is basic principles. At the time the *Lermanosi* came into being, we would have done the same, but we blunted the issue in two ways: we avoided competition with you by leaving the area. . . ."

Here Meure interrupted, "Which postponed but did not solve."

"Exactly. Translated the problem into a different arena, larger scale in both space and time. Within ourselves, we made the avoidance of internal competition a cult essential by incorporating it into our family structure, always striving to better systems to ingest socially the outlander, the stranger, the Ler from steadily farther away. You, in turn, borrowed in part from us and made homogenization of population one of your goals. And in both cases, these things have worked to greater or lesser degree. To the contrary, here, these mad klesh have not sidestepped the issue, but have leaped directly into it—and chosen the path of internal competition. Selfness, sense of self, here will be extremely strong, more than you or I have ever seen. That the Haydar did not mark us prey comes from that: no one here will assume ignorance of this basic tenet on our part. It is much as Flerdistar has said—they think our sense of self, our confidence, if you will, is too great to fear them, and without fear, there is no game. That we came on a starship, which they saw, is of no moment whatsoever. They know other creatures live in the universe, but they think it's just like here on a larger scale: murder, mayhem, massacre, and the weak in selfness gather into masses."

"Why do you tell me these things?"

"I will be candid. I mean no offense. You are an innocent. That is not a bad thing of itself. But you are also active, you move around, see things, peek into things, get involved. As here." Here Clellendol gestured behind him toward the wagon. "Those two, the boy who came with you, and the slender girl; do you think either of them would walk here to see an eratzenaster up close? You know it's virtually helpless on the ground, regardless of what it does when airborne. You can see it directly. But they wait in the same place they were left this morning. And the woman with whom you seem to have formed an association . . ."

"Seem to have is correct. We have had little together."

"Just so. She is shocked, but you will recover and adapt. Mind, if she lives here fifty years, she won't like it, but she'll manage. That is her nature. But these three are not going to upset anything. You may. Before the landing. Flerdistar was the key member of this group; this was her project, her thesis, if you will. Now the thesis is unimportant."

"I understand that."

"I know you do. You are the only one who does. And the things you will do here are pivotal. You, sooner or later, are going to upset some balance point. I see it as my task to retard your entry into events beyond your capabilities."

"You see this, Clellendol, and do not want the position for yourself?"

"It can't be mine. This is, all appearances to the contrary, a *Human* planet, in the most ancient sense of the word. All the old demons are alive and well here, walking about naked and proud. I know many things—to what you would say a point beyond my age in years, but when it's all said and done, I remain, after that, a Ler thief. I have no instincts for the job and I have no knowledge of the internal field. But you do. And are active enough to learn to use them. These people, these Haydars and these halfbreed embasses and their servants, and all the others, they are all innocent, too, in a sense. You and they fit each other."

Meure said nothing. Clellendol let that sink in, and then added, "Of course, there is the matter of Flerdistar as well; there will have to be those who integrate her into their deeds despite herself. She, for all her disagreeable nature, is like yourself, an innocent activist, only she has purpose, and if unrestrained, could awaken things here I do not wish to see awakened."

"Understandable, that. With her pursuit of history she will reawaken legend-memories of the Warriors. They are gone, but I would suppose to a klesh it would make little difference . . ."

"Although not the whole of it, that is enough for now. So, then: let us for the present associate and please listen to me."

"So that I can be . . . retarded, until the moment for release?"

Clellendol spoke more sternly, "You are not an arrow, but a disturber of equilibriums. My wish is that we survive here."

"Until the *Ilini Visk* comes?"

"You know little of the Spsom?"

"Very little. A little, from school. I have seen them, heard some tales. I know more of what I have seen."

"Meure Schasny, I must enlighten you in this regard: the Spsom are possessed of an elaborate sense of humor, of which we see little. They find many things amusing, that we would find terrifying, or sorrowful. You may recall, back on the hill before the ship blew, that Vdhitz thought it was funny that Shchifr had set the power system to explode. Well, so it has been with the tale of the *Ilini Visk*."

"In what way?"

"Flerdistar does not know them as well as she thinks she does. She knows the Spsom language well enough, but she knows very little *about* them. That is why I am here. I know, for example, that the *Ilini Visk* is a ghost ship from the Spsom past . . . all people have such legends, and humans are particularly rich in them, The Wandering Jew, The Flying Dutchman . . . *Ilini Visk* is such a vessel of legend among the Spsom. Vdhitz told Flerdistar that, and she had spread it to us all. What Vdhitz was actually saying . . ."

". . . was that only ghosts heard us."

"Was that only ghosts would come to rescue us. They heard us all right, but they won't come. Those Spsom would think it humorous that

Shchifr lost his ship against his own better judgment, all for the higher payment he'd get from a charter instead of tramping it around."

It was completely dark, now, and Meure was certain that Clellendol could not see his face, but he was equally sure of what was showing on it. Marooned on Monsalvat. . . .

Clellendol said, "I think we'll be rescued, despite all that. Spsom have their humor, but their civilization is older than ours, both Ler and Human put together. And they are not barbarians. My own feeling is that the warship will go down, for repairs, and come here. Less than a year. Maybe no more than a season. Moreover, I think Vdhitz knows it. It's in character. He also knows I know. It's his joke on Flerdistar and the perils of thinking you know more than you do."

"Does she know?"

"No. Not yet. I am saving it for the proper moment. I suspect Vdhitz is also savoring punch lines as well and is waiting for the proper timing. As far as I am concerned, it can stay that way for the time. Now . . . let us join the others." Clellendol looked to the small fire the Haydar had made, where tall shadows were beginning to stride back and forth, as if readying, preparing themselves. The Haydar seemed nervous, wishing for action, although none spoke a word, and their movements made no noise. Only one seemed to remain relatively still, one tall shape, graceful and slender, who stood facing the fire, directly opposite Meure and Clellendol, head bowed, her face deep in the shadows of her hood. Her hands fidgeted with what seemed to be a small bag made of leather.

There seemed to be more Haydar present now than had been gathered about the wagon during the day; they seemed to materialize out of the shadows. Meure thought they were the ones who had been gone through the day, but he did not speculate upon what they might have been doing. The Spsom were there, and their slave, and the Humans and Ler were also approaching the group about the fire, urged in part by Flerdistar and their desire not to be left alone on the plains of Ombur.

Flerdistar joined Meure and Clellendol, whispering excitedly, "The one who calls himself Morgin tells me that events have been so extraordinary today that they are going to call for a divination by the girl . . . what's the more, they don't care that we watch, which is something I wouldn't expect in primitives."

Clellendol commented, "Perhaps they're not primitive. . . ."

The girl's face clouded with a most unhappy expression and she answered, "Of course they are—the wildest sort of barbarians and anthropophages too!"

"On this planet, Human society is old, and was imposed upon the native life-forms. The Klesh were considered to have low potential for survival, yet they have survived, even prospered, after their own fashion, with no help from either of their would-be helpers. There is either something operant here which we don't see yet, or can't perceive, or there is a highly sophisticated system of order in force; perhaps all three."

"I think you are reading data into random numbers."

Clellendol responded mildly, conversationally, "You have been trained to realize the condition of the past through its shadows in the present; not the less have I been trained to be suspicious about that same present, to perceive traps and snares. Just so can I tell you that I *know* we have already set off several alarms and telltales during the course of the day and our landing here: an entity—whether creature, organization, or thing—has become aware of us and observes us. I have the suspicion that it may have known we were coming. This—if true—falls into patterns of risk-assumption I do not wish to follow yet."

Flerdistar accepted the correction without retort, "Possible, possible, indeed. Talking to Morgin, I can sense something unnatural in their pasts."

"An event?"

"No, a presence. The sense of it is . . . smeared out through time, that's the way I'd say it. I'm only getting a little of it just yet, so I've had to allow for considerable error. That's all I'd say now."

"Remain alert, if you will, and share with me, as it was intended that we do."

"So I will. Now hush; they are to begin their rite."

The Haydars had ceased their pacing and settled into a loose circle about the small fire. Only the girl remained standing, still holding her head bowed, deep in thought, or trance. Meure also noticed, on the far side of the fire, that some non-Haydar had joined the tribal circle: Morgin and his party, and the Spsom.

The girl moved slowly around the fire, avoiding it while giving the impression that she was unaware of it, stopping before one Haydar who sat alone, separated from the others by a gap of respect.

Flerdistar whispered, barely audibly, "The girl now readies herself, and approaches the leader. Ringuid Coam Mallam. She will speak for the spirit world. This is a chancy time for us, for he will do what she says . . . Mallam has requested a divination, and he must abide by the oracle."

The girl said something, to Mallam, but Meure couldn't make out the words. An introduction, a preamble?

Flerdistar continued. "Now she makes the invocation; she mentions certain divine beings known to her, and others, possibly demons, or revered persons from the past. And at the end, she invokes a St. Zermille . . . now she holds the bag up, now she lowers it, and dumps it before Mallam, so that he may see the disposition of its contents . . . something white."

Meure peered through the darkness, dazzled by the fire. What had fallen on the ground looked like bones.

"Now she speaks again . . . she enumerates the basic configurations, which Mallam knows as well as she. The objects are bones from the hand and fingers of a sacrifice, I think of one of their prey tribes . . . no. I hear it, now. The bones are of one of their people, her predecessor. Now she studies the positions. She points, and Mallam follows, agrees. They are to go on a hunt . . . tonight. The Spsom will accompany them; they are to be initiated. Under no circumstances must they leave this band, the Dagazaram. If they do, misfortune. Now she comes to the rest, and says as firmly that the others, which is us, must depart immediately, not to be harmed or hunted. Something about a talisman . . . I can't make it out. Mallam concurs, and they discuss how to do it. The girl isn't clear on this. Her reading only gives what to do, not how to accomplish it. Mallam presses her now. He wants to take us somewhere, a place I don't know. She looks at the bones and says no. It's not far enough. He mentions another place, Medlight. No. She is under some strain, now. She ventures a suggestion, another place I don't know, something about flying. Mallam is angry, but controlled. It is resolved. She kneels to retrieve the bones, and the others stand . . . something else is going to happen, something dark . . ."

Meure did not really wish to see anything dark, but he could not look away, either. Now the Haydar were getting to their feet, slowly, but still maintaining the loose circle. They were all staring intently at the girl, while she carefully retrieved the bones from their places. She finished, and sat back on her heels, as if exhausted, her head thrown back, her eyes closed. Then she seemed to come to herself again, and slowly got to her feet, carefully avoiding looking at any one of the surrounding group. They were all watching her intently as she replaced the bones in the little bag, and pulled the string. The divination was over.

Meure decided he'd seen enough, and slipped behind Clellendol and Flerdistar, to move to the place where the wagon had been left. He did not look at the fire, or the girl, or the tribe, but he could see out of the corner of his eyes that they were still standing motionless, silent. He moved through the dark, unseen. All eyes were on the circle.

He walked across the springy turf to the wagon, where the Sumpters were half-reclining in their harness, unconcerned. Meure wished to avoid the Sumpters, beasts who looked like men, or men who had become bestial. He didn't know which. He stopped at the back of the wagon and looked out over the starlit plains rolling away to the east. Behind him, he could hear now fragments of conversation, motion. The firelight began to fade, as if it were being put out. He listened, despite his best intentions: nothing had happened. Meure breathed deeply. Now they were going to move again. Flying, Flerdistar had said. Probably a rattling fast run in the cart of Morgin, although it didn't exactly look like it had been built for speed. . . .

He heard the Sumpters suddenly start, snorting, rattling their harness. The wagon moved a little, creaking against its hand-brake. There was a soft noise, and when he turned to look around the corner of Morgin's wagon, he saw a darkness obscuring the dying fire, a tall, spare form approaching, one hand on the wagon's edge to steady herself, and Meure Schasny felt his hair prickling along the back of his neck, and ice running in his heart. He stopped.

She came within arm's-reach before she seemed to be aware of him. Meure stood absolutely still, afraid to move. He had no idea what these wild Haydars might do, oracle or no. Besides, she might be immune from her own words, might be under another oracle. This was a mythic figure before him, not a person he could comprehend, easily.

Tenguft was tall, about half a head taller or more than him; and at that she was slightly slumped, not at her full height. Meure could not make out any details of her, close as she was, for the darkness obscured everything.

She seemed to become aware of him slowly, as if still in the oracular trance. He could sense she was, however, staring at him intently. Meure wanted to turn and run, but he knew he had better not.

She studied him for a long moment, then said, in a soft, breathy voice, "You, it is to be." Meure heard the words, strange, but he thought he understood her. She continued, "Come with me. Now, fly. Tonight." She said something else, wearily, but Meure didn't understand the words. Only something about "Incana." Where they were going?

Tenguft extended her hand, took Meure's arm to guide him. The contact was light, the feel of the hand unexpectedly soft, but he could sense steel under the softness, and impulses held rigidly in check. What? He was sure of it. Did she want to hunt him, and was restraining herself? She started him off, with her, repeating the word again. "Come." They walked around the wagon.

Meure now saw that there was a different air to the place they had been: the Haydar and the two Spsom were in one group, all staring at the girl and himself with opaque, flinty stares that he found intensely uncomfortable. . . . The Ler elders were standing disconsolately with Morgin and his associates, to the side. Other Haydar were walking among the flying creatures, prodding them with the butts of their spears, speaking to them in harsh, peremptory tones.

From the group close by the eratzenasters, Flerdistar hurried to meet Meure and the Haydar seeress. She spoke quickly, breathlessly, "We are being split up! Morgin is sending the Elders with his servants! He is turning over his function here to one among the Haydar who is also of that office, and going with us. We two, and you four Humans, plus Morgin and the Vfzyekhr will fly . . . northeast, to another land, Incana. A place they call 'Cucany.' It's a fortress, or a castle."

Meure asked, "Fly? In what? Do we whistle up an aircraft?"

"No," she said. "On those things." A tug on his elbow reminded Meure that someone was guiding him. Other Haydar were gesturing at the grounded Eratzenasters, moving Audiart, Halander, Ingraine. It was clear they did not wish to go.

Flerdistar and Clellendol were unceremoniously hustled off toward the beasts, now grumbling and making jerky, awkward motions as they were abused into wakefulness by the suddenly impatient Haydars. Flerdistar had time to say one more thing before they were separated, "Schasny, be careful. I think you have become part of some kind of rite . . ." Her voice trailed off. Meure and Tenguft were now beside the large one she had ridden in the evening.

The tall girl gestured. "Up." Meure reached to the semirigid surface, the leading edge of the aft wing, touched it. It was covered in a microfine fuzz, and felt cool to the touch. It, the skin, moved slightly, as if sliding over a harder structure beneath. On all fours, moving with extreme care, he negotiated the slope to the spine of the creature, which was slightly depressed, and bare of all coverings. The skin felt looser. Tenguft bounded onto the Eratzenaster, and mounted with an odd spanning locomotion, graceful from much practice, but also gawky and awkward. She settled herself just aft of the narrowest part of the creature, moving experimentally up and down, bouncing to find the right place. Her motions were transmitted through the creature's members, making it rock and vibrate slightly. Now she tossed her hood back with an abrupt motion of her head, and turned to glare at Meure. She made a peremptory gesture with her right hand, to a spot behind her. "Here."

Meure clambered forward along the spine to the girl, and settled himself close behind her, not touching her. She reached behind herself with one of her long arms, and pulled Meure up against her; then she reached with the other arm, took his hands and placed them across her thighs to the Eratzenaster's skin in front of her. She bent his fingers into the cool, flexible surface. She said, "Hold here." She did not wait to see that he had done so, but released her grip on him and slapped the creature hard across the spine.

Meure gripped instinctively and the Eratzenaster lurched forward, getting its drooping wingtips clear of the ground, then using them to help it along.

Tenguft was still sitting upright, looking back to see that the others were up and moving; Meure ventured a quick look. He saw others, precariously mounted, alone, holding on for their lives, while the Haydar stood aside and hooted encouragement and instructions to them. All the larger beasts had riders, but the smaller ones were up and moving, too. Apparently the whole flock flew together.

The girl tensed her body, dug her heels into the stretched membrane connecting the wings, and leaned forward. Meure moved with her, feeling the thing beneath him begin increasing its speed, turning slightly to find the correct azimuth, then heading into the wind. There was a breeze, he realized, and he felt it increase. He was also acutely conscious of the girl's body he was pressed against; he could feel the muscles beneath the thin cloak she wore, feel the heat of the wiry body. Her scent was sun warmed, oily, aromatic and very slightly sweet at the same time.

Tenguft looked back at her passenger over her shoulder, a broad grin opening her lips to reveal white teeth that gleamed in the starlight. She slapped the Eratzenaster again and its awkward, loping pace increased, and Meure could hear a rhythmic, dry sound from underneath. He felt now tendons beginning to move in the creature's structure. It felt as if more than four limbs were moving, but he couldn't be certain. Now it began to bound, making a rocking motion, springing along. The wings began making synchronized motions; the wind now became uncomfortable. Meure could see little directly forward, for the girl was in the way, but it seemed as if they were approaching a rise, a low ridgeline. The Eratzenaster now began working its body violently, struggling for speed; they seemed to leap forward, the ground rose to the ridgeline, the wings beating violently, grabbing at air, a thrust, a lurch, a falling sensation, and Meure, from his vantage point near the thin middle of the creature, saw the ground sliding away underneath him.

The motions of the Eratzenaster were labored, carrying two as it was, and it gained altitude slowly, beating its wings in their odd syncopated rhythm. The wind in Meure's face became cold. It seemed they were moving to the east. He held on tightly. He felt muscles move in the hard body against him, shoulder and arm, buttock and leg. Now they began a slow, shallow turn to the north with almost no bank. He could feel Tenguft still pounding the creature's spine, urging it to greater speed. The flexing motions increased, and the wind hurt. He averted his face, and leaned closer to the girl. The motions became more violent, then the rhythm changed abruptly. Meure risked a glance ahead into the slipstream and saw the forward wings now set, opened wide in a shallow dihedral, the tips opened to wring the last gram of lift, while behind and under him, the rear wings thrust powerfully. The motion was violent, and he pressed as close to the girl as he could, feeling the contours of her body. She pressed herself down, almost prone. She moved, adjusting to him. Meure pressed himself against her, and felt a strong visceral pleasure in the motion. Tenguft turned slightly, although she could no longer turn enough to see him, and squeezed with the muscles of her hips. The message was direct and unmistakable, and required no words, which would have been torn away in the blast of the slipstream anyway. Then she returned her attention to guiding the Eratzenaster.

In the night of Monsalvat they flew, apparently not at any great altitude, although the speed with which the creatures flew seemed very great, judging by the blast of the slipstream and the violent motions of the aft wings, which made his perch feel unbalanced and precarious. He dared not look around to see if the others were keeping up, although now and again Tenguft would steer their mount from side to side so that she could see behind her. Meure guessed they were keeping up, for she did not divert from their northward course.

He sensed a darkened, empty land, the swales and rolling prairies of Ombur, passing beneath them. There was an area that seemed jumbled and rugged, canyons and gullies, and the land fell away and a great darkness spread beneath them. There was a chill dampness in the air, and the odor of a river; a large one, apparently, for these sensations continued for some time. Then the dampness faded, and a resinous scent replaced it. Meure could not make out any details in the country beneath, but it seemed more irregular than Ombur. They increased their altitude, and made slow detours around hills. The land seemed to be rising. Now they were passing over an inhabited land, for occasionally Meure could see yellowish lights, which were invariably extinguished as they passed overhead; but these were few, and scattered.

Now the scale of the hills increased, became low mountains separated by broad, open valleys. Tenguft made no attempt to fly over them, but followed the valleys as the openings presented themselves. The mountains were curiously isolated, in many cases steep and scarped. Meure's eyes were becoming adjusted to the starlight, and he could see more clearly to the sides. Many of the hills and mountains seemed to be crowned with structures, some large, some small. Castles? Fortresses? Some were nothing more than stone towers, others huts, and some more substantial. There were no lights below.

Meure sensed the Eratzenaster pitching up slightly, felt their speed decrease a bit; they were climbing, slowing. The forward wings still remained outstretched. Meure ventured a quick look over the girl's shoulder, and saw a great bulk ahead, surmounted by a dark, blocky mass, with pinpoints of yellow light in it. The mountain seemed to be steeper on the side they were approaching it from, swooping up from the broad valley floor, peaking like a wave, and falling off to the north more gradually.

The girl turned and shouted over her shoulder, "Cucany!" Now they were just below the mountain peak, turning onto it from the center of the valley, a shallow left turn. Meure's eyes were now adjusted enough to the darkness to make out the place they were making for; more or less, a fortress atop a long mountain that faced the valley in a steep scarp. He couldn't make out fine details of the structure, but it seemed to be a blocky castle or fortress that had developed whole families of erratic projecting additions, almost grown on like lichens on a brick: shelves, turrets, towers of several mismatched styles and shapes; apartments, balconies. There was no city or town or anything resembling one about the structure—if there was a town here, the town was the fortress.

The Eratzenaster continued the long and shallow turn to the left, maintaining its altitude and dropping its pace somewhat. Now they were just below the summit of the mountain, looking up at the fortress; now they were turning back the way they had come, apparently to land somewhere else. Their mount now stopped the beating of its rear wings and set them, like the front pair, for maximum lift, pitching its nose down to keep airspeed up. Meure risked a look behind him, to his left; and there the others were, strung out in a loose line formation, all turning behind them and setting their wings into glide shapes. Meure could see on most of the larger ones irregular protuberances along the spines between the wings: their passengers. The riderless Eratzenasters continued to climb and began making playful, gliding passes beside the burdened ones before following the lead beast down.

Their speed now lost its driving force and the airblast gave up some of its violence. He felt Tenguft's body tensing and working again, instructing and guiding the creature they flew on. Now the glide angle pitched down more steeply, but the creature set its wings so that its speed did not build up. Meure sensed a definite holding-back, a pause, before they committed for grounding. The noise of the wind abated, too. Tenguft leaned around and shouted back, "Watch now; then stop!"

Meure shouted back, "People there?"

She answered, "No people; Korsors! Dromoni! Maybe a Selander!"

Meure did not inquire of the nature of the forms she mentioned. He reflected that on Monsalvat, not all Humans were human, and that there were probably stranger shapes on the planet than Haydar and Sumpters.

Now their mount, still holding back, slowing, made a sweep over the dark ground below, moving subtly from side to side. Apparently satisfied, it made an abrupt series of motions with its rear wings, rocking them from side to side rapidly; then it flattened out its wings and pitched down hard, a motion that almost threw Meure. He grasped tightly, pressed closer to the girl. The dark ground below rushed up at them slantwise, fast. Meure began to see quick flashes of details, bushes, small trees, a watercourse, and the Eratzenaster pitched up and began beating its rear wings rapidly, shallowly. They began to settle, and the front wings started beating, now in an entirely different rhythm from their takeoff beat; the ground rushed up at them as the Eratzenaster made its final approach descent. At the last possible moment, both pairs of wings beating wildly, it broke its fall into an awkward glide, stalled out, and made contact, slowing itself with the unseen limbs of the underside.

Tenguft did not release her hold on the creature until it was almost completely stopped; then she abruptly sat back, throwing one leg over the side. "Off!" And she ran lightly down the leading edge of the right rear wing. Meure followed her, half-falling. All around them the others were landing in their semi-controlled crashes, dropping out of the sky like leaves in the Autumn. Meure saw Morgin the Embasse climbing most ungracefully off his mount, stumbling as his feet hit the ground. He did not wait, but ran to where the others were still huddling on their mounts, and began urging them off. Tenguft was doing the same. Meure followed them and ran to one of the Eratzenasters they had missed, calling, "Get down! They want all of us off!"

The rider sat up and began clambering down, like someone in a trance. Meure could see from the shape that it was Audiart; the last few steps to the ground, he had to help her. Standing, she was shivering. It was then that he noticed that he was suddenly hot, almost overheated. Of course, the air had cooled him, and he hadn't noticed.

Now the others were all off, and Tenguft ran from beast to beast, slapping them on the wingtips, tugging at them, but making as little sound as possible; and one by one, reluctantly, they began scuttling along the ground, climbing awkwardly over irregular places, and one by one, springing into the air, beating the dark night with their leathern wings. Meure watched them depart as they climbed into the night, wheeling back around to the southwest, climbing higher than they had when they had come, noiselessly, then fading dark spots, and then lost in the starry background.

Tenguft led them to a small, bare knoll, from which they had a good view of the surrounding countryside, and indicated that they should remain where they were. Morgin took Flerdistar aside and spoke earnestly with her. The Ler girl gained her feet and approached Meure.

"I come to you first. Morgin says that we are to remain here for the night; we will go to the city tomorrow. The Haydar will not approach a strongpoint at night. In those places they shoot first, and Morgin makes me to understand that in Incana, that may be the best policy. Morgin also says for me to tell you that you must do as the girl says, no matter how odd it may seem. . . ."

At the end, she trailed off suggestively in a manner Meure was not sure he liked. She returned to her place, between Morgin and Clellendol and the Vfzyekhr. Meure stood where he was, uncertainly. Tenguft, satisfied that all were placed as she wanted them, now turned to Meure, coming down the hill to him. He watched the spare, tall figure approaching him, a persona of mystery and power. And violence, he added. But he also remembered the tense feel of her wiry body when they had ridden the wind, and the suggestive motions she had made, once; and when she motioned for him to follow her, away from the knoll, he thought he knew something of what she had in mind, although he could not, for the life of himself, imagine why.

6

"There is, of course, extreme danger in coming into contact with a demon of a malignant or unintelligent nature. It should, however, be said that such demons only exist for imperfectly initiated magicians."

—A.C.

TWO SUNS CLEARED the horizon and illuminated the land of Incana, dispelling the dawn twilight, replacing blue shadows with a winy tangerine light; Meure, breakfastless, found himself toiling up a steepening slope toward an enigmatic structure which became more, not less, peculiar as he drew closer to it. The others climbed the slope with zeal or lassitude as befitted their basic dispositions; Clellendol deliberate and careful, Morgin tiredly, Halander and Ingraine awkwardly and reluctantly, Flerdistar quite beyond her limits physically but grimly determined to go upward and see it all. The Vfzyekhr climbed easily, as if on an outing. Tenguft. . . .

Tenguft moved up the slope warily, always watching, listening; pause: then a step, another, pause, listen, look. She watched the lowlands behind them out of the corner of her eyes, never leaving it entirely, never losing the air of a predator in a strange land. The orange cast to the light seemed to dull her, as it brightened the air, the rocks, the scrubby vegetation, waving slightly in a light, cool breeze. It had not been thus in the night, when she had let her robe fall away from her and calmly walked into the icy stream at the foot of the valley, calmly motioning to Meure that he join her. He had been chilled by the water and intimidated by the half-wild, intense tall girl, more so by her manner, which became surprisingly passive past a point he was not sure had passed. Nor had she spoken any words at all, not since they had dismounted the Eratzenaster, but the sounds she had made deep in her throat would haunt his memory forever.

Audiart came last, going slowly and laboriously; she was not made for clambering over pathless mountains and made no apologies for her pace.

Now above him, Tenguft halted, motioning the others to stop as well, while she scanned the structure looming at the top of the slope. Meure found a secure place, and took the time to look as well.

Now he did not have the panoramic view from the air, wheeling high over the valley, nor the long, dim night-view from the valley floor. Now, in the bright tangerine morning of Monsalvat, he could only see one side of it, and it no longer looked quaint, eccentric, barbarian. To the contrary, it looked ever more grim, although it still retained its erratic air of improvisation. The basic lines of the structure leaned inward, from a many-sided foundation merging with the rock of the mountain, then gradually becoming more or less square. It had, Meure suspected, once been rather flat-roofed. No longer. Now superstructures covered it like lichens on a rotten log; galleries, complete with tiled roofs, turrets, balconies, many connected with masonry staircases, covered or uncovered. Projecting cupolas leaned far out into empty space, some with great open spaces staring out into the air, others closed tightly up with only slit windows for illumination, or outlook. Higher up, it became more erratic, the turrets fading upwards into minarets, watchtowers, some complete with crenelations and embrasures.

Clellendol negotiated what Meure thought to be a particularly difficult section of scree and joined him. Clellendol, too, had been looking upward, at the strongpoint Cucany.

"Look yonder," Clellendol gestured toward the rising suns. "You can see more of these castles on the peaks, all around us."

Meure looked in the direction the Ler youth had indicated. Far up the valley, true enough, was another castle perched atop another peak, as precarious, if not more so, in its site. Meure also saw something flickering, a reflection, or sheen, about the dark mass of the distant castle. "What's the light, there?"

Clellendol shaded his eyes and watched for a moment. "A heliograph, sending code; it's regularly modulated. I can't read it, of course. I should imagine that there's an answer up there in Cucany on the sunlit side."

Meure looked up to Cucany, but couldn't make out any movement, or indeed, any sign that the fortress was even inhabited.

Clellendol ventured, "I don't see much evidence on this slope that they *do* much, up there, but everything suggests that they observe and comment; make no mistake: they've been watching us since we came out of the brush before dawn. I can tell by watching the Haydar girl, if by nothing else; her attention is now about seven-eighths on the city, or fortress, or whatever it is."

"She was not afraid by the river, last night."

"Curious, is it not? Perhaps whatever she feared will not approach water, although I cannot imagine it . . . but never mind. There is much here which will prove beyond my experience." Then he changed the subject. "And you—I trust you are learning to follow the wave of the present, to get into the flow of it."

"I feel much out of my depth here, to be candid. I am being offered much, but the reasons don't make a coherent whole. It's as if I were being guided to something out of the ordinary, for reasons I can't see."

"As you know, those were my feelings earlier. I am more suspicious now, as well." He glanced upward to the outcrop where Tenguft was sitting warily, her hawk profile outlined against the lighter tan color of the walls of Cucany. "That one, now; Morgin told us last night that Haydars do not enter Incana voluntarily. There is no specific prohibition, indeed, there is no government as such to prohibit them. And as you see, the land is open. But they do not come here except in extraordinary circumstances. They fear these people, these Kurbish Windfowlers, as they call themselves. Morgin either does not know, or is being reticent; but there is something about the past, and something these people did. Flerdistar is trying to plumb it."

"I see . . . but she brings us to a land she fears . . ."

"She has brought you, not us. We simply have no other place to go, and since she's on the way anyway . . . Moreover, Haydars are known for their refusal to enter any permanent structure. They consider such things to affront the spirit world; therefore a city is unclean; a fortress more so, since it is its permanence that distinguishes it. Yet I do believe she will walk into that pile up there to deliver you."

"To whom?"

"I am asking myself, 'to what? There is no people in the universe without a fear, or fears. Therefore to override hers she must be enacting a powerful shamanistic role, which is already hers within the Haydar tribe."

Tenguft stood and motioned to the rest of the party. It was time to move on. Clellendol stood, and turned to leave, saying quietly over his shoulder, "Still and all, friend, you must go forward, for here and now you own no back into which to retreat, as we might say in the House of the Thieves."

Meure said, also standing, "But I am the least of those to set out blindly."

"We seem to have gathered little choice, you the least of us. So go forward with faith; and with eyes open . . . you know that on the sea, one can still go anywhere one wants, even though the wind only blows one way, but in a canyon one can only go where the stream leads. But there are streams and there are streams."

"What is the meaning of that?"

"Some courses have carved themselves; others are guided by the skillful arrangement of rockpiles to either side, to provide a given destination. This thing we are on seems unnatural, all the more so with every step we go farther into it. It becomes . . ." Here Clellendol hesitated, then continued, ". . . as if it didn't make any difference whether we could see it or not. It will even become obvious to you in time. I sound like I'm telling you to become a willing sacrifice, but I'm not; you are to be given your chance. You must take it and act innocently, which is to say, unpredictably. Only there lies safety, in unsafety."

Then he turned and began climbing, and would say no more. Meure followed, looking back to see if the others were climbing again after their brief stop. They were, and most were already past him. He looked up the mountain, and began climbing.

Rested a little, at first they made good progress, but they soon slowed, doing progressively less walking and more climbing. The slope became steeper, and dislodged pebbles now rattled down the mountainside for a considerable distance before stopping. Meure could hear them clearly in the calm air, bouncing and ringing on the stones below. He did not look back, or down.

He did not look up; now Cucany seemed close enough to reach upward a little and touch . . . In reality, the foundation courses were still a few meters higher than them. But he was now close enough to see the structure in detail. There was nothing particularly modern or sophisticated about its construction: heavy basal courses of dressed stone, laid without mortar, skillfully, but not extremely so. Above that began the masonry, timbers and rubble, projecting braces of stone and wood. The masonry had weathered to warm pastel tan, and the wood to a silverybrown. Some of the balconies and hanging galleries were almost directly above them, soaring into the aqua-blue sky.

And Tenguft was nowhere in sight.

Now he was at the base of the castle, and saw there was a tiny, precarious ledge that ran erratically about the base, disappearing to the east around a projection of the walls. To the left, it followed a spine of the mountain upwards, up a flight of rude steps, at the top of which Tenguft awaited them, looking not at them, but out over the empty landscape, the tremendous open distances of Incana. Meure looked where she was looking: to the east, mountains rose in isolated peaks and ridgelines like waves in a frozen sea, a dun sea illuminated by an orange star. Near the horizon, he thought he could make out the shimmer of heat waves, or a mirage forming, but he could not be sure. The expanse of distance was hypnotic; the horizon seemed much farther away than he knew it had to be from the size of the planet. And he also saw that what Clellendol had said was true: almost every point of high ground held a structure of one size or another. And that in a good number of them, a flickering, pulsing point of light could be glimpsed, a silvery flickering like sunlight being reflected off an unstable surface, perhaps water, although not necessarily so. Meure felt very uncomfortable, and wondered if he was catching some of Tenguft's wariness; or perhaps it was the overpowering nearness of this fortress atop a bare and uncultivated mountain, with little sign of habitation in the land, save the enigmatic castles. Inside, they watched, and discussed, and consulted with other castles. . . . Out of the corner of his eyes he could now sense the horizon flickering of the heliographs, first one, then another, then others.

Tenguft waited for the rest of them to come up on the path, and then continued up the rude stone steps, following the line of the last outcrop. Meure followed her.

The stairs made a few more blind turns, always upward, and then ended in a smallish stone-flagged porch, facing a tall, narrow doorway shaped in an ogive arch. Tall doors of dark wood and black iron barred the way. Beside the door, a stone gargoyle projected a leering, slavering face into space; stylized drops from its lolling tongue hung down: apparently a bell-pull. Tenguft pulled on the cord without hesitation. They heard nothing within, and waited passively.

It was only a few moments before movement could be heard inside, in response to the doorbell; there was an immanent thumping and knocking, as if a bolt were being slowly withdrawn, and then the arched, tall doors opened on a figure even more curious than Tenguft and the Haydars, if such a thing were possible.

At first Meure saw a tall, spare figure wearing a helmet or headdress. Its body was concealed under a long black robe not dissimilar to the loose robes of the Haydars. Like them, it seemed slender and tall, the headdress adding to its height so that it seemed as tall as the Haydar girl. As far as he could see, it carried no arms of any kind. The headdress, however, attracted all his attention: It was as wide as the shoulders and easily twice as tall as the head within. It was shaped most curiously, being built up of a number of superimposed prisms; from a point resting on the upper chest, it rose upward in straight lines to points just above the shoulders—these apparently supported the weight of the contraption. From the shoulder points, small shelves, triangular, stepped back at a rising angle to meet another prism shape, which was a continuation of the opening for the face. This inner prism rose to a height above the head and also terminated in a sharp point. Seen from the side, the lines of the helmet formed a diagonal cross shape. The top was filled in with triangles, points down. The face opening lozenge-shaped, a continuation of the outer lines of the figure. The colors of it were arresting, too: the sides were a bright, deep red, while the rooflike top triangles were painted a flat black.

A face could be seen inside, but only dimly, for the overhang of the helmet blocked most of the light; the face was heavily shadowed. Whatever was inside seemed bearded, and the eyes were outlined with greenish-white circles, that glowed? Glowed. Fluorescent paint. Meure suppressed an urge to idiotic laughter. Suppressed it because the attitude of Tenguft displayed unmistakable submission.

Morgin nodded politely to the silent figure, and turned to the members of the party. He said, very seriously, "You see before you the Noble Molio Azendarach, Phanet of Dzoz Cucany. You are his guests, but do not take the word lightly, for travelers are few now in the land Incana and hospitality is not offered to all. Proceed forward, then, with respect."

The helmeted person, Azendarach, made a slight motion, a subtle nod, and motioned for them to follow; having done so, he turned and proceeded into the depths of the castle without waiting to see if they were following. Morgin went first, followed by Tenguft and Meure. The rest came after.

Another helmeted figure slid out of the shadows by the door, to close it behind them, but they had little time to see the second one, save that his helmet seemed almost as large and impossible in shape as Azendarach's. The Phanet was moving on, down a high-arched corridor which was in strong contrast to the openness and light outside, for it was dark and gloomy, the ceiling fading into shadows.

Azendarach led them a ways along the dark hallway, and then turned into a narrow way, climbing a steep stairwell. Inside, there seemed to be the same construction as the outside—masonry over rubble braced by half-timbers sunk into the material.

Now they climbed the awkward stairwell through many abrupt turns until they were thoroughly confused as to direction. The stair was interrupted frequently by small landings with narrow doors fronting on them. None were open, and no sound could be heard; it was as if the castle were uninhabited. Yet the doors were well-maintained, and the sills were swept clean. People lived in Cucany, true enough; it seemed that they were very quiet about it.

The stairs continued upward, sometimes almost too steeply to be called stairs; rather more like ladders. Azendarach maintained the same pace, whether walking on the level, or on the sharpest ascents, always holding his carriage so that the helmet did not wobble or misalign itself in any way.

At the last, they emerged onto a broad landing where the ascent ended. All were breathing hard from the climb, save the Phanet, who was opening the iron-bound door with great concentration. While he was manipulating the mechanism, Tenguft leaned to Meure and whispered, "Wizards! Beware!" After she said it, she straightened and shivered slightly.

Azendarach opened the door and allowed it to stand ajar for them to enter. Light flooded into the dim landing from an enormous room alive with the play of light. The contrast was blinding at first.

They were obviously high up in the castle, or Dzoz, as Morgin had called it, probably near its highest point. This room appeared to be a single large area, with curtained alcoves along the walls; where there were no curtains, the walls were whitewashed carefully to a uniform flat white. One side was entirely open to the air, and seemed to be one of the projecting galleries Meure had seen from the ground. Facing the south, generally, it curved far out in a smooth line unbroken by supports. Its sill was even more curious, being a pool of water. The roof was stepped back slightly. There was no furniture in the room, save some antique cabinets or wardrobes along the walls, in the curtained sections, and cushions scattered around the floor, which was of flagstones. Air from the breeze outside whispered in the corners of the room, and light played there, some from the bright-dun landscape stretching away to the horizons, and from reflections from the wind-ruffled pool along the sill.

Another helmeted figure emerged from a curtained alcove and made motions of deference to Azendarach. They spoke then, ignoring the visitors, but Meure listened alertly. To his surprise, their speech was more understandable than Tenguft's, although to her ears it probably sounded archaic and cryptic.

Azendarach said, in a thin reedy voice, almost like nasal whispering, "What are the reports, Erisshauten?"

The one called Erisshauten answered, "Phanet, Dzoz Soltro relayed through Kormendy and Endrode that a party of Lagostomes attempted to pass Vakiflar Narrows, but were repulsed and punished. Dzoz Veszid and Orkeny in the Eastmarch report empty reflections. Lisbene likewise. Midre, Andely and Lachryma report through Malange Gather that a party of Eratzenasters departed the Reach for the Ombur, exiting above Torskule. Atropope had an incident with Korsors. Potale Dzoz has reflections, but they are not clear and a more expert reader has been summoned. . . . shall we dispatch Romulu Bedetdznatsch?"

"What was their nature, at Potale?"

"Continuing, but weak. They want an evening reading . . ."

"Understandable . . . but we may not spare Bedetdznatsch. We will read tonight; have Onam Hareschacht posted from Lisbene. If he leaves now he can be there in time."

"Your will, Phanet," replied the man, and he turned and returned into the alcove from whence he had emerged.

The prism-shaped helmet turned back to them, and once again the eye-circles stared out of the darkness of the helmet at them.

Azendarach said, almost whispering, "These are the riders of the ship of space?"

Tenguft answered, straining to match the phrasing of the Phanet, "These people and a thing for which I have no word . . ."

". . . No matter. We have taken knowledge of it."

". . . were the dunnage. Those who owned it remained with my people, now of the Ombur."

"Just so. I understand. I have read of it in the prodromic current; and so has its profluence been. We did not believe, for there is much that passes understanding in the reflections. Yet they continued so, even to their meeting of the Venatic People, on Ombur. And they were to be here, and so indeed are they here. We shall continue the eutaxy."

Meure suspected he was in the presence of a madman, or a lunatic cultist, or perhaps both. Neither were improbable on Monsalvat.

Apparently Azendarach divined his uneasiness, for he now said, "The

Kurbish Windfowlers of Incana are reputed the strangest folk of all Aceldama, which you will know as Monsalvat." He nodded the heavy helmet toward Tenguft. "That child of open spaces, of the night, and murder, who is no small thing at the arts herself, and who practices divination using the hand-bones of the left hand of her own mother, given to her willingly, I might add, she fears for her very sanity in the halls of Cucany. But consider, civilized creatures. I call you creatures for I know that all are not human. Some of you are of the kind of the ancient enemy, he who made us as we are. Have no fear! For we know the ends of the things of the past, and the Warriors are vanished, faded away. Whatever vendetta might be left over we have more than expiated against one another these millennia. But consider, I say: Incana *is* an empty land, but no man will march on it, not even the pestiferous Lagostomes. We neither expand, enslave, nor disturb the rest of others with our machinations. We mine the peaks, we grow things in the roof gardens, we trade, we gather the wild things, we limit ourselves . . . altogether good neighbors. But," here his voice rose in volume, "we read truth in the reflections of the light of this world, and consult, and act, and if we are right, then if some say, 'there walk wizards on the parapet,' then so let it be as they will say."

"And so Bedetdznatsch and I so read what has come to pass. Here, in an isolated Dzoz in an empty land, and that one such would be brought to us who would dare what we dare not to ourselves. One from *Outside*. Embasse, tell him."

Morgin said, "History. Only one man ever tried to unify this planet, knowing that to be the necessary precondition to our rejoining our human fellows. He lived long ago, and was called many things, but his name was Cretus the Scribe. He was not a soldier, or a warrior, but one who could put things together. He started at a location, by the great river of Kepture, which no longer exists, but he finished here, in Incana, in Cucany. The great work was under way, and even the mad Lagos were restrained once from their breedings, and then there was no more. Cretus expired, the heirs fell to disagreements, and the empire vanished. The Windfowlers from Inner Incana remained true to his memory, but the rest fled like scavenger beetles in the dawn. Here is where the Scribe worked, counselled, plotted, built. Here, below ground, is where his dust remains, and an artifact he used. He was the last of his Klesh-kind, and only a quadroon of that was his in truth. He had no tribe, no land, no hetman, no loyalty but to his own vision. He had a thing he saw visions in, which no one else knew how to use, or wouldn't. It is widely accepted that the guardians of the world saw fit to strike him down for stealing their secrets of the future . . . that is what the people know of it."

They were interrupted by a young boy, obviously an apprentice, who wore only a light open framework about his head instead of the full rigor of the opaque helmet. The boy issued forth from the same alcove Erisshauten had come from, without asking permission, bowed with his hands hidden in his sleeves, and said, in a high voice, "My lord Phanet, the Cellar Chamberlain Trochanter advises me that all is in readiness."

Azendarach nodded acknowledgment, dismissed the boy with a gesture. Close on the boy's departure returned Erisshauten from whatever observation point he occupied.

Erisshauten announced, "Phanet, Dzoz Potale respectfully withdraws their request for the boon of interpretation. They aver that their reading is now clear, to be passed to the Master Reader without delay. It is this: 'Say that they say to do it now.' "

"That is all?"

"Just so they sent, M'Lord Phanet. They said that there was rapid clearing during our last series of transmissions."

The Phanet shook his headdress from side to side slowly, a universal gesture of unsureness. He sighed audibly, then said, "I cannot doubt a clear reading, for they are rare, and even the inexperienced lad at Potale can read a clear; nevertheless, I would wonder why we read no such message here . . . ?" He trailed off, musing, seemingly innocently.

Erisshauten began to evidence sighs of nervousness. He spoke, now rapidly, "Perhaps, your surety, it might lie in the practices of our own reader, the Noble Bedetdznatsch. Having read at dawn, and having performed the 'clearing mind of distraction by horizoning' exercise, he now takes his rest in his chambers."

Azendarach chuckled to himself, and said, expansively, "So, indeed. And I suppose the apprentices read in the day."

"I should not venture to comment upon the practices of the Noble Bedetdznatsch, but it does sound highly probable that such might conceivably be the case."

"Well, we shall not disturb old Romulu. Doubtless he has earned some freedom from opprobrium. Ready the chamber, then. I shall read."

"Begging M'Lord's pardon, but . . . in the presence of outlanders?"

" 'Now' must be verified. There is risk in what we would try."

"As you instruct, then." Erisshauten then fussily began to prepare the chamber for what they called a reading. First he latched the doors from inside, then he carefully arranged the cushions and throws on the floor.

Azendarach stood aside and waited without comment. Erisshauten then walked gingerly to the parapet, peering owlishly outside, determining the angle of the suns. Then he returned, went to another alcove, and extracted an iron rod with a crank, which appeared to be pivoted at its concealed end. This he began turning; the mechanism this operated worked without noise whatsoever, indicating long use and careful maintenance, but the effects were immediately apparent. A section of the roof over the parapet began withdrawing into the supporting structure, allowing the orange sunlight of the two suns to flood into the room.

Azendarach now seemed remote, uninterested. He looked off into space, at noplace. Meure could not be sure, but his eyes seemed to have an unfocused look. Azendarach said, in a monotone, "What is the mode?"

Erisshauten answered, "Coming up on Broadside, M'Lord Azendarach. Best possible conditions there are, clear sky, no wind."

Azendarach did not acknowledge that he had heard. Erisshauten continued cranking the handle. Now, besides the light streaming into the room from the sunlight, more light appeared, as if from an artificial source. Meure looked up, to the low ceiling, but saw only a reflection from the pool of water along the parapet. The pool was there to throw a reflection of the sun onto the ceiling, or perhaps the walls, according to the time of day. The room became very bright.

Now Azendarach carefully got down to the floor, and laid himself out, with as much dignity as he could manage. The purpose of the odd headdress now seemed clearer: it was to minimize distraction and reduce the flux of light. The chamber was so bright that it was uncomfortable, and the visitors squinted.

Erisshauten motioned to the visitors for quiet. Azendarach stretched out, relaxed, became quiescent. Stared at the reflection of the suns on the ceiling. Meure felt uncomfortable. Omens! These damn Klesh read omens at the least provocation, in front of others, and they seemed to consider such behavior normal. He supposed that most of them used some method; they could conceivably meet necromancers, geomancers, palmists, dreg-readers of several classifications, dependant upon the beverage employed, fire-leapers, the whole gamut. He risked a glance at Clellendol and Flerdistar. They stood respectfully, also accepting the behavior without comment.

Now he looked at the reflections on the ceiling; it was a reflection of the suns, side by side. Broadside, Erisshauten had called it. The image was not perfectly still, but wavered ever so slightly, in sharp, nervous little movements. The image conveyed nothing intelligible to Meure. The time was now midafternoon.

Azendarach watched the reflections for some time, without gesture or sound, or indeed any sign of consciousness. Then, abruptly, he waved to Erisshauten and began getting to his feet. He seemed to have some difficulty in doing so, and Audiart stepped forward, her hand extended, as if to offer assistance, but she stopped quickly. On one knee, Molio Azendarach fixed her with a glance of malign intent, so that she looked away, and stepped back, avoiding the imprint of those glow-rimmed eyes.

Azendarach gained his feet, while Erisshauten proceeded with the operation of closing the parapet roof. When he had finished, the Phanet said, "Yes, it is so, just so. I would rate the uncertainty factor at Purple. The admonishment is clearly to proceed."

Erisshauten commented, "I will so inform Trochanter."

"Very appropriate. And also as you do so, remember that our guests will require sustenance."

"Aye, I will see to it, as you have said before."

Erisshauten indicated that they should follow him, and set off without ceremony, save silence. The members of the group hesitated a moment, then fell in behind him. Erisshauten led them from the chamber of Molio Azendarach, out onto the landing, and then down, down, quickly turning off at a landing just below, and boring down into the bowels of the castle through ways much different from the way they had entered. Meure, pausing at the door before starting down the steep stairwell, glanced back once—and saw Azendarach standing at the edge of open space, staring out into the afternoon light and the distances, his hands carefully folded behind him, apparently deep in thought. What thought? What weighty decision lay in feeding strangers? Or that the omens should be consulted, unless all these Klesh people were hagridden with them?

Then he turned and followed the others down, catching up with the end of the line, the ridiculous slave creature from Vfzyekhr, struggling with the stairs which were too great a step for its short legs.

They rapidly lost any sense of direction in the narrow warrens of Cucany; they traversed short corridors, went through ponderous wooden doors framed in black iron, which latched behind them. Light came from iron lanterns, burning an oil which made little soot, or from shafts cleverly let down into the body of the castle. And always down. Meure could not recall a single instance in which they went up. Nor were they greeted by any inhabitant along the way—it seemed the castle was inhabited only by those they had met in the upper chamber, and ghosts. They heard no noises, no conversations, no sound of life whatsoever. But judging by the passages they traversed, the castle had to be honeycombed, riddled with ways.

The scent and feel of the air changed subtly; a faint dusty odor gave way to a damper smell, and it felt damp. Meure tried to compare how far up they had climbed against how far down they had come, and decided that they were now below ground level. Still, the inner walls were of masonry, rubble, timbers of a heavy, coarse wood. Down one more stair, almost steep enough to warrant a ladder, and they reached a level where the walls were stone. There were fewer intersections.

Erisshauten led them to a room of moderate dimensions, furnished with plain tables and benches, motioned to the benches, and departed. Presently, another person appeared, still wearing one of the prism-shaped headdresses of Incana, bearing bowls of what appeared to be a stew or goulash. The food was steaming hot. The steward set the tables, left and returned with huge clay pots of a light, but very bitter beer. They all looked uncertainly at the lamplit hall, the rough tables, the bowls and jugs, and sat down to eat, one by one. Satisfied that all were setting to the fare, the steward left.

They were all hungry, and began at once, slowly at first, then faster, as the bland taste of the stew began to fill them. The beer tasted odd, too, but it seemed to fit the food. All seemed correct, all were eating, even Morgin and the Haydar girl, although in their cases they ate very sparingly, almost reluctantly. Nothing seemed out of place, unless it was the distance that their hosts kept from them. Meure concentrated on the bland stew and the beer; it might be some time before they had such an opportunity again.

The steward looked in once more, saw empty bowls, and refilled them, also refilling the beer-pots. Yes, indeed, all did seem well. There was no sign of hostile intent in the steward's manner whatsoever. Meure attacked his new helping with gusto. Underneath the bland taste of it, there seemed to be a subtle flavor he couldn't quite identify, but which he began to enjoy. And he saw the others were similarly engaged, and that was good. This was turning out to be less hazardous than he had imagined. Shortly, he imagined, they would be led to plain but serviceable pallets somewhere in the castle, and would spend the night. That sounded like a very good idea, even better than the food, for, now that he thought of it, he was very fatigued from the adventures of the last few days—he wasn't sure how many since they had abandoned the ship, but it seemed like a long time. He tried to imagine how long, for something didn't quite fit, that it, the feel of the time, seemed longer than his recollection of the number of days involved.

He looked around at the others. The Vfzyekhr had curled up in Audiart's lap and seemed to be asleep. Well enough that! Slaves would learn to sleep whenever they could, if half of what one heard about the Spsom could be credited. He saw that Morgin and Tenguft had not taken seconds, and were sitting, quietly aloof, their eyes drooping. What odd people, not to take advantage of hospitality. The others continued, just as he did, but in slow-motion, as if suspended in syrup. He turned the beer-pot up and drank it clean. Flerdistar was across the table from him, staring at her bowl with a most comical, wall-eyed expression on her thin and homely face, although now Meure thought to see some previously hidden charm in the aristocratic Ler girl. He looked again at the plain face, the pale skin; the thin, boyish body. The watery eyes. That was how she ought to be, he thought, but she didn't look that way now, even though she was acting very odd. Now he could see some of the intensity of her inner personality animating the physical features. Yes, of course. She would possess extravagant emotions, and would probably be fond of all sorts of odd practices. He saw her in other lights now; saw the thin mouth as a giver of hard kisses and fierce, passionate words in the dark. How could he have thought of her as plain, even homely. Clellendol was a fool for ignoring her.

The Ler girl pushed her bowl away and laid her head down on her arm, her eyes open, staring, but after a moment they closed, separately. Her mouth opened, and he could see her teeth behind the thin lower lip, white and pink. He felt emboldened, full of confidence. Yes. Tonight. If Clellendol wouldn't he would. Right! It was then that he discovered he couldn't seem to put his intent into motion. He wanted to get up and join Flerdistar, but somehow he couldn't move his legs properly. In fact, he could barely keep his head up. He looked around, and saw the most curious sight; all were settling at their places, their heads drooping over the table. And the oil lamps were so bright now! Even Morgin and Tenguft, although upright, seemed disconnected, not conscious. Only Clellendol, who was sliding off his bench with exaggerated care. Meure laughed. Let him! Now he could discern what Meure had in mind, with his superior intuition, such as Ler were supposed to have. And he would come to him and tell him, after the blustering manner of Cervitan, to leave the girl alone. Hah! It was not to be so!

Meure watched Clellendol crawling on his hands and knees around the table to him, as if it were the hardest thing he had ever done in his life. Each step forward was like climbing a mountain. It was fascinating. At last, Clellendol reached Meure's place, and struggled to support himself on the bench. Clearly, he was failing to do so. Meure leaned close; if could do no harm. Why, he'd even tell him what he had in mind. What the hell: he could watch, if so inclined. He leaned down until their heads were almost touching. Clellendol tried to look up, but couldn't make his eyes look high enough. And then he spoke, and it was not what Meure expected to hear.

"...We've been drugged ... be careful ... beware Cretus. Don't look at it, whatever it is ..."

But then the Ler boy could say no more, for he was sliding to the cold floor, with just enough coordination left to keep his head from bumping.

Meure laid his head on his arm and thought about that for a moment. He closed his eyes, because the light from the lamps was so bright, it hurt. *Don't look at it.* Flerdistar? That didn't sound right. Cretus? Why beware a man dead thousands of years, however long it was. Cretus was gone, something for Flerdistar to worry over. Drugged? Well, now, he'd have to look into that. That wasn't hospitable at all, but he supposed that the matter would keep until tomorrow ...

Nightfall occurred coincident with the phase of the Sun Bitirme which the savants among the Windfowlers called, among the society of the Elect, *manefranamosi*, which they thought meant "broadening" in the ancient Singlespeech of their once-masters.* This was when one of the pair was rounding the limb of the other, suggesting an ovoid shape; the pair of stars, already broadened by the atmosphere, distorted by uneven refraction, and their orange light reddened further, assumed a bizarre, floating shape on the edge of the world, seemingly stopping for a moment, and then sinking unnaturally rapidly. This condition, with just the precise degree of ovality, precisely at the moment of sundown, augered in general success for deeds of questionable virtue, in the system affected by the Windfowlers. No doubt, for others somewhere on the four continents of Monsalvat, such an event might well have contrary interpretations.

---

*What the Klesh thought was Singlespeech was actually the degenerate form of that tongue as spoken on the planet Dawn. The correct construction would have been "mafranemosi (felor)," with the word for star, "felor," understood, but not said.

*   *   *

No light illuminated the cellar refectory of Dzoz Cucany except the oil lanterns hung along the walls, with a slight added gleam coming from a pair of such lamps suspended from an iron standard carried by a helmeted and robed figure whose headdress identified him as Eddo Erisshauten. There were others; one, in the most angular prism-shaped headdress, was Molio Azendarach. Another carried a rotund figure beneath the dark robes, and answered to the cognomen of Romulu Bedetdznatsch. A fourth was doorward of the castle.

They entered in the refectory with a gait suggestive of two opposites: great ceremony, and the furtiveness of sneakthieves. They came in procession, but they watched the sleeping, drugged guests carefully lest any one of them show signs of awareness. Morgin still sat bolt upright, but his eyes were half-closed, and his breathing was slow and regular. Tenguft, likewise, also sat upright yet, but her eyes were closed. The procession, led by Erisshauten, wound into the cellar, filing to that side of the bench where sat Schasny. There they gathered in conclave, conferring in almost inaudible whispers.

Azendarach whispered, "The inhalation will awaken him?"

The doorward answered, "Certainty. The subject will be ambulatory, but will have little will, other than to perform as he is instructed, and the instructions are not difficult. It is nothing new, this procedure," he added petulantly. "We have done this before."

Azendarach answered, after a long hesitation, ". . . As you say, so it is. But this one, now, this one is of the offworld *gorgensuchen**, and who knows what he might be carrying in his bloodline."

Bedetdznatsch interjected, "The underservant reported that the subject was more resistant than the others, but that his lapsing was well within the calculated tolerances. We should anticipate, if anything, only another failure."

"It is possible that he might have done it willingly. The drug may be a factor in our past failures."

"The concomitant use of the ingestant and the inhalant stupefies the will and renders the subject suggestible; so much is rote from the phar-

---

*A word impossible to translate simply. It meant, more or less, "the descendant of persons who deliberately perverted their racial ancestry and destiny." Moreover, who continued to do so. It was a word filled with connotations of shivery horror and singularly repulsive deviance.

macopoeia; even persons resistant to hypnosis perform marvels in the attained state. Remember, the drug was resorted to for the reason that no one would even look at it otherwise."

"We are, naturally, equally prepared for the other possibility?"

All moved their helmets ponderously, signifying affirmatively. Erisshauten summarized. "In the event of successful transfer, we must destroy the device immediately and overpower the subject so that we may interrogate him at our leisure, without fear."

Azendarach mused, "I fear this, each time we try it. I like it not, even though it was read in the reflection generations ago and reverified again and again. We are to attempt to revive the personality of Cretus the Scribe in the body of a subject. After that, nothing. No advice, no instructions, suggestions, absolutely blank. The best omenreaders have plied their trade and get no reading of advantage or disadvantage, blame or unblame."

Bedetdznatsch corrected the Phanet, politely, "Your pardon, m'lord, but the reading is always 'advantage/disadvantage, no blame.' "

The reply was icy. "In my workbook, that is the import of the null reading."

Bedetdznatsch whispered, "Of course, of course. But within a concept in which inaction is a form of action, and indecisiveness a form of decision, then a null reading has its wording and commands the same respect as the others. And we cannot overlook that this particular one was delineated. 'One will be brought from the offworlds. Use him next.' This is the one, according to the Embasse."

"The Embasse also said that the Star-boat crashed very close to the country of the Lagostomes. He could have been for them to use."

"They couldn't have done much. Only we possess the talisman. No, things have worked to bring the subject here. The reflections so read, and so it has been. I have faith."

"Mine is not in question. I am fearful, when I receive what can only be interpreted as specific instructions from the omens, and no resultant is revealed at the culmination of those actions. And no way has been found to weasel it out, either."

Bedetdznatsch mused, "Rapmanchelein the Mystic was reputed to have inquired in the reflections of their origin, to wit, were the omens, of God. In his opinion the interpretation was a negation of that idea. That is, while his sanity remained. He spent the remainder of his short life, muttering, 'they laugh their laughs, they do,' and sometimes, 'one in many, many in one.' I would not think of wondering what the source is.

For the time, I will accept that it is not communication with the One, but perhaps something lesser, at least familiar with Aceldama."

Azendarach added, "And the region surrounding it, out how far we can't even guess. We read the instruction many days before the Ship could have landed here."

Erisshauten agreed, emphatically, "Yes, many days, indeed. One wonders, for a certainty."

Azendarach turned away from the group and looked at Schasny, reflectively. Finally he said, still looking at the unconscious body slumped at his place at the table, "We should be able to control that one in the event the transfer works . . . dare we mention the rest here?"

The doorward said, "This level is supposed to be free of bane or omen. All experiments conducted here approximate random to the extent we have been able to perform and record them. The conclusion is that this level is blind. . . ."

"No one knows why the readings suggest the reactivation of Cretus the Scribe. But in the archives it was reported that he was known to be not only a reader, but an activant. That implies control, or cooperation with some affective entity. If our suspicions are accurate, then we will possess either a key to our dreams, or else a powerful bargaining tool to work toward that. But it will have to be fast. We must not let him get away from us this time, eh? Like those fools of the old Incana, long ago, let him get away from them."

He stopped, as if the idea were too powerful to submit to the tyranny of mere words. He shook his head. "These adventurers and charismatics come along and think the world's their own toy to pull down or set straight! And setting straighter it's always needed, correct enough; but for it practical men are needed to guide the repairing hand, else all be broken along the way. *They* had the right idea, then. They insulated him in routines and functions and repetitious acts and got him pointed in the right direction. It's all in the archives. But they left him one way out. We must leave this one no way out, if it works. And then we'll subdue this proud Cretus. With fire and iron, if need be . . . What shall we have him set to rights first, my fellows?"

Bedetdznatsch muttered, "Potale has long been a hotbed of heterodoxy and should be brought to heel."

The doorward ventured, "Rid the wide world of Eratzenasters. And their riders. My cousin was taken."

Erisshauten said, thoughtfully, "The Lagostomes will provide ample manpower, properly instructed, for ourselves and associates to subdue Kepture; we can work from there."

"Let it begin, then."

Erisshauten withdrew from his robe a vial containing a clear liquid. This he poured onto a towel handed him for the purpose. The solution appeared to have no discernible scent. Then he seized Schasny roughly by the hair and covered the boy's face with the saturated towel. At first, there was no change; Schasny gave no indication whatsoever that he perceived what was being done to him. Then his eyes began moving under the lids, and he opened his eyes. Erisshauten removed the towel, and the boy sat upright unassisted. He asked no questions, nor did he look around, although he seemed alert enough.

Azendarach said sharply, "Test him!"

Erisshauten asked the boy, "What is your name?"

He answered tonelessly, "Meure Wendrin Schasny."

"Give your age and planet of origin."

"I was born on Tancred; I have twenty Tancred years. The correction factor for Tancred is .962215."

Azendarach asked, "What is a correction factor?"

The boy answered in the same toneless voice, "It is a ratio between a planetary year and the year of the suspected planet of origin. The period has been verified independently by biometric means, so the system need not be found to prove the concept. It provides a means to equate ages among persons from different planets, for statistical purposes, and also legal purposes."

The Incanans looked at one another. Azendarach asked, "The existence of such a concept suggests a community of many planets. How many are there inhabited by humans like us?"

Schasny emitted a short giggle. "None."

Azendarach asked, "How many inhabited by those like you?"

"I don't know."

"More than twenty?"

"Yes."

"More than a hundred?"

"Yes."

Azendaach looked at his companions. "That's a lot of people."

Erisshauten commented, "Homogenized *Gorgensuchen*. One Klesh would be worth any ten or twenty. They have not had to survive against their fellow Humans in the manner we have. They will reward equality and conformity. We pursue excellence. There is no correspondence between the two systems. We will gain an initial advantage at first, then enter a period of stalemate. After a time, their will will weaken and we will gain the victory. This will come later. Now, first things first."

Azendarach said to Schasny, "What is your desire?"

"I have no desire."

"Then arise and come with me."

He got to his feet, unsteadily, assisted by the doorward, who turned him in the direction he should go The group left the refectory and passed through a small kitchen, Azendarach leading. Bedetdznatsch and Erisshauten bringing up the rear.

Bedetdznatsch whispered to Erisshauten, "Molio's not such an alert watchman as one might need."

"Precautions have been taken."

"I have it from my morning reading that this one will take."

"You kept that quiet, didn't you?"

"Azendarach assumed the Phaneterie by chicanery; he may read according to his abilities to do so."

"They say each reader sees a different truth, both ways. You know the saying."

"Aye, what you can see and what it says. I know: they can change, they can. I've caught 'em changing with the students, more than once."

"You know more?"

"They don't like Molio."

"Why?"

"Too much peace, not enough war. He's a parlor-Phanet, a politician, such as the filthy Lagos follow."

"Well, from what I hear, Cretus'll change all that. All the accounts say he was fond of action. Took the council almost ten years to get him under control. We'll accomplish that tonight. Or we'll put the legend to sleep for good."

"I'll give you a foretelling . . ."

"It's supposed to be bad luck."

"Throw that! Luck is made, not waited for. So all I'll say is give him room, not a lot, and be wary, but if Cretus makes the first move, let him make it."

"He'll get Azendarach, then?"

"There's a big uncertainty factor in it, but it looks like that's the probability."

"What's the uncertainty factor?"

"Orange."

"You're dreaming, not reading. Orange lies within the norm of random variation."

"I admit it was weak, but I say it was there."

"Very well. But attend! These steps are bad."

Now they were at the end of a long passageway they had been traversing, starting down a steep stairs deeper into the native rock. Erisshauten's caution was not in error; the stairs were dark, wet and treacherous, making several changes in direction and pitch; not enough to make a landing, but enough to make one stumble. At the end, they descended into a small chamber, quite bare, which led into a larger one. The lanterns they carried cast a yellow, flickering light to the dusty, underground rooms.

Azendarach was explaining to Meure what he must do; "You are to carry this lantern, and enter that room. There, you will find a shining object made of wire. You will pick it up and look at it in the light. While you are looking at it, you must try to imagine, and remember what you see."

"That is all?"

"That is all. If you see nothing, you will replace the object in the place where it was."

"Am I a fortuneteller now?"

"You may be a fortune bringer. Now!"

Azendarach and the doorward flanked Schasny and led him into the room, carefully averting their eyes from something out of sight to the left, using the headdresses to great advantage, as if they had been designed just for this purpose, to let one see where one was going, blocking the sight of something. The others lagged a little, hanging back at the doorway.

They saw Schasny, moving like a sleepwalker, look for something, and locate it; he reached for it, bending, and picked up something shining and glittering, something from which Bedetdznatsch and Erisshauten alike averted their eyes. Holding the object with one hand, and the lantern with the other, the boy looked blankly at the object for what seemed like an extended time; so far this had been identical to scores of other times. But this time began to go differently, and in a way none of them expected, without preparatory gesture, or motion, Schasny rapidly squeezed the object with the hand holding it, breaking up its shining glitters and transforming it into an uninteresting wad of metallic fibers. It was done fast. And then all hell broke loose.

---

*" 'Motion about a point is iniquity' . . . and 'Torsion is iniquity.'
I understand that every disturbance, which makes manifestation
possible, implies deviation from perfection."*

—A.C.

T HERE HAD BEEN a passage of time so long that years could not serve
to measure it; centuries would not suffice, for there would have
been too many of them. And if the double star Bitirme had been visible
from any other planet as a member of a constellation, then that constellation would have changed shape to the naked eye.

For one who called himself Cretus the Scribe there was no time, and
the courses of the stars in space had no meaning for him. He was here;
and then he was . . . *here.*

Cretus entered the chamber at the bottom of the stairs, carefully latch-
ing the door behind him. Not so much for security, he told himself
wryly, because they could break it down in minutes, but for the little reassurance that he'd have a short privacy for what had to be done. The
chamber was a storage closet, a good locker for times of siege. Empty
now, the shelves bare, damp-smelling, dusty. There was a crate on the
stone floor. Cretus placed the lantern he was carrying on the shelf,
absent-mindedly, and then pulled the crate over to him. He sat, looking
back up at the lantern, as if verifying its relative position.

He thought, *about now, they'll find out I'm gone.* He knew how it
would go after that; they'd not waste time worrying about how he
got past the guards, supposedly his protectors, but would check the
gates of the stronghold Cucany, and find out that none had passed.
But they'd put out a patrol anyway, supplemented with the filthy

Derques*, and with daylight, there'd be a Haydar or two to cover the ground. No, they wouldn't be fooled long; they'd imagine he was somewhere in the stronghold yet, and they'd start looking. Very thoroughly, a room at a time. They were thorough, that was a fact. And that thoroughness would of necessity slow them down a little. Long enough, he supposed.

He reached into the plain robe he was wearing, and withdrew an object, shining and glittering in the lamplight, now in its inactive shape, mostly flattened into a shape that was disclike and toroidal at the same time. He looked at it carelessly; it didn't matter now, folded as it was. He could do nothing with it until it was opened up.

The object was, to his knowledge, the last *Skazenache* in existence, just as he was the last Zlat. And at that, not a true-zlat, but a quadroon-zlat. One-fourth, that somehow had bred true. But he did not delude himself; he had looked deeply into time and the symbol that told stories which he now held in his hand, and he knew his appearance and zlat ways were only one expression of a probability formula that no one could change. The terrible magic wrought by the Warriors in the deeps of yesterday was coming unravelled in some of its parts, and the Zlat trait was being absorbed back into the common ruck and squabble. He also knew that the genetic distribution expanded its base by a factor of two each generation. Were he to sire one more true-zlat, son or daughter, they would only have one-eighth zlat in them. One could not maintain a pure line by oneself.

Cretus sighed. He had seen much, but he was not, so he imagined, much of a philosopher. A faint smile flickered across the sharp features, the deepset eyes, the lines and hollows of his face, the half-shaven stubble that had been his trademark. He thought, *it's this, now: I couldn't do anything for my people, because my people are gone, one by one. At least I could do for myself. At the least I could help the others keep their identity, and put a stop to this absurd racecrossing. What foolishness! To populate*

---

*Derques were a form of Klesh far removed from the original human form. A Derque supported its weight on its arms, which were greatly strengthened. The hands were atrophied into footlike appendages. The original legs were much reduced, and the former feet served as organs of manipulation. Derques were reputed to be less sentient than the average animal, and this was not merely another of the myriad racial slurs of Monsalvat, but carried more than a bit of truth. Derques in fact did roam wild in Chengurune, serving as scavengers. A Klesh Radah called the Ularid Khoze captured them and trained them as scenthounds, paralleling the free Haydar who were visually-guided predators.

this world with bastards! Even half-breeds detested the idea, and would seek others like them to form the cores of future tribes. But I am a victim of my own program, am I not? "Cretus,' they cry, 'who saved us." *Who had unified all of Kepture that counted, first from a base in Ombur, and then here in Incana.*

And who had felt his grasp leading men slowly leached away by government, by counsellors, by servants and toadies and politicians and professional hangers-on, who always waited for a leader to ride behind as long as they survived . . . and who they now cherished like a prisoner, to deflect along the shabby paths such running-Derques always wanted. What trash! He had offered them the stars, in time, ultimately. And all they wanted was something they could feel today: a woman, money, an eyrie in the castle with a view. But they couldn't seem to grasp the first step, that all Monsalvat had to be wielded into a whole of component Klesh races, everyone to his part, stronger than all the rest put together. Like crystals in a matrix. He had seen that.

He had seen much with his storyteller, once he had learned it was for more than telling stories; lives from the past, worlds and their inhabitants spread across the sky, old humans, new humans, more, stranger creatures, some odd indeed. He had nothing but the Klesh experience to judge the universe by, and he suspected that it was an erroneous view, but he didn't know where the error was. And there were the others, whose location and nature, kind and numbers were vague, shifting, unstable. Nothing remained the same but that they spoke, indirectly or not at all. They had suggested (was it he, she, or it had suggested?) this way out, *into* the storyteller to wait for another time, another body. More than once he had rejected the idea out of hand. Zlats had never used the device that way, so his grandmother had told him. Never. It was the unclean way. His skin crawled. Cretus, who had terrified many in his climb from street urchin to titular ruler of most of Kepture, was himself terrified by what he thought to do.

They'd protect him until they found the right one, eh? That's what they (he, she, it) said. But how long, that's the rub. Only that all these coattail riders will all be dead, and that they'd be considerably discomfited by his absence, since their only genuine foreteller would be gone. Cretus had learned to fine-tune his *Skazenache* to the immediate worldline and the immediate future. And who could win battles against one who could read the future, and not only choose the ground, as he'd learned on the streets, but could choose the time of engagement as well?

He unfolded the device into a shining spherical object made of metallic wires, with thousands of tiny beads strung along them, made a series of adjustments, now concentrating, not careless or off-hand at all, and *looked* at it, face curiously empty of expression. Then back. He nodded, as if he had seen more or less what he expected to see".

It was time to do it. His chamberlains were not far away, proceeding with thoroughness. Cretus took a deep breath and exhaled slowly. To be gone, this agile body, and what would he continue in? A fat publican? A child? Perhaps a woman? Now that would be something. He smiled to himself.

A last odd thought occurred to him, and he stood up to look about the storeroom. A mirror, that as what was needed. A mirror. He was not vain, but he wanted to have a last look. And there, by the door, on the bottom shelf. Cracked, and the frame damaged, to be sure, but serviceable enough, if dusted. He retrieved the mirror and dusted it with his sleeve. Then he sat it at the back of the shelf, opposite him, sat back on the crate, and shook the storytell out, returning it to its null-setting. There was infinity set into it now. No escape. He looked at the mirror, and the mirror looked at him. He saw no more than he expected to; a street-tough, cynical face, bony and sharp, a little tired around the eyes.

He looked around, alarmed. The oddest sensation, as if he were being watched . . . the feeling faded, returned, then faded again. *Damn, I'm making excuses.*

He held the device in his lap, so he couldn't drop it, and looked into it. This time, the images didn't come swimming into his mind like an unusually-clear dream. There was nothing but the emptiness of the spaces between the wires. He couldn't *see* anything. He knew it was hopeless to force it; it couldn't be forced. He thought to daydream, to relax, the room grew dim a little; was the lantern running out of oil? Infinity. He had not dared to contemplate it before, but it seemed there was just a lot of nothing to it. Nothing. Crap and damnation! It wasn't working at all. He chuckled. The old tales and warnings of the Zlats were just that: old tales. The damn thing wouldn't work, it couldn't . . .

. . . his mind had been wandering, hadn't it? To the storytell. Try again. But there was something odd now. The light was brighter, and he was standing, holding the lantern in his hand, and the storytell in the other. *Must have gone to sleep*, he thought ruefully, and they have caught up with me. The light hurt his eyes, it was too bright. Someone was in the room with him, behind him, keeping him between the device and them. He could sense them, hear them breathing. The door was open and there were more outside. He didn't dare look. His mind felt fogged, dulled by something, a drug. Cretus wasn't sure. Something reeled drunkenly in the adyt of his mind, a vertigo. Had it been that simple? Had it worked? He didn't know and couldn't ask. But he thought, *there's one way to test it, and that's to bet all on one throw. I don't know when I am, but I'll bet they don't want an uncontrolled Cretus among them, whenever they are.*

He felt the fingers holding the storytell, felt the wires against his skin. Sharp and cold. They would cut. He needed something to break down the fog he seemed to be in. It was distracting. He could think, but he wasn't sure he could act.

How many with him? More than one, for sure, in the room. Two definitely. A third? No, they were outside. Two. He could do it, if they were sloppy. He hoped they were.

Cretus squeezed the storytell as hard as he could, feeling the wire cut into his hand, feeling the pain come rippling up his arm like a madman's shout, shooting sparks, and he crumpled it up into a shapeless mass, never to be used again. *To hell with it! If it didn't work, then my only escape's to the streets. And if it did, then transfer's occurred and we don't need the poor bastard who went-within. So long, sucker.*

First these two. Then the door. Cretus lifted one leg and let himself start to fall, away from the door, letting his arm trail behind him, and letting the lantern begin to drop. As he started moving, he started a turn to see his associates. Who would it be? Asc? Shlar? Osper Udle the First Servant?

They came into view, still drunkenly, although the pain of the cut helped clear some of the fog. He saw strangers with elaborate headgear which obscured their heads. But their faces were open, if shadowed and oddly painted. They had expressions of disappointment and disgust, as best he could tell. They thought he was fainting.

Now! He snapped out of the fall and let inertia swing the heavy iron lantern around under him, with a snap, and he threw it at the larger one's face-opening. The range was intimate, he could not miss, even with this clumsy, soft body. *(What the hell? Did I come out in a woman's body?)* The lantern struck, bottom first, direct hit. There was a satisfying, solid sound. That one was down. The other started forward, then hesitated, as if he might try to run. *Run where, you fool? I'm blocking the only way out of this dead end!* Cretus continued his motion, feinted to the side, and the other took the bait. Cretus stepped out, as if to trip him, and the other opened up. He backhandedly threw the crumpled mass of the storytell at the other's genitals. Another hit, but, not a knockdown. The man grimaced, covering himself. Cretus stepped into him, extending his left hand rigidly, stabbing upward at a point just below the breastbone. The man crumpled over his hand, making retching sounds. Cretus chopped the neck exposed by the unsteady helmet falling forwards, hard, once, and as he slid to the stone floor, he flipped him over with his foot. As the body landed, rolling, he stamped on the windpipe, just to be sure. The other man he had hit with the lantern lay silent, crumpled in a corner. Dead? Looked that way. *That's two down.*

The first one didn't appear to have a weapon, and there was no time to rummage through the robes for one. But the other had a small sword in a sheath inside the robe, the hilt protruding through a slit. This Cretus took, straddling the body. By now the ones outside were reacting, sure enough. But now he had a weapon. Let them come!

One came into the storeroom, sword exposed, but Cretus could see he knew little enough of how to use it, and wearing one of those clumsy helmets to boot. The third man was pushing at the door with his free hand as if he anticipated Cretus closing it. Good. Cretus lunged for the door, as if to do just that. The third man pushed harder, opening himself up to Cretus' stroke without even a parry. Over the shoulders of the third, he saw the fourth, who was now looking about in total panic. What had become of the stronghold? Had they turned it into a roadhouse for tipsy wanderers and itinerant peddlers? This last one decided to run for it. *Oh, no. That one must not get away. He'll have to talk.* Cretus stepped over the body blocking the doorway, and started after him. The man had discarded his headdress, but had collided with the edge of the jamb leading to a set of stairs in their right position, and was only just now starting up. Seemed old and out of shape. Cretus raced to the stairs, seized a rising foot and pulled. A bulky mass responded, slowly at first, but like all things that fall, swiftly enough in the end. The fourth rolled back into the chamber with no ceremony at all.

Him Cretus rolled over, straddled, and laid the edge of the sword across the soft, jowly throat.

Cretus grinned down at the old man, jerking the sword suggestively, watching the dull edge indent the skin of the neck.

"Yes, it's dull, but even a fool can cut with a dull edge if he pushes hard enough."

The old man shook his head, apparently not understanding his words. They had sounded muddled, unreal, even to himself.

The old man said, shakily, "Who are you?"

"Cretus, of course! Now I don't care who you are. But I want to know when this is."

"When?"

"When! Is this place called Cucany, in Incana?"

The old man nodded.

"What year is it? I know it's been years by the look of the hats you wear."

"The year is that of the Korsor*."

"Does anyone number years sequentially?"

"Records are kept and years are marked as being so many from notable events, such as the assumption of a new Phanet, or a widespread natural event, or a war."

"I am Cretus, but I do not know what a Phanet is. Therefore the office came after me. How long have Phanets ruled Incana?"

"A long time, longer than I could say. Centuries, many. That is very far back, more than two thousand years."

"You knew about Cretus, but you do not know how long you've waited?"

"All I know is what I have read, been told, and seen. Cretus is known all over Aceldama; all men know Cretus."

"How is it that the *Skazenache* did not change any in that time?"

"The artifact? I do not know, save that it is said that it was handled only during the beholdings; at any rate, it doesn't appear to tarnish or rot. We do not know how to operate it, so it has been handled carefully . . ."

"A lot of good that's come to. I closed it, permanently. If you live to return to this place, come get it and melt it down; it's a valuable metal, pure like gold, but harder and it takes hell's own fires to melt it."

Cretus relaxed, stood up from the old man. He said, "Now lead me out of here. There were four of your hoodheads down here. Where are the others?"

The old man struggled to prop himself up on his elbows. "The others?"

"The rest of you. The guards, the attendants. You people don't go far without them. If you waited a millennium for a man from the past, it's a good bet you're not common folk. So where are they?"

* Part of a fifteen-year cycle which equated with a fifteen-month year. The Aceldaman calendar was solar, matched to the star-groupings visible along the plane of the ecliptic. The small moon was ignored.

While the old man stumbled, trying to make up his mind, Cretus allowed himself to relax a little, for the first time. *Now, this was going correctly, indeed. I come to the future, whenever the hell it is, and instead of steely men of power I meet priestly mumbo-jumbo and incompetents. Damn! They probably need me more than they did . . . then. Yesterday? An hour ago? Centuries, he had said. That he did. More than two thousand years! Well enough. This body seems young, a little soft, male now that I care to notice it; it will stand hardening, and tempering to suit my style. And then, why then, we'll do it again, only this time we'll do it right, won't we, dear. We won't ever let us get tangled in a million threads again, oh, no. This time they'll feel the whip and the boot. They all want country villas and the love of nubile mistresses, but the only love they'll discover will be the kiss of the lash.*

The old man said, now standing, "There was a servant in the refectory above, at the head of the stairs. In the dining hall proper, there were off-worlders, of which you were once one. They should still be sleeping; they were drugged. What will you do with me?"

Cretus indicated the stairs with the point of the sword. "You can earn my pleasure by showing me the door out of Cucany. I was on my way to leave before, I believe, but I was interrupted."

"You will leave Incana, my lord?"

"Ombur lacked the concern of scope to carry out any program. Nomads! Worthless! Incana lacked will. What do they now call the land east of here, facing the Inner Sea?"

"Intance."

"I do not know the name." Cretus said it in an ordinary tone, but the old man, Bedetdznatsch, did not miss the hatred in his eyes, nor the lurid flame that lurked there. He thought, *To what purpose we have brought this demon to life again I cannot fathom. But he must be controlled, or killed outright. There is nothing in this world, this time, which would within him restrain him. If there ever was. He will build something he wants in this time, but he'll pull down the whole world to do it. If he'd walk out of here and put his wits up against the whole world, he'd have to be supremely confident or crazy . . . he had done it before, so went the legends.* The thought made Bedetdznatsch half-crazy with fear. But another thought intruded. *There's one consolation if we can kill him. Control is out of the question. And that's that he's cut off his escape route by destroying the artifact. Cretus is mortal, now, and we can rid the world of him for good. And let the past remain with the past. We want no saviors and changers!*

Cretus relaxed some more. *This was going to be simple. The old man was terrified, and slow to boot. He could do this half-asleep.*

Then something curious happened. Cretus saw himself raise the sword, to look at it. He had not done it, but there it was. He tried to stop it, but he suddenly felt he couldn't control the movement of his limbs; there was resistance. He staggered, and tried to keep an eye on the old man, who had noticed that something was amiss, but was still indecisive. He fell back heavily against the wall, still fighting for control, and now he heard from far away, somewhere deep in his mind, another set of voices, memories, something rapidly rising to the surface, emerging, parting. . . .

Meure Schasny found himself standing against a damp wall in a cellar, holding a sword, facing a man he remembered as Bedetdznatsch, who was looking at him with an expression of stark terror. Schasny tried to speak, stammered out, "How did I get here? Where are the others?"

To answer him, Bedetdznatsch turned and bolted up the stairs madly, robes flapping.

Schasny stood where he was, looking at the sword as if he'd never seen one. He hadn't actually seen a real sword before, and this one had blood on it. He felt unreal, drugged, half-stupefied, and when his mind wandered a little, he heard a voice inside him, speaking urgently, in words he could barely understand. The walls swung unsteadily. It seemed important somehow, but the words were in the way. He probed at it, but to no result; he relaxed and inwardly turned away from it, and then it came, pure ideas that something strung into words for him, like remembering a dream.

"STOP FIGHTING ME. YOU IDIOT! GIVE ME BACK MOTOR CONTROL! I/WE HAVE TO CATCH THAT OLD MAN SO WE CAN GET OUT OF HERE!"

Meure's skin crawled. He knew he was going crazy. He ventured, timidly, *Who are you? What are you? Are you me?*

This time the ideas came clearer, and he started moving toward the stairs, seemingly against his will, or *around* it, that seemed the more accurate word.

"That's right, relax a little, let me help you run!" Meure sensed an urgency to the odd voice, and a sense of truth in it, so he did as it suggested, feeling at the same time an impossible sense of separation-yet-unity with the odd, harsh voice, that spoke in his own recalled timbres and rhythms. Like a cinema, a newscast, where a speaker was orating powerfully, but in another language, and there was a lag, while the translator caught up with the sense of it, all the time the original figure mouthing wildly on the screen, waving his arms, spittle fly-

ing, urging what unnamed multitudes to what unknown deeds of valor or atrocity. He felt himself move, but he had nothing to do with it:

"Good, now. There's a lot to tell, but first we have to get out of this pile. They are going to kill you, do you know? You will want to live, and I, dear, have a most inordinate desire to remain corporate. But later. You've released enough control now, so I'm going to put you to sleep for a while. Then we'll get acquainted. You won't like it, but neither do I, and neither one of us can do anything about it." Meure felt comfortable and reassured. The delayed, lagging sense of meaning carried an undertone of a sharp assessment of facts, and realistic plans of action. On that note, he faded out.

Cretus flexed his muscles, and made a motion like brushing cobwebs from his eyes. He thought, swiftly, *Didn't work quite rightly, did it? Well, no cure for that. First things first. That old buzzard will be raising the alarm even now while I stop to explain things to this mooncalf. Well, I'll show him some paces, now, and put this soft body through some changes.*

Cretus bounded up the stairs two at a time, pausing at the top only to be sure it was the same, and that no additional passages had been hewn since he had come down this way . . . how many years ago? He felt the edges of the boy's own memories, and found nothing. He had no memory of coming down the stairs. Cretus ran down the passageway, passed through a small cookroom, right. This had been the dungeons before. And into a larger common room beyond. Now he stopped and looked around, for there were changes. A lot of changes, in fact, the common room hardly looked the same at all. And there were a lot of strangers in it. He looked them over carefully . . . there was only one High Klesh present, a girl, a Haydar by the look of her, and . . . Cretus' skin crawled. First-folk! The creators. Strange oaths flickered through his mind like summer lightning: *Hell's highest demons! Valdflar the Oathbreaker! Sammar, who lied and polished the cobblestones of the underworld. What did they here?*

Nothing looked right in this room. All these people were asleep, but at odd positions that said they were down fast . . . probably drugged . . . yes, that would explain why the boy had no memory of the stairs. Why drugged? It all began connecting. No time to waste, though. And he'd have to talk to one of them. There was a seasoned-looking man among the company, with gray hair, and the features of no identifiable breed. Cretus hesitated, weighing choices. He didn't trust mixers at all, but even less did he trust Haydars, and Lermen would be useless. This old man, now, he looked like a native.

Cretus walked around the table, noting a young Ler sprawled on the floor, and stretched out on the bench, a smallish, white-furred creature he was unfamiliar with. He stood beside the one he had selected, and started to touch him. Then he stopped. *No. Not a mixer, first contact. I don't know what he is, therefore I don't know how he'll react. Now this Haydar girl, I know what she'll do. That's the virtue of having knowable types: we can adopt a known position from the start.*

Cretus turned and touched the girl lightly. Like all her kind, she was spare and stringy to the touch, her flesh being mostly muscle and tendon. She also seemed to be the one least drugged. The eyelids moved, wandered, opened. Closed, then opened again. The girl looked around, then to Cretus. The expression on her face suggested relief at first, but something must have tripped her hair-trigger hunting perceptions, for her expression rapidly changed to one of fear. *Whatever she had done with this one, there was someone else looking out of the eyes, now, setting the muscles of the face differently. He knew that, could feel it. He also knew that Haydars perceived all moving things that were alive as either co-hunters, or meat. And if co-hunters, then there were leader and led. It was all fairly simple. He knew what to do.*

He spoke first, "We are trapped and must escape this place of stones to continue the hunt. I know you to be a Haydar of the ancient High Klesh, one who does not mix the flesh, and I know you to be a noblewoman of high resolve, therefore I ask your good arm and eye, that our enemies may feel the thunderbolt. Is it to be so?" And suiting action to word, he gently put the point of the sword at her throat.

Tenguft swallowed, and said, haltingly, "I cannot deny one who invokes strong bonds in the language of the dead, that is spoken no more on this sad world, save by the initiates and the high. Are you a demon? They said. . . ."

"I am not a demon, although doubtless many would think me so. Come with me, then. There will be many of the helmeted ones to break through."

"These others must go also."

"There is need for haste. We cannot guide such a large party, especially those not willing to fight, or unable."

She shook her head, with great effort. "No. They must go. I have sworn a bond on their safety. I am responsible."

"Then I will speak of secret things, that the wisewoman of the Haydar see in the firelight by the bones of their mother's left hand: I am Cretus and I have returned to reclaim my world. I see that you still obey that custom from the deeps of time; I read it in your face. Four accompanied this body to the chamber below, who were to capture me or kill me. They failed, but I did not succeed, either. One escaped me, and is now spreading the tale, recruiting his armsmen. There is no way out of this chamber but up, and we must assume they hold it now. Can these fight?"

"I do not know. They are offworlders and Firstfolk from beyond the stars. The one with the gray hair is an embasse, and he may not be attacked."

"Not good. It will be hard, this way."

"You invoke a force I cannot disobey; yet I will not leave these. It is honorable to die in such circumstances."

That was that. No point in forcing her further. Haydar who survived the trials of adolescence would no longer have a fear of death. It was just another option.

"Demon or Cretus, I respect your obligations. But know that I am a Hierarch of the Ludi, that I have seen Sara Damassou with my own eyes, and walked along the Falaise."

"If you are Cretus, of whom it is spoken, you are not of this world but of the past. Who was your master in the trial of truth?"

"Tarso Emi Koussi."

She had tested him, and he had given an answer that rang of the far past, and men who stood mighty in the legends of the People. And Sara Damassou, the only city the Haydars had ever lived in, the Forbidden One, the Holy Place, was no more and none knew where it had been.

"E-eyeh! Let it be so! Let us awaken these strangers and depart this place. It has come as was told to me, and I would have you speak of these things with my people. It is said of old that the Haydar were high in the councils of Cretus, and would that it be so again."

"Indeed."

Together, they set to the task of awakening the others, then, some easily, others with more difficulty, but after a time, all were conscious again, and Tenguft had explained the situation to them all. And not once had Cretus felt anything from his unwilling host. He tensed himself slightly, hoping that he would not until they could get out of this castle. Then there would have to be some arrangement made, without doubt, although there was no precedent for it anywhere in Cretus' memory.

8

"Unless we live in the present, we do not live at all."
—A.C.

WHEN THEY WERE all awake, Cretus explained briefly, borrowing the words and speech from Meure's memories; he spoke with wry authority and a fine sense of irony which left no doubt in any of their imaginations what he might do. And the situation was clearly as he described it; no one could argue against the necessity of escaping the castle immediately.

Clellendol regained his thief's ways, and assessed the situation they found themselves in. He observed, to Cretus-Meure, "We are far down in the rock. Then we shall have to go back up the narrow way, which they can challenge, no doubt."

Cretus thought a moment before answering. At last, he said, "They can. And I know no secret adyts, at least not near this level, such as we might use. And I assume that the inhabitants have delved more since my days. More, certain passages I remember may be blocked up, or be useless. No, the way out is not in stealth. But the narrow ways can work for us, too. And it also may be that they will not risk a direct confrontation; they do not know what I can do—or can't."

"You have lost the ability to read the future, that is true."

"I used it seldom, even in the first. My power was in decision and persuasion, in risktaking, and in minimizing losses. My opponents were dogmatists and safety-firsters. When I had the power to do so, I crushed them; when I did not, I manipulated their weaknesses until I could neutralize them, and deal with them at leisure. And besides, reading the future is uncomfortable; we do not have the reference for it, to understand what we see, so it is deadly; that is why I stopped early. And because also . . . that I saw that the act itself was just another system to build surety, as was theirs; so I returned to the ways I knew best. And what I have seen here so far gives me hope that we can get out of here without too much trouble."

Then he indicated that they should begin, and set out, up the stairs and passageways of Dzoz Cucany. Cretus-Meure led the way, and Tenguft covered the rear at his direction. Close behind Cretus came Clellendol and Flerdistar. At first, the Vfzyekhr walked with Tenguft, but as they entered the maze of tunnels, it unobtrusively moved forward to stay close to Cretus. It remained silent, and made no gestures or noticeable motions, yet it fell in behind Cretus quickly.

For a time, they followed a route that was the exact reverse of the way they had come; Clellendol could verify this: the memory matched the present exactly. But soon, Cretus turned off into a darkened section, which began to change level rapidly. This passage seemed abandoned, judging from rubble and debris scattered along the floor. Their only light was a lantern carried by Flerdistar.

Clellendol ventured, "This air is live; flowing. There is a draught. Therefore the passage is open, even though it seems closed-off, disused."

Cretus-Meure answered, half to himself, "I searched his mind and found that the way you came to the Durance Level had not intersected the Grand Corridor. This way is the ancient Guards way, and through it we should emerge at the main door. They will be looking for us higher up."

"Why? If I were them, I would strive to contain a party such as ours as far down as possible."

"They will think that I wish to hunt them down, and take possession of Cucany. They have built the higher structures, and so they will wish to meet me on their ground. It does not occur to mem that I only wish to get out of Cucany, and indeed all Incana, as fast as possible. By the time that falls into their minds, we will be at the door . . . this structure was made to keep invaders out, not escapees in, once they get to the door."

"Why didn't you just leave, before?"

"I had become more than a leader; I was a talisman for their continued survival. So they kept me busy, filled my hours with issues, loaded me down with hangers-on, sycophants, toadies, counsellors of the Reach of Incana, and the like. It is that way with all power; you set forces in motion which later come to direct you, begin controlling your actions . . . I saw that they would not move beyond Kepture, once they had it consolidated. That was all they wanted; the rest could come later, if their successors thought it worthwhile. They kept to the fine line, and by that I gradually became a prisoner . . . so I found this way, which is the trying of another time. Perhaps the situation now will be a matrix more readily bent to the original goal."

From the back of the line came a sibilant sound, from the Haydar girl. They fell silent, immediately.

Tenguft came forward to join Cretus-Meure and Clellendol, her hawk profile casting predatory shadows on the ancient stone walls. Now that the loyalty problem was temporarily solved and there was no contest between her will and Cretus', she had entered totally into the web of action. Now she whispered, but it was the oddest whisper Cretus had ever heard, for it had almost no volume, but it carried perfectly and none of the words were distorted. She said, "Above us, in the stone, men running, all together, in step. From behind, then overhead, and no longer do I hear them."

Cretus looked upward at the low ceiling, as if trying to see through it, remembering, trying to recover the layout of Dzoz Cucany. He said, after a moment, "It seems too early for them to reinforce the gate, but it could be possible . . . I wouldn't have given the old one enough credit to think that fast."

Clellendol ventured, "Perhaps he could have turned over matters to an underling with more initiative."

"Perhaps. In any event, the way we will come should lead us to the entry-corridor; and there will be only a few steps to the door."

"If things have not changed there, too, in a thousand years or more," added Morgin. To this Cretus did not respond.

There was more of the passage, much more going up and down, more of the narrow ways favored by the castledwellers of Incana, in many places partially blocked by rubble. In one place they had difficulty getting through, and they had to move some blocks fallen from the ceiling. Instead of leaving them lie, however, Tenguft carefully placed the moved blocks back on the pile of rubble, balancing them so they would fall at the slightest disturbance.

The passage now ascended abruptly through a series of short, debris-filled stairwells set at odd angles, and terminated at a small landing fronting on a panel which appeared to slide in a set of grooves in the lintel, and the sill. There was no handle on this side, and the dust on the floor gave no evidence of ever having been disturbed.

Cretus now whispered, "This appears to have been rebuilt since my day."

Morgin observed, "And not designed for exit, either."

Clellendol said, "Hst! Let me study this! Once we start to open it, it will have to be fast. That slab will make a lot of noise."

They would have continued to discuss the problem, save for the fact that at that moment a dull rumbling sounded up the stairwell behind them. Tenguft turned sharply, her mouth open, teeth gleaming. She drew a knife from beneath the folds of her robe. For a time there were some indistinct noises from below, but they soon faded.

Cretus asked, "Accident?"

Tenguft shook her head. "No. Something comes. Not soldiers. They rattle, and tread heavily. There was no metal-sound, but something live was moving after the blocks fell, I fear."

Cretus said, "Tenguft, you said you heard footfalls behind us and above us, but not ahead, yes?"

"It ended above us, and a little ahead. Then there was a sliding sound, like stone grating on stone, like a great millwheel. Be still!"

They all stood rigidly, not daring to breathe. Tenguft leaned out over the stairwell, ear turned down. Then she turned back, her pupils dilated to empty black pits and the muscles of her face working with fear.

Cretus shook her roughly, and whispered sharply, "What do you hear, hunts-woman?"

"In the darkness, something moving, making a shuffling sound, I hear the pad of its feet, the brushing of its fur on the stones, O *bi leberim, ao Dehir sherda!*" Her agitation was so great she lapsed at the end into the secret hunt-language of the Haydars.

Cretus turned to Morgin. "Speak, Embasse. What does this mad-woman say!"

Morgin drew his own knife. "She says a Korsor comes. If you have weapons, prepare to use them now, for we must kill it, or be killed by it."

Cretus exclaimed, "Ai! Now I know; somewhere they opened a cage, to let a night-devil track us. That is why these pits have no exit from this side. Prepare for madness and fight for your lives!"

At the bottom of the stairs the darkness moved, and something immense and heavy and densely black solidified into form, a thing so large that when it turned the last curve of the stairs, the front seemed halfway up while the rear was still in darkness. It neither waited nor threatened, but climbed the stairs like a destroying demon, and in an instant was among them. They all shrank back to the edges of the landing, seeing only blurred impressions of parts of the creature: something heavy and strong, black-furred. There were eyes, and stabbing teeth, and claws.

Cretus it sought, and Cretus it found immediately, following its nose. Cretus raised the blade, although he knew it to be futile; his blade would only prick it. And the Vfzyekhr stepped within the circle of the monster's embrace and laid its hand on the throat of the Korsor, and the beast stopped.

Now they could see it: the tiny Vfzyekhr standing before the Korsor, a mountain of darkness. Bearlike it was in general shape, but there were many differences. It was in build as supple as a panther, and there was no fat on it whatsoever. The fur was a dull, flat black with no shine at all, and the muzzle had none of the doglike heaviness of the true bear, but was smooth and tapered. The skull was low, spreading out behind the brow ridges, but it was large and spacious. The eyes were set deep under shelved ridges of bone, and were seemingly covered by an iridescent film which showed shifting colors in the lamplight like oil on a wet roadway. Its presence and scent filled the landing: a pungent, musky odor from its body, and a raw-meat odor from its jaws.

The Vfzyekhr slowly turned, still touching the Korsor, and moved to the sliding panel. Allowing its touch to slide down the throat to the belly, still keeping contact, the Vfzyekhr caused somehow the Korsor to stand on its hind legs, and catch the edges of the panel in its claws. Then the panel began to slide open, enough to admit one human at a time. Then the small, white-furred creature slowly led the Korsor back to the stairs.

Cretus recovered first. "Through the door, you idiots! It will turn the Korsor loose!"

On shaking legs they filed from the landing through the slit, into an anteroom, and from there into the great hall, which stood empty. The guard room was immediately to their right, and beyond it, a simple wooden door with a bar across it. They ran to the empty room and slipped the bar from the door. Cretus hurried them out, through the narrow door, into the night. One by one they ran out into the darkness, down the stairs to the ground. There was wind, and a chill in the air.

Tenguft came last to the door, and stood by Cretus. "The furry one is still within with the Korsor."

"What is that little one, that it can stop a Korsor with the touch of the hand?"

"I know it not. The Spsom brought it with them from beyond the stars; it is their pet, or their slave, or perhaps something else we do not understand."

"What are Spsom?"

"A spaceship came. It was theirs. Star-folk they are. And they hunt. They remained behind, in Ombur. My charge was that the little one was to be 'as if people.' It speaks not."

"Shall we leave it? I fear a Korsor, just as you, but I fear more that-which-stops-a-Korsor."

"I cannot. And, I do not know if it can be left." The Vfzyekhr emerged from the guardroom, looked down the grand hall, and then joined them at the entrance. It came to Cretus-Meure and grasped his hand like a small child. Cretus lifted the creature effortlessly, and set it on his hip, cradling it under his arm. He looked down at it and said, "Little one, we are in great debt to you." The Vfzyekhr said nothing, but it held on tightly. Cretus closed the door.

Cretus mused, "I wonder what it did with the Korsor?"

Tenguft answered, "We heard no noise, no cries of pain. Perhaps the Korsor now seeks other prey, for once it tracks, the hunt must culminate. How they pent it up is beyond my scope, but I . . ." She let the sentence trail off, looking sharply at Cretus. Something was wrong.

Cretus-Meure staggered on the last step, and was now looking about in the darkness crazily. The Vfzyekhr squirmed, freed itself, and dropped to the ground, where it took no further notice of what was now obviously Meure Schasny, not Cretus the Scribe.

The others continued walking into the darkness beyond the dim lighting of the porch of Dzoz Cucany. Tenguft took Meure by the elbow, bent and looked closely at his eyes, which were staring blankly into nothing. She said, softly, "Who are you . . . ?"

"Meure . . . I think," he began uncertainly. "I have been asleep, or not here, or something. I don't know. Why are we outside?"

She began, "There was something in the food, that made us dulled. I slept, but when I woke, I could not move of my own will. Then you came back, but it was not you. Another looked out of your eyes, and he named himself Cretus, the one they were trying to bring back. He spoke of things which I know *you* do not know, so that I knew it was not you . . . The others we awakened, and he led us through the stone to the door and we escaped. Now we must leave this place, before they recover and set the Korsor on us again."

"What is a Korsor?"

"You do not remember it, or the slave of the Spsom stopping it?"

"No. It's . . . there is something there, but I can't reach it. Like a dream you know you had, but you can't remember."

"You must remember. You must try; Cretus could remember things from your memory. True, it seemed he had to work at it, but he could recall from your memory how we came through the castle to the place where we were."

"I feel something there, but it's quiet now. I . . . talked with him, once, I remember that. He forced me to . . . then nothing. But now I can't feel him like then. It's like . . . something's wrong with him. There is a presence there, but it's veiled in layers I can't see through."

Tenguft was still carrying her knife openly. Now she grasped the blade and handed it to Meure. "Here. You must take this."

"Why?"

"I consulted the oracle when we were with my people. The vision was strong, not to be denied, one that foreshadowed my footsteps, my every act. I saw it, and could not but live it out."

"Can you not turn aside from a vision?"

"You are an offworlder and not one of the people, therefore I take no offense at your question. I cannot even frame such a question in my mind. To turn from such a revealed course. . . . I dare not force those-who-see to become manifest, to clothe themselves in flesh; they change. But see: I saw my way, and I walked in that path, and now I am free of it, this minute. I did not know it before, but I knew it would come. Now I am free. Now you must go your way."

"What is my way?"

"To meet Cretus the Scribe. I have done that which I was constrained to do; thus and thus. So it was shown to me, and so I have done. But that I may be something more than a wind that has blown you to a strange house without warmth of fire, or to evil, I press my own knife to you. Take it! I took it in tongs living from the fire, and quenched it with my own hands, and as its light faded I laid upon it and my spear deep secrets only I know; therefore it will aid you. More I cannot give, and remain what I have been and am to be." She breathed deeply, and stood erect and tall against the light from the dark bulk of the castle, and her eyes were darker than the night.

Meure took the proffered knife by the hilt; it was made of many strips of leather wound around the tang of the blade. A rude weapon, one that had doubtless been used before. He looked at it intently for a long moment, almost as if he hoped some of what she put into it might speak to him. The spirits remained silent. Meure looked up, and felt a chill air moving against his face.

He said, "I know now much of which you have spoken. But I do not know why. As you said, to meet Cretus. So, then. I have met him, and it answers no questions. I do not know what he wants."

"Nor do I, beyond escaping from Cucany."

"Then you will return to Ombur?"

"Yes. We will go that way, and what will come to be will be."

"What of the rest of us?"

"I was commanded to bring you here and return you safely within the limits of my power. Thus I will do."

"And me?"

"You are no longer one of them, and I cannot protect you. You must become a hunter on your own account."

Meure felt a shiver pass along his body, one that ended in a sudden spasm of laughter. "Fine, then. I will take my first step. I will walk with you and your party for a time. But let us be gone from Cucany, and this whole land of towers and empty places. I sense that this spirit from the far past needs at least to meet some people from the present." So saying, he began walking into the darkness, where waited the others.

Tenguft followed him, and only one thing did she say: "It is said that of old Cretus was no prophet of the waste places, but one who went straightly into the press and the throng."

Meure said back over his shoulder, "And the Haydar? Are you a throng?"

She answered, curiously submissive, "We are but bands of hunters on the face of the wide world."

"Are there cities on this world?"

"In Chengurune the Great, and in Cantou, there are said to be cities . . . I know only Kepture. In this land are settled places, ports, trade-junctions, forts and castles."

"What about Glordune, the forth continent?"

"There are no cities in Glordune. But there is a place in Kepture where many gather."

"Where?"

"At the Mouth of Vast are the lands of the Lagostomes, and it is said that by the river docks can be found the sweepings and ends, and scraps of all peoples."

"Can we go there?"

"You can, if you will, but I will not take you. They are a vile people.

We hunt them, and all true men of Kepture strive to keep them pent in the Low Country."

"Do they have a city?"

"Their whole land is city. There is nothing like it anywhere else. Ask of the Embasse; he comes and goes as he pleases."

At the end, she had seemed offended that he had shown any interest at all. And she had recommended him to Morgin with the distaste one would use for someone who performed a vital, but to her, a completely degrading act. But they were a long way from the mouth of Vast, and had more immediate problems for the moment. Meure felt a stirring in himself that he could not quiet. A stirring that was, for the moment, only a potential; but he wondered, at the same, if perhaps he would wind up there, whether he willed or not.

"The word of a Magus is always a falsehood. For it is a creative word; there would be no object in uttering it if it merely stated an existing fact in nature. The task of a Magus is to make his word, the expression of his will, come true. It is the most formidable labor the mind can conceive."

—A.C.

THE GREAT RIVER of Kepture, the Vast, began its journey to the sea toward the west, from the east of the continent, in a range of hills separating Incana from the land to the east, Intance. Except for the hills which separated Incana from Intance, the Vast was the border separating Incana from all other lands, as it passed westward, turned south, and finally ran back to the east for a shorter space before turning once more to the south and its delta between the two landmasses comprising Kepture. Within a frame of reference which could survey all known planets, Monsalvat was not a notable world in its landforms, nor was Kepture an impressive continent; likewise, the river Yast set no records. But it was the greatest river on the planet, and in its season struck awe into the Klesh who lived along its banks.

Meure vaguely remembered crossing the river; a greater darkness had passed beneath them as they had flown through the night; there had been nothing below to fix the eye on, no reference: the surface below had darkened, and dropped away, and later rose again into the dry hills of Incana.

Under one's own power on the surface, however, a viewer saw the great river of Kepture in different perspectives: from a low barge in the midst of its flow, it stretched away glassily to vague, low shores, or along its length, unbroken to the horizon. There was a current, requiring the bargemen, hybrids of unknown parentage, to take no action. The river was unruffled and wave less, but its calm surface was dark and opaque, and was pocked with upwellings, dimples, curious little whirlpools which appeared and vanished without apparent cause. There was an odor of something long-dead, and the sunlight lent no sparkle to the stagnant surface. It was the very image of a river in Hell.

No one had hindered their departure from Incana; for five days they had walked through an empty, unpopulated land, with the ridges and hills each crowned with a Dzoz of greater or lesser size. The land around them had been vibrant with the messages of heliographs, but they had neither been pursued, harassed, nor stopped. They had reached the river in sight of one of the castles, but such folk as lived along the Great River ignored it, and disregarded the influence of those who lived within.

Passage across the Vast was prohibitively expensive, owing, so the bargemen averred, to the labor of rowing the distance in the absence of wind. On the other hand, passage down the river was free, and should the Ombur bank be handy, they could debark as Circumstances warranted. There was one barge currently in commission, due to leave, and so they boarded it, after bartering some trinkets Flerdistar and Clellendol had apparently hidden. Morgin procured some loaves of stale bread for them, on the strength of his office as Embasse, but without either Prote or Bagman, it was clear Morgin's influence was limited.

As for Tenguft, the bargemen-mongrels kept a respectful distance, but they were not awed by one Haydar. A band might have sent them into the water, howling with fear, but one alone? Let her pass, while they bided their time, for the Great River brought everything to the outcast bargemen.

There was a haze over the double sun, a film that Tenguft said meant rain. Meure sat atop a pile of faggots and watched the sullen flow of the river. The Haydar girl sat at the opposite end, chin on hands folded upon one knee, staring into the distance. The others had left him alone since the incidents at the castle, although Cretus had made no more overt manifestations.

Flerdistar and Clellendol climbed up on the pile beside him. The Ler girl broke the silence first. "Have you had any contact?"

Meure looked at her for a time before answering. "No. Not in so many words. He's there, all right; but not there, too. I think it's an effort for him to control me."

She nodded, as if she understood. "I see . . . that's an experience I have no words for."

Meure smiled, for once, finding her studiousness amusing. "Oh, yes, there aren't any. It's definitely out of the ordinary, rather unspeakable. You know that since he's the outsider, he is invisible to me . . . I mean, I can sense that he's there, but I can't catch any of his thought or memory. But he can see all of mine; I can tell where he's been, what things he's been poking through, because those memories are changed, somehow; as if they had been re-recorded. I suppose in time he could become me if he wanted, but that's not his way."

Clellendol picked up the thought and continued it, "And so Cretus could mimic you so perfectly we'd not know the difference."

"Right. But like I said, that's not his way. He doesn't want to become me."

Clellendol said, "Then you could become him."

"Not that, either. That would produce two Cretuses. I could suppress him entirely then. That's why he hides from me. While he learns."

"Learns what?"

"All about the universe we know, that he doesn't know and never did. Also Time. He wants to know how long it's been."

Flerdistar asked, "Does he know? Do you?"

"No, and no. Only that it's been a very long span of time, and that there's been little or no change in the nature of the Klesh."

She said, "That bothers me; for a long time it was so obvious that I overlooked it, but it's there, none the less. These people seem to remain essentially static, advancing neither politically nor technologically."

Clellendol added, "That and the prevalence of omens and fortune-tellers; they seem to be everywhere, and they also seem to work better than the usual sort one meets. . . . Morgin tells me that it's like that everywhere. The method varies, but the consultation is done and the answers are given. Except when a Prote is being used, the creature the Embasses use for perception and communication."

Flerdistar said, "It would seem we have two things to occupy our attentions, besides the original two—to resolve our old question, and get off this planet."

Meure looked at her incredulously. "You mean you still have those in mind?"

"I could hardly forget them. But the Spsom behavior was not to Clellendol's liking."

Clellendol explained, "It is true that Spsom are essentially carnivorous, and that they hunt. *However* . . . in their natural habitat, they prey on small game, and they are not built for heavy encounters. Moreover, they are inordinately curious, and they seek out Human contacts, the more bizarre the better. That they would stay with the Haydar, while we were off adventuring, makes no sense, especially when they let the Vfzyekhr go with us . . . we don't know exactly what the relationship is between those two races, but they simply don't let them go on their own. Flerdistar reads the past and smells a rat; I read the present and smell another. The Spsom wanted to stay in the same vicinity of the crash site."

Flerdistar finished, "Which means that a Spsom ship will come for us, sooner or later. And as for the other problem, the one we came here to resolve . . . That's not over, either."

"How could you ever hope to revive that, after what you've seen?" Meure stared at the girl blankly.

"All secrets leave their traces. We have always known that things were not as history had them, for us, the New People, but never what the true picture was. I said to you on the ship that we finally traced the echoes of that discontinuity to this world. We *know* that the truth was on this world at one time; and we *know* that historical truths like that leave traces stamped into the very gesture-language, of the people who hide them, willingly or no. And at the last, as a reader of the past, I can feel the answer just as certainly as you can feel the presence of Cretus. It is here." Here she gestured with a hand all around the barge and the leaden, brassy water of the sullen river. "Here, all around us, if I could but get it out."

Meure said, "Which of our problems do you think will resolve itself first?"

Clellendol said, "Something on this world suppresses change. There are known rates of change for Humans, wherever you find them. When change does not occur, you look for the mechanism causing that lack. I am very concerned about it, because it implies a power on a planet-wide scale. It could be a natural effect, in which case we should not want to blunder into it. On the other hand, it might be something shaped by design. Then we are dealing with an entity, or entities. There is much here that strains probabilities; the lack of change, the success of omens, the isolation by stressed space, of the planet, preventing contact or effective integration with other worlds. And, like you and the Liy Flerdistar, while I can see that my problem's there, I can't resolve it any better than the two of you."

Meure felt his way along another tack. "About change, among Humans; I am not conscious of any lack of change . . ." He realized as he said it that he had just demonstrated the validity of Clellendol's concept. "At least, I know of no great changes in the people I'd heard of. And remember, I come from a colonial world. We had change, in the New Lands Program."

Clellendol answered, "So Tancred is a pioneer world, settled a few generations back, still being exploited. That I know. What about this fact, that for every new world Humans discover and exploit, they abandon three others, either to Ler, or some non-Human sentient, or in some cases, not all that rare, to the wind. Change is going on indeed, on a grand scale. Now Humans do everything right, but it doesn't work for them."

Meure laughed, "But it's right there: that we're right, according to your lights. Maybe we shouldn't be!"

"We are now discussing sanity itself," exclaimed Flerdistar.

Meure didn't answer her, but instead abruptly turned his head at an odd angle, and then looked about the landscape with a piercing glance quite at odds with his usual relaxed manner. Then he seemed to shudder, and resumed his normal appearance. Still, he kept silent, with his head cocked, as if listening.

After a time, he said, "Yes, that's right, though; it is no great secret. We have long envied the Second People and their ways. You get a steadier progression without the horrific ups and downs we seemed so attracted to in our history. And we always knew that *you* considered Humans primitive, uncontrolled, rude, unpotentialized. So gradually we quieted down, stabilized ourselves, concerned ourselves with homely things close to us. I had thought it was working."

Clellendol said, "That's the trouble with an interplanetary civilization. The consciousness of the far islands is lost. That's why there is a colonization program . . . but it has not halted the decline; only slowed it. What has been done has not been enough."

Flerdistar interrupted, "Was that Cretus, just now?"

"Yes. He's been listening to us. He left me a message to deliver to the two of you to add to your list of things to worry about. Clellendol: you said something was suppressing change here and isolating Monsalvat. Consider this—that we got in, and that a chain of circumstances leads from outside this stellar area right to Cretus."

"Cretus said that."

"Yes, and that he has his suspicions as well; that is why he is staying as hidden as he can. He says I screen him. From what, he doesn't say.

But he said that his troubles in his original life commenced when he began to suspect the true nature of what Monsalvat harbors." Meure paused, and added, "I really don't like what he is suggesting at all. If it's true, none of this has been accidental; but not one of us knows to what purpose. Not him either."

Flerdistar asked, "What is it Monsalvat harbors?"

"I don't know. *He* doesn't know, although I sense that he has seen much more that we would like to know as well. It was not on Dawn, with the Klesh when they were made in the deeps of time, it did not come here with them. Somehow, they awakened it, here. But it was not of Dawn."

"Cretus has seen Dawn? Impossible. He can't have been an Original; Morgin talked about him, and Cretus appeared historically after the naming of lands."

"He looked. The thing that caused the transfer of him into me; with that he could see other places, other times. . . . He looked back to see where the Klesh had come from."

"Then he knows what we have come to hear." There was unmistakable triumph in the Ler girl's voice.

Meure smiled. "Perhaps. But until certain questions are resolved, he is as cautious of you as he is of Monsalvat."

Flerdistar assumed a more haughty posture, and said, "Neither you nor Cretus know to what lengths we would go to attain the final resolution."

Meure stood now, and looked down on Flerdistar and Clellendol as from a great height. And at that moment, they could not be sure which persona was speaking, for he said, "And you do not know what things Cretus has already done, over lesser issues than this one. He who was once Lord of Incana and All Kepture, come there from the street-wisdom of mongrelhood, will protect his refuge. And demand not of him, that he not demand more of you in return. For the moment, leave Cretus and your secret alone; he is capable of setting forces in motion we cannot imagine, the less control."

Clellendol said, with some heat, "He is mortal. Cut him, and he bleeds; strike him, and he pains. If worse comes to worse, he can be killed."

Meure now said, with chilling assurance, "Do not make the mistake of imagining either one of you could measure up to that." Then he softened a little, and said, almost apologetically, "You must not force him to activate before his time. Let it be! He knows what he must do."

Meure turned, climbed down, and went to stand by the side of the barge, looking out over the greasy reflections on the water. Flerdistar said to Clellendol, in an undertone, "It is clear to me what this Cretus wants; do you see it?"

Clellendol answered her, "This whole thing has been arranged to get Cretus the Scribe off Monsalvat. By whom or what, I cannot imagine, but it must not be permitted to happen. He is a unique type—a master of historical currents."

"Just so. And not only can he ride those currents, but he can, so it appears, steer them, and probably create them as well. He was schooled deeply in the barbarities of Klesh existence. The Humans will follow him into blood and iron again."

"It would, so to speak, solve their problem."

"Probably. But create others. This Cretus is an upsetter, and I want none of it; we have learned to do without them. I agree; Cretus must not be permitted to leave this earth; yet there are secrets we'd have of him before it comes to that, isn't it so?"

Clellendol turned his face, so that there would be no gesture accompanying the words, an innately Ler mannerism,* but his agreement was spoken: "Zha' armeshero," which was an affirmative that left little doubt, if any.† Clellendol would array against Cretus all that he possessed of the Ninth House of Thieves.

Now the great burden of Cretus pressed down heavily upon Meure, so that there was a darkness and a weight behind his eyes; and Cretus, who saw all things through the eyes and nerves of Meure, also felt these things and felt in his heart a kindliness, an affection, for one who had been given a burden unasked and undeserved, but yet bore it as bravely as he could according to his lights. And, bodiless invader though he was, Cretus contrived a way to speak more directly with him who bore him, as though they were separate.

This speech, if speech it could be called, passed faster than could be done with words, for it was made of raw thoughts, as were in men's minds before they invented words to symbolize and transmit them. Yet it was speechlike, in that it was directed thought, consciously shaped, not merely unedited and uncontrolled mind-stuff. And there was much that Cretus did not say.

---

*Ler gestures were muted, where present at all.

†Singlespeech, approximately, "It is indeed (most)-agreed." Past Indicative Passive Participle, superior comparison. Zha' is emphatic.

Of the many griefs of the Klesh he spoke in summary, but did not dwell upon those things; likewise he spoke of the brutal weeding which had made the original Klesh pure racial types in the beginning. And of the time before that, when the pre-Klesh had been just orindary Humans, men and women, the Klesh only said, "That is now forgotten and unknown, since we cannot reach it—the Time Before the Beginning. Of that we know not, therefore we care not."

And when they had been freed of the Warriors, awaiting the great ships that would take them from the planet Dawn to some new home far away in the stars, they gathered, in their many shapes and colors, and said among one another, "We were slaves without hope of salvation, *since we were slaves for the sake of slavery*, not even for a real purpose, however shabby. Freedom, we had ceased to dream of it. Now, we are free, and though we were made pureblooded through no will of our own, pure we are, and pure we remain, and pure we shall remain by our own hands, for it was the mixed men who were weak and allowed the corrupt Warriors to enslave them and mold their forms like wax. Thus they set chains on them. Thereby let each cleave to his and her own kind; let it be so until the end of time!" And it was so. And they then all spoke strong and blood-curdling oaths that never again, whatever befell them, would any Klesh, even the least as the strongest, endure what had befallen them in the pits of the Warriors.

They were taken to the planet the Mixed men called Monsalvat. And they also learned to call it Aceldama, a place to bury strangers, learning that word from the awed and incredulous administrators who came to guide them, meaning well, no doubt, but failing as quickly as those who might have meant evil. There, some flourished, even as others weakened, faded, and their lines failed and their lights went out and they were no more. Most of all they needed, and longed for, stern teachers of men; but the Ler feared them, thinking of the Warriors, no doubt, and of optative revenges by the Klesh. And just so the men, who were from the stars, feared them, seeing their tumults and the strife, and so both drew back, missing much, and thereby withdrew altogether. And so abandoned, the Klesh made do, and settled down to the long night.

In which, they suspected, they were not alone. Monsalvat was an old world; of that there was no lack of ample geological evidence, as discovered by the star-men, and the Klesh saw no reason to doubt their conclusions, for they flew through space, did they not? But nowhere were artifacts found, no ruins, nor any trace of any kind that speaking creatures had ever walked its surface. Here was an ideal planet, and one that echoed to the boundless silences of time throughout the ages, its native life forms few and bearing no trace of evolutionary relationship to one another. A world so old that the first explorers said that Monsalvat had known flowering plants before there was a Solar System. And there was no one.

But there was something to the clarity of the air, ripples just below the threshold of perception, motions seen out of the corners of one's eyes, lights in the forest, and the undoubted success of fortune-tellers and omen-readers. Here, the oracle spoke. And there was a brooding presence that could not be denied, even though the form it took could neither be defined nor perceived, a something older than the darkness, older than man, perhaps older than time itself . . . It seemed not to notice them that they could tell, and they hoped not to notice it, or them. And for a time, one could forget it, but always, in the back of the mind, there never failed the suspicion that one was being watched, and always the sensation was strongest at the most intense moments; so that in the midst of a great battle, when the horns called and the swords struck fire against their cutting edges, so it was that the heroes always paused, at the last moment before the battle-lust took them, and saluted, with their raised weapons, to the one unseen who was not to be named, and then fell to their deadly work.

Now in the beginning, the Klesh perceived that the type called Zlat could see farther than any of them, and they accorded them special place on Monsalvat; the advisers and counselors of chiefs and princes they became. But their service quickly separated them from one another, and their confidants cared little for the maintenance of any tribe save their own, so that in the course of their service, the Zlats faded slowly as a race, having to undertake long and perilous journeys for a bride or husband. Many had no descendant, and others mingled with other Klesh types, so that in the end they faded, and vanished. That some in that end stooped to evil deeds and false counsel cannot be denied, but however it was, they passed from the world, and were forgotten, with their secrets. Save in a few forgotten places, the Zlat Rada was gone.

Those few pockets lingered on a little longer, but in time, they too became single wanderers, itinerant fortune-tellers and omen-readers, and so mixed with half-breeds, renegades and worse, and so ended their line.

A generation after the end that was thought, there was born a boy, who by his marks was pure Zlat. His life was a chancy one, and soon he was orphaned by the incessant wars and mayhems of Monsalvat; he was eventually taken in by an old woman who claimed to be also a Zlat, and who possessed the artifact which lent them their far-sight, the *Skazenach*, the wire tangle through which the user could see places and times distant from himself, seemingly in the guise of stories and epics told on the settings of the *Skazenach** made by an ancient tradition.

The old woman took the boy to the fens of Yast, in the far delta of the great river of Kepture, where they made a living smoking meats, and the old woman cast fortunes for the nomads who came down from the heights of Ombur. Originally, the boy was sickly, and good for little in the camps of the nomads save for fetching water, and so he came to be called, in the common speech of those parts, Sano Hanzlator, which is bad Singlespeech, but which means, more or less, "Waterboy Last-Zlat."†

In time, the old woman's time came, and she died, having instructed him in the ways of the *Skazenach*; and she taught him in secret, and swore him to secrecy also, for the *Skazenach* was the most powerful of all oracles, and the possessor of one would be hounded for reading until he had no life left of his own, whatsoever.

Now the boy was grown almost to manhood, and the sickliness had been replaced by a grim wiriness. He left the delta camps of the nomads, and drifted north, to the great city Yastian, a city grown exceedingly large, a vast mixing-pot where all breeds met and mingled and detestation hung in the air, stronger in its reek than the odor of the swamps. There were bravoes and tarts, ruined beggars and kings, wise men and fools alike, the rich and the educated, the ignorant and the poor. There were also princes and fastidious clerks. Evil was done in the light as well as in the dark, and a single life was worth less than nothing. But being a fetchboy for the fierce nomads, and the letters he had learned of the old woman, and his secret oracle, all stood him well there, and Sano became a scribe, transcribing petitions beside the palace wall.

The boy Sano in the city survived and grew, even prospering after his

---

*The word is distorted Singlespeech, and means, "Betold-things." The correct form is, "maskazemoni nakhon," meaning those things which are spoken of in tales.

†Hanzlator = "last-Zlat" is correct, but Sano for "Waterboy" is the wildest sort of colloqualism. Literally, it would correctly mean, "most waterlike (in action)," an adverbial form.

own fashion, for he was wont to waste nothing and live frugally; and as he grew he came to understand many things from the life of the city in which he was immersed. He came to understand that the great secret, the only one worth knowing, was not that life consisted of haves and have-nots, but that it consisted of doers and seers, the rub being that the seers seemed unable to do, and the doers unable to see. That was the great secret and the division of men, Klesh not the less. And more he saw clearly: that the Klesh would never advance farther than they were at that moment, if they failed to learn that they must cooperate with one another, learn to complement one another, instead of endlessly striving to outdo one another; and that the pride of *Rada* that they took on so readily was but still another trap from which there was in the end no escape, since each remembered the crimes done to all, even to the whole of the past.

Therefore in all his time, he studied, he dreamed, he planned. He looked within, through his *Skazenach*, many times and places, becoming skilled in aiming and directing his thought through the symbolisms of the device. And his aim became no less than to built the Klesh peoples into a great people, such as they could be, but not by mixing them, which they would never countenance, but by constructing a component system of interlocking dependencies, all respected, all needed.

Now in Yastian the City there was a place somewhat below the palace where orators were wont to go and speak to the people, and to that place Sano went to deliver his message to whomever might give ear. When at last he had spoken, many of those there mocked him, saying, "Sano the Scribe will deliver us from ourselves. And even as now. "Whereupon he stepped down, saying, "Then I will be Waterboy Last-Zlat the Scribe no longer, but will come to you again as an avatar of Cretus, a fell hero of the old days*, but I will yet be a scribe until the last day." The mob hooted, and tried to stone him, unsuccessfully.

Sano, now Cretus, left the city of the delta and walked westward up into the land Ombur, where his words fell on sympathetic ears, but went, by and large, without action. So he crossed the great river Vast northward into Incana, where some listened, and acted, too. And first in Incana, it began to come together, not without strife, nor yet without war, but come it did, and soon all nations began to crumble before the newfound

---

*"Cretus" is a contraction of Koror Trethus, lit., "fear of the lance."

strength they seemed to possess as if by magic. But there was no sorcery, but varied skills being used together in concert for the first time in the history of Monsalvat. And at the last, Cretus commanded great variegated armies, and they marched over Kepture where they would.

Now there is something which must be told, which is part of the story of Cretus the scribe as well (and it was along these lines that Meure felt most surely that Cretus was withholding something of it, not out of a desire for secrecy, but out of a requirement to protect Meure from something Cretus feared to face directly). From the beginning of his labors, which took in twenty of the years of Monsalvat, Cretus had been accustomed to consult his own oracle, and act thereupon, and it had not failed him, not once. But as Kepture neared complete assimilation, and the war at last neared its end, and even Yastian in its delta lands submitted, Cretus began to feel a subtle change in the oracle.

And in the circumstances around him as well. The counselors and advisers and court flunkies were closing in; he knew this to be natural, and moved to counter this trend, following the correct course: and while it slowed the clotting of the great dynamic empire, it was only by a little. It was as if something offstage were purposely guiding all those people to a common end. And as he realized, or suspected this, he also saw that while they had indeed gained all Kepture, the remaining three continents were as far away as other planets, and getting no closer; and that the invasion of Chengurune had been postponed so long that by now they must be waiting on the beaches for them, to repulse the first overseas invasion in the history of the planet.

There was more that disturbed him; his own oracle was becoming unreliable, unsteady, as if something was distorting it even as he worked it. The visions it provoked were unclear and vague, and he began to distrust them, for they always seemed to lead to the path of more war, and more blood, and even more strife. Then he used one of the ways of his people and consulted their oracle, and the oracle told him that *within*, as he knew the way, he would find rest, and be called again.

—*Is that all?*

—No, not all. Nothing is ever all of it. But mostly. Yet when I came again, it was to a world that had changed. Almost like another planet, but I knew that it was Monsalvat/Aceldama, and that a great, vast time had passed. The empire came and went, and left little enough behind it. But there was an equilibrium among the peoples, a quiet, as if my war had been the last great one. What was it like, all those centuries? Like a moment, in which I thought I felt some ripples, and then I was you.

—*You think transfer was tried other times?*

—Yes. But no one knows how we Klesh armor ourselves, save other Klesh. It wouldn't take, because it couldn't—we won't accept transference, because we hate too strongly. We feel everything too strongly. So it brought a Mixed man from the stars to me so that . . .

—*So that you would stir things up again.*

—I'll say it the old way: *Tasi mapravemo zha'*. Most correctly so. So that I would try to rebuild the Empire with strife where none is now; therefore I hide from it. In bringing me back, it has given a place to hide from it, where there was none before. But you are exposed, of course; I will help you as I may. (Here, the stream of onrushing thought paused for a second, as if considering something Meure could not see, or perhaps just wandering. He could not tell.) . . . yes. It wants strife, so much I know. I know well; I have looked through the *Skazenach* all the way back, to the beginning, and beyond it. Ha! Beyond the beginning, I say! I know the secret of the Ler, and what a joke it is; what fools they have been. St. Zermille, our Lady of Monsalvat, protector of the weak, defender of the defenseless, Sister of Mercy, on a planet whose people confuse the word justice with revenge, and forget the difference. But we knew all along, and they were the ones who were misled. And knowing that we were right on that one, I wonder how many other things about this place we've been right about? Yes, about that. I know it's there. And yet, in a way I can't tell you, it isn't there . . . (And here, the thought almost faded out, as if Cretus was only musing to himself) . . . and the strife it wants I'll bring to it, if I can find it before it finds me.

—*You keep saying "it".* . . .

—I think that we are almost as hard for it to perceive as it is to us; but it can cause long-range events, large-current movements among the people. It can reach far, but it seems difficult for it to undertake fine detail work, except through the persuasions of the oracles it uses. . . .

—*It sounds almost like a God, but I.* . . .

—This isn't religion we're talking about . . . I'm not even sure it's alive, in the sense we'd call something alive, like a person or an animal or a plant.

—*But you talk about it perceiving; that's life, isn't it? And it causing things to happen* . . .

—Many things perceive, and even regulations can cause things to happen. Your machines have will and awareness, some of them, but for all that they are not alive. At any rate, the last time I looked, they weren't. The last time I looked . . . I looked across time and space to where a young man sat in a tower and wrote verses to the night. It doesn't matter where it was . . . or when, relative to you and I and now on Monsalvat the cursed. This he said aloud, repeating it until it felt right to him, and some of his words were strange, but I understood and remembered: "Language is a chemical phenomenon, with atoms and molecules and complex superstructures, that, in a proper environment aided by proper stimuli, become replicating structures which lead to life-forms. Phonemes into words into ideas into chains of things. At the present, we who think are but in the bare-planet stage of life; the life-forms of the future are unknown to us who are to be their matrix, but in the future beautiful burning tigers will stalk through the nighted forests of our minds." What do you think of that, hah? That things can assume life within our very thoughts!? Then do not be so quick to draw the line between the living and the dead . . . There are life forms, and there are other life forms. Size and scale, rates of time vary, perceptions vary, I am Cretus, what you think is a barbarian, but I know that to a creature who sees with radio waves, men are invisible, ghosts who probably aren't there. Yes?

—*You are a barbarian. Where did you learn these things?*

—I may be a barbarian, boy, but I was an emperor. An emperor can do what he damn well pleases: he can stupefy himself with drugs, he can wallow abed with the court whores. . . .

—*He can indulge in gluttony, which is the only sin.*

—Very perceptive, that! Take it further, now that you've said it! All valid thoughts are endless chains, but you must follow them out as far as you can; there lies mastery.

—*Drugs, women, drink, food: just refinements . . . That the medium changes does not change the nature of the act.*

—Keep going!

—*One in power practices other indulgences beside those of the senses . . . I see, it still remains the same: Some fondle the position, and others the work that maintains it. Still others concentrate on the manipulations of power, plots, strategies . . .*

—Possessions, routines, obedience, flattery. The list is virtually endless, without changing the nature of it. And the others expect it of you and press upon you to seek those indulgences. I sought ways to avoid those traps. So much is basically natural, a part of us. It was when I escaped those fates that the pressure became unnatural, and at that point

I was sure that there was an exterior . . . something . . . manipulating the people around me. Not by individual control, but by a kind of bending of the behavioral space to steepen the natural impulse. It damn near revealed itself, but it realized that I could then see its traces and was closing on its actuality; then it became more concealed. Shortly thereafter, I saw that the end was at hand in that time. I took what it offered, as a truce, because I could do no more there . . .

The voice stopped then, and remained quiet, as if it had admitted something unintended. Then it continued.

—So I know this about it: it isn't a God, because it has limited perceptions and makes mistakes. It is a life-form, not a machine, however odd it may seem to us, and it is single, not one of a kind of which there are others. It has continuation, but not reproduction, which suggests a kind of colony organism. But all that is nothing: what counts is that it has a single nature and it is fixed, immobile.

Meure could not deny the gloating he heard in the voice. And Cretus caught the fugitive thought, as well.

—That's correct. It is large, very large, but it is highly vulnerable. So much so that if I can touch it, I can kill it. And I intend to.

—*And you're going to use me as bait for it.*

—Not quite so. I am you, now. Rest assured that I will not recklessly endanger our mutual house. And remember this: it's hard to find, but I know that it can't move. I know that, now; because if it could have left, it would have. There are better opportunities for strife elsewhere. It's tied *here.*

—*It came here and was trapped, like you Klesh were?*

—No. Wait, I say that without knowing. If it came from elsewhere, it was very long ago. No, it has been here from the beginning. It is native, as far as I have been able to see.

—*I see it bringing others to it. It brought me.*

—And the Ler under circumstances that. . . . yes, I see. You are one step ahead now. It will bring the new contenders; the Mixed men from the stars, the Ler, those star-creatures.

—*And you-I are to ignite the mixture.*

—It would be here, of course. But I have an objection: though I do not care that the offworlders fight among themselves, I can see easily enough that it would be the end of the Klesh.

—*And the strife will not be limited to Monsalvat. I object to that.*

—Well you should, if you respect your origins; for it does not care about events outside. Only that they happen here.

—*There has not been in history a major interstellar war. Minor actions, yes, but nothing where the survival of a race or a planet was in question.*

—At the least, then, we can agree: you must let me do this thing.

—*We have little choice. Neither it nor the Ler will allow us to leave Monsalvat. And I fear what you might do there if you did leave.*

—You will keep me here, too? You will volunteer to remain on this most deadly world? Then you will assuredly need my help to survive here, now, for this has never been a gentle world. Up to now, you have been under the protection of a force, but that has now been accomplished which was intended, and I can no longer be sure it will protect you as fully as it has. Since Cucany, things have been easy. Do not be fooled by that ease. It has given me time to integrate myself into you. Now it will prod us a little.

—*You never did say what your indulgence was when you ruled.*

—To know what happened to us, why . . . and if there were any others. I will keep them to myself. Those times will not come again. I had my turn, and unlike others, was able to walk away from it.

And, abruptly, not finishing the thought-pattern, the Cretus presence withdrew, faded out, vanished. Meure felt freer than he had since the castle; Cretus must have gone deep within, to hide, or perhaps to sulk. He felt free; still, he knew he would never be entirely free of Cretus. There was no way he knew to reverse the thing that had happened to him. And he wondered, deep in his own thoughts, how they would eventually come to terms with each other. It seemed there was no way out.

"It is hard to explain, and harder to learn, that truth abides in the inmost sanctuary of the soul and may not be told, either by speech or by silence; yet all attempts to interpret it distort it progressively as they adapt themselves to the perceptions of the mind, and become sheer caricatures by the time they are translated into terms of bodily sensation. Now the reality of things depends on their truth, and thus it is that it is not a philosophical paradox but a matter of experience that the search for truth teaches us to distrust appearances exactly in proportion as they are positive."

—A.C.

WHILE MEURE HAD been holding his internal conversation with the shade of Cretus, he had ignored the flow of perceptual events outside; and why not? For time on the river was a repetition of endless sameness, and within the group, relationships were now fixed.

But someone was standing beside him at the edge of the barge, who had come silently, unobtrusively. Ingraine Deffy, the other girl from the *Ffstretsha.*

Meure was fond of girls without desiring to possess them; still, he could appreciate how this slight girl, Ingraine, could incite possessiveness: seen from a distance, she was merely a pretty girl of no great distinction, not entirely real. Close by, however, she had a beauty that was remarkable—something not quite human anymore. Overall, she was fragile and delicate in appearance, with clear, almost translucent skin; and what he could see of her features had been drawn with a hand free of hesitation or doubt. Ignoring a slight childishness which the fineness of her features suggested, she was almost perfect, even after their escapades since the grounding of the ship.

Meure was not city-quick, after what he thought was the manner of

Cretus, but neither was he an innocent yokel; he was perceptive enough on his own to see with his own senses that Ingraine was not as young as she appeared, nor had she been discomfited by some of the harsh exertions they had been through. He could see easily that she would inspire protectiveness by her appearance alone, whether she actually needed it or not. And that, having been favored by beauty, she had made herself the final adjustments in mannerisms to fit herself into a specific interaction with the people around her; feeling subliminally the undertow of others' emotions, she had turned herself to them, to her advantage. Now he wondered, what was the advantage?

He felt acutely uncomfortable; Meure and Halander had been only casual acquaintances, not particularly friends, and he had claimed her early aboard the ship. This action on her part could only cause problems which he did not care to add to what he thought were excessive complications.

Now she was here, when before she had scarcely noticed him, looking out over the water dreamily, brushing her soft brown hair out of her eyes, pursing her delicate, full lips pensively.

What had Cretus said? *Thoughts are endless chains, but you must follow them as far as you can.* He accepted without question that he would have to learn from Cretus. What did that learning tell him now? That Ingraine, sensing the stronger Cretus personality, had switched allegiances at the first appropriate moment . . . she could mean more trouble than all he had experienced on Monsalvat up to this moment. It was a most delicate moment; he felt, without looking, the beginnings of malice in Halander; what did the others feel? Tenguft? Audiart? Indeed, what about Cretus? Glancing about, internally and externally, he sensed withdrawal. He was on his own.

She asked, softly, as if for his ears alone, "What are you thinking about now?"

"I was thinking, as a fact, just now, why me? I had not hoped for so much adventure when I signed on the *Ffstretsha*, on Tancred."

She mused, "Yes, isn't it terrible, what's happened to us? Do you think we'll ever be rescued from this . . . Monsalvat?"

"Myself, I believe the worst; but the Ler think that a Spsom craft will come here, after all. If we can survive until then, they will surely pick us up." *Why had she hesitated over the word,* Monsalvat?

"But they sided with those hunters, so quickly."

"They think, only to allow them to remain close to the crash site; presumably the hypersensitive perceptions of the Haydar will warn them when the new ship arrives. In the meantime, they can enjoy themselves with a little sport, while they're waiting."

"While we wonder from minute to minute whether we'll be alive or not; I thought those hunters were preparing to eat us. And why didn't they?"

"They act under a system of oracles and revelations, as I understand it. The best way to say it is that their spirits told them to pack us off to that castle. Besides . . . I don't think they'd actually eat us: we're not 'game,' apparently. They might have disposed of us as excess baggage by dumping us somewhere, or selling us to another tribe. Who knows. We are certainly no threat to them, and they know that easily enough . . . of what we've seen so far, they appear to be the best. At the least, the most honorable, even though they are wild. I wish we had more of them with us where we are going."

"I thought we were going down this vile river only because it was away from the land of castles. Where are we going?"

Now Meure was wary, although he tried not to show it; Ingraine had spoken at the last to Cretus, not to him, Meure Schasny. Cretus-Meure had led them to the river and the barge; Cretus knew what lay at the place where the pestilential river drowned itself in the stormy gulf between the two southern peninsulas of Kepture, knew it far better than any of them, even Tenguft. And if he was bound there, to what purpose? Ingraine sensed that the land was just itself, but a city was a bridge to somewhere else, something else, change. He said, only, "To a city."

"Do they actually have cities on this planet?"

"So I am told, although they will not be cities as I have seen them. Like something from the dim past." Now he sought to deflect her. "Were you from Tancred?"

Ingraine shook her head briefly, as if shaking cobwebs away, sending waves flowing down her hair. "No. Didn't you know? Well, no matter— I suppose it never got around to you. I came aboard on Flordeluna."

Meure turned slightly away to conceal his surprise. "That's . . ."

She finished the sentence, ". . . a long way off. I know."

"Where did Audiart come from? Flordeluna?"

"She didn't tell you?"

"No. I hadn't asked . . ."

"She was there when I boarded. She hasn't told me, either. She has some mannerisms which suggest . . . perhaps a world like Tancred, something a bit out of the way."

Meure took no offense. He knew Tancred was more than a bit out of the way. But Flordeluna was on the far side of the central group; if Audiart came from a colony planet like Tancred, then it would be, very likely, on the far side, adjoining Spsom space. He asked, "You were hired on by the Ler as we were?"

"Hired, yes. Not as you were. She and I were aboard when the Ler girl entered the *Ffstretsha;* we could have left the ship or taken employment with the Ler party . . . it was on a Ler world and I did not care to be so stranded." She finished with some heat, as if there was something offensive to her about a world inhabited solely by Ler.

"Was there not a Transition?"*

"On Lickrepent? Indeed there was, but you would not care to have to work your way out of it. I did not." Here Ingraine looked coyly sidelong at Meure under her eyelashes. "I prefer not to work any harder than absolutely necessary, and so I thought being a scull for Ler aristocrats was better than slogging it in Transiton. I did not reckon on the disasters that have befallen us along the way, but all in all, things have not turned out badly so far . . . I will certainly have a tale to tell!" Here she shook out her hair again and smiled up at the sky.

Meure thought, here stands a slight girl who looks like she should yet be in school, yet she is experienced enough to set out tramping rides alone across space, obviously an individual of considerable verve . . . Still, dangerous. Audiart had offered and given of herself with no thought of tomorrow; Tenguft had used him for some incomprehensible purpose, but had allowed him to share in it, however brief it had been; this one would have a price, which he was not sure he could pay. Or would. Not the least of which would be surrender to Cretus . . . He was not entirely sure Cretus would wish to pay, either, whatever it was. He was one who liked no restraints or obligations. But at the same time, looking at the smooth skin of her throat, at the slender body under the borrowed Ler overshirt, he could not but imagine. Meure looked around guiltily. He was acutely uncomfortable. And Cretus, of course, would sit back and let him make his own choices, and probably vicariously watch as well.

Halander was glaring at them from the bow, making small, indecisive movements. He continued glancing around at the others. Tenguft ignored the whole proceeding. Audiart caught his eye and looked away, with an odd flicker of sadness, or so Meure thought. As if she were worried for him, rather than jealous of the girl. He felt pressure

*Contraction of "Transient-town," a common adjunct of spaceports.

to act, to make a decision. The only thing was, any way he moved, he would make an enemy, and he could afford no more. Cretus, however benign, had to be counted an enemy, and one such as no man ever had before.

One of the bargemen hybrids suddenly called out to the others, and began to jabber excitedly; the others hurriedly joined him at the stern, facing west, back up the river, where they conferred earnestly and gestured wildly at something out over the water which Meure couldn't quite make out.

The bargemen became more excited, and one climbed up on the rail and began shouting at the passengers. Meure looked hard up the river, but he could see no cause for their erratic behavior . . . there was an irregular spot far back up the river, seemingly moving toward them, but he could make out no details. It seemed to be moving, or changing its orientation. He could not make out a shape at all.

The bargeman who had climbed up on the rail emitted a long, doleful hoot that echoed across the water, an expression of emotions too complex to frame in speech, and then stepped over the side and began swimming for the nearer shore to the south. The remaining bargemen hesitated, looking fearfully first up the river, then at one another, then at the barge. Then, one by one, they, too, began climbing over the side, and swimming for the shore. The river had become ominously still, its surface like molten glass. The bargemen scarcely made ripples as they entered the water and began stroking mightily.

They all looked at each other uncertainly. The bargemen had abandoned the barge! Morgin had been dozing, but now he ran to stern to see what it was that caused such panic. Meure and Ingraine also hurried to join Morgin. They passed Tenguft, who hadn't changed position, but was looking intently up the river from under her deep brows.

South of the barge, between the barge and the south shore, the Ombur side of the Great River, the bargemen were still swimming for the shore; there was a sudden sucking sound and a swirl of water, and there was one bargeman less. Meure felt his scalp crawling. What was it, there, coming toward them that would make bargemen who supposedly knew the river brave it? The others took no notice whatsoever, but kept on making for the Ombur shore.

Now they stood by the stern rail and looked up the river; something was approaching, coming toward the barge, an irregular something which would not resolve into a perceptible shape, suspended somewhat above the surface without visible force. Meure looked at Morgin; Morgin looked back, blankly; here was something of Monsalvat beyond the experience of an Embasse.

Tenguft slid down from the pile of faggots, a silky, wary motion, and stood slightly behind Meure looking very intently at the approaching object. Meure looked at her also, but she did not return the gesture; she was watching.

Meure turned back to the object; it was closer now, still approaching, still suspended above the water without visible effort. He tried harder to make it out, but something about it continued to elude resolution. It was brownish in color, but it seemed to have no single outline, nor stable shape. It *changed* somehow, constantly; but it also possessed an inexplicable vagueness of size, for it seemed both very large and far way, and simultaneously small and close, no matter how it occluded the backgound it moved against. It was nothing he could classify into any known category.

He glanced again at Tenguft; the Haydar girl was still looking at the object, her lips tightly compressed. Meure asked her, "What is that? Why did they fear it?"

She answered, not looking at him, speaking tonelessly and softly, as if she wished not to disturb some delicate equilibrium, "I have heard of such things in the most ancient of tales, but I have not ever seen one myself, nor has anyone I have known. Our rites exist to prevent this appearance of such demons. It is not good that we see it now; it is a sign of dire events."

Meure insisted, "What is it?"

She continued, "The *Lami* Sari Au Ardebe faced one alone for the sake of the tribe Tahiret; Gambir 'Am-seleb the holy man called upon one to end the holy war N'Guil-Ellem; Imrem Galtaru was said to have entered into association with one, but he was no longer of the Haydar after that, and was pursued as game by the great among the People— without success or trophy, indeed, many a fine warrior of the Haydar learned truth untelling in that quest. . . ."

"You mean they saw, but they could not speak of it?"

Morgin tactfully interrupted, "She means that the great warriors vanished in a manner strongly suspected of bringing great shame upon them . . ."

Tenguft interrupted Morgin, ". . . Ebdalla Yamsa returned to Illili without his spear, crawling on the ground in his fear. The people gave him the truth, and hunted after Imrem the unholy no more. His memory be cursed. But we do not forget, and we do not seek that-which-has-no-name; and what it does here is beyond me. I have not called it, and Morgin the Embasse does not know how, indeed, those who carry a Prote cannot see one."

The object, now measured against its background, seemed to have approached the barge closely, almost within stone-throwing distance. Its motion had ceased, save for that slight drift necessary to keep it near the barge, but not its mutability; its outline wavered constantly, and its shape and internal features shifted too rapidly for anything of detail to be made out. Meure strained at it, trying to grasp enough of it to make up an image, but he could not. It was as if the thing were mutating at a rate too great for his senses to discern any single state of it. It made no sound. And although he saw no evidence to support the suspicion, he strongly felt that it was a living thing, however imprecise it was, rather than a machine. Or a part of something alive. Where had that idea come from?

A voice issued from the thing, that echoed as if coming from a great distance, but also as if very close by from a tiny mechanism: "Where is Cretus?"

Tenguft raised her spear. "Cretus is not here! Begone! We are pilgrims driven by the oracle of Dossolem; I cast it, I read, I know! There is no place for you in it!"

It said, "Not so, Haydar. I give the reading. Cretus casts a shadow I can sense. For cycles he eludes me, and I do not know a way to that place. But his shadow moves in this time. I know the commotion at Cucany and the Invigilator speaks of it. They fear me much there. But Cretus is gone, casting his shadow. I seek the presence."

Meure said, "Cretus is not here. There is no such person!"

The thing seemed to regard Meure for the first time, although there was no perceptible change in its shifting mutability. It was a long moment shifting its attention, but Meure felt a great mass behind the object, a great momentum, a pressure. It said, "You I perceive, who move to Monsalvat. But the shadow you cast, it is of the cast of Cretus."

"Cretus attempted to possess me but I cast him forth! You must look elsewhere!"

"Can there be error? Not so, I review the course, and I follow the shadow of Cretus. There is a mistake but he is here; he must mingle his shadow in the I-ness—yes, it is so; he is all shadow now, a unit!" The thing moved slowly, closer to the barge. It was coming for Meure and Cretus.

Meure wanted desperately to be free of Cretus, but he felt a greater fear of this anomalous thing that he did of Cretus; what could it do to him extricating Cretus from him? Without particular thought he brought forth the knife Tenguft had given him, and threw it at the center of the object. The knife went truly and impacted point-first on the object, but it came back exactly along the same course to the hand that had thrown it, while Meure made the exact motions of throwing it, but in reverse order. He threw it again; this time it was off a bit, the blade moving as it came near the thing.

The knife was deflected off the surface, and was propelled violently into the river below the object, making a powerful splash which splashed water back up upon the object. A great gout of steam appeared and began to whirl rapidly about the object, making a hissing sound that grew in volume rapidly, reached a peak, and faded out rather suddenly, as if moving away. The whirling cloud dissipated, and there was nothing behind it. Whatever the apparition had been, it was gone.

Meure did not know if his act had been responsible; he thought that he had contributed to some instability in the thing; and thus it had withdrawn. But it would probably come again. He looked at the river surface, when the knife had entered the water. That was gone, forever; he hoped Tenguft thought it had been to good use. At the spot there was a swirling, as if something massive was moving just below the surface, and then, that, too, was gone.

It was afternoon, but the sunlight was waning under a high, filmy layer, through some illusion of the light and the reflections off the river, the light altered from its normal tangerine color to a greasy beige, a color, Meure thought, of repulsive substances. The mood was clearly one of apprehension and foreboding, and after the visit of the apparition, all fell silent. By shared impulses, each drifted off to maintain watch over the river, should it appear again.

The twilight deepened into a melancholy, depthless gray-blue tone, an oily, poisonous color, and the distant shorelines faded into first indistinguishability, then invisibility. Morgin and Tenguft distributed hard crusts and flasks of water, and as night fell, all found a shelter from the dampness that had come to the air, and slept a fitful sleep.

It was not yet light when something moved beside Meure, or a noise awoke him, and he awakened; a warm presence was beside him, one of the girls. He could not tell who it was, exactly, for she was wrapped up in a section of coarse cloth found on the barge. He thought it was probably not Tenguft; that one had a bony angularity about her that even heavy cloth would not obscure. Half asleep, he opened his eyes warily, suspiciously sniffed the damp air.

There was dense fog, not rising from the river, but pressing down upon it from above. There was no motion, either of the boat or of the fog; every surface was covered with a fine film of dew. There was also a different scent to the air, something laid over the persistent miasma of the dank water. It was weak, yet, hidden by the river's ripe odor, but it was there—smoke, and a pungent, toasty odor, but a stale one. They were nearing some kind of settled place. Meure looked for lights, but saw none; still, the darkness wasn't total. Something was illuminating the fog, although faintly.

He listened; the girl was breathing regularly, but he sensed she was not asleep. Waiting. Far away, muffled by the fog and distorted by the overripe airs over the greasy water, came a suggestion of sound, a rhythmic tapping that proceeded for a time, and then was silent. He could also hear, at slightly less volume, the girl's breathing. The suggestion of body warmth. The tapping began again, sounding fractionally nearer, and continued.

Meure breathed deeply, and leaned against the warm bundle to his left, feeling his heartbeat increase; who was it? Where on the barge was Halander? The tapping became irregular and slow, as if deliberating each stroke, then picked up its old pattern again, now a little faster. He moved his arm, to enfold the warm body. The girl moved suddenly, rolling over and straddling Meure, at the same time moving the coarse cloth around behind her so that it fell over them and covered them. Good, he thought; that she knew the necessity for concealment. But the folds and heavy weight of it made motion difficult and distorted perception. He felt a hot wetness on his neck, moving, on his collarbone, a sharp bite; he felt cool skin where his hands moved, and the clumsy long tails of the borrowed overshirts sliding upwards almost without effort, making him realize, curiously, that it was because they had been designed to do just that.

She spoke no words, no endearments; neither did he. Somehow, he thought words would shatter what was happening, deflect it into a mere entertainment. He searched with his mouth, found an ear, a neck, a finely-boned shoulder, which he kissed lightly, feeling hot breath and cool legs, and their first shy contacts, delicate pressures, and their bodies slid together easily. They seemed to rest together at an odd position, but this seemed to have no effect; the little motions they could make seem magnified a hundredfold. There was no sensation of weight or force, just instincts which happened of themselves, sensations, wet, light skin-kisses, things he did without thinking of them, and a sudden, unanticipated hot relief matched in her an instant later by a timeless moment in which she pressed her body against his and held her breath; he listened, and he could not recall when the tapping had stopped.

They did not move for a long time, feeling their heartbeats and breathing falling back to their normal rates. He could feel hers distinctly. Meure savored the sensations of the girl's body, the slender wiriness of her, the warm spots, where they had touched the longest; cool spots they revealed by their shiftings. A sharp, flowery tone to her scent, the way her hands moved, one under him, the other holding the ball of his shoulder . . . but he thought there was an odd pressure to that hand, as she steadied herself to move, still adjusting, still moving her body against his, as the hand pressed on his shoulder at three points instead of two. He experimentally flexed his own right hand, resting lightly on the girl's buttocks; it was difficult to set his own hand that way, because he couldn't rotate his little finger far enough outward. A sudden suspicion nagged him, and with his other hand he reached for the girl's hair, feeling his way around the cloth that covered them, feeling. The hair was short, straight, and silky-fine. Flerdistar.

Meure struggled with the cloth, finally managing to pull away enough of it to expose their faces, to a light which had now taken on a faint bluish tone not there before. He looked directly into a thin, intense pale face whose lips were now curved, slightly open, in a faint smile that held absolutely no affection whatsoever.

"The proof of a man's prowess lies in the invisible influence which he has had on generations of men."

—A.C.

MEURE HARDLY DARED to move, or to make any sound whatsoever. Not even to look around; he listened, trying to pierce the predawn bluish murk. All around him, but faraway and delicately faint, so as to vanish at the slightest rustle, lay a texture of noises, not at all like the silences and windsongs of the wilderness. He listened for the tapping he had heard earlier; at first he could not hear it, but after a time it returned, now much weaker, almost one with the background. The river slapped the sides of the barge with small wavelets like hands, irregularly. He could not escape the impression that he was in the midst of a large settlement, isolated from it by the colossal flood of the river. And aboard the barge there was no sound whatsoever. This did not comfort him; he suspected that Clellendol could move soundlessly in the dark if he so desired. But on the ship he had denied having an interest in Flerdistar, and Meure had seen him ignore or deny her more than once since then.

Flerdistar seemed to read his worries. She leaned close, and said, in his ear, "No one has seen. I know; I can move in the nightside almost as quietly as Clellen. We have trained together for some time, and I have learned much of him."

Meure said, quietly, "And him, of you?"

"Thus, and thus. But he knows not the ways I have learned to reconstruct the past out of the noise of the present; there's a finer trick than slipping through the night and stealing. Have no apprehensions on that score. There is only one past-reader here."

"What about Cretus?"

"Cretus is one no longer, whatever he has seen in his own past. But of him I will be able to see the truth, that we have searched for so long . . . And of the here and now," and here she moved her hips suggestively, "you need not fear. Within my age cycle there is no jealousy to speak of for such events as these, and the circumstances of Clellendol and I . . ." She paused, either searching for a word, or reluctant to utter one. She straightened a little, and said, with some of the old authority he had seen her use, "He does not care what I do, or with whom. Surely you can perceive that as well."

"I do."

"And consider that Morgin is past his prime, and that Halander is a mooncalf . . ."

Meure interjected, ". . . And that I have Cretus."

"True. But not the sole reason, never fear. And also you must learn that I can rid you of Cretus, if you allow me to."

"How can you do that?"

"There are ways to manipulate states of existence like his. It is part of my training; we theorized that there was an entity here like him, so that we tried to reconstruct its characteristics from what we could learn of the planet and the trail of rumors which have come from here over the years . . . And having done so, we also developed certain practices to isolate and contain the entity."

Meure felt a spasm of humor, but his position would not permit him to laugh. He moved, shifted her weight, and chuckled. "And all that work for Cretus. . . . and you can't even get to him. Nor can he get to you."

Flerdistar leaned close to him again, and said, coldly, "We erred in that we missed the identity-persona in its exact state. We did not know Cretus; nevertheless, I can do so."

Meure shook his head. "You have erred further. Cretus is powerless— a creature of his times, no more. A man of the past. I admit to having become a victim of a singular misfortune, but he is nowhere near the elemental you seem to think he is. There is another entity here that has kept the whole planet at bay for thousands of years . . ."

"I know." She cut him off. "I saw the thing over the water. Although I don't think I saw the same thing you did. And I tell you—as a past-reader, what I am, that I can feel Cretus inside you, however well he hides, generating the kind of waves he makes right now. So much of the past vanishes into the backscatter, so soon. If you could but understand how insignificant most of your lives are! The whole of millions of existences adds up to nothing but a contributory tone in the background. But there are some you can read across time. Some of these identities can be resolved to personae known in recorded history, although their effects are different from what we imagined they were. Others . . . there is no trace of them, no name, no record, nothing, only the fact that they existed and that they changed the flow of time. At the beginning of the Ler, when we were created, there was a Human, just before that, who has deflected the entire course of Human history—a major turn in the long run. We know he existed, I have sensed his influence myself—finding him is one of our exercises. In a sense, he is more real to me than you are, now. But not once have our best been able to inrelate who he was in the real world, what his name was, where he lived, who were his descendants . . . he possessed the great mana, the power . . . and we think that he didn't even know it. We think that he didn't even care . . . He is one of the strongest in the pre-space period, although there are some further back who are very hard to read but who are as strong. But that one: he was obscure and unknown in his own time. Cretus, on the other hand, burns across my perceptions like some flaming comet! I must desensitize my perceptions in order to register him properly!"

"What is it that Cretus does that makes him so . . . visible to you?"

"It is difficult to explain; you are of necessity not knowledgeable of the correct terminology or concepts; there is essentially not enough time to construct them in you. Nevertheless . . . what makes a life-form sentient, thinking, intelligent, as we say, is the way in which it stores the information necessary for it to act and endure. Many creatures store a program internally; thus is instinct; more advanced types reduced the instinctual preprogramming and rely on coding and evaluation and storage from the environment to the individual. At a higher level yet comes the ability to communicate pertinent segments of this data—this is the first great leap forward, and it is a major effort. Finally we reach the highest level, at which vast amounts of data are not stored in the individual, but in an abstract body of information accessible to all. We call this culture—our basic instructions, values, habits, standards of judgments, knowledge.

"The whole system here is based upon information and how it is stored and used, how one accesses it. To change behavior, it is only a matter of changing the informational base. You can see that to change the course of a people is a very great task—we find that these cultural entities follow courses of their own, according to laws pertinent to them. But in Human history we find . . . deviations along the sometimes abrupt changes in course. It is as if one were following the course of a star in space, and then it veers, for no reason you can see . . . some phe-

nomenon perturbs its course. In the case of the star, the anomaly is resolved to an heretofore-invisible object; in the culture, the culture itself
produces the disturbances."

Meure softly disengaged himself and said, "So far, I see; but could not
the theory be unfinished? It would seem that a more finished version
would also predict these . . . changes."

"We have followed that line of development; it leads nowhere. In
fact, it leads to severe logical contradictions that render the entire concept meaningless. Instead, what we find is that certain individuals gain,
at random intervals, the ability to change key sections of the overall assumptions, apparently by means of a process we do not understand."

"Are such people born to this? Genetics? Or is it that they learn to
do it."

"The research we have done so far indicates both: the ability is inborn, but the facility to use it, consciously or unconsciously, is *learned*.
Moreover, they act for no foreseeable reason. For example, as a Human
culture approaches a hazard, a savior does not automatically arise, necessarily. Sometimes there is none; other times, one appears, too early.
Some appear too late."

"You know early Human history . . . was Hitler one of these people?"

"Wrong. That one is an example of another phenomenon, even more
complex . . . currents on the flow of assumptions lead to what we call
nodes, which attract and capture exemplars. Apparently the node governs behavior to a fine degree. If we could go back in time and remove
the physical person Hitler before his rise to power, we would find that
another would snap into his place. That would be very dangerous, indeed, could it be done, for the next victim of the node might stand up
to it better than the original. Hitler lost his great chance because he was
flawed for the use of the node . . . it is a truism that political types tend
to be node-fillers, rather than changers, magi, powers, whatever you
should call them. Of course, there are exceptions . . ."

"Cretus, for example?"

"So much would seem to be the case."

"And what of the Lerfolk? What do you see in your history?"

". . . We work with an even larger component of culture than you, a
picture of finer resolution. That would suggest that our stream would
be more difficult to change, but in fact, according to this system, it
means that for us, we have no random event, or happenstance; with us,
it is simply Will and Idea. Anyone can alter the course whenever they
please. The result is that . . ."

". . . You change constantly?"

"Wrong again! That we don't deflect the course at all. We are terrified of that act, because we cannot foresee to what it would lead. Only
once in our history has one so seized the balance of the pendulum, and
at that, the deflection was infinitesimal. Even so, the shock of it echoes
through us yet. It is a contradiction implicit in that event that I am here
to investigate, to resolve." She lay on her side with one bare thigh extended across Meure's knees. Now she moved her leg over his, slowly,
softly. "I and this trip, here to Monsalvat, are the culmination of generations of work . . ."

"And you're going to dig Cretus out, whatever it takes . . . I am sorry;
I have not tried to deceive you, but what you have gotten so far is just
Meure Schasny, neither more nor less. What we just did was a . . . wonderful thing, nevertheless it was me, and not Cretus, who was your
lover."

"I did not entangle my body with yours to tempt Cretus to come
forth. At the first, that is unreasonable, for it would be the promise of
joy, not the joy itself, that would tempt him, or you. I hope you will give
him to me because of this in part, but I came for my own reasons, too."
She breathed deeply. "Accept, ask not."

"I would know something. I am tired of groping in a fog, being used
for others' purposes . . ."

"You possess a rare quality we call in my speech *wurwan*, which is
best translated 'innocence.' . . . You accept what is offered you."

Here Flerdistar stopped, as if collecting her thoughts. Perhaps she
would have elaborated further, but she did not. A voice from nearby on
the deck of the barge interrupted her. "It might be more truthful to suggest, however impolitely, that the reason closer to reality lies in the fact
that even a princess may lack suitors of the preferred numbers and
types, and might be led to seek farther afield than would be the usual
practice."

Meure turned and looked behind him, and found, as he expected,
Clellendol, sitting on the rail, shrouded in streamers of fog. The light
had brightened noticeably, but it was still not yet day; visibility close to
the water, horizontally, was clearing in bits and vague open lanes, which
still led nowhere. Above, however, the fog was, if anything, thicker. Its
color was still bluish, but there was a hint in it of an orange dawn somewhere around the curve of the world.

Clellendol looked off across the water. All around them was a growing texture of sounds, wafted and misdirected by the odd atmospherics:

sounds of animals, creakings, clatters, odd snatches of conversation, or calls. Somewhere, someone was singing an aimless tune, of which Meure could not quite make out the melody, or the words. It, too, faded. Clellendol spoke abstractly, as if to no one in particular, "You may have no cause to feel concern on my account; at the least, you have a certain gratitude of me, as this at last relieves me of a responsibility which I did not want."

Meure looked at Flerdistar, and then back at Clellendol. In the short interval, he had vanished back into the other part of the barge.

Flerdistar said, "There would seem to be no mystery here; Clellendol simply doesn't like me, nor has he ever . . . that is a mild way of putting it."

"Odd, then, that a mission of such importance would depend upon such an ill-matched crew. I know that your elders are fairly rigorous in their organizations . . ."

"We were pressed into it, by what we knew and conjectured about the surface conditions of Monsalvat, and by . . . that was what I was trying to tell you, along the way. Somehow, we were getting a dual reading from the trails that lead here: a Ler laid a heavy hand on this planet once, which is an event not repeated elsewhere. But the reading is . . . offset, somehow, as if that person weren't here. And then there was Cretus. Of course, we hadn't the name; but all the evidence told us that we'd find that out almost as soon as we landed, for here was the exceptional situation: a changer who was also a political figure."

She took a deep breath. "It helps if you know the Tarot, here . . ."

"I have heard of it. I am not a practitioner."

"It is an ancient Human device. There are three levels of power in the types of cards—the ordinary numbers, the court cards, and the trumps. We have refined the system further, and believe that each persona corresponds to a card identity in the, Tarot deck. So that ordinary people favor the ordinary numbers, and exceptional members of their number assume the identities of the court cards, which relate in part to the signs of the old earth zodiac, and essences of similar influence. Trumps are those who can change. They are rare. But what is even rarer is a single personality containing two trump identities; Cretus is such a person."

"Go on. What are the personae of Cretus?"

"According to my reading of the data, Cretus is a composite of two identities. The Magus, and the Hanged Man . . . there is much friction there, for the Magus holds power over the four elements, but the Hanged Man willingly sacrifices himself. There is in this system a pattern of flow, and in this case it is direct, but the sources and junctions add up wrongly along that path, so that inevitably, violence and accident are a by-product of that state."

Meure reflected a moment, and said, "If any Ler can change things, as you say, then all Ler are trumps, in this system of reference."

"That is so . . . but we do not attain multiple-trump identities."

Meure said, "Then let me guess, although I do not know the system well . . ."

"I will tell you, although it is a secret thing; I am trump nine—The Hermit. Clellendol is trump fourteen—Art. But there is a thing which I read here that I had not before: besides Cretus, there is another double-trump on this planet, even just now beginning to come into influence . . . I have wondered if it was that thing that approached the barge. But it was not that one."

"What are its identities?"

"Cretus, being trump one plus trump twelve, controls all nodes directly and indirectly, save two . . . . this other identity is trump zero, The Fool, and trump two, The High Priestess. That Identity controls everything Cretus does, plus the two he does not; and they both originate from the prime node . . . Where Cretus is a direct line of two segments, this other is split in two directions, with the Fool as the dominant side, although as I sense it, the High Priestess is the visible part. The dualities of this planet disturb and confuse me . . . things are moving to completion here fast, but I cannot see them."

Meure said, "Perhaps you are used to seeing these things from a distance, extracted out of the noise of Time; you may be too close to events."

"Perhaps you are right, there . . . but I cannot tell you how confusing it is. From a distance, it all seems to lead to an identity, which I can easily correlate to Cretus. But there's this other one, who is potentially stronger than Cretus, and could overpower him. But I could not see that one from distance, yet I know it is here. And it is aware of that which we do; it's an eye, seeking, open, but not yet fully aware. It has not yet focussed upon us, or anything I can see."

"Perhaps it's that creature, after all . . ."

"That creature, as you call it, has no identity whatsoever. Cretus in his own body could wish it out of existence. He fears it because he doesn't know the method."

"You do."

Flerdistar turned away, abruptly. Meure touched her shoulder. "What is it?"

"How did you know that?"

"I . . . guessed, from what you said. How could you know Cretus didn't know the way, unless you knew it yourself?"

"I know it, but I can't do it. This is a Human planet, and the governing system here is Human. I am, like all of us, a single trump and have the power, but it is only over my own society."

"Then you could tell Cretus how. . . ."

"Yes, if the Meure Schasny would allow him to do it . . ."

"I believe we have a common ground, Flerdistar; I think I could speak for Cretus without fear of contradiction, that he would speak freely of the things he knows about your people if you were to tell him how to erase his enemy. Thus things will resolve themselves in the easiest way."

Flerdistar looked at Meure fearfully. "What do *you* want, now?"

Meure shook his head, sadly. "I just want to go home and be left alone."

"So do we all, indeed. But the currents we swim in do not allow it . . . I sense it in the currents about us; the wind whispers of it, and the night-demons sing of it in their rites. I can almost see it, but it remains hidden, a potential coming onto the world. It is . . . Meure! The coming of Cretus to this time awakened it!"

"The thing over the water?"

"Something perhaps worse, but stronger for certain." She began moving under the tarpaulin, disengaging herself from Meure and their cover. She emerged into the bluish predawn fog, and brushed her overshirt down over pale legs.

She said, "Something is disturbing me, and so I will now leave you. I must go and meditate upon these circumstances." She abruptly turned-away and walked quickly to the far rail, where she stared aimlessly out over the water, not looking back at Meure once.

Meure felt a fatigue creeping over him, but he knew sleep would not come. Something was stirring in him, too, but he could not identify it; Cretus? He thought not. Cretus had a certain *flavor* to his presence, and that essense also contaminated thoughts in himself influenced by Cretus. No, this wasn't Cretus, but it defied identification.

He slipped out from under the tarpaulin and set out toward the front of the barge. He felt an urge to talk to someone. Perhaps he could find someone awake. As he passed along the walkway down the side, he passed Tenguft, huddled beside a rude crate in an angular, uncomfortable position, but she was obviously asleep, and somehow he felt it wasn't her he wanted to talk to now; from one mystery to another; she would tell him horrific tales of the deeds of the Haydars, or worse, describe demons in the Haydar pantheon. No.

He reached the front. There he immediately found Clellendol, who was awake, but withdrawn and sullen. Not far away, Meure saw Halander, alone. Alone? He looked about for the two girls, Audiart and Ingraine. They were nowhere to be seen. Meure continued looking, circling the whole circumference of the barge, peering in every possible place. He found the Vfzyekhr in a tool box in a corner, its fur much the worse for wear.

Meure returned to the front of the barge, feeling a sense of unreality gathering about him. The girls were gone, without a trace or sound. Vanished. And when he came again into sight of Halander, Meure could see that Halander was staring at him with bloodshot, blank eyes. And the light around them was losing its blue color in favor of a ruddier shade. Day was coming. And Meure could see patches of water, farther away. The fog was lifting.

Meure started to speak to Halander, but something stopped him. Something in the boy Meure thought he had known had snapped, broken. Something had changed forever: this creature in front of him was no longer Dreve Halander.

It spoke in a rasping growl that made Meure's skin crawl, and also caught the attention of Morgin and Clellendol. Behind him, he sensed Tenguft come awake instantly. Meure felt pressure. Halander said, "You. You said come on this ship, and it came here. You wanted them all for yourself, when you saw them on the ship. Audiart you took, and you lured Ingraine. And when you had had your fill of them, they weren't enough, so you took the one no one wants, and let her practice her arts on you. And the girls, our own kind, you heaved overboard. Pervert! Monster!" The boy shifted position into a crouch, fingers twitching in anticipation.

Something moved in the edge of Meure's vision; Clellendol drew a knife, and offered it to Meure. Meure acted without hesitation: he waved the offer back. Halander chose that moment to spring.

Meure met the first rush and grappled Halander, saying, "Listen to me, you fool! I lured no one and threw no one overboard. I asked for none of this!"

Halander hissed between clenched teeth, "You killed them, you pervert, and you called to a demon of this planet to possess you, to teach you secrets from the past of this filthy world. Everyone has sat back and let his happen, watched it happen, and liked what they saw. These changling freaks, this mutant witchwoman from a tribe of savages who eat human flesh, this arranger of murder. But not I!"

Halander burst through Meure's arms and seized his throat, to choke him. Meure felt the same disassociation he had felt when he had noticed the girls were missing. A cool, analytical mood. There was neither fear nor panic. He was being choked. Noted. There was a cure for that. He stepped inside Halander's stance, and leaned back, hard. He began to fall; as he started falling, he let his body bend at the knees, drawing them up. Halander followed, still holding tightly to his grip, unwilling to release his victim.

Now they were falling together, and Meure's knees were up and ready; almost too late Halander saw what was coming: either release his grip, or hold it and be thrown. He released Meure and, off-balance, staggered forward over Meure clumsily. Meure landed on his back, rolling first to the side, then to a poised crouch, ready for Halander's next rush. It never came. Halander lurched to the rail, and seemed to try to lever himself up on the side of the barge to spring back, but he clumsily allowed his momentum to carry him too far up onto the low rail, and he went on over the side, hesitating only briefly at the top. A sullen splash told that he was in the water.

Meure rushed to the rail to try to help Halander back aboard, remembering all too well the fate of the bargeman. Clellendol and Morgin joined him. Tenguft did not, but said, "Nay! Do not save him! He is now under the power of the Changer! His course is written."

The three of them looked at the smooth, greasy surface, and saw Halander treading water, making no attempt to regain the barge. He was already beyond their reach, and drifting farther away. He glared back at them with the eyes of a madman. He began mouthing incoherent curses, fragments of expletives, none completed. His motions in the water became more agitated, and foam appeared at the corners of his mouth. Meure felt sick. What was happening to Halander? Suddenly Halander's face stopped its mad working, and assumed an expression of intense curiosity and wondering; he looked around himself, peering this way and that, looking at the water. Then his head slid under the water abruptly, leaving only a slight rippling behind to show where it had been. There was turbulence in the water, and then that, too, faded.

Meure felt sick with horror. A friend, a potential enemy, vanished, without a trace, or indeed a reason.

He stepped back and turned away from those at the rail. Beside the far rail, he saw Flerdistar, who was looking at him as if he were a

stranger. And Tenguft had remained in her place, but now she was pointing, gesturing to the space around them, crying, "Look, an omen! The
murk is the color of blood!"

Meure looked, and it was so. Sunrise was flushing the fogbanks of the
river with an orange-brown tone. And the fog was lifting off the water
as if it were delaminating, peeling up vertically, dissipating, fading. Day
and clarity were upon them. Meure looked in astonishment at the scene
that was opening up to them all: There, in all directions about the drifting barge, a city was appearing; a city of low, ramshackle buildings, narrow, dirty lanes, smoke and swirling clouds of filth. And in whatever
direction they looked, it seemed to go on like that forever, to the limits
of the horizons. It looked like a hallucination from the deepest nightmares of forbidden drugs. An enormous city of a depth of poverty far
beyond anything Meure could have imagined in his wildest dreams.

Tenguft announced, "Behold Yastian, the city of the Lagostomes! See
and understand why the Haydar seek the empty places!"

Meure felt the presence of Cretus, but it was a light touch. He was
looking, through Meure's eyes. And the emotion from Cretus was even
stranger than the one he felt himself: Cretus was struck dumb, appalled
by the vast stinking city they saw about them. He was dismayed, and for
the first time in Meure's recollection, completely at a loss for what to
do. The phantom withdrew.

Meure felt Cretus withdraw, and felt safe enough, private enough, to
think to himself, *What the hell good does it do one to be possessed when
the possessing spirit quails from the reality he himself has precipitated us all
into?* It was the most bitter thought Meure could remember having. But
there was a resolve hitherto unknown contained in that, as well.

"Vitriol: Sulfuric Acid, H_2SO_4."
"VITRIOL: Visita Interiora Terrae, Rectificando Invenies Occultum Lapidem: 'Visit the interior parts of the Earth: by rectification thou shalt find the hidden stone.' The Lapis or alchemical stone is the True Self, which can only be found by rectifying one's attitude, by seeking inwards."

—A.C.

FOR THE MOMENT, the barge continued to drift with the main current of the river; there may have been other channels, for there was a suggestion of water all around, of distant canals and wharves. Meure could make out a mast, a mooring, a rickety derrick lashed together with bulky ropes, beyond the first line of buildings. Folk were up and about, stirring at their tasks, although there seemed to be no great urgency in their motions. He could see them moving along the shore, or an occasional rowboat stroking lethargically close to the shore. They seemed to take no great notice of the barge, although he thought they seemed to note their presence.

Meure asked Morgin about this. He now knew that Morgin was widely traveled, for a native of Monsalvat, and also that Morgin had visited Yastian often. Morgin now stood leaning over the rail, looking at the city with great attentiveness, and acknowledged Meure's question immediately, without looking directly at him.

"Do they know we're here? Indeed they do, but it's of no great moment to them. The Lagostomes . . . I must explain their ways to you, and to our Haydar friend was well, if she will be so good as to stifle her disgust for a time . . . good, I have your attentions. Well, you see, in certain circumstances, they are nervous, excitable; I should describe them as both volatile and explosive, irrational and highly susceptible to mob-fever. In other occasions, they display the opposite virtues, exactly: they move through life with a placidity and a resignation which is astounding, and in that mood they are difficult to provoke. Then, also, they are totally self-contained, and almost immune from the influences of others."

"Are there other states? And when do they adopt them?"

"No, to the first question. Gratitude to St. Zermille for that, at the least. As for the second . . . there is no rule I could tell or teach you simply. Circumstances change, and they adopt what they think is the proper mode instinctively, according to transition rules known only to them. I am accounted as skillful as any outlander in the use of Lago mood, but I could not impersonate one successfully . . . As to why this peculiar condition exists, I would suppose it to relate to the condition of their lives, which are strict and disciplined in the extreme. They are severely overpopulated for the land they inhabit, and that land is a poor one for resource. They surmount the difficulty by an exercise of truly steely self-control. The other mode releases the tensions, thus built up. Occasions exist within their social framework for the exercise of both in appropriate amounts. Here I must caution you: if a person performs what they recognize as a transition-act, that person can transform a staid and boring meeting of religious elders into a mass riot in a twinkling, which moreover will propagate. The only fortunate thing about this is that in the excitement, you may be overlooked. Also, the original cause is forgotten quickly, for the sake of action. Normally, the action will die of itself after a time, when a certain number have discharged their pent-up emotions."

Morgin ran his hand through the brushy stubble which covered his scalp, and continued, "Below the initiation of change level, they perceive the fading impulse, but do not act upon it. It, however, registers on the Lago consciousness, and they are aware of distant events in their society to an astonishing degree of accuracy, as they pick up the fading echoes of transitions. This perception includes what most people would regard as normal, ah, sexual activity, so I must caution you here not to respond to sexual invitations, and . . . er, innuendoes, so to speak, as you might be inclined to do by natural inclination; such events will precipitate consequences which will amaze you to the ends of your days."

Meure said, "You said 'aware of distant events.' . . . Telepathy?"

"No. Crowd-instinct, plus a hair-trigger sensitivity to very small cues in behavior, so most believe. By the way, I mean to ignore all sexual invitations, including those attachments which you might have with each other—such events are inflammatory."

Clellendol had been listening, and now he asked, "How is it that these overstressed people manage to reproduce and retain a viable society, then? How does one initiate a family?"

Morgin looked pained. "Like everyone else, they seem to manage their restrictions one way or another. Actually, they utilize an ingenious method, involving highly secluded establishments, where the necessary performances take place . . . At any rate, it is my hope that you not see them in their release state; they are difficult enough as it is. The last time I was here, to preside over certain discussions, and to provide a Prote, it resulted in an attempt at my life. Nothing is sacred to Lagos, outside their own mores. They do not honor Embasses—only tolerate them, and in addition, they consult no oracles, which is the most unthinkable condition of all." Morgin shook his head, disbelievingly, as if no people could be so uncivilized.

Meure had a sudden thought, and followed it. "Why not consult oracles?"

"They say that in ancient times, they followed an oracle to the land Yastian, where they were trapped . . ."

Meure said, "If that's true, then it's almost as if something wanted them where they are . . . Who held these lands before the Lagostomes?"

Morgin mused, "Yastian, by definition, is the land of the River Yast. Peoples have come and gone. Yastian always has carried the stigma of a dumping-ground for the scraps and rag-ends of the peoples, from all four continents. They sojourned here, and they passed on, on their way to oblivion . . . There is still a foreign quarter, in the neighborhood of the Great Docks, where exiles gather, but they are, all in all, few in numbers. Oh, indeed, you might well see all sorts there—Kurbs from the hinterlands of Incana, Aurismen, Meors from the Ombur and perhaps even Seagove; Maosts from Boigne, Garlinds from Intance and Far Nasp, which is just across the river-bottoms, to the east. Clones from Chengurune, for they are great seamen, and other races. I believe one even sees Haydar on occasion."

Tenguft asked, "They would not attack me here, when they could smother my spirit with their vile numbers?"

"No, most definitely. At least not while you were here. You see, such an event would ignite the desire to settle every grudge each Lago had; the result would be carnage on a grand scale: of a fact, many Lagos would be killed, while the menace of the Haydar predation would only be diminished by one, hardly worth the price. No, you are safe—here. And since you can call Eratzenasters from the sky, I doubt if they would set brigands on us, either, although such events are probable."

Meure stood by the rail for a time, looking out upon the panorama of the city-state Yastian, the noisome city. Finally, he said, thoughtfully, "Cretus had once an impulse to come here; rather, to *return* here, since he grew up in the delta. But things have changed, so I believe, and Cretus shrinks from his future, our present. I see little we can do with such a people, save walk carefully and avoid entanglements with them. I share Tenguft's distaste for them. All the same, I do not wish to return to Incana, either, and Ombur is not a hospitable land."

Flerdistar said, softly, "There is no need for us to leave Kepture. We know that what we seek is here."

Meure looked sidelong at her, and said, almost inaudibly, "What you seek is where I am, and that is wherever I go: to Chengurune, Cantou, Glordune, or seek the sea-people on the face of the World Sea." The words came almost without having to think of them, although as he said them, they had a strange, alien taste on his tongue. Then, to Morgin, "You know your way about this place better than any of us; where should we debark?"

Morgin thought for a while, then said, "There would be no great profit in landing hereabouts . . . come, let us man these clumsy sweeps and steer as best we may for a proper channel. I will try to guide us toward the foreign quarter."

Clellendol said, "At least that is good. I would like to smell some sea air for a change."

Morgin said, "Do not hope, yet, for the sea. The Great Docks are nowhere near open water, and in Yastian is no boundary between land and sea, only a gradual change. You will only see the Blue Sea if you leave Kepture."

Clellendol added, "And also I have not forgotten the Spsom and their hoped-for rescue. No, it is not my intent to leave Kepture. I want to be where they can find us, when they come, not off somewhere else, roaming all over Monsalvat."

"Nor I," said Meure resignedly. "Now. Where are those sweeps?"

Morgin turned from the rail and sought for, and shortly found, a locker which contained crude navigational gear: sectional masts, ragged sails in much need of repair, and sweeps for the steering of the clumsy craft. These last he distributed among those remaining, save the

Vfzyekhr, who was too small to use one, and they began moving the barge according to Morgin's directions.

For the remainder of the day, they worked at positioning the barge as Morgin instructed them; although the Embasse seemed somewhat vague at times about landmarks, as the day wore on he grew more sure of himself. They did not make for any particular point, so it seemed, but rather Morgin tried to maneuver the barge so as to be moved by certain currents. Once, he commented, "This is Upper Yastian; things in the water are fairly constant. One can figure out where the currents are without too much difficulty. Below, however, the matter is something of a different quality: the currents seems to develop a mind of their own. We will not attempt that part, and I hope to hit the edge of the foreign quarter, at the least. Thus we will be spared the hazards of the river, as well as the hazards of travel across Yastian among a pure Lago population."

Flerdistar commented, straining with an oar much too large for her fragile build, "I admit to confusion over your attitude; you seem to dislike the tribes you serve. Is that not a contradiction?"

Morgin answered plainly, without heat, "It is custom that the Embasse be of mixed-blood, thereby miscastes also have their chance to survive, where they would not otherwise. But as we wander, we also see all the *Radah* within the limits of our wanderings . . . Each people of this planet thinks themselves set above all others in quality, whereas the truth is that each seems to emphasize certain traits at the expense of others. Some are simple and easy; others are rigorous and most difficult. None have uncovered a universal truth. I myself came to Kepture from Chengurune, and so am somewhat more impatient than most. Yet I have my preferences. You offworlders and Kleshmakers may think them arbitrary or arcane, but they are mine nonetheless: personally, I never have difficulties with the Haydar. They are, in my estimation, a brave and honorable people. Yet it is sometimes hard to strike agreements over territory with them, owing to their nomadic ways. Here today, gone tomorrow. They are also fond of violence to excess."

He continued, "I would not wish to be an Aurisman, nor live like one, yet they are attentive to Embasses. Kurbs I find over-civilized and arbitrary in the extreme, but they have the quality of constancy—they remain the same this year as last. Garlinds are enamored of chaos . . . I could continue, of course, but the central point is that all have some virtue. Save the Lagostomes: they change everything they touch forever. They utterly ruin land for future use, which is why they remain confined to the delta . . ."

While Morgin continued to declaim upon the negative values of the Lagostomes, Meure watched the city-state slowly drifting past, also observing the people when the barge drifted close by the shore.

As he did so, his anticipations slowly sank. Like Cretus and Morgin both, as he saw them, he could see no redeeming feature. This was not the place to be stranded, nor were these people the material from which to fashion the new millenium . . . Odd, that thought. It felt Cretusish, but he could not detect any leakage. Cretus was firmly hidden, completely withdrawn.

And the rest? Well, the Haydar certainly had a place, and as Cretus said, they had been "high in his esteem," and he in theirs. Otherwise . . . no. Not even the Haydar! He saw it! It came unbidden, unasked, but he saw it, clearly! He had reviewed each race he had met on Monsalvat, Lagostome, Haydar, Kurb, Rivermen, and Lagostomes again, and what he had learned of each of them, and he saw something of what Flerdistar had spoken of: Cretus *had* been a great character out of history, for he had set his influence and his logos upon the whole planet. Yes! They had attained it, once, under Cretus. Meure saw plainly that had Cretus endured and continued, he would have fused the warring factions of Monsalvat into the most dynamic human society ever fashioned. But he also saw that when this development was arrested in midstream, as it were, it had functioned upon the unique social conditions of Monsalvat like a virus, *to which the population of Monsalvat had developed a perfect immunity*, which went far to explain its changelessness, at least to a level from which it could be maneuvered into complete stasis by something else.

That was why Cretus had withdrawn: they were all immune to him now, something unforeseen by Cretus, or the entity who had manipulated events to bring Cretus back. And what was it Flerdistar had said? Another identity, a double-trump personality, coming into action . . . things moving quickly to completion?

The thought-pattern started moving, flowing. Meure could feel the answer coming; and there was a block. Something stopped him. He could not follow it.

He looked at the passing river shore, trying to redistract himself. Meure saw poverty of the most oppressive flowing past them, and more, it was a poverty without honor or chance to escape. The brownish river water washed flaccidly against a muddy shoreline, or against stained and rotting levees and pilings, while the people behind those borders moved about their affairs listlessly, or just sat and stared, or moved among one another carefully, carefully, more fearful of igniting one another than they were of the conditions about them that oppressed them. He saw it. Nothing held them here but themselves. They had built a mental-social refuge, which had become a prison. It was their values that made them distrusted and hated.

Meure looked hard at the reeking panorama of wretched huts, trash idly piled in random heaps, the careful motions, the ragged children which according to Morgin were procreated outside the home, which would go far to explain the extraordinary similarity of appearance among Lagos—they had the widest genetic base of any population on the planet.

Meure knew.

—*Cretus!*

There was silence and emptiness. No sense of presence at all. He tried again, this time more strongly.

—*Cretus! Cretus, the Scribe! Come forth! You hear with my ears, so you know as I do, what can be done!*

One instant it was not there. Then it was.

—I hear. The "voice" was tired, resigned.

—*Magus and Hanged Man, she said. And what am I?*

—A most deadly combination, so I now see. I, too, know that ancient theory. My vice, you see; I looked far, I saw *Her,* and I saw beyond her as well, back to the beginning. I should have guessed it, but it's my nature, what I am, not to guess, do you see . . . that's why the transfers never took before: you can only transfer personality among likes, or upward, up the hierarchy. A double-trump personality could only shift to another double-trump. And to think that the entity projected itself across space to bring you, to house me. Pardon me, but I must laugh to myself over that one. It has unleashed doom upon Monsalvat. You will change it more than I, and the entity will go, too. The Ler girl has seen far into it. I am, as she said, Magus and Hanged Man. The numbers are one and twelve. My symbol is their sum, thirteen: Unity.

—*And what are mine, Manipulator of Symbols and Giver of Oneself to a Unfied Cause?*

—You know, nor would you ask. The Fool and the High Priestess. Zero and two. Equals two. Innocence of action and innocence of thought. Motiveless, resultless, energy. But Monsalvat lives on stasis.

—No more.

—You dare not ignite these pestiferous Lagos!

—I will ignite them, you control them.

—You have an escape, if you will but wait for it.

—I no longer believe in escapes. I was brought here to stay here, forever. Do you think for a moment that that thing will permit any ship to approach this planet, with us on it? We have to go forward, now.

—As soon as it learns what you have in mind, it may send you back without a ship, directly, though it would cost a lot of lives to do so . . . It may not be able to deal with us, on the other hand. I know it's not a God, or anything like that; it has limitations, although they are hard enough to find.

—It sent a manifestation of itself, but it couldn't perceive you . . .

—I don't believe it can perceive you, either, directly, though it can discern your effects. I mean, it knows something's there. That may be the adept's camouflage which my presence lends you: we muddy each other's image for it.

—And for others as well.

—Ah, well, it's just as you say, sure enough. Horny little beast, she didn't know who she was having, or why she was there in the first place . . . the light of a double star blinds those who have learned to see by the light of one.

—However it was, she wants something of you, she came across the oceans of space to get it; I am not the source of these rumors about the Ler of long ago.

—However polite the greeting, it always comes down to the matter at hand.

—As you say, the matter at hand. How is it you are the source? And what it is you've seen?

—To the first, I am not so much source, as focus. We Klesh always knew something, do you understand . . . something from the old days that was never spoken of directly.

—Something from Dawn?

—Aye. Dawn. And who knows where *they* heard it. The Warriors were . . . secretive about it, so I understand. But it was before the Klesh, the secret, it was . . . but you can't keep a secret like that entirely shut up; you see, the Warriors performed a crime, and they never stopped trying to justify it among themselves, and so perhaps the very first slaves overheard something, and added it to other bits and scraps later on, and so in the slave grapevine, it was known. And if you had the power to look into a window upon all space and time, what question would you ask, Meure Schnasy, what would you look for? The most important thing in the world to you, out of the basic facts of your life. And so did I. I looked through the *Skazenache*, I did; many times. I kept having to go further back, further and further. I have seen the exodus from Dawn on the great ships, the Great Warriors caged up and glaring like wild animals, the Klesh fearful; I saw the *Radahim* made out of human stock that the Warriors sifted, one by one; some had uses, some had esthetics, and some were just caprice: that was toward the end. I saw the Warriors make their first captures, I saw them find Dawn.

—*What they did, it was not on Dawn?*

—No. Before that. In a period when they were exiled and wandering, lost and trying to lose themselves, long years, visiting unknown planets, trying to find a place that suited their temperament.

—*What?*

—I am hanging on to life by one thread, and that's the one. And as soon as you know it, you'll sell me to her, you will . . . and so it was that I became the focus of what she's perceived out of the past, her past. I spread the story. We needed something to believe in, even an irony: Our Lady of Monsalvat.

—*St. Zermille, that I've heard them call on?*

—I invented St. Zermille. I, Cretus, will tell you that. If you can guess it yourself . . .

—*I would rather have you tell me; just as I would have you tell me what happened to the girls. Why was no one concerned? I wanted to ask, but everyone seemed to know except me.*

—And I wondered if you'd noticed. They were here, and then gone. It happens all the time; not as if an everyday thing, but often enough. It was so in my day, when I was a buck, and I would look no farther. Of course, ordinary foul play might be suspect, so you, say, might think. But not Morgin or Tenguft or I: we are natives. Not you or Flerdistar—you were otherwise occupied. This leaves the unfortunate boy, whom we cannot question, and Clellendol, who is so perplexed he is ashamed to ask. Him, a criminal, and a crime was performed under his nose. No—I do not wonder, because of what I remember. You would not suspect anything because you did not know what to look for. For example . . . the auburn-haired girl? Clearly, unmistakably a Medge or Urige. The other one? An Ellar of Holastri, which is an island off the southern tip of Glordune.

—*That raises more questions than foul play. It is not the most simple explanation.*

—Occam's razor, eh? Yes, I know about it. Well, that all depends upon what you know about environments, like Aceldama.

—*They were parts of it?*

—No. It can't hold a steady state in the world we perceive. No, they are, or were, or will be, real enough, real flesh and blood. It took them . . . or takes, or will take; and puts them out, under some control. Since there's a strain involved from the original, all it has to do is relax, as it were, and they return to the place from whence they came. I regard it as a most sinister symptom that this happened—it has dispensed with indirect controls.

—*That's not logical! If it could do that, then it could just reach out and pick who it wanted and transfer them here.*

—Wrong. First, it doesn't have fine control enough to work like that at a distance. Only here, and then, not all the time. Second, you would know it, and resist, which would make the transfer operation in Cucany worthless . . . No, it's as I've told you, it's control is very crude, and cruder with distance. When it came, I tried to perceive it, and saw a little—I am half in the shadow-world, anyway. It's been doing this for centuries, trying to lure the right type here. It made mistakes, you see. It helped the Klesh stay more intractable than they actually were, which frightened the others off, and it hemmed me in. . . .

—*I suppose you will say that it made up Flerdistar and Clellendol and the Spsom as well.*

—No—but it's been attracting them for a long time. I suppose you could say that it's kept an issue alive, that without which, there would be no Flerdistar, and without her and her family group, no expedition to Monsalvat . . .

—*But the space-stresses, the storms . . .*

—You got here in one piece, didn't you? And the ship you came in was broken, wasn't it? I tell you, you must exercise caution! It wants strife. What we provide for it isn't enough . . . you see, when I was alive, what I did to Monsalvat was instill a certain order into things; that remained, at least. It stopped me too soon, but in actuality it was just right—for us. To you, Monsalvat seems chaotic, but to me it's actually quite orderly now, much better than the old days. At least I did that! But for it, it's boring, like it was before the Klesh came! No, I'm sure of it: it is leading you into a trap. You must not set these Lagos off. I see repercussions that will echo across time. It's prodding you, even though it can no longer perceive you directly: that is a measure of its urgency. Even at the risk of serious consequences to itself. It brought you here to set things back as they were, and that must not be.

—*Still the Hanged Man?*

—I am what I am. And you must be as true to yourself. The Fool can bring any consequences, and The High Priestess possesses uncorrupted original wisdom. Already Flerdistar can feel your influence on this world, though she's a pastreader—she's getting backscatter from the future . . .

—*I can refuse to act!*

—Fool! That's an action as well! Then you'll be led into one situation after another, until you do the right thing . . . you lose all initiative along that path, which means that you'll do what it wants. And don't think that it will save you after it has used you to ignite the change it wants—you're just a catalyst. You have value until the moment, and afterwards, nothing. It doesn't care if it kills you in the process or not.

—*What about you?*

—What so? It has already discovered what we know, that I can't do anything anymore. So it is with all men out of time. We are all creatures of our own times, and none other . . . think of the irony of the entity: it brings me back, and I'm useless for this world, this now-world. Then it turns out that the vehicle is stronger than the cargo. Then it loses both of us in the interference we create. Now it is tampering with reality to the extent of its powers, even when there is potential there to destroy it. You can be anything you want: you can be Monsalvat's deliverer, or you can be an Emperor of Hell, for a short time.

—*We already have Brotherhood of Mankind, out there where I came from. It hasn't done us much good, so it seems.*

—Cain slew Abel, in the oldest story, and so much for Brotherhood. Your ancient Kleshlike forebears had the right idea. But peoples can work together, once they have the vision. So lead us! Finish the thing I tried to start! And we will go out and return to Man and teach, and all men will grow strange and wonderful—it's our diversity and our mutability that is our selfness—we've chased rainbows of ideology for millennia, but they have been wrong! All we have to be is ourselves, and work together. We all have different shapes, but we have congruent dreams; it will be that way, no matter how odd we become. Look how far Derques have gone.

—*I've heard of Derques, but not seen one.*

—What?

—*No, I remember them. I've seen them, somewhere, but I can't place it . . . yes, I remember them: they are odd Humans who walk on their hands and swing their bodies between their arms. Their legs and feet are atrophied and used as hands. They are not native to Kepture, but are sometimes brought here from . . . ah, Ch . . . Chengurune. Now it's coming . . . I can remember: men with robes and cowls atop a hill, in the wind, there's a pack of them, moving restlessly, and the men show them some scrap of cloth. They take it, show it to each other, holding it with their feet, which are hands. They are ugly brutes, grimacing and grunting, capering about; their shoulders are grown into their necks, and their faces are long; ugly, ugly. Now they begin to bound off down the trail, swinging both arms at once, and using their arses as a third foot, tossing bits of dirt in the air in their excitement. They are hunting someone! A fugitive; he escaped me and I set the Derques on him . . . That's not my memory!*

There was no answer from Cretus.

—*Gone hiding again? No matter, that: if I can remember Derques, I can remember the rest of it, what I need to know to buy free. . . .*

It was a little like trying to remember something he had forgotten, and also a little like trying to visualize numbers while working a mathematics exercise in his head. And a little unlike anything else. At first, he got results, but it was uncontrolled: a flash image, this, that. He remembered things Cretus had thought memorable, the details we all remember without trying to do so. Meure remembered the color of afternoon sunlight on a sun-heated wall of stucco, amber-colored, a time when the city was just coming alive, and he, Cretus, anticipated nightfall and its darkness-blessed opportunities for larceny and vice. He remembered Nomads by a campfire deep in the fens, mysterious figures in dark robes who muttered among themselves in an incomprehensible jargon. He remembered a great battle, the end of it, men surrendering, others counting the fallen, while he stood on a hill overlooking a winedark sea, and one of the captains struggled up the hill and reported that it had gone just like he had said, and he saluted, not without a trace of awe, and returned, and he looked out over the violet sea into the unknowable Northern Ocean, and the deep blue light that flowed over it.

There was no key, it seemed. He could not control the chains of association. Things fell into his head, and fell out again, leaving disconnected echoes of themselves; the harder he reached, the more random the memories came, and the more erratic the duration of each scene became. Some were just instants—others lasted minutes, so it seemed. Still others were disconnected pictures, that made no sense at all.

Then there was a long one, a scene that must have made a deep impression on Cretus, for it lasted long and was recalled in meticulous detail. It was simple, in its own way—a view of a city through an open window, but there was something odd about it. Meure strained, a great force of will, and managed to halt the changeover of the memories. Now he had one. But there was an oddity about it, and he, Meure, didn't know what it was. Now he remembered as if it were his own, and he tried to see what was so extraordinary about this scene. Cretus remembered it as odd, alien.

The architecture of the city was unconventional, but that was not it. *That* didn't bother Cretus at all. But it bothered Meure: it was a city of slender towers, all set at different heights, all composed of ornate rococo cupolas set atop columnar bases of differing degrees of slenderness. Between some of the structures airy walkways were stretched, seemingly defying gravity, for he could not see how they were supported; there was traffic moving on the ways as well, but he could not make out any details of the figures. They were dark blots, moving, apparently walking or gliding with a motion rather like dancing, or skating, all without haste, very esthetically, as if Time had no substance. The creatures seemed manlike in general shape, but they were oddly jointed. Men? Meure couldn't tell. But Cretus wasn't bothered at all. He accepted that.

It was day, in the city. The sun was shining brightly in a clear blue sky, he could see it through the window, backlighting the scene . . . and it was a single star. That was what Cretus thought was the most alien feature of the scene he was looking at. It must have been a scene from his early use of the *Skazenache:* another world, perhaps another time, future, past, who knew. Now he had the association he wanted, a key to the vault within.

There still was no presence, but a voice seemed to whisper bodilessly in his mind, "This is the world Erspa, a planet located in the Greater Magellanic Cloud, a hundred million years in the past. It was the first time I tried to see another world inhabited by sentient beings, but neither Human nor Ler. I was astounded at the appearance of their sun. It looked incomplete, unfinished, naked. I have seen different shapes of living, reasoning flesh, but nothing so odd as that first time."

The voice faded. Now Meure had one association, and he pursued it. Now the images stayed longer, and were clearer, but they become very odd indeed. Meure saw empty planets illuminted by the violet glare of giant stars, doomed to oblivion hardly before decently cooling off. He saw things that swam, and others that flew; still others loped, strode, or hopped. Then, after many of the odd scenes had gone by him, he remembered seeing a Klesh, in the light of a single sun. Now he had the association he had been looking for, and he followed it, watching every scene closely, pressing for the conclusion.

He got the whispered rumor immediately, and it stunned him so much he almost lost the chain-thread he was following. But before he had time to digest the import of it, the source of the rumor Flerdistar had tracked across space and time, he skipped a score of similar images, that were Cretus' tracks back into the past, and then the final scene came without warning, and unfolded to Meure, as it had to Cretus. Everything was there, nothing was left out. And the oddest thing about it was that the memory was of a person telling the true story, as if to an audience. Perhaps it had been Cretus' viewpoint that had left that impression. But the memory was of someone talking directly to Cretus. And then Meure understood everything about the curious history of the Ler, and the Warriors, and the travails of the Klesh.

He was so surprised (for it was, actually, a simple story, despite its details), that he said, aloud, "So that's what it was, all the time."

Flerdistar, wrestling with a sweep much too large for her, turned and said, "What did you say?"

And with his mind still flickering and reverberating with the spillout of the memories of Cretus the Scribe, he looked at the Ler girl as if awakening from a deep sleep, and answered, "It was nothing. Nothing at all." And it was true: it was nearly nothing, considered in comparison with an uncountable number of acts, intentions, initiations, beginnings. Nearly nothing! But the consequences of that one act had left standing waves across time. Meure felt disoriented and deconceptualized. Nothing he had learned to assume about the consequentiality of acts, about the value of actions, had remained true after what he had 'remembered' from the memories of Cretus. He felt the conceptual universe shift along some unknown axis, adjusting to the new information, integrating it, although now it was the rest of what he thought he knew that shifted, rather than the new data. And then, prepared, initiated, ready, the realization following the exposure came rumbling through his mind, and he did not try to inhibit it, or deflect it. It, too, was a simple thing, almost nothing, but with consequences. It was: living creatures, being imperfect, unfinished, possess a flaw in their perceptions and reasonings which permits them to assign an entirely unrealistic set of weighted values upon their acts, so that what they think is a major decision, actually has close to zero value in the reality which includes the dimension of Time, and acts which seem unimportant, or even virtually nonexistent, assume major significance in that dimension. Oh, there was nothing wrong with the Theory of Causality—things were caused, all right—that was true beyond a shadow of a doubt. It was just that all reasoning creatures tended to assign the wrong values to the wrong acts. It was true, what the old stories had suggested, their authors half guessing even as they approached the real truth—that the death of a butterfly out of its sequence would determine the results of an election, and the form of government, and whether millions of those creatures would live or die, millions of years after the inconsequential butterfly. That the way a wind blows on a certain day would set the course of an empire spanning Time. That an enormous commercial enterprise, spanning whole planetary systems, would vanish overnight, engulfed by its competitors and its creditors, because one insignificant manager of one operation could not manage his own mouth.

Cretus had seen that, and the examples that were its foundation, in his view through the *Skazenache*, and for that reason had left his work incomplete, short of its great triumph. He didn't care what his subjects might say, or historians from any planet or any period in time, before him or after him. That was truly inconsequential; what mattered to him were the things which seemed insignificant now, meaningless, valueless: the way a servant plied his broom; the way a low-ranking minister looked out the window; and even smaller things whose presence he could guess, but which he could not see. From that data base, he had concluded that it was time to disengage, that any of his idea at all be retained, for if he stayed where he was, not only would the idea fail, but its opposite would rise again in greater strength. *For Cretus to hold on to his Empire to the end, no matter what, would have the consequence that Monsalvat would become so filled with pride and rage and alienation that no society at all would be possible, and that the Klesh of that planet would disintegrate, and die off, and one by one, gutter and go out.* But to step off the stage, voluntarily, at that moment, would hold things somewhat as they were, and freeze them, for perhaps another to take up thousands of years in the future. *He could only win by surrendering: that was what his study of consequentiality told him.*

Now Meure understood Cretus very well. He understood what Cretus had done, half-consciously at that. He understood the nature of things, because he had seen an excellent example not to be denied. He had seen and understood the secret of the Klesh. He had seen that Cretus had used his knowledge to map out a rough outline of his unseen enemy, the Entity. And now Meure felt a greater weight than Cretus bearing down upon him; now he himself knew what Flerdistar had come light-years to find, but he did not know the consequences of giving her that information. Or, for that matter, of not giving it to her. But he felt the weight of his decision multiplying, magnifying itself in resonances across time and space: what he told her, and when, would have results. That much was certain. And that was the least of the decisions he had to make!

13

"There is no such thing as history. The facts, even were they available, are too numerous to grasp. A selection must be made; and this can only be onesided, because the selector is enclosed in the same network of time and space as his subject."

—A.C.

THE DOUBLE SUNS of Monsalvat had sunk below the western rises leading to Ombur when Morgin announced that it appeared they would reach a section of the foreign quarter; how he knew was not apparent, as the city drifting past them had not seemingly changed, save to grow slightly more dense; in place of hovels and shacks, and seedy tumbledown sheds given over to all sorts of questionable enterprises, there were now small blocks of flats, with lethargic inhabitants leaning out of frameless windows, staring into space. There were also what seemed to be small factories, scrap yards, dumps. Peddlers roamed the street, hawking various articles of food and commerce, with measured cadences, almost as if moving to a rhythm Meure could not either hear or imagine. It looked both dreary and impossible. The prevailing emotion was despair.

Now that the river had divided itself up into the myriad channels of the delta proper, the width of each stream was narrower, and they were drifting closer to the littered streets, and could see the inhabitants better. The Lagostomes in their city did not look any better than the ones he could remember from the incident alongside the vanished *Ffstretsha*: if anything, the ones who had come out after the ship had seemed to be better-dressed. They wore rags and tatters and castoffs whose original identity had long since been lost. Occasionally, one saw a rare individual in slightly better order, but that was seldom. A pervasive effluvia filled the air, of too many people, too long unwashed, mixed with all the substances which had been gathered by the Great River; waste, organic chemicals, other things not so readily identifiable.

Meure wondered what the others thought of it. For himself, he felt a great bottomless dismay; there was nothing in his experience or knowledge like this. Monsalvat seemed to be a way of life humanity had tried hard to forget. He said as much to Morgin, sharing one of the sweeps with the middle-aged Embasee.

Morgin ruminated long upon an answer, or perhaps whole families of answers. Finally, he replied, "I know Kepture and Chengurune by direct experience, Glordune by repute, which is adequate for my purposes, and Cantou by longing, which I do not expect to attain. Kepture is . . . rather harsher, shall we say, then Chengurune, but not quite so abrupt and unforgiving as Glordune. But these are differences of degree, not of kind. All peoples I have known seem to live lives of greater or lesser complexity, all deriving something valuable from the reality they inhabit. I have heard you off-worlders speak of things and thought that things sound more peaceable on your worlds, and it is a wonder to me, for even in Cantou, men strive and hate and slay. And in Glordune? Ah, that is beyond even some of us Aceldamans." He shook his head, as if something was beyond his ability to describe it.

And then continued, "But equally so, you have not lived as one of us." He favored Meure with a sidelong leer. "You saw the girl, who had taken up with the other boy? She seemed of the lineaments of the Ellar, and they are a most curious people, even for Glordune; all their lives, they make up, in their heads, an astonishing epic of some imaginary world, full of amazing events, monsters, magic, flashing swords, deeds of great valor and heroism. These personal legends are embroidered in fantastic detail—the more bizarre the better, and constructed according to a literary canon I could not begin to describe, it is so complicated and arbitrary. All this, you understand, in total secrecy: the epic is never committed to paper, nor is it repeated to anyone. Then, when the Ellar feels the approach of death, they summon friends and enemies alike, and all gather to hear the recitation of the Deathsong. And the Ellar do no expire until they have finished their story.

"I heard one in my life, and if I never hear another, I could vanish into eternity content. These stories are like nothing anyone has ever heard before, and they stir the blood with ancient longings; as a fact, after hearing one, the Ellar are prone to go out and perform some amazing feat.

"I heard the Deathsong from a mariner who had been the sole survivor of a shipwreck; he lay on the beach of Chengurune and recounted the real-world events first to us who had found him, broken and cast up. Those events made an epic in themselves: pirates, sea-demons, storms, Eratzenasters—astonishing! But those things were unimportant to him: he had to have an audience for the real epic he was to tell. We sent to the town for the people, that he might recite it, and not make his transition unhallowed. He was broken, tattered and bleeding, and quite beyond help, but he hung on until the people came, and then told his story.

"A man, more dead than alive, spoke from one dusk until the next, of events so ferocious it made his real-world tale seem like an ordinary trip to the market. And we sat there and listened, completely in his spell, neither eating, nor fornicating, nor moving restlessly until he had finished, which he did by including an elaborate curse upon all not of the Ellar blood. The curse I have long since forgotten; who listens to curses, when they flow like the air, everywhere? But the tale . . . ? I will never forget it, though I could not recount it if I tried; a savant in the crowd told me afterward that there were seventeen main plots in it, interwoven together in a manner impossible to unravel . . . spaceships were but the least of it. The Ellar live in small stone houses upon a rocky island, and cultivate things that grow on vines. By all accounts, they are rather poor and modest, except when attacked."

Meure said, "Then the girl Ingraine, whatever her real name was . . ."

"Most likely it was."

". . . had one of these stories in her all the time?"

"Of course."

"But it would have been unfinished . . ."

"According to the lore of the Ellar, Deathsongs of the young are reputed to be the best."

"I could almost understand that."

"There is one thing more to them . . . that they act out in their real lives, as best as they are able, a role selected from their personal epic. It is a major portion of the Ellar way to attempt to discern the outlines of that role and react properly to it. Such efforts fail, of course, but they occupy the Ellar well enough; I have not heard them complain of boredom."

"Cretus has told me that she was an Ellar, brought by an entity which oppresses Monsalvat . . . then she could have done so willingly."

"If she was a spy, I should suspect enthusiastic cooperation in such a proceeding . . . neither you nor Halander, of course, would appear in her Deathsong, in a form you would recognize, if at all."

"You didn't seem concerned about her disappearance."

Morgin shrugged, a gesture he could *see* Cretus making. "People disappear, occasionally, that's a fact. Not everyone, nor even many, but some. I was not surprised . . . anyone on Monsalvat who seems unexplainable seems to vanish, sooner or later. Had it been one of you offworlders, I would have been surprised. Or the Haydar girl."

"Why Tenguft?"

"Haydar are never out of place, such is my experience."

Now Morgin turned his attention back to the sweep, as if he had spent too much time with Meure. But Meure understood what Morgin had been trying to tell him about Monsalvat: that its humanity was not muted and tamed. That if in Yastian there were pits of despair, in the hearts of the Ellar there lurked a poetry of soul-stirring complexity, an *Iliad* and an *Odyssey* waiting behind every pair of eyes . . . Cretus let an image through, and Meure recalled, that all the Ellar were small and delicate of physique, as Ingraine had been; slender, pale, self-contained, self-sufficient. A people who travelled little, who had fled from the tumults of Glordune to their rocky island, and who went no further, no matter what. Morgin had used them as a symbol for Monsalvat, and Meure could sense Cretus' agreement with that. The rest of the people . . . Meure understood that there was much in excess on Monsalvat, that the excesses and crimes had been trimmed, so to speak, from civilized humanity; but humanity had only one Homer, while on a small rocky island between the Inner Sea and the Outer Ocean, there was an entire tribe of them. What could an integrated Ellar have brought to Monsalvat, and what might they have brought to all men? And so it was with the rest. Perhaps, Morgin's opinion to the contrary, even the Lagostomes. . . .

Clellendol interrupted his thoughts. "Truly, I am in my own, here."

Flerdistar added, disrespectfully, "A blind dog in a meatmarket would serve as excellent comparison."

Clellendol answered, unconcernedly, "A historian on a planet where people remember oaths of revenge forever would not be far off the mark, either. But here, this city! I can hardly wait to land. It seethes with crime, of the most refined sorts."

Meure asked, "How can you tell that? Not that they don't look criminal to me, but then again, so do they all."

"I detect furtiveness, collusion, intrigue; it is in their motions, their gestures. I will need to get closer to discern the exactness, of course, but one can feel it in the air. There is burglary and chicanery here on a scale heretofore unknown! Cheating, conniving, and the taking of unfair advantages; all are represented in this paragon of vice!"

Meure said, "All those qualities you have enumerated; those would seem excellent reasons for avoiding such people—indeed, so feel the majority of the natives, so I hear."

Flerdistar added, advising caution, "And so much I would say as well. My ability allows me to feel the eddies stirred up by the mighty of this planet, in Time . . . but what I have felt does not make me wish to plunge into that stream and interact with such characters! To the contrary! Here we are the other way toward chaos, much too far to suit me—I only wish now to derive what I came to seek, and depart this planet. The wardens were correct an age ago: Monsalvat is no place for a civilized creature."

Meure said, "And so you are wise to wish no contact with the elementals, here; but to observe or communicate, you must contact some or many of them. How is it that you are affected here? You, Flerdistar, are losing your nerve at the last moment, and you, Clellendol, are gaining too much. Your purpose in being here at all is unraveling."

Flerdistar looked downward at the planks. "You must not speak of such things."

Clellendol muttered, "You are becoming a creature of this world too much for my liking."

"We are all merely responding to something archaic that has been preserved here and nowhere else; it was bred out of you at the start, and it's been slowly cultured out of *us*. But all legitimacies carry the seed germ of their destruction by themselves, if retained intact. That's just the problem: nowhere but here has the ancient dichotomy been retained; the paradox. And, yes, I feel it stir something in me, I didn't know I had."

Clellendol said, "Galloping across the plains with a spear in one hand and an anatomical trophy in the other; or contributing to someone else's trophies? So much does not strike me as the goal of civilized Humans."

Meure replied, "The image is wrong from the beginning; for I am no Haydar, and they do not gallop, but ride Eratzenasters. And I know that neither here, nor on the Human worlds, has Man attained to his generic civilization. Not ever! It hasn't come yet! That is the great secret. Even now with so much Time behind us, it hasn't come yet! Spaceships and technology? They have buried it, not brought it closer."

Clellendol mocked Meure, "So here we have just another antitech."

"Because I said it was not the best answer as a whole system, does not mean I take a stand against it. You Ler are said to be folk of subtle distinctions: where in that is the subtlety?"

Clellendol asked, "Who speaks thus to us? Is it Cretus, or is it Meure Schasny, who could hardly lift his eyes from the floor not so long ago?"

Meure laughed, almost to himself. "For the moment, I am me, which is to say, Meure . . . although I am becoming less certain that such a distinction would be meaningful. And as for change . . . one is said to survive according to how one reacts to changing circumstances. Flerdistar, that is what we have lost, your people and mine: we have lost the ability to dance on the wind, instead, we built little closed cells in which change could be exempted. You say it yourself, with every statement you make: Ler culture hasn't changed for centuries, if at all. Since the originals left the Home planet, I suspect. And you said, no Ler would make any change, because they were afraid of consequences. But we inhabit a sea of consequences, and you read the waves on the surface of that sea. The faster the adaptation, the higher the creature. But building hermetically sealed closed environments does not increase adaptability."

Morgin cautioned them, "I sense dispute! This must now cease, as we are nearing our landing, and your words will doubtless unsettle some Lago, who will commit some atrocity."

Meure said, "Of course you are right. But would this not be reduced somewhat with foreigners present, as in the quarter we are in?"

Morgin said, "The foreigners are a minority, and of diverse background. There is not a single, coherent ideal to oppose and negate the Lago way; all this accomplishes is to make them more edgy, and less predictable. Soon we will land; we should find a place to run to earth until we can determine what is what. I have not the Embasse's protection, now."

"Do you know of such a place?"

"I know of several by repute. None of them are places I would choose in normal circumstances. We shall try."

Meure said, "And now I have another question, Master Morgin. How shall we get ourselves out of this city, into better lands? I know we cannot stay here forever, nor do I wish it."

Morgin scratched his scalp thoughtfully. "We have a Thief in our company, who claims to relish the aura of Crime exuded by the Lagos . . . And you have a most fearsome spirit locked up inside you; it might be worth consideration to allow these two identities to perambulate somewhat . . . There is no other way I know of to escape Yastian, save by this manner. I have no more good will left to draw on, and you cannot expect donations for a party which includes a Haydar, or First-folk . . . if you have not faced unpleasant choices before in your lives, you must prepare to face them now."

Meure observed, "You are casual enough about the choice you present us: Steal or Starve."

Morgin shrugged, "As an Embasse, I have spent my life telling lies of greater or lesser moment, for the good of all the people. I would act similarly to save my own neck as well. You may safely assume that all whom you meet here will already have made that decision. The ones who have elected to stand upon morality you will not meet."

Flerdistar asked, "They are not about much, then?"

Morgin again shrugged. "They are not alive, Lady. Not in Yastian."

With some currency they obtained through Morgin's sale of the barge and everything on it, at last, long after dark had fallen, they were able to secure an adjoining collection of poor rooms at the back of what would loosely qualify as an inn. They allowed Morgin to make the choices, although all of the places they had seen seemed equally bad. It seemed Morgin was using some standard other than cleanliness or style to select a place.

Indeed, he had told them after they were settled for the night, "One picks his place here with care, so it is; although you will not see so many open disputes in Yastian, when dark falls it is wise to seek shelter in an easily defended location, deregarding such niceties as comfort, or price, low or high . . . there are prowlers about in the nights, and they suffer neither resistance nor the bearing of tales, in short, they kill first, as silently as possible. I had heard of this place from certain outland bloods operating here temporarily, and believe it as good as any we could find . . . With a large, mixed party such as us, they will doubtless suspect a spectacular crime in the offing, and will leave us exceptionally alone. This place also provides street-wardens throughout the day and night— part of the tariff, so we should have a little space to breathe."

But that space was little enough. Morgin projected that the barge would translate very roughly into something less than a week*, allowing enough "extra money to get them safely out of the land of the Lagos-tomes and into either Ombur, or Far Nasp, on the opposite side of the

*The "week" on Monsalvat was of six days.

delta. Clellendol immediately went down to the tavern on the street floor, to orient himself for possible opportunities to practice his skill.

The rest of them settled down to rest for the night, with Tenguft volunteering to keep the night watch. Morgin found an obscure corner pallet and fell asleep instantly.

Meure was tired, but sleep would not come; he felt uneasy and agitated, for no cause he could determine. He knew he was not particularly concerned with safety, for he trusted Tenguft's hair-fine perceptions without question. Still, he knew from what he had seen of Yastian that it possessed distrusts no amount of confidence could still. Evening—sundown, had been typical of the city: the double suns had not set behind a horizon of faraway landforms or vegetation, but had slunk, bloated and gross, behind ramshackle buildings. From no point in the city proper could one see actual open land; and even the air itself seemed changed. Filled with a greasy, almost imperceptible haze, it distorted colors, washing them out, and shapes seen through it in the distance wavered and floated, appearing and disappearing.

Inland from the wharves, the physical condition of the city did not improve. Meure had seen no indication whatsoever that wealthy people formed a quarter of their own, or, for that matter, existed. Morgin had assured him that they were few, and so retiring as to be almost invisible. Meure had been somewhat surprised at that, for from the poverty he had expected to see evidence of at least part of a leisure class, but apparently in Yastian things had progressed much further than that; originally there had been a stratified class society, but that structure had eroded away long ago, by the operation of a sociological equivalent to Gresham's Law: once the low classes reach a certain majority percentage, their values swamp the entire society. A wealthy class was only possible where there was something left over for the poorest. Yastian had passed the nothing-left-over point early in its Lagostome history.

The foreigners Meure had expected to see had not materialized. He had imagined that the foreign quarter would have a raffish cosmopolitanism about it, with odd crowds, fragments of uncouth speech, restaurants catering to various ethnic identities. Instead, he caught quick glimpses of occasional persons, about which it could only be said that they were not Lagostomes. He had seen, in short, what appeared to him to be rather ordinary people, if somewhat furtive.

Meure knew his perceptions were not wrong—it was the data base he was using to interpret what he saw that was the problem. He himself didn't recognize the types he saw, and even the Cretus memories seemed uncertain. Cretus' picture of the tribes and septs of Kepture and other continents was an old memory—far back in the past. Also, Meure felt that he was seeing less than pure types, as well, for who else would wind up stranded in a vile city hated by all the rest of the planet, the city and its inhabitants. The hybrids, quadroons, octoroons and worse of the whole planet.

Cretus had remained quiet so far. Meure thought that his companion was now merely still, not so withdrawn as before, presumably observing rather than hiding out of dismay. He hoped he could keep Cretus quiet a little longer, for it would not do for him to take over in this place unless conditions were just right. Or required. He wished it, and had the curious feeling that it was so because of that, that somehow he was controlling Cretus. If it were true, he could be grateful for it, and might yet figure out a way to survive this experience.

The Vfzyekhr had settled itself down by Meure's hip, and after a long and elaborate toilet, gone to sleep, as soundly as Morgin. Now it was just Meure and Flerdistar again.

In the thick atmosphere of Yastian by night, light was refracted and muted, and so a steady glow illuminated the bare rooms, and Meure could see well enough; he suspected the diffusing effect of the city air helped Flerdistar and Clellendol rather than hindered them, as they would be able to see better in this half-light. Out in the open spaces, he had noticed that they were particularly careful about moving about after dark. He could see Flerdistar, by the window, facing it from her pallet, but not specifically looking out at anything; her face was blank and expressionless.

She abruptly rose and came over to sit beside Meure. She began speaking immediately, as if voicing something that had long been on her mind. "I had not wished to face this before . . . but it seems that someone must. Another expedition to Monsalvat has failed, and the remnants will have to decide what they are to do next; whether to wait upon a dubious rescue, or embark upon a hazardous future."

Meure said, "You cannot be said to have failed until you fail to get the information you have sought off Monsalvat."

"We have no ship, so I cannot go in person; we have no communications off-planet, so I cannot send it. Moreoever, I don't have the answer to take or send, and our party of people—so well equipped and intentioned at the first, is now reduced to three, and one of those—you—is steadily growing more alien under my eyes, more frightening."

Meure laughed in a low tone, relaxed. "So you think Cretus is taking over? I can put you at rest on that account: Cretus is not me, and you would spot the difference immediately."

"Not Cretus. Something . . . worse I don't know . . . the present, the past, the future; they're all mixed up on this planet, and I'm finding it difficult to untangle the traces. I sense them, but I can't tell if they are from the past or the future. Shadowy powers moving, manipulating, in the background, point sources, which are people or people-like entities. Diffuse sources, or rather, one diffuse source, which I imagine is the entity; it is not coherent, but turbulent, sometimes many, sometimes one."

"Anything else?"

"Yes. I have feared to tell you, for the consequences."

"I don't understand."

"I . . . can't tell you how it works, but I *know* it: something I do initiates a major change here. I do something, and immediately there's a shift . . . in the world-lines. It's as if I create a character in History, but I can't see past that character into what it does; it masks the consequences, or blocks them."

Meure said, "Like an eclipse, where a smaller close body can obscure a larger distant one?"

"Like that, yes."

"How do you know *you* cause it?"

"This will be even harder to explain . . . but when I set out on this path, many years ago, I felt it weakly, even then. It became stronger with every step I took nearer here. It has now become so strong I can't see around it . . . the past and the future reverberate with echoes here, and somehow I myself am a momentary flicker in the time-line of this planet, and then unimaginable things happen; or I could deliberately thwart that by removing myself from life, because I don't know what it is that I do that sets it off. I can't see acts so well—only Powers."

"Having glimpsed Time, you now fear consequences of every act? That is no way to go forward, surely you know that, and do not need me to tell you. You could ultimately wind up a catatonic in a corner, fearing every act, and still be had by time, for that might be the thing that set it off. Nay! You must act as you would!"

"What I set off here makes Monsalvat different. All these barbarian cultures, preserved here as if in amber, they all vanish. What replaces them I don't understand at all."

"Surely not immediately, as if by Magic."

"No. It takes years, generations."

"Monsalvat could stand change; it is long overdue for it."

"You speak with more than an echo of Cretus."

"There are things Cretus desires, with which I agree, and would work with him to attain, without shame . . . what replaces the state of Monsalvat as it is now?"

"I think a civilization which is opaque to history-readers such as I . . ."

"So you fear to act, for fear of removing by improvement values of intolerance and hatred, because those acts perpetuate quaint barbarians for you to study at your leisure? Or that your profession be eliminated, while the rest of us slowly become relics of a former skill in adaptibility and survival? Now you are something less than lacking in courage."

She replied, with equal heat to match his, "It is not those selfish things, but the fear for my whole people that stays me! We become enclosed, limited, curiosities . . . obscure, forgotten. We go on, but our stream is lessened. I will be remembered for this."

"In a sense, if you can read it, then you already are."

"Hmph. Time-paradoxes are idle play of every schoolchild!"

"And I will remind you once that a paradox exists solely because of incomplete perception, and for no other reason." And Meure stopped himself suddenly, afraid to say more, because of what it was revealing to him as the words unfolded. Because never in his life had he explored a paradox, created one, or thought about them. What he had just said, while no less true for that, was as uncharacteristic of him as it was possible to be. And it didn't feel like Cretus, either. That was the worst part.

A shadow detached itself from the other shadows in the dim room and floated silently to where they sat. The shadow approached, moved suddenly, and lapsed into an angular shape; Tenguft. She whispered, harshly, "On the stairs. Two come!"

Meure listened but for a moment he heard nothing. He had not expected to. Then he heard scuffling, steps. Whoever was coming was neither slinking nor skulking, but coming openly, and he said as much to Tenguft. Nevertheless she drifted away from them to take up a position by the door, silent and invisible and deadly.

The steps came to the door, and there was a rattling at the latch, which opened the door, and in came Clellendol, assisting someone or something, they couldn't make out who in the light.

Clellendol said, whispering over his shoulder as he half-dragged his companion in, "Light, give us light, a little."

Tenguft secured and lit the reeking oil lamp, and by its flickering yellow light they saw whom Clellendol had brought: the Spsom Vdhitz, apparently none the better for his travels.

Vdhitz was not, apparently, fatally injured, but for the moment he was beyond speaking a Human language coherently. They made him comfortable, all the same, while he made half-hearted attempts to form Human speech formants. Flerdistar leaned close, and sputtered something in Vdhitz's ear in his own tongue. Afterwards, he returned to his own language, which Fleridstar translated in pauses as Vdhitz spoke, haltingly.

It was a tale that unfolded as a descending series of disasters and misfortunes. Things went bad, and then worse. The Bagman and the servant had started for Medlight, as they and Morgin had agreed, assuming Morgin would catch up with them later, there, or farther on, at Utter Semerend, with the Ler elders in tow. Then Jemasmy returned, to report the Prote gone—who knew where? The disappearance of a Prote being a serious matter, they applied to Afanasy for a reading, using his Prote, upon which circumstances Jemasmy found his also departed—again, who could say where. The party departed for the west with foreboding, and Benne-the-Clone mounted and assembled upon its place on the wagon the powerful ballista with which he had such deadly expertise. Afanasy went with them, along with a buck called Tallou.

Mallam had studiously ignored these proceedings, but after they had left, he sent a small party to follow at a distance, sensing something on the wind. Mallam proved correct, if somewhat tardy. The following party returned with a tale of woe and heroic striving against great odds: Jemasmy's group had been jumped by the same Meor pack which had followed them up from the Delta, apparently circling far around the south. The Haydar had arrived at the end, too late to help, but they told a hair-raising tale, seen from a distance, of two Haydar covering Benne, while he dealt out deaths to the Meor with a speed and a resolve they had not seen before in one not of the blood of the hunt. Like lightning-bolts his darts flew among the Meor, and he did not miss, swinging the clumsy weapon to aim and loading and cocking simultaneously. But in the end, there were enough Meors, and not enough Bennes, Afanasys,

Tallous . . . The relief party, led by Zermo Lafma, extracted a certain revenge upon the Meor band, but of course it was too late.

Lafma had allowed some of the Meors to escape, so as to spread the tale, and Mallam had them set out in the Hunt for these remainders, so as to leave the number to one witness. In the ensuing fray, somewhat south of the Yastian-Medlight track, Shchifr took a Meor dart and was killed. Perhaps it was the presence of aliens among them that stiffened the Meors, but they fought and stood their ground. Mallam had his revenge, but it cost him an amount he thought dear. Too dear; he had lost almost half his band, the Prote had abandoned Afanasy, and their spirit-woman had gone off into Incana on the word of the oracle. Segedine called down the Eratzenasters, to depart for the northwest, and the band they had left. They would have taken Vdhitz, for he had accounted himself competent in the fray with the Meors, despite his relative light weight and fragile build, but the Eratzenasters would have none of him, bucking and snorting and making odd blowing sounds from a concealed orifice along their undersides that made the Haydar warriors nervous and jumpy.

It was clearly an impossible situation: Rhardous N'hodos was called upon to make divination, and the portents were bad. They had a thousand kilometers to fly, perhaps farther, and to walk was clearly not advised. They were not convinced, further, that they could gain acceptance of Vdhitz by the other Haydar. Some muttered that the alien was bad fortune to them.

So Vdhitz left, and shortly afterward saw the band airborne upon the gruesome Eratzenasters . . . some stragglers circled back for a time, to keep him in sight, but in the end they turned back to the northwest and faded from sight.

Vdhitz hid by day and traveled by night across the wastes of Ombur, moving east toward the only place he knew anything about, Yastian. It was a city, and should there be a rescue attempt, it would be an obvious place to start for the rescuers. But in Ombur, night was no less hazardous than day: Korsors prowled the wastes, and other things as well, things that could be heard, but not seen. He became acquainted with fear. He saw things that were transitory and mutable, but emitted no sound, nor scent. It was puzzling. Vdhitz felt watched. But he could also feel the Vfzyekhr drawing him to that place, for the small furry creatures were not entirely slaves of the Spsom, but partners in a complex relationship for which no Human or Ler concept existed. Part of this relationship involved odd forms of telepathy, but only where certain combinations of Spsom and Vfyzekhr were assembled . . . he had wondered that the Vfyzekhr had gone to Incana with the Haydar girl, for Humans were not known to have exploitable telepathic ability, and the Ler were known to have none at all, save through their unique, and non-telepathic Multichannel Language, which acted like telepathy, but wasn't, being propagated by ordinary sound waves.

He starved and suffered; Ombur was Dry Steppe, with little open water, and little game. The Korsors and other nameless things that co-habited in the wastes haunted his wakefulness and his dreams alike. Men, stranger men than he had ever heard of, hunted him by day and by night, drawn by his alienness, his un-belonging to the land. And the adventure had passed—and what was left was a slender hope that in the mongrel diversity of the docks of Yastian he could remain alive, until a Spsom ship came again. One would come—the alternative was un-thinkable.

In the marshes he left his pursuers behind, and came to the city, and made his way by night to the foreign quarter. That journey was worth ten across Ombur; the city was deadlier than the wastes. Still he con-tinued, trading something of himself for survival, and wondering every moment when his supply of tradable Vdhitzness was going to run out, for no creature ever knowns his own resources until the moment, the exact moment, of unchangeable failure. Test to destruction.

A trace element vital to the Spsom metabolism was lacking, or at best in insufficient concentration. That problem had begun immediately upon their landing, but it became more apparent in Ombur, more so in Yastian. He had finally allowed himself to be exhibited with a traveling circus that was now passing through this part of the Delta, representing a type of Klesh never before seen in this part of the world. Clellendol had picked up his rumor-trail on the street, immediately, and run the rumor to earth. How he had secured Vdhitz was not said.

Meure listened to this story and heard hopelessness in it, and mount-ing pressure on him. Things were coming together fast now, and he hardly could imagine what to do . . . Then he laughed to himself. *Of course I know what to do. The only question is, do I dare do it?*

He stepped off into space, as it were, with a sense of abandon to the flow of time, and somewhere offstage, on the periphery of his imagina-tion, or perceptions, something shuddered at the necessity of what it now had to do. Meure said, "Ask him what it is exactly that the Vfzyekhr does, Flerdistar."

She looked oddly into Meure's eyes, and the sudden authority that had come into his voice. But she turned without comment and put the question to Vdhitz, in his own sputtering speech. After a time, the answer came, marked by faltering and hesitations, first on the part of the Spsom, and then with Flerdistar's translation.

But the answer went: "They are not animals, as they seem, but rather the other extreme, the relics of a race which was once both sapient and great, long ago, before Spsom, before man. Perhaps before everything . . . (*Not before everything*, went off a silent alarm in the back of Meure's head, but he already suspected that answer.) . . . No one knows how they came to be the way they are . . . the way the Spsom found them. They themselves had forgotten, and did not wish to remember. They had had everything, so the Spsom scientists deduced. Telepathy was only the foundation of what they had become; they were on the edge of becoming totally free of material life-support whatsoever. Then, they . . . changed themselves, and declined, voluntarily. But they retained some things, or shadows of former abilities, as they never attained complete control."

She continued, haltingly, ". . . This is difficult for me to understand . . . it seems that they can still communicate, telepathically, but not their own thoughts . . . they are not aware of what passes . . . like a part of an assembly of communcations equipment, but only when the proper stimulus is present, which is, in Vdhitz's concept, at least two Spsom at each end . . . they don't know how it works, they never discovered the propagation medium, but it proved to be instantaneous, as far as they could detect, and unlimited in distance.

"They became, not so much oppressors, but guardians, preserving the Vfzyekhr carefully, for they were few. There were hints to the Spsom Vfzyekhr-students that their former power had been great indeed, and they feared greatly any reawakening of that, as oppression might cause, so they invited them along, as it were, and gave them the piping to clean to give the bored creatures something to do, something within the bounds they had set for themselves. . . . The Spsom told other races they met that the Vfzyekhr were their slaves, but the relationship's not like that at all; they maintain a spacefaring culture solely because of the Vfzyekhr, and in actual fact have no way to coerce them, should it come to that . . . and now with only one Spsom on the planet, the communications ability is gone . . . It's too late, that we know this. If we had known, we could have preserved Shchifr for a complete circuit . . . we could have brought an army in here, if needed . . . all for nothing, now."

Meure ventured, "There are two Klesh here; there are two Ler; why not them?"

"Vdhitz has said that between the 'components' there must be a certain empathy, a sense of sharing . . . at a threshold level. Use of the Vfzyekhr capability then increases this radically. We saw no sexual relationships suggested among the Spsom because . . . transmission so empathizes the participants that they become a social unit similar to a family . . . they tune to each other. There's no sex in it—it occurs several steps up the hierarchy of needs, and pre-empts that, along with several other drives . . . sexual experience among the 'components' distorts and prohibits use of the Vfzyekhr, because sex itself is multiplex and includes negative factors that upset the resonances . . . apparently this explains the Klesh end of it, and us as well . . . the use magnifies things among the group, so that Morgin's fear of Tenguft would no longer be rationalized away, but would dominate Morgin's personality. Like that. I would not attempt it with Clellendol after what I have heard . . ."

Meure nodded. "But I am twofold, unsexual, and our conflicts have been resolved, more or less . . ."

Flerdistar started violently, and said, "No!"

Vdhitz apparently understood some of what was going on, and he began making a series of gestures. Flerdistar said, "See? He says no as well. You do not know the consequences of such an act. At the least, if it worked, you would be put in direct communication with a Spsom Crew-entity. No! The potential for loss is too great. The experience could make both of you raving madmen. You and Cretus have to get along—you've been forced to it."

"What is any relationship but that it's forced to it by one circumstance or another, *whatever we say*. You institute selfishness into the core of your social order, Flerdistar, and the Klesh set up a racial selfishness in place of it, similarly. But Cretus was a mixed-blood, a remnant of a departed Klesh Rada. No . . . I think it's the only course. Now ask Vdhitz how it's done."

Vdhitz said a few words, and then turned away. Flerdistar translated, "He says it's just Will and Idea, and physical proximity. The Spsom unit holds hands with the Vfzyekhr in a circle . . . sometimes they just sit close together."

Meure looked for the creature, momentarily, and found that it had not moved from where it had settled for the night: by his hip. He looked down at the ball of off-white fur. Was it sleeping? He did not, he realized, know anything about its temperament. He felt, gently, along the body, curled up in rest; it was not so different from the basic physical shape of a Human, or a Spsom: two arms, two legs, a head, a body . . . By Meure's prodding, the Vfzyekhr stirred restlessly, and turned under Meure's touch. Then, as if realizing something, or sensing something, it turned to face Meure, although there was not much of a face to look at. Just fur, and suggestions. Deep within the thick fur that covered the face Meure thought he caught a suggestion of something dark and shiny, like eyes, reflecting the light from deep in sockets protected by bone, flesh, fur. Something disturbing looking at him. The Vfzyekhr moved, to stand on Meure's knees, and faced him directly; he felt a disturbing sensation of being under acute observation. What was it Vdhitz had said? Will and Idea? Will and Idea.

But how did one wish the unimaginable? He dragged Cretus with him, wishing . . . what did he want? To communicate? To whom? Who was available? Some Home-planet Spsom Communcations relay team? A tramp freighter across the universe? Cretus, overlooking Meure's memories, suggested, *Try Thlecsne Ischt, the warship. We could use fire-power, and rations for the long furry one. His kind will* . . .

Meure concurred, wished, tried. Will and Idea.

Cretus wished, too. They made an effort, together.

Then they heard voices. No, not voices. Meure's mind substituted voices for what he was sensing. It, they, were not voices, but raw thought-stuff, but with no soft edges. It was precision, steely, ruthless, all-powerful; and once connected, grew stronger without effort on his part. Will and Idea.

Something was waking up.

He/They heard: *Threshold attained, empathy index 7A4X551 AT&* (a string of symbols totally meaningless to Meure, so his mind substituted a coded number in place of the reality, which was untranslatable) *require adjust to #*+555DF$aa-3—feasible, now executing synchrony, to contact unit 9923 A445-F, initiation will commence upon attainment of level A* . . .

There was no pain, no fear, no foreknowledge. Instantly, both Meure Schasny and Cretus the Scribe ceased, ended, terminated, and to themselves, vanished.

14

"The idea of the Universe in the mind of a modern mathematician is singularly reminiscent of the ravings of William Blake."
—A.C.

THESIS, ANTITHESIS, SYNTHESIS. A persona was formed who did not exist before, but yet who possessed two complete memories of all events perceived by those two persons who went into its formation; to it, there was no break in continuity, no sense of change, abrupt or otherwise, but the natural culmination of events. In the same sense that it was quite neither Cretus nor Meure, it was also both of them, combined. At the first, it was not particularly conscious of a named-identity for itself, but it was totally aware that it was a unique being, possibly with unique powers. And where before the two had suspected a great Game being played out far above them, on the borders of perception, this new persona suddenly perceived the whole Game, the players, and dealt itself into a hand, all in the single first instant of its existence. It became aware. And simultaneously became something to become aware *of.*

There was no time to waste; these first moments required realization, but more, action and initiatives based on that realization. These things had to come before naming.

He saw a room in a pestilential city on the planet Monsalvat, dimly, as a faded hologram. There were concerned people there, people who were entangled with him intricately, who were afraid that they had set something in motion to cause harm. Yes, harm. There would be change, and it would be seen by some as negative, a change in state.

He was, in the primal perception, aware of the vast network across the universe maintained by the Spsom-Vfzyekhr gestalt: a four-dimensional continuum of glowing nodes spread across the darkness. But there was, of course, much more. Entities, beings, odd composite sapient forms . . . some contact was possible, he could see, and between other sets, antipathies. Space was distorted from what he thought it would seem like in this projection. Things did not fit, here, their distances in light-years. His target contact, for example, aboard the Spsom Warship *Thlecsne Ishcht*, in flight between the stars, which showed as dull pockmarks, had a shimmering quality, as if its place were somehow indistinct. There, but not now, really. Other places-points showed a specificity, a hard glitter. Far away, so it seemed, there was an odd pattern, unique. He could focus on it, examine it in detail, just by wishing it so: it was uncontestably alien. Alien to him, and alien to the norms of the network he had tapped into. Something was wrong (?), malfunctioning (?), contrary-to-expected-progressions (?). Moreover, it was aware of him, and moving sluggishly with a sideways-sliding motion which he could not translate into the physical world of human bodies. It moved, in this perception, but he sensed or guessed that it did not move at all, physically. But however it occurred, he was aware that it intended to threaten him.

He had *Thlecsne Ishcht*. To the transponder-entity aboard, he sent, *Bring the ship to Monsalvat and do what is necessary to rescue the survivors of Ffstretsha. And subdue a hostile entity which has been preying on the people of this planet.*

Thlecsne answered, *We come in strength, and are prepared for violence. As before when we tried to approach, we are experiencing flight difficulty. This time we are stressed for it.*

He: *I will attempt to weaken that influence. It is caused. You are part of this network; it is the alien presence at coordinates 23@¢#+667, which is* either on this world or immediately adjacent to it.

The presence aboard *Thlecsne Ishcht* sent back: *You are seeing at magnitude G. We cannot perceive at that level. All we see are the other Spsom points, indistinct patchy areas, and you. You are not Spsom. What are you, and how did you tap into the Vfzyekhr network?*

He said: *I/We are/were Human. I now, under this method of data transmission, appear to have gained a single nature, but I do not know what that nature is, nor if it is lasting. I am now going to a higher level, to contact an alien entity threatening our mutual effort. You must take all Spsom terminals off this network for a time, as there is perceptual danger to your system. Have your Vfzyekhr use pattern 2#3, shadowing and filtration applicable. If I do not recontact you, enter this planetary system and destroy the entity. The Vfzyekhr can locate it.*

Now he broke contact with the *Thlecsne Ishcht*, and tuned his Vfzyekhr contact up into a higher band, higher, higher still. It protested, like long-disused machinery, being forced into configurations close to the limits of its own parameters. He sensed, far back in the Vfzyekhr collective consciousness, a protest. But it responded. They responded. The Spsom gestalt vanished, and was replaced by other receptions he did not understand, or could not resolve enough to comprehend. The universe was full of aware, communicating entities. And the Vfzyekhr were his only key to it.

His target entity now became the center of attention, and as he progressed up the abstraction ladder, he found he could begin to understand it. But perception and understanding, in this conceptual universe, involved contact, and interaction. There was great danger now of losing . . . what? Losing his nerve, and being subsumed into the entity now facing him with calculating malevolence.

Far back in one of the two life-lines he possessed, there had been a contact with a projection of this entity; that had held a superstitious quality, a dreamlike unreality, a tentative instability. Contact now differed greatly; the entity existed, if the word could be used at all, on a conceptual, communicative plane. It had roots in physical reality, but they were tenuous, deceptive, almost invisible, after the fashion of fungi. And inasmuch as the visible part of the fungus was only a fruiting body thrown out by the real structure of subsurface filaments, so then the physical manifestations of the entity on Monsalvat were not the thing itself, but contact-bodies, temporary sensors, communicative devices grown by an advanced colony organism to interact with creatures it deemed primitive and inferior.

That much he could not directly perceive; what he could not translate was where it was in what little physical body it had left.

Of course not, it broadcast at him. And in that directed communication he realized again the danger he was in, for if Monsalvat was within the influence of the entity, here, within a communications concept, he was existing within its proper domain. He felt single and whole, but at the same time the echoes of Cretus and Meure, the old individuals, still rang, and of course there was the Vfzyekhr, whose amplification powers made this contact possible. They together were a shaky threefold organism, held together by a Vfzyekhr performing near its limits, while the entity was . . . he strained to focus down, to *see* . . . thousands, no, millions of units, no, more than that, linked, interconnected. And those parts were not individual wills, with their own conceptual lives to match against one another, but fitted parts, each smoothly matched into the enormous construct of the whole.

At last, it sent, *I can speak directly with one I labored over so long to bring back from the house of the dead.*

The Meure portion contributed, *And also one whom you brought from afar to serve as a new container for the Cretus you brought back. But neither of us has gratitude for what you have done to us, or to the people on Monsalvat.*

It replied, *What of that? Even artificial and temporary as you are now, you have attained an exalted state; in that, you will come to comprehend that when you become as I am, you live through the actions of others. Animals are unsatisfactory, because they have no idea of Time. Likewise, organisms similar to me have the power to be aware of me, resist me, perhaps attack me. No, the men of Monsalvat, full of glorious passions, hates, revenges, detestations they were both convenient, and at the perfect state of intelligence. Loneliness and boredom increase with awareness. Physical limitations hamper the climb into this state, so they become reduced, so one can reach farther and farther . . . no, We'll not give up on Monsalvat. All those knives, and so handy to use. No, that won't change. And since you couldn't come to me physically even if you knew where my basic units were, there's little enough you can do to change things.*

He sent, *What about me/us, then?*

The transfer didn't work, and the two of you were stuck in Limbo. Now, to contact me, you have further integrated with another being; this process is not reversible. As for the entity you have become, I have no use for that; you are aware of me. You will have to adjust to your new state . . .

What are you?

A community, a colony, a gestalt . . . long ago, very long ago, I was made up of units who had individual wills . . .

Humanoid?

Not particularly. Although my units had bones, organs, limbs and all require appurtenances. Life follows basic patterns; only the details vary. But the universe has physical limits. The only way around these limits is to stop trying to beat them in their own domains. To see, to realize, is all. It is not necessary to actually go to a planet to perceive it . . . and once we understood what we had to do, we started it in process. We took control of our planetary ecology, to tune it perfectly to us, and we undertook to guide our ongoing evolution into forms that would maximize the intercommunication and reduce the friction of individual wills. This goal was attained before your planet, the home of Man, had life forms.

He asked, *You say we and I. Which is it, properly?*

How interesting! No contact body ever asked before. It is both, of course.

I do not exist in the physical universe; we are an assembly of creatures which can be seen, felt, weighed, measured, and anything else one would care to perform upon them. In fact, it is possible for entities such as myself to . . . transfer to another base population, where conditions permit. This is the only sort of long-range mobility I have. We, as we are now, have none, except local movements on the planetary surface.

You have not done so . . .

No. But it would cause problems. The base population would lose me; this is a form of budding, where the bud is the continuation form and the stock is the infant. The base population would retain the physical base of an entity like myself, and would grow another. Such a creature would not share my learned cautions.

And you want no competition. Obvious and understandable.

You, it said, are a creature of movement, which means you are immobile with respect to Time. Conditions are reversed with forms like myself. My intent, as you would translate it, for Monsalvat, is to transfer my selfness there once the base population has reached a certain level . . . they would be space-mobile, under my guidance, and then I will be mobile in both realms.

(Aha, he thought. It's not on Monsalvat, because it said, "transfer my selfness there.") And he said, *Spread and multiply?*

No, came the answer. *Once transfer was done, we'd eliminate the old base population, and travel together . . . density to a certain level is a requisite of this kind of existence.*

(Aha, again, he thought, shielding the idea. It has to have a large population, probably confined to a single planet. Otherwise it would have already invested Monsalvat. At least with a beachhead.) *Why move?*

The long view of time. Stellar systems eventually lose their habitability to any life-form. I shall be forced to leave this system in order to continue . . . I had quite given up hope until the Klesh came.

(Now he thought deeply. Why did it have to have a Human-Klesh vector?) *You control an entire ecology, an evolutionary sequence; re-evolve your original host population.*

All life forms, however powerful, have limits. That is one of mine. I can make forms coalesce, and specialize them, but I cannot renew to the old form, or evolve forward. You would call my host form so highly evolved as to be degenerate, a side-branch. I cannot make marble, only make statues of what marble I find. My Hosts, we are individually small creatures, grass and seed eaters, who are the distant descendants of what I might call "Stem Epiprimates," somewhat better integrated than the creators of the Klesh.

But you'll be coming down, to transfer here, to the Klesh . . .

True. But I won't let them go so far, either. They'll retain an ability to make technology, so we can move . . .

He said, *That's like the transfer you did with Cretus-me.*

Cretus was an experiment, that's true. I discovered him in Time, and laboriously tracked him down in space. And you, too, after others failed.

Have you thought that the same thing could happen again? That the Klesh-Monsalvat host might possess some concealed, untested strength? That it could turn on you and exploit you, with your knowledge of Time, your ability to move in its medium? I cannot see any beneficial effects of such an entity. It would impose change upon the universe in the same sense that I am going to impose change upon the Klesh . . .

What kind of change? There was a note of alarm in its contact, now.

To start with, I'll make them immune to you. Human legend is filled with the fear of demons. You'll do, well enough, although you're not exactly what I have always had in mind . . .

And for the first time, the eagerness for contact which had characterized the entity was gone. He probed, he listened, he searched. But for a time, there was silence, darkness.

He ventured, *I see . . . things like you were what we called demons. But those attempts never worked, or. . . .*

It responded, *No or. They never worked. I know. I have seen. Transfer has never been done successfully. It's always been tried from too great a physical distance . . . they were running out of time on their origin-worlds and had no nearby possible host.*

One race turned back from what you are, a third part of him contributed.

More than one, it answered. *Those I have seen as well. One of them is now the switching part of your collective entity. But they had my experience to draw on, and they saw before their forms were past the evolutionary point of no return. We had contact, ago as you would say it, there as I would say it.*

What was another?

Those whose ship brought you here.

Ths Spsom?

Indeed the Spsom. They feared amalgamation more than the Vfzyekhr, and so in time they forgot it . . . until they met the Vfzyekhr, and enough remained to key the association. By forming the communications network they do together, they mutually protect one another from going further again along that path of development.

What of Humans; of Ler; of Klesh?

The situation will seem paradoxical to you, so I will explain: all sentient populations develop toward unity. That process is an analogue of the way individual cells become multicellular creatures. So much is the general rule. There are exceptions. The Ler do not develop this way, because all their combinational drive has been translated into an equal society of perfect individuals within the limitations and attributes they have. The original DNA manipulators did not know this, and did it unaware. In turn, the Ler have influenced mainstream humanity by social feedback into a similar, but artificial, state. On the other hand, the Klesh, isolated from both by accident, and later deliberately so by me, are far into large-scale integration.

—But the races detest one another!

Never mind what they say. It's what they do. They react to one another in well-defined patterns. These patterns are the precursors to the large-scale integrations necessary to attain an awareness like mine.

Or, become the host for one.

Just so. To one other point, the Klesh are reachable, and many of them exhibit threshold sensitivity. Cretus, for example, although it was his forebears who first caught my attention. I was almost too late.

Cretus fought you . . .

Some of that. He had his own ideas, as well . . . at the least, he set up conditions where I could implant remote sensors on Monsalvat, and prevent things from falling back further. It costs me a great deal to maintain those sensors there; they are like myself, not completely material, although they seem so at your perceptual level.

A Cretus part of him said, *Protes.*

Correct. The word itself is from an ancient Human word, protean. That is why they could never discover how Protes communicated. They don't; they are parts of me. There is no waveform between them, but a continuous state of being.

Protes were before Cretus.

And I am a creature of Time. I planted them before Cretus, so they would be there to use after him. It was both the most I could do, and the only thing I could do approaching direct intervention.

That's the best you can do in the material universe.

It's the only stable form I can attain in the material universe.

He would have asked it more, thinking to let it ramble and reveal itself; he knew it was nearby, near enough to come within range of the weapons of *Thlecsne Ishcht*, whatever they were. But suddenly the perceptual universe he was sharing with the entity vanished. It did not fade out, or withdraw; it was shut off, switched off. And he had lost contact with his dim outside reference as well! He was walled up in Limbo, a nowhere, a no when.

A tiny voice spoke to him then, exquisitely faint, yet also of a piercing clarity so precise that he could have heard it over the hum and drill of the noises of the city, and of the entity's universe. Then everything had been shut off for another reason. The voice told him.

"We," it said, "are now drawing upon the resource of the entire Vfzyekhr population to shield you from that. It is shrewd rather than intelligent, but it is beginning to suspect you are trying to find out where it is. We know it from long ago, when we found it, or it us, and knowing it, turned back from becoming an entity like it. It is currently located on the second planet of this system, or based there. But this is a creature of Time, and so it anticipates you by commencing transfer now. During this duration-sequence, it will be establishing control of its new base population, and other functions will lapse. Already the warship finds clear space, and approaches under full power. The entity, as you call it, is settling upon the population of the city we are in, before you can set them off. But it must be stopped, for the aberrant Human population of this planet will increase its power by a factor of two to the tenth. Then it can move out of this system where it has been pent."

He thought, "I thought it grew here."

"It is native to this system. But long ago it tried to move out. It was the firstborn within this cycle of creation, and the strongest. All other entities like it united to block it. There in your reference started the process. But you have the craftiness of Cretus and the dreams of Meure, and you have the ordinary weapons of *Thlecsne Ishcht* to use upon it, if need be. When you contact the entity again, you will have only a clear channel to it, and one other to *Thlecsne*. They will be mutually shielded from each other—secure. Even I-we will not be in contact. All I-we will see is what happens. If you fail, then we act." And as the voice spoke, he could sense a growing power behind it, a swelling of multitudes, as suppressed abilities lain dormant and forgotten for centuries, millennia, geological ages, began to awaken once more. The voice faded, faded, grew distant, and suddenly winked out.

Then the perception of the entity returned, and with it, superimposed on it, a sense of the warship. But only he could see them both. They were mutually invisible to each other.

He thought, *it's on the second planet—Catharge, but it's already started transfer here, to Monsalvat. But to what population? It could be anywhere on the four continents, anywhere.* But as he desperately tried to recall all

the lore of Monsalvat he knew, from Cretus and Meure alike, one fact
seemed to stand out. That nowhere on the planet was there enough of
any one group to dominate even a single continent. That the Embasses,
though widespread, were mixed bloods and few in numbers. There was
nowhere for it to go . . . except here, to Yastian, to the teeming numbers
of the Lagostomes, individually weak, but properly organized and motivated, unbeatable. And only they seemed to have the remarkable empathy for crowd-emotion that they did. He thought, *The nerve of the
damned thing! It has to be here, right here, and under our very noses. But
what will we give to stop it?* The Meure part of him was unsure, but Cretus had no such ambiguities.

He put the connection aside for a moment. Returning to the world
was like dreaming. He saw through a distorting glass. He arose, carrying
the Vfzyekhr, and made his way to the window, ignoring the others, who
stared blankly at him. He looked out into the night of the city. And
though each point of light in that city was weak, by itself, together they
made enough light to block the light of the stars. He found himself
yearning for the clean uplands of Incana, the rolling swales of Ombur,
wind in his face. Here at last was the real giver of visions, or oracle, who
had been tinkering with Monsalvat for uncounted years. And coming
here itself, at last.

The city of the Lagostomes had not quieted with nightfall, but it was
quiet now, for no reason. It was as if everyone had stopped in those moments, paused, and anticipated . . . something. They were waiting for
something. He could almost feel it, himself; a hidden emotion, a desire
to let go, to flow with the collective will, to do what *they* wanted and
said. Something heavy and lethargic was settling upon this land from
out of the sky they could not see, something whispering to them sub-
thought, *I come to release you, I come giving freedom at last, license to shout
and slay, to eat and breed as one will. I will make you the great people, who
will go to the stars, who will live forever . . .* and on and on it went, promising, promising, the heart-balm to a losing, desperate people. It was
hardly perceptible, but the more deadly for that. Words would have
made even the Lagos suspicious. This was something more than propa-
ganda. Of course they answered, unknowing. *Yes, Master, we are thy people. Verily we come unto you.* It was happening even as he watched.

The air grew heavy with expectancy. He turned, to motion to Tenguft, now fighting the influence of the thing himself. She responded as
if in slow motion. Dreamily she arose, and drifted to the window, not
fast enough. She should have moved instantly. The window overlooked

a small court, where people were gathering, looking guilty at one another, and up at the sky, waiting. Here he would strike, whatever the cost. He would throw the spear of Tenguft at one of those in the center of the yard, and let precipitate what would among the volatile Lagostomes.

He felt a sharp jolt along his nervous system, like a shock, followed by a pain and an emotion he could not name. And the entity spoke, blotting out his perception of the present: *The ship came with fire, and has done great damage. My units panic with the fright of it, and this has made a difficulty. It is no matter. I am now budded. Let them gnaw at the bare bones of Catharge. In moments a great fist will rise into the sky and erase that metal thing. These people have great strength, and with them I shall bend space. I could not know until I felt them with the touch. We will not need to train these to build spaceships. Wielded by me, they already have the native power to reach out and have the ships brought to us, there is no limit to what shall be mine.*

He tried to contact the *Thlecsne Ishcht*, felt the channel open momentarily, then close again. It was as if there had been no need to *say* it.

There was a glow on the horizon, in the East, where one had not been before. A growing flame, rising out of the East. Something was approaching at furious speed. And in the city below, flickers of alien emotions began racing back and forth among the Lagostomes. The glow became a fireball, white-hot, burning, flaring across the sky like some meteor of incredible size. It came faster than the sound could catch its passage, growing, and the people cringed, and it stopped, dead, directly overhead, looming over the waiting city like the angel of Death. The fire of its passage flared, bloomed, and went out, leaving behind in its place the awful shape of the *Thlecsne Ishcht*, its tubes now glowing from the intense heat of its passage. The light from it cast shadows in the streets below. It seemed to be at low altitude, hovering by some unknown means. Lights, burning actinic points of light began to flicker and sparkle along the network of the tubes surrounding the slipper form of it. And the sound of its passage arrived and smote the streets and alleys and canals of Yastian. Below, people were thrown off their feet by the blow. Glass fell out of windows, and fragile sheds collapsed in turning heaps of dust.

He sent at it, *It is not to be here, now. The ship is here and ready to do worse than it did on Catharge, whatever it did. We will not allow you the Lagostomes, nor Monsalvat, nor the Klesh. As we love and revere all life, we would not hound you to oblivion but we will prevent your parasitizing us. If we are to have an overmind, we will grow our own.* Then he waited for an answer.

For a time, there was none, although he could sense dimly something happening out of sight, offstage. Dire events, no doubt. There was a subtle perception of great energy transfers, roiling currents, struggle and strife. He hoped the entity was having difficulty with the Lagostomes. Yet he could not tell what exactly was going on; everything was muffled, indistinct, distant, and growing fainter.

Then everything cleared once more, and the entity spoke.

Betrayed! Trapped! And its signal was fading even as it sent that.

???

Cretus! I prodded Cretus until he became aware of me in his limited way, and he disengaged himself. But he promoted a stability which I took for preparation, when the right catalyst came again. Now I know what he did. He created a dormant, primitive multicellular consciousness, which I awakened in trying to transfer to it. I transferred here and let the other go, and the warship disorganized my old base population. They run wild now. And here now, the organism resists me, while the fear of the ship disrupts it. And another entity moves in Time to block that avenue. Fading. . . .

The transmission had become very weak at the end, halting, strangled, he would have said, had it been words. Choking on its own plots. And he sensed the Vfzyekhr shifting down from its higher levels, letting itself go, fading, too. It sent, *It is gone. We should have dealt thus with it the first time, but we thought what we did was enough.*

It, the Vfzyekhr mass consciousness, had briefly willed itself into existence, but now it was letting itself fall back into the oblivion from whence it had come. It had awakened with his prodding. . . . The Spsom had not responded at all.

He sent, *No! Not yet! I know neither what to do nor where to begin.*

Even as he sent, it was dissolving, disassociating back into its component parts, rustic, simple, rare folk who occasionally went to space with a race with whom they had formed a telepathic symbiosis *to prevent its natural formation and continuation.*

A last answer floated out of it: *You are Cretus who has been tamed by a persona-substance not available on Monsalvat: lead yourself. You know what to do. The spark still lives on Monsalvat, your people's ability to bypass the trap of the overmind. Strive . . .* and he could no longer receive it.

And with the quiet, came the end of the Vfzyekhr contact: it winked out an instant later, with a finality that told him he would never have it again. They, it—whatever it or they was or were—had locked him out, forever. Now he was left as the contact had made him, an unpredicted fusion of two disparate personalities. There was no model for this, no legends, no tales; he would have to feel his way along the road to come, blindly, sensing, reacting, building his own working diagram of the universe, and of the men who must know of what they so closely missed.

He was in a shabby room, still dimly lit from the glow of lights from outside. And outside, there was the sound of confusion and tumult, of despair and panic. He saw the others, looking at him, and in their eyes he read something of his own strangeness to them. He thought that it would do to be careful, and deliberate, for of his words and actions he felt the stirrings of a newer conceptual universe being created; events would radiate from this room, this moment in Time, in ever-expanding circles, sometimes assuming strange forms. He would need to choose his moments carefully.

He looked down at the Vfzyekhr, that had set up the contact that had fused him, touched it absent-mindedly, as if for reassurance. The creature was cool and did not move. It was dead. Whether this was so from its overextending itself, or voluntary, he knew this to be the underling of the last intent of the Vfzyekhr collective: that he would never again have access to the power he had gained to energize a system that had once turned itself off. He stroked the still form lovingly, feeling a great sadness. And thought, *They have paid their admission and intiation fees many times over, and still do not demand, nor compel. Now mine begin.*

Clellendol leaned closely, and said, "Morgin and I have been watching the people from the window; they are agitated enough, but not reacting at all like the Lagostomes of old, so Morgin says. They seem to have lost their sentitivity to one another. There is a general tendency to abandon this particular neighborhood, arid after a bit, it should be safe to venture outside."

"Where is the ship, now?"

"Not far. The Lagos ran from it, and it is clearing an area for landing, now, not far away. They seem to know someone is nearby they should look for . . ."

"Let them finish their work. Afterward, we will go to them."

"And we can leave, at last."

"You and Flerdistar can leave . . . there is much I have to do here that has been unfinished."

Flerdistar now settled beside him, wonderingly, and said, "Something happened to you, to us . . ."

He answered, suddenly tired beyond his ability to ignore, "To all of us; the waves of the past must pass through a place, here, that will mute their clamor . . ."

"Who are you? Cretus, or is it Meure Schasny?"

"It is neither, and it is both."

"How shall we call you?"

"As you will; or according to what I do."

"What have you come to do?"

"To help find the way we have lost, I think . . . I will bring a message to those who will listen; some will."

"I know not what to call one such."

"There is no need. Say 'Cretus,' that something be continued from that which could have been, but never forget that the other is an equal part, too."

"You will remain on Monsalvat?"

"Just so. It will begin here better than anywhere else . . . they can come here now. The stormy spaces about Monsalvat are smooth, and the terrible oracles are gone. It will truly become what its name means—'Mountain of Salvation,' rather than what we have called it— 'Place to Bury strangers.' "

Flerdistar snorted skeptically. "Salvation! And from what? Salvation is to save."

"From our worst enemy—you and I alike: ourselves. I will lead my people, here, and we will show the way . . . to be truly Human."

"What powers have you gained, that you could do this thing?"

"In terms of what you mean of power, I have not gained, but lost. Yet by that, I have become unique."

"As you are in your duality."

"Former. I am one, now."

"And so Monsalvat will again know the tread of the armies of Cretus . . ."

"Not that, again. This must be grown, not forced; cultivated with the loving care of the husbandman."

"I do not miss that inference; the husbandman culls, prunes, burns clippings, eradicates pests."

"Indeed that is; and so will I . . . but we will learn to do those things for ourselves. We need no master; we know the way already, but we fear it because it is simple, direct."

She said, cynically, "And the millennium will come, no doubt."

"Neither you nor I will see it; but Historian, you will see change of this day, far from now."

She said, "I have sensed it beforetimes, that it was coming; is it truly to have been this simple?"

He thought then back to his contact with the Entity, with the Vfzyekhr collective overmind, with hints and visions of the other lights that were, farther away than they had found yet, but they too would come in the future and the men that were to be must be ready for *that* . . . He said, finally, "Simple? Yes, simple, like the matter of timing in music, that meets the median between clashing noise and pedantic formalism, that perfect timing, and the funniest part of it all is that much of the time it's mostly by accident."

"An accident?"

"It's so simple, and so hard to say; the words aren't right. Now we will make them so. It is accidental, random; also it is implicit-consequence of everything that has happened here since the beginning of Time. This system, with its dual stars, teaches us much about the nature of things: everything seems to possess dual aspect at the first level of penetration. That the universe appears accidental and predestined at the same time is not so much a measure of the qualities of the universe, but of the limitation of the perceptive system applied to it."

"You are rather more oracular than the Entity, now. They have not lost their oracle here, only traded."

"They never had one, nor have they one now. Do you not understand what you saw here, what you perceive of this world's past? That thing was no oracle. In that conceptual framework, it was not an oracle, but a demon, a succubus, that had fastened upon this world to suck it dry. It manipulated to the extent of its powers, for its advantage. They have traded a taker for a giver. It was almost to have been that way before, when Cretus walked in his own body, but for the thwarting by the Entity. Fear not. History will not speak here of the days to come, as the conquests of a conqueror, whose name lives on in infamy; but they will note something happened here that changed Men forever, and they will never know who did it. You said it: Monsalvat will become opaque to your kind of analysis in History. First Monsalvat, then the rest. We will be pariahs no longer, and I will be anonymous, a face, a body that wanders. They will know me by my words, and the dreams I launch them onto."

Morgin now leaned near, and said, softly, "You have spoken for the offworlders who do not know, but I see your meaning as a native. You will need a knowledgeable companion on your long road . . . and a scribe to record a scribe's words."

He smiled, a gesture barely visible in the dim light. "You will never catch it as it is to be . . . but I will be grateful for your knowledge. Come with me, then."

He got up, pausing to lay the Vfzyekhr softly on the pallet. Tenguft towered over him, and she said, in a throaty voice, a tone he had not heard in her for a long time, "I, too, will come. As Morgin knows people, so do I know the markers of the world itself. And of course," she added slyly, "you should not have to worry over finding a new woman every night, either."

"You know this is going into the darkness."

"Just so. I know the path well; the way of the Haydar warrior is into the darkness of unknowing. Otherwise, why would there be warriors. Any city-man can walk in the light among the known."

"Let it be so, then. But in this is neither fame nor glory. Just hard strokes."

"But we will change it all. I understand. Forever. The rest does not matter. I see that much I have known and loved will pass from sight—and for others, too. But I also know that all we have done before has been the illusion of change, that in our hearts we were still beasts, no matter that some lived in the bellies of machines . . ."

He looked out the window now and saw the *Thlecsne Ishcht* settling onto a place not far away, still clearing the ramshackle buildings under it with what seemed to be swift strokes of light. At each stroke, there was no fire, only dust and debris. The people had long since cleared that part of the city. He made a gesture curiously like a shrug, and said, "Come along, then. It's time."

"The art of progress is to keep intact the Eternal."

"Complete mystery surrounds the question of the origin of this system; any theory which satisfies the facts demands assumptions which are completely absurd."

—A.C.

THEY MADE THEIR way to the ship in silence, not because they each had nothing to say, but that they each had too much to say; or that what was there would not fit the words they had to say it.

By the time they had reached the place where the *Thlecsne Ishcht* was to ground itself, it had completed its clearing process and was resting lightly on the bare ground. The ship was not shut down now as the Meure Schasny of long ago had first seen it resting on the field by Kundre, on Tancred. Here, it rested lightly, its bulk not quite touching the earth. It did not move, but they could sense that there was little holding its power leashed. And along the lengths of the tubes that surrounded its basic shape, infinitesimally remote colored sparks crawled spiral paths, like burning fuses.

It had been night; but now, far away across the flats and the river steamings, the eastern sky was beginning to color slightly. He thought, *There, over the hills of Intance or Nasp, the sky will be pale over the black seas, clearer than here. And now the shimmer you always caught out of the corner of your eye will be gone. Forever. We saw it so long, not knowing what it was, that we managed to forget it. Only offworlders were troubled by it, and thought things were watching them. Something was there, that we suppressed. And like a man, leaning on a wall, we'll fall now that the wall is gone, unless we build another one—or recover our proper balance.* And in his mind, before *thought*, he knew which one was the only acceptable choice.

Ferocious-appearing Spsom, dressed in what passed for uniforms among them, swarmed down the boarding-ladder, to retrieve Vdhitz, and take the still form of the Vfzyekhr from Tanguft, who had carried it to the ship, back to its own kind. Clellendol hesitated for a moment, but a moment only. He glanced at Flerdistar, at the rest of them, and climbed the ladder into the ship. The part he had come for was over. He was merely a passenger now.

Flerdistar stepped onto the first rung, steadying herself with a thin hand on the safety rail, pausing uncertainly. She said, "I came to study the past—instead I received an answer about the future, which I neither knew existed, nor wanted to know."

Cretus said, "Once you learn to hear answers, you hear all kinds of answers to questions you have not yet asked; this is as it should be, but it is hard to live with at first."

"I did not learn the answer to my project query."

"You haven't asked it plainly enough."

"Written history says Sanjirmil led the Warriors, as did the legends of the Warriors themselves. But through Monsalvat we suspected that this was not the truth. What was the truth, and why did it come through here?"

"As the Cretus of old, I spent much time with the *Skazenache*, learning the mastery of it. Once I saw a thing I did not understand, not at all. It was so odd I memorized the settings so I could come back to it— something extremely difficult, even for a master of the instrument. Later, when I had learned to interpret what I was seeing, I turned the *Skazenache* to those settings again . . . and the scene was replayed.

". . . it was odd because after I had learned all the major part of the legends about the Warriors and the Klesh, I found that I was looking at Sanjirmil herself, at great age. But listen: she was on another world—not Dawn. And she was acting, in this scene, as if she expected that someone would be able to see her—somehow."

Flerdistar asked, "What . . . ?" but Cretus held up a hand, gently, to hold her question.

"She spoke aloud, in simple Singlespeech, as if reciting. Now you will hear it from me as I-Cretus saw and heard it. When the First Ship was to have left home, Sanjirmil was the leader of a minority faction of your people who wished to exercise domination over the Humans. She was one of the elite—the flying crew, and so was not seen on the first part of the voyage. And when the mutiny occurred, and that faction stole the ship, those Ler who were left behind assumed it was she who had led them.

"Not so. She had changed. Her views were part of a mental dysfunction caused by an overload she received as a child; and after her actions had set everything in motion beyond the point of no return, she was cured, by one who loved her greatly. The cure set her mind right again, and removed the radical view she had cultivated from her, but it also removed her ability to fly the ship. She kept to her quarters and secluded herself, doing some minor astrogating, some teaching, and trying to undermine the very thing she herself had started.

"As she was at the age of the onset of fertility, she entered into family relationships after the manner of your people. She had her two children on the first world your people landed on. And raised them there. She led a gentle, retiring life, indeed, almost a secretive one, practicing all the virtues of the Ler and trying quietly to obviate the evil she had done so much to invent in an earlier part of her life."

Flerdistar said, "This modest person you are speaking of, this paragon of Ler virtues, is credited in Ler history with the invention of our own sort of evil, as a force. She is an historical character whose shadow casts itself longer than any other. She made us what we are now. And you say she recited that she retired?"

"Did you think I would not verify all that she said? Or that I could not? It was as astounding to me as to you. And afterwards, I did verify it. I studied Sanjirmil off and on for almost ten years. I know more about her life, almost, than she did herself.

"But of course, things do not always go as we want them to; where before she had been a Power, a shaper, in her affliction, cured she was a simple woman of the people, and the Mana was gone. She could no longer steer history. The conspiracy simmered underground, was passed from mouth to mouth, in secret covens . . . and almost a generation later, a band of desperate amateurs stole the ship and took off into space, marooning the majority faction, now colonists.

"They took her with them, since she was the prophetess of their whole movement, the one who started it—before any of them had been born. They only knew that she was Sanjirmil the Great. But it was against her will that she went; they kidnapped her when she resisted, knowing in their hearts they could not leave without their own legendary source, knowing that they could not endure the shame of having their own prophet denounce them, perhaps even seek revenge upon them.

"But her cure had been too complete; she proved no more able to justify the Sanjirmil of old aboard the ship again, then she had while raising her family. They had their talisman, well enough—but it was a talisman that would not accept anything short of complete surrender, and the return of the ship. They were at an impasse of the worst sort: she wouldn't cooperate, and they couldn't take her back, and to have killed her outright would have made them totally depraved, and to their credit, they at least saw that in that future.

"So, on their way away outward from their place, in their rush to the darkness of the Rim, they passed a curious planetary system, with a choice of habitable worlds within it. One proved to be a gentle and pleasant world, more or less, and so they landed there, and labored for a time, to build her a house by the shore, and left her tools, and seeds, and some animals. This world had no intelligent life, and was bare and lonely; here they could honor her with a small castle, but they could also abandon her there in good conscience, knowing she would never betray them. This world was so far out they knew it would never be found while any artifact of hers existed—they didn't know where it was for sure, themselves. Besides, she was then Elder phase, and couldn't have all that much time left, anyway. And so, after doing her honors, they departed, and left Sanjirmil on an uninhabited planet, whose location was not known and soon forgotten—mislaid—by its discoverers.

"But when she had been cured, it had been complete. Sanjirmil was then, I think, probably the sanest Human or near-Human, or Ler that has ever been. Alone in a stone castle by an empty sea, caught at last by the thing she had created and then abandoned, and at last fought, she did not despair, but called on strengths she had possessed all her life. She survived. First, the first year. Then a second. Then it got a little easier; she was falling into the rhythm of the planet.

"She expanded her little country, began exploring the land about her. She learned about certain dangerous forms of life, and how to avoid them. She took long excursions along the seashore, explored the interior. She had been overstressed, for the ship. But as a generalist, as a survivor, she was superb; she recreated a community, and all its necessary handicrafts, totally within herself. Hope she had none, but she would not give up, even where there was none to see it.

"She lost count of the years, for she could not know what they were in the years of the home planet. It no longer mattered. Her hair was streaked with gray when they left her; it went all gray, then white. She became careful of her strength, and stayed closer to her castle. It was then that she thought something was stirring, something aware, but unseen, unknowable, something evil, something had had been, for all practical purposes, dead. At first she dismissed it as hallucination, or simple old age and loneliness. But it continued, and the impressions became stronger. It began to leave traces she could objectively measure. Even doubting herself, she devised subtle little test-traps for it. It became the major objective of what remained of her life—to prove this suspicion a real, although subtle thing, or a figment of her own failing mind and body.

"She finally decided that whatever it was, it was real, not a phantom, and that somehow it was intelligent, powerful, and awakening. She feared it, but in a very limited way, she communicated with it; enough to hope that a day would come when someone would be able to look across time and space and see her who had set the events in motion that would lead to that person's vision. And so she set a particular scene, when she told this whole story, so that someone would know it, no matter whether the Warriors, as they had called themselves, continued or ended. And in the end she had the victory over them, for the Warriors are indeed gone, them and their line alike, and the lie they told of her, that she was their prophet, their leader, their ideal. She told me, and I. . . ."

Flerdistar said. "You as Cretus alone, long ago, spread the tale over Monsalvat. . . ."

"Edited, changed a little, embroidered to fit the people it served. . . ."

". . . That Sanjirmil. . . ."

"St. Zermille, our Lady of Monsalvat."

. . . though a Ler, had hated the Warriors and would love the victims of their persecutions."

"Just so."

"A fine tale, that, Cretus. Good for your people, and the answer I came for. All is well! But why here? What makes her important to Monsalvat?" And even as she said it, she knew. Her face shouted it. She knew.

"They left her here, on Monsalvat. She lived in the west by the Great Ocean, in the land we call now Warvard. Not so far from the Ombur. And she awoke the Entity who still lived on Catharge . . . and told me how to recognize it, and escape its influences. It could distort space and time, but somehow it couldn't deflect that message she arranged as one of her last acts, nor could it perceive it except dimly . . . it was through her that I disengaged, knowing that my dream could go no further as long as it was awake and alive, and that I could not reach it. . . ."

He had let it trail off, but now he continued again, "She walked into the sea and went for a swim, and the Great Ocean took her. And the seasons and the waves and the years slowly undid what she had done there by the sea, and the traces of it grew dim, and then invisible to un-trained eyes. And then they came, the Warriors and their former slaves, who built, and tore down, and built again. And governors, and colonists, and all traces of her were erased. And why should anyone have thought to look for her here? They all thought she had gone with the Warriors—but when they were taken off Dawn, no Warrior mentioned her grave, nor any memorial to her, or indeed anything of her. No—it was here she lived her last days. And so we made her a saint, and I suppose in a way, that it's true, after all . . . in the end, a long way around, she did save us, and show us the way. For what I now reveal is not Cretus, nor Meure, but what she told me long ago—what we all must do. I have known it all this time, but could not transmit the idea of it. Now, after these final strokes—I can. And through me, she will at last expiate her crimes of centuries ago. She thought it all out—she had nothing else to do, and she was the only Ler at that time who was totally mind-clean—purged and humble. She had the clear sight that I lacked, even though I had a great dream. I was dreamer enough to recognize hers was the greater."

Flerdistar took an uncertain step on the ladder, words beyond her.

He said, as if in parting, "Say these things that you have heard and seen here to your sponsors, to your people . . . that you no longer will have to probe subtle concepts and study dusty manuscripts to travel to her who was your greatest seer, but that we will bring her to you, after a time, and that our lives will change, and we all will grow strange and wonderful and we'll look at all that went before this, here, as the initi-ation we had to have accomplished. Good-bye."

Flerdistar obeyed without thinking about it, walking up the inclined ladder into the belly of the *Thlecsne Ishcht*, without looking back.

And the ladder folded back into the ship, and it was covered and the hull became smooth and without seam. It lifted, moving hardly at all at first, then faster, rotating to a different heading, orienting itself accord-ing to the unseen Captain and astrogator, rising into a sky gone rosy-fingered with the approach of dawn, yet also with that tincture of tangerine that was the mark of Monsalvat and its double star—Bitirme. Noiselessly, and the sparkles along the tubing faded, and the ship rose, and diminished, and moved away, becoming a dark smudge, a spot, and then nothing.

It was said of the three remaining behind, by those who made it their business to watch all events in Yastian, that they remained in the cleared area for a short time, but then left. And that in the day that followed, made their way to the great docks along the south end of the foreign quarter, where they spoke with several captains, and at last went aboard a ship rigged with flowing triangular sails, and crewed by slender men who wore striped, form-fitting shirts and turbans, and whose faces were thin and skins shiny brown, identifying them as of the Radah Horisande, the dreaded pirate-mariners of Glordune.

There were those who averred that the three were welcomed there, with the grim reserve characteristic of that Klesh Radah, and that afterwards, the Glordune ship dropped its mooring lines and began drifting down the estuary, toward the sea. And as it faded into the growing dark of evening over the marshes, that they could be seen by the rail for a long time, as if relaxing, and that strange songs floated back over the water, not the usual bloodthirsty chants attributed to the Horisande by their few survivors. These things were noted, and put away in the press of daily events, but not forgotten; they were remembered as proper portents when after many passages of the double suns across the floor of the Inner Sea, many sums of such passages, Cretus the Scribe returned to Kepture, last of all the continents. But that is another tale, which may be summarized by the saying, there came a great change from the East. Which finished its course in Kepture, where it started, and passed onward, to all men and salamanders and gnomes.